Arthur Mervyn;
or,
Memoirs of the Year 1793

with Related Texts

Charles Brockden Brown

ARTHUR MERVYN;
or,
MEMOIRS OF THE YEAR 1793

with Related Texts

Edited, with an Introduction and Notes, by
Philip Barnard and Stephen Shapiro

Hackett Publishing Company, Inc.
Indianapolis/Cambridge

Copyright © 2008 by Hackett Publishing Company, Inc.

13 12 11 10 09 08   1 2 3 4 5 6

For further information, please address
  Hackett Publishing Company, Inc.
  P.O. Box 44937
  Indianapolis, IN 46244-0937

  www.hackettpublishing.com

Cover design by Abigail Coyle
Text design by Carrie Wagner
Composition by Professional Book Compositors
Printed at Edwards Brothers, Inc.

The text of *Arthur Mervyn; or, Memoirs of the Year 1793* included in this edition was provided by the University of Virginia Library's Electronic Text Center.

Library of Congress Cataloging-in-Publication Data

Brown, Charles Brockden, 1771–1810.
  Arthur Mervyn; or, Memoirs of the year 1793 ; with related texts \ Charles Brockden Brown ; edited, with an introduction and notes, by Philip Barnard and Stephen Shapiro.
    p.cm.
  Includes bibliographical references.
  ISBN 978-0-87220-922-0 (alk. paper) — ISBN 978-0-87220-921-3 (pbk. : alk. paper)
1. Young men--Fiction.   2. Physicians—Fiction.   3. Yellow fever—Fiction.   4. Swindlers andswindling—Fiction.   5. Murder—Fiction.   6. Philadelphia (Pa.)—Fiction.   I. Barnard, Philip,1951–   II. Shapiro, Stephen, 1964–   III. Title.   IV. Title: Arthur Mervyn.
V. Title: Memoirs of the year 1793.
PS1134.A32 2008
813'.2—dc22

                                                      2007039790

CONTENTS

Acknowledgments   vii

Introduction   ix

A Note on the Text   xlv

Arthur Mervyn; or, Memoirs of the Year 1793   1

Related Texts:

A. By Charles Brockden Brown:

1. "Walstein's School of History. From the German of
    Krants of Gotha" (August–September 1799)   331

2. "The Difference between History and Romance"
    (April 1800)   340

3. Two Statements on the Modern Novel: 343
    a) "Romances" (January 1805)   343
    b) Excerpt from "Terrific Novels" (April 1805)   344

4. "The Man at Home—No. XI" (April 1798)   345

5. "Portrait of an Emigrant" (June 1799)   350

6. "What Is a *Jew*?" (November 1800)   355

7. Excerpts from "On the Consequences of Abolishing the
    Slave Trade to the West Indian Colonies"
    (November 1805)   358

B. Literary and Cultural Context:

8. William Birch, "Plan of the City of Philadelphia" (1800)   365

Contents

9. William Godwin, excerpts from *Enquiry Concerning Political Justice* (1793)   366

10. Mary Wollstonecraft, excerpts from *Letters Written during a Short Residence in Sweden, Norway, and Denmark* (1796)   373

11. Laurence Sterne, excerpt from *A Sentimental Journey through France and Italy* (1768)   377

12. Mathew Carey, excerpts from *A Short Account of the Malignant Fever, Lately Prevalent in Philadelphia* (1793)   380

13. Absalom Jones and Richard Allen, excerpt from *A Narrative of the Proceedings of the Black People during the Late Awful Calamity in Philadelphia in the Year 1793* (1794)   388

14. Three Abolitionist Addresses from Brown's Circle: 400
    a) Theodore Dwight, excerpts from *An Oration* (May 1794)   402
    b) Elihu Hubbard Smith, excerpts from *A Discourse* (April 1798)   403
    c) Samuel Miller, excerpts from *A Discourse* (April 1797)   407

15. Two Perspectives on Slavery from *The Monthly Magazine*:   410
    a) "H.L.," excerpt from "Thoughts on the Probable Termination of Negro Slavery in the United States of America" (February 1800)   411
    b) William Eton, excerpts from "Interesting Account of the Character and Political State of the Modern Greeks" (May 1800)   411

16. Benjamin Nones vs. the *Gazette*:   413
    a) "An Observer," excerpts from "For the Gazette of the United States" (August 5, 1800)   415
    b) Benjamin Nones, "To the Printer of the Gazette of the U.S." (August 13, 1800)   417

17. Lydia Maria Child, excerpts from *Isaac T. Hopper: A True Life* (1853)   420

Bibliography and Works Cited   427

ACKNOWLEDGMENTS

We thank the Department of English, University of Kansas, and the Department of English and Comparative Literary Studies, University of Warwick, for support throughout the preparation of this volume. The staffs of the University of Kansas Libraries and the Spencer Research Library rare book collection have been helpful sources of textual materials. Richard Clements of the Spencer Library has been especially generous in his help with ongoing work on Brown, facilitating access to materials that have contributed to this edition and related work for the Charles Brockden Brown Scholarly Edition.

For access to their digitized text of the first editions of *Arthur Mervyn*, we acknowledge and thank the University of Virginia Libraries and their Early American Fiction Collection project. The analysis of textual data provided by S. W. Reid in the 1980 Kent State Bicentennial Edition of the novel has been a valuable source of information for our work.

For great generosity in sharing his knowledge of Philadelphia's eighteenth-century urban space and social structure, and unfailing willingness to entertain questions, we recognize and thank Billy G. Smith. His suggestions and responses to queries have been invaluable. Likewise, Anthony Corbeill has been generous with advice and insights concerning Brown's Latin usage and Latinisms.

We are thoroughly indebted to the community of scholars who work on Brown and early modern culture, and to colleagues in the Charles Brockden Brown Society, whose insights and advice have helped form our ideas about and approach to this and other writings by Brown. On a long view, the path leading to this edition began with Henry Sussman and Leslie Fiedler, whose enthusiasm for *Arthur Mervyn* was infectious in the best sense of the word.

For guidance and support with the editorial process at Hackett, we thank Rick Todhunter, an extraordinarily supportive editor. Carrie Wagner, Christina Kowalewski, and Abigail Coyle have been essential contributors for the book's design and the quality of its text.

Personal thanks and Woldwinite relations of reason and desire link us to Anne Schwan, Cheryl Lester, and Julia Barnard.

*****

Dr. Elihu Hubbard Smith, one of Brown's closest friends, died from yellow fever in September 1798 while treating its victims during that year's New York outbreak. In the days before his own death, Smith, assisted by Brown, personally cared for the fever-stricken visiting physician Giambattista Scandella, who also died after staying behind to care for others. Brown memorialized these physicians in the figure of the selfless Maravegli in *Arthur Mervyn*'s Chapter 16.

In the context of this novel, we similarly want to commemorate the memory of Dr. Carlo Urbani (1956–2003), who first identified severe acute respiratory syndrome (SARS) as a fatally contagious disease and provided early warning that saved thousands, possibly millions, of lives. Urbani's dedication to care led to his own death from SARS. In light of Smith's Woldwinite beliefs, we can also recall that the onset of SARS was structurally related to the coercive urbanization of rural workers by contemporary global market forces, as Mike Davis explains in *The Monster at Our Door: The Global Threat of Avian Flu* (Verso, 2005).

INTRODUCTION

Tremendous times! Wars, Pestilence, Earthquakes, etc . . .

—Elizabeth Drinker, *The Diary of Elizabeth Drinker* (October 24, 1793)

But, as in medicine there is a species of complaint in the bowels which works its own cure, and, leaving the body healthy, gives an invigorated tone to the system, so there is in politics: and whilst the agitation of its regeneration continues, the excrementitious humours exuding from the contaminated body will excite a general dislike and contempt for the nation; and it is only the philosophical eye, which looks into the nature and weighs the consequences of human actions, that will be able to discern the cause, which has produced so many dreadful effects.

—Mary Wollstonecraft, *An Historical and Moral View of the Origin and Progress of the French Revolution* (1794, I.522)

Although it is commonly treated and read as a single, continuous tale, Charles Brockden Brown's *Arthur Mervyn; or, Memoirs of the Year 1793* is actually two novels in one. It consists of a first novel that was published as a full-length work in its own right sometime between March and May 1799 (the first nine chapters were previously serialized in June–August 1798) and a "sequel," as its author understood it, which appeared as *Arthur Mervyn; or, Memoirs of the Year 1793. Second Part* in September or possibly early October 1800, after Brown had published two other full-length novels in the interim. Taken as a whole, in both its parts, *Arthur Mervyn* is one of the seven novelistic works that Brown published in a remarkable burst of literary activity between 1798 and 1801 and one of the high points in the interrelated sequence of novels that is still the best-known aspect of his prolific literary career.

Even by the standards of Brown's other novels, all characterized by formal and conceptual complexity, *Arthur Mervyn* involves an impressive range of references and addresses a far-reaching set of questions. Generally known as an influential classic of American gothic and urban literature, the novel memorializes the epic Philadelphia yellow fever epidemic of 1793 and develops a series of interconnected subplots that connect the outbreak with the upheavals of the revolutionary era and the murderous financial networks of Atlantic slavery. While the tale's surface action traces the social progress of an individual farm boy, Arthur Mervyn, as he leaves the country and faces the challenges of a corrupt commercial city before deciding to become a doctor and entering a concluding romance with a cosmopolitan refugee, its subplots and back-stories relate Mervyn's experiences and development to the momentous events of the year 1793 and suggest an engaged political response to the challenges they imply.

This introduction is intended to orient the reader to the world of *Arthur Mervyn* by providing some tools for understanding Brown and his novel. We will outline and provide background for the novel's primary themes in order to draw the reader's attention to them and open them up for discussion. A sketch of Brown's life and the novel's late 1790s context, and a discussion of Brown's understanding of novels as instruments of political education and enlightenment, will provide general background. Information on central motifs—the 1793 yellow fever epidemic, the revolutionary turmoil of the Haitian and French Revolutions, which brought waves of émigrés and refugees to Brown's Philadelphia, and references to eighteenth-century theories of commerce, sensibility, race, and abolition—will lead to a discussion of how the novel develops and explores its primary social, economic, psychological, and political concerns.

Brown's Life and the Context of the 1790s

Brown was born into a Philadelphia Quaker merchant family on January 17, 1771. Philadelphia, the capital of the newly formed United States during the 1790s and then the largest, wealthiest, most culturally and politically diverse city in North America, was his home for most of his life. Beginning in the mid-1790s and particularly during the intense 1797–1800 period when he was writing his novels, however, Brown also lived in New York and moved in a cosmopolitan circle of young upper-class intellectuals who circulated and debated the latest medical-scientific, political, and cultural information and produced writings on a wide variety of subjects.

Growing up a Philadelphia Quaker (members of The Religious Society of Friends are commonly known as "Quakers" or "Friends"), Brown was shaped by that community's history of dissenting relations to mainstream Protestant and Anglo-American culture, and by Philadelphia's importance as both a political center and a major port connected with Atlantic and global mercantile networks. Brown had a classical education at the elite Friends' Latin School in Philadelphia and briefly taught at the Friends' Grammar School in the early 1790s but, unlike his male friends in the New York circle, he did not attend a university, since many Quakers and other dissenters in the United States and England did not patronize the educational institutions that served dominant Protestant groups. Although Brown's adult years led him from his Philadelphia origins to the intellectual world of the radical Enlightenment, his Quaker background nonetheless marks his development in fundamental ways. Progressive

Quaker traditions and doctrines concerning egalitarianism and equal authority for women in the Quaker community contributed to Brown's lifelong commitment to women's education and equality. Similarly, Quaker leadership in antislavery organization is part of the background for the implicit and explicit reflections on slavery in *Arthur Mervyn* and other writings. Interestingly, after having grown up as Quakers in the increasingly diversified Philadelphia of the late eighteenth century, Brown and all his siblings married non-Quakers. Consequently, Brown was formally dissociated from the Quaker meeting in Philadelphia when he married Elizabeth Linn, daughter of a Presbyterian minister, in 1804.

Growing up the fourth of five brothers and seven surviving siblings in a merchant family,[1] Brown's life was shaped by the mercantile culture of Philadelphia during the revolutionary era. The merchant careers of Brown's father and four brothers made him intimately familiar with the circum-Atlantic import-export commerce that was the main business of Philadelphia's port and with the mercantile and financial institutions, practices, and legal concerns that are dramatized in *Arthur Mervyn*.[2] Brown's father Elijah, who, like the novel's central character Arthur, came to Philadelphia as a young man from Chester County, Pennsylvania, had a checkered business career mainly as a conveyancer, a broker and manager for real estate, mortgage, and other transactions. In 1770, as a young man, Elijah had voyaged as supercargo, or family commercial representative, on merchant ventures to the West Indies on behalf of his brother-in-law Richard Waln. Much like the complex legal and illegal schemes involving colonial trade restrictions that play an important role in this novel, Elijah's West Indian transactions involved smuggling and other quasilegal strategies for evading the Townshend Acts, which taxed American imports at the time.[3] In 1777–1778, during the American Revolution, he was arrested and interned in Virginia as one of a group of Quakers deemed "dangerous to the State" because they refused on religious grounds to sign oaths of allegiance. In 1784, he was humiliatingly imprisoned for debt. Through all this, the father struggled to continue in business, partly sustained by the real estate holdings and financial interests of Brown's maternal aunt, Elizabeth Armitt.

Brown's older brothers Joseph and James, and the youngest brother, Elijah, Jr.—like the Thetford brothers in this novel—were import-export merchants who bought interest shares in ocean ventures as early as the 1780s. Joseph traveled frequently to

---

[1] Kafer, *Charles Brockden Brown's Revolution*, provides the numbers we use here, that is, five brothers and two sisters who survived to adulthood, plus three siblings who died at birth or in early infancy (45, 210, n36, 221, n25).

[2] See the accounts of Brown family business interests in Warfel, *Charles Brockden Brown*, 16–18, 23, 204; Clark, *Charles Brockden Brown*, 108–09, 194–95; and Kafer, 26–37, 45–46, 162, 214, n15.

[3] Kafer, 30–32. The Townshend Acts (1767) were an attempt to tax imports to the British North American colonies that aroused widespread colonial resistance and anger; they constitute a significant element of the context that led to the American Revolution ten years later. Smuggling and other forms of resistance to the acts were common.

the Caribbean, Northwestern Europe, the Mediterranean, and the Levant to oversee his shipping interests; he died in Flanders in 1807 on one of these voyages.[4] Charles himself became a reluctant partner in the family import-export firm, James Brown and Co., from late 1800 (just as he was finishing *Second Part*) to the firm's dissolution in 1806. Brown's brother Armitt also worked in key financial and banking institutions, first in the Treasury Department (where he was a clerk for Alexander Hamilton in the early 1790s) and later at the Bank of Pennsylvania. Thus *Arthur Mervyn*'s detailed backdrop concerning colonial trade networks and the culture of commerce—inheritances lost and disputed, debt and bankruptcy imprisonment, risky export investments, long-distance credit transfers and banking practices, and revolutionary era trade restrictions and insurance technicalities—are drawn not just from Brown's wider knowledge of the world around him, but also from his own family business background and first-hand experience.

Although his family intended for him to become a lawyer, Brown abandoned his Philadelphia law apprenticeship in 1793 and moved toward the circle of young, New York-based intellectuals who helped launch his literary career and, with Brown as one of their group, enacted progressive Enlightenment ideals of conversation, intellectual inquiry, and companionship.[5] The key figure in this group was Elihu Hubbard Smith (1771–1798), a Yale-educated physician who met Brown in Philadelphia in 1790 and played a crucial role in encouraging his literary ambitions. Aspects of Smith's life, including his efforts to treat yellow fever victims and progressive political and social ideas, figure as models for characters and events in this and several other Brown novels. Smith was an abolitionist and deist dedicated to progressive sociopolitical engagement.[6] His early death occurred while he and Brown were sharing an apartment and helping treat yellow fever victims during the New York yellow fever epidemic of 1798.

The New York group included a number of young male professionals who called themselves The Friendly Club along with female relatives and friends who were equally invested in progressive intellectual exchange and enlightened models for

---

[4] Warfel, 16–18.

[5] For discussions of this circle, see Waterman, *Republic of Intellect:* and Teute, "A 'Republic of Intellect'" and "The Loves of the Plants." The diaries of William Dunlap and Elihu Hubbard Smith provide detailed records of Brown's activities and relations within this circle.

[6] Deism was a progressive eighteenth-century response to Christianity. It affirmed the existence of a "supreme being" but rejected revelation, supernatural doctrines, and any notion of divine intervention in human affairs. Reason and science, rather than scripture and dogma, were the basis for religious belief. Late eighteenth-century writers often adopted a deistic stance as part of their general secular and rationalist critique of earlier institutions. Deism was associated with "natural religion" and the well-known metaphor of the deity as a "clock-maker" who creates the universe but makes no further intervention in it. Many leaders of the American revolutionary generation were deists, notably Benjamin Franklin and Thomas Jefferson. See Walters, *Rational Infidels: The American Deists.*

same-sex and other-sex companionship. This progressive model of companionship based on "reason and desire"[7] expressed through a "republic of letters" is a crucial context for Brown's astonishing burst of novel writing between 1798 and 1801. As one of this circle, Brown developed his knowledge of like-minded British radical-democratic writers of the period—above all William Godwin and Mary Wollstonecraft (whose books were already in Brown's household as a youth, before he met Smith)—as well as medical and physiological knowledges drawn from the Scottish Enlightenment (notably Erasmus Darwin), the French Naturalists, and other streams of Enlightenment thought. The circle was committed to abolitionist activism and many of the male members of the group were officers in abolition societies.[8] The circle's interest in similar groups of progressive British thinkers was strong enough that they established contact through correspondence with scientist Erasmus Darwin (via Smith), novelist Thomas Holcroft, and Godwin himself (via Dunlap and Godwin's ward Thomas Cooper, an actor who emigrated to the U.S. and moved in Brown's circles). Thus Brown's interest in European developments led him to participate in a network of like-minded endeavors, but his progressive, modernizing ideals meant that he felt little or no need to emulate Europe or the past as a superior culture.

If Brown's intellectual circle in New York constitutes one part of the context for his burst of novel writing, the other crucial element in this context is the explosive political atmosphere of the revolutionary 1790s as it culminated in the antirevolutionary backlash of 1797–1800. July 1793 to July 1794, the time period of this novel's action, was a crucial moment in the interrelated processes of the French Revolution (1789–1798), the Haitian Revolution (1791–1804), and events leading to the Irish uprisings of 1796–1798. Refugees from these revolutionary events filled the streets of 1790s Philadelphia and New York with émigrés of every stripe and color, from Royalist French aristocrats and planters from the Caribbean fleeing ongoing revolutions to enslaved "French negroes" or "wild Irish" revolutionary activists and intellectuals. By the end of the decade a severe reaction against the progressive ideals of the revolutionary era spread through the Atlantic world and was especially powerful in England, Germany, and the recently formed United States. During the administration of the second U.S. president, John Adams (1796–1800), the ruling Federalist party presided over an authoritarian, partisan response to real and imagined threats of revolutionary subversion and potential conflict with France.[9] Enacting the now-infamous Alien and Sedition Acts (1798), for example, Federalists made it illegal to criticize the Adams administration and legitimated the arrest and deportation of those deemed "dangerous" state enemies (i.e., French and Irish radicals). Paranoid

---

[7] Teute, "The Loves of the Plants."

[8] See "Three Abolitionist Addresses from Brown's Circle" and excerpts from Brown's "On the Consequences of Abolishing the Slave Trade to the West Indian Colonies" in this volume's Related Texts.

[9] See the discussions of this backlash and its implications in Cotlar, "The Federalists' Transatlantic Cultural Offensive of 1798"; Fischer, *The Revolution of American Conservatism*; Miller, *Crisis in Freedom: The Alien and Sedition Acts;* and Elkins and McKitrick, *The Age of Federalism.*

countersubversive fantasies about conspiracies led by mysterious groups like the Illuminati (a European secret society ostensibly plotting to overthrow Christian government), as well as elite panic about newly articulated ideals of universal democracy, including female equality and slave emancipation, contributed to this crisis.[10] Although these excesses led to the Federalists' defeat and the election of their Democratic-Republican opponent Jefferson in the 1800 election that occurred just weeks after the appearance of *Second Part*, the larger early romantic, culturally conservative wave announced by this convulsion put an end to the revolutionary era and laid the foundations for the more staid cultural order of the early nineteenth century. The many slaves, bound servants, free blacks, and laboring-class whites who figure for the most part namelessly throughout *Arthur Mervyn* embody the period's tectonic shift toward new modes of class and ethno-racial social organization. Arthur Mervyn himself, as a disinherited Scots-Irish youth who survives exposure to the city's mercantile corruption and fever before ending as a future doctor engaged to a Jewish refugee from revolutionary turmoil, embodies Brown's intervention in debates about the possible futures of U.S. society in the revolutionary aftermath.

Brown's efforts to establish himself as a writer were impressive indeed. After several years of experimentation with literary narratives that remained unfinished, Brown's novelistic phase began with the 1798 feminist dialogue *Alcuin* and continued unabated through the composition of eight novels by late 1801. In addition to these novels, Brown was editing the New York *Monthly Magazine* and publishing numerous essays, tales, and reviews. As noted earlier, the four "gothic" novels for which Brown is best known—*Wieland, Ormond, Arthur Mervyn*, and *Edgar Huntly*—were all published between September 1798 and September 1799 (*Second Part* appeared in September 1800), and there was a period in 1798 when all four were underway at once. Although Cold War era commentators often presented Brown as a writer who renounces his literary and progressive political ideals when he stops publishing novels in 1801, a more plausible explanation for his subsequent shift toward other forms of writing is that his novels did not make money, the particular conditions that fueled the intense novelistic burst from 1798 to 1801 changed (who could sustain such a rhythm of production?), and he became interested in new literary outlets. Like his older counterpart Godwin in England, Brown moves away from the novel because he feels it no longer offers an effective mode of argumentation in the increasingly conservative cultural and political environment that emerges after 1800. Had Brown lived longer, he might conceivably have returned to novel writing, as Godwin did in the later 1810s.

Brown's later literary career builds continuously on the novels and earlier writings. Between 1801 and his death from tuberculosis in 1810, Brown edited two important periodicals: *The Literary Magazine* (1803–1807)—a literary and cultural miscellany

---

[10] On the countersubversive fantasies that were a basic element of this crisis, see Hofstadter, *The Paranoid Style*; Wood, "Conspiracy and the Paranoid Style"; and White, "The Value of Conspiracy Theory."

that renewed his experience with the earlier *Monthly Magazine* and that he filled with his own essays and fiction—and *The American Register* (1807–1809), a historical and political periodical that featured Brown's "Annals of Europe and America," a comprehensive narrative of Napoleonic-era geopolitics. In addition, he undertook a novel-length, experimental historical fiction known as *The Historical Sketches* (1803–1806) that was published posthumously, a now-lost play, and several lengthy, quasinovelistic pamphlets on expansion into the Louisiana territory and Jefferson's embargo policies (1803, 1809). These writings continue Brown's career-long concern with the link between historical and fictional ("romance") writing, and extend the earlier program of "reason and desire" that makes writing an instrument of progressive, educational principles in the public sphere. Rather than dramatizing the ways individuals are shaped by social pressures and crisis contexts, as he did in his novels, the later Brown explores forms of historical narrative and the larger historical world that made up the allusive backdrop of the earlier fiction. The critical perspective on global webs of imperial commerce, colonialism, and slavery that figures behind the frauds and fortunes of *Arthur Mervyn*, for example, becomes explicit and is explored in detail in the later histories and essays.

The Woldwinite Writers and Brown's Novelistic Method

The world of Brown's novels, with their gothic emotional intensities, disorienting psychosocial violence, and imbedded backstories and subplots, may be difficult to sort out on first encounter. Understanding some basics about Brown's primary intellectual and political sources and his well-defined novelistic method, however, can help the reader understand features of his novels that might otherwise seem difficult to grasp.

Unlike many authors of eighteenth-century fiction, Brown had a well-developed methodology and set of themes for writing novels. His method draws on and further develops the ideas of the British radical-democratic writers of the period. Brown's enthusiastic reception of these Woldwinite[11] ("Anglo-Jacobin") writers—above all Mary Wollstonecraft, William Godwin, Thomas Holcroft, Robert Bage, Helen Maria Williams, and Thomas Paine—undergirds his entire literary project after the

---

[11] We use the term "Woldwinite" to highlight, through an abbreviation of Wollstonecraft and Godwin, this group's special place among the British radical democrats of the 1790s. The term "Godwinians" erases the crucial role of Wollstonecraft and other women in this group, a role that was particularly important for Brown and many other writers. Similarly, these British writers are also discussed as "Jacobins" or "Anglo-Jacobins," a name used by opponents to link them to the most authoritarian and partisan faction of the French Revolution, but the group explicitly rejected the "Jacobin" position in favor of its own distinct set of cultural-political positions. For studies of literary Woldwinism, see: Clemit, *The Godwinian Novel;* Kelly, *The English Jacobin Novel 1780–1805* and *English Fiction of the Romantic Period, 1789–1830;* Butler, *Jane Austen and the War of Ideas;* and J. M. S. Tompkins, *The Popular Novel in England, 1770–1800.*

mid-1790s. The British "Dissenter" culture of highly educated middle-class professionals and the clubs and academies from which these writers emerged was the wider context of Brown's own Philadelphia Quaker community. Brown was exposed to the Woldwinite writers through his father's copies of their works even before he moved into the New York circle and explored their writings in greater detail.[12]

The Woldwinite agenda rests on three basic arguments that draw together the main strands of knowledge and critique in the late, radical Enlightenment. Drawing on well-established eighteenth-century arguments and themes, such as associative sentiment (the idea that emotions are communicated from one individual to another and may be used to encourage constructive, progressive behavior), these arguments sum up this group's rejection of the pre-revolutionary order, and their conviction that social progress may be achieved by altering dominant ways of thinking through peaceful cultural means such as literature. First, the social order of the old regime (monarchy and feudalism) is to be rejected because it is artificial and illegitimate, violating the natural equality of humanity by imposing coercive hierarchies of caste and faith. Second, given that the old regime maintained its domination through an obscurantist mythology of territorialized race, priestly tricks, and a politics of secret plots, conspiracies, and lies, a new social order will require the development of more rational, constructive, and transparent institutions and practices. Third, the illustration of progressive behavior in print and other media will multiply to generate larger social transformation because society works through chains of associative sentiment and emulation. These cultural relays will generate progressive change since the illustration of virtuous behaviors and results will spread through imitation, as each person learns new and improved ways of acting by observing others. Proceeding from these assumptions, the Woldwinites' critique leads to their antistatism, their distrust of institutions, and their use of cultural forms such as literature to advance their program. Because they believed in the natural propulsion of cooperative behavior and the guidance of critical reason, these writers see social change as resulting from the amplification of transformed local, interpersonal or intersubjective relations. Thus, as we say today, the personal is political.

In their assumption that global historical change begins from the bottom up with the premeditated transformation of relations among a small circle, the Woldwinites are an early instance of cultural avant-gardism that aims to develop means of worldly social revolution through arts and manners rather than political parties or state institutions. In contemporary terms, the Woldwinites introduce a relatively straightforward, albeit limited, idea of environmental or social construction, the notion that individuals are shaped or conditioned by their social environments and circumstances. Their ideas about social construction are limited in that they position themselves as innocent participants and do not always recognize the dilemmas implicit in their own social program (particularly its assumptions about sentiment, benevolence,

---

[12] For the Woldwinite writings in Brown's household, see Warfel, 17–18, 27; Clark, 16; Kafer, 46, 66–72.

and associative imitation) and insofar as they direct their critique mainly at the hierarchical inequalities of the old regime while neglecting the emergent structures of liberal capitalism. Brown adopts their environmentalist argument but also, as a second-wave Woldwinite, recognizes that their ideas about social construction and action are incomplete. His fiction attempts to think through these limitations and their implications in ways that we will explore in greater detail when we turn to the plot of *Arthur Mervyn* in what follows.

Building on these basic Woldwinite ideas, Brown's fictional method is articulated in several key essays on narrative technique and the social role of the novel that appear at the height of his novelistic phase, most notably "Walstein's School of History" (August–September 1799) and "The Difference between History and Romance" (April 1800).[13] To summarize this method, we can say that Brown's novels combine elements of history and fiction, placing his characters in situations of social and historical distress as a means of engaging a wider audience with considerations of progressive behavior. His novels explore how common, disempowered subjects such as Arthur Mervyn respond to damaging social conditions caused by defects in dominant ideas and practices. Through their interconnected patterns of socially conditioned behavior, dramatic suspense, and gothic intensities, Brown's fictions urge readers to reflect on how to overcome corruption in order to construct a more "virtuous," more equal and fulfilling society.

This approach begins with Brown's understanding of the relation between historical and fictional ("romance") writing. History and fiction, he argues, are not different because one deals with factual and the other with fictional materials. Rather, they are intrinsically connected as two sides of one coin: history describes and documents the results of actions, while fiction investigates the possible motives and circumstances that cause these actions. Fictions are thus narrative experiments that tease out possible preconditions for historical events or behaviors and that reason through social problems presented as hypothetical situations; they are a form of conjectural or counterfactual history. Whereas history describes events, romance analyzes and projects the probable causes, conditions, and preconditions of events. The "Walstein" essay builds on this distinction and develops a threefold plan for novel writing, providing a fuller account of the rationale and essential themes that inform Brown's fiction. Indeed, "Walstein" is keyed directly to *Arthur Mervyn* and provides implicit commentary on it. The essay's closing paragraphs illustrate Brown's method with a thinly disguised plot outline for *Mervyn's* first part. The historian Walstein combines history and romance in such a way as to promote "moral and political" engagement while rejecting universal truths, stressing the situatedness of engaged political response in noble and classical figures such as the Roman statesman Cicero. Walstein's pupil Engel then modernizes and develops the theory by adding that a romance, to be effective in today's world, must be addressed to a wide popular audience and draw its characters not from the elite but from the same lower-status groups that will read

---

[13] These essays are included in this volume's Related Texts.

and be moved by the work. History and romance alike must address issues and situations familiar to their modern audience, notably the common inequalities arising from relations of sex and property. Thus a modern literature will insert ordinary individuals like Arthur Mervyn, rather than elite actors like Cicero, into crisis situations in which they must negotiate contemporary conflicts involving money and erotic desire or gender relations. Finally, a thrilling style and form are crucial, since a romance capable of moving its audience to considerations of progressive action must, as Brown writes, "be so arranged as to inspire, at once, curiosity and belief, to fasten the attention, and thrill the heart." In this manner, Brown's method uses the twists and turns of his plots, and dramatic settings such as yellow fever epidemics, as ways to illustrate and think through interrelated social problems and encourage an engaged response to them.

Woldwinite Perspectives in *Arthur Mervyn*

Brown's use of Woldwinite ideas is particularly evident in *Arthur Mervyn*, for this novel (or "romance," to be precise) highlights plot points and arguments openly drawn from the group's two best-known fictions, William Godwin's *Things as They Are; or The Adventures of Caleb Williams* (1794) and Thomas Holcroft's *Anna St. Ives* (1792). From *Caleb Williams*, Brown takes the tale of a secretary who finds that his investigation into the mysterious criminality of Falkland, his noble employer, leads to his own implication in deceit, to his subsequent incrimination, and to his being relentlessly pursued; the ensuing series of adventures provides a socially progressive exposé of inequality and political problems in England. From *Anna St. Ives*, Brown takes a socially progressive misalliance—a romance between an upper-class woman and a plebian man—as well as the dramatic decision to burn forged money. *Arthur Mervyn*'s relation to Godwin's fiction has long been recognized, but the relation to Holcroft is equally significant. In the period preceding Godwin's seminal publication of *Enquiry Concerning Political Justice and Its Influence on Modern Morals and Happiness* (1793), the most complete statement of Woldwinite principles, he and Holcroft had intensive discussions that were crucial in the development of that landmark work. Since Godwin himself recognized Holcroft's romance as an earlier fictional emplotting of the political science he was about to summarize in the *Enquiry*, Godwin's treatise may also be read as an attempt to systematize the ideas first portrayed in *Anna St. Ives*. That book's plot revolves around the successful attempt by Anna St. Ives, the daughter of the manor, and Frank Henley, the gardener's son, to overcome the class prejudice that would prevent their marriage, the demonic machinations of her libertine aristocrat brother, and the grasping avarice of Henley's father. Almost literally talking each other into having the confidence to break through obsolete, yet still-powerful barriers of status difference, Anna and Frank express rationalized desire for each other and insist that the marriage of two virtuous people can provide a beacon for emulation and function as a first step toward a generally more perfect civil society. Holcroft's tale expresses a generally optimistic belief that conversational sincerity among friends can transform negative erotic passion into a socially productive performance and that a small cultural vanguard can catalyze larger historical transformation in ways that political economy and legislation cannot.

Although Brown's novels and their endings are usually relatively pessimistic or critical in tone, *Arthur Mervyn* provides the exception to this rule with a positive resolution that seems to affirm Holcroft and Godwin's earlier faith in the possibility of progressive change. *Arthur Mervyn*'s plot ends with the ribald foreshadowing of sexual union between Arthur and the heiress Achsa Fielding, an ending that is markedly different from the moody tone of anomie and marginalization that closes Brown's other tales. The other novels, from *Wieland* (August 1798) to *Jane Talbot* (December 1801), present these kinds of personal and social outcomes in far more troubling terms. Seen in the context of his other fictions, then, *Arthur Mervyn* relies on the behavioral predicates of Woldwinite thinking even more clearly than its companion novels, as Brown crafts a tale that is remarkably positive about the central character's ability to flourish, learn, and provide worthy models for emulation.

As suggested in the "Walstein's School" essay, Brown presents *Arthur Mervyn* as a tale about an untutored individual's response to a socially corrupt environment, following the Woldwinite slogan that humans are mainly conditioned by their social context rather than individual inclinations or inherited traits. Mervyn begins the novel as a disinherited Scots-Irish youth who enters the commercial city, survives the challenges of yellow fever and mercantile deceit, decides to become a physician and help those around him, and finally marries and looks forward to his future as a member of the professional classes. Although one generation of literary critics, trained within a modernist dedication to plumbing the psychic depths of literary characters, devoted great energy to evaluating the relative authenticity of Mervyn's inner self as he negotiates Philadelphia's cultural landscape,[14] Brown, as he makes clear, is not primarily interested in psychologizing or epistemological kinds of questions. We might say that, rather than understanding social structures by reference to problematic individual perceptions, Brown clarifies problematic individual perceptions by reference to social structures. The novel's characters are mainly bearers of social positions, and their often unstable mental processes are the results of manifold pressures and "circumstances," as the Woldwinites might put it, bearing down upon them. Mervyn, for example, is quite literally stripped down and disoriented as he enters Philadelphia so that Brown can dramatize the ways that social pressures and crises will shape and challenge him. The enlightened, and notably female-centric, circle of women and men that Mervyn builds around him as he labors to help others in the *Second Part* is

---

[14] Cold War era discussions focusing on Mervyn's authenticity (with the implication that Brown is emphasizing psychologistic or skeptical epistemological models) include Warner Berthoff, "Adventures of the Young Man: An Approach to Charles Brockden Brown" (1957); Brancaccio, "Studied Ambiguity: *Arthur Mervyn* and the Problem of the Unreliable Narrator" (1970); Russo, "The Chameleon of Convenient Vice: A Study of the Narrative of *Arthur Mervyn*" (1974); Bell, "'The Double-Tongued Deceiver': Sincerity and Duplicity in the Novels of Charles Brockden Brown" (1974); and Elliott, "Narrative Unity and Moral Resolution in *Arthur Mervyn*" (1981).

precisely the kind of forward-looking group working to overcome obsolete social distinctions that Brown and his friends learned about and themselves enacted in their activities during the 1790s. The way Brown explains the fictional origins of the narrative (at the end of Chapter II.22), which is organized by the frame narrator Dr. Stevens for the first three-fourths of the novel and subsequently by Mervyn beginning in Chapter II.16, makes the novel itself an exemplary production of such enlightened modes of cooperation, designed, in the manner described in "Walstein's School of History," to encourage further emulation and public awareness of the problems it addresses.

Fever and Urban Crisis

Arthur Mervyn's best-known feature is its representation of the Philadelphia yellow fever epidemic of August–October 1793, which appears in Chapters 15–23 of the novel's first part and is closely related to the novel's influential depiction of the city's dense urban landscape. The novel follows the epidemic's timeline and urban topography precisely, from its beginnings in Water Street by the city's wharves in mid-August to its peak mortality rate of over one hundred deaths a day around October 9–13, the moment when Mervyn returns to the city to search for Wallace in Chapter 15. These chapters and the rest of the novel provide carefully chosen glimpses of particular aspects of the epidemic, such as the work of free blacks as nurses and undertakers or the emergency Bush-Hill hospital, which was organized in September as civil order broke down and thousands of refugees fled the city.[15] In connection with the emphasis on Caribbean commerce and slave revolt that runs through the novel's backstories, the novel alludes to particular Caribbean physicians who played significant roles in debates over fever treatment and the public response to the emergency, such as Jean Devèze and Edward Stevens, the likely source of the name that Brown introduces in Chapter 4 of *Second Part* for the novel's frame narrator.[16] The novel's depiction of the fever was sufficiently notable for contemporaries that it prompted

---

[15] For general accounts of the epidemic, see Powell, *Bring Out Your Dead: The Great Plague of Yellow Fever in Philadelphia in 1793*; and the web-based resources in Arnebeck, *Destroying Angel: Benjamin Rush, Yellow Fever and the Birth of Modern Medicine* (www.geocities.com/bobarnebeck/fever1793.html). For historical discussions of the fever's social and political implications, see the essays in Estes and Smith, eds., *A Melancholy Scene of Devastation: The Public Response to the 1793 Philadelphia Yellow Fever Epidemic*; Kornfield, "Crisis in the Capital: The Cultural Significance of Philadelphia's Great Yellow Fever Epidemic"; and Taylor, *"We Live in the Midst of Death": Yellow Fever, Moral Economy, and Public Health in Philadelphia, 1793–1805*.

[16] Since the historical Dr. Edward Stevens was appointed U.S. Consul to Haiti in early 1799, timing suggests that his reemergence on the public scene at that juncture was a factor in Brown's use of this name in *Second Part* (September 1800). On Edward Stevens, see Day, *Edward Stevens*, and Chernow, *Alexander Hamilton*. On Jean Devèze, see Powell, *Bring Out Your Dead* and Arnebeck, *Destroying Angel*.

journalist Mathew Carey, author of the most popular account of the epidemic (see the excerpts from Carey in this volume's Related Texts), to write that *Arthur Mervyn* "gives a vivid and terrifying picture, probably not too highly coloured, of the horrors of that period" and later served as a model for Mary Shelley's depiction of an apocalyptic plague in her novel *The Last Man* (1826; Shelley had previously turned to Brown before beginning *Frankenstein* in 1818).[17]

In considering the fever's place in the novel, it is important to bear in mind that these well-known chapters take on their full significance in connection with the novel's underlying concerns with commercial corruption, Caribbean slave revolution and abolition, and the larger social transformations of the revolutionary 1790s. As Shelley understood, fever figures in *Arthur Mervyn* as a dramatic condensation of the period's multifaceted experience of social crisis and transformation. It constitutes a spectacular crisis context in which Brown dramatizes the effects of social behaviors and institutions.[18] The disease had great social and political consequences in the eighteenth-century Atlantic world, especially as it devastated imperial armies attempting to regain control over valuable sugar colonies after the Haitian Revolution, and Brown and his circle were well-read in the period's literature on it. Brown himself lived through several epidemics and survived the disease when he caught it in August 1798, during the same New York epidemic that killed his close friend Dr. Elihu Hubbard Smith and associate Dr. Giambattista Scandella, whom Brown memorializes as the heroic Maravegli in Chapter 16 of *Arthur Mervyn*. Brown likely began composition of the novel's fever scenes shortly after his 1798 experience of the disease, and earlier that same year he had already begun a series of narratives, which would culminate in *Arthur Mervyn*, that emphasize yellow fever epidemics as dramatic settings.[19]

---

[17] For more on Mary Shelley's response to Brown, see Shapiro, "I Could Kiss Him One Minute and Kill Him the Next!"; and Steinman, "Transatlantic Cultures: Godwin, Brown, and Mary Shelley."

[18] Numerous later writers have used the 1793 epidemic in related ways, up to and including a recent spate of narratives and children's stories published at the beginning of the twenty-first century. Recent treatments generally focus on the epidemic's significance as a watershed moment for the Philadelphia free black community, part of the context for the emergence of the first African American public institutions. Most notable are John Edgar Wideman's fictions: the story collection *Fever* (1989), the novel *The Cattle Killing* (1996), and the related story "Ascent by Balloon from the Yard of Walnut Street Jail" (1996), all of which explore the moment's significance for African American experience. The recent emergence of children's narratives about the epidemic is a related phenomenon. See Ellen Norman Stern, *The French Physician's Boy; a Story of Philadelphia's 1793 Yellow Fever Epidemic* (2001; fictionalizing the story of David Nassy, a Sephardic Caribbean doctor who worked in Philadelphia during the epidemic); Laurie Halse Anderson, *Fever 1793* (2002); and Jim Murphy, *An American Plague: The True and Terrifying Story of the Yellow Fever Epidemic of 1793* (2003).

[19] Brown's interrelated fever narratives, all from 1798–1799, are the essay series "The Man at Home" (February–April 1798), the novel *Ormond; or, The Secret Witness* (January 1799), and *Arthur Mervyn's* first part (March or April 1799). The eleventh installment of "The Man at Home," later republished as "Pestilence and Bad Government Compared," is a separate fever narrative distinct from the larger fever setting of the series in which it appears and is included in the Related

Although the actual cause and nature of yellow fever were not understood at this time (scientific understanding of the fever was established only in the early twentieth century), the disease itself is a viral hemorrhagic fever carried by *Aedes aegypti* mosquitoes, a plague that probably entered Atlantic culture with the African slave trade that figures in so many of this novel's backstories. Late-summer yellow fever epidemics were a periodic feature of life in North American cities at this time, but the 1793 Philadelphia episode became the best known and most frequently invoked of all in American accounts.[20] This was partly because of its sheer magnitude and devastation (about 5,000 died, and about 17,000 fled the city, whose population was roughly 55,000 at that time)[21] but also, just as importantly, because it became a flashpoint for struggle over the function of public institutions (such as the hospitals and prisons depicted in *Arthur Mervyn*) and over attitudes about race, class, and immigration that intersected with the period's partisan anxieties. Because the disease's etiology and transmission by mosquitoes were not yet understood, for example, many debates racialized the fever, supposing that its nature and virulence varied according to race and that Africans were less susceptible than Europeans. A variant xenophobic fantasy even speculated that the French might be less susceptible than Anglos and other Protestant Europeans. The city's free blacks were on the front lines of emergency care, often pressed into service as nurses and undertakers on the mistaken assumption that they were immune to contagion. The arguments in this volume's Related Texts from Mathew Carey's popular account of the fever and from the reply to his racialization of the debate by African American ministers Absalom Jones and Richard Allen are now frequently studied elements of the contemporary literature.

Early debates about the origin of the fever were almost immediately politicized: a xenophobic contagion school believed the fever was contagious and resulted from the importation of infected goods and French, African, and other "foreigners," while a miasma (or environmental) school recognized that the fever was not contagious and argued that it was caused by poor urban design and hygiene. Scientifically speaking, both were far from the mark but partly accurate in intuitive terms. The mosquitoes that carry the disease were transported by shipping vessels from the Caribbean; but since the disease is not contagious and mosquitoes require warm stagnant water for breeding, the city's filthy docks, abysmal hygienic conditions, and late summer heat created ideal conditions for the outbreak. Similarly, ongoing debates about different approaches to medical treatment (between advocates of vigorous purging and

---

Texts here. For a summary of the available information on Brown's experience of the fever and its relation to the composition of *Arthur Mervyn*, see Grabo, "Historical Essay."

[20] The 1793 Philadelphia event was the worst of many on the U.S. Atlantic seaboard during these years (Philadelphia 1793, 1797, 1798, 1799, 1802; New York 1791, 1795, 1798, 1805; Baltimore 1794; New Haven 1794; Boston 1798).

[21] Statistics concerning the 1793 epidemic vary significantly in different sources; we use numbers from Estes and Smith, *A Melancholy Scene of Devastation*.

bloodletting versus a rest-and-fluids school) became highly partisanized and led to widely publicized libel and malpractice suits after a later 1798 outbreak.[22]

In addition to medically focused concerns, innovative responses to the public care emergency created by the epidemic had other important sociopolitical implications. As Brown suggests with the novel's interrelated subplots, efforts to cope with the emergency on all levels took place within the larger revolution-driven context of the year 1793, when Philadelphia was receiving large numbers of refugees from the French and Haitian Revolutions. The private property of a Loyalist was seized by an ad hoc committee of previously marginalized merchants and craftsmen to set up a hospital, the Bush-Hill facility, dramatized in the novel's Chapter 18. The laboring poor and nonwhites who could not afford to flee both used the crisis context to exert newly found collective authority in the absence of city elites, and died and suffered at far higher rates than the gentry elite who routinely waited out yellow fever epidemics in their country homes. The power vacuum that was created when the local, state, and national governments adjourned and abandoned the capital in early September, as the epidemic reached crisis proportions, gave political have-nots and previously marginalized class, trade, and ethno-racial groups sudden political opportunities to assert themselves in ways that were hitherto unavailable in the United States. This is one of the reasons that 1793 was also a year that saw the rise of new Democratic-Republican societies, which played an important role in the decade's subsequent political landscape.[23] George Lesher, for example, owner of the tavern that Mervyn visits in Chapter 3 on his first arrival in the city, was a well-known participant in these societies. The breakdown of civil order and social debates that occurred during the Philadelphia epidemic did not match the political turbulence of the French Revolution and Terror (1793 saw the executions of Louis XVI and Marie Antoinette, and the September 1793–July 1794 period of the "Reign of Terror" corresponds closely to the novel's July 1793–July 1794 time frame) or the Haitian violence that drove thousands of planters to flee that colony with black and mixed-race companions, servants, and slaves. However, the multiple struggles connected with this yellow fever epidemic are also distant parts of the same Atlantic waves of class, race, and ideological conflict that had their epicenters in these other sources of turmoil. Beyond the immediate and clinical dimensions of the epidemic, it is these wider social

---

[22] On the politicization of fever debates, see Pernick, "Politics, Parties, and Pestilence: Epidemic Yellow Fever in Philadelphia and the Rise of the First Party System"; Miller, "Passions and Politics: The Multiple Meanings of Benjamin Rush's Treatment for Yellow Fever"; and the other essays included in Estes and Smith, eds., *A Melancholy Scene of Devastation*. The polemical Nones-Gazette exchange included in the Related Texts contains echoes of these fever-related libel suits and pamphlet wars.

[23] The Nones-Gazette exchange included in this volume's Related Texts takes place around racially charged responses to a Democratic-Republican Society meeting. On the ad hoc committees and extragovernmental efforts to cope with the breakdown of civil institutions, see Powell, *Bring Out Your Dead*. For the emergence of the democratic clubs, see Foner, *The Democratic-Republican Societies, 1790–1800;* and Koschnik, "The Democratic Societies of Philadelphia and the Limits of the American Public Sphere, circa 1793–1795."

struggles and "mysteries" of early U.S. and Atlantic social order that are literalized in the novel's presentation of the fever, for example when Mervyn is struck on the head by a mysterious black figure in a mirror scene in Chapter 16, which underlines the racial components and tensions of U.S. identity categories, or when the contagionist-environmentalist debate is explained to Mervyn by the enlightened character Medlicote in the first part's Chapter 18.[24] Seen from this perspective, Mervyn's decision to become a doctor and his ongoing medical training in *Second Part* are only the most evident aspect of his response to the fever and of the novel's engagement with the events of 1793.

The Vice of Commerce, the Heart of the City

Given the prevalence of fraud, vengeful creditors, and a range of mercantile concerns throughout the novel, it is not difficult to see that the underlying social malady that surfaces during the fever is corruption tied to commerce.[25] The early modern rise and revaluation of commerce—making a once-marginalized and suspect dimension of the social order into the central concern and structuring principle of the modern state—is a frequently told story and a crucial context for understanding *Arthur Mervyn*. Throughout the eighteenth century, writers and academics increasingly revalued commerce, providing new arguments about its nature and implications, and Brown's novel responds to these debates on several levels. At the end of the Middle Ages and beginning of the early modern period, commerce was generally viewed with suspicion and conceptualized with ancient ideas from Greco-Roman antiquity and the early Christian tradition. Although it was functionally and pragmatically clear that mercantile commerce was increasingly necessary for modernizing societies—monarchies and the Catholic church alike required the revenues that the merchant class generated and managed, if only to underwrite their internecine wars and imperial adventures—nevertheless in a doctrinal or "official" sense commercial institutions and practices were still considered morally questionable and culturally foreign to the late feudal order that prevailed up to the age of revolution in the late eighteenth century. The outsider status of merchants was amplified when early modern commerce utilized the kinds of long-distance networks maintained by religious

---

[24] On the first part's twinned mirror scenes and their relation to the novel's wider concern with race and masculinist civic identity, see Smith-Rosenberg, "Black Gothic: The Shadowy Origins of the American Bourgeoisie."

[25] For perspectives on the novel's focus on commerce and corruption, see Baker, *Securing the Commonwealth: Debt, Speculation, and Writing in the Making of Early America*; Cohen, "*Arthur Mervyn* and His Elders: The Ambivalence of Youth in the Early Republic"; Hinds, *Private Property: Charles Brockden Brown's Gendered Economics of Virtue*; Samuels, "Plague and Politics in 1793: *Arthur Mervyn*"; Smith-Rosenberg, "Black Gothic"; Tompkins, *Sensational Designs: The Cultural Work of American Fiction, 1790–1860*; and Weyler, *Intricate Relations: Sexual and Economic Desire in American Fiction, 1789–1814*.

and ethnic trading "nations" such as Jews and Armenians, communities whose very disadvantages—their political marginalization (outside the nation-state) and far-flung geographical exile and dispersal—worked to advantage when their family-based networks allowed them to safeguard the flow of money, credit, and commodities between distant regions.

By the eighteenth century, the social groups most closely associated with trade were coalescing to form a more self-aware commercial urban middle class, the bourgeoisie (derived from *bourg* or burgh, for "town").[26] As the early bourgeoisie gained prominence, it increasingly sought to replace older and mainly disapproving ideas and language concerning commerce with newer and more positive frames so as to lend commerce greater legitimacy and social status and to use ethical assumptions about marketplace behavior as a means of securing commodity and credit transfers in an age that still lacked strong national and international laws for policing and protecting trade. The steady efforts of representative bourgeois figures such as Benjamin Franklin, the most iconic early American booster of commercial society, gradually revised prevailing ideas about commerce to present it as a positive, modernizing force that could replace the "old regime" with forward-looking, presumably more egalitarian social energies and principles. In short, one of the great transformations of Brown's era was to legitimate commerce as a basic feature of the social order, transforming an age-old suspicion of moneymaking into a wholehearted celebration of its potential to generate new values and social relations. It is only after the revolutionary age that moneymaking has generally been regarded in Western societies as a "good" and honorable thing and that the forces involved in commerce have become conceptualized in political and cultural doctrines as liberalism, "possessive individualism," and so on.

A key aspect of this proliferating defense of commerce was the claim that while individual men may be harmfully selfish or greedy, the *collective* or overall result of commerce is to increase social fairness, harmony, and moral advancement. Many writers put forward aspects of these claims, but the Edinburgh writers of the "Scottish School," such as Adam Ferguson and Adam Smith, were especially influential in shaping these arguments into what, by the end of the century, began to appear as a coherent common sense. Ferguson, in *An Essay on the History of Civil Society* (1767), argues that human social development can be divided into ascending stages, from savagery and barbarism to civilization. The highest, "civilized" stage is commercial society because commerce epitomizes the evolution from a violence-based system of dominating concrete territory and property to a more advanced or "polite" form of social intercourse organized by a "moral community" of traders who trust one another, peacefully circulating intangible goods like credit. Because the nature of commerce and finance relies on virtual goods that cannot be forcibly handled (abstract values notated by money, credit, interest, etc.), commerce depends on inculcating a sense of shame and guilt regarding nonpayment of debts, a new morality that differs

---

[26] See Wallerstein, "The Bourgeois(ie) as Concept and Reality."

from the warrior caste's belief that might makes right. For Ferguson, a commercial society run by the middle classes is the most "civilized" type; commercial society is therefore "civil," rather than military-feudal, society.

Adam Smith, still largely considered one of the authoritative writers on free market economics, provides a further explanation for the mechanics of bourgeois society. In *An Inquiry into the Nature and Causes of the Wealth of Nations* (1776), Smith holds that humans are naturally selfish and that we trade to satisfy our own desires, rather than for any general or common benefit. Yet for us to receive the goods we desire, we must be able to satisfy someone else's desires and convince them to trust and trade with us. As two traders learn that they achieve their own satisfaction only by helping others satisfy their partners in the mutual exchange of goods, they learn to moderate their otherwise aggressive and mistrustful behavior. The marketplace becomes a sphere in which men come together to teach each other how to trade peacefully in ways that are, in principle, different from belligerent exploitation by nobles and priests, whose institutions merely reinforce hierarchy and submission. The market-place is thus a classroom of pacifism that balances and gradually corrects men's bullying animosity toward one another. Smith famously calls this regulating force the "invisible hand" of the market that trains humans softly, rather than by smacking them into sense. Although many later, neoliberal thinkers claim that Smith legiti-mates and celebrates a fundamentally individualistic model of competition, such claims profoundly misread his arguments. For eighteenth-century writers, competi-tion is a passion-driven action that should be moderated, not amplified, by the civi-lizing fellow feeling of commerce. For Smith, Ferguson, and others, mercantile exchange provides both an experience and a model of a more polite and amiable so-ciety. In their thinking, each round of successful trade not only leads on to the next but also has a multiplier effect in establishing a larger, peaceful sphere of commerce. Ultimately, in this model, commerce's upward spiral creates a global domain in which the bourgeoisie functions as the dominant force in a new world of interna-tionalized business, displacing the aristocracy and institutional religion, and driving a gradual evolution toward new and better forms of government.

These widely held claims came under attack by the end of the eighteenth century and throughout the nineteenth. The Scottish thinkers' assumptions about ever-in-creasing trade and about the market's tendency to regulate itself harmoniously were challenged initially by figures such as Thomas Malthus, and later by utilitarians such as Jeremy Bentham and John Stuart Mill. These writers claimed that the market's tendency to expand would soon bump up against the limits of natural resources and that the collision between consumer demand and the supply of goods would force negative social changes (an early instance of twenty-first-century concerns about overconsumption and global warming). These post-Smith writers saw crisis and ex-ploitation, rather than cooperation and progress, as the main drivers of sociohistori-cal change and as the characteristic features of commercial society. Karl Marx, for example, later suggested that modern commerce stems from a desire to accumulate profit through exchange that structurally produces human misery and not, as Smith had argued, from mutually satisfying and cooperative trading. If profits result when one group (the wealthy bourgeoisie) cheats and exploits another (the wage workers, women, colonial slaves, and other lower-status groups who supply them with labor and a market for their goods), then the expansion of commerce creates new emergencies of survival, not their prevention. In this argument, the nature of commerce further depends on its ever-increasing mysteriousness, which makes the source of profit in exploitative production more difficult to see and understand. For Marx, the invisible hand of the marketplace was the hidden hand of class warfare waged by the very bourgeois who celebrated themselves as peaceful agents of cooperation and progress.

The language of Marx's critique of Smith was, of course, not historically available to Brown. Nevertheless, Brown stands as another early dissenter from the belief systems of Ferguson and Smith, and his arguments connect with those of Marx and other critics of Smith in significant ways. Brown's depiction of a Philadelphia that is profoundly deranged by the activity of its mercantile elites differentiates him from the Woldwinite writers on whom he otherwise depends for arguments concerning social processes and the path toward a more perfect society. Although the careers of the Woldwinite writers coincide with the early stages of the Industrial Revolution, they rarely focus on the mechanics of commercial society.[27] They see the greatest obstacle to the creation of an egalitarian world as the then dominant order of the landed elites and institutionalized religion (nobles and priests, the sword and the cross, what Stendhal calls the red and the black). For example, while Holcroft's *Anna St. Ives* lampoons the entrepreneurial aspirations of Frank Henley's father (the gardener's efforts to get St. Ives to borrow money from him to finance landscaping is presented mainly for comic effect rather than as a substantial concern), the real threat lies with Anna's aristocratic brother and not with the emerging bourgeoisie. Similarly, Caleb Williams in Godwin's novel must fear the gentry landlord Falkland, but not the representatives of rising mercantile forces.

Writing from the social context of 1790s Philadelphia and New York, Brown shifts the Woldwinites' focus on the old aristocracy of landed elites to an examination of the rising merchant elite and new wealth of the early American republic. Rather than dramatizing Mervyn's entry into Philadelphia's world of commerce as an experience of fellow feeling and Franklinesque opportunity, Brown's narrative describes arrival in the city as a disorienting fall into webs of deceit and manipulation. Arriving at night and walking down the iconic thoroughfare of Philadelphia's Market Street in Chapter 3, Mervyn emphasizes gleaming street lamps and other urban improvements that were a point of pride for Benjamin Franklin, who cited their creation as a

---

[27] Of the Woldwinites, Mary Wollstonecraft is perhaps the most notable for a concern with speculation, commercial intrigue, and the economic dimensions of the revolution debates of the 1790s; see, for example, the excerpts from her *Letters Written during a Short Residence in Sweden, Norway, and Denmark* (1796) in this volume's Related Texts. Thomas Paine's *Agrarian Justice* (1795–1796), his most explicit work on class relations and socioeconomic structures, was also significant for Brown.

civic achievement.[28] The novel presents these lamps and their marketplace setting in a very different manner, however, when Mervyn cites lines from Milton's *Paradise Lost* that describe the blazing lamps of Pandaemonium in Hell and winds up at Lesher's tavern in the city's "Hell-Town" district. When the magical glare of the city's bright lights is examined more closely, Brown seems to suggest, it reveals a self-absorbed and almost demonic underworld. The source of this subterranean vice is the city's merchants, whose business, in this novel, is mainly to devise new ways to defraud each other. While Welbeck's counterfeits and lies in the novel's first part are the most obvious example, the novel as a whole makes it clear that his acts are more routine than not and that merchants like Thetford, or higher agents of commerce such as Old Thetford and Jamieson, in the novel's *Second Part*, are even more dangerous than Welbeck. Mervyn's first encounter with commercial "benevolence," when the clerk Wallace meets him in Lesher's tavern and offers him a meal and a room to sleep in, turns out to be a prank with potentially serious consequences. As Mervyn realizes he has been tricked and locked in a young couple's room in Chapter 4, he narrowly escapes being shot and circumstantially incriminated as a thief. Certainly Mervyn has a talent for getting boxed into situations by being in the wrong place at the wrong time. Yet Brown's Woldwinite belief that human character is created by social circumstances, however, means that the basic problem is not that Mervyn has accidentally met damaged individuals, but that the individuals he meets have been taught to behave in damaged ways because of their social environment.

The immediate victims of commercial misdeeds are the wives and daughters of the commercial class. The novel's women, from Clemenza Lodi to Achsa Fielding, bear the initial burden of mercantile corruption, in the first instance as the ones who are left to pick up the pieces when men go broke, as they often do in this novel. Mercantile lust for goods and profits is literalized in the relentless seduction of women by male merchants, often resulting in illegitimate pregnancy. In the plot's many seductions and pregnancies, women are commonly treated as little more than objects to be consumed, a point Brown underscores in *Second Part* by highlighting recourse to prostitution by the novel's middle-class women. Even in a decade when the best-known American novels focused on related tales of seduction and ruin, this novel is notably replete with repeated episodes of seduction, pregnancy, suicide, and madness, all presented as systemic tragedies tied back to mercantile dynamics.[29]

As historian Fernand Braudel memorably put it: "Towns are like electric transformers. They increase tension, accelerate the rhythm of exchange and constantly

---

[28] Franklin discusses the Market Street pavement and street lamps ("the Idea of enlightening all the City") in "Part Three" of the *Autobiography* in the passages around the paragraph beginning "After some time I drew a Bill for Paving the City."

[29] For the "Seduction Novels" of the 1790s, which form the general U.S. novelistic context for this and other novels by Brown, see the discussions in Davidson, *Revolution and the Word*; Dillon, *The Gender of Freedom*; Samuels, *Romances of the Republic*; Stern, *The Plight of Feeling*; and Weyler, *Intricate Relations*.

recharge human life."[30] Implicitly recognizing the urban mechanics of commerce, and linking commerce and its corruption to the representation of modern urban space, *Arthur Mervyn* helps inaugurate the nineteenth-century literary genre of urban gothic, a genre in which the city's superficial chaos makes it initially difficult to perceive its structuring and deeply commercial, systematizing order. Mervyn's experience of commercial vice is also, necessarily, an experience of its urban landscape and spatial networks. One of the novel's most arresting images, Dr. Stevens' reflection in Chapter II.4 on the "horrible corruption" of the body of Captain Watson, buried beneath a Society Hill mansion and encircled by a hidden fortune based on Caribbean slavery, locates this hellish image of commercial vice at the very foundation of the city's elite residential area, in the figural heart of the city. Thus the novel parallels the biological corruption of the fever and the subterranean urban commercial corruption of the Atlantic social order, literalized in the novel's web of streets, basements, mansions, markets, hidden attic spaces, and the wider regional topography that links the city's commerce to worldwide imperial networks. The subsequent tradition of nineteenth-century urban gothic tales—including the sensationalist "boulevard novels" of the 1840s, such as George Lippard's 1844 best seller *The Quaker City, or, The Monks of Monk Hall*, a novel dedicated to and clearly influenced by Brown—often argue that the metropolis' social dysfunction emanates from the covert influence of secret organizations and abnormal vices that infiltrate civil society like a cancerous virus. *Arthur Mervyn*'s complicated set of interweaving backstories certainly makes readers yearn for a master code that could explain the mystery in simple terms of conspiratorial agency or grotesque abnormality. But Brown, like Marx, suggests that the urban hieroglyph is best deciphered by following the money trail to discover that it is the nature of civil society itself, as formed by the commercial classes, that is the source of the social crime the novel registers.[31]

If commercial trust and credit are fragile in *Arthur Mervyn*, the problem lies not in financial instruments or institutions as such but with the men whose behavior ought

---

[30] Braudel, *Civilization and Capitalism: 15th–18th Century*, I, 479.

[31] *Mervyn* the novel and Mervyn the name reappear across the landscape of nineteenth-century literature in allusions and references that suggest that Brown's novel was a significant precedent for later versions of urban gothic. Brown's character is referenced with another "Arthur Mervyn" in Walter Scott's *Guy Mannering* (1815) and with two reformer-and-deist characters, both named "Arthur Dermoyne" in Lippard's *Empire City* (1849–1850) and *New York: Its Upper Ten and Lower Million* (1853). The name recurs in Britain in Samuel Carter's "Arthur Mervyn, A Tale of the Peasantry," a long poem of rural dissent set in 1795 that appeared in Carter's *Midnight Effusions* (1848); and Richard Ainsworth's romance *The Life and Adventures of Mervyn Clitheroe* (1851, 1858). In France, the name "Mervyn" makes a notable appearance attached to the naïve youth who is seduced, murdered, and flung across the urban landscape in book 6 of Lautréamont's protosurrealist *Chants of Maldoror* (1868) in scenes that are well known as a landmark avant-garde pastiche and destruction of the century's conventional urban gothic potboilers. Mervyn and Achsa's deflated twentieth-century avatars, urban Woldwinites no longer, are the repulsive suburbanites Achsa and Marvin in "Nude Croquet" (1957), a tale by Leslie Fiedler. For Fiedler's commentary on *Arthur Mervyn*, see his *Love and Death in the American Novel*.

to secure their underlying value.[32] The Woldwinites and Brown did not have a labor theory of value, which sees value as generated by the amount of work invested in the making of a commodity. They did recognize, however, that mediums of money are not the source of wealth but rather annotations or measures of the value of human social relations. When Welbeck convinces Mervyn that a fortune in banknotes has been forged, and then dizzily tries to convince him otherwise in Chapter 23, readers may wonder which statement is true. But from a Woldwinite perspective, the money is fraudulent in either case because its value depends on human reliability and transparency; in a world of deceptive men, there is no such thing as noncounterfeit currency. *Arthur Mervyn* thus charts the correspondence of virtue to value through the mutable characters of Welbeck and the novel's other merchants. When Welbeck floats through the cotillions and counting houses of the mercantile world in part one, he is selfish and destructive. When he falls within the sphere of Mervyn and Stevens, inside the debtor's prison in *Second Part*, Welbeck unexpectedly delivers back to Mervyn the missing bills of credit that Mervyn will return to their owners. From a Woldwinite perspective, the message here is that even the most corrupt individual may be reformed if placed in the proper environment.

Atlantic Slavery, the Crime Committed in Common

Responding to this question about the underlying origin of commercial wealth and behaviors—about "the causes of appearances" that Mervyn contemplates in Chapter 7 as he reflects on his new urban environment—Brown develops his strongest critique of commercial vice by systematically linking the novel's frauds, fortunes, and other commercial activity back to their roots in Atlantic slavery. Whereas Smith, Ferguson, and others argued that commercial contact and exchange were inherently civilizing, Brown's novel, through its coordinated web of subplots, juxtaposes these contemporary claims for commerce with the actual practice of Atlantic trade and its dependence on slavery, or in other words on the profit-driven kidnapping, rape, and coercion involved in the capture of Africans and their misery-inducing transportation to the Caribbean and United States.

In the most significant development to emerge in recent studies of this novel, scholars have increasingly explored the implications of the fact that virtually all of *Arthur Mervyn's* financial dealings and searches for escaped value have their common origins

---

[32] For the period's culture of commerce and its relation to the novel's representations of unreliability and deception, see, for example, Ditz, "Secret Selves, Credible Personas: The Problematics of Trust and Public Display in the Writing of Eighteenth-Century Philadelphia Merchants" and "Shipwrecked; or, Masculinity Imperiled: Mercantile Representations of Failure and Gendered Self in Eighteenth-Century Philadelphia"; and Mann, *Republic of Debtors: Bankruptcy in the Age of American Independence*, which discusses the Prune Street debtor's prison that figures as an important setting in *Second Part*.

in slavery, in slave labor on Caribbean sugar and coffee plantations.[33] The novel's embedded subplots imply a virtual primer on Caribbean slavery and slave revolution, tying the novel's Philadelphia action to the period's slave economy and its implications throughout the wider circum-Atlantic world. Slavery not only generates the wealth that allows the novel's merchants to practice their guile but also provides the initial context for events that set off cycles of violence that begin far away but literally come home to roost in the novel's domestic relationships and spaces, which are filled with luxurious goods purchased with the profits of slavery and its associated economy. Welbeck, for example, is linked to slavery via his origins in Liverpool, capital of the period's slave trade, and his arrival in the U.S. via Charleston, the de facto capital of the U.S. slave industry in the period. The stolen wealth and circumstances leading to Welbeck's seduction and ruin of Clemenza Lodi originate in Caribbean slavery and slave revolt (in Chapter 10) because the Lodi family fortune was first imperiled and set into motion when the elder Lodi was assassinated on the French sugar island of Guadeloupe by a slave he had refused to free. Similarly, the Maurice family fortune that circulates in *Second Part* is set into motion by anxieties over slave uprising in British-controlled Jamaica and motivates the trip to Baltimore during which Mervyn reflects on slavery during the novel's stagecoach scene in Chapter II.17.

The Haitian Revolution (1791–1804) proceeded through a complicated series of often contradictory events, but its overall effect was to establish, for the first time, the rights of former slaves to self-control over their bodies and the lands on which they labored. In the wake of the French Revolution's call for "liberty, equality, and fraternity" (that is: freedom from the old regime of nobles and the Church, egalitarian citizenship, and open access to civil society), the mixed-race and black slaves of the French Caribbean rose up to demand their emancipation as well. This black revolution threatened European and U.S. systems of power on many levels, with many implications.[34] First, it deprived France of the island's tremendous profits from the sale of sugar in the global marketplace, thus threatening France's ability to pay for its

---

[33] See Christopherson, *The Apparition in the Glass* (1993); Goddu, *Gothic America: Narrative, History, and Nation* (1997); Smith-Rosenberg, "Black Gothic" (2000); Mackenthun, *Fictions of the Black Atlantic in American Foundational Literature* (2004); Doolen, *Fugitive Empire: Locating Early American Imperialism* (2005); Goudie, *Creole America: The West Indies and the Formation of Literature and Culture in the New Republic* (2006). Our discussion in what follows draws from Shapiro, *The Culture and Commerce of the Early American Novel: Reading the Atlantic World-System* (2008).

[34] For the Caribbean revolution and its repercussions in the U.S. in the 1790s, see Blackburn, "Haiti, Slavery, and the Age of Democratic Atlantic Revolution"; Davis, "American Equality and Foreign Revolutions"; Dubois, *A Colony of Citizens: Revolution & Slave Emancipation in the French Caribbean, 1787–1804*; Geggus, *Slavery, War, and Revolution: The British Occupation of Saint Domingue, 1793–1798*; Linebaugh and Rediker, *The Many-Headed Hydra: Sailors, Slaves, Commoners, and the Hidden History of the Revolutionary Atlantic*; Nash, "Reverberations of Haiti in North America: Black Saint Dominguans in Philadelphia"; and White, *"A Flood of Impure Lava": Saint Dominguan Refugees in the United States, 1791–1820*.

military defense against the British during the Revolutionary and Napoleonic Wars. Second, it sparked unrest and fear in other Caribbean slave populations, thereby threatening British imperial interests as well. Britain tried to take advantage of the opportunity to occupy Haiti, but it lost tens of thousands of troops to yellow fever plagues in the unsuccessful attempt. While *Arthur Mervyn*'s action occurs in 1793 Philadelphia, Brown was well aware of the fever's devastating effects on the British army that sought to reestablish slavery in Haiti in the years between 1793 and 1798, when he began composing the novel. In this context, fever became a protector of liberty by functioning as a defense against foreign invasion. Third, the struggles in Haiti and related Anglo-French shipping restrictions were part of the context that allowed American merchants to establish the "reexport" economy of the 1790s. Their status as neutrals in revolutionary era Anglo-French conflicts allowed them to trade more actively in Caribbean goods. This increased traffic in the profitable goods of consumer sensation (primarily sugar and its main byproduct rum) was an important driver for the U.S. economy and its crises during the 1790s, bringing astonishing profits to American merchants in ways that shook up traditional hierarchies and allowed previously marginal or unknown merchants to become wealthy or, in some cases, fabulously wealthy. Welbeck's sudden arrival in the novel's Philadelphia is comprehensible to other merchants because it corresponds to the abrupt appearance of other nouveau riche "Nabobs" who were profiting from Caribbean trade and fleeing Caribbean unrest.[35]

The final major consequence of the Haitian Revolution, from the novel's Philadelphia perspective, was to increase U.S. exposure to political, economic, and cultural consequences of ongoing European geopolitical conflicts, despite George Washington's presidential desire to isolate the United States. The Caribbean conflict produced waves of white, mixed-race, and black refugees who fled the Haitian violence for North American cities in 1793. As Brown suggests in *Arthur Mervyn* and related pieces such as "Portrait of an Emigrant" (included in this volume's Related Texts), these refugees brought radically different visual and behavioral styles to their new homes. Although often impoverished by revolutionary turmoil, the mostly professional and elite Catholic émigrés of the planter class brought new modes of behavior, dress, food, and sexual display to Philadelphia, accelerating the culture's development toward consumerism and displays of luxury that had been discouraged by earlier Quaker and other Anglo elites. Further, the exiles brought mixed-race mistresses and mixed-race relationships that were far more common in the Caribbean than in North American settings. The heightened visibility of mixed-race relationships in the city, subsequent to this influx of francophone refugees, may be part of the context for

---

[35] See Dun, "'What Avenues of Commerce, Will You, Americans, Not Explore!': Commercial Philadelphia's Vantage onto the Early Haitian Revolution"; Chew, "Certain Victims of an International Contagion: The Panic of 1797 and the Hard Times of the Late 1790s in Baltimore"; and the aforementioned articles by Ditz.

Brown's affirmation of mixed-race unions in the novel's concluding romance between Arthur and the dark-skinned Achsa Fielding.[36]

Haitian émigrés to Philadelphia came from all four of the island's main racialized groups: wealthy white plantation owners, middling whites, African slaves, and a mixed-race population that was often free and had increasingly come to own their own plantations and black slaves. Just as wealthy nineteenth-century Americans married their daughters to bankrupted European nobility for the latter's aura or cultural capital, many wealthy mixed-race property owners married their daughters to less wealthy whites so that their grandchildren would gain the social prestige of whiteness. Many of these mixed-race women joined the émigrés, fleeing a revolution that in its early phases pitted mulattos against black slaves, and in Philadelphia these women often continued their search for white lovers or marriage partners. Haitian slaves, the "French negroes" that U.S. slave owners feared would seed rebellion among their own "human property," likewise arrived in significant numbers along with their owners.

In *Arthur Mervyn*, the effects of the Haitian Revolution and its reorganization of the U.S. and Atlantic economies disturb the profits that flow from the Caribbean plantations, forcing the capital previously fixed in Caribbean land and slaves to become remonetarized and perilously transmitted through commercial networks of credit, bills of exchange, import-export voyaging, and so on. As this fugitive wealth is set into motion through the period's channels of credit transfers, it appears to be nearly without ownership and thus open for the taking, for example when Welbeck appropriates the Lodi family fortune from the dying younger Lodi in Chapter 10, when Captain Watson is buried with the Maurice family fortune hidden on his body in Chapter 12, or when Mervyn carries half of the Lodi fortune on his person and destroys it on a momentary impulse in Chapter 23. The identity of the implicitly absent exchange partner who lies behind this wealth, the personal agent who ought to stabilize trade and stand at its origin to guarantee its motion, is that of the slave him or herself, who does not achieve satisfaction in trade, as Adam Smith had claimed, because he or she is the very object being traded.

In this light, Brown's more complete response to the earlier-mentioned contagion-environmentalism debate is implicit in his treatment of the novel's cast of characters tied to the Caribbean slave economy—a large group that includes Welbeck, Wortley, the Lodi family, Captains Watson and Williams, the Thetford and Maurice families, and, implicitly, the Claverings, Wentworths, and Mervyn himself—and their experience of the threat of slave rebellion and its consequences for the moral economy of commerce. Brown reformulates the question about yellow fever's origin by suggesting, with the novel's action, that the city's corruption is produced by a damaged social environment. The novel's underlying social malady is caused by the importation of violence against Africans, by a diseased environment in which the carriers of

---

[36] For more on Brown's representation of mixed-race relationships, see the "Portrait of an Emigrant" sketch, as well as the Brown-edited excerpts on slavery from *The Monthly Magazine*, both included in the Related Texts.

destruction are not African bodies, not French refugees, but the merchants who traffic in the goods provided by slaves.

The novel's events also allow Brown to comment on closely related questions concerning the important post-fever pamphlet controversy between Mathew Carey and African American ministers Absalom Jones and Richard Allen. The city's free blacks were on the front lines of public response to the epidemic, and when Carey accused black undertakers of extortion and theft, the ministers replied with examples of the steadfast credibility and generosity of the city's blacks during the epidemic by way of contrast to the selfish and destructive behaviors of whites. Mervyn both recounts and hears analogous tales of white selfishness and cruelty in scenes that always include free black workers and servants who have stayed behind to help. The chief example here is the character Medlicote and his black servant Austin, whose knowledge and self-possession in Chapter 17's fever scenes are developed as a learning experience for Mervyn and in obvious contrast to the destructive panic and selfishness of the merchant Thetford and his clerk Wallace.[37]

Enacting Abolition, Ending with Achsa

If one strand links together the key groups in Brown's life—his childhood friends among the tightly knit Quakers, his adult associates in the New York circle, and later Philadelphia associates—it is a common commitment to the immediate abolition of slavery. Perhaps more than any other single issue, abolition provided Brown's circles with a direct, concrete goal and demand for the betterment of human society. During the 1803–1806 years when he was primarily occupied with editing and writing articles for *The Literary Magazine and American Register,* for example, Brown planned with lifelong friend Thomas Pym Cope, a wealthy Quaker businessman and civic activist, to write an abolitionist *History of Slavery,* but the project was never brought to fruition.[38] Eighteenth-century abolitionism involved a spectrum of ideas and approaches to slavery, but the positions that Brown and others in his New York group marked out, in a series of writings and speeches, are remarkable for their militant critiques of slavery and of underlying prejudices concerning race and racial

---

[37] See the excerpts from Carey and Jones-Allen included in the Related Texts. For the pamphlet controversy and its importance for the emergence of the city's free black institutions, see Nash, *Forging Freedom: The Formation of Philadelphia's Black Community, 1720–1840*; Brooks, "The Early American Public Sphere and the Emergence of a Black Print Counterpublic"; Will, "Liberalism, Republicanism, and Philadelphia's Black Elite in the Early Republic: The Social Thought of Absalom Jones and Richard Allen"; and Lapsansky, "'Abigail, a Negress': The Role and Legacy of African Americans in the Yellow Fever Epidemic" in Estes and Smith, *A Melancholy Scene of Devastation.*

[38] On Cope's commission to Brown and efforts to provide him with abolitionist society records to help in this project, see *Philadelphia Merchant: The Diary of Thomas P. Cope, 1800–1851,* 137–139, 182, 192. Cope writes, on February 19, 1803, "Having lately, in the name of myself & colleagues, given C.B.B. the offer of writing the History of Slavery, he has this day accepted of it & is to proceed with all dispatch in that interesting undertaking" (139).

typology. A synthesis of their positions, as illustrated in the excerpts from the abolition addresses and other texts included in this volume's Related Texts, provides dramatic contrasts with the emergent affirmation of biological racialism that is a familiar
feature of the period's thinking.

Brown's circle sees slavery in radical-Enlightenment terms as an illegitimate use of
force that typifies premodern societies but that is not part of any eternal human
order. As the forcible capture of individuals who should be free, slavery has no foundation in rational law. Although slavery has existed in older social formations in classical antiquity and feudalism, its prior existence neither justifies it nor provides any
rationale for its continuation. A gradual approach to the abolition of slavery simply
delays right and ultimately inevitable action. No past order, such as that invoked in
Christian claims for African enslavement based on the curse of Noah's child, has any
legitimacy on this question. Explicitly rejecting biological categories of race that were
gaining prominence in late eighteenth-century arguments for polygenesis, the idea
that separate races of humans exist and consequently that some are inferior to others,
Brown's circle argued that there is only one human race. If New World slaves appear
lazy or shiftless, as slavery advocates claim, they counter that this is simply an expression of the degraded life slaves have experienced. Once slaves are granted the conditions of dignity, this change of circumstances will gradually change their behavior.
Slave uprisings in Haiti and elsewhere, for Brown's group, are the predictable expression of the human desire for freedom, events that are not dissimilar from the energies
that motivated the American and French Revolutions. Drawing illustrations from
earlier hierarchies of unjust domination, for example in the Turkish occupation of
Greece, the history of Western Europe, and prior modes of slavery, Brown and his associates argue that there is no fundamental difference in kind between Africans and
European peoples, who were likewise subordinated at different times in forms of co-
erced labor ranging from slavery to serfdom. The arguments of Brown and his circle
affirm that Europeans are not intrinsically superior to Africans and indeed that the
reverse argument could just as easily be made, given the sophistication of early modern African societies.

Calls for abolition are inherently models for what should be done to repair the
damage of slavery. Here Brown's associates were clear: rather than advocate repatriation or recolonization, for the removal of Africans from a presumptively white U.S.
culture (a position that was put forward by writers from Thomas Jefferson to Harriet
Beecher Stowe), Brown and his circle felt that former slaves should be integrated into
existing U.S. civil society through education, full and immediate enfranchisement
into the privileges and protective rights of democratic citizenship, and a process of
interracial union that they hoped would progressively remove racializing distinctions
through miscegenation.

What are the implications of these abolitionist arguments for reading *Arthur Mervyn*?
While previous commentators have differed in their interpretations of the novel's
stance concerning slavery and race, and significant interpretations have argued that
Brown's novel is symptomatic of the period's emerging ideas about biological racialism
and polygenesis, our discussion in what follows takes the position that the novel is part

of and consistent with the larger system of arguments that Brown and his circle articulated in their antislavery addresses and other writings. We can approach the question by looking more closely at the novel's treatment of sympathy and its role in Mervyn's rise to middle-class status as well as at Brown's decision to conclude the novel with a romance between Mervyn and Achsa Fielding and, finally, by examining the interesting possibility that the novel refers to early Underground Railroad activity.

As Mervyn makes his way through Philadelphia's circles of mercantile corruption, questions related to ethno-racial status and abolition seem to become increasingly prominent in the narrative. For most of the novel's first part, Mervyn's tale poses the question: What happens if we abandon older social hierarchies based on family bloodlines and localized, monoethnic community ties? When Mervyn's Scots-Irish father disinherits his son and violates class boundaries by marrying the formerly indentured Betty Lawrence, a woman beneath his rank, Mervyn is expelled from his country home and discovers the paradoxical freedom of modernity, the precarious status of free-floating individuals set loose by the relentless dissolution of traditional community structures: "I was become, in my own conceptions, an alien and an enemy to the roof under which I was born" (Chapter 2). The now-landless Mervyn slinks toward the city's commerce and bright lights, like so many displaced farmers throughout modern history, and quickly realizes that he has precious few resources that might prevent him from descending even lower on the food chain of status groups. Mervyn's birth status was never high, but it was just high enough that he must fear losing its privileges as he flirts with abject poverty or unfreedom in bound labor, a possibility that surfaces immediately as he encounters the consequences of his new rootlessness in Chapters 2–5. On the one hand, Mervyn's newfound freedom looks like a poisoned gift that may destine him to a life of downward mobility in a pitiless commercial order. On the other, as he experiences the quasimagical transformations and disorientation created by urban commerce, Mervyn giddily entertains the possibility and fantasy that, once uprooted from the fixed referents of his rural background, he may float higher in the social realm, especially as the chaos of the fever epidemic and revolution scrambles the fixed structures of society.

Mervyn's aspirational energies proceed through two sequential and ultimately mutually exclusive strategies. The first, less successful one involves Mervyn's commitment to the optics of sympathy and sensibility, the eighteenth-century complex of ideas concerning immediate, physical-emotional ("sympathetic") bonds and responses between individuals that are often held to represent modern egalitarian relationships that supplant older hierarchical models of interaction. In Woldwinite and other late eighteenth-century narratives, bonds of sympathy are commonly linked to themes of visuality and problems of interpretation based on physical appearance, as is the case in *Arthur Mervyn*.[39] Shorn of family and other traditional relations,

---

[39] For the visual dimension of this complex of ideas in Woldwinite and other period fictions, see Johnson, *Equivocal Beings: Politics, Gender, and Sentimentality in the 1790s;* Juengel, "Godwin, Lavater, and the Pleasures of Surface"; and Rivers, *Face Value: Physiognomical Thought and the Legible Body in Marivaux, Lavater, Balzac, Gautier, and Zola.*

Mervyn rejects the option of physical labor and relies instead on the cultural capital of his good looks and bookish manners as they magnetize and charm the city's bourgeoisie. The strategy of "looks" becomes a class strategy that Mervyn uses to improve his position, as middle-class professionals literally *see* him as one of their own, despite his natal origins.[40] This visual sympathy is often literalized as Mervyn capitalizes on his uncanny physical resemblance to other promising young bourgeois men, such as Clavering or Clemenza's brother Vincentio Lodi. Even more broadly, Mervyn's ability to generate a sympathetic response to his face and body creates crucial opportunities, for example in the novel's first scene when his appearance is a key factor in Dr. Stevens' seemingly spontaneous enthusiasm for the unknown individual he sees lying ill on the pavement in front of his home. The benevolent Stevens continually defends Mervyn on the basis of his "sympathetic" appearance and self-representation, and stands in his support against skeptics like the creditor Wortley or the parochial matron Mrs. Althorpe, who insist that Mervyn should be evaluated according to older, more conventionalized grids of bloodlines and reputation. Perhaps because Mervyn's ascent is so dependent on this visualized logic of sympathy, he himself adopts and employs the approach to interpretation it implies, echoing and amplifying Stevens' dedication to this mode of relationship. The culmination of Mervyn's moral evaluation of others by means of an almost voyeuristic surveillance occurs in *Second Part*'s Chapter 17, during the stagecoach journey to Baltimore, as Mervyn gazes at the coach's other passengers: a Creole Frenchman, his pet monkey, and two female blacks. In this key scene, as several commentators have noted, the force of watching illustrates how quickly sympathetic viewing can become a means of projecting codes of racial taxonomy, a means of categorizing and classifying humans as if they were objects of natural history.[41]

While sympathetic codes, conveyed primarily through vision, are Mervyn's initial social strategy for empowerment and relating to others in the city, the novel suggests that they soon prove inadequate and even counterproductive. As the novel traces Mervyn's movement through the city's webs of commercial corruption, it illustrates the weaknesses and potential for structural prejudice and deception inherent in sympathetic or sentimental reflexes, in the absence of any rational consideration of their nature and implications. The overall trajectory of Welbeck's story, from his initial masquerade and theatrical deceptions to his murderous decline and final magnanimous gesture in *Second Part*, underlines the unreliability of appearances and, by implication, sympathy's inadequacy as a response to changing conditions and social

---

[40] A similar tactic appears in the contemporary, "true-life" Mervyn-like rogue's tale, *Memoirs of Stephen Burroughs* (1798).

[41] For the iconic passage from Laurence Sterne's *Sentimental Journey* that Brown references in Mervyn's stagecoach scene, see this volume's Related Texts and the discussion in Ellis, *The Politics of Sensibility*. For discussions of Mervyn's stagecoach scene and its implications for understanding Brown's perspective on new codes of racial typology, see Mackenthun, *Fictions of the Black Atlantic*; Goudie, *Creole America*; Doolen, *Fugitive Empire*; Waterman, *Republic of Intellect*; and Shapiro, *The Culture and Commerce of the Early American Novel*.

relations. The "causes of appearances" turn out not to be accessible through immediate impressions. Ultimately, the novel implies, sympathy produces results that are little better than the older mechanism of social status, for it assigns fixed identities that cannot be changed or improved.

As the inadequacy of "sympathetic" codes becomes increasingly evident, Mervyn gradually gains awareness of a second and more successful mode of new relations, and discovers that a "revolution" is occurring in his thinking and consciousness. Sometimes, with this oft-repeated image, Mervyn simply means epiphanies or sudden realizations, but, in the novel's *Second Part*, particularly after the introduction of the refugee and émigré character Achsa Fielding in Chapter II.12, the "revolution" taking place in Mervyn's mind seems to become related ever more clearly to the aftershocks of the Haitian and French Revolutions as they reach the shores of the early U.S.[42]

Mervyn's new modes of thinking and new approach to social relation appear most dramatically in the novel's conclusion, in the romance that affirms the émigré Achsa Fielding and at the same time overturns readerly expectations that Mervyn will marry the virginal Eliza Hadwin. The tremendous contrast between these two characters appears immediately in the differences between their associated origins. Whereas Hadwin initially appears on an idealized Chester County farm run by a benevolent agrarian patriarch, Fielding makes her entrance as a mysterious exile in a lurid, middle-class brothel run by an intemperate urban matriarch (Mrs. Villars' name evokes *ville* or city). A multitude of readers and critics, beginning with Brown's friend and biographer William Dunlap and the British poet Percy Shelley, have been perplexed, even angered, by Brown's anticonventional choice to end the novel by pairing Mervyn with a dark-skinned and decidedly nonvirginal ethno-racial other who seems to condense the novel's previous reflections on gendered relations of power, slavery, revolution, and troubled commercial networks.[43] The question of why Brown chose to end the novel with this pairing becomes even more intriguing when we consider that Brown's initial plan, noted in a letter to his brother James in early 1799, was to conclude *Second Part* with a marriage between Mervyn and

---

[42] Mervyn's references to "revolutions" in his thinking or perception occur in Chapters 8, 20, II.7, II.9, II.11, and II.13. See especially the key passage in II.9 where Mervyn articulates the transformation of his thinking on the potentials of urban professional life.

[43] Dunlap, in his *Life of Charles Brockden Brown* (II, 40), interprets the conclusion as an abandonment of Eliza, which is manifestly not the case: ". . . Eliza Hadwin is the most worthy and artless and interesting creature of the author's creation, but in the conclusion she is abandoned both by hero and author, in a manner as unexpected as disgusting." Thomas Love Peacock, reporting Shelley's enthusiasm for Brown, writes that Shelley was particularly impressed with Brown's female characters, except for Achsa: "The transfer of the hero's affections from a simple peasant girl to a rich Jewess, displeased Shelley extremely, and he could only account for it on the ground that it was the only way in which Brown could bring his story to an uncomfortable conclusion" ("Memoir of Percy Bysshe Shelley," 409–10).

Eliza.[44] Why, readers have asked, other than greed for her wealth, does Brown have Mervyn choose the exiled and conventionally unattractive Achsa Fielding over the younger and clearly infatuated Eliza Hadwin?

Very late in the novel, in *Second Part*'s Chapter 23, Brown surprises the reader with the unexpected revelation that Achsa is a "Portuguese" or Sephardic Jew.[45] The revelation is intended to startle the reader in narrative terms but also occurs so late in the novel and with so little foreshadowing that the reader may wonder when, exactly, Brown decided to give Arthur's new romantic partner her Jewish ethnicity. Timing suggests that a likely context for the decision to make Achsa Jewish is the August 1800 newspaper polemic between Jewish democratic activist Benjamin Nones and Federalist journalists who attacked him and other activists with racial and other slurs as part of the period's partisan newspaper wars. Nones' well-known reply to his anonymous attackers is a landmark statement of Jewish identity in the U.S., and explicitly relates that community's struggles to those of other disenfranchised groups who sought inclusion in citizen status during the revolutionary period. By ending with Achsa, Brown highlights the period's "Jewish question," the debate about citizenship rights for Jews that asked whether a "foreign" and historically disenfranchised race could share citizen status within Christian republics.[46] By developing Achsa's backstory with a combination of allusions and references to Mary Wollstonecraft's troubled life story and the struggle for citizen status by the period's Jews, Brown makes Achsa a bearer of revolutionary era struggles for both gender and ethno-racial emancipation. By making Achsa Jewish, in other words, Brown takes a progressive position in immediate and more distant debates about race, citizenship, and gender that were occurring around him as he concluded the novel.[47]

There may be an even stronger reading of Achsa's role in the novel's conclusion to consider, however, if we connect it with the repeated emphasis on her "tawny" skin, a period codeword for black or mixed-race persons. As he teases Mervyn and encourages

---

[44] Brown's letter of February 15, 1799 to his brother James, written just after finishing the novel's first part, explains his initial plan for a "sequel" to continue the plot lines of the first volume. Much of what he projected in that letter changed by the time he wrote *Second Part,* particularly the conventionalized, helpless roles for women and his plan for ending the story with a marriage between Arthur and Eliza. Referring to the Hadwin sisters, Brown writes that the Mervyn of this plan "relieves the two helpless females from their sorrows and fears. Marriage with the youngest; the death of the elder by a consumption and grief, leaves him in possession of competence, and the rewards of virtue."

[45] For a discussion of Achsa as a Jewish character, see Harap, "Fracture of a Stereotype: Charles Brockden Brown's Achsa Fielding."

[46] See "Benjamin Nones vs. the *Gazette*" in this volume's Related Texts.

[47] For the 1790s Philadelphia Jewish community, as well as the partisan, racialized context for the Nones-Gazette exchange and similar episodes, see Pencak, *Jews and Gentiles in Early America, 1654–1800*; Wolf and Whiteman, *The History of the Jews of Philadelphia from Colonial Times to the Age of Jackson*; Nathans, "A Much-Maligned People: Jews on and off the Stage in the Early American Republic"; and Schappes, "Reaction and Anti-Semitism, 1795–1800."

him to propose to Achsa in *Second Part*'s Chapter 24, for example, Stevens underlines her Africanized appearance by describing her as "unsightly as a *night-hag*, tawney as a Moor, the eye of a gypsey." The novel associates Achsa with blackness on several explicit and implicit levels. Beyond the "tawney" skin noted by Mervyn and Stevens, Achsa's Sephardic background may or may not imply Afro-Caribbean ethno-racial potentials, since the Sephardic trading networks from which Achsa emerges and which established the first Jewish communities in North America arrived via Portuguese and Dutch Caribbean slave colonies such as Curaçao and Suriname, where social mixture and interracial unions produced a subgroup of mulatto or black "Portuguese" Jews who, in turn, provoked early modern debates about Jewish identity and race in Amsterdam and London.[48] Achsa's positive association with African models is inscribed more allusively in affirmative Miltonic citations at the beginning of *Second Part*'s Chapter 22 that balance out the more ominous Milton references that Mervyn developed as he entered the city in Chapter 3. Whereas the novel's opening citations from Milton drew on his depiction of Hell in *Paradise Lost*, Achsa's concluding citations turn to Milton's *Comus* and *Il Penseroso* to suggest an unconventional role for herself, not as a helpmate or subordinated partner for Mervyn but as a powerful black figure of intellectualized desire who can guide his further development. Reversing the surface message of Milton's *Comus* by quoting from the swarthy Comus, rather than the chaste Lady, Achsa appropriates an invitation to erotic, non-Christian otherness that implies that Mervyn should marry her rather than the virginal and inexperienced Eliza Hadwin. Alluding to *Il Penseroso*, Achsa identifies herself with that poem's African, non-Christian muse, suggestively leading the pensive Mervyn toward an improved understanding of and engagement with the commercial and revolutionary social relations he has been exploring throughout the novel. In this light, the final romance between Mervyn and Fielding enacts the kinds of innovative relations that Brown's closest friends in abolitionist circles were arguing for: interracial sexual union and miscegenation as a means for overcoming phobic responses to ethno-racial others.[49]

If we approach *Arthur Mervyn* as a text grounded both in Woldwinite desires to break with unexamined patterns in order to change the cultural environment and

---

[48] For the Sephardic background that informs Achsa's story, see Israel, *Diasporas with a Diaspora: Jews, Crypto-Jews and the World Maritime Empires*; Yogev, *Diamonds and Coral: Anglo-Dutch Jews and Eighteenth-Century Trade*; Endelman, *The Jews of Georgian England, 1714–1830: Tradition and Change in a Liberal Society*; and Malino, *The Sephardic Jews of Bordeaux: Assimilation and Emancipation in Revolutionary and Napoleonic France*. For the debate on race and color that occurred within the Sephardic community after racial mixture in Caribbean colonies, see Kaplan, "Political Concepts in the World of the Portuguese Jews of Amsterdam during the Seventeenth Century: The Problem of Exclusion and the Boundaries of Self-Identity."

[49] In this volume's Related Texts, see Brown's "Portrait of an Emigrant," "What Is a *JEW*?" and the excerpts from "On the Consequences of Abolishing the Slave Trade to the West Indian Colonies," as well as "Three Abolitionist Addresses from Brown's Circle" and "Two Perspectives on Slavery from *The Monthly Magazine*."

reform existing institutions, and in critical and even militant arguments regarding slavery and its aftermath, we can situate the text as an early and remarkable contribution to abolitionist fiction. The novel inverts the typical function of urban gothic, which shocks its readers with tales of corruption only to restore the conventions of "normal" society in conclusion. In Brown's tale of urban vice, it is so-called normal commercial society itself that is disturbing, in its largely unacknowledged dependence on Atlantic slavery and unquestioned set of related inequalities and prejudices regarding class, gender, and race. As historian Caroll Smith-Rosenberg argues, "Achsa Fielding's embodied fusion of the white middle-class man's two defining others (women / blacks) requires us to recognize not only the white middle-class man's dependence on them both to define and stabilize his own subjectivity but also their mutual interdependence. Only by tracing their complex triangularity will we begin to understand the ways power is produced, reproduced, and deployed in America's bourgeois world."[50] Rather than reinforcing dominant categories, the novel's final romance seems to suggest, there may be a way out of this mundane hell, or at least a way to moderate its damage.

Signposting the Underground Railroad

The novel's relation to militant antislavery arguments may be even more concrete, however, if we consider the possibility that *Arthur Mervyn* alludes to a very specific abolitionist project for black liberation: the Underground Railroad, which helped runaway slaves elude their masters and live as free individuals.

Arthur Mervyn's first part ends with an intentionally intriguing omission, a secret that begs to be deciphered and leaves the reader wondering what it might imply. Just paragraphs before the end of the volume—and in this connection we need to remember that the first part had no sequel when it was published in early 1799, making this passage the end of the entire novel at that time—as he describes his attempts to escape hospitalization during his last moments in Welbeck's rented mansion, Mervyn explains that he discovered a hidden attic crawl space. He tells his listeners, Dr. Stevens and his wife Eliza, that he hid in this "recess" momentarily and that "one studious of concealment, might rely on its protection with unbounded confidence." Mervyn says that he saw startling and very significant objects in this crawl space but then refuses to explain what they were, dramatically insisting that "at present, it appears to be my duty to pass them over in silence." The novel never explains what Mervyn sees and infers in the crawl space or why he feels duty bound to keep this information secret. Given the emphasis Mervyn has already placed on honesty and keeping secrets under ethical obligation, however, it is worthwhile to consider what he might go to such lengths to suggest but not explain clearly.

Is Brown suggesting that Mervyn has stumbled across a hiding place for runaway slaves on the Underground Railroad? Throughout the 1790s, Philadelphia was a

---

[50] Smith-Rosenberg, "Black Gothic," 260.

magnet for runaway slaves who sought protection among the city's large free black population and in proximity to its mostly Quaker abolition activists. Besides everything else, the year 1793 was a critical moment in the history of U.S. slavery, the year that the first Fugitive Slave Act was signed into law by George Washington. This act provided a legal mechanism allowing runaway slaves to be apprehended in northern free states and returned to their masters. Abolitionists and leaders of the city's free black community, including the Reverends Absalom Jones and Richard Allen, had publicly and unsuccessfully opposed the Act. After they were defeated on the legislative front, they turned their energy to expanding the activity of the Underground Railroad, which hid escaped slaves from the pursuit of slave catchers.

Although the Underground Railroad seems to have existed in embryonic, improvised form for decades, it took on a more organized structure in the 1790s. The crucial figure in its 1790s development was Isaac Hopper (1771–1852), a Philadelphia Quaker tailor who was a member of the Pennsylvania Abolition Society (PAS) and a key activist in the period's antislavery efforts. From his own accounts, commissioned and republished by Lydia Maria Child years later, we know that in the 1790s Hopper used a variety of means, both legal and illegal, to help fugitives challenge their slave status openly or to elude slave owners or slave catchers and escape northward. Hopper was famous for his detailed knowledge of Pennsylvania's slave laws, which he used to force the manumission of slaves who had lived openly in the state for a period of six months. Hopper was also a key figure in building bridges between the Philadelphia free black community, the middle-class, professional members of the PAS, and farmers in the outlying counties who cooperated in the process of moving runaways into and out of Philadelphia. Hopper's tailor shop became an unofficial antislavery office where threatened individuals and their friends could find help, and he became well known for his emergency interventions in sometimes violent situations involving the attempted recapture of fugitive slaves.

Brown could not have been unaware of Hopper's activity. They were the same age and circulated in the same circles of Quaker abolitionists, and Hopper had considerable notoriety as a result of his activities. Hopper's workshop and home on Philadelphia's South Second Street was only a few doors from Brown's own family address during the 1790s. If Brown grew up in a Philadelphia that still had open-air slave auctions off Market Street, he also saw free blacks congregate around Hopper's doorway planning illegal opposition to slavery and heard accounts of the often dramatic incidents in which Hopper became involved. By all accounts, Hopper was not someone easily overlooked. A gregarious man with a magnetic and idiosyncratic personality, he was well known for his ability to confront and disarm hostility with his quick wits, and to use his opponents' conventional expectations to his own advantage, much as Arthur Mervyn does in *Second Part* as he confounds Mrs. Althorpe, Philip Hadwin, and Mrs. Villars (Chapters II.2, II.10, and II.11–12).[51]

---

[51] For more on Hopper, see the excerpts from his tales in Related Texts, and Meaders, "Kidnapping Blacks in Philadelphia: Isaac Hopper's Tales of Oppression."

During the 1793 yellow fever epidemic, both slave catchers and fugitives attempted to use the confusion of the moment to their advantage, and the city's urban space was a field for their attempts to discover and elude one another. It is therefore likely that Hopper and his associates used the event as a cover to transport slaves at a time when government structures were suspended and when remaining city officials, many of whom were abolitionists themselves, were preoccupied with other pressing matters and would have turned a blind eye even if they had been aware of efforts to obstruct and evade the Fugitive Slave Act. A scenario of active resistance to recapture may help clarify what seems initially to be one of the most racially mysterious episodes in the novel. When Mervyn enters a house searching for the clerk Wallace during the fever in Chapter 16, he sees the mirrored reflection of a scarred African in livery, who strikes him unconscious. Is this violence unmotivated aggression on the part of an undisciplined black, in the kind of scenario suggested in Mathew Carey's accusations, or is it a rational, albeit hasty act of self-defense against a possible slave catcher? Mervyn, at this point, is behaving like a slave catcher as he roams through houses unannounced searching for a man who might be avoiding discovery. The black figure's facial scars may be the trace of an injury, a whipping, or possibly an African ceremonial marking, all of which suggest the man's former status as a slave. From this perspective, this individual instance of black violence may recall the wider view of black revolutionary struggle articulated by Theodore Dwight, Brown's New York Friendly Club associate. In his abolition address, Dwight memorably insists that slave violence against plantation owners in Haiti is simply the "language of freedom; but . . . also the language of truth . . . Indeed, from individuals, the spirit is generally communicated to states, and from states to nations."[52]

The more time Mervyn spends in Philadelphia, the more he begins to perceive the "causes of appearances" and the structure of the city's activities, especially as these relate to networks of commercial crime and fraud. But the same is true of Mervyn's developing perceptions of racism and racial domination. On his first arrival in the city, Mervyn seems to regard blacks as little more than the invisible furniture of his middle-class contacts. As the tale progresses and culminates with his impending marriage to the dark-skinned Achsa, Mervyn becomes increasingly aware of the unfreedom that afflicts the blacks and women around him and moves toward an ever greater understanding of the implications of the racial domination that is part of Philadelphia's commercial order. Mervyn initially seeks primarily to survive, rise, and ingratiate himself, to participate in bourgeois freedom and privilege through the mechanism of sympathy. But as he learns more about the world he inhabits, the novel's subtitle, "Memoirs of the Year 1793," comes to refer to more than that year's famous epidemic and more even than the momentous events of the Haitian and French Revolutions. By the novel's conclusion it refers to the revolution in Mervyn's thinking and consciousness regarding race and slavery, as he increasingly seems to

---

[52] See excerpts from Dwight's *Oration* in this volume's Related Texts, "Three Abolitionist Addresses from Brown's Circle."

reject the common sense of racial difference and its retarding influences by uniting himself with the nonwhite Achsa and possibly by refusing to divulge secrets of the early Underground Railroad. By the end of *Arthur Mervyn*, Brown has used the core set of Woldwinite beliefs to craft a programmatic story of property and sex about how individuals might overcome class, gender, and racial prejudice and communicate their changing consciousness to others. Linking narrative tension to international political and social activism, Brown crafts a political romance that deserves to make young Mervyn an iconic figure, like John Steinbeck's Tom Joad, who illustrates how the rural poor can teach urban elites something about the concrete enactment of political liberty.

A NOTE ON THE TEXT

Arthur Mervyn; or, Memoirs of the Year 1793 was first published in book form some-time between March 7 and May 21, 1799 by Hugh Maxwell in Philadelphia. The first nine chapters of the book edition previously appeared as nine installments in James Watters' Philadelphia-based *Weekly Magazine* from June to August 1799. After Brown became dissatisfied with Maxwell, he sought out another, New York publisher for the sequel, and *Arthur Mervyn, Second Part* was subsequently first published by George F. Hopkins sometime in September, possibly early October 1800.

The Kent State "Bicentennial" edition of *Arthur Mervyn*, published in 1980, is the modern scholarly text of the novel and provides a Textual Essay and List of Emenda-tions that document copy-text variants and provide a rationale for selecting between variants in the serialized and book versions of the early chapters.

This Hackett edition does not refer to the serialized chapters but uses the first print-ings of the novel's two parts as its copy-text, silently correcting their typographical er-rors. We regularize the first editions' irregular dashes and ellipses and, like all modern editions, we have removed the quotation marks that are used irregularly in Maxwell's first part, making both parts consistent with Hopkins' rendering of quoted speech. We have not modernized or regularized spellings or names, since these present no problem for the contemporary reader. Like other modern editions, we have elimi-nated the repetition of the title over each chapter heading and certain typographical accidentals.

For a full discussion of the novel's textual history, see the textual essay, notes, and appendices by S. W. Reid in the Kent State edition.

Similarly, this volume's Related Texts are drawn from first or, where indicated, other contemporary printings, and are not modernized.

Note on Chapter References

Because the novel was published in distinct parts, it has two sets of chapter numbers beginning at 1. Some editions have numbered the chapters consecutively, 1 to 48, ef-facing the difference between the first part and its sequel. Since various ways of writ-ing "*Second Part*'s Chapter 1" are bulky and laborious, we have adopted the solution of referring to chapters in *Second Part* with a roman numeral II. Thus in our Intro-duction, footnotes, and Related Texts, "Chapter 1" indicates the first part's Chapter 1, and "II.1" indicates *Second Part*, Chapter 1.

ARTHUR MERVYN:

OR,

MEMOIRS

OF THE

YEAR 1793.

BY THE AUTHOR OF WIELAND; AND ORMOND,
OR THE SECRET WITNESS.

COPY-RIGHT SECURED.

PHILADELPHIA:

PRINTED AND PUBLISHED BY H. MAXWELL,
NO. 3, LÆTITIA COURT—AND SOLD BY MESSRS.
T. DOBSON, R. CAMPBELL, H. AND P. RICE,
A. DICKINS, AND THE PRINCIPAL
BOOKSELLERS IN THE NEIGH-
BOURING STATES.

1799.

PREFACE

THE evils of pestilence[1] by which this city has lately been afflicted will probably form an æra in its history. The schemes of reformation and improvement to which they will give birth, or, if no efforts of human wisdom can avail to avert the periodical visitations of this calamity, the change in manners and population which they will produce, will be, in the highest degree, memorable. They have already supplied new and copious materials for reflection to the physician and the political economist. They have not been less fertile of instruction to the moral observer, to whom they have furnished new displays of the influence of human passions and motives.[2]

Amidst the medical and political discussions which are now afloat in the community relative to this topic, the author of these remarks has ventured to methodize his own reflections, and to weave into an humble narrative, such incidents as appeared to him most instructive and remarkable among those which came within the sphere of his own observation. It is every one's duty to profit by all opportunities of inculcating on mankind the lessons of justice and humanity. The influences of hope and fear, the trials of fortitude and constancy, which took place in this city, in the autumn of 1793, have, perhaps, never been exceeded in any age. It is but just to snatch some of these from oblivion, and to deliver to posterity a brief but faithful sketch of the condition of this metropolis during that calamitous period. Men only require to be made acquainted with distress for their compassion and their charity to be awakened. He that depicts, in lively colours, the evils of disease and poverty, performs an eminent service to the sufferers, by calling forth benevolence in those who are able to afford relief, and he who pourtrays examples of disinterestedness and intrepidity, confers on virtue the notoriety and homage that are due to it, and rouses in the spectators, the spirit of salutary emulation.[3]

---

[1] "Pestilence": the novel is organized around the Philadelphia yellow fever epidemic of August–November 1793. Fever outbreaks were common in the eighteenth century, but particularly intense in the 1790s when they accompanied and amplified the chaos of the decade's revolutionary upheavals. Thus the novel dramatizes the local effects of an Atlantic crisis context familiar to Brown's readers and the object of much public debate and analysis. See the Introduction for more on the epidemic and the novel's relation to debates about it.

[2] "Passions and motives": Brown separates medical controversies (concerning the fever's origin and treatment) and political debates (concerning its international scope and implications for foreign and domestic relations) from his purpose as a romancer. As a romancer, or novelist, Brown uses the fever setting to investigate issues of cultural sociology and provide examples of progressive behavior and ideas; he asks why people act as they do (under specific historical pressures, such as the epidemic and commercial crises used as the setting here) and exhibits "lessons of justice and humanity."

[3]"Spirit of salutary emulation": in keeping with his plan for novel or "romance" writing, Brown provides a model of virtue and hopes that his readers will copy the healthy, enlightened actions

In the following tale a particular series of adventures is brought to a close; but these are necessarily connected with the events which happened subsequent to the period here described. These events are not less memorable than those which form the subject of the present volume,[4] and may hereafter be published either separately or in addition to this.

C. B. B.

---

represented in the narrative. See the discussion of Brown's novelistic method in the Introduction and "Walstein's School of History" in Related Texts.

[4] "Present volume": the preface refers to part one only, which appeared in March–May 1799. Brown suggests he may write a second volume to develop situations and plotlines not resolved here, which in fact he did. The *Second Part* appeared as a "sequel" to the first eighteen months later in September 1800. For more on the relation of the two parts, see Introduction and notes 23.5 and II.1.1.

ARTHUR MERVYN;
OR, MEMOIRS OF THE YEAR 1793

Chapter I

I WAS resident in this city during the year 1793. Many motives contributed to detain me, though departure was easy and commodious, and my friends were generally solicitous for me to go. It is not my purpose to enumerate these motives, or to dwell on my present concerns and transactions, but merely to compose a narrative of some incidents with which my situation made me acquainted.[1]

Returning one evening, somewhat later than usual, to my own house, my attention was attracted, just as I entered the porch, by the figure of a man, reclining against the wall at a few paces distant. My sight was imperfectly assisted by a far-off lamp; but the posture in which he sat, the hour, and the place immediately suggested the idea of one disabled by sickness. It was obvious to conclude that his disease was pestilential. This did not deter me from approaching and examining him more closely.

He leaned his head against the wall, his eyes were shut, his hands clasped in each other, and his body seemed to be sustained in an upright position merely by the cellar door against which he rested his left shoulder. The lethargy into which he was sunk, seemed scarcely interrupted by my feeling his hand and his forehead. His throbbing temples and burning skin indicated a fever, and his form, already emaciated, seemed to prove that it had not been of short duration.

There was only one circumstance that hindered me from forming an immediate determination in what manner this person should be treated. My family consisted of my wife and a young child. Our servant maid had been seized three days before by the reigning malady, and, at her own request, had been conveyed to the hospital. We ourselves enjoyed good health, and were hopeful of escaping with our lives. Our measures for this end had been cautiously taken and carefully adhered to. They did not consist in avoiding the receptacles of infection, for my office required me to go daily into the midst of them; nor in finding the house with the exhalations of gun-powder, vinegar, or tar. They consisted in cleanliness, reasonable exercise, and wholesome

---

[1] "My situation made me acquainted": the narrator is an enlightened physician who has remained in Philadelphia during the fever epidemic to treat individuals. He benevolently takes the fever-stricken Mervyn into his household and creates a frame for the novel's first part by listening to Mervyn relate his story up to the point of their meeting. Throughout the first part he remains unnamed. Brown often introduces characters well before their names appear; in this case, Dr. Stevens' name is not given until Chapter 4 of *Second Part*. For Stevens' name and its first appearance, see note II.4.5.

diet.[2] Custom had likewise blunted the edge of our apprehensions. To take this person into my house, and bestow upon him the requisite attendance, was the scheme that first occurred to me. In this, however the advice of my wife was to govern me.[3]

I mentioned the incident to her. I pointed out the danger which was to be dreaded from such an inmate. I desired her to decide with caution, and mentioned my resolution to conform myself implicitly to her decision. Should we refuse to harbour him, we must not forget that there was an hospital to which he would, perhaps, consent to be carried, and where he would be accommodated in the best manner the times would admit.

Nay, said she, talk not of hospitals. At least let him have his choice. I have no fear about me, for my part, in a case where the injunctions of duty are so obvious. Let us take the poor unfortunate wretch into our protection and care, and leave the consequences to Heaven.

I expected and was pleased with this proposal. I returned to the sick man, and, on rousing him from his stupor, found him still in possession of his reason. With a candle near, I had opportunity of viewing him more accurately.

His garb was plain, careless, and denoted rusticity: His aspect was simple and ingenuous, and his decayed visage still retained traces of uncommon, but manlike beauty. He had all the appearances of mere youth, unspoiled by luxury and uninured to misfortune. I scarcely ever beheld an object which laid so powerful and sudden a claim to my affection and succour.[4]

You are sick, said I, in as cheerful a tone as I could assume. Cold bricks and night airs are comfortless attendants for one in your condition. Rise, I pray you, and come into the house. We will try to supply you with accommodations a little more suitable.

---

[2] "Cleanliness, reasonable exercise, and wholesome diet": Stevens' hygienic precautions and treatments imply that the fever is not contagious and lean toward enlightened or scientific views of prevention rather than irrational hearsay or folklore. Stevens' "non-contagionist" approach and treatments are close to those favored by Caribbean physicians familiar with yellow fever, rather than invasive techniques chosen by local physicians who had less experience with the illness and tended to rely on printed accounts of it. These safeguards were also those of Brown and his circle of physician friends, many of whom remained in New York and Philadelphia during fever epidemics to care for the ill, and some of whom, like Brown's close friend Dr. Elihu Hubbard Smith, died while treating the illness.

[3] "The advice of my wife was to govern me": Stevens' egalitarian partnership and reasoned dialogue with his wife, Eliza Stevens, here and throughout the novel, is another sign of his enlightened values. Progressive association and conversation between men and women is a feature of the circle Mervyn builds around himself in *Second Part* and was a crucial element of Brown's intellectual circle in New York in the late 1790s. The Bush-Hill hospital to which Stevens refuses to send Mervyn is described in Chapter 18.

[4] "So powerful and sudden a claim to my affection and succor": Stevens repeatedly makes judgments based on empathetic perception of facial and bodily appearance. His language and actions thereby evoke eighteenth-century codes of sensibility and sympathy, which run throughout the novel, as well as contemporary debates about physiognomy (interpreting character through facial and physical structure).

Sensibility and sympathy are important concepts that were much debated in eighteenth-century culture and frequently referenced by Brown. They identify an immediate emotional-physical

At this address he fixed his languid eyes upon me. What would you have, said he. I am very well as I am. While I breathe, which will not be long, I shall breathe with more freedom here than elsewhere. Let me alone—I am very well as I am.

Nay, said I, this situation is unsuitable to a sick man. I only ask you to come into my house and receive all the kindness that it is in our power to bestow. Pluck up courage and I will answer for your recovery, provided you submit to directions, and do as we would have you. Rise, and come along with me. We will find you a physician and a nurse, and all we ask in return is good spirits and compliance.

Do you not know, he replied, what my disease is? Why should you risk your safety for the sake of one whom your kindness cannot benefit, and who has nothing to give in return?

There was something in the style of this remark, that heightened my prepossession in his favour, and made me pursue my purpose with more zeal. Let us try what we can do for you, I answered. If we save your life, we shall have done you some service, and as for recompence, we will look to that.

It was with considerable difficulty that he was persuaded to accept our invitation. He was conducted to a chamber, and the criticalness of his case requiring unusual attention, I spent the night at his bed-side.

My wife was encumbered with the care both of her infant and her family. The charming babe was in perfect health. But her mother's constitution was frail and delicate. We simplified the household duties as much as possible, but still these duties were considerably burthensome to one not used to the performance, and luxuriously educated.[5] The addition of a sick man, was likely to be productive of much fatigue. My engagements would not allow me to be always at home, and the state of my patient and the remedies necessary to be prescribed were attended with many noxious and disgustful circumstances. My fortune would not allow me to hire assistance. My wife, with feeble frame and a mind shrinking, on ordinary occasions, from such offices with fastidious scrupulousness, was to be his only or principal nurse.

My neighbours were fervent in their well-meant zeal, and loud in their remonstrances on the imprudence and rashness of my conduct. They called me presumptuous and cruel in exposing my wife and child, as well as myself, to such imminent hazard, for the sake of one too who most probably was worthless, and whose disease had doubtless been, by negligence or mistreatment, rendered incurable.

I did not turn a deaf ear to these censurers. I was aware of all the inconveniences and perils to which I thus spontaneously exposed myself. No one knew better the value of that woman whom I called mine, or set an higher price upon her life, her

---

connection with or response to other individuals, often celebrated as replacing older, pre-revolutionary or aristocratic modes of deference with new, more modern and implicitly egalitarian models for interpersonal behavior and cooperation. The doctor sympathetically believes that Mervyn deserves to be treated in a "higher" manner than his laboring-class clothes might suggest. For another example, see note 16.6.

[5] "Luxuriously educated": Stevens implies that their servants have left them during the fever and that his wife will be performing some of the servants' tasks.

health, and her ease. The virulence and activity of this contagion, the dangerous condition of my patient, and the dubiousness of his character, were not forgotten by me; but still my conduct in this affair received my own entire approbation. All objections on the score of my friend were removed by her own willingness and even solicitude to undertake the province. I had more confidence than others in the vincibility of this disease, and in the success of those measures which we had used for our defence against it. But, whatever were the evils to accrue to us, we were sure of one thing; namely, that the consciousness of having neglected this unfortunate person, would be a source of more unhappiness than could possibly redound from the attendance and care that he would claim.

The more we saw of him, indeed, the more did we congratulate ourselves on our proceeding. His torments were acute and tedious, but in the midst even of delirium, his heart seemed to overflow with gratitude, and to be actuated by no wish but to alleviate our toil and our danger. He made prodigious exertions to perform necessary offices for himself. He suppressed his feelings and struggled to maintain a cheerful tone and countenance, that he might prevent that anxiety which the sight of his sufferings produced in us. He was perpetually furnishing reasons why his nurse should leave him alone, and betrayed dissatisfaction whenever she entered his apartment.

In a few days, there were reasons to conclude him out of danger; and in a fortnight, nothing but exercise and nourishment were wanting to complete his restoration. Meanwhile nothing was obtained from him but general information, that his place of abode was Chester County,[6] and that some momentous engagement induced him to hazard his safety by coming to the city in the height of the epidemic.

He was far from being talkative. His silence seemed to be the joint result of modesty and unpleasing remembrances. His features were characterised by pathetic seriousness, and his deportment by a gravity very unusual at his age. According to his own representation, he was no more than eighteen years old, but the depth of his remarks indicated a much greater advance. His name was Arthur Mervyn. He described himself as having passed his life at the plough-tail and the threshing-floor: as being destitute of all scholastic instruction; and as being long since bereft of the affectionate regards of parents and kinsmen.

---

[6] "His place of abode was Chester Country": Chester County is immediately west and southwest of Philadelphia. Almost all of Arthur's movements take place in these two locales. At this time Chester County consisted primarily of farms and rural settlements with a predominantly Anglo, German, and Scots-Irish population and a southern border that was much disputed until legally fixed in 1774 as the Mason-Dixon line, after the southern part of the county had been split off into Maryland. After Pennsylvania abolished slavery in 1780, this southern boundary became part of the Pennsylvania border between free and slave states. Originally one of the three counties created at the state's founding in 1682 by William Penn, it was reduced in size by the 1790s after parts were used to create newer counties. Brown's father Elijah grew up in Nottingham, in the part of southern Chester County that was later divided by the Mason-Dixon line, and came to Philadelphia to begin a merchant career in the 1750s.

When questioned as to the course of life which he meant to pursue,[7] upon his recovery, he professed himself without any precise object. He was willing to be guided by the advice of others, and by the lights which experience should furnish. The country was open to him, and he supposed that there was no part of it in which food could not be purchased by his labour. He was unqualified, by his education, for any liberal profession. His poverty was likewise an insuperable impediment. He could afford to spend no time in the acquisition of a trade. He must labour, not for future emolument, but for immediate subsistence. The only pursuit which his present circumstances would allow him to adopt was that which, he was inclined to believe, was likewise the most eligible. Without doubt, his experience was slender, and it seemed absurd to pronounce concerning that of which he had no direct knowledge; but so it was, he could not out root from his mind the persuasion that to plough, to sow, and to reap were employments most befitting a reasonable creature, and from which the truest pleasure and the least pollution would flow. He contemplated no other scheme than to return, as soon as his health should permit, into the country, seek employment where it was to be had, and acquit himself in his engagements with fidelity and diligence.

I pointed out to him various ways in which the city might furnish employment to one with his qualifications. He had said that he was somewhat accustomed to the pen. There were stations in which the possession of a legible hand was all that was requisite. He might add to this a knowledge of accompts, and thereby procure himself a post in some mercantile or public office.[8]

To this he objected, that experience had shewn him unfit for the life of a penman. This had been his chief occupation for a little while, and he found it wholly incompatible with his health. He must not sacrifice the end for the means. Starving was a disease preferable to consumption. Besides, he laboured merely for the sake of living, and he lived merely for the sake of pleasure. If his tasks should enable him to live, but at the same time, bereave him of all satisfaction, they inflicted injury and were to be shunned as worse evils than death.

---

[7] "When questioned . . . pursue": this initial question about Mervyn's future, prompting reflections about how city and country life are related to virtue and vice or to different options for personal advancement and the pursuit of "justice and humanity," are pursued throughout the rest of the novel. The relation between city and country, explored in the novel as the first link in a larger mercantile chain connecting Philadelphia with the rest of the Atlantic world, both refers to and revises familiar period oppositions between civic-republican virtue (often allegorized as paternalist agrarian independence, through the image of the "yeoman" farmer) and emerging models of liberal progress (which idealize the world of commerce, making cities the home of civilizing and uplifting market exchange). In this sense, the novel can be read as a Woldwinite critique of both "republican" and "liberal" models as they are presented in key texts of the period, such as Crèvecoeur's *Letters from an American Farmer* (1782); Jefferson's *Notes on the State of Virginia* (1784); and Franklin's *Autobiography* (1793).

[8] "Mercantile or public office": Mervyn's language and writing skills qualify him for employment as a clerk or secretary.

I asked to what species of pleasure he alluded, with which the business of a clerk was inconsistent.

He answered, that he scarcely knew how to describe it. He read books when they came in his way. He had lighted upon few, and, perhaps, the pleasure they afford him was owing to their fewness; yet he confessed that a mode of life which entirely forbade him to read, was by no means to his taste. But this was trivial. He knew how to value the thoughts of other people, but he could not part with the privilege of observing and thinking for himself. He wanted business which would suffer at least nine-tenths of his attention to go free. If it afforded agreeable employment to that part of his attention which it applied to its own use, so much the better; but if it did not, he should not repine. He should be content with a life whose pleasures were to its pains as nine are to one. He had tried the trade of a copyist, and in circumstances more favourable than it was likely he should ever again have an opportunity of trying it, and he had found that it did not fulfil the requisite conditions. Whereas the trade of ploughman was friendly to health, liberty, and pleasure.

The pestilence, if it may so be called, was now declining. The health of my young friend allowed him to breathe the fresh air and to walk.—A friend of mine, by name Wortley, who had spent two months from the city, and to whom, in the course of a familiar correspondence, I had mentioned the foregoing particulars, returned from his rural excursion. He was posting, on the evening of the day of his arrival, with a friendly expedition, to my house, when he overtook Mervyn going in the same direction. He was surprised to find him go before him into my dwelling, and to discover, which he speedily did, that this was the youth whom I had so frequently mentioned to him. I was present at their meeting.

There was a strange mixture in the countenance of Wortley, when they were presented to each other. His satisfaction was mingled with surprise, and his surprise with anger. Mervyn, in his turn, betrayed considerable embarrassment. Wortley's thoughts were too earnest on some topic to allow him to converse. He shortly made some excuse for taking leave, and, rising, addressed himself to the youth with a request that he would walk home with him. This invitation, delivered in a tone which left it doubtful whether a compliment or menace were meant, augmented Mervyn's confusion. He complied without speaking, and they went out together;—my wife and I were left to comment upon the scene.

It could not fail to excite uneasiness. They were evidently no strangers to each other. The indignation that flashed from the eyes of Wortley, and the trembling consciousness of Mervyn were unwelcome tokens. The former was my dearest friend, and venerable for his discernment and integrity. The latter appeared to have drawn upon himself the anger and disdain of this man. We already anticipated the shock which the discovery of his unworthiness would produce.

In an half hour Mervyn returned. His embarrassment had given place to dejection. He was always serious, but his features were now overcast by the deepest gloom. The anxiety which I felt would not allow me to hesitate long.

Arthur, said I, something is the matter with you. Will you not disclose it to us? Perhaps you have brought yourself into some dilemma out of which we may help you to escape. Has any thing of an unpleasant nature passed between you and Wortley?

The youth did not readily answer. He seemed at a loss for a suitable reply. At length he said, that something disagreeable had indeed passed between him and Wortley. He had had the misfortune to be connected with a man by whom Wortley conceived himself to be injured. He had borne no part in inflicting this injury, but had nevertheless been threatened with ill treatment if he did not make disclosures which indeed it was in his power to make, but which he was bound, by every sanction, to withhold. This disclosure would be of no benefit to Wortley. It would rather operate injuriously than otherwise; yet it was endeavoured to be wrested from him by the heaviest menaces.—There he paused.

We were naturally inquisitive as to the scope of these menaces; but Mervyn intreated us to forbear any further discussion of this topic. He foresaw the difficulties to which his silence would subject him. One of its most fearful consequences would be the loss of our good opinion. He knew not what he had to dread from the enmity of Wortley. Mr. Wortley's violence was not without excuse. It was his mishap to be exposed to suspicions which could only be obviated by breaking his faith. But, indeed, he knew not whether any degree of explicitness would confute the charges that were made against him; whether, by trampling on his sacred promise, he should not multiply his perils instead of lessening their number. A difficult part had been assigned to him: by much too difficult for one, young, improvident, and inexperienced as he was.

Sincerity, perhaps, was the best course. Perhaps, after having had an opportunity for deliberation, he should conclude to adopt it; meanwhile he intreated permission to retire to his chamber. He was unable to exclude from his mind ideas which yet could, with no propriety, at least at present, be made the theme of conversation.

These words were accompanied with simplicity and pathos, and with tokens of unaffected distress.

Arthur, said I, you are master of your actions and time in this house. Retire when you please; but you will naturally suppose us anxious to dispel this mystery. Whatever shall tend to obscure or malign your character will of course excite our solicitude. Wortley is not short-sighted or hasty to condemn. So great is my confidence in his integrity that I will not promise my esteem to one who has irrecoverably lost that of Wortley. I am not acquainted with your motives to concealment, or what it is you conceal, but take the word of one who possesses that experience which you complain of wanting, that sincerity is always safest.

As soon as he had retired, my curiosity prompted me to pay an immediate visit to Wortley. I found him at home. He was no less desirous of an interview, and answered my inquiries with as much eagerness as they were made.

You know, said he, my disastrous connection with Thomas Welbeck. You recollect his sudden disappearance last July,[9] by which I was reduced to the brink of ruin. Nay,

---

[9] "Last July": July 1793, just before the yellow fever outbreak. This date supplies a reference point for the novel's timeline in the novel's *Second Part* (see note II.19.4).

I am, even now, far from certain that I shall survive that event. I spoke to you about the youth who lived with him, and by what means that youth was discovered to have crossed the river in his company on the night of his departure. This is that very youth.

This will account for my emotion at meeting him at your house: I brought him out with me. His confusion sufficiently indicated his knowledge of transactions between Welbeck and me. I questioned him as to the fate of that man. To own the truth, I expected some well digested lie; but he merely said, that he had promised secrecy on that subject, and must therefore be excused from giving me any information. I asked him if he knew, that his master, or accomplice, or whatever was his relation to him, absconded in my debt? He answered that he knew it well; but still pleaded a promise of inviolable secrecy as to his hiding place. This conduct justly exasperated me, and I treated him with the severity which he deserved. I am half ashamed to confess the excesses of my passion; I even went so far as to strike him. He bore my insults with the utmost patience. No doubt the young villain is well instructed in his lesson. He knows that he may safely defy my power.—From threats I descended to entreaties. I even endeavoured to wind the truth from him by artifice. I promised him a part of the debt if he would enable me to recover the whole. I offered him a considerable reward if he would merely afford me a clue by which I might trace him to his retreat; but all was insufficient. He merely put on an air of perplexity and shook his head in token of non-compliance.

Such was my friend's account of this interview. His suspicions were unquestionably plausible; but I was disposed to put a more favourable construction on Mervyn's behaviour. I recollected the desolate and pennyless condition in which I found him, and the uniform complacency and rectitude of his deportment for the period during which we had witnessed it. These ideas had considerable influence on my judgment, and indisposed me to follow the advice of my friend, which was to turn him forth from my doors that very night.

My wife's prepossessions[10] were still more powerful advocates of this youth. She would vouch, she said, before any tribunal, for his innocence; but she willingly concurred with me in allowing him the continuance of our friendship on no other condition than that of a disclosure of the truth. To entitle ourselves to this confidence we were willing to engage, in our turn, for the observance of secrecy, so far that no detriment should accrue from this disclosure to himself or his friend.

Next morning at breakfast, our guest appeared with a countenance less expressive of embarrassment than on the last evening. His attention was chiefly engaged by his own thoughts, and little was said till the breakfast was removed. I then reminded him of the incidents of the former day, and mentioned that the uneasiness which thence arose to us had rather been increased than diminished by time.

It is in your power, my young friend, continued I, to add still more to this uneasiness, or to take it entirely away. I had no personal acquaintance with Thomas

---

[10] "Prepossessions": "the condition of being favourably predisposed towards a person or thing" (OED e.g., *Oxford English Dictionary*).

Welbeck. I have been informed by others that his character, for a certain period, was respectable, but that, at length, he contracted large debts and, instead of paying them, absconded. You, it seems, lived with him. On the night of his departure you are known to have accompanied him across the river, and this, it seems, is the first of your re-appearance on the stage. Welbeck's conduct was dishonest. He ought doubtless to be pursued to his asylum and be compelled to refund his winnings. You confess yourself to know his place of refuge, but urge a promise of secrecy. Know you not that to assist, or connive at the escape of this man was wrong? To have promised to favour his concealment and impunity by silence was only an aggravation of this wrong. That, however, is past. Your youth, and circumstances, hitherto unexplained, may apologize for that misconduct, but it is certainly your duty to repair it to the utmost of your power. Think whether by disclosing what you know, you will not repair it.

I have spent most of last night, said the youth, in reflecting on this subject. I had come to a resolution, before you spoke, of confiding to you my simple tale. I perceive in what circumstances I am placed, and that I can keep my hold of your good opinion only by a candid deportment. I have indeed given a promise which it was wrong, or rather absurd, in another to exact and in me to give; yet none but considerations of the highest importance would persuade me to break my promise. No injury will accrue from my disclosure to Welbeck. If there should, dishonest as he was, that would be a sufficient reason for my silence. Wortley will not, in any degree, be benefited by any communication that I can make. Whether I grant or withhold information, my conduct will have influence only on my own happiness, and that influence will justify me in granting it.

I received your protection when I was friendless and forlorn. You have a right to know whom it is that you protected. My own fate is connected with the fate of Welbeck, and that connection, together with the interest you are pleased to take in my concerns, because they are mine, will render a tale worthy of attention which will not be recommended by variety of facts or skill in the display of them.

Wortley, though passionate, and, with regard to me, unjust, may yet be a good man; but I have no desire to make him one of my auditors. You, Sir, may, if you think proper, relate to him afterwards what particulars concerning Welbeck it may be of importance for him to know; but at present, it will be well if your indulgence shall support me to the end of a tedious but humble tale.

The eyes of my Eliza sparkled with delight at this proposal. She regarded this youth with a sisterly affection and considered his candour, in this respect, as an unerring test of his rectitude. She was prepared to hear and to forgive the errors of inexperience and precipitation. I did not fully participate in her satisfaction, but was nevertheless most zealously disposed to listen to his narrative.

My engagements obliged me to postpone this rehearsal till late in the evening. Collected then round a cheerful hearth, exempt from all likelihood of interruption from without, and our babe's unpractised senses, shut up in the sweetest and profoundest sleep, Mervyn, after a pause of recollection, began.

Chapter II

MY natal soil is Chester County.[1] My father had a small farm on which he has been able, by industry, to maintain himself and a numerous family. He has had many children, but some defect in the constitution of our mother has been fatal to all of them but me. They died successively as they attained the age of nineteen or twenty, and, since I have not yet reached that age, I may reasonably look for the same premature fate. In the spring of last year my mother followed her fifth child to the grave, and three months afterwards died herself.

My constitution has always been frail, and, till the death of my mother, I enjoyed unlimited indulgence. I cheerfully sustained my portion of labour, for that necessity prescribed; but the intervals were always at my own disposal, and in whatever manner I thought proper to employ them, my plans were encouraged and assisted. Fond appellations, tones of mildness, solicitous attendance when I was sick, deference to my opinions, and veneration for my talents compose the image which I still retain of my mother. I had the thoughtlessness and presumption of youth, and now that she is gone my compunction is awakened by a thousand recollections of my treatment of her. I was indeed guilty of no flagrant acts of contempt or rebellion. Perhaps her deportment was inevitably calculated to instil into me a froward and refractory spirit. My faults, however, were speedily followed by repentance, and in the midst of impatience and passion, a look of tender upbraiding from her was always sufficient to melt me into tears and make me ductile to her will. If sorrow for her loss be an atonement for the offences which I committed during her life, ample atonement has been made.

My father is a man of slender capacity, but of a temper easy and flexible. He was sober and industrious by habit. He was content to be guided by the superior intelligence of his wife. Under this guidance he prospered; but when that was withdrawn, his affairs soon began to betray marks of unskilfulness and negligence. My understanding, perhaps, qualified me to counsel and assist my father, but I was wholly unaccustomed to the task of superintendence. Besides, gentleness and fortitude did not descend to me from my mother, and these were indispensable attributes in a boy who desires to dictate to his grey-headed parent. Time, perhaps, might have conferred dexterity on me, or prudence on him, had not a most unexpected event given a different direction to my views.

Betty Lawrence was a wild girl from the pine forests of New-Jersey. At the age of ten years she became a bound servant[2] in this city, and, after the expiration of her time, came into my father's neighbourhood in search of employment. She was hired in our

---

[1] "Chester County": see note 1.6 on Arthur's identification with Chester County.

[2] "Bound servant": a bound or "indentured" servant was a (usually white) worker bound by legal contract to an employer for four to seven years in order to pay off a debt, an apprenticeship, or passage to a new home. This form of servitude was common at this time, but in its last phases. It marks an individual as unfree, although not a slave, and places them just above (black) slaves at the bottom of the social order; bond servants could be sold at auction as they came off Atlantic ships in this period. Thus the union between Mervyn's father, a free landowner, and Betty Lawrence, from a lower

family as milk-maid and market woman. Her features were coarse, her frame robust, her mind totally unlettered, and her morals defective in that point in which female excellence is supposed chiefly to consist. She possessed superabundant health and good humour, and was quite a supportable companion in the hay-field or the barn-yard.

On the death of my mother, she was exalted to a somewhat higher station. The same tasks fell to her lot; but the time and manner of performing them were, in some degree, submitted to her own choice. The cows and the dairy were still her province; but in this no one interfered with her, or pretended to prescribe her measures. For this province she seemed not unqualified, and as long as my father was pleased with her management, I had nothing to object.

This state of things continued, without material variation, for several months. There were appearances in my father's deportment to Betty, which excited my reflections, but not my fears. The deference which was occasionally paid to the advice or the claims of this girl, was accounted for by that feebleness of mind which degraded my father, in whatever scene he should be placed, to be the tool of others. I had no conception that her claims extended beyond a temporary or superficial gratification.

At length, however, a visible change took place in her manners. A scornful affectation and awkward dignity began to be assumed. A greater attention was paid to dress, which was of gayer hues and more fashionable texture. I rallied her on these tokens of a sweetheart, and amused myself with expatiating to her on the qualifications of her lover. A clownish fellow[3] was frequently her visitant. His attentions did not appear to be discouraged. He therefore was readily supposed to be the man. When pointed out as the favourite, great resentment was expressed, and obscure insinuations were made that her aim was not quite so low as that. These denials I supposed to be customary on such occasions, and considered the continuance of his visits as a sufficient confutation of them.

I frequently spoke of Betty, her newly acquired dignity, and of the probable cause of her change of manners to my father. When this theme was started, a certain coldness and reserve overspread his features. He dealt in monosyllables and either laboured to change the subject or made some excuse for leaving me. This behaviour, though it occasioned surprise, was never very deeply reflected on. My father was old, and the mournful impressions which were made upon him by the death of his wife, the lapse of almost half a year seemed scarcely to have weakened. Betty had chosen her partner, and I was in daily expectation of receiving a summons to the wedding.

One afternoon this girl dressed herself in the gayest manner and seemed making preparations for some momentous ceremony. My father had directed me to put the

---

status group, is perceived as demeaning. The novel features many characters, above all Mervyn himself, who are marked by disenfranchisement, low ethno-racial or gender status, servitude, and poverty and who explicitly or implicitly struggle to improve their rank and opportunities in the tumultuous social conditions of the 1790s. See notes 2.10, 5.5, and II.14.3 for more on Mervyn's brushes with servant status.

[3] "A clownish fellow": a "clown" in this period is a rustic, a rural worker.

horse to the chaise.[4] On my inquiring whither he was going, he answered me, in general terms, that he had some business at a few miles distance. I offered to go in his stead, but he said that was impossible. I was proceeding to ascertain the possibility of this when he left me to go to a field where his workmen were busy, directing me to inform him when the chaise was ready, to supply his place, while absent, in overlooking the workmen.

This office was performed; but before I called him from the field I exchanged a few words with the milk-maid, who sat on a bench, in all the primness of expectation and decked with the most gaudy plumage. I rated her imaginary lover for his tardiness, and vowed eternal hatred to them both for not making me a bride's attendant. She listened to me with an air in which embarrassment was mingled sometimes with exultation, and sometimes with malice. I left her at length, and returned to the house not till a late hour. As soon as I entered, my father presented Betty to me as his wife, and desired she might receive that treatment from me which was due to a mother.

It was not till after repeated and solemn declarations from both of them that I was prevailed upon to credit this event. Its effect upon my feelings may be easily conceived. I knew the woman to be rude, ignorant, and licentious. Had I suspected this event I might have fortified my father's weakness and enabled him to shun the gulf to which he was tending; but my presumption had been careless of the danger. To think that such an one should take the place of my revered mother was intolerable.

To treat her in any way not squaring with her real merits; to hinder anger and scorn from rising at the sight of her in her new condition, was not in my power. To be degraded to the rank of her servant, to become the sport of her malice and her artifices was not to be endured. I had no independent provision; but I was the only child of my father, and had reasonably hoped to succeed to his patrimony.[5] On this hope I had built a thousand agreeable visions. I had meditated innumerable projects which the possession of this estate would enable me to execute. I had no wish beyond the trade of agriculture, and beyond the opulence which an hundred acres would give.

These visions were now at an end. No doubt her own interest would be, to this woman, the supreme law, and this would be considered as irreconcilably hostile to mine. My father would easily be moulded to her purpose, and that act easily extorted from him which should reduce me to beggary. She had a gross and perverse taste. She had a numerous kindred, indigent and hungry. On these his substance would speedily be lavished. Me she hated, because she was conscious of having injured me, because she knew that I held her in contempt, and because I had detected her in an illicit intercourse with the son of a neighbour.

The house in which I lived was no longer my own, nor even my father's. Hitherto I had thought and acted in it with the freedom of a master, but now I was become, in my own conceptions, an alien and an enemy to the roof under which I was born.

---

[4] "Chaise": a small carriage.

[5] "Patrimony": an inheritance; literally a paternal inheritance, passed down from the father in a patriarchal social system.

Every tie which had bound me to it was dissolved or converted into something which repelled me to a distance from it. I was a guest whose presence was borne with anger and impatience.

I was fully impressed with the necessity of removal, but I knew not whither to go, or what kind of subsistence to seek. My father had been a Scottish emigrant,[6] and had no kindred on this side of the ocean. My mother's family lived in New-Hampshire, and long separation had extinguished all the rights of relationship in her offspring. Tilling the earth was my only profession, and to profit by my skill in it, it would be necessary to become a day-labourer in the service of strangers; but this was a destiny to which I, who had so long enjoyed the pleasures of independence and command, could not suddenly reconcile myself. It occurred to me that the city might afford me an asylum. A short day's journey would transport me into it. I had been there twice or thrice in my life, but only for a few hours each time. I knew not an human face, and was a stranger to its modes and dangers. I was qualified for no employment, compatible with a town-life, but that of the pen. This, indeed, had ever been a favourite tool with me, and though it may appear somewhat strange, it is no less true that I had had nearly as much practice at the quill as at the mattock.[7] But the sum of my skill lay in tracing distinct characters. I had used it merely to transcribe what others had written, or to give form to my own conceptions. Whether the city would afford me employment, as a mere copyist, sufficiently lucrative, was a point on which I possessed no means of information.

My determination was hastened by the conduct of my new mother. My conjectures as to the course she would pursue with regard to me had not been erroneous. My father's deportment, in a short time, grew sullen and austere. Directions were given in a magisterial tone, and any remissness in the execution of his orders, was rebuked with an air of authority. At length these rebukes were followed by certain intimations that I was now old enough to provide for myself; that it was time to think of some employment by which I might secure a livelihood; that it was a shame for me to spend my youth in idleness; that what he had gained was by his own labour; and I must be indebted for my living to the same source.

---

[6] "Scottish emigrant": this is the first mention of Mervyn's "Scottish" background. In *Second Part,* Chapter II.2, the father's name will be given as "Sawny," a pejorative nickname for someone of Scottish ethnicity (note II.2.3). The implication is that Mervyn's family is ethnically "Scots-Irish" or Protestant Irish, like the characters Clithero in Brown's novel *Edgar Huntly* or Frank Carwin in *Wieland*. In cultural terms, Mervyn is a displaced Protestant Irishman of the type whose truthfulness and experience were commonly interrogated and devalued by the period's Anglo-Quaker elites. At this time the Scots-Irish were considered a separate and inferior race or ethnicity, situated near the bottom of the Euro-American social hierarchy. Since the mother is from New Hampshire, the implication is that she may come from more "civilized" Anglo stock, making Mervyn a child of mixed ethnicity.

[7] "Mattock": "A tool similar to a pick but with a point or chisel edge at one end of the head and an adze-like blade at the other, used for breaking up hard ground, grubbing up trees, etc." (OED).

These hints were easily understood. At first, they excited indignation and grief. I knew the source whence they sprung, and was merely able to suppress the utterance of my feelings in her presence. My looks, however, were abundantly significant, and my company became hourly more insupportable. Abstracted from these considerations, my father's remonstrances[8] were not destitute of weight. He gave me being, but sustenance ought surely to be my own gift. In the use of that for which he had been indebted to his own exertions, he might reasonably consult his own choice. He assumed no control over me: he merely did what he would with his own, and so far from fettering my liberty, he exhorted me to use it for my own benefit, and to make provision for myself.

I now reflected that there were other manual occupations besides that of the plough. Among these none had fewer disadvantages than that of carpenter or cabinet-maker. I had no knowledge of this art; but neither custom, nor law, nor the impenetrableness of the mystery required me to serve a seven years' apprenticeship to it. A master in this trade might possibly be persuaded to take me under his tuition: two or three years would suffice to give me the requisite skill. Meanwhile my father would, perhaps, consent to bear the cost of my maintenance. Nobody could live upon less than I was willing to do.

I mentioned these ideas to my father; but he merely commended my intentions without offering to assist me in the execution of them. He had full employment, he said, for all the profits of his ground. No doubt if I would bind myself to serve four or five years, my master would be at the expence of my subsistence. Be that as it would, I must look for nothing from him. I had shewn very little regard for his happiness: I had refused all marks of respect to a woman who was entitled to it from her relation to him. He did not see why he should treat as a son one who refused what was due to him as a father. He thought it right that I should henceforth maintain myself. He did not want my services on the farm, and the sooner I quitted his house the better.

I retired from this conference with a resolution to follow the advice that was given. I saw that henceforth I must be my own protector, and wondered at the folly that detained me so long under his roof. To leave it was now become indispensable, and there could be no reason for delaying my departure for a single hour. I determined to bend my course to the city. The scheme foremost in my mind was to apprentice myself to some mechanical trade.[9] I did not overlook the evils of constraint and the dubiousness as to the character of the master I should choose. I was not without hopes

---

[8] "Remonstrances": strenuous objections or complaints.

[9] "Mechanical trade": a "mechanic" in this period is a worker with a particular skill or trade, thus a more specialized laborer than a farmer. Achieving this status usually required a monetary fee or indentured service to the "master" craftsmen who trained the apprentice. Mervyn reconsiders this scheme at the beginning of Chapter 5, after his first introduction to the city (note 5.1).

that accident would suggest a different expedient, and enable me to procure an immediate subsistence without forfeiting my liberty.[10]

I determined to commence my journey the next morning. No wonder the prospect of so considerable a change in my condition should deprive me of sleep. I spent the night ruminating on the future, and in painting to my fancy the adventures which I should be likely to meet. The foresight of man is in proportion to his knowledge. No wonder that in my state of profound ignorance, not the faintest preconception should be formed of the events that really befel me. My temper was inquisitive, but there was nothing in the scene to which I was going from which my curiosity[11] expected to derive gratification. Discords and evil smells, unsavoury food, unwholesome labour, and irksome companions, were, in my opinion, the unavoidable attendants of a city.

My best clothes were of the homeliest texture and shape. My whole stock of linen consisted of three check shirts. Part of my winter evening's employment, since the death of my mother, consisted in knitting my own stockings. Of these I had three pair, one of which I put on, and the rest I formed, together with two shirts, into a bundle. Three quarter-dollar pieces composed my whole fortune in money.[12]

---

[10] "Without forfeiting my liberty": since Arthur's father refuses to support him and even suggests in the previous paragraph that he should "bind [him]self to serve four or five years," he is now faced with the same options of servitude and degraded social rank that defined Betty Lawrence earlier. Here he considers the real possibility of becoming a bound servant and trading his status as a free citizen for employment and subsistence. With no inheritance or professional class status to make him a free property holder, Mervyn has no more economic capital than the lowest white laborer or servant.

[11] "Curiosity": curiosity is a keyword in eighteenth-century debates about history and the pursuit of knowledge, particularly among the Woldwinite writers, who are Brown's primary models, and Brown frequently uses it to motivate his protagonists in ways that relate to these debates. The term has an ambivalent meaning: it reflects the Enlightenment desire to learn, but can also lead to unchecked excess. Both are in evidence throughout this novel. Like the protagonist Caleb in William Godwin's novel *Caleb Williams* (1794), a crucial precedent here, Mervyn's "inquisitive" temper leads him to both knowledge and gothic experiences of social corruption.

[12] "Money": this tiny sum soon fades in comparison with the fortunes won and lost in the novel's frauds and other transactions. Calculated relative to the consumer price index then and now, one 1790 dollar is equivalent to about 22 dollars at the beginning of the twenty-first century.

Chapter III

I ROSE at the dawn, and without asking or bestowing a blessing, sallied forth into the high road to the city which passed near the house. I left nothing behind, the loss of which I regretted. I had purchased most of my own books with the product of my own separate industry, and their number being, of course, small, I had, by incessant application, gotten the whole of them by rote. They had ceased, therefore, to be of any further use. I left them, without reluctance, to the fate for which I knew them to be reserved, that of affording food and habitation to mice.

I trod this unwonted path with all the fearlessness of youth. In spite of the motives to despondency and apprehension, incident to my state, my heels were light and my heart joyous. Now, said I, I am mounted into man.[1] I must build a name and a fortune for myself. Strange if this intellect and these hands will not supply me with an honest livelihood. I will try the city in the first place; but if that should fail, resources are still left to me. I will resume my post in the corn-field and threshing-floor, to which I shall always have access, and where I shall always be happy.

I had proceeded some miles on my journey, when I began to feel the inroads of hunger. I might have stopped at any farm-house, and have breakfasted for nothing. It was prudent to husband, with the utmost care, my slender stock; but I felt reluctance to beg as long as I had the means of buying, and I imagined, that coarse bread and a little milk would cost little even at a tavern, when any farmer was willing to bestow them for nothing. My resolution was farther influenced by the appearance of a sign-post. What excuse could I make for begging a breakfast with an inn at hand and silver in my pocket?

I stopped, accordingly, and breakfasted. The landlord was remarkably attentive and obliging, but his bread was stale, his milk sour, and his cheese the greenest imaginable. I disdained to animadvert [2]on these defects, naturally supposing that his house could furnish no better.

---

[1] "I am mounted into man": Mervyn's self-empowerment through rejection of paternal authority (ironic here, since he is about to learn just how fragile his position really is) is an iconic Enlightenment act of rebellion and independence, a self-appropriation of authority that appears frequently in the writing of the Atlantic revolutionary age. The prime U.S. example is Benjamin Franklin's *Autobiography*, first published in 1793, the year of this novel's action; British examples are Thomas Holcroft's *Anna St. Ives* (1792) and Godwin's *Caleb Williams* (1794). The previous chapter's drama of paternal impotence, to be recalled and further developed in Chapter II.14, provides motivation and justification for Mervyn's desire to find his way as a rational individual, an enlightened citizen. Rightful social authority and order were commonly symbolized as fatherly authority and deference in early modern culture; but this novel, like Brown's others, consistently represents the old regime of patriarchal order as flawed, tyrannical, and backward. The matriarchal overtones of Mervyn's enlightened social circle in *Second Part* thus amount to a principled negation of paternalist assumptions and values.

[2] "Animadvert": censure or criticize negatively.

Having finished my meal, I put, without speaking, one of my pieces into his hand. This deportment I conceived to be highly becoming, and to indicate a liberal and manly spirit. I always regarded with contempt a scrupulous maker of bargains. He received the money with a complaisant obeisance. Right, said he. *Just* the money, Sir. You are on foot, Sir. A pleasant way of travelling, Sir. I wish you a good day, Sir.—So saying he walked away.

This proceeding was wholly unexpected. I conceived myself entitled to at least three-fourths of it in change. The first impulse was to call him back, and contest the equity of his demand, but a moment's reflection shewed me the absurdity of such conduct. I resumed my journey with spirits somewhat depressed. I have heard of voyagers and wanderers in deserts, who were willing to give a casket of gems for a cup of cold water. I had not supposed my own condition to be, in any respect, similar; yet I had just given one third of my estate for a breakfast.

I stopped at noon at another inn. I counted on purchasing a dinner for the same price, since I meant to content myself with the same fare. A large company was just sitting down to a smoking banquet. The landlord invited me to join them. I took my place at the table, but was furnished with bread and milk. Being prepared to depart, I took him aside. What is to pay? said I.—Did you drink anything, Sir?—Certainly. I drank the milk which was furnished.—But any liquors, Sir?—No.

He deliberated a moment and then assuming an air of disinterestedness, 'Tis our custom to charge dinner and club, but as you drank nothing, we'll let the club go. A mere dinner is half-a-dollar, Sir.

He had no leisure to attend to my fluctuations. After debating with myself on what was to be done, I concluded that compliance was best, and leaving the money at the bar resumed my way.

I had not performed more than half my journey, yet my purse was entirely exhausted. This was a specimen of the cost incurred by living at an inn. If I entered the city, a tavern must, at least for some time, be my abode, but I had not a farthing remaining to defray my charges. My father had formerly entertained a boarder for a dollar per week, and, in a case of need, I was willing to subsist upon coarser fare, and lie on an harder bed than those with which our guest had been supplied. These facts had been the foundation of my negligence on this occasion.

What was now to be done? To return to my paternal mansion[3] was impossible. To relinquish my design of entering the city and to seek a temporary asylum, if not permanent employment, at some one of the plantations, within view, was the most obvious expedient. These deliberations did not slacken my pace. I was almost

---

[3] "Paternal mansion": "mansion" here means simply a dwelling or structure, not a luxurious home marking high status, as in the Philadelphia setting. Nevertheless, the intentional ambivalence of terms like "paternal mansion" or "my estate," five paragraphs earlier in "I had given one third of my estate for a breakfast," provides an ironic, dryly economic perspective on Mervyn's new independence and lack of patrimony.

unmindful of my way, when I found I had passed Schuylkill at the upper bridge.[4] I was now within the precincts of the city and night was hastening. It behoved me to come to a speedy decision.

Suddenly I recollected that I had not paid the customary toll at the bridge: neither had I money wherewith to pay it. A demand of payment would have suddenly arrested my progress; and so slight an incident would have precluded that wonderful destiny to which I was reserved. The obstacle that would have hindered my advance, now prevented my return. Scrupulous honesty did not require me to turn back and awaken the vigilance of the toll gatherer. I had nothing to pay, and by returning I should only double my debt. Let it stand, said I, where it does. All that honour enjoins is to pay when I am able.

I adhered to the cross ways, till I reached Market-street.[5] Night had fallen, and a triple row of lamps presented a spectacle enchanting and new. My personal cares were, for a time, lost in the tumultuous sensations with which I was now engrossed. I had never visited the city at this hour. When my last visit was paid I was a mere child. The novelty which environed every object was, therefore, nearly absolute. I proceeded with more cautious steps, but was still absorbed in attention to passing objects. I reached the market-house, and, entering it, indulged myself in new delight and new wonder.

I need not remark that our ideas of magnificence and splendour are merely comparative; yet you may be prompted to smile when I tell you that, in walking through this avenue, I, for a moment, conceived myself transported to the hall "pendent with many a row of starry lamps and blazing crescents fed by naptha and asphaltos."[6] That

---

[4] "Upper bridge": in the 1790s three "floating" or pontoon bridges crossed the Schuylkill River into Philadelphia from Chester County in the west. The lower two were at Gray's Ferry, site of the present-day Gray's Ferry Avenue Bridge, and at Market Street, site of the first permanent bridge across the Schuylkill in 1800 and the present-day Market Street Bridge. The "upper bridge" where Mervyn crosses was north of Market Street at the foot of the hill ("Fair-Mount") where the present-day Philadelphia Museum of Art is located, and connected with Callowhill and Vine Streets. The site was earlier known as "Scull's Ferry" and corresponds to the present-day Spring Garden Street Bridge. In the 1780s, Thomas Paine identified the need for an iron bridge across the Schuylkill with progressive efforts to improve the city. See period sketches of this stretch of the river in Foster, *Captain Watson's Travels in America*.

[5] "Market-street": Mervyn reaches the main thoroughfare and central axis of early Philadelphia, a 100-foot wide boulevard running east-west between the Schuylkill and Delaware rivers. As he enters the city he walks unawares past the residences and institutions of the town and nation's elite. As president in 1793, for example, George Washington's official residence was on Market Street between Fifth and Sixth.

[6] "Naptha and asphaltos": as Mervyn walks through three blocks of covered market buildings running down the middle of Market Street from Fourth to Front, illuminated by interior lamps, he conveys his amazement by loosely quoting John Milton's *Paradise Lost*, Book I (1667). These buildings were familiar features of everyday life in Philadelphia in this period and condense its urban development into a single image. The passage Mervyn quotes describes the lamps that illuminate Pandaemonium, the vast golden palace where Satan calls the fallen angels together: "Within, her

this transition from my homely and quiet retreat, had been affected in so few hours, wore the aspect of miracle or magic.

I proceeded from one of these buildings to another, till I reached their termination in Front-street.[7] Here my progress was checked, and I sought repose to my weary limbs by seating myself on a stall. No wonder some fatigue was felt by me, accustomed as I was to strenuous exertions, since, exclusive of the minutes spent at breakfast and dinner, I had travelled fifteen hours and forty-five miles.

I began now to reflect, with some earnestness, on my condition. I was a stranger, friendless, and moneyless. I was unable to purchase food and shelter, and was wholly unused to the business of begging. Hunger was the only serious inconvenience to which I was immediately exposed. I had no objection to spend the night in the spot where I then sat. I had no fear that my visions would be troubled by the officers of police. It was no crime to be without a home; but how should I supply my present cravings and the cravings of tomorrow?

At length it occurred to me that one of our country neighbours was probably at this time in the city. He kept a store as well as cultivated a farm. He was a plain and well meaning man, and should I be so fortunate as to meet him, his superior knowledge of the city might be of essential benefit to me in my present forlorn circumstances. His generosity might likewise induce him to lend me so much as would purchase one meal. I had formed the resolution to leave the city next day and was astonished at the folly that had led me into it; but, meanwhile, my physical wants must be supplied.

Where should I look for this man? In the course of conversation I recollected him to have referred to the place of his temporary abode. It was an inn, but the sign, or the name of the keeper, for some time withstood all my efforts to recall them.

At length I lighted on the last. It was Lesher's tavern.[8] I immediately set out in

---

ample spaces, o'er the smooth / And level pavement; from the archèd roof / Pendant by subtle magic many a row / Of starry lamps and blazing cressets fed / With *naphtha* and *asphaltus* yielded light / As from a sky" (I, 725–30).

Comparing the city's iconic central marketplace to marvelous structures raised in hell, the quotation foreshadows a context of urban corruption and vicious, subterranean struggles within market society, rather than one of redemption like the Puritan image of a City on a Hill. On the market buildings that ran down the center of Market Street (then officially High Street) see Gilchrist, "Market Houses in High Street." For other important Milton citations near the end of the novel, see notes II.22.1 and II.22.2. Throughout *Arthur Mervyn*, glimmering lights act as a sympathetic fallacy foreshadowing disaster.

[7] "Front-street": a north-south street primarily of offices and warehouses at the foot of Market Street, running parallel to the Delaware River waterfront and docks, and the primary locus of the import-export trade that plays a crucial role in the action that follows. The intersection of Front and Market was the ground zero and nerve center of mercantile commerce and finance in 1790s Philadelphia and the core of the city's urban density. At the time *Arthur Mervyn* was published, Brown's family import-export firm, James Brown & Co., had its office at 33 South Front Street.

[8] "Lesher's Tavern": George Lesher's tavern at 94 North Second (between Arch and Race), at "The Sign of the Bethlehem and New-York Stages" since it was the terminus of a daily service to and from these and other cities. The area north of Market Street near Second or Third and Race was known

search of it. After many inquiries I at last arrived at the door. I was preparing to enter the house when I perceived that my bundle was gone. I had left it on the stall where I had been sitting. People were perpetually passing to and fro. It was scarcely possible not to have been noticed. No one that observed it would fail to make it his prey. Yet it was of too much value to me, to allow me to be governed by a bare probability. I resolved to lose not a moment in returning.

With some difficulty I retraced my steps, but the bundle had disappeared. The clothes were, in themselves, of small value, but they constituted the whole of my wardrobe; and I now reflected that they were capable of being transmuted, by the pawn or sale of them, into food. There were other wretches as indigent as I was, and I consoled myself by thinking that my shirts and stockings might furnish a seasonable covering to their nakedness; but there was a relique concealed within this bundle, the loss of which could scarcely be endured by me. It was the portrait of a young man who died three years ago at my father's house, drawn by his own hand.

He was discovered one morning in the orchard with many marks of insanity upon him. His air and dress bespoke some elevation of rank and fortune. My mother's compassion was excited, and, as his singularities were harmless, an asylum was afforded him, though he was unable to pay for it. He was constantly declaiming, in an incoherent manner, about some mistress who had proved faithless. His speeches seemed, however, like the rantings of an actor, to be rehearsed by rote or for the sake of exercise. He was totally careless of his person and health, and by repeated negligences of this kind, at last contracted a fever of which he speedily died. The name which he assumed was Clavering.

He gave no distinct account of his family, but stated in loose terms that they were residents in England, high born and wealthy. That they had denied him the woman whom he loved and banished him to America, under penalty of death if he should dare to return, and that they had refused him all means of subsistence in a foreign land. He predicted, in his wild and declamatory way, his own death. He was very skilful at the pencil, and drew this portrait a short time before his dissolution, presented it to me, and charged me to preserve it in remembrance of him. My mother loved the youth because he was amiable and unfortunate, and chiefly, because she fancied a very powerful resemblance between his countenance and mine.[9] I was too

---

as "Hell-Town" for its concentration of brothels and taverns, frequented mainly by sailors and servants. By the time the novel was written, gentrification was changing this older association, although a stretch of row houses at Third and Race was still known by the "Hell-Town" name many years later. The city was filled with taverns (one for every twenty-five adult males in this period), but Mervyn looks for Mr. Capper at one that is associated with contemporary Democratic-Republican society organizations. George Lesher was a member of the progressive Democratic Society of Pennsylvania, and the tavern was in the news in 1798–1799 as a society meeting place. Brown's Philadelphia address in the late 1790s was on the same street as this tavern, but in a more respectable area at 119 South Second (a property owned by his wealthy aunt Elizabeth Armitt).

[9] "A very powerful resemblance between his countenance and mine": in Chapters 7 and following, Mervyn's uncanny resemblance to Clavering becomes a plot motif advancing his relation to the

young to build affection on any rational foundation. I loved him, for whatever reason, with an ardour unusual at my age, and which this portrait had contributed to prolong and to cherish.

In thus finally leaving my home, I was careful not to leave this picture behind. I wrapt it in paper in which a few elegiac stanzas[10] were inscribed in my own hand and with my utmost elegance of penmanship. I then placed it in a leathern case, which, for greater security, was deposited in the centre of my bundle. It will occur to you, perhaps, that it would be safer in some fold or pocket of the clothes which I wore. I was of a different opinion and was now to endure the penalty of my error.

It was in vain to heap execrations[11] on my negligence, or to consume the little strength left to me in regrets. I returned once more to the tavern and made inquiries for Mr. Capper, the person whom I have just mentioned as my father's neighbour. I was informed that Capper was now in town; that he had lodged, on the last-night, at this house; that he had expected to do the same to-night, but a gentleman had called ten minutes ago, whose invitation to lodge with him to-night had been accepted. They had just gone out together. Who, I asked, was the gentleman? The landlord had no knowledge of him: he knew neither his place of abode nor his name. . . . Was Mr. Capper expected to return hither in the morning?—No, he had heard the stranger propose to Mr. Capper to go with him into the country to-morrow, and Mr. Capper, he believed, had assented.

This disappointment was peculiarly severe. I had lost, by my own negligence, the only opportunity that would offer of meeting my friend. Had even the recollection of my loss been postponed for three minutes, I should have entered the house, and a meeting would have been secured. I could discover no other expedient to obviate the present evil. My heart began now, for the first time, to droop. I looked back, with nameless emotions, on the days of my infancy. I called up the image of my mother. I reflected on the infatuation of my surviving parent, and the usurpation of the detestable Betty with horror. I viewed myself as the most calamitous and desolate of human beings.

---

characters Welbeck and Mrs. Wentworth (Clavering's aunt). This doubling is itself doubled in Mervyn's similar uncanny resemblance to the younger Vincentio Lodi, which is his initial link to the merchant Welbeck beginning in Chapter 5 (see note 9.2). These uncanny likenesses are elements of a wider pattern of doubling and repetition that structures the novel's first part. A motif of twin-like doubling and resemblance also underlies the plot of Brown's novel *Memoirs of Stephen Calvert*, which was serialized in between this novel's two parts from June 1799 to June 1800. The itinerant Clavering is taken in by Mervyn's mother in a manner similar to the way Mervyn is welcomed in *Second Part* by other older, benevolent women such as Eliza Stevens, Mrs. Wentworth, and, finally, Achsa Fielding.

[10] "Elegiac stanzas": in keeping with his affection for poetry and Milton, Mervyn has composed verses and carefully written them on the paper in which he wraps Clavering's portrait. Elegiac verse is any verse written in elegiac meter (couplets with alternating rhythm) and not necessarily poetry of grief and mourning, although the predominant association in the 1790s is with the tone of melancholy exemplified by Thomas Gray's 1768 "Elegy Written in a Country Churchyard."

[11] "Execrations": curses.

At this time I was sitting in the common room. There were others in the same apartment, lounging, or whistling, or singing. I noticed them not, but leaning my head upon my hand, I delivered myself up to painful and intense meditation. From this I was roused by some one placing himself on the bench near me and addressing me thus: Pray Sir, if you will excuse me, who was the person whom you were looking for just now? Perhaps I can give you the information you want. If I can, you will be very welcome to it.—I fixed my eyes with some eagerness on the person that spoke. He was a young man, expensively and fashionably dressed, whose mien was considerably prepossessing, and whose countenance bespoke some portion of discernment.[12] I described to him the man whom I sought. I am in search of the same man myself, said he, but I expect to meet him here. He may lodge elsewhere, but he promised to meet me here at half after nine. I have no doubt he will fulfil his promise, so that you will meet the gentleman.

I was highly gratified by this information, and thanked my informant with some degree of warmth. My gratitude he did not notice, but continued: In order to beguile expectation, I have ordered supper. Will you do me the favour to partake with me, unless indeed you have supped already? I was obliged, somewhat awkwardly, to decline his invitation, conscious as I was that the means of payment were not in my power. He continued however to urge my compliance, till at length it was, though reluctantly, yielded. My chief motive was the certainty of seeing Capper.

My new acquaintance was exceedingly conversible, but his conversation was chiefly characterized by frankness and good humour. My reserves gradually diminished, and I ventured to inform him, in general terms, of my former condition and present views. He listened to my details with seeming attention, and commented on them with some judiciousness. His statements, however, tended to discourage me from remaining in the city.

Meanwhile the hour passed and Capper did not appear. I noticed this circumstance to him with no little solicitude. He said that possibly he might have forgotten or neglected his engagement. His affair was not of the highest importance, and might be readily postponed to a future opportunity. He perceived that my vivacity was greatly damped by this intelligence. He importuned me to disclose the cause. He made himself very merry with my distress, when it was at length discovered. As to the expence of supper, I had partaken of it at his invitation, he therefore should of course be charged with it. As to lodging, he had a chamber and a bed which he would insist upon my sharing with him.

---

[12] "He was a young man . . . some portion of discernment": this character is Wallace, another young man from Chester County, who has become a clerk for the merchant Thetford. He remains a mysterious figure at this point and will not be named until Chapter 14 but plays a key role in connecting Mervyn to the Hadwin family in the remainder of the novel. In this first encounter with Wallace, Brown foreshadows the merchant clerk's ambiguous adherence to the standards of a commercial moral community.

My faculties were thus kept upon the stretch of wonder. Every new act of kindness in this man surpassed the fondest expectation that I had formed. I saw no reason why I should be treated with benevolence. I should have acted in the same manner if placed in the same circumstances; yet it appeared incongruous and inexplicable. I know whence my ideas of human nature were derived. They certainly were not the offspring of my own feelings. These would have taught me that interest and duty were blended in every act of generosity.

I did not come into the world without my scruples and suspicions. I was more apt to impute kindnesses to sinister and hidden than to obvious and laudable motives. I paused to reflect upon the possible designs of this person. What end could be served by this behaviour? I was no subject of violence or fraud. I had neither trinket nor coin to stimulate the treachery of others. What was offered was merely lodging for the night. Was this an act of such transcendent disinterestedness as to be incredible? My garb was meaner than that of my companion, but my intellectual accomplishments were at least upon a level with his. Why should he be supposed to be insensible to my claims upon his kindness. I was a youth destitute of experience, money, and friends; but I was not devoid of all mental and personal endowments. That my merit should be discovered, even on such slender intercourse, had surely nothing in it that shocked belief.[13]

While I was thus deliberating, my new friend was earnest in his solicitations for my company. He remarked my hesitation, but ascribed it to a wrong cause. Come, said he, I can guess your objections and can obviate them. You are afraid of being ushered into company; and people who have passed their lives like you have a wonderful antipathy to strange faces; but this is bed-time with our family, so that we can defer your introduction to them till to-morrow. We may go to our chamber without being seen by any but servants.

I had not been aware of this circumstance. My reluctance flowed from a different cause, but now that the inconveniences of ceremony were mentioned, they appeared to me of considerable weight. I was well pleased that they should thus be avoided, and consented to go along with him.

We passed several streets and turned several corners. At last we turned into a kind of court which seemed to be chiefly occupied by stables. We will go, said he, by the back way into the house. We shall thus save ourselves the necessity of entering the parlour, where some of the family may still be.

My companion was as talkative as ever, but said nothing from which I could gather any knowledge of the number, character, and condition of his family.

---

[13] "That my merit should be discovered . . . had surely nothing in it that shocked belief": Mervyn is anxious about how his low social status will determine his relations to others and naively hopes that intrinsic "merit" may be visible apart from his embodied status as a poor Scots-Irish youth newly arrived in the city.

Chapter IV

WE arrived at a brick wall through which we passed by a gate into an extensive court or yard. The darkness would allow me to see nothing but outlines. Compared with the pigmy dimensions of my father's wooden hovel, the buildings before me were of gigantic loftiness. The horses were here far more magnificently accommodated than I had been. By a large door we entered an elevated hall. Stay here, said he, just while I fetch a light.

He returned, bearing a candle, before I had time to ponder on my present situation.

We now ascended a stair-case, covered with painted canvas. No one whose inexperience is less than mine, can imagine to himself the impressions made upon me by surrounding objects. The height to which this stair ascended, its dimensions, and its ornaments, appeared to me a combination of all that was pompous and superb.

We stopped not till we had reached the third story. Here my companion unlocked and led the way into a chamber. This, said he, is my room: Permit me to welcome you into it.

I had no time to examine this room before, by some accident, the candle was extinguished. Curse upon my carelessness, said he. I must go down again and light the candle. I will return in a twinkling. Meanwhile you may undress yourself and go to bed. He went out, and, as I afterwards recollected, locked the door behind him.

I was not indisposed to follow his advice, but my curiosity would first be gratified by a survey of the room. Its height and spaciousness were imperfectly discernible by star-light, and by gleams from a street lamp. The floor was covered with a carpet, the walls with brilliant hangings; the bed and windows were shrouded by curtains of a rich texture and glossy hues. Hitherto I had merely read of these things. I knew them to be the decorations of opulence, and yet as I viewed them, and remembered where and what I was on the same hour the preceding day, I could scarcely believe myself awake or that my senses were not beguiled by some spell.

Where, said I, will this adventure terminate? I rise on the morrow with the dawn and speed into the country. When this night is remembered, how like a vision will it appear! If I tell the tale by a kitchen fire, my veracity will be disputed. I shall be ranked with the story tellers of Shirauz and Bagdad.[1]

Though busied in these reflections, I was not inattentive to the progress of time. Methought my companion was remarkably dilatory. He went merely to re-light his

---

[1] "I shall be ranked with the story-tellers of Shirauz and Bagdad": like his amazement at Market Street or at the luxurious surroundings of an urban mansion in the next chapter, Mervyn's introduction to the urban world constructed by commerce is described here as an experience of disorientation and shock, of extreme, quasimagical transformations. To provide an analogy, Mervyn alludes to the magical visions, fantastic structures, and extravagant luxuries in the popular eighteenth-century genre of "oriental tales," European fictions set in exotic Middle Eastern or Muslim locales. A landmark gothic fiction like Thomas Beckford's *Vathek* (1782) is a good example of how the period uses the trappings of oriental tales to register the shock of personal and social transformation. Shirauz or Shiraz is a city in southwest Iran that was capital of Persia in the eighteenth century.

candle, but certainly he might, during this time, have performed the operation ten times over. Some unforeseen accident might occasion his delay.

Another interval passed and no tokens of his coming. I began now to grow uneasy. I was unable to account for his detention. Was not some treachery designed? I went to the door and found that it was locked. This heightened my suspicions. I was alone, a stranger, in an upper room of the house. Should my conductor have disappeared, by design or by accident, and some one of the family should find me here, what would be the consequence? Should I not be arrested as a thief and conveyed to prison? My transition from the street to this chamber would not be more rapid than my passage hence to a gaol.

These ideas struck me with panick. I revolved them anew, but they only acquired greater plausibility. No doubt I had been the victim of malicious artifice. Inclination, however, conjured up opposite sentiments and my fears began to subside. What motive, I asked, could induce an human being to inflict wanton injury? I could not account for his delay, but how numberless were the contingencies, that might occasion it?

I was somewhat comforted by these reflections, but the consolation they afforded was short-lived. I was listening with the utmost eagerness to catch the sound of a foot, when a noise was indeed heard, but totally unlike a step. It was human breath struggling, as it were, for passage. On the first effort of attention it appeared like a groan. Whence it arose I could not tell. He that uttered it was near; perhaps in the room.

Presently the same noise was again heard, and now I perceived that it came from the bed. It was accompanied with a motion like some one changing his posture. What I at first conceived to be a groan, appeared now to be nothing more than the expiration of a sleeping man. What should I infer from this incident? My companion did not apprise me that the apartment was inhabited. Was his imposture a jestful or a wicked one?

There was no need to deliberate. There were no means of concealment or escape. The person would sometime awaken and detect me. The interval would only be fraught with agony and it was wise to shorten it. Should I not withdraw the curtain, awake the person, and encounter at once all the consequences of my situation? I glided softly to the bed, when the thought occurred, May not the sleeper be a female?

I cannot describe the mixture of dread and of shame which glowed in my veins. The light in which such a visitant would be probably regarded by a woman's fears, the precipitate alarms that might be given, the injury which I might unknowingly inflict or undeservedly suffer, threw my thoughts into painful confusion. My presence might pollute a spotless reputation or furnish fuel to jealousy.[2]

---

[2] "My presence might pollute a spotless reputation or furnish fuel to jealousy": the second of many expressions of concern with female sexuality as a sign of virtue and its perceived or real absence. Whereas Mervyn condemned the loose sexuality of lower-class Betty Lawrence, now he expresses automatic respect and deference toward the sexual reputation of an upper-class female. This is the first of Mervyn's numerous illicit entries into women's spaces.

Still, though it were a female, would not least injury be done by gently interrupting her slumber? But the question of sex still remained to be decided. For this end I once more approached the bed and drew aside the silk. The sleeper was a babe. This I discovered by the glimmer of a street lamp.

Part of my solicitudes were now removed. It was plain that this chamber belonged to a nurse or a mother. She had not yet come to bed. Perhaps it was a married pair and their approach might be momently expected. I pictured to myself their entrance and my own detection. I could imagine no consequence that was not disastrous and horrible, and from which I would not, at any price, escape. I again examined the door, and found that exit by this avenue was impossible. There were other doors in this room. Any practicable expedient in this extremity was to be pursued. One of these was bolted. I unfastened it and found a considerable space within. Should I immure myself in this closet? I saw no benefit that would finally result from it. I discovered that there was a bolt on the inside which would somewhat contribute to security. This being drawn no one could enter without breaking the door.

I had scarcely paused when the long expected sound or footsteps were heard in the entry. Was it my companion or a stranger? If it were the latter, I had not yet mustered courage sufficient to meet him. I cannot applaud the magnanimity of my proceeding, but no one can expect intrepid or judicious measures from one in my circumstances. I stepped into the closet and closed the door. Some one immediately after, unlocked the chamber door. He was unattended with a light. The footsteps, as they moved along the carpet, could scarcely be heard.

I waited impatiently for some token by which I might be governed. I put my ear to the key-hole, and at length heard a voice, but not that of my companion, exclaim, somewhat above a whisper, Smiling cherub! safe and sound, I see. Would to God my experiment may succeed and that thou mayest find a mother where I have found a wife! There he stopped. He appeared to kiss the babe and presently retiring locked the door after him.[3]

These words were capable of no consistent meaning. They served, at least, to assure me that I had been treacherously dealt with. This chamber, it was manifest, did not belong to my companion. I put up prayers to my deity that he would deliver me from these toils. What a condition was mine? Immersed in palpable darkness! shut up in this unknown recess! lurking like a robber![4]

---

[3] "Locked the door after him": in this scene Mervyn overhears the corrupt merchant Walter Thetford and gathers information that is crucial in understanding the larger web of frauds that soon surrounds him. Before revealing information about his business frauds, Thetford deposits a foundling, or abandoned baby, in his bedroom to be discovered by his wife, who is in deep emotional distress after losing her own baby. Mervyn encounters Thetford publicly in Chapter 8 and realizes then that Thetford was the same person he overheard in this scene.

[4] "Lurking like a robber!": the first of several coffin-like enclosures. Each of these experiences is accompanied by Mervyn's fear of incrimination because he is unwittingly in the wrong place at the wrong time. See Chapter 12 for a subsequent example of the "terrors of imprisonment and accusation."

My meditations were disturbed by new sounds. The door was unlocked, more than one person entered the apartment, and light streamed through the key-hole. I looked; but the aperture was too small and the figures passed too quickly to permit me the sight of them. I bent my ear and this imparted some more authentic information.

The man, as I judged by the voice, was the same who had just departed. Rustling of silk denoted his companion to be female. Some words being uttered by the man, in too low a key to be overheard, the lady burst into a passion of tears. He strove to comfort her by soothing tones and tender appellations. How can it be helped, said he. It is time to resume your courage. Your duty to yourself and to me requires you to subdue this unreasonable grief.

He spoke frequently in this strain, but all he said seemed to have little influence in pacifying the lady. At length, however, her sobs began to lessen in vehemence and frequency. He exhorted her to seek for some repose. Apparently she prepared to comply, and conversation was, for a few minutes, intermitted.

I could not but advert to the possibility that some occasion to examine the closet in which I was immured, might occur. I knew not in what manner to demean myself if this should take place. I had no option at present. By withdrawing myself from view I had lost the privilege of an upright deportment. Yet the thought of spending the night in this spot was not to be endured.

Gradually I began to view the project of bursting from the closet, and trusting to the energy of truth and of an artless tale, with more complacency. More than once my hand was placed upon the bolt, but withdrawn by a sudden faltering of resolution. When one attempt failed, I recurred once more to such reflections as were adapted to renew my purpose.

I preconcerted the address which I should use. I resolved to be perfectly explicit: To withhold no particular of my adventures from the moment of my arrival. My description must necessarily suit some person within their knowledge. All I should want was liberty to depart; but if this were not allowed, I might at least hope to escape any ill treatment, and to be confronted with my betrayer. In that case I did not fear to make him the attester of my innocence.

Influenced by these considerations, I once more touched the lock. At that moment the lady shrieked, and exclaimed Good God! What is here? An interesting conversation ensued. The object that excited her astonishment was the child. I collected from what passed that the discovery was wholly unexpected by her. Her husband acted as if equally unaware of this event. He joined in all her exclamations of wonder and all her wild conjectures. When these were somewhat exhausted he artfully insinuated the propriety of bestowing care upon the little foundling. I now found that her grief had been occasioned by the recent loss of her own offspring. She was, for some time, averse to her husband's proposal, but at length was persuaded to take the babe to her bosom and give it nourishment.

This incident had diverted my mind from its favourite project, and filled me with speculations on the nature of the scene. One explication was obvious, that the husband was the parent of this child, and had used this singular expedient to procure for it the maternal protection of his wife. It would soon claim from her all the fondness which she entertained for her own progeny. No suspicion probably had yet, or would hereafter, occur with regard to its true parent. If her character be distinguished by the usual attributes of women, the knowledge of this truth may convert her love into hatred. I reflected with amazement on the slightness of that thread by which human passions are led from their true direction. With no less amazement did I remark the complexity of incidents by which I had been impowered to communicate to her this truth. How baseless are the structures of falsehood, which we build in opposition to the system of eternal nature. If I should escape undetected from this recess, it will be true that I never saw the face of either of these persons, and yet I am acquainted with the most secret transaction of their lives.[5]

My own situation was now more critical than before. The lights were extinguished and the parties had sought repose. To issue from the closet now would be eminently dangerous. My councils were again at a stand and my designs frustrated. Meanwhile the persons did not drop their discourse, and I thought myself justified in listening. Many facts of the most secret and momentous nature were alluded to. Some allusions were unintelligible. To others I was able to affix a plausible meaning, and some were palpable enough. Every word that was uttered on that occasion is indelibly imprinted on my memory. Perhaps the singularity of my circumstances and my previous ignorance of what was passing in the world, contributed to render me a greedy listener. Most that was said I shall overlook, but one part of the conversation it will be necessary to repeat.

A large company had assembled that evening at their house. They criticised the character and manners of several. At last the husband said, What think you of the Nabob?[6] Especially when he talked about riches? How artfully he incourages the notion of his poverty! Yet not a soul believes him. I cannot for my part account for that scheme of his. I half suspect that his wealth flows from a bad source, since he is so studious of concealing it.

Perhaps, after all, said the lady, you are mistaken as to his wealth.

Impossible, exclaimed the other. Mark how he lives. Have I not seen his bank account. His deposits, since he has been here, amount to not less than half a million.

---

[5] "I never saw the face of either of these persons, and yet I am acquainted with the most secret transaction of their lives": since it implies that a secret may not be legible on the faces of people we meet, Mervyn's comment introduces doubts about judgment of character through visual appearances.

[6] "Nabob": a rich man, a grandee, originally a merchant who acquired a fortune in colonial commerce with India. Here, as in many eighteenth-century writings, the word conveys contempt for an emergent social category of newly enriched colonial merchants competing for respectability with older money and other sectors of mercantile wealth. Thetford is referring to Thomas Welbeck, already mentioned in Chapter 1 as the man who defrauded Wortley, and uses the word because he takes Welbeck for a social-climbing moneybags displaced to Philadelphia by colonial unrest. The word comes to English via Portuguese or Spanish from Urdu *Nawab*, a provincial governor or administrator.

Heaven grant that it be so, said the lady with a sigh. I shall think with less aversion of your scheme. If poor Tom's fortune be made, and he not the worse, or but little the worse on that account, I shall think it on the whole best.

That, replied he, is what reconciles me to the scheme. To him thirty thousand are nothing.[7]

But will he not suspect you of some hand in it?

How can he? Will I not appear to lose as well as himself? Tom is my brother, but who can be supposed to answer for a brother's integrity: but he cannot suspect either of us. Nothing less than a miracle can bring our plot to light. Besides, this man is not what he ought to be. He will, some time or other, come out to be a grand impostor. He makes money by other arts than bargain and sale. He has found his way, by some means, to the Portuguese treasury.[8]

Here the conversation took a new direction, and after some time, the silence of sleep ensued.

Who, thought I, is this nabob who counts his dollars by half millions, and on whom, it seems as if some fraud was intended to be practised. Amidst their wariness and subtlety how little are they aware that their conversation has been overheard! By means as inscrutable as those which conducted me hither, I may hereafter be enabled to profit by this detection of a plot. But, meanwhile, what was I to do? How was I to effect my escape from this perilous asylum?

After much reflection it occurred to me that to gain the street without exciting their notice was not utterly impossible. Sleep does not commonly end of itself, unless at a certain period. What impediments were there between me and liberty which I could not remove, and remove with so much caution as to escape notice? Motion and sound inevitably go together, but every sound is not attended to. The doors of the closet and the chamber did not creak upon their hinges. The latter might be locked. This I was able to ascertain only by experiment. If it were so, yet the key was probably in the lock and might be used without much noise.

---

[7] "To him thirty thousand are nothing": the scheme to defraud Welbeck for the benefit of Thetford's younger brother Thomas is explained at greater length in Chapter 11. Very large sums are at stake in the novel's commercial transactions. This amount is equivalent to millions in the early twenty-first century. There is no single correct measure of historical value conversion, and gauging equivalents requires different metrics for different contexts. Calculated relative to consumer price index then and now (the minimum equivalent), $30,000 in 1790 equals $661,000 in 2005. Relative to average unskilled wage compensation then and now (a more functional measure), $30,000 in 1790 equals $12.745 million in 2005. To put this in context, in 1798 the mean value of a home in Pennsylvania was $248; the mean value of a dwelling and lot in the center of Philadelphia, the wealthiest and most expensive city on the continent, was $1,741. Explanations and supporting statistics for historical conversions of dollar value, and a do-it-yourself calculator are available at http://www.measuringworth.com/uscompare. For real estate values in 1790s Philadelphia, see Shammas, "The Space Problem in Early United States Cities."

[8] "Portuguese treasury": the reader learns in Chapter 10 that this wealth is stolen from the dying son of Vincentio Lodi, whose "money consisted in Portuguese gold" (see note 10.6).

I waited till their slow and hoarser inspirations shewed them to be both asleep. Just then, on changing my position, my head struck against some things which depended from the ceiling of the closet. They were implements of some kind which rattled against each other in consequence of this unlucky blow. I was fearful lest this noise should alarm, as the closet was little distant from the bed. The breathing of one instantly ceased, and a motion was made as if the head were lifted from the pillow. This motion, which was made by the husband, awaked his companion, who exclaimed, What is the matter?

Something, I believe, replied he, in the closet. If I was not dreaming, I heard the pistols strike against each other as if some one was taking them down.

This intimation was well suited to alarm the lady. She besought him to ascertain the matter. This to my utter dismay he at first consented to do, but presently observed that probably his ears had misinformed him. It was hardly possible that the sound proceeded from them. It might be a rat, or his own fancy might have fashioned it.— It is not easy to describe my trepidations while this conference was holding. I saw how easily their slumber was disturbed. The obstacles to my escape were less surmountable than I had imagined.

In a little time all was again still. I waited till the usual tokens of sleep were distinguishable. I once more resumed my attempt. The bolt was withdrawn with all possible slowness but I could by no means prevent all sound. My state was full of inquietude and suspense; my attention being painfully divided between the bolt and the condition of the sleepers. The difficulty lay in giving that degree of force which was barely sufficient. Perhaps not less than fifteen minutes were consumed in this operation. At last it was happily effected and the door was cautiously opened.

Emerging as I did from utter darkness, the light admitted into three windows, produced to my eyes, a considerable illumination. Objects which, on my first entrance into this apartment, were invisible, were now clearly discerned. The bed was shrouded by curtains, yet I shrunk back into my covert, fearful of being seen. To facilitate my escape I put off my shoes. My mind was so full of objects of more urgent moment that the propriety of taking them along with me never occurred. I left them in the closet.

I now glided across the apartment to the door. I was not a little discouraged by observing that the key was wanting. My whole hope depended on the omission to lock it. In my haste to ascertain this point, I made some noise which again roused one of the sleepers. He started and cried Who is there?

I now regarded my case as desperate and detection as inevitable. My apprehensions, rather than my caution, kept me mute. I shrunk to the wall, and waited in a kind of agony for the moment that should decide my fate.

The lady was again roused. In answer to her inquiries, her husband said that some one he believed was at the door, but there was no danger of their entering, for he had locked it and the key was in his pocket.

My courage was completely annihilated by this piece of intelligence. My resources were now at an end. I could only remain in this spot, till the morning light, which could be at no great distance, should discover me. My inexperience disabled me from estimating all the perils of my situation. Perhaps I had no more than temporary inconveniences to dread. My intention was innocent, and I had been betrayed into my present situation, not by my own wickedness but the wickedness of others.

I was deeply impressed with the ambiguousness which would necessarily rest upon my motives, and the scrutiny to which they would be subjected. I shuddered at the bare possibility of being ranked with thieves. These reflections again gave edge to my ingenuity in search of the means of escape. I had carefully attended to the circumstances of their entrance. Possibly the act of locking had been unnoticed; but, was it not likewise possible that this person had been mistaken? The key was gone. Would this have been the case if the door were unlocked?

My fears, rather than my hopes, impelled me to make the experiment. I drew back the latch and, to my unspeakable joy, the door opened.

I passed through and explored my way to the stair-case. I descended till I reached the bottom. I could not recollect with accuracy the position of the door leading into the court, but by carefully feeling along the wall with my hands, I at length discovered it. It was fastened by several bolts and a lock. The bolts were easily withdrawn, but the key was removed. I knew not where it was deposited. I thought I had reached the threshold of liberty, but here was an impediment that threatened to be insurmountable.

But if doors could not be passed, windows might be unbarred. I remembered that my companion had gone into a door on the left hand, in search of a light. I searched for this door. Fortunately it was fastened only by a bolt. It admitted me into a room which I carefully explored till I reached a window. I will not dwell on my efforts to unbar this entrance. Suffice it to say that, after much exertion and frequent mistakes, I at length found my way into the yard, and thence passed into the court.[9]

---

[9] "And thence passed into the court": Mervyn exits the same kitchen window in the same manner at the beginning of Chapter 17 at the height of the yellow fever epidemic. The doubling of spaces and movements in Mervyn's two trips to the city is another element of the first part's repetition and mirroring. See note 17.1 for his second experience of this same space.

Chapter V

NOW I was once more on public ground. By so many anxious efforts had I disengaged myself from the perilous precincts of private property. As many stratagems as are usually made to enter an house, had been employed by me to get out of it. I was urged to the use of them by my fears; yet so far from carrying off spoil, I had escaped with the loss of an essential part of my dress.

I had now leisure to reflect. I seated myself on the ground and reviewed the scenes through which I had just passed. I began to think that my industry had been misemployed. Suppose I had met the person on his first entrance into his chamber? Was the truth so utterly wild as not to have found credit? Since the door was locked, and there was no other avenue; what other statement but the true one would account for my being found there? This deportment had been worthy of an honest purpose. My betrayer probably expected that this would be the issue of his jest. My rustic simplicity, he might think, would suggest no more ambiguous or elaborate expedient. He might likewise have predetermined to interfere if my safety had been really endangered.

On the morrow the two doors of the chamber and the window below would be found unclosed. They will suspect a design to pillage, but their searches will terminate in nothing but in the discovery of a pair of clumsy and dusty shoes in the closet. Now that I was safe I could not help smiling at the picture which my fancy drew of their anxiety and wonder. These thoughts, however, gave place to more momentous considerations.

I could not image to myself a more perfect example of indigence than I now exhibited. There was no being in the city on whose kindness I had any claim. Money I had none, and what I then wore comprised my whole stock of moveables. I had just lost my shoes, and this loss rendered my stockings of no use. My dignity remonstrated against a bare-foot pilgrimage, but to this, necessity now reconciled me. I threw my stockings between the bars of a stable window, belonging, as I thought, to the mansion I had just left. These, together with my shoes, I left to pay the cost of my entertainment.

I saw that the city was no place for me. The end that I had had in view, of procuring some mechanical employment,[1] could only be obtained by the use of means, but what means to pursue I knew not. This night's perils and deceptions gave me a distaste to a city life, and my ancient occupations rose to my view enhanced by a thousand imaginary charms. I resolved forthwith to strike into the country.

The day began now to dawn. It was Sunday, and I was desirous of eluding observation. I was somewhat recruited by rest though the languors of sleeplessness oppressed me. I meant to throw myself on the first lap of verdure I should meet, and indulge in sleep that I so much wanted. I knew not the direction of the streets; but followed that which I first entered from the court, trusting that, by adhering steadily to one course,

---

[1] "Mechanical employment": Mervyn reconsiders the plan he devised in Chapter 2 (note 2.9) of seeking an apprenticeship or indenture in an artisanal craft.

I should sometime reach the fields. This street, as I afterwards found, tended to Schuylkill, and soon extricated me from houses. I could not cross this river without payment of toll. It was requisite to cross it in order to reach that part of the country whither I was desirous of going, but how should I effect my passage? I knew of no ford, and the smallest expence exceeded my capacity. Ten thousand guineas and a farthing were equally remote from nothing, and nothing was the portion allotted to me.

While my mind was thus occupied, I turned up one of the streets which tend northward. It was, for some length, uninhabited and unpaved. Presently I reached a pavement, and a painted fence, along which a row of poplars was planted. It bounded a garden into which a knot-hole permitted me to pry. The inclosure was a charming green, which I saw appended to an house of the loftiest and most stately order. It seemed like a recent erection, had all the gloss of novelty, and exhibited, to my unpractised eyes, the magnificence of palaces. My father's dwelling did not equal the height of one story, and might be easily comprised in one fourth of those buildings which here were designed to accommodate the menials. My heart dictated the comparison between my own condition and that of the proprietors of this domain. How wide and how impassible was the gulf by which we were separated! This fair inheritance had fallen to one who, perhaps, would only abuse it to the purposes of luxury, while I, with intentions worthy of the friend of mankind, was doomed to wield the flail and the mattock.

I had been intirely unaccustomed to this strain of reflection. My books had taught me the dignity and safety of the middle path, and my darling writer abounded with encomiums on rural life. At a distance from luxury and pomp I viewed them, perhaps, in a just light. A nearer scrutiny confirmed my early prepossessions, but at the distance at which I now stood, the lofty edifices, the splendid furniture, and the copious accommodations of the rich, excited my admiration and my envy.

I relinquished my station and proceeded, in an heartless mood, along the fence. I now came to the mansion itself. The principal door was entered by a stair-case of marble. I had never seen the stone of Carrara,[2] and wildly supposed this to have been dug from Italian quarries. The beauty of the poplars, the coolness exhaled from the dew-besprent bricks, the commodiousness of the seat which these steps afforded, and the uncertainty into which I was plunged respecting my future conduct, all combined to make me pause. I sat down on the lower step and began to meditate.

By some transition it occurred to me that the supply of my most urgent wants might be found in some inhabitant of this house. I needed at present a few cents; and what were a few cents to the tenant of a mansion like this. I had an invincible aversion to the calling of a beggar, but I regarded with still more antipathy the vocation of a thief; to this alternative, however, I was now reduced. I must either steal or beg; unless, indeed, assistance could be procured under the notion of a loan. Would a stranger refuse to lend the pittance that I wanted? Surely not, when the urgency of my wants were explained.

---

[2] "Stone of Carrara": fine marble from Carrara, in Tuscany, a renowned source of marble since the time of ancient Rome.

I recollected other obstacles. To summon the master of the house from his bed, perhaps, for the sake of such an application, would be preposterous. I should be in more danger of provoking his anger than exciting his benevolence. This request might, surely, with more propriety be preferred to a passenger. I should, probably, meet several before I should arrive at Schuylkill.

A servant just then appeared at the door, with bucket and brush. This obliged me, much sooner than I intended, to decamp. With some reluctance I rose and proceeded.—This house occupied the corner of the street, and I now turned this corner towards the country. A person, at some distance before me, was approaching in an opposite direction.

Why, said I, may I not make my demand of the first man I meet? This person exhibits tokens of ability to lend.[3] There is nothing chilling or austere in his demeanour.

The resolution to address this passenger was almost formed; but the nearer he advanced, my resolves grew less firm. He noticed me not till he came within a few paces. He seemed busy in reflection, and had not my figure caught his eye; or had he merely bestowed a passing glance upon me, I should not have been sufficiently courageous to have detained him. The event however was widely different.

He looked at me and started. For an instant, as it were, and till he had time to dart at me a second glance, he checked his pace. This behaviour decided mine, and he stopped on perceiving tokens of a desire to address him. I spoke, but my accents and air sufficiently denoted my embarrassments.

I am going to solicit a favour, which my situation makes of the highest importance to me, and which I hope it will be easy for you, Sir, to grant. It is not an alms but a loan that I seek; a loan that I will repay the moment I am able to do it. I am going to the country, but have not wherewith to pay my passage over Schuylkill, or to buy a morsel of bread. May I venture to request of you, Sir, the loan of six pence? As I told you, it is my intention to repay it.

I delivered this address, not without some faltering, but with great earnestness. I laid particular stress upon my intention to refund the money. He listened with a most inquisitive air. His eye perused me from head to foot.

After some pause, he said, in a very emphatic manner, Why into the country? Have you family? Kindred? Friends?

No, answered I, I have neither. I go in search of the means of subsistence. I have passed my life upon a farm, and propose to die in the same condition.

Whence have you come?

I came yesterday from the country, with a view to earn my bread in some way, but have changed my plan and propose now to return.

---

[3] "Tokens of ability to lend": the first appearance of Thomas Welbeck, a corrupt commercial adventurer who will become the most central figure in the first part's action after Mervyn. He has already been mentioned by name in Chapter 1 (as the businessman who defrauded Wortley) and as the "Nabob" (being defrauded in turn by Thetford) in the conversation Mervyn overheard in Chapter 4 while hidden in the bedroom.

Why have you changed it? In what way are you capable of earning your bread?

I hardly know, said I. I can, as yet, manage no tool, that can be managed in the city, but the pen. My habits have, in some small degree, qualified me for a writer. I would willingly accept employment of that kind.

He fixed his eyes upon the earth, and was silent for some minutes. At length, recovering himself, he said, Follow me to my house. Perhaps something may be done for you. If not, I will lend you six-pence.

It may be supposed that I eagerly complied with the invitation. My companion said no more, his air bespeaking him to be absorbed by his own thoughts, till he reached his house, which proved to be that at the door of which I had been seated. We entered a parlour together.

Unless you can assume my ignorance and my simplicity, you will be unable to conceive the impressions that were made by the size and ornaments of this apartment. I shall omit these impressions, which, indeed, no descriptions could adequately convey, and dwell on incidents of greater moment. He asked me to give him a specimen of my penmanship. I told you that I had bestowed very great attention upon this art. Implements were brought and I sat down to the task. By some inexplicable connection a line in Shakspeare occurred to me, and I wrote

"My poverty, but not my will consents"[4]

The sentiment conveyed in this line powerfully affected him, but in a way which I could not then comprehend. I collected from subsequent events that the inference was not unfavourable to my understanding or my morals. He questioned me as to my history. I related my origin and my inducements to desert my father's house. With respect to last night's adventures I was silent. I saw no useful purpose that could be answered by disclosure, and I half suspected that my companion would refuse credit to my tale.

There were frequent intervals of abstraction and reflection between his questions. My examination lasted not much less than an hour. At length he said, I want an amanuensis or copyist. On what terms will you live with me?

I answered that I knew not how to estimate the value of my services. I knew not whether these services were agreeable or healthful. My life had hitherto been active. My constitution was predisposed to diseases of the lungs and the change might be hurtful. I was willing, however, to try and to content myself for a month or a year, with so much as would furnish me with food, clothing, and lodging.

'Tis well, said he, You remain with me as long and no longer than both of us please. You shall lodge and eat in this house. I will supply you with clothing,[5] and your task

---

[4] "Consents": *Romeo and Juliet*, V.i.75. The line occurs when Romeo asks a starving apothecary to sell him mortal poison. The pharmacist delivers the line by way of rationalizing or justifying the fatal exchange. By "inexplicably" citing the line, Mervyn unwittingly suggests that Welbeck is enmeshed in secret plots involving illegitimate sexual desires and tragic deaths, all of which is true.

[5] "You shall lodge and eat . . . I will supply you with clothing": standard provisions of an indenture contract, bringing Mervyn close to servant status.

will be to write what I dictate. Your person, I see, has not shared much of your attention. It is in my power to equip you instantly in the manner which becomes a resident in this house. Come with me.

He led the way into the court behind and thence into a neat building, which contained large wooden vessels and a pump: There, said he, you may wash yourself, and when that is done, I will conduct you to your chamber and your wardrobe.

This was speedily performed, and he accordingly led the way to the chamber. It was an apartment in the third story, finished and furnished in the same costly and superb style with the rest of the house. He opened closets and drawers which overflowed with clothes and linen of all and of the best kinds. These are yours, said he, as long as you stay with me. Dress yourself as likes you best. Here is every thing your nakedness requires. When dressed you may descend to breakfast. With these words he left me.

The clothes were all in the French style, as I afterwards, by comparing my garb with that of others, discovered. They were fitted to my shape with the nicest precision. I bedecked myself with all my care. I remembered the style of dress used by my beloved Clavering. My locks were of shining auburn, flowing and smooth like his. Having wrung the wet from them, and combed, I tied them carelessly in a black riband. Thus equipped I surveyed myself in a mirror.

You may imagine, if you can, the sensations which this instantaneous transformation produced. Appearances are wonderfully influenced by dress. Check shirt, buttoned at the neck, an awkward fustian coat, check trowsers and bare feet were now supplanted by linen and muslin, nankeen coat striped with green, a white silk waistcoat elegantly needle-wrought, casimer[6] pantaloons, stockings of variegated silk, and shoes that in their softness, pliancy, and polished surface vied with sattin. I could scarcely forbear looking back to see whether the image in the glass, so well proportioned, so galant, and so graceful, did not belong to another. I could scarcely recognize any lineaments[7] of my own. I walked to the window. Twenty minutes ago, said I, I was traversing that path a barefoot beggar; now I am thus. Again I surveyed myself. Surely some insanity has fastened on my understanding. My senses are the sport of dreams. Some magic that disdains the cumbrousness of nature's progress has

---

[6] "Fustian . . . nankeen . . . casimer": fabrics were a major investment in the households of this period and a basic signifier of social status. Thus Mervyn is detailing an amazing transformation as he dons luxury garments that identify him with an elite household and make it possible for him to circulate in "respectable" society. "Fustian" is a heavy, homespun cloth that implies rural poverty. Radicalized laborers in nineteenth-century England consciously wore fustian as a sign of working-class solidarity, but it is unlikely the same connotation existed in the 1790s. "Nankeen" is a yellow cotton cloth originally imported from Nanking, China, and thus a luxurious Asian product of commercial empire. Similarly, "casimer" (or cassimere) is another expensive fabric, "a thin fine twilled woollen cloth used for men's clothes" (OED). The startling makeover is one more of the quasimagical transformations Mervyn experiences as he enters the world of commerce.

[7] "Lineaments": "distinctive features or characteristics" (OED).

wrought this change. I was roused from these doubts by a summons to breakfast, obsequiously delivered by a black servant.[8]

I found Welbeck, (for I shall henceforth call him by his true name) at the breakfast table. A superb equipage of silver and china was before him. He was startled at my entrance. The change in my dress seemed for a moment to have deceived him. His eye was frequently fixed upon me with unusual steadfastness. At these times there was inquietude and wonder in his features.

I had now an opportunity of examining my host. There was nicety but no ornament in his dress. His form was of the middle height, spare, but vigorous and graceful. His face was cast, I thought, in a foreign mould.[9] His forehead receded beyond the usual degree in visages which I had seen. His eyes large and prominent, but imparting no marks of benignity and habitual joy. The rest of his face forcibly suggested the idea of a convex edge. His whole figure impressed me with emotions of veneration and awe. A gravity that almost amounted to sadness invariably attended him when we were alone together.

He whispered the servant that waited, who immediately retired. He then said, turning to me, A lady will enter presently, whom you are to treat with the respect due to my daughter. You must not notice any emotion she may betray at the sight of you, nor expect her to converse with your; for she does not understand your language. He had scarcely spoken when she entered. I was seized with certain misgivings and flutterings which a clownish education[10] may account for. I so far conquered my timidity, however, as to snatch a look at her. I was not born to execute her portrait. Perhaps the turban[11] that wreathed her head, the brilliant texture and inimitable folds of her drapery, and nymphlike port, more than the essential attributes of her person, gave splendour to the celestial vision. Perhaps it was her snowy hues and the cast, rather

---

[8] "A black servant": this paragraph's episode of mirror gazing is repeated with crucial differences in Chapter 16 (see note 16.2) during the fever. In both instances, Mervyn's self-absorption and literal "reflection" on his own identity includes an African other and thus condenses important features of the class and ethno-racial tensions that Mervyn negotiates throughout the novel as he constructs a middle-class identity and seeks to understand "the causes behind appearances." For more on the mirror scenes, see Smith-Rosenberg, "Black Gothic."

[9] "Foreign mould": examining Welbeck's head according to physiognomical conventions, Mervyn concludes that he looks "foreign," which carries a hint of Mediterranean or other "exotic" ethnicity in this context, since Mervyn's neighbors in Chester County are primarily Anglo, German, Welsh, or Scots-Irish farmers. Wondering later if Welbeck could have an Italian daughter, Mervyn notes that he has "foreign lineaments in his countenance."

[10] "Clownish education": lack of experience as a country dweller.

[11] "Turban": in her first entrance, Clemenza Lodi wears a fashionable turban in the French style. The clothing at Welbeck's, as Mervyn noted of his servant's livery, is "all in the French style," whose cultural associations were amplified in the 1790s by the arrival of thousands of French and Haitian refugees in Philadelphia. After 1793, "French" coding in Philadelphia carried overtones of European social revolution and Caribbean slave revolt.

than the position of her features,[12] that were so prolific of enchantment: or perhaps the wonder originated only in my own ignorance.

She did not immediately notice me. When she did she almost shrieked with surprise. She held up her hands, and gazing upon me, uttered various exclamations which I could not understand. I could only remark that her accents were thrillingly musical. Her perturbations[13] refused to be stilled. It was with difficulty that she withdrew her regards from me. Much conversation passed between her and Welbeck, but I could comprehend no part of it. I was at liberty to animadvert on the visible part of their intercourse. I diverted some part of my attention from my own embarrassments, and fixed it on their looks.

In this art, as in most others, I was an unpractised simpleton. In the countenance of Welbeck, there was somewhat else than sympathy with the astonishment and distress of the lady; but I could not interpret these additional tokens. When her attention was engrossed by Welbeck, her eyes were frequently vagrant or downcast; her cheeks contracted a deeper hue; and her breathing was almost prolonged into a sigh. These were marks on which I made no comments at the time. My own situation was calculated to breed confusion in my thoughts and awkwardness in my gestures. Breakfast being finished, the lady, apparently at the request of Welbeck, sat down to a piano forte.

Here again I must be silent. I was not wholly destitute of musical practice and musical taste. I had that degree of knowledge which enabled me to estimate the transcendent skill of this performer. As if the pathos of her touch were insufficient, I found after some time that the lawless jarrings of the keys were chastened by her own more liquid notes. She played without a book, and though her base might be preconcerted, it was plain that her right-hand notes were momentary and spontaneous inspirations. Meanwhile Welbeck stood, leaning his arms on the back of a chair near her, with his eyes fixed on her face. His features were fraught with a meaning which I was eager to interpret but unable.

I have read of transitions effected by magic: I have read of palaces and deserts which were subject to the dominion of spells: Poets may sport with their power, but I am certain that no transition was ever conceived more marvellous and more beyond the reach of foresight than that which I had just experienced. Heaths vexed by a midnight storm may be changed into an hall of choral nymphs and regal banqueting;[14]

---

[12] "Snowy hues and the cast . . . of her features": Mervyn emphasizes Clemenza's skin color and the way she holds her body.

[13] "Perturbations": disturbance, anxiety.

[14] "Heaths vexed by a midnight storm . . . regal banqueting": the image of a midnight storm changed into a regal banquet recalls the ending of John Milton's court masque *Comus*, which will be cited by Achsa Fielding in Chapter II.22. See notes II.22.1 and 2 for the implications of this reference. Once again, Mervyn describes the shocking "transitions" he experiences as he enters commercial society as quasimagical transformations.

forest glades may give sudden place to colonnades and carnivals, but he whose senses are deluded finds himself still on his natal earth. These miracles are contemptible when compared with that which placed me under this roof and gave me to partake in this audience. I know that my emotions are in danger of being regarded as ludicrous by those who cannot figure to themselves the consequences of a limited and rustic education.

Chapter VI

IN a short time the lady retired. I naturally expected that some comments would be made on her behaviour, and that the cause of her surprise and distress on seeing me, would be explained, but Welbeck said nothing on that subject. When she had gone, he went to the window and stood for some time occupied, as it seemed, with his own thoughts. Then he turned to me and, calling me by my name, desired me to accompany him up stairs. There was neither cheerfulness nor mildness in his address, but neither was there any thing domineering or arrogant.

We entered an apartment on the same floor with my chamber, but separated from it by a spacious entry. It was supplied with bureaus, cabinets, and book-cases. This, said he, is your room and mine; but we must enter it and leave it together. I mean to act not as your master but your friend. My maimed hand, so saying he shewed me his right hand, the forefinger of which was wanting, will not allow me to write accurately or copiously. For this reason I have required your aid, in a work of some moment. Much haste will not be requisite, and as to the hours and duration of employment, these will be seasonable and short.

Your present situation is new to you and we will therefore defer entering on our business. Meanwhile you may amuse yourself in what manner you please. Consider this house as your home and make yourself familiar with it. Stay within or go out, be busy or be idle, as your fancy shall prompt: Only you will conform to our domestic system as to eating and sleep: the servants will inform you of this. Next week we will enter on the task for which I designed you. You may now withdraw.

I obeyed this mandate with some awkwardness and hesitation. I went into my own chamber not displeased with an opportunity of loneliness. I threw myself on a chair and resigned myself to those thoughts which would naturally arise in this situation. I speculated on the character and views of Welbeck. I saw that he was embosomed in tranquility and grandeur. Riches, therefore, were his; but in what did his opulence consist, and whence did it arise? What were the limits by which it was confined, and what its degree of permanence? I was unhabituated to ideas of floating or transferable wealth.[1] The rent of houses and lands was the only species of property which was, as yet, perfectly intelligible: My previous ideas led me to regard Welbeck as the proprietor of this dwelling and of numerous houses and farms. By the same cause I was fain to suppose him enriched by inheritance, and that his life had been uniform.

I next adverted to his social condition. This mansion appeared to have but two inhabitants besides servants. Who was the nymph who had hovered for a moment in my sight? Had he not called her his daughter? The apparent difference in their ages

---

[1] "Unhabituated to ideas of floating or transferable wealth": Mervyn has no experience or knowledge of the cosmopolitan world of commerce and finance capital, the world of Welbeck, Thetford, Wortley, and others like the speculators Old Thetford and Jamieson who appear in *Second Part*. Mervyn gradually penetrates the web of fraud and deceit that joins these characters as he learns to negotiate the pitfalls of the commercial world.

would justify this relation; but her guise, her features, and her accents were foreign. Her language I suspected strongly to be that of Italy. How should he be the father of an Italian? But were there not some foreign lineaments in his countenance?

This idea seemed to open a new world to my view. I had gained from my books, confused ideas of European governments and manners. I knew that the present was a period of revolution and hostility. Might not these be illustrious fugitives from Provence or the Milanese?[2] Their portable wealth, which may reasonably be supposed to be great, they have transported hither. Thus may be explained the sorrow that veils their countenance. The loss of estates and honours; the untimely death of kindred, and perhaps of his wife, may furnish eternal food for regrets. Welbeck's utterance, though rapid and distinct, partook, as I conceived, in some very slight degree of a foreign idiom.[3]

Such was the dream that haunted my undisciplined and unenlightened imagination. The more I revolved it the more plausible it seemed. On this supposition every appearance that I had witnessed was easily solved—unless it were their treatment of me. This, at first, was a source of hopeless perplexity. Gradually, however, a clue seemed to be afforded. Welbeck had betrayed astonishment on my first appearance. The lady's wonder was mingled with distress. Perhaps they discovered a remarkable resemblance between me and one who stood in the relation of son to Welbeck and of brother to the lady. This youth might have perished on the scaffold or in war. These, no doubt, were his clothes. This chamber might have been reserved for him, but his death left it to be appropriated to another.

I had hitherto been unable to guess at the reason why all this kindness had been lavished on me. Will not this conjecture sufficiently account for it? No wonder that this resemblance was enhanced by assuming his dress.

Taking all circumstances into view, these ideas were not, perhaps, destitute of probability. Appearances naturally suggested them to me. They were, also, powerfully enforced by inclination. They threw me into transports of wonder and hope. When I dwelt upon the incidents of my past life, and traced the chain of events, from the death of my mother to the present moment, I almost acquiesced in the notion that some beneficent and ruling genius had prepared my path for me. Events which, when foreseen, would most ardently have been deprecated, and when they happened

---

[2] "Fugitives from Provence or the Milanese?": Provence is a region in southeastern France along the Mediterranean; Milan was in 1793 capital of the Habsburg (Austrian) kingdom of Lombardy in what is now northern Italy, and the Milanese is immediately east of Provence. These areas are mentioned repeatedly in the course of the novel. Here, Mervyn wonders if Welbeck and Clemenza are refugees from revolutionary turmoil in these areas, since 1790s Milan (like Philadelphia) was a destination for émigré aristocrats and others fleeing the French Revolution. Provence also contains the Venaissin, an area linked to Achsa Fielding's deceased husband, and to revolutionary turmoil in Chapter II.23 (note II.23.12). In 1796 Napoleon conquered Milan and "liberated" it from Habsburg rule. The theme of Milanese instability and regime change also recurs with Vincentio Lodi's romance-like backstory, related in Chapters 10 and 13 (see notes 10.8 and 13.8).

[3] "Foreign idiom": besides "looking foreign" (note 5.9), Welbeck "sounds foreign."

were accounted in the highest degree luckless, were now seen to be propitious. Hence I inferred the infatuation of despair and the folly of precipitate conclusions.

But what was the fate reserved for me? Perhaps Welbeck would adopt me for his own son. Wealth has ever been capriciously distributed. The mere physical relation of birth is all that intitles us to manors and thrones. Identity itself frequently depends upon a casual likeness or an old nurse's imposture. Nations have risen in arms, as in the case of the Stewarts, in the cause of one,[4] the genuineness of whose birth has been denied and can never be proved. But if the cause be trivial and falacious, the effects are momentous and solid. It ascertains our portion of felicity and usefulness, and fixes our lot among peasants or princes.

Something may depend upon my own deportment. Will it not behove me to culti-vate all my virtues and eradicate all my defects? I see that the abilities of this man are venerable. Perhaps he will not lightly or hastily decide in my favour. He will be gov-erned by the proofs that I shall give of discernment and integrity. I had always been exempt from temptation and was therefore undepraved, but this view of things had a wonderful tendency to invigorate my virtuous resolutions. All within me was exhila-ration and joy.

There was but one thing wanting to exalt me to a dizzy height and give me place among the stars of heaven. My resemblance to her brother had forcibly affected this lady: but I was not her brother. I was raised to a level with her and made a tenant of the same mansion. Some intercourse would take place between us. Time would lay level impediments and establish familiarity, and this intercourse might foster love and terminate in—*marriage!*[5]

These images were of a nature too glowing and expensive to allow me to be longer inactive. I sallied forth into the open air. This tumult of delicious thoughts in some time subsided and gave way to images relative to my present situation. My curiosity was awake. As yet I had seen little of the city, and this opportunity for observation was not to be neglected. I therefore coursed through several streets, attentively ex-amining the objects that successively presented themselves.

---

[4] "Nations have risen in arms, as in the case of the Stewarts, in the cause of one": Mervyn refers to rumors about a foundling replacing a stillborn child, which challenged the birth legitimacy of Prince James Francis Edward Stuart (1688–1766, aka "The Old Pretender" as opposed to his more famous son Bonnie Prince Charlie, "The Young Pretender"), a key figure in the storied House of Stuart. Mervyn's point is that the supposed legitimacy of inheritance and ownership is often fraud-ulent. Appearances can be good enough to establish property rights and actual bloodlines may not matter, as in the case of the foundling that Thetford introduced into his wife's bedroom in Chapter 4. If Mervyn "looks like" Welbeck's son (or Clemenza's brother), the mere resemblance may be enough to legitimate an inheritance. Obviously Mervyn indulges in this fantasy of magical wealth and status after losing his own modest inheritance or "patrimony."

[5] "*Marriage!*": In the course of the novel, Mervyn fantasizes about marrying three successive women, each attached to a troubled inheritance: the exotic but ruined commercial heiress Clemenza Lodi, the Quaker farm girl Eliza Hadwin, who also loses an inheritance (beginning in Chapter 13), and fi-nally Achsa Fielding (beginning in Chapters II.21–22), another exotic commercial heiress who be-comes his fiancée and muse in the conclusion of *Second Part*.

At length, it occurred to me to search out the house in which I had lately been immured. I was not without hopes that at some future period I should be able to comprehend the allusions and brighten the obscurities that hung about the dialogue of last night.

The house was easily discovered. I reconnoitred the court and gate through which I had passed. The mansion was of the first order in magnitude and decoration. This was not the bound of my present discovery, for I was gifted with that confidence which would make me set on foot inquiries in the neighbourhood. I looked around for a suitable medium of intelligence. The opposite and adjoining houses were small and apparently occupied by persons of an indigent class. At one of these was a sign denoting it to be the residence of a taylor. Seated on a bench at the door was a young man, with coarse uncombed locks, breeches knee-unbuttoned, stockings ungartered, shoes slip-shod and unbuckled, and a face unwashed, gazing stupidly from hollow eyes. His aspect was embellished with good nature though indicative of ignorance.

This was the only person in sight. He might be able to say something concerning his opulent neighbour. To him, therefore, I resolved to apply. I went up to him and, pointing to the house in question, asked him who lived there?

He answered, Mr. Mathews.

What is his profession: his way of life?

A gentleman. He does nothing but walk about.

How long has he been married?

Married! He is not married as I know on. He never has been married. He is a bachelor.

This intelligence was unexpected. It made me pause to reflect whether I had not mistaken the house. This, however, seemed impossible. I renewed my questions.

A bachelor, say you? Are you not mistaken?

No. It would be an odd thing if he was married. An old fellow, with one foot in the grave—Comical enough for him to *git* a *vife*.

An old man? Does he live alone? What is his family?

No he does not live alone. He has a niece that lives with him. She is married and her husband lives there too.[6]

What is his name?

I don't know: I never heard it as I know on.

What is his trade?

He's a marchant: he keeps a store somewhere or other; but I don't no where.

How long has he been married?

About two years. They lost a child lately. The young woman was in a huge taking about it. They says she was quite crazy some days for the death of the child: And she is not quite out of *the dumps* yet. To be sure the child was a sweet little thing; but

---

[6] "She is married and her husband lives there too": The "young man," probably a tailor's apprentice, is describing Walter Thetford and his wife, the couple Mervyn overheard in their bedroom in Chapter 4.

they need not make such a rout about it. I'll warn they'll have enough of them before they die.

What is the character of the young man? Where was he born and educated? Has he parents or brothers?

My companion was incapable of answering these questions, and I left him with little essential addition to the knowledge I already possessed.

Chapter VII

AFTER viewing various parts of the city; intruding into churches;[1] and diving into alleys, I returned. The rest of the day I spent chiefly in my chamber, reflecting on my new condition; surveying my apartment, its presses and closets; and conjecturing the causes of appearances.

At dinner and supper I was alone. Venturing to inquire of the servant where his master and mistress were, I was answered that they were engaged. I did not question him as to the nature of their engagement, though it was a fertile source of curiosity.

Next morning, at breakfast, I again met Welbeck and the lady. The incidents were nearly those of the preceding morning, if it were not that the lady exhibited tokens of somewhat greater uneasiness. When she left us Welbeck sank into apparent meditation. I was at a loss whether to retire or remain where I was. At last, however, I was on the point of leaving the room, when he broke silence and began a conversation with me.

He put questions to me, the obvious scope of which was to know my sentiments on moral topics. I had no motives to conceal my opinions, and therefore delivered them with frankness. At length he introduced allusions to my own history, and made more particular inquiries on that head. Here I was not equally frank; yet I did not fain any thing, but merely dealt in generals. I had acquired notions of propriety on this head, perhaps somewhat fastidious. Minute details, respecting our own concerns, are apt to weary all but the narrator himself. I said thus much and the truth of my remark was eagerly assented to.

With some marks of hesitation and after various preliminaries, my companion hinted that my own interest, as well as his, enjoined upon me silence to all but himself, on the subject of my birth and early adventures. It was not likely, that while in his service, my circle of acquaintance would be large or my intercourse with the world frequent; but in my communication with others he requested me to speak rather of others than of myself. This request, he said, might appear singular to me, but he had his reasons for making it, which it was not necessary, at present, to disclose, though, when I should know them, I should readily acknowledge their validity.

I scarcely knew what answer to make. I was willing to oblige him. I was far from expecting that any exigence[2] would occur, making disclosure my duty. The employment was productive of pain more than of pleasure, and the curiosity that would uselessly seek a knowledge of my past life, was no less impertinent than the loquacity that would uselessly communicate that knowledge. I readily promised, therefore, to adhere to his advice.

This assurance afforded him evident satisfaction; yet it did not seem to amount to quite as much as he wished. He repeated in stronger terms, the necessity there was for

---

[1] "Intruding into churches": Mervyn's urban tourism will be recalled in *Second Part* as incriminating circumstantial evidence of his wayward character (see note II.2.7).

[2] "Exigence": an urgent necessity, a pressing demand.

caution. He was far from suspecting me to possess an impertinent and talkative disposition, or that in my eagerness to expatiate on my own concerns, I should over-step the limits of politeness. But this was not enough. I was to govern myself by a persuasion that the interests of my friend and myself would be materially affected by my conduct.

Perhaps I ought to have allowed these insinuations to breed suspicion in my mind; but conscious as I was of the benefits which I had received from this man; prone, from my inexperience, to rely upon professions and confide in appearances; and un-aware that I could be placed in any condition, in which mere silence respecting my-self could be injurious or criminal, I made no scruple to promise compliance with his wishes. Nay, I went farther than this; I desired to be accurately informed as to what it was proper to conceal. He answered that my silence might extend to every thing an-terior to my arrival in the city, and my being incorporated with his family. Here our conversation ended and I retired to ruminate on what had passed.

I derived little satisfaction from my reflections. I began now to perceive inconve-niencies that might arise from this precipitate promise. Whatever should happen in consequence of my being immured in the chamber, and of the loss of my clothes and of the portrait of my friend, I had bound myself to silence. These inquietudes, how-ever, were transient. I trusted that these events would operate auspiciously; but my curiosity was now awakened[3] as to the motives which *Welbeck* could have for exact-ing from me this concealment? To act under the guidance of another, and to wander in the dark, ignorant whither my path tended, and what effects might flow from my agency, was a new and irksome situation.

From these thoughts I was recalled by a message from Welbeck. He gave me a folded paper which he requested me to carry to No . . . South Fourth Street.[4] In-quire, said he, for Mrs. Wentworth, in order merely to ascertain the house, for you need not ask to see her; merely give the letter to the servant and retire. Excuse me for imposing this service upon you. It is of too great moment to be trusted to a common messenger; I usually perform it myself, but am at present otherwise engaged.

I took the letter and set out to deliver it. This was a trifling circumstance, yet my mind was full of reflections on the consequences that might flow from it. I remem-bered the directions that were given, but construed them in a manner different, per-haps, from Welbeck's expectations or wishes. He had charged me to leave the billet

---

[3] "Curiosity was now awakened": again Mervyn is motivated by curiosity to find "the causes of ap-pearances," as he puts it in the chapter's first paragraph. See notes 2.11 and 9.1 on the novel's wider emphasis on curiosity.

[4] "South Fourth Street": Wentworth lives near Welbeck and Achsa Fielding, in a wealthy area close to major civic institutions. South Fourth Street was at the heart of city's elite residential and civic patterns at this time, in a neighborhood known as "Society Hill." Many "gentlemen" and genteel widows lived in this area, which was close to the city's major government buildings, banks, churches, and the new prison complex between Walnut and Prune that is emphasized in *Second Part*. Mervyn returns to South Fourth Street during the fever, in Chapter 15 (see note 15.6).

with the servant who happened to answer my summons; but had he not said that the message was important, insomuch that it could not be intrusted to common hands?[5] He had permitted, rather than enjoined, me to dispense with seeing the lady, and this permission I conceived to be dictated merely by regard to my convenience. It was incumbent on me, therefore, to take some pains to deliver the script into her own hands.

I arrived at the house and knocked. A female servant appeared. Her mistress was up stairs; she would tell her if I wished to see her, and meanwhile invited me to enter the parlour. I did so; and the girl retired to inform her mistress that one waited for her— I ought to mention that my departure from the directions which I had received was, in some degree, owing to an inquisitive temper. I was eager after knowledge, and was disposed to profit by every opportunity to survey the interior of dwellings and converse with their inhabitants.

I scanned the walls, the furniture, the pictures. Over the fire-place was portrait in oil of a female. She was elderly and matron-like. Perhaps she was the mistress of this habitation, and the person to whom I should immediately be introduced. Was it a casual suggestion, or was there an actual resemblance between the strokes of the pencil which executed this portrait and that of Clavering? However that be, the sight of this picture revived the memory of my friend and called up a fugitive suspicion that this was the production of his skill.

I was busily revolving this idea when the lady herself entered. It was the same whose portrait I had been examining. She fixed scrutinizing and powerful eyes upon me. She looked at the superscription of the letter which I presented, and immediately resumed her examination of me. I was somewhat abashed by the closeness of her observation and gave tokens of this state of mind which did not pass unobserved. They seemed instantly to remind her that she behaved with too little regard to civility. She recovered herself and began to peruse the letter. Having done this, her attention was once more fixed upon me. She was evidently desirous of entering into some conversation, but seemed at a loss in what manner to begin. This situation was new to me and was productive of no small embarrassment. I was preparing to take my leave when she spoke, though not without considerable hesitation.

This letter is from Mr. Welbeck—you are his friend—I presume—perhaps—a relation?

I was conscious that I had no claim to either of these titles, and that I was no more than his servant. My pride would not allow me to acknowledge this, and I merely said—I live with him at present Madam.

---

[5] "Could not be entrusted to common hands": Mervyn's nervous concern with Welbeck's phrase about not entrusting the note to a "common messenger" or "common hands" betrays his anxiety about his new status as a servant, an anxiety he confesses (to the reader only) a few paragraphs farther on when Mrs. Wentworth questions him about his identity. As Welbeck explains in Chapter 11, he entrusts the note to Mervyn as part of his scheme to defraud Mrs. Wentworth because he wants her to see Mervyn's resemblance to Clavering.

I imagined that this answer did not perfectly satisfy her; yet she received it with a certain air of acquiescence. She was silent for a few minutes, and then, rising, said— Excuse me, Sir, for a few minutes. I will write a few words to Mr. Welbeck.—So saying she withdrew.

I returned to the contemplation of the picture. From this, however, my attention was quickly diverted by a paper that lay on the mantle. A single glance was sufficient to put my blood into motion. I started and laid my hand upon the well-known pacquet. It was that which inclosed the portrait of Clavering!

I unfolded and examined it with eagerness. By what miracle came it hither? It was found, together with my bundle, two nights before. I had despaired of ever seeing it again, and yet, here was the same portrait inclosed in the self-same paper! I have forborne to dwell upon the regret, amounting to grief, with which I was affected in consequence of the loss of this precious relique. My joy on thus speedily and unexpectedly regaining it, is not easily described.

For a time I did not reflect that to hold it thus in my hand was not sufficient to intitle me to repossession. I must acquaint this lady with the history of this picture, and convince her of my ownership. But how was this to be done? Was she connected in any way, by friendship or by consanguinity, with that unfortunate youth. If she were, some information as to his destiny would be anxiously sought. I did not, just then, perceive any impropriety in imparting it. If it came into her hands by accident still it will be necessary to relate the mode in which it was lost in order to prove my title to it.

I now heard her descending footsteps and hastily replaced the picture on the mantle. She entered, and presenting me a letter, desired me to deliver it to Mr. Welbeck. I had no pretext for deferring my departure; but was unwilling to go without obtaining possession of the portrait. An interval of silence and irresolution succeeded. I cast significant glances at the spot where it lay and at length, mustered up my strength of mind, and pointing to the paper—Madam, said I, *there* is something which I recognize to be mine—I know not how it came into your possession, but so lately as the day before yesterday, it was in mine. I lost it by a strange accident, and as I deem it of inestimable value, I hope you will have no objection to restore it.—

During this speech the lady's countenance exhibited marks of the utmost perturbation—Your picture! she exclaimed, You lost it! How? Where? Did you know that person? What has become of him?—

I knew him well, said I. That picture was executed by himself. He gave it to me with his own hands; and, till the moment I unfortunately lost it, it was my dear and perpetual companion.

Good Heaven! she exclaimed with increasing vehemence, where did you meet with him? What has become of him? Is he dead or alive?

These appearances sufficiently shewed me that Clavering and this lady were connected by some ties of tenderness. I answered that he was dead; that my mother and myself were his attendants and nurses, and that this portrait was his legacy to me.

This intelligence melted her into tears, and it was some time before she recovered strength enough to resume the conversation. She then inquired When and where was it that he died? How did you lose this portrait? It was found wrapt in some coarse clothes, lying in a stall in the market-house, on Saturday evening. Two negro women, servants of one of my friends, strolling through the market, found it and brought it to their mistress, who, recognizing the portrait, sent it to me. To whom did that bundle belong? Was it yours?

These questions reminded me of the painful predicament in which I now stood. I had promised Welbeck to conceal from every one my former condition; but to explain in what manner this bundle was lost, and how my intercourse with Clavering had taken place was to violate this promise. It was possible, perhaps, to escape the confession of the truth by equivocation. Falsehoods were easily invented, and might lead her far away from my true condition; but I was wholly unused to equivocation. Never yet had a lie polluted my lips. I was not weak enough to be ashamed of my origin. This lady had an interest in the fate of Clavering, and might justly claim all the information which I was able to impart. Yet to forget the compact which I had so lately made, and an adherence to which might possibly be, in the highest degree, beneficial to me and to Welbeck—I was willing to adhere to it, provided falsehood could be avoided.

These thoughts rendered me silent. The pain of my embarrassment amounted almost to agony. I felt the keenest regret at my own precipitation in claiming the picture. Its value to me was altogether imaginary. The affection which this lady had borne the original, whatever was the source of that affection, would prompt her to cherish the copy, and, however precious it was in my eyes, I should cheerfully resign it to her.

In the confusion of my thoughts an expedient suggested itself sufficiently inartificial and bold—It is true, Madam; what I have said. I saw him breathe his last. This is his only legacy. If you wish it I willingly resign it; but this is all that I can now disclose. I am placed in circumstances which render it improper to say more.

These words were uttered not very distinctly, and the lady's vehemence hindered her from noticing them. She again repeated her interrogations, to which I returned the same answer.

At first she expressed the utmost surprise at my conduct. From this she descended to some degree of asperity.[6] She made rapid allusions to the history of Clavering. He was the son of the gentleman who owned the house in which Welbeck resided.[7] He was the object of immeasurable fondness and indulgence. He had sought permission to travel, and this being refused by the absurd timidity of his parents, he had twice been frustrated in attempting to embark for Europe clandestinely. They ascribed his disappearance to a third and successful attempt of this kind, and had exercised

---

[6] "Asperity": sharpness or roughness; here, anger or bitterness.

[7] "The gentleman who owned the house in which Welbeck resided": Wentworth explains that Welbeck's rented mansion is owned by Clavering's father, presumably Wentworth's brother or brother-in-law since she is Clavering's aunt. The ownership of this house comes up again in Chapter 4 of *Second Part* (see note II.4.2).

anxious and unwearied diligence in endeavouring to trace his footsteps. All their efforts had failed. One motive for their returning to Europe was the hope of discovering some traces of him, as they entertained no doubt of his having crossed the ocean. The vehemence of Mrs. Wentworth's curiosity as to those particulars of his life and death may be easily conceived. My refusal only heightened this passion.

Finding me refractory[8] to all her efforts she at length dismissed me in anger.

---

[8] "Refractory": stubborn or unmanageable.

Chapter VIII

THIS extraordinary interview was now passed. Pleasure as well as pain attended my reflections on it. I adhered to the promise I had improvidently given to Welbeck, but had excited displeasure, and perhaps suspicion in the lady. She would find it hard to account for my silence. She would probably impute it to perverseness, or imagine it to flow from some incident connected with the death of Clavering, calculated to give a new edge to her curiosity.

It was plain that some connection subsisted between her and Welbeck. Would she drop the subject at the point which it had now attained? Would she cease to exert herself to extract from me the desired information, or would she not rather make Welbeck a party in the cause, and prejudice my new friend against me? This was an evil proper, by all lawful means, to avoid. I knew of no other expedient than to confess to him the truth, with regard to Clavering, and explain to him the dilemma in which my adherence to my promise had involved me.

I found him on my return home and delivered him the letter with which I was charged. At the sight of it surprise, mingled with some uneasiness appeared in his looks. What! said he, in a tone of disappointment, you then saw the lady?

I now remembered his directions to leave my message at the door, and apologized for my neglecting them by telling my reasons. His chagrin vanished, but not without an apparent effort, and he said that all was well; the affair was of no moment.

After a pause of preparation, I intreated his attention to something which I had to relate. I then detailed the history of Clavering and of my late embarrassments. As I went on his countenance betokened increasing solicitude. His emotion was particularly strong when I came to the interrogatories of Mrs. Wentworth in relation to Clavering; but this emotion gave way to profound surprise when I related the manner in which I had eluded her inquiries. I concluded with observing, that when I promised forbearance on the subject of my own adventures, I had not foreseen any exigence which would make an adherence to my promise difficult or inconvenient; that, if his interest was promoted by my silence, I was still willing to maintain it and requested his directions how to conduct myself on this occasion.

He appeared to ponder deeply and with much perplexity on what I had said. When he spoke there was hesitation in his manner and circuity in his expressions, that proved him to have something in his thoughts which he knew not how to communicate. He frequently paused; but my answers and remarks, occasionally given, appeared to deter him from the revelation of his purpose. Our discourse ended, for the present, by his desiring me to persist in my present plan; I should suffer no inconveniencies from it, since it would be my own fault if an interview again took place between the lady and me; meanwhile he should see her and effectually silence her inquiries.

I ruminated not superficially or briefly on this dialogue. By what means would he silence her inquiries? He surely meant not to mislead her by fallacious representations? Some inquietude now crept into my thoughts. I began to form conjectures as to the nature of the scheme to which my suppression of the truth was to be thus made subservient. It seemed as if I were walking in the dark and might rush into snares or drop into pits before I was aware of my danger.[1] Each moment accumulated my doubts and I cherished a secret foreboding that the event would prove my new situation to be far less fortunate than I had, at first, fondly believed. The question now occurred, with painful repetition, Who and what was Welbeck? What was his relation to this foreign lady? What was the service for which I was to be employed?

I could not be contented without a solution of these mysteries. Why should I not lay my soul open before my new friend? Considering my situation, would he regard my fears and my surmises as criminal? I felt that they originated in laudable habits and views. My peace of mind depended on the favourable verdict which conscience should pass on my proceedings. I saw the emptiness of fame and luxury when put in the balance against the recompense of virtue. Never would I purchase the blandishments of adulation and the glare of opulence at the price of my honesty.

Amidst these reflections the dinner-hour arrived. The lady and Welbeck were present. A new train of sentiments now occupied my mind. I regarded them both with inquisitive eyes. I cannot well account for the revolution which had taken place in my mind. Perhaps it was a proof of the capriciousness of my temper, or it was merely the fruit of my profound ignorance of life and manners. Whencever it arose, certain it is that I contemplated the scene before me with altered eyes. Its order and pomp was no longer the parent of tranquility and awe. My wild reveries of inheriting this splendour and appropriating the affections of this nymph, I now regarded as lunatic hope and childish folly. Education and nature had qualified me for a different scene. This might be the mask of misery and the structure of vice.

My companions as well as myself were silent during the meal. The lady retired as soon as it was finished. My inexplicable melancholy increased. It did not pass unnoticed by Welbeck, who inquired, with an air of kindness, into the cause of my visible dejection. I am almost ashamed to relate to what extremes my folly transported me. Instead of answering him I was weak enough to shed tears.

This excited afresh his surprise and his sympathy. He renewed his inquiries; my heart was full, but how to disburthen it I knew not. At length, with some difficulty, I expressed my wishes to leave his house and return into the country.

What, he asked, had occurred to suggest this new plan? What motive could incite me to bury myself in rustic obscurity? How did I purpose to dispose of myself? Had some new friend sprung up more able or more willing to benefit me than he had been?

No, I answered, I have no relation who would own me, or friend who would protect. If I went into the country it would be to the toilsome occupations of a day-labourer; but even that was better than my present situation.

---

[1] "Walking in the dark . . . danger": rather than the airy, magical, or fantasy fulfilling transformations Mervyn imagines on arrival in the city in Chapters 3–6 and rejects in the next paragraph, images such as sleepwalking and falling into subterranean pits now begin to suggest entrapment in Welbeck's deceptions and frauds. At novel's end, in Chapter II.25, Mervyn suffers a sleepwalking episode.

This opinion, he observed, must be newly formed. What was there irksome or offensive in my present mode of life.

That this man condescended to expostulate with me; to dissuade me from my new plan; and to enumerate the benefits which he was willing to confer, penetrated my heart with gratitude. I could not but acknowledge that leisure and literature, copious and elegant accommodation were valuable for their own sake; that all the delights of sensation and refinements of intelligence were comprised within my present sphere; and would be nearly wanting in that to which I was going; I felt temporary compunction for my folly, and determined to adopt a different deportment. I could not prevail upon myself to unfold the true cause of my dejection, and permitted him therefore to ascribe it to a kind of homesickness; to inexperience; and to that ignorance which, on being ushered into a new scene, is oppressed with a sensation of forlornness. He remarked that these chimeras[2] would vanish before the influence of time, and company, and occupation. On the next week he would furnish me with employment; meanwhile he would introduce me into company where intelligence and vivacity would combine to dispel my glooms.

As soon as we separated, my disquietudes returned. I contended with them in vain and finally resolved to abandon my present situation. When and how this purpose was to be effected I knew not. That was to be the theme of future deliberation.

Evening having arrived, Welbeck proposed to me to accompany him on a visit to one of his friends. I cheerfully accepted the invitation and went with him to your friend Mr. Wortley's. A numerous party was assembled, chiefly of the female sex.[3] I was introduced by Welbeck by the title of *a young friend of his*. Notwithstanding my embarrassment I did not fail to attend to what passed on this occasion. I remarked that the utmost deference was paid to my companion, on whom his entrance into this company appeared to operate like magic. His eye sparkled;[4] his features expanded into a benign serenity; and his wonted reserve gave place to a torrent-like and overflowing elocution.

---

[2] "Chimeras": "an unreal creature of the imagination; a mere wild fancy" (OED). Brown and many writers of the Enlightenment use the term with a progressive or radical inflection to mean delusive, irrational, or "unenlightened" conclusions based on false premises or the illogical linkage of cause and effect.

[3] "A numerous party . . . chiefly of the female sex": Welbeck and Mervyn put in a brief appearance at a soirée hosted by Wortley, a friend of Dr. Stevens and one of the businessmen centrally involved in the novel's network of commercial frauds. The predominance of women may hint that these are prostitutes and that Wortley is not the entirely upstanding businessman he claims to be when challenging Mervyn to Dr. Stevens. Welbeck is notably promiscuous, as Mervyn discovers a few pages later in this chapter and in Chapter 9. A more knowing Mervyn will initiate Clemenza's rescue from a brothel in Chapters II.11–16, but the relatively naïve Mervyn of the early chapters may not notice discrete signs of the commerce around him.

[4] "His eyes sparkled": Welbeck's glimmering, seductive eyes and theatrical mask of well-being contradict the notion that character can be gauged from facial appearance and bodily comportment. In the next paragraph Mervyn notes that this appearance "was mere dissimulation."

I marked this change in his deportment with the utmost astonishment. So great was it, that I could hardly persuade myself that it was the same person. A mind thus susceptible of new impressions must be, I conceived, of a wonderful texture. Nothing was further from my expectations than that this vivacity was mere dissimulation and would take its leave of him when he left the company; yet this I found to be the case. The door was no sooner closed after him than his accustomed solemnity returned. He spake little, and that little was delivered with emphatical and monosyllabic brevity.

We returned home at a late hour, and I immediately retired to my chamber, not so much from the desire of repose as in order to enjoy and pursue my own reflections without interruption.

The condition of my mind was considerably remote from happiness. I was placed in a scene that furnished fuel to my curiosity. This passion is a source of pleasure, provided its gratification be practicable. I had no reason, in my present circumstances, to despair of knowledge; yet suspicion and anxiety beset me. I thought upon the delay and toil which the removal of my ignorance would cost, and reaped only pain and fear from the reflection.

The air was remarkably sultry. Lifted sashes and lofty ceilings were insufficient to attemper it. The perturbation of my thoughts affected my body, and the heat which oppressed me, was aggravated, by my restlessness, almost into fever.[5] Some hours were thus painfully past, when I recollected that the bath, erected in the court below, contained a sufficient antidote to the scorching influence of the atmosphere.

I rose, and descended the stairs softly, that I might not alarm Welbeck and the lady, who occupied the two rooms on the second floor. I proceeded to the bath, and filling the reservoir with water, speedily dissipated the heat that incommoded me. Of all species of sensual gratification, that was the most delicious; and I continued for a long time, laving[6] my limbs and moistening my hair. In the midst of this amusement, I noticed the approach of day, and immediately saw the propriety of returning to my chamber. I returned with the same caution which I had used in descending; my feet were bare, so that it was easy to proceed unattended by the smallest signal of my progress.

I had reached the carpetted staircase, and was slowly ascending, when I heard, within the chamber that was occupied by the lady, a noise, as of some one moving. Though not conscious of having acted improperly, yet I felt reluctance to be seen. There was no reason to suppose that this sound was connected with the detection of me, in this situation; yet I acted as if this reason existed, and made haste to pass the door and gain the second flight of steps.

I was unable to accomplish my design, when the chamber door slowly opened, and Welbeck, with a light in his hand, came out. I was abashed and disconcerted at this

---

[5] "Almost into fever": the language in this and following passages, emphasizing the "sultry" atmosphere and unbearable heat, sets the stage for the yellow fever scenes that begin in Chapter 13.

[6] "Laving": washing.

interview. He started at seeing me; but discovering in an instant who it was, his face assumed an expression in which shame and anger were powerfully blended. He seemed on the point of opening his mouth to rebuke me; but suddenly checking himself, he said, in a tone of mildness, How is this?—Whence come you?

His emotion seemed to communicate itself, with an electrical rapidity, to my heart. My tongue faltered while I made some answer. I said, I had been seeking relief from the heat of the weather, in the bath. He heard my explanation in silence; and, after a moment's pause, passed into his own room, and shut himself in. I hastened to my chamber.

A different observer might have found in these circumstances no food for his suspicion or his wonder. To me, however, they suggested vague and tumultuous ideas.

As I strode across the room I repeated, This woman is his daughter. What proof have I of that? He once asserted it; and has frequently uttered allusions and hints from which no other inference could be drawn. The chamber from which he came, in an hour devoted to sleep, was hers. For what end could a visit like this be paid? A parent may visit his child at all seasons, without a crime. On seeing me, methought his features indicated more than surprise. A keen interpreter would be apt to suspect a consciousness of wrong. What if this woman be not his child! How shall their relationship be ascertained?

I was summoned at the customary hour to breakfast. My mind was full of ideas connected with this incident. I was not endowed with sufficient firmness to propose the cool and systematic observation of this man's deportment. I felt as if the state of my mind could not but be evident to him; and experienced in myself all the confusion which this discovery was calculated to produce in him. I would have willingly excused myself from meeting him; but that was impossible.

At breakfast, after the usual salutations, nothing was said. For a time I scarcely lifted my eyes from the table. Stealing a glance at Welbeck, I discovered in his features nothing but his wonted gravity. He appeared occupied with thoughts that had no relation to last night's adventure. This encouraged me; and I gradually recovered my composure. Their inattention to me allowed me occasionally to throw scrutinizing and comparing glances at the face of each.

The relationship of parent and child is commonly discoverable in the visage; but the child may resemble either of its parents, yet have no feature in common with both. Here outlines, surfaces, and hues were in absolute contrariety. That kindred subsisted between them was possible, notwithstanding this dissimilitude; but this circumstance contributed to envenom my suspicions.

Breakfast being finished, Welbeck cast an eye of invitation to the piano forte. The lady rose to comply with his request. My eye chanced to be, at that moment, fixed on her. In stepping to the instrument some motion or appearance awakened a thought in my mind, which affected my feelings like the shock of an earthquake.

I have too slight acquaintance with the history of the passions to truly explain the emotion which now throbbed in my veins. I had been a stranger to what is called love. From subsequent reflection, I have contracted a suspicion, that the sentiment with which I regarded this lady was not untinctured from this source, and that hence arose the turbulence of my feelings, on observing what I construed into marks of pregnancy. The evidence afforded me was slight; yet it exercised an absolute sway over my belief.

It was well that this suspicion had not been sooner excited. Now civility did not require my stay in the apartment, and nothing but flight could conceal the state of my mind. I hastened, therefore, to a distance, and shrouded myself in the friendly secrecy of my own chamber.

The constitution of my mind is doubtless singular and perverse; yet that opinion, perhaps, is the fruit of my ignorance. It may by no means be uncommon for men to *fashion* their conclusions in opposition to evidence and *probability*, and so as to feed their malice and subvert their happiness. Thus it was, in an eminent degree, in my case. The simple fact was connected, in my mind, with a train of the most hateful consequences. The depravity of Welbeck was inferred from it. The charms of this angelic woman were tarnished and withered. I had formerly surveyed her as a precious and perfect monument, but now it was a scene of ruin and blast.

This had been a source of sufficient anguish; but this was not all. I recollected that the claims of a parent had been urged. Will you believe that these claims were now admitted, and that they heightened the iniquity of Welbeck into the blackest and most stupendous of all crimes? These ideas were necessarily transient. Conclusions more conformable to appearances succeeded. This lady might have been lately reduced to widowhood. The recent loss of a beloved companion would sufficiently account for her dejection, and make her present situation compatible with duty.

By this new train of ideas I was somewhat comforted. I saw the folly of precipitate inferences, and the injustice of my atrocious imputations,[7] and acquired some degree of patience in my present state of uncertainty. My heart was lightened of its wonted burthen, and I laboured to invent some harmless explication of the scene that I had witnessed the preceding night.

At dinner Welbeck appeared as usual, but not the lady. I ascribed her absence to some casual indisposition, and ventured to inquire into the state of her health. My companion said she was well, but that she had left the city for a month or two, finding the heat of summer inconvenient where she was. This was no unplausible reason for retirement. A candid mind would have acquiesced in this representation, and found in it nothing inconsistent with a supposition respecting the cause of appearances favourable to her character; but otherwise was I affected. The uneasiness which had flown for a moment returned, and I sunk into gloomy silence.

From this I was roused by my patron, who requested me to deliver a billet, which he put into my hand, at the counting-house of Mr. Thetford, and to bring him an answer. This message was speedily performed. I entered a large building by the river side. A spacious apartment presented itself, well furnished with pipes and

---

[7] "Imputations": accusations.

hogsheads.[8] In one corner was a smaller room, in which a gentleman was busy at writing. I advanced to the door of the room, but was there met by a young person, who received my paper, and delivered it to him within. I stood still at the door; but was near enough to overhear what would pass between them.

The letter was laid upon the desk, and presently he that sat at it lifted his eyes, and glanced at the superscription. He scarcely spoke above a whisper, but his words, nevertheless, were clearly distinguishable. I did not call to mind the sound of his voice, but his words called up a train of recollections.

Lo! said he, carelessly, this from the *Nabob!*

An incident so slight as this was sufficient to open a spacious scene of meditation. This little word, half whispered in a thoughtless mood, was a key to unlock an extensive cabinet of secrets. Thetford was probably indifferent whether his exclamation were overheard. Little did he think on the inferences which would be built upon it.

The Nabob! By this appellation had some one been denoted in the chamber-dialogue, of which I had been an unsuspected auditor.[9] The man who pretended poverty, and yet gave proofs of inordinate wealth; whom it was pardonable to defraud of thirty thousand dollars; first, because the loss of that sum would be trivial to one opulent as he; and secondly, because he was imagined to have acquired this opulence by other than honest methods. Instead of forthwith returning home, I wandered into the fields, to indulge myself in the new thoughts which were produced by this occurrence.

I entertained no doubt that the person alluded to was my patron. No new light was thrown upon his character; unless something were deducible from the charge vaguely made, that his wealth was the fruit of illicit practices. He was opulent, and the sources of his wealth were unknown, if not to the rest of the community, at least to Thetford. But here had a plot been laid. The fortune of Thetford's brother was to rise from the success of artifices, of which the credulity of Welbeck was to be the victim. To detect and to counterwork this plot was obviously my duty. My interference might now indeed be too late to be useful; but this was at least to be ascertained by experiment.

How should my intention be effected? I had hitherto concealed from Welbeck my adventures at Thetford's house. These it was now necessary to disclose, and to mention the recent occurrence. My deductions, in consequence of my ignorance, might be erroneous; but of their truth his knowledge of his own affairs would enable him to

---

[8] "Hogsheads": large barrels or casks with standardized capacities for basic commodities such as tobacco, rum, molasses, or rice. Hogsheads were the standard shipping containers of early-modern maritime networks, and shipping ventures were often advertised according to how many hundreds of barrels they would carry. Thetford is an import-export merchant (like Brown's brothers) and thus his "counting-house" is both a business office and a shipping warehouse full of these barrels, almost inevitably located on Front or Water Street along the wharves and docks.

[9] "An unsuspected auditor": see note 4.6 on the scene in which Mervyn overhears Thetford use the term "Nabob" and learns of his plot to defraud Welbeck.

judge. It was possible that Thetford and he, whose chamber-conversation I had over-heard, were different persons. I endeavoured in vain to ascertain their identity by a comparison of their voices. The words lately heard, my remembrance did not enable me certainly to pronounce to be uttered by the same organs.

This uncertainty was of little moment. It sufficed that Welbeck was designated by this appellation, and that therefore he was proved to be the subject of some fraudu-lent proceeding. The information that I possessed it was my duty to communicate as expeditiously as possible. I was resolved to employ the first opportunity that offered for this end.

My meditations had been ardently pursued, and, when I recalled my attention, I found myself bewildered among fields and fences. It was late before I extricated my-self from unknown paths, and reached home.

I entered the parlour; but Welbeck was not there. A table, with tea-equipage for one person was set; from which I inferred that Welbeck was engaged abroad. This belief was confirmed by the report of the servant. He could not inform me where his mas-ter was, but merely that he should not take tea at home. This incident was a source of vexation and impatience. I knew not but that delay would be of the utmost mo-ment to the safety of my friend. Wholly unacquainted as I was with the nature of his contracts with Thetford, I could not decide whether a single hour would not avail to obviate the evils that threatened him. Had I known whither to trace his footsteps, I should certainly have sought an immediate interview; but, as it was, I was obliged to wait with what patience I could collect for his return to his own house.

I waited hour after hour in vain. The sun declined, and the shades of evening de-scended; but Welbeck was still at a distance.

Chapter IX

WELBECK did not return though hour succeeded hour till the clock struck ten. I inquired of the servants, who informed me that their master was not accustomed to stay out so late. I seated myself at a table, in the parlour, on which there stood a light, and listened for the signal of his coming, either by the sound of steps on the pavement without or by a peal from the bell. The silence was uninterrupted and profound, and each minute added to my sum of impatience and anxiety.

To relieve myself from the heat of the weather, which was aggravated by the condition of my thoughts, as well as to beguile this tormenting interval, it occurred to me to betake myself to the bath. I left the candle where it stood, and imagined that even in the bath, I should hear the sound of the bell which would be rung upon his arrival at the door.

No such signal occurred, and, after taking this refreshment, I prepared to return to my post. The parlour was still unoccupied, but this was not all; the candle I had left upon the table was gone. This was an inexplicable circumstance. On my promise to wait for their master, the servants had retired to bed. No signal of any one's entrance had been given. The street door was locked and the key hung at its customary place, upon the wall. What was I to think? It was obvious to suppose that the candle had been removed by a domestic; but their footsteps could not be traced, and I was not sufficiently acquainted with the house to find the way, especially immersed in darkness, to their chamber. One measure, however, it was evidently proper to take, which was to supply myself, anew, with a light. This was instantly performed; but what was next to be done?

I was weary of the perplexities in which I was embroiled. I saw no avenue to escape from them but that which led me to the bosom of nature and to my ancient occupations. For a moment I was tempted to resume my rustic garb, and, on that very hour, to desert this habitation. One thing only detained me; the desire to apprize my patron of the treachery of Thetford. For this end I was anxious to obtain an interview; but now I reflected that this information, could, by other means be imparted. Was it not sufficient to write him briefly these particulars, and leave him to profit by the knowledge? Thus, I might, likewise, acquaint him with my motives for thus abruptly and unseasonably deserting his service.

To the execution of this scheme pen and paper were necessary. The business of writing was performed in the chamber on the third story. I had been hitherto denied access to this room. In it was a show of papers and books. Here it was that the task, for which I had been retained, was to be performed; but I was to enter it and leave it only in company with Welbeck. For what reasons, I asked, was this procedure to be adopted?

The influence of prohibitions and an appearance of disguise in awakening curiosity are well known.[1] My mind fastened upon the idea of this room with an unusual

---

[1] "The influence . . . in awakening curiosity, are well known": curiosity draws Mervyn into webs of commercial corruption and vice. Here the relation between the curious young Mervyn and his

degree of intenseness. I had seen it but for a moment. Many of Welbeck's hours were spent in it. It was not to be inferred that they were consumed in idleness. What then was the nature of his employment over which a veil of such impenetrable secrecy was cast?

Will you wonder that the design of entering this recess was insensibly formed? Possibly it was locked, but its accessibleness was likewise possible. I meant not the commission of any crime. My principal purpose was to procure the implements of writing, which were elsewhere not to be found. I should neither unseal papers nor open drawers. I would merely take a survey of the volumes and attend to the objects that spontaneously presented themselves to my view. In this there surely was nothing criminal or blameworthy. Meanwhile I was not unmindful of the sudden disappearance of the candle. This incident filled my bosom with the inquietudes of fear and the perturbations of wonder.

Once more I paused to catch any sound that might arise from without. All was still. I seized the candle and prepared to mount the stairs. I had not reached the first landing when I called to mind my midnight meeting with Welbeck at the door of his daughter's chamber. The chamber was now desolate; perhaps it was accessible; if so no injury was done by entering it. My curiosity was strong, but it pictured to itself no precise object. Three steps would bear me to the door. The trial, whether it was fastened, might be made in a moment; and I readily imagined that something might be found within to reward the trouble of examination. The door yielded to my hand and I entered.

No remarkable object was discoverable. The apartment was supplied with the usual furniture. I bent my steps towards a table over which a mirror was suspended. My glances, which roved with swiftness from one object to another, shortly lighted on a miniature portrait that hung near. I scrutinized it with eagerness. It was impossible to overlook its resemblance to my own visage.[2] This was so great that, for a moment, I imagined myself to have been the original from which it had been drawn. This flattering conception yielded place to a belief merely of similitude between me and the genuine original.

The thoughts which this opinion was fitted to produce were suspended by a new object. A small volume, that had, apparently, been much used, lay upon the toilet. I opened it, and found it to contain some of the Dramas of Apostolo Zeno.[3] I turned

---

corrupt mercantile patron Welbeck draws on the relation between young Caleb and corrupt aristocratic patron Falkland in William Godwin's radical novel of social critique, *Caleb Williams* (1794). See notes 2.11 and 7.3 on the development of this motif. For more on the novel's relation to Godwin and *Caleb Williams*, see the Introduction.

[2] "Resemblance to my own visage": Mervyn is startled by his uncanny resemblance to the portrait of the younger Vincentio Lodi, bother of Clemenza. Welbeck confirms this resemblance in Chapter 11, and it repeats Mervyn's resemblance to the deceased Clavering, noted earlier from Chapter 3 (see note 3.9).

[3] "Apostolo Zeno": (1668–1750), a Venetian writer known for innovative melodramas, early journalism, and librettos for composers such as Scarlatti, Vivaldi, and Handel.

over the leaves; a written paper saluted my sight. A single glance informed me that it was English.[4] For the present I was insensible to all motives that would command me to forbear. I seized the paper with an intention to peruse it.

At that moment a stunning report was heard. It was loud enough to shake the walls of the apartment, and abrupt enough to throw me into tremours. I dropped the book and yielded for a moment to confusion and surprise. From what quarter it came, I was unable accurately to determine; but there could be no doubt, from its loudness, that it was near, and even in the house. It was no less manifest that the sound arose from the discharge of a pistol. Some hand must have drawn the trigger. I recollected the disappearance of the candle from the room below. Instantly a supposition darted into my mind which made my hair rise and my teeth chatter.

This, I said, is the deed of Welbeck. He entered while I was absent from the room; he hied to his chamber; and, prompted by some unknown instigation, has inflicted on himself death! This idea had a tendency to palsy my limbs and my thoughts. Some time past in painful and tumultuous fluctuation. My aversion to this catastrophe, rather than a belief of being, by that means, able to prevent or repair the evil, induced me to attempt to enter his chamber. It was possible that my conjectures were erroneous.

The door of his room was locked. I knocked; I demanded entrance in a low voice; I put my eye and my ear to the key-hole and the crevices; nothing could be heard or seen. It was unavoidable to conclude that no one was within; yet the effluvia[5] of gunpowder was perceptible.

Perhaps the room above had been the scene of this catastrophe. I ascended the second flight of stairs. I approached the door. No sound could be caught by my most vigilant attention. I put out the light that I carried, and was then able to perceive that there was light within the room. I scarcely knew how to act. For some minutes I paused at the door. I spoke, and requested permission to enter. My words were succeeded by a death-like stillness. At length I ventured softly to withdraw the bolt; to open and to advance within the room. Nothing could exceed the horror of my expectation; yet I was startled by the scene that I beheld.

In a chair, whose back was placed against the front wall, sat Welbeck. My entrance alarmed him not, nor roused him from the stupor into which he was plunged. He rested his hands upon his knees, and his eyes were rivetted to something that lay, at the distance of a few feet before him, on the floor. A second glance was sufficient to inform me of what nature this object was. It was the body of a man, bleeding, ghastly, and still exhibiting the marks of convulsion and agony!

---

[4] "English": Mervyn recalls this sheet of paper, inserted in Clemenza's book, when he searches for Clemenza at Mrs. Villars' brothel in *Second Part*; see note II.11.3.

[5] "Effluvia": an "effluvium" is a stream of particles producing a smell, usually unpleasant. The word seems to appear here in an associative way, since gunpowder odors were thought to ward off yellow fever and this somewhat technical term is used repeatedly to describe yellow fever odors and emanations in the novel's fever scenes beginning in Chapter 15. The term appeared frequently in the period's yellow fever writings.

I shall omit to describe the shock which a spectacle like this communicated to my unpractised senses. I was nearly as panic-struck and powerless as Welbeck himself. I gazed, without power of speech, at one time, at Welbeck. Then I fixed terrified eyes on the distorted features of the dead. At length, Welbeck, recovering from his reverie, looked up, as if to see who it was that had entered. No surprise, no alarm, was betrayed by him on seeing me. He manifested no desire or intention to interrupt the fearful silence.

My thoughts wandered in confusion and terror. The first impulse was to fly from the scene; but I could not be long insensible to the exigencies of the moment. I saw that affairs must not be suffered to remain in their present situation. The insensibility or despair of Welbeck required consolation and succour. How to communicate my thoughts, or offer my assistance, I knew not. What led to this murderous catastrophe; who it was whose breathless corpse was before me; what concern Welbeck had in producing his death; were as yet unknown.

At length he rose from his seat, and strode at first with faltering, and then with more steadfast steps, across the floor. This motion seemed to put him in possession of himself. He seemed now, for the first time, to recognize my presence. He turned to me and said in a tone of severity:

How now! What brings you here?

This rebuke was unexpected. I stammered out in reply, that the report of the pistol had alarmed me, and that I came to discover the cause of it.

He noticed not my answer, but resumed his perturbed steps, and his anxious, but abstracted looks. Suddenly he checked himself, and glancing a furious eye at the corse, he muttered, Yes, the die is cast. This worthless and miserable scene shall last no longer. I will at once get rid of life and all its humiliations.

Here succeeded a new pause. The course of his thoughts seemed now to become once more tranquil. Sadness, rather than fury, overspread his features; and his accent, when he spoke to me, was not faltering, but solemn.

Mervyn, said he, you comprehend not this scene.[6] Your youth and inexperience make you a stranger to a deceitful and flagitious[7] world. You know me not. It is time that this ignorance should vanish. The knowledge of me and of my actions may be of use to you. It may teach you to avoid the shoals on which my virtue and my peace have been wrecked; but to the rest of mankind it can be of no use. The ruin of my fame is, perhaps, irretrievable; but the height of my iniquity need not be known. I perceive in you a rectitude and firmness worthy to be trusted; promise me, therefore, that not a syllable of what I tell you shall ever pass your lips.

---

[6] "You comprehend not this scene": from this point to the end of Chapter 11, Welbeck narrates his complicated backstory, providing the outline of his crimes and essential information on the origin, development, and Caribbean slavery context of the commercial frauds that drive the novel's plot. Now Mervyn begins to learn the real relations behind the appearances he has seen to this point. The frauds that Welbeck explains in his backstory will continue to unravel and occupy Mervyn in *Second Part*.

[7] "Flagitious": "extremely wicked or criminal: heinous, villainous" (OED).

I had lately experienced the inconvenience of a promise; but I was now confused, embarrassed, ardently inquisitive as to the nature of this scene, and unapprized of the motives that might afterwards occur, persuading or compelling me to disclosure. The promise which he exacted was given. He resumed:

I have detained you in my service, partly for your own benefit, but chiefly for mine. I intended to inflict upon you injury, and to do you good. Neither of these ends can I now accomplish, unless the lessons which my example may inculcate shall inspire you with fortitude, and arm you with caution.

What it was that made me thus, I know not. I am not destitute of understanding. My thirst of knowledge, though irregular, is ardent. I can talk and can feel as virtue and justice prescribe; yet the tenor of my actions has been uniform. One tissue of iniquity and folly has been my life; while my thoughts have been familiar with enlightened and disinterested principles. Scorn and detestation I have heaped upon myself. Yesterday is remembered with remorse. To-morrow is contemplated with anguish and fear; yet every day is productive of the same crimes and of the same follies.

I was left, by the insolvency of my father (a trader of Liverpool),[8] without any means of support, but such as labour should afford me. Whatever could generate pride, and the love of independence, was my portion. Whatever can incite to diligence was the growth of my condition; yet my indolence was a cureless disease; and there were no arts too sordid for me to practise.

I was content to live on the bounty of a kinsman. His family was numerous, and his revenue small. He forebore to upbraid me, or even to insinuate the propriety of providing for myself; but he empowered me to pursue any liberal or mechanical profession which might suit my taste. I was insensible to every generous motive. I laboured to forget my dependent and disgraceful condition, because the remembrance was a source of anguish, without being able to inspire me with a steady resolution to change it.

I contracted an acquaintance with a woman who was unchaste, perverse and malignant. Me, however, she found it no difficult task to deceive. My uncle remonstrated against the union. He took infinite pains to unveil my error, and to convince me that wedlock was improper for one destitute, as I was, of the means of support, even if the object of my choice were personally unexceptionable.

His representations were listened to with anger. That he thwarted my will, in this respect, even by affectionate expostulation, cancelled all that debt of gratitude which I owed to him. I rewarded him for all his kindness by invective and disdain, and hastened to complete my ill-omened marriage. I had deceived the woman's father by assertions of possessing secret resources. To gratify my passion I descended to dissimulation and falsehood. He admitted me into his family, as the husband of his child;

---

[8] "A trader of Liverpool": Welbeck's Liverpool origin links him to the slave-based commercial economy that underlies the novel's financial frauds and fortunes and is thus a first link in the novel's web of references to slavery and slave revolt or resistance. Liverpool's rise to prosperity was based on slavery: in the last half of the eighteenth century, it became the primary trading and finance port for the African slave trade and its ships dominated the slave routes.

but the character of my wife and the fallacy of my assertions were quickly discovered. He denied me accommodation under his roof, and I was turned forth to the world to endure the penalty of my rashness and my indolence.

Temptation would have moulded me into any villainous shape. My virtuous theories and comprehensive erudition would not have saved me from the basest of crimes. Luckily for me, I was, for the present, exempted from temptation. I had formed an acquaintance with a young American captain.[9] On being partially informed of my situation, he invited me to embark with him for his own country. My passage was gratuitous. I arrived, in a short time, at Charleston,[10] which was the place of his abode.

He introduced me to his family, every member of which was, like himself, imbued with affection and benevolence. I was treated like their son and brother. I was hospitably entertained until I should be able to select some path of lucrative industry. Such was my incurable depravity, that made no haste to select my pursuit. An interval of inoccupation succeeded, which I applied to the worst purposes.

My friend had a sister, who was married; but, during the absence of her husband resided with her family. Hence originated our acquaintance. The purest of human hearts and the most vigorous understanding were hers. She idolized her husband, who well deserved to be the object of her adoration. Her affection for him, and her general principles, appeared to be confirmed beyond the power to be shaken. I sought her intercourse without illicit views; I delighted in the effusions of her candour and the flashes of her intelligence; I conformed, by a kind of instinctive hypocrisy, to her views; I spoke and felt from the influence of immediate and momentary conviction. She imagined she had found in me a friend worthy to partake in all her sympathies, and forward all her wishes. We were mutually deceived. She was the victim of self-delusion; but I must charge myself with practising deceit both upon myself and her.

I reflect with astonishment and horror on the steps which led to her degradation and to my calamity. In the high career of passion all consequences were overlooked.

---

[9] "American captain": this is Captain Amos Watson, whose married sister Welbeck will shortly seduce, impregnate, and ruin. Watson is the man Welbeck has just shot; he will be named and will reappear at the end of Welbeck's narrative in Chapter 11. In *Second Part*, the financial implications of Watson's murder will be extended to include another family fortune tied to Caribbean slavery and slave revolt.

[10] "Charleston": Charleston was the primary North American port for the landing and sale of African slaves, and thus commonly associated with slavery by period writers. Hector St. Jean de Crèvecoeur's *Letters from an American Farmer* (1782), for example, contains a famous scene depicting the gothicized torture of a rebellious slave in Charleston, and the antislavery poem "A Negro's Lamentation," published in the Brown-edited *Monthly Magazine* (November 1800) is set there. Brown was also familiar with Carolinian slave wealth through its many Philadelphia connections. Brown's oldest merchant brother Joseph worked for a time from Edenton, South Carolina, and so many of the wealthiest Charleston plantation families had mansions in an exclusive stretch of Philadelphia's Eighth Street that it was popularly known as "planter's row."

She was the dupe of the most audacious sophistry and the grossest delusion. I was the slave of sensual impulses and voluntary blindness. The effect may be easily conceived. Not till symptoms of pregnancy began to appear were our eyes opened to the ruin which impended over us.

Then I began to revolve the consequences, which the mist of passion had hitherto concealed. I was tormented by the pangs of remorse, and pursued by the phantom of ingratitude. To complete my despair, this unfortunate lady was apprised of my marriage with another woman; a circumstance which I had anxiously concealed from her. She fled from her father's house at a time when her husband and brother were hourly expected. What became of her I knew not. She left behind her a letter to her father, in which the melancholy truth was told.[11]

Shame and remorse had no power over my life. To elude the storm of invective and upbraiding; to quiet the uproar of my mind, I did not betake myself to voluntary death. My pusillanimity[12] still clung to this wretched existence. I abruptly retired from the scene, and, repairing to the port, embarked in the first vessel which appeared. The ship chanced to belong to Wilmington, in Delaware,[13] and here I sought out an obscure and cheap abode.

I possessed no means of subsistence. I was unknown to my neighbours, and desired to remain unknown. I was unqualified for manual labour by all the habits of my life; but there was no choice between penury and diligence—between honest labour and criminal inactivity. I mused incessantly on the forlornness of my condition. Hour after hour passed, and the horrors of want began to encompass me. I sought with eagerness for an avenue by which I might escape from it. The perverseness of my nature led me on from one guilty thought to another. I took refuge in my customary sophistries, and reconciled myself at length to a scheme of—*forgery!*

---

[11] "The melancholy truth was told": the briefly narrated seduction of Watson's married sister, like that of Clemenza Lodi, repeats the typical plot points of seduction-and-ruin narratives that were made famous in Samuel Richardson's *Clarissa* (1748) and supplied the basic frame for the well-known U.S. "seduction novels" of the 1790s, such as Susanna Rowson's *Charlotte Temple* (1791, the first U.S. best seller) or Hannah Foster's *The Coquette* (1797). Brown's readers were familiar with the way such scenarios of virtue-vice and middle-class identity evoke larger networks of gender, class, and commercial relations. The repeated linkage of seduction and exploitation in *Arthur Mervyn*'s backstories also serves to underline the dominated status of women, a structural feature of social relations that is emphasized by Brown's narrative method of analyzing society through basic relations of "sex" and "property" (see "Walstein's School of History" in Related Texts).

[12] "Pusillanimity": "lack of courage or fortitude . . . cowardliness" (OED).

[13] "Wilmington, in Delaware": twenty-five miles southwest of Philadelphia.

Chapter X

HAVING ascertained my purpose, it was requisite to search out the means by which I might effect it. These were not clearly or readily suggested. The more I contemplated my project, the more numerous and arduous its difficulties appeared. I had no associates in my undertaking. A due regard to my safety and the unextinguished sense of honour[1] deterred me from seeking auxiliaries and co-agents. The esteem of mankind was the spring of all my activity, the parent of all my virtue and all my vice. To preserve this, it was necessary that my guilty projects should have neither witness nor partaker.

I quickly discovered that to execute this scheme demanded time, application and money, none of which my present situation would permit me to devote to it. At first, it appeared that an attainable degree of skill and circumspection would enable me to arrive, by means of counterfeit bills, to the pinnacle of affluence and honour. My error was detected by a closer scrutiny, and I, finally, saw nothing in this path but enormous perils and insurmountable impediments.

Yet what alternative was offered me. To maintain myself by the labour of my hands, to perform any toilsome or prescribed task, was incompatible with my nature. My habits debarred me from country occupations. My pride regarded as vile and ignominious drudgery any employment which the town could afford. Meanwhile, my wants were as urgent as ever and my funds were exhausted.

There are few, perhaps, whose external situation resembled mine, who would have found in it any thing but incitements to industry and invention. A thousand methods of subsistence, honest but laborious, were at my command, but to these I entertained an irreconcilable aversion. Ease and the respect attendant upon opulence I was willing to purchase at the price of ever-wakeful suspicion and eternal remorse; but, even at this price, the purchase was impossible.

The desperateness of my condition became hourly more apparent. The further I extended my view, the darker grew the clouds which hung over futurity. Anguish and infamy appeared to be the inseparable conditions of my existence. There was one mode of evading the evils that impended. To free myself from self-upbraiding and to shun the persecutions of my fortune was possible only by shaking off life itself.

One evening, as I traversed the bank of the creek, these dismal meditations were uncommonly intense. They at length terminated in a resolution to throw myself into

---

[1] "Unextinguished sense of honour": Welbeck's obsession with "honour" and reputation and his aversion to labor hark back to pre-revolutionary aristocratic codes of behavior and class status. He describes this obsession as his "ruling passion" at the end of this chapter. Rather than considering the effects of his actions on others or in a larger social sense, Welbeck's concern is to maintain elite status and reputation or "esteem." As opposed to Mervyn's "modern" and enlightened rise, as the novel develops, from rural poverty to urban professional status and progressive social relations, Welbeck repeatedly emphasizes his hatred of any form of labor or solidarity within larger groups. His destructive combination of quasiaristocratic entitlement and mercantile selfishness makes him an apt representative of contemporary trading elites and commercial corruption.

the stream. The first impulse was to rush instantly to my death, but the remembrance of papers, lying at my lodgings, which might unfold more than I desired to the curiosity of survivors, induced me to postpone this catastrophe till the next morning.

My purpose being formed, I found my heart lightened of its usual weight. By you it will be thought strange, but it is nevertheless true, that I derived from this new prospect, not only tranquility but cheerfulness. I hastened home. As soon as I entered, my land-lord informed me that a person had been searching for me in my absence. This was an unexampled incident and forboded me no good. I was strongly persuaded that my visitant had been led hither not by friendly, but hostile purposes. This persuasion was confirmed by the description of the stranger's guize and demeanour given by my land-lord. My fears instantly recognized the image of Watson, the man by whom I had been so eminently benefitted, and whose kindness I had compensated by the ruin of his sister and the confusion of his family.

An interview with this man was less to be endured than to look upon the face of an avenging deity. I was determined to avoid this interview, and for this end, to execute my fatal purpose within the hour. My papers were collected with a tremulous hand, and consigned to the flames. I then bade my land-lord inform all visitants that I should not return till the next day, and once more hastened towards the river.

My way led past the Inn where one of the stages from Baltimore was accustomed to stop. I was not unaware that Watson had possibly been brought in the coach which had recently arrived, and which now stood before the door of the Inn. The danger of my being descried or encountered by him as I passed did not fail to occur. This was to be eluded by deviating from the main street.

Scarcely had I turned a corner for this purpose when I was accosted by a young man whom I knew to be an inhabitant of the town, but with whom I had hitherto had no intercourse but what consisted in a transient salutation. He apologized for the liberty of addressing me, and, at the same time, inquired if I understood the French language.

Being answered in the affirmative, he proceeded to tell me, that in the stage, just arrived, had come a passenger, a youth who appeared to be French, who was wholly unacquainted with our language, and who had been seized with a violent disease.

My informant had felt compassion for the forlorn condition of the stranger, and had just been seeking me at my lodgings, in hope that my knowledge of French would enable me to converse with the sick man, and obtain from him a knowledge of his situation and views.

The apprehensions I had precipitately formed, were thus removed and I readily consented to perform this service. The youth was, indeed, in a deplorable condition. Besides the pains of his disease, he was overpowered by dejection. The inn-keeper, was extremely anxious for the removal of his guest. He was by no means willing to sustain the trouble and expense of a sick or a dying man, for which it was, scarcely probable that he should ever be reimbursed. The traveller had no baggage and his dress betokened the pressure of many wants.

My compassion for this stranger was powerfully awakened. I was in possession of a suitable apartment, for which I had no power to pay the rent that was accruing, but my inability in this respect was unknown, and I might enjoy my lodgings unmolested for some weeks. The fate of this youth would be speedily decided, and I should be left at liberty to execute my first intentions before my embarrassments should be visibly increased.

After a moment's pause, I conducted the stranger to my home, placed him in my own bed, and became his nurse. His malady was such as is known in the tropical islands, by the name of the Yellow or Malignant Fever,[2] and the physician who was called speedily pronounced his case desperate.

It was my duty to warn him of the death that was hastening, and to promise the fulfillment of any of his wishes, not inconsistent with my present situation. He received my intelligence with fortitude, and appeared anxious to communicate some information respecting his own state. His pangs and his weakness scarcely allowed him to be intelligible. From his feeble efforts and broken narrative I collected thus much concerning his family and fortune.

His father's name was Vincentio Lodi. From a Merchant at Leghorn,[3] he had changed himself into a planter in the Island of Guadaloupe.[4] His Son, had been sent, at an early age, for the benefits of education to Europe. The young Vincentio was, at length, informed by his father, that, being weary of his present mode of existence, he had determined to sell his property, and transport himself to the United States. The son was directed to hasten home, that he might embark, with his father, on this voyage.

The summons was cheerfully obeyed. The youth on his arrival at the Island found preparation making for the funeral of his father. It appeared that the elder Lodi had flattered one of his slaves with the prospect of his freedom, but had, nevertheless, included this slave in the sale that he had made of his estate. Actuated by revenge, the

---

[2] "Yellow or Malignant Fever": the first naming of the disease. "Malignant" was used as commonly as "yellow" to describe the illness, for example in Mathew Carey's *A Short Account of the Malignant Fever* (see excerpts in this volume's Related Texts).

[3] "Leghorn": the Italian city Livorno. As the main port for Florence, Livorno was tightly connected to global markets, including the Mediterranean and Atlantic slave trades, and traffic in illicit and contraband goods. It was a cosmopolitan center with significant populations of trading "nations," such as Armenians and Sephardic Jews, who facilitated mercantile links. Many Sephardim came to the city after the Spanish expulsion of the Jews in 1492 and were influential in managing the financing and operation of New World sugar plantations (see note II.23.4).

[4] "Guadeloupe": a French Caribbean colony, the wealthiest sugar colony after Haiti and Jamaica, involved in the novel's networks of commerce and slave revolution. In 1790, when Guadeloupe's planter elites refused new laws from Paris concerning equal rights, civil war broke out between monarchists (plantation owners) and republicans (*petits blancs* or poor whites). Slaves and free people of color took both sides of the conflict. The monarchists ultimately regained control, but in 1793, the year of the novel's action, widespread slave rebellion broke out, forcing the planters to ask the British to occupy the island and put down the insurrection. Even during the larger revolutionary wars that opposed them throughout the period, British and French colonial elites remained united against Caribbean slave revolts and cooperated to suppress them.

slave assassinated Lodi in the open street and resigned himself, without a struggle, to the punishment which the law had provided for such a deed.[5]

The property had been recently transferred, and the price was now presented to young Vincentio by the purchaser. He was, by no means, inclined to adopt his father's project, and was impatient to return with his inheritance, to France. Before this could be done, the conduct of his father had rendered a voyage to the continent indispensable.

Lodi had a daughter, whom, a few weeks previous to his death, he had intrusted to an American Captain, for whom, he had contracted a friendship. The vessel was bound to Philadelphia, but the conduct she was to pursue, and the abode she was to select, on her arrival, were known only to the father, whose untimely death involved the son in considerable uncertainty with regard to his sister's fate. His anxiety on this account induced him to seize the first conveyance that offered. In a short time he landed at Baltimore.

As soon as he recovered from the fatigues of his voyage, he prepared to go to Philadelphia. Thither his baggage was immediately sent under the protection of a passenger and countryman. His money consisted in Portuguese gold,[6] which, in pursuance of advice, he had changed into Bank-notes. He besought me, in pathetic terms, to search out his sister, whose youth and poverty and ignorance of the language and manners of the country might expose her to innumerable hardships. At the same time, he put a pocket-book and small volume into my hand, indicating, by his countenance and gestures, his desire that I would deliver them to his sister.

His obsequies being decently performed, I had leisure to reflect upon the change in my condition which this incident had produced. In the pocket-book were found bills to the amount of twenty thousand dollars.[7] The volume proved to be a manuscript,

---

[5] "Punishment . . . for such a deed": the assassination of the elder Lodi by a vengeful slave condenses the dynamics of slave revolution in the 1790s. This assassination and the slave unrest it represents are key motivating factors in the web of subplots that explain the surface action of the novel, leading to links between the ruined Lodi family, Welbeck, the Thetfords, and the now-murdered trader and captain Watson (for Watson, see note 9.9). Thus a desperate Caribbean slave's assassination of his master is one of the first links in the chain of causes and effects that shapes Mervyn's experiences in the city.

[6] "Portuguese gold": Welbeck was earlier linked to "Portuguese" riches (note 4.8). This gold is not bullion but money (specie) that could circulate in the U.S. at this time. The U.S. mint (then being organized in Philadelphia) did not begin producing U.S. coinage until 1794; in the interim, the Foreign Coin Act of February 9, 1793 made gold coinage from Portugal, Spain, Britain, and France legal tender in the U.S. beginning on July 1 of that year. These new currency flows are one of the financial concerns that parallel the novel's time frame (see Mathew Carey's description of the city's financial fragility in Related Texts). Brown's brother Armitt worked as a clerk in the Treasury Department and in Philadelphia banks while Alexander Hamilton was engineering the new currency system.

[7] "Twenty thousand dollars": calculated relative to the consumer price index then and now (a minimum estimate), $20,000 in 1790 equals $407,000 in 2005; relative to average unskilled wage compensation then and now, $20,000 in 1790 equals $6.55 million in 2005. See note 4.7 for conversion of dollar values.

written by the elder Lodi in Italian, and contained memoirs of the Ducal house of Visconti, from whom the writer believed himself to have lineally descended.[8]

Thus had I arrived, by an avenue so much beyond my foresight, at the possession of wealth. The evil which impelled me to the brink of suicide, and which was the source, though not of all, yet of the larger portion of my anguish, was now removed. What claims to honour or to ease were consequent on riches, were, by an extraordinary fortune, now conferred upon me.

Such, for a time, were my new born but transitory raptures. I forgot that this money was not mine. That it had been received under every sanction of fidelity, for another's use. To retain it was equivalent to robbery. The sister of the deceased was the rightful claimant; it was my duty to search her out, and perform my tacit, but sacred obligations, by putting the whole into her possession.

This conclusion was too adverse to my wishes, not to be strenuously combatted. I asked, what it was that gave man the power of ascertaining the successor to his property? During his life, he might transfer the actual possession, but if vacant at his death, he, into whose hands accident should cast it, was the genuine proprietor. It is true, that the law had sometimes otherwise decreed, but in law, there was no validity, further than it was able by investigation and punishment, to enforce its decrees; But would the law extort this money from me?

It was rather by gesture than by words that the will of Lodi was imparted. It was the topic of remote inferences and vague conjecture rather than of explicit and unerring declarations. Besides if the lady were found, would not prudence dictate the reservation of her fortune to be administered by me, for her benefit? Of this her age and education had disqualified herself. It was sufficient for the maintenance of both. She would regard me as her benefactor and protector. By supplying all her wants and watching over her safety without apprizing her of the means, by which I shall be enabled to do this, I shall lay irresistible claims to her love and her gratitude.

Such were the sophistries by which reason was seduced and my integrity annihilated. I hastened away from my present abode. I easily traced the baggage of the deceased to an inn, and gained possession of it. It contained nothing but clothes and books. I then instituted the most diligent search after the young lady. For a time, my exertions were fruitless.

---

[8] "Visconti . . . believed himself to have lineally descended": Welbeck emphasizes the imaginary or arbitrary nature of aristocratic lineages and ownership, echoing Mervyn's comment about the House of Stuart in Chapter 6 (note 6.4). The House of Visconti was an Italian noble family that ruled Milan from 1227 to 1427, when a short-lived republic arose. In 1450, the House of Sforza, related by marriage to the Visconti, seized power and ruled Milan to 1535, when power passed to the Austrian-Spanish Habsburgs after military conflicts with France that took place in Provence and Lombardy. Lodi is the name of a town and province in Lombardy, part of the territory controlled by the Visconti and Sforza, and thus the implied origin of the Lodi family name. *Arthur Mervyn* repeatedly references these regions and their political unrest: see notes 6.2, 13.8, II.23.12.

Meanwhile, the possessor of this house thought proper to embark with his family for Europe.[9] The sum which he demanded for his furniture, though enormous, was precipitately paid by me. His servants were continued in their former stations, and in the day, at which he relinquished the mansion, I entered on possession.

There was no difficulty in persuading the world that Welbeck was a personage of opulence and rank. My birth and previous adventures it was proper to conceal. The facility with which mankind are misled in their estimate of characters, their proneness to multiply inferences and conjectures will not be readily conceived by one destitute of my experience. My sudden appearance on the stage, my stately reserve, my splendid habitation and my circumspect deportment were sufficient to intitle me to homage. The artifices that were used to unveil the truth, and the guesses that were current respecting me, were adapted to gratify my ruling passion.

I did not remit my diligence to discover the retreat of Mademoiselle Lodi;[10] I found her, at length, in the family of a kinsman of the Captain under whose care she had come to America. Her situation was irksome and perilous. She had already experienced the evils of being protectorless and indigent, and my seasonable interference snatched her from impending and less supportable ills.

I could safely unfold all that I knew of her brother's history, except the legacy which he had left. I ascribed the diligence with which I had sought her to his death-bed injunctions, and prevailed upon her to accept from me the treatment which she would have received from her brother, if he had continued to live, and if his power to benefit had been equal to my own.

Though less can be said in praise of the understanding, than of the sensibilities of this woman, she is one, whom, no one could refrain from loving, though placed in situations far less favourable to the generation of that sentiment, than mine. In habits of domestic and incessant intercourse, in the perpetual contemplation of features animated by boundless gratitude and ineffable sympathies, it could not be expected that either she or I should escape enchantment.

---

[9] "Possessor of this house . . . embark with his family for Europe": with the money stolen from the Lodis in Wilmington, Delaware, Welbeck rents a mansion in Philadelphia from Clavering's father (see notes 7.7 and II.4.2), complete with furniture and staff, where he can launder his past and masquerade as part of the merchant elite, "a person of opulence and rank." The father has left for Europe to look for Clavering, wrongly believing that Clavering made good on his prior thwarted attempts to travel there. This is the increasingly gothic building where Welbeck and Arthur are located at this point in the plot, in and around which much of the first part's action occurs.

[10] "Mademoiselle Lodi": although her family is spread across an international commercial network linking the Caribbean, France, Italy, and the U.S., Clemenza speaks Italian and would ordinarily be called Signorina. By using the French name for an unmarried woman, Welbeck assimilates her to the "French" cultural coding of his new mansion and staff (see note 5.11). In the atmosphere of the 1790s, such "French" coding is generally opposed to the British-aligned interests of the U.S. Federalist elite.

The poison was too sweet not to be swallowed with avidity by me. Too late I remembered that I was already enslaved by inextricable obligations.[11] It was easy to have hidden this impediment from the eyes of my companion, but here my integrity refused to yield. I can, indeed, lay claim to little merit on account of this forbearance. If there had been no alternative between deceit and the frustration of my hopes, I should doubtless have dissembled the truth with as little scruple on this, as on a different occasion, but I could not be blind to the weakness of her with whom I had to contend.

---

[11] "Enslaved by inextricable obligations": in other words, Welbeck is still married to the profligate wife he abandoned in Liverpool (Chapter 9) and rationalizes his exploitation of Clemenza on the grounds that marrying her would constitute bigamy.

Chapter XI

MEANWHILE large deductions had been made from my stock of money, and the remnant would be speedily consumed by my present mode of life. My expences far exceeded my previous expectations. In no long time I should be reduced to my ancient poverty, which the luxurious existence that I now enjoyed, and the regard due to my beloved and helpless companion, would render more irksome than ever. Some scheme to rescue me from this fate, was indispensable; but my aversion to labour, to any pursuit, the end of which was merely gain, and which would require application and attention continued undiminished.

I was plunged anew into dejection and perplexity. From this I was somewhat relieved by a plan suggested by Mr. Thetford.[1] I thought I had experience of his knowledge and integrity, and the scheme that he proposed seemed liable to no possibility of miscarriage. A ship was to be purchased, supplied with a suitable cargo, and dispatched to a port in the West-Indies. Loss from storms and enemies was to be precluded by insurance. Every hazard was to be enumerated, and the ship and cargo valued at the highest rate. Should the voyage be safely performed, the profits would be double the original expense. Should the ship be taken or wrecked, the insurers would have bound themselves to make ample, speedy, and certain indemnification—Thetford's brother, a wary and experienced trader, was to be the supercargo.[2]

All my money was laid out upon this scheme. Scarcely enough was reserved to supply domestic and personal wants. Large debts were likewise incurred. Our caution had, as we conceived, annihilated every chance of failure. Too much could not be expended on a project so infallible; and the vessel, amply fitted and freighted, departed on her voyage.

An interval, not devoid of suspense and anxiety, succeeded. My mercantile inexperience made me distrust the clearness of my own discernment, and I could not but remember that my utter and irretrievable destruction was connected with the failure

---

[1] "A plan suggested by Mr. Thetford": together with earlier hints about this plot in Chapters 4 and 8 (notes 4.7, 8.9) and Mervyn's reasoning about it in Chapter 14 (note 14.9), this chapter provides the explanation of Thetford's scheme to defraud Welbeck. Following Welbeck's theft of Lodi's fortune, explained in the previous chapter, the Thetford fraud deepens and complicates the web of subplots outlining commercial corruption. The plan is to defraud Welbeck (of wealth itself obtained by fraud) by luring him to invest in a reexport voyage. Thetford and his brother recuperate Welbeck's investment for themselves by manipulating insurance regulations and revolutionary era restrictions concerning Caribbean shipping and the threat of slave revolt. Further twists and implications of the Thetford fraud will be developed in *Second Part* (see note II.3.15).

[2] "Supercargo": the representative of a merchant who accompanies a trading voyage and supervises the cargo's sale to prevent fraud, often a close family relation of the investing merchant. Family members often fulfilled this function due to the trust required and to prevent collusion with the ship's captain. In this case, supercargo Thomas Thetford, younger brother of the Walter Thetford proposing the investment scheme, uses his supercargo position to ensure that the fraud succeeds. The primary goal of the fraud, as Thetford notes in Chapter 4, is to gain the capital required to establish his younger brother Thomas as a merchant exporter in his own right.

of my scheme. Time added to my distrust and apprehensions. The time, at which tidings of the ship were to be expected, elapsed without affording any information of her destiny. My anxieties, however, were to be carefully hidden from the world. I had taught mankind to believe, that this project had been adopted more for amusement than gain; and the debts which I had contracted, seemed to arise from willingness to adhere to established maxims, more than from the pressure of necessity.

Month succeeded month, and intelligence was still withheld. The notes which I had given for one third of the cargo, and for the premium of insurance, would shortly become due. For the payment of the former, and the cancelling of the latter, I had relied upon the expeditious return, or the demonstrated loss of the vessel. Neither of these events had taken place.

My cares were augmented from another quarter. My companion's situation now appeared to be such, as, if our intercourse had been sanctified by wedlock, would have been regarded with delight.[3] As it was, no symptoms were equally to be deplored. Consequences, as long as they were involved in uncertainty, were extenuated or overlooked; but now, when they became apparent and inevitable, were fertile of distress and upbraiding.

Indefinable fears, and a desire to monopolize all the meditations and affections of this being, had induced me to perpetuate her ignorance of any but her native language, and debar her from all intercourse with the world. My friends were of course inquisitive respecting her character, adventures, and particularly her relation to me. The consciousness how much the truth redounded to my dishonour, made me solicitous to lead conjecture astray. For this purpose I did not discountenance the conclusion that was adopted by some, that she was my daughter. I reflected, that all dangerous surmizes would be effectually precluded by this belief.

These precautions afforded me some consolation in my present difficulties. It was requisite to conceal the lady's condition from the world. If this should be ineffectual, it would not be difficult to divert suspicion from my person. The secrecy that I had practised would be justified, in the apprehension of those to whom the personal condition of Clemenza should be disclosed, by the feelings of a father.

Meanwhile, it was an obvious expedient to remove the unhappy lady to a distance from impertinent observers. A rural retreat, lonely, and sequestered, was easily procured, and hither she consented to repair. This arrangement being concerted, I had leisure to reflect upon the evils which every hour brought nearer, and which threatened to exterminate me.

My inquietudes forbade me to sleep, and I was accustomed to rise before day, and seek some respite in the fields. Returning from one of these unseasonable rambles, I chanced to meet you. Your resemblance to the deceased Lodi, in person and visage, is remarkable. When you first met my eye, this similitude startled me. Your subsequent appeal to my compassion was cloathed in such terms, as formed a powerful contrast with your dress, and prepossessed me greatly in favour of your education and capacity.

---

[3] "Situation . . . regarded with delight": Clemenza's pregnancy, first noted in Chapter 8.

In my present hopeless condition, every incident, however trivial, was attentively considered, with a view to extract from it some means of escaping from my difficulties. My love for the Italian girl, in spite of all my efforts to keep it alive, had begun to languish. Marriage was impossible and had now, in some degree, ceased to be desirable. We are apt to judge of others by ourselves. The passion, I now found myself disposed to ascribe chiefly to fortuitous circumstances; to the impulse of gratitude, and the exclusion of competitors; and believed that your resemblance to her brother, your age, and personal accomplishments, might, after a certain time, and in consequence of suitable contrivances, on my part, give a new direction to her feelings. To gain your concurrence, I relied upon your simplicity, your gratitude, and your susceptibility to the charms of this bewitching creature.

I contemplated, likewise, another end. Mrs. Wentworth is rich. A youth who was once her favourite, and designed to inherit her fortunes, has disappeared, for some years, from the scene. His death is most probable, but of that there is no satisfactory information. The life of this person, whose name is Clavering, is an obstacle to some designs which had occurred to me in relation to this woman. My purposes were crude and scarcely formed. I need not swell the catalogue of my errors by expatiating upon them. Suffice it to say, that the peculiar circumstances of your introduction to me, led me to reflections on the use that might be made of your agency, in procuring this lady's acquiescence in my schemes. You were to be ultimately persuaded to confirm in her the belief that her nephew was dead. To this consummation it was indispensible to lead you by slow degrees, and circuitous paths. Meanwhile, a profound silence, with regard to your genuine history, was to be observed; and to this forbearance, your consent was obtained with more readiness than I expected.[4]

There was an additional motive for the treatment you received from me. My personal projects and cares had hitherto prevented me from reading Lodi's manuscript; a slight inspection, however, was sufficient to prove that the work was profound and eloquent. My ambition has panted, with equal avidity, after the reputation of literature and opulence. To claim the authorship of this work was too harmless and specious a stratagem, not to be readily suggested. I meant to translate it into English, and to enlarge it by enterprising incidents of my own invention. My scruples to assume the merit of the original composer, might thus be removed. For this end, your assistance as an amanuensis would be necessary.

You will perceive, that all these projects depended on the seasonable arrival of intelligence from. . . . The delay of another week would seal my destruction. The silence might arise from the foundering of the ship, and the destruction of all on board. In this case, the insurance was not forfeited, but payment could not be obtained within a year. Meanwhile, the premium and other debts must be immediately discharged, and this was beyond my power. Meanwhile I was to live in a manner that would not belie my pretensions; but my coffers were empty.

---

[4] "Expected": the paragraph provides Welbeck's explanation for why he had Mervyn deliver a message to Mrs. Wentworth (see note 7.5).

I cannot adequately paint the anxieties with which I have been haunted. Each hour has added to the burthen of my existence, till, in consequence of the events of this day, it has become altogether insupportable. Some hours ago, I was summoned by Thetford to his house. The messenger informed me that tidings had been received of my ship. In answer to my eager interrogations, he could give no other information than that she had been captured by the British. He was unable to relate particulars.

News of her safe return would, indeed, have been far more acceptable; but even this information was a source of infinite congratulation. It precluded the demand of my insurers. The payment of other debts might be postponed for a month, and my situation be the same as before the adoption of this successless scheme. Hope and joy were reinstated in my bosom, and I hasted to Thetford's compting house.

He received me with an air of gloomy dissatisfaction. I accounted for his sadness by supposing him averse to communicate information, which was less favourable than our wishes had dictated. He confirmed, with visible reluctance, the news of her capture. He had just received letters from his brother, acquainting him with all particulars, and containing the official documents of this transaction.

This had no tendency to damp my satisfaction, and I proceeded to peruse with eagerness, the papers which he put into my hand. I had not proceeded far when my joyous hopes vanished. Two French mulattoes[5] had, after much solicitation, and the most solemn promises to carry with them no articles which the laws of war decree to be contraband, obtained a passage in the vessel. She was speedily encountered by a privateer, by whom every receptacle was ransacked. In a chest, belonging to the Frenchmen, and which they had affirmed to contain nothing but their clothes, were found two sabres, and other accoutrements of an officer of cavalry. Under this pretence, the vessel was captured and condemned, and this was a cause of forfeiture, which had not been provided against in the contract of insurance.[6]

---

[5] "French mulattoes": a key event leading up to the Haitian Revolution was the uprising of "mulattos" (free people of color) in late 1790 outside of Cap François. The three-quarters white son of a trader, Ogé, happened to be in Paris in 1789 at the outbreak of the French Revolution. Ogé petitioned the National Assembly to extend emancipation rights to the free people of color in the colonies (but not slaves). Believing that the Assembly had done so, Ogé returned to Haiti, had arms smuggled in from New Orleans, and began an uprising of free blacks. The revolt was defeated and Ogé brutally executed.

[6] "The contract of insurance": combined with Mervyn's reflection on the incident in Chapter 14 (see note 14.9), this paragraph provides the key details of the Thetford brother's fraud. By shipping contraband weapons on board the Thetfords' vessel, the mixed-race smugglers (implicitly involved in slave revolt) violate the ship's neutrality and the vessel is seized by the British navy. The violation of neutrality is a political event not covered by the ship's commercial insurance contract, and consequently Welbeck's investment is forfeit or lost. Thetford's younger brother Thomas, traveling with the ship as supercargo, will be able to repurchase the impounded ship and cargo at a "fifth or a tenth of its real value" (note 14.9), and recover an immense profit. Welbeck loses his investment (all of the remaining Lodi fortune that he possesses) because of the terms of the insurance contract. As Mervyn realizes in Chapter 14, all of this implies that the Thetfords have "planted" the contraband as a means by which to have the ship and cargo, paid for by Welbeck, impounded and resold to themselves for a fraction of their value.

By this untoward event my hopes were irreparably blasted. The utmost efforts were demanded to conceal my thoughts from my companion. The anguish that preyed upon my heart was endeavoured to be masked by looks of indifference. I pretended to have been previously informed by the messenger, not only of the capture, but of the cause that led to it, and forbore to expatiate upon my loss, or to execrate the authors of my disappointment. My mind, however, was the theatre of discord and agony, and I waited with impatience for an opportunity to leave him.

For want of other topics, I asked by whom this information had been brought. He answered, that the bearer was Captain Amos Watson, whose vessel had been forfeited, at the same time, under a different pretence. He added, that my name being mentioned, accidentally, to Watson, the latter had betrayed marks of great surprise, and been very earnest in his inquiries respecting my situation. Having obtained what knowledge Thetford was able to communicate, the captain had departed, avowing a former acquaintance with me, and declaring his intention of paying me a visit.

These words operated on my frame like lightning. All within me was tumult and terror, and I rushed precipitately out of the house. I went forward with unequal steps, and at random. Some instinct led me into the fields, and I was not apprized of the direction of my steps, till, looking up, I found myself upon the shore of Schuylkill.

Thus was I, a second time, overborne by hopeless and incurable evils. An interval of motley feelings, of specious artifice, and contemptible imposture, had elapsed since my meeting with the stranger at Wilmington. Then my forlorn state had led me to the brink of suicide. A brief and feverish respite had been afforded me, but now was I transported to the verge of the same abyss.

Amos Watson was the brother of the angel whom I had degraded and destroyed. What but fiery indignation and unappeasable vengeance could lead him into my presence? With what heart could I listen to his invectives? How could I endure to look upon the face of one, whom I had loaded with such atrocious and intolerable injuries?

I was acquainted with his loftiness of mind: his detestation of injustice, and the whirl-wind passions that ingratitude and villainy like mine were qualified to awaken in his bosom. I dreaded not his violence. The death that he might be prompted to inflict was no object of aversion. It was poverty and disgrace, the detection of my crimes, the looks and voice of malediction and upbraiding, from which my cowardice shrunk.

Why should I live? I must vanish from that stage which I had lately trodden. My flight must be instant and precipitate. To be a fugitive from exasperated creditors, and from the industrious revenge of Watson, was an easy undertaking; but whither could I fly, where I should not be pursued by the phantoms of remorse, by the dread of hourly detection, by the necessities of hunger and thirst? In what scene should I be exempt from servitude and drudgery? Was my existence embellished with enjoyments that would justify my holding it, encumbered with hardships, and immersed in obscurity?

There was no room for hesitation. To rush into the stream before me, and to put an end at once to my life and the miseries inseparably linked with it, was the only proceeding which fate had left to my choice. My muscles were already exerted for this end, when the helpless condition of Clemenza was remembered. What provision could I make against the evils that threatened her? Should I leave her utterly forlorn and friendless? Mrs. Wentworth's temper was forgiving and compassionate. Adversity had taught her to participate, and her wealth enabled her to relieve distress. Who was there by whom such powerful claims to succour and protection could be urged as by this desolate girl? Might I not state her situation in a letter to this lady, and urge irresistible pleas for the extension of her kindness to this object?

These thoughts made me suspend my steps. I determined to seek my habitation once more, and having written and deposited this letter, to return to the execution of my fatal purpose. I had scarcely reached my own door, when some one approached along the pavement. The form, at first, was undistinguishable, but by coming, at length, within the illumination of a lamp, it was perfectly recognized.

To avoid this detested interview was now impossible. Watson approached and accosted me. In this conflict of tumultuous feelings I was still able to maintain an air of intrepidity. His demeanour was that of a man who struggles with his rage. His accents were hurried, and scarcely articulate. I have ten words to say to you, said he; lead into the house, and to some private room. My business with you will be dispatched in a breath.

I made him no answer, but led the way into my house, and to my study. On entering this room, I put the light upon the table, and turning to my visitant, prepared, silently to hear, what he had to unfold. He struck his clenched hand against the table with violence. His motion was of that tempestuous kind, as to overwhelm the power of utterance, and found it easier to vent itself in gesticulations than in words. At length, he exclaimed,

It is well. Now has the hour, so long, and so impatiently demanded by my vengeance, arrived. Welbeck! Would that my first words could strike thee dead! They will so, if thou hast any title to the name of man.

My sister is dead:[7] dead of anguish and a broken heart. Remote from her friends; in a hovel; the abode of indigence and misery.

Her husband is no more. He returned after long absence, a tedious navigation, and vicissitudes of hardships. He flew to the bosom of his love; of his wife. She was gone; lost to him, and to virtue. In a fit of desperation, he retired to his chamber, and dispatched himself. This is the instrument with which the deed was performed.

Saying this, Watson took a pistol from his pocket, and held it to my head. I lifted not my hand to turn aside the weapon. I did not shudder at the spectacle, or shrink from his approaching hand. With fingers clasped together, and eyes fixed upon the floor, I waited till his fury was exhausted. He continued:

All passed in a few hours. The elopement of his daughter—the death of his son. O! my father! Most loved, and most venerable of men! To see thee changed into a maniac! Haggard and wild! Deterred from outrage on thyself and those around thee, by fetters and stripes! What was it that saved me from a like fate? To view this hideous

---

7 "My sister is dead": Watson refers to Welbeck's seduction and ruin of his sister, which Welbeck explained to Mervyn in Chapter 9 (see note 9.11).

ruin, and to think by whom it was occasioned! Yet not to become frantic like thee, my father; or not destroy myself like thee my brother! My friend!—

No. For this hour was I reserved; to avenge your wrongs and mine in the blood of this ungrateful villain.

There, continued he, producing a second pistol, and tendering it to me, there is thy defence. Take we opposite sides of this table, and fire at the same instant.

During this address I was motionless. He tendered the pistol, but I unclasped not my hands to receive it.

Why do you hesitate? resumed he. Let the chance between us be equal, or fire you first.

No, said I, I am ready to die by your hand. I wish it. It will preclude the necessity of performing the office for myself. I have injured you, and merit all that your vengeance can inflict. I know your nature too well, to believe that my death will be perfect expiation. When the gust of indignation is past, the remembrance of your deed will only add to your sum of misery; yet I do not love you well enough to wish that you would forbear. I desire to die, and to die by another's hand rather than my own.

Coward! exclaimed Watson, with augmented vehemence. You know me too well, to believe me capable of assassination. Vile subterfuge! Contemptible plea! Take the pistol and defend yourself. You want not the power or the will; but, knowing that I spurn at murder, you think your safety will be found in passiveness. Your refusal will avail you little. Your fame, if not your life, is at my mercy. If you faulter now, I will allow you to live, but only till I have stabbed your reputation.

I now fixed my eyes stedfastly upon him, and spoke. How much a stranger are you to the feelings of Welbeck! How poor a judge of his cowardice! I take your pistol, and consent to your conditions.

We took opposite sides of the table. Are you ready? he cried, fire!

Both triggers were drawn at the same instant. Both pistols were discharged. Mine was negligently raised. Such is the untoward chance that presides over human affairs; such is the malignant destiny by which my steps have ever been pursued. The bullet whistled harmlessly by me. Levelled by an eye that never before failed, and with so small an interval between us. I escaped, but my blind and random shot took place in his heart.

There is the fruit of this disastrous meeting. The catalogue of death is thus completed. Thou sleepest Watson! Thy sister is at rest, and so art thou. Thy vows of vengeance are at an end. It was not reserved for thee to be thy own and thy sister's avenger.[8] Welbeck's measure of transgressions is now full, and his own hand must execute the justice that is due to him.

---

[8] "Vengeance . . . avenger": Watson's obsession with revenge (here patriarchal vengeance for the dishonor of a female relative) is an irrational passion that backfires and leads to his own death. In much Woldwinite and other fiction of this period, dueling and revenge exemplify regressive and irrational determinations of justice by force, rather than modern, middle-class adjudication through law. In *Enquiry Concerning Political Justice* (1793), a crucial text for Brown (see the Related Texts in this volume), William Godwin writes that dueling "was originally invented by barbarians for the gratification of revenge" (Book II, ch. 2, appendix II, "Of Duelling").

Chapter XII

SUCH was Welbeck's tale listened to by me with an eagerness in which every faculty was absorbed. How adverse to my dreams were the incidents that had just been related! The curtain was lifted, and a scene of guilt and ignominy disclosed where my rash and inexperienced youth had suspected nothing but loftiness and magnanimity.

For a while the wondrousness of this tale kept me from contemplating the consequences that awaited us. My unfledged fancy had not hitherto soared to this pitch. All was astounding by its novelty, or terrific by its horror. The very scene of these offences partook, to my rustic apprehension, of fairy splendour, and magical abruptness. My understanding was bemazed, and my senses were taught to distrust their own testimony.

From this musing state I was recalled by my companion, who said to me in solemn accents. Mervyn! I have but two requests to make. Assist me to bury these remains, and then accompany me across the river. I have no power to compel your silence on the acts that you have witnessed. I have meditated to benefit, as well as to injure you; but I do not desire that your demeanour should conform to any other standard than justice. You have promised, and to that promise I trust.

If you chuse to fly from this scene, to withdraw yourself from what you may conceive to be a theatre of guilt or peril, the avenues are open; retire unmolested and in silence. If you have a man-like spirit, if you are grateful for the benefits bestowed upon you, if your discernment enables you to see that compliance with my request will intangle you in no guilt, and betray you into no danger, stay, and aid me in hiding these remains from human scrutiny.

Watson is beyond the reach of further injury. I never intended him harm, though I have torn from him his sister and friend, and have brought his life to an untimely close. To provide him a grave, is a duty that I owe to the dead and to the living. I shall quickly place myself beyond the reach of inquisitors and judges, but would willingly rescue from molestation or suspicion those whom I shall leave behind.

What would have been the fruit of deliberation, if I had had the time or power to deliberate, I know not. My thoughts flowed with tumult and rapidity. To shut this spectacle from my view was the first impulse; but to desert this man, in a time of so much need, appeared a thankless and dastardly deportment. To remain where I was, to conform implicitly to his direction, required no effort. Some fear was connected with his presence, and with that of the dead; but, in the tremulous confusion of my present thoughts, solitude would conjure up a thousand phantoms.

I made no preparation to depart. I did not verbally assent to his proposal. He interpreted my silence into acquiescence. He wrapt the body in the carpet, and then lifting one end, cast at me a look which indicated his expectations, that I would aid him in lifting this ghastly burthen. During this process, the silence was unbroken.

I knew not whither he intended to convey the corpse. He had talked of burial, but no receptacle had been provided. How far safety might depend upon his conduct in this particular, I was unable to estimate. I was in too heartless[1] a mood to utter my doubts. I followed his example in raising the corpse from the floor.

He led the way into the passage and down stairs. Having reached the first floor, he unbolted a door which led into the cellar. The stairs and passage were illuminated by lamps, that hung from the ceiling, and were accustomed to burn during the night. Now, however, we were entering dark-some and murky recesses.

Return, said he, in a tone of command, and fetch the light. I will wait for you.

I obeyed. As I returned with the light, a suspicion stole into my mind, that Welbeck had taken this opportunity to fly; and that on regaining the foot of the stairs, I should find the spot deserted by all but the dead. My blood was chilled by this image. The momentary resolution it inspired was to follow the example of the fugitive, and leave the persons, whom the ensuing day might convene on this spot, to form their own conjectures as to the cause of this catastrophe.

Meanwhile, I cast anxious eyes forward. Welbeck was discovered in the same place and posture in which he had been left, lifting the corpse and its shroud in his arms he directed me to follow him. The vaults beneath were lofty and spacious. He passed from one to the other till we reached a small and remote cell. Here he cast his burthen on the ground. In the fall, the face of Watson chanced to be disengaged from its covering. Its closed eyes and sunken muscles were rendered, in a tenfold degree, ghastly and rueful by the feeble light which the candle shed upon it.

This object did not escape the attention of Welbeck. He leaned against the wall and folding his arms resigned himself to reverie. He gazed upon the countenance of Watson but his looks denoted his attention to be elsewhere employed.

As to me, my state will not be easily described. My eye roved fearfully from one object to another. By turns it was fixed upon the murdered person and the murderer. The narrow cell in which we stood, its rudely fashioned walls and arches, destitute of communication with the external air, and its palpable dark scarcely penetrated by the rays of a solitary candle, added to the silence which was deep and universal, produced an impression on my fancy which no time will obliterate.

Perhaps my imagination was distempered by terror. The incident which I am going to relate may appear to have existed only in my fancy. Be that as it may, I experienced all the effects which the fullest belief is adapted to produce. Glancing vaguely at the countenance of Watson, my attention was arrested by a convulsive motion in the eye-lids. This motion increased, till, at length the eyes opened, and a glance, languid but wild, was thrown around. Instantly they closed, and the tremulous appearance vanished.[2]

---

[1] "Heartless": "destitute of courage, enthusiasm, or energy . . . disheartened, dejected" (OED).

[2] "Tremulous appearance vanished": the possibility of premature burial foreshadows Mervyn's close call during the epidemic in Chapter 16, and his suffocating entrapment in the mysterious attic crawl space in Chapter 23.

I started from my place and was on the point of uttering some involuntary exclamation. At the same moment. Welbeck seemed to recover from his reverie.

How is this! said he. Why do we linger here? Every moment is precious. We cannot dig for him a grave with our hands. Wait here, while I go in search of a spade.

Saying this, he snatched the candle from my hand, and hasted away. My eye followed the light as its gleams shifted their place upon the walls and ceilings, and gradually vanishing, gave place to unrespited gloom. This proceeding was so unexpected and abrupt, that I had no time to remonstrate against it. Before I retrieved the power of reflection, the light had disappeared and the foot-steps were no longer to be heard.

I was not, on ordinary occasions, destitute of equanimity,[3] but, perhaps the imagination of man is naturally abhorrent of death, until tutored into indifference by habit. Every circumstance combined to fill me with shuddering and panick. For a while, I was enabled to endure my situation by the exertions of my reason. That the lifeless remains of an human being are powerless to injure or benefit, I was thoroughly persuaded. I summoned this belief to my aid, and was able, if not to subdue, yet to curb my fears. I listened to catch the sound of the returning foot-steps of Welbeck, and hoped that every new moment would terminate my solitude.

No signal of his coming was afforded. At length it occurred to me that Welbeck had gone with no intention to return. That his malice had seduced me hither to encounter the consequences of his deed. He had fled and barred every door behind him. This suspicion may well be supposed to overpower my courage, and to call forth desperate efforts for my deliverance.

I extended my hands and went forward. I had been too little attentive to the situation and direction of these vaults and passages, to go forward with undeviating accuracy. My fears likewise tended to confuse my perceptions and bewilder my steps. Notwithstanding the danger of encountering obstructions, I rushed towards the entrance with precipitation.

My temerity[4] was quickly punished. In a moment, I was repelled by a jutting angle of the wall, with such force that I staggered backward and fell. The blow was stunning, and when I recovered my senses, I perceived that a torrent of blood was gushing from my nostrils. My clothes were moistened with this unwelcome effusion, and I could not but reflect on the hazard which I should incur by being detected in this recess, covered by these accusing stains.

This reflection once more set me on my feet, and incited my exertions. I now proceeded with greater wariness and caution. I had lost all distinct notions of my way. My motions were at random. All my labour was to shun obstructions and to advance whenever the vacuity would permit. By this means, the entrance was at length found, and after various efforts, I arrived, beyond my hopes, at the foot of the stair-case.

I ascended, but quickly encountered an insuperable impediment. The door at the stair-head, was closed and barred. My utmost strength was exerted in vain, to break

---

[3] "Equanimity": "calmness and composure, especially in difficult situations" (OED).

[4] "Temerity": audacity, boldness, rashness, or recklessness.

the lock or the hinges. Thus were my direst apprehensions fulfilled. Welbeck had left me to sustain the charge of murder; to obviate suspicions the most atrocious and plausible that the course of human events is capable of producing.

Here I must remain till the morrow; till some one can be made to overhear my calls and come to my deliverance. What effects will my appearance produce on the spectator! Terrified by phantoms and stained with blood shall I not exhibit the tokens of a maniac as well as an assassin?

The corpse of Watson will quickly be discovered. If previous to this disclosure I should change my blood-stained garments and withdraw into the country, shall I not be pursued by the most vehement suspicions and, perhaps, hunted to my obscurest retreat by the ministers of justice? I am innocent, but my tale however circumstantial or true, will scarcely suffice for my vindication. My flight will be construed into a proof of incontestable guilt.

While harassed by these thoughts my attention was attracted by a faint gleam cast upon the bottom of the staircase. It grew stronger, hovered for a moment in my sight, and then disappeared. That it proceeded from a lamp or candle, borne by some one along the passages, was no untenable opinion, but was far less probable than that the effulgence was meteorous.[5] I confided in the latter supposition and fortified myself anew against the dread of preternatural dangers. My thoughts reverted to the contemplation of the hazards and suspicions which flowed from my continuance in this spot.

In the midst of my perturbed musing, my attention was again recalled by an illumination like the former. Instead of hovering and vanishing, it was permanent. No ray could be more feeble, but the tangible obscurity to which it succeeded rendered it conspicuous as an electrical flash. For a while I eyed it without moving from my place, and in momentary expectation of its disappearance.

Remarking its stability, the propriety of scrutinizing it more nearly, and of ascertaining the source whence it flowed, was at length suggested. Hope, as well as curiosity, was the parent of my conduct. Though utterly at a loss to assign the cause of this appearance, I was willing to believe some connection between that cause and the means of my deliverance.

I had scarcely formed the resolution of descending the stair, when my hope was extinguished by the recollection that the cellar had narrow and grated windows, through which light from the street might possibly have found access. A second recollection supplanted this belief, for in my way to this stair-case, my attention would have been solicited, and my steps, in some degree, been guided by light coming through these avenues.

Having returned to the bottom of the stair, I perceived every part of the long-drawn passage illuminated. I threw a glance forward, to the quarter whence the rays seemed to proceed, and beheld, at a considerable distance, Welbeck in the cell which I had left, turning up the earth with a spade.

---

[5] "Meteorous": resembling a meteor or, in other words, a glowing and moving light.

After a pause of astonishment, the nature of the error which I had committed rushed upon apprehension. I now perceived that the darkness had misled me to a different stair-case from that which I had originally descended, It was apparent that Welbeck intended me no evil, but had really gone in search of the instrument which he had mentioned.

This discovery overwhelmed me with contrition and shame, though it freed from the terrors of imprisonment and accusation. To return to the cell which I had left, and where Welbeck was employed in his disastrous office, was the expedient which regards to my own safety unavoidably suggested.

Welbeck paused at my approach, and betrayed a momentary consternation at the sight of my ensanguined visage.[6] The blood, by some inexplicable process of nature, perhaps by the counteracting influence of fear, had quickly ceased to flow. Whether the cause of my evasion, and of my flux of blood, was guessed, or whether his attention was withdrawn, by more momentous objects, from my condition, he proceeded in his task in silence.

A shallow bed, and a slight covering of clay was provided for the hapless Watson. Welbeck's movements were hurried and tremulous. His countenance betokened a mind engrossed by a single purpose, in some degree, foreign to the scene before him. An intensity and fixedness of features, that conspicuous, were led me to suspect the subversion of his reason.

Having finished the task, he threw aside his impliment. He then put into my hand a pocket-book, saying it belonged to Watson, and might contain something serviceable to the living. I might make what use of it I thought proper. He then remounted the stairs and, placing the candle on a table in the hall, opened the principal door and went forth. I was driven, by a sort of mechanical impulse, in his footsteps. I followed him because it was agreeable to him and because I knew not whither else to direct my steps.

The streets were desolate and silent. The watchman's call remotely and faintly heard, added to the general solemnity. I followed my companion in a state of mind not easily described. I had no spirit even to inquire whither he was going. It was not till we arrived at the water's edge that I persuaded myself to break silence. I then began to reflect on the degree in which his present schemes might endanger Welbeck or myself. I had acted long enough a servile and mechanical part; and been guided by blind and foreign impulses. It was time to lay aside my fetters, and demand to know whither the path tended in which I was importuned to walk.

Meanwhile I found myself intangled among boats and shipping. I am unable to describe the spot by any indisputable tokens. I know merely that it was the termination of one of the principal streets. Here Welbeck selected a boat and prepared to enter it. For a moment I hesitated to comply with his apparent invitation. I stammered out an interrogation. Why is this? Why should we cross the river? What service can I do for you? I ought to know the purpose of my voyage before I enter it.

---

[6] "Ensanguined visage": bloodied face.

He checked himself and surveyed me for a minute in silence. What do you fear? said he. Have I not explained my wishes? Merely cross the river with me, for I cannot navigate a boat by myself. Is there any thing arduous or mysterious in this undertaking? we part on the Jersey shore, and I shall leave you to your destiny. All I shall ask from you will be silence, and to hide from mankind what you know concerning me.

He now entered the boat and urged me to follow his example. I reluctantly complied. I perceived that the boat contained but one oar and that was a small one. He seemed startled and thrown into great perplexity by this discovery. It will be impossible, said he, in a tone of panic and vexation, to procure another at this hour; what is to be done?

This impediment was by no means insuperable. I had sinewy arms and knew well how to use an oar for the double purpose of oar and rudder. I took my station at the stern, and quickly extricated the boat from its neighbours and from the wharves. I was wholly unacquainted with the river. The bar,[7] by which it was incumbered, I knew to exist, but in what direction and to what extent it existed, and how it might be avoided in the present state of the tide I knew not. It was probable, therefore, unknowing as I was of the proper tract, that our boat would speedily have grounded.

My attention, meanwhile, was fixed upon the oar. My companion sat at the prow and was in a considerable degree unnoticed. I cast eyes occasionally at the scene which I had left. Its novelty, joined with the incidents of my condition, threw me into a state of suspense and wonder which frequently slackened my hand, and left the vessel to be driven by the downward current. Lights were sparingly seen, and these were perpetually fluctuating, as masts, yards, and hulls were interposed, and passed before them. In proportion as we receded from the shore, the clamours seemed to multiply, and the suggestion that the city was involved in confusion and uproar, did not easily give way to maturer thoughts. *Twelve* was the hour cried, and this ascended at once from all quarters, and was mingled with the baying of dogs, so as to produce trepidation and alarm.

From this state of magnificent and awful feeling, I was suddenly called by the conduct of Welbeck. We had scarcely moved two hundred yards from the shore,[8] when he plunged into the water. The first conception was that some implement or part of the boat had fallen overboard. I looked back and perceived that his seat was vacant. In my first astonishment I loosened my hold of the oar, and it floated away. The surface was smooth as glass and the eddy occasioned by his sinking was scarcely visible. I had not time to determine whether this was designed or accidental. Its suddenness deprived me of the power to exert myself for his succour. I wildly gazed around me in hopes of seeing him rise. After some time my attention was drawn, by the sound of agitation in the water, to a considerable distance.

---

[7] "Bar": a sand or mud bar near the river's surface. These bars and two low, sandy islands (Windmill and Smith's islands) ran parallel to the Philadelphia docks a few hundred yards from shore, opposite the southern part of the city.

[8] "Two hundred yards from the shore": at Philadelphia the Delaware is about a half mile or 800–900 yards wide.

It was too dark for any thing to be distinctly seen. There was no cry for help. The noise was like that of one vigorously struggling for a moment, and then sinking to the bottom. I listened with painful eagerness, but was unable to distinguish a third signal. He sunk to rise no more.

I was, for a time, inattentive to my own situation. The dreadfulness, and unexpectedness of this catastrophe occupied me wholly. The quick motion of the lights upon the shore, shewed me that I was borne rapidly along with the tide. How to help myself, how to impede my course, or to regain either shore, since I had lost the oar, I was unable to tell. I was no less at a loss to conjecture whither the current, if suffered to control my vehicle, would finally transport me.

The disappearance of lights and buildings, and the diminution of the noises, acquainted me that I had passed the town.[9] It was impossible longer to hesitate. The shore was to be regained by one way only, which was swimming. To any exploit of this kind, my strength and my skill were adequate. I threw away my loose gown; put the pocket-book of the unfortunate Watson in my mouth, to preserve it from being injured by moisture; and committed myself to the stream.

I landed in a spot incommoded with mud and reeds. I sunk knee-deep into the former, and was exhausted by the fatigue of extricating myself. At length I recovered firm ground, and threw myself on the turf to repair my wasted strength, and to reflect on the measures which my future welfare enjoined me to pursue.

What condition was ever parallel to mine? The transactions of the last three days resembled the monstrous creations of delirium. They were painted with vivid hues on my memory; but so rapid and incongruous were these transitions, that I almost denied belief to their reality. They exercised a bewildering and stupifying influence on my mind, from which the meditations of an hour were scarcely sufficient to relieve me. Gradually I recovered the power of arranging my ideas, and forming conclusions.

Welbeck was dead. His property was swallowed up, and his creditors left to wonder at his disappearance. All that was left, was the furniture of his house, to which Mrs. Wentworth would lay claim, in discharge of the unpaid rent. What now was the destiny that awaited the lost and friendless Mademoiselle Lodi. Where was she concealed? Welbeck had dropped no intimation by which I might be led to suspect the place of her abode. If my power, in other respects, could have contributed aught to her relief, my ignorance of her asylum had utterly disabled me.

But what of the murdered person? He had suddenly vanished from the face of the earth. His fate and the place of his interment would probably be suspected and ascertained. Was I sure to escape from the consequences of this deed? Watson had relatives and friends. What influence on their state and happiness his untimely and mysterious fate would possess, it was obvious to inquire. This idea led me to the recollection of his pocket-book. Some papers might be there explanatory of his situation.

---

[9] "I had passed the town": Mervyn drifts south of the eighteenth-century city, which was only urbanized to an area just beyond South (then Cedar) Street. He abandons the boat and swims to the river's west bank to come ashore in marshlands presumably somewhere near the present-day location of the Walt Whitman bridge.

I resumed my feet. I knew not where to direct my steps. I was dropping with wet, and shivering with the cold. I was destitute of habitation and friend. I had neither money, nor any valuable thing in my possession. I moved forward, mechanically and at random. Where I landed was at no great distance from the verge of the town. In a short time I discovered the glimmering of a distant lamp. To this I directed my steps, and here I paused to examine the contents of the pocket-book.

I found three bank-notes, each of fifty dollars, inclosed in a piece of blank paper. Beside these were three letters, apparently written by his wife, and dated at Baltimore. They were brief, but composed in a strain of great tenderness, and containing affecting allusions to their child. I could gather from their date and tenor, that they were received during his absence on his recent voyage; that her condition was considerably necessitous, and surrounded by wants which their prolonged separation had increased.

The fourth letter was open, and seemed to have been very lately written. It was directed to Mrs. Mary Watson. He informed her in it of his arrival at Philadelphia from St. Domingo; of the loss of his ship and cargo;[10] and of his intention to hasten home with all possible expedition. He told her that all was lost but one hundred and fifty dollars, the greater part of which he should bring with him, to relieve her more pressing wants. The letter was signed, and folded, and superscribed, but unsealed.

A little consideration shewed me, in what manner it became me, on this occasion, to demean myself. I put the bank-notes in the letter, and sealed it with a wafer;[11] a few of which were found in the pocket-book. I hesitated sometime whether I should add any thing to the information which the letter contained, by means of a pencil which offered itself to my view; but I concluded to forbear. I could select no suitable terms in which to communicate the mournful truth. I resolved to deposit this letter at the post-office, where I knew letters could be left at all hours.

My reflections at length, reverted to my own condition. What was the fate reserved for me? How far my safety might be affected by remaining in the city, in consequence of the disappearance of Welbeck, and my known connection with the fugitive, it was impossible to foresee. My fears readily suggested innumerable embarrassments and inconveniences which would flow from this source. Besides, on what pretence should I remain? To whom could I apply for protection or employment? All avenues, even to subsistence, were shut against me. The country was my sole asylum. Here, in exchange for my labour, I could at least purchase food, safety, and repose. But if my choice pointed to the country, there was no reason for a moment's delay. It would be

---

[10] "St. Domingo . . . loss of his ship and cargo": St. Domingo is Haiti, the site of ongoing slave revolution. A wave of ships containing thousands of refugees from St. Domingo arrived in Philadelphia in summer 1793 at the same moment the narrative is taking place. Thus Watson's disastrous trading voyage is another link to Caribbean slave revolution and its aftershocks in Philadelphia. In Chapter II.3, the backstory concerning Watson's voyage will be expanded to include a secret money belt containing the fortune of the Maurice family, likewise based on Caribbean slave labor. For the continuation of Watson's backstory see note II.3.11.

[11] "Wafer": a small disk of flour mixed with gum or gelatin, used for sealing letters.

prudent to regain the fields, and be far from this detested city before the rising of the sun.

Meanwhile I was chilled and chaffed by the clothes that I wore. To change them for others, was absolutely necessary to my ease. The clothes which I wore were not my own, and were extremely unsuitable to my new condition. My rustic and homely garb was deposited in my chamber at Welbeck's. These thoughts suggested the design of returning thither. I considered, that, probably, the servants had not been alarmed. That the door was unfastened, and the house was accessible. It would be easy to enter and retire without notice; and this, not without some waverings and misgivings, I presently determined to do.

Having deposited my letter at the office, I proceeded to my late abode. I approached, and lifted the latch with caution. There were no appearances of any one having been disturbed. I procured a light in the kitchen, and hied softly and with dubious foot-steps to my chamber. There I disrobed, and resumed my check shirt, and trowsers, and fustian coat. This change being accomplished, nothing remained but that I should strike into the country with the utmost expedition.

In a momentary review which I took of the past, the design for which Welbeck professed to have originally detained me in his service, occurred to my mind. I knew the danger of reasoning loosely on the subject of property. To any trinket, or piece of furniture in this house, I did not allow myself to question the right of Mrs. Wentworth; a right accruing to her in consequence of Welbeck's failure in the payment of his rent; but there was one thing which I felt an irresistible desire, and no scruples which should forbid me, to possess, and that was, the manuscript to which Welbeck had alluded, as having been written by the deceased Lodi.

I was well instructed in Latin, and knew the Tuscan language[12] to be nearly akin to it. I despaired not of being at sometime able to cultivate this language, and believed that the possession of this manuscript might essentially contribute to this end, as well as to many others equally beneficial. It was easy to conjecture that the volume was to be found among his printed books, and it was scarcely less easy to ascertain the truth of this conjecture. I entered, not without tremulous sensations, into the apartment which had been the scene of the disastrous interview between Watson and Welbeck. At every step I almost dreaded to behold the spectre of the former rise before me.

Numerous and splendid volumes were arranged on mahogany shelves,[13] and screened by doors of glass. I ran swiftly over their names, and was at length so fortunate as to light upon the book of which I was in search. I immediately secured it, and

---

[12] "Tuscan language": a dialect of Italian. Mervyn's comment about Latin is accurate; Tuscan was closer to Latin than other Italian dialects and became basic to the formation of modern Italian after use by major figures such as Dante, Petrarch, and Machiavelli.

[13] "Mahogany shelves": in this period mahogany is an expensive hardwood imported from the Caribbean, commonly advertised as "St. Domingo mahogany." Even in details, the novel evokes commodity chains linking wealth and luxury in Philadelphia to slave-based colonial production in the West Indies.

leaving the candle extinguished on a table in the parlour, I once more issued forth into the street. With light steps and palpitating heart I turned my face towards the country. My necessitous condition I believed would justify me in passing without payment the Schuylkill bridge, and the eastern sky began to brighten with the dawn of morning not till I had gained the distance of nine miles from the city.

Such is the tale which I proposed to relate to you. Such are the memorable incidents of five days of my life; from which I have gathered more instruction than from the whole tissue of my previous existence. Such are the particulars of my knowledge respecting the crimes and misfortunes of Welbeck; which the insinuations of Wortley, and my desire to retain your good opinion, have induced me to unfold.

Chapter XIII

MERVYN's pause allowed his auditors to reflect on the particulars of his narration, and to compare them with the facts, with a knowledge of which, their own observation had supplied them.[1] My profession introduced me to the friendship of Mrs. Wentworth, by whom, after the disappearance of Welbeck, many circumstances respecting him had been mentioned. She particularly dwelt upon the deportment and appearance of this youth, at the single interview which took place between them, and her representations were perfectly conformable to those which Mervyn had himself delivered.

Previously to this interview Welbeck had insinuated to her that a recent event had put him in possession of the truth respecting the destiny of Clavering. A kinsman of his had arrived from Portugal, by whom this intelligence had been brought. He dexterously eluded her intreaties to be furnished with minuter information, or to introduce this kinsman to her acquaintance. As soon as Mervyn was ushered into her presence, she suspected him to be the person to whom Welbeck had alluded, and this suspicion his conversation had confirmed. She was at a loss to comprehend the reasons of the silence which he so pertinaciously maintained.

Her uneasiness, however, prompted her to renew her solicitations. On the day subsequent to the catastrophe related by Mervyn, she sent a messenger to Welbeck, with a request to see him. Gabriel, the black servant, informed the messenger that his master had gone into the country for a week. At the end of the week, a messenger was again dispatched with the same errand. He called and knocked, but no one answered his signals. He examined the entrance by the kitchen, but every avenue was closed. It appeared that the house was wholly deserted.

These appearances naturally gave birth to curiosity and suspicion. The house was repeatedly examined, but the solitude and silence within continued the same. The creditors of Welbeck, were alarmed by these appearances, and their claims to the property remaining in the house were precluded by Mrs. Wentworth, who, as owner of the mansion, was legally entitled to the furniture, in place of the rent which Welbeck had suffered to accumulate.

On examining the dwelling, all that was valuable and portable, particularly linen and plate, was removed. The remainder was distrained,[2] but the tumults of pestilence succeeded and hindered it from being sold. Things were allowed to continue in their former situation, and the house was carefully secured. We had no leisure to

---

[1] "Mervyn's pause . . . had supplied them": Dr. Stevens interrupts Mervyn's narrative for six paragraphs at this point, dividing the first volume into two main sections: Mervyn's first visit to the city and experience of commercial corruption (Chapters 2–12) and his second visit and experience of physical corruption in the yellow fever epidemic (Chapters 13–23). Mervyn's second narrative occupies the remainder of the first part, and Stevens' frame narrative will be resumed at the beginning of *Second Part*.

[2] "Distrained": a legal term meaning to seize property for unpaid rent or debts.

form conjectures on the causes of this desertion. An explanation was afforded us by the narrative of this youth. It is probable that the servants, finding their master's absence continue, had pillaged the house and fled.

Meanwhile, though our curiosity with regard to Welbeck was appeased, it was obvious to inquire by what series of inducements and events Mervyn was reconducted to the city and led to the spot where I first met with him. We intimated our wishes in this respect, and our young friend readily consented to take up the thread of his story and bring it down to the point that was desired. For this purpose, the ensuing evening was selected. Having, at an early hour, shut ourselves up from all intruders and visitors, he continued as follows:

I have mentioned that, by sun-rise, I had gained the distance of many miles from the city. My purpose was to stop at the first farm-house, and seek employment as a day-labourer. The first person whom I observed was a man of placid mien and plain garb. Habitual benevolence was apparent amidst the wrinkles of age. He was traversing his buck-wheat field and measuring, as it seemed, the harvest that was now nearly ripe.

I accosted him with diffidence, and explained my wishes. He listened to my tale with complacency, inquired into my name and family, and into my qualifications for the office to which I aspired. My answers were candid and full.

Why, said he, I believe thou[3] and I can make a bargain. We will, at least, try each other for a week or two. If it does not suit our mutual convenience we can change. The morning is damp and cool, and thy plight does not appear the most comfortable that can be imagined. Come to the house and eat some breakfast.

The behaviour of this good man filled me with gratitude and joy. Methought I could embrace him as a father, and entrance into his house, appeared like return to a long-lost and much-loved home. My desolate and lonely condition appeared to be changed for paternal regards and the tenderness of friendship.

These emotions were confirmed and heightened by every object that presented itself under this roof. The family consisted of Mrs. Hadwin, two simple and affectionate girls, his daughters, and servants. The manners of this family, quiet, artless, and cordial, the occupations allotted, me, the land by which the dwelling was surrounded, its pure airs, romantic walks, and exhaustless fertility, constituted a powerful contrast to the scenes which I had left behind, and were congenial with every dictate of my understanding and every sentiment that glowed in my heart.

My youth, mental cultivation, and circumspect deportment entitled me to deference and confidence. Each hour confirmed me in the good opinion of Mr. Hadwin, and in the affections of his daughters. In the mind of my employer, the simplicity of the husbandman and the devotion of the Quaker were blended with humanity and intelligence. The sisters, Susan and Eliza, were unacquainted with calamity and vice, through the medium of either observation or books. They were strangers to the benefits of an elaborate education, but they were endowed with curiosity and

---

[3] Hadwin's plain clothing and use of the second person familiar ("thou") marks him as a Quaker, a member of the Society of Friends.

discernment, and had not suffered their slender means of instruction to remain unimproved.

The sedateness of the elder formed an amusing contrast with the laughing eye and untamable vivacity of the younger: but they smiled and they wept in unison. They thought and acted in different but not discordant keys. On all momentous occasions, they reasoned and felt alike. In ordinary cases, they separated, as it were, into different tracks; but this diversity was productive, not of jarring, but of harmony.

A romantic and untutored disposition like mine, may be supposed liable to strong impressions from perpetual converse with persons of their age and sex. The elder was soon discovered to have already disposed of her affections. The younger was free, and somewhat that is more easily conceived than named, stole insensibly upon my heart. The images that haunted me at home and abroad, in her absence and her presence gradually coalesced into one shape, and gave birth to an incessant train of latent palpitations and indefinable hopes.[4] My days were little else than uninterrupted reveries, and night only called up phantoms more vivid and equally enchanting.

The memorable incidents which had lately happened scarcely counterpoised my new sensations or diverted my contemplations from the present. My views were gradually led to rest upon futurity, and in that I quickly found cause of circumspection and dread. My present labours were light and were sufficient for my subsistence in a single state; but wedlock was the parent of new wants and of new cares. Mr. Hadwin's possessions were adequate to his own frugal maintenance, but divided between his children would be too scanty for either. Besides this division could only take place at his death, and that was an event whose speedy occurrence was neither desirable nor probable.

Another obstacle was now remembered. Hadwin was the consciencious member of a sect, which forbade the marriage of its votaries with those of a different communion.[5] I had been trained in an opposite creed, and imagined it impossible that I should ever become a proselyte[6] to Quakerism. It only remained for me to feign conversion, or to root out the opinions of my friend, and win her consent to a secret marriage. Whether hypocrisy was eligible was no subject of deliberation. If the possession of all that ambition can conceive, were added to the transports of union with Eliza Hadwin, and offered as the price of dissimulation, it would have been instantly rejected. My external goods were not abundant nor numerous, but the consciousness

---

[4] "Latent palpitations and indefinable hopes": as he did with Clemenza Lodi, Mervyn quickly becomes infatuated with Eliza Hadwin and fantasizes about marrying her. Eliza is the second woman he falls in love with (after Clemenza, and before Achsa Fielding at the end of *Second Part*).

[5] "Different communion": Quakers were "disassociated" or expelled from their religious community if they married outside their faith, an increasingly common event in this period. Brown and all his siblings, for example, were "disassociated" after marrying non-Quakers. Arthur's eventual union with the Jewish Achsa Fielding will heighten this focus on intermarriage between people from different, religious, social, and ethno-racial backgrounds.

[6] "Proselyte": a convert.

of rectitude was mine, and, in competition with this, the luxury of the heart and of the senses, the gratifications of boundless ambition and inexhaustible wealth were contemptible and frivolous.[7]

The conquest of Eliza's errors was easy; but to introduce discord and sorrow into this family was an act of the utmost ingratitude and profligacy. It was only requisite for my understanding clearly to discern, to be convinced of the insuperability of this obstacle. It was manifest, therefore, that the point to which my wishes tended was placed beyond my reach.

To foster my passion, was to foster a disease destructive either of my integrity or my existence. It was indispensable to fix my thoughts upon a different object, and to debar myself even from her intercourse. To ponder on themes foreign to my darling image, and to seclude myself from her society, at hours which had usually been spent with her, were difficult tasks. The latter was the least practicable. I had to contend with eyes, which alternately wondered at, and upbraided me for my unkindness. She was wholly unaware of the nature of her own feelings, and this ignorance made her less scrupulous in the expression of her sentiments.

Hitherto I had needed not employment beyond myself and my companions. Now my new motives made me eager to discover some means of controling and beguiling my thoughts. In this state, the manuscript of Lodi occurred to me. In my way hither, I had resolved to make the study of the language of this book, and the translation of its contents into English, the business and solace of my leisure. Now this resolution was revived with new force.

My project was perhaps singular. The ancient language of Italy possessed a strong affinity with the modern. My knowledge of the former, was my only means of gaining the latter. I had no grammar or vocabulary to explain how far the meanings and inflections of Tuscan words varied from the Roman dialect. I was to ponder on each sentence and phrase; to select among different conjectures the most plausible, and to ascertain the true, by patient and repeated scrutiny.

This undertaking, phantastic and impracticable as it may seem, proved upon experiment, to be within the compass of my powers. The detail of my progress would be curious and instructive. What impediments, in the attainment of a darling purpose, human ingenuity and patience are able to surmount; how much may be done by strenuous and solitary efforts; how the mind, unassisted, may draw forth the principles of inflection and arrangement; may profit by remote, analogous, and latent similitudes, would be forcibly illustrated by my example; but the theme, however attractive, must, for the present, be omitted.

My progress was slow; but the perception of hourly improvement afforded me unspeakable pleasure. Having arrived near the last pages, I was able to pursue, with little interruption, the thread of an eloquent narration. The triumph of a leader of outlaws over the popular enthusiasm of the Milanese, and the claims of neighbouring

---

[7] "Contemptible and frivolous": although he fantasizes about Eliza and an unscrupulous "secret marriage," Mervyn rejects the kind of seduction plot that Welbeck indulges in repeatedly.

potentates, were about to be depicted. The *Condottiero* Sforza,[8] had taken refuge from his enemies in a tomb; accidentally discovered amidst the ruins of a Roman fortress in the Appenine. He had sought this recess for the sake of concealment, but found in it a treasure, by which he would be enabled to secure the wavering and venal faith of that crew of ruffians that followed his standard, provided he fell not into the hands of the enemies who were now in search of him.

My tumultuous curiosity was suddenly checked by the following leaves being glewed together at the edges. To dissever them without injury to the written spaces was by no means easy. I proceeded to the task, not without precipitation. The edges were torn away, and the leaves parted.

It may be thought that I took up the thread where it had been broken; but no. The object that my eyes encountered, and which the cemented leaves had so long concealed, was beyond the power of the most capricious or lawless fancy to have prefigured; yet it bore a shadowy resemblance to the images with which my imagination was previously occupied. I opened, and beheld—*a bank-note!*

To the first transports of surprise, the conjecture succeeded that the remaining leaves, cemented together in the same manner, might inclose similar bills. They were hastily separated, and the conjecture was verified. My sensations, at this discovery, were of an inexplicable kind. I gazed at the notes in silence. I moved my finger over them; held them in different positions; read and re-read the name of each sum, and the signature; added them together, and repeated to myself—*Twenty thousand dollars!* They are mine, and by such means!

This sum would have redeemed the falling fortunes of Welbeck. The dying Lodi was unable to communicate all the contents of this inestimable volume. He had divided his treasure, with a view to its greater safety, between this volume and his pocket-book.[9] Death hasted upon him too suddenly to allow him to explain his precautions. Welbeck had placed the book in his collection, purposing sometime to peruse it; but deterred by anxieties, which the perusal would have dissipated, he rushed to desperation and suicide, from which some evanescent contingency, by unfolding this treasure to his view, would have effectually rescued him.

But was this event to be regretted? This sum, like the former, would probably have been expended in the same pernicious prodigality. His career would have continued sometime longer, but his inveterate habits would have finally conducted his existence to the same criminal and ignominious close.

---

[8] "*Condotierre* Sforza": the elder Lodi's manuscript returns to the history of political instability around early modern Milan. The "Condotierre Sforza" is Francesco I Sforza, founder of the Sforza dynasty who displaced the Visconti as rulers of Milan. Condottieri were mercenary warlords and the Sforzas embraced force and intrigue as political tools: their adopted name is from Italian *sforzare*, to exert force. For earlier allusions to this setting, see notes 6.2 and 10.8.

[9] "Between this volume and his pocket-book": this means the younger Lodi was transporting a family fortune or patrimony of $40,000 total when he died, divided into the $20,000 he revealed and entrusted to Welbeck and another $20,000 secreted in the pages of his father's manuscript. See note 10.7 on the value of this sum and note 21.2 for its later confirmation.

But the destiny of Welbeck was accomplished. The money was placed, without guilt or artifice, in my possession. My fortune had been thus unexpectedly and wonderously propitious. How was I to profit by her favour? Would not this sum enable me to gather round me all the instruments of pleasure? Equipage, and palace, and a multitude of servants; polished mirrors, splendid hangings, banquets, and flatterers, were equally abhorrent to my taste, and my principles. The accumulation of knowledge, and the diffusion of happiness, in which riches may be rendered eminently instrumental, were the only precepts of duty, and the only avenues to genuine felicity.

But what, said I, is my title to this money? By retaining it, shall I not be as culpable as Welbeck? It came into his possession as it came into mine, without a crime; but my knowledge of the true proprietor is equally certain, and the claims of the unfortunate stranger are as valid as ever. Indeed, if utility, and not law, be the measure of justice, her claim, desolate and indigent as she is, unfitted, by her past life, by the softness and the prejudices of her education, for contending with calamity, is incontestible.

As to me, health and diligence will give me, not only the competence which I seek, but the power of enjoying it. If my present condition be unchangeable, I shall not be unhappy. My occupations are salutary and meritorious; I am a stranger to the cares as well as to the enjoyment of riches; abundant means of knowledge are possessed by me, as long as I have eyes to gaze at man and at nature, as they are exhibited in their original forms or in books. The precepts of my duty cannot be mistaken. The lady must be sought and the money be restored to her.

Certain obstacles existed to the immediate execution of this scheme. How should I conduct my search? What apology should I make for withdrawing thus abruptly, and contrary to the terms of an agreement into which I had lately entered, from the family and service of my friend and benefactor, Hadwin?

My thoughts were called away from pursuing these inquiries by a rumour, which had gradually swelled to formidable dimensions; and which, at length, reached us in our quiet retreats. The city, we were told, was involved in confusion and panick, for a pestilential disease had begun its destructive progress.[10] Magistrates and citizens were flying to the country. The numbers of the sick multiplied beyond all example; even in the pest affected cities of the Levant. The malady was malignant, and unsparing.

The usual occupations and amusements of life were at an end. Terror had exterminated all the sentiments of nature. Wives were deserted by husbands, and children by parents. Some had shut themselves in their houses, and debarred themselves from all communication with the rest of mankind. The consternation of others had destroyed their understanding, and their misguided steps hurried them into the midst of the danger which they had previously laboured to shun. Men were seized by this disease in the streets; passengers fled from them; entrance into their own dwellings was denied to them; they perished in the public ways.

---

[10] "Pestilential disease . . . progress": the first mention of the Philadelphia epidemic.

The chambers of disease were deserted, and the sick left to die of negligence. None could be found to remove the lifeless bodies.[11] Their remains, suffered to decay by piece-meal, filled the air with deadly exhalations, and added tenfold to the devastation.

Such was the tale, distorted and diversified a thousand ways, by the credulity and exaggeration of the tellers. At first I listened to the story with indifference or mirth. Methought it was confuted by its own extravagance. The enormity and variety of such an evil made it unworthy to be believed. I expected that every new day would detect the absurdity and fallacy of such representations. Every new day, however, added to the number of witnesses, and the consistency of the tale, till, at length, it was not possible to withhold my faith.

---

[11] "None could be found to remove the lifeless bodies": as part of this reported catalogue of the fever's devastation, Mervyn notes the need for undertakers and nurses that was filled by members of the free black community. For more on this and related aspects of the epidemic, see the Introduction and Related Texts.

Chapter XIV

THIS rumour was of a nature to absorb and suspend the whole soul. A certain sublimity is connected with enormous dangers, that imparts to our consternation or our pity, a tincture of the pleasing.[1] This, at least, may be experienced by those who are beyond the verge of peril. My own person was exposed to no hazard. I had leisure to conjure up terrific images, and to personate the witnesses and sufferers of this calamity. This employment was not enjoined upon me by necessity, but was ardently pursued, and must therefore have been recommended by some nameless charm.

Others were very differently affected. As often as the tale was embellished with new incidents, or inforced by new testimony, the hearer grew pale, his breath was stifled by inquietudes, his blood was chilled and his stomach was bereaved of its usual energies. A temporary indisposition was produced in many. Some were haunted by a melancholy bordering upon madness, and some, in consequence of sleepless panics, for which no cause could be assigned, and for which no opiates could be found, were attacked by lingering or mortal diseases.

Mr. Hadwin was superior to groundless apprehensions. His daughters, however, partook in all the consternation which surrounded them. The eldest had, indeed, abundant reason for her terror. The youth to whom she was betrothed, resided in the city. A year previous to this, he had left the house of Mr. Hadwin, who was his uncle, and had removed to Philadelphia, in pursuit of fortune.

He made himself clerk to a merchant, and by some mercantile adventures in which he had successfully engaged, began to flatter himself with being able, in no long time, to support a family. Meanwhile, a tender and constant correspondence was maintained between him and his beloved Susan. This girl was a soft enthusiast, in whose bosom devotion and love glowed with an ardour that has seldom been exceeded.

The first tidings of the *yellow fever*, was heard by her with unspeakable perturbation. Wallace was interrogated, by letter,[2] respecting its truth. For a time, he treated it as a vague report. At length, a confession was extorted from him that there existed a pestilential disease in the city, but, he added, that it was hitherto confined to one quarter, distant from the place of his abode.

---

[1] "A tincture of the pleasing": referring to a paradox frequently discussed in eighteenth-century aesthetics, Mervyn observes that horrific, gothic events can be simultaneously terrifying and pleasing to readers or listeners as long as the beholder is not actually in danger. With this acknowledgment of "nameless charm" of narrated suffering and horror, Brown may be warning his readers—us—about alternative uses and perceptions of gothic narratives. In essays on his question (see the relevant excerpts in Related Texts), Brown argues that aesthetic effects are secondary to ethical concerns, that effects of terror in gothic narratives should be secondary to the political use of these narratives in educating their audience about enlightened ideas and values concerning social relations.

[2] "Wallace was interrogated, by letter": as Mervyn realizes by the end of this chapter, Wallace, Susan's first cousin and betrothed, is the young man who tricked him by shutting him in Thetford's bedroom in Chapter 3 (note 3.12); this is the first appearance of his name. Like Mervyn, Wallace has drifted to the city in hopes of escaping rural economic pressures.

The most pathetic intreaties, were urged by her that he would withdraw into the country. He declared his resolution to comply when the street in which he lived should become infected, and his stay should be attended with real danger. He stated how much his interests depended upon the favour of his present employer, who had used the most powerful arguments to detain him, but declared that, when his situation should become, in the least degree, perillous, he would slight every consideration of gratitude and interest, and fly to *Malverton*.[3] Meanwhile, he promised to communicate tidings of his safety, by every opportunity.

Belding, Mr. Hadwin's next neighbour, though not uninfected by the general panic, persisted to visit the city daily with his *market-cart*. He set out by sun-rise, and usually returned by noon. By him a letter was punctually received by Susan. As the hour of Belding's return approached, her impatience and anxiety increased. The daily epistle was received and read, in a transport of eagerness. For a while, her emotion subsided, but returned with augmented vehemence at noon on the ensuing day.

These agitations were too vehement for a feeble constitution like hers. She renewed her supplications to Wallace to quit the city. He repeated his assertions of being, hitherto, secure, and his promise of coming when the danger should be imminent. When Belding returned, and, instead of being accompanied by Wallace, merely brought a letter from him, the unhappy Susan would sink into fits of lamentation and weeping, and repel every effort to console her with an obstinacy that partook of madness. It was, at length, manifest, that Wallace's delays would be fatally injurious to the health of his mistress.

Mr. Hadwin had hitherto been passive. He conceived that the intreaties and remonstrances of his daughter were more likely to influence the conduct of Wallace, than any representations which he could make. Now, however, he wrote the contumacious[4] Wallace a letter, in which he laid his commands upon him to return in company with Belding, and declared that by a longer delay, the youth would forfeit his favour.

The malady had, at this time, made considerable progress. Belding's interest at length yielded to his fears, and this was the last journey which he proposed to make. Hence our impatience for the return of Wallace was augmented; since, if this opportunity were lost, no suitable conveyance might again be offered him.

Belding set out, as usual, at the dawn of day. The customary interval between his departure and return was spent by Susan, in a tumult of hopes and fears. As noon approached her suspense arose to a pitch of wildness and agony. She could scarcely be restrained from running along the road, many miles, towards the city; that she might, by meeting Belding half way, the sooner ascertain the fate of her lover. She stationed herself at a window which overlooked the road along which Belding was to pass.

---

[3] "*Malverton*": the name of the Hadwin's farm. The name recalls that of Malvern, a small Chester County town twenty-five miles west of Philadelphia, initially settled by Welsh Quakers.

[4] "Contumacious": stubbornly disobedient.

Her sister, and her father, though less impatient, marked, with painful eagerness, the first sound of the approaching vehicle. They snatched a look at it as soon as it appeared in sight. Belding was without a companion.

This confirmation of her fears, overwhelmed the unhappy Susan. She sunk into a fit, from which, for a long time, her recovery was hopeless. This was succeeded by paroxysms of a furious insanity, in which she attempted to snatch any pointed implement which lay within her reach, with a view to destroy herself.[5] These being carefully removed, or forcibly wrested from her, she resigned herself to sobs and exclamations.

Having interrogated Belding, he informed us that he occupied his usual post in the market place; that heretofore, Wallace had duly sought him out, and exchanged letters; but, that on this morning, the young man had not made his appearance; though Belding had been induced, by his wish to see him, to prolong his stay in the city, much beyond the usual period.

That some other cause than sickness had occasioned this omission, was barely possible. There was scarcely room for the most sanguine[6] temper to indulge an hope. Wallace was without kindred, and probably without friends, in the city. The merchant, in whose service he had placed himself, was connected with him by no consideration but that of interest. What then must be his situation when seized with a malady which all believed to be contagious; and the fear of which, was able to dissolve the strongest ties that bind human beings together?

I was personally a stranger to this youth. I had seen his letters, and they bespoke, not indeed any great refinement or elevation of intelligence, but a frank and generous spirit, to which I could not refuse my esteem; but his chief claim to my affection consisted in his consanguinity[7] to Mr. Hadwin, and his place in the affections of Susan. His welfare was essential to the happiness of those, whose happiness had become essential to mine. I witnessed the outrages of despair in the daughter, and the symptoms of a deep, but less violent grief, in the sister and parent. Was it not possible for me to alleviate their pangs? Could not the fate of Wallace be ascertained?

This disease assailed men with different degrees of malignity. In its worst form perhaps it was incurable; but in some of its modes, it was doubtless conquerable by the skill of physicians, and the fidelity of nurses. In its least formidable symptoms, negligence and solitude would render it fatal.

Wallace might, perhaps, experience this pest in its most lenient degree: but the desertion of all mankind; the want, not only of medicines, but of food, would

---

[5] "Destroy herself": prefiguring her eventual breakdown, Susan nearly goes mad and commits suicide. Along with the previous suicidal impulses of Welbeck, Watson, the husband of Watson's ruined sister, and others, this is one of the many instances of suicide and suicidal impulses in *Arthur Mervyn*.

[6] "Sanguine": hopeful, confident of success; literally, of a flushed or bloody complexion and the moods associated with it.

[7] "Consanguinity": family kinship, blood relations.

irrevocably seal his doom. My imagination was incessantly pursued by the image of this youth, perishing alone, and in obscurity; calling on the name of distant friends, or invoking, ineffectually, the succour of those who were near.

Hitherto distress had been contemplated at a distance, and through the medium of a fancy delighting to be startled by the wonderful, or transported by sublimity. Now the calamity had entered my own doors, imaginary evils were supplanted by real, and my heart was the seat of commiseration and horror.

I found myself unfit for recreation or employment. I shrouded myself in the gloom of the neighbouring forest, or lost myself in the maze of rocks and dells. I endeavoured, in vain, to shut out the phantoms of the dying Wallace, and to forget the spectacle of domestic woes. At length, it occurred to me to ask, May not this evil be obviated, and the felicity of the Hadwins re-established? Wallace is friendless and succourless; but cannot I supply to him the place of protector and nurse? Why not hasten to the city, search out his abode, and ascertain whether he be living or dead? If he still retain life, may I not, by consolation and attendance, contribute to the restoration of his health, and conduct him once more to the bosom of his family?

With what transports will his arrival be hailed? How amply will their impatience and their sorrow be compensated by his return! In the spectacle of their joys, how rapturous and pure will be my delight! Do the benefits which I have received from the Hadwins demand a less retribution than this?

It is true, that my own life will be endangered; but my danger will be proportioned to the duration of my stay in this seat of infection. The death or the flight of Wallace may absolve me from the necessity of spending one night in the city. The rustics who daily frequent the market are, as experience proves, exempt from this disease; in consequence, perhaps, of limiting their continuance in the city to a few hours. May I not, in this respect, conform to their example, and enjoy a similar exemption?

My stay, however, may be longer than the day. I may be condemned to share in the common destiny. What then? Life is dependent on a thousand contingencies, not to be computed or foreseen. The seeds of an early and lingering death are sown in my constitution. It is vain to hope to escape the malady by which my mother and my brothers have died. We are a race, whose existence some inherent property has limited to the short space of twenty years. We are exposed, in common with the rest of mankind, to innumerable casualties; but if these be shunned, we are unalterably fated to perish by *consumption*.[8] Why then should I scruple to lay down my life in the cause of virtue and humanity? It is better to die, in the consciousness of having offered an heroic sacrifice; to die by a speedy stroke, than by the perverseness of nature, in ignominious inactivity, and lingering agonies.

These considerations determined me to hasten to the city. To mention my purpose to the Hadwins would be useless or pernicious. It would only augment the sum of their present anxieties. I should meet with a thousand obstacles in the tenderness and terror of Eliza, and in the prudent affection of her father. Their arguments I should

---

[8] *"Consumption"*: tuberculosis.

be condemned to hear, but should not be able to confute; and should only load myself with imputations of perverseness and temerity.

But how else should I explain my absence? I had hitherto preserved my lips untainted by prevarication or falsehood. Perhaps there was no occasion which would justify an untruth; but here, at least, it was superfluous or hurtful. My disappearance, if effected without notice or warning, will give birth to speculation and conjecture; but my true motives will never be suspected, and therefore will excite no fears. My conduct will not be charged with guilt. It will merely be thought upon with some regret, which will be alleviated by the opinion of my safety, and the daily expectation of my return.

But, since my purpose was to search out Wallace, I must be previously furnished with directions to the place of his abode, and a description of his person. Satisfaction on this head was easily obtained from Mr. Hadwin; who was prevented from suspecting the motives of my curiosity, by my questions being put in a manner apparently casual. He mentioned the street, and the number of the house.

I listened with surprise. It was an house with which I was already familiar. He resided, it seems, with a merchant. Was it possible for me to be mistaken?

What, I asked, was the merchant's name?

Thetford.

This was a confirmation of my first conjecture. I recollected the extraordinary means by which I had gained access to the house and bed-chamber of this gentleman. I recalled the person and appearance of the youth by whose artifices I had been intangled in the snare. These artifices implied some domestic or confidential connection between Thetford and my guide. Wallace was a member of the family. Could it be he by whom I was betrayed?

Suitable questions easily obtained from Hadwin a description of the person and carriage of his nephew. Every circumstance evinced the identity of their persons. Wallace, then, was the engaging and sprightly youth whom I had encountered at Lesher's; and who, for purposes not hitherto discoverable, had led me into a situation so romantic and perilous.

I was far from suspecting that these purposes were criminal. It was easy to infer that his conduct proceeded from juvenile wantonness, and a love of sport. My resolution was unaltered by this disclosure; and having obtained all the information which I needed, I secretly began my journey.

My reflections, on the way, were sufficiently employed in tracing the consequences of my project; in computing the inconveniences and dangers to which I was preparing to subject myself; in fortifying my courage against the influence of rueful sights and abrupt transitions; and in imagining the measures which it would be proper to pursue in every emergency.

Connected as these views were with the family and character of Thetford, I could not but sometimes advert to those incidents which formerly happened. The mercantile alliance between him and Welbeck was remembered; the allusions which were made to the condition of the latter in the chamber-conversation, of which I was an unsuspected auditor; and the relation which these allusions might possess with subsequent occurrences. Welbeck's property was forfeited. It had been confided to the care of Thetford's brother. Had the case of this forfeiture been truly or thoroughly explained? Might not contraband articles have been admitted through the management, or under the connivance of the brothers; and might not the younger Thetford be furnished with the means of purchasing the captured vessel and her cargo; which, as usual, would be sold by auction at a fifth or tenth of its real value?[9]

Welbeck was not alive to profit by the detection of this artifice, admitting these conclusions to be just. My knowledge will be useless to the world; for by what motives can I be influenced to publish the truth; or by whom will my single testimony be believed, in opposition to that plausible exterior, and, perhaps, to that general integrity which Thetford has maintained? To myself it will not be unprofitable. It is a lesson on the principles of human nature; on the delusiveness of appearances; on the perviousness[10] of fraud; and on the power with which nature has invested human beings over the thoughts and actions of each other.

Thetford and his frauds were dismissed from my thoughts, to give place to considerations relative to Clemenza Lodi, and the money which chance had thrown into my possession. Time had only confirmed my purpose to restore these bills to the rightful proprietor, and heightened my impatience to discover her retreat. I reflected, that the means of doing this were more likely to suggest themselves at the place to which I was going than elsewhere. I might, indeed, perish before my views, in this respect, could be accomplished. Against these evils, I had at present no power to provide. While I lived, I would bear perpetually about me the volume and its precious contents. If I died, a superior power must direct the course of this as of all other events.

---

[9] "A fifth or a tenth of its real value": Mervyn connects the dots, realizing that the Thetfords conspired to have the vessel seized so they could recover it at a huge profit, defrauding Welbeck. This paragraph provides the final details explaining the Thetford fraud (see notes 11.5 and 6 for the initial explanation in Chapter 11).

[10] "Perviousness": "the quality of being pervious, penetrability" (OED), in other words, the fact that fraud can be seen through and defeated.

Chapter XV

THESE meditations did not enfeeble my resolution, or slacken my pace. In proportion as I drew near the city, the tokens of its calamitous condition became more apparent. Every farm-house was filled with supernumerary[1] tenants; fugitives from home; and haunting the skirts of the road, eager to detain every passenger with inquiries after news. The passengers were numerous; for the tide of emigration was by no means exhausted. Some were on foot, bearing in their countenances the tokens of their recent terror, and filled with mournful reflections on the forlornness of their state. Few had secured to themselves an asylum; some were without the means of paying for victuals or lodging for the coming night; others, who were not thus destitute, yet knew not whither to apply for entertainment, every house being already over-stocked with inhabitants, or barring its inhospitable doors at their approach.

Families of weeping mothers, and dismayed children, attended with a few pieces of indispensable furniture, were carried in vehicles of every form. The parent or husband had perished; and the price of some moveable, or the pittance handed forth by public charity, had been expended to purchase the means of retiring from this theatre of disasters; though uncertain and hopeless of accommodation in the neighbouring districts.

Between these and the fugitives whom curiosity had led to the road, dialogues frequently took place, to which I was suffered to listen. From every mouth the tale of sorrow was repeated with new aggravations. Pictures of their own distress, or of that of their neighbours, were exhibited in all the hues which imagination can annex to pestilence and poverty.

My preconceptions of the evil now appeared to have fallen short of the truth. The dangers into which I was rushing, seemed more numerous and imminent than I had previously imagined. I wavered not in my purpose. A panick crept to my heart, which more vehement exertions were necessary to subdue or control; but I harboured not a momentary doubt that the course which I had taken was prescribed by duty. There was no difficulty or reluctance in proceeding. All for which my efforts were demanded, was to walk in this path without tumult or alarm.

Various circumstances had hindered me from setting out upon this journey as early as was proper. My frequent pauses to listen to the narratives of travellers, contributed likewise to procrastination. The sun had nearly set before I reached the precincts of

---

[1] "Supernumerary": excessive in number, unnecessary. Just as Philadelphia was flooded with international refugees fleeing revolutionary instability in Europe and the Caribbean, by early September Chester County and the entire mid-Atlantic region were flooded with around 17,000 refugees fleeing the urban epidemic. Many were refused shelter or even attacked by fearful locals, while wealthy families were able to leave Philadelphia for country homes as civil order broke down in the city. President George Washington first withdrew to Germantown, an area on high ground seven miles north of the city, then abandoned the capital altogether for Mount Vernon. The local and national governments—both situated in Philadelphia at this time—adjourned and abandoned the city on 10 and 11 September, 1793. See Powell, *Bring Out Your Dead*.

the city. I pursued the track which I had formerly taken, and entered High-street[2] after night-fall. Instead of equipages and a throng of passengers, the voice of levity and glee, which I had formerly observed, and which the mildness of the season would, at other times, have produced, I found nothing but a dreary solitude.

The market-place, and each side of this magnificent avenue were illuminated, as before, by lamps; but between the verge of Schuylkill and the heart of the city, I met not more than a dozen figures; and these were ghost-like,[3] wrapt in cloaks, from behind which they cast upon me glances of wonder and suspicion; and, as I approached, changed their course, to avoid touching me. Their clothes were sprinkled with vinegar; and their nostrils defended from contagion by some powerful perfume.

I cast a look upon the houses, which I recollected to have formerly been, at this hour, brilliant with lights, resounding with lively voices, and thronged with busy faces. Now they were closed, above and below; dark, and without tokens of being inhabited. From the upper windows of some, a gleam sometimes fell upon the pavement I was traversing, and shewed that their tenants had not fled, but were secluded or disabled.

These tokens were new, and awakened all my panicks. Death seemed to hover over this scene, and I dreaded that the floating pestilence had already lighted on my frame. I had scarcely overcome these tremors, when I approached an house, the door of which was open, and before which stood a vehicle, which I presently recognized to be an *hearse*.

The driver was seated on it. I stood still to mark his visage, and to observe the course which he proposed to take. Presently a coffin, borne by two men, issued from the house. The driver was a negro, but his companions were white.[4] Their features were marked by ferocious indifference to danger or pity. One of them as he assisted in thrusting the coffin into the cavity provided for it, said, I'll be damned if I think the poor dog was quite dead.[5] It wasn't the *fever* that ailed him, but the sight of the

---

[2] "High-street": the official name for Market Street at this time. British convention is that every city's main (shopping) street is formally or informally named High Street. By the mid-eighteenth century, Market Street was the commonly used name based on the market buildings down the center of the wide boulevard, but the official name was not changed until 1858. Mervyn's second visit to the city revisits many of the same locales as the first in new circumstances. For Mervyn's first visit to Market or High Street, see note 3.5.

[3] "Ghost-like": the image recalls Mervyn's first description of High (Market) Street using lines from Milton's scene of Pandaemonium in Hell. The allusion has now become literal.

[4] "The driver was a negro, but his companions were white": black figures in the fever chapters reflect the important, and contested, role that the free black community played in the public response to the epidemic. At the height of the fever, when civil order collapsed, free black community members were among the first lay volunteers to help in combating the epidemic (see Powell, *Bring Out Your Dead*, 94–101). Many worked as undertakers and nurses, roles that are illustrated here and in the following chapters. Controversy followed these efforts when Mathew Carey's popular account of the epidemic claimed that blacks often drove up prices for their services or stole from the sick. Black leaders Absalom Jones and Richard Allen defended their community in a landmark pamphlet published January 1794. See excerpts from these accounts in Related Texts

[5] "If the poor dog was quite dead": this corpse is the body of Thetford.

girl and her mother on the floor. I wonder how they all got into that room. What carried them there?

The other surlily muttered, Their legs to be sure.

But what should they hug together in one room for?

To save us trouble to be sure.

And I thank them with all my heart; but damn it, it wasn't right to put him in his coffin before the breath was fairly gone. I thought the last look he gave me, told me to stay a few minutes.

Pshaw! He could not live. The sooner dead the better for him; as well as for us. Did you mark how he eyed us, when we carried away his wife and daughter? I never cried in my life, since I was knee-high, but curse me if I ever felt in better tune for the business than just then. Hey! continued he, looking up, and observing me standing a few paces distant, and listening to their discourse, What's wanted? Any body dead?

I stayed not to answer or parly, but hurried forward. My joints trembled, and cold drops stood on my forehead. I was ashamed of my own infirmity; and by vigorous efforts of my reason, regained some degree of composure. The evening had now advanced, and it behoved me to procure accommodation at some of the inns.

These were easily distinguished by their *signs*, but many were without inhabitants. At length, I lighted upon one, the hall of which was open, and the windows lifted. After knocking for some time, a young girl appeared, with many marks of distress. In answer to my question, she answered that both her parents were sick, and that they could receive no one. I inquired, in vain, for any other tavern at which strangers might be accommodated. She knew of none such; and left me, on some one's calling to her from above, in the midst of my embarrassment. After a moment's pause, I returned, discomforted and perplexed, to the street.

I proceeded, in a considerable degree, at random. At length, I reached a spacious building, in Fourth-Street,[6] which the sign-post shewed me to be an inn. I knocked loudly and often at the door. At length, a female opened the window of the second story, and, in a tone of peevishness, demanded what I wanted? I told her that I wanted lodging.

Go hunt for it somewhere else, said she; you'll find none here. I began to expostulate; but she shut the window with quickness, and left me to my own reflections.

I began now to feel some regret at the journey I had taken. Never, in the depth of caverns or forests, was I equally conscious of loneliness. I was surrounded by the habitations of men; but I was destitute of associate or friend. I had money, but an horse shelter, or a morsel of food, could not be purchased. I came for the purpose of relieving others, but stood in the utmost need myself. Even in health my condition

---

[6] "Fourth-Street": this Inn is on the same street as Mrs. Wentworth's mansion, located on "South Fourth Street" in Chapter 7. The allusion is likely to the Indian Queen, one of the city's best-known establishments (the meeting place in earlier years of Franklin's Junto club, for example), on Fourth Street just south of Chestnut. The Indian Queen is mentioned by name in Chapter 9 of Brown's novel *Ormond; or, The Secret Witness*, which also features action set in the yellow fever epidemic. *Ormond* appeared in January 1799, just two or three months before *Arthur Mervyn*.

was helpless and forlorn; but what would become of me, should this fatal malady be contracted. To hope that an asylum would be afforded to a sick man, which was denied to one in health, was unreasonable.

The first impulse which flowed from these reflections, was to hasten back to *Malverton;* which, with sufficient diligence, I might hope to regain before the morning light. I could not, methought, return upon my steps with too much speed. I was prompted to run, as if the pest was rushing upon me, and could be eluded only by the most precipitate flight.

This impulse was quickly counteracted by new ideas. I thought with indignation and shame on the imbecility of my proceeding. I called up the images of Susan Hadwin, and of Wallace. I reviewed the motives which had led me to the undertaking of this journey. Time had, by no means, diminished their force. I had, indeed, nearly arrived at the accomplishment of what I had intended. A few steps would carry me to Thetford's habitation. This might be the critical moment, when succour was most needed, and would be most efficacious.

I had previously concluded to defer going thither till the ensuing morning; but why should I allow myself a moment's delay? I might at least gain an external view of the house, and circumstances might arise, which would absolve me from the obligation of remaining an hour longer in the city. All for which I came might be performed; the destiny of Wallace be ascertained; and I be once more safe within the precincts of *Malverton* before the return of day.

I immediately directed my steps towards the habitation of Thetford. Carriages bearing the dead were frequently discovered. A few passengers likewise occurred, whose hasty and perturbed steps, denoted their participation in the common distress. The house, of which I was in quest, quickly appeared. Light, from an upper window, indicated that it was still inhabited.

I paused a moment to reflect in what manner it became me to proceed. To ascertain the existence and condition of Wallace was the purpose of my journey. He had inhabited this house; and whether he remained in it, was now to be known. I felt repugnance to enter, since my safety might, by entering, be unawares and uselessly endangered. Most of the neighbouring houses were apparently deserted. In some there were various tokens of people being within. Might I not inquire, at one of these, respecting the condition of Thetford's family? Yet why should I disturb them by inquiries so impertinent, at this unseasonable hour? To knock at Thetford's door, and put my questions to him who should obey the signal, was the obvious method.

I knocked dubiously and lightly. No one came. I knocked again, and more loudly; I likewise drew the bell. I distinctly heard its distant peals. If any were within, my signal could not fail to be noticed. I paused, and listened, but neither voice nor footsteps could be heard. The light, though obscured by window curtains, which seemed to be drawn close, was still perceptible.

I ruminated on the causes that might hinder my summons from being obeyed. I figured to myself nothing but the helplessness of disease, or the insensibility of death. These images only urged me to persist in endeavouring to obtain admission. Without weighing the consequences of my act, I involuntarily lifted the latch. The door yielded to my hand, and I put my feet within the passage.

Once more I paused. The passage was of considerable extent, and at the end of it I perceived light as from a lamp or candle. This impelled me to go forward, till I reached the foot of a stair-case. A candle stood upon the lowest step.

This was a new proof that the house was not deserted. I struck my heel against the floor with some violence; but this, like my former signals, was unnoticed. Having proceeded thus far, it would have been absurd to retire with my purpose uneffected. Taking the candle in my hand, I opened a door that was near. It led into a spacious parlour, furnished with profusion and splendour. I walked to and fro, gazing at the objects which presented themselves; and involved in perplexity, I knocked with my heel louder than ever;[7] but no less ineffectually.

Notwithstanding the lights which I had seen, it was possible that the house was uninhabited. This I was resolved to ascertain, by proceeding to the chamber which I had observed, from without, to be illuminated. This chamber, as far as the comparison of circumstances would permit me to decide, I believed to be the same in which I had passed the first night of my late abode in the city. Now was I, a second time, in almost equal ignorance of my situation, and of the consequences which impended exploring my way to the same recess.

I mounted the stair. As I approached the door of which I was in search, a vapour, infectious and deadly, assailed my senses. It resembled nothing of which I had ever before been sensible. Many odours had been met with, even since my arrival in the city, less supportable than this. I seemed not so much to smell as to taste the element that now encompassed me. I felt as if I had inhaled a poisonous and subtle fluid, whose power instantly bereft my stomach of all vigour. Some fatal influence appeared to seize upon my vitals; and the work of corrosion and decomposition to be busily begun.[8]

For a moment, I doubted whether imagination had not some share in producing my sensation; but I had not been previously panick-struck; and even now I attended to my own sensations without mental discompose. That I had imbibed this disease was not to be questioned. So far the chances in my favour were annihilated. The lot of sickness was drawn.

Whether my case would be lenient or malignant; whether I should recover or perish, was to be left to the decision of the future. This incident, instead of appalling me, tended rather to invigorate my courage. The danger which I feared had come. I might enter with indifference, on this theatre of pestilence. I might execute without

---

[7] "Louder than ever": Mervyn stamps his foot to announce his presence in a dangerous situation, but this action also underlines the repetition of the setting. The first time he was in this house, as he notes in the next paragraph, he was trapped in Thetford's bedroom and left his shoes behind to escape noiselessly.

[8] "Fatal influence . . . busily begun": unlike Dr. Stevens in Chapter 1, Mervyn at this point believes that bad air (the "effluvia" mentioned four paragraphs farther on) is the cause of the plague. The enlightened Maravegli persuades him to take a more rational, enlightened approach in Chapter 17 (see note 17.5)

faultering, the duties that my circumstances might create. My state was no longer hazardous; and my destiny would be totally uninfluenced by my future conduct.

The pang with which I was first seized, and the momentary inclination to vomit, which it produced, presently subsided. My wholesome feelings, indeed, did not revisit me, but strength to proceed was restored to me. The effluvia became more sensible as I approached the door of the chamber. The door was ajar; and the light within was perceived. My belief, that those within were dead, was presently confuted by a sound, which I first supposed to be that of steps moving quickly and timorously across the floor. This ceased, and was succeeded by sounds of different, but inexplicable import.

Having entered the apartment, I saw a candle on the hearth. A table was covered with vials and other apparatus of a sick chamber. A bed stood on one side, the curtain of which was dropped at the foot, so as to conceal any one within. I fixed my eyes upon this object. There were sufficient tokens that some one lay upon the bed. Breath, drawn at long intervals; mutterings scarcely audible; and a tremulous motion in the bedstead, were fearful and intelligible indications.

If my heart faultered, it must not be supposed that my trepidations arose from any selfish considerations. Wallace only, the object of my search, was present to my fancy. Pervaded with remembrance of the Hadwin's; of the agonies which they had already endured; of the despair which would overwhelm the unhappy Susan, when the death of her lover should be ascertained; observant of the lonely condition of this house, whence I could only infer that the sick had been denied suitable attendance; and reminded by the symptoms that appeared, that this being was struggling with the agonies of death; a sickness of the heart, more insupportable than that which I had just experienced stole upon me.

My fancy readily depicted the progress and completion of this tragedy. Wallace was the first of the family on whom the pestilence had seized. Thetford had fled from his habitation. Perhaps, as a father and husband, to shun the danger attending his stay, was the injunction of his duty. It was questionless the conduct which selfish regards would dictate. Wallace was left to perish alone; or, perhaps, which indeed was a supposition somewhat justified by appearances, he had been left to the tendence of mercenary wretches; by whom, at this desperate moment he had been abandoned.

I was not mindless of the possibility that these forebodings, specious as they were, might be false. The dying person might be some other than Wallace. The whispers of my hope were, indeed, faint; but they, at least, prompted me to snatch a look at the expiring man. For this purpose, I advanced and thrust my head within the curtain.

Chapter XVI

THE features of one whom I had seen so transiently as Wallace, may be imagined to be not easily recognized, especially when those features were tremulous and deathful. Here, however, the differences were too conspicuous to mislead me. I beheld one to whom I could recollect none that bore resemblance. Though ghastly and livid, the traces of intelligence and beauty were undefaced. The life of Wallace was of more value to a feeble individual, but surely the being that was stretched before me and who was hastening to his last breath was precious to thousands.[1]

Was he not one in whose place I would willingly have died? The offering was too late. His extremities were already cold. A vapour, noisome and contagious, hovered over him. The flutterings of his pulse had ceased. His existence was about to close amidst convulsion and pangs.

I withdrew my gaze from this object, and walked to a table. I was nearly unconscious of my movements. My thoughts were occupied with contemplations of the train of horrors and disasters that pursue the race of man. My musings were quickly interrupted by the sight of a small cabinet the hinges of which were broken and the lid half-raised. In the present state of my thoughts, I was prone to suspect the worst. Here were traces of pillage. Some casual or mercenary attendant, had not only contributed to hasten the death of the patient, but had rifled his property and fled.

This suspicion would, perhaps, have yielded to mature reflections, if I had been suffered to reflect. A moment scarcely elapsed, when some appearance in the mirror, which hung over the table, called my attention. It was a human figure, nothing could be briefer than the glance that I fixed upon this apparition, yet there was room enough for the vague conception to suggest itself, that the dying man had started from his bed and was approaching me. This belief was, at the same instant, confuted, by the survey of his form and garb. One eye, a scar upon his cheek, a tawny skin, a form grotesquely misproportioned, brawny as Hercules, and habited in livery, composed, as it were, the parts of one view.[2]

---

[1] "The being . . . stretched before me . . . precious to thousands": as Mervyn learns at the end of this chapter, this dying man is Maravegli, a Venetian physician stricken while attempting to save others. In this character Brown pays homage to Giambattista Scandella, a physician from Veneto who fell ill with yellow fever in New York in September 1798. Brown's friend and roommate, Dr. Elihu Hubbard Smith, already ill with the fever, tended Scandella and brought him to the apartment he shared with Brown, where both Scandella and Smith died in Brown's presence within days. See the discussion of Brown's experience of the fever in the Introduction. On Maravegli-Scandella, see Clark, *Charles Brockden Brown*, 126–27; Grabo, "Historical Essay," 453–54; and Pace, "Giambattista Scandella and His American Friends."

[2] "One eye . . . one view": in the mirror Mervyn glimpses an African in "livery," or servant's uniform. In the period's codes, "tawny" means a light "black" skin. The scar may be the trace of an injury, a whipping, or a tribal marking, suggesting the man's former experience of slavery. This episode doubles the mirrored self-contemplation that Mervyn enacted on his entry into Welbeck's service in Chapter 5 and repeats, now in a more violent form, that moment's uncanny condensation of class, gender, and ethno-racial tensions (see note 5.8).

To perceive, to fear, and to confront this apparition were blended into one sentiment. I turned towards him with the swiftness of lightning, but my speed was useless to my safety. A blow upon my temple was succeeded by an utter oblivion of thought and of feeling. I sunk upon the floor prostrate and senseless.

My insensibility might be mistaken by observers for death, yet some part of this interval was haunted by a fearful dream. I conceived myself lying on the brink of a pit whose bottom the eye could not reach. My hands and legs were fettered, so as to disable me from resisting two grim and gigantic figures, who stooped to lift me from the earth. Their purpose methought was to cast me into this abyss. My terrors were unspeakable, and I struggled with such force, that my bonds snapt and I found myself at liberty. At this moment my senses returned and I opened my eyes.

The memory of recent events was, for a time, effaced by my visionary horrors. I was conscious of transition from one state of being to another, but my imagination was still filled with images of danger. The bottomless gulf and my gigantic persecutors were still dreaded. I looked up with eagerness. Beside me I discovered three figures, whose character or office were explained by a coffin of pine-boards which lay upon the floor. One stood with hammer and nails in his hand, as ready to replace and fasten the lid of the coffin, as soon as its burthen should be received.

I attempted to rise from the floor, but my head was dizzy and my sight confused. Perceiving me revive, one of the men, assisted me to regain my feet. The mist and confusion presently vanished, so as to allow me to stand unsupported and to move. I once more gazed at my attendants, and recognized the three men, whom I had met in High-Street, and whose conversation I have mentioned that I over-heard. I looked again upon the coffin. A wavering recollection of the incidents that led me hither and of the stunning blow which I had received, occurred to me. I saw into what error, appearances had misled these men, and shuddered to reflect, by what hairbreadth means I had escaped being buried alive.

Before the men had time to interrogate me, or to comment upon my situation, one entered the apartment whose habit and mein tended to incourage me. The stranger was characterized by an aspect full of composure and benignity, a face in which the serious lines of age were blended with the ruddiness and smoothness of youth, and a garb that bespoke that religious profession, with whose benevolent doctrines the example of Hadwin had rendered me familiar.[3]

On observing me on my feet, he betrayed marks of surprise and satisfaction. He addressed me in a tone of mildness.

Young man, said he, what is thy condition? Art thou sick? If thou art, thou must consent to receive the best treatment which the times will afford. These men will convey thee to the hospital at Bush-Hill.[4]

---

[3] "With whose benevolent doctrines the example of Hadwin had rendered me familiar": in other words, as his use of "thee" and "thou" indicates, Mr. Estwick is a Quaker like the Hadwins.

[4] "Bush-Hill": Bush-Hill, on higher ground just east of Fair-Mount, the present-day location of the Philadelphia Museum of Art, was the location of a mansion converted into an emergency hospital

The mention of that contagious and abhorred receptacle, inspired me with some degree of energy. No, said I, I am not sick, a violent blow reduced me to this situation. I shall presently recover strength enough to leave this spot, without assistance.

He looked at me, with an incredulous but compassionate air: I fear thou dost deceive thyself or me. The necessity of going to the hospital is much to be regretted, but on the whole it is best. Perhaps, indeed, thou hast kindred or friends who will take care of thee.

No, said I; neither kindred nor friends. I am a stranger in the city. I do not even know a single being.

Alas! returned the stranger with a sigh, thy state is sorrowful—but how camest thou hither? continued he, looking around him, and whence comest thou?

I came from the country. I reached the city, a few hours ago. I was in search of a friend who lived in this house.

Thy undertaking was strangely hazardous and rash: but who is the friend thou seekest? Was it he who died in that bed, and whose corpse has just been removed?

The men now betrayed some impatience; and inquired of the last comer, whom they called Mr. Estwick, what they were to do. He turned to me, and asked if I were willing to be conducted to the hospital?

I assured him that I was free from disease, and stood in no need of assistance; adding, that my feebleness was owing to a stunning blow received from a ruffian on my temple. The marks of this blow were conspicuous, and after some hesitation he dismissed the men; who, lifting the empty coffin on their shoulders, disappeared.

He now invited me to descend into the parlour: for, said he, the air of this room is deadly. I feel already as if I should have reason to repent of having entered it.

He now inquired into the cause of those appearances which he had witnessed. I explained my situation as clearly and succinctly as I was able.

After pondering, in silence, on my story:—I see how it is, said he: the person whom thou sawest in the agonies of death was a stranger. He was attended by his servant and an hired nurse. His master's death being certain, the nurse was dispatched by the servant to procure a coffin. He probably chose that opportunity to rifle his master's trunk, that stood upon the table. Thy unseasonable entrance interrupted him; and he designed, by the blow which he gave thee, to secure his retreat before the arrival of an hearse. I know the man, and the apparition thou hast so well described, was his.[5] Thou sayest that a friend of thine lived in this house—Thou hast come too late to be of service. The whole family have perished—Not one was suffered to escape.

This intelligence was fatal to my hopes. It required some efforts to subdue my rising emotions. Compassion not only for Wallace, but for Thetford, his father, his wife and his child; caused a passionate effusion of tears. I was ashamed of this useless and

---

for tending fever victims. Wallace describes conditions at Bush-Hill in Chapter 18 when he relates his fever experience to Mervyn.

[5] "The apparition . . . was his": Estwick hypothesizes that Mervyn was attacked by the dead man's servant. Again, responses to black nurses and volunteers became the subject of an important pamphlet debate in the fever's aftermath. See the excerpts from Carey, and Jones and Allen in Related Texts.

child-like sensibility; and attempted to apologize to my companion. The sympathy, however, had proved contagious, and the stranger turned away his face to hide his own tears.[6]

Nay, said he, in answer to my excuses, there is no need to be ashamed of thy emotion. Merely to have known this family, and to have witnessed their deplorable fate, is sufficient to melt the most obdurate[7] heart. I suspect that thou wast united to some one of this family, by ties of tenderness like those which led the unfortunate *Maravegli* hither.

This suggestion was attended, in relation to myself, with some degree of obscurity; but my curiosity was somewhat excited by the name that he had mentioned. I inquired into the character and situation of this person, and particularly respecting his connection with this family.

Maravegli, answered he, was the lover of the eldest daughter and already betrothed to her. The whole family, consisting of helpless females, had placed themselves under his peculiar guardianship. Mary Walpole and her children enjoyed in him an husband and a father.

The name of Walpole, to which I was a stranger, suggested doubts which I hastened to communicate. I am in search, said I, not of a female friend, though not devoid of interest in the welfare of Thetford and his family. My principal concern is for a youth, by name, Wallace.

He looked at me with surprise. Thetford! this is not his abode. He changed his habitation some weeks previous to the *fever*. Those who last dwelt under this roof were an English woman, and seven daughters.

This detection of my error somewhat consoled me. It was still possible that Wallace was alive and in safety. I eagerly inquired whither Thetford had removed, and whether he had any knowledge of his present condition.

They had removed to number . . . , in Market-Street. Concerning their state he knew nothing. His acquaintance with Thetford was imperfect. Whether he had left the city or had remained, he was wholly uninformed.

It became me to ascertain the truth in these respects. I was preparing to offer my parting thanks to the person by whom I had been so highly benefitted; since, as he now informed, it was by his interposition that I was hindered from being inclosed alive in a coffin. He was dubious of my true condition, and peremptorily commanded the followers of the hearse to desist. A delay of twenty minutes, and some medical application, would, he believed, determine whether my life was extinguished or suspended. At the end of this time, happily, my senses were recovered.

Seeing my intention to depart he inquired why, and whither I was going? Having heard my answer. Thy design resumed he, is highly indiscrete and rash. Nothing will

---

[6] "Sensibility . . . sympathy . . . hide his own tears": in this example of associative sensibility, Estwick weeps sympathetically in response to Mervyn's sympathetic response to the story Estwick has just related. Sympathy functions here as its advocates claim it ought to by circulating to affect a chain of listeners and readers. Implicitly, we ourselves should be moved to emulate this compassion, completing the circuit enacted by the novel.

[7] "Obdurate": hardened, "resistant or insensible to moral influence" (OED).

sooner generate this fever than fatigue and anxiety. Thou hast scarcely recovered from the blow so lately received. Instead of being useful to others this precipitation will only disable thyself. Instead of roaming the streets and inhaling this unwholesome air, thou hadst better betake thyself to bed and try to obtain some sleep. In the morning, thou wilt be better qualified to ascertain the fate of thy friend, and afford him the relief which he shall want.

I could not but admit the reasonableness of these remonstrances, but where should a chamber and bed be sought? It was not likely that a new attempt to procure accommodation at the Inns would succeed better than the former.

Thy state, replied he, is sorrowful. I have no house to which I can lead thee. I divide my chamber and even my bed with another, and my landlady could not be prevailed upon to admit a stranger. What thou wilt do, I know not. This house has no one to defend it. It was purchased and furnished by the last possessor, but the whole family, including mistress, children and servants, were cut off in a single week. Perhaps, no one in America can claim the property. Meanwhile plunderers are numerous and active. An house thus totally deserted, and replenished with valuable furniture will, I fear, become their prey. To-night, nothing can be done towards rendering it secure, but staying in it. Art thou willing to remain here till the morrow?

Every bed in the house has probably sustained a dead person. It would not be proper, therefore, to lie in any one of them. Perhaps, thou mayest find some repose upon this carpet. It is, at least, better than the harder pavement, and the open air.

This proposal, after some hesitation, I embraced. He was preparing to leave me, promising, if life were spared to him, to return early in the morning. My curiosity respecting the person whose dying agonies I had witnessed, prompted me to detain him a few minutes.

Ah! said he, this perhaps, is the only one of many victims to this pestilence whose loss the remotest generations may have reason to deplore. He was the only descendent of an illustrious house of Venice. He has been devoted from his childhood to the acquisition of knowledge and the practice of virtue. He came hither, as an enlightened observer, and after traversing the country, conversing with all the men in it eminent for their talents or their office; and collecting a fund of observations, whose solidity and justice have seldom been paralleled, he embarked, three months ago, for Europe.

Previously to his departure, he formed a tender connection with the eldest daughter of this family. The mother and her children had recently arrived from England. So many faultless women, both mentally and personally considered, it was not my fortune to meet with before. This youth well deserved to be adopted into this family. He proposed to return with the utmost expedition to his native country, and after the settlement of his affairs, to hasten back to America, and ratify his contract with Fanny Walpole.

The ship in which he embarked, had scarcely gone twenty leagues to sea, before she was disabled by a storm, and obliged to return to port. He posted to New-York, to gain a passage in a packet shortly to sail. Meanwhile this malady prevailed among us. Mary Walpole was hindered by her ignorance of the nature of that evil which assailed us, and the counsel of injudicious friends, from taking the due precautions for her safety. She hesitated to fly till flight was rendered impracticable. Here death added to the helplessness and distraction of the family. They were successively seized and destroyed by the same pest.

Maravegli was apprised of their danger. He allowed the packet to depart without him, and hastened to the rescue of the Walpoles from the perils which encompassed them. He arrived in this city time enough to witness the interment of the last survivor. In the same hour he was seized himself by this disease: the catastrophe is known to thee.

I will now leave thee to thy repose. Sleep is no less needful to myself than to thee; for this is the second night which has past without it—Saying this, my companion took his leave.

I now enjoyed leisure to review my situation. I experienced no inclination to sleep. I lay down for a moment, but my comfortless sensations and restless contemplations would not permit me to rest. Before I entered this roof, I was tormented with hunger, but my craving had given place to inquietude and loathing. I paced, in thoughtful and anxious mood, across the floor of the apartment.

I mused upon the incidents related by Estwick, upon the exterminating nature of this pestilence, and on the horrors of which it was productive. I compared the experience of the last hours, with those pictures which my imagination had drawn in the retirements of *Malverton*. I wondered at the contrariety that exists between the scenes of the city and the country; and fostered with more zeal than ever, the resolution to avoid those seats of depravity and danger.

Concerning my own destiny, however, I entertained no doubt. My new sensations assured me that my stomach had received this corrosive poison. Whether I should die or live was easily decided. The sickness which assiduous attendance and powerful prescriptions might remove, would, by negligence and solitude, be rendered fatal: but from whom could I expect medical or friendly treatment?

I had indeed a roof over my head. I should not perish in the public way: but what was my ground for hoping to continue under this roof? My sickness being suspected, I should be dragged in a cart to the hospital; where I should, indeed die; but not with the consolation of loneliness and silence. Dying groans were the only music, and livid corpses were the only spectacle to which I should there be introduced.

Immured[8] in these dreary meditations, the night passed away. The light glancing through the window awakened in my bosom a gleam of cheerfulness. Contrary to my expectations, my feelings were not more distempered, notwithstanding my want of sleep, than on the last evening. This was a token that my state was far from being so desperate as I suspected. It was possible, I thought, that this was the worst indisposition to which I was liable.

Meanwhile the coming of Estwick was impatiently expected. The sun arose, and the morning advanced, but he came not. I remembered that he talked of having rea-

---

[8] "Immured": literally walled in, trapped, enclosed, surrounded.

son to repent his visit to this house. Perhaps, he likewise, was sick, and that this was the cause of his delay. This man's kindness had even my love. If I had known the way to his dwelling, I should have hastened thither, to inquire into his condition, and to perform for him every office that humanity might enjoin, but he had not afforded me any information on that head.

Chapter XVII

IT was now incumbent on me to seek the habitation of Thetford. To leave this house accessible to every passenger appeared to be imprudent. I had no key by which I might lock the principal door. I therefore bolted it on the inside, and passed through a window, the shutters of which I closed, though I could not fasten after me. This led me into a spacious court, at the end of which was a brick wall, over which I leaped into the street. This was the means by which I had formerly escaped from the same precincts.[1]

The streets, as I passed, were desolate and silent. The largest computation made the number of fugitives two-thirds of the whole people; yet, judging by the universal desolation, it seemed, as if the solitude were nearly absolute. That so many of the houses were closed, I was obliged to ascribe to the cessation of traffic, which made the opening of their windows useless, and the terror of infection, which made the inhabitants seclude themselves from the observation of each other.

I proceeded to search out the house to which Estwick had directed me, as the abode of Thetford. What was my consternation when I found it to be the same, at the door of which the conversation took place, of which I had been an auditor on the last evening.[2]

I recalled the scene, of which a rude sketch had been given by the *hearse-men*. If such were the fate of the master of the family, abounding with money and friends, what could be hoped for the moneyless and friendless Wallace? The house appeared to be vacant and silent; but these tokens might deceive. There was little room for hope; but certainty was wanting, and might, perhaps, be obtained by entering the house. In some of the upper rooms a wretched being might be immured; by whom the information, so earnestly desired, might be imparted, and to whom my presence might bring relief; not only from pestilence, but famine. For a moment, I forgot my own necessitous condition; and reflected not that abstinence had already undermined my strength.

I proceeded to knock at the door. That my signal was unnoticed, produced no surprize. The door was unlocked, and I opened. At this moment my attention was attracted by the opening of another door near me. I looked, and perceived a man issuing forth from an house at a small distance.

It now occurred to me, that the information which I sought might possibly be gained from one of Thetford's neighbours. This person was aged, but seemed to have lost neither cheerfulness nor vigour. He had an air of intrepidity and calmness. It soon appeared that I was the object of his curiosity. He had, probably, marked my deportment through some window of his dwelling, and had come forth to make inquiries into the motives of my conduct.

---

[1] "Escaped from the same precincts": Mervyn escaped the same house in the same manner after his first night in Philadelphia in Chapter 4 (see note 4.9).

[2] "The same . . . last evening": this is the same house where Mervyn heard the black undertaker commenting on the death of a man and his family in Chapter 15 (see note 15.5). The following explanation by the enlightened character Medlicote clarifies the events of that passage, explaining that the dead man in question was Thetford.

He courteously saluted me. You seem, said he, to be in search of some one. If I can afford you the information you want, you will be welcome to it.

Encouraged by this address, I mentioned the name of Thetford; and added my fears that he had not escaped the general calamity.

It is true, said he. Yesterday himself, his wife, and his child were in an hopeless condition. I saw them in the evening, and expected not to find them alive this morning. As soon as it was light, however, I visited the house again; but found it empty. I suppose they must have died, and been removed in the night.

Though anxious to ascertain the destiny of Wallace, I was unwilling to put direct questions. shuddered, while I longed to know the truth.

Why, said I, falteringly, did he not seasonably withdraw from the city? Surely he had the means of purchasing an asylum in the country.

I can scarcely tell you, he answered. Some infatuation appeared to have seized him. No one was more timorous; but he seemed to think himself safe, as long as he avoided contact with infected persons. He was likewise, I believe, detained by a regard to his interest. His flight would not have been more injurious to his affairs, than it was to those of others; but gain was, in his eyes, the supreme good. He intended ultimately to withdraw; but his escape to-day, gave him new courage to encounter the perils of to-morrow. He deferred his departure from day to day, till it ceased to be practicable.

His family, said I, was numerous. It consisted of more than his wife and children. Perhaps these retired in sufficient season.

Yes, said he; his father left the house at an early period. One or two of the servants likewise forsook him. One girl, more faithful and heroic than the rest, resisted the remonstrances of her parents and friends, and resolved to adhere to him in every fortune. She was anxious that the family should fly from danger, and would willingly have fled in their company; but while they stayed, it was her immovable resolution not to abandon them.

Alas, poor girl! She knew not of what stuff the heart of Thetford was made. Unhappily, she was the first to become sick. I question much whether her disease was pestilential. It was, probably, a slight indisposition; which, in a few days, would have vanished of itself, or have readily yielded to suitable treatment.

Thetford was transfixed with terror. Instead of summoning a physician, to ascertain the nature of her symptoms, he called a negro and his cart from Bush-Hill. In vain the neighbours interceded for this unhappy victim. In vain she implored his clemency, and asserted the lightness of her indisposition. She besought him to allow her to send to her mother, who resided a few miles in the country, who would hasten to her succour, and relieve him and his family from the danger and trouble of nursing her.

The man was lunatic with apprehension.[3] He rejected her intreaties, though urged in a manner that would have subdued an heart of flint. The girl was innocent, and

---

[3] "Lunatic with apprehension": Medlicote's description of Thetford's panic and criminal selfishness follows Jones and Allen's defense of black workers in response to Mathew Carey's charges of black theft and extortion during the epidemic (see excerpts in Related Texts). Jones and Allen point out

amiable, and courageous, but entertained an unconquerable dread of the hospital. Finding intreaties ineffectual, she exerted all her strength in opposition to the man who lifted her into the cart.

Finding that her struggles availed nothing, she resigned herself to despair. In going to the hospital, she believed herself led to certain death, and to the sufferance of every evil which the known inhumanity of its attendants could inflict. This state of mind, added to exposure to a noon-day sun, in an open vehicle; moving, for a mile, over a rugged pavement, was sufficient to destroy her. I was not surprised to hear that she died the next day.

This proceeding was sufficiently iniquitous; yet it was not the worst act of this man. The rank and education of the young woman, might be some apology for negligence; but his clerk, a youth who seemed to enjoy his confidence, and to be treated by his family, on the footing of a brother or son, fell sick on the next night, and was treated in the same manner.

These tidings struck me to the heart. A burst of indignation and sorrow filled my eyes. I could scarcely stifle my emotion sufficiently to ask, Of whom, sir, do you speak? Was the name of the youth—his name—was—

His name was Wallace. I see that you have some interest in his fate. He was one whom I loved. I would have given half my fortune to procure him accommodation under some hospitable roof. His attack was violent; but still, his recovery, if he had been suitably attended, was possible. That he should survive removal to the hospital, and the treatment he must receive when there, was not to be hoped.

The conduct of Thetford was as absurd as it was wicked. To imagine this disease to be contagious was the height of folly; to suppose himself secure, merely by not permitting a sick man to remain under his roof, was no less stupid; but Thetford's fears had subverted his understanding.[4] He did not listen to arguments or supplications. His attention was incapable of straying from one object. To influence him by words was equivalent to reasoning with the deaf.

Perhaps the wretch was more to be pitied than hated. The victims of his implacable caution, could scarcely have endured agonies greater than those which his pusillanimity inflicted on himself. Whatever be the amount of his guilt, the retribution has been adequate. He witnessed the death of his wife and child, and last night was the close of his own existence. Their sole attendant was a black woman; whom, by fre-

---

that while some blacks may have acted improperly, the improprieties of white Philadelphians were far more serious in every way. Coming after Estwick's implied accusation against a servant (see note 16.5), the discussion therefore echoes Jones and Allen's reply to Carey. Given that Medlicote's virtue and intelligence are unquestioned and function to correct Arthur's less knowledgeable perspective, this sequence suggests Brown may be ventriloquizing Jones and Allen, echoing their argument and implying that their position in the debate is the more accurate and reasonable one.

[4] "Thetford's fears had subverted his understanding": recalling Mervyn's comments about irrational panic at the beginning of Chapter 13, Medlicote's account of Thetford's selfish and dangerous behavior provides another caution about the rational need to resist anxiety and fear mongering and pursue cooperative efforts for mutual aid instead.

quent visits, I endeavoured, with little success, to make diligent in the performance of her duty.

Such, then, was the catastrophe of Wallace. The end for which I journeyed hither was accomplished. His destiny was ascertained; and all that remained was to fulfil the gloomy predictions of the lovely, but unhappy Susan. To tell them all the truth, would be needlessly to exasperate her sorrow. Time, aided by the tenderness and sympathy of friendship, may banish her despair, and relieve her from all but the witcheries of melancholy.

Having disengaged my mind from these reflections, I explained to my companion in general terms, my reasons for visiting the city, and my curiosity respecting Thetford. He inquired into the particulars of my journey and, the time of my arrival. When informed that I had come in the preceding evening, and had passed the subsequent hours without sleep or food, he expressed astonishment and compassion.

Your undertaking, said he, has certainly been hazardous. There is poison in every breath which you draw, but this hazard has been greatly increased by abstaining from food and sleep. My advice is to hasten back into the country; but you must first take some repose and some victuals. If you pass Schuylkill before night-fall, it will be sufficient.

I mentioned the difficulty of procuring accommodation on the road. It would be most prudent to set out upon my journey so as to reach *Malverton* at night. As to food and sleep they were not to be purchased in this city.

True, answered my companion, with quickness, they are not to be bought, but I will furnish you with as much as you desire of both for nothing. That is my abode, continued he, pointing to the house, which he had lately left. I reside with a widow lady and her daughter, who took my counsel, and fled in due season. I remain to moralize upon the scene, with only a faithful black, who makes my bed, prepares my coffee, and bakes my loaf. If I am sick, all that a physician can do, I will do for myself, and all that a nurse can perform, I expect to be performed by *Austin*.

Come with me, drink some coffee, rest a while on my matrass, and then fly, with my benedictions on your head.

These words were accompanied by features disembarrassed and benevolent. My temper is alive to social impulses, and I accepted his invitation, not so much because I wished to eat or to sleep, but because I felt reluctance to part so soon with a being, who possessed so much fortitude and virtue.

He was surrounded by neatness and plenty. Austin added dexterity to submissiveness. My companion, whose name I now found to be Medlicote, was prone to converse, and commented on the state of the city like one whose reading had been extensive and experience large. He combatted an opinion which I had casually formed, respecting the origin of this epidemic, and imputed it, not to infected substances imported from the east or west, but to a morbid constitution of the atmosphere, owing wholly, or in part to filthy streets, airless habitations and squalid persons.[5]

---

[5] "He combatted an opinion . . . squalid persons": the enlightened Medlicote corrects Mervyn's uninformed ideas about the fever and takes sides in contemporary debates about its origins. In an era

As I talked with this man, the sense of danger was obliterated, I felt confidence revive in my heart, and energy revisit my stomach. Though far from my wonted health, my sensation grew less comfortless, and I found myself to stand in no need of repose.

Breakfast being finished, my friend pleaded his daily engagements as reasons for leaving me. He counselled me to strive for some repose, but I was conscious of incapacity to sleep. I was desirous of escaping, as soon as possible, from this tainted atmosphere and reflected whether any thing remained to be done respecting Wallace.

It now occurred to me that this youth must have left some clothes and papers, and, perhaps, books. The property of these was now vested in the Hadwins. I might deem myself, without presumption, their representative or agent. Might I not take some measures for obtaining possession, or at least, for the security of these articles?

The house and its furniture was tenantless and unprotected. It was liable to be ransacked and pillaged by those desperate ruffians, of whom many were said to be hunting for spoil, even at a time like this. If these should overlook this dwelling, Thetford's unknown successor or heir might appropriate the whole. Numberless accidents might happen to occasion the destruction or embezzlement of what belonged to Wallace, which might be prevented by the conduct which I should now pursue.

Immersed in these perplexities, I remained bewildered and motionless. I was at length roused by some one knocking at the door. Austin obeyed the signal, and instantly returned, leading in—Mr. Hadwin![6]

I know not whether this unlooked-for interview excited on my part, most grief or surprize. The motive of his coming was easily divined. His journey was on two accounts superfluous. He whom he sought was dead. The duty of ascertaining his condition, I had assigned to myself.

I now perceived and deplored the error of which I had been guilty, in concealing my intended journey from my patron. Ignorant of the part I had acted, he had rushed into the jaws of this pest, and endangered a life unspeakably valuable to his children and friends. I should doubtless have obtained his grateful consent to the project which I had conceived; but my wretched policy had led me into this clandestine path. Secrecy may seldom be a crime. A virtuous intention may produce it; but surely it is always erroneous and pernicious.[7]

---

before the actual cause and nature of the fever were understood, the two leading theories opposed contagionists, who believed the disease was spread by contagion and probably arrived with infected produce and persons from the Caribbean, and proponents of the "miasma" or environmental theory, who recognized that it was not contagious and argued that it arose from local unsanitary conditions. As he educates Mervyn about the fever, Medlicote takes the more progressive stance, which was also endorsed by Brown's circle. For more on the fever debates, see Introduction.

[6] "Mr. Hadwin!": a passage in Chapter II.7 will explain that this meeting takes place in October 1793, thus placing the novel's fever scenes in the epidemic's deadliest days. Between October 9 and 13, according to Carey's *Short Account of the Malignant Fever*, the mortality rate reached its peak with over one hundred victims daily. For the passage that specifies this time frame, see note II.7.2.

[7] "Secrecy . . . pernicious.": Mervyn repeats the standard Woldwinite belief that secrecy is bad in itself. The Woldwinites reject the belief that actions can be judged on their intentions. To be virtuous,

My friend's astonishment at the sight of me, was not inferior to my own. The causes which led to this unexpected interview were mutually explained. To soothe the agonies of his child, he consented to approach the city, and endeavour to procure intelligence of Wallace. When he left his house, he intended to stop in the environs, and hire some emissary, whom an ample reward might tempt to enter the city, and procure the information which was needed.

No one could be prevailed upon to execute so dangerous a service. Averse to return without performing his commission, he concluded to examine for himself. Thetford's removal to this street was known to him; but, being ignorant of my purpose, he had not mentioned this circumstance to me, during our last conversation.

I was sensible of the danger which Hadwin had incurred by entering the city. Perhaps, my knowledge or the inexpressible importance of his life, to the happiness of his daughters, made me aggravate his danger. I knew that the longer he lingered in this tainted air, the hazard was increased. A moment's delay was unnecessary. Neither Wallace nor myself were capable of being benefitted by his presence.

I mentioned the death of his nephew, as a reason for hastening his departure. I urged him in the most vehement terms to remount his horse and to fly; I endeavoured to preclude all inquiries respecting myself or Wallace; promising to follow him immediately, and answer all his questions at *Malverton*. My importunities were inforced by his own fears, and after a moment's hesitation, he rode away.

The emotions produced by this incident, were, in the present critical state of my frame, eminently hurtful. My morbid indications suddenly returned. I had reason to ascribe my condition to my visit to the chamber of Maravegli, but this, and its consequences, to myself, as well as the journey of Hadwin, were the fruits of my unhappy secrecy.

I had always been accustomed to perform my journeys on foot. This, on ordinary occasions, was the preferable method, but now I ought to have adopted the easiest and swiftest means. If Hadwin had been acquainted with my purpose he would not only have approved, but would have allowed me the use of an horse. These reflections were rendered less pungent by the recollection that my motives were benevolent, and that I had endeavoured the benefit of others by means, which appeared to me most suitable.

Meanwhile, how was I to proceed? What hindered me from pursuing the foot-steps of Hadwin with all the expedition which my uneasiness, of brain and stomach would allow? I conceived that to leave any thing undone, with regard to Wallace, would be absurd. His property might be put under the care of my new friend. But how was it to be distinguished from the property of others? It was, probably, contained in trunks, which was designated by some label or mark. I was unacquainted with his

---

an act must also produce good effects, and secrecy prevents good intentions from being realized. Brown presents this theme in his short story "Lesson on Concealment; or, Memoirs of Mary Selwyn" (March 1800).

chamber, but, by passing from one to the other, I might finally discover it. Some token, directing my foot-steps, might occur, though at present unforeseen.

Actuated by these considerations. I once more entered Thetford's habitation. I regretted that I had not procured the counsel or attendance of my new friend, but some engagements, the nature of which he did not explain, occasioned him to leave me as soon as breakfast was finished.

Chapter XVIII

I WANDERED over this deserted mansion, in a considerable degree, at random. Effluvia of a pestilential nature, assailed me from every corner. In the front room of the second story, I imagined that I discovered vestiges of that catastrophe which the past night had produced. The bed appeared as if some one had recently been dragged from it. The sheets were tinged with yellow, and with that substance which is said to be characteristic of this disease, the gangrenous or black vomit. The floor exhibited similar stains.

There are many, who will regard my conduct as the last refinement of temerity, or of heroism. Nothing, indeed, more perplexes me than a review of my own conduct. Not, indeed, that death is an object always to be dreaded, or that my motive did not justify my actions; but of all dangers, those allied to pestilence, by being mysterious and unseen, are the most formidable. To disarm them of their terrors, requires the longest familiarity. Nurses and physicians soonest become intrepid or indifferent; but the rest of mankind recoil from the scene with unconquerable loathing.

I was sustained, not by confidence of safety, and a belief of exemption from this malady, or by the influence of habit, which inures us to all that is detestable or perilous, but by a belief that this was as eligible an avenue to death as any other; and that life is a trivial sacrifice in the cause of duty.

I passed from one room to the other. A portmanteau,[1] marked with the initials of Wallace's name, at length, attracted my notice. From this circumstance I inferred, that this apartment had been occupied by him. The room was neatly arranged, and appeared as if no one had lately used it. There were trunks and drawers. That which I have mentioned, was the only one that bore marks of Wallace's ownership. This I lifted in my arms with a view to remove it to Medlicote's house.

At that moment, methought I heard a foot-step slowly and lingeringly ascending the stair. I was disconcerted at this incident. The foot-step had in it a ghost-like solemnity and tardiness. This phantom vanished in a moment, and yielded place to more humble conjectures. A human being approached, whose office and commission were inscrutable. That we were strangers to each other was easily imagined; but how would my appearance, in this remote chamber, and loaded with another's property, be interpreted? Did he enter the house after me, or was he the tenant of some chamber hitherto unvisited; whom my entrance had awakened from his trance and called from his couch?

In the confusion of my mind, I still held my burthen uplifted. To have placed it on the floor, and encountered this visitant, without this equivocal token about me, was the obvious proceeding. Indeed, time only could decide whether these foot-steps tended to this, or to some other apartment.

My doubts were quickly dispelled. The door opened, and a figure glided in. The portmanteau dropped from my arms, and my heart's-blood was chilled. If an apparition

---

[1] "Portmanteau": "a case or bag for carrying clothing and other belongings when travelling" (OED).

of the dead were possible, and that possibility I could not deny, this was such an apparition. A hue, yellowish and livid; bones, uncovered with flesh; eyes, ghastly, hollow, woebegone, and fixed in an agony of wonder upon me; and locks, matted and negligent, constituted the image which I now beheld. My belief of somewhat preternatural in this appearance, was confirmed by recollection of resemblances between these features and those of one who was dead. In this shape and visage, shadowy and death-like as they were, the lineaments of Wallace, of him who had misled my rustic simplicity on my first visit to this city, and whose death I had conceived to be incontestably ascertained, were forcibly recognized.

This recognition, which at first alarmed my superstition, speedily led to more rational inferences. Wallace had been dragged to the hospital. Nothing was less to be suspected than that he would return alive from that hideous receptacle, but this was by no means impossible. The figure that stood before me, had just risen from the bed of sickness, and from the brink of the grave. The crisis of his malady had passed, and he was once more entitled to be ranked among the living.

This event, and the consequences which my imagination connected with it, filled me with the liveliest joy. I thought not of his ignorance of the causes of my satisfaction, of the doubts to which the circumstances of our interview would give birth, respecting the integrity of my purpose. I forgot the artifices by which I had formerly been betrayed, and the embarrassments which a meeting with the victim of his artifices would excite in him; I thought only of the happiness which his recovery would confer upon his uncle and his cousins.

I advanced towards him with an air of congratulation, and offered him my hand. He shrunk back, and exclaimed in a feeble voice, Who are you? What business have you here?

I am the friend of Wallace, if he will allow me to be so. I am a messenger from your uncle and cousins at *Malverton* I came to know the cause of your silence, and to afford you any assistance in my power.

He continued to regard me with an air of suspicion and doubt. These I endeavoured to remove by explaining the motives that led me hither. It was with difficulty that he seemed to credit my representations. When thoroughly convinced of the truth of my assertions, he inquired with great anxiety and tenderness concerning his relations; and expressed his hope that they were ignorant of what had befallen him.

I could not encourage his hopes, I regretted my own precipitation in adopting the belief of his death. This belief, had been uttered with confidence, and without stating my reasons for embracing it, to Mr. Hadwin. These tidings would be borne to his daughters, and their grief would be exasperated to a deplorable, and, perhaps, to a fatal degree.

There was but one method of repairing or eluding this mischief. Intelligence ought to be conveyed to them of his recovery. But where was the messenger to be found? No one's attention could be found disengaged from his own concerns. Those who were able or willing to leave the city had sufficient motives for departure, in relation to themselves. If vehicle or horse were procurable for money, ought it not to be secured for the use of Wallace himself, whose health required the easiest and speediest conveyance from this theatre of death?

My companion was powerless in mind as in limbs. He seemed unable to consult upon the means of escaping from the inconveniences by which he was surrounded. As soon as sufficient strength was regained, he had left the hospital. To repair to *Malverton* was the measure which prudence obviously dictated; but he was hopeless of effecting it. The city was close at hand; this was his usual home; and hither his tottering, and almost involuntary steps had conducted him.

He listened to my representations and councils, and acknowledged their propriety. He put himself under my protection and guidance, and promised to conform implicitly to my directions. His strength had sufficed to bring him thus far, but was now utterly exhausted. The task of searching for a carriage and horse devolved upon me.

In effecting this purpose, I was obliged to rely upon my own ingenuity and diligence. Wallace, though so long a resident in the city, knew not to whom I could apply, or by whom carriages were let to hire. My own reflections taught me, that this accommodation was most likely to be furnished by innkeepers, or that some of those might at least inform me of the best measures to be taken. I resolved to set out immediately on this search. Meanwhile, Wallace was persuaded to take refuge in Medlicote's apartments; and to make, by the assistance of Austin, the necessary preparation for his journey.

The morning had now advanced. The rays of a sultry sun had a sickening and enfeebling influence, beyond any which I had ever experienced. The drought of unusual duration had bereft the air and the earth of every particle of moisture. The element which I breathed appeared to have stagnated into noxiousness and putrifaction. I was astonished at observing the enormous diminution of my strength. My brows were heavy, my intellects benumbed, my sinews enfeebled, and my sensations universally unquiet.

These prognostics were easily interpreted. What I chiefly dreaded was, that they would disable me from executing the task which I had undertaken. I summoned up all my resolution, and cherished a disdain of yielding to this ignoble destiny. I reflected that the source of all energy, and even of life, is seated in thought; that nothing is arduous to human efforts; that the external frame will seldom languish, while actuated by an unconquerable soul.

I fought against my dreary feelings, which pulled me to the earth. I quickened my pace, raised my drooping eye-lids, and hummed a cheerful and favourite air. For all that I accomplished during this day, I believe myself indebted to the strenuousness and ardour of my resolutions.

I went from one tavern to another. One was deserted; in another the people were sick, and their attendants refused to hearken to my inquiries or offers; at a third, their horses were engaged. I was determined to prosecute my search as long as an inn or a livery-stable remained unexamined, and my strength would permit.

To detail the events of this expedition, the arguments and supplications which I used to overcome the dictates of avarice and fear, the fluctuation of my hopes and my incessant disappointments, would be useless. Having exhausted all my expedients in-effectually, I was compelled to turn my weary steps once more to Medlicote's lodgings.

My meditations were deeply engaged by the present circumstances of my situation. Since the means which were first suggested, were impracticable, I endeavoured to in-vestigate others. Wallace's debility made it impossible for him to perform this jour-ney on foot: but would not his strength and his resolution suffice to carry him beyond Schuylkill? A carriage or horse, though not to be obtained in the city, could, without difficulty, be procured, in the country. Every farmer had beasts for burthen and draught. One of these might be hired at no immoderate expense, for half a day.

This project appeared so practicable and so specious,[2] that I deeply regretted the time and the efforts which had already been so fruitlessly expended. If my project, however, had been mischievous, to review it with regret, was only to prolong and to multiply its mischiefs. I trusted that time and strength would not be wanting to the execution of this new design.

On entering Medlicote's house, my looks, which, in spite of my languors, were sprightly and confident, flattered Wallace with the belief that my exertions had suc-ceeded. When acquainted with their failure, he sunk as quickly into hopelessness. My new expedient was heard by him with no marks of satisfaction. It was impossible, he said, to move from this spot by his own strength. All his powers were exhausted by his walk from Bush-Hill.

I endeavoured, by arguments and railleries,[3] to revive his courage. The pure air of the country would exhilirate him into new life. He might stop at every fifty yards, and rest upon the green sod. If overtaken by the night, we would procure a lodging, by address and importunity; but if every door should be shut against us, we should at least, enjoy the shelter of some barn, and might diet wholsomely upon the new-laid eggs that we should find there. The worst treatment we could meet with, was better than continuance in the city.

These remonstrances had some influence, and he at length consented to put his ability to the test. First, however, it was necessary to invigorate himself by a few hours rest. To this, though with infinite reluctance, I consented.

This interval allowed him to reflect upon the past, and to inquire into the fate of Thetford and his family. The intelligence, which Medlicote had enabled me to afford him, was heard with more satisfaction than regret. The ingratitude and cruelty with which he had been treated, seemed to have extinguished every sentiment, but hatred and vengeance. I was willing to profit by this interval to know more of Thetford, than I already possessed. I inquired why Wallace, had so perversely neglected the ad-vice of his uncle and cousin, and persisted to brave so many dangers when flight was so easy.

I cannot justify my conduct, answered he. It was in the highest degree, thoughtless and perverse. I was confident and unconcerned as long as our neighbourhood was

---

[2] "Specious": outwardly plausible or attractive, but of little real value.

[3] "Raillerires": good-humored teasing.

free from disease, and as long as I forbore any communication with the sick; yet I should have withdrawn to Malverton, merely to gratify my friends, if Thetford had not used the most powerful arguments to detain me. He laboured to extenuate the danger.

Why not stay, said he, as long as I and my family stay? Do you think that we would linger here, if the danger were imminent. As soon as it becomes so, we will fly. You know that we have a country-house prepared for our reception. When we go, you shall accompany us. Your services at this time are indispensable to my affairs. If you will not desert me, your salary next year shall be double; and that will enable you to marry your cousin immediately. Nothing is more improbable than that any of us should be sick, but if this should happen to you, I plight my honour that you shall be carefully and faithfully attended.

These assurances were solemn and generous. To make Susan Hadwin my wife was the scope of all my wishes and labours. By staying I should hasten this desirable event, and incur little hazard. By going, I should alienate the affections of Thetford; by whom, it is but justice to acknowledge, that I had hitherto been treated with un-exampled generosity and kindness; and blast all the schemes I had formed for rising into wealth.

My resolution was by no means stedfast. As often as a letter from *Malverton* arrived, I felt myself disposed to hasten away, but this inclination was combated by new ar-guments and new intreaties of Thetford.

In this state of suspense, the girl by whom Mrs. Thetford's infant was nursed, fell sick. She was an excellent creature, and merited better treatment than she received. Like me, she resisted the persuasions of her friends, but her motives for remaining were disinterested and heroic.[4]

No sooner did her indisposition appear, than she was hurried to the hospital. I saw that no reliance could be placed upon the assurances of Thetford. Every considera-tion gave way to his fear of death. After the girl's departure, though he knew that she was led by his means to execution,—yet he consoled himself with repeating and be-lieving her assertions, that her disease was not *the fever*.

I was now greatly alarmed for my own safety. I was determined to encounter his anger and repel his persuasions; and to depart with the market-man, next morning. That night, however, I was seized with a violent fever. I knew in what manner patients were treated at the hospital, and removal thither was to the last degree abhorred.

The morning arrived, and my situation was discovered. At the first intimation, Thetford rushed out of the house, and refused to re-enter it till I was removed. I knew not my fate, till three ruffians made their appearance at my bed-side, and com-municated their commission.

---

[4] "Mrs. Thetford's infant . . . heroic": this is the foundling Thetford brought into his bedroom se-cretly in Chapter 4 to allay his wife's grief after the loss of her own newborn (see note 4.3), and the selfless servant who tried to stay behind and help is the girl killed by Thetford's "lunatic" panic in Chapter 17 (see note 17.3). Thetford's greed and selfishness lead to the death of his own family and thwarts the benevolence of those who try to help them.

I called on the name of Thetford and his wife. I intreated a moment's delay, till I had seen these persons, and endeavoured to procure a respite from my sentence. They were deaf to my intreaties, and prepared to execute their office by force. I was delirious with rage and with terror. I heaped the bitterest execrations on my murderer; and by turns, invoked the compassion, and poured a torrent of reproaches on the wretches whom he had selected for his ministers. My struggles and outcries were vain.

I have no perfect recollection of what passed till my arrival at the hospital. My passions, combined with my disease, to make me frantic and wild. In a state like mine, the slightest motion could not be indured without agony. What then must I have felt, scorched and dazled by the sun, sustained by hard boards, and borne for miles over a rugged pavement?

I cannot make you comprehend the anguish of my feelings. To be disjointed and torn piece-meal by the rack, was a torment inexpressibly inferior to this. Nothing excites my wonder, but that I did not expire before the cart had moved three paces.

I knew not how, or by whom I was moved from this vehicle. Insensibility came at length to my relief. After a time I opened my eyes, and slowly gained some knowledge of my situation.[5] I lay upon a mattress, whose condition proved that an half-decayed corpse had recently been dragged from it. The room was large, but it was covered with beds like my own. Between each, there was scarcely the interval of three feet. Each sustained a wretch, whose groans and distortions, bespoke the desperateness of his condition.

The atmosphere was loaded by mortal stenches. A vapour, suffocating and malignant, scarcely allowed me to breathe. No suitable receptacle was provided for the evacuations produced by medicine or disease. My nearest neighbour was struggling with death, and my bed, casually extended, was moist with the detestable matter which had flowed from his stomach.

You will scarcely believe that, in this scene of horrors, the sound of laughter should be overheard. While the upper rooms of this building, are filled with the sick and the dying, the lower apartments are the scene of carrousals and mirth. The wretches who are hired, at enormous wages, to tend the sick and convey away the dead, neglect their duty and consume the cordials, which are provided for the patients, in debauchery and riot.

A female visage, bloated with malignity and drunkenness, occasionally looked in. Dying eyes were cast upon her, invoking the boon, perhaps, of a drop of cold water, or her assistance to change a posture which compelled him to behold the ghastly writhings or deathful *smile* of his neighbour.

The visitant had left the banquet for a moment, only to see who was dead. If she entered the room, blinking eyes and reeling steps, shewed her to be totally unqualified for ministering the aid that was needed. Presently, she disappeared and others as-

---

[5] "Some knowledge of my situation": what follows is Wallace's account of the Bush-Hill emergency hospital.

cended the stair-case, a coffin was deposited at the door, the wretch, whose heart still quivered, was seized by rude hands, and dragged along the floor into the passage.

O! how poor are the conceptions which are formed, by the fortunate few, of the sufferings to which millions of their fellow beings are condemned. This misery was more frightful, because it was seen to flow from the depravity of the attendants. My own eyes only would make me credit the existence of wickedness so enormous. No wonder that to die in garrets and cellars and stables unvisited and unknown, had, by so many, been preferred to being brought hither.

A physician cast an eye upon my state. He gave some directions to the person who attended him. I did not comprehend them,[6] they were never executed by the nurses, and if the attempt had been made, I should probably have refused to receive what was offered. Recovery was equally beyond my expectations and my wishes. The scene which was hourly displayed before me, the entrance of the sick, most of whom perished in a few hours, and their departure to the graves prepared for them, reminded me of the fate to which I, also, was reserved.

Three days passed away, in which every hour was expected to be the last. That, amidst an atmosphere so contagious and deadly, amidst causes of destruction hourly accumulating, I should yet survive, appears to me nothing less than miraculous. That of so many conducted to this house, the only one who passed out of it alive, should be myself, almost surpasses my belief.

Some inexplicable principle rendered harmless those potent enemies of human life. My fever subsided and vanished. My strength was revived, and the first use that I made of my limbs, was to bear me far from the contemplation and sufferance of those evils.

---

[6] "I did not comprehend them": since this Bush-Hill physician speaks a language Wallace cannot understand, the passage seems to allude to Dr. Jean Devèze. Devèze was a French practitioner who came to Philadelphia from Haiti, where he had survived yellow fever himself and gained extensive experience treating it. Like the knowledgeable character Medlicote in the previous chapter, he rejected contagionist theory and attributed it to "ignorance and party influence" (see Pernick, "Politics, Parties, and Pestilence:"). He arrived in Philadelphia as a refugee from the Haitian slave revolution on August 7 just as the epidemic began and was appointed head of staff at Bush-Hill on September 20, as the epidemic reached its height. For more on Devèze and his role in the institutional response to the fever, see Powell, *Bring Out Your Dead*.

Chapter XIX

HAVING gratified my curiosity in this respect, Wallace proceeded to remind me of the circumstances of our first interview. He had entertained doubts whether I was the person, whom he had met at Lesher's. I acknowledged myself to be the same, and inquired, in my turn, into the motives of his conduct on that occasion.

I confess, said he, with some hesitation, I meant only to sport with your simplicity and ignorance. You must not imagine, however, that my stratagem was deep-laid and deliberately executed. My professions at the tavern were sincere. I meant not to injure but to serve you. It was not till I reached the head of the stair-case, that the mischievous contrivance occurred. I foresaw nothing, at the moment, but ludicrous mistakes and embarrassment. The scheme was executed almost at the very moment it occurred.

After I had returned to the parlour, Thetford charged me with the delivery of a message in a distant quarter of the city. It was not till I had performed this commission, and had set out on my return, that I fully revolved the consequences likely to flow from my project.

That Thetford and his wife would detect you in their bed-chamber was unquestionable. Perhaps, weary of my long delay, you would have fairly undressed and gone to bed. The married couple would have made preparation to follow you, and when the curtain was undrawn, would discover a robust youth, fast asleep, in their place. These images, which had just before excited my laughter, now produced a very different emotion. I dreaded some fatal catastrophe from the fiery passions of Thetford. In the first transports of his fury he might pistol you, or, at least, might command you to be dragged to prison.

I now heartily repented of my jest and hastened home that I might prevent, as far as possible, the evil effects that might flow from it. The acknowledgment of my own agency in this affair, would at least, transfer Thetford's indignation to myself to whom it was equitably due.

The married couple had retired to their chamber, and no alarm or confusion had followed. This was an inexplicable circumstance. I waited with impatience till the morning should furnish a solution of the difficulty. The morning arrived. A strange event, had, indeed, taken place in their bed-chamber. They found an infant asleep in their bed. Thetford had been roused twice in the night, once by a noise in the closet and, afterwards, by a noise at the door.

Some connection between these sounds and the foundling, was naturally suspected. In the morning the closet was examined, and a coarse pair of shoes was found on the floor. The chamber door, which Thetford had locked in the evening, was discovered to be open, as likewise a window in the kitchen.

These appearances were a source of wonder and doubt to others, but were perfectly intelligible to me. I rejoiced that my stratagem had no more dangerous consequence, and admired the ingenuity and perseverance with which you had extricated yourself from so critical a state.

This narrative was only the verification of my own guesses. Its facts were quickly supplanted in my thoughts by the disastrous picture he had drawn of the state of the hospital. I was confounded and shocked by the magnitude of this evil. The cause of it was obvious. The wretches whom money could purchase, were of course, licentious and unprincipled, superintended and controlled they might be useful instruments, but that superintendence could not be bought.[1]

What qualities were requisite in the governor of such an institution? He must have zeal, diligence and perseverance. He must act from lofty and pure motives. He must be mild and firm, intrepid and compliant. One perfectly qualified for the office it is desirable, but not possible, to find. A dispassionate and honest zeal in the cause of duty and humanity, may be of eminent utility. Am I not endowed with this zeal? Cannot my feeble efforts obviate some portion of this evil?

No one has hitherto claimed this disgustful and perilous situation. My powers and discernment are small, but if they be honestly exerted they cannot fail to be somewhat beneficial.

The impulse, produced by these reflections, was to hasten to the City-hall, and make known my wishes.[2] This impulse was controlled by recollections of my own indisposition, and of the state of Wallace. To deliver this youth to his friends was the strongest obligation. When this was discharged, I might return to the city, and acquit myself of more comprehensive duties.

Wallace had now enjoyed a few hours rest, and was persuaded to begin the journey. It was now noon-day, and the sun darted insupportable rays. Wallace was more sensible than I of their unwholesome influence. We had not reached the suburbs, when his strength was wholly exhausted, and had I not supported him, he would have sunk upon the pavement.

My limbs were scarcely less weak, but my resolutions were much more strenuous than his. I made light of his indisposition, and endeavoured to persuade him that his vigour would return in proportion to his distance from the city. The moment we should reach a shade, a short respite would restore us to health and cheerfulness.

Nothing could revive his courage or induce him to go on. To return or to proceed was equally impracticable. But, should he be able to return, where should he find a

---

[1] "Superintendance . . . bought": Mervyn argues that commercial self-interest alone cannot produce the orientation to the common good that is necessary for the well-being of public institutions. In fact, operations at Bush-Hill were gradually improved by the work of Devèze and his staff. See Powell, *Bring Out Your Dead*.

[2] "Make known my wishes": Mervyn's civic impulse to volunteer as manager of Bush-Hill hospital signals his decision to become a physician in *Second Part* but also reminds the reader of his youthful naïveté, since he does not yet possess the knowledge and experience that allowed actual physicians like Elihu Hubbard Smith, Giambattista Scandella, Jean Devèze, and Edward Stevens, all alluded to in the novel (see notes 1.2, 16.1, 18.6, II.4.5), to play constructive roles in medical responses to the fever. Mervyn will begin to amass this knowledge and experience as he "rises" toward middle-class status and builds an egalitarian circle of like-minded benevolent friends in the novel's *Second Part*.

retreat! The danger of relapse was imminent: his own chamber at Thetford's was un-occupied. If he could regain this house, might I not procure him a physician and per-form for him the part of nurse.

His present situation was critical and mournful. To remain in the street, exposed to the malignant fervours of the sun, was not to be endured. To carry him in my arms, exceeded my strength. Should I not claim the assistance of the first passenger that appeared?

At that moment a horse and chaise passed us. The vehicle proceeded at a quick pace. He that rode in it might afford us the succour that we needed. He might be persuaded to deviate from his course and convey the helpless Wallace to the house we had just left.

This thought instantly impelled me forward. Feeble as I was, I even ran with speed, in order to overtake the vehicle. My purpose was effected with the utmost difficulty. It fortunately happened that the carriage contained but one person, who stopped at my request. His countenance and guise was mild and encouraging.

Good friend, I exclaimed, here is a young man too indisposed to walk. I want him carried to his lodgings. Will you, for money or for charity, allow him a place in your chaise, and set him down where I shall direct? Observing tokens of hesitation, I con-tinued, you need have no fears to perform this office. He is not sick, but merely fee-ble. I will not ask twenty minutes, and you may ask what reward you think proper.

Still he hesitated to comply. His business, he said, had not led him into the city. He merely passed along the skirts of it, whence he conceived that no danger would arise. He was desirous of helping the unfortunate, but he could not think of risque-ing his own life, in the cause of a stranger, when he had a wife and children de-pending on his existence and exertions, for bread. It gave him pain to refuse, but he thought his duty to himself and to others required that he should not hazard his safety by compliance.

This plea was irresistable. The mildness of his manner shewed, that he might have been overpowered by persuasion or tempted by reward. I would not take advantage of his tractability;[3] but should have declined his assistance, even if it had been spon-taneously offered. I turned away from him in silence, and prepared to return to the spot where I had left my friend. The man prepared to resume his way.

In this perplexity, the thought occurred to me, that, since this person was going into the country, he might, possibly, consent to carry Wallace along with him. I confided greatly in the salutary influence of rural airs. I believed that debility constituted the whole of his complaint; that continuance in the city might occasion his relapse, or, at least, procrastinate his restoration.

I once more addressed myself to the traveller, and inquired in what direction, and how far he was going. To my unspeakable satisfaction, his answer informed me, that his home lay beyond Mr. Hadwin's, and that his road carried him directly past that

---

[3] "Tractability": openness to persuasion, compliance, direction.

gentleman's door. He was willing to receive Wallace into his chaise, and to leave him at his uncle's.

This joyous and auspicious occurrence surpassed my fondest hopes. I hurried with the pleasing tidings to Wallace, who eagerly consented to enter the carriage. I thought not at the moment of myself, or how far the same means of escaping from my danger might be used. The stranger could not be anxious on my account; and Wallace's dejection and weakness may apologize for his not soliciting my company, or expressing his fears for my safety. He was no sooner seated, than the traveller hurried away. I gazed after them, motionless and mute, till the carriage turning a corner, passed beyond my sight.

I had now leisure to revert to my own condition, and to ruminate on that series of abrupt and diversified events that had happened, during the few hours which had been passed in the city: the end of my coming was thus speedily and satisfactorily accomplished. My hopes and fears had rapidly fluctuated; but, respecting this young man, had now subsided into calm and propitious certainty. Before the decline of the sun, he would enter his paternal roof, and diffuse ineffable joy throughout that peaceful and chaste asylum.

This contemplation, though rapturous and soothing speedily gave way to reflections on the conduct which my duty required, and the safe departure of Wallace, afforded me liberty to pursue. To offer myself as a superintendent of the hospital was still my purpose. The languors of my frame might terminate in sickness, but this event it was useless to anticipate. The lofty scite and pure airs of Bush-Hill might tend to dissipate my languors and restore me to health. At least, while I had power, I was bound to exert it to the wisest purposes. I resolved to seek the City-hall immediately, and, for that end, crossed the intermediate fields which separated Sassafras from Chesnut-Street.[4]

More urgent considerations had diverted my attention from the money which I bore about me, and from the image of the desolate lady to whom it belonged. My intentions, with regard to her, were the same as ever; but now it occurred to me, with new force, that my death might preclude an interview between us, and that it was prudent to dispose, in some useful way, of the money which would otherwise be left to the sport of chance.[5]

The evils which had befallen this city were obvious and enormous. Hunger and negligence had exasperated the malignity and facilitated the progress of the pestilence. Could this money be more usefully employed than in alleviating these evils?

---

[4] "Intermediate fields . . . Chesnut-Street". Walking from Sassafras (now Race) Street on the northwest side of the city, to City Hall at Fifth and Chestnut, Mervyn crosses open fields. In 1793, urban development extended only to about Eighth Street. Areas west of that point were still open countryside with dirt paths and scattered estates.

[5] "The sport of chance": Mervyn thinks again of Clemenza and the enormous sum of money he found in Lodi's manuscript, resolving to use the money benevolently if he cannot return it to Clemenza.

During my life, I had no power over it, but my death would justify me in prescribing the course which it should take.

How was this course to be pointed out? How might I place it, so that I should effect my intentions without relinquishing the possession during my life.

These thoughts were superseded by a tide of new sensations. The weight that incommoded my brows and my stomach was suddenly increased. My brain was usurped by some benumbing power, and my limbs refused to support me. My pulsations were quickened, and the prevalence of fever could no longer be doubted.

Till now, I had entertained a faint hope, that my indisposition would vanish of itself. This hope was at an end. The grave was before me, and my projects of curiosity or benevolence were to sink into oblivion. I was not bereaved of the powers of reflection. The consequences of lying in the road, friendless and unprotected, were sure. The first passenger would notice me, and hasten to summon one of those carriages which are busy night and day, in transporting its victims to the hospital.

This fate was, beyond all others, abhorrent to my imagination. To hide me under some roof, where my existence would be unknown and unsuspected, and where I might perish unmolested and in quiet, was my present wish. Thetford's or Medlicote's might afford me such an asylum, if it were possible to reach it.

I made the most strenuous exertions; but they could not carry me forward more than an hundred paces. Here I rested on steps, which, on looking up, I perceived to belong to Welbeck's house.

This incident was unexpected. It led my reflections into a new train. To go farther, in the present condition of my frame, was impossible. I was well acquainted with this dwelling. All its avenues were closed. Whether it had remained unoccupied since my flight from it, I could not decide. It was evident that, at present, it was without inhabitants. Possibly it might have continued in the same condition in which Welbeck had left it. Beds of sofas might be found, on which a sick man might rest, and be fearless of intrusion.

This inference was quickly overturned by the obvious supposition, that every avenue was bolted and locked. This, however, might not be the condition of the bath-house, in which there was nothing that required to be guarded with unusual precautions. I was suffocated by inward, and scorched by external heat; and the relief of bathing and drinking, appeared inestimable.

The value of this prize, in addition to my desire to avoid the observation of passengers, made me exert all my remnant of strength. Repeated efforts at length enabled me to mount the wall; and placed me, as I imagined, in security. I swallowed large draughts of water as soon as I could reach the well.

The effect was, for a time, salutary and delicious. My fervours were abated, and my faculties relieved from the weight which had lately oppressed them. My present condition was unspeakably more advantageous than the former. I did not believe that it could be improved, till, casting my eye vaguely over the building, I happened to observe the shutters of a lower window partly opened.

Whether this was occasioned by design or by accident there was no means of deciding. Perhaps, in the precipitation of the latest possessor, this window had been overlooked. Perhaps it had been unclosed by violence, and afforded entrance to a robber. By what means soever it had happened, it undoubtedly afforded ingress to me. I felt no scruple in profiting by this circumstance. My purposes were not dishonest. I should not injure or purloin any thing. It was laudable to seek a refuge from the well-meant persecutions of those who governed the city. All I sought was the privilege of dying alone.

Having gotten in at the window. I could not but remark that the furniture and its arrangements had undergone no alteration in my absence. I moved softly from one apartment to another, till at length I entered, that which had formerly been Welbeck's bed-chamber.

The bed was naked of covering. The cabinets and closets exhibited their fastenings broken. Their contents were gone. Whether these appearances had been produced by midnight robbers or by the ministers of law, and the rage of the creditors of Welbeck, was a topic of fruitless conjecture.

My design was now effected. This chamber should be the scene of my disease and my refuge from the charitable cruelty of my neighbours. My new sensations, conjured up the hope that my indisposition might prove a temporary evil. Instead of pestilential or malignant fever it might be an harmless intermittent. Time would ascertain its true nature, meanwhile I would turn the carpet into a coverlet, supplying my pitcher with water, and administered without sparing, and without fear, that remedy which was placed within my reach.

Chapter XX

I LAID myself on the bed and wrapped my limbs in the folds of the carpet. My thoughts were restless and perturbed. I was once more busy in reflecting on the conduct which I ought to pursue, with regard to the bank-bills. I weighed with scrupulous attention, every circumstance that might influence my decision. I could not conceive any more beneficial application of this property, than to the service of the indigent, at this season of multiplied distress, but I considered that if my death were unknown, the house would not be opened or examined till the pestilence had ceased, and the benefits of this application would thus be partly or wholly precluded.

This season of disease, however, would give place to a season of scarcity. The number and wants of the poor, during the ensuing winter, would be deplorably aggravated. What multitudes might be rescued from famine and nakedness by the judicious application of this sum?

But how should I secure this application? To inclose the bills in a letter, directed to some eminent citizen or public officer, was the obvious proceeding. Both of these conditions were fulfilled in the person of the present chief magistrate. To him, therefore, the packet was to be sent.

Paper and the implements of writing were necessary for this end. Would they be found, I asked, in the upper room? If that apartment, like the rest which I had seen, and its furniture had remained untouched, my task would be practicable, but if the means of writing were not to be immediately procured, my purpose, momentous and dear as it was, must be relinquished.

The truth, in this respect, was easily, and ought immediately to be ascertained. I rose from the bed which I had lately taken, and proceeded to the *study*. The entries and stair cases were illuminated by a pretty strong twilight. The rooms, in consequence of every ray being excluded by the closed shutters, were nearly as dark as if it had been midnight. The rooms into which I had already passed, were locked, but its key was in each lock. I flattered myself that the entrance into the *study* would be found in the same condition. The door was shut but no key was to be seen. My hopes were considerably damped by this appearance, but I conceived it to be still possible to enter, since, by chance or by design, the door might be unlocked.

My fingers touched the lock, when a sound was heard as if a bolt, appending to the door on the inside, had been drawn. I was startled by this incident. It betokened that the room was already occupied by some other, who desired to exclude a visitor. The unbarred shutter below was remembered, and associated itself with this circumstance. That this house should be entered by the same avenue, at the same time, and this room should be sought, by two persons was a mysterious concurrence.

I began to question whether I had heard distinctly. Numberless inexplicable noises are apt to assail the ear in an empty dwelling. The very echoes of our steps are unwonted and new. This perhaps was some such sound. Resuming courage, I once more applied to the lock. The door, in spite of my repeated efforts, would not open.

My design was too momentous to be readily relinquished. My curiosity and my fears likewise were awakened. The marks of violence, which I had seen on the closets and cabinets below, seemed to indicate the presence of plunderers. Here was one who laboured for seclusion and concealment.

The pillage was not made upon my property. My weakness would disable me from encountering or mastering a man of violence. To solicit admission into this room would be useless. To attempt to force my way would be absurd. These reflections prompted me to withdraw from the door, but the uncertainty of the conclusions I had drawn, and the importance of gaining access to this apartment, combined to check my steps.

Perplexed as to the means I should employ, I once more tried the lock. This attempt was fruitless as the former. Though hopeless of any information to be gained by that means, I put my eye to the key-hole. I discovered a light different from what was usually met with at this hour. It was not the twilight which the sun, imperfectly excluded, produces, but gleams, as from a lamp; yet gleams were fainter and obscurer than a lamp generally imparts.

Was this a confirmation of my first conjecture? Lamp-light at noon-day, in a mansion thus deserted, and in a room which had been the scene of memorable and disastrous events, was ominous. Hitherto no direct proof had been given of the presence of an human being. How to ascertain his presence, or whether it were eligible by any means, to ascertain it, were points on which I had not deliberated.

I had no power to deliberate. My curiosity, impelled me to call—Is there any one within? Speak.

These words were scarcely uttered, when some one exclaimed, in a voice, vehement but half-smothered—Good God!—

A deep pause succeeded. I waited for an answer: for somewhat to which this emphatic invocation might be a prelude. Whether the tones were expressive of surprise or pain, or grief, was, for a moment dubious. Perhaps the motives which led me to this house, suggested the suspicion, which, presently succeeded to my doubts, that the person within was disabled by sickness. The circumstances of my own condition took away the improbability from this belief. Why might not another be induced like me to hide himself in this desolate retreat? might not a servant, left to take care of the house, a measure usually adopted by the opulent at this time, be seized by the reigning malady? Incapacitated for exertion, or fearing to be dragged to the hospital, he has shut himself in this apartment. The robber, it may be, who came to pillage, was overtaken and detained by disease. In either case, detection or intrusion would be hateful, and would be assiduously eluded.

These thoughts had no tendency to weaken or divert my efforts to obtain access to this room. The person was a brother in calamity, whom it was my duty to succour and cherish to the utmost of my power. Once more I spoke:—

Who is within? I beseech you answer me. Whatever you be, I desire to do you good and not injury. Open the door and let me know your condition. I will try to be of use to you.

I was answered by a deep groan, and by a sob counteracted and devoured as it were by a mighty effort. This token of distress thrilled to my heart. My terrors wholly disappeared, and gave place to unlimited compassion. I again intreated to be admitted, promising, all the succour or consolation which my situation allowed me to afford.

Answers were made in tones of anger and impatience, blended with those of grief— I want no succour—vex me not with your entreaties and offers. Fly from this spot: Linger not a moment lest you participate my destiny and rush upon your death.

These, I considered merely as the effusions of delirium, or the dictates of despair. The style and articulation denoted the speaker to be superior to the class of servants. Hence my anxiety to see and to aid him was increased. My remonstrances were sternly and pertinaciously repelled. For a time, incoherent and impassioned exclamations flowed from him. At length, I was only permitted to hear, strong aspirations and sobs, more eloquent and more indicative of grief than any language.

This deportment filled me with no less wonder than commiseration. By what views this person was led hither, by what motives induced to deny himself to my intreaties, was wholly incomprehensible. Again, though hopeless of success, I repeated my request to be admitted.

My perseverance seemed now to have exhausted all his patience, and he exclaimed, in a voice of thunder—Arthur Mervyn! Begone. Linger but a moment and my rage, tyger-like, will rush upon you and rend you limb from limb.

This address petrified me. The voice that uttered this sanguinary menace, was strange to my ears. It suggested no suspicion of ever having heard it before. Yet my accents had betrayed me to him. He was familiar with my name. Notwithstanding the improbability of my entrance into this dwelling, I was clearly recognized and unhesitatingly named!

My curiosity and compassion were in no wise diminished, but I found myself compelled to give up my purpose—I withdrew reluctantly from the door, and once more threw myself upon my bed. Nothing was more necessary in the present condition of my frame, than sleep; and sleep had, perhaps, been possible, if the scene around me had been less pregnant with causes of wonder and panic.

Once more I tasked my memory in order to discover, in the persons with whom I had hitherto conversed, some resemblance in voice or tones, to him whom I had just heard. This process was effectual. Gradually my imagination called up an image, which now, that it was clearly seen, I was astonished had not instantly occurred. Three years ago, a man, by name Colvill, came on foot, and with a knapsack on his back, into the district where my father resided. He had learning and genius, and readily obtained the station for which only he deemed himself qualified; that of a school-master.

His demeanour was gentle and modest; his habits, as to sleep, food, and exercise, abstemious and regular. Meditation in the forest, or reading in his closet, seemed to constitute, together with attention to his scholars, his sole amusement and employment. He estranged himself from company, not because society afforded no pleasure, but because studious seclusion afforded him chief satisfaction.

No one was more idolized by his unsuspecting neighbours. His scholars revered him as a father, and made under his tuition a remarkable proficiency. His character seemed open to boundless inspection, and his conduct was pronounced by all to be faultless.

At the end of a year the scene was changed. A daughter of one of his patrons, young, artless and beautiful, appeared to have fallen a prey to the arts of some detestable seducer. The betrayer was gradually detected, and successive discoveries shewed that the same artifices had been practised, with the same success upon many others. Colvill was the arch-villain. He retired from the storm of vengeance that was gathering over him, and had not been heard of since that period.

I saw him rarely, and for a short time, and I was a mere boy. Hence, the failure to recollect his voice, and to perceive that the voice of him, immured in the room above, was the same with that of Colvill. Though I had slight reasons for recognizing his features, or accents, I had abundant cause to think of him with detestation, and pursue him with implacable revenge, for the victim of his acts, she whose ruin was first detected, was—*my sister.*[1]

This unhappy girl, escaped from the upbraidings of her parents, from the contumelies of the world, from the goadings of remorse, and the anguish flowing from the perfidy and desertion of Colvill, in a voluntary death. She was innocent and lovely. Previous to this evil, my soul was linked with her's by a thousand resemblances and sympathies, as well as by perpetual intercourse from infancy, and by the fraternal relation. She was my sister, my preceptress and friend, but she died—her end was violent, untimely, and criminal!—I cannot think of her without heart-bursting grief, of her destroyer, without a rancour which I know to be wrong, but which I cannot subdue.

When the image of Colvill rushed, upon this occasion, on my thought, I almost started on my feet. To meet him, after so long a separation, here, and in these circumstances, was so unlooked-for and abrupt an event, and revived a tribe of such hateful impulses and agonizing recollections, that a total revolution seemed to have been effected in my frame. His recognition of my person, his aversion to be seen, his ejaculation of terror and surprise on first hearing my voice, all contributed to strengthen my belief.

How was I to act? My feeble frame could but illy second my vengeful purposes; but vengeance, though it sometimes occupied my thoughts, was hindered by my reason,[2] from leading me in any instance, to outrage or even to upbraiding.

All my wishes with regard to this man, were limited to expelling his image from my memory, and to shunning a meeting with him. That he had not opened the door at my bidding, was now a topic of joy. To look upon some bottomless pit, into which I was about to be cast headlong, and alive, was less to be abhorred than to look upon the face of Colvill. Had I known that he had taken refuge in this house, no power should have compelled me to enter it. To be immersed in the infection of the hospital, and to be hurried, yet breathing and observant, to my grave, was a more supportable fate.

---

[1] "*My sister*": The backstory concerning Colvill provides another seduction plot and another of the novel's many suicides when Mervyn's sister takes her own life.

[2] "Vengeance . . . was hindered by my reason": Mervyn appeals to reason, resisting the desire for revenge that blinds and ruins so many other characters in the course of the novel. See note 11.8, for example, on Captain Watson's fatal obsession with revenge. In the following paragraph Mervyn instead affirms progressive principles associated with sympathy and benevolence as rational alternatives.

I dwell, with self-condemnation and shame, upon this part of my story. To feel extraordinary indignation at vice, merely because we have partaken in an extraordinary degree, of its mischiefs, is unjustifiable. To regard the wicked with no emotion but pity, to be active in reclaiming them, in controlling their malevolence, and preventing or repairing the ills which they produce, is the only province of duty. This lesson, as well as a thousand others, I have yet to learn; but I despair of living long enough for that or any beneficial purpose.

My emotions with regard to Colvill, were erroneous, but omnipotent. I started from my bed, and prepared to rush into the street. I was careless of the lot that should befall me, since no fate could be worse than that of abiding under the same roof with a wretch spotted with so many crimes.

I had not set my feet upon the floor before my precipitation was checked by a sound from above. The door of the study was cautiously and slowly opened. This incident admitted only of one construction, supposing all obstructions removed. Colvill was creeping from his hiding place, and would probably fly with speed from the house. My belief of his sickness was now confuted.[3] An illicit design was congenial with his character and congruous with those appearances already observed.

I had no power or wish to obstruct his flight. I thought of it with transport and once more threw myself upon the bed, and wrapped my averted face in the carpet. He would probably pass this door, unobservant of me, and my muffled face would save me from the agonies connected with the sight of him.

The foot-steps above were distinguishable, though it was manifest that they moved with lightsomeness and circumspection. They reached the stair and descended. The room in which I lay, was, like the rest, obscured by the closed shutters. This obscurity now gave way to a light, resembling that glimmering and pale reflection which I had noticed in the study. My eyes, though averted from the door, were disengaged from the folds which covered the rest of my head, and observed these tokens of Colvill's approach, flitting on the wall.

My feverish perturbations increased as he drew nearer. He reached the door, and stopped. The light rested for a moment. Presently he entered the apartment. My emotions suddenly rose to an height that would not be controlled. I imagined that he approached the bed, and was gazing upon me. At the same moment, by an involuntary impulse, I threw off my covering, and, turning my face, fixed my eyes upon my visitant.

It was as I suspected. The figure, lifting in his right hand a candle, and gazing at the bed, with lineaments and attitude, bespeaking fearful expectation and tormenting doubts, was now beheld. One glance communicated to my senses all the parts of this terrific vision. A sinking at my heart, as if it had been penetrated by a dagger, seized me. This was not enough, I uttered a shriek, too rueful and loud not to have startled the attention of the passengers, if any had, at that moment been passing the street.

---

[3] "Confuted": proven wrong.

Heaven seemed to have decreed that this period should be filled with trials of my equanimity and fortitude. The test of my courage was once more employed to cover me with humiliation and remorse. This second time, my fancy conjured up a spectre, and I shuddered as if the grave were forsaken and the unquiet dead haunted my pillow.

The visage and the shape had indeed preternatural attitudes, but they belonged, not to Colvill, but to—WELBECK.

Chapter XXI

HE whom I had accompanied to the midst of the river; whom I had imagined that I saw sink to rise no more, was now before me. Though incapable of precluding the groundless belief of preternatural visitations, I was able to banish the phantom almost at the same instant at which it appeared. Welbeck had escaped from the stream alive; or had, by some inconceivable means, been restored to life.

The first was the most plausible conclusion. It instantly engendered a suspicion, that his plunging into the water was an artifice, intended to establish a belief of his death. His own tale had shewn him to be versed in frauds, and flexible to evil. But was he not associated with Colvill; and what, but a compact in iniquity, could bind together such men?

While thus musing, Welbeck's countenance and gesture displayed emotions too vehement for speech. The glances that he fixed upon me were unstedfast and wild. He walked along the floor, stopping at each moment, and darting looks of eagerness upon me. A conflict of passions kept him mute. At length, advancing to the bed, on the side of which I was now sitting, he addressed me.

What is this? Are you here? In defiance of pestilence, are you actuated by some demon to haunt me, like the ghost of my offences, and cover me with shame? What have I to do with that dauntless, yet guileless front? With that foolishly, confiding, and obsequious, yet erect and unconquerable spirit? Is there no means of evading your pursuit? Must I dip my hands, a second time, in blood; and dig for you a grave by the side of Watson?

These words were listened to with calmness. I suspected and pitied the man, but I did not fear him. His words and his looks were indicative less of cruelty than madness. I looked at him with an air compassionate and wistful. I spoke with mildness and composure.

Mr. Welbeck, you are unfortunate and criminal. Would to God I could restore you to happiness and virtue; but though my desire be strong, I have no power to change your habits or rescue you from misery.

I believed you to be dead. I rejoice to find myself mistaken. While you live, there is room to hope that your errors will be cured; and the turmoils, and inquietudes that have hitherto beset your guilty progress, will vanish by your reverting into better paths.

From me you have nothing to fear. If your welfare will be promoted by my silence on the subject of your history, my silence shall be inviolate. I deem not lightly of my promises. They are given and shall not be recalled.

This meeting was casual.[1] Since I believed you to be dead, it could not be otherwise. You err, if you suppose that any injury will accrue to you from my life; but you need not discard that error. Since my death is coming, I am not averse to your adopting the belief that the event is fortunate to you.

---

[1] "Casual": "produced by chance; accidental" (OED).

Death is the inevitable and universal lot. When or how it comes, is of little moment. To stand, when so many thousands are falling around me, is not to be expected. I have acted an humble and obscure part in the world, and my career has been short; but I murmur not at the decree that makes it so.

The pestilence is now upon me. The chances of recovery are too slender to deserve my confidence. I came hither to die unmolested, and at peace. All I ask of you is to consult your own safety by immediate flight; and not to disappoint my hopes of concealment, by disclosing my condition to the agents of the hospital.

Welbeck listened with the deepest attention. The wildness of his air disappeared, and gave place to perplexity and apprehension.

You are sick, said he, in a tremulous tone, in which terror was mingled with affection. You know this, and expect not to recover. No mother, nor sister, nor friend will be near to administer food, or medicine, or comfort; yet you can talk calmly; can be thus considerate of others—of me; whose guilt has been so deep, and who has merited so little at your hands!

Wretched coward! Thus miserable as I am, and expect to be, I cling to life. To comply with your heroic counsel, and to fly; to leave you thus desolate and helpless, is the strongest impulse. Fain would I resist it but cannot.

To desert you would be flagitious and dastardly beyond all former acts, yet to stay with you is to contract the disease and to perish after you.

Life, burthened as it is, with guilt and ignominy, is still dear—yet you exhort me to go; you dispense with my assistance. Indeed, I could be of no use, I should injure myself and profit you nothing. I cannot go into the city and procure a physician or attendant. I must never more appear in the streets of this city. I must leave you then—He hurried to the door. Again, he hesitated. I renewed my intreaties that he would leave me; and encouraged his belief that his presence might endanger himself without conferring the slightest benefit upon me.

Whither should I fly? The wide world contains no asylum for me. I lived but on one condition. I came hither to find what would save me from ruin—from death. I find it not. It has vanished. Some audacious and fortunate hand has snatched it from its place, and now my ruin is complete. My last hope is extinct.

Yes. Mervyn! I will stay with you. I will hold your head. I will put water to your lips. I will watch night and day by your side. When you die, I will carry you by night to the neighbouring field: will bury you, and water your grave with those tears that are due to your incomparable worth and untimely destiny. Then I will lay myself in your bed and wait for the same oblivion.

Welbeck seemed now no longer to be fluctuating between opposite purposes. His tempestuous features subsided into calm. He put the candle, still lighted on the table, and paced the floor with less disorder than at his first entrance.

His resolution was seen to be the dictate of despair. I hoped that it would not prove invincible to my remonstrances. I was conscious that his attendance might preclude, in some degree, my own exertions, and alleviate the pangs of death; but these consolations might be purchased too dear. To receive them at the hazard of his life would be to make them odious.

But if he should remain, what conduct would his companion pursue? Why did he continue in the study when Welbeck had departed? By what motives were those men led hither? I addressed myself to Welbeck.

Your resolution to remain is hasty and rash. By persisting in it, you will add to the miseries of my condition; you will take away the only hope that I cherished. But, however you may act, Colvill or I must be banished from this roof. What is the league between you? Break it, I conjure you; before his frauds have involved you in inextricable destruction.

Welbeck looked at me with some expression of doubt.

I mean, continued I, the man whose voice I heard above. He is a villain and be-trayer. I have manifold proofs of his guilt. Why does he linger behind you? However you may decide, it is fitting that he should vanish.

Alas! said Welbeck, I have no companion; none to partake with me in good or evil. I came hither alone.

How? exclaimed I. Whom did I hear in the room above? Some one answered my in-terrogations and intreaties, whom I too certainly recognized. Why does he remain?

You heard no one but myself. The design that brought me hither, was to be accom-plished without a witness. I desired to escape detection, and repelled your solicita-tions for admission in a counterfeited voice.

That voice belonged to one from whom I had lately parted. What his merits or de-merits are, I know not. He found me wandering in the forests of New-Jersey. He took me to his home. When seized by a lingering malady, he nursed me with fidelity, and tenderness. When somewhat recovered, I speeded hither; but our ignorance of each other's character and views was mutual and profound.

I deemed it useful to assume a voice different from my own. This was the last which I had heard, and this arbitrary and casual circumstance decided my choice.

This imitation was too perfect, and had influenced my fears too strongly, to be eas-ily credited. I suspected Welbeck of some new artifice to baffle my conclusions and mislead my judgment. This suspicion, however, yielded to his earnest and repeated declarations. If Colvill were not here, where had he made his abode? How came friendship and intercourse between Welbeck and him? By what miracle escaped the former from the river, into which I had imagined him forever sunk?

I will answer you, said he, with candour. You know already too much for me to have any interest in concealing any part of my life. You have discovered my existence, and the causes that rescued me from destruction may be told without detriment to my person or fame.

When I leaped into the river, I intended to perish. I harboured no previous doubts of my ability to execute my fatal purpose. In this respect I was deceived. Suffocation would not come at my bidding. My muscles and limbs rebelled against my will. There was a mechanical repugnance to the loss of life which I could not vanquish. My struggles might thrust me below the surface, but my lips were spontaneously shut and excluded the torrent from my lungs. When my breath was exhausted, the efforts that kept me at the bottom were involuntarily remitted, and I rose to the surface.

I cursed my own pusillanimity. Thrice I plunged to the bottom and as often rose again. My aversion to life swiftly diminished, and at length, I consented to make use of my skill in swimming, which has seldom been exceeded, to prolong my existence. I landed in a few minutes on the Jersey shore.

This scheme being frustrated, I sunk into dreariness and inactivity. I felt as if no dependence could be placed upon my courage, as if any effort I should make for self-destruction would be fruitless; yet existence was as void as ever of enjoyment and embellishment. My means of living were annihilated. I saw no path before me. To shun the presence of mankind was my sovereign wish. Since I could not die, by my own hands. I must be content to crawl upon the surface, till a superior fate should permit me to perish.

I wandered into the centre of the wood. I stretched myself on the mossy verge of a brook, and gazed at the stars till they disappeared. The next day was spent with little variation. The cravings of hunger were felt, and the sensation was a joyous one, since it afforded me the practicable means of death. To refrain from food was easy, since some efforts would be needful to procure it, and these efforts should not be made. Thus was the sweet oblivion for which I so earnestly panted, placed within my reach.

Three days of abstinence, and reverie, and solitude succeeded. On the evening of the fourth, I was seated on a rock, with my face buried in my hands. Some one laid his hand upon my shoulder. I started and looked up. I beheld a face, beaming with compassion and benignity. He endeavoured to extort from me the cause of my solitude and sorrow. I disregarded his intreaties, and was obstinately silent.

Finding me invincible in this respect, he invited me to his college, which was hard by. I repelled him at first, with impatience and anger, but he was not to be discouraged or intimidated. To elude his persuasions I was obliged to comply. My strength was gone and the vital fabric was crumbling into pieces. A fever raged in my veins, and I was consoled by reflecting that my life was at once assailed by famine and disease.

Meanwhile, my gloomy meditations experienced no respite. I incessantly ruminated on the events of my past life. The long series of my crimes arose daily and afresh to my imagination. The image of Lodi was recalled, his expiring looks and the directions which were mutually given respecting his sister's and his property.

As I perpetually revolved these incidents, they assumed new forms, and were linked with new associations. The volume written by his father, and transferred to me by tokens, which were now remembered to be more emphatic than the nature of the composition seemed to justify, was likewise remembered. It came attended by recollections respecting a volume which I filled, when a youth, with extracts from the Roman and Greek poets. Besides this literary purpose I likewise used to preserve the bank-bills, with the keeping or carriage of which I chanced to be intrusted. This image led me back to the leather-case containing Lodi's property, which was put into my hands at the same time with the volume.

These images now gave birth to a third conception, which darted on my benighted understanding like an electrical flash. Was it possible that part of Lodi's property might be inclosed within the leaves of this volume? In hastily turning it over. I recollected to have noticed leaves whose edges by accident or design adhered to each other. Lodi, in speaking of the sale of his father's West-Indian property, mentioned that the sum obtained for it, was forty thousand dollars.[2] Half only of this sum had been discovered by me. How had the remainder been appropriated? Surely this volume contained it.

The influence of this thought was like the infusion of a new soul into my frame. From torpid and desperate, from inflexible aversion to medicine and food, I was changed in a moment into vivacity and hope, into ravenous avidity for whatever could contribute to my restoration to health.

I was not without pungent regrets and racking fears. That this volume would be ravished away by creditors or plunderers, was possible. Every hour might be that which decided my fate. The first impulse was to seek my dwelling and search for this precious deposit.

Meanwhile, my perturbations and impatience only exasperated my disease. While chained to my bed, the rumour of pestilence was spread abroad. This event, however, generally calamitous, was propitious to me, and was hailed with satisfaction. It multiplied the chances that my house and its furniture would be unmolested.

My friend was assiduous and indefatigable in his kindness. My deportment, before and subsequent to the revival of my hopes, was incomprehensible, and argued nothing less than insanity. My thoughts were carefully concealed from him, and all that he witnessed was contradictory and unintelligible.

At length, my strength was sufficiently restored. I resisted all my protector's importunities, to postpone my departure till the perfect confirmation of my health. I designed to enter the city at midnight, that prying eyes might be eluded; to bear with me a candle and the means of lighting it, to explore my way to my ancient study, and to ascertain my future claim to existence and felicity.

I crossed the river this morning. My impatience would not suffer me to wait till evening. Considering the desolation of the city, I thought I might venture to approach thus near, without hazard of detection. The house, at all its avenues was closed. I stole into the back-court. A window-shutter proved to be unfastened. I entered, and discovered closets and cabinets, unfastened and emptied of all their contents. At this spectacle my heart sunk. My books, doubtless, had shared the common destiny. My blood throbbed with painful vehemence as I approached the study and opened the door.

My hopes, that languished for a moment, were revived by the sight of my shelves, furnished as formerly. I had lighted my candle below, for I desired not to awaken observation and suspicion, by unclosing the windows. My eye eagerly sought the spot where I remembered to have left the volume. Its place was empty. The object of all my hopes had eluded my grasp, and disappeared forever.

---

[2] "Forty thousand dollars": Welbeck's memory confirms the total value of Lodi's Caribbean fortune, half of which Mervyn discovered in Chapter 13 (see note 13.9). Mervyn is still carrying this $20,000 on his person.

To paint my confusion, to repeat my execrations on the infatuation, which had rendered, during so long a time, that it was in my possession, this treasure useless to me, and my curses of the fatal interference which had snatched away this prize, would be only aggravations of my disappointment and my sorrow. You found me in this state, and know what followed.

Chapter XXII

THIS narrative threw new light on the character of Welbeck. If accident had given him possession of this treasure, it was easy to predict on what schemes of luxury and selfishness it would have been expended. The same dependence on the world's erroneous estimation, the same devotion to imposture, and thoughtlessness of futurity, would have constituted the picture of his future life, as had distinguished the past.

This money was another's. To retain it for his own use was criminal. Of this crime he appeared to be as insensible as ever. His own gratification was the supreme law of his actions. To be subjected to the necessity of honest labour, was the heaviest of all evils, and one from which he was willing to escape by the commission of suicide.

The volume which he sought was mine. It was my duty to restore it to the rightful owner, or, if the legal claimant could not be found, to employ it in the promotion of virtue and happiness. To give it to Welbeck was to consecrate it to the purpose of selfishness and misery. My right, legally considered, was as valid as his.

But if I intended not to resign it to him, was it proper to disclose the truth, and explain by whom the volume was purloined from the shelf? The first impulse was to hide this truth: but my understanding had been taught, by recent occurrences, to question the justice, and deny the usefulness of secrecy in any case. My principles were true; my motives were pure: Why should I scruple to avow my principles, and vindicate my actions?

Welbeck had ceased to be dreaded or revered. That awe which was once created by his superiority of age, refinement of manners and dignity of garb, had vanished. I was a boy in years, an indigent and uneducated rustic, but I was able to discern the illusions of power and riches, and abjured every claim to esteem that was not founded on integrity. There was no tribunal before which I should faulter in asserting the truth, and no species of martyrdom which I would not cheerfully embrace in its cause.

After some pause, I said: cannot you conjecture in what way this volume has disappeared?

No: he answered with a sigh. Why, of all his volumes, this only should have vanished, was an inexplicable enigma.

Perhaps, said I, it is less important to know how it was removed, than by whom it is now possessed.

Unquestionably: and yet, unless that knowledge enables me to regain the possession it will be useless.

Useless then it will be, for the present possessor will never return it to you.

Indeed, replied he, in a tone of dejection, your conjecture is most probable. Such a prize is of too much value to be given up.

What I have said, flows not from conjecture, but from knowledge. I know that it will never be restored to you.

At these words, Welbeck looked at me with anxiety and doubt—You *know* that it will not! Have you any knowledge of the book! Can you tell me what has become of it?

Yes, after our separation on the river, I returned to this house. I found this volume and secured it, you rightly suspected its contents. The money was there.

Welbeck started as if he had trodden on a mine of gold. His first emotion was rapturous, but was immediately chastised by some degree of doubt. What has become of it? Have you got it? Is it entire? Have you it with you?

It is unimpaired. I have got it, and shall hold it as a sacred trust for the rightful proprietor.

The tone with which this declaration was accompanied, shook the new born confidence of Welbeck. The rightful Proprietor! true, but I am he. To me only it belongs and to me, you are, doubtless, willing to restore it.

Mr. Welbeck! It is not my desire to give you perplexity or anguish; to sport with your passions. On the supposition of your death, I deemed it no infraction of justice to take this manuscript. Accident unfolded its contents. I could not hesitate to chuse my path. The natural and legal successor of Vincentio Lodi is his sister. To her, therefore, this property belongs, and to her only will I give it.

Presumptuous boy! And this is your sage decision. I tell you that I am the owner, and to me you shall render it. Who is this girl! childish and ignorant! Unable to consult and to act for herself on the most trivial occasion. Am I not, by the appointment of her dying brother, her protector and guardian? Her age produces a legal incapacity of property. Do you imagine that so obvious an expedient, as that of procuring my legal appointment as her guardian, was overlooked by me? If it were neglected, still my title to provide her subsistance and enjoyment is unquestionable.[1]

Did I not rescue her from poverty and prostitution and infamy? Have I not supplied all her wants with incessant solicitude? Whatever her condition required has been plenteously supplied. This dwelling and its furniture, was hers, as far as a rigid jurisprudence would permit. To prescribe her expences and govern her family, was the province of her guardian.

You have heard the tale of my anguish and despair. Whence did they flow but from the frustration of schemes, projected for her benefit, as they were executed with her money and by means which the authority of her guardian fully justified. Why have I encountered this contagious atmosphere, and explored my way, like a thief, to this recess, but with a view to rescue her from poverty and restore to her, her own?

Your scruples are ridiculous and criminal. I treat them with less severity, because your youth is raw and your conceptions crude. But if, after this proof of the justice of my claim, you hesitate to restore the money, I shall treat you as a robber, who has plundered my cabinet and refused to refund his spoil.

These reasonings were powerful and new. I was acquainted with the rights of guardianship. Welbeck had, in some respects, acted as the friend of this lady. To vest

---

[1] "My title . . . is unquestionable": Welbeck's legalistic and tyrannical appeal to paternal authority in dismissing a woman's right to property and independence, and Mervyn's impulse to defend that right, will be repeated in similar terms in *Second Part*, Chapter 10, when Mervyn confronts Philip Hadwin over Eliza Hadwin's inheritance (see note II.10.8).

himself with this office, was the conduct which her youth and helplessness prescribed to her friend. His title to this money, as her guardian, could not be denied.

But how was this statement compatible with former representations? No mention had then been made of guardianship. By thus acting, he would have thwarted all his schemes for winning the esteem of mankind, and fostering the belief which the world entertained of his opulence and independence.

I was thrown, by these thoughts, into considerable perplexity. If his statement were true, his claim to this money was established, but I questioned its truth. To intimate my doubts of his veracity, would be to provoke abhorrence and outrage.

His last insinuation was peculiarly momentous. Suppose him the fraudulent possessor of this money, shall I be justified in taking it away by violence under pretence of restoring it to the genuine proprietor, who, for aught I know, may be dead, or with whom, at least, I may never procure a meeting? But will not my behaviour on this occasion, be deemed illicit? I entered Welbeck's habitation at midnight, proceeded to his closet, possessed myself of portable property, and retired unobserved. Is not guilt imputable to an action like this?

Welbeck waited with impatience for a conclusion to my pause. My perplexity and indecision did not abate, and my silence continued. At length, he repeated his demands, with new vehemence. I was compelled to answer. I told him, in few words, that his reasonings had not convinced me of the equity of his claim, and that my determination was unaltered.

He had not expected this inflexibility from one in my situation. The folly of opposition, when my feebleness and loneliness were contrasted with his activity and resources, appeared to him monstrous and glaring, but his contempt was converted into rage and fear when he reflected that this folly might finally defeat his hopes. He had probably determined to obtain the money, let the purchase cost what it would, but was willing to exhaust pacific expedients before he should resort to force. He might likewise question whether the money was within his reach: I had told him that I had it, but whether it was now about me, was somewhat dubious; yet, though he used no direct inquiries, he chose to proceed on the supposition of its being at hand. His angry tones were now changed into those of remonstrance and persuasion.

Your present behaviour, Mervyn, does not justify the expectation I had formed of you. You have been guilty of a base theft. To this you have added the deeper crime of ingratitude, but your infatuation and folly are, at least, as glaring as your guilt. Do you think I can credit your assertions that you keep this money for another, when I recollect that six weeks[2] have passed since you carried it off? Why have you not sought the owner and restored it to her? If your intentions had been honest, would you have suffered so long a time to elapse without doing this? It is plain, that you designed to keep it for your own use.

---

[2] "Six weeks": Mervyn sought out Lodi's manuscript the day after Watson was shot and buried in Chapter 12. For the timeline of Watson's murder, see notes 1.9 and II.19.4.

But whether this were your purpose or not, you have no longer power to restore it or retain it. You say that you came hither to die. If so, what is to be the fate of the money? In your present situation you cannot gain access to the lady. Some other must inherit this wealth. Next to *Signora Lodi*, whose right can be put in competition with mine? But if you will not give it to me, on my own account, let it be given in trust for her. Let me be the bearer of it to her own hands. I have already shewn you that my claim to it, as her guardian, is legal and incontrovertible, but this claim, I wave. I will merely be the executor of your will. I will bind myself to comply with your directions by any oath, however solemn and tremendous, which you shall prescribe.

As long as my own heart acquitted me, these imputations of dishonesty affected me but little. They excited no anger, because they originated in ignorance, and were rendered plausible to Welbeck, by such facts as were known to him. It was needless to confute the charge by elaborate and circumstantial details.

It was true that my recovery was, in the highest degree, improbable, and that my death would put an end to my power over this money; but had I not determined to secure its useful application, in case of my death? This project was obstructed by the presence of Welbeck, but I hoped that his love of life would induce him to fly. He might wrest this volume from me by violence, or he might wait till my deaths should give him peaceable possession. But these, though probable events, were not certain, and would, by no means, justify the voluntary surrender. His strength, if employed for this end, could not be resisted; but then it would be a sacrifice, not to choice, but necessity.

Promises were easily given, but were surely not to be confided in. Welbeck's own tale, in which it could not be imagined that he had aggravated his defects, attested the frailty of his virtue. To put into his hands, a sum like this, in expectation of his delivering it to another, when my death would cover the transaction with impenetrable secrecy, would be, indeed, a proof of that infatuation which he thought proper to impute to me.

These thoughts influenced my resolutions, but they were revolved in silence. To state them verbally was useless. They would not justify my conduct in his eyes. They would only exasperate dispute, and impel him to those acts of violence which I was desirous of preventing. The sooner this controversy should end, and my measure be freed from the obstruction of his company, the better.

Mr. Welbeck, said I, my regard to your safety compels me to wish that this interview should terminate. At a different time, I should not be unwilling to discuss this matter. Now it will be fruitless. My conscience points out to me too clearly the path I should pursue for me to mistake it. As long as I have power over this money I shall keep it for the use of the unfortunate lady, whom I have seen in this house. I shall exert myself to find her, but if that be impossible, I shall appropriate it in a way, in which you shall have no participation.

I will not repeat the contest that succeeded between my forbearance and his passions. I listened to the dictates of his rage and his avarice in silence. Astonishment, at my inflexibility, was blended with his anger. By turns he commented on the guilt and

155

on the folly of my resolutions. Sometimes his emotions would mount into fury, and he would approach me in a menacing attitude, and lift his hand as if he would exterminate me at a blow. My languid eyes, my cheeks glowing, and my temples throbbing with fever, and my total passiveness, attracted his attention and arrested his stroke. Compassion would take place of rage, and the belief be revived that remonstrances and arguments would answer his purpose.

Chapter XXIII

THIS scene lasted, I know not how long. Insensibly the passions and reasonings of Welbeck assumed a new form. A grief, mingled with perplexity, overspread his countenance. He ceased to contend or to speak. His regards were withdrawn from me, on whom they had hitherto been fixed; and wandering or vacant, testified a conflict of mind, terrible beyond any that my young imagination had ever conceived.

For a time, he appeared to be unconscious of my presence. He moved to and fro with unequal steps, and with gesticulations, that possessed an horrible but indistinct significance. Occasionally he struggled for breath, and his efforts were directed to remove some choking impediment.

No test of my fortitude had hitherto occurred equal to that to which it was now subjected. The suspicion which this deportment suggested was vague and formless. The tempest which I witnessed was the prelude of horror. These were throes which would terminate in the birth of some gigantic and sanguinary[1] purpose. Did he meditate to offer a bloody sacrifice? Was his own death or was mine to attest the magnitude of his despair, or the impetuosity of his vengeance?

Suicide was familiar to his thoughts. He had consented to live but on one condition: that of regaining possession of this money. Should I be justified in driving him, by my obstinate refusal, to this fatal consummation of his crimes? Yet my fear of this catastrophe was groundless. Hitherto he had argued and persuaded, but this method was pursued because it was more eligible than the employment of force, or than procrastination.

No. These were tokens that pointed to me. Some unknown instigation was at work within him, to tear away his remnant of humanity, and fit him for the office of my murderer. I knew not how the accumulation of guilt could contribute to his gratification or security. His actions had been partially exhibited and vaguely seen. What extenuations or omissions had vitiated his former or recent narrative; how far his actual performances were congenial with the deed which was now to be perpetrated, I knew not.

These thoughts lent new rapidity to my blood. I raised my head from the pillow, and watched the deportment of this man, with deeper attention. The paroxysm which controlled him, at length, in some degree subsided. He muttered, Yes. It must come. My last humiliation must cover me. My last confession must be made. To die, and leave behind me this train of enormous perils, must not be.

O Clemenza! O Mervyn! Ye have not merited that I should leave you a legacy of persecution and death. Your safety must be purchased at what price my malignant destiny will set upon it. The cord of the executioner, the note of everlasting infamy, is better than to leave you beset by the consequences of my guilt. It must not be.

Saying this, Welbeck cast fearful glances at the windows and door. He examined every avenue and listened. Thrice he repeated this scrutiny. Having, as it seemed,

---

[1] "Sanguinary": bloody, bloodthirsty.

ascertained that no one lurked within audience, he approached the bed. He put his mouth close to my face. He attempted to speak, but once more examined the apartment with suspicious glances.

He drew closer, and at length, in a tone, scarcely articulate and suffocated with emotion, he spoke: Excellent but fatally obstinate youth! Know at least the cause of my importunity. Know at least the depth of my infatuation and the enormity of my guilt.

The bills—Surrender them to me, and save yourself from persecution and disgrace. Save the woman whom you wish to benefit, from the blackest imputations; from hazard to her life and her fame; from languishing in dungeons; from expiring on the gallows!—

The bills—O save me from the bitterness of death. Let the evils, to which my miserable life has given birth terminate here and in myself. Surrender them to me, for—

There he stopped. His utterance was choked by terror. Rapid glances were again darted at the windows and door. The silence was uninterrupted except by far-off sounds, produced by some moving carriage. Once more, he summoned resolution, and spoke:

Surrender them to me, for—*they are forged.*

Formerly I told you, that a scheme of forgery had been conceived. Shame would not suffer me to add, that my scheme was carried into execution. The bills were fashioned, but my fears contended against my necessities, and forbade me to attempt to exchange them. The interview with Lodi saved me from the dangerous experiment. I enclosed them in that volume, as the means of future opulence, to be used when all other, and less hazardous resources should fail.

In the agonies of my remorse, at the death of Watson, they were forgotten. They afterwards recurred to recollection. My wishes pointed to the grave; but the stroke that should deliver me from life, was suspended only till I could hasten hither, get possession of these papers, and destroy them.

When I thought upon the chances that should give them an owner; bring them into circulation; load the innocent with suspicion; and lead them to trial, and, perhaps, to death, my sensations were fraught with agony: earnestly as I panted for death, it was necessarily deferred till I had gained possession of and destroyed these papers.

What now remains? You have found them. Happily they have not been used. Give them, therefore, to me, that I may crush at once the brood of mischiefs which they could not but generate.

This disclosure was strange. It was accompanied with every token of sincerity. How had I tottered on the brink of destruction! If I had made use of this money, in what a labyrinth of misery might I not have been involved! My innocence could never have been proved. An alliance with Welbeck could not have failed to be inferred. My career would have found an ignominious close; or, if my punishment had been transmuted into slavery and toil, would the testimony of my conscience have supported me?

I shuddered at the view of those disasters from which I was rescued by the miraculous chance which led me to this house. Welbeck's request was salutary to me, and honourable to himself. I could not hesitate a moment in compliance. The notes were enclosed in paper, and deposited in a fold of my clothes. I put my hand upon them.

My motion and attention was arrested at the instant, by a noise which arose in the street. Foot-steps were heard upon the pavement before the door, and voices, as if busy in discourse. This incident was adapted to infuse the deepest alarm into myself and my companion. The motives of our trepidation were, indeed, different, and were infinitely more powerful in my case than in his. It portended to me nothing less than the loss of my asylum, and condemnation to an hospital.

Welbeck hurried to the door, to listen to the conversation below. This interval was pregnant with thought. That impulse which led my reflections from Welbeck to my own state, past away in a moment, and suffered me to meditate anew upon the terms of that confession which had just been made.

Horror at the fate which this interview had enabled me to shun, was uppermost in my conceptions. I was eager to surrender these fatal bills. I held them for that purpose in my hand, and was impatient for Welbeck's return. He continued at the door; stooping, with his face averted, and eagerly attentive to the conversation in the street.

All the circumstances of my present situation tended to arrest the progress of thought, and chain my contemplations to one image; but even now there was room for foresight and deliberation. Welbeck intended to destroy these bills. Perhaps he had not been sincere; or, if his purpose had been honestly disclosed, this purpose might change when the bills were in his possession. His poverty and sanguineness of temper, might prompt him to use them.

That this conduct was evil and would only multiply his miseries, could not be questioned. Why should I subject his frailty to this temptation? The destruction of these bills was the loudest injunction of my duty; was demanded by every sanction which bound me to promote the welfare of mankind.

The means of destruction were easy. A lighted candle stood on a table, at the distance of a few yards. Why should I hesitate a moment to annihilate so powerful a cause of error and guilt. A passing instant was sufficient. A momentary lingering might change the circumstances that surrounded me, and frustrate my project.

My languors were suspended by the urgencies of this occasion. I started from my bed and glided to the table. Seizing the notes with my right hand, I held them in the flame of the candle, and then threw them, blazing, on the floor.[2]

The sudden illumination was perceived by Welbeck. The cause of it appeared to suggest itself as soon. He turned, and marking the paper where it lay, leaped to the

---

[2] "Seizing the notes . . . blazing, on the floor": Brown borrows this dramatic motif and volume-ending plot twist from Thomas Holcroft's *Anna St. Ives* (1792), the first important Woldwinite or radical-democratic novel of the 1790s and a major influence on Brown and his circle. At the end of that novel (Letter CXXVIII), protagonist Frank Henley throws £4,000 worth of banknotes into a fireplace to keep them from villainous Coke Clifton. On Brown's use of Holcroft in *Arthur Mervyn*, see the Introduction and Shapiro, "I Could Kiss Him One Minute and Kill Him the Next!" Eliza Hadwin will burn her father's will in a parallel gesture in Chapter II.8 (see note II.8.1).

spot, and extinguished the fire with his foot. His interposition was too late. Only enough of them remained to inform him of the nature of the sacrifice.

Welbeck now stood, with limbs trembling, features aghast, and eyes glaring upon me. For a time he was without speech. The storm was gathering in silence, and at length burst upon me. In a tone menacing and loud, he exclaimed:

Wretch! What have you done?

I have done justly. These notes were false. You desired to destroy them that they might not betray the innocent. I applauded your purpose, and have saved you from the danger of temptation by destroying them myself.

Maniac! Miscreant! To be fooled by so gross an artifice! The notes were genuine. The tale of their forgery was false, and meant only to wrest them from you. Execrable and perverse idiot! Your deed has sealed my perdition. It has sealed your own. You shall pay for it with your blood. I will slay you by inches. I will stretch you as you have stretched me, on the rack.

During this speech, all was frenzy and storm in the countenance and features of Welbeck. Nothing less could be expected than that the scene would terminate in some bloody catastrophe. I bitterly regretted the facility with which I had been deceived, and the precipitation of my sacrifice. The act, however lamentable, could not be revoked. What remained, but to encounter or endure its consequences with unshrinking firmness?

The contest was too unequal. It is possible that the frenzy which actuated Welbeck might have speedily subsided. It is more likely that his passions would have been satiated with nothing but my death. This event was precluded by loud knocks at the street-door, and calls by some one on the pavement without, of—Who is within? Is any one within?

These noises gave a new direction to Welbeck's thoughts. They are coming said he. They will treat you as a sick man and a thief. I cannot desire you to suffer a worse evil than they will inflict. I leave you to your fate. So saying, he rushed out of the room.

Though confounded and stunned by this rapid succession of events, I was yet able to pursue measures for eluding these detested visitants. I first extinguished the light, and then, observing that the parley in the street continued and grew louder, I sought an asylum in the remotest corner of the house. During my former abode here, I noticed, that a trap door opened in the ceiling of the third story, to which you were conducted by a movable stair or ladder. I considered that this, probably, was an opening into a narrow and darksome nook, formed by the angle of the roof. By ascending, drawing after me the ladder, and closing the door, I should escape the most vigilant search.

Enfeebled as I was by my disease, my resolution rendered me strenuous. I gained the uppermost room, and mounting the ladder, found myself at a sufficient distance from suspicion. The stair was hastily drawn up, and the door closed. In a few minutes, however, my new retreat proved to be worse than any for which it was possible to change it. The air was musty, stagnant, and scorchingly hot. My breathing became difficult, and I saw that to remain here ten minutes, would unavoidably produce suffocation.

My terror of intruders had rendered me blind to the consequences of immuring myself in this chearless recess. It was incumbent on me to extricate myself as speedily as possible. I attempted to lift the door. My first effort was successless. Every inspiration[3] was quicker, and more difficult than the former. As my terror, so my strength and my exertions increased. Finally my trembling hand lighted on a nail that was imperfectly driven into the wood, and which by affording me a firmer hold, enabled me at length to raise it, and to inhale the air from beneath.

Relieved from my new peril, by this situation, I bent an attentive ear through the opening with a view to ascertain if the house had been entered or if the outer door was still beset, but could hear nothing. Hence I was authorized to conclude, that the people had departed, and that I might resume my former station without hazard.

Before I descended, however, I cast a curious eye over this recess—It was large enough to accommodate an human being. The means by which it was entered were easily concealed. Though narrow and low, it was long, and were it possible to contrive some inlet for the air, one studious of concealment, might rely on its protection with unbounded confidence.

My scrutiny was imperfect by reason of the faint light which found its way through the opening, yet it was sufficient to set me afloat on a sea of new wonders and subject my fortitude to a new test—

Here Mervyn paused in his narrative. A minute passed in silence and seeming indecision. His perplexities gradually disappeared, and he continued.

I have promised to relate the momentous incidents of my life, and have hitherto been faithful in my enumeration. There is nothing which I more detest than equivocation and mystery. Perhaps, however, I shall now incur some imputation of that kind. I would willingly escape the accusation, but confess that I am hopeless of escaping it.

I might indeed have precluded your guesses and surmises by omitting to relate what befel me from the time of my leaving my chamber till I regained it. I might deceive you by asserting that nothing remarkable occurred, but this would be false, and every sacrifice is trivial which is made upon the altar of sincerity. Beside, the time may come when no inconvenience will arise from minute descriptions of the objects which I now saw and of the reasonings and inferences which they suggested to my understanding. At present, it appears to be my duty to pass them over in silence, but it would be needless to conceal from you that the interval, though short, and the scrutiny, though hasty, furnished matter which my curiosity devoured with unspeakable eagerness, and from which consequences may hereafter flow, deciding on my peace and my life.[4]

---

[3] "Inspiration": intake of breath, breathing.

[4] "Deciding on my peace and life": the novel never explains what Mervyn sees and infers in the attic crawl space or why he feels duty bound to keep this information secret. Given the emphasis Mervyn has placed on honesty and keeping secrets under ethical obligation, this omission may not be a mere oversight. For more on this scene and its possible relation to the novel's concern with slavery, see the Introduction.

Nothing however occurred which could detain me long in this spot. I once more sought the lower story and threw myself on the bed which I had left. My mind was thronged with the images flowing from my late adventures. My fever had gradually increased, and my thoughts were deformed by inaccuracy and confusion.

My heart did not sink when I reverted to my own condition. That I should quickly be disabled from moving, was readily perceived. The fore-sight of my destiny was stedfast and clear. To linger for days in this comfortless solitude, to ask in vain, not for powerful restoratives or alleviating cordials, but for water to moisten my burning lips, and abate the torments of thirst; ultimately, to expire in torpor or phrenzy, was the fate to which I looked forward, yet I was not terrified. I seemed to be sustained by a preternatural energy. I felt as if the opportunity of combating such evils was an enviable privilege, and though none would witness my victorious magnanimity, yet to be conscious that praise was my due, was all that my ambition required.

These sentiments were doubtless tokens of delirium. The excruciating agonies which now seized upon my head, and the cord which seemed to be drawn across my breast, and which, as my fancy imagined, was tightened by some forcible hand, with a view to strangle me, were incompatible with sober and coherent views.

Thirst was the evil which chiefly oppressed me. The means of relief were pointed out by nature and habit. I rose and determined to replenish my pitcher at the well. It was easier, however, to descend than to return. My limbs refused to bear me, and I sat down upon the lower step of the stair-case. Several hours had elapsed since my entrance into this dwelling, and it was now night.

My imagination now suggested a new expedient. Medlicote was a generous and fearless spirit. To put myself under his protection, if I could walk as far as his lodgings, was the wisest proceeding which I could adopt. From this design, my incapacity to walk thus far, and the consequences of being discovered in the street, had hitherto deterred me. These impediments were now, in the confusion of my understanding, overlooked or despised, and I forthwith set out upon this hopeless expedition.

The doors communicating with the court, and through the court, with the street, were fastened by inside bolts. These were easily withdrawn, and I issued forth with alacrity and confidence. My perturbed senses and the darkness hindered me from discerning the right way. I was conscious of this difficulty, but was not disheartened. I proceeded, as I have since discovered, in a direction different from the true, but hesitated not, till my powers were exhausted, and I sunk upon the ground. I closed my eyes, and dismissed all fear, and all fore-sight of futurity. In this situation I remained some hours, and should probably have expired on this spot, had not I attracted your notice, and been provided under this roof, with all that medical skill, and the tenderest humanity could suggest.[5]

---

[5] "Had not I attracted your notice . . . suggest": Mervyn addresses his listeners, the still-unnamed Dr. Stevens and Eliza Stevens, as his story comes full circle, in narrative terms, ending the novel's first part by bringing the action up to the scene with which the novel began. The reader now

In consequence of your care, I have been restored to life and to health. Your conduct was not influenced by the prospect of pecuniary recompence, of service, or of gratitude. It is only in one way that I am able to heighten the gratification which must flow from reflection on your conduct—by shewing that the being whose life you have prolonged, though uneducated, ignorant and poor, is not profligate and worthless, and will not dedicate that life which your bounty has given, to mischievous or contemptible purposes.

---

understands the events that led the feverish Mervyn to Stevens' doorstep on the novel's first page. *Second Part* will move Arthur's story into the future.

The plot summary Brown incorporated into his essay "Walstein's School of History" (included in the Related Texts), published September 1799, four or five months after this volume, sketches Mervyn's adventures to this point and confirms that his turn to civic concerns in Chapters 19–23 signals an emerging desire to become a physician. That summary and Brown's February 1799 remarks in a letter to his brother James about possible elements of the sequel indicate that much of *Second Part*'s plot and certainly its conclusion were undecided when he finished this volume.

ARTHUR MERVYN

OR,

MEMOIRS

OF

THE YEAR 1793.

SECOND PART.

BY THE AUTHOR OF WIELAND, ORMOND, HUNTLEY, &c.

NEW-YORK:

PRINTED AND SOLD BY GEORGE F. HOPKINS,
AT WASHINGTON'S HEAD, 136, PEARL-STREET.

1800.

Chapter I

HERE ended the narrative of Mervyn.[1] Surely its incidents were of no common kind. During this season of pestilence, my opportunities of observation had been numerous, and I had not suffered them to pass unimproved. The occurrences which fell within my own experience bore a general resemblance to those which had just been related, but they did not hinder the latter from striking on my mind with all the force of novelty. They served no end, but as vouchers for the truth of the tale.[2]

Surely the youth had displayed inimitable and heroic qualities. His courage was the growth of benevolence and reason, and not the child of insensibility and the nursling of habit.[3] He had been qualified for the encounter of gigantic dangers by no laborious education. He stept forth upon the stage, unfurnished, by anticipation or experience, with the means of security against fraud; and yet, by the aid of pure intentions, had frustrated the wiles of an accomplished and veteran deceiver.

I blessed the chance which placed the youth under my protection. When I reflected on that tissue of nice contingences which led him to my door, and enabled me to save from death a being of such rare endowments, my heart overflowed with joy, not unmingled with regrets and trepidation. How many have been cut off by this disease, in their career of virtue and their blossom-time of genius! How many deeds of heroism and self-devotion are ravished from existence, and consigned to hopeless oblivion!

I had saved the life of this youth. This was not the limit of my duty or my power. Could I not render that life profitable to himself and to mankind? The gains of my profession were slender; but these gains were sufficient for his maintainance as well as my own. By residing with me, partaking my instructions, and reading my books, he would, in a few years, be fitted for the practice of physic.[4] A science, whose truths are so conducive to the welfare of mankind, and which comprehends the whole system of nature, could not but gratify a mind so beneficent and strenuous as his.

---

[1] "Here ended the narrative of Mervyn": the novel's *Second Part* is not simply a continuation of part one but a "sequel" (Brown's own term in letters about the novel) that develops its characters and situations in new ways. *Second Part* appeared eighteen months after the first, in September 1800, and after Brown had published two more novels (*Edgar Huntly* and *Stephen Calvert*) in the interval.

[2] "Vouchers for the truth of the tale": Dr. Stevens (still unnamed after the entire first part) continues to supply the frame narrative during the first five chapters of the *Second Part*, providing an objective, enlightened perspective that tests and confirms the veracity of Mervyn's narrative. Mervyn's honesty, confirmed and improved in exchange with others like Stevens, can be used as a token of exchange (a voucher) to gain inclusion within the wider moral community of civil society.

[3] "Benevolence and reason, and not . . . habit.": Stevens implicitly rejects the hierarchy of ascribed status and innate predispositions, as well as the idea that an individual's social destiny is determined by embodied features such as gender and racial identities.

[4] "The practice of physic": medical practice.

This scheme occurred to me as soon as the conclusion of his tale allowed me to think. I did not immediately mention it; since the approbation[5] of my wife, of whose concurrence, however, I entertained no doubt, was previously to be obtained. Dismissing it, for the present, from my thoughts, I reverted to the incidents of his tale.

The lady whom Welbeck had betrayed and deserted, was not unknown to me. I was but too well acquainted with her fate. If she had been single in calamity, her tale would have been listened to with insupportable sympathy; but the frequency of the spectacle of distress, seems to lessen the compassion with which it is reviewed. Now that those scenes are only remembered, my anguish is greater than when they were witnessed. Then every new day was only a repetition of the disasters of the foregoing. My sensibility, if not extinguished, was blunted; and I gazed upon the complicated ills of poverty and sickness with a degree of unconcern, on which I should once have reflected with astonishment.

The fate of Clemenza Lodi was not, perhaps, more signal than many which have occurred. It threw detestable light upon the character of Welbeck, and showed him to be more inhuman than the tale of Mervyn had evinced him to be. That man, indeed, was hitherto imperfectly seen. The time had not come which should fully unfold the enormity of his transgressions and the complexity of his frauds.

There lived in a remote quarter of the city a woman, by name Villars,[6] who passed for the widow of an English officer. Her manners and mode of living were specious. She had three daughters, well trained in the school of fashion, and elegant in person, manners and dress. They had lately arrived from Europe, and for a time, received from their neighbors that respect to which their education and fortune appeared to lay claim.

The fallacy of their pretensions slowly appeared. It began to be suspected that their subsistence was derived not from pension or patrimony, but from the wages of pollution.[7] Their habitation was clandestinely frequented by men who were unfaithful to their secret; one of these was allied to me by ties, which authorized me in watching his steps and detecting his errors, with a view to his reformation.[8] From him I obtained a knowledge of the genuine character of these women.

A man like Welbeck, who was the slave of depraved appetites,[9] could not fail of being quickly satiated with innocence and beauty. Some accident introduced him to

---

[5] "Approbation": approval. As he did at the beginning of the novel's first part (see note 1.3), Stevens indicates an enlightened respect for his wife's thinking and partnership.

[6] "Villars": this passage introduces the name and character of Mrs. Villars, a brothel madam who plays an important role in *Second Part*. Besides sounding like "villain," it is notable that the name is a common place name in France, cognate with *village* or *ville* (city).

[7] "Wages of pollution": prostitution.

[8] "With a view to his reformation": as he uses surveillance as a tool for the moral reform of a young relative, also possibly a physician (see the comments four paragraphs farther on), Stevens acquires information about Villars' brothel.

[9] "Slave of depraved appetites": essentially addicted to vicious passions, in this case sexual pleasure.

the knowledge of this family, and the youngest daughter found him a proper subject on which to exercise her artifices. It was to the frequent demands made upon his purse, by this woman, that part of the embarrassments in which Mervyn found him involved, are to be ascribed.

To this circumstance must likewise be imputed his anxiety to transfer to some other the possession of the unhappy stranger. Why he concealed from Mervyn his connection with Lucy Villars, may be easily imagined. His silence, with regard to Clemenza's asylum, will not create surprise, when it is told that she was placed with Mrs. Villars. On what conditions she was received under this roof, cannot be so readily conjectured. It is obvious, however, to suppose that advantagewas to be taken of her ignorance and weakness, and that they hoped, in time, to make her an associate in their profligate schemes.

The appearance of pestilence, meanwhile, threw them into panick, and they hastened to remove from danger. Mrs. Villars appears to have been a woman of no ordinary views. She stooped to the vilest means of amassing money; but this money was employed to secure to herself and her daughters the benefits of independence. She purchased the house which she occupied in the city, and a mansion in the environs, well built and splendidly furnished. To the latter, she and her family, of which the Italian girl was now a member, retired at the close of July.

I have mentioned that the source of my intelligence was a kinsman, who had been drawn from the paths of sobriety and rectitude, by the impetuosity of youthful passions. He had power to confess and deplore, but none to repair his errors. One of these women held him by a spell which he struggled in vain to dissolve, and by which, in spite of resolutions and remorses, he was drawn to her feet, and made to sacrifice to her pleasure, his reputation and his fortune.

My house was his customary abode during those intervals in which he was persuaded to pursue his profession. Some time before the infection began its progress, he had disappeared. No tidings was received of him, till a messenger arrived intreating my assistance. I was conducted to the house of Mrs. Villars, in which I found no one but my kinsman. Here it seems he had immured himself from my enquiries, and on being seized by the reigning malady, had been deserted by the family, who, ere they departed, informed me by a messenger of his condition.

Despondency combined with his disease to destroy him. Before he died, he informed me fully of the character of his betrayers. The late arrival, name and personal condition of Clemenza Lodi were related. Welbeck was not named, but was described in terms, which, combined with the narrative of Mervyn, enabled me to recognize the paramour of Lucy Villars in the man whose crimes had been the principal theme of our discourse.

Mervyn's curiosity was greatly roused when I intimated my acquaintance with the fate of Clemenza. In answer to his eager interrogations, I related what I knew. The tale plunged him into reverie. Recovering, at length, from his thoughtfulness, he spoke.

Her condition is perilous. The poverty of Welbeck will drive him far from her abode. Her profligate protectors will entice her or abandon her to ruin. Cannot she be saved?

I know not, answered I, by what means.

The means are obvious. Let her remove to some other dwelling. Let her be apprized of the vices of those who surround her. Let her be intreated to fly. The will need only be inspired, the danger need only be shown, and she is safe, for she will remove beyond its reach.

Thou art an adventurous youth. Who wilt thou find to undertake the office? Who will be persuaded to enter the house of a stranger, seek without an introduction the presence of this girl, tell her that the house she inhabits is an house of prostitution, prevail on her to believe the tale, and persuade her to accompany him? Who will open his house to the fugitive? Whom will you convince that her illicit intercourse with Welbeck, of which the opprobrious tokens[10] cannot be concealed, has not fitted her for the company of prostitutes, and made her unworthy of protection? Who will adopt into their family, a stranger, whose conduct has incurred infamy, and whose present associates have, no doubt, made her worthy of the curse?

True. These are difficulties which I did not foresee. Must she then perish! Shall not something be done to rescue her from infamy and guilt?

It is neither in your power nor in mine to do any thing.

The lateness of the hour put an end to our conversation and summoned us to repose. I seized the first opportunity of imparting to my wife the scheme which had occurred, relative to our guest; with which, as I expected, she readily concurred. In the morning, I mentioned it to Mervyn. I dwelt upon the benefits that adhered to the medical profession, the power which it confers of lightening the distresses of our neighbors, the dignity which popular opinion annexes to it, the avenue which it opens to the acquisition of competence, the freedom from servile cares which attends it, and the means of intellectual gratification with which it supplies us.

As I spoke, his eyes sparkled with joy.[11] Yes, said he with vehemence, I willingly embrace your offer. I accept this benefit, because I know that if my pride should refuse it, I should prove myself less worthy than you think, and give you pain, instead of that pleasure which I am bound to confer. I would enter on the duties and studies of my new profession immediately, but somewhat is due to Mr. Hadwin and his daughters. I cannot vanquish my inquietudes respecting them, but by returning to Malverton and ascertaining their state with my own eyes. You know in what circumstances I parted with Wallace and Mr. Hadwin. I am not sure, that either of them ever reached home, or that they did not carry the infection along with them. I now find myself sufficiently strong to perform the journey, and proposed to have acquainted you, at this interview, with my intentions. An hour's delay is superfluous, and I hope

---

[10] "Opprobrious": shameful. The "tokens" are shameful signs of Clemenza's pregnancy, first noted in Chapters 8 and 11 (note 11.3).

[11] "His eyes sparkled with joy": Mervyn accepts Stevens' offer to oversee his medical training, opening his path to professional status and respectability. The phrasing may imply a hint of ambiguity regarding Mervyn's "vehemence" and joy for readers who recall Welbeck's "sparkling" eyes and duplicity at Wortley's soirée in Chapter 8 (see note 8.4).

you will consent to my setting out immediately. Rural exercise and air, for a week or fortnight, will greatly contribute to my health.

No objection could be made to this scheme. His narrative had excited no common affection in our bosoms for the Hadwins.[12] His visit could not only inform us of their true state, but would dispel that anxiety which they could not but entertain respecting our guest. It was a topic of some surprize that neither Wallace nor Hadwin had returned to the city, with a view to obtain some tidings of their friend. It was more easy to suppose them to have been detained by some misfortune, than by insensibility or indolence. In a few minutes Mervyn bade us adieu, and set out upon his journey, promising to acquaint us with the state of affairs, as soon as possible after his arrival. We parted from him with reluctance, and found no consolation but in the prospect of his speedy return.

During his absence, conversation naturally turned upon those topics which were suggested by the narrative and deportment of this youth. Different conclusions were formed by his two auditors. They had both contracted a deep interest in his welfare, and an ardent curiosity as to those particulars which his unfinished story had left in obscurity. The true character and actual condition of Welbeck, were themes of much speculation. Whether he were dead or alive, near or distant from his ancient abode, was a point on which neither Mervyn, nor any of those with whom I had means of intercourse, afforded any information. Whether he had shared the common fate, and had been carried by the collectors of the dead from the highway or the hovel to the pits opened alike for the rich and the poor, the known and the unknown; whether he had escaped to a foreign shore, or were destined to re-appear upon this stage, were questions involved in uncertainty.

The disappearance of Watson would, at a different time, have excited much enquiry and suspicion; but as this had taken place on the eve of the epidemic, his kindred and friends would acquiesce, without scruple, in the belief that he had been involved in the general calamity, and was to be numbered among the earliest victims. Those of his profession usually resided in the street where the infection began,[13] and where its ravages had been most destructive; and this circumstance would corroborate the conclusions of his friends.

I did not perceive any immediate advantage to flow from imparting the knowledge I had lately gained to others. Shortly after Mervyn's departure to Malverton, I was visited by Wortley. Enquiring for my guest, I told him that, having recovered his health, he had left my house. He repeated his invectives[14] against the villainy of

---

[12] "Affection . . . for the Hadwins": Mervyn's narrative sparks an experience of associative sentiment and encourages benevolent cooperation, as the Stevens feel a new bond of affection and community with the Hadwins, whom they have never met.

[13] "His profession usually resided in the street where the infection began": captains and merchants kept their offices close to the wharves, and the epidemic began around a sailor's lodging house in Water Street, a narrow street running between Front Street and the wharves. See Powell, *Bring Out Your Dead*, 8–29.

[14] "Invectives": denunciations, attacks.

Welbeck, his suspicions of Mervyn, and his wishes for another interview with the youth. Why had I suffered him to depart, and whither had he gone?

He has gone for a short time into the country. I expect him to return in less than a week, when you will meet with him here as often as you please, for I expect him to take up his abode in this house.

Much astonishment and disapprobation were expressed by my friend. I hinted that the lad had made disclosures to me, which justified my confidence in his integrity. These proofs of his honesty were not of a nature to be indiscriminately unfolded. Mervyn had authorized me to communicate so much of his story to Wortley, as would serve to vindicate him from the charge of being Welbeck's copartner in fraud; but this end would only be counteracted by an imperfect tale, and the full recital, though it might exculpate Mervyn, might produce inconveniences by which this advantage would be outweighed.

Wortley, as might be naturally expected, was by no means satisfied with this statement. He suspected that Mervyn was a wily imposter; that he had been trained in the arts of fraud, under an accomplished teacher; that the tale which he had told to me, was a tissue [15] of ingenious and plausible lies; that the mere assertions, however plausible and solemn, of one like him, whose conduct had incurred such strong suspicions, were unworthy of the least credit.

It cannot be denied, continued my friend, that he lived with Welbeck at the time of his elopement; that they disappeared together; that they entered a boat, at Pine-Street wharf, at midnight; that this boat was discovered by the owner in the possession of a fisherman at Red-bank,[16] who affirmed that he had found it stranded near his door, the day succeeding that on which they disappeared. Of all this, I can supply you with incontestible proof. If, after this proof, you can give credit to his story, I shall think you made of very perverse and credulous materials.

The proof you mention, said I, will only enhance his credibility. All the facts which you have stated, have been admitted by him. They constitute an essential portion of his narrative.

What then is the inference? Are not these evidences of a compact between them? Has he not acknowledged this compact in confessing that he knew Welbeck was my debtor; that he was apprized of his flight, but that, (what matchless effrontery!) he had promised secrecy, and would, by no means, betray him? You say he means to return; but of that I doubt. You will never see his face more. He is too wise to thrust himself again into the noose: but I do not utterly despair of lighting upon Welbeck.

---

[15] "Tissue": an interconnected network.

[16] "Red-bank": a small settlement on the New Jersey side of the Delaware River just south of the eighteenth-century city and opposite the present-day Philadelphia shipyards and Philadelphia International Airport. This is where Mervyn's boat drifted ashore after he abandoned it in Chapter 12 (see note 12.8).

Old Thetford, Jamieson and I, have sworn to hunt him through the world.[17] I have strong hopes that he has not strayed far. Some intelligence has lately been received, which has enabled us to place our hounds upon the scent. He may double and skulk; but if he does not fall into our toils[18] at last, he will have the agility and cunning, as well as the malignity of devils.

The vengeful disposition thus betrayed by Wortley, was not without excuse. The vigor of his days had been spent in acquiring a slender capital: his diligence and honesty had succeeded, and he had lately thought his situation such as to justify marriage with an excellent woman, to whom he had for years been betrothed, but from whom his poverty had hitherto compelled him to live separate. Scarcely had this alliance taken place, and the full career of nuptial enjoyments begun, when his ill fate exposed him to the frauds of Welbeck, and brought him, in one evil hour, to the brink of insolvency.

Jamieson and Thetford, however, were rich, and I had not till now been informed that they had reasons for pursuing Welbeck with peculiar animosity. The latter was the uncle of him whose fate had been related by Mervyn, and was one of those who employed money, not as the medium of traffic, but as in itself a commodity. He had neither wines nor cloths, to transmute into silver. He thought it a tedious process to exchange to day, one hundred dollars for a cask or bale, and to-morrow exchange the bale or cask for an hundred *and ten* dollars. It was better to give the hundred for a piece of paper, which, carried forthwith to the money changers, he could procure an hundred twenty-three and three-fourths. In short, this man's coffers were supplied by the despair of honest men and the stratagems of rogues.[19] I did not immediately suspect how this man's prudence and indefatigable attention to his own interest should allow him to become the dupe of Welbeck.

What, said I, is old Thetford's claim upon Welbeck?

It is a claim, he replied, that, if it ever be made good, will doom Welbeck to imprisonment and wholsome labor for life.

How? Surely it is nothing more than debt.

---

[17] "Old Thetford, Jamieson and I, have sworn to hunt him through the world": although Stevens is fond of him, the creditor Wortley, already an antagonist of Mervyn's in the first volume, now takes on a more developed role as a malevolent agent of finance capital. The vengeful pursuit of debtors is a repeated theme in the novel's *Second Part*, and here Wortley introduces and combines with the characters Old Thetford (uncle of the Walter Thetford who organized the Caribbean fraud against Welbeck) and Jamieson, two speculators who are condemned as vengeful and unscrupulous commercial predators two paragraphs farther on. On the irrationality of revenge motivation, see notes 11.8 and 20.2.

[18] "double and skulk...toils": a toil is "a trap or snare for wild beasts" (OED). Welbeck will double back on his tracks like a hunted animal to hide in Philadelphia.

[19] "The despair of honest men and the stratagems of rogues": the financial speculation and mysteries of "floating wealth" at which Mervyn marveled in Chapter 6 (note 6.1) are condemned as destructive, predatory practices.

Have you not heard? But that is no wonder. Happily you are a stranger to mercantile anxieties and revolutions. Your fortune does not rest on a basis which an untoward blast may sweep away, or four strokes of a pen may demolish. That hoary dealer in suspicions[20] was persuaded to put his hand to three notes for eight hundred dollars each. The *eight* was then dexterously prolonged to eigh*teen;* they were duly deposited in time and place, and the next day Welbeck was credited for fifty-three hundred and seventy-three, which an hour after, were *told out* to his messenger. Hard to say whether the old man's grief, shame or rage be uppermost. He disdains all comfort but revenge, and that he will procure at any price. Jamieson, who deals in the same *stuff* with Thetford, was outwitted in the same manner, to the same amount, and on the same day.[21]

This Welbeck must have powers above the common rate of mortals. Grown grey in studying the follies and the stratagems of men, these veterans were overreached. No one pities them. 'Twere well if his artifices had been limited to such, and he had spared the honest and the poor. It is for his injuries to men who have earned their scanty subsistence without forfeiting their probity, that I hate him, and shall exult to see him suffer all the rigors of the law. Here Wortley's engagements compelled him to take his leave.

---

[20] "Hoary dealer in suspicions": Old Thetford's gaming of the market (based on "suspicions" and informed guesses) merits a subtle allusion to the devil, as Wortley distinguishes what he considers honest profit, generated by production or trade in tangible commodities, from disreputable profit, generated by interest on credit or the exchange of money alone. As bad as Welbeck may be, the implication is that Thetford and Jamieson are worse and have merely been bested at their own cynical and unethical practices.

[21] "Outwitted in the same manner . . . on the same day": one knave has swindled two more, using a simple check fraud. Welbeck persuades Old Thetford and Jamieson to invest or lend him $2,400 each in three checks of $800. He forges a "1" in front of each "8," transforming 800 into 1,800 and producing $5,400 in each case, or a gross of $10,800. Minus $27 in fees for each transaction ($9 per check), Welbeck's forgery nets $5,373 from each investor, a net profit of $10,746.

Chapter II

WHILE musing upon these facts, I could not but reflect with astonishment on the narrow escapes which Mervyn's virtue had experienced. I was by no means certain that his fame or his life was exempt from all danger, or that the suspicions which had already been formed respecting him, could possibly be wiped away. Nothing but his own narrative, repeated with that simple but nervous eloquence, which we had witnessed, could rescue him from the most heinous charges. Was there any tribunal that would not acquit him on merely hearing his defence?

Surely the youth was honest. His tale could not be the fruit of invention; and yet, what are the bounds of fraud? Nature has set no limits to the combinations of fancy. A smooth exterior, a show of virtue, and a specious tale, are, a thousand times, exhibited in human intercourse by craft and subtlety. Motives are endlessly varied, while actions continue the same; and an acute penetration may not find it hard to select and arrange motives, suited to exempt from censure any action that an human being can commit.

Had I heard Mervyn's story from another, or read it in a book, I might, perhaps, have found it possible to suspect the truth; but, as long as the impression, made by his tones, gestures and looks, remained in my memory, this suspicion was impossible. Wickedness may sometimes be ambiguous, its mask may puzzle the observer; our judgment may be made to faulter and fluctuate, but the face of Mervyn is the index of an honest mind. Calm or vehement, doubting or confident, it is full of benevolence and candor. He that listens to his words may question their truth, but he that looks upon his countenance when speaking, cannot withhold his faith.[1]

It was possible, however, to find evidence, supporting or confuting his story. I chanced to be acquainted with a family, by name Althorpe, who were natives of that part of the country where his father resided. I paid them a visit, and, after a few preliminaries, mentioned, as if by accident, the name of Mervyn. They immediately recognized this name as belonging to one of their ancient neighbors. The death of the wife and sons, and the seduction of the only daughter by Colvill, with many pathetic incidents connected with the fate of this daughter, were mentioned.

This intelligence induced me to inquire of Mrs. Althorpe, a sensible and candid woman,[2] if she were acquainted with the recent or present situation of this family.

---

[1] "He that listens to his words . . . cannot withhold his faith": this paragraph is another example of Stevens' trust in sympathetic codes of bodily performance ("his tones, gestures and looks," "the face of Mervyn") as opposed to the merely formal content of speech (rumors or the ill-informed opinions of Wortley or Mrs. Althorpe) or writing (official or journalistic records).

[2] "Sensible and candid woman": in the remainder of the chapter Stevens interrogates Mrs. Althorpe, chosen as an apparently "sensible" and "ancient" (long-standing) neighbor of the Mervyn family, as to Mervyn's character. Her answers paint a malicious picture of Mervyn but also suggest her own class- and culture-bound inability to comprehend Mervyn and the codes she claims to interpret. Althorpe judges on appearances and sees Mervyn as a "strange being" who violates her highly conventional assumptions and prejudices. Mervyn responds to Althorpe's accusations in Chapter II.14.

I cannot say much, she answered, of my own knowledge. Since my marriage, I am used to spend a few weeks of summer, at my father's, but am less inquisitive than I once was into the concerns of my old neighbors. I recollect, however, when there, last year, during *the fever*, to have heard that Sawny[3] Mervyn had taken a second wife; that his only son, a youth of eighteen, had thought proper to be highly offended with his father's conduct, and treated the new mistress of the house with insult and contempt. I should not much wonder at this, seeing children are so apt to deem themselves unjustly treated by a second marriage of their parent, but it was hinted that the boy's jealousy and discontent was excited by no common cause. The new mother was not much older than himself, had been a servant of the family, and a criminal intimacy[4] had subsisted between her, while in that condition, and the son. Her marriage with his father was justly accounted by their neighbors a most profligate and odious transaction.[5] The son, perhaps, had, in such a case, a right to scold, but he ought not to have carried his anger to such extremes as have been imputed to him. He is said to have grinned upon her with contempt, and even to have called her *strumpet*[6] in the presence of his father and of strangers.

It was impossible for such a family to keep together. Arthur took leave one night to possess himself of all his father's cash, mount the best horse in his meadow, and elope. For a time, no one knew whither he had gone. At last, one was said to have met with him in the streets of this city, metamorphosed from a rustic lad into a fine gentleman. Nothing could be quicker than this change, for he left the country on a Saturday morning, and was seen in a French frock and silk stockings, going into Christ's Church[7] the next day. I suppose he kept it up with an high hand, as long as his money lasted.

---

[3] "Sawny": the first appearance of Mervyn's father's name, a pejorative nickname for someone of Scottish ethnicity. This name and the description of the father as a "Scotch peasant" (see p. 179) again imply that Mervyn's family is likely "Scots-Irish" or Protestant Irish and that Mervyn is positioned, like important characters in other Brown novels, as a wandering, displaced Irishman whose experience and truthfulness are interrogated and devalued by dominant Anglo-Quaker groups (the matron Mrs. Althorpe in this instance) who consider themselves ethnically distinct from and superior to this population. For the first passages on Mervyn's Scots-Irish ethnicity, see note 2.6.

[4] "Criminal intimacy": sexual relations outside marriage. Mrs. Althorpe accuses Mervyn of an affair with Betty Lawrence, the former indentured servant and "wild girl" who became his mother-in-law in Chapter 2.

[5] "A most profligate and odious transaction": in other words, prostitution or a cynical arrangement bordering on prostitution.

[6] "*Strumpet*": prostitute.

[7] "Christ's Church": the first Episcopal church in the U.S., located at Second and Market Streets. This church was a bastion of the city's Anglo-Protestant social elites; Washington, for example, attended services there. The implication is that Mrs. Althorpe does not understand Philadelphia's urban culture very well because, as a high place of the Anglophile elite, first Loyalist and then conservative-Federalist, Christ Church is the last place anyone would wear the "French" clothing she describes. Mervyn passes just a few yards from this church on his first night walk into the city in the scene where he quotes Milton's *Paradise Lost* (see note 3.6).

My father paid us a visit last week, and among other country news, told us that Sawny Mervyn had sold his place. His wife had persuaded him to try his fortune in the Western Country. The price of his hundred acres here would purchase a thousand there, and the man being very gross and ignorant, and withall, quite a simpleton, found no difficulty in perceiving that a thousand are ten times more than an hundred. He was not aware that a rood of ground upon Schuylkill is ten fold better than an acre on the Tenessee.[8]

The woman turned out to be an artful profligate. Having sold his ground and gotten his money, he placed it in her keeping, and she, to enjoy it with the more security, ran away to the city; leaving him to prosecute his journey to Kentucky, moneyless and alone. Sometime after, Mr. Althorpe and I were at the play, when he pointed out to me a groupe of females in an upper box, one of whom was no other than Betty Laurence. It was not easy to recognize, in her present gaudy trim, all flaunting with ribbons and shining with trinkets, the same Betty who used to deal out pecks of potatoes and superintend her basket of cantilopes in the Jersey market,[9] in paste-board bonnet and linsey petticoat.[10] Her companions were of the infamous class. If Arthur were still in the city, there is no doubt that the mother and son might renew the ancient terms[11] of their acquaintance.

The old man, thus robbed and betrayed, sought consolation in the bottle, of which he had been at all times over-fond. He wandered from one tavern to another till his credit was exhausted, and then was sent to jail, where, I believe, he is likely to continue till his death. Such, my friend, is the history of the Mervyns.

What proof, said I, have you of the immoral conduct of the son? of his mistreatment of his mother, and his elopement with his father's horse and money?

I have no proof but the unanimous report of Mervyn's neighbors. Respectable and honest men have affirmed, in my hearing, that they have been present when the boy treated his mother in the way that I have described. I was, besides, once in company

---

[8] "Tenessee": the Tennessee River, running from eastern Tennessee and northern Alabama to western Kentucky, where it joins the Mississippi River. True to his class and ethnic grouping, Mervyn's father joins the Scots-Irish dispersion from the coastal states into the trans-Appalachian frontier regions that were the object of land speculation by coastal financial elites. Althorpe dismisses this class of people as simpletons, and her contempt is echoed a generation later in Washington Irving's well-known "Legend of Sleepy Hollow" (1820). In that tale, elite narrator Diedrich Knickerbocker echoes Althorpe when he mocks the lower-class Ichabod Crane, as an itinerant parasite on gentry elites who foolishly dreams of joining the Scots-Irish diaspora and owning land in "Kentucky, Tennessee, or the Lord knows where."

[9] "Jersey market": held twice weekly in the covered market buildings on Market Street between Front and Second, ostensibly featuring the produce of New Jersey farmers. See Gilchrist, "Market Houses in High Street."

[10] "Paste-board bonnet and linsey petticoat": cheap materials. Linsey is a coarse fabric worn by the poor, workers, and slaves.

[11] "Ancient terms": since Betty's companions are "of the infamous class" or prostitutes, this is a euphemistic way to claim that Mervyn paid for sex with her.

with the old man, and heard him bitterly inveigh against his son, and charge him with the fact of stealing his horse and money. I well remember that tears rolled from his eyes while talking on the subject. As to his being seen in the city the next day after his elopement, dressed in a most costly and fashionable manner, I can doubt that as little as the rest, for he that saw him was my father, and you who know my father, know what credit is due to his eyes and his word. He had seen Arthur often enough not to be mistaken, and described his appearance with great exactness. The boy is extremely handsome, give him his due; has dark hazle eyes, auburn hair, and very elegant proportions. His air and gate have nothing of the clown in them. Take away his jacket and trowsers, and you have as spruce a fellow as ever came from dancing-school or college. He is the exact picture of his mother, and the most perfect contrast to the sturdy legs, squat figure, and broad, unthinking, sheepish face of the father[12] that can be imagined. You must confess that his appearance here is a pretty strong proof of the father's assertions. The money given for these clothes could not possibly have been honestly acquired. It is to be presumed that they were bought or stolen, for how else should they have been gotten?

What was this lad's personal deportment during the life of his mother, and before his father's second marriage?

Very little to the credit of his heart or his intellects. Being the youngest son, the only one who at length survived, and having a powerful resemblance to herself, he became the mother's favorite. His constitution was feeble, and he loved to stroll in the woods more than to plow or sow. This idleness was much against the father's inclination and judgment; and, indeed, it was the foundation of all his vices. When he could be prevailed upon to do any thing it was in a bungling manner, and so as to prove that his thoughts were fixed on any thing except his business. When his assistance was wanted he was never to be found at hand. They were compelled to search for him among the rocks and bushes, and he was generally discovered sauntering along the bank of the river, or lolling in the shade of a tree. This disposition to inactivity and laziness, in so young a man, was very strange. Persons of his age are rarely fond of work, but then they are addicted to company, and sports, and exercises. They ride, or shoot, or frolic; but this being moped away his time in solitude, never associated with other young people, never mounted an horse but when he could not help it, and never fired a gun or angled for a fish in his life. Some people supposed him to be half an idiot, or, at least, not to be in his right mind; and, indeed, his conduct was so very perverse and singular, that I do not wonder at those who accounted for it in this way.

But, surely, said I, he had some object of pursuit. Perhaps he was addicted to books.

Far from it. On the contrary, his aversion to school was as great as his hatred of the plough. He never could get his lessons or bear the least constraint. He was so much

---

[12] "Sheepish face of the father": Althorpe evokes a litany of stereotypes about Scottish bodies to contrast Sawny's "sturdy legs, squat figure, and broad, unthinking sheepish face" to Mervyn's "spruce" and "elegant proportions," supposedly inherited from the mother. This censorious contrast may imply that Althorpe thinks the mother is not herself Scots-Irish, making Mervyn a mixed-ethnicity child.

indulged by his mother at home, that tasks and discipline of any kind were intolerable. He was a perpetual truant; till the master one day attempting to strike him, he ran out of the room and never entered it more. The mother excused and countenanced his frowardness,[13] and the foolish father was obliged to give way. I do not believe he had two month's schooling in his life.

Perhaps, said I, he preferred studying by himself, and at liberty. I have known boys endowed with great curiosity and aptitude to learning, who never could endure set tasks, and spurned at the pedagogue and his rod.

I have known such likewise, but this was not one of them. I know not whence he could derive his love of knowledge or the means of acquiring it. The family were totally illiterate. The father was a Scotch peasant, whose ignorance was so great that he could not sign his name. His wife, I believe, could read, and might sometimes decypher the figures in an almanac, but that was all. I am apt to think that the son's ability was not much greater.[14] You might as well look for silver platters or marble tables in his house, as for a book or a pen.

I remember calling at their house one evening in the winter before last. It was intensely cold; and my father, who rode with me, having business with Sawney Mervyn, we stopped a minute at his gate; and, while the two old men were engaged in conversation, I begged leave to warm myself by the kitchen fire. Here, in the chimney-corner, seated on a block, I found Arthur busily engaged in *knitting stockings!* I thought this a whimsical employment for a young active man. I told him so, for I wanted to put him to the blush; but he smiled in my face, and answered, without the least discomposure, just as whimsical a business for a young active woman. Pray, did you never knit a stocking?

Yes; but that was from necessity. Were I of a different sex, or did I possess the strength of a man, I should rather work in my field or study my book.

Rejoice that you are a woman, then, and are at liberty to pursue that which costs least labor and demands most skill. You see, though a man, I use your privilege, and prefer knitting yarn to threshing my brain with a book or the barn-floor with a flail.

I wonder, said I contemptuously, you do not put on the petticoat as well as handle the needle.

Do not wonder, he replied: it is because I hate a petticoat incumbrance as much as I love warm feet. Look there (offering the stocking to my inspection) is it not well done?

I did not touch it, but sneeringly said, excellent! I wonder you do not apprentice yourself to a taylor.

He looked at me with an air of ridiculous simplicity and said, how prone the woman is to *wonder*. You call the work excellent, and yet *wonder* that I do not make

---

[13] "Frowardness": the quality of being "perverse, difficult to deal with, hard to please; refractory, ungovernable" or generally "naughty" (OED).

[14] "The son's ability was not much greater": Stevens can note that Althorpe is badly mistaken about Mervyn's language skills and love of writing.

myself a slave to improve my skill! Did you learn needle-work from seven year's squatting on a taylor's board? Had you come to me, I would have taught you in a day.

I was taught at school.

And paid your instructor?

To be sure.

'Twas liberty and money, thrown away. Send your sister, if you have one, to me, and I will teach her without either rod or wages. Will you?

You have an old and a violent antipathy, I believe, to any thing like a school.

True. It was early and violent. Had not you?

No. I went to school with pleasure; for I thought to read and write were accomplishments of some value.

Indeed? Then I misunderstood you just now. I thought you said, that, had you the strength of a man, you should prefer the plough and the book to the needle. Whence, supposing you a female, I inferred that you had a woman's love for the needle and a fool's hatred of books.

My father calling me from without, I now made a motion to go. Stay, continued he with great earnestness, throwing aside his knitting apparatus, and beginning in great haste to pull off his stockings, Draw these stockings over your shoes. They will save your feet from the snow while walking to your horse.

Half angry, and half laughing, I declined the offer. He had drawn them off, however, and holding them in his hand, be persuaded, said he; only lift your feet, and I will slip them on in a trice.

Finding me positive in my refusal, he dropped the stockings; and, without more ado, caught me up in his arms, rushed out of the room, and, running barefoot through the snow, set me fairly on my horse. All was done in a moment, and before I had time to reflect on his intentions. He then seized my hand, and, kissing it with great fervor, exclaimed, a thousand thanks to you for not accepting my stockings. You have thereby saved yourself and me the time and toil of drawing on and drawing off. Since you have taught me to wonder, let me practice the lesson in wondering at your folly, in wearing worsted shoes and silk stockings at a season like this. Take my counsel, and turn your silk to worsted and your worsted to leather. Then may you hope for warm feet and dry. What! Leave the gate without a blessing on your counsellor?

I spurred my horse into a gallop, glad to escape from so strange a being.[15] I could give you many instances of behaviour equally singular, and which betrayed a mixture of shrewdness and folly, of kindness and impudence, which justified, perhaps, the common notion that his intellects were unsound. Nothing was more remarkable than his impenetrability to ridicule and censure. You might revile him for hours, and

---

[15] "So strange a being": Althorpe is mystified by Mervyn's ironic manner, which makes fun of her stereotypical expectations for masculine behavior. Mervyn's ability to parry and resist such expectations, anticipating an antagonist's conventional thinking and turning it against them, is repeated in his confrontation with Philip Hadwin in Chapter II.10.

he would listen to you with invincible composure. To awaken anger or shame in him was impossible. He would answer, but in such a way as to show him totally unaware of your true meaning. He would afterwards talk to you with all the smiling affability and freedom of an old friend. Every one despised him for his idleness and folly, no less conspicuous in his words than his actions; but no one feared him, and few were angry with him, till after the detection of his commerce with Betty, and his inhuman treatment of his father.

Have you good reasons for supposing him to have been illicitly connected with that girl?

Yes. Such as cannot be discredited. It would not be proper for me to state these proofs. Nay, he never denied it. When reminded, on one occasion, of the inference which every impartial person would draw from appearances, he acknowledged, with his usual placid effrontery, that the inference was unavoidable. He even mentioned other concurring and contemporary incidents, which had eluded the observation of his censurer, and which added still more force to the conclusion. He was studious to palliate the vices of this woman as long as he was her only paramour; but after her marriage with his father, the tone was changed. He confessed that she was tidy, notable, industrious; but, then, she was a prostitute. When charged with being instrumental in making her such, and when his companions dwelt upon the depravity of reviling her for vices which she owed to him: True, he would say, there is depravity and folly in the conduct you describe. Make me out, if you please, to be a villain. What then? I was talking not of myself, but of Betty. Still this woman is a prostitute. If it were I that made her such, with more confidence may I make the charge. But think not that I blame Betty. Place me in her situation, and I should have acted just so. I should have formed just such notions of my interest, and pursued it by the same means. Still, say I, I would fain have a different woman for my father's wife, and the mistress of this family.

Chapter III

THIS conversation was interrupted by a messenger from my wife, who desired my return immediately. I had some hopes of meeting with Mervyn, some days having now elapsed since his parting from us, and not being conscious of any extraordinary motives for delay. It was Wortley, however, and not Mervyn, to whom I was called.

My friend came to share with me his suspicions and inquietudes respecting Welbeck and Mervyn. An accident had newly happened which had awakened these suspicions afresh. He desired a patient audience while he explained them to me. These were his words:[1]

To-day a person presented me a letter from a mercantile friend at Baltimore. I easily discerned the bearer to be a sea captain. He was a man of sensible and pleasing aspect, and was recommended to my friendship and counsel in the letter which he brought. The letter stated that a man, by name Amos Watson, by profession a mariner, and a resident at Baltimore, had disappeared in the summer of last year,[2] in a mysterious and incomprehensible manner. He was known to have arrived in this city from Jamaica, and to have intended an immediate journey to his family, who lived at Baltimore; but he never arrived there, and no trace of his existence has since been discovered. The bearer had come to investigate, if possible, the secret of his fate, and I was earnestly intreated to afford him all the assistance and advice in my power, in the prosecution of his search. I expressed my willingness to serve the stranger, whose name was Williams; and, after offering him entertainment at my house, which was thankfully accepted, he proceeded to unfold to me the particulars of this affair. His story was this.

On the 20th of last June, I arrived, said he, from the West-Indies, in company with captain Watson. I commanded the ship in which he came as a passenger, his own ship being taken and confiscated by the English.[3] We had long lived in habits of strict friendship, and I loved him for his own sake, as well as because he had married my sister. We landed in the morning, and went to dine with Mr. Keysler, since dead,

---

[1] "These were his words": this chapter unfolds new developments in the backstory of Captain Amos Watson, who was shot and buried in Welbeck's mansion in the first part; most notably revelations about another lost family fortune based on Caribbean slavery. Ultimately, this information and its implications will motivate Mervyn's trip to Baltimore in Chapters II.17–20. What follows is reported narrative from Stevens' friend Wortley and the sea captain Ephraim Williams, brother-in-law of the murdered Captain Watson.

[2] "Summer of last year": as Mervyn's wintertime journey to the Hadwin farm will reveal in Chapters II.6–7, it is now winter, early 1794. With the onset of cold weather, the epidemic is in the past.

[3] "Confiscated by the English": like the vessel seized in the Thetford fraud, Watson's ship is taken by the British in the context of Caribbean revolutionary struggle. Throughout the revolutionary wars of the 1790s, the English and French harassed each other's fleets and Caribbean trade networks. U.S.-based merchants like Watson and the Thetfords (and Brown's family) were able to make stupendous profits during these years by reexporting Caribbean goods as "neutrals" but were exposed to catastrophic losses by seizure in this context as well.

but who then lived in Water-Street.[4] He was extremely anxious to visit his family, and having a few commissions to perform in the city, which would not demand more than a couple of hours, he determined to set out next morning in the stage. Meanwhile, I had engagements which required me to repair with the utmost expedition to New-York. I was scarcely less anxious than my brother to reach Baltimore, where my friends also reside, but there was an absolute necessity of going eastward. I expected, however, to return hither in three days, and then to follow Watson home. Shortly after dinner we parted; he to execute his commissions, and I to embark in the mail-stage.

In the time prefixed I returned. I arrived early in the morning, and prepared to depart again at noon. Meanwhile, I called at Keysler's. This is an old acquaintance of Watson's and mine; and, in the course of talk, he expressed some surprize that Watson had so precipitately deserted his house. I stated the necessity there was for Watson's immediate departure *southward*, and added, that no doubt my brother[5] had explained this necessity.

Why, said Keysler, it is true, Captain Watson mentioned his intention of leaving town early next day; but then he gave me reason to expect that he would sup and lodge with me that night, whereas he has not made his appearance since. Beside his trunk was brought to my house. This, no doubt, he intended to carry home with him, but here it remains still. It is not likely that in the hurry of departure his baggage was forgotten. Hence, I inferred that he was still in town, and have been puzzling myself these three days with conjectures, as to what is become of him. What surprizes me more is, that, on enquiring among the few friends which he has in this city, I find them as ignorant of his motions as myself. I have not, indeed, been wholly without apprehensions that some accident or other has befallen him.

I was not a little alarmed by this intimation. I went myself, agreeably to Keysler's directions, to Watson's friends, and made anxious enquiries, but none of them had seen my brother since his arrival. I endeavored to recollect the commissions which he designed to execute, and, if possible, to trace him to the spot where he last appeared. He had several packets to deliver, one of which was addressed to Walter Thetford. Him, after some enquiry, I found out, but unluckily he chanced to be in the country. I found, by questioning a clerk[6] who transacted his business in his absence, that a person, who answered the minute description which I gave of Watson, had been there on the day on which I parted with him, and had left papers relative to the capture of one of Thetford's vessels by the English.[7] This was the sum of the information he was able to afford me.

---

[4] "Water-Street": the waterfront street where the epidemic began, previously mentioned in this part's Chapter 1 (see note II.1.13).

[5] "Brother": used loosely, since Watson is Williams' brother-in-law.

[6] "A clerk": likely Wallace, since he was employed by Thetford as a clerk.

[7] "By the English": this is the seizure arranged by the Thetfords as part of their conspiracy to defraud Welbeck, discussed in Chapters 11 and 14 of the first part. See notes 11.6 and 14.9 on that conspiracy.

I then applied to three merchants for whom my brother had letters. They all acknowledged the receipt of these letters, but they were delivered through the medium of the post-office.[8]

I was extremely anxious to reach home. Urgent engagements compelled me to go on without delay. I had already exhausted all the means of enquiry within my reach, and was obliged to acquiesce in the belief, that Watson had proceeded homeward at the time appointed, and left, by forgetfulness or accident, his trunk behind him. On examining the books kept at the stage offices, his name no where appeared, and no conveyance by water had occurred during the last week. Still the only conjecture I could form, was that he had gone homeward.

Arriving at Baltimore, I found that Watson had not yet made his appearance. His wife produced a letter, which, by the post mark, appeared to have been put into the office at Philadelphia, on the morning after our arrival, and on which he had designed to commence his journey. This letter had been written by my brother, in my presence, but I had dissuaded him from sending it, since the same coach that should bear the letter, was likewise to carry himself. I had seen him put it unwafered in his pocket-book, but this letter, unaltered in any part, and containing money which he had at first intended to enclose in it, was now conveyed to his wife's hand. In this letter he mentioned his design of setting out for Baltimore, on the *twenty-first*, yet, on that day the letter itself had been put into the office.

We hoped that a short time would clear up this mystery, and bring the fugitive home, but from that day till the present, no atom of intelligence has been received concerning him. The yellow-fever, which quickly followed, in this city, and my own engagements have hindered me, till now, from coming hither and resuming the search.

My brother was one of the most excellent of men. His wife loved him to distraction, and, together with his children, depended for subsistence upon his efforts. You will not, therefore, be surprized that his disappearance excited, in us, the deepest consternation and distress; but I have other, and peculiar reasons for wishing to know his fate. I gave him several bills of exchange[9] on merchants of Baltimore, which I had re-

---

[8] "Post-office": these are the three letters Mervyn deposited at the post office after the boat episode in Chapter 12 of the first part. The fourth letter, containing $150, which Mervyn sealed and sent to Watson's wife at the same time, is recalled two paragraphs farther on. Welbeck gave Mervyn Watson's "pocket-book" containing the letters and money after they buried Watson beneath Welbeck's mansion.

[9] "Bills of exchange": an early-modern credit instrument different from money or checks. Historian Fernand Braudel refers to them as "the key weapon in the armoury of merchant capitalism." Watson was entrusted with three of these bills by his brother-in-law Captain Williams. Merchants commonly used bills of exchange that required another payer (a wealthier merchant) to make payment to the named payee; the payer would "discount" the bill, taking a percentage of the whole as a commission. Bills of exchange were an important feature of the period's market circuits and often involved a chain of transactions. Redeeming such bills at discount would be one element of the financial trade practiced by men at the top of the mercantile food chain, such as Old Thetford and

ceived in payment of my cargo, in order that they might, as soon as possible, be presented and accepted. These have disappeared with the bearer. There is likewise another circumstance that makes his existence of no small value.

There is an English family, who formerly resided in Jamaica, and possessed an estate of great value, but who, for some years, have lived in the neighborhood of Baltimore. The head of this family died a year ago, and left a widow and three daughters. The lady tho't it eligible to sell her husband's property in Jamaica, the Island becoming hourly more exposed to the chances of war and revolution,[10] and transfer it to the United States, where she purposes henceforth to reside. Watson had been her husband's friend, and his probity and disinterestedness being well known, she entrusted him with legal powers to sell this estate. This commission was punctually performed, and the purchase money was received. In order to confer on it the utmost possible security, he rolled up four bills of exchange, drawn upon opulent merchants of London, in a thin sheet of lead, and depositing this roll in a leathern girdle, fastened it round his waist, and under his clothes; a second set he gave to me, and a third he dispatched to Mr. Keysler, by a vessel which sailed a few days before him. On our arrival in this city, we found that Keysler had received those transmitted to him, and which he had been charged to keep till our arrival. They were now produced and, together with those which I had carried, were delivered to Watson. By him they were joined to those in the girdle,[11] which he still wore, conceiving this method of conveyance to be safer than any other, and, at the same time, imagining it needless, in so short a journey as remained to be performed, to resort to other expedients.

The sum which he thus bore about him, was no less than ten thousand pounds sterling.[12] It constituted the whole patrimony of a worthy and excellent family, and the loss of it reduces them to beggary. It is gone with Watson, and whither Watson has gone, it is impossible even to guess.

Jamieson. On bills of exchange, see Braudel, *Civilization and Capitalism* 2.142–48, 3.66–67, and 3.243–45.

[10] "Jamaica . . . exposed to . . . war and revolution": like the Lodi fortune described in the first part, the Maurice family fortune is tied to Caribbean slave economy and destabilized by the waves of revolutionary slave insurrection now reaching Philadelphia. Jamaica was the second most lucrative sugar colony after Haiti and, although it did not have a full-scale revolution like Haiti, the threat of insurrection leads the Maurices to sell their plantation there and transfer their money northward. This is a secondary wave, since after the Haitian revolt began in 1791, many Haitian planters initially fled to Jamaica and transferred their money to that island for safekeeping. For the revolutionary context in Jamaica, see Geggus, "Jamaica and the Saint Domingue Slave Revolt."

[11] "Four bills of exchange . . . a second set . . . a third . . . joined to those in the girdle": in addition to the bills of exchange he carried on behalf of brother-in-law Williams, Watson was also entrusted with the value of the Maurices' Jamaican plantation, carried in yet more bills of exchange. To lower the risk of transporting an immense sum, Watson divided the Maurice bills into three sets, which he reassembled in Philadelphia and was carrying secretly on his own body in a money belt when he was buried beneath Welbeck's mansion.

[12] "Ten thousand pounds sterling": a British pound was worth 4.5 dollars at this time, making this sum about 45,000 1793 dollars.

You may now easily conceive, Sir, the dreadful disasters which may be connected with this man's fate, and with what immeasurable anxiety his family and friends have regarded his disappearance. That he is alive, can scarcely be believed, for in what situation could he be placed in which he would not be able and willing to communicate some tidings of his fate to his family?

Our grief has been unspeakably aggravated by the suspicions which Mrs. Maurice and her friends have allowed themselves to admit. They do not scruple to insinuate, that Watson, tempted by so great a prize, has secretly embarked for England, in order to obtain payment for these bills, and retain the money for his own use.

No man was more impatient of poverty than Watson, but no man's honesty was more inflexible. He murmured at the destiny that compelled him to sacrifice his ease, and risk his life upon the ocean in order to procure the means of subsistence; and all the property which he had spent the best part of his life in collecting, had just been ravished away from him by the English; but if he had yielded to this temptation at any time, it would have been on receiving these bills at Jamaica. Instead of coming hither, it would have been infinitely more easy and convenient to have embarked directly for London; but none, who thoroughly knew him, can, for a moment, harbor a suspicion of his truth.

If he be dead, and if the bills are not to be recovered, yet, to ascertain this, will, at last, serve to vindicate his character. As long as his fate is unknown, his fame will be loaded with the most flagrant imputations, and if these bills be ever paid in London these imputations will appear to be justified. If he has been robbed, the robber will make haste to secure the payment, and the Maurices may not unreasonably conclude that the robber was Watson himself. Many other particulars were added by the stranger, to show the extent of the evils flowing from the death of his brother, and the loss of the papers which he carried with him.

I was greatly at a loss, continued Wortley, what directions or advice to afford this man. Keysler, as you know, died early of the pestilence; but Keysler was the only resident in this city with whom Williams had any acquaintance. On mentioning the propriety of preventing the sale of these bills in America, by some public notice, he told me that this caution had been early taken; and I now remembered seeing the advertisement, in which the bills had been represented as having been lost or stolen in this city, and a reward of a thousand dollars[13] was offered to any one who should restore them. This caution had been published in September, in all the trading towns from Portsmouth to Savannah, but had produced no satisfaction.

I accompanied Williams to the mayor's office, in hopes of finding in the records of his proceedings, during the last six months, some traces of Watson, but neither these records nor the memory of the magistrate, afforded us any satisfaction. Watson's friends had drawn up, likewise, a description of the person and dress of the fugitive, an account of the incidents attending his disappearance, and of the papers which he

---

[13] "Advertisement . . . a thousand dollars": such advertisements were commonly published up and down the seaboard, announcing searches and rewards for runaway slaves, bound servants, or criminals. The $1,000 reward will become a topic of discussion in Chapter II.19.

had in his possession, with the manner in which these papers had been secured. These had been already published in the Southern newspapers, and have been just reprinted in our own. As the former notice had availed nothing, this second expedient was thought necessary to be employed.

After some reflection, it occurred to me that it might be proper to renew the attempt which Williams had made to trace the footsteps of his friend to the moment of his final disappearance. He had pursued Watson to Thetford's, but Thetford himself had not been seen, and he had been contented with the vague information of his clerk. Thetford and his family, including his clerk, had perished, and it seemed as if this source of information was dried up. It was possible, however, that old Thetford might have some knowledge of his nephew's transactions, by which some light might chance to be thrown upon this obscurity. I therefore called on him, but found him utterly unable to afford me the light that I wished. My mention of the packet which Watson had brought to Thetford, containing documents respecting the capture of a certain ship, reminded him of the injuries which he had received from Welbeck, and excited him to renew his menaces and imputations on that wretch. Having somewhat exhausted this rhetoric, he proceeded to tell me what connection there was between the remembrance of his injuries and the capture of this vessel.

This vessel and its cargo were, in fact, the property of Welbeck. They had been sent to a good market and had been secured by an adequate insurance. The value of this ship and cargo, and the validity of the policy he had taken care to ascertain by means of his two nephews, one of whom had gone out supercargo. This had formed his inducement to lend his three notes to Welbeck, in exchange for three other notes, the whole amount of which included the *equitable interest* of *five per cent. per month* on his own loan. For the payment of these notes, he by no means relied, as the world foolishly imagined, on the seeming opulence and secret funds of Welbeck. These were illusions too gross to have any influence on him. He was too old a bird to be decoyed into the net by *such* chaff.[14] No; his nephew, the supercargo, would of course receive the produce of the voyage, and so much of this produce as would pay his debt. He had procured the owner's authority to intercept its passage from the pocket of his nephew to that of Welbeck. In case of loss, he had obtained a similar security upon the policy. Jamieson's proceedings had been the same with his own, and no affair in which he had ever engaged, had appeared to be more free from hazard than this. Their calculations, however though plausible, were defeated. The ship was taken and condemned, for a cause which rendered the insurance ineffectual.

I bestowed no time in reflecting on this tissue of extortions and frauds, and on that course of events which so often disconcerts the stratagems of cunning.[15] The names

---

[14] "Chaff": worthless husks, from the proverbial "an old bird is not caught with chaff."

[15] "This tissue of extortions and frauds . . . disconcerts the stratagems of cunning": in other words, given what Old Thetford has just explained about his calculations and losses in the same voyage in which Welbeck was defrauded, the Thetford brothers have successfully defrauded their uncle and Jamieson as well. Walter Thetford has died in the epidemic, so the entire sum remains with his younger brother Thomas (the supercargo) in the Caribbean.

of Welbeck and Watson were thus associated together, and filled my thoughts with restlessness and suspicion. Welbeck was capable of any wickedness. It was possible an interview had happened between these men, and that the fugitive had been someway instrumental in Watson's fate. These thoughts were mentioned to Williams, whom the name of Welbeck threw into the utmost perturbation. On finding that one of this name had dwelt in this city, and, that he had proved a villain, he instantly admitted the most dreary forebodings.

I have heard, said Williams, the history of this Welbeck a score of times from my brother. There formerly subsisted a very intimate connection between them. My brother had conferred upon one whom he thought honest, innumerable benefit, but all his benefits had been repaid by the blackest treachery. Welbeck's character and guilt had often been made the subject of talk between us, but, on these occasions, my brother's placid and patient temper forsook him. His grief for the calamities which had sprung from this man, and his desire of revenge, burst all bounds, and transported him to a pitch of temporary frenzy. I often enquired in what manner he intended to act, if a meeting should take place between them. He answered, that doubtless he should act like a maniac, in defiance of his sober principles, and of the duty which he owed his family.[16]

What, said I, would you stab or pistol him?

No! I was not born for an assassin. I would upbraid him in such terms as the furious moment might suggest, and then challenge him to a meeting, from which either he or I should not part with life. I would allow time for him to make his peace with Heaven, and for me to blast his reputation upon earth, and to make such provision for my possible death, as duty and discretion would prescribe.

Now, nothing is more probable than that Welbeck and my brother have met. Thetford would of course mention his name and interest in the captured ships, and hence the residence of this detested being in this city, would be made known. Their meeting could not take place without some dreadful consequence. I am fearful that to that meeting we must impute the disappearance of my brother.

---

[16] "Act like a maniac, in defiance of his sober principles . . . family": Williams correctly infers Watson's actual fate and renews the novel's emphasis on the irrational and destructive consequences of revenge motivation. For the earlier critique of vengeance, see notes 11.8, 20.2, II.1.17.

Chapter IV

HERE was new light thrown upon the character of Welbeck, and new food administered to my suspicions.[1] No conclusion could be more plausible than that which Williams had drawn; but how should it be rendered certain? Walter Thetford, or some of his family, had possibly been witnesses of something, which, added to our previous knowledge, might strengthen or prolong that clue, one end of which seemed now to be put into our hands; but Thetford's father-in-law was the only one of his family who, by seasonable flight from the city, had escaped the pestilence. To him, who still resided in the country, I repaired with all speed, accompanied by Williams.

The old man being reminded, by a variety of circumstances, of the incidents of that eventful period was, at length, enabled to relate that he had been present at the meeting which took place between Watson and his son Walter, when certain packets were delivered by the former, relative, as he quickly understood, to the condemnation of a ship in which Thomas Thetford had gone supercargo. He had noticed some emotion of the stranger, occasioned by his son's mentioning the concern which Welbeck had in the vessel. He likewise remembered the stranger's declaring his intention of visiting Welbeck, and requesting Walter to afford him directions to his house.

Next morning at the breakfast table, continued the old man, I adverted to yesterday's incidents, and asked my son how Welbeck had borne the news of the loss of his ship. He bore it, says Walter, as a man of his wealth ought to bear so trivial a loss. But there was something very strange in his behaviour, says my son, when I mentioned the name of the captain who brought the papers; and when I mentioned the captain's design of paying him a visit, he stared upon me, for a moment, as if he were frighted out of his wits, and then, snatching up his hat, ran furiously out of the house. This was all my son said upon that occasion; but, as I have since heard, it was on that very night, that Welbeck absconded from his creditors.

I have this moment returned from this interview with old Thetford. I come to you, because I thought it possible that Mervyn, agreeably to your expectations, had returned, and I wanted to see the lad once more. My suspicions with regard to him have been confirmed, and a warrant was this day issued for apprehending him as Welbeck's accomplice.

I was startled by this news. My friend, said I, be cautious how you act, I beseech you. You know not in what evils you may involve the innocent. Mervyn I know to be blameless; but Welbeck is indeed, a villain. The latter I shall not be sorry to see brought to justice, but the former, instead of meriting punishment is entitled to rewards.

---

[1] "My suspicions": in the first three paragraphs of this chapter, Stevens reflects on Wortley's information and collects new clues concerning Watson's disappearance from Walter Thetford's father-in-law. Wortley breaks back in abruptly with "I have this moment returned" in paragraph four, initiating a heated dialogue between Wortley and Stevens.

So you believe, on the mere assertion of the boy, perhaps, his plausible lies might produce the same effect upon me, but I must stay till he thinks proper to exert his skill. The suspicions to which he is exposed will not easily be obviated; but if he has any thing to say in his defence, his judicial examination will afford him the suitable opportunity. Why are you so much afraid to subject his innocence to this test? It was not till you heard his tale, that your own suspicions were removed. Allow me the same privilege of unbelief.

But you do me wrong, in deeming me the cause of his apprehension. It is Jamieson and Thetford's work, and they have not proceeded on shadowy surmises and the impulses of mere revenge. Facts have come to light of which you are wholly unaware, and which, when known to you, will conquer even your incredulity as to the guilt of Mervyn.

Facts? Let me know them, I beseech you. If Mervyn has deceived me, there is an end to my confidence in human nature. All limits to dissimulation, and all distinctions between vice and virtue will be effaced. No man's word, no force of collateral evidence shall weigh with me an hair.

It was time, replied my friend, that your confidence in smooth features and fluent accents should have ended long ago. Till I gained from my present profession, some knowledge of the world, a knowledge which was not gained in a moment, and has not cost a trifle, I was equally wise in my own conceit; and, in order to decide upon the truth of any one's pretensions, needed only a clear view of his face and a distinct hearing of his words. My folly, in that respect, was only to be cured, however, by my own experience, and I suppose your credulity will yield to no other remedy. These are the facts.

Mrs. Wentworth, the proprietor of the house in which Welbeck lived,[2] has furnished some intelligence respecting Mervyn, whose truth cannot be doubted, and which furnishes the strongest evidence of a conspiracy between this lad and his employer. It seems, that, some years since, a nephew of this lady left his father's family clandestinely, and has not been heard of since. This nephew was intended to inherit her fortunes, and her anxieties and enquiries respecting him have been endless and incessant. These, however, have been fruitless. Welbeck, knowing these circumstances, and being desirous of substituting a girl whom he had moulded for his purpose, in place of the lost youth, in the affections of the lady while living, and in her testament when dead, endeavored to persuade her that the youth had died in some foreign country. For this end, Mervyn was to personate a kinsman of Welbeck who

---

[2] "Proprietor of the house in which Welbeck lived": Wortley is close but not correct in this assertion, since Wentworth only collects the rent on behalf of the mansion's owner, her brother. Wentworth herself explained in the first part's Chapter 7 that Clavering's father (her brother) owns the house (note 7.7). This could be an inconsistency on Brown's part, but more likely hints that Wortley's information is incomplete and not entirely accurate, and that he is prone to unverified assumptions and "imputations," as Stevens eventually concludes. Although Wortley angrily lectures Stevens after he asks for proof of Wortley's accusations ("Facts? Let me know them, I beseech you."), the very first "fact" that he offers is mistaken. The passage also clarifies the earlier explanation of Welbeck's attempt to use Mervyn in defrauding Mrs. Wentworth.

had just arrived from Europe, and who had been a witness of her nephew's death. A story was, no doubt, to be contrived, where truth should be copied with the most exquisite dexterity, and the lady, being prevailed upon to believe the story, the way was cleared for accomplishing the remainder of the plot.

In due time, and after the lady's mind had been artfully prepared by Welbeck, the pupil made his appearance; and, in a conversation full of studied ambiguities, assured the lady, that her nephew was dead. For the present he declined relating the particulars of his death, and displayed a constancy and intrepidity in resisting her intreaties, that would have been admirable in a better cause. Before she had time to fathom this painful mystery, Welbeck's frauds were in danger of detection, and he and his pupil suddenly disappeared.

While the plot was going forward, there occurred an incident which the plotters had not foreseen or precluded, and which possibly might have created some confusion or impediment in their designs. A bundle was found one night in the street, consisting of some coarse clothes, and containing, in the midst of it, the miniature portrait of Mrs. Wentworth's nephew. It fell into the hands of one of that lady's friends, who immediately dispatched the bundle to her. Mervyn, in his interview with this lady, spied the portrait on the mantle-piece. Led by some freak of fancy, or some web of artifice, he introduced the talk respecting her nephew, by boldly claiming it as his; but, when the mode in which it had been found was mentioned, he was disconcerted and confounded, and precipitately withdrew.

This conduct, and the subsequent flight of the lad, afforded ground enough to question the truth of his intelligence respecting her nephew; but it has since been confuted, in a letter just received from her brother in England. In this letter she is informed, that her nephew had been seen by one who knew him well, in Charleston; that some intercourse took place between the youth and the bearer of the news, in the course of which the latter had persuaded the nephew to return to his family, and that the youth had given some tokens of compliance. The letter-writer, who was father to the fugitive, had written to certain friends at Charleston, intreating them to use their influence with the runaway to the same end, and, at any rate, to cherish and protect him. Thus, I hope you will admit that the duplicity of Mervyn is demonstrated.

The facts which you have mentioned, said I, after some pause, partly correspond with Mervyn's story; but the last particular is irreconcileably repugnant to it. Now, for the first time, I begin to feel that my confidence is shaken. I feel my mind bewildered and distracted by the multitude of new discoveries which have just taken place. I want time to revolve them slowly, to weigh them accurately, and to estimate their consequences fully. I am afraid to speak; fearing, that, in the present trouble of my thoughts, I may say something which I may afterwards regret. I want a counsellor; but you, Wortley, are unfit for the office.[3] Your judgment is unfurnished with the

---

[3] "Unfit for the office": Stevens refuses to jump to conclusions, rejecting Wortley as too emotional and prone to hasty judgments to supply reliable counsel. Instead he consults his wife, placing confidence

same materials; your sufferings have soured your humanity and biassed your candor. The only one qualified to divide with me these cares, and aid in selecting the best mode of action, is my wife. She is mistress of Mervyn's history; an observer of his conduct during his abode with us; and is hindered, by her education and temper, from deviating into rigor and malevolence. Will you pardon me, therefore, if I defer commenting on your narrative till I have had an opportunity of reviewing it and comparing it with my knowledge of the lad, collected from himself and from my own observation.

Wortley could not but admit the justice of my request, and after some desultory conversation we parted. I hastened to communicate to my wife the various intelligence which I had lately received. Mrs. Althorpe's portrait of the Mervyns contained lineaments which the summary detail of Arthur did not enable us fully to comprehend. The treatment which the youth is said to have given to his father; the illicit commerce that subsisted between him and his father's wife; the pillage of money and his father's horse, but ill accorded with the tale which we had heard, and disquieted our minds with doubts, though far from dictating our belief.

What, however, more deeply absorbed our attention, was the testimony of Williams and of Mrs. Wentworth. That which was mysterious and inscrutable to Wortley and the friends of Watson, was luminous to us. The coincidence between the vague hints, laboriously collected by these enquirers, and the narrative of Mervyn, afforded the most cogent attestation of the truth of that narrative.

Watson had vanished from all eyes, but the spot where rested his remains was known to us. The girdle spoken of by Williams, would not be suspected to exist by his murderer. It was unmolested, and was doubtless buried with him. That which was so earnestly sought, and which constituted the subsistence of the Maurices, would probably be found adhering to his body. What conduct was incumbent upon me who possessed this knowledge?

It was just to restore these bills to their true owner; but how could this be done without hazardous processes and tedious disclosures? To whom ought these disclosures to be made? By what authority or agency could these half-decayed limbs be dug up, and the lost treasure be taken from amidst the horrible corruption[4] in which it was immersed?

This ought not to be the act of a single individual. This act would entangle him in a maze of perils and suspicions, of concealments and evasions, from which he could not hope to escape with his reputation inviolate. The proper method was through the agency of the law. It is to this that Mervyn must submit his conduct. The story

---

in a woman shaped by rational education. Once again Stevens places more faith in rational, acquired behaviors than in embodied qualities such as gender, age, or social status.

[4] "Lost treasure . . . horrible corruption": the novel's elaborate juxtaposition of social and bodily corruption is condensed into the arresting gothic image of a decomposing corpse encircled by the "treasure" of a Jamaican plantation. "Let none admire / That riches grow in hell; that soil may best / Deserve the precious bane" (Milton, *Paradise Lost*, I: 690–92).

which he told to me he must tell to the world. Suspicions have fixed themselves upon him, which allow him not the privilege of silence and obscurity. While he continued unknown and unthought of, the publication of his story would only give unnecessary birth to dangers; but now dangers are incurred which it may probably contribute to lessen, if not to remove.

Meanwhile the return of Mervyn to the city was anxiously expected. Day after day passed and no tidings were received. I had business of an urgent nature which required my presence in Jersey, but which, in the daily expectation of the return of my young friend, I postponed a week longer than rigid discretion allowed. At length I was obliged to comply with the exigence, and left the city, but made such arrangements that I should be apprized by my wife of Mervyn's return with all practicable expedition.

These arrangements were superfluous, for my business was dispatched, and my absence at an end, before the youth had given us any tokens of his approach. I now remembered the warnings of Wortley, and his assertions that Mervyn had withdrawn himself forever from our view. The event had hitherto unwelcomely coincided with these predictions, and a thousand doubts and misgivings were awakened.

One evening, while preparing to shake off gloomy thoughts by a visit to a friend, some one knocked at my door, and left a billet containing these words:

> "*Dr. Stevens*[5] *is requested to come immediately to
> the Debtors' Apartments in Prune Street.*"

This billet was without signature. The hand writing was unknown, and the precipitate departure of the bearer, left me wholly at a loss with respect to the person of the

---

[5] "Dr. Stevens": the first appearance of Stevens' name. Brown frequently introduces characters before the appearance of their names (e.g., Wallace, Thetford, or Achsa Fielding in this novel), and Stevens is the extreme example. Despite the character's centrality, no name was ever provided in the first part, and now the long-delayed name appears at the moment Stevens assumes an active role in Mervyn's efforts toward benevolence.

While the novel makes no direct allusion, it is likely that Brown intended the name to evoke associations with Dr. Edward Stevens, a well-known physician and diplomat in 1790s Philadelphia and Haiti. Stevens was a St. Croix native and lifelong close friend (possibly the secret half-brother) of Alexander Hamilton. His Caribbean origins and experience prepared him to play central and progressive roles in both the 1793 fever epidemic (where he was a leading medical authority and debated Benjamin Rush in the press on styles of treatment) and U.S. diplomatic responses to the Haitian Revolution (he was U.S. Consul-General to St. Domingue, 1799–1801, and became notable for dealing with black revolutionary leader Toussaint L'Ouverture as an equal).

Although literary scholarship does not discuss Edward Stevens in this connection, a writer as well informed about contemporary medicine and politics as Brown was certainly aware of him. Brown had several links to the Hamilton circle that included Stevens via his brother Armitt (once a clerk to Hamilton) and his friend and future brother-in-law John Blair Linn (a former law apprentice with Hamilton). Since Stevens' name was back in the public eye after his February 1799 appointment as consul, timing suggests that Brown chose the name as he was writing *Second Part* in late 1799–early 1800 as another means of reiterating links between the novel's crucial contexts of fever and slave revolution.

writer, or the end for which my presence was required. This uncertainty only hastened my compliance with the summons.

The evening was approaching—a time when the prison[6] doors are accustomed to be shut and strangers to be excluded. This furnished an additional reason for dispatch. As I walked swiftly along, I revolved the possible motives that might have prompted this message. A conjecture was soon formed, which led to apprehension and inquietude.

One of my friends, by name Carlton, was embarrassed with debts which he was unable to discharge. He had lately been menaced with arrest, by a creditor not accustomed to remit any of his claims. I dreaded that this catastrophe had now happened, and called to mind the anguish with which this untoward incident would overwhelm his family. I knew his incapacity to take away the claim of his creditor by payment, or to soothe him into clemency by supplication.

So prone is the human mind to create for itself distress, that I was not aware of the uncertainty of this evil till I arrived at the prison. I checked myself at the moment when I opened my lips to utter the name of my friend, and was admitted without particular enquiries. I supposed that he by whom I had been summoned hither would meet me in the common room.

The apartment was filled with pale faces and withered forms. The marks of negligence and poverty were visible in all; but few betrayed, in their features or gestures, any symptoms of concern on account of their condition. Ferocious gaiety, or stupid indifference, seemed to sit upon every brow. The vapour from an heated stove, mingled with the fumes of beer and tallow that were spilled upon it, and with the tainted breath of so promiscuous a crowd,[7] loaded the stagnant atmosphere. At my first transition from the cold and pure air without, to this noxious element, I found it difficult to breathe. A moment, however, reconciled me to my situation, and I looked anxiously round to discover some face which I knew.

Almost every mouth was furnished with a segar, and every hand with a glass of porter. Conversation, carried on with much emphasis of tone and gesture, was not wanting. Sundry groupes, in different corners, were beguiling the tedious hours at

---

[6] "The prison": Prune Street debtor's prison was part of the large and historically innovative Walnut Street Prison complex bounded by Fifth and Sixth Streets, and Walnut and Prune (now Locust). The debtor's prison building was separate from the main buildings and faced south onto Prune Street. Many Europeans interested in penal reform visited and reported on this complex, as did Brown and his circle, who toured the prison on numerous occasions. Because of Brown's familiarity with new theories on the social role of prisons, Benjamin Rush recommended him in 1803 as a likely author for a history of Prison Reform.

[7] "Ferocious gaiety . . . so promiscuous a crowd": the conditions at Prune Street described here and in Chapter II.13 are accurate. Since debtors paid for their own food and other amenities, and had easier access to visitors than ordinary criminals in the main building, a freewheeling atmosphere prevailed. Liquor sales in the jail's main room were brisk, and business opportunities were such that prostitutes commonly procured their own incarceration at Prune Street in order to work inside the jail. See Bruce Mann, *Republic of Debtors*, 87–98.

whist. Others, unemployed, were strolling to and fro, and testified their vacancy of thought and care by humming or whistling a tune.

I fostered the hope, that my prognostics had deceived me. This hope was strengthened by reflecting that the billet received was written in a different hand from that of my friend. Meanwhile I continued my search. Seated on a bench, silent and aloof from the crowd, his eyes fixed upon the floor, and his face half concealed by his hand, a form was at length discovered which verified all my conjectures and fears. Carlton was he.

My heart drooped, and my tongue faultered, at this sight. I surveyed him for some minutes in silence. At length, approaching the bench on which he sat, I touched his hand and awakened him from his reverie. He looked up. A momentary gleam of joy and surprize was succeeded by a gloom deeper than before.

It was plain that my friend needed consolation. He was governed by an exquisite sensibility to disgrace. He was impatient of constraint. He shrunk, with fastidious abhorrence, from the contact of the vulgar and the profligate. His constitution was delicate and feeble. Impure airs, restraint from exercise, unusual aliment, unwholesome or incommodious accommodations, and perturbed thoughts, were, at any time, sufficient to generate disease and to deprive him of life.

To these evils he was now subjected. He had no money wherewith to purchase food. He had been dragged hither in the morning. He had not tasted a morsel since his entrance. He had not provided a bed on which to lie; or enquired in what room, or with what companions, the night was to be spent.

Fortitude was not among my friend's qualities. He was more prone to shrink from danger than encounter it, and to yield to the flood rather than sustain it; but it is just to observe that his anguish, on the present occasion, arose not wholly from selfish considerations. His parents were dead, and two sisters were dependent on him for support. One of these was nearly of his own age. The other was scarcely emerged from childhood. There was an intellectual as well as a personal resemblance between my friend and his sisters. They possessed his physical infirmities, his vehement passions, and refinements of taste; and the misery of his condition was tenfold increased, by reflecting on the feelings which would be awakened in them by the knowledge of his state, and the hardships to which the loss of his succour would expose them.

Chapter V

IT was not in my power to release my friend by the payment of his debt; but, by contracting with the keeper of the prison for his board, I could save him from famine; and, by suitable exertions, could procure him lodging as convenient as the time would admit. I could promise to console and protect his sisters, and, by cheerful tones and frequent visits, dispel some part of the evil which encompassed him.

After the first surprize had subsided, he enquired by what accident this meeting had been produced. Conscious of my incapacity to do him any essential service, and unwilling to make me a partaker in his miseries, he had forborne to inform me of his condition.

This assurance was listened to with some wonder. I showed him the billet. It had not been written by him. He was a stranger to the penmanship. None but the attorney and officer were apprized of his fate. It was obvious to conclude, that this was the interposition of some friend, who, knowing my affection for Carlton, had taken this mysterious method of calling me to his succour.

Conjectures, as to the author and motives of this interposition, were suspended by more urgent considerations. I requested an interview with the keeper, and enquired how Carlton could be best accommodated.

He said, that all his rooms were full but one, which, in consequence of the dismission[1] of three persons in the morning, had at present but one tenant. This person had lately arrived, was sick, and had with him, at this time, one of his friends. Carlton might divide the chamber with this person. No doubt his consent would be readily given; though this arrangement, being the best, must take place whether he consented or not.

This consent I resolved immediately to seek, and, for that purpose, desired to be led to the chamber. The door of the apartment was shut. I knocked for admission. It was instantly opened, and I entered. The first person who met my view was—Arthur Mervyn.

I started with astonishment. Mervyn's countenance betrayed nothing but satisfaction at the interview. The traces of fatigue and anxiety gave place to tenderness and joy. It readily occurred to me that Mervyn was the writer of the note which I had lately received. To meet him within these walls, and at this time, was the most remote and undesirable of all contingences. The same hour had thus made me acquainted with the kindred and unwelcome fate of two beings whom I most loved.

I had scarcely time to return his embrace, when, taking my hand, he led me to a bed that stood in one corner. There was stretched upon it one whom a second glance enabled me to call by his name, though I had never before seen him. The vivid portrait which Mervyn had drawn was conspicuous in the sunken and haggard visage before me. This face had, indeed, proportions and lines which could never be forgotten or

---

[1] "Dismission": release, discharge, setting free.

mistaken. Welbeck, when once seen or described, was easily distinguished from the rest of mankind. He had stronger motives than other men for abstaining from guilt, the difficulty of concealment or disguise being tenfold greater in him than in others, by reason of the indelible and eye-attracting marks which nature had set upon him.

He was pallid and emaciated. He did not open his eyes on my entrance. He seemed to be asleep; but, before I had time to exchange glances with Mervyn, or to enquire into the nature of the scene, he awoke. On seeing me he started, and cast a look of upbraiding on my companion. The latter comprehended his emotion and endeavored to appease him.

This person, said he, is my friend. He is likewise a physician; and, perceiving your state to require medical assistance, I ventured to send for him.

Welbeck replied, in a contemptuous and indignant tone, thou mistakest my condition, boy. My disease lies deeper than his scrutiny will ever reach. I had hoped thou wert gone. Thy importunities are well meant, but they aggravate my miseries.

He now rose from the bed, and continued, in a firm and resolute tone, you are intruders into this apartment. It is mine, and I desire to be left alone.

Mervyn returned, at first, no answer to this address. He was immersed in perplexity. At length, raising his eyes from the floor, he said, my intentions are indeed honest, and I am grieved that I want the power of persuasion. To-morrow, perhaps, I may reason more cogently with your despair, or your present mood may be changed. To aid my own weakness I will entreat the assistance of this friend.

These words roused a new spirit in Welbeck. His confusion and anger encreased. His tongue faultered as he exclaimed, good God! what mean you? Headlong and rash as you are, you will not share with this person your knowledge of me?— Here he checked himself, conscious that the words he had already uttered tended to the very end which he dreaded. This consciousness, added to the terror of more ample disclosures, which the simplicity and rectitude of Mervyn might prompt him to make, chained up his tongue, and covered him with dismay.

Mervyn was not long in answering—I comprehend your fears and your wishes. I am bound to tell you the truth. To this person your story has already been told. Whatever I have witnessed under your roof, whatever I have heard from your lips, have been faithfully disclosed to him.

The countenance of Welbeck now betrayed a mixture of incredulity and horror. For a time his utterance was stifled by his complicated feelings.

It cannot be. So enormous a deed is beyond thy power. Thy qualities are marvellous. Every new act of thine outstrips the last, and belies the newest calculations. But this—this perfidy exceeds—This outrage upon promises, this violation of faith, this blindness to the future is incredible. There he stopped; while his looks seemed to call upon Mervyn for a contradiction of his first assertion.

I know full well how inexpiably stupid or wicked my act will appear to you, but I will not prevaricate or lie. I repeat, that every thing is known to him. Your birth; your early fortunes; the incidents at Charleston and Wilmington; your treatment of the brother and sister; your interview with Watson, and the fatal issue of that interview—I have told him all, just as it was told to me.

Here the shock that was felt by Welbeck overpowered his caution and his strength. He sunk upon the side of the bed. His air was still incredulous, and he continued to gaze upon Mervyn. He spoke in a tone less vehement.

And hast thou then betrayed me? Hast thou shut every avenue to my return to honor? Am I known to be a seducer and assassin? To have meditated all crimes, and to have perpetrated the worst?

Infamy and death are my portion. I know they are reserved for me; but I did not think to receive them at thy hands, that under that innocent guise there lurked a heart treacherous and cruel. But go; leave me to myself. This stroke has exterminated my remnant of hope. Leave me to prepare my neck for the halter, and my lips for this last, and bitterest cup.

Mervyn struggled with his tears and replied, all this was foreseen, and all this I was prepared to endure. My friend and I will withdraw, as you wish; but to-morrow I return; not to vindicate my faith or my humanity; not to make you recant your charges, or forgive the faults which I seem to have committed, but to extricate you from your present evil, or to arm you with fortitude.

So saying he led the way out of the room. I followed him in silence. The strangeness and abruptness of this scene left me no power to assume a part in it. I looked on with new and indescribable sensations. I reached the street before my recollection was perfectly recovered. I then reflected on the purpose that had led me to Welbeck's chamber. This purpose was yet unaccomplished. I desired Mervyn to linger a moment while I returned into the house. I once more enquired for the keeper, and told him I should leave to him the province of acquainting Welbeck with the necessity of sharing his apartment with a stranger. I speedily rejoined Mervyn in the street.

I lost no time in requiring an explanation of the scene that I had witnessed. How became you once more the companion of Welbeck? Why did you not inform me by letter of your arrival at Malverton, and of what occurred during your absence? What is the fate of Mr. Hadwin and of Wallace?

Alas! said he, I perceive, that, though I have written, you have never received my letters. The tale of what has occurred since we parted is long and various. I am not only willing but eager to communicate the story, but this is no suitable place. Have patience till we reach your house. I have involved myself in perils and embarrassments from which I depend upon your counsel and aid to release me.

I had scarcely reached my own door, when I was overtaken by a servant, whom I knew to belong to the family in which Carlton and his sisters resided. Her message, therefore, was readily guessed. She came, as I expected, to enquire for my friend, who had left his home in the morning with a stranger, and had not yet returned. His absence had occasioned some inquietude, and his sister had sent this message to me, to procure what information respecting the cause of his detention I was able to give.

My perplexity hindered me, for some time, from answering. I was willing to communicate the painful truth with my own mouth. I saw the necessity of putting an end to her suspence, and of preventing the news from reaching her with fallacious aggravations or at an unseasonable time.

I told the messenger, that I had just parted with Mr. Carlton, that he was well, and that I would speedily come and acquaint his sister with the cause of his absence.

Though burning with curiosity respecting Mervyn and Welbeck, I readily postponed its gratification till my visit to Miss Carlton was performed. I had rarely seen this lady; my friendship for her brother, though ardent, having been lately formed, and chiefly matured by interviews at my house. I had designed to introduce her to my wife, but various accidents had hindered the execution of my purpose. Now consolation and counsel was more needed than ever, and delay or reluctance in bestowing it would have been, in an high degree, unpardonable.

I therefore parted with Mervyn, requesting him to await my return, and promising to perform the engagement which compelled me to leave him with the utmost dispatch. On entering Miss Carlton's apartment, I assumed an air of as much tranquillity as possible. I found the lady seated at a desk, with pen in hand and parchment before her. She greeted me with affectionate dignity, and caught from my countenance that cheerfulness of which on my entrance she was destitute.

You come, said she, to inform me what has made my brother a truant to-day. Till your message was received I was somewhat anxious. This day he usually spends in rambling through the fields, but so bleak and stormy an atmosphere I suppose would prevent his excursion. I pray, sir, what is it detains him?

To conquer my embarrassment, and introduce the subject by indirect and cautious means, I eluded her question, and casting an eye at the parchment, how now? said I; this is strange employment for a lady. I knew that my friend pursued this trade, and lived by binding fast the bargains which others made, but I knew not that the pen was ever usurped by his sister.

The usurpation was prompted by necessity. My brother's impatient temper and delicate frame unfitted him for this trade. He pursued it with no less reluctance than diligence, devoting to the task three nights in the week and the whole of each day. It would long ago have killed him, if I had not bethought myself of sharing his tasks. The pen was irksome and toilsome at first, but use has made it easy, and far more eligible than the needle, which was formerly my only tool.[2]

This arrangement affords my brother opportunities of exercise and recreation, without diminishing our profits; and my time, though not less constantly, is more agreeably, as well as more lucratively, employed than formerly.

I admire your reasoning. By this means provision is made against untoward accidents. If sickness should disable him, you are qualified to pursue the same means of support.

At these words the lady's countenance changed. She put her hand on my arm and said, in a fluttering and hurried accent, is my brother sick?

---

[2] "The needle, which was formerly my only tool": as the exchange beginning with this observation indicates, Miss Carlton exemplifies female independence, strength, and entry into the commercial marketplace of ideas. She eventually joins Mervyn's enlightened social circle in Chapter II.16.

No. He is in perfect health. My observation was an harmless one. I am sorry to observe your readiness to draw alarming inferences. If I were to say, that your scheme is useful to supply deficiencies, not only when your brother is disabled by sickness, but when thrown, by some inhuman creditor, into jail, no doubt you would perversely and hastily infer that he is now in prison.

I had scarcely ended the sentence, when the piercing eyes of the lady were anxiously fixed upon mine. After a moment's pause, she exclaimed—The inference, indeed, is too plain. I know his fate. It has long been foreseen and expected, and I have summoned up my equanimity to meet it. Would to Heaven he may find the calamity as light as I should find it; but I fear his too irritable spirit.

When her fears were confirmed, she started out into no vehemence of exclamation. She quickly suppressed a few tears which would not be withheld, and listened to my narrative of what had lately occurred, with tokens of gratitude.

Formal consolation was superfluous. Her mind was indeed more fertile than my own in those topics which take away its keenest edge from affliction. She observed that it was far from being the heaviest calamity which might have happened. The creditor was perhaps vincible by arguments and supplications. If these should succeed, the disaster would not only be removed, but that security from future molestation, be gained, to which they had for a long time been strangers.

Should he be obdurate, their state was far from being hopeless. Carlton's situation allowed him to pursue his profession. His gains would be equal, and his expences would not be augmented. By their mutual industry they might hope to amass sufficient to discharge the debt at no very remote period.

What she chiefly dreaded was the pernicious influence of dejection and sedentary labor on her brother's health. Yet this was not to be considered as inevitable. Fortitude might be inspired by exhortation and example, and no condition precluded us from every species of bodily exertion. The less inclined he should prove to cultivate the means of deliverance and happiness within his reach, the more necessary it became for her to stimulate and fortify his resolution.

If I were captivated by the charms of this lady's person and carriage, my reverence was excited by these proofs of wisdom and energy. I zealously promised to concur with her in every scheme she should adopt for her own or her brother's advantage; and after spending some hours with her, took my leave.

I now regretted the ignorance in which I had hitherto remained respecting this lady. That she was, in an eminent degree, feminine and lovely, was easily discovered; but intellectual weakness had been rashly inferred from external frailty. She was accustomed to shrink from observation, and reserve was mistaken for timidity. I called on Carlton only when numerous engagements would allow, and when by some accident, his customary visits had been intermitted. On those occasions, my stay was short, and my attention chiefly confined to her brother. I now resolved to atone for my ancient negligence, not only by my own assiduities, but by those of my wife.

On my return home, I found Mervyn and my wife in earnest discourse. I anticipated the shock which the sensibility of the latter would receive from the tidings which I had to communicate respecting Carlton. I was unwilling, and yet perceived the necessity, of disclosing the truth. I desired to bring these women, as soon as possible, to the knowledge of each other, but the necessary prelude to this was an acquaintance with the disaster that had happened.

Scarcely had I entered the room, when Mervyn turned to me and said, with an air of anxiety and impatience—Pray, my friend, have you any knowledge of Francis Carlton?

The mention of this name by Mervyn, produced some surprize. I acknowledged my acquaintance with him.

Do you know in what situation he now is?

In answer to this question, I stated by what singular means his situation had been made known to me, and the purpose, from the accomplishment of which, I had just returned. I enquired, in my turn, whence originated this question?

He had overheard the name of Carlton in the prison. Two persons were communing in a corner, and accident enabled him to catch this name, though uttered by them in an half whisper, and to discover that the person talked about, had lately been conveyed thither.

This name was not now heard for the first time. It was connected with remembrances that made him anxious for the fate of him to whom it belonged. In discourse with my wife, this name chanced to be again mentioned, and his curiosity was roused afresh. I was willing to communicate all that I knew, but Mervyn's own destiny was too remarkable not to absorb all my attention, and I refused to discuss any other theme till that were fully explained. He postponed his own gratification to mine, and consented to relate the incidents that had happened from the moment of our separation till the present.

Chapter VI

AT parting with you, my purpose was to reach the abode of the Hadwins as speedily as possible. I travelled therefore with diligence. Setting out so early, I expected, though on foot, to reach the end of my journey before noon. The activity of muscles is no obstacle to thought. So far from being inconsistent with intense musing, it is, in my own case, propitious to that state of mind.

Probably no one had stronger motives for ardent meditation than I. My second journey to the city was prompted by reasons, and attended by incidents, that seemed to have a present existence. To think upon them, was to view, more deliberately and thoroughly, objects and persons that still hovered in my sight. Instead of their attributes being already seen, and their consequences at an end, it seemed as if a series of numerous years and unintermitted contemplation were requisite to comprehend them fully, and bring into existence their most momentous effects.[1]

If men be chiefly distinguished from each other by the modes in which attention is employed, either on external and sensible objects, or merely on abstract ideas and the creatures of reflection, I may justly claim to be enrolled in the second class. My existence is a series of thoughts rather than of motions. Ratiocination and deduction leave my senses unemployed. The fulness of my fancy renders my eye vacant and inactive. Sensations do not precede and suggest, but follow and are secondary to the acts of my mind.

There was one motive, however, which made me less inattentive to the scene that was continually shifting before and without me than I am wont to be. The loveliest form which I had hitherto seen, was that of Clemenza Lodi. I recalled her condition as I had witnessed it, as Welbeck had described, and as you had painted it. The past was without remedy; but the future was, in some degree, within our power to create and to fashion. Her state was probably dangerous. She might already be forlorn, beset with temptation or with anguish; or danger might only be approaching her, and the worst evils be impending ones.

I was ignorant of her state. Could I not remove this ignorance? Would not some benefit redound to her from beneficent and seasonable interposition?

You had mentioned that her abode had lately been with Mrs. Villars, and that this lady still resided in the country. The residence had been sufficiently described, and I perceived that I was now approaching it. In a short time I spied its painted roof and five chimnies through an avenue of *catalpas*.[2]

---

[1] "Their most momentous effects": Mervyn continues to consider and realize the complex implications of what he has seen and experienced in the city.

[2] "*Catalpas*": *Catalpa longissima*, a tall shade tree with heart-shaped leaves, originally from the Caribbean sugar colonies, that became popular in early modern gardening when it was imported and cultivated in Europe and North America. It is also known as St. Domingo or French oak (OED) and sometimes as Haitian Oak or Jamaica Oak. Row planting implies an ornamental, cultivated use, not a wild variety. Some of the elite country homes around Philadelphia had elaborate gardens and greenhouses with botanical specimens from all over the world.

When opposite the gate which led into this avenue, I paused. It seemed as if this moment were to decide upon the liberty and innocence of this being. In a moment I might place myself before her, ascertain her true condition, and point out to her the path of honor and safety. This opportunity might be the last. Longer delay might render interposition fruitless.

But how was I to interpose? I was a stranger to her language, and she was unacquainted with mine. To obtain access to her, it was necessary only to demand it. But how should I explain my views and state my wishes when an interview was gained? And what expedient was it in my power to propose?

Now, said I, I perceive the value of that wealth which I have been accustomed to despise. The power of eating and drinking, the nature and limits of existence and physical enjoyment, are not changed or enlarged by the increase of wealth. Our corporeal and intellectual wants are supplied at little expence; but our own wants are the wants of others, and that which remains, after our own necessities are obviated, it is always easy and just to employ in relieving the necessities of others.

There are no superfluities[3] in my store. It is not in my power to supply this unfortunate girl with decent rayment and honest bread. I have no house to which to conduct her. I have no means of securing her from famine and cold.

Yet, though indigent and feeble, I am not destitute of friends and of home. Cannot she be admitted to the same asylum to which I am now going? This thought was sudden and new. The more it was revolved, the more plausible it seemed. This was not merely the sole expedient, but the best that could have been suggested.

The Hadwins were friendly, hospitable, unsuspicious. Their board, though simple and uncouth, was wholesome and plenteous. Their residence was sequestered and obscure, and not obnoxious to impertinent enquiries and malignant animadversion.[4] Their frank and ingenuous temper would make them easy of persuasion, and their sympathies were prompt and overflowing.

I am nearly certain, continued I, that they will instantly afford protection to this desolate girl. Why shall I not anticipate their consent, and present myself to their embraces and their welcomes in her company?

Slight reflection showed me, that this precipitation was improper. Whether Wallace had ever arrived at Malverton? whether Mr. Hadwin had escaped infection? whether his house were the abode of security and quiet, or a scene of desolation? were questions yet to be determined. The obvious and best proceeding was to hasten forward, to afford the Hadwins, if in distress, the feeble consolations of my friendship; or, if their state were happy, to procure their concurrence to my scheme respecting Clemenza.

Actuated by these considerations, I resumed my journey. Looking forward, I perceived a chaise and horse standing by the left hand fence, at the distance of some

---

[3] "Superfluities": more than is necessary, excess.

[4] "Not obnoxious . . . animadversion": in other words, the Villars house is hidden from prying eyes and wagging tongues. "Animadversion" is warning, censure, or blame.

hundred yards. This object was not uncommon or strange, and, therefore, it was scarcely noticed. When I came near, however, methought I recognized in this carriage the same in which my importunities had procured a seat for the languishing Wallace, in the manner which I have formerly related.

It was a crazy[5] vehicle and old fashioned. When once seen it could scarcely be mistaken or forgotten. The horse was held by his bridle to a post, but the seat was empty. My solicitude with regard to Wallace's destiny, of which he to whom the carriage belonged might possibly afford me some knowledge, made me stop and reflect on what measures it was proper to pursue.

The rider could not be at a great distance from this spot. His absence would probably be short. By lingering a few minutes an interview might be gained, and the uncertainty and suspense of some hours be thereby precluded. I therefore waited, and the same person whom I had formerly encountered made his appearance, in a short time, from under a copse that skirted the road.

He recognized me with more difficulty than attended my recognition of him. The circumstances, however, of our first meeting were easily recalled to his remembrance. I eagerly enquired when and where he had parted with the youth who had been, on that occasion, entrusted to his care.

He answered, that, on leaving the city and inhaling the purer air of the fields and woods, Wallace had been, in a wonderful degree, invigorated and refreshed. An instantaneous and total change appeared to have been wrought in him. He no longer languished with fatigue or fear, but became full of gaiety and talk.

The suddenness of this transition; the levity with which he related and commented on his recent dangers and evils, excited the astonishment of his companion, to whom he not only communicated the history of his disease, but imparted many anecdotes of a humorous kind. Some of these my companion repeated. I heard them with regret and dissatisfaction. They betokened a mind vitiated by intercourse with the thoughtless and depraved of both sexes, and particularly with infamous and profligate women.[6]

My companion proceeded to mention, that Wallace's exhilaration lasted but for a short time, and disappeared as suddenly as it had appeared. He was seized with deadly sickness, and insisted upon leaving the carriage, whose movements shocked his stomach and head to an insupportable degree. His companion was not void of apprehensions on his own account, but was unwilling to desert him, and endeavored to encourage him. His efforts were vain. Though the nearest house was at the distance of some hundred yards, and though it was probable that the inhabitants of this house would refuse to accommodate one in his condition, yet Wallace could not be prevailed on to proceed; and, in spite of persuasion and remonstrance, left the carriage and threw himself on the grassy bank beside the road.

---

[5] "Crazy": "full of cracks . . . liable to break apart or fall to pieces" (OED).

[6] "Infamous and profligate women": prostitutes.

This person was not unmindful of the hazard which he incurred by contact with a sick man. He conceived himself to have performed all that was consistent with duty to himself and to his family; and Wallace, persisting in affirming that, by attempting to ride farther, he should merely hasten his death, was at length left to his own guidance.

These were unexpected and mournful tidings. I had fondly imagined, that his safety was put beyond the reach of untoward accidents. Now, however, there was reason to suppose him to have perished by a lingering and painful disease, rendered fatal by the selfishness of mankind, by the want of seasonable remedies, and exposure to inclement airs. Some uncertainty, however, rested on his fate. It was my duty to remove it, and to carry to the Hadwins no mangled and defective tale. Where, I asked, had Wallace and his companion parted?

It was about three miles further onward. The spot and the house within view from the spot, were accurately described. In this house it was possible that Wallace had sought an asylum, and some intelligence respecting him might be gained from its inhabitants. My informant was journeying to the city, so that we were obliged to separate.

In consequence of this man's description of Wallace's deportment, and the proofs of a dissolute and thoughtless temper which he had given, I began to regard his death as an event less deplorable. Such an one was unworthy of a being so devoutly pure, so ardent in fidelity and tenderness as Susan Hadwin. If he loved, it was probable that in defiance of his vows, he would seek a different companion. If he adhered to his first engagements, his motives would be sordid, and the disclosure of his latent defects might produce more exquisite misery to his wife, than his premature death or treacherous desertion.

The preservation of this man, was my sole motive for entering the infected city, and subjecting my own life to the hazards, from which my escape may almost be esteemed miraculous. Was not the end disproportioned to the means? Was there arrogance in believing my life a price too great to be given for his?

I was not, indeed, sorry for the past. My purpose was just, and the means which I selected, were the best my limited knowledge applied. My happiness should be drawn from reflection on the equity of my intentions. That these intentions were frustrated by the ignorance of others, or my own, was the consequence of human frailty. Honest purposes, though they may not bestow happiness on others, will, at least, secure it to him who fosters them.

By these reflections my regrets were dissipated, and I prepared to rejoice alike, whether Wallace should be found to have escaped or to have perished. The house to which I had been directed was speedily brought into view. I enquired for the master or mistress of the mansion, and was conducted to a lady of a plain and housewifely appearance.

My curiosity was fully gratified. Wallace, whom my description easily identified, had made his appearance at her door on the evening of the day on which he left the city. The dread of *the fever* was descanted[7] on with copious and rude eloquence. I

---

[7] "Descanted": talked at length in a boring fashion.

supposed her eloquence on this theme to be designed to apologize to me for her refusing entrance to the sick man. The peroration,[8] however, was different. Wallace was admitted, and suitable attention paid to his wants.

Happily, the guest had nothing to struggle with but extreme weakness. Repose, nourishing diet, and salubrious airs restored him in a short time to health.[9] He lingered under this roof for three weeks, and then, without any professions of gratitude, or offers of pecuniary remuneration, or information of the course which he determined to take, he left them.

These facts, added to that which I had previously known, threw no advantageous light upon the character of Wallace. It was obvious to conclude, that he had gone to Malverton, and thither there was nothing to hinder me from following him.

Perhaps, one of my grossest defects is a precipitate temper. I chuse my path suddenly, and pursue it with impetuous expedition. In the present instance, my resolution was conceived with unhesitating zeal, and I walked the faster that I might the sooner execute it. Miss Hadwin deserved to be happy. Love was in her heart the all-absorbing sentiment. A disappointment there was a supreme calamity. Depravity and folly must assume the guise of virtue before it can claim her affection. This disguise might be maintained for a time, but its detection must inevitably come, and the sooner this detection takes place the more beneficial it must prove.

I resolved to unbosom myself, with equal and unbounded confidence, to Wallace and his mistress. I would chuse for this end not the moment when they were separate, but that in which they were together. My knowledge, and the sources of my knowledge, relative to Wallace, should be unfolded to the lady with simplicity and truth. The lover should be present, to confute, to extenuate, or to verify the charges.

During the rest of the day these images occupied the chief place in my thoughts. The road was miry and dark, and my journey proved to be more tedious and fatiguing than I expected. At length, just as the evening closed, the well-known habitation appeared in view. Since my departure, winter had visited the world, and the aspect of nature was desolate and dreary. All around this house was vacant, negligent, forlorn. The contrast between these appearances and those which I had noticed on my first approach to it, when the ground and the trees were decked with the luxuriance and vivacity of summer, was mournful, and seemed to foretoken ill. My spirits drooped as I noticed the general inactivity and silence.

I entered, without warning, the door that led into the parlour. No face was to be seen or voice heard. The chimney was ornamented, as in summer, with evergreen shrubs. Though it was now the second month of frost and snow, fire did not appear to have been lately kindled on this hearth.

---

[8] "Peroration": a speech or, in this usage, the concluding part of a speech that sums up its content.

[9] "Repose, nourishing diet, and salubrious airs . . . to health": Mervyn alludes to theories (like those embraced by the character Medlicote and historical figures such as Elihu Hubbard Smith, Edward Stevens, and Jean Devèze) that the fever is not contagious and is best treated with hygienic measures. For more on theories about yellow fever and its treatment, see the Introduction. This is Wallace's last appearance in the novel's action; future mentions imply that he died sometime after this point.

This was a circumstance from which nothing good could be deduced. Had there been those to share its comforts, who had shared them on former years, this was the place and hour at which they commonly assembled. A door on one side led, through a narrow entry, into the kitchen. I opened this door, and passed towards the kitchen.

No one was there but an old man, squatted in the chimney-corner. His face, though wrinkled, denoted undecayed health and an unbending spirit. An homespun coat, leathern breeches wrinkled with age, and blue yarn hose, were well suited to his lean and shrivelled form. On his right knee was a wooden bowl, which he had just replenished from a pipkin of hasty-pudding still smoking on the coals; and in his left hand a spoon, which he had, at that moment, plunged into a bottle of molasses that stood beside him.

This action was suspended by my entrance. He looked up and exclaimed, hey day! who's this that comes into other people's houses without so much as saying "by your leave?" What's thee business? Who's thee want?[10]

I had never seen this personage before. I supposed it to be some new domestic, and enquired for Mr. Hadwin.

Ah! replied he with a sigh, William Hadwin. Is it him thee wants? Poor man! He is gone to rest many days since.

My heart sunk within me at these tidings. Dead, said I, do you mean that he is dead?—This exclamation was uttered in a tone of some vehemence. It attracted the attention of some one who was standing without, who immediately entered the kitchen. It was Eliza Hadwin. The moment she beheld me she shrieked aloud, and, rushing into my arms, fainted away.

The old man dropped his bowl; and, starting from his seat, stared alternately at me and at the breathless girl. My emotion, made up of joy, and sorrow, and surprize, rendered me for a moment powerless as she. At length, he said, I understand this. I know who thee is, and will tell her thee's come. So saying he hastily left the room.

---

[10] "Who's thee want?": dialect speech identifies the speaker as lower-class and uneducated. As in Mervyn's first encounter with the Hadwins (Chapter 13) or the enlightened Medlicote (Chapter 16), use of "thee" and "thou" indicates the speaker is a Quaker. But whereas the Hadwins, Estwick, and Medlicote used the forms correctly, this character, Old Caleb, uses only "thee," even when "thou" or "thy" is correct.

Chapter VII

IN a short time this gentle girl recovered her senses. She did not withdraw herself from my sustaining arm, but, leaning on my bosom, she resigned herself to passionate weeping. I did not endeavor to check this effusion, believing that its influence would be salutary.

I had not forgotten the thrilling sensibility and artless graces of this girl. I had not forgotten the scruples which had formerly made me check a passion whose tendency was easily discovered. These new proofs of her affection were, at once, mournful and delightful. The untimely fate of her father and my friend pressed with new force upon my heart, and my tears, in spite of my fortitude, mingled with hers.

The attention of both was presently attracted by a faint scream, which proceeded from above. Immediately tottering footsteps were heard in the passage, and a figure rushed into the room, pale, emaciated, haggard, and wild. She cast a piercing glance at me, uttered a feeble exclamation, and sunk upon the floor without signs of life.

It was not difficult to comprehend this scene. I now conjectured, what subsequent enquiry confirmed, that the old man had mistaken me for Wallace, and had carried to the elder sister the news of his return. This fatal disappointment of hopes that had nearly been extinct, and which were now so powerfully revived, could not be endured by a frame verging to dissolution.

This object recalled all the energies of Eliza, and engrossed all my solicitude. I lifted the fallen girl in my arms; and, guided by her sister, carried her to her chamber. I had now leisure to contemplate the changes which a few months had made in this lovely frame. I turned away from the spectacle with anguish, but my wandering eyes were recalled by some potent fascination, and fixed in horror upon a form which evinced the last stage of decay. Eliza knelt on one side, and, leaning her face upon the bed, endeavored in vain to smother her sobs. I sat on the other motionless, and holding the passive and withered hand of the sufferer.

I watched with ineffable solicitude the return of life. It returned, at length, but merely to betray symptoms that it would speedily depart forever. For a time my faculties were palsied,[1] and I was made an impotent spectator of the ruin that environed me. This pusillanimity quickly gave way to resolutions and reflections better suited to the exigencies of the time.

The first impulse was to summon a physician, but it was evident that the patient had been sinking by slow degrees to this state, and that the last struggle had begun. Nothing remained but to watch her while expiring, and perform for her, when dead, the rites of interment. The survivor was capable of consolation and of succour. I went to her and drew her gently into another apartment. The old man, tremulous and wonderstruck, seemed anxious to perform some service. I directed him to kindle a fire in Eliza's chamber. Meanwhile I persuaded my gentle friend to remain in this

---

[1] "Palsied": paralyzed with tremors.

chamber, and resign to me the performance of every office which her sister's condition required. I sat beside the bed of the dying till the mortal struggle was past.

I perceived that the house had no inhabitant beside the two females and the old man. I went in search of the latter, and found him crouched as before, at the kitchen fire, smoking his pipe. I placed myself on the same bench, and entered into conversation with him.

I gathered from him that he had, for many years, been Mrs. Hadwin's servant. That lately he had cultivated a small farm in this neighborhood for his own advantage. Stopping one day in October,[2] at the tavern, he heard that his old master had lately been in the city, had caught *the fever*, and after his return had died with it. The moment he became sick, his servants fled from the house, and the neighbors refused to approach it. The task of attending his sick bed, was allotted to his daughters, and it was by their hands that his grave was dug, and his body covered with earth. The same terror of infection existed after his death as before, and these hapless females were deserted by all mankind.

Old Caleb was no sooner informed of these particulars, than he hurried to the house, and had since continued in their service. His heart was kind, but it was easily seen that his skill extended only to execute the directions of another. Grief for the death of Wallace,[3] and her father, preyed upon the health of the elder daughter. The younger became her nurse, and Caleb was always at hand to execute any orders, the performance of which was on a level with his understanding. Their neighbors had not withheld their good offices, but they were still terrified and estranged by the phantoms of pestilence.

During the last week Susan had been too weak to rise from her bed, yet such was the energy communicated by the tidings that Wallace was alive, and had returned, that she leaped upon her feet and rushed down stairs. How little did that man deserve so strenuous and immortal an affection.

I would not allow myself to ponder on the sufferings of these women. I endeavored to think only of the best expedients for putting an end to these calamities. After a moment's deliberation, I determined to go to an house at some miles distance; the dwelling of one, who, though not exempt from the reigning panic, had shewn more generosity towards these unhappy girls than others. During my former abode in this district, I had ascertained his character, and found him to be compassionate and liberal.

Overpowered by fatigue and watching, Susan was no sooner relieved by my presence, of some portion of her cares, than she sunk into profound slumber. I directed Caleb to watch the house till my return, which should be before midnight, and then set out for the dwelling of Mr. Ellis.

---

[2] "October": this passage places the Philadelphia meeting of Mervyn and Mr. Hadwin in October 1793, at the height of the epidemic. See note 17.6 on the timing of that encounter.

[3] "The death of Wallace": this is the only assertion of Wallace's death; he does not appear in the novel again. The last chapter explained that Wallace disappeared from the house of the woman who bravely sheltered him without thanking her (see note II.7.9), but there is no further explanation of his fate.

The weather was temperate and moist, and rendered the footing of the meadows extremely difficult. The ground that had lately been frozen and covered with snow, was now changed into gullies and pools, and this was no time to be fastidious in the choice of paths. A brook, swelled by the recent *thaw*, was likewise to be passed. The rail which I had formerly placed over it by way of bridge, had disappeared, and I was obliged to wade through it. At length I approached the house to which I was going.

At so late an hour, farmers and farmer's servants are usually abed, and their threshold is entrusted to their watch-dogs. Two belonged to Mr. Ellis, whose ferocity and vigilance were truly formidable to a stranger, but I hoped that in me they would recognize an old acquaintance, and suffer me to approach. In this I was not mistaken. Though my person could not be distinctly seen by star-light, they seemed to scent me from afar, and met me with a thousand caresses.

Approaching the house, I perceived that its tenants were retired to their repose. This I expected, and hastened to awaken Mr. Ellis, by knocking briskly at the door. Presently he looked out of a window above, and in answer to his enquiries, in which impatience at being so unseasonably disturbed, was mingled with anxiety, I told him my name, and entreated him to come down and allow me a few minutes conversation. He speedily dressed himself, and opening the kitchen door, we seated ourselves before the fire.

My appearance was sufficiently adapted to excite his wonder; he had heard of my elopement from the house of Mr. Hadwin, he was a stranger to the motives that prompted my departure, and to the events that had befallen me, and no interview was more distant from his expectations than the present. His curiosity was written in his features, but this was no time to gratify his curiosity. The end that I now had in view, was to procure accommodation for Eliza Hadwin in this man's house. For this purpose it was my duty to describe with simplicity and truth, the inconveniences which at present surrounded her, and to relate all that had happened since my arrival.

I perceived that my tale excited his compassion, and I continued with new zeal to paint to him the helplessness of this girl. The death of her father and sister left her the property of this farm. Her sex and age disqualified her for superintending the harvest-field and the threshing-floor; and no expedient was left, but to lease the land to another, and, taking up her abode in the family of some kinsman or friend, to subsist, as she might easily do, upon the rent. Meanwhile her continuance in this house was equally useless and dangerous, and I insinuated to my companion the propriety of immediately removing her to his own.

Some hesitation and reluctance appeared in him, which I immediately ascribed to an absurd dread of infection. I endeavored, by appealing to his reason, as well as to his pity, to conquer this dread. I pointed out the true cause of the death of the elder daughter, and assured him the youngest knew no indisposition but that which arose from distress. I offered to save him from any hazard that might attend his approaching the house, by accompanying her hither myself. All that her safety required was that his doors should not be shut against her when she presented herself before them.

Still he was fearful and reluctant; and, at length, mentioned that her uncle resided not more than sixteen miles farther; that he was her natural protector, and he dared to say would find no difficulty in admitting her into his house. For his part, there might be reason in what I said, but he could not bring himself to think but that there was still some danger of *the fever*. It was right to assist people in distress, to be sure; but to risk his own life he did not think to be his duty. He was no relation of the family, and it was the duty of relations to help each other. Her uncle was the proper person to assist her, and no doubt he would be as willing as able.

The marks of dubiousness and indecision which accompanied these words, encouraged me in endeavoring to subdue his scruples. The increase of his aversion to my scheme kept pace with my remonstrances, and he finally declared that he would, on no account, consent to it.

Ellis was by no means hard of heart. His determination did not prove the coldness of his charity, but merely the strength of his fears. He was himself an object more of compassion than of anger; and he acted like the man, whose fear of death prompts him to push his companion from the plank which saved him from drowning, but which is unable to sustain both. Finding him invincible to my entreaties, I thought upon the expedient which he suggested of seeking the protection of her uncle. It was true, that the loss of parents had rendered her uncle her legal protector. His knowledge of the world; his house, and property, and influence would, perhaps, fit him for this office in a more eminent degree than I was fitted. To seek a different asylum might, indeed, be unjust to both, and, after some reflection, I not only dismissed the regret which Ellis's refusal had given me, but even thanked him for the intelligence and counsel which he had afforded me. I took leave of him, and hastened back to Hadwin's.

Eliza, by Caleb's report, was still asleep. There was no urgent necessity for awakening her; but something was forthwith to be done with regard to the unhappy girl that was dead. The proceeding incumbent on us was obvious. All that remained was to dig a grave, and to deposit the remains with as much solemnity and decency as the time would permit. There were two methods of doing this. I might wait till the next day; till a coffin could be made and conveyed hither; till the woman, whose trade it was to make and put on the habiliments assigned by custom to the dead, could be sought out and hired to attend; till kindred, friends, and neighbors could be summoned to the obsequies; till a carriage were provided to remove the body to a burying-ground, belonging to a meetinghouse, and five miles distant; till those, whose trade it was to dig graves, had prepared one, within the sacred inclosure, for her reception; or, neglecting this toilsome, tedious, and expensive ceremonial, I might seek the grave of Hadwin, and lay the daughter by the side of her parent.

Perhaps I was wrong in my preference of the latter mode. The customs of burial may, in most cases, be in themselves proper. If the customs be absurd, yet it may be generally proper to adhere to them; but, doubtless, there are cases in which it is our duty to omit them. I conceived the present case to be such an one.[4]

---

[4] "I conceived the present case to be such an one": Mervyn's rational calculation of benefits and consequences leads him to ignore conventional rituals and "groundless superstition" (four paragraphs

The season was bleak and inclement. Much time, labor, and expence would be required to go through the customary rites. There was none but myself to perform these, and I had not the suitable means. The misery of Eliza would only be prolonged by adhering to these forms; and her fortune be needlesly diminished; by the expences unavoidably to be incurred.

After musing upon these ideas for some time, I rose from my seat, and desired Caleb to follow me. We proceeded to an outer shed where farmers' tools used to be kept. I supplied him and myself with a spade, and requested him to lead me to the spot where Mr. Hadwin was laid.

He betrayed some hesitation to comply, and appeared struck with some degree of alarm, as if my purpose had been to molest, instead of securing, the repose of the dead. I removed his doubts by explaining my intentions, but he was scarcely less shocked, on discovering the truth, than he had been alarmed by his first suspicions. He stammered out his objections to my scheme. There was but one mode of burial he thought that was decent and proper, and he could not be free to assist me in pursuing any other mode.

Perhaps Caleb's aversion to the scheme might have been easily overcome, but I reflected that a mind like his was at once flexible and obstinate. He might yield to arguments and entreaties, and act by their immediate impulse; but the impulse passed away in a moment; old and habitual convictions were resumed, and his deviation from the beaten track would be merely productive of compunction.[5] His aid, on the present occasion, though of some use, was by no means indispensible. I forbore to solicit his concurrence, or even to vanquish the scruples he entertained against directing me to the grave of Hadwin. It was a groundless superstition that made one spot more suitable for this purpose than another. I desired Caleb, in a mild tone, to return to the kitchen, and leave me to act as I thought proper. I then proceeded to the orchard.

One corner of this field was somewhat above the level of the rest. The tallest tree of the groupe grew there, and there I had formerly placed a bench, and made it my retreat at periods of leisure. It had been recommended by its sequestered situation, its luxuriant verdure, and profound quiet. On one side was a potatoe field, on the other a *melon-patch;* and before me, in rows, some hundreds of apple trees. Here I was accustomed to seek the benefits of contemplation, and study the manuscripts of Lodi. A few months had passed since I had last visited this spot. What revolutions had since occurred, and how gloomily contrasted was my present purpose with what had formerly led me hither!

---

farther on) in burying Susan's body. This attitude reverses the burial of Watson that occurred in Chapters 11–12 of the first part.

[5] "Compunction": doubts, misgivings, reluctance. Mervyn judges that the laboring-class Caleb is not amenable to the rational persuasion that should characterize relations among middle-class professionals.

In this spot I had hastily determined to dig the grave of Susan. The grave was dug. All that I desired was a cavity of sufficient dimensions to receive her. This being made, I returned to the house, lifted the corpse in my arms, and bore it without delay to the spot. Caleb seated in the kitchen, and Eliza asleep in her chamber, were wholly unapprised of my motions. The grave was covered, the spade reposited under the shed, and my seat by the kitchen fire resumed in a time apparently too short for so solemn and momentous a transaction.

I look back upon this incident with emotions not easily described. It seems as if I acted with too much precipitation; as if insensibility, and not reason, had occasioned that clearness of conceptions, and bestowed that firmness of muscles, which I then experienced. I neither trembled nor wavered in my purpose. I bore in my arms the being whom I had known and loved, through the whistling gale and intense darkness of a winter's night; I heaped earth upon her limbs, and covered them from human observation, without fluctuations or tremors, though not without feelings that were awful and sublime.

Perhaps some part of my stedfastness was owing to my late experience, and some minds may be more easily inured to perilous emergencies than others. If reason acquires strength only by the diminution of sensibility, perhaps it is just for sensibility to be diminished.

Chapter VIII

THE safety of Eliza was the object that now occupied my cares. To have slept, after her example, had been most proper, but my uncertainty with regard to her fate, and my desire to conduct her to some other home, kept my thoughts in perpetual motion. I waited with impatience till she should awake and allow me to consult with her on plans for futurity.

Her sleep terminated not till the next day had arisen. Having recovered the remembrance of what had lately happened, she enquired for her sister. She wanted to view once more the face, and kiss the lips, of her beloved Susan. Some relief to her anguish she expected to derive from this privilege.

When informed of the truth, when convinced that Susan had disappeared forever, she broke forth into fresh passion. It seemed as if her loss was not hopeless or compleat as long as she was suffered to behold the face of her friend and to touch her lips. She accused me of acting without warrant and without justice; of defrauding her of her dearest and only consolation; and of treating her sister's sacred remains with barbarous indifference and rudeness.

I explained in the gentlest terms the reasons of my conduct. I was not surprized or vexed, that she, at first, treated them as futile, and as heightening my offence. Such was the impulse of a grief, which was properly excited by her loss. To be tranquil and stedfast, in the midst of the usual causes of impetuosity and agony, is either the prerogative of wisdom that sublimes itself above all selfish considerations, or the badge of giddy and unfeeling folly.

The torrent was at length exhausted. Upbraiding was at an end; and gratitude, and tenderness, and implicit acquiescence in any scheme which my prudence should suggest, succeeded. I mentioned her uncle as one to whom it would be proper, in her present distress, to apply.

She started and betrayed uneasiness at this name. It was evident that she by no means concurred with me in my notions of propriety; that she thought with aversion of seeking her uncle's protection. I requested her to state her objections to this scheme, or to mention any other which she thought preferable.

She knew no body. She had not a friend in the world but myself. She had never been out of her father's house. She had no relation but her uncle Philip, and he—she could not live with him. I must not insist upon her going to his house. It was not the place for her. She should never be happy there.

I was, at first, inclined to suspect in my friend some capricious and groundless antipathy. I desired her to explain what in her uncle's character made him so obnoxious. She refused to be more explicit, and persisted in thinking that his house was no suitable abode for her.

Finding her, in this respect, invincible, I sought for some other expedient. Might she not easily be accommodated as a boarder in the city, or some village, or in a remote quarter of the country? Ellis, her nearest and most opulent neighbor, had refused to receive her; but there were others who had not his fears. There were others, within the compass of a day's journey, who were strangers to the cause of Hadwin's death; but would it not be culpable to take advantage of that ignorance? Their compliance ought not to be the result of deception.

While thus engaged, the incidents of my late journey recurred to my remembrance, and I asked, is not the honest woman, who entertained Wallace, just such a person as that of whom I am in search? Her treatment of Wallace shews her to be exempt from chimerical fears, proves that she has room in her house for an occasional inmate.

Encouraged by these views, I told my weeping companion, that I had recollected a family in which she would be kindly treated; and that, if she chose, we would not lose a moment in repairing thither. Horses, belonging to the farm, grazed in the meadows, and a couple of these would carry us in a few hours to the place which I had selected for her residence. On her eagerly assenting to this proposal, I enquired in whose care, and in what state, our present habitation should be left.

The father's property now belonged to the daughter. Eliza's mind was quick, active, and sagacious; but her total inexperience gave her sometimes the appearance of folly. She was eager to fly from this house, and to resign herself and her property, without limitation or condition, to my controul. Our intercourse had been short, but she relied on my protection and counsel as absolutely as she had been accustomed to do upon her father's.

She knew not what answer to make to my enquiry. Whatever I pleased to do was the best. What did I think ought to be done?

Ah! thought I, sweet, artless, and simple girl! how wouldst thou have fared, if Heaven had not sent me to thy succour? There are beings in the world who would make a selfish use of thy confidence; who would beguile thee at once of innocence and property. Such am not I. Thy welfare is a precious deposit, and no father or brother could watch over it with more solicitude than I will do.

I was aware that Mr. Hadwin might have fixed the destination of his property, and the guardianship of his daughters, by will. On suggesting this to my friend, it instantly reminded her of an incident that took place after his last return from the city. He had drawn up his will, and gave it into Susan's possession, who placed it in a drawer, whence it was now taken by my friend.

By this will his property was now found to be bequeathed to his two daughters; and his brother, Philip Hadwin, was named executor, and guardian to his daughters till they should be twenty years old. This name was no sooner heard by my friend, than she exclaimed, in a tone of affright, executor! My uncle! What is that? What power does that give him?

I know not exactly the power of executors. He will, doubtless, have possession of your property till you are twenty years of age. Your person will likewise be under his care till that time.

Must he decide where I am to live?

He is vested with all the power of a father.

This assurance excited the deepest consternation. She fixed her eyes on the ground, and was lost, for a time, in the deepest reverie. Recovering, at length, she said, with a sigh, what if my father had made no will?

In that case, a guardian could not be dispensed with, but the right of naming him would belong to yourself.

And my uncle would have nothing to do with my affairs?

I am no lawyer, said I; but I presume all authority over your person and property would devolve upon the guardian of your own choice.

Then I am free. Saying this, with a sudden motion, she tore in several pieces the will, which, during this dialogue, she had held in her hand, and threw the fragments into the fire.[1]

No action was more unexpected to me than this. My astonishment hindered me from attempting to rescue the paper from the flames. It was consumed in a moment. I was at a loss in what manner to regard this sacrifice. It denoted a force of mind little in unison with that simplicity and helplessness which this girl had hitherto displayed. It argued the deepest apprehensions of mistreatment from her uncle. Whether his conduct had justified this violent antipathy, I had no means of judging. Mr. Hadwin's choice of him, as his executor, was certainly one proof of his integrity.

My abstraction was noticed by Eliza, with visible anxiety. It was plain, that she dreaded the impression which this act of seeming temerity had made upon me. Do not be angry with me, said she; perhaps I have been wrong, but I could not help it. I will have but one guardian and one protector.

The deed was irrevocable. In my present ignorance of the domestic history of the Hadwins, I was unqualified to judge how far circumstances might extenuate or justify the act. On both accounts, therefore, it was improper to expatiate upon it.

It was concluded to leave the care of the house to honest Caleb; to fasten closets and drawers, and, carrying away the money which was found in one of them, and which amounted to no inconsiderable sum, to repair to the house formerly mentioned. The air was cold; an heavy snow began to fall in the night; the wind blew tempestuously; and we were compelled to confront it.

In leaving her dwelling, in which she had spent her whole life, the unhappy girl gave way afresh to her sorrow. It made her feeble and helpless. When placed upon the horse, she was scarcely able to maintain her seat. Already chilled by the cold, blinded by the drifting snow, and cut by the blast, all my remonstrances were needed to inspire her with resolution.

I am not accustomed to regard the elements, or suffer them to retard or divert me from any design that I have formed. I had overlooked the weak and delicate frame of my companion, and made no account of her being less able to support cold and fatigue than myself. It was not till we had made some progress in our way, that I began

---

[1] "Threw the fragments into the fire": acting as a "free" person, Eliza figuratively breaks her patriarchal bonds and adopts the same bold strategy Mervyn used in the finale of the first part, when he burned $20,000 to keep it from Welbeck. Both scenes draw this plot motif from Thomas Holcroft's *Anna St. Ives* (1792), the first major British radical-democratic novel of the 1790s. See note 23.2 for more on Brown's use of this motif and reference to Holcroft. Since their acts parallel each other, Eliza's decision reveals a "force of mind" (in the next paragraph) much like Mervyn's own, and an independent spirit that will be developed in the next chapter. This newly revealed side of Eliza makes her another female seeking independence and rational improvement, like Miss Carlton in Chapter II.5.

to view, in their true light, the obstacles that were to be encountered. I conceived it, however, too late to retreat, and endeavored to push on with speed.

My companion was a skilful rider, but her steed was refractory and unmanageable. She was able, however, to curb his spirit till we had proceeded ten or twelve miles from Malverton. The wind and the cold became too violent to be longer endured, and I resolved to stop at the first house which should present itself to my view, for the sake of refreshment and warmth.

We now entered a wood of some extent, at the termination of which I remembered that a dwelling stood. To pass this wood, therefore, with expedition, was all that remained before we could reach an hospitable asylum. I endeavored to sustain, by this information, the sinking spirits of my companion. While busy in conversing with her, a blast of irresistible force twisted off the highest branch of a tree before us. It fell in the midst of the road, at the distance of a few feet from her horse's head. Terrified by this accident, the horse started from the path, and, rushing into the wood, in a moment threw himself and his rider on the ground, by encountering the rugged stock of an oak.

I dismounted and flew to her succour. The snow was already dyed with the blood which flowed from some wound in her head, and she lay without sense or motion. My terrors did not hinder me from anxiously searching for the hurt which was received, and ascertaining the extent of the injury. Her forehead was considerably bruised; but; to my unspeakable joy, the blood flowed from the nostrils, and was, therefore, to be regarded as no mortal symptom.

I lifted her in my arms, and looked around me for some means of relief. The house at which I proposed to stop was upwards of a mile distant. I remembered none that was nearer. To place the wounded girl on my own horse, and proceed gently to the house in question, was the sole expedient; but, at present, she was senseless, and might, on recovering, be too feeble to sustain her own weight.

To recall her to life was my first duty; but I was powerless, or unacquainted with the means. I gazed upon her features, and endeavored, by pressing her in my arms, to inspire her with some warmth. I looked towards the road, and listened for the wished-for sound of some carriage that might be prevailed on to stop and receive her. Nothing was more improbable than that either pleasure or business would induce men to encounter so chilling and vehement a blast. To be lighted on by some traveller was, therefore, an hopeless event.

Meanwhile, Eliza's swoon continued, and my alarm increased. What effect her half-frozen blood would have in prolonging this condition, or preventing her return to life, awakened the deepest apprehensions. I left the wood, still bearing her in my arms, and re-entered the road, from the desire of descrying, as soon as possible, the coming passenger. I looked this way and that, and again listened. Nothing but the sweeping blast, rent and falling branches, and snow that filled and obscured the air, were perceivable. Each moment retarded the course of my own blood and stiffened my sinews, and made the state of my companion more desperate. How was I to act? To perish myself or see her perish was an ignoble fate; courage and activity were still able to avert it. My horse stood near, docile and obsequious; to mount him and to proceed on my way, holding my lifeless burthen in my arms, was all that remained.

At this moment my attention was called by several voices, issuing from the wood. It was the note of gaiety and glee; presently a sleigh, with several persons of both sexes, appeared, in a road which led through the forest into that in which I stood. They moved at a quick pace, but their voices were hushed and they checked the speed of their horses on discovering us. No occurrence was more auspicious than this; for I relied with perfect confidence on the benevolence of these persons, and as soon as they came near, claimed their assistance.

My story was listened to with sympathy, and one of the young men, leaping from the sleigh, assisted me in placing Eliza in the place which he had left. A female, of sweet aspect and engaging manners, insisted upon turning back and hastening to the house, where it seems her father resided, and which the party had just left. I rode after the sleigh, which in a few minutes arrived at the house.

The dwelling was spacious and neat, and a venerable man and woman, alarmed by the quick return of the young people, came forth to know the cause. They received their guest with the utmost tenderness, and provided her with all the accommodations which her condition required. Their daughter relinquished the scheme of pleasure in which she had been engaged, and, compelling her companions to depart without her, remained to nurse and console the sick.

A little time shewed that no lasting injury had been suffered. Contusions, more troublesome than dangerous, and easily curable by such applications as rural and traditional wisdom has discovered, were the only consequences of the fall. My mind, being relieved from apprehensions on this score, had leisure to reflect upon the use which might be made of the present state of things.

When I marked the structure of this house, and the features and deportment of its inhabitants, methought I discerned a powerful resemblance between this family and Hadwin's. It seemed as if some benignant power had led us hither as to the most suitable asylum that could be obtained; and in order to supply, to the forlorn Eliza, the place of those parents and that sister she had lost, I conceived, that, if their concurrence could be gained, no abode was more suitable than this. No time was to be lost in gaining this concurrence. The curiosity of our host and hostess, whose name was Curling, speedily afforded me an opportunity to disclose the history and real situation of my friend. There were no motives to reserve or prevarication. There was nothing which I did not faithfully and circumstantially relate. I concluded with stating my wishes that they would admit my friend as a boarder into their house.

The old man was warm in his concurrence. His wife betrayed some scruples; which, however, her husband's arguments and mine removed. I did not even suppress the tenor and destruction of the will, and the antipathy which Eliza had conceived for her uncle, and which I declared myself unable to explain. It presently appeared that Mr. Curling had some knowledge of Philip Hadwin and that the latter had acquired the repute of being obdurate and profligate. He employed all means to accomplish his selfish ends, and would probably endeavor to usurp the property which his brother had left. To provide against his power and his malice would be particularly incumbent on us, and my new friend readily promised his assistance in the measures which we should take to that end.

Chapter IX

THE state of my feelings may be easily conceived to consist of mixed, but on the whole, of agreeable sensations. The death of Hadwin and his elder daughter could not be thought upon without keen regrets. These it were useless to indulge, and were outweighed by reflections on the personal security in which the survivor was now placed. It was hurtful to expend my unprofitable cares upon the dead, while there existed one to whom they could be of essential benefit, and in whose happiness they would find an ample compensation.

This happiness, however, was still incomplete. It was still exposed to hazard, and much remained to be done before adequate provision was made against the worst of evils, poverty. I now found that Eliza, being only fifteen years old, stood in need of a guardian, and that the forms of law required that some one should make himself her father's administrator. Mr. Curling being tolerably conversant with these subjects, pointed out the mode to be pursued, and engaged to act on this occasion as Eliza's friend.

There was another topic on which my happiness, as well as that of my friend, required us to form some decision. I formerly mentioned, that during my abode at Malverton, I had not been insensible to the attractions of this girl. An affection had stolen upon me, for which, it was easily discovered, that I should not have been denied a suitable return. My reasons for stifling these emotions, at that time, have been mentioned. It may now be asked, what effect subsequent events had produced on my feelings, and how far partaking and relieving her distresses, had revived a passion which may readily be supposed to have been, at no time, entirely extinguished.

The impediments which then existed, were removed. Our union would no longer risk the resentment or sorrow of her excellent parent. She had no longer a sister to divide with her the property of the farm, and make what was sufficient for both, when living together, too little for either separately. Her youth and simplicity required, beyond most others, a legal protector, and her happiness was involved in the success of those hopes which she took no pains to conceal.

As to me, it seemed at first view, as if every incident conspired to determine my choice. Omitting all regard to the happiness of others, my own interest could not fail to recommend a scheme by which the precious benefits of competence and independence might be honestly obtained. The excursions of my fancy had sometimes carried me beyond the bounds prescribed by my situation, but they were, nevertheless, limited to that field to which I had once some prospect of acquiring a title.[1] All

---

[1] "That field . . . acquiring a title": that is, it could be in Mervyn's self-interest to marry Eliza and thereby gain the "title" or status of an independent property owner that he lost when his father disowned him in Chapter 2 of the first part (note 2.5). Mervyn could selfishly appropriate Eliza's property by marrying her, according to the marriage laws of the time, but he renounces this path to advancement or independence. In the remainder of the chapter he explains his decision to pursue a future as a cosmopolitan urban professional instead. Brown's "Memoirs of Carwin" (Part 7)

I wanted for the basis of my gaudiest and most dazzling structures, was an hundred acres of plough-land and meadow. Here my spirit of improvement, my zeal to invent and apply new maxims of household luxury and convenience, new modes and instruments of tillage, new arts connected with orchard, garden and cornfield, were supplied with abundant scope. Though the want of these would not benumb my activity, or take away content, the possession would confer exquisite and permanent enjoyments.

My thoughts have ever hovered over the images of wife and children with more delight than over any other images. My fancy was always active on this theme, and its reveries sufficiently extatic and glowing; but since my intercourse with this girl, my scattered visions were collected and concentered. I had now a form and features before me, a sweet and melodious voice vibrated in my ear, my soul was filled, as it were, with her lineaments and gestures, actions and looks.[2] All ideas, possessing any relation to beauty or sex, appeared to assume this shape. They kept an immoveable place in my mind, they diffused around them an ineffable complacency. Love is merely of value as a prelude to a more tender, intimate and sacred union. Was I not in love, and did I not pant after the irrevocable bonds, the boundless privileges of wedlock?

The question which others might ask, I have asked myself. Was I not in love? I am really at a loss for an answer. There seemed to be irresistible weight in the reasons why I should refuse to marry, and even forbear to foster love in my friend. I considered my youth, my defective education and my limited views. I had passed from my cottage into the world. I had acquired even in my transient sojourn among the busy haunts of men, more knowledge than the lucubrations[3] and employments of all my previous years had conferred. Hence I might infer the childlike immaturity of my understanding, and the rapid progress I was still capable of making. Was this an age to form an irrevocable contract; to chuse the companion of my future life, the associate of my schemes of intellectual and benevolent activity?[4]

I had reason to contemn my own acquisitions; but were not those of Eliza still more slender? Could I rely upon the permanence of her equanimity and her docility to my instructions? What qualities might not time unfold, and how little was I qualified to estimate the character of one, whom no vicissitude or hardship had approached before the death of her father? Whose ignorance was, indeed, great, when it could justly be said even to exceed my own.

---

rejects this kind of marriage in even plainer terms, arguing that it amounts to the theft of a woman's wealth and makes her a "domestic slave" subject to the "absolute power" of her husband.

[2] "Lineaments and gestures, actions and looks": Mervyn repeats Stevens' emphasis on the surface of the body and associative sentiment as an index to character that breaks with older notions of ascribed status.

[3] "Lucubrations": studies, originally nocturnal study or meditation.

[4] "My schemes of intellectual and benevolent activity": Mervyn adopts and repeats Dr. Stevens' emphasis on motivations of "benevolence and reason" in the first paragraphs of *Second Part* (see note II.1.3).

Should I mix with the world, enrol myself in different classes of society; be a witness to new scenes; might not my modes of judging undergo essential variations? Might I not gain the knowledge of beings whose virtue was the gift of experience and the growth of knowledge? Who joined to the modesty and charms of woman, the benefits of education, the maturity and steadfastness of age, and with whose character and sentiments my own would be much more congenial than they could possibly be with the extreme youth, rustic simplicity and mental imperfections of Eliza Hadwin?

To say truth, I was now conscious of a revolution in my mind.[5] I can scarcely assign its true cause. No tokens of it appeared during my late retreat to Malverton. Subsequent incidents, perhaps, joined with the influence of meditation, had generated new views. On my first visit to the city, I had met with nothing but scenes of folly, depravity and cunning. No wonder that the images connected with the city, were disastrous and gloomy; but my second visit produced somewhat different impressions. Maravegli, Estwick, Medlicote and you, were beings who inspired veneration and love. Your residence appeared to beautify and consecrate this spot, and gave birth to an opinion that if cities are the chosen seats of misery and vice, they are likewise the soil of all the laudable and strenuous productions of mind.[6]

My curiosity and thirst of knowledge had likewise received a new direction. Books and inanimate nature were cold and lifeless instructors. Men, and the works of men, were the objects of rational study, and our own eyes only could communicate just conceptions of human performances.[7] The influence of manners, professions and social institutions, could be thoroughly known only by direct inspection.

---

[5] "A revolution in my mind": this sentence introduces a crucial passage explaining the transformation Mervyn has experienced to this point and outlining new principles and desires that will guide his actions in the remainder of the novel. Addressing Stevens directly, Mervyn explains that his "curiosity" (see notes 2.11, 7.3, 9.1) and "thirst of knowledge" have turned toward new goals and that he now plans to pursue rational self-improvement through study and direct engagement with human relations ("the influence of manners, professions, and social institutions"). Mervyn's approach to visual observation ("our eyes only could communicate just perceptions") and rational improvement here takes on a somewhat different coloration than Stevens'. Mervyn explicitly links his studies to the project of contemplating and improving social relations in general (using all forms of knowledge) in contrast to Stevens' more restricted emphasis on medical knowledge and care for individuals. This passage and chapter initiate a significant departure from Brown's original plot outline, notably by abandoning his original plan to have Mervyn marry Eliza Hadwin. For more on the sense of this "revolution" in Mervyn's mind and Brown's plot decisions for *Second Part*, see the Introduction.

[6] "Productions of mind": Mervyn rejects the notion he entertained in the first part that cities are primarily pools of vice, arguing that cities are also the location of human enlightenment and the place where interpersonal conversation and improvement occurs with a density and circulation not possible in the countryside.

[7] "Human performances": rejecting impersonal books and nature, which cannot "converse" with humans, Mervyn emphasizes the observation of society as a form of direct engagement with human relations. See Godwin's similar argument in Related Texts.

Competence, fixed property and a settled abode, rural occupations and conjugal pleasures, were justly to be prized; but their value could be known, and their benefits fully enjoyed only by those who have tried all scenes; who have mixed with all classes and ranks; who have partaken of all conditions; and who have visited different hemispheres and climates and nations. The next five or eight years of my life, should be devoted to activity and change; it should be a period of hardship, danger and privation; it should be my apprenticeship to fortitude and wisdom, and be employed to fit me for the tranquil pleasures and steadfast exertions of the remainder of my life.

In consequence of these reflections, I determined to suppress that tenderness which the company of Miss Hadwin produced, to remove any mistakes into which she had fallen, and to put it out of my power to claim from her more than the dues of friendship. All ambiguities, in a case like this, and all delays were hurtful. She was not exempt from passion, but this passion I thought was young, and easily extinguished.

In a short time her health was restored, and her grief melted down into a tender melancholy. I chose a suitable moment, when not embarrassed by the presence of others, to reveal my thoughts. My disclosure was ingenuous and perfect. I laid before her the whole train of my thoughts, nearly in the order, though in different and more copious terms than those in which I have just explained them to you. I concealed nothing. The impression which her artless lovelines had made upon me at Malverton; my motives for estranging myself from her society; the nature of my present feelings with regard to her, and my belief of the state of her heart; the reasonings into which I had entered; the advantages of wedlock and its inconveniences; and, finally, the resolution I had formed of seeking the city, and perhaps, of crossing the ocean, were minutely detailed.

She interrupted me not, but changing looks, blushes, flutterings and sighs, shewed her to be deeply and variously affected by my discourse. I paused for some observation or comment. She seemed conscious of my expectation, but had no power to speak. Overpowered, at length, by her emotions, she burst into tears.

I was at a loss in what manner to construe these symptoms. I waited till her vehemence was somewhat subsided, and then said—what think you of my schemes? Your approbation is of some moment; do you approve of them or not?

This question excited some little resentment, and she answered—you have left me nothing to say. Go and be happy; no matter what becomes of me. I hope I shall be able to take care of myself.

The tone in which this was said, had something in it of upbraiding. Your happiness, said I, is too dear to me to leave it in danger. In this house you will not need my protection, but I shall never be so far from you, as to be disabled from hearing how you fared, by letter, and of being active for your good. You have some money which you must husband well. Any rent from your farm cannot be soon expected; but what you have got, if you remain with Mr. Curling, will pay your board and all other expences for two years; but you must be a good economist. I shall expect, continued I, with a serious smile, a punctual account of all your sayings and doings. I must know how every minute is employed, and every penny is expended, and if I find you erring, I must tell you so in good round terms.

These words did not dissipate the sullenness which her looks had betrayed. She still forebore to look at me, and said—I do not know how I should tell you every thing. You care so little about me that—I should only be troublesome. I am old enough to think and act for myself, and shall advise with no body but myself.

That is true, said I. I shall rejoice to see you independent and free. Consult your own understanding, and act according to its dictates. Nothing more is wanting to make you useful and happy. I am anxious to return to the city; but, if you will allow me, will go first to Malverton, see that things are in due order, and that old Caleb is well. From thence, if you please, I will call at your uncle's, and tell him what has happened. He may, otherwise, entertain pretensions and form views, erroneous in themselves and injurious to you. He may think himself entitled to manage your estate. He may either suppose a will to have been made, or may actually have heard from your father, or from others, of that which you burnt, and in which he was named executor. His boisterous and sordid temper may prompt him to seize your house and goods, unless seasonably apprised of the truth; and, when he knows the truth, he may start into rage, which I shall be more fitted to encounter than you. I am told that anger transforms him into a ferocious madman. Shall I call upon him?

She shuddered at the picture which I had drawn of her uncle's character; but this emotion quickly gave place to self-upbraiding, for the manner in which she had repelled my proffers of service. She melted once more into tears and exclaimed:

I am not worthy of the pains you take for me. I am unfeeling and ungrateful. Why should I think ill of you for despising me, when I despise myself?

You do yourself injustice, my friend. I think I see your most secret thoughts; and these, instead of exciting anger or contempt, only awaken compassion and tenderness. You love; and must, therefore, conceive my conduct to be perverse and cruel. I counted on your harboring such thoughts. Time only and reflection will enable you to see my motives in their true light. Hereafter you will recollect my words, and find them sufficient to justify my conduct. You will acknowledge the propriety of my engaging in the cares of the world, before I sit down in retirement and ease.

Ah! how much you mistake me! I admire and approve of your schemes. What angers and distresses me is, that you think me unworthy to partake of your cares and labors; that you regard my company as an obstacle and incumbrance; that assistance and counsel must all proceed from you; and that no scene is fit for me, but what you regard as slothful and inglorious.

Have I not the same claims to be wise, and active, and courageous as you?[8] If I am ignorant and weak, do I not owe it to the same cause that has made you so; and will not the same means which promote your improvement be likewise useful to me? You desire to obtain knowledge, by travelling and conversing with many persons, and studying many sciences; but you desire it for yourself alone. Me, you think poor, weak, and contemptible; fit for nothing but to spin and churn. Provided I exist, am

---

[8] "Have I not the same claims . . . as you?": Eliza articulates the claims of Wollstonecraftian feminism, pressing Mervyn toward greater awareness of the implications of her subordinated position.

screened from the weather, have enough to eat and drink, you are satisfied. As to strengthening my mind and enlarging my knowledge, these things are valuable to you, but on me they are thrown away. I deserve not the gift.

This strain, simple and just as it was, was wholly unexpected. I was surprized and disconcerted. In my previous reasonings I had certainly considered her sex as utterly unfitting her for those scenes and pursuits, to which I had destined myself. Not a doubt of the validity of my conclusion had insinuated itself; but now my belief was shaken, though it was not subverted. I could not deny, that human ignorance was curable by the same means in one sex as in the other;[9] that fortitude and skill was of no less value to one than to the other.

Questionless, my friend was rendered, by her age and inexperience, if not by sex, more helpless and dependent than I; but had I not been prone to overrate the difficulties which I should encounter? Had I not deemed unjustly of her constancy and force of mind? Marriage would render her property joint, and would not compel me to take up my abode in the woods, to abide forever in one spot, to shackle my curiosity, or limit my excursions.

But marriage was a contract awful and irrevocable. Was this the woman with whom my reason enjoined me to blend my fate, without the power of dissolution? Would no time unfold qualities in her which I did not at present suspect, and which would evince an incurable difference in our minds? Would not time lead me to the feet of one who more nearly approached that standard of ideal excellence which poets and romancers had exhibited to my view?

These considerations were powerful and delicate. I knew not in what terms to state them to my companion, so as to preclude the imputation of arrogance or indecorum. It became me, however, to be explicit, and to excite her resentment rather than mislead her judgment. She collected my meaning from a few words, and, interrupting me, said:

How very low is the poor Eliza in your opinion! We are, indeed, both too young to be married. May I not see you, and talk with you, without being your wife? May I not share your knowledge, relieve your cares, and enjoy your confidence, as a sister might do? May I not accompany you in your journeys and studies, as one friend accompanies another? My property may be yours; you may employ it for your benefit and mine; not because you are my husband, but my friend. You are going to the city. Let me go along with you. Let me live where you live. The house that is large enough to hold you, will hold me. The fare that is good enough for you will be luxury to me. Oh! let it be so, will you? You cannot think how studious, how thoughtful, how inquisitive I will be. How tenderly I will nurse you when sick; it is possible you may be

---

[9] "In one sex as in the other": Eliza's desire for opportunities of "strengthening my mind and enlarging my knowledge," just paragraphs after Mervyn expresses the same goal, requires Mervyn and the reader alike to acknowledge gendered double standards. The passage offers another of the novel's arguments for women's rights and Woldwinite feminism, and another parallel between Eliza and Mervyn after their similar decisions to burn valuable papers in Chapters 23 and II.8.

sick, you know, and no one in the world will be half so watchful and affectionate as I shall be. Will you let me?

In saying this, her earnestness gave new pathos to her voice. Insensibly she put her face close to mine, and, transported beyond the usual bounds of reserve, by the charms of that picture which her fancy contemplated, she put her lips to my cheek, and repeated, in a melting accent, will you let me?

You, my friends, who have not seen Eliza Hadwin, cannot conceive what effect this entreaty was adapted to produce in me. She has surely the sweetest voice, the most speaking features, and most delicate symetry, that ever woman possessed. Her guileless simplicity and tenderness made her more enchanting. To be the object of devotion to an heart so fervent and pure, was, surely, no common privilege. Thus did she tender me herself; and was not the gift to be received with eagerness and gratitude?

No. I was not so much a stranger to mankind as to acquiesce in this scheme. As my sister or my wife, the world would suffer us to reside under the same roof; to apply, to common use, the same property; and daily to enjoy the company of each other; but she was not my sister, and marriage would be an act of the grossest indiscretion. I explained to her, in few words, the objections to which her project was liable.

Well, then, said she, let me live in the next house, in the neighborhood, or, at least, in the same city. Let me be where I may see you once a day, or once a week, or once a month. Shut me not wholly from your society, and the means of becoming, in time, less ignorant and foolish than I now am.[10]

After a pause, I replied, I love you too well not to comply with this request. Perhaps the city will be as suitable a residence as any other for you, as it will, for some time, be most convenient to me. I shall be better able to watch over your welfare, and supply you with the means of improvement, when you are within a small distance. At present, you must consent to remain here, while I visit your uncle, and afterwards go to the city. I shall look out for you a suitable lodging, and inform you when it is found. If you then continue in the same mind, I will come, and, having gained the approbation of Mr. Curling, will conduct you to town. Here ended our dialogue.

---

[10] "The means of becoming . . . less foolish and ignorant": Eliza's desire for improvement rivals Mervyn's own and she succeeds in her argument for a mode of different-sex friendship and association outside of marriage that is unconventional for the time. The enlightened social circle Mervyn gathers around him at the end of the novel will be characterized by progressive but unconventional bonds of rational friendship across sexes.

Chapter X

THOUGH I had consented to this scheme, I was conscious that some hazards attended it. I was afraid of calumny,[1] which might trouble the peace or destroy the reputation of my friend. I was afraid of my own weakness, which might be seduced into an indiscreet marriage, by the charms or sufferings of this bewitching creature. I felt that there was no price too dear to save her from slander. A fair fame is of the highest importance to a young female, and the loss of it but poorly supplied by the testimony of her own conscience. I had reason for tenfold solicitude on this account, since I was her only protector and friend. Hence, I cherished some hopes, that time might change her views, and suggest less dangerous schemes. Meanwhile, I was to lose no time in visiting Malverton and Philip Hadwin.

About ten days had elapsed since we had deserted Malverton. These were days of successive storms, and travelling had been rendered inconvenient. The weather was now calm and clear, and, early in the morning that ensued the dialogue which I have just related, I set out on horseback.

Honest Caleb was found, eating his breakfast, nearly in the spot where he had been first discovered. He answered my enquiries by saying that two days after our departure, several men had come to the house, one of whom was Philip Hadwin. They had interrogated him as to the condition of the farm, and the purpose of his remaining on it. William Hadwin they knew to have been sometime dead, but where were the girls, his daughters?

Caleb answered that Susy, the eldest, was likewise dead.

These tidings excited astonishment. When died she, and how, and where was she buried?

It happened two days before, and she was buried, he believed, but could not tell where.

Not tell where? By whom then was she buried?

Really, he could not tell. Some strange man came there just as she was dying. He went to the room, and when she was dead, took her away, but what he did with the body was more than he could say, but he had a notion that he buried it. The man staid till the morning and then went off with Lizzy, leaving him to keep house by himself. He had not seen either of them, nor indeed, a single soul since.

This was all the information that Caleb could afford the visitants. It was so lame and incredible that they began to charge the man with falsehood, and to threaten him with legal animadversion. Just then, Mr. Ellis entered the house, and being made acquainted with the subject of discourse, told all that he himself knew. He related the midnight visit which I had paid him, explained my former situation in the

---

[1] "Calumny": libel, slander, false charges. Mervyn rightly worries that Eliza will be slandered or considered disrespectable because of her unconventional relationship with him. Relative to the period's norms, her desires for independence and a free life as an unmarried female constitute "dangerous schemes."

family, and my disappearance in September. He stated the advice he had given me to carry Eliza to her uncle's, and my promise to comply with his counsel. The uncle declared he had seen nothing of his niece, and Caleb added, that when she set out, she took the road that led to town.

These hints afforded grounds for much conjecture and suspicion. Ellis now mentioned some intelligence that he had gathered respecting me in a late journey to _____. It seems I was the son of an honest farmer in that quarter, who married a tidy girl of a milk maid, that lived with him. My father had detected me in making some atrocious advances to my mother-in-law, and had turned me out of doors. I did not go off, however, without rifling his drawer of some hundreds of dollars, which he had laid up against a rainy day. I was noted for such pranks, and was hated by all the neighbors for my pride and laziness. It was easy by comparison of circumstances, for Ellis to ascertain that Hadwin's servant Mervyn was the same against whom such hearty charges were laid.

Previously to this journey, he had heard of me from Hadwin, who was loud in praise of my diligence, sobriety and modesty. For his part, he had always been cautious of giving countenance to vagrants, that came from nobody knew where, and worked their way with a plausible tongue. He was not surprised to hear it whispered that Betsey Hadwin had fallen in love with the youth, and now, no doubt, he had persuaded her to run away with him. The heiress of a fine farm was a prize not to be met with every day.

Philip broke into rage at this news; swore that if it turned out so, his niece should starve upon the town, and that he would take good care to baulk[2] the lad. His brother he well knew had left a will, to which he was executor, and that this will, would in good time, be forth coming. After much talk and ransacking the house, and swearing at his truant niece, he and his company departed, charging Caleb to keep the house and its contents for his use. This was all that Caleb's memory had retained of that day's proceedings.

Curling had lately commented on the character of Philip Hadwin. This man was totally unlike his brother, was a noted brawler and bully, a tyrant to his children, a plague to his neighbors, and kept a rendezvous for drunkards and idlers, at the sign of the Bull's Head,[3] at _____. He was not destitute of parts,[4] and was no less dreaded for cunning than malignity. He was covetous, and never missed an opportunity of overreaching his neighbor. There was no doubt that his niece's property would be

---

[2] "Baulk": hinder, frustrate, foil.

[3] "Bull's Head": a common name for taverns and inns in the eighteenth century. Chester County had two inns by this name in the 1780s–1790s, located in the nearly adjoining townships of West Nantmeal and Honey Brook, both forty-five miles from Philadelphia in the western part of the county. Like several other taverns in the area, the Bull's Head in Honey Brook was renamed the "General Wayne" shortly after the death of "Mad" Anthony Wayne (1745–1796), a general who defeated a confederation of Native American warriors at the Battle of Fallen Timbers in 1794.

[4] "Parts": talents, abilities, capabilities.

embezzled, should it ever come into his hands, and any power which he might obtain over her person would be exercised to her destruction. His children were tainted with the dissoluteness of their father, and marriage had not repaired the reputation of his daughters, or cured them of depravity; this was the man whom I now proposed to visit.

I scarcely need to say that the calumny of Betty Lawrence gave me no uneasiness. My father had no doubt been deceived, as well as my father's neighbors, by the artifices of this woman. I passed among them for a thief and a profligate, but their error had hitherto been harmless to me. The time might come which should confute the tale, without my efforts. Betty, sooner or later would drop her mask, and afford the antidote to her own poisons, unless some new incident should occur to make me hasten the catastrophe.

I arrived at Hadwin's house. I was received with some attention as a guest. I looked among the pimpled visages that filled the piazza,[5] for that of the landlord, but found him in an inner apartment with two or three more, seated round a table. On intimating my wish to speak with him alone, the others withdrew.

Hadwin's visage had some traces of resemblance to his brother; but the meek, placid air, pale cheeks and slender form of the latter were powerfully contrasted with the bloated arrogance, imperious brow and robust limbs of the former.[6] This man's rage was awakened by a straw; it impelled him in an instant to oaths and buffetings, and made his life an eternal brawl. The sooner my interview with such a personage should be at an end, the better. I therefore explained the purpose of my coming as fully and in as few words as possible.

Your name, Sir, is Philip Hadwin. Your brother William, of Malverton, died lately and left two daughters. The youngest only is now alive, and I come, commissioned from her, to inform you, that as no will of her father's is extant, she is preparing to administer to his estate. As her father's brother, she thought you entitled to this information.

The change which took place in the countenance of this man, during this address, was remarkable, but not easily described. His cheeks contracted a deeper crimson, his eyes sparkled, and his face assumed an expression in which curiosity was mingled with rage. He bent forwards and said, in an hoarse and contemptuous tone, pray, is your name Mervyn?

I answered, without hesitation, and as if the question were wholly unimportant, yes; my name is Mervyn.

God damn it! You then are the damn'd rascal—(but permit me to repeat his speech without the oaths, with which it was plentifully interlarded. Not three words were uttered without being garnished with a—God damn it! damnation! I'll be damn'd to

---

[5] "Piazza": a porch or, sometimes, a covered walkway between a main building and an outbuilding.

[6] "Robust limbs of the former": the great difference between the two Hadwin brothers (Mervyn earlier notes "this man is totally unlike his brother") is another implicit rejection of the idea that character can be determined by one's lineage and "breeding." Philip Hadwin's anger, swearing, and use of "you" rather than "thou" also indicates that, unlike his brother, he does not follow Quaker practices of calm behavior.

hell if—and the like energetic expletives.) You then are the rascal that robbed Billy's house; that ran away with the fool his daughter; persuaded her to burn her father's will, and have the hellish impudence to come into this house! But I thank you for it. I was going to look for you—you've saved me trouble. I'll settle all accounts with you here. Fair and softly, my good lad! If I don't bring you to the gallows—If I let you escape without such a dressing! Damned impudence! Fellow! I've been at Malverton. I've heard of your tricks; so! finding the will not quite to your mind, knowing that the executor would baulk your schemes, you threw the will into the fire; you robbed the house of all the cash, and made off with the girl!—The old fellow saw it all, and will swear to the truth.

These words created some surprize. I meant not to conceal from this man the tenor[7] and destruction of the will, nor even the measures which his niece had taken or intended to take. What I supposed to be unknown to him appeared to have been communicated by the talkative Caleb, whose mind was more inquisitive and less sluggish than first appearances had led me to imagine. Instead of moping by the kitchen fire, when Eliza and I were conversing in an upper room, it now appeared that he had reconnoitred our proceedings through some key-hole or crevice, and had related what he had seen to Hadwin.

Hadwin proceeded to exhaust his rage in oaths and menaces. He frequently clenched his fist, and thrust it in my face, drew it back as if to render his blow more deadly; ran over the same series of exclamations on my impudence and villainy, and talked of the gallows and the whipping-post; enforced each word by the epithets—*damnable* and *hellish*—closed each sentence with—and be curst to you!

There was but one mode for me to pursue; all forcible opposition to a man of his strength was absurd. It was my province to make his anger confine itself to words, and patiently to wait till the paroxism should end or subside of itself. To effect this purpose, I kept my seat, and carefully excluded from my countenance every indication of timidity and panick on the one hand, and of scorn and defiance on the other. My look and attitude were those of a man who expected harsh words, but who entertained no suspicion that blows would be inflicted.

I was indebted for my safety to an inflexible adherence to this medium. To have strayed, for a moment, to either side would have brought upon me his blows. That he did not instantly resort to violence inspired me with courage, since it depended on myself whether food should be supplied to his passion. Rage must either progress or decline, and since it was in total want of provocation, it could not fail of gradually subsiding.

My demeanor was calculated to damp the flame, not only by its direct influence but by diverting his attention from the wrongs which he had received, to the novelty of my behaviour. The disparity in size and strength between us was too evident to make him believe that I confided in my sinews for my defence; and since I betrayed neither contempt nor fear; he could not but conclude that I trusted to my own integrity or to his moderation. I seized the first pause in his rhetorick to enforce this sentiment.

---

[7] "Tenor": contents, the substance or meaning of something written or spoken.

You are angry, Mr. Hadwin, and are loud in your threats, but they do not frighten me. They excite no apprehension or alarm, because I know myself able to convince you that I have not injured you. This is an inn, and I am your guest. I am sure I shall find better entertainment than blows. Come, continued I, smiling, it is possible that I am not so mischievous a wretch as your fancy paints me. I have no claims upon your niece but that of friendship, and she is now in the house of an honest man, Mr. Curling, where she proposes to continue as long as is convenient.

It is true that your brother left a will, which his daughter burnt in my presence, because she dreaded the authority which that will gave you, not only over her property, but person. It is true that on leaving the house, she took away the money which was now her own, and which was necessary to subsistence. It is true that I bore her company, and have left her in an honest man's keeping. I am answerable for nothing more. As to you, I meant not to injure you; I advised not the burning of the will. I was a stranger till after that event, to your character. I knew neither good nor ill of you. I came to tell you all this, because, as Eliza's uncle, you had a right to the information.

So! you come to tell me that she burnt the will, and is going to administer—to what, I beseech you? to her father's property? Aye, I warrant you; but take this along with you, that property is mine; land, house, stock, every thing. All is safe and snug under cover of a mortgage, to which Billy was kind enough to add a bond. One was sued, and the other *entered up*, a week ago.[8] So that all is safe under my thumb, and the girl may whistle or starve for me. I shall give myself no concern about the strumpet. You thought to get a prize; but, damn me, you've met with your match in me. Phil. Haddin's not so easily choused,[9] I promise you. I intended to give you this news, and a drubbing into the bargain; but you may go, and make haste. She burnt the will, did she; because I was named in it—and sent you to tell me so? Good souls! It was kind of you, and I am bound to be thankful. Take her back news of the mortgage; and, as for you, leave my house. You may go scot free this time; but I pledge my word for a sound beating when you next enter these doors. I'll pay it you with interest. Leave my house, I say!

A mortgage, said I, in a low voice, and affecting not to hear his commands, that will be sad news for my friend. Why, sir, you are a fortunate man. Malverton is an excellent spot; well watered and manured; newly and completely fenced; not a larger barn in the county; oxen, and horses, and cows in the best order; I never sat eyes on a finer orchard. By my faith, sir, you are a fortunate man. But, pray, what have you for dinner? I am hungry as a wolf. Order me a beef-steak, and some potation or other. The bottle there—it is cyder, I take it; pray, push it to this side. Saying this, I stretched

---

[8] "*Entered up,* a week ago": like Welbeck's legalistic arguments about being Clemenza's guardian in the first part (see note 22.1), Philip Hadwin's greed and disregard for a woman's property and possible independence are expressed in legalistic claims (mortgages, bonds, guardianship) to patriarchal authority.

[9] "Choused": cheated, tricked, swindled, defrauded.

out my hand towards the bottle which stood before him.

I confided in the power of a fearless and sedate manner. Methought that as anger was the food of anger, it must unavoidably subside in a contest with equability. This opinion was intuitive, rather than the product of experience, and perhaps, I gave no proof of my sagacity in hazarding my safety on its truth. Hadwin's character made him dreaded and obeyed by all. He had been accustomed to ready and tremulous submission from men far more brawny and robust than I was, and to find his most vehement menaces and gestures, totally ineffectual on a being so slender and diminutive, at once wound up his rage and excited his astonishment. One motion counteracted and suspended the other. He lifted his hand, but delayed to strike. One blow, applied with his usual dexterity, was sufficient to destroy me. Though seemingly careless, I was watchful of his motions, and prepared to elude the stroke by shrinking or stooping. Meanwhile, I stretched my hand far enough to seize the bottle, and pouring its contents into a tumbler, put it to my lips.

Come, sir, I drink your health, and wish you speedy possession of Malverton. I have some interest with Eliza, and will prevail on her to forbear all opposition and complaint. Why should she complain? While I live, she shall not be a beggar. No doubt, your claim is legal, and therefore ought to be admitted. What the law gave, the law has taken away. Blessed be the dispensers of law—excellent cyder! open another bottle, will you, and I beseech hasten dinner, if you would not see me devour the table.

It was just, perhaps, to conjure up the demon avarice to fight with the demon anger. Reason alone, would, in such a contest, be powerless, but, in truth, I spoke without artifice or disguise. If his claim were legal, opposition would be absurd and pernicious. I meant not to rely upon his own assertions, and would not acknowledge the validity of his claim, till I had inspected the deed. Having instituted suits, this was now in a public office, and there the inspection should be made. Meanwhile, no reason could be urged why I should part from him in anger, while his kindred to Eliza, and his title to her property, made it useful to secure his favor. It was possible to obtain a remission of his claims, even when the law enforced them; it would be imprudent at least to diminish the chances of remission by festering his wrath and provoking his enmity.

What, he exclaimed, in a transport of fury, a'n't I master of my own house? Out, I say!

These were harsh terms, but they were not accompanied by gestures and tones so menacing as those which had before been used. It was plain that the tide, which so lately threatened my destruction, had begun to recede. This encouraged me to persist.

Be not alarmed, my good friend, said I, placidly and smiling. A man of your bone need not fear a pigmy like me. I shall scarcely be able to dethrone you in your own castle, with an army of hostlers, tapsters, and cooks at your beck. You shall still be master here, provided you use your influence to procure me a dinner.

His acquiescence in a pacific system, was extremely reluctant and gradual. He laid aside one sullen tone and wrathful look after the other; and, at length, consented not only to supply me with a dinner, but to partake of it with me. Nothing was more a topic of surprize to himself, than his forbearance. He knew not how it was. He had never been treated so before. He was not proof against entreaty and submission; but

I had neither supplicated nor submitted. The stuff that I was made of was at once damnably tough and devilishly pliant.[10] When he thought of my impudence, in staying in his house after he had bade me leave it, he was tempted to resume his passion. When he reflected on my courage, in making light of his anger, notwithstanding his known impetuosity and my personal inferiority, he could not withhold his esteem. But my patience under his rebukes, my unalterable equanimity, and my ready consent to the validity of his claims, soothed and propitiated him.

An exemption from blows and abuse was all that I could gain from this man. I told him the truth, with regard to my own history, so far as it was connected with the Hadwins. I exhibited, in affecting colours, the helpless condition of Eliza; but could extort from him nothing but his consent, that, if she chose, she might come and live with him. He would give her victuals and clothes for so much house-work as she was able to do. If she chose to live elsewhere, he promised not to molest her, or intermeddle in her concerns. The house and land were his by law, and he would have them.

It was not my province to revile, or expostulate with him. I stated what measures would be adopted by a man who regarded the interest of others more than his own; who was anxious for the welfare of an innocent girl, connected with him so closely by the ties of kindred, and who was destitute of what is called natural friends. If he did not cancel, for her sake, his bond and mortgage, he would, at least, afford her a frugal maintainance. He would extend to her, in all emergences, his counsel and protection.

All that, he said, was sheer nonsense. He could not sufficiently wonder at my folly, in proposing to him to make a free gift of an hundred rich acres, to a girl too who scarcely knew her right hand from her left; whom the first cunning young rogue, like myself, would *chouse* out of the whole, and take herself into the bargain. But my folly was even surpassed by my impudence, since, as the *friend* of this girl, I was merely petitioning on my own account. I had come to him, whom I never saw before, on whom I had no claim, and who, as I well knew, had reason to think me a sharper, and modestly said—"Here's a girl who has no fortune. I am greatly in want of one. Pray, give her such an estate that you have in your possession. If you do, I'll marry her, and take it into my own hands." I might be thankful that he did not answer such a petition with an horse-whipping. But if he did not give her his estate, he might extend to her, forsooth, his counsel and protection. That I've offered to do, continued he. She may come and live in my house, if she will. She may do some of the family work. I'll discharge the chamber-maid to make room for her. Lizzy, if I remember right, has a

---

[10] "Damnably tough and devilishly pliant": Hadwin is frustrated by Mervyn's ability to turn conventional expectations and prejudices to his advantage. The same ability angered and bewildered the matron Mrs. Althorpe in Chapter II.2 (see note II.2.15). Mervyn's strategy of calculated "pacific" equanimity may also refer to the well-documented style of interaction and intervention favored by Quaker abolition activist Isaac Hopper in the 1790s. See the account of Isaac Hopper in Related Texts.

pretty face. She can't have a better market for it than as chamber-maid to an inn. If she minds her p's and q's she may make up a handsome sum[11] at the year's end.

I thought it time to break off the conference; and, my dinner being finished, took my leave; leaving behind me the character of *a queer sort of chap.* I speeded to the prothonotary's[12] office, which was kept in the village, and quickly ascertained the truth of Hadwin's pretensions. There existed a mortgage, with bond and warrant of attorney, to so great an amount as would swallow up every thing at Malverton. Furnished with these tidings, I prepared, with a drooping heart, to return to Mr. Curling's.

---

[11] "Can't have a better market for it . . . handsome sum": Hadwin implies that a pretty girl can do well as a chambermaid, with a vulgar implication that she could make money on the side as a prostitute.

[12] "Prothonotary": chief clerk, recorder, or principal notary of a court; the keeper of public records in a village like this.

Chapter XI

THIS incident necessarily produced a change in my views with regard to my friend. Her fortune consisted of a few hundreds of dollars, which, frugally administered, might procure decent accommodation in the country. When this was consumed, she must find subsistence in tending the big-wheel or the milk-pail, unless fortune should enable me to place her in a more favorable situation. This state was, in some respects, but little different from that in which she had spent the former part of her life; but, in her father's house, these employments were dignified by being, in some degree, voluntary, and relieved by frequent intervals of recreation and leisure. Now they were likely to prove irksome and servile, in consequence of being performed for hire, and imposed by necessity. Equality, parental solicitudes, and sisterly endearments would be wanting to lighten the yoke.

These inconveniences, however, were imaginary. This was the school in which fortitude and independence were to be learned. Habit, and the purity of rural manners, would, likewise, create a-new those ties which death had dissolved. The affections of parent and sister would be supplied by the fonder and more rational attachments of friendship. These toils were not detrimental to beauty or health. What was to be dreaded from them was their tendency to quench the spirit of liberal curiosity; to habituate the Person to bodily, rather than intellectual, exertions; to supersede, and create indifference or aversion to the only instruments of rational improvement, the pen and the book.

This evil, however, was at some distance from Eliza. Her present abode was quiet and serene. Here she might enjoy domestic pleasures and opportunities of mental improvement, for the coming twelvemonth at least. This period would, perhaps, be sufficient for the formation of studious habits. What schemes should be adopted, for this end, would be determined by the destiny to which I myself should be reserved.

My path was already chalked out, and my fancy now pursued it with uncommon pleasure. To reside in your family; to study your profession;[1] to pursue some subordinate or casual mode of industry, by which I might purchase leisure for medical pursuits, for social recreations, and for the study of mankind on your busy and thronged stage, was the scope of my wishes. This destiny would not hinder punctual correspondence and occasional visits to Eliza. Her pen might be called into action, and her mind be awakened by books, and every hour be made to add to her stores of knowledge and enlarge the bounds of her capacity.

I was spiritless and gloomy when I left—, but reflections on my future lot, and just views of the situation of my friend, insensibly restored my cheerfulness. I arrived at Mr. Curling's in the evening, and hastened to impart to Eliza the issue of my commission. It gave her uneasiness, merely as it frustrated the design, on which she had

---

[1] "Your family . . . your profession": addressing his mentor Dr. Stevens, Mervyn refers back to the "revolution" and transformation of his thinking in Chapter II.9 (see note II.9.5) revealing his plans to become a physician like Stevens and, more widely, devote himself to "the study of mankind." After his negotiation with Eliza, she too is dedicated to "opportunities of mental improvement."

fondly mused, of residing in the city. She was somewhat consoled by my promises of being her constant correspondent and occasional visitor.

Next morning I set out on my journey hither, on foot. The way was not long; the weather, though cold, was wholesome and serene. My spirits were high, and I saw nothing in the world before me but sunshine and prosperity. I was conscious that my happiness depended not on the revolutions of nature or the caprice of man. All without was, indeed, vicissitude and uncertainty; but within my bosom was a centre not to be shaken or removed. My purposes were honest and steadfast. Every sense was the inlet of pleasure, because it was the avenue to knowledge; and my soul brooded over the world of ideas, and glowed with exultation at the grandeur and beauty of its own creations.

This felicity was too rapturous to be of long duration. I gradually descended from these heights; and the remembrance of past incidents, connected with the images of your family, to which I was returning, led my thoughts into a different channel. Welbeck and the unhappy girl whom he had betrayed; Mrs. Villars and Wallace were recollected a-new. The views which I had formed, for determining the fate and affording assistance to Clemenza, were recalled. My former resolutions, with regard to her, had been suspended by the uncertainty in which the fate of the Hadwins was, at that time, wrapped. Had it not become necessary wholly to lay aside these resolutions?

That, indeed, was an irksome conclusion. No wonder that I struggled to repel it; that I fostered the doubt whether money was the only instrument of benefit; whether caution, and fortitude, and knowledge were not the genuine preservatives from evil. Had I not the means in my hands of dispelling her fatal ignorance of Welbeck and of those with whom she resided? Was I not authorized by my previous, though slender, intercourse, to seek her presence?

Suppose I should enter Mrs. Villars' house, desire to be introduced to the lady, accost her with affectionate simplicity, and tell her the truth? Why be anxious to smooth the way; why deal in apologies, circuities and inuendoes? All these are feeble and perverse refinements, unworthy of an honest purpose and an erect spirit. To believe her inaccessible to my visit, was absurd. To wait for the permission of those whose interest it might be to shut out visitants, was cowardice. This was an infringement of her liberty, which equity and law equally condemned. By what right could she be restrained from intercourse with others? Doors and passages may be between her and me. With a purpose such as mine, no one had a right to close the one or obstruct the other. Away with cowardly reluctances and clownish scruples, and let me hasten this moment to her dwelling.

Mrs. Villars is the portress[2] of the mansion. She will probably present herself before me, and demand the reason of my visit. What shall I say to her? The truth. To faulter,

---

[2] "Portress": "a woman who acts as a porter or doorkeeper, esp. in a nunnery" (OED). Villars oversees a house that is at once a brothel and an elite female space filled with expensive aesthetic objects implying cosmopolitan sophistication.

or equivocate, or dissemble to this woman, would be wicked. Perhaps her character has been misunderstood and maligned. Can I render her a greater service than to apprize her of the aspersions that have rested on it, and afford her the opportunity of vindication? Perhaps she is indeed selfish and profligate; the betrayer of youth and the agent of lasciviousness. Does she not deserve to know the extent of her errors and the ignominy of her trade? Does she not merit the compassion of the good and the rebukes of the wise? To shrink from the task, would prove me cowardly and unfirm. Thus far, at least, let my courage extend.

Alas! Clemenza is unacquainted with my language. My thoughts cannot make themselves apparent but by words, and to my words she will be able to affix no meaning. Yet is not that an hasty decision? The venison from the dramas of Zeno which I found in her toilet was probably hers, and proves her to have a speculative knowledge of our tongue.[3] Near half a year has since elapsed, during which she has dwelt with talkers of English, and consequently could not fail to have acquired it. This conclusion is somewhat dubious, but experiment will give it certainty.

Hitherto I had strolled along the path at a lingering pace. Time enough, methought, to reach your threshold between sun-rise and moonlight, if my way had been three times longer than it was. Yon were the pleasing phantoms that hovered before me, and beckoned me forward. What a total revolution had occurred in the course of a few seconds, for thus long did my reasonings with regard to Clemenza and the Villars require to pass through my understanding, and escape, in half muttered soliloquy, from my lips. My muscles trembled with eagerness, and I bounded forward with impetuosity. I saw nothing but a vista of catalpas, leafless, loaded with icicles, and terminating in four chimneys and a painted roof. My fancy outstripped my footsteps, and was busy in picturing faces and rehearsing dialogues. Presently I reached this new object of my pursuit, darted through the avenue, noticed that some windows of the house were unclosed, drew thence an hasty inference that the house was not without inhabitants, and knocked, quickly and loudly, for admission.

Some one within crept to the door, opened it with seeming caution, and just far enough to allow the face to be seen. It was the timid, pale and unwashed face of a girl who was readily supposed to be a servant, taken from a cottage, and turned into a bringer of wood and water, and a scourer of tubs and trenchers. She waited in timorous silence the delivery of my message. Was Mrs. Villars at home?

No: she was gone to town.

Were any of her daughters within?

She could not tell; she believed—she thought—which did I want? Miss Hetty or Miss Sally?

Let me see Miss Hetty. Saying this, I pushed gently against the door. The girl, half reluctant, yielded way; I entered the passage, and putting my hand on the lock of a door that seemed to lead into a parlour—is Miss Hetty in this room?

---

[3] "A speculative knowledge of our tongue": Mervyn recalls that he found an English translation in Clemenza's copy of Zeno's plays. For that scene, which also precedes a dramatic confrontation and a gunshot, see note 9.4.

No: there was nobody there.

Go call her then. Tell her there is one who wishes to see her on important business. I will wait for her coming in this room. So saying, I opened the door, and entered the apartment, while the girl withdrew to perform my message.

The parlour was spacious and expensively furnished, but an air of negligence and disorder was every where visible. The carpet was wrinkled and unswept; a clock on the table, in a glass frame, so streaked and spotted with dust as scarcely to be transparent, and the index motionless, and pointing at four instead of nine; embers scattered on the marble hearth, and tongs lying on the fender with the handle in the ashes; an harpsicord, uncovered, one end loaded with *scores*, tumbled together in a heap, and the other with volumes of novels and plays, some on their edges, some on their backs, gaping open by the scorching[4] of their covers; rent; blurred; stained; blotted; dog-eared; tables awry; chairs crouding each other; in short, no object but indicated the neglect or ignorance of domestic neatness and economy.

My leisure was employed in surveying these objects, and in listening for the approach of Miss Hetty. Some minutes elapsed, and no one came. A reason for delay was easily imagined, and I summoned patience to wait. I opened a book; touched the instrument; surveyed the vases on the mantle-tree; the figures on the hangings, and the print of Apollo and the Sybil, taken from Salvator,[5] and hung over the chimney. I eyed my own shape and garb in the mirror and asked how my rustic appearance would be regarded by that supercilious and voluptuous being to whom I was about to present myself.

Presently the latch of the door was softly moved, it opened, and the simpleton, before described, appeared. She spoke, but her voice was so full of hesitation, and so

---

[4] "Scorching": becoming detached, peeled back, possibly from being read too close to a candle or fire or from sweaty handling by anxious customers. The texts could also be the kind of French pornographic tales that circulated in Philadelphia during the 1790s with the influx of French and Haitian refugees. The description of "chairs crouding" also suggests an overly close, lascivious contact between (female and male) sitters.

[5] "The print of Apollo and the Sibyl, taken from Salvator": a reproduction of an etching by Roman painter and writer Salvator Rosa (1615–1673). Commonly known as "Salvator," the artist became stylish in eighteenth-century British and American circles, especially in revolutionary era literary developments. Primarily known for "wild" or "picturesque" landscapes (influential in gothic novels like Brown's own *Edgar Huntly*), he made several painting and print versions of the encounter between Apollo and the Cumaean sibyl (Greek for prophetess). The sibyl at Cumae (near Naples) was a guide into the underworld. As narrated in Ovid's *Metamorphoses*, the source of Salvator's scene, the sibyl guides Aeneas through the underworld and explains to him her distressed situation and suffering. Long before, Apollo offered the sibyl a thousand years of life but poisoned his gift by denying her youth when she refused to have sex with him, making her shrivelled and smaller in stature (an exaggerated version of the description of Achsa in the novel's last chapters). The print referred to here does not feature a landscape but represents the still-voluptuous sibyl welcoming Apollo, who sits in anticipation holding a lyre. This is an apt image for a brothel, since it can be read as a parable warning that beauty and happiness may be lost in resisting the demands of male sexual desire.

near a whisper, that much attention was needed to make out her words; Miss Hetty was not at home—she was gone to town with her *mistiss*.

This was a tale not to be credited. How was I to act? She persisted in maintaining the truth of it.— Well then, said I, at length, tell Miss Sally that I wish to speak with her. She will answer my purpose just as well.

Miss Sally was not at home neither. She had gone to town too. They would not be back, she did not know when: not till night, she supposed. It was so indeed, none of them wasn't at home: none but she and Nanny in the kitchen—indeed'n there wasn't.

Go tell Nanny to come here—I will leave my message with her. She withdrew, but Nanny did not receive the summons, or thought proper not to obey it. All was vacant and still.

My state was singular and critical. It was absurd to prolong it; but to leave the house with my errand unexecuted, would argue imbecility and folly. To ascertain Clemenza's presence in this house, and to gain an interview, were yet in my power. Had I not boasted of my intrepidity in braving denials and commands, when they endeavored to obstruct my passage to this woman? But here were no obstacles nor prohibitions. Suppose the girl had said truth, that the matron and her daughters were absent, and that Nanny and herself were the only guardians of the mansion. So much the better. My design will not be opposed. I have only to mount the stair, and go from one room to another, till I find what I seek.

There was hazard, as well as plausibility, in this scheme. I thought it best once more to endeavor to extort information from the girl, and persuade her to be my guide to whomsoever the house contained. I put my hand to the bell and rung a brisk peal. No one came. I passed into the entry, to the foot of a stair-case, and to a back window. Nobody was within hearing or sight.

Once more I reflected on the rectitude of my intentions, on the possibility that the girl's assertions might be true, on the benefits of expedition, and of gaining access to the object of my visit without interruption or delay. To these considerations was added a sort of charm, not easily explained, and by no means justifiable, produced by the very temerity and hazardness accompanying this attempt. I thought, with scornful emotions, on the bars and hindrances which pride and caprice, and delusive maxims of decorum,[6] raise in the way of human intercourse. I spurned at these semblances and substitutes of honesty, and delighted to shake such fetters into air, and trample such impediments to dust. I wanted to see an human being, in order to promote her happiness. It was doubtful whether she was within twenty paces of the spot where I stood. The doubt was to be solved. How? By examining the space. I forthwith proceeded to examine it. I reached the second story. I approached a door that was closed I knocked; after a pause, a soft voice said, who is there?

---

[6] "Delusive maxims of decorum": useless principles of propriety or conventional behavior. As he did when burying Susan Hadwin or confronting Philip Hadwin, Mervyn ignores conventional rituals and behaviors in favor of direct action and strategy grounded in rational plans for benevolence. This scene and its continuation in the next chapter verge at moments on a comic exaggeration of Mervyn's perseverance in frankness and honesty.

The accents were as musical as those of Clemenza, but were in other respects, different.[7] I had no topic to discuss with this person. I answered not, yet hesitated to withdraw. Presently the same voice was again heard; what is it you want? Why don't you answer? Come in!—I complied with the command, and entered the room.

It was deliberation and foresight that led me hither, and not chance or caprice. Hence, instead of being disconcerted or vanquished by the objects that I saw, I was tranquil and firm. My curiosity, however, made me a vigilant observer. Two females, arrayed with voluptuous negligence, in a manner adapted to the utmost seclusion, and seated in a careless attitude, on a sofa, were now discovered.

Both darted glances at the door. One, who appeared to be the youngest, no sooner saw me, than she shrieked, and starting from her seat, betrayed, in the looks which she successively cast upon me, on herself and on the chamber, whose apparatus[8] was in no less confusion than that of the apartment below, her consciousness of the unseasonableness of this meeting.

The other shrieked likewise, but on her it seemed to be the token of surprize, rather than that of terror. There was, probably, somewhat in my aspect and garb that suggested an apology for this intrusion, as arising from simplicity and mistake. She thought proper, however, to assume the air of one offended, and looking sternely— How now, fellow, said she, what is this? Why come you hither?

This questioner was of mature age, but had not passed the period of attractiveness and grace. All the beauty that nature had bestowed was still retained, but the portion had never been great. What she possessed was so modelled and embellished by such a carriage and dress, as to give it most power over the senses of the gazer. In proportion, however, as it was intended and adapted to captivate those, who know none but physical pleasures, it was qualified to breed distaste and aversion in me.

I am sensible how much error may have lurked in this decision. I had brought with me the belief of their being unchaste; and seized, perhaps, with too much avidity, any appearance that coincided with my prepossessions. Yet the younger by no means inspired the same disgust; though I had no reason to suppose her more unblemished than the elder. Her modesty seemed unaffected, and was by no means satisfied, like that of the elder, with defeating future curiosity. The consciousness of what had already been exposed filled her with confusion, and she would have flown away, if her companion had not detained her by some degree of force. What ails the girl? There's nothing to be frightened at. Fellow! she repeated, what brings you here?

I advanced and stood before them. I looked steadfastly, but, I believe, with neither effrontery nor anger, on the one who addressed me. I spoke in a tone serious and emphatical. I come for the sake of speaking to a woman, who formerly resided in this

---

[7] "But were in other respects, different": this inviting and "musical" voice is the first appearance of Achsa Fielding, Mervyn's future betrothed, who remains unnamed in the following scene as the younger of the two women. The older woman is Lucy Villars.

[8] "Apparatus": material elements or arrangements; in other words, the room's furnishings and contents.

house, and probably resides here still. Her name is Clemenza Lodi. If she be here, I request you to conduct me to her instantly.

Methought I perceived some inquietude, a less imperious and more inquisitive air, in this woman, on hearing the name of Clemenza. It was momentary, and gave way to peremptory looks. What is your business with her? And why did you adopt this mode of enquiry? A very extraordinary intrusion! Be good enough to leave the chamber. Any questions proper to be answered, will be answered below.

I meant not to intrude or offend. It was not an idle or impertinent motive that led me hither. I waited below for some time after soliciting an audience of you, through the servant. She assured me you were absent, and laid me under the necessity of searching for Clemenza Lodi myself, and without a guide. I am anxious to withdraw, and request merely to be directed to the room which she occupies.

I direct you, replied she in a more resolute tone, to quit the room and the house.

Impossible, madam, I replied, still looking at her earnestly, leave the house without seeing her! You might as well enjoin me to pull the Andes on my head! To walk barefoot to Peking! Impossible!

Some solicitude was now mingled with her anger. This is strange insolence! unaccountable behaviour!—be gone from my room! will you compel me to call the gentlemen?

Be not alarmed, said I, with augmented mildness. There was indeed compassion and sorrow at my heart, and these must have somewhat influenced my looks. Be not alarmed—I came to confer a benefit, not to perpetrate an injury. I came not to censure or expostulate with you, but merely to counsel and aid a being that needs both; all I want is to see her. In this chamber I sought not you, but her. Only lead me to her, or tell me where she is. I will then rid you of my presence.

Will you compel me to call those who will punish this insolence as it deserves?

Dearest madam! I compel you to nothing. I merely supplicate. I would ask you to lead me to these gentlemen, if I did not know that there are none but females in the house. It is you who must receive and comply with my petition. Allow me a moment's interview with Clemenza Lodi. Compliance will harm you not, but will benefit her. What is your objection?

This is the strangest proceeding! the most singular conduct! Is this a place fit to parley with you? I warn you of the consequence of staying a moment longer. Depend upon it, you will sorely repent it.

You are obdurate, said I, and turned towards the younger, who listened to this discourse in tremors and panick. I took her hand with an air of humility and reverence. Here, said I, there seems to be purity, innocence and condescension. I took this house to be the temple of voluptuousness. Females, I expected to find in it, but such only as traded in licentious pleasures; specious, perhaps not destitute of talents, beauty and address, but dissolute and wanton; sensual and avaricious; yet, in this countenance and carriage there are tokens of virtue. I am born to be deceived, and the semblance of modesty is readily assumed. Under this veil, perhaps, lurk a tainted heart and depraved appetites. Is it so?

She made me no answer, but somewhat in her looks seemed to evince that my favorable prepossessions were just. I noticed likewise that the alarm of the elder was greatly increased by this address to her companion. The thought suddenly occurred that this girl might be in circumstances not unlike those of Clemenza Lodi; that she was not apprized of the character of her associates, and might by this meeting be rescued from similar evils.

This suspicion filled me with tumultuous feelings. Clemenza was for a time forgotten. I paid no attention to the looks or demeanor of the elder, but was wholly occupied in gazing on the younger. My anxiety to know the truth, gave pathos and energy to my tones, while I spoke:

Who, where, what are you? Do you reside in this house? Are you a sister or daughter in this family, or merely a visitant? Do you know the character, profession and views of your companions? Do you deem them virtuous, or know them to be profligate? Speak! tell me, I beseech you!

The maiden confusion which had just appeared in the countenance of this person, now somewhat abated. She lifted her eyes, and glanced by turns at me and at her who sat by her side. An air of serious astonishment overspread her features, and she seemed anxious for me to proceed. The elder, meanwhile, betrayed the utmost alarm, again upbraided my audacity, commanded me to withdraw, and admonished me of the danger I incurred by lingering.

I noticed not her interference, but again entreated to know of the younger her true state. She had no time to answer me, supposing her not to want the inclination, for every pause was filled by the clamorous importunities and menaces of the other. I began to perceive that my attempts were useless to this end, but the chief, and most estimable purpose, was attainable. It was in my power to state the knowledge I possessed, through your means, of Mrs. Villars and her daughters. This information might be superfluous, since she to whom it was given, might be one of this licentious family. The contrary, however, was not improbable, and my tidings, therefore, might be of the utmost moment to her safety.

A resolute, and even impetuous manner, reduced my incessant interruptor to silence. What I had to say I compressed in a few words, and adhered to perspicuity and candor with the utmost care. I still held the hand that I had taken, and fixed my eyes upon her countenance with a steadfastness that hindered her from lifting her eyes.

I know you not; whether you be dissolute or chaste, I cannot tell. In either case, however, what I am going to say will be useful. Let me faithfully repeat what I have heard. It is mere rumor, and I vouch not for its truth. Rumor as it is, I submit it to your judgment, and hope that it may guide you into paths of innocence and honor.

Mrs. Villars and her three daughters are English women, who supported for a time an unblemished reputation, but who, at length, were suspected of carrying on the trade of prostitution. This secret could not be concealed forever. The profligates who frequented their house, betrayed them. One of them who died under their roof, after they had withdrawn from it into the country, disclosed to his kinsman, who attended his death bed, their genuine character.

The dying man likewise related incidents in which I am deeply concerned. I have been connected with one by name Welbeck. In his house I met an unfortunate girl, who was afterwards removed to Mrs. Villars's. Her name was Clemenza Lodi. Residence in this house, under the controul of a woman like Mrs. Villars and her daughters, must be injurious to her innocence, and from this controul I now come to rescue her.

I turned to the elder, and continued: By all that is sacred, I adjure you to tell me whether Clemenza Lodi be under this roof! if she be not, whither has she gone? To know this, I came hither, and any difficulty or reluctance in answering, will be useless; till an answer be obtained, I will not go hence.

During this speech, anger had been kindling in the bosom of this woman. It now burst upon me in a torrent of opprobrious epithets. I was a villain, a calumniator, a thief. I had lurked about the house, till those whose sex and strength enabled them to cope with me, had gone. I had entered these doors by fraud. I was a wretch, guilty of the last excesses of insolence and insult.

To repel these reproaches, or endure them, was equally useless. The satisfaction that I sought was only to be gained by searching the house. I left the room without speaking. Did I act illegally in passing from one story and one room to another? Did I really deserve the imputations of rashness and insolence? My behaviour, I well know, was ambiguous and hazardous, and perhaps wanting in discretion, but my motives were unquestionably pure. I aimed at nothing but the rescue of an human creature from distress and dishonor.

I pretend not to the wisdom of experience and age; to the praise of forethought or subtlety. I chuse the obvious path, and pursue it with headlong expedition. Good intentions, unaided by knowledge, will, perhaps, produce more injury than benefit, and therefore, knowledge must be gained, but the acquisition is not momentary; is not bestowed unasked and untoil'd for; meanwhile, we must not be unactive because we are ignorant. Our good purposes must hurry to performance, whether our knowledge be greater or less.

Chapter XII

TO explore the house in this manner was so contrary to ordinary rules, that the design was probably wholly unsuspected by the women whom I had just left. My silence, at parting, might have been ascribed by them to the intimidating influence of invectives and threats. Hence I proceeded in my search without interruption.

Presently I reached a front chamber in the third story. The door was ajar. I entered it on tiptoe. Sitting on a low chair by the fire, I beheld a female figure, dressed in a negligent, but not indecent manner. Her face in the posture in which she sat was only half seen. Its hues were sickly and pale, and in mournful unison with a feeble and emaciated form. Her eyes were fixed upon a babe, that lay stretched upon a pillow at her feet. The child, like its mother, for such she was readily imagined to be, was meagre and cadaverous. Either it was dead, or could not be very distant from death.

The features of Clemenza were easily recognized, though no contrast could be greater, in habit and shape, and complexion, than that which her present bore to her former appearance. All her roses had faded, and her brilliances vanished. Still, however, there was somewhat fitted to awaken the tenderest emotions. There were tokens of inconsolable distress.

Her attention was wholly absorbed by the child. She lifted not her eyes, till I came close to her, and stood before her. When she discovered me, a faint start was perceived. She looked at me for a moment, then putting one spread hand before her eyes, she stretched out the other towards the door, and waving it in silence, as if to admonish me to depart.

This motion, however emphatical, I could not obey. I wished to obtain her attention, but knew not in what words to claim it. I was silent. In a moment she removed her hand from her eyes, and looked at me with new eagerness. Her features bespoke emotions, which, perhaps, flowed from my likeness to her brother, joined with the memory of my connection with Welbeck.

My situation was full of embarrassment. I was by no means certain that my language would be understood. I knew not in what light the policy and dissimulation of Welbeck might have taught her to regard me. What proposal, conductive to her comfort and her safety, could I make to her?

Once more she covered her eyes, and exclaimed in a feeble voice, go away! be gone!

As if satisfied with this effort, she resumed her attention to her child. She stooped and lifted it in her arms, gazing, meanwhile, on its almost lifeless features with intense anxiety. She crushed it to her bosom, and again looking at me, repeated, go away! go away! Be gone!

There was somewhat in the lines of her face, in her tones and gestures, that pierced to my heart. Added to this, was my knowledge of her condition; her friendlessness; her poverty; the pangs of unrequited love; and her expiring infant. I felt my utterance choaked, and my tears struggling for passage. I turned to the window, and endeavored to regain my tranquillity.

What was it, said I, that brought me hither? The perfidy of Welbeck must surely have long since been discovered. What can I tell her of the Villars which she does not already know, or of which the knowledge will be useful? If their treatment has been just, why should I detract from their merit? If it has been otherwise, their own conduct will have disclosed their genuine character. Though voluptuous themselves, it does not follow that they have labored to debase this creature. Though wanton, they may not be inhuman.

I can propose no change in her condition for the better. Should she be willing to leave this house, whither is it in my power to conduct her? O that I were rich enough to provide food for the hungry, shelter for the houseless, and raiment for the naked.

I was roused from these fruitless reflections by the lady, whom some sudden thought induced to place the child in its bed, and rising to come towards me. The utter dejection which her features lately betrayed, was now changed for an air of anxious curiosity. Where, said she, in her broken English, where is Signior Welbeck?

Alas! returned I, I know not. That question might, I thought, with more propriety be put to you than me.

I know where he be; I fear where he be.

So saying, the deepest sighs burst from her heart. She turned from me, and going to the child, took it again into her lap. Its pale and sunken cheek was quickly wet with the mother's tears, which, as she silently hung over it, dropped fast from her eyes.

This demeanor could not but awaken curiosity, while it gave a new turn to my thoughts. I began to suspect that in the tokens which I saw, there was not only distress for her child, but concern for the fate of Welbeck. Know you, said I, where Mr. Welbeck is? Is he alive? Is he near? Is he in calamity?

I do not know if he be alive. He be sick. He be in prison. They will not let me go to him. And—Here her attention and mine was attracted by the infant, whose frame, till now motionless, began to be tremulous. Its features sunk into a more ghastly expression. Its breathings were difficult, and every effort to respire produced a convulsion harder than the last.

The mother easily interpreted these tokens. The same mortal struggle seemed to take place in her feature as in those of her child. At length her agony found way in a piercing shriek. The struggle in the infant was past. Hope looked in vain for a new motion in its heart or its eyelids. The lips were closed, and its breath was gone, forever!

The grief which overwhelmed the unhappy parent, was of that outrageous and desperate kind which is wholly incompatible with thinking. A few incoherent motions and screams, that rent the soul, were followed by a deep swoon. She sunk upon the floor, pale and lifeless as her babe.

I need not describe the pangs which such a scene was adapted to produce in me. These were rendered more acute by the helpless and ambiguous situation in which I was placed. I was eager to bestow consolation and succour, but was destitute of all means. I was plunged into uncertainties and doubts. I gazed alternately at the infant and its mother. I sighed. I wept. I even sobbed. I stooped down and took the lifeless hand of the sufferer. I bathed it with my tears, and exclaimed, Ill-fated woman! unhappy mother! what shall I do for thy relief? How shall I blunt the edge of this calamity, and rescue thee from new evils?

At this moment the door of the apartment was opened, and the youngest of the women whom I had seen below, entered. Her looks betrayed the deepest consternation and anxiety. Her eyes in a moment were fixed by the decayed form and the sad features of Clemenza. She shuddered at this spectacle, but was silent. She stood in the midst of the floor, fluctuating and bewildered. I dropped the hand that I was holding, and approached her.

You have come, said I, in good season. I know you not, but will believe you to be good. You have an heart, it may be, not free from corruption, but it is still capable of pity for the miseries of others. You have an hand that refuses not its aid to the unhappy. See; there is an infant dead. There is a mother whom grief has, for a time, deprived of life. She has been oppressed and betrayed; been robbed of property and reputation—but not of innocence. She is worthy of relief. Have you arms to receive her? Have you sympathy, protection, and a home to bestow upon a forlorn, betrayed and unhappy stranger? I know not what this house is; I suspect it to be no better than a brothel. I know not what treatment this woman has received. If, when her situation and wants are ascertained, will you supply her wants? Will you rescue her from evils that may attend her continuance here?

She was disconcerted and bewildered by this address. At length she said—All that has happened, all that I have heard and seen is so unexpected, so strange, that I am amazed and distracted. Your behaviour I cannot comprehend, nor your motive for making this address to me. I cannot answer you, except in one respect. If this woman has suffered injury, I have had no part in it. I knew not of her existence, nor her situation till this moment; and whatever protection or assistance she may justly claim, I am both able and willing to bestow. I do not live here, but in the city. I am only an occasional visitant in this house.

What then, I exclaimed, with sparkling eyes and a rapturous accent,[1] you are not profligate; are a stranger to the manners of this house, and a detester of these manners? Be not a deceiver, I entreat you. I depend only on your looks and professions, and these may be dissembled.

These questions, which indeed argued a childish simplicity, excited her surprize. She looked at me, uncertain whether I was in earnest or in jest. At length she said, your language is so singular, that I am at a loss how to answer it. I shall take no pains to find out its meaning, but leave you to form conjectures at leisure. Who is this woman, and how can I serve her? After a pause, she continued—I cannot afford her any immediate assistance, and shall not stay a moment longer in this house. There (putting a card in my hand) is my name and place of abode. If you shall have any

---

[1] "Sparkling eyes and a rapturous accent": Mervyn's breathless exchange with Achsa Fielding takes on a note of blinded, eroticized perception. "Sparkling eyes" recall Welbeck's unreliable, eroticized seeming in Chapter 8 (note 8.4) and Mervyn's own eagerness as he accepts Stevens' offer of medical training at the outset of *Second Part* (note II.1.11). The intense visual connection in Mervyn's second contact with Achsa ("I depend only on your looks") prefigures the important coding of her eyes in Chapter II.23 (note II.23.3), where they supply the key to her hidden ethnic identity in the novel's finale.

proposals to make, respecting this woman, I shall be ready to receive them in my own house. So saying, she withdrew.

I looked wistfully after her, but could not but assent to her assertion, that her presence here would be more injurious to her than beneficial to Clemenza. She had scarcely gone, when the elder woman entered. There was rage, sullenness, and disappointment in her aspect. These, however, were suspended by the situation in which she discovered the mother and child. It was plain that all the sentiments of woman were not extinguished in her heart. She summoned the servants and seemed preparing to take such measures as the occasion prescribed. I now saw the folly of supposing that these measures would be neglected, and that my presence could not essentially contribute to the benefit of the sufferer. Still, however, I lingered in the room, till the infant was covered with a cloth, and the still senseless parent was conveyed into an adjoining chamber. The woman then, as if she had not seen me before, fixed scowling eyes upon me, and exclaimed, thief! villain! why do you stay here?

I mean to go, said I, but not till I express my gratitude and pleasure, at the sight of your attention to this sufferer. You deem me insolent and perverse, but I am not such; and hope that the day will come when I shall convince you of my good intentions.

Begone! interrupted she, in a more angry tone. Begone this moment, or I will treat you as a thief. She now drew forth her hand from under her gown, and showed a pistol. You shall see, she continued, that I will not be insulted with impunity. If you do not vanish, I will shoot you as a robber.

This woman was far from wanting a force and intrepidity worthy of a different sex. Her gestures and tones were full of energy. They denoted an haughty and indignant spirit. It was plain that she conceived herself deeply injured by my conduct; and was it absolutely certain that her anger was without reason? I had loaded her house with atrocious imputations, and these imputations might be false. I had conceived them upon such evidence as chance had provided, but this evidence, intricate and dubious as human actions and motives are, might be void of truth.

Perhaps, said I, in a sedate tone, I have injured you; I have mistaken your character. You shall not find me less ready to repair, than to perpetrate, this injury. My error was without malice, and—

I had not time to finish the sentence, when this rash and enraged woman thrust the pistol close to my head and fired it. I was wholly unaware that her fury would lead her to this excess. It was a sort of mechanical impulse that made me raise my hand, and attempt to turn aside the weapon. I did this deliberately and tranquilly, and without conceiving that any thing more was intended by her movement than to intimidate me. To this precaution, however, I was indebted for life. The bullet was diverted from my forehead to my left ear, and made a slight wound upon the surface, from which the blood gushed in a stream.

The loudness of this explosion, and the shock which the ball produced in my brain, sunk me into a momentary stupor.[2] I reeled backward, and should have fallen had

---

[2] "Stupor": Mervyn's third blow to the head. The first two occur in the first part as he buries Watson (Chapter 12) and is struck by the mirrored figure during the fever (Chapter 16).

not I supported myself against the wall. The sight of my blood instantly restored her reason. Her rage disappeared, and was succeeded by terror and remorse. She clasped her hands, and exclaimed—Oh! what, what have I done? My frantic passion has destroyed me.

I needed no long time to shew me the full extent of the injury which I had suffered and the conduct which it became me to adopt. For a moment I was bewildered and alarmed, but presently perceived that this was an incident more productive of good than of evil. It would teach me caution in contending with the passions of another, and shewed me that there is a limit which the impetuosities of anger will sometimes overstep. Instead of reviling my companion, I addressed myself to her thus:

Be not frighted. You have done me no injury, and I hope will derive instruction from this event. You rashness had like to have sacrificed the life of one who is your friend, and to have exposed yourself to infamy and death, or, at least, to the pangs of eternal remorse. Learn, from hence, to curb your passions, and especially to keep at a distance from every murderous weapon, on occasions when rage is likely to take place of reason.

I repeat that my motives in entering this house were connected with your happiness as well as that of Clemenza Lodi. If I have erred, in supposing you the member of a vile and pernicious trade, that error was worthy of being rectified, but violence and invective tend only to confirm it. I am incapable of any purpose that is not beneficent; but, in the means that I use and in the evidence on which I proceed, I am liable to a thousand mistakes. Point out to me the road by which I can do you good, and I will cheerfully pursue it.

Finding that her fears had been groundless, as to the consequences of her rashness, she renewed, though with less vehemence than before, her imprecations on my intermeddling and audacious folly. I listened till the storm was nearly exhausted, and then, declaring my intention to re-visit the house, if the interest of Clemenza should require it, I resumed my way to the city.

Chapter XIII

WHY, said I, as I hasted forward, is my fortune so abundant in unforeseen occurrences? Is every man, who leaves his cottage and the impressions of his infancy behind him, ushered into such a world of revolutions and perils as have trammelled my steps? or, is my scene indebted for variety and change to my propensity to look into other people's concern, and to make their sorrows and their joys mine?

To indulge an adventurous spirit, I left the precincts of the barn-door, enlisted in the service of a stranger and encountered a thousand dangers to my virtue under the disastrous influence of Welbeck. Afterward my life was set at hazard in the cause of Wallace, and now am I loaded with the province of protecting the helpless Eliza Hadwin and the unfortunate Clemenza. My wishes are fervent, and my powers shall not be inactive in their defence, but how slender are these powers!

In the offers of the unknown lady there is, indeed, some consolation for Clemenza. It must be my business to lay before my friend Stevens the particulars of what has befallen me, and to entreat his directions how this disconsolate girl may be most effectually succoured. It may be wise to take her from her present abode, and place her under some chaste and humane guardianship, where she may gradually lose remembrance of her dead infant and her specious betrayer. The barrier that severs her from Welbeck must be high as heaven and insuperable as necessity.

But, soft![1] Talked she not of Welbeck? Said she not that he was in prison and was sick? Poor wretch! I thought thy course was at an end; that the penalty of guilt no longer weighed down thy heart. That thy misdeeds and thy remorses were buried in a common and obscure grave; but it seems thou art still alive.

Is it rational to cherish the hope of thy restoration to innocence and peace? Thou art no obdurate criminal; hadst thou less virtue, thy compunctions would be less keen. Wert thou deaf to the voice of duty, thy wanderings into guilt and folly would be less fertile of anguish. The time will perhaps come, when the measure of thy transgressions and calamities will overflow, and the folly of thy choice will be too conspicuous to escape thy discernment. Surely, even for such transgressors as thou, there is a salutary power in the precepts of truth and the lessons of experience.

But, thou art imprisoned and art sick. This, perhaps, is the crisis of thy destiny. Indigence and dishonour were the evils, to shun which thy integrity and peace of mind have been lightly forfeited. Thou hast found that the price was given in vain; that the hollow and deceitful enjoyments of opulence and dignity were not worth the purchase; and that, frivolous and unsubstantial as they are, the only path that leads to them is that of honesty and diligence. Thou art in prison and art sick; and there is

---

[1] "But soft!": in this passage Mervyn begins his on-again off-again use of the stylized language of enlightened sentiment and sensibility commonly associated with the writers such as Laurence Sterne, a tendency which becomes more pronounced after he assumes control of the narrative in Chapter II.16. Poetically charged usage ("But soft!"), sentence structure ("Talked she not of Welbeck?"), and the rhetorically intensified "thee" and "thou" in the following paragraphs signal the shift. For subsequent allusions to Sterne, see notes II.17.3, II.23.1, II.25.4.

none to cheer thy hour with offices of kindness, or uphold thy fainting courage by the suggestions of good counsel. For such as thou the world has no compassion. Mankind will pursue thee to the grave with execrations. Their cruelty will be justified or palliated, since they know thee not. They are unacquainted with the goadings of thy conscience and the bitter retributions which thou art daily suffering: they are full of their own wrongs, and think only of those tokens of exultation and complacency which thou wast studious of assuming in thy intercourse with them. It is I only that thoroughly know thee, and can rightly estimate thy claims to compassion.

I have somewhat partaken of thy kindness, and thou meritest some gratitude at my hands. Shall I not visit and endeavor to console thee in thy distress? Let me, at least, ascertain thy condition, and be the instrument in repairing the wrongs which thou hast inflicted. Let me gain, from contemplation of thy misery, new motives to sincerity and rectitude.

While occupied by these reflections, I entered the city. The thoughts which engrossed my mind related to Welbeck. It is not my custom to defer till tomorrow what can be done to-day. The destiny of man frequently hangs upon the lapse of a minute. I will stop, said I, at the prison; and, since the moment of my arrival may not be indifferent, I will go thither with all possible haste. I did not content myself with walking, but, regardless of the comments of passengers, hurried along the way at full speed.

Having enquired for Welbeck, I was conducted through a dark room, crouded with beds, to a staircase. Never before had I been in a prison. Never had I smelt so noisome an odour, or surveyed faces so begrimed with filth and misery. The walls and floors were alike squallid and detestable. It seemed that in this house existence would be bereaved of all its attractions; and yet those faces, which could be seen through the obscurity that encompassed them, were either void of care or distorted with mirth.

This, said I, as I followed my conductor, is the residence of Welbeck. What contrasts are these to the repose and splendor, pictured walls, glossy hangings, gilded sofas, mirrors that occupied from cieling to floor, carpets of Tauris,[2] and the spotless and transcendent brilliancy of coverlets and napkins, in thy former dwelling? Here brawling and the shuffling of rude feet are eternal. The air is loaded with the exhalations of disease and the fumes of debauchery. Thou art cooped up in airless space, and, perhaps, compelled to share thy narrow cell with some stupid ruffian. Formerly, the breezes were courted by thy lofty windows. Aromatic shrubs were scattered on thy hearth. Menials, splendid in apparel, shewed their faces with diffidence in they apartment, trod lightly on thy marble floor, and suffered not the sanctity of silence to be troubled by a whisper. Thy lamp shot its rays through the transparency of alabaster, and thy fragrant lymph flowed from vases of porcelain. Such were formerly the decorations of thy hall, the embellishments of thy existence; but now—alas!—

---

[2] "Carpets of Tauris": Tauris or Tabriz, an important Persian (now Iranian) city near the Caspian Sea, noted for fine carpets and still a major manufacturing and cultural center in the twenty-first century. Persian carpets are another luxury commodity linking 1790s Philadelphia to worldwide commercial networks.

We reached a chamber in the second story. My conductor knocked at the door. No one answered. Repeated knocks were unheard or unnoticed by the person within. At length, lifting a latch, we entered together.

The prisoner lay upon the bed, with his face turned from the door. I advanced softly, making a sign to the keeper to withdraw. Welbeck was not asleep, but merely buried in reverie. I was unwilling to disturb his musing, and stood with my eyes fixed upon his form. He appeared unconscious that any one had entered.

At length, uttering a deep sigh, he changed his posture, and perceived me in my motionless and gazing attitude. Recollect in what circumstances we had last parted. Welbeck had, no doubt, carried away with him from that interview a firm belief that I should speedily die. His prognostic, however, was fated to be contradicted.

His first emotions were those of surprize. These gave place to mortification and rage. After eyeing me for some time, he averted his glances, and that effort which is made to dissipate some obstacle to breathing shewed me that his sensations were of the most excruciating kind. He laid his head upon the pillow, and sunk into his former musing. He disdained, or was unable, to utter a syllable of welcome or contempt.

In the opportunity that had been afforded me to view his countenance, I had observed tokens of a kind very different from those which used to be visible. The gloomy and malignant were more conspicuous. Health had forsaken his cheeks, and taken along with it those flexible parts, which formerly enabled him to cover his secret torments and insidious purposes, beneath a veil of benevolence and cheerfulness. Alas! said I, loud enough for him to hear me, here is a monument of ruin. Despair and mischievous passions are too deeply rooted in this heart for me to tear them away.

These expressions did not escape his notice. He turned once more and cast sullen looks upon me. There was somewhat in his eyes that made me shudder. They denoted that his reverie was not that of grief, but of madness. I continued, in a less steadfast voice than before:

Unhappy Clemenza! I have performed thy message. I have visited him that is sick and in prison. Thou hadst cause for anguish and terror, even greater cause than thou imaginedst. Would to God that thou wouldst be contented with the report which I shall make; that thy misguided tenderness would consent to leave him to his destiny, would suffer him to die alone; but that is a forbearance which no eloquence that I possess will induce thee to practise. Thou must come, and witness for thyself.

In speaking thus, I was far from foreseeing the effects which would be produced on the mind of Welbeck. I was far from intending to instil into him a belief that Clemenza was near at hand, and was preparing to enter his apartment: yet no other images but these would, perhaps, have roused him from his lethargy and awakened that attention which I wished to awaken. He started up and gazed fearfully at the door.

What! he cried. What! Is she here? Ye powers that have scattered woes in my path, spare me the sight of her! But from this agony I will rescue myself. The moment she appears I will pluck out these eyes and dash them at her feet.

So saying, he gazed with augmented eagerness upon the door. His hands were lifted to his head, as if ready to execute his frantic purpose. I seized his arm, and besought him to lay aside his terror, for that Clemenza was far distant. She had no intention, and besides was unable, to visit him.

Then I am respited. I breathe again. No; keep her from a prison. Drag her to the wheel or to the scaffold; mangle her with stripes; torture her with famine; strangle her child before her face, and cast it to the hungry dogs that are howling at the gate; but—keep her from a prison. Never let her enter these doors.—There he stopped; his eyes being fixed on the floor, and his thoughts once more buried in reverie. I resumed:

She is occupied with other griefs than those connected with the fate of Welbeck. She is not unmindful of you: she knows you to be sick and in prison; and I came to do for you whatever office your condition might require, and I came at her suggestion. She, alas! has full employment for her tears in watering the grave of her child.

He started. What! dead? Say you that the child is dead?

It is dead. I witnessed its death. I saw it expire in the arms of its mother; that mother whom I formerly met under your roof blooming and gay, but whom calamity has tarnished and withered. I saw her in the rayment of poverty, under an accursed roof; desolate; alone; unsolaced by the countenance or sympathy of human beings; approached only by those who mock at her distress, set snares for her innocence, and push her to infamy. I saw her leaning over the face of her dying babe.

Welbeck put his hands to his head and exclaimed: curses on thy lips, infernal messenger! Chant elsewhere thy rueful ditty! Vanish! if thou wouldst not feel in thy heart fangs red with blood less guilty than thine.

Till this moment the uproar in Welbeck's mind appeared to hinder him from distinctly recognizing his visitant. Now it seemed as if the incidents of our last interview suddenly sprung up in his remembrance.

What! This is the villain that rifled my cabinet, the maker of my poverty and of all the evils which it has since engendered! That has led me to a prison! Execrable fool! you are the author of the scene that you describe, and of horrors without number and name. To whatever crimes I have been urged since that interview, and the fit of madness that made you destroy my property, they spring from your act; they flowed from necessity, which, had you held your hand at that fateful moment, would never have existed.

How dare you thrust yourself upon my privacy? Why am I not alone? Fly! and let my miseries want, at least, the aggravation of beholding their author. My eyes loathe the sight of thee! My heart would suffocate thee with its own bitterness! Begone!

I know not, I answered, why innocence should tremble at the ravings of a lunatic; why it should be overwhelmed by unmerited reproaches! Why it should not deplore the errors of its foe, labor to correct those errors, and—

Thank thy fate, youth, that my hands are tied up by my scorn; thank thy fate that no weapon is within reach. Much has passed since I saw thee, and I am a new man. I am no longer inconstant and cowardly. I have no motives but contempt to hinder me from expiating the wrongs which thou hast done me in thy blood. I disdain to take thy life. Go; and let thy fidelity, at least, to the confidence which I have placed in thee, be inviolate. Thou hast done me harm enough, but canst do, if thou wilt, still more. Thou canst betray the secrets that are lodged in thy bosom, and rob me of the comfort of reflecting that my guilt is known but to one among the living.

This suggestion made me pause, and look back upon the past. I had confided this man's tale to you. The secrecy, on which he so fondly leaned, was at an end. Had I acted culpably or not?

But why should I ruminate, with anguish and doubt, upon the past? The future was within my power, and the road of my duty was too plain to be mistaken. I would disclose to Welbeck the truth, and cheerfully encounter every consequence. I would summon my friend to my aid, and take his counsel in the critical emergency in which I was placed. I ought not to rely upon myself alone in my efforts to benefit this being, when another was so near whose discernment, and benevolence, and knowledge of mankind, and power of affording relief were far superior to mine.

Influenced by these thoughts, I left the apartment without speaking; and, procuring pen and paper, dispatched to you the billet which brought about our meeting.

Chapter XIV

MERVYN'S auditors allowed no pause in their attention to this story. Having ended, a deep silence took place. The clock which stood upon the mantle, had sounded twice the customary *larum*,[1] but had not been heard by us. It was now struck a third time. It was *one*. Our guest appeared somewhat startled at this signal, and looked, with a mournful sort of earnestness, at the clock. There was an air of inquietude about him, which I had never observed in an equal degree before.

I was not without much curiosity respecting other incidents than those which had just been related by him; but after so much fatigue as he had undergone, I thought it improper to prolong the conversation.

Come, said I, my friend, let us to bed. This is a drowsy time, and after so much exercise of mind and body, you cannot but need some repose. Much has happened in your absence, which is proper to be known to you, but our discourse will be best deferred till tomorrow. I will come into your chamber by day-dawn, and unfold to you my particulars.

Nay, said he, withdraw not on my account. If I go to my chamber, it will not be to sleep, but to meditate, especially after your assurance that something of moment has occurred in my absence. My thoughts, independently of any cause of sorrow or fear, have received an impulse which solitude and darkness will not stop. It is impossible to know too much for our safety and integrity, or to know it too soon. What has happened?

I did not hesitate to comply with his request, for it was not difficult to conceive that, however tired the limbs might be, the adventures of this day would not be easily expelled from the memory at night. I told him the substance of the conversation with Mrs. Althorpe. He smiled at these parts of the narrative which related to himself; but when his father's depravity and poverty were mentioned, he melted into tears.

Poor wretch! I that knew thee in thy better days, might have easily divined this consequence. I foresaw thy poverty and degradation in the same hour that I left thy roof. My soul drooped at the prospect, but I said, it cannot be prevented, and this reflection was an antidote to grief, but now that thy ruin is complete, it seems as if some of it were imputable to me, who forsook thee when the succour and counsel of a son were most needed. Thou art ignorant and vicious, but thou art my father still. I see that the sufferings of a better man than thou art would less afflict me than thine. Perhaps it is still in my power to restore thy liberty and good name, and yet—that is a fond wish. Thou art past the age when the ignorance and groveling habits of a human being are susceptible of cure—There he stopt, and after a gloomy pause, continued:

I am not surprised or afflicted at the misconceptions of my neighbors, with relation to my own character. Men must judge from what they see: they must build their

---

[1] "*Larum*": alarm. The period term for a timepiece that sounds the hours is "larum clock" or "larum watch."

conclusions on their knowledge. I never saw in the rebukes of my neighbors, any thing but laudable abhorrence of vice. They were not eager to blame, to collect materials of censure rather than of praise. It was not me whom they hated and despised. It was the phantom that passed under my name, which existed only in their imagination, and which was worthy of all their scorn and all their enmity.

What I appeared to be in their eyes, was as much the object of my own disapprobation as of theirs. Their reproaches only evinced the rectitude of their decisions, as well as of my own. I drew from them new motives to complacency. They fortified my perseverance in the path which I had chosen as best; they raised me higher in my own esteem; they hightened the claims of the reproachers themselves to my respect and my gratitude.

They thought me slothful, incurious, destitute of knowledge, and of all thirst of knowledge, insolent and profligate. They say that in the treatment of my father, I have been ungrateful and inhuman. I have stolen his property, and deserted him in his calamity. Therefore they hate and revile me. It is well: I love them for these proofs of their discernment and integrity. Their indignation at wrong is the truest test of their virtue.

It is true that they mistake me, but that arises from, the circumstances of our mutual situation. They examined what was exposed to their view: they grasped at what was placed within their reach. To decide contrary to appearances; to judge from what they know not, would prove them to be brutish and not rational, would make their decision of no worth, and render them, in their turn, objects of neglect and contempt.

It is true that I hated school; that I sought occasions of absence, and finally, on being struck by the master, determined to enter his presence no more. I loved to leap, to run, to swim, to climb trees, and to clamber up rocks, to shroud myself in thickets, and stroll among woods, to obey the impulse of the moment, and to prate or be silent, just as my humor prompted me. All this I loved more than to go to and fro in the same path, and at stated hours, to look off and on a book, to read just as much, and of such a kind, to stand up and be seated, just as another thought proper to direct. I hated to be classed, cribbed, rebuked and feruled[2] at the pleasure of one, who, as it seemed to me, knew no guide in his rewards but caprice, and no prompter in his punishments but passion.

It is true that I took up the spade and the hoe as rarely, and for as short a time, as possible. I preferred to ramble in the forest and loiter on the hill: perpetually to change the scene; to scrutinize the endless variety of objects; to compare one leaf and pebble with another; to pursue those trains of thought which their resemblances and differences suggested; to enquire what it was that gave them this place, structure, and form were more agreeable employments than plowing and threshing.

My father could well afford to hire labor. What my age and my constitution enabled me to do could be done by a sturdy boy, in half the time, with half the toil, and

---

[2] "Feruled": smacked with a ferule (a cane or stick). Mervyn rebels against the verbal and physical abuse schoolchildren routinely experienced in the period's classrooms. The abusive teacher is Colvill, seducer of Mervyn's sister, mentioned again seven paragraphs farther on.

with none of the reluctance. The boy was a bond servant,[3] and the cost of his clothing and food was next to nothing. True it is, that my service would have saved him even this expence, but my motives for declining the effort were not hastily weighed or superficially examined. These were my motives:

My frame was delicate and feeble. Exposure to wet blasts and vertical suns was sure to make me sick. My father was insensible to this consequence; and no degree of diligence would please him, but that which would destroy my health. My health was dearer to my mother than to me. She was more anxious to exempt me from possible injuries than reason justified; but anxious she was, and I could not save her from anxiety, but by almost wholly abstaining from labor. I thought her peace of mind was of some value and that, if the inclination of either of my parents must be gratified at the expence of the other, the preference was due to the woman who bore me; who nursed me in disease; who watched over my safety with incessant tenderness; whose life and whose peace were involved in mine. I should have deemed myself brutish and obdurately wicked to have loaded her with fears and cares merely to smooth the brow of a froward old man, whose avarice called on me to sacrifice my ease and my health, and who shifted to other shoulders the province of sustaining me when sick, and of mourning for me when dead.

I likewise believed that it became me to reflect upon the influence of my decision on my own happiness; and to weigh the profits flowing to my father from my labor, against the benefits of mental exercise, the pleasures of the woods and streams, healthful sensations, and the luxury of musing. The pecuniary profit was petty and contemptible. It obviated no necessity. It purchased no rational enjoyment. It merely provoked, by furnishing the means of indulgence, an appetite from which my father was not exempt. It cherished the seeds of depravity in him, and lessened the little stock of happiness belonging to my mother.

I did not detain you long, my friends, in pourtraying my parents, and recounting domestic incidents, when I first told you my story. What had no connection with the history of Welbeck and with the part that I have acted upon this stage, I thought it proper to omit. My omission was likewise prompted by other reasons. My mind is ennervated and feeble like my body. I cannot look upon the sufferings of those I love without exquisite pain. I cannot steel my heart by the force of reason, and by submission to necessity; and, therefore, too frequently employ the cowardly expedient of endeavoring to forget what I cannot remember without agony.

I told you that my father was sober and industrious by habit, but habit is not uniform. There were intervals when his plodding and tame spirit gave place to the malice and fury of a demon. Liquors were not sought by him, but he could not withstand entreaty, and a potion that produced no effect upon others changed him into a maniac.

---

[3] "Bond servant": as a free property owner, Mervyn's father was wealthy enough to have a (white) indentured servant. Mervyn can avoid rough physical labor because the boy can be forced to do it instead. See note 2.2 for more on bond servant status.

I told you that I had a sister, whom the arts of a villain destroyed.[4] Alas! the work of her destruction was left unfinished by him. The blows and contumelies of a misjudging and implacable parent, who scrupled not to thrust her, with her new-born infant, out of doors; the curses and taunts of unnatural brothers left her no alternative but death—But I must not think of this; I must not think of the wrongs which my mother endured in the person of her only and darling daughter.

My brothers were the copyists of the father, whom they resembled in temper and person. My mother doated on her own image in her daughter and in me. This daughter was ravished from her by self-violence, and her other children by disease. I only remained to appropriate her affections and fulfil her hopes. This alone had furnished a sufficient reason why I should be careful of my health and my life, but my father's character supplied me with a motive infinitely more cogent.

It is almost incredible, but, nevertheless, true, that the only being whose presence and remonstrances had any influence on my father, at moments when his reason was extinct, was myself. As to my personal strength, it was nothing; yet my mother's person was rescued from brutal violence: he was checked, in the midst of his ferocious career, by a single look or exclamation from me. The fear of my rebukes had even some influence in enabling him to resist temptation. If I entered the tavern, at the moment when he was lifting the glass to his lips, I never weighed the injunctions of decorum, but, snatching the vessel from his hand, I threw it on the ground. I was not deterred by the presence of others; and their censures, on my want of filial respect and duty, were listened to with unconcern. I chose not to justify myself by expatiating on domestic miseries, and by calling down that pity on my mother, which I knew would only have increased her distress.

The world regarded my deportment as insolent and perverse to a degree of insanity.[5] To deny my father an indulgence which they thought harmless, and which, indeed, was harmless in its influence on other men; to interfere thus publicly with his social enjoyments, and expose him to mortification and shame, was loudly condemned; but my duty to my mother debarred me from eluding this censure on the only terms on which it could have been eluded. Now it has ceased to be necessary to conceal what passed in domestic retirements, and I should willingly confess the truth before any audience.

At first my father imagined, that threats and blows would intimidate his monitor. In this he was mistaken, and the detection of this mistake impressed him with an involuntary reverence for me, which set bounds to those excesses which disdained any

---

[4] "A sister, whom the arts of a villain destroyed": in Chapter 20 Mervyn explained that his sister committed suicide after her seduction by Colvill, the corrupt schoolmaster who later sheltered Welbeck in New Jersey. On Colvill, see note 20.1.

[5] "Insolent and perverse to a degree of insanity": Mervyn's lack of deference to his father is incomprehensible to those around him, even if technically justified in this quasiclinical context of alcohol abuse and domestic violence. For more on the novel's rejection of paternal authority, established in the opening chapters, see note 3.1.

other controul. Hence, I derived new motives for cherishing a life which was useful, in so many ways, to my mother.

My condition is now changed. I am no longer on that field to which the law, as well as reason, must acknowledge that I had some right, while there was any in my father. I must hazard my life, if need be, in the pursuit of the means of honest subsistence. I never spared myself while in the service of Mr. Hadwin; and, at a more inclement season, should probably have incurred some hazard by my diligence.

These were the motives of my *idleness*—for, my abstaining from the common toils of the farm passed by that name among my neighbors; though, in truth, my time was far from being wholly unoccupied by manual employments, but these required less exertion of body or mind, or were more connected with intellectual efforts. They were pursued in the seclusion of my chamber or the recesses of a wood. I did not labor to conceal them, but neither was I anxious to attract notice. It was sufficient that the censure of my neighbors was unmerited to make me regard it with indifference.

I sought not the society of persons of my own age, not from sullen or unsociable habits but merely because those around me were totally unlike myself. Their tastes and occupations were incompatible with mine. In my few books, in my pen, in the vegetable and animal existences around me, I found companions who adapted their visits and intercourse to my convenience and caprice, and with whom I was never tired of communing.

I was not unaware of the opinion which my neighbors had formed of my being improperly connected with Betty Lawrence. I am not sorry that I fell into company with that girl. Her intercourse has instructed me in what some would think impossible to be attained by one who had never haunted the impure recesses of licentiousness in a city. The knowledge, which residence in this town for ten years gave her audacious and inquisitive spirit, she imparted to me. Her character, profligate and artful, libidinous and impudent, and made up of the impressions which a city life had produced on her coarse but active mind, was open to my study, and I studied it.

I scarcely know how to repel the charge of illicit conduct, and to depict the exact species of intercourse subsisting between us. I always treated her with freedom, and sometimes with gaiety. I had no motives to reserve. I was so formed that a creature like her had no power over my senses. That species of temptation adapted to entice me from the true path was widely different from the artifices of Betty. There was no point at which it was possible for her to get possession of my fancy. I watched her while she practised all her tricks and blandishments, just as I regarded a similar deportment in the *animal salax ignavumque*[6] who inhabits the stye. I made efforts to pursue my observations unembarrassed; but my efforts were made, not to restrain desire, but to suppress disgust. The difficulty lay, not in withholding my caresses, but in forbearing to repulse her with rage.

---

[6] "*Animal salax ignavumque*": Latin for "lecherous and lazy animal." Mervyn's Latinate comparison may allude to theories in physiognomy that character is legible in physical resemblance to animals; so that if a person looks like a hog, known to be gluttonous and lazy, then that person is likewise gluttonous and lazy (see Rivers, *Face Value*, 22–23). Betty is, after all, "ruddy, smooth, and plump."

Decorum, indeed, was not outraged, and all limits were not overstept, at once. Dubious advances were employed; but, when found unavailing, were displaced by more shameless and direct proceedings. She was too little versed in human nature to see that her last expedient was always worse than the preceding; and that, in proportion as she lost sight of decency, she multiplied the obstacles to her success.

Betty had many enticements in person and air. She was ruddy, smooth, and plump. To these she added—I must not say what, for it is strange to what lengths a woman destitute of modesty will sometimes go. But all her artifices availing her not at all in the contest with my insensibilities, she resorted to extremes which it would serve no good purpose to describe in this audience. They produced not the consequences she wished, but they produced another which was by no means displeasing to her. An incident one night occurred, from which a sagacious observer deduced the existence of an intrigue. It was useless to attempt to rectify his mistake, by explaining appearances, in a manner consistent with my innocence. This mode of explication implied a *continence* in me which he denied to be possible. The standard of possibilities, especially in vice and virtue, is fashioned by most men after their own character. A temptation which this judge of human nature knew that *he* was unable to resist, he sagely concluded to be irresistible by any other man, and quickly established the belief among my neighbors that the woman who married the father had been prostituted to the son. Though I never admitted the truth of this aspersion, I believed it useless to deny, because no one would credit my denial, and because I had no power to disprove it.

Chapter XV

WHAT other enquiries were to be resolved by our young friend, we were now, at this late hour, obliged to postpone till the morrow. I shall pass over the reflections which a story like this would naturally suggest, and hasten to our next interview.

After breakfast next morning, the subject of last night's conversation was renewed. I told him that something had occurred in his absence, in relation to Mrs. Wentworth and her nephew, that had perplexed us not a little. My information is obtained, continued I, from Wortley; and it is nothing less, than that young Clavering, Mrs. Wentworth's nephew, is, at this time, actually alive.

Surprise, but none of the embarrassment of guilt, appeared in his countenance at these tidings. He looked at me as if desirous that I should proceed.

It seems, added I, that a letter was lately received by this lady from the father of Clavering, who is now in Europe. This letter reports that this son was lately met with in Charleston, and relates the means which old Mr. Clavering had used to prevail upon his son to return home; means, of the success of which he entertained well grounded hopes. What think you?

I can only reject it, said he, after some pause, as untrue. The father's correspondent may have been deceived. The father may have been deceived, or the father may conceive it necessary to deceive the aunt, or some other supposition, as to the source of the error, may be true; but an error it surely is. Clavering is not alive. I know the chamber where he died, and the withered pine under which he lies buried.

If she be deceived, said I, it will be impossible to rectify her error.

I hope not. An honest front and a straight story will be sufficient.

How do you mean to act?

Visit her without doubt, and tell her the truth. My tale will be too circumstantial and consistent to permit her to disbelieve.

She will not hearken to you. She is too strongly prepossessed against you to admit you even to an hearing.

She cannot help it. Unless she lock her door against me, or stuff her ears with wool, she must hear me. Her prepossessions are reasonable, but are easily removed by telling the truth. Why does she suspect me of artifice? Because I seemed to be allied to Welbeck, and because I disguised the truth. That she thinks ill of me is not her fault, but my misfortune; and, happily for me, a misfortune easily removed.

Then you will try to see her.

I will see her, and the sooner the better. I will see her to-day; this morning; as soon as I have seen Welbeck, whom I shall immediately visit in his prison.

There are other embarrassments and dangers of which you are not aware. Welbeck is pursued by many persons whom he has defrauded of large sums. By these persons you are deemed an accomplice in his guilt, and a warrant is already in the hands of officers for arresting you wherever you are found.

In what way, said Mervyn, sedately, do they imagine me a partaker of his crime?

I know not. You lived with him. You fled with him. You aided and connived at his escape.

Are these crimes?

I believe not, but they subject you to suspicion.

To arrest and to punishment?

To detention for a while, perhaps. But these alone cannot expose you to punishment.

I thought so. Then I have nothing to fear.

You have imprisonment and obloquy, at least, to dread.

True; but they cannot be avoided but by my exile and skulking out of sight—evils infinitely more formidable. I shall, therefore, not avoid them. The sooner my conduct be subjected to scrutiny, the better. Will you go with me to Welbeck?

I will go with you.

Enquiring for Welbeck of the keeper of the prison, we were informed that he was in his own apartment very sick. The physician, attending the prison, had been called, but the prisoner had preserved an obstinate and scornful silence; and had neither explained his condition, nor consented to accept any aid.

We now went, alone, into his apartment. His sensibility seemed fast ebbing, yet an emotion of joy was visible in his eyes at the appearance of Mervyn. He seemed likewise to recognize in me his late visitant, and made no objection to my entrance.

How are you this morning? said Arthur, seating himself on the bed-side, and taking his hand. The sick man was scarcely able to articulate his reply—I shall soon be well. I have longed to see you. I want to leave with you a few words. He now cast his languid eyes on me. You are his friend, he continued. You know all. You may stay.—

There now succeeded a long pause, during which he closed his eyes, and resigned himself as if to an oblivion of all thought. His pulse under my hand was scarcely perceptible. From this in some minutes he recovered, and fixing his eyes on Mervyn, resumed, in a broken and feeble accent:

Clemenza! You have seen her. Weeks ago, I left her in an accursed house: yet she has not been mistreated. Neglected and abandoned indeed, but not mistreated. Save her Mervyn. Comfort her. Awaken charity for her sake.

I cannot tell you what has happened. The tale would be too long—too mournful. Yet, in justice to the living, I must tell you something. My woes and my crimes will be buried with me. Some of them, but not all.

Ere this, I should have been many leagues upon the ocean, had not a newspaper fallen into my hands while on the eve of embarkation. By that I learned that a treasure was buried with the remains of the ill-fated Watson. I was destitute. I was unjust enough to wish to make this treasure my own. Prone to think I was forgotten, or numbered with the victims of pestilence, I ventured to return under a careless disguise. I penetrated to the vaults of that deserted dwelling by night. I dug up the bones of my friend, and found the girdle and its valuable contents, according to the accurate description that I had read.

I hastened back with my prize to Baltimore, but my evil destiny overtook me at last. I was recognized by emissaries of Jamieson, arrested and brought hither, and here shall I consummate my fate and defeat the rage of my creditors by death. But first—

Here Welbeck stretched out his left hand to Mervyn, and, after some reluctance, shewed a roll of lead.

Receive this, said he. In the use of it, be guided by your honesty and by the same advertisement that furnished me the clue by which to recover it.[1] That being secured, the world and I will part forever. Withdraw, for your presence can help me nothing.

We were unwilling to comply with his injunction, and continued some longer time in his chamber, but our kind intent availed nothing. He quickly relapsed into insensibility, from which he recovered not again, but next day expired. Such, in the flower of his age, was the fate of Thomas Welbeck.

Whatever interest I might feel in accompanying the progress of my young friend, a sudden and unforeseen emergency compelled me again to leave the city. A kinsman, to whom I was bound by many obligations, was suffering a lingering disease, and imagining, with some reason, his dissolution to be not far distant, he besought my company and my assistance, to sooth, at least, the agonies of his last hour. I was anxious to clear up the mysteries which Arthur's conduct had produced, and to shield him, if possible, from the evils which I feared awaited him. It was impossible, however, to decline the invitation of my kinsman, as his residence was not a day's journey from the city. I was obliged to content myself with occasional information, imparted by Mervyn's letters, or those of my wife.

Meanwhile, on leaving the prison, I hasted to inform Mervyn of the true nature of the scene which had just passed. By this extraordinary occurrence, the property of the Maurices was now in honest hands. Welbeck, stimulated by selfish motives, had done that which any other person would have found encompassed with formidable dangers and difficulties. How this attempt was suggested or executed, he had not informed us, nor was it desirable to know. It was sufficient that the means of restoring their own to a destitute and meritorious family were now in our possession.

Having returned home, I unfolded to Mervyn all the particulars respecting Williams and the Maurices, which I had lately learned from Wortley.[2] He listened with deep attention, and my story being finished, he said: In this small compass, then, is the patrimony and subsistence of a numerous family. To restore it to them is the obvious proceeding—but how? Where do they abide?

Williams and Watson's wife live in Baltimore, and the Maurices live near that town. The advertisements alluded to by Wortley, and which are to be found in any newspaper, will inform us; but first, are we sure that any or all of these bills are contained in this covering?

---

[1] "By which to recover it": Welbeck has retrieved the gruesome "girdle" that secrets the "treasure" belonging to Captain Williams and the Maurice family (note II.4.4). As he dies, Welbeck performs a generous deed prompted by Mervyn's benevolent example, and entrusts the money to him. This final act seems to confirm the novel's earlier implication that, even with his spectacular personal faults, Welbeck is not as damaging to society as the business elite and purely mercantile values personified by Thetford, Old Thetford, and Jamieson, and that in a society populated by individuals like Mervyn, the Welbecks of the world might be influenced to become more virtuous.

[2] "Lately learned from Wortley": in other words, Stevens passes on to Mervyn the information he learned in Chapter II.3, concerning the money from Williams and the Maurice family that Watson was carrying on his person when he was buried beneath Welbeck's house in the novel's first part.

The lead was now unrolled, and the bills which Williams had described were found inclosed. Nothing appeared to be deficient. Of this, however, we were scarcely qualified to judge. Those that were the property of Williams might not be entire, and what would be the consequence of presenting them to him, if any had been embezzled by Welbeck?

This difficulty was obviated by Mervyn, who observed that the advertisement, describing these bills, would afford us ample information on this head. Having found out where the Maurices and Mrs. Watson live, nothing remains but to visit them and put an end, as far as lies in my power, to their inquietudes.

What! Would you go to Baltimore?

Certainly. Can any other expedient be proper? How shall I otherwise insure the safe conveyance of these papers?

You may send them by post.

But why not go myself?

I can hardly tell, unless your appearance on such an errand, may be suspected likely to involve you in embarrassments.

What embarrassments? If they receive their own, ought they not to be satisfied?

The enquiry will naturally be made as to the manner of gaining possession of these papers. They were lately in the hands of Watson, but Watson has disappeared. Suspicions are awake respecting the cause of his disappearance. These suspicions are connected with Welbeck, and Welbeck's connection with you is not unknown.

These are evils, but I see not how an ingenuous and open conduct is adapted to increase these evils. If they come, I must endure them.

I believe your decision is right. No one is so skilful an advocate in a cause, as he whose cause it is. I rely upon your skill and address, and shall leave you to pursue your own way. I must leave you for a time, but shall expect to be punctually informed of all that passes. With this agreement we parted, and I hastened to perform my intended journey.

Chapter XVI

I AM glad, my friend, thy nimble pen has got so far upon its journey. What remains of my story may be dispatched in a trice. I have just now some vacant hours, which might possibly be more usefully employed, but not in an easier manner or more pleasant. So, let me carry on thy thread.[1]

First, let me mention the resolutions I had formed at the time I parted with my friend. I had several objects in view. One was a conference with Mrs. Wentworth: another was an interview with her whom I met with at Villars's. My heart melted when I thought upon the desolate condition of Clemenza, and determined me to direct my first efforts for her relief. For this end I was to visit the female who had given me a direction to her house. The name of this person is Achsa Fielding,[2] and she lived, according to her own direction, at No. 40, Walnut-Street.[3]

I went thither without delay. She was not at home. Having gained information from the servant, as to when she might be found, I proceeded to Mrs. Wentworth's. In going thither my mind was deeply occupied in meditation; and, with my usual carelessness of forms, I entered the house and made my way to the parlour, where an interview had formerly taken place between us.

Having arrived, I began, though somewhat unseasonably, to reflect upon the topics with which I should introduce my conversation, and particularly the manner in which I should introduce myself. I had opened doors without warning, and traversed passages without being noticed. This had arisen from my thoughtlessness. There was

---

[1] "Let me carry on thy thread": the last section of the novel begins at this point, as Mervyn takes over the narrative from Stevens. Whereas Mervyn's story to this point has been reported discourse transmitted though Stevens, organized by Stevens' frame narrative, now it reaches the reader directly, written by Mervyn himself.

[2] "Achsa Fielding": the first appearance of Achsa's name. Achsa is the daughter of Caleb in *Joshua* 15:16–19 and *1 Chronicles* 2:49. Caleb gives her in marriage to the victorious Othniel. Fielding may evoke associations with the name of novelist Henry Fielding (1707–1754).

[3] "No. 40, Walnut-Street": the only specific address given in the novel, was the southeast corner of Second and Walnut, in a respectable but not exclusive area only three houses north of Brown's own family address at 117–119 South Second. City directories and census records list 40–42 Walnut as the property of Sharp Delany, then the city's port collector (official in charge of customs duties), and Achsa's use of the address implies that she rents or boards there (Mervyn refers to her "lodgings" later in this chapter). The 1790 census lists "6 free males age 16+" and 7 "free white females" in the "household," indicating that Delany had boarders. Across the street, at no. 46 Walnut, was another house with both white and black boarders.

In 1777, during the American War of Independence, Delany was on a four-person committee that drew up a (proscription) list of mainly Quaker men who were deemed "dangerous to the State" (because they refused an oath of allegiance on religious grounds) and subsequently exiled to an internment camp in Virginia. Brown's father Elijah was one of the Quakers thus arrested and exiled in the winter of 1777–1778 (see Kafer, *Charles Brockden Brown's Revolution*). See Achsa's reference to revolutionary proscriptions at note II.23.16, and Brown's comparison of yellow fever and proscriptions in "The Man at Home," in Related Texts.

no one within hearing or sight. What was next to be done? Should I not return softly to the outer door, and summon the servant by knocking?

Preparing to do this, I heard a footstep in the entry which suspended my design. I stood in the middle of the floor, attentive to these movements, when presently the door opened, and there entered the apartment Mrs. Wentworth herself! She came, as it seemed, without expectation of finding any one there. When, therefore, the figure of a man caught her vagrant attention, she started and cast an hasty look towards me.

Pray! (in a peremptory tone) how came you here, sir? and what is your business?

Neither arrogance, on the one hand; nor humility, upon the other, had any part in modelling my deportment. I came not to deprecate anger, or exult over distress. I answered, therefore, distinctly, firmly, and erectly.

I came to see you, madam, and converse with you; but, being busy with other thoughts, I forgot to knock at the door. No evil was intended by my negligence, though propriety has certainly not been observed. Will you pardon this intrusion, and condescend to grant me your attention?

To what? What have you to say to me? I know you only as the accomplice of a villain in an attempt to deceive me. There is nothing to justify your coming hither, and I desire you to leave the house with as little ceremony as you entered it.

My eyes were lowered at this rebuke, yet I did not obey the command. Your treatment of me, madam, is such as I appear to you to deserve. Appearances are unfavorable to me, but those appearances are false. I have concurred in no plot against your reputation or your fortune. I have told you nothing but the truth. I came hither to promote no selfish or sinister purpose. I have no favor to entreat, and no petition to offer, but that you will suffer me to clear up those mistakes which you have harbored respecting me.

I am poor. I am destitute of fame and of kindred. I have nothing to console me in obscurity and indigence, but the approbation of my own heart and the good opinion of those who know me as I am. The good may be led to despise and condemn me. Their aversion and scorn shall not make me unhappy; but it is my interest and my duty to rectify their error if I can. I regard your character with esteem. You have been mistaken in condemning me as a liar and impostor, and I came to remove this mistake. I came, if not to procure your esteem, at least, to take away hatred and suspicion.

But this is not all my purpose. You are in an error in relation not only to my character, but to the situation of your nephew Clavering. I formerly told you that I saw him die; that I assisted at his burial; but my tale was incoherent and imperfect, and you have since received intelligence to which you think proper to trust, and which assures you that he is still living. All I now ask is your attention, while I relate the particulars of my knowledge.

Proof of my veracity or innocence may be of no value in your eyes, but the fate of your nephew ought to be known to you. Certainty, on this head, may be of much importance to your happiness, and to the regulation of your future conduct. To hear me patiently can do you no injury, and may benefit you much. Will you permit me to go on?

During this address, little abatement of resentment and scorn was visible in my companion.

I will hear you, she replied. Your invention may amuse if it does not edify. But, I pray you, let your story be short.

I was obliged to be content with this ungraceful concession, and proceeded to begin my narration. I described the situation of my father's dwelling. I mentioned the year, month, day, and hour of her nephew's appearance among us. I expatiated minutely on his form, features, dress, sound of his voice, and repeated his words. His favorite gestures and attitudes were faithfully described.

I had gone but a little way in my story, when the effects were visible in her demeanor which I expected from it. Her knowledge of the youth, and of the time and manner of his disappearance, made it impossible for me, with so minute a narrative, to impose upon her credulity. Every word, every incident related, attested my truth, by their agreement with what she herself previously knew.

Her suspicions and angry watchfulness was quickly exchanged for downcast looks, and stealing tears, and sighs difficultly repressed. Meanwhile, I did not pause, but described the treatment he received from my mother's tenderness, his occupations, the freaks of his insanity, and, finally, the circumstances of his death and funeral.

Thence I hastened to the circumstances which brought me to the city; which placed me in the service of Welbeck, and obliged me to perform so ambiguous a part in her presence. I left no difficulty to be solved and no question unanticipated.

I have now finished my story, I continued, and accomplished my design in coming hither. Whether I have vindicated my integrity from your suspicions, I know not. I have done what in me lay to remove your error; and, in that, have done my duty.— What more remains? Any enquiries you are pleased to make, I am ready to answer. If there be none to make, I will comply with your former commands, and leave the house with as little ceremony as I entered it.

Your story, she replied, has been unexpected. I believe it fully, and am sorry for the hard thoughts which past appearances have made me entertain concerning you.

Here she sunk into mournful silence. The information, she at length resumed, which I have received from another quarter respecting that unfortunate youth, astonishes and perplexes me. It is inconsistent with your story, but it must be founded on some mistake, which I am, at present, unable to unravel. Welbeck, whose connection has been so unfortunate to you—

Unfortunate! Dear Madam! How unfortunate? It has done away a part of my ignorance of the world in which I live. It has led me to the situation in which I am now placed. It has introduced me to the knowledge of many good people. It has made me the witness and the subject of many acts of beneficence and generosity. My knowledge of Welbeck has been useful to me. It has enabled me to be useful to others. I look back upon that allotment of my destiny which first led me to his door, with gratitude and pleasure.

Would to Heaven, continued I, somewhat changing my tone, intercourse with Welbeck had been as harmless to all others as it has been to me: that no injury to fortune and fame, and innocence and life, had been incurred by others greater than has fallen upon my head. There is one being, whose connection with him has not been utterly dissimilar in its origin and circumstances to mine, though the catastrophe has, indeed, been widely and mournfully different.

And yet, within this moment, a thought has occurred from which I derive some consolation and some hope. You, dear madam, are rich. These spacious apartments, this plentiful accommodation are yours. You have enough for your own gratification and convenience, and somewhat to spare. Will you take to your protecting arms to your hospitable roof an unhappy girl whom the arts of Welbeck have robbed of fortune, reputation and honor, who is now languishing in poverty, weeping over the lifeless remains of her babe, surrounded by the agents of vice, and trembling on the verge of infamy?

What can this mean? replied the lady. Of whom do you speak?

You shall know her. You shall be apprized of her claims to your compassion. Her story, as far as is known to me, I will faithfully repeat to you. She is a stranger; an Italian; her name is Clemenza Lodi.—

Clemenza Lodi! Good Heaven! exclaimed Mrs. Wentworth; why, surely—it cannot be. And yet— Is it possible that you are that person?

I do not comprehend you, madam.

A friend has related a transaction of a strange sort. It is scarcely an hour since she told it me. The name of Clemenza Lodi was mentioned in it, and a young man of most singular deportment was described.—But tell me how you were engaged on Thursday morning?

I was coming to this city from a distance. I stopped ten minutes at the house of—

Mrs. Villars?

The same. Perhaps you know her and her character. Perhaps you can confirm or rectify my present opinions concerning her. It is there that the unfortunate Clemenza abides. It is thence that I wish her to be speedily removed.

I have heard of you; of your conduct upon that occasion.

Of me? answered I eagerly. Do you know that woman? So saying, I produced the card which I had received from her, and in which her name was written.

I know her well. She is my countrywoman and my friend.

Your friend? Then she is good—she is innocent— she is generous. Will she be a sister, a protectress to Clemenza? Will you exhort her to a deed of charity? Will you be, yourself, an example of beneficence? Direct me to Miss Fielding, I beseech you. I have called on her already, but in vain, and there is no time to be lost.

Why are you so precipitate? What would you do?

Take her away from that house instantly—bring her hither—place her under your protection—give her Mrs. Wentworth for a counsellor—a friend—a mother. Shall I do this? Shall I hie thither to-day, this very hour—now? Give me your consent, and she shall be with you before noon.

By no means, replied she, with earnestness. You are too hasty. An affair of so much importance cannot be dispatched in a moment. There are many difficulties and doubts to be first removed.

Let them be reserved for the future. Withhold not your helping hand till the struggler has disappeared forever. Think on the gulph that is already gaping to swallow her. This is no time to hesitate and faulter. I will tell you her story, but not now; we will postpone it till to-morrow; and first secure her from impending evils. She shall tell it you herself. In an hour I will bring her hither, and she herself shall recount to you her sorrows. Will you let me?

Your behaviour is extraordinary. I can scarcely tell whether this simplicity be real or affected. One would think that your common sense would shew you the impropriety of your request. To admit under my roof a woman, notoriously dishonoured, and from an infamous house—

My dearest madam! How can you reflect upon the situation without irresistible pity? I see that you are thoroughly aware of her past calamity and her present danger. Do not these urge you to make haste to her relief? Can any lot be more deplorable than hers? Can any state be more perilous? Poverty is not the only evil that oppresses, or that threatens her. The scorn of the world, and her own compunction, the death of the fruit of her error and the witness of her shame, are not the worst. She is exposed to the temptations of the profligate; while she remains with Mrs. Villars, her infamy accumulates; her further debasement is facilitated; her return to reputation and to virtue is obstructed by new bars.

How know I that her debasement is not already complete and irremediable? She is a mother but not a wife. How came she thus? Is her being Welbeck's prostitute no proof of her guilt?

Alas! I know not. I believe her not very culpable; I know her to be unfortunate; to have been robbed and betrayed. You are a stranger to her history. I am myself imperfectly acquainted with it.

But let me tell you the little that I know. Perhaps my narrative may cause you to think of her as I do.

She did not object to this proposal, and I immediately recounted all that I had gained from my own observations, or from Welbeck himself, respecting this forlorn girl. Having finished my narrative, I proceeded thus:—

Can you hesitate to employ that power which was given you for good ends to rescue this sufferer? Take her to your home; to your bosom; to your confidence. Keep aloof those temptations which beset her in her present situation. Restore her to that purity which her desolate condition, her ignorance; her misplaced gratitude and the artifices of a skilful dissembler have destroyed, if it be destroyed; for how know we under what circumstances her ruin was accomplished? With what pretences or appearances, or promises she was won to compliance?

True. I confess my ignorance; but ought not that ignorance to be removed before she makes a part of my family?

O no! It may be afterwards removed. It cannot be removed before. By bringing her hither you shield her, at least, from future and possible evils. Here you can watch her conduct and sift her sentiments conveniently and at leisure. Should she prove worthy of your charity, how justly may you congratulate yourself on your seasonable efforts in her cause? If she prove unworthy, you may then demean yourself according to her demerits.

I must reflect upon it.—To-morrow—

Let me prevail on you to admit her at once, and without delay. This very moment may be the critical one. To-day, we may exert ourselves with success, but to-morrow, all our efforts may be fruitless. Why fluctuate, why linger, when so much good may be done, and no evil can possibly be incurred? It requires but a word from you; you need not move a finger. Your house is large. You have chambers vacant and convenient. Consent only that your door shall not be barred against her; that you will treat her with civility; to carry your kindness into effect; to persuade her to attend me hither and to place herself in your care, shall be my province.

These, and many similar entreaties and reasonings, were ineffectual. Her general disposition was kind, but she was unaccustomed to strenuous or sudden exertions. To admit the persuasions of such an advocate to so uncommon a scheme as that of sharing her house with a creature, thus previously unknown to her, thus loaded with suspicion and with obloquy, was not possible.

I at last forbore importunity, and requested her to tell me when I might expect to meet with Miss Fielding at her lodgings? Enquiry was made to what end I sought an interview? I made no secret of my purpose.

Are you mad, young man? she exclaimed. Mrs. Fielding has already been egregiously imprudent. On the faith of an ancient slight acquaintance with Mrs. Villars in Europe, she suffered herself to be decoyed into a visit. Instead of taking warning by numerous tokens of the real character of that woman, in her behaviour, and in that of her visitants, she consented to remain there one night. The next morning took place that astonishing interview with you which she has since described to me. She is now warned against the like indiscretion. And pray, what benevolent scheme would you propose to her?

Has she property? Is she rich?

She is. Unhappily, perhaps, for her, she is absolute mistress of her fortune, and has neither guardian nor parent to controul her in the use of it.

Has she virtue? Does she know the value of affluence and a fair fame? And will not she devote a few dollars to rescue a fellow-creature from indigence and infamy and vice? Surely she will. She will hazard nothing by the boon. I will be her almoner.[4] I will provide the wretched stranger with food and raiment and dwelling, I will pay for all, if Miss Fielding, from her superfluity will supply the means. Clemenza shall owe life and honor to your friend, till I am able to supply the needful sum from my own stock.

While thus speaking, my companion gazed at me with steadfastness—I know not what to make of you. Your language and ideas are those of a lunatic. Are you acquainted with Mrs. Fielding?

Yes. I have seen her two days ago, and she has invited me to see her again.

And on the strength of this acquaintance, you expect to be her almoner? To be the medium of her charity?

---

[4] "Almoner": an official who distributes money to the poor.

I desire to save her trouble; to make charity as light and easy as possible. 'Twill be better if she perform those offices herself. 'Twill redound more to the credit of her reason and her virtue. But I solicit her benignity only in the cause of Clemenza. For her only do I wish at present to call forth her generosity and pity.

And do you imagine she will entrust her money to one of your age and sex, whom she knows so imperfectly, to administer to the wants of one whom she found in such an house as Mrs. Villars's? She never will. She mentioned her imprudent engagement to meet you, but she is now warned against the folly of such confidence.

You have told me plausible stories of yourself and of this Clemenza. I cannot say that I disbelieve them, but I know the ways of the world too well to bestow implicit faith so easily. You are an extraordinary young man. You may possibly be honest. Such an one as you, with your education and address, may possibly have passed all your life in an hovel; but it is scarcely credible, let me tell you. I believe most of the facts respecting my nephew, because my knowledge of him before his flight, would enable me to detect your falsehood; but there must be other proofs besides an innocent brow and a voluble tongue to make me give full credit to your pretensions.

I have no claim upon Welbeck which can embarrass you. On that score, you are free from any molestation from me or my friends. I have suspected you of being an accomplice in some vile plot, and am now inclined to acquit you, but that is all that you must expect from me, till your character be established by other means than your own assertions. I am engaged at present, and must therefore request you to put an end to your visit.

This strain was much unlike the strain which preceded it. I imagined, by the mildness of her tone and manners, that her unfavorable prepossessions were removed, but they seemed to have suddenly regained their pristine force. I was somewhat disconcerted by this unexpected change. I stood for a minute silent and irresolute.

Just then a knock was heard at the door, and presently entered that very female whom I had met with at Villars's. I caught her figure as I glanced through the window. Mrs. Wentworth darted at me many significant glances, which commanded me to withdraw; but with this object in view, it was impossible.

As soon as she entered, her eyes were fixed upon me. Certain recollections naturally occurred at that moment, and made her cheeks glow. Some confusion reigned for a moment, but was quickly dissipated. She did not notice me, but exchanged salutations with her friend.

All this while I stood near the window, in a situation not a little painful. Certain tremors which I had not been accustomed to feel, and which seemed to possess a mystical relation to the visitant, disabled me at once from taking my leave, or from performing any useful purpose by staying. At length, struggling for composure, I approached her, and shewing her the card she had given me, said:—

Agreeably to this direction, I called, an hour ago, at your lodgings. I found you not. I hope you will permit me to call once more. When shall I expect to meet you at home?

Her eyes were cast on the floor. A kind of indirect attention was fixed on Mrs. Wentworth, serving to intimidate and check her. At length she said, in an irresolute voice, I shall be at home this evening.

And this evening, replied I, I will call to see you. So saying, I left the house.

This interval was tedious; but was to be endured with equanimity. I was impatient to be gone to Baltimore, and hoped to be able to set out by the dawn of next day. Meanwhile, I was necessarily to perform something with respect to Clemenza.

After dinner I accompanied Mrs. Stevens to visit Miss Carlton. I was eager to see a woman who could bear adversity in the manner which my friend had described.

She met us at the door of her apartment. Her seriousness was not abated by her smiles of affability and welcome.—My friend! whispered I, How truly lovely is this Miss Carlton! Are the heart and the intelligence within worthy of these features?

Yes, they are. Your account of her employments; of her resignation to the ill fate of the brother whom she loves, proves that they are.

My eyes were rivetted to her countenance and person, I felt uncontroulable eagerness to speak to her, and to gain her good opinion.

You must know this young man, my dear Miss Carlton, said my friend, looking at me: He is my husband's friend, and professes a great desire to be yours. You must not treat him as a mere stranger, for he knows your character and situation already, as well as that of your brother.

She looked at me with benignity.—I accept his friendship willingly and gratefully, and shall endeavor to convince him that his good opinion is not misplaced.

There now ensued a conversation somewhat general, in which this young woman shewed a mind vigorous from exercise and unembarrassed by care. She affected no concealment of her own condition, of her wants, or her comforts. She laid no stress upon misfortunes, but contrived to deduce some beneficial consequence to herself, and some motive for gratitude to Heaven, from every wayward incident that had befallen her.

This demeanor emboldened me, at length, to enquire into the cause of her brother's imprisonment, and the nature of his debt.

She answered frankly and without hesitation. It is a debt of his father's, for which he made himself responsible during his father's life. The act was generous but imprudent, as the event has shewn; though, at the time, the unhappy effects could not be foreseen.

My father, continued she, was arrested by his creditor, at a time when the calmness and comforts of his own dwelling were necessary to his health. The creditor was obdurate, and would release him upon no condition but that of receiving a bond from my brother, by which he engaged to pay the debt at several successive times and in small portions. All these instalments were discharged with great difficulty indeed, but with sufficient punctuality, except the last, to which my brother's earnings were not adequate.

How much is the debt?

Four hundred dollars.

And is the state of the creditor such as to make the loss of four hundred dollars of more importance to him than the loss of liberty to your brother?

She answered, smiling, that is a very abstract view of things. On such a question, you and I might, perhaps, easily decide in favor of my brother; but would there not be some danger of deciding partially? His conduct is a proof of his decision, and there is no power to change it.

Will not argument change it? Methinks in so plain a case I should be able to convince him. You say he is rich and childless. His annual income is ten times more than this sum. Your brother cannot pay the debt while in prison; whereas, if at liberty, he might slowly and finally discharge it. If his humanity would not yield, his avarice might be brought to acquiesce.

But there is another passion which you would find it somewhat harder to subdue, and that is his vengeance.[5] He thinks himself wronged, and imprisons my brother, not to enforce payment, but to inflict misery. If you could persuade him that there is no hardship in imprisonment, you would speedily gain the victory; but that could not be attempted consistently with truth. In proportion to my brother's suffering is his gratification.

You draw an odious and almost incredible portrait.

And yet such an one as would serve for the likeness of almost every second man we meet.

And is such your opinion of mankind? Your experience must surely have been of a rueful tenor to justify such hard thoughts of the rest of your species.

By no means. It has been what those whose situation disables them from looking further than the surface of things, would regard as unfortunate; but if my goods and evils were equitably balanced, the former would be the weightiest. I have found kindness and goodness in great numbers, but have likewise met prejudice and rancor in many. My opinion of Farquhar is not lightly taken up. I have seen him yesterday, and the nature of his motives in the treatment of my brother was plain enough.

Here this topic was succeeded by others, and the conversation ceased not till the hour had arrived on which I had preconcerted to visit Mrs. Fielding. I left my two friends for this purpose.

I was admitted to Mrs. Fielding's presence without scruple or difficulty. There were two females in her company, and one of the other sex, well dressed, elderly, and sedate persons. Their discourse turned upon political topics, with which, as you know, I have but slight acquaintance. They talked of fleets and armies, of Robespierre and Pitt,[6] of whom I had only a newspaper knowledge.

---

[5] "Passion . . . vengeance": another of the novel's subnarratives concerning irrational vengeance and debt. For more, see notes 11.8, 20.2, II.1.17, and II.3.16.

[6] "Of fleets and armies, of Robespierre and Pitt": that is, the ongoing wars between the two great powers of the 1790s, monarchical England (Prime Minister William Pitt) and revolutionary France (Maximilien Robespierre, head of the Committee for Public Safety that directed the government in 1793–1794). These revolutionary wars and their global consequences are the larger geopolitical context of the shipping investments, frauds, Caribbean slave revolution, and widespread Atlantic unrest underlying the novel's local action. Fielding's informed conversation on current world politics marks her as able and willing to contemplate topics beyond stereotypical female concerns and as much better educated and informed than Mervyn. Her backstory in Chapter II.23 develops her ties to European revolutionary turmoil and Robespierre's significance for her former husband.

In a short time the women rose, and, huddling on their cloaks, disappeared, in company with the gentleman. Being thus left alone with Mrs. Fielding, some embarrassment was mutually betrayed. With much hesitation, which, however, gradually disappeared, my companion, at length, began the conversation.

You met me lately, in a situation, sir, on which I look back with trembling and shame, but not with any self-condemnation. I was led into it without any fault, unless a too hasty confidence may be stiled a fault. I had known Mrs. Villars in England, where she lived with an untainted reputation, at least; and the sight of my countrywoman, in a foreign land, awakened emotions, in the indulgence of which I did not imagine there was either any guilt or any danger. She invited me to see her at her house with so much urgency and warmth, and solicited me to take a place immediately in a chaise in which she had come to the city that I too incautiously complied.

You are a stranger to me, and I am unacquainted with your character. What little I have seen of your deportment, and what little I have lately heard concerning you from Mrs. Wentworth, do not produce unfavorable impressions; but the apology I have made was due to my own reputation, and should have been offered to you whatever your character had been. There she stopped.

I came not hither, said I, to receive an apology. Your demeanor, on our first interview, shielded you sufficiently from any suspicions or surmises that I could form. What you have now mentioned was likewise mentioned by your friend, and was fully believed upon her authority. My purpose, in coming, related not to you but to another. I desired merely to interest your generosity and justice on behalf of one, whose destitute and dangerous condition may lay claim to your compassion and your succour.

I comprehend you, said she, with an air of some perplexity. I know the claims of that person.

And will you comply with them?

In what manner can I serve her?

By giving her the means of living.

Does she not possess them already?

She is destitute. Her dependence was wholly placed upon one that is dead, by whom her person was dishonored and her fortune embezzled.

But she still lives. She is not turned into the street. She is not destitute of home.

But what an home?

Such as she may chuse to remain in.

She cannot chuse it. She must not chuse it. She remains through ignorance, or through the incapacity of leaving it.

But how shall she be persuaded to a change?

I will persuade her. I will fully explain her situation. I will supply her with a new home.

You would persuade her to go with you, and to live at a home of your providing, and on your bounty?

Certainly.

Would that change be worthy of a cautious person? Would it benefit her reputation? Would it prove her love of independence?

My purposes are good. I know not why she should suspect them. But I am only anxious to be the instrument. Let her be indebted to one of her own sex, of unquestionable reputation. Admit her into this house. Invite her to your arms. Cherish and console her as your sister.

Before I am convinced that she deserves it? And even then, what regard shall I, young, unmarried, independent, affluent, pay to my own reputation in harboring a woman in these circumstances?

But you need not act yourself. Make me your agent and almoner. Only supply her with the means of subsistence through me.

Would you have me act a clandestine part? Hold meetings with one of your sex, and give him money for a purpose which I must hide from the world? Is it worth while to be a dissembler and impostor? And will not such conduct incur more dangerous surmises and suspicions, than would arise from acting openly and directly? You will forgive me for reminding you like wise that it is particularly incumbent upon those in my situation to be circumspect in their intercourse with men and with strangers. This is the second time that I have seen you. My knowledge of you is extremely dubious and imperfect, and such as would make the conduct you prescribe to me, in an high degree, rash and culpable. You must not, therefore, expect me to pursue it.

These words were delivered with an air of firmness and dignity. I was not insensible to the truth of her representations. I confess, said I, what you have said makes me doubt the propriety of my proposal: yet I would fain be of service to her. Cannot you point out some practicable method?

She was silent and thoughtful, and seemed indisposed to answer my question.

I had set my heart upon success in this negociation, continued I, and could not imagine any obstacle to its success; but I find my ignorance of the world's ways much greater than I had previously expected. You defraud yourself of all the happiness redounding from the act of making others happy. You sacrifice substance to shew, and are more anxious to prevent unjust aspersions from lighting on yourself, than to rescue a fellow-creature from guilt and infamy.

You are rich, and abound in all the conveniences and luxuries of life. A small portion of your superfluity would obviate the wants of a being not less worthy than yourself. It is not avarice or aversion to labor that makes you withhold your hand. It is dread of the sneers and surmises of malevolence and ignorance.

I will not urge you further at present. Your determination to be wise should not be hasty. Think upon the subject calmly and sedately, and form your resolution in the course of three days. At the end of that period I will visit you again. So saying, and without waiting for comment or answer, I withdrew.

Chapter XVII

I MOUNTED the stage-coach at day-break the next day, in company with a sallow Frenchman from Saint Domingo,[1] his fiddle-case, an ape, and two female blacks. The Frenchman, after passing the suburbs, took out his violin and amused himself with humming to his own *tweedle-tweedle*. The monkey now and then mounched an apple, which was given to him from a basket by the blacks, who gazed with stupid wonder, and an exclamatory *La! La!* upon the passing scenery; or chattered to each other in a sort of open-mouthed, half-articulate, monotonous, and sing-song jargon.

The man looked seldom either on this side or that; and spoke only to rebuke the frolicks of the monkey, with a Tenez! Dominique! Prenez garde! Diable noir![2]

As to me my thought was busy in a thousand ways. I sometimes gazed at the faces of my *four* companions, and endeavored to discern the differences and samenesses between them. I took an exact account of the features, proportions, looks, and gestures of the monkey, the Congolese, and the Creole-Gaul. I compared them together, and examined them apart. I looked at them in a thousand different points of view, and pursued, untired and unsatiated, those trains of reflections which began at each change of tone, feature, and attitude.[3]

I marked the country as it successively arose before me, and found endless employment in examining the shape and substance of the fence, the barn and the cottage, the aspect of earth and of heaven. How great are the pleasures of health and of mental activity.

My chief occupation, however, related to the scenes into which I was about to enter. My imaginations were, of course, crude and inadequate; and I found an uncommon gratification in comparing realities, as they successively occurred, with the pictures which my wayward fancy had depicted.

---

[1] "Saint Domingo": Haiti.

[2] "Tenez! Dominique! Prenez garde! Diable noir!": "Hold on now! Dominique! Watch out (behave yourself)! Black devil!" Because the monkey's name plays on European names for Haiti (Saint Domingo or Domingue), the Creole's efforts to control the restless pet may allude to the island's ongoing black revolution, to planter elites' increasingly futile efforts to control Domingan slaves. See Brown's essay "On the Consequences of Abolishing the Slave Trade in the West Indian Colonies" in Related Texts.

[3] "Each change of tone, feature, and attitude": beginning with the iconic pet and his Creole master, the stagecoach scene uses the sympathetic gaze the novel has associated with rational sensibility to spark an implicit reflection on slavery. The setting and details seem reminiscent of the pet starling that prompts a polemic against Atlantic slavery in Laurence Sterne's influential *Sentimental Journey through France and Italy* (1768). In that narrative, the appearance of a caged starling that cries "I can't get out—I can't get out" leads to a series of reflections on liberty and an empathetic identification with "the millions of my fellow creatures born to no inheritance but slavery" (see this passage in the Related Texts here). As a travel narrative, Sterne's novel was commonly associated with stagecoach settings, for example in the progressive invocation of "the divine Sterne" in the opening scene (Letter I) of Holcroft's *Anna St. Ives,* another source for this novel. For Mervyn's stylistic aping of Sterne, see notes II.13.1, II.23.1, and II.25.4.

I will not describe my dreams. My proper task is to relate the truth. Neither shall I dwell upon the images suggested by the condition of the country through which I passed.[4] I will confine myself to mentioning the transactions connected with the purpose of my journey.

I reached Baltimore at night. I was not so fatigued, but that I could ramble through the town. I intended, at present, merely the gratification of a stranger's curiosity. My visit to Mrs. Watson and her brother I designed should take place on the morrow. The evening of my arrival I deemed an unseasonable time.

While roving about, however, it occurred to me that it might not be impolitic to find the way to their habitation even now. My purposes of general curiosity would equally be served whichever way my steps were bent; and, to trace the path to their dwelling, would save me the trouble of enquiries and interrogations to-morrow.

When I looked forward to an interview with the wife of Watson, and to the subject which would be necessarily discussed at that interview, I felt a trembling and misgiving at my heart. Surely, thought I, it will become me to exercise immeasurable circumspection and address; and yet how little are these adapted to the impetuosity and candor of my nature.

How am I to introduce myself? What am I to tell her? That I was a sort of witness to the murder of her husband? That I received from the hand of his assassin the letter which I afterwards transmitted to her? and, from the same hands, the bills contained in his girdle?

How will she start and look aghast? What suspicions will she harbor? What enquiries shall be made of me? How shall they be disarmed and eluded, or answered? Deep consideration will be necessary before I trust myself to such an interview. The coming night shall be devoted to reflection upon this subject.

From these thoughts I proceeded to enquiries for the street mentioned in the advertisement, where Mrs. Watson was said to reside. The street and, at length, the habitation, was found. Having reached a station opposite, I paused and surveyed the mansion. It was a wooden edifice of two stories; humble, but neat. You ascended to the door by several stone steps. Of the two lower windows, the shutters of one were closed, but those of the other were open. Though late in the evening, there was no appearance of light or fire within.

Beside the house was a painted fence, through which was a gate leading to the back of the building. Guided by the impulse of the moment, I crossed the street to the gate, and, lifting the latch, entered the paved alley, on one side of which was a paled fence, and on the other the house, looking through two windows into the alley.

The first window was dark like those in front; but at the second a light was discernible. I approached it, and, looking through, beheld a plain but neat apartment, in which parlour, kitchen, and nursery seemed to be united. A fire burnt cheerfully in the chimney, over which was a tea-kettle. On the hearth sat a smiling and playful

---

[4] "Images suggested by the condition of the country through which I passed": that is, reflections on a state in which slavery is legal.

cherub of a boy, tossing something to a black girl who sat opposite, and whose inno-cent and regular features wanted only a different hue to make them beautiful. Near it, in a rocking hair, with a sleeping babe in her lap, sat a female figure in plain but neat and becoming attire. Her posture permitted half her face to be seen, and saved me from any danger of being observed.

This countenance was full of sweetness and benignity, but the sadness that veiled its lustre was profound. Her eyes were now fixed upon the fire and were moist with the tears of remembrance, while she sung, in low and scarcely audible strains, an artless lullaby.

This spectacle exercised a strange power over my feelings. While occupied in medi-tating on the features of the mother, I was unaware of my conspicuous situation. The black girl having occasion to change her situation, in order to reach the ball which was thrown at her, unluckily caught a glance of my figure through the glass. In a tone of half surprize and half terror she cried out—O! see dare! a man!

I was tempted to draw suddenly back, but a second thought shewed me the impro-priety of departing thus abruptly, and leaving behind me some alarm. I felt a sort of necessity for apologizing for my intrusion into these precincts, and hastened to a door that led into the same apartment. I knocked. A voice somewhat confused bade me enter. It was not till I opened the door and entered the room that I fully saw in what embarrassments I had incautiously involved myself.

I could scarcely obtain sufficient courage to speak, and gave a confused assent to the question—"Have you business with me, sir?" She offered me a chair, and I sat down. She put the child, not yet awakened, into the arms of the black, who kissed it and rocked it in her arms with great satisfaction, and, resuming her seat, looked at me with inquisitiveness mingled with complacency.

After a moment's pause, I said—I was directed to this house as the abode of Mr. Ephraim Williams.[5] Can he be seen, madam?

He is not in town at present. If you will leave a message with me, I will punctually deliver it.

The thought suddenly occurred, whether any more was needful than merely to leave the bills suitably enclosed, as they already were, in a pacquet. Thus all painful explanations might be avoided, and I might have reason to congratulate myself on his seasonable absence. Actuated by these thoughts, I drew forth the pacquet, and put it into her hand, saying, I will leave this in your possession, and must earnestly request you to keep it safe until you can deliver it into his own hands.

Scarcely had I said this before new suggestions occurred. Was it right to act in this clandestine and mysterious manner? Should I leave these persons in uncertainty

---

[5] "Mr. Ephraim Williams": the enlightened sea captain Williams, brother-in-law of Watson, who told the story of Watson's link to the Maurice fortune in Chapter II.3. Watson's widow, the mother in this scene, is his sister, and he will become Mervyn's friend after meeting him in Chapter II.19. There does not seem to be any reference to the Ephraim Williams, Jr. (1715–1755) for whom Williams College was named in 1793.

respecting the fate of an husband and a brother? What perplexities, misunderstandings, and suspences might not grow out of this uncertainty; and ought they not to be precluded at any hazard to my own safety or good name?

These sentiments made me involuntarily stretch forth my hand to retake the pacquet. This gesture, and other significances in my manners, joined to a trembling consciousness in herself, filled my companion with all the tokens of confusion and fear. She alternately looked at me and at the paper. Her trepidation increased, and she grew pale. These emotions were counteracted by a strong effort.

At length she said faulteringly, I will take good care of them, and will give them to my brother.

She rose and placed them in a drawer, after which she resumed her seat.

On this occasion all my wariness forsook me. I cannot explain why my perplexity and the trouble of my tho'ts were greater upon this than upon similar occasions. However it be, I was incapable of speaking, and fixed my eyes upon the floor. A sort of electrical sympathy pervaded my companion, and terror and anguish were strongly manifested in the glances which she sometimes stole at me. We seemed fully to understand each other without the aid of words.

This imbecility could not last long. I gradually recovered my composure and collected my scattered thoughts. I looked at her with seriousness, and steadfastly spoke—Are you the wife of Amos Watson?

She started.—I am, indeed. Why do you ask? Do you know any thing of —? There her voice failed.

I replied with quickness, yes. I am fully acquainted with his destiny.

Good God! she exclaimed in a paroxysm of surprize, and bending eagerly forward, my husband is then alive. This pacquet is from him. Where is he? When have you seen him?

'Tis a long time since.

But where, where is he now? Is he well? Will he return to me?

Never.

Merciful Heaven! looking upwards and clasping her hands, I thank thee at least for his life! But why has he forsaken me? Why will he not return?

For a good reason, said I with augmented solemnity, he will never return to thee. Long ago was he laid in the cold grave.

She shrieked; and, at the next moment, sunk in a swoon upon the floor. I was alarmed. The two children shrieked, and ran about the room terrified and unknowing what they did. I was overwhelmed with somewhat like terror, yet I involuntarily raised the mother in my arms, and cast about for the means of recalling her from this fit.

Time to effect this had not elapsed, when several persons, apparently Mrs. Watson's neighbors, and raised by the outcries of the girls, hastily entered the room. They looked at me with mingled surprize and suspicion; but my attitude, being that not of an injurer but helper; my countenance, which shewed the pleasure their entrance, at this critical moment, afforded me; and my words, in which I besought their assistance, and explained, in some degree, and briefly, the cause of those appearances, removed their ill thoughts.

Presently, the unhappy woman, being carried by the new-comers into a bed-room adjoining, recovered her sensibility. I only waited for this. I had done my part. More information would be useless to her, and not to be given by me, at least, in the present audience, without embarrassment and peril. I suddenly determined to withdraw, and this, the attention of the company being otherwise engaged, I did without notice. I returned to my inn, and shut myself up in my chamber. Such was the change which, undesigned, unforeseen, an half an hour had wrought in my situation. My cautious projects had perished in their conception. That which I had deemed so arduous, to require such circumspect approaches, such well concerted speeches was done.

I had started up before this woman as if from the pores of the ground. I had vanished with the same celerity, but had left her in possession of proofs sufficient that I was neither spectre nor demon. I will visit her, said I, again. I will see her brother, and know the full effect of my disclosure. I will tell them all that I myself know. Ignorance would be no less injurious to them than to myself; but, first, I will see the Maurices.

Chapter XVIII

NEXT morning I arose betimes, and equipped myself without delay. I had eight or ten miles to walk, so far from the town being the residence of these people; and I forthwith repaired to their dwelling. The persons whom I desired to see were known to me only by name, and by their place of abode. It was a mother and her three daughters to whom I now carried the means not only of competence but riches; means which they, no doubt, had long ago despaired of regaining, and which, among all possible messengers, one of my age and guise would be the least suspected of being able to restore.

I arrived, through intricate ways, at eleven o'clock, at the house of Mrs. Maurice. It was a neat dwelling, in a very fanciful and rustic style, in the bosom of a valley, which, when decorated by the verdure and blossoms of the coming season, must possess many charms. At present it was naked and dreary.

As I approached it, through a long avenue, I observed two female figures, walking arm-in-arm and slowly to and fro, in the path in which I now was. These, said I, are daughters of the family. Graceful, well-dressed, fashionable girls they seem at this distance. May they be deserving of the good tidings which I bring.—Seeing them turn towards the house, I mended my pace, that I might overtake them and request their introduction of me to their mother.

As I more nearly approached, they again turned; and, perceiving me, they stood as if in expectation of my message. I went up to them.

A single glance, cast at each, made me suspect that they were not sisters; but, somewhat to my disappointment, there was nothing highly prepossessing in the countenance of either. They were what is every day met with, though less embellished by brilliant drapery and turban, in markets and streets. An air, somewhat haughty, somewhat supercilious, lessened still more their attractions. These defects, however, were nothing to me.

I enquired, of her that seemed to be the elder of the two, for Mrs. Maurice.

She is indisposed, was the cold reply.

That is unfortunate. Is it not possible to see her?

No—with still more gravity.

I was somewhat at a loss how to proceed. A pause ensued. At length, the same lady resumed—What's your business? You can leave your message with me.

With no body but her. If she be not *very* indisposed—

She is very indisposed, interrupted she peevishly. If you cannot leave your message, you may take it back again, for she must not be disturbed.

This was a singular reception. I was disconcerted and silent. I knew not what to say. Perhaps, I at last observed, some other time—

No, with increasing heat, no other time. She is more likely to be worse than better. Come, Betsy, said she, taking hold of her companion's arm; and, hieing into the house, shut the door after her, and disappeared. I stood, at the bottom of the steps, confounded at such strange and unexpected treatment. I could not withdraw till my purpose was accomplished. After a moment's pause, I stepped to the door, and pulled the bell. A Negro came, of a very unpropitious aspect, and opening the door, looked at me in silence. To my question, was Mrs. Maurice to be seen? he made some answer, in a jargon which I could not understand; but his words were immediately followed by an unseen person within the house—Mrs. Maurice can't be seen by any body. Come in, Cato, and shut the door. This injunction was obeyed by Cato without ceremony.

Here was a dilemma! I came with ten thousand pounds[1] in my hands to bestow freely on these people, and such was the treatment I received. I must adopt, said I, a new mode.

I lifted the latch, without a second warning, and, Cato having disappeared, went into a room, the door of which chanced to be open, on my right hand. I found within the two females whom I had accosted in the portico. I now addressed myself to the younger—This intrusion, when I have explained the reason of it, will, I hope, be forgiven. I come, madam—

Yes, interrupted the other, with a countenance suffused by indignation, I know very well whom you come from, and what it is that prompts this insolence, but your employer shall see that we have not sunk so low as he imagines. Cato! Bob! I say.

My employer, madam! I see you labor under some great mistake. I have no employer. I come from a great distance. I come to bring intelligence of the utmost importance to your family. I come to benefit and not to injure you.

By this time, Bob and Cato, two sturdy blacks, entered the room. Turn this person, said the imperious lady, regardless of my explanations, out of the house. Don't you hear me? she continued, observing that they looked one upon the other and hesitated.

Surely, madam, said I, you are precipitate. You are treating like an enemy one who will prove himself your mother's best friend.

Will you leave the house? she exclaimed, quite beside herself with anger. Villains! why don't you do as I bid you?

The blacks looked upon each other, as if waiting for an example. Their habitual deference for every thing *white*, no doubt, held their hands from what they regarded as a profanation. At last Bob said, in a whining, beseeching tone—Why, missee, massa buckra[2] wanna go for doo, dan he wanna go fo' wee.

The lady now burst into tears of rage. She held out her hand, menacingly. Will you leave the house?

Not willingly, said I, in a mild tone. I came too far to return with the business that brought me unperformed. I am persuaded, madam, you mistake my character and my views. I have a message to deliver your mother which deeply concerns her and

---

[1] "Ten thousand pounds": on this money and its dollar value, see note II.3.12.

[2] "Buckra": black slang for a white person. Originally from Igbo "beke" (white man) and Caribbean patois (the "jargon" Mervyn can't understand a few paragraphs earlier), the term first gained currency in English during the 1790s in the context of Caribbean slave revolt. The term figures centrally in an antislavery poem "The Negro's Lamentation," that was published in the Brown-edited *Monthly Magazine* in November, 1800. The poem concludes: "*Buckra*, for want of gold, / The lovely nymph inflexibly has sold / To some rich planter, man of high renown, / *Who haunts vendues to knock poor Negroes down!*"

your happiness, if you are her daughter. I merely wished to see her, and leave with her a piece of important news; news in which her fortune is deeply interested.

These words had a wonderful effect upon the young lady. Her anger was checked. Good God! she exclaimed, are you Watson?

No: I am only Watson's representative, and come to do all that Watson could do if he were present.

She was now importunate to know my business.

My business lies with Mrs. Maurice. Advertisements, which I have seen, direct me to her, and to this house, and to her only shall I deliver my message.

Perhaps, said she, with a face of apology, I have mistaken you. Mrs. Maurice is my mother. She is really indisposed, but I can stand in her place on this occasion.

You cannot represent her in this instance. If I cannot have access to her now, I must go; and shall return when you are willing to grant it.

Nay, replied she, she is not, perhaps, so very sick but that—I will go, and see if she will admit you.— So saying, she left me for three minutes; and returning said, her mother wished to see me.

I followed up stairs, at her request; and, entering an ill-furnished chamber, found, seated in an arm-chair, a lady seemingly in years, pale and visibly infirm. The lines of her countenance were far from laying claim to my reverence. It was too much like the daughter's.

She looked at me, at my entrance, with great eagerness, and said, in a sharp tone, Pray, friend, what is it you want with me? Make haste; tell your story, and begone.

My story is a short one, and easily told. Amos Watson was your agent in Jamaica. He sold an estate belonging to you, and received the money.

He did, said she, attempting ineffectually to rise from her seat, and her eyes beaming with a significance that shocked me—He did, the villain, and purloined the money to the ruin of me and my daughters. But if there be justice on earth it will overtake him. I trust, I shall have the pleasure one day—I hope to hear he's hanged. Well, but go on, friend. He *did* sell it, I tell you.

He sold it for ten thousand pounds, I resumed, and invested this sum in bills of exchange. Watson is dead. These bills came into my hands. I was lately informed, by the public papers, who were the real owners, and have come from Philadelphia with no other view than to restore them to you. There they are, continued I, placing them in her lap, entire and untouched.

She seized the papers, and looked at me and at her daughter, by turns, with an air of one suddenly bewildered. She seemed speechless, and growing suddenly more ghastly pale, leaned her head back upon the chair. The daughter screamed, and hastened to support the languid parent, who difficultly articulated—O! I am sick; sick to death. Put me on the bed.

I was astonished and affrighted at this scene. Some of the domestics, of both colours, entered, and gazed at me with surprize. Involuntarily I withdrew, and returned to the room below into which I had first entered, and which I now found deserted.

I was for some time at a loss to guess at the cause of these appearances. At length it occurred to me that joy was the source of the sickness that had seized Mrs. Maurice.

The abrupt recovery of what had probably been deemed irretrievable, would naturally produce this effect upon a mind of a certain texture.

I was deliberating, whether to stay or go, when the daughter entered the room, and, after expressing some surprize at seeing me, whom she supposed to have retired, told me that her mother wished to see me again before my departure. In this request there was no kindness. All was cold, supercilious, and sullen. I obeyed the summons without speaking.

I found Mrs. Maurice seated in her arm-chair, much in her former guise. Without desiring me to be seated, or relaxing ought in her asperity of looks and tones—Pray, friend, how did you *come by* these papers?

I assure you, madam, they were honestly *come by*, answered I, sedately and with half a smile; but, if the whole is there that was missing, the mode and time in which they came to me is matter of concern only to myself. Is there any deficiency?

I'm not sure. I don't know much of these matters. There may be less. I dare say there is. I shall know that soon. I expect a friend of mine every minute who will look them over. I don't doubt you can give a good account of yourself.

I doubt not but I can—to those who have a right to demand it. In this case, curiosity must be very urgent indeed, before I shall consent to gratify it.

You must know this is a suspicious case. Watson, to be sure, embezzled the money: to be sure, you are his accomplice.

Certainly, said I, my conduct, on this occasion, proves that. What I have brought to you, of my own accord; what I have restored to you, fully and unconditionally, it is plain Watson embezzled and that I was aiding in the fraud. To restore what was never stolen always betrays the thief. To give what might be kept without suspicion is, without doubt, arrant knavery.—To be serious, madam, in coming thus far, for this purpose, I have done enough; and must now bid you farewel.

Nay, don't go yet. I have something more to say to you. My friend I'm sure will be here presently. There he is, noticing a peal upon the bell. Polly, go down, and see if that's Mr. Somers. If it is, bring him up. The daughter went.

I walked to the window absorbed in my own reflections. I was disappointed and dejected. The scene before me was the unpleasing reverse of all that my fancy, while coming hither, had foreboded. I expected to find virtuous indigence and sorrow lifted, by my means, to affluence and exultation. I expected to witness the tears of gratitude and the caresses of affection. What had I found? Nothing but sordidness, stupidity, and illiberal suspicion.

The daughter staid much longer than the mother's patience could endure. She knocked against the floor with her heel. A servant came up.—Where's Polly, you slut? It was not you, hussey, that I wanted. It was her.

She is talking in the parlour with a gentleman.

Mr. Somers, I suppose; hay! fool! Run with my compliments to him, wench. Tell him, please walk up.

It is not Mr. Somers, ma'am.

No! Who then, saucebox? What gentleman can have any thing to do with Polly?

I don't know, ma'am.

Who said you did, impertinence? Run, and tell her I want her this instant.

The summons was not delivered, or Polly did not think proper to obey it. Full ten minutes of thoughtful silence on my part, and of muttered vexation and impatience on that of the old lady, elapsed before Polly's entrance. As soon as she appeared, the mother began to complain bitterly of her inattention and neglect; but Polly, taking no notice of her, addressed herself to me, and told me that a gentleman below wished to see me. I hastened down, and found a stranger, of a plain appearance, in the parlour. His aspect was liberal and ingenuous; and I quickly collected from his discourse that this was the brother-in-law of, Watson and the companion of his last voyage.

Chapter XIX

MY eyes sparkled with pleasure at this unexpected interview, and I willingly confessed my desire to communicate all the knowledge of his brother's destiny which I possessed. He told me, that, returning late to Baltimore on the last evening, he found his sister in much agitation and distress, which, after a time, she explained to him. She likewise put the pacquets I had left into his hands.

I leave you to imagine, continued he, my surprize and curiosity at this discovery. I was, of course, impatient to see the bearer of such extraordinary tidings. This morning, enquiring for one of your appearance at the taverns, I was, at length, informed of your arrival yesterday in the stage; of your going out alone in the evening; of your subsequent return; and of your early departure this morning. Accidentally I lighted on your footsteps; and, by suitable enquiries on the road, have finally traced you hither.

You told my sister her husband was dead. You left with her papers that were probably in his possession at the time of his death. I understand from Miss Maurice that the bills belonging to her mother, have just been delivered to her. I presume you have no objection to clear up this mystery.

To you I am anxious to unfold every thing. At this moment, or at any time, but the sooner, the more agreeable to me, I will do it.

This, said he, looking around him, is no place; there is an inn not an hundred yards from this gate, where I have left my horse; will you go thither? I readily consented, and calling for a private apartment, I laid before this man every incident of my life connected with Welbeck and Watson; my full, circumstantial and explicit story, appeared to remove every doubt which he might have entertained of my integrity.

In Williams, I found a plain good man, of a temper confiding and affectionate. My narration being finished, he expressed, by unaffected tokens, his wonder and his grief on account of Watson's destiny. To my enquiries, which were made with frankness and fervor, respecting his own and his sister's condition, he said, that the situation of both was deplorable till the recovery of this property. They had been saved from utter ruin, from beggary and a jail, only by the generosity and lenity of his creditors, who did not suffer the suspicious circumstances attending Watson's disappearance to outweigh former proofs of his probity. They had never relinquished the hopes of receiving some tidings of their kinsman.

I related what had just passed in the house of Mrs. Maurice, and requested to know from him the history and character of this family.

They have treated you, he answered, exactly as any one who knew them would have predicted. The mother is narrow, ignorant, bigotted, and avaricious. The eldest daughter, whom you saw, resembles the old lady in many things. Age, indeed, may render the similitude complete. At present, pride and ill-humor are her chief characteristics.

The youngest daughter has nothing in mind or person in common with her family. Where they are irrascible, she is patient; where they are imperious, she is humble; where they are covetous, she is liberal; where they are ignorant and indolent, she is studious and skilful. It is rare, indeed, to find a young lady more amiable than Miss Fanny Maurice, or who has had more crosses and afflictions to sustain.

The eldest daughter always extorted the supply of her wants, from her parents, by threats and importunities; but the younger could never be prevailed upon to employ the same means, and, hence, she suffered inconveniences which, to any other girl, born to an equal rank, would have been, to the last degree, humiliating and vexatious. To her they only afforded new opportunities for the display of her most shining virtues—fortitude and charity. No instance of their sordidness or tyranny ever stole a murmur from her. For what they had given, existence and a virtuous education, she said they were entitled to gratitude. What they withheld was their own, in the use of which they were not accountable to her. She was not ashamed to owe her subsistence to her own industry, and was only held, by the pride of her family—in this instance their pride was equal to their avarice—from seeking out some lucrative kind of employment. Since the shock which their fortune sustained, by Watson's disappearance, she has been permitted to pursue this plan, and she now teaches music in Baltimore for a living. No one, however, in the highest rank, can be more generally respected and caressed than she is.

But will not the recovery of this money make a favorable change in her condition?

I can hardly tell; but I am inclined to think it will not. It will not change her mother's character. Her pride may be awakened anew, and she may oblige Miss Fanny to relinquish her new profession, and that will be a change to be deplored.[1]

What good has been done, then, by restoring this money?

If pleasure be good, you must have conferred a great deal on the Maurices; upon the mother and two of the daughters, at least. The only pleasure, indeed, which their natures can receive. It is less than if you had raised them from absolute indigence, which has not been the case, since they had wherewithal to live upon beside their Jamaica property. But how, continued Williams, suddenly recollecting himself, have you claimed the reward promised to him who should restore these bills?

What reward?

No less than a thousand dollars.[2] It was publicly promised under the hands of Mrs. Maurice and of Hemming, her husband's executor.

Really, said I, that circumstance escaped my attention, and I wonder that it did; but is it too late to repair the evil?

Then you have no scruple to accept the reward?

Certainly not. Could you suspect me of so strange a punctilio[3] as that?

Yes; but I know not why. The story you have just finished taught me to expect some unreasonable refinement upon that head.—To be hired, to be bribed to do our duty is supposed by some to be degrading.

---

[1] "A change to be deplored": with her fortune returned, the "bigotted" Mrs. Maurice may force her enlightened daughter to stop working and living independently. Her regressive ideas about social status define wages as demeaning, and female independence as undesirable. Her "imperious" approach to parental authority recalls the behavior of Welbeck and Philip Hadwin (notes 22.1, II.10.8).

[2] "A thousand dollars": Williams noted this reward offer in Chapter II.3 (note II.3.13).

[3] "Punctilio": excessive concern about small matters or technicalities; as Williams puts it, "unreasonable refinement."

This is no such bribe to me. I should have acted just as I have done, had no recompence been promised. In truth, this has been my conduct, for I never once thought of the reward; but now that you remind me of it, I would gladly see it bestowed. To fulfil their engagements, in this respect, is no more than justice in the Maurices. To one, in my condition, the money will be highly useful. If these people were poor, or generous and worthy, or if I myself were already rich, I might less repine at their withholding it; but, things being as they are with them and with me, it would, I think, be gross injustice in them to withhold, and in me to refuse.

That injustice, said Williams, will, on their part, I fear, be committed. 'Tis pity you first applied to Mrs. Maurice. Nothing can be expected from her avarice, unless it be wrested from her by a lawsuit.

That is a force which I shall never apply.

Had you gone first to Hemming's, you might, I think, have looked for payment. He is not a mean man. A thousand dollars he must know is not much to give for forty thousand. Perhaps, indeed, it may not yet be too late. I am well known to him, and if you please, will attend you to him in the evening, and state your claim.

I thankfully accepted this offer, and went with him accordingly. I found that Hemmings had been with Mrs. Maurice in the course of the day; had received from her intelligence of this transaction, and had entertained the expectation of a visit from me for this very purpose.

While Williams explained to him the nature of my claim, he scanned me with great intentness. His austere and inflexible brow, afforded me little room to hope for success, and this hopelessness was confirmed by his silence and perplexity, when Williams had made an end.

To be sure, said he, after some pause, the contract was explicit. To be sure, the conditions on Mr. Mervyn's side have been performed. Certain it is, the bills are entire and complete, but Mrs. Maurice will not consent to do her part, and Mrs. Maurice, to whom the papers were presented, is the person, by whom, according to the terms of the contract, the reward must be paid.

But Mrs. Maurice, you know, sir, may be legally compelled to pay, said Williams.

Perhaps she may; but I tell you plainly, that she never will do the thing without compulsion. Legal process, however, in this case, will have other inconveniences besides delay. Some curiosity will naturally be excited, as to the history of these papers. Watson disappeared a twelve month ago.[4] Who can avoid asking, where have these papers been deposited all this while, and how came this person in possession of them?

That kind of curiosity, said I, is natural and laudable, and gladly would I gratify it. Disclosure or concealment in that case, however, would no wise affect my present claim. Whether a bond, legally executed, shall be paid, does not depend upon

---

[4] "Watson disappeared a twelve month ago": if Hemmings' calculation is accurate, it is now June or July 1794. In the novel's first chapter, Wortley noted that Welbeck disappeared suddenly (subsequent to Watson's murder) in July 1793 (see note 1.9).

determining whether the payer is fondest of boiled mutton or roast beef. Truth, in the first case, has no connection with truth in the second. So far from eluding this curiosity; so far from studying concealment, I am anxious to publish the truth.

You are right, to be sure, said Hemmings. Curiosity is a natural, but only an incidental consequence in this case. I have no reason for desiring that it should be an unpleasant consequence to you.

Well, sir, said Williams, you think that Arthur Mervyn has no remedy in this case but the law.

Mrs. Maurice, to be sure, will never pay but on compulsion. Mervyn should have known his own interest better. While his left hand was stretched out to give, his right should have been held forth to receive. As it is, he must be contented with the aid of law. Any attorney will prosecute on condition of receiving *half the sum* when recovered.

We now rose to take our leave, when, Hemmings desiring us to pause a moment, said, to be sure, in the utmost strictness of the terms of our promise, the reward was to be paid by the person who received the papers; but it must be owned that your claim, at any rate, is equitable. I have money of the deceased Mr. Maurice in my hands. These very bills are now in my possession. I will therefore pay you your due, and take the consequences of an act of justice on myself. I was prepared for you. Sign that receipt, and there is a *check*[5] for the amount.

---

[5] "*Check*": by receiving a check that he can produce at a bank for cash, Mervyn has a less common, but far more stable means of exchanging capital than the "bills of exchange" on which the Maurices had to depend.

Chapter XX

THIS unexpected and agreeable decision was accompanied by an invitation to supper, at which we were treated by our host with much affability and kindness. Finding me the author of Williams's good fortune, as well as Mrs. Maurice's, and being assured by the former of his entire conviction of the rectitude of my conduct, he laid aside all reserve and distance with regard to me. He enquired into my prospects and wishes, and professed his willingness to serve me.

I dealt with equal unreserve and frankness. I am poor, said I. Money for my very expences hither, I have borrowed from a friend, to whom I am, in other respects, much indebted, and whom I expect to compensate only by gratitude and future services.

In coming hither, I expected only an increase of my debts; to sink still deeper into poverty; but happily the issue has made me rich. This hour has given me competence, at least.

What! call you a thousand dollars competence?

More than competence. I call it an abundance.[1] My own ingenuity, while I enjoy health, will enable me to live. This I regard as a fund, first to pay my debts, and next to supply deficiencies occasioned by untoward accidents or ill health, during the ensuing three or four years, at least.

We parted with this new acquaintance at a late hour, and I accepted Williams's invitation to pass the time I should spend at Baltimore, under his sister's roof. There were several motives for prolonging this stay. What I had heard of Miss Fanny Maurice, excited strong wishes to be personally acquainted with her. This young lady was affectionately attached to Mrs. Watson, by whose means my wishes were easily accomplished.

I never was in habits of reserve, even with those whom I had no reason to esteem. With those who claimed my admiration and affection, it was impossible to be incommunicative. Before the end of my second interview, both these women were mistresses of every momentous incident of my life, and of the whole chain of my feelings and opinions, in relation to every subject, and particularly in relation to themselves. Every topic disconnected with these, is comparatively lifeless and inert.

I found it easy to win their attention, and to render them communicative in their turn. As full disclosures as I had made without condition or request, my enquiries and example easily obtained from Mrs. Watson and Miss Maurice. The former related every event of her youth, and the circumstances leading to her marriage. She depicted the character of her husband, and the whole train of suspences and inquietudes occasioned by his disappearance. The latter did not hide from me her opinions upon any important subject, and made me thoroughly acquainted with her actual situation.

---

[1] "An abundance": Mervyn will be able to live on $1,000 while he pursues his medical studies. Laborers in the 1790s typically earned wages in the range of $200–$300 per year. For historical value conversions, see note 4.7.

This intercourse was strangely fascinating. My heart was buoyed up by a kind of intoxication. I now found myself exalted to my genial element, and began to taste the delights of existence. In the intercourse of ingenious and sympathetic minds,[2] I found a pleasure which I had not previously conceived.

The time flew swiftly away, and a fortnight passed almost before I was aware that a day had gone by. I did not forget the friends whom I had left behind, but maintained a punctual correspondence with Stevens, to whom I imparted all occurrences.

The recovery of my friend's kinsman, allowed him in a few days to return home. His first object was the consolation and relief of Carlton, whom, with much difficulty, he persuaded to take advantage of the laws in favor of insolvent debtors. Carlton's only debt was owing to his uncle, and by rendering up every species of property, except his clothes and the implements of his trade, he obtained a full discharge. In conjunction with his sister, he once more assumed the pen, and being no longer burthened with debts he was unable to discharge, he resumed, together with his pen, his cheerfulness. Their mutual industry was sufficient for their decent and moderate subsistence.

The chief reason for my hasty return, was my anxiety respecting Clemenza Lodi. This reason was removed by the activity and benevolence of my friend. He paid this unfortunate stranger a visit at Mrs. Villars's. Access was easily obtained, and he found her sunk into the deepest melancholy. The recent loss of her child, the death of Welbeck, of which she was soon apprized, her total dependence upon those with whom she was placed, who, however, had always treated her without barbarity or indecorum, were the calamities that weighed down her spirit.

My friend easily engaged her confidence and gratitude, and prevailed upon her to take refuge under his own roof.[3] Mrs. Wentworth's scruples, as well as those of Mrs. Fielding, were removed by his arguments and entreaties, and they consented to take upon themselves, and divide between them, the care of her subsistence and happiness. They condescended to express much curiosity respecting me, and some interest in my welfare, and promised to receive me on my return, on the footing of a friend.

With some reluctance, I at length bade my new friends farewell, and returned to Philadelphia. Nothing remained, before I should enter on my projected scheme of study and employment, under the guidance of Stevens, but to examine the situation of Eliza Hadwin with my own eyes, and if possible, to extricate my father from his unfortunate situation.

---

[2] "The intercourse of ingenious and sympathetic minds": after establishing friendships with Mrs. Stevens and Miss Carlton in Chapter II.16, Mervyn's sympathetic, rational connection with Mrs. Watson and Fanny Maurice extends his circle of enlightened conversation. The predominance of women in this circle gives it a progressive and matriarchal cast that Mervyn intensifies when he starts calling Achsa "mamma" even as he falls in love with her in the following chapters.

[3] "Refuge under his own roof": Mervyn's campaign to save Clemenza Lodi has succeeded. She leaves Villars' to live in Dr. Stevens' household (like Mervyn), and Mervyn's circle of friends provides for her support. This is the novel's resolution of Clemenza's narrative and the final mention of her character.

My father's state had given me the deepest concern. I figured to myself his condition, besotted by brutal appetites, reduced to beggary, shut up in a noisome prison, and condemned to that society which must foster all his depraved propensities. I revolved various schemes for his relief. A few hundreds would take him from prison, but how should he be afterwards disposed of? How should he be cured of his indolent habits? How should he be screened from the contagion of vicious society? By what means, consistently with my own wants, and the claims of others, should I secure to him an acceptable subsistence?

Exhortation and example were vain. Nothing but restraint would keep him at a distance from the haunts of brawling and debauchery. The want of money would be no obstacle to prodigality and waste. Credit would be resorted to as long as it would answer his demand. When that failed, he would once more be thrown into a prison; the same means to extricate him would be to be repeated, and money be thus put into the pockets of the most worthless of mankind, the agents of drunkenness and blasphemy, without any permanent advantage to my father, the principal object of my charity.

Though unable to fix on any plausible mode of proceeding, I determined, at least, to discover his present condition. Perhaps, something might suggest itself, upon the spot, suited to my purpose. Without delay I proceeded to the village of Newtown,[4] and alighting at the door of the prison, enquired for my father.

Sawny Mervyn you want, I suppose, said the keeper. Poor fellow! He came into limbo in a crazy condition, and has been a burthen on my hands ever since. After lingering along for some time, he was at last kind enough to give us the slip. It is just a week since he drank his last pint—and *died.*

I was greatly shocked at this intelligence. It was some time before my reason came to my aid, and shewed me that this was an event, on the whole, and on a disinterested and dispassionate view, not unfortunate. The keeper knew not my relation to the deceased, and readily recounted the behaviour of the prisoner and the circumstances of his last hours.

I shall not repeat the narrative. It is useless to keep alive the sad remembrance. He was now beyond the reach of my charity or pity; and since reflection could answer no beneficial end to him, it was my duty to divert my thoughts into different channels, and live henceforth for my own happiness and that of those who were within the sphere of my influence.

I was now alone in the world, so far as the total want of kindred creates solitude. Not one of my blood, nor even of my name, were to be found in this quarter of the world. Of my mother's kindred I knew nothing. So far as friendship or service might be claimed from them, to me they had no existence. I was destitute of all those benefits which flow from kindred, in relation to protection, advice or property. My

---

[4] "Newtown": a village in Bucks County, about thirty miles northeast of Philadelphia, founded 1684 by William Penn. In 1793, Newtown was the Bucks County seat. Mervyn's father has been transported there for its jail.

inheritance was nothing. Not a single relique or trinket in my possession constituted a memorial of my family. The scenes of my childish and juvenile days were dreary and desolate. The fields which I was wont to traverse, the room in which I was born, retained no traces of the past. They were the property and residence of strangers, who knew nothing of the former tenants, and who, as I was now told, had hastened to new-model and transform every thing within and without the habitation.

These images filled me with melancholy, which, however, disappeared in proportion as I approached the abode of my beloved girl. Absence had endeared the image of my *Bess*—I loved to call her so—to my soul. I could not think of her without a melting softness at my heart, and tears in which pain and pleasure were unaccountably mingled. As I approached Curling's house, I strained my sight, in hopes of distinguishing her form through the evening dusk.

I had told her of my purpose, by letter. She expected my approach at this hour, and was stationed, with a heart throbbing with impatience, at the road side, near the gate. As soon as I alighted, she rushed into my arms.

I found my sweet friend less blithsome and contented than I wished. Her situation, in spite of the parental and sisterly regards which she received from the Curlings, was mournful and dreary to her imagination. Rural business was irksome, and insufficient to fill up her time. Her life was tiresome, and uniform and heavy.

I ventured to blame her discontent, and pointed out the advantages of her situation. Whence, said I, can these dissatisfactions and repinings arise?

I cannot tell, said she; I don't know how it is with me. I am always sorrowful and thoughtful. Perhaps, I think too much of my poor father and of Susan, and yet that can't be it neither, for I think of them but seldom; not half as much as I ought, perhaps. I think of nobody almost, but you. Instead of minding my business, or chatting and laughing with Peggy Curling, I love to get by myself—to read, over and over, your letters, or to think how you are employed just then, and how happy I should be if I were in Fanny Maurice's place.

But it is all over now; this visit rewards me for every thing. I wonder how I could ever be sullen or mopeful. I will behave better, indeed I will, and be always, as now, a most happy girl.

The greater part of three days was spent in the society of my friend, in listening to her relation of all that had happened during my absence, and in communicating, in my turn, every incident which had befallen myself. After this I once more returned to the city.

Chapter XXI

I NOW set about carrying my plan of life into effect. I began with ardent zeal and unwearied diligence the career of medical study. I bespoke the counsels and instructions of my friend; attended him on his professional visits, and acted, in all practicable cases, as his substitute. I found this application of time more pleasurable than I had imagined. My mind gladly expanded itself, as it were, for the reception of new ideas. My curiosity grew more eager, in proportion as it was supplied with food, and every day added strength to the assurance that I was no insignificant and worthless being; that I was destined to be *something* in this scene of existence, and might sometime lay claim to the gratitude and homage of my fellow-men.

I was far from being, however, monopolized by these pursuits. I was formed on purpose for the gratification of social intercourse. To love and to be loved; to exchange hearts, and mingle sentiments with all the virtuous and amiable, whom my good fortune had placed within the circuit of my knowledge, I always esteemed my highest enjoyment and my chief duty.

Carlton and his sister, Mrs. Wentworth and Achsa Fielding, were my most valuable associates beyond my own family. With all these my correspondence was frequent and unreserved, but chiefly with the latter. This lady had dignity and independence, a generous and enlightened spirit beyond what her education had taught me to expect. She was circumspect and cautious in her deportment, and was not prompt to make advances or accept them. She withheld her esteem and confidence until she had full proof of their being deserved.

I am not sure that her treatment of me was fully conformable to her rules. My manners, indeed, as she once told me, she had never met with in another. Ordinary rules were so totally overlooked in my behaviour, that it seemed impossible for any one who knew me to adhere to them. No option was left but to admit my claims to friendship and confidence, instantly, or to reject them altogether.

I was not conscious of this singularity. The internal and undiscovered character of another, weighed nothing with me in the question, whether they should be treated with frankness or reserve. I felt no scruple on any occasion, to disclose every feeling and every event. Any one who could listen, found me willing to talk. Every talker found me willing to listen. Every one had my sympathy and kindness, *without* claiming it, but I *claimed* the kindness and sympathy of every one.[1]

Achsa Fielding's countenance bespoke, I thought, a mind worthy to be known and to be loved. The first moment I engaged her attention, I told her so. I related the little story of my family, spread out before her all my reasonings and determinations, my notions of right and wrong, my fears and wishes. All this was done with sincerity and fervor, with gestures, actions and looks, in which I felt as if my whole soul was

---

[1] "Sympathy of every one": the unorthodox approach to social relations Mervyn sums up here, and which he has been practicing throughout the *Second Part,* amounts to a rejection of conventional status distinctions (based on class, gender, or race) and an insistence on immediate, egalitarian, and mutually benevolent standards of exchange.

visible. Her superior age, sedateness and prudence, gave my deportment a filial freedom and affection, and I was fond of calling her "*mamma.*"

I particularly dwelt upon the history of my dear country girl; painted her form and countenance; recounted our dialogues, and related all my schemes for making her wise and good and happy. On these occasions my friend would listen to me with the mutest attention. I shewed her the letters I received, and offered her for her perusal, those which I wrote in answer, before they were sealed and sent.

On these occasions she would look by turns on my face and away from me. A varying hue would play upon her cheek, and her eyes[2] were fuller than was common of meaning.

Such and such, I once said, are my notions; now what do *you* think?

Think! emphatically, and turning somewhat aside, she answered, that you are the most—*strange* of human creatures.

But tell me, I resumed, following and searching her averted eyes, am I right; would you do thus? Can you help me to improve my girl? I wish you knew the bewitching little creature. How would that heart overflow with affection and with gratitude towards you. She should be your daughter. No—you are too nearly of an age for that.[3] A sister: her *elder* sister you should be. *That*, when there is no other relation, includes them all. Fond sisters you would be, and I the fond brother of you both.

My eyes glistened as I spoke. In truth, I am in that respect, a mere woman. My friend was more powerfully moved. After a momentary struggle, she burst into tears.

Good Heaven! said I, what ails you? Are you not well?

Her looks betrayed an unaccountable confusion, from which she quickly recovered—it was folly to be thus affected. Something ailed me I believe, but it is past— But come; you want some lines of finishing the description of the *Boa* in La Cepide.[4]

True. And I have twenty minutes to spare. Poor Franks[5] is very ill indeed, but he cannot be seen till nine. We'll read till then.

---

[2] "Varying hue . . . eyes": Mervyn closely observes Fielding's facial skin and eyes to detect when she might be agitated, foreshadowing his discovery of her hidden ethnicity.

[3] "Too nearly of an age for that": Chapter II.9 gave Eliza's age as fifteen; Chapter II.23 reveals that Achsa is twenty-six.

[4] "The *Boa* in La Cepide": as part of his medical-scientific training, Mervyn studies the French language discussion of the boa constrictor snake in the writings of Etienne de la Ville, compte de Lacépède (1756–1825), an important zoologist and member of the revolutionary assembly in Paris known for his work on classifying fish and reptiles. His *Histoire naturelle des reptiles* appeared in 1789, the first year of the revolution. Like Achsa's former husband in Chapter II.23, Lacépède was an assembly member who was forced to flee Paris because he opposed Robespierre's faction during the 1793–1794 "Reign of Terror."

[5] "Poor Franks": apparently one of Mervyn's first patients or other associate, mentioned only here. Given the coming clarification of Achsa's Jewish ethnicity, the detail is possibly significant in that Franks was perhaps the most widely known elite Jewish family name in eighteenth-century Philadelphia and New York. The Franks were a long-established and wealthy merchant family spread between London, New York, and Philadelphia, the only elite Ashkenazim in the Philadelphia

Thus on the wings of pleasure and improvement past my time; not without some hues, occasionally of a darker tint. My heart was now and then detected in sighing. This occurred when my thoughts glanced at the poor Eliza, and measured, as it were, the interval between us. We are too—*too* far apart, thought I.

The best solace on these occasions was the company of Mrs. Fielding; her music, her discourse, or some book which she set me to rehearsing to her. One evening, when preparing to pay her a visit, I received the following letter from my Bess.

TO A. MERVYN.

Curling's, May 6, 1794.

WHERE does this letter you promised me, stay all this while? Indeed, Arthur, you torment me more than I deserve, and more than I could ever find it in my heart to do you. You treat me cruelly. I must say so, though I offend you. I must write, though you do not deserve that I should, and though I fear I am in a humor not very fit for writing. I had better go to my chamber and weep: weep at your—*unkindness*, I was going to say; but, perhaps, it is only forgetfulness: and yet what can be more unkind than forgetfulness? I am sure I have never forgotten you. Sleep itself, which wraps all other images in forgetfulness, only brings you nearer, and makes me see you more distinctly.

But where can this letter stay?—O! that—hush! foolish girl! If a word of that kind escape thy lips, Arthur will be angry with thee; and then, indeed, thou mightst weep in earnest. *Then* thou wouldst have some cause for thy tears. More than once already has he almost broken thy heart with his reproaches. Sore and weak as it now is, any new reproaches would assuredly break it quite.

I *will* be content. I will be as good an housewife and dairy-woman, stir about as briskly, and sing as merrily as Peggy Curling. Why not? I am as young, as innocent, and enjoy as good health.— Alas! she has reason to be merry. She has father, mother, brothers; but I have none.—And he that was all these, and more than all these, to me, has—*forgotten* me.

But, perhaps, it is some accident that hinders. Perhaps Oliver left the market earlier than he used to do; or you mistook the house; or, perhaps, some poor creature was sick, was taken suddenly ill, and you were busy in chafing his clay-cold limbs; it fell to you to wipe the clammy drops from his brow. Such things often happen; don't

---

community at this time; many married Gentiles and supported England during the Revolution (the city's only elite Jewish family to do so). Rebecca Franks was a renowned Philadelphia society belle in the 1770s–1780s and married a British officer. Colonel Isaac Franks, on the other hand, was a continental officer and aide to Washington, whose Germantown home was later used by Washington as an emergency residence and headquarters during the 1793 fever epidemic.

they, Arthur, to people of your trade, and some such thing has happened now; and that was the reason you did not write.

And if so, shall I repine at your silence? O no! At such a time the poor Bess might easily be, and ought to be forgotten. She would not deserve your love, if she could repine at a silence brought about this way.

And O! May it be so! May there be nothing worse than this. If the sick man—see, Arthur, how my hand trembles. Can you read this scrawl? What is always bad, my fears make worse than ever.

I must not think that. And yet, if it be so, if my friend himself be sick, what will become of me? Of me, that ought to cherish you and comfort you; that ought to be your nurse. Endure for you your sickness, when she cannot remove it.

O! that—I *will* speak out—O! that this strange scruple had never possessed you. Why should I *not* be with you? Who can love you and serve you as well as I? In sickness and health, I will console and assist you. Why will you deprive yourself of such a comforter, and such an aid as I would be to you?

Dear Arthur, think better of it. Let me leave this dreary spot, where, indeed, as long as I am thus alone, I can enjoy no comfort. Let me come to you. I will put up with any thing for the sake of seeing you, tho' it be but once a day. Any garret or cellar in the dirtiest lane or darkest alley, will be good enough for me. I will think it a palace, so that I can *but* see you now and then.

Do not refuse—do not argue with me, so fond you always are of arguing! My heart is set upon your compliance. And yet, dearly as I prize your company, I would not ask it, if I thought there was any thing improper. You say there is, and you talk about it in a way that I do not understand. For my sake, you tell me, you refuse, but let me entreat you to comply for my sake.

Your pen cannot teach me like your tongue. You write me long letters, and tell me a great deal in them, but my soul droops when I call to mind your voice and your looks, and think how long a time must pass before I see you and hear you again. I have no spirit to think upon the words and paper before me. My eye and my thought wander far away.

I bethink me how many questions I might ask you; how many doubts you might clear up if you were but within hearing. If you were but close to me; but I cannot ask them here. I am too poor a creature at the pen, and, some how or another, it always happens, I can only write about myself or about you. By the time I have said all this, I have tired my fingers, and when I set about telling you how this poem and that story have affected me, I am at a loss for words; I am bewildered and bemazed as it were.

It is not so when we talk to one another. With your arm about me, and your sweet face close to mine, I can prattle forever. Then my heart overflows at my lips. After hours thus spent, it seems as if there were a thousand things still to be said. Then I can tell you what the book has told me. I can repeat scores of verses by heart, though I heard them only once read, but it is because *you* have read them to me.

Then there is nobody here to answer my questions. They never look into books. They hate books. They think it waste of time to read. Even Peggy, who you say has naturally a strong mind, wonders what I can find to amuse myself in a book. In her playful mood, she is always teazing me to lay it aside.

I do not mind her, for I like to read; but if I did not like it before, I could not help doing so ever since you told me that nobody could gain your love who was not fond of books. And yet, though I like it on that account, more than I did, I don't read somehow so earnestly, and understand so well as I use to do, when my mind was all at ease; always frolicksome, and ever upon *tiptoe*, as I may say.

How strangely, (have you not observed it?) I am altered of late; I that was ever light of heart, the very soul of gaiety, brim full of glee—am now, demure as our old *tabby*—and not half as wise. Tabby had wit enough to keep her paws out of the coals, whereas poor I have—but no matter what. It will never come to pass, I see that. So many reasons for every thing! Such looking forward! Arthur, are not men sometimes too *wise* to be happy?

I am now *so* grave. Not one smile can Peggy sometimes get from me, though she tries for it the whole day. But I know how it comes. Strange, indeed, if losing father and sister, and thrown upon the wide world, penniless and *friendless* too, now that *you* forget me; I should continue to smile. No. I never shall smile again. At least while I stay here, I never shall, I believe.

If a certain somebody suffer me to live with him—*near* him, I mean: perhaps the sight of him as he enters the door, perhaps the sound of his voice, asking—"where is my Bess?"—might produce a smile. Such a one as the very thought produces now—yet not, I hope, so transient, and so quickly followed by a tear. Women are born, they say, to trouble, and tears are given them for their relief. 'Tis all very true.

Let it be as I wish, will you? If Oliver bring not back good tidings, if he bring not a letter from thee, or thy letter still refuses my request—I don't know what may happen. Consent, if you love your poor girl.

E.H.

Chapter XXII

THE reading of this letter, though it made me mournful, did not hinder me from paying the visit I intended. My friend noticed my discomposure.

What, Arthur, thou are quite the "penseroso"[1] to night. Come, let me cheer thee with a song. Thou shalt have thy favorite ditty:—She stepped to the instrument, and with more than airy lightness, touched and sung:

> Now knit hands and beat the ground
> In a light, fantastic round,
> Till the tell-tale sun descry
> Our conceal'd solemnity.[2]

Her music, though blithsome and aerial, was not sufficient for the end. My cheerfulness would not return even at her bidding. She again noticed my sedateness, and enquired into the cause.

This girl of mine, said I, has infected me with her own sadness. There is a letter I have just received—she took it and began to read.

Meanwhile, I placed myself before her, and fixed my eyes steadfastly upon her features. There is no book in which I read with more pleasure, than the face of woman. *That* is generally more full of meaning, and of better meaning too, than the hard and inflexible lineaments of man, and *this* woman's face has no parallel.

---

[1] "Penseroso": a brooding or melancholy person and an allusion to John Milton's poem "Il Penseroso" (1631–1632), which celebrates melancholy as pensive or intellectual contemplation. Achsa prepares her song from Milton's *Comus* with this quip, and both allusions provide suggestive indirect commentary on Arthur and Achsa's budding relationship. Achsa's dark skin becomes a factor in the next chapter, so it is perhaps notable here that the goddess Melancholy, muse to the "Penseroso," is black ("Wisdom's hue") and likened to legendary African beauties such as the tragic Ethiopian queen Cassiopeia: "Black, but such as in esteem / Prince Memnon's sister might beseem, / Or that starr'd Ethiop queen that strove / To set her beauty's praise above / The sea-nymphs, and their powers offended" (ll. 17–21). Mervyn begins to call Achsa his "mother and deity" when he kisses her later in this chapter, and characterizes his devotion to her as "worship" and "idolatry." For the novel's first quotation from Milton upon Mervyn's arrival in the city, see note 3.6.

[2] "Solemnity": Achsa tries to distract Arthur by singing (and changing) lines from Milton's *Comus* (1634). The lines in Milton are "And to the tell-tale Sun descry / Our concealed solemnity. / Come, knit hands, and beat the ground, / In a light fantastic round" (ll. 141–44).

Comus, who speaks these lines inviting the listener to a sensual dance, is the debauched son of Bacchus and Circe. He embodies sensual pleasure, excess, and non-Christian otherness, all associated with dark, Eastern regions ("tawny sands," "dun shades," an "ebon chair"). With the knowledge from his mother Circe, who turned Odysseus' men into pigs with a magic potion, Comus attempts to seduce a virtuous (Western) lady by drugging her with an "orient liquor" that makes humans animalistic and prone to "roll with pleasure in a sensual sty" (like Mervyn's Latin description of Betty Lawrence in Chapter II.14), but the lady triumphs by resisting and escaping this foreign temptation. The scenario shares many themes with *Arthur Mervyn*, notably virtue exemplified by chastity and corruption figured in illegitimate erotic encounters and deceptions "that cheat the eye with blear illusion."

She read it with visible emotion. Having gone through it, she did not lift her eye from the paper, but continued silent, as if buried in thought. After some time, for I would not interrupt the pause, she addressed me thus:

This girl seems to be very anxious to be with you.

As much as I am that she should be so.—My friend's countenance betrayed some perplexity. As soon as I perceived it, I said, why are you thus grave? Some little confusion appeared as if she would not have her gravity discovered. There again, said I, new tokens in your face, my good mamma, of something which you will not mention. Yet, sooth to say, this is not your first perplexity. I have noticed it before, and wondered. It happens only when my *Bess* is introduced. Something in relation to her it must be, but what I cannot imagine. Why does *her* name, particularly, make you thoughtful; disturbed; dejected?—There now—but I must know the reason. You don't agree with me in my notions of this girl, I fear, and you will not disclose your thoughts.

By this time, she had gained her usual composure, and without noticing my comments on her looks, said: Since you are both of one mind, why does she not leave the country?

That cannot be, I believe. Mrs. Stevens says it would be disreputable. I am no proficient in etiquette, and must, therefore, in affairs of this kind, be guided by those who are. But would to Heaven, I were truly her father or brother. Then all difficulties would be done away.

Can you seriously wish that?

Why no. I believe it would be more rational to wish that the world would suffer me to act the fatherly or brotherly part, without the relationship.

And is that the only part you wish to act towards this girl?

Certainly, the only part.

You surprize me. Have you not confessed your love for her?

I *do* love her. There is nothing upon earth more dear to me than my *Bess*.

But love is of different kinds. She was loved by her father—

Less than by me. He was a good man, but not of lively feelings. Besides, he had another daughter, and they shared his love between them, but she has no sister to share *my* love. Calamity too, has endeared her to me; I am all her consolation, dependence and hope, and nothing, surely, can induce me to abandon her.

Achsa's performance, however, reverses or rewrites the poem's implications for Mervyn. The lines she sings are those of Comus, not the virtuous Lady, and thus she allusively exchanges conventional ideals of female chastity and sexual passivity for an affirmation of assertive erotic play, inauthentic identity, and non-Christian otherness. Her identification with Comus and complaint against pensive seriousness telegraph her own "dark" exoticism and hint that Mervyn ought to follow his erotic desires by marrying her, rather than her virginal rival Eliza Hadwin. When Mervyn later rushes to propose to Achsa on a midnight field, he figuratively accepts this rewriting of his "favorite ditty," affirming the lure of sexual desire and ethnic otherness in a figure associated with intellectual elevation.

Her reliance upon you, for happiness, replied my friend, with a sigh, is plain enough.

It is: but why that sigh? And yet I understand it. It remonstrates with me on my incapacity for her support. I know it well, but it is wrong to be cast down. I have youth, health and spirits, and ought not to despair of living for my own benefit and hers; but you sigh again, and it is impossible to keep my courage when *you* sigh. Do tell me what you mean by it?

You partly guessed the cause. She trusts to you for happiness, but I somewhat suspect she trusts in vain.

In vain! I beseech you tell me why you think so.

You say you love her—why then not make her your wife?

My wife! Surely her extreme youth, and my destitute condition, will account for that.

She is fifteen: the age of delicate fervor; of inartificial love, and suitable enough for marriage. As to your condition, you may live more easily together than apart. She has no false taste or perverse desires to gratify. She has been trained in simple modes and habits. Besides, that objection can be removed another way. But are these all your objections?

Her youth I object to, merely in connection with her mind. She is too little improved to be my wife. She wants that solidity of mind; that maturity of intelligence which ten years more may possibly give her, but which she cannot have at this age.

You are a very prudential youth; then you are willing to wait ten years for a wife?

Does that follow? Because my Bess will not be qualified for wedlock, in less time, does it follow that I must wait for her?

I spoke on the supposition that you loved her.

And that is true; but love is satisfied with studying her happiness as her father or brother. Some years hence, perhaps in half a year, for this passion, called wedded, or *marriage-wishing* love, is of sudden growth, my mind may change, and nothing may content me but to have Bess for my wife. Yet I do not expect it.

Then you are determined against marriage with this girl.

Of course; until that love comes which I feel not now; but which, no doubt, will come, when Bess has had the benefit of five or eight years more, unless previously excited by another.

All this is strange, Arthur. I have heretofore supposed that you actually loved (I mean with the *marriage-seeking* passion) your *Bess*.

I believe I once did; but it happened at a time when marriage was improper; in the life of her father and sister, and when I had never known in what female excellence consisted. Since that time my happier lot has cast me among women so far above Eliza Hadwin; so far above, and so widely different from any thing which time is likely to make her, that I own, nothing appears more unlikely than that I shall ever love her.

Are you not a little capricious in that respect, my good friend? You have praised your *Bess* as rich in natural endowments; as having an artless purity and rectitude of mind, which somewhat supersedes the use of formal education; as being full of sweetness and tenderness, and in her person a very angel of loveliness.

All that is true. I never saw features and shape so delicately beautiful; I never knew so young a mind so quick sighted and so firm; but, nevertheless, she is not the creature whom I would call my *wife*. My bosom slave; counsellor; friend; the mother; the pattern; the tutress of my children must be a different creature.

But what are the attributes of this *desirable* which Bess wants?

Every thing she wants. Age, capacity, acquirements, person, features, hair, complexion, all, all are different from this girl's.

And pray of what kind may they be?

I cannot pourtray them in words—but yes, I can:—The creature whom I shall worship:—it sounds oddly, but, I verily believe, the sentiment which I shall feel for my wife, will be more a kin to worship than any thing else. I shall never love, but such a creature as I now image to myself, and *such* a creature will deserve, or almost deserve, worship—but this creature, I was going to say, must be the exact counterpart, my good mamma—of *yourself*.

This was said very earnestly, and with eyes and manners that fully expressed my earnestness: perhaps my expressions were unwittingly strong and emphatic, for she started and blushed, but the cause of her discomposure, whatever it was, was quickly removed, and she said:

Poor Bess! This will be sad news to thee!

Heaven forbid! said I, of what moment can my opinions be to her?

Strange questioner that thou art. Thou knowest that her gentle heart is touched with love. See how it shews itself in the tender and inimitable strain of this epistle. Does not this sweet ingenuousness bewitch you?

It does so, and I love, beyond expression, the sweet girl; but my love is in some inconceivable way, different from the passion which that *other* creature will produce. She is no stranger to my thoughts. I will impart every thought over and over to her. I question not but I shall make her happy without forfeiting my own.

Would marriage with her, be a forfeiture of your happiness?

Not absolutely, or forever, I believe. I love her company. Her absence for a long time is irksome. I cannot express the delight with which I see and hear her. To mark her features, beaming with vivacity; playful in her pleasures; to hold her in my arms, and listen to her prattle; always musically voluble; always sweetly tender, or artlessly intelligent—and this you will say is the dearest privilege of marriage: and so it is; and dearly should I prize it; and yet, I fear my heart would droop as often as that *other* image should occur to my fancy. For then, you know, it would occur as something never to be possessed by me.

Now this image might, indeed, seldom occur. The intervals, at least, would be serene. It would be my interest to prolong these intervals as much as possible, and my endeavors to this end, would, no doubt, have some effect. Besides, the bitterness of this reflection would be lessened by contemplating, at the same time, the happiness of my beloved girl.

I should likewise have to remember, that to continue unmarried, would not necessarily secure me the possession of the *other* good—

But these reflections, my friend (broke she in upon me) are of as much force to induce you to marry, as to reconcile you to marriage already contracted.

Perhaps they are. Assuredly, I have not a hope that the *fancied* excellence will ever be mine. Such happiness is not the lot of humanity, and is, least of all, within my reach.

Your diffidence, replied my friend, in a timorous accent, has not many examples; but your character, without doubt, is all your own, possessing all and disclaiming all, is, in few words, your picture.

I scarcely understand you. Do you think I ever shall be happy to that degree which I have imagined. Think you I shall ever meet with an exact copy of *yourself!*

Unfortunate you will be, if you do not meet with many better. Your Bess, in personals, is, beyond measure, *my* superior, and in mind, allowing for difference in years, quite as much so.

But that, returned I, with quickness and fervor, is not the object. The very counterpart of *you* I want; neither worse nor better, nor different in any thing. Just such form, such features, such hues. Just that melting voice, and above all, the same habits of thinking and conversing. In thought, word and deed; gesture, look and form, that rare and precious creature whom I shall love, must be your resemblance. Your—

Have done with these comparisons, interrupted she, in some hurry, and let us return to the country girl, thy Bess.

You once, my friend, wished me to treat this girl of yours as my sister. Do you know what the duties of a sister are?

They imply no more kindness or affection than you already feel toward my Bess. Are you not her sister?

I ought to have been so. I ought to have been proud of the relation you ascribe to me, but I have not performed any of its duties. I blush to think upon the coldness and perverseness of my heart. With such means as I possess, of giving happiness to others, I have been thoughtless and inactive to a strange degree; perhaps, however, it is not yet too late. Are you still willing to invest me with all the rights of an elder sister over this girl? And will she consent, think you?

Certainly, she will; she has.

Then the first act of sistership, will be to take her from the country; from persons on whose kindness she has no natural claim, whose manners and characters are unlike her own, and with whom no improvement can be expected, and bring her back to her sister's house and bosom, to provide for her subsistence and education, and watch over her happiness.

I will not be a nominal sister. I will not be a sister by halves. *All* the rights of that relation I will have, or none. As for you, you have claims upon her, on which I must be permitted to judge, as becomes the elder sister, who, by the loss of all other relations, must occupy the place, possess the rights, and fulfil the duties of father, mother and brother.

She has now arrived at an age, when longer to remain in a cold and churlish soil, will stunt her growth and wither her blossoms. We must hasten to transplant her to a genial element, and a garden well enclosed. Having so long neglected this charming plant, it becomes me henceforth to take her wholly to myself.

And now, for it is no longer in her or your power to take back the gift, since she is fully mine, I will charge you with the office of conducting her hither. I grant it to you as a favor. Will you go?

Go! I will fly! I exclaimed, in an extacy of joy, on pinions swifter than the wind. Not the lingering of an instant will I bear. Look! one, two, three—thirty minutes after nine. I will reach Curling's gate by the morn's dawn. I will put my girl into a chaise, and by noon, she shall throw herself into the arms of her sister. But first, shall I not, in some way, manifest my gratitude?

My senses were bewildered, and I knew not what I did. I intended to kneel, as to my mother or my deity, but, instead of that, I clasped her in my arms, and kissed her lips fervently. I staid not to discover the effects of this insanity, but left the room and the house, and calling for a moment at Stevens's, left word with the servant, my friend being gone abroad, that I should not return till the morrow.

Never was a lighter heart, a gaiety more overflowing, and more buoyant than mine. All cold from a boisterous night, at a chilly season, all weariness from a rugged and miry road, were charmed away. I might have ridden, but I could not brook delay, even the delay of enquiring for and equipping an horse. I might thus have saved myself fatigue, and have lost no time, but my mind was in too great a tumult for deliberation and forecast. I saw nothing but the image of my girl, whom my tidings would render happy.

The way was longer than my fond imagination had foreseen. I did not reach Curling's till an hour after sun-rise. The distance was full thirty-five miles. As I hastened up the green lane leading to the house, I spied my Bess passing through a covered way, between the dwelling and kitchen. I caught her eye. She stopped and held up her hands, and then ran into my arms.

What means my girl? Why this catching of the breath? Why this sobbing? Look at me my love. It is Arthur, he who has treated you with forgetfulness, neglect and cruelty.

O! do not, she replied, hiding her face with her hand. One single reproach, added to my own, will kill me. That foolish, wicked letter—I could tear my fingers for writing it.

But, said I, I will kiss them—and put them to my lips. They have told me the wishes of my girl. They have enabled me to gratify her wishes. I have come to carry thee this very moment to town.

Lord bless me, Arthur—said she, lost in a sweet confusion, and her cheeks, always glowing, glowing still more deeply—indeed, I did not mean—I meant only—I will stay here—I would rather stay—

It grieves me to hear that, said I, with earnestness, I thought I was studying our mutual happiness.

It grieves you? Don't say so. I would not grieve you for the world—but, indeed, indeed, it is too soon. Such a girl as I, am not yet fit to—live in your city. Again she hid her glowing face in my bosom.

Sweet consciousness! Heavenly innocence! Thought I; may Achsa's conjectures prove false!—You have mistaken my design, for I do not intend to carry you to town with such a view as you have hinted—but merely to place you with a beloved friend;

with Achsa Fielding, of whom already you know so much, where we shall enjoy each other's company without restraint or intermission.

I then proceeded to disclose to her the plan suggested by my friend, and to explain all the consequences that would flow from it. I need not say that she assented to the scheme. She was all rapture and gratitude. Preparations for departure were easily and speedily made. I hired a chaise of a neighboring farmer, and, according to my promise, by noon the same day, delivered the timid and bashful girl into the arms of her new sister.

She was received with the utmost tenderness, not only by Mrs. Fielding, but by all my friends. Her affectionate heart was encouraged to pour forth all its feeling as into the bosom of a mother. She was reinspired with confidence. Her want of experience was supplied by the gentlest admonitions and instructions. In every plan for her improvement, suggested by her new *mamma*, for she never called her by any other name, she engaged with docility and eagerness; and her behaviour and her progress exceeded the most sanguine hopes that I had formed, as to the softness of her temper and the acuteness of her genius.

Those graces which a polished education, and intercourse with the better classes of society, are adapted to give, my girl possessed, in some degree, by a native and intuitive refinement and sagacity of mind. All that was to be obtained from actual observation and instruction, was obtained without difficulty; and in a short time, nothing but the affectionate simplicity and unperverted feelings of the country girl, bespoke the original condition.—

What art so busy about, Arthur? Always at thy pen of late. Come, I must know the fruit of all this toil and all this meditation. I am determined to scrape acquaintance with Haller and Lineus.[3] I will begin this very day. All one's friends you know should be our's. Love has made many a patient, and let me see if it cannot, in my case, make a physician. But first, what is all this writing about?

Mrs. Wentworth has put me upon a strange task—not disagreeable, however, but such as I should, perhaps, have declined, had not the absence of my Bess, and her mamma, made the time hang somewhat heavy. I have, oftener than once, and far more circumstantially than now, told her my adventures, but she is not satisfied. She wants a written narrative, for some purpose which she tells me she will disclose to me hereafter.

Luckily, my friend Stevens has saved me more than half the trouble.[4] He has done me the favor to compile much of my history with his own hand. I cannot imagine

---

[3] "Haller and Lineus": Swiss physiologist Albrecht von Haller (1708–1777) and Swedish physician and zoologist Carl Linnaeus (1707–1778), a founder of modern biological nomenclature and ecology; two major scientists of the Enlightenment included in Mervyn's studies. Eliza's appetite for knowledge and improvement again parallels Mervyn's own.

[4] "My friend Stevens has saved me more than half the trouble": the passage clarifies the novel's final structure and the fictional context of its composition. Answering Eliza's question two paragraphs earlier, "what is all this writing about," Mervyn explains that Mrs. Wentworth asked him to record his story (implicitly so that others can benefit from it) and clarifies the relation between the narrative written by himself (Chapters II.16 and following) and the frame narrative by Dr. Stevens that

what could prompt him to so wearisome an undertaking; but he says that adventures and a destiny so singular as mine ought not to be abandoned to forgetfulness like any vulgar and *every-day* existence. Besides, when he wrote it, he suspected that it might be necessary to the safety of my reputation and my life, from the consequences of my connection with Welbeck. Time has annihilated that danger. All enmities and all suspicions are buried with that ill-fated wretch. Wortley has been won by my behaviour, and confides in my integrity now as much as he formerly suspected it. I am glad, however, that the task was performed. It has saved me a world of writing. I had only to take up the broken thread, and bring it down to the period of my present happiness, and this was done, just as you tripped along the entry this morning.

To bed, my friend, it is late, and this delicate frame is not half so able to encounter fatigue as a youth spent in the hay-field and the dairy might have been expected to be.

I will, but let me take these sheets along with me. I will read them, that I am determined, before I sleep, and watch if you have told the whole truth.

Do so, if you please; but remember one thing. Mrs. Wentworth requested me to write not as if it were designed for her perusal, but for those who have no previous knowledge of her or of me. 'Twas an odd request. I cannot imagine what she means by it, but she never acts without good reason, and I have done so. And now withdraw, my dear, and farewel.

---

precedes it. Thus, in a fictional sense, the final narrative that we read is a collaboration, a byproduct and extension of the rational conversation and progressive cooperation produced by the social circle Mervyn has built up over the course of *Second Part* (a benevolent circle that now includes Dr. Stevens, Mrs. Wentworth, Miss Carlton and her brother, Achsa, and Eliza, as well as Mrs. Watson, Fanny Maurice, and captain Williams in Baltimore). After the narrative takes written form, it can circulate and the "examples" it provides can encourage further rational benevolence and improvement in us, its readers, as indicated in the novel's Preface (see note 0.3 in the Preface). For earlier clarifications of the narrative structure, see notes 1.1, II.1.2, and II.16.1.

Chapter XXIII

MOVE on, my quill! wait not for my guidance. Reanimated with thy master's spirit, all-airy light! An hey day rapture! A mounting impulse sways him: lifts him from the earth.

I must, cost what it will, rein in this upward-pulling, forward-urging—what shall I call it? But there are times, and now is one of them, when words are poor.[1]

It will not do—Down this hill, up that steep; thro' this thicket, over that hedge—I have *labored* to fatigue myself: To reconcile me to repose; to lolling on a sofa; to poring over a book, to any thing that might win for my heart a respite from these throbs; to deceive me into a few *tolerable* moments of forgetfulness.

Let me see: they tell me this is Monday night. Only three days yet to come! If thus restless to day; if my heart thus bounds till its mansion scarcely can hold it, what must be my state to morrow! What next day! What as the hour hastens on; as the sun descends; as my hand touches her in sign of wedded unity, of love without interval; of concord without end.

I must quell these tumults. They will disable me else. They will wear out all my strength. They will drain away life itself. But who could have thought! So soon! Not three months since I first set eyes upon her. Not three weeks since our plighted love, and only three days to terminate suspense and give me *all*.

I must compel myself to quiet: to sleep. I must find some refuge from anticipations so excruciating. All extremes are agonies. A joy like this is too big for this narrow tenement. I must thrust it forth; I must bar and bolt it out for a time, or these frail walls will burst asunder. The pen is a pacifyer. It checks the mind's career; it circumscribes her wanderings. It traces out, and compels us to adhere to one path. It ever was my friend. Often it has blunted my vexations; hushed my stormy passions; turned my peevishness to soothing; my fierce revenge to heart-dissolving pity.

Perhaps it will befriend me now. It may temper my impetuous wishes; lull my intoxication: and render my happiness supportable: And, indeed, it has produced partly this effect already. My blood, within the few minutes thus employed, flows with less destructive rapidity. My thoughts range themselves in less disorder—And now that the conquest is effected, what shall I say? I must continue at the pen, or shall immediately relapse.

What shall I say? Let me look back upon the steps that led me hither. Let me recount preliminaries. I cannot do better.

And first as to Achsa Fielding—to describe this woman.

To recount, in brief, so much of her history as has come to my knowledge, will best account for that zeal, almost to idolatry, with which she has, ever since I thoroughly knew her, been regarded by me.

---

[1] "There are times . . . when words are poor": Mervyn's impatience for marriage and sexual union, expressed in Sterne-like outbursts of eroticized "sentimental" rhetoric, recalls the suggestive references to Milton at the beginning of the previous chapter and provides an affirmative context for the revelation of Achsa's painful backstory in what follows.

Never saw I one to whom the term *lovely* more truly belonged. And yet, in stature she is too low; in complection, dark and almost sallow; and her eyes, though black and of piercing lustre, has a cast, which I cannot well explain. It lessens without destroying their lustre and their force to charm; but all personal defects are outweighed by her heart and her intellect. There is the secret of her power[2] to entrance the soul of the listener and beholder. It is not only when she sings that her utterance is musical. It is not only when the occasion is urgent and the topic momentous that her eloquence is rich and flowing. They are always so.

I had vowed to love her and serve her, and been her frequent visitant, long before I was acquainted with her past life. I had casually picked up some intelligence, from others, or from her own remarks. I knew very soon that she was English by birth, and had been only a year and an half in America; that she had scarcely passed her twenty-fifth year, and was still embellished with all the graces of youth; that she had been a wife; but was uninformed whether the knot had been untied by death or divorce: That she possessed considerable, and even splendid fortune; but the exact amount, and all beside these particulars, were unknown to me till some time after our acquaintance was begun.

One evening, she had been talking very earnestly on the influence annexed, in Great Britain, to birth, and had given me some examples of this influence. Meanwhile, my eyes were fixed steadfastly on hers. The peculiarity in their expression never before affected me so strongly. A vague resemblance to something seen elsewhere, on the same day, occurred, and occasioned me to exclaim, suddenly in a pause of her discourse—

As I live, my good mamma, those eyes of yours have told me a secret. I almost think they spoke to me; and I am not less amazed at the strangeness than at the distinctness of their story.

And pry'thee what have they said?

Perhaps I was mistaken. I might have been deceived by a fancied voice, or have confounded one word with another near akin to it; but let me die, if I did not think they said that you were—*a Jew*.

At this sound, her features were instantly veiled with the deepest sorrow and confusion. She put her hand to her eyes, the tears started and she sobbed. My surprise at this effect of my words,[3] was equal to my contrition. I besought her to pardon me, for having thus unknowingly, alarmed and grieved her.

---

[2] "The secret of her power": describing Achsa's ability to charm the eye and spirit despite her small stature, dark complection, and black eyes, Mervyn recalls the allusion to "Il Penseroso" in the last chapter and the black-appearing goddess Melancholy, who inspires devotion in that work (note II.22.1), as well as Acha's ventriloquism of Comus. Like Milton's intellectual deity, Achsa is not conventionally joyous but a figure who invites contemplation, and whose "musical" charm can "though mine ear / Dissolve me into ecstasies" ("Il Penseroso," ll. 164–65).

[3] "My surprise at this effect of my words": presented as a shock and a painful secret Achsa has been afraid to disclose, the revelation of her Jewish and nonwhite ethnicity is calculated to surprise the reader, coming so late in the novel. See the Introduction and Related Texts for more on Brown's

After she had regained some composure, she said, you have not offended, Arthur. Your surmise was just and natural, and could not always have escaped you. Connected with that word are many sources of anguish, which time has not, and never will, dry up; and the less I think of past events, the less will my peace be disturbed. I was desirous that you should know nothing of me, but what you see; nothing but the present and the future, merely that no allusions might occur in our conversation, which will call up sorrows and regrets that will avail nothing.

I now perceive the folly of endeavoring to keep you in ignorance, and shall therefore, once for all, inform you of what has befallen me, that your enquiries and suggestions may be made, and fully satisfied at once, and your curiosity have no motive for calling back my thoughts to what I ardently desire to bury in oblivion.

My father was indeed a *jew*, and one of the most opulent of his nation in London. A Portuguese by birth, but came to London when a boy.[4] He had few of the moral or external qualities of Jews. For I suppose there is some justice in the obloquy that follows them so closely. He was frugal without meanness, and cautious in his dealings, without extortion. I need not fear to say this, for it was the general voice.[5]

---

decision to identify the character as Jewish and nonwhite, possibly in response to the Benjamin Nones newspaper exchange on politicized anti-Semitic and antiblack slurs that appeared at the same time Brown was finishing the novel in August 1800.

[4] "A Portuguese by birth, but came to London as a boy": this means that Achsa is a Sephardic or "Portuguese" Jew, not that her father was necessarily born in that country. Sephardim are Jews of Spanish and Portuguese heritage; a community that was expelled from those countries in the 1490s, pursued by the Inquisition, and often converted to avoid persecution. These converts, like Achsa, were then variously known as marranos, conversos, "Portuguese" Jews, or crypto-Jews, i.e., "hidden" Jews (*marrano* was literally "pig" or "swine" in Spanish and Portuguese). Many fled to mercantile centers such as Amsterdam, London, and Leghorn, or across the Spanish border to Bordeaux in France, where they built family-based trading firms and worldwide maritime commercial networks much like the ones this novel describes from a Philadelphia vantage point. Sephardic trade networks were especially important in Portuguese and Dutch Caribbean or South American slave colonies such as Curaçao and Suriname, where social mixture and interracial unions produced a subgroup of mulatto or black "Portuguese" Jews, who in turn provoked debates about Jewish identity and race in Amsterdam and London. The earliest Jewish communities in North America were small groups of "Portuguese" Sephardim from these Caribbean colonies who were expelled as a result of new colonial regulations in 1654. Sephardic professionals and merchants dominated Jewish life and institutions in the U.S. before the 1820s, when Ashkenazim or Central European Jews began to immigrate in large numbers. The great majority of the small elite Jewish communities in Philadelphia and New York in the 1790s were Sephardic, and Brown and his circle had Sephardic friends and professional associates. For more on the implications of Achsa's background, see the Introduction.

[5] "It was the general voice": Achsa's apologetic efforts to meet and counter stereotypes concerning Jews and money seem pointedly ironic in this novel's larger context, which presents Anglo-dominated commercial and imperial networks as gothic webs of theft, fraud, embezzlement, and chronic corruption, and implies that much "legitimate" wealth is blood money based on murderous slave labor. In this connection, recall how Anglo financiers Old Thetford and Jamieson were condemned as greater villains than Welbeck at the beginning of *Second Part* (notes II.1.19–21).

Me, an only child, and of course, the darling of my parents, they trained up in the most liberal manner. My education was purely English. I learned the same things and of the same masters with my neighbors. Except frequenting their church and repeating their creed, and partaking of the same food, I saw no difference between them and me. Hence I grew more indifferent, perhaps, than was proper to the distinctions of religion. They were never enforced upon me. No pains were taken to fill me with scruples and antipathies. They never stood, as I may say, upon the threshold: They were often thought upon but were vague, and easily eluded or forgotten.

Hence it was that my heart too readily admitted impressions, that more zeal and more parental caution would have saved me from. They could scarcely be avoided, as my society was wholly English; and my youth, my education and my father's wealth made me an object of much attention. And the same causes that lulled to sleep my own watchfulness, had the same effect upon that of others. To regret or to praise this remissness, is now too late. Certain it is, that my destiny, and not a happy destiny, was fixed by it.

The fruit of this remissness was a passion for one, who fully returned it. Almost as young as I, who was only sixteen; he knew as little as myself, what obstacles the difference of our births was likely to raise between us. His father, Sir Ralph Fielding, a man nobly born, high in office, splendidly allied, could not be expected to consent to the marriage of his eldest son, in such green youth, to the daughter of an alien, a Portuguese, a Jew; but these impediments were not seen by my ignorance, and were overlooked by the youth's passion.

But strange to tell, what common prudence would have so confidently predicted, did not happen. Sir Ralph had a numerous family, likely to be still more so; had but slender patrimony: the income of his offices nearly made up his all. The young man was headstrong, impetuous, and would probably disregard the inclinations of his family. Yet the father would not consent but on one condition, that of my admission to the English church.

No very strenuous opposition to these terms could be expected from me. At so thoughtless an age, with an education so unfavorable to religious impressions; swayed likewise, by the strongest of human passions; made somewhat impatient by the company I kept, of the disrepute and scorn to which the Jewish nation are every where condemned, I could not be expected to be very averse to the scheme.

My fears, as to what my father's decision would be, were soon at an end. He loved his child too well to thwart her wishes in so essential a point. Finding in me no scruples, no unwillingness, he thought it absurd to be scrupulous for me. My own heart having abjured my religion, it was absurd to make any difficulty about a formal renunciation. These were his avowed reasons for concurrence, but time shewed that he had probably other reasons, founded, indeed, in his regard for my happiness, but such, as if they had been known, would probably have strengthened into invincible, the reluctance of my lover's family.

No marriage was ever attended with happier presages. The numerous relations of my husband, admitted me with the utmost cordiality, among them. My father's tenderness was unabated by this change, and those humiliations to which I had before been exposed, were now no more; and every tie was strengthened, at the end of a year, by the feelings of a *mother*. I had need, indeed, to know a season of happiness, that I might be fitted to endure the sad reverses that succeeded. One after the other my disasters came, each one more heavy than the last, and in such swift succession, that they hardly left me time to breathe.

I had scarcely left my chamber, I had scarcely recovered my usual health, and was able to press with true fervor, the new and precious gift to my bosom, when melancholy tidings came—I was in the country, at the seat of my father-in-law, when the messenger arrived.

A shocking tale it was! and told abruptly, with every unpitying aggravation. I hinted to you once, my father's death. The *kind* of death—O! my friend! It was horrible.[6] He was then a placid venerable old man; though many symptoms of disquiet had long before been discovered by my mother's watchful tenderness. Yet none could suspect him capable of such a deed; for none, so carefully had he conducted his affairs, suspected the havock that mischance had made of his property.

I, that had so much reason to love my father—I will leave you to imagine how I was affected by a catastrophe so dreadful, so unlooked-for. Much less could I suspect the cause of his despair; yet he had foreseen his ruin before my marriage; had resolved to defer it for his daughter's and his wife's sake, as long as possible, but had still determined not to survive the day that should reduce him to indigence. The desperate act was thus preconcerted—thus deliberate.

The true state of his affairs was laid open by his death. The failure of great mercantile houses at Frankfort and Liege[7] was the cause of his disasters. Thus were my prospects shut in. That wealth, which no doubt, furnished the chief inducement with my husband's family to concur in his choice, was now suddenly exchanged for poverty.

Bred up, as I had been, in pomp and luxury; conscious that my wealth was my chief security from the contempt of the proud and bigotted, and my chief title to the station to which I had been raised, and which I the more delighted in because it enabled me to confer so great obligations on my husband. What reverse could be harder than this, and how much bitterness was added by it to the grief, occasioned by the violent end of my father!

Yet, loss of fortune, though it mortified my pride, did not prove my worst calamity. Perhaps it was scarcely to be ranked with evils, since it furnished a touchstone by

---

[6] "The kind of death . . . was horrible": Achsa's father commits suicide, exposed by bankruptcy to the "contempt of the proud and the bigotted" three paragraphs farther on.

[7] "Great mercantile houses at Frankfort and Liege": Frankfurt and Liege (in present-day Belgium) were mercantile and banking centers in the orbit of Amsterdam. Achsa's father is ruined in the financial crisis of 1780–1783 that brought down the Amsterdam-based credit system of northern Europe, sparked the Batavian Revolution, and prompted a capital flight that confirmed London as the new center of Atlantic finance networks. The region suffered spectacular bankruptcies, many among Sephardic merchants who played a key role in the Dutch-based credit system. For the 1780–1783 crisis, see Braudel, *Civilization and Capitalism,* 3:266–76.

which my husband's affections were to be tried; especially as the issue of the trial was auspicious; for my misfortune seemed only to heighten the interest which my character had made for me in the hearts of all that knew me. The paternal regards of Sir Ralph had always been tender, but that tenderness seemed now to be redoubled.

New events made this consolation still more necessary. My unhappy mother!—She was nearer to the dreadful scene when it happened. Had no surviving object to beguile her sorrow; was rendered, by long habit, more dependent upon fortune than her child.

A melancholy always mute was the first effect upon my mother. Nothing could charm her eye, or her ear. Sweet sounds that she once loved, and especially when her darling child was the warbler, were heard no longer. How, with streaming eyes, have I sat and watched the dear lady, and endeavored to catch her eye, to rouse her attention!—But I must not think of these things.

But even this distress was little in comparison with what was to come. A frenzy thus mute, motionless and vacant, was succeeded by fits, talkative, outrageous, requiring incessant superintendance, restraint, and even violence.[8]

Why led you me thus back to my sad remembrances? Excuse me for the present. I will tell you the rest some other time; to-morrow.

To-morrow, accordingly, my friend resumed her story.

Let me now make an end, said she, of my mournful narrative, and never, I charge you, do any thing to revive it again.

Deep as was my despondency, occasioned by these calamities, I was not destitute of some joy. My husband and my child were lovely and affectionate. In their caresses, in their welfare, I found peace; and might still have found it, had there not been—But why should I open afresh, wounds which time has imperfectly closed? But the story must have sometime been told to you, and the sooner it is told and dismissed to forgetfulness, the better.

My ill fate led me into company with a woman too well known in the idle and dissipated circles. Her character was not unknown to me. There was nothing in her features or air to obviate disadvantageous prepossessions. I sought not her intercourse; I rather shunned it, as unpleasing and discreditable, but she would not be repulsed. Self invited, she made herself my frequent guest; took unsolicited part in my concerns; did me many kind offices; and, at length, in spite of my counter inclination, won upon my sympathy and gratitude.

No one in the world, did I fondly think, had I less reason to fear than Mrs. Waring. Her character excited not the slightest apprehension for my own safety. She was upwards of forty,[9] no wise remarkable for grace or beauty; tawdry in her dress; accus-

---

[8] "And even violence": Achsa's mother sinks into chronic depression and madness. Several of the novel's mothers (e.g., Clemenza, Thetford's and Watson's wives) suffer related depressions, although the context of ethno-racial prejudice Achsa describes is an additional factor in the disintegration of her family network.

[9] "Upwards of forty": whereas Mrs. Waring is nearly forty, Achsa and her husband are presumably around twenty at this time, since they married when both were sixteen years old. The description of Waring recalls that of Mrs. Villars in Chapter II.11.

tomed to render more conspicuous the traces of age by her attempts to hide them; the mother of a numerous family, with a mind but slenderly cultivated; always careful too to save appearances; studiously preserving distance with my husband, and he, like myself, enduring, rather than wishing her society. What could I fear from the arts of such an one?

But alas! the woman had consummate address.—Patience too, that nothing could tire. Watchfulness that none could detect. Insinuation the wiliest and most subtle. Thus wound she herself into my affections, by an unexampled perseverance in seeming kindness; by tender confidence; by artful glosses of past misconduct; by self-rebukes and feigned contritions.

Never were stratagems so intricate, dissimulation so profound! But still, that such an one should seduce my husband; young; generous; ambitious; impatient of contumely and reproach, and surely not indifferent; before this fatal intercourse, not indifferent to his wife and child!—Yet, so it was!

I saw his discontents; his struggles; I heard him curse this woman, and the more deeply for my attempts, unconscious as I was of her machinations, to reconcile them to each other, to do away what seemed a causeless indignation, or antipathy against her. How little I suspected the nature of the conflict in his heart, between a new passion and the claims of pride; of conscience and of humanity; the claims of a child and a wife; a wife already in affliction, and placing all that yet remained of happiness, in the firmness of his virtue; in the continuance of his love; a wife, at the very hour of his meditated flight, full of terrors at the near approach of an event, whose agonies demand a double share of an husband's supporting; encouraging love—

Good Heaven! For what evils are some of thy creatures reserved! Resignation to thy decree, in the last, and most cruel distress, was, indeed, an hard task.

He was gone. Some unavoidable engagement calling him to Hamburgh was pleaded. Yet to leave me at such an hour! I dared not upbraid, nor object. The tale was so specious! The fortunes of a friend depended on his punctual journey. The falsehood of his story too soon made itself known. He was gone, in company with his detested paramour!

Yet, though my vigilance was easily deceived, it was not so with others. A creditor, who had his bond for three thousand pounds, pursued, and arrested him at Harwich.[10] He was thrown into prison, but his companion, let me, at least, say that in her praise, would not desert him. She took lodging near the place of his confinement, and saw him daily. That, had she not done it, and had my personal condition allowed, should have been my province.

Indignation and grief hastened the painful crisis with me. I did not weep that the second fruit of this unhappy union saw not the light. I wept only that this hour of agony, was not, to its unfortunate mother, the last.

---

[10] "Harwich": a small port in Essex on the southeast coast of England, providing primarily ferries and shipping to the Netherlands. Fielding's imprisonment for a £3,000 debt is the last of the novel's many subplots concerning debt, bankruptcy, and commercial failure.

I felt not anger; I had nothing but compassion for Fielding. Gladly would I have re-called him to my arms and to virtue: I wrote, adjuring him by all our past joys, to re-turn; vowing only gratitude for his new affection, and claiming only the recompence of seeing him restored to his family; to liberty; to reputation.

But alas! Fielding had a good, but a proud, heart. He looked upon his error with re-morse; with self-detestation, and with the fatal belief that it could not be retrieved; shame made him withstand all my reasonings and persuasions, and in the hurry of his feelings, he made solemn vows that he would, in the moment of restored liberty, abjure his country and his family forever. He bore indignantly the yoke of his new at-tachment, but he strove in vain to shake it off. Her behaviour, always yielding, doat-ing, supplicative, preserved him in her fetters. Though upbraided, spurned and banished from his presence, she would not leave him, but by new efforts and new ar-tifices, soothed, appeased, and won again, and kept his tenderness.

What my entreaties were unable to effect, his father could not hope to accomplish. He offered to take him from prison; the creditor offered to cancel the bond, if he would return to me; but this condition he refused. All his kindred, and one who had been his bosom friend from childhood, joined in beseeching his compliance with these conditions; but his pride, his dread of my merited reproaches; the merits and dissuasions of his new companion, whose sacrifices for his sake had not been small, were obstacles which nothing could subdue.

Far, indeed, was I from imposing these conditions. I waited only till, by certain arrangements, I could gather enough to pay his debts, to enable him to execute his vow; empty would have been my claims to his affection, if I could have suffered, with the means of his deliverance in my hands, my husband to remain a moment in prison.

The remains of my father's vast fortune, was a jointure of a thousand pounds a year, settled on my mother, and after her death, on me. My mother's helpless condition put this revenue into my disposal. By this means was I enabled, without the knowl-edge of my father-in-law, or my husband, to purchase the debt, and dismiss him from prison. He set out instantly, in company with his paramour, to France.

When somewhat recovered from the shock of this calamity, I took up my abode with my mother. What she had was enough, as you, perhaps, will think, for plentiful subsistence, but to us, with habits of a different kind, it was little better than poverty. That reflection, my father's memory, my mother's deplorable state, which every year grew worse, and the late misfortune, were the chief companions of my thoughts.

The dear child, whose smiles were uninterrupted by his mother's afflictions, was some consolation in my solitude. To his instruction and to my mother's wants, all my hours were devoted. I was sometimes not without the hope of better days. Full as my mind was of Fielding's merits, convinced by former proofs of his ardent and generous spirit, I trusted that time and reflection would destroy that spell by which he was now bound.

For some time, the progress of these reflections was not known. In leaving England, Fielding dropped all correspondence and connection with his native country. He parted with the woman at Rouen, leaving no trace behind him by which she might follow him, as she wished to do. She never returned to England, but died a twelve month afterwards in Switzerland.

As to me, I had only to muse day and night upon the possible destiny of this beloved fugitive.[11] His incensed father cared not for him. He had cast him out of his paternal affections, ceased to make enquiries respecting him, and even wished never to hear of him again. My boy succeeded to my husband's place in his grand-father's affections, and in the hopes and views of the family; and his mother wanted nothing which their compassionate and respectful love could bestow.

Three long and tedious years passed away, and no tidings were received. Whether he were living or dead, nobody could tell. At length, an English traveller, going out of the customary road from Italy, met with Fielding, in a town in the Venaissin.[12] His manners, habit and language, had become French. He seemed unwilling to be recognized by an old acquaintance, but not being able to avoid this, and becoming gradually familiar, he informed the traveller of many particulars in his present situation. It appeared that he had made himself useful to a neighboring *Seigneur*, in whose *chateau* he had long lived on the footing of a brother. France he had resolved to make his future country, and among other changes for that end, he had laid aside his English name, and taken that of his patron, which was *Perrin*. He had endeavored to

---

[11] "The possible destiny of this beloved fugitive": given all the particulars—Achsa's futile and humiliating efforts to pursue a reckless, ungrateful husband, despite the husband's persistence in abandoning a pregnant Achsa for a woman twice her age (even after her desperate efforts to help him), only to disappear and become involved in murky revolutionary intrigues in what follows—this aspect of Achsa's narrative seems to draw in spirit and detail on William Godwin's account of Mary Wollstonecraft's embarrassing rejection and abandonment by revolutionary era adventurer Gilbert Imlay. Godwin's candid *Memoir of the Author of a Vindication of the Rights of Woman* caused tremendous controversy when it violated conventions about narrating women's lives in 1798, just as Brown began this novel, and Brown and his circle read the *Memoir* with great interest. The narrative shocked conservative readers by detailing Wollstonecraft's weaknesses and humiliation in failed relationships that take place against a similar backdrop of revolutionary and financial turmoil. Similarly, Achsa's backstory reveals unflattering and disturbing episodes but asks the reader to view an imperfect yet strong, admirable, intellectual, and long-suffering heroine with rational sympathy. The stories situate the subject's shortcomings within a larger rational view of her merits and explain how a male admirer can "worship" and desire a figure who appears troubled and unattractive from a conventional standpoint.

[12] "Venaissin": the Comtat Venaissin was a former papal territory around Avignon and Carpentras in the Provence-Alps region of southern France. As a papal territory, a separate enclave within France from 1274 to 1789, the Venaissin provided better conditions for Jews than the French monarchy before the revolution and attracted a sizeable Jewish community. This group was around 10% of the region's urban population and had its own Judeo-Provençal dialect. Once revolutionary France began to emancipate Jews in 1790–1791, the Venaissan Jewish community massively supported annexation and struggles broke out over the extension of citizenship to Jews (there were attempts to maintain degrading old regime regulations requiring Jews to wear yellow hats and live in segregated areas, for example). While Achsa's husband is not himself Jewish, it is notable that he travels to a Jewish enclave in Provence, changes his name, and acquires "all the rights of a French citizen" at the same time that the Venaissin's Jews struggle for similar emancipation.

compensate himself for all other privations, by devoting himself to rural amusements and to study.

He carefully shunned all enquiries respecting me, but when my name was mentioned by his friend, who knew well all that had happened, and my general welfare, together with that of his son, asserted, he shewed deep sensibility, and even consented that I should be made acquainted with his situation.

I cannot describe the effect of this intelligence on me. My hopes of bringing him back to me, were suddenly revived. I wrote him a letter, in which I poured forth my whole heart; but his answer contained avowals of all his former resolutions, to which time had only made his adherence more easy. A second and third letter were written, and an offer made to follow him to his retreat, and share his exile; but all my efforts availed nothing. He solemnly and repeatedly renounced all the claims of an husband over me, and absolved me from every obligation as a wife.

His part in this correspondence, was performed without harshness or contempt. A strange mixture there was of pathos and indifference; of tenderness and resolution. Hence I continually derived hope, which time, however, brought no nearer to certainty.

At the opening of the revolution, the name of Perrin appeared among the deputies to the constituent assembly, for the district in which he resided. He had thus succeeded in gaining all the rights of a French citizen; and the hopes of his return became almost extinct; but that, and every other hope, respecting him, has since been totally extinguished by his marriage with Marguerite D'Almont, a young lady of great merit and fortune, and a native of Avignon.[13]

A long period of suspence was now at an end, and left me in a state almost as full of anguish as that which our first separation produced. My sorrows were increased by my mother's death, and this incident freeing me from those restraints upon my motions which before existed, I determined to come to America.

My son was now eight years old,[14] and his grandfather claiming the province of his instruction, I was persuaded to part with him, that he might be sent to a distant school. Thus was another tie removed, and in spite of the well meant importunities of my friends, I persisted in my scheme of crossing the ocean.

---

[13] "Marguerite D'Almont . . . a native of Avignon": Fielding, now named Perrin, marries a woman from the Venaissin. Avignon was administratively distinct from the surrounding Comtat, but part of the same papal enclave. Instead of a married woman taking the name of her husband in the patrilineal manner, Fielding reverses the procedure and adopts his new wife's name, becoming Perrin d'Almont (as Achsa notes shortly). By contrast, Achsa never reveals her Sephardic family name and uses only Fielding, the Anglo name that is hers by marriage. In his *Memoir*, Godwin notes how the displaced and wandering Wollstonecraft for a time ambiguously retained the name Imlay after her former husband disappeared in revolutionary France with another woman.

[14] "Eight years old": if Achsa's son was eight when she left England in 1792 (the beginning of the chapter notes Achsa has been in the U.S. for eighteen months now, and the novel is ending in June–July 1794), her marriage to Fielding occurred in 1783–1784. Her father's suicide, "eight years" in the past two paragraphs farther on, occurred in 1786.

I could not help, at this part of her narration, expressing my surprise, that any motives were strong enough to recommend this scheme.

It was certainly a freak of despair. A few months would, perhaps, have allayed the fresh grief, and reconciled me to my situation; but I would not pause or deliberate. My scheme was opposed by my friends, with great earnestness. During my voyage, affrighted by the dangers which surrounded me, and to which I was wholly unused, I heartily repented of my resolution; but now, methinks, I have reason to rejoice at my perseverance. I have come into a scene and society so new, I have had so many claims made upon my ingenuity and fortitude, that my mind has been diverted in some degree from former sorrows. There are even times when I wholly forget them, and catch myself indulging in cheerful reveries.

I have often reflected with surprise on the nature of my own mind. It is eight years since my father's violent death. How few of my hours since that period, have been blessed with serenity! How many nights and days, in hateful and lingering succession, have been bathed in tears and tormented with regrets! That I am still alive with so many causes of death, and with such a slow consuming malady, is surely to be wondered at.

I believe the worst foes of man, at least of men in grief, are solitude and idleness. The same eternally occurring round of objects, feeds his disease, and the effects of mere vacancy and uniformity, is sometimes mistaken for those of grief. Yes, I am glad I came to America. My relations are importunate for my return, and till lately, I had some thoughts of it; but I think now, I shall stay where I am, for the rest of my days.[15]

Since I arrived, I am become more of a student than I used to be. I always loved literature, but never, till of late, had a mind enough at ease, to read with advantage. I now find pleasure in the occupation which I never expected to find.

You see in what manner I live. The letters which I brought secured me a flattering reception from the best people in your country; but scenes of gay resort had nothing to attract me, and I quickly withdrew to that seclusion in which you now find me. Here, always at leisure, and mistress of every laudable means of gratification, I am not without the belief of serene days yet to come.

I now ventured to enquire what were her latest tidings of her husband.

At the opening of the revolution, I told you he became a champion of the people. By his zeal and his efforts he acquired such importance as to be deputed to the National Assembly. In this post he was the adherent of violent measures, till the subversion of monarchy; and then, when too late for his safety, he checked his career.

And what has since become of him?

She sighed deeply. You were yesterday reading a list of the proscribed under Robespierre. I checked you. I had good reason. But this subject grows too painful, let us change it.

---

[15] "Importunate for my return . . . rest of my days": although Achsa's ex-in-laws want her to return to England, she states here that she prefers to stay in Philadelphia. If Achsa and Mervyn were to travel to England after their marriage, they would enter an aristocratic realm in England. The question of a voyage to Europe is left unresolved at novel's end (see note II.25.4).

Some time after I ventured to renew this topic; and discovered that Fielding, under his new name of Perrin d'Almont, was among the outlawed deputies[16] of last year*, and had been slain in resisting the officers sent to arrest him. My friend had been informed that his *wife* Philippine d'Almont, whom she had reason to believe, a woman of great merit, had eluded persecution, and taken refuge in some part of America.[17] She had made various attempts, but in vain, to find out her retreat. Ah! said I, you must commission me to find her. I will hunt her through the continent from Penobscot to Savanna. I will not leave a nook unsearched.

---

[16] "A list of the proscribed under Robespierre . . . list of outlawed deputies": Girondin revolutionaries condemned by the dictatorial Robespierre during the "Reign of Terror" (September 5, 1793–July 28, 1794). Robespierre led the Jacobin faction that initiated the Terror, and the Terror ended when he himself was executed with twenty-one followers in 1794 (the event, known as "Thermidor," was a crucial turning point in the revolution). Thus his name, for the English Woldwinites and Brown, evokes partisan extremism and the tragic blocking of progressive change, while the Girondins are frequently invoked as heroic progressive models. Brown's novel *Ormond* (January 1799) also expresses solidarity with Girondin figures in their struggle against Robespierre.

* 1793. [Brown's footnote, the novel's only original footnote].

[17] "Refuge in some part of America": Achsa's benevolent and forgiving efforts to locate and aid Marguerite (aka Philippine) d'Almont, now brought low as a political refugee, recall her prior willingness to help Clemenza and Eliza. Brown's novel *Ormond* also features mutually supportive groups of refugee and radical women who search for each other after separation during tumultuous revolutionary events. This character, the woman that Achsa's former husband married after resurfacing in the Comtat Venaissin, is identified by two names (possibly an oversight on Brown's part): Marguerite (fourteen paragraphs earlier) and now Philippine.

Chapter XXIV

NONE will be surprized, that to a woman thus unfortunate and thus deserving, my heart willingly rendered up all its sympathies; that as I partook of all her grief, I hailed, with equal delight, those omens of felicity which now, at length, seemed to play in her fancy.

I saw her often, as often as my engagements would permit, and oftener than I allowed myself to visit any other. In this I was partly selfish. So much entertainment, so much of the best instruction did her conversation afford me, that I never had enough of it.

Her experience had been so much larger than mine, and so wholly different, and she possessed such unbounded facility of recounting all she had seen and felt, and absolute sincerity and unreserve in this respect, were so fully established between us, that I can imagine nothing equally instructive and delightful with her conversation.

Books are cold, jejune,[1] vexatious in their sparingness of information at one time, and their impertinent loquacity at another. Besides, all they chuse to give, they give at once; they allow no questions; offer no further explanations, and bend not to the caprices of our curiosity. They talk to us behind a screen. Their tone is lifeless and monotonous. They charm not our attention by mute significances of gesture and looks. They spread no light upon their meaning by cadences and emphasis and pause.

How different was Mrs. Fielding's discourse! So versatile; so bending to the changes of occasion; so obsequious to my curiosity, and so abundant in that very knowledge in which I was most deficient, and on which I set the most value, the knowledge of the human heart; of society as it existed in another world, more abundant in the varieties of customs and characters, than I had ever had the power to witness.

Partly selfish I have said my motives were, but not wholly so, as long as I saw that my friend derived pleasure, in her turn, from my company. Not that I could add directly to her knowledge or pleasure, but that expansion of heart, that ease of utterance and flow of ideas which always were occasioned by my approach, were sources of true pleasure of which she had been long deprived, and for which her privation had given her a higher relish than ever.

She lived in great affluence and independence, but made use of her privileges of fortune chiefly to secure to herself the command of her own time. She had been long ago tired and disgusted with the dull and fulsome uniformity and parade of the playhouse and ball-room. Formal visits were endured as mortifications and penances, by which the delights of privacy and friendly intercourse were by contrast increased. Music she loved, but never sought it in place of public resort, or from the skill of mercenary performers, and books were not the least of her pleasures.

As to me, I was wax in her hand. Without design and without effort, I was always of that form she wished me to assume. My own happiness became a secondary

---

[1] "Jejune": scanty, meager, unsatisfying to the mind. For similar remarks on the superiority of direct conversation and social observation to books, see the excerpts from Godwin's *Political Justice* in Related Texts.

passion, and her gratification the great end of my being. When with her, I thought not of myself. I had scarcely a separate or independent existence, since my senses were occupied by her, and my mind was full of those ideas which her discourse communicated. To meditate on her looks and words, and to pursue the means suggested by my own thoughts, or by her, conducive, in any way, to her good, was all my business.

What a fate, said I, at the conclusion of one of our interviews, has been yours. But, thank Heaven, the storm has disappeared before the age of sensibility has gone past, and without drying up every source of happiness. You are still young: all your powers unimpaired; rich in the compassion and esteem of the world; wholly independent of the claims and caprices of others; amply supplied with that mean of usefulness, called money; wise in that experience which only adversity can give. Past evils and sufferings, if incurred and endured without guilt, if called to view without remorse, make up the materials of present joy. They cheer our most dreary hours with the whispered accents of "well done," and they heighten our pleasures into somewhat of celestial brilliancy, by furnishing a deep, a ruefully deep contrast.

From this moment, I will cease to weep for you. I will call you the happiest of women. I will share with you your happiness by witnessing it—but that shall not content me. I must someway contribute to it. Tell me how I shall serve you? What can I do to make you happier? Poor am I in every thing but zeal, but still I may do something. What—pray tell me what can I do?

She looked at me with sweet and solemn significance. What it was exactly, I could not divine, yet I was strangely affected by it. It was but a glance, instantly withdrawn. She made me no answer.

You must not be silent; you *must* tell me what I can do for you. Hitherto I have done nothing. All the service is on your side. Your conversation has been my study, a delightful study, but the profit has only been mine. Tell me how I can be grateful— my voice and manner, I believe, seldom belye my feelings. At this time, I had almost done what a second thought made me suspect to be unauthorized. Yet I cannot tell why. My heart had nothing in it but reverence and admiration. Was she not the substitute of my lost mamma. Would I not have clasped that beloved shade? Yet the two beings were not just the same, or I should not, as now, have checked myself, and only pressed her hand to my lips.

Tell me, repeated I, what can I do to serve you? I read to you a little now, and you are pleased with my reading. I copy for you when you want the time. I guide the reins for you when you chuse to ride. Humble offices, indeed, though, perhaps, all that a raw youth like me can do for you; but I can be still more assiduous. I can read several hours in the day, instead of one. I can write ten times as much as now.

Are you not my lost mamma come back again? And yet, not *exactly* her, I think. Something different; something better, I believe, if that be possible. At any rate, methinks I would be wholly yours. I shall be impatient and uneasy till every act, every thought, every minute, someway does you good.

How! said I—her eye still averted, seemed to hold back the tear with difficulty, and she made a motion as if to rise—have I grieved you? Have I been importunate? Forgive me if I have offended you.

Her eyes now overflowed without restraint. She articulated with difficulty—Tears are too prompt with me of late; but they did not upbraid you. Pain has often caused them to flow, but now it—is—*pleasure.*

What an heart must yours be, I resumed. When susceptible of such pleasures, what pangs must formerly have rent it!—But you are not displeased, you say, with my importunate zeal. You will accept me as your own in every thing. Direct me: prescribe to me. There must be *something* in which I can be of still more use to you: some way in which I can be wholly yours—

Wholly mine! she repeated, in a smothered voice, and rising—leave me, Arthur. It is too late for you to be here. It was wrong to stay so late.

I have been wrong, but how too late! I entered but this moment. It is twilight still: Is it not?

No—it is almost twelve. You have been here a long four hours; short ones, I would rather say—but indeed you must go.

What made me so thoughtless of the time! But I will go, yet not till you forgive me. I approached her with a confidence, and for a purpose at which, upon reflection, I am not a little surprised, but the being called Mervyn is not the same in her company and in that of another. What is the difference, and whence comes it? Her words and looks engross me. My mind wants room for any other object. But why enquire whence the difference? The superiority of her merits and attractions to all those whom I knew, would surely account for my fervor. Indifference, if I felt it, would be the only just occasion of wonder.

The hour was, indeed too late, and I hastened home. Stevens was waiting my return with some anxiety. I apologized for my delay, and recounted to him what had just passed. He listened with more than usual interest. When I had finished,

Mervyn, said he, you seem not to be aware of your present situation. From what you now tell me, and from what you have formerly told me, one thing seems very plain to me.

Pry'thee, what is it?

Eliza Hadwin—do you wish—could you bear to see her the wife of another?

Five years hence I will answer you. Then my answer may be—"No: I wish her only to be mine." Till then, I wish her only to be my pupil, my ward, my sister.

But these are remote considerations: they are bars to marriage, but not to love. Would it not molest and disquiet you to observe in her a passion for another?

It would, but only on her own account: not on mine. At a suitable age it is very likely I may love her, because, it is likely, if she holds on in her present career, she will then be worthy, but, at present, though I would die to ensure her happiness, I have no wish to ensure it by marriage with her.

Is there no other whom you love?

No. There is one worthier than all others; one whom I wish the woman who shall be my wife to resemble in all things.

And who is this model?

You know I can only mean Achsa Fielding.

If you love her likeness, why not love herself?

319

I felt my heart leap.—What a thought is that! Love her I *do* as I love my God; as I love virtue. To love her in another sense, would brand me for a lunatic.

To love her as a woman, then, appears to you an act of folly.

In me it would be worse than folly. 'Twould be frenzy.

And why?

Why? Really, my friend, you astonish me. Nay, you startle me—for a question like that implies a doubt in you whether I have not actually harbored the tho't.

No, said he, smiling, presumtuous though you be, you have not, to be sure, reached so high a pitch. But still, though I think you innocent of so heinous an offence, there is no harm in asking why you might not love her, and even seek her for a wife.

Achsa Fielding *my wife!* Good Heaven!—The very sound threw my soul into unconquerable tumults.—Take care, my friend, continued I, in beseeching accents, you may do me more injury than you conceive, by even starting such a thought.

True, said he, as long as such obstacles exist to your success; so many incurable objections; for instance, she is six years older than you—[2]

That is an advantage. Her age is what it ought to be.

But she has been a wife and mother already.

That is likewise an advantage. She has wisdom, because she has experience. Her sensibilities are stronger, because they have been exercised and chastened. Her first marriage was unfortunate. The purer is the felicity she will taste in a second! If her second choice be propitious, the greater her tenderness and gratitude.

But she is a foreigner: independent of controul, and rich.

All which, are blessings to herself and to him for whom her hand is reserved; especially if like me, he is indigent.

But then she is unsightly as a *night-hag,* tawney as a moor,[3] the eye of a gypsey, low in stature, contemptibly diminutive, scarcely bulk enough to cast a shadow as she walks, less luxuriance than a charred log, fewer elasticities than a sheet pebble.

Hush! hush! blasphemer!—and I put my hand before his mouth—have I not told you that in mind, person and condition, she is the type after which my enamored fancy has modelled my wife.

O ho! Then the objection does not lie with you. It lies with her, it seems. She can find nothing in you to esteem! And pray, for what faults do you think she would reject you?

I cannot tell. That she can ever balance for a moment, on such a question, is incredible. *Me! me!* That Achsa Fielding should think of me!

---

[2] "Six years older than you": the previous chapter noted that Achsa has "scarcely passed her twenty-fifth year." Arthur is therefore nineteen or twenty years old and was eighteen or nineteen during the events of the first part.

[3] "Unsightly as a *night-hag,* tawney as a moor": Stevens is using a degree of irony or "jest," as he puts it shortly, to tease Mervyn but also recalling earlier comments about Achsa's dark skin as he uses the period's code words for Africans. "Tawny" also described the skin of the African Mervyn glimpsed in the mirror just before he was struck on the head during the fever epidemic (note 16.2).

Incredible, indeed! You who are loathsome in your person, an ideot in your understanding, a villain in your morals! deformed! withered! vain, stupid and malignant. That such an one should chuse *you* for an idol!

Pray, my friend, said I, anxiously, jest not. What mean you by an hint of this kind?

I will not jest then, but will soberly enquire, what faults are they which make this lady's choice of you so incredible? You are younger than she, though no one, who merely observed your manners, and heard you talk, would take you to be under thirty. You are poor; are these impediments?

I should think not. I have heard her reason with admirable eloquence, against the vain distinctions of property and nation and rank. They were once of moment in her eyes; but the sufferings, humiliations and reflections of years, have cured her of the folly. Her nation[4] has suffered too much by the inhuman antipathies of religious and political faction; she, herself, has felt so often the contumelies of the rich, the highborn, and the bigotted, that—

Pry'thee then, what dost imagine her objections to be?

Why—I don't know. The thought was so aspiring; to call her *my wife*, was an height of bliss; the very far-off view of which made my head dizzy.

An height, however, to attain which you suppose only her consent, her love, to be necessary?

Without doubt, her love is indispensible.

Sit down, Arthur, and let us no longer treat this matter lightly. I clearly see the importance of this moment to this lady's happiness and yours. It is plain that you love this woman. How could you help it? A brilliant skin is not her's; nor elegant proportions; nor majestic stature; yet no creature had ever more power to bewitch. [5] Her manners have grace and dignity that flow from exquisite feeling, delicate taste, and the quickest and keenest penetration. She has the wisdom of men and of books. Her sympathies are enforced by reason, and her charities regulated by knowledge. She has a woman's age, fortune more than you wish, and a spotless fame. How could you fail to love her?

You, who are her chosen friend, who partake her pleasures, and share her employments, on whom she almost exclusively bestows her society and confidence, and to whom she thus affords the strongest of all indirect proofs of impassioned esteem. How could you, with all that firmness to love, joined with all that discernment of her excellence, how could you escape the enchantment?

You have not thought of marriage. You have not suspected your love. From the purity of your mind, from the idolatry with which this woman has inspired you, you have imaged no delight beyond that of enjoying her society as you now do, and have never fostered an hope beyond this privilege.

---

[4] "Her nation": Mervyn uses the term "nation" in its older sense of identifying ethnic groups, not the more modern one of citizenship.

[5] "A brilliant skin is not her's . . . bewitch": a final emphasis on Achsa's dark skin and capacity to seduce or bewitch, recalling her earlier alignment with figures in Milton's "Comus" and "Il Penseroso" (see notes II.22.1–2).

How quickly would this tranquillity vanish, and the true state of your heart be evinced, if a rival should enter the scene and be entertained with preference; then would the seal be removed, the spell be broken, and you would awaken to terror and to anguish.

Of this, however, there is no danger. Your passion is not felt by you alone. From her treatment of you, your diffidence disables you from seeing, but nothing can be clearer to me than, that she loves you.

I started on my feet. A flush of scorching heat flowed to every part of my frame. My temples began to throb like my heart. I was half delirious, and my delirium was strangely compounded of fear and hope, of delight and of terror.

What have you done, my friend? You have overturned my peace of mind. Till now the image of this woman has been followed by complacency and sober rapture; but your words have dashed the scene with dismay and confusion. You have raised up wishes and dreams and doubts, which possess me in spite of my reason,

Good God! You say she loves; loves *me!* me, a boy in age; bred in clownish ignorance; scarcely ushered into the world; more than childishly unlearned and raw; a barn-door simpleton; a plow-tail, kitchen-hearth, turnip-hoeing novice! She, thus splendidly endowed; thus allied to nobles; thus gifted with arts, and adorned with graces; that she should chuse me, me for the partner of her fortune; her affections; and her life! It cannot be. Yet, if it were; if your guesses should—prove—Oaf! madman! To indulge so fatal a chimera! So rash a dream!

My friend! my friend! I feel that you have done me an irreparable injury. I can never more look her in the face. I can never more frequent her society. These new thoughts will beset and torment me. My disquiet will chain up my tongue. That overflowing gratitude; that innocent joy, unconscious of offence, and knowing no restraint, which have hitherto been my titles to her favor, will fly from my features and manners. I shall be anxious, vacant and unhappy in her presence. I shall dread to look at her, or to open my lips lest my mad and unhallowed ambition should betray itself.

Well, replied Stevens, this scene is quite new. I could almost find it in my heart to pity you. I did not expect this; and yet from my knowledge of your character, I ought, perhaps, to have foreseen it. This is a necessary part of the drama. A joyous certainty, on these occasions, must always be preceded by suspenses and doubts, and the close will be joyous in proportion as the preludes are excruciating. Go to bed, my good friend, and think of this. Time and a few more interviews with Mrs. Fielding, will, I doubt not, set all to rights.

Chapter XXV

I WENT to my chamber, but what different sensations did I carry into it, from those with which I had left it a few hours before. I stretched myself on the mattress and put out the light; but the swarm of new images that rushed on my mind, set me again instantly in motion. All was rapid, vague and undefined, wearying and distracting my attention. I was roused as by a divine voice, that said:—"Sleep no more: Mervyn shall sleep no more."[1]

What chiefly occupied me was a nameless sort of terror. What shall I compare it to? Methinks, that one falling from a tree, overhanging a torrent, plunged into the whirling eddy, and gasping and struggling while he sinks to rise no more, would feel just as I did then. Nay, some such image actually possessed me. Such was one of my reveries, in which suddenly I stretched my hand, and caught the arm of a chair. This act called me back to reason, or rather gave my soul opportunity to roam into a new track equally wild.

Was it the abruptness of this vision that thus confounded me! was it a latent error in my moral constitution, which this new conjuncture drew forth into influence? These were all the tokens of a mind lost to itself; bewildered; unhinged; plunged into a drear insanity.

Nothing less could have prompted so phantastically—for midnight as it was, my chamber's solitude was not to be supported. After a few turns across the floor, I left the room, and the house. I walked without design and in an hurried pace. I posted straight to the house of Mrs. Fielding. I lifted the latch, but the door did not open. It was, no doubt, locked.

How comes this, said I, and looked around me. The hour and occasion were unthought of. Habituated to this path, I had taken it spontaneously. How comes this? repeated I. Locked upon *me!* but I will summon them, I warrant me—and rung the bell, not timidly or slightly, but with violence. Some one hastened from above. I saw the glimmer of a candle through the key-hole.

Strange, thought I, a candle at noon day!—The door was opened, and my poor Bess, robed in a careless and a hasty manner, appeared. She started at sight of me, but merely because she did not, in a moment, recognize me.—Ah! Arthur, is it you? Come in. My mamma has wanted you these two hours. I was just going to dispatch Philip to tell you to come.

Lead me to her, said I.

---

[1] "Sleep no more: Mervyn shall sleep no more": a reference to *Macbeth*, II.ii.32–40: "Methought I heard a voice cry 'Sleep no more! / Macbeth does murder sleep', the innocent sleep . . . Balm of hurt minds / great nature's second course / Chief nourisher in life's feast." The ominous voice announcing sleep disturbance as a sign of unresolved anxiety or guilt introduces Mervyn's gothic nightmare about being "stabbed to the heart" by Achsa's ghostly husband. The "nameless sort of terror" that accompanies this imaginary revenant, preceded by a scantily clothed Eliza, suggests a host of anxieties about Mervyn's decision to propose marriage to Achsa and about the haunting force of massive historical trauma involved in Achsa's and her dead husband's life stories.

She led the way into the parlor.—"Wait a moment here: I will tell her you are come"—and she tripped away.

Presently a step was heard. The door opened again, and then entered a man. He was tall, elegant, sedate to a degree of sadness: Something in his dress and aspect that bespoke the foreigner; the Frenchman.

What, said he, mildly, is your business with my wife? She cannot see you instantly, and has sent me to receive your commands.

Your *wife!* I want Mrs. Fielding.

True; and Mrs. Fielding is my wife. Thank Heaven I have come in time to discover her, and claim her as such.

I started back. I shuddered. My joints slackened, and I stretched my hand to catch something by which I might be saved from sinking on the floor. Meanwhile, Fielding changed his countenance into rage and fury. He called me villain! bad me avaunt! and drew a shining steel from his bosom, with which he stabbed me to the heart. I sunk upon the floor, and all, for a time, was darkness and oblivion! At length, I returned as it were to life. I opened my eyes. The mists disappeared, and I found myself stretched upon the bed in my own chamber. I remembered the fatal blow I had received. I put my hand upon my breast; the spot where the dagger entered. There were no traces of a wound. All was perfect and entire. Some miracle had made me whole.

I raised myself up. I re-examined my body. All around me was hushed, till a voice from the pavement below, proclaimed that it was "past three o'clock."

What, said I, has all this miserable pageantry, this midnight wandering, and this ominous interview, been no more than—*a dream!*

It may be proper to mention, in explanation of this scene, and to shew the thorough perturbation of my mind, during this night, intelligence gained some days after from Eliza. She said, that about two o'clock, on this night, she was roused by a violent ringing of the bell. She was startled by so unseasonable a summons. She slept in a chamber adjoining Mrs. Fielding's, and hesitated whether she should alarm her friend, but the summons not being repeated, she had determined to forbear.

Added to this, was the report of Mrs. Stevens, who, on the same night, about half an hour after I and her husband had retired, imagined that she heard the street-door opened and shut, but this being followed by no other consequence, she supposed herself mistaken. I have little doubt, that, in my feverish and troubled sleep, I actually went forth, posted to the house of Mrs. Fielding, rung for admission, and shortly after, returned to my own apartment.[2]

This confusion of mind was somewhat allayed by the return of light. It gave way to more uniform, but not less rueful and despondent perceptions. The image of Achsa filled my fancy, but it was the harbinger of nothing but humiliation and sorrow. To outroot the conviction of my own unworthiness, to persuade myself that I was

---

[2] "Returned to my own apartment": Mervyn was sleepwalking. See note 8.1 on this motif.

regarded with the tenderness that Stevens had ascribed to her, that the discovery of my thoughts would not excite her anger and grief, I felt to be impossible.

In this state of mind, I could not see her. To declare my feelings would produce indignation and anguish; to hide them from her scrutiny was not in my power: yet, what would she think of my estranging myself from her society? What expedient could I honestly adopt to justify my absence, and what employment could I substitute for those precious hours hitherto devoted to her.

This afternoon, thought I, she has been invited to spend at Stedman's country house on Schuylkill.[3] She consented to go, and I was to accompany her. I am fit only for solitude. My behaviour, in her presence, will be enigmatical, capricious and morose. I must not go: Yet, what will she think of my failure? Not to go will be injurious and suspicious.

I was undetermined. The appointed hour arrived. I stood at my chamber window, torn by variety of purposes, and swayed alternately by repugnant arguments. I several times went to the door of my apartment, and put my foot upon the first step of the stair-case, but as often paused, reconsidered and returned to my room.

In these fluctuations the hour passed. No messenger arrived from Mrs. Fielding, enquiring into the cause of my delay. Was she offended at my negligence? Was she sick and disabled from going, or had she changed her mind? I now remember her parting words at our last interview. Were they not susceptible of two constructions? She said my visit was too long, and bad me begone. Did she suspect my presumption, and is she determined thus to punish me?

This terror added anew to all my former anxieties. It was impossible to rest in this suspense. I would go to her. I would lay before her all the anguish of my heart: I would not spare myself. She shall not reproach me more severely than I will reproach myself. I will hear my sentence from her own lips, and promise unlimited submission to the doom of separation and exile, which she will pronounce.

---

[3] "Stedman's country house on Schuylkill": an estate or "villa," as Arthur will call it, on the Schuylkill River just west of the city's urbanized area. Members of the city elite maintained country homes along this scenic stretch, within easy reach of the urbanized center, some with elaborate ornamental and botanical gardens that were open to strolling visitors.

The name may allude to Alexander Stedman and his son Charles, members of the "gentlemen" class of Philadelphia's colonial mercantile, legal, and political elite. Alexander Stedman's fortune was partly based on trade in German indentured labor, functionally similar to the Atlantic slave trade insofar as it involved the transportation and sale of unfree laborers. In 1777–1778, Stedman father and son were both arrested as part of the group, which included Brown's father Elijah and other Quakers, who were deemed "dangerous to the State" and exiled to an internment camp in Virginia (see note II.16.3). While the Quaker elites were arrested because of their neutrality and refusal to swear oaths on religious grounds, the Stedmans were Tory Loyalists, much like the Jewish Franks family mentioned in note II.21.5. Charles served under British General Howe during the revolution, and the Stedman family emigrated to Britain after independence; Alexander died in 1794, the same year his son published the *History of the Origin, Progress, and Termination of the American War*, which became the standard British-centric account of the conflict.

I went forthwith to her house. The drawing-room and summer-house was empty. I summoned Philip the footman—his mistress was gone to Mr. Stedman's.

How?—To Stedman's?—In whose company?

Miss Stedman and her brother called for her in the carriage, and persuaded her to go with them.

Now my heart sunk, indeed! Miss Stedman's *brother!* A youth, forward, gallant and gay! Flushed with prosperity, and just returned from Europe, with all the confidence of age, and all the ornaments of education! She has gone with him, though pre-engaged to me! Poor Arthur, how art thou despised!

This information only heightened my impatience. I went away, but returned in the evening. I waited till eleven, but she came not back. I cannot justly paint the interval that passed till next morning. It was void of sleep. On leaving her house, I wandered into the fields. Every moment increased my impatience. She will probably spend the morrow at Stedman's, said I, and possibly the next day. Why should I wait for her return? Why not seek her there, and rid myself at once of this agonizing suspense? Why not go thither now? This night, wherever I spend it, will be unacquainted with repose. I will go, it is already near twelve, and the distance is more than eight miles. I will hover near the house till morning, and then, as early as possible, demand an interview.

I was well acquainted with Stedman's Villa, having formerly been there with Mrs. Fielding. I quickly entered its precincts. I went close to the house; looked mournfully at every window. At one of them a light was to be seen, and I took various stations to discover, if possible, the persons within. Methought once I caught a glimpse of a female, whom my fancy easily imagined to be Achsa. I sat down upon the lawn, some hundred feet from the house, and opposite the window whence the light proceeded. I watched it, till at length some one came to the window, lifted it, and leaning on her arms, continued to look out.

The preceding day had been a very sultry one; the night, as usual after such a day, and the fall of a violent shower, was delightfully serene and pleasant. Where I stood, was enlightened by the moon. Whether she saw me or not, I could hardly tell, or whether she distinguished any thing but a human figure.

Without reflecting on what was due to decorum and punctilio, I immediately drew near the house. I quickly perceived that her attention was fixed. Neither of us spoke, till I had placed myself directly under her; I then opened my lips, without knowing in what manner to address her. She spoke first, and in a startled and anxious voice—

Who is that?

Arthur Mervyn: he that was two days ago your friend.

Mervyn! What is it that brings you here at this hour? What is the matter? What has happened? Is any body sick?

All is safe—all are in good health.

What then do you come hither for at such an hour?

I meant not to disturb you: I meant not to be seen.

Good Heavens! How you frighten me. What can be the reason of so strange—

Be not alarmed. I meant to hover near the house till morning, that I might see you as early as possible.

For what purpose?

I will tell you when we meet, and let that be at five o'clock; the sun will then be risen; in the cedar grove under the bank; till when, farewel.

Having said this, I prevented all expostulation, by turning the angle of the house, and hastening towards the shore of the river. I roved about the grove that I have mentioned. In one part of it is a rustic seat and table, shrouded by trees and shrubs, and an intervening eminence, from the view of those in the house. This I designed to be the closing scene of my destiny.

Presently, I left this spot and wandered upward through embarrassed and obscure paths, starting forward or checking my pace, according as my wayward meditations governed me. Shall I describe my thoughts?—Impossible! It was certainly a temporary loss of reason; nothing less than madness could lead into such devious tracts, drag me down to so hopeless, helpless, panickful a depth, and drag me down so suddenly; lay waste, as at a signal, all my flourishing structures, and reduce them in a moment to a scene of confusion and horror.

What did I fear? What did I hope? What did I design? I cannot tell; my glooms were to retire with the night. The point to which every tumultuous feeling was linked was the coming interview with Achsa. That was the boundary of fluctuation and suspense. Here was the sealing and ratification of my doom.

I rent a passage through the thicket, and struggled upward till I reached the edge of a considerable precipice; I laid me down at my length upon the rock, whose cold and hard surface I pressed with my bared and throbbing breast. I leaned over the edge; fixed my eyes upon the water and wept—plentifully; but why?

May *this* be my heart's last beat, if I can tell why.

I had wandered so far from Stedman's, that when roused by the light, I had some miles to walk before I could reach the place of meeting. Achsa was already there. I slid down the rock above, and appeared before her. Well might she be startled at my wild and abrupt appearance.

I placed myself, without uttering a word, upon a seat opposite to her, the table between, and crossing my arms upon the table, leaned my head upon them, while my face was turned towards and my eyes fixed upon hers, I seemed to have lost the power and the inclination to speak.

She regarded me, at first, with anxious curiosity; after examining my looks, every emotion was swallowed up in terrified sorrow. For God's sake!—what does all this mean? Why am I called to this place? What tidings, what fearful tidings do you bring?

I did not change my posture or speak. What, she resumed, could inspire all this woe? Keep me not in this suspense, Arthur; these looks and this silence shocks and afflicts me too much.

Afflict you? said I, at last: I come to tell you, what, now that I am here, I cannot tell—there I stopped.

Say what, I entreat you. You seem to be very unhappy—such a change—from yesterday!

Yes! From yesterday: all then was a joyous calm, and now all is—but then I knew not my infamy, my guilt—

What words are these, and from you Arthur? Guilt is to you impossible. If purity is to be found on earth, it is lodged in your heart. What have you done?

I have dared—how little you expect the extent of my daring. That such as I should look upwards with this ambition.

I now stood up, and taking her hands in mine, as she sat, looked earnestly in her face—I come only to beseech your pardon. To tell you my crime, and then disappear forever; but first let me see if there be any omen of forgiveness. Your looks—they are kind; heavenly; compassionate still. I will trust them, I believe: and yet—letting go her hands, and turning away.—This offence is beyond the reach even of *your* mercy.

How beyond measure these words and this deportment distress me! Let me know the worst; I cannot bear to be thus perplexed.

Why, said I, turning quickly round, and again taking her hands, that Mervyn, whom you have honored and confided in, and blessed with your sweet regards, has been—

What has he been? Divinely amiable, heroic in his virtue, I am sure. What else has he been?

This Mervyn has imagined, has dared—Will you forgive him?

Forgive you what? Why don't you speak? Keep not my soul in this suspense.

He has dared—But do not think that I am he. Continue to look as now, and reserve your killing glances, the vengeance of those eyes as for one that is absent.—Why, what—You weep, then, at last. That is a propitious sign. When pity drops from the eyes of our judge, then should the suppliant approach. Now, in confidence of pardon, I will tell you: This Mervyn, not content with all you have hitherto granted him, has dared—to *love* you; nay, to think of you, as of *his wife!*

Her eye sunk beneath mine, and disengaging her hands, covered her face with them.

I see my fate, said I, in a tone of despair. Too well did I predict the effect of this confession; but I will go—*and unforgiven.*

She now partly uncovered her face. The hand withdrawn from her cheek, was stretched towards me. She looked at me.

Arthur! I *do* forgive thee.—With what accents was this uttered! With what looks! The cheek that was before pale with terror, was now crimsoned over by a different emotion, and delight swam in her eye.

Could I mistake? My doubts, my new-born fears made me tremble, while I took the offered hand.

Surely—faultered I, I am not—I cannot be—so blessed.

There was no need of words. The hand that I held, was sufficiently eloquent. She was still silent.

Surely, said I, my senses deceive me. A bliss like this cannot be reserved for me. Tell me, once more— set my doubting heart at rest.—

She now gave herself to my arms—I have not words—Let your own heart tell you, you have made your Achsa—

At this moment, a voice from without, it was Miss Stedman's, called—Mrs. Fielding! where are you?

My friend started up, and in a hasty voice, bade me begone! You must not be seen by this giddy girl. Come hither this evening, as if by my appointment, and I will return with you.—She left me in a kind of trance. I was immoveable. My reverie was too delicious;—but let me not attempt the picture. If I can convey no image of my state, previous to this interview, my subsequent feelings are still more beyond the reach of my powers to describe.

Agreeably to the commands of my mistress, I hastened away, evading paths which might expose me to observation. I speedily made my friends partake of my joy, and passed the day in a state of solemn but confused rapture. I did not accurately pourtray the various parts of my felicity. The whole rushed upon my soul at once. My conceptions were too rapid, and too comprehensive to be distinct.

I went to Stedman's in the evening. I found in the accents and looks of my Achsa new assurances that all which had lately past, was more than a dream. She made excuses for leaving the Stedmans sooner than ordinary, and was accompanied to the city by her friend. We dropped Mrs. Fielding at her own house, and thither, after accompanying Miss Stedman to her own home, I returned, upon the wings of tremulous impatience.—

Now could I repeat every word of every conversation that has since taken place between us; but why should I do that on paper? Indeed it could not be done. All is of equal value, and all could not be comprised but in many volumes. There needs nothing more deeply to imprint it on my memory; and while thus reviewing the past, I should be iniquitously neglecting the present. What is given to the pen, would be taken from her; and that, indeed, would be—but no need of saying what it would be, since it is impossible.

I merely write to allay these tumults which our necessary separation produces; to aid me in calling up a little patience, till the time arrives, when our persons, like our minds, shall be united forever. That time—may nothing happen to prevent—but nothing can happen. But why this ominous misgiving just now? My love has infected me with these unworthy terrors, for she has them too.

This morning I was relating my dream to her. She started, and grew pale. A sad silence ensued the cheerfulness that had reigned before—why thus dejected, my friend?

I hate your dream. It is a horrid thought. Would to God it had never occurred to you. Why surely you place no confidence in dreams.

I know not where to place confidence; not in my present promises of joy—and she wept. I endeavored to soothe or console her. Why, I asked, did she weep.

My heart is sore. Former disappointments were so heavy; the hopes which were blasted, were so like my present ones, that the dread of a like result, will intrude upon my thoughts. And now your dream! Indeed, I know not what to do. I believe I ought still to retract—ought, at least, to postpone an act so irrevocable.

Now was I obliged again to go over in my catalogue of arguments to induce her to confirm her propitious resolution to be mine within the week. I, at last, succeeded, even in restoring her serenity and beguiling her fears by dwelling on our future happiness.

Our houshold, while we staid in America—in a year or two we hie to Europe—[4] should be *thus* composed. Fidelity and skill and pure morals, should be sought out, and enticed, by generous recompences, into our domestic service. Duties should be light and regular.—Such and such should be our amusements and employments abroad and at home, and would not this be true happiness?

O yes—If it may be so.

It shall be so; but this is but the humble outline of the scene; something is still to be added to complete our felicity.

What more can be added?

What more? Can Achsa ask what more? She who has not been *only* a wife—

But why am I indulging this pen-prattle? The hour she fixed for my return to her is come, and now take thyself away, quill. Lie there, snug in thy leathern case, till I call for thee, and that will not be very soon. I believe I will abjure thy company till all is settled with my love. Yes: I *will* abjure thee, so let *this* be thy last office, till Mervyn has been made the happiest of men.

THE END

---

[4] "—in a year or two we hie to Europe—": these plans may well change, since, at the end of Chapter II.23, Achsa was relieved to find refuge from her traumatic past and declared "I shall stay where I am for the rest of my days" (see note II.23.15). Nevertheless, such cosmopolitan ambitions reflect Mervyn's newly improved resources and social status and provide a final telling contrast with his modest and troubled origins in Chester Country. The closing flurry of dashes, poeticized language ("we hie to Europe") and erotic suggestiveness (in the novel's last paragraph) are a final tip of the hat to Laurence Sterne, possibly a bemused hint that the "sentimental education" of this young bourgeois is only beginning.

RELATED TEXTS

1. Charles Brockden Brown, "Walstein's School of History. From the German of Krants of Gotha." *The Monthly Magazine and American Review* 1:5 (August–September 1799).

Published in August–September 1799, at the height of Brown's novelistic phase and in between Arthur Mervyn's *two parts (March 1799 and September 1800), "Walstein's School of History" is an important fictionalized essay in which Brown articulates his plan for novel writing, identifying both the rationale for his novels and the themes and techniques he will use to construct them.*

Along with "The Difference between History and Romance," which develops further remarks on the close relation of historical and "romance" narratives that is a central point in this essay, this is a key document for understanding Brown's aims and methods in writing fiction. It also arguably establishes Brown as the first modern U.S. literary critic in the sense of one who explores how texts construct meaning and function in society rather than simply asserting the relative merits of literary productions judged against an imaginary standard of excellence.

The essay's theory of novel writing is directly keyed to Arthur Mervyn *and provides an implicit commentary on it; the closing paragraphs illustrate the new theory with a thinly disguised plot outline for* Arthur Mervyn's *first part. The story of "Olivo Ronsica," set in the German city of Weimar during the chaos and disease created by the Thirty Years' War (1618–1648), transposes the 1790s sociopolitical unrest and epidemic of* Arthur Mervyn's *Philadelphia setting to a roughly analogous conjuncture at the origin of the modern nation-state system, underlining Brown's larger historical vision and his characteristic manner of alluding to large-scale parallels and patterns in early modern history. Additionally, the outline suggests that Brown had not yet finalized plans for the* Second Part *when this essay was published since it summarizes the first part but provides only the vaguest of indications that Mervyn-Ronsica's story may have further developments.*

The essay's fictional framework concerns the literary productions of Walstein, a professor of history at Jena, and his leading student Engel. Brown's choice of the name Walstein and other elements of the frame likely refer to the work of Friedrich Schiller (1759–1805), a professor of history and philosophy at Jena and a major figure of the late Enlightenment, whose progressive fictions, histories, dramas, and doctrines about art were well known to Brown and his friends. Schiller's 1791–1793 History of the Thirty Years' War, *for example, appeared in English translation in 1799; "Walstein" is an alternate English spelling in the period for Wallenstein, a general that Schiller writes about in that history and in several plays; and the setting in Jena and Weimar recalls several 1799* Monthly Magazine *articles by Brown and his circle on Schiller and August von Kotzebue (1761–1819), another contemporary German writer associated with these cities and their cultural institutions.*

Brown derives the essay's approach to novel writing from primarily British Woldwinite models, but the Schillerian frame implicitly joins these two related currents of late Enlightenment thinking about progressive historical and fictional storytelling.

In the essay, Walstein provides a first model for the progressive novel by combining history and romance in such a way as to promote "moral and political" engagement while rejecting universal truths: the novel provides models for benevolent action and makes its readers active observers of the social world around them. Walstein's fictions concern classical or elite figures such as the Roman orator Cicero (whose death marked the end of the Roman republic) and Portugal's Marquis de Pombal (an Enlightenment reformer and civic leader).

Engel modernizes Walstein's model by adding that a romance, to be effective in today's world, must be addressed to a wide popular audience and draw its characters and dilemmas not from the elite but from the same lower-status groups (women, laborers, servants, etc.) that will read and be moved by the work. Engel insists that history and romance alike should address issues and situations familiar to their modern audiences, notably the common inequalities arising from sex and property. Thus Engel's modern romances will insert ordinary individuals like "Olivo Ronsica," or Arthur Mervyn into situations of stress resulting from contemporary tensions and inequalities related to money and other property relations, and erotic desire and other forms of personal relations. Finally, Engel adds that a thrilling style is also necessary if modern fictions are to hold their readers' interest and move them toward progressive values and behaviors.

*****

WALSTEIN was professor of history at Jena, and, of course, had several pupils. Nine of them were more assiduous in their attention to their tutor than the others. This circumstance came at length to be noticed by each other, as well as by Walstein, and naturally produced goodwill and fellowship among them. They gradually separated themselves from the negligent and heedless crowd, cleaved to each other, and frequently met to exchange and compare ideas. Walstein was prepossessed in their favor by their studious habits, and their veneration for him. He frequently admitted them to exclusive interviews, and, laying aside his professional dignity, conversed with them on the footing of a friend and equal.

Walstein's two books were read by them with great attention. These were justly to be considered as exemplifications of his rules, as specimens of the manner in which history was to be studied and written.

No wonder that they found few defects in the model; that they gradually adopted the style and spirit of his composition, and, from admiring and contemplating, should, at length, aspire to imitate. It could not but happen, however, that the criterion of excellence would be somewhat modified in passing through the mind of each; that each should have his peculiar modes of writing and thinking.

All observers, indeed, are, at the first and transient view, more affected by resemblances than differences. The works of Walstein and his disciples were hastily ascribed to the same hand. The same minute explication of motives, the same indissoluble and well-woven tissue of causes and effects, the same unity and coherence of design, the same power of engrossing the attention, and the same felicity, purity, and compactness of style are conspicuous in all.

There is likewise evidence, that each had embraced the same scheme of accounting for events, and the same notions of moral and political duty. Still, however, there were marks of difference in the different nature of the themes that were adopted, and of the purpose which the productions of each writer seemed most directly to promote.

We may aim to exhibit the influence of some moral or physical cause, to enforce some useful maxim, or illustrate some momentous truth. This purpose may be more or less simple, capable of being diffused over the surface of an empire or a century, or of shrinking into the compass of a day, and the bounds of a single thought.

The elementary truths of morals and politics may merit the preference: our theory may adapt itself to, and derive confirmation from whatever is human. Newton and Xavier, Zengis and William Tell, may bear close and manifest relation to the system we adopt, and their fates be linked, indissolubly, in a common chain.

The physician may be attentive to the constitution and diseases of man in all ages and nations. Some opinions, on the influence of a certain diet, may make him eager to investigate the physical history of every human being. No fact, falling within his observation, is useless or anomalous. All sensibly contribute to the symmetry and firmness of some structure which he is anxious to erect. Distances of place and time, and diversities of moral conduct, may, by no means, obstruct their union into one homogeneous mass.

I am apt to think that the moral reasoner may discover principles equally universal in their application, and giving birth to similar coincidence and harmony among characters and events. Has not this been effected by WALSTEIN?

Walstein composed two works. One exhibited, with great minuteness, the life of Cicero; the other, that of the Marquis of Pombal. What link did his reason discover, or his fancy create between times, places, situations, events, and characters so different? He reasoned thus:—

Human society is powerfully modified by individual members. The authority of individuals sometimes flows from physical incidents; birth, or marriage, for example. Sometimes it springs, independently of physical relation, and, in defiance of them, from intellectual vigor. The authority of kings and nobles exemplifies the first species of influence. Birth and marriage, physical, and not moral incidents, entitle them to rule.

The second kind of influence, that flowing from intellectual vigor, is remarkably exemplified in Cicero and Pombal. In this respect they are alike.

The mode in which they reached eminence, and in which they exercised power, was different, in consequence of different circumstances. One lived in a free, the other in a despotic state. One gained it from the prince, the other from the people. The end of both, for their degree of virtue was the same, was the general happiness. They promoted this end by the best means which human wisdom could suggest. One cherished, the other depressed the aristocracy. Both were right in their means as in their end; and each, had he exchanged conditions with the other, would have acted like that other.

Walstein was conscious of the uncertainty of history. Actions and motives cannot be truly described. We can only make approaches to the truth. The more attentively we observe mankind, and study ourselves, the greater will this uncertainty appear, and the farther shall we find ourselves from truth.

This uncertainty, however, has some bounds. Some circumstances of events, and some events, are more capable of evidence than others. The same may be said of motives. Our guesses as to the motives of some actions are more probable than the guesses that relate to other actions. Though no one can state the motives from which any action has flowed, he may enumerate motives from which it is quite certain, that the action did *not* flow.

The lives of Cicero and Pombal are imperfectly related by historians. An impartial view of that which history has preserved makes the belief of their wisdom and virtue more probable than the contrary belief.

Walstein desired the happiness of mankind. He imagined that the exhibition of virtue and talents, forcing its way to sovereign power, and employing that power for the national good, was highly conducive to their happiness.

By exhibiting a virtuous being in opposite conditions, and pursuing his end by the means suited to his own condition, he believes himself displaying a model of right conduct, and furnishing incitements to imitate that conduct, supplying men not only with knowledge of just ends and just means, but with the love and the zeal of virtue.

How men might best promote the happiness of mankind in given situations, was the problem that he desired to solve. The more portraits of human excellence he was able to exhibit the better; but his power in this respect was limited. The longer his life and his powers endured the more numerous would his portraits become. Futurity, however, was precarious, and, therefore, it behoved him to select, in the first place, the most useful theme.

His purpose was not to be accomplished by a brief or meagre story. To illuminate the understanding, to charm curiosity, and sway the passions, required that events should be copiously displayed and artfully linked, that motives should be vividly depicted, and scenes made to pass before the eye. This has been performed. Cicero is made to compose the story of his political and private life from his early youth to his flight from Astura, at the coalition of Antony and Octavius. It is addressed to Atticus, and meant to be the attestor of his virtue, and his vindicator with posterity.

The style is energetic, and flows with that glowing impetuosity which was supposed to actuate the writer. Ardent passions, lofty indignation, sportive elegance, pathetic and beautiful simplicity, take their turns to control his pen, according to the nature of the theme. New and striking portraits are introduced of the great actors on the stage. New lights are cast upon the principal occurrences. Everywhere are marks of profound learning, accurate judgment, and inexhaustible invention. Cicero here exhibits himself in all the forms of master, husband, father, friend, advocate, pro-consul, consul, and senator.

To assume the person of Cicero, as the narrator of his own transactions, was certainly an hazardous undertaking. Frequent errors and lapses, violations of probability, and incongruities in the style and conduct of this imaginary history with the genuine productions of Cicero, might be reasonably expected, but these are not found. The more conversant we are with the authentic monuments, the more is our admiration at the felicity of this imposture enhanced.

The conspiracy of Cataline is here related with abundance of circumstances not to be found in Sallust. The difference, however, is of that kind which results from a deeper insight into human nature, a more accurate acquaintance with the facts, more correctness of arrangement, and a deeper concern in the progress and issue of the story. What is false, is so admirable in itself, so conformable to Roman modes and sentiments, so self-consistent, that one is almost prompted to accept it as the gift of inspiration.

The whole system of Roman domestic manners, of civil and military government, is contained in this work. The facts are either collected from the best antiquarians, or artfully deduced from what is known, or invented with a boldness more easy to admire than to imitate. Pure fiction is never employed but when truth was unattainable.

The end designed by Walstein, is no less happily accomplished in the second, than in the first performance. The style and spirit of the narrative is similar; the same skill in the exhibition of characters and deduction of events, is apparent; but events and characters are wholly new. Portugal, its timorous populace, its besotted monks, its jealous and effeminate nobles, and its cowardly prince, are vividly depicted. The narrator of this tale is, as in the former instance, the subject of it. After his retreat from court, Pombal consecrates his leisure to the composition of his own memoirs.

Among the most curious portions of this work, are those relating to the constitution of the inquisition, the expulsion of the Jesuits, the earthquake, and the conspiracy of Daveiro.

The Romish religion, and the feudal institutions, are the causes that chiefly influence the modern state of Europe. Each of its kingdoms and provinces exhibits the operations of these causes, accompanied and modified by circumstances peculiar to each. Their genuine influence is thwarted, in different degrees, by learning and commerce. In Portugal, they have been suffered to produce the most extensive and unmingled mischiefs. Portugal, therefore, was properly selected as an example of moral and political degeneracy, and as a theatre in which virtue might be shewn with most advantage, contending with the evils of misgovernment and superstition.

In works of this kind, though the writer is actuated by a single purpose, many momentous and indirect inferences will flow from his story. Perhaps the highest and lowest degrees in the scale of political improvement have been respectively exemplified by the Romans and the Portuguese. The pictures that are here drawn, may be considered as portraits of the human species, in two of the most remarkable forms.

There are two ways in which genius and virtue may labor for the public good: first by assailing popular errors and vices, argumentatively and through the medium of books; secondly by employing legal or ministerial authority to this end.

The last was the province which Cicero and Pombal assumed. Their fate may evince the insufficiency of the instrument chosen by them, and teach us, that a change of national opinion is the necessary prerequisite of revolutions.

ENGEL, the eldest of Walstein's pupils, thought, like his master, that the narration of public events, with a certain license of invention, was the most efficacious of moral instruments. Abstract systems, and theoretical reasonings, were not without their use, but they claimed more attention than many were willing to bestow. Their influence, therefore, was limited to a narrow sphere. A mode by which truth could be conveyed to a great number, was much to be preferred.

Systems, by being imperfectly attended to, are liable to beget error and depravity. Truth flows from the union and relation of many parts. These parts, fallaciously connected and viewed separately, constitute error. Prejudice, stupidity, and indolence, will seldom afford us a candid audience, are prone to stop short in their researches, to remit, or transfer to other objects their attention, and hence to derive new motives to injustice, and new confirmations in folly from that which, if impartially and accurately examined, would convey nothing but benefit.

Mere reasoning is cold and unattractive. Injury rather than benefit proceeds from convictions that are transient and faint; their tendency is not to reform and enlighten, but merely to produce disquiet and remorse. They are not strong enough to resist temptation and to change the conduct, but merely to pester the offender with dissatisfaction and regret.

The detail of actions is productive of different effects. The affections are engaged, the reason is won by incessant attacks; the benefits which our system has evinced to be possible, are invested with a seeming existence; and the evils which error was proved to generate, exchange the fleeting, misty, and dubious form of inference, for a sensible and present existence.

To exhibit, in an eloquent narration, a model of right conduct, is the highest province of benevolence. Our patterns, however, may be useful in different degrees. Duties are the growth of situations. The general and the statesman have arduous duties to perform; and to teach them their duty is of use: but the forms of human society allow few individuals to gain the station of generals and statesmen. The lesson, therefore, is reducible to practice by a small number; and, of these, the temptations to abuse their power are so numerous and powerful, that a very small part, and these, in a very small degree, can be expected to comprehend, admire, and copy the pattern that is set before them.

But though few may be expected to be monarchs and ministers, every man occupies a station in society in which he is necessarily active to evil or to good. There is a sphere of some dimensions, in which the influence of his actions and opinions is felt. The causes that fashion men into instruments of happiness or misery, are numerous, complex, and operate upon a wide surface. Virtuous activity may, in a thousand ways, be thwarted and diverted by foreign and superior influence. It may seem best to purify the fountain, rather than filter the stream; but the latter is, to a certain degree, within our power, whereas, the former is impracticable. Governments and general education, cannot be rectified, but individuals may be somewhat fortified against their influence. Right intentions may be instilled into them, and some good may be done by each within his social and domestic province.

The relations in which men, unendowed with political authority, stand to each other, are numerous. An extensive source of these relations, is property. No topic can engage the attention of man more momentous than this. Opinions, relative to property, are the immediate source of nearly all the happiness and misery that exist among mankind. If men were guided by justice in the acquisition and disbursement, the brood of private and public evils would be extinguished.

To ascertain the precepts of justice, and exhibit these precepts reduced to practice, was, therefore, the favorite task of Engel. This, however, did not constitute his whole scheme. Every man is encompassed by numerous claims, and is the subject of intricate relations. Many of these may be comprised in a copious narrative, without infraction of simplicity or detriment to unity.

Next to property the most extensive source of our relations is sex. On the circumstances which produce, and the principles which regulate the union between the sexes, happiness greatly depends. The conduct to be pursued by a virtuous man in those situations which arise from sex, it was thought useful to display.

Fictitious history has, hitherto, chiefly related to the topics of love and marriage. A monotony and sentimental softness have hence arisen that have frequently excited contempt and ridicule. The ridicule, in general, is merited; not because these topics are intrinsically worthless or vulgar, but because the historian was deficient in knowledge and skill.

Marriage is incident to all; its influence on our happiness and dignity, is more entire and lasting than any other incident can possess. None, therefore, is more entitled to discussion. To enable men to evade the evils and secure the benefits of this state, is to consult, in an eminent degree, their happiness.

A man, whose activity is neither aided by political authority nor by the *press*, may yet exercise considerable influence on the condition of his neighbours, by the exercise of intellectual powers. His courage may be useful to the timid or the feeble, and his knowledge to the ignorant, as well as his property to those who want. His benevolence and justice may not only protect his kindred and his wife, but rescue the victims of prejudice and passion from the yoke of those domestic tyrants, and shield the powerless from the oppression of power, the poor from the injustice of the rich, and the simple from the stratagems of cunning.

Almost all men are busy in acquiring subsistence or wealth by a fixed application of their time and attention. Manual or mental skill is obtained and exerted for this end. This application, within certain limits, is our duty. We are bound to choose that species of industry which combines most profit to ourselves with the least injury to others; to select that instrument which, by most speedily supplying our necessities, leaves us at most leisure to act from the impulse of benevolence.

A profession, successfully pursued, confers power not merely by conferring property and leisure. The skill which is gained, and which, partly or for a time, may be exerted to procure subsistence, may, when this end is accomplished, continue to be exerted for the common good. The pursuits of law and medicine, enhance our power over the liberty, property, and health of mankind. They not only qualify us for imparting benefit, by supplying us with property and leisure, but by enabling us to obviate, by intellectual exertions, many of the evils that infest the world.

Engel endeavored to apply these principles to the choice of a profession, and to point out the mode in which professional skill, after it has supplied us with the means of subsistence, may be best exerted in the cause of general happiness.

Human affairs are infinitely complicated. The condition of no two beings is alike. No model can be conceived, to which our situation enables us to conform. No situation can be imagined perfectly similar to that of an actual being. This exact similitude is not required to render an imaginary portrait useful to those who survey it. The usefulness, undoubtedly, consists in suggesting a mode of reasoning and acting somewhat similar to that which is ascribed to a feigned person; and, for this end, some similitude is requisite between the real and imaginary situation; but that similitude is not hard to produce. Among the incidents which invention will set before us, those are to be culled out which afford most scope to wisdom and virtue, which are most analogous to facts, which most forcibly suggest to the reader the parallel between his state and that described, and most strongly excite his desire to act as the feigned personages act. These incidents must be so arranged as to inspire, at once, curiosity and belief, to fasten the attention, and thrill the heart. This scheme was executed in the life of "Olivo Ronsica."

Engel's principles inevitably led him to select, as the scene and period of his narrative, that in which those who should read it, should exist. Every day removed the reader farther from the period, but its immediate readers would perpetually recognize the objects, and persons, and events, with which they were familiar.

Olivo is a rustic youth, whom domestic equality, personal independence, agricultural occupations, and studious habits, had endowed with a strong mind, pure taste, and unaffected integrity. Domestic revolutions oblige him to leave his father's house in search of subsistence. He is destitute of property, of friends, and of knowledge of the world. These are to be acquired by his own exertions, and virtue and sagacity are to guide him in the choice and the use of suitable means.

Ignorance subjects us to temptation, and poverty shackles our beneficence. Olivo's conduct shows us how temptation may be baffled, in spite of ignorance, and benefits be conferred in spite of poverty.

He bends his way to Weimar. He is involved, by the artifices of others, and, in consequence of his ignorance of mankind, in many perils and perplexities. He forms a connection with a man of a great and mixed, but, on the whole, a vicious character. Semlits is introduced to furnish a contrast to the simplicity and rectitude of Olivo, to exemplify the misery of sensuality and fraud, and the influence which, in the present system of society, vice possesses over the reputation and external fortune of the good.

Men hold external goods, the pleasures of the senses, of health, liberty, reputation, competence, friendship, and life, partly by virtue of their own wisdom and activity. This, however, is not the only source of their possession. It is likewise dependent on physical accidents, which human foresight cannot anticipate, or human power prevent. It is also influenced by the conduct and opinions of others.

There is no external good, of which the errors and wickedness of others may not deprive us. So far as happiness depends upon the retention of these goods, it is held at the option of another. The perfection of our character is evinced by the transient or slight influence which privations and evils have upon our happiness, on the skillfulness of those exertions which we make to avoid or repair disasters, on the diligence and success with which we improve those instruments of pleasure to ourselves and to others which fortune has left in our possession.

Richardson has exhibited in Clarissa, a being of uncommon virtue, bereaved of many external benefits by the vices of others. Her parents and lover conspire to destroy her fortune, liberty, reputation, and personal sanctity. More talents and address cannot be easily conceived, than those which are displayed by her to preserve and to regain these goods. Her efforts are vain. The cunning and malignity with which she had to contend, triumphed in the contest.

Those evils and privations she was unable to endure. The loss of fame took away all activity and happiness, and she died a victim to errors, scarcely less opprobrious and pernicious, than those of her tyrants and oppressors. She misapprehended the value of parental approbation and a fair fame. She depreciated the means of usefulness and pleasure of which fortune was unable to deprive her.

Olivo is a different personage. His talents are exerted to reform the vices of others, to defeat their malice when exerted to his injury, to endure, without diminution of his usefulness or happiness, the injuries which he cannot shun.

Semlits is led, by successive accidents, to unfold his story to Olivo, after which they separate. Semlits is supposed to destroy himself, and Olivo returns into the country.

A pestilential disease, prevalent throughout the north of Europe, at that time (1630), appears in the city. To ascertain the fate of one connected, by the ties of kindred and love, with the family in which Olivo resides, and whose life is endangered by residence in the city, he repairs thither, encounters the utmost perils, is seized with the reigning malady, meets, in extraordinary circumstances, with Semlits, and is finally received into the house of a physician, by whose skill he is restored to health, and to whom he relates his previous adventures.

He resolves to become a physician, but is prompted by benevolence to return, for a time, to the farm which he had lately left. The series of ensuing events, are long, intricate, and congruous, and exhibit the hero of the tale in circumstances that task his fortitude, his courage, and his disinterestedness.

Engel has certainly succeeded in producing a tale, in which are powerful displays of fortitude and magnanimity; a work whose influence must be endlessly varied by varieties of character and situation of the reader, but, from which, it is not possible for any one to rise without some degree of moral benefit, and much of that pleasure which always attends the emotions of curiosity and sympathy.

2. Charles Brockden Brown, "The Difference between History and Romance." *The Monthly Magazine and American Review* 2:4 (April 1800).

Together with "Walstein's School of History," and appearing just a few months after it, this essay outlines the basic interrelation of history and fiction writing that Brown assumes in his novels and later historical writings, and helps explain how the novels are intended to educate readers and move them to greater awareness of their social surroundings. Likening the social relations investigated by historians and romancers to the physical relations studied by key early modern scientists such as Isaac Newton (astronomer and physicist who first outlined the theory of gravity), Carl Linnaeus (founder of modern biological taxonomy and ecology), and William Herschel (astronomer who discovered infrared radiation and pioneered advanced telescope technologies such as interferometry), Brown argues that novelists and historians alike are, or should be, social scientists who use narrative to explore their social order and its history and to educate their readers about it. Note that Haller and Linnaeus, two of the landmark scientists mentioned in the essay, are part of the reading that Arthur Mervyn undertakes during his medical studies in the novel's Second Part.*

The essay rejects the common notion that history and fiction are different because one deals with factual and the other with fictional materials. Rather, Brown argues, history and fiction are best understood as two sides of one coin: history describes and documents the results of actions, while fiction investigates the possible conditions and motives that cause these actions. Whereas the historian establishes facts about events and behaviors, the "romancer" is more concerned with asking why and how the events and behaviors took place. Thus the writing of romance (Brown's kind of novel) deals in conjecture about the causes and consequences of social actions and events. This imaginative conjecture is useful because it helps clarify the ways in which seemingly unique or personal events and acts (such as individual experiences and responses to the yellow fever epidemic in Arthur Mervyn*) are actually conditioned, although not narrowly determined, by larger social forces.*

The difference between history as documentation and romance as interpretation also allows Brown to develop an implicit distinction between "romance" and "novel." Brown's definition here situates romance as the kind of narrative that educates readers and helps them grasp the social processes in which they are embedded. Unlike the nineteenth century's contrast between realism and romance, where romance allows the imaginative flight of fancy from the mundane world (this is the way romance is understood in Nathaniel Hawthorne's prefaces of the 1850s, for example), Brown situates the "novel" as a fiction that seeks to amuse a passive reader and "romance" as a fiction that seeks to train the reader as an active interpreter and interrogator of society. When Brown writes in this novel's preface that his fiction dramatizes a social crisis and responses to it "in the spirit of salutary emulation," he is indicating that he has designed the work as a romance, not a novel.

Most basically, then, Brown's ideas about "the difference between history and romance" imply that Arthur Mervyn's tale should be read as an exploration of the causes of contem-

porary events and behaviors, rather than simply as a "terrific" tale of sensational wonder (see the excerpt from "Terrific Novels" for Brown's definition of that variety of narrative).

*****

HISTORY and romance are terms that have never been very clearly distinguished from each other. It should seem that one dealt in fiction, and the other in truth; that one is a picture of the *probable* and certain, and the other a tissue of untruths; that one describes what *might* have happened, and what has *actually* happened, and the other what never had existence.

These distinctions seem to be just; but we shall find ourselves somewhat perplexed, when we attempt to reduce them to practice, and to ascertain, by their assistance, to what class this or that performance belongs.

Narratives, whether fictitious or true, may relate to the processes of nature, or the actions of men. The former, if not impenetrable by human faculties, must be acknowledged to be, hitherto, very imperfectly known. Curiosity is not satisfied with viewing facts in their disconnected state and natural order, but is prone to arrange them anew, and to deviate from present and sensible objects, into speculations on the past or future; it is eager to infer from the present state of things, their former or future condition.

The observer or experimentalist, therefore, who carefully watches, and faithfully enumerates the appearances which occur, may claim the appellation of historian. He who adorns these appearances with cause and effect, and traces resemblances between the past, distant, and future, with the present, performs a different part. He is a dealer, not in certainties, but probabilities, and is therefore a romancer.

An historian will relate the noises, the sights, and the smells that attend an eruption of Vesuvius. A romancer will describe, in the first place, the *contemporary* ebullitions and inflations, the combustion and decomposition that take place in the bowels of the earth. Next he will go to the origin of things, and describe the centrical, primary, and secondary orbs composing the universe, as masses thrown out of an immense volcano called *chaos*. Thirdly, he will paint the universal dissolution that is hereafter to be produced by the influence of volcanic or internal fire.

An historian will form catalogues of stars, and mark their positions at given times. A romancer will arrange them in *clusters* and dispose them in *strata*, and inform you by what influences the orbs have been drawn into sociable knots and circles.

An electrical historian will describe appearances that happen when hollow cylinders of glass and metal are placed near each other, and the former is rubbed with a cloth. The romancer will replenish the space that exists between the sun and its train of planetary orbs, with a fluid called electrical; and describe the modes in which this fluid finds its way to the surface of these orbs through the intervenient atmosphere.

Historians can only differ in degrees of diligence and accuracy, but romancers may have more or less probability in their narrations. The same man is frequently both historian and romancer in the compass of the same work. Buffon, Linneus, and Herschel, are examples of this union. Their observations are as diligent as their theories are adventurous. Among the historians of nature, Haller was, perhaps, the most diligent: among romancers, he that came nearest to the truth was Newton.

It must not be denied that, though history be a term commonly applied to a catalogue of natural appearances, as well as to the recital of human actions, romance is chiefly limited to the latter. Some reluctance may be felt in calling Buffon and Herschel romancers, but that name will be readily conferred on Quintus Curtius and Sir Thomas More. There is a sufficient analogy, however, between objects and modes, in the physical and intellectual world, to justify the use of these distinctions in both cases.

Physical objects and appearances sometimes fall directly beneath our observation, and may be truly described. The duty of the *natural* historian is limited to this description. *Human* actions may likewise be observed, and be truly described. In this respect, the actions of *voluntary* and *involuntary* agents, are alike, but in other momentous respects they differ.

Curiosity is not content with noting and recording the *actions* of men. It likewise seeks to know the *motives* by which the agent is impelled to the performance of these actions; but motives are modifications of thought which cannot be subjected to the senses. They cannot be certainly known. They are merely topics of conjecture. Conjecture is the weighing of probabilities; the classification of probable events, according to the measure of probability possessed by each.

Actions of different men or, performed at different times, may be alike; but the motives leading to these actions must necessarily vary. In guessing at these motives, the knowing and sagacious will, of course, approach nearer to the truth than the ignorant and stupid; but the wise and the ignorant, the sagacious and stupid, when busy in assigning motives to actions, are not *historians* but *romancers*.

The motive is the cause, and therefore the antecedent of the action; but the action is likewise the cause of subsequent actions. Two contemporary and (so to speak) adjacent actions may both be faithfully described, because both may be witnessed; but the connection between them, that quality which constitutes one the effect of the other, is mere matter of conjecture, and comes with the province, not of *history*, but *romance*.

The description of human actions is of moment merely as they are connected with motives and tendencies. The delineation of tendencies and motives implies a description of the action; but the action is describable without the accompaniment of tendencies and motives.

An action may be simply described, but such descriptions, though they alone be historical, are of no use as they stand singly and disjoined from tendencies and motives, in the page of the historian or the mind of the reader. The writer, therefore, who does not blend the two characters, is essentially defective. It is true, that facts simply described, may be connected and explained by the reader; and that the describer may, at least, claim the merit of supplying the builder with materials. The merit of him who drags stones together, must not be depreciated; but must not be compared with him who hews these stones into just proportions, and piles them up into convenient and magnificent fabrics.

That which is done beneath my own inspection, it is possible for me certainly to know and exactly to record; but that which is performed at a distance, either in time or place, is the theme of foreign testimony. If it be related by me, I relate not what I have witnessed, but what I derived from others who were witnesses. The subject of my senses is merely the existence of the record, and not the deed itself which is recorded. The truth of the action can be weighed in no scales but those of probability.

A voluntary action is not only connected with cause and effect, but is itself a series of motives and incidents subordinate and successive to each other. Every action differs from every other in the number and complexity of its parts, but the most simple and brief is capable of being analyzed into a thousand subdivisions. If it be witnessed by others, probabilities are lessened in proportion as the narrative is circumstantial.

These principles may be employed to illustrate the distinction between history and romance. If history relate what is true, its relations must be limited to what is known by the testimony of our senses. Its sphere, therefore, is extremely narrow. The facts to which we are immediate witnesses, are, indeed, numerous; but time and place merely connect them. Useful narratives must comprise facts linked together by some other circumstance. They must, commonly, consist of events, for a knowledge of which the narrator is indebted to the evidence of others. This evidence, though accompanied with different degrees of probability, can never give birth to certainty. How wide, then, if romance be the narrative of mere probabilities, is the empire of romance? This empire is absolute and undivided over the motives and tendencies of human actions. Over actions themselves, its dominion, though not unlimited, is yet very extensive.

X.

3. Two Statements on the Modern Novel:

a) Charles Brockden Brown, "Romances." *The Literary Magazine and American Register* 3:16 (January 1805).

In this article on "romances," which in this case means the novel-like narratives that flourished from the Middle Ages to the 1600s, Brown reiterates the need for contemporary forms of art to focus on themes that are relevant for contemporary audiences. Works of the past may have been tremendous achievements, but their usefulness for the modern reader is limited because new historical conditions demand new ideas and modes of behavior. Brown's argument here suggests that there is no unchanging or eternal, transhistorical standard for values, ideas, or behaviors. The lessons of one age may not be useful for another. Like his contemporaries William Godwin and Thomas Paine, Brown remains skeptical about worshipping past forms of art, society, and government.

*****

A TALE, agreeable to truth and nature or, more properly speaking, agreeable to our *own* conceptions of truth and nature, may be long, but cannot be tedious. Cleopatra

343

and Cassandra by no means referred to an ideal world; they referred to the manners and habits of the age in which they were written; names and general incidents only were taken from the age of Alexander and Caesar. In that age, therefore, they were not tedious, but the more delighted was the reader the longer the banquet was protracted. In after times, when taste and manners were changed, the tale became tedious, because it was deemed unnatural and absurd, and it would have been condemned as tedious, and treated with neglect, whether it filled ten pages or ten volumes.

Cleopatra and Cassandra are no greater violations of historical veracity and probability, and no more drawn from an ideal world, than Johnson's Rasselas, Hawkesworth's Almoran and Hamet, or Fenelon's Telemachus. In all these, names and incidents, and some machinery, are taken from a remote age and nation, but the manners and sentiments are modeled upon those of the age in which the works were written, as those of the Scuderis were fashioned upon the habits of their own age. The present unpopularity of the romances of the fifteenth and sixteenth centuries is not owing to the satires of Cervantes or of Boileau, but to the gradual revolution of human manners and national taste.

The "*Arabian Nights*" delight us in childhood, and so do the chivalrous romances; but, in riper age, if enlightened by education, we despise what we formerly revered. Individuals, whose minds have been uncultivated, continue still their attachment to those marvelous stories. And yet, must it not be ascribed rather to change of manners than to any other cause, that we neglect and disrelish works which gave infinite delight to Sir Philip Sidney, Sir Walter Raleigh, and Sir Thomas More, to Sully and Daubigne: men whose knowledge of Augustan models, and delight in them, was never exceeded, and the general vigor and capacity of whose minds has never been surpassed.

The works that suited former ages are now exploded by us. The works that are now produced, and which accommodate themselves to our habits and taste, would have been utterly neglected by our ancestors: and what is there to hinder the belief, that they, in their turn, will fall into oblivion and contempt at some future time. We naturally conceive our own habits and opinions the standard of rectitude; but their rectitude, admitting our claim to be just, will not hinder them from giving way to others, and being exploded in their turn.

b) Charles Brockden Brown, excerpt from "Terrific Novels." *The Literary Magazine and American Register* 3:19 (April 1805).

This passage illustrates Brown's criticism of conventional gothic style and helps explain, by contrast, how his own use of the gothic is oriented toward the representation of modern life. Today the term "gothic" generally describes narratives that use the supernatural to excite fear and suspense in their audience. But in this essay, Brown judges such narratives by their motivation rather than by their form, themes, or effect on their audience. Brown calls novels that use sensational devices of mystery simply to create suspense "terrific" ones because they are intended to generate sensations of terror, rather than a sense of excellence.

In keeping with his general emphasis on the development of modern forms suited to modern social conditions, Brown criticizes conventional gothic's emphasis on premodern superstitions rather than the anxieties and stresses of contemporary life. As opposed to castles, monks, and superstitions, Brown's version of the gothic, in Arthur Mervyn *and his other novels, highlights scenarios and themes that his readers might actually experience: bankruptcy, impoverishment, vulnerability to illnesses like yellow fever, psychological symptoms of extreme anxiety and stress such as somnambulism, the threat of rape, and so on.*

*****

THE Castle of Otranto laid the foundation of a style of writing, which was carried to perfection by Mrs. Radcliff, and which may be called the *terrific style*. The great talents of Mrs. Radcliff made some atonement for the folly of this mode of composition, and gave some importance to exploded fables and childish fears, by the charms of sentiment and description; but the multitude of her imitators seem to have thought that description and sentiment were impertinent intruders, and by lowering the mind somewhat to its ordinary state, marred and counteracted those awful feelings, which true genius was properly employed in raising. They endeavour to keep the reader in a constant state of tumult and horror, by the powerful engines of trapdoors, back stairs, black robes, and pale faces: but the solution of the enigma is ever too near at hand, to permit the indulgence of supernatural appearances. A well-written scene of a party at snap-dragon would exceed all the fearful images of these books. There is, besides, no *keeping* in the author's design: fright succeeds to fright, and danger to danger, without permitting the unhappy reader to draw his breath, or to repose for a moment on subjects of character or sentiment.

4. Charles Brockden Brown, "The Man at Home.—No. XI." *The Weekly Magazine of Original Essays, Fugitive Pieces, and Interesting Intelligence* 1:11 (April 14, 1798).

Brown used yellow fever, as both a motif underlining social corruption and a setting for dramatizing social behaviors, in a group of related fictions and essays published in the year leading up to Arthur Mervyn'*s first part. Yellow fever figures centrally in his novel* Ormond; or, The Secret Witness, *published in January 1799, two or three months before the first part of* Arthur Mervyn, *and in the following short sketch, which first appeared as one installment of Brown's 1798 essay series "The Man at Home." Brown republished the same piece in 1806 with minor changes and a new, more suggestive title, "Pestilence and Bad Government Compared" (*Literary Magazine *6:39, December 1806).*

Given the way this sketch ends by prefiguring what in Arthur Mervyn *would have been a marriage between Mervyn and an Eliza Hadwin who successfully inherits her father's farm (which was in fact Brown's original plan for Second Part, as Brown noted in a letter to his brother James), it seems to be an experimental draft or outline for aspects of the later romance. As the sketch highlights the historical contexts and conditions that structure the lovers' meeting, it emphasizes Brown's point that a personal tale has to be read in the context of its sociopolitical environment. An additional contrast suggests other shifts in Brown's later thinking about the design of the novel. The later work divides the sketch's single character Wallace into two figures, Arthur and Wallace, and, similarly, the sketch's single female object splits into Eliza Hadwin and Achsa Fielding. This doubling of characters suggests that Brown felt that using only domestic characters, as he does in this sketch, would fail to convey the novel's larger international concerns.*

In Arthur Mervyn *the fever's primary sociopolitical parallel is the mercantile corruption based on Atlantic slavery, which spreads a deadly poison through that novel's collective body politic. In this sketch, the sociopolitical parallel is state terrorism, manifested in a politically motivated doctrine of "security," which in reality amounts to a calculated abandonment of legal restraints and suppression of civil liberties allowing partisan proscriptions and executions. The story also prefigures Brown's closely related and more spectacular tale of governmental force, "Thessalonica, A Roman Story" (May 1799). The parallel between the dangers of yellow fever and state terrorism perpetrated in the name of "security" can clearly be read in terms of France's 1793–1794 "Reign of Terror" (referenced in Achsa Fielding's backstory), in which Jacobin political leaders guillotined those accused of being enemies to the French people, who were in reality simply the political opposition to the current government. But Brown's narrative echoes more closely to home in its implicit references to the U.S. revolutionary proscriptions of Tories and neutrals in 1777–1778 (these were important to Brown personally because they resulted in the internment of his own father) and to the better-known 1798–1801 abandonment of constitutional civil liberties in the U.S. Alien and Sedition Acts, which were enacted as repressive, partisan measures during the same years Brown was writing his novels.*

The sketch begins by describing the negative effects of unregulated sympathy, when the sight of misery prompts a sentimental response of suicide. The piece ends, though, by suggesting that we are not doomed to repeat the traumas of history if we rationally overcome unreasonable prejudices and bigotry. The sketch encourages the reader to weigh the similarities and differences between the medical damage of malignant fevers and the political-social damage of "malignant passions"—the parallel effects of "Pestilence and Bad Government," as the later title has it—and implicitly enacts the kind of ethical, socially engaged use of narrative to provoke awareness of contemporary social conditions and their implications that Brown outlines in his essays "Walstein's School of History" and "The Difference between History and Romance."

✶✶✶✶✶

WHAT a series of calamities is the thread of human existence? I have heard of men who, though free themselves from any uncommon distress, were driven to suicide by reflecting on the misery of others. They employed their imagination in running over the catalogue of human woes, and were so affected by the spectacle, that they willingly resorted to death to shut it from their view. No doubt their minds were constituted after a singular manner. We are generally prone, when objects chance to present to us their gloomy side, to change their position, till we hit upon the brightest of its aspects.

I was lately perusing, in company with my friends Harrington and Wallace, the history of intestine commotions, in one of the ancient republics. It was one of the colonies of Magna Græcia.[1] The nation comprehended a commercial city, peopled by eighty thousand persons, with a small territory annexed. Two factions were for a long time contending for the sovereignty. On one occasion, the party that had hitherto been undermost, obtained the upper place. The maxims by which they intended to deport themselves were, for some time, unknown. That they would revenge themselves on their adversaries, in any signal or atrocious way, was by no means, expected. Time, however, soon unfolded their characters and views.

The annalist proceeds to describe the subsequent events with great exactness of time, place, and number; but exhibits none of those general views which fill the reader's imagination, and translate him to the scene of action. His details, however, are, on that account, the more valuable, since the dullest reader, when possessed of these materials, will stand in no need of foreign aid to *circumstantialize* the picture.

The ordinary course and instruments of judicature were esteemed inadequate to their purposes, for these would not allow them to select their victims in sufficient numbers, and with sufficient dispatch. They therefore erected a secret tribunal, and formed a band of three hundred persons, who should execute, implicitly, the decrees of this tribunal. These judges were charged with the punishment of those who had been guilty of crimes against the state. They set themselves to the vigorous performance of their office.

On other occasions it has been usual to subject to some appearance of trial the objects of persecution; to furnish them with an intelligible statement of their offences; to summon them to an audience of their judges; and to found their sentence on some evidence real or pretended; but these rulers were actuated by no other impulse than vengeance. The members of the tribunal were convened, daily, for no other purpose than to form a catalogue of those who should be forthwith sacrificed.

The avenues to the hall where they were assembled were guarded by the troop before mentioned. Having executed this business of the day, the officers of the band of executioners were summoned, and the fatal list was put into their hands. The work of death began at night-fall. This season was adopted to render their proceedings more terrible. For this end, likewise, it was ordered that no warning should be given to the men whose names were inscribed upon this roll, but by the arrival of the messengers at their door.

These, dressed in peculiar uniform, marched by night to the sounds of harsh and lamentable music, through the streets of the mute and affrighted city. They stopped

---

[1] Latin for "Greater Greece," the area at the southernmost part of the Italian peninsula that was colonized by Greek settlers in the eighth century BCE and absorbed into the Roman Republic at the time of the Pyrrhic War (280–275 BCE).

at the appointed door, and admission being gained, peaceably or by violence, they proceeded, in silence, to the performance of their commission. The bow-string was displayed; the victim torn from his bed, from the arms of his wife, from the embraces of his children, was strangled in an instant; and the breathless corpse, left upon the spot where it had fallen. They retired, without any interruption to their silence, and ended not their circuit till the catalogue was finished.

To inflict punishment was the intention of these judges, but they considered that our own death is not, in all instances, the greatest evil that we can suffer. We would sometimes willingly purchase the safety of others at the price of our own existence. The tribunal therefore conducted itself by a knowledge of the characters of those whom its malice had selected. Sometimes the criminal remained untouched, but he was compelled to witness the destruction of some of his family. Sometimes his wife, sometimes his children were strangled before his eyes. Sometimes, after witnessing the agonies of all that he loved, the sentence was executed on himself.

The nature of this calamity was adapted to inspire the utmost terror. No one was apprized of his fate. The list was inscrutable to every eye but that of the tribunal. The adherents to the ruling faction composed about one-third of the inhabitants. These of course were secure. If they did not triumph in the confusion of their foes, they regarded it with unconcern.

The rage and despair which accompanied the midnight progress of the executioners, scarcely excited their attention. Their revels and their mirth suffered no abatement.

It was asked in vain, by the sufferers, when the power which thus scattered death and dismay was to end. No answer was returned. They were left to form their judgment on the events that arose. Night succeeded night; but the murders, instead of lessening, increased in number. Many admitted the persuasion that a total extermination of the fallen party was intended. For a considerable period every circumstance contributed to heighten this persuasion. It was observed that the list continued gradually to swell, till the number of executions in a single night amounted to no less than two hundred.

It were worthy of some eloquent pen to describe this state of things. Surely never did the depravity of human passions more conspicuously display itself than on this stage. The most vigorous efforts were made to shake off this dreadful yoke, but the tyrants had previously armed their adherents, and guarded every avenue to a revolution, with the utmost care. The city-walls and gates served to stop the fugitives, and none but the members of the triumphant faction were suffered to go out. Policy required that those who furnished the city with provisions should be unmolested in their entrances and exits. In no variation of circumstances, indeed, had the wretched helots any thing to fear. No change in their condition could possibly be for the worse.

It will hardly be believed that this state of things continued for so long a period as four months. During this time, vengeance did not pause for a single night. At the expiration of this period, suddenly, and without warning, the nightly visitations ceased, and the tribunal was dissolved. The world were permitted to discover what limits had been assigned to the destruction. On counting up the slain, it appeared that six thousand persons had perished, and, consequently, that the purpose of the tyrants had been, not the indiscriminate massacre, but, merely the decimation of their adversaries.

Having finished the perusal of this tale, I could not forbear expatiating to my friends on the enormity of these evils, and thanking the destiny that had reserved us for a milder system of manners—"Not so fast," said Harrington. "You forget that the very city of which we are inhabitants, no longer ago than 1793, suffered evils nearly parallel to those that are here described. In some respects the resemblance is manifest and exact. In the inscrutability of the causes that produced death; the duration of the calamity; and the proportional number of the slain, the cases are parallel. Our condition was worse inasmuch as the lingerings and agonies of fever are worse than the expeditious operation of the bow-string. We had to encounter the miseries of neglect and want. The cessation of all lucrative business, and the sealing up of most of the sources of subsistence, were disadvantages peculiar to ourselves. Against these may be put in the balance the misery which haunts the oppressors, and those aggravations of distress flowing from a knowledge that the authors of our calamities are men like ourselves, whom, perhaps, our own folly has armed against us. The evils which infest human society flow either from causes beyond our power to scrutinize, or from the license of malignant passions. It would require a delicate hand to adjust truly the balance between these opposite kinds of evil. Suppose tyranny and plague, as in these cases, to destroy the same numbers in the same time, which has produced the greatest quantity of suffering? It is not easy to decide, but I am apt to think that the miseries of plague must be allowed to preponderate."

"The cases," said Wallace, "seem to me to have very little resemblance. If I had been an inhabitant of the Greek colony, I see not how I should have been benefited by this state of affairs, whereas the yellow fever was, to me, the most fortunate event that could have happened. I kept a store, as you know, in Water Street. I am young, and then was then so poor that my stock, small as it was, was obtained upon credit. I was obliged to exert the most unremitting industry to procure myself the means of living, and the very means by which I sought to live, had like to have destroyed me. My frail constitution could not support the inconveniences of inactivity and bad air. My health was rapidly declining, and I could not afford to relinquish my business. The yellow fever, however, compelled to me relinquish it for a while.

"I took cheap lodgings in the neighbourhood of Lancaster. Country air and exercises completely reinstated me in the possession of health, but this was not all, for I formed an acquaintance with a young lady, who added three hundred pounds a year, to youth, beauty, and virtue. This acquaintance soon ripened into love, and now you see me one of the happiest of men. A lovely wife, a plentiful fortune, health, and leisure are the ingredients of my present lot, and for all these am I indebted to the yellow fever."

5. Charles Brockden Brown, "Portrait of an Emigrant. Extracted from a Letter." *The Monthly Magazine and American Review* 1:3 (June 1799).

Despite its brevity, "Portrait of an Emigrant" brings together a complex set of positions on progressive politics and social history, especially concerning race. The immediate context for Brown's sketch is the 1793 flood of French refugees who arrived in U.S. port cities, notably Philadelphia, after fleeing the increasingly violent black slave revolution in Haiti. White French Creole (colony-born) refugees in this group, along with native-born French political exiles arriving from France to escape Jacobin rule, had an immediate impact on American culture far out of proportion to their relatively small numbers as an emigrant group. Unlike the mainly agricultural and laboring-class background of earlier and larger northern European emigrant groups such as the Germans and Scots-Irish, these Francophone exiles of the 1790s belonged largely to the middle class and planter elites and consequently tended to be more literate, financially comfortable, and less familiar with manual labor than other groups. With little experience in crafts, the refugees scrambled to survive by helping to establish a market for consumer pleasures—often involving the commercialization of physical appearance and behavior—as hairdressers, dressmakers, cooks, dance instructors, booksellers, and music and theater performers.

As they brought a new code of manners and personal dress styles to the plainer, predominately Protestant cultures of American cities, the French strangers were arguably important catalysts or accelerators in this period's shift from self-sufficient, agrarian, household economies toward more modern patterns in which individuals fashion their identity, not by adherence to family or village origins but through consumer choices in clothes, books, and other cultural commodities. Not only did these French immigrants make new kinds of consumer objects and behaviors available to Americans, they also embodied and modeled for locals a radically new mentality involving comfort with lifestyles based on a consumer economy, an orientation that is dramatically different from Puritan ideals of asceticism or Quaker moderation. Brown's "Portrait" begins by highlighting the experience of this transformation and then turns to an implicit claim for the abolition of slavery and the affirmation of a postslavery society based on miscegenation and a "mulatto" culture of racial mixture.

The narrator opens the sketch by emphasizing that social experience is contingent on the changing historical environment, highlighting the Woldwinite claim that we are determined more by cultural environment than by the accident of birth into a particular family and location. Explaining that he has been asked to speak with Mrs. K, the narrator claims that while the undereducated might not know history and political debates, their familiarity with the world around them nevertheless makes them insightful commentators on the shifts in everyday social history, what Brown calls "the romance of real life." While the woman's tales of her urban neighborhood might seem trivial, the narrator suggests that as an example of the opinions and attitudes of a newly urbanized population (like Arthur Mervyn himself), her thinking ought to be viewed as an index to historical transformation and a model for virtuous activity more important than the writings and legislation of political elites. By respectfully listening to and learning from the uneducated female observer, the narrator affirms the need for a more socially inclusive, egalitarian history from the bottom up.

Mrs. K discusses the everyday behavior of a white Haitian refugee, M. de Lisle (de l'isle = "from the island"; Lisle is also a Brown family name on the maternal side), who is openly and unashamedly living with a mixed-race (or mulatto) woman from the French colony. Such a coupling was common in Haiti, where an increasingly wealthy segment of mixed-race property owners would marry their daughters to white men so that their grandchildren would gain the privileges of whiteness in the colonies. The black slave uprising, however, has forced them to flee, losing their wealth in the process. But instead of holding a revenge grudge against unruly blacks after arriving in 1793, they show benevolence by adopting what is, as indicated by her dialect speech, a black child orphaned possibly by yellow fever. Rather than wallowing in self-pity for their lost status, the couple instead enjoys life, taking pleasure in each other's spirited conversation, and live what appears to be a purely consumer-oriented lifestyle, ordering all their meals in and avoiding manual labor by paying for washing and ignoring housecleaning. Contrary to conventional readerly expectations that Mrs. K will condemn the couple's behavior as shiftless and unacceptable, she instead envies their joie de vivre *and insists that "the French are the only people that know how to live." Instead of being shocked by their foreignness and different sexual morality (there is a hint that the woman may be a kept mistress who occasionally dabbles in prostitution), Mrs. K is comfortable with these "exiles and strangers." The implied purpose of the conversation, then, is not so much to document the cultural otherness and racial intermixture of the French, as to record and amplify the affirmative response of the common American. It is Mrs. K's newly emergent cosmopolitanism that the narrator wants to highlight, as she provides evidence of a larger historical shift of mentalities that makes the case for a peaceful and in fact desirable move toward a mixed-race, postslavery society.*

As in many of Brown's writings, seemingly random details and references work together to reinforce the surface meaning of the sketch. The de Lisles order their food from Etienne ("Chrétien") Simonet, a French émigré from Montargis who had a patisserie and catering business on South Second Street near Lombard. Simonet belonged to St. John's Masonic Lodge, which was presided over by Dr. Jean Devèze, a Creole physician who played a leading role at Bush-Hill hospital during the 1793 yellow fever epidemic and is referred to in Arthur Mervyn.

The mention of Madame de Lisle's acting in Lailson's circus seemingly dates the conversation to April–July 1797. In 1797–1798, French immigrant Philip Lailson established the city's largest circus at Fifth and Prune Streets (across from the debtor's prison described in Arthur Mervyn*) and staged shows that combined equestrian tricks, burlesque, ballet, pantomimes, and plays. In May 1797, Brown's close friends William Dunlap, Elihu Hubbard Smith, and Samuel Latham Mitchill came to Philadelphia to participate in a convention of state abolition societies. With Brown they attended Lailson's circus during the period when it staged plays, and they may well have seen a piece called* The American Heroine *featuring actors such as Madame de Lisle.*

This was an adaptation of George Coleman's tremendously successful Inkle and Yarico *(1787), a tale about an English merchant, Inkle, who is shipwrecked on a Caribbean is-*

land and saved by the beautiful aborigine Yarico, who shields him from her people's anger. They exchange marriage vows, but Inkle later decides to sell his Indian wife into slavery, raising the price when he learns she is pregnant. Coleman's play was widely received as an abolitionist attack on mercantile greed and is now recognized as a significant part of the cultural push toward the successful British campaign to abolish slavery. Coleman was also familiar to Brown and his friends as the author of The Iron Chest (1796), a stage version of William Godwin's novel Caleb Williams (1793), a primary model for Arthur Mervyn. As she acts in Lailson's productions, then, Madame de Lisle may be employed in more than simply frivolous entertainment; she may be contributing to a popular art form that conveys progressive political messages to a wide audience. This cultural strategy follows Brown's own as outlined in "Walstein's School of History," a Related Text here.

The sketch may also involve one further allusion and intervention. During Lailson's short run, Susanna Rowson, author of the Francophobic Charlotte Temple, a Tale of Truth (U.K. publication 1791, U.S. republication 1794), was in the last stages of her acting career and appeared at Lailson's, to somewhat bad reviews, in a play titled The Harlequin Mariner. Critic Steven Epley has recently argued that the great success of Charlotte Temple was based on Rowson's repackaging of Inkle and Yarico's thematic elements in ways that stripped the source narrative of its abolitionist political purpose. Thus Brown's affirmative characterization of the de Lisles may signal an oblique criticism of Rowson's brand of xenophobic entertainment and declining career as an actor; for at this time Brown and Smith were interested participants in their friend William Dunlap's rival career and (at that time) successful management of the New Park Theatre in New York.

*****

I CALLED, as you desired, on Mrs. K————. We had considerable conversation. Knowing, as you do, my character and her's, you may be somewhat inquisitive as to the subject of our conversation. You may readily suppose that my inquiries were limited to domestic and every-day incidents. The state of her own family, and her servants and children being discussed, I proceeded to inquire into the condition of her neighbours. It is not in large cities as it is in villages. Those whose education does not enable and accustom them to look abroad, to investigate the character and actions of beings of a distant age and country, are generally attentive to what is passing under their own eye. Mrs. K———— never reads, not even a newspaper. She is unacquainted with what happened before she was born. She is equally a stranger to the events that are passing in distant nations, and to those which ingross the attention and shake the passions of the statesmen and politicians of her own country; but her mind, nevertheless, is far from being torpid or inactive. She speculates curiously and even justly on the objects that occur within her narrow sphere.

Were she the inhabitant of a village, she would be mistress of the history and character of every family within its precincts; but being in a large city,* her knowledge is

---

* Philadelphia.

confined chiefly to her immediate neighbours; to those who occupy the house on each side and opposite. I will not stop to inquire into the reason of this difference in the manners of villagers and citizens. The fact has often been remarked, though seldom satisfactorily explained. I shall merely repeat the dialogue which took place on my inquiry into the state of the family inhabiting the house on the right hand and next to her's.

"M'Culey," said she, "who used to live there, is gone."

"Indeed! and who has taken his place?"

"A Frenchman and his wife. His wife, I suppose her to be, though he is a man of fair complexion, well formed, and of genteel appearance; and the woman is half negro. I suppose they would call her a mestee. They came last winter from the West-Indies, and miserably poor I believe; for when they came into this house they had scarcely any furniture besides a bed, and a chair or two, and a pine table. They shut up the lower rooms, and lived altogether in the two rooms in the second story."

"Of whom does the family consist?"

"The man and woman, and a young girl, whom I first took for their daughter, but I afterwards found she was an orphan child, whom, shortly after their coming here, they found wandering in the streets; and, though poor enough themselves, took her under their care."

"How do they support themselves?"

"The man is employed in the compting-house of a French merchant of this city. What is the exact sort of employment, I do not know, but it allows him to spend a great deal of his time at home. The woman is an actress in Lailson's pantomimes. In the winter she scarcely ever went out in the day-time, but now that the weather is mild and good she walks out a great deal."

"Can you describe their mode of life, what they eat and drink, and how they spend their time?"

"I believe I can. Most that they do can be seen from our windows and yard, and all that they say can be heard. In the morning every thing is still till about ten o'clock. Till that hour they lie a-bed. The first sign that they exist, is given by the man, who comes half dressed, to the back window; and lolling out of it, smokes two or three segars, and sometimes talks to a dog that lies on the out-side of the kitchen door. After sometime passed in this manner he goes into the room over the kitchen, takes a loaf of bread from the closet, and pours out a tumbler of wine; with these he returns to the front room, but begins as soon as he has hold of them, to gnaw at one and sip from the other. This constitutes their breakfast. In half an hour they both re-appear at the window. They throw out crums of bread to the dog, who stands below with open mouth to receive it; and talk sometimes to him and sometimes to each other. Their tongues run incessantly; frequently they talk together in the loudest and shrillest tone imaginable. I thought, at first, they were quarrelsome; but every now and then they burst into laughter, and it was plain that they were in perfect good humour with each other.

"About twelve o'clock the man is dressed, and goes out upon his business. He returns at three. In the mean time the lady employs herself in washing every part of her body, and putting on a muslin dress, perfectly brilliant and clean. Then she either lolls at the window, and sings without intermission, or plays on a guitar. She is certainly a capital performer and singer. No attention is paid to house or furniture. As to rubbing tables, and sweeping and washing floors, these are never thought of. Their house is in a sad condition, but she spares no pains to make her person and dress clean.

"The man has scarcely entered the house, when he is followed by a black fellow, with bare head and shirt tucked up at his elbows, carrying on his head a tray covered with a white napkin. This is their dinner, and is brought from *Simonet's*. After dinner the man takes his flute, on which he is very skilful; and the woman either sings or plays in concert till evening approaches: some visitants then arrive, and they all go out together to walk. We hear no more of them till next morning."

"What becomes of the girl all this time?"

"She eats, sings, dresses, and walks with them. She often comes into our house, generally at meal times; if she spies any thing she likes, she never conceals her approbation. 'O my, how good *dat* must be! Me wish me had some: will you *gif* me some?' She is a pretty harmless little thing, and one cannot refuse what she asks.

"Next day after they came into this house, the girl, in the morning, while our servant was preparing breakfast, entered the kitchen—'O my!' said she to me, 'what you call dem tings?'

'Buckwheat cakes.'

'Ahah! buckawit cake! O my! how good dey must be! Me likes—will you give me one?'

"Next morning she came again, and we happened to be making *muffins.*' 'O my!' cried she, 'you be always baking and baking! What you call dem dere?'

'Muffins.'

'Mofeen? O my! me wish for some, me do.'

"Afterwards she was pretty regular in her visits. She was modest, notwithstanding; and, seeming to be half-starved, we gave her entertainment as often as she claimed it."

"Are not these people very happy?"

"Very happy. When together they are for ever chattering and laughing, or playing and singing in concert. How the man is employed when separate we do not certainly know; but the woman, it seems, is continually singing, and her hands, if not employed in adorning her own person, are playing the guitar. I am apt to think the French are the only people that know how to live. These people, though exiles and strangers, and subsisting on scanty and precarious funds, move on smoothly and at ease. Household cares they know not. They breakfast upon bread and wine, without the ceremony of laying table, and arranging platters and cups. From the trouble of watching and directing servants they are equally exempt. Their cookery is performed abroad. Their clothes are washed in the same way. The lady knows no manual employment but the grateful one of purifying and embellishing her own person. The intervals are consumed in the highest as well as purest sensual enjoyments, in music, in which she appears to be an adept, and of which she is passionately enamoured. When the air is serene and bland, she repairs to the public walks, with muslin handkerchief in one hand, and parti-coloured *parasol* in the other. She is always accompanied by men anxious to please her, busy in supplying her with amusing topics, and listening with complacency and applause to her gay effusions and her ceaseless volubility.

"I have since taken some pains to discover the real situation of this family. I find that the lady was the heiress of a large estate in St. Domingo, that she spent her youth in France, where she received a polished education, and where she married her present companion, who was then in possession of rank and fortune, but whom the revolution has reduced to indigence. The insurrection in St. Domingo destroyed their property in that island. They escaped with difficulty to these shores in 1793, and have since subsisted in various modes and places, frequently pinched by extreme poverty, and sometimes obliged to solicit public charity; but retaining, in every fortune, and undiminished, their propensity to talk, laugh and sing—their flute and their guitar."

Nothing is more ambiguous than the motives that stimulate men to action. These people's enjoyments are unquestionably great. They are innocent: they are compatible, at least, with probity and wisdom, if they are not the immediate fruits of it. Constitutional gaiety may account for these appearances; but as they may flow, in one case, from the absence of reflection and foresight, they may likewise, in another instance, be the product of justice and benevolence.

It is our duty to make the best of our condition; to snatch the good that is within our reach, and to nourish no repinings on account of what is unattainable. The gratifications of sense, of conjugal union, and of social intercourse, are among the highest in the scale; and these are as much in the possession of *de Lisle* and his wife, as of the most opulent and luxuriant members of the community.

As to mean habitation and scanty furniture, their temper or their reason enables them to look upon these things as trifles. They are not among those who witnessed their former prosperity, and their friends and associates are unfortunate like themselves. Instead of humiliation and contempt, adversity has probably given birth to sympathy and mutual respect.

His profession is not laborious; and her's, though not respectable according to our notions, is easy and amusing. Her life scarcely produces any intermission of recreation and enjoyment. Few instances of more unmingled and uninterrupted felicity can be found; and yet these people have endured, and continue to endure, most of the evils which the imagination is accustomed to regard with most horror; and which would create ceaseless anguish in beings fashioned on the model of my character, or of yours. Let you and I grow wise by the contemplation of their example.

B.

6. Charles Brockden Brown, "What Is a *Jew*?" *The Monthly Magazine and American Review* 3:5 (November 1800).

Published two months after Brown ended Arthur Mervyn *with the dramatic revelation of Achsa Fielding's Jewish ethnicity and preparations for Arthur and Achsa's implicitly interracial union, this short piece is another example of the way Brown frames questions about social history and race in ways that are decidedly antiessentialist or critical of ex-clusionary ethno-racial categories and stereotyping. Additionally, and typically for Brown, the piece approaches religion as a negative social and historical institution, implicitly re-jecting orientation to scriptural authority as superstition.*

The primarily Sephardic Jewish communities in 1790s North America were small, but the question of Jewish identity during these years had a philosophical and political im-portance far out of proportion to the actual size of the period's Jewish populations. In rev-olutionary France and throughout the British and Dutch-Portuguese Atlantic world, discussions of Jewish identity and emancipation (1791 in France, 1796 in the Nether-lands) often inaugurated and rehearsed subsequent debates about the category of citizen-ship and its applicability to nondominant groups, that is, women and nonwhites. Brown's character Achsa is designed to be an innovative "citizen" in both categories. Jewish iden-tity was thus an important and widely rehearsed topic in this period, at a time when ethno-racial categories were, on the one hand, being revised in terms of Enlightenment and revolutionary ideals concerning a more pluralistic and tolerant social order and, on the other, becoming hardened and transformed into essentialist cages as nineteenth-century codes of biological, parascientific racialism began to emerge as a dominant dis-course.

Brown writes the article as an editorial voice at the Monthly Magazine, *responding to a possibly fictional letter titled "Queries Concerning the Jews," by "Biblicus," in the mag-azine's September issue. Whereas that query, perhaps written by Brown in order to stage his reply, frames Jewish identity as an essentialist and transhistorical category assumed by those who would use the Bible as their authority for categorizing other social groups, Brown's response rejects such an understanding, approaching the notion of Jewishness with a series of analytical questions that dissolve Biblicus' problematic assumptions, transform-ing an essentialist category into a historical name and question that will require critical-historical investigation to be adequately understood.*

Brown pointedly does not even attempt to answer the titular query "What is a JEW?" implying that Biblicus' effort to define identity in this way is basically a question wrongly posed. Note how the first paragraph instead suggests that historical and political questions concerning "the present state of the Jews," that is, their civil emancipation in republics and historical status as a persecuted ethno-racial group in monarchies, are actually more worthy of consideration. Refusing to answer Biblicus, Brown asks his readers to think crit-ically about how their own unexamined assumptions and reliance on the claims of tradi-tional institutions frame their common sense.

Additionally, Brown writes this article in the wake of the August 1800 Benjamin Nones statement on politicized anti-Semitism, also included in this volume's Related Texts. Nones' statement is likely part of the immediate context for Brown's decision to make Achsa's character Jewish and undertake an article like this one, but both Nones and Brown are also responding to a wider and well-documented pattern of politicized attacks on Jews in the partisan infighting of the 1790s. Brown frequently returned to related treatments of Jewish identity and history during the 1803–1807 years of his Literary Magazine *and his posthumously published* Historical Sketches.

✶✶✶✶✶

To the Editor of the Monthly Magazine.

Sir,

IN addition to the queries inserted in your former number, concerning the present state of the Jews, and which are well worth consideration, I beg leave to propose one which seems to be of no small importance, and which, perhaps, it is requisite to decide in the first place. This question is—

What is a Jew?

Suppose a man and his wife, whose parents respectively were of the Hebrew nation and opinions, to be convinced of the truth of the Christian faith, and to throw off all the rules and practices that usually distinguish the followers of Moses, are such persons and their immediate posterity, trained up in their father's new religion, Jews?

Suppose a man, a Delaware Indian, for instance, to adopt the law of Moses and the prophets, in exclusion of the New Testament, does such a man become a Jew?

Or is this appellation confined to those who can trace their genealogy somewhat backward, and find it to be unmixed with the blood of the *aboriginal* inhabitants of any country but Palestine, and *likewise* who conform to the ritual of Moses, in exclusion of any later system?

If his claim to this appellation arise from his *opinions,* it may seem that a Jew may be distinguished from another man with tolerable precision. Any man, in this case, is a Jew who believes and practices (exclusively) the law of Moses. But it is an obvious inquiry—what *is* the law, and the prophets? What interpretation of the Hebrew writings is the true one?

While *opinion* is the standard, it is obvious that no man is either Jew or Christian in a strict and proper sense, who finds in the scriptures what is not there; who ascribes to Moses and Christ doctrines and practices which they never approved.

A rational Christian must believe that his *own* construction of the Hebrew writings is the only true one; that every reputed Jew is merely a Jew in name; that he totally mistakes the meaning of the sacred books, and is as far from being a genuine worshipper of *the God of Israel,* as a Mahometan or Hindoo. In embracing christianity, the rational man believes that he is fulfilling the law and the prophets, and is conforming strictly to the directions of Jehovah and his servant Moses.

But admitting that the creed of a proper Jew must *exclude* a belief in Christ, that negative alone does not make a Jew. Unless we admit a man to be what he chooses to call himself, we must confer the name of Jew only on him whose positive constructions of the law are true.

There are three sects of reputed or nominal Jews. One confines its faith to the pentateuch; another adheres exclusively to the *mishna,* or body of Rabbinical traditions; a third sect embraces, at once, the mishna and the pentateuch. Now, which of these is the Jew?

Does the rejector of the books of Moses deserve this name? Among those whose guide is Moses, there is as great a variety of sects, in proportion to their number, as among Christians. Which of these sects contains the pure, unadulterated Jew?

These remarks show the difficulties which attend the subject, if we make opinion the criterion of Jew*ism*.

If, on the contrary, we consider this as a national distinction, we shall be obliged to load, with all the obligations and penalties of Jewism, thousands and millions who are descended from Jewish proselytes to the Christian faith. This people are, in reality, a miserable remnant, who owe the present fewness of their numbers to wide and incessant desertions. The miracle connected with the separate existence of the Jews, does not consist in the number having never been *impaired* by desertions, but that the persecution and contempt pursuing them for so many ages, have not occasioned the conversion, and consequent disappearance, of the *whole*.

The Inquisition has had wonderful influence in lessening the number of reputed Jews, not by executions, but by forced or feigned conversions. A great number of the Portuguese nobility are descendants, in the fourth or fifth generation, from Jews, proselyted by the fear of exile, fire, and the wheel, and bear the tokens of their origin in their features.

If we confine this appellation to one who is at once of the Hebrew nation and the Hebrew faith, we shall still be involved in considerable difficulty; for how shall a Jew's genealogy be ascertained? How shall we discover that some reputed Jew is not descended from a Christian proselyte to Judaism, who has been incorporated, by marriage or adoption, at some time or another, with the nation? If descent be the standard, then the convert of St. Paul, and all his posterity, are Jews, as well as he whose father abandoned the fraternity last year; and the reputed Jew, whose ancestor three centuries ago become a proselyte to Judaism, is no Jew.

If opinion be the standard, then a convert to any form of Christianity ceases to be a Jew; and an aboriginal American becomes a Jew by circumcision or profession.

If opinion and descent together make a Jew, then it is impossible to ascertain the genuineness of a Jew. If indefinite pedigree be not necessary to make a Jew, what number of generations must pass before he acquires all the penalties and privileges annexed to this people? Are they five, ten, fifteen, or twenty generations? And where is to be found the tree of any Jew's pedigree?

In short, Mr. Editor, before I answer any of your correspondent's queries, I should be glad to know what a Jew is.

QUERIST.

7. Charles Brockden Brown, excerpts from "On the Consequences of Abolishing the Slave Trade to the West Indian Colonies." *The Literary Magazine and American Register* 4:26 (November 1805).

In this essay, Brown rejects the idea that Africans are intrinsically inferior to Europeans and rejects as nonsensical racialist physiognomic claims that differences in physical appearances between ethnic groups can be used to hierarchize them. Throughout the piece he recapitulates the arguments of 1790s abolitionists in his circle; see "Three Abolitionist Addresses" in Related Texts. Drawing on early sociological conventions developed in the period's Scottish Enlightenment in works such as Adam Ferguson's Essay on the History of Civil Society *(1767), Brown argues for the progressive amelioration of conditions and opportunities for ex-slaves, which would produce their empowering self-control and integration into American society (rather than repatriation to Africa) by means that include interracial marriage.*

Brown's repeated claim that African slaves exist in a lower state of civilization sounds more ominous than it ought to contemporary readers because we hear the term "civilization" as evaluating the behavior of ethnic or national groups. For eighteenth-century writers like Brown, however, "civilization" is not an essential, permanent characteristic or achievement of certain groups, but rather a stage (or mode) of social organization that is historically mutable. In this sense, Brown does consider some civilizations as better than others in that enlightened and egalitarian societies are better than feudal ones run by warrior and priestly castes. In this tradition, the creation of a "civil society" is a historical process of "civil-ization." This contrast between civilizations has nothing to do with place or ethno-racial origins. If African slaves act badly, this is because, as Brown and Godwin insist, humans are products of their social environment and the conditions of slavery are inherently degrading. In Arthur Mervyn, *Mervyn himself considers that he is in need of civilization through greater experience with different societies.*

Throughout the piece, Brown labors to compare the current state of African slavery to that of medieval Europe with its serf labor. Just as Europeans could only create the Enlightenment after their mass emancipation from conditions of bound labor, Africans will also be transformed by the abolition of slavery, a point proven by the almost spontaneous ability of independent Haiti to challenge European military and social technologies. The point of Brown's comparison is to remind his readers that their own not-so-distant ancestors were more similar to than different from Africans. Indeed, Brown emphasizes that even in Africa, the farther away we go from the coastlines of Atlantic slavery and its brutalizing mercantile flesh trade, the more we see evidence of (Muslim) civilization. By the second half of the eighteenth-century, English and French explorers were slowly making their way into Africa's interior, where they reported on its complex societies. It was one of the dubious achievements of later, nineteenth-century European writers to erase the prior century's recognition of African achievements and reverse the prior progressive definition of civilization into its more commonly understood quasiaristocratic and racist sense.

*****

THE probable fate of the negro race in the American colonies, is an interesting subject at all times, in a merely speculative view. It comprehends various questions of high importance in the philosophy of man; it touches on the destinies of a large portion of the species, on the event to be expected from the grandest and most cruel experiment that ever was tried upon human nature; the sudden and violent transportation of immense multitudes of savages to distant regions and new climates, and their forcible and instantaneous exposure to a state of comparative civilization.[. . .]

[. . .] Till the slave trade is at once boldly and totally abolished (for in the present circumstances delay is not prudence; it is rashness, in fact, though it may result, like many other kinds of temerity, from real cowardice); till the root of all the evil is hardily struck at, and the main, universal cause of all danger destroyed, an hour's quiet cannot be expected in the slave colonies, nor any sensible alleviation of the manifold evils which crowd the picture of West Indian society.[. . .]

That the bad qualities ascribed to the negroes, often with great justice, belong rather to their habits than to their nature, and are derived either from the low state of civilization in which the whole race at present is placed, or from the manifold hardships of their situation in the colonies, is not only consistent with analogy, but is deducible from facts. The travellers who have visited interior Africa, where the influence of the slave-trade is much less felt than on the west coast, assure us, that the natural dispositions of the negro race are mild, gentle, and amiable in a high degree: that, far from wanting ingenuity, they have made no contemptible progress in the arts; and have even united into political societies of great extent and complicated structure, notwithstanding the obstacles arising from their remote situation, and their want of water-carriage: that their disposition to voluntary and continued exertions of body and mind, their capacity of industry, the great promoter of all human improvement, is not inferior to the same principle in other tribes, in similar situations: in fine, that they have the same propensity to improve both their condition, their faculties, and their virtues, conspicuous in the human character over all the rest of the world. Let us compare the general circumstances of any European nation; the character, both for talents and virtues of its inhabitants, at two distant periods. How remarkable is the contrast between them! Little more than a century ago, Russia was covered with hordes of barbarians; cheating, drinking, brutal lust, and ferocious rage, were as well known, and as little blamed, among the nobles of the czar's court, as the more polished and mitigated forms of the same vices are at this day in Petersburgh; literature never appeared among its inhabitants; and you might travel several days journey, without meeting a man, even among the higher classes, qualified for one moment's rational conversation. . . . Though the various circumstances of *external* improvement will not totally conceal, even at this day, and among the first classes, the *"vestigia ruris,"*[1] yet no one can deny that the stuff of which Russians are made has been greatly and fundamentally improved; that their capacities and virtues rapidly unfolding, as their habits have been changed, and their communication with the rest of mankind extended. A century ago, it would have been just as miraculous to read a tolerable Russian poem, or find a society of Boyars[2] where a rational person could spend his time with satisfaction, as it would be at this day, to find the same

---

[1] *"Vestigia ruris"*: vestiges or traces of the rustic past. From Horace, *Epistles* 2.1.160: *Sed in longum tamen ævum Manserunt, hodieque manent* vestigia ruris ". . . yet for many a year lived on, and still live on, traces of our rustic past" (Loeb tr. H. R. Fairclough). The phrase from Horace was well known to Brown's Latinate readership and a way of saying something like "primitive cultural origins."

[2] "Boyars": the highest rank of the Russian aristocracy in the early modern period.

prodigies at Houssa or Tombuctoo:[3] and those who argue about races, and despise the effect of circumstances, would have had the same right to decide upon the fate of all the Russias, from an inspection of the Calmuc skull,[4] as they now have to condemn all Africa to everlasting barbarism, from the craniums, colour, and wool of its inhabitants. If we allow that there will always be a sensible difference between the negro and the European, yet why should we suppose that this disparity will be greater than between the Sclavonian and Gothic nations?[5] No one denies that all the families of mankind are capable of great improvement. And though, after all, some tribes should remain inferior to others, it would be ridiculous on that account to deny the possibility of greatly civilizing even the most untoward tribe, or the importance of the least considerable advances which it may be capable of making. That the progress of any race of men, or of the whole species, in the various branches of virtue and power, must be infinite, was never maintained by sound reasoners. But that this progress is indefinite; that no limit can be assigned to its extent or acceleration, is beyond all reasonable controversy.

The superiority of a negro in the interior of Africa to one on the Slave Coast[6] is notorious. The enemies of the slave-trade reasonably impute the degeneracy of the maritime tribes to that baneful commerce. Its friends have, on the other hand, deduced from thence an argument against the negro character, which, say they, is not improved by intercourse with civilized nations. But the *fact* is admitted. Mr. Park observed it in the north, and Mr. Barrow in the tribes south of the line, who increase in civilization as you leave the Slave Coast.[7] Compare the accounts given by these travellers, of the skill, the industry, the excellent moral qualities of the Africans in Houssa and Tombuctoo, &c., with the pictures that have been drawn of the same race, living in all the barbarity which the supply of slave ships requires; you will be convinced that the negro is as much improved by a change of circumstances as the white. The state of slavery is in no case favourable to improvement; yet, compare the Creole negro with the imported slave, and you will find that even the most debasing form of

---

[3] "Houssa . . . Tombuctoo": African cities that are Gao and Timbuktu, Mali. Both were important Muslim trading cities.

[4] "Calmuc skull": now spelled Kalmyk, from Kalmykia, an area near the Caspian Sea, as of the 2000s a part of the Russian Federation bordering Georgia and Azerbaijan. Brown seems to be lampooning the physiognomical work of Johan Caspar Lavatar (1741–1801), which he knew from the 1794 American edition of Lavater's *Essays on Physiognomy . . . abridged from Mr. Holcroft's translation* (Boston). There Lavater sequentially compares the skull shapes of a Dutchman (as normative European), a Calmuc (as Eurasian), and an Ethiopian (as African).

[5] "Sclavonian and Gothic nations": immediately referring to the Slavic and Germanic peoples but, more broadly, the difference between Western and Eastern Europe.

[6] "Slave Coast": the coastal region of current Togo, Benin, and Nigeria.

[7] "Mr. Park . . . and Mr. Barrow": Mungo Park (1771–1806), Scottish explorer of interior Africa and author of *Travels in the Interior Districts of Africa in the Years 1795, 1796 and 1797* (London, 1799); John Barrow (1764–1848), a British diplomat who served during the late 1790s in what is today South Africa; author of *Travels into the Interior of South Africa* (London, 1802).

servitude, though it necessarily eradicates most of the moral qualities of the African, has not prevented him from profiting intellectually by the intercourse of more civilized men. The war of St. Domingo reads us a memorable lesson; negroes organizing immense armies; laying plans of campaigns and sieges, which, if not scientific, have at least been successful against the finest European troops; arranging forms of government, and even proceeding some length in executing the most difficult of human enterprizes; entering into commercial relations with foreigners, and conceiving the idea of alliances; acquiring something like a maritime force, and, at any rate, navigating vessels in the tropical seas, with as much skill and foresight as that complicated operation requires.

This spectacle ought to teach us the effects of circumstances upon the human faculties, and prescribe bounds to that arrogance, which would confine to one race, the characteristics of the species. We have torn those men from their country, on the vain pretence, that their nature is radically inferior to our own. We have treated them so as to stunt the natural growth of their virtues and their reason. Our efforts have partly succeeded; for the West Indian, like all other slaves, has copied some of the tyrant's vices. But their ingenuity has advanced apace, under all disadvantages; and the negroes are already so much improved, that, while we madly continue to despise them, and to justify the crimes which have transplanted them, it has really become doubtful how long they will suffer us to exist in the islands.

[. . .] There is nothing in the physical or moral constitution of the negro, which renders him an exception to the general character of the species, and prevents him from improving in all estimable qualities, when placed in favourable circumstances. Nay, under all possible disadvantages, *we* see the progress he is capable of making, whether insulated by the deserts of Africa, or surrounded by the slave factories of Europeans, or groaning under the cruelties of the West Indian system. This progress will be accelerated in proportion as those impediments are removed; while Africa is civilized by legitimate commerce with the more polished nations of the world, the negroes already in the West Indies will rapidly improve, as soon as the abolition shall begin to ameliorate their treatment.

It will not be long before milder treatment will increase the productive powers of negro labour. [. . .] The history of all Europe demonstrates the effects which the mild treatment of the labouring orders naturally produces on the value of their industry.

The proprietors of Hungary, almost immediately after the reform of Maria Theresa,[8] began to feel the salutary consequences of the limitations of the corvées[9] due from their peasants. When, instead of full power over the whole of the serf's

---

[8] "Reform of Maria Theresa": the enlightened Habsburg Queen of Hungary and Bohemia 1740–1780. In 1771 Maria Theresa gave peasants land tenure and abolished the "Robot Patent," an oppressive feudal peasant rent that allowed nobles to monopolize land.

[9] "Corvées": unpaid mass labor; the corvée was a feudal institution, an annual tax paid through labor (by serfs or villeins) for the landowner to whom they were bound. By extension the word is used to described the mass forced labor used in prefeudal eras to build immense projects like the great pyramids of Egypt or the Great Wall of China.

labour, the lord could only take two days in each week, he found those two worth much more than all the seven had been before; though at the same time, he lost the right of retaining the peasant on his ground against his will. If such mitigations are favourable to the master, still more advantageous must they be to the slave. [. . .] The new mode of treatment would render *universal* task-work, not only an easy, but a necessary improvement. And when these changes shall have been effected slowly, and with the consent of all proprietors, not taken by vote, but freely given by each individual; will not the lower orders in the islands be exactly in the state of the *ascripti glebæ*[10] under the milder feudal governments of the old world? It is but one step to make them *coloni partiarii*,[11] or serf tenants paying a proportion of their crops to the lord. Such they are already in some parts of Spanish and Portuguese America, where the richest ores and pearls are obtained, by means of this very contract between the master and his slave. Nor does it much signify in what form the last change of all shall then be effected by the total emancipation of the negro. He will, by this natural gradation, have become civilized to a certain degree, and fully capable of enjoying the station of a free man, for which all are fitted by nature. In the course of time, we may hope to see the same relaxation of prejudice against him among the whites, which has made the European baron cease to look down upon his serf as an inferior animal. The mixture even of the races, is a thing by no means impossible, and will remove the only pretext that can remain for supposing the West Indian society, as new-modelled by the abolition, to be in the smallest degree different from the society in Europe, after the successors of the Romans ceased to procure slaves in commerce.

---

[10] "*Ascripti glebæ*": in Latin literally those "bound to the soil" or earth, the lowest class of serf laborers in the feudal system; "villeins" with no property of their own.

[11] "*Coloni partiarii*": a class of serf laborers (literally "sharers in the plantation" or share farmers) in late Roman and medieval feudalism who could own property themselves and were thus one step better off than villainage workers. Sometimes glossed with the old French derived "métayage" or as "sharecroppers." Adam Smith discusses the transition to *coloni partiarii* status in *Wealth of Nations* III.2 (1776), in a passage on slavery that also mentions the Quaker-driven abolition of slavery in Pennsylvania. Friedrich Engels discusses this transition with similar side comparisons to modern and U.S. race slavery in Chapter 8 of *The Origin of the Family, Private Property, and the State* (1884).

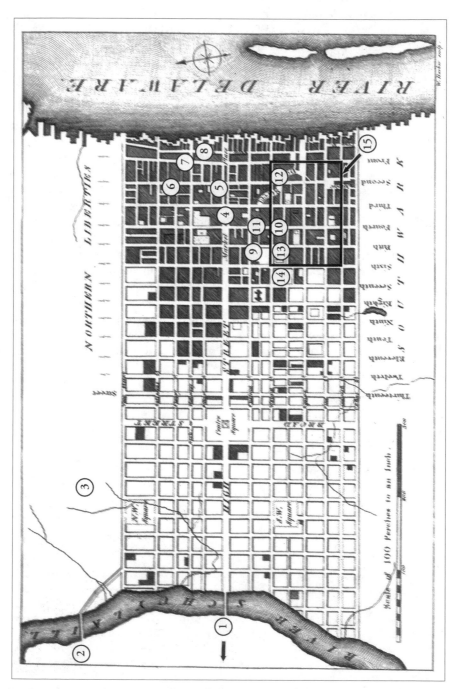

Map courtesy the Library Company of Philadelphia.

1. Chester County (Ch. 2)
2. Upper bridge across the Schuylkill (Ch. 3)
3. Bush-Hill Emergency Hospital (Ch. 17)
4. High Street Market Houses (Ch. 3; also site of "Jersey Market" in Ch. II.2)
5. Christ Church (just above North Second and Market; Chapter II.2)
6. Lesher's Tavern (94 North Second, between Arch and Race; Ch. 3)
7. Front Street (Ch. 3);
8. Water Street (Ch. II.3);
9. City Hall (Ch. 19);
10. South Fourth Street (Mrs. Wentworth's residence; Ch. 7)
11. Indian Queen Inn (on South Fourth, likely the Inn mentioned in Ch. 17)
12. No. 40, Walnut Street (Achsa Fielding's address; Ch. II.16);
13. Prune Street Debtor's Prison (Ch. II.4);
14. Washington Square, known as Congo Square, a meeting place for slaves, and a burial field for laboring-class yellow fever victims;
15. Society Hill neighborhood (homes of Welbeck, Thetford, and Mrs. Wentworth)

8. William Birch, "Plan of the City of Philadelphia" (1800).

The map reproduced here was originally printed in William Birch & Sons' The City of Philadelphia . . . as it appeared in the Year 1800, a book of etchings or urban "views" that was published at the same moment as Arthur Mervyn. Birch's book was an important visual representation of Philadelphia's self-consciously "modern" urban space and provides many points of comparison with Brown's literary depiction. Birch's plates are available for viewing on websites and may provide an interesting accompaniment to the novel; see, for example, Birch's views from within the market houses on Market Street that are described with quotations from Milton in the novel's Chapter 3.

Birch's views idealize the city and its urban space as an orderly, hygienic realm that is notably free of crowds and the poor; somewhat like the promotional views that accompany today's urban development and architectural projects. Whereas Birch visualizes a tranquil and "improved" metropolis whose visible prosperity is based on an implicitly uplifting commerce, Brown's novel articulates the city's social spaces and commercial links to the Atlantic world in very different terms.

The version of Birch's map provided here gives the reader a basic idea of the city's situation between the Schuylkill and Delaware rivers and indicates how the urbanized area as of the 1790s was roughly a triangle with its base along the Delaware River and its peak at about Eighth and Market Streets; streets were projected all the way to the Schuylkill but as yet remained undeveloped west of this urbanized core. This version of the map is additionally coded to indicate other locales that figure in Arthur Mervyn, such as the Bush-Hill hospital, the Upper crossing of the Schuylkill, or the Society Hill neighborhood in which much of the novel's urban action takes place.

The Birch map is scaled at "100 Perches to an Inch." A "perch" or "rod" was a unit of measurement standardized in the eighteenth century to five and one half yards, or five and three tenths meters. The distance along High (Market) Street between the Delaware and Schuylkill Rivers is approximately two miles.

9. William Godwin, excerpts from *Enquiry Concerning Political Justice and Its Influence on Modern Morals and Happiness* (1793).

William Godwin (1756–1836) was at the center of British progressive politics in the 1790s. His Enquiry Concerning Political Justice *is a key work of the Woldwinite circle, the most complete articulation of its social principles and program. Along with Mary Wollstonecraft and Thomas Paine, Godwin was tremendously popular and influential among the college-educated young men who formed the core of Brown's associates. These writings operate as the common sense and moral compass for Brown's group, who corresponded with Godwin as early as 1796.*

Brown had access to Political Justice *in several editions. These excerpts follow the second (1796) edition in the Philadelphia printing by Bioren and Madan, the edition Brown probably used during his novelistic years. The excerpts insist on the social degradation and psychic damage caused by inequalities of wealth, the obligation to struggle for social reform through rational improvements, the power of benevolence as it acts through associative sentiment, and the importance of intimate conversation and transparency of personal motivation in setting the stage for larger social and historical transformations.*

*****

Book I (*Of the Powers of Man Considered in His Social Capacity*), Chapter III: *Spirit of Political Institutions*

Two of the greatest abuses relative to the interior policy of nations, which at this time prevail in the world, consist in the irregular transfer of property, either first by violence, or secondly by fraud. If among the inhabitants of any country there existed no desire in one individual to possess himself of the substance of another, or no desire so vehement and restless as to prompt him to acquire it by means inconsistent with order and justice, undoubtedly in that country guilt could scarcely be known but by report. If every man could with perfect facility obtain the necessaries of life, and, obtaining them, feel no uneasy craving after its superfluities, temptation would lose its power. Private interest would visibly accord with public good; and civil society become what poetry has feigned of the golden age. Let us enquire into the principles to which these abuses are indebted for their existence.

First then it is to be observed that, in the most refined states of Europe, the inequality of property has risen to an alarming height. Vast numbers of their inhabitants are deprived of almost every accommodation that can render life tolerable or secure. Their utmost industry scarcely suffices for their support. The women and children lean with an insupportable weight upon the efforts of the man, so that a large family has in the lower orders of life become a proverbial expression for an uncommon degree of poverty and wretchedness. If sickness, or some of those casualties which are perpetually incident to an active and laborious life, be added to these burdens, the distress is yet greater.

It seems to be agreed that in England there is less wretchedness and distress than in most of the kingdoms of the continent. In England the poors' rates amount to the sum of two millions sterling per annum. It has been calculated that one person in seven of the inhabitants of this country derives at some period of his life assistance from this fund. If to this we add the persons who, from pride, a spirit of independence, or the want of a legal settlement, though in equal distress receive no such assistance, the proportion will be considerably increased.

I lay no stress upon the accuracy of this calculation; the general fact is sufficient to give us an idea of the greatness of the abuse. The consequences that result are placed beyond the reach of contradiction. A perpetual struggle with the evils of poverty, if frequently ineffectual, must necessarily render many of the sufferers desperate. A painful feeling of their oppressed situation will itself deprive them of the power of surmounting it. The superiority of the rich, being thus unmercifully exercised, must inevitably expose them to reprisals; and the poor man will be induced to regard the state of society as a state of war, an unjust combination, not for protecting every man in his rights and securing to him the means of existence, but for engrossing all its advantages to a few favoured individuals, and reserving for the portion of the rest want, dependence and misery.

A second source of those destructive passions by which the peace of society is interrupted is to be found in the luxury, the pageantry and magnificence with which enormous wealth is usually accompanied. Human beings are capable of encountering with cheerfulness considerable hardships when those hardships are impartially shared with the rest of the society, and they are not insulted with the spectacle of indolence and ease in others, no way deserving of greater advantages than themselves. But it is a bitter aggravation of their own calamity, to have the privileges of others forced on their observation, and, while they are perpetually and vainly endeavouring to secure for themselves and their families the poorest conveniences, to find others revelling in the fruits of their labours. This aggravation is assiduously administered to them under most of the political establishments at present in existence. There is a numerous class of individuals who, though rich, have neither brilliant talents nor sublime virtues; and, however highly they may prize their education, their affability, their superior polish and the elegance of their manners, have a secret consciousness that they possess nothing by which they can so securely assert their pre-eminence and keep their inferiors at a distance as the splendour of their equipage, the magnificence of their retinue and the sumptuousness of their entertainments. The poor man is struck with this exhibition; he feels his own miseries; he knows how unwearied are his efforts to obtain a slender pittance of this prodigal waste; and he mistakes opulence for felicity. He cannot persuade himself that an embroidered garment may frequently cover an aching heart.

A third disadvantage that is apt to connect poverty with discontent consists in the insolence and usurpation of the rich. If the poor man would in other respects compose himself in philosophic indifference, and, conscious that he possesses every thing that is truly honourable to man as fully as his rich neighbour, would look upon the rest as beneath his envy, his neighbour will not permit him to do so. He seems as if he could never be satisfied with his possessions unless he can make the spectacle of them grating to others; and that honest self-esteem, by which his inferior might otherwise attain to tranquillity, is rendered the instrument of galling him with oppression and injustice. In many countries justice is avowedly made a subject of solicitation, and the man of the highest rank and most splendid connections almost infallibly carries his cause against the unprotected and friendless. In countries where this shameless practice is not established, justice is frequently a matter of expensive purchase, and the man with the longest purse is proverbially victorious. A consciousness of these facts must be expected to render the rich little cautious of offence in his dealings with the poor, and to inspire him with a temper overbearing, dictatorial and tyrannical. Nor does this indirect oppression satisfy his despotism. The rich are in all such countries directly or indirectly the legislators of the state; and of consequence are perpetually reducing oppression into a system, and depriving the poor of that little commonage of nature which might otherwise still have remained to them.

*****

Book I, Chapter IV: *The Characters of Men Originate in Their External Circumstances*

Under this branch of the subject I shall attempt to prove two things: first, that the actions and dispositions of mankind are the offspring of circumstances and events, and not of any original determination that they bring into the world; and, secondly, that the great stream of our voluntary actions essentially depends, not upon the direct and immediate impulses of sense, but upon the decisions of the understanding.

*****

Book I, Chapter V: *The Voluntary Actions of Men Originate in Their Opinions*

The corollaries respecting political truth, deducible from the simple proposition, which seems clearly established by the reasonings of the present chapter, that the voluntary actions of men are in all instances conformable to the deductions of their understanding, are of the highest importance. Hence we may infer what are the hopes and prospects of human improvement. The doctrine which may be founded upon these principles may perhaps best be expressed in the five following propositions: sound reasoning and truth, when adequately communicated, must always be victorious over error: sound reasoning and truth are capable of being so communicated: truth is omnipotent: the vices and moral weakness of man are not invincible: man is perfectible, or in other words susceptible of perpetual improvement.

*****

Book II (*Principals of Society*), Chapter IV: *Of Personal Virtue and Duty*

In the first sense I would define virtue to be any action or actions of an intelligent being proceeding from kind and benevolent intention, and having a tendency to contribute to general happiness. Thus defined, it distributes itself under two heads; and, in whatever instance either the tendency or the intention is wanting, the virtue is incomplete. An action, however pure may be the intention of the agent, the tendency of which is mischievous, or which shall merely be nugatory and useless in its character, is not a virtuous action. Were it otherwise, we should be obliged to concede the appellation of virtue to the most nefarious deeds of bigots, persecutors and religious assassins, and to the weakest observances of a deluded superstition. Still less does an action, the consequences of which shall be supposed to be in the highest degree beneficial, but which proceeds from a mean, corrupt and degrading motive, deserve the appellation of virtue. A virtuous action is that, of which both the motive and the tendency concur to excite our approbation.

*****

Book IV (*Of the Operation of Opinion in Societies and Individuals*), Chapter I: *Of Resistance*

The strong hold of government has appeared hitherto to have consisted in seduction. However imperfect might be the political constitution under which they lived, mankind have ordinarily been persuaded to regard it with a sort of reverential and implicit respect. The privileges of Englishmen, and the liberties of Germany, the splendour of the most Christian, and the solemn gravity of the Catholic king, have each afforded a subject of exultation to the individuals who shared, or thought they shared, in the advantages these terms were conceived to describe. Each man was accustomed to deem it a mark of the peculiar kindness of providence that he was born in the country, whatever it was, to which he happened to belong. The time may come which shall subvert these prejudices. The time may come when men shall exercise the piercing search of truth upon the mysteries of government, and view without prepossession the defects and abuses of the constitution of their country. Out of this new order of things a new series of duties will arise. When a spirit of impartiality shall prevail, and loyalty shall decay, it will become us to enquire into the conduct which such a state of thinking shall make necessary. We shall then be called upon to maintain a true medium between blindness to injustice and calamity on the one hand, and an acrimonious spirit of violence and resentment on the other. It will be the duty of such as shall see these subjects in the pure light of truth to exert themselves for the effectual demolition of monopolies and usurpation; but effectual demolition is not the offspring of crude projects and precipitate measures. He who dedicates himself to these may be suspected to be under the domination of passion, rather than benevolence. The true friend of equality will do nothing unthinkingly, will cherish no wild schemes of uproar and confusion, and will endeavour to discover the mode in which his faculties may be laid out to the greatest and most permanent advantage.

The whole of this question is intimately connected with the enquiry which has necessarily occupied a share in the disquisitions of all writers on the subject of government, concerning the propriety and measures of resistance. "Are the worst government and best equally entitled to the toleration and forbearance of their subjects? Is there no case of political oppression that will authorize the persons who suffer it to take up arms against their oppressors? Or, if there be, what is the quantity of oppression at the measure of which insurrections begin to be justifiable? Abuses will always exist, for man will always be imperfect; what is the nature of the abuse which it would be pusillanimous to oppose by words only, and which true courage would instruct us was to be endured no longer?"

No question can be conceived more important than this. In the examination of it philosophy almost forgets its nature; it ceases to be speculation, and becomes an actor. Upon the decision, according as it shall be decided in the minds of a bold and resolute party, the existence of thousands may be suspended. The speculative enquirer, if he live in a state where abuse is notorious and grievances frequent, knows not, while he weighs the case in the balance of reason, how far that which he attempts to describe is already realized in the apprehension of numbers of his countrymen. Let us enter upon the question with the seriousness which so critical an inquiry demands.

Resistance may have its source in the emergencies either of the public or the individual. "A nation," it has commonly been said, "has a right to shake off any authority that is usurped over it." This is a proposition that has generally passed without question, and certainly no proposition can appear more plausible. But, if we examine it minutely, we shall find that it is attended with equivocal circumstances. What do we mean by a nation? Is the whole people concerned in this resistance, or only a part? If the whole be prepared to resist, the whole is persuaded of the injustice of the usurpation. What sort of usurpation is that which can be exercised by one or a few persons over a whole nation universally disapproving of it? Government is founded in opinion. Bad government deceives us first, before it fastens itself upon us like an incubus, oppressing all our efforts. A nation in general must have learned to respect a king and a house of lords, before a king and a house of lords can exercise any authority over them. If a man or a set of men, unsanctioned by any previous prejudice in their favour, pretend to exercise sovereignty in a country, they will become objects of derision rather than of serious resistance. Destroy the existing prejudice in favour of any of our present institutions, and they will fall into similar disuse and contempt.

✶✶✶✶✶

Book IV, Chapter III: *Of Political Associations*

Books have by their very nature but a limited operation; though, on account of their permanence, their methodical disquisition, and their easiness of access, they are entitled to the foremost place. The number of those who almost wholly abstain from reading is exceedingly great. Books, to those by whom they are read, have a sort of constitutional coldness. We review the arguments of an "insolent innovator" with sullenness, and are unwilling to expand our minds to take in their force. It is with difficulty that we obtain the courage to strike into untrodden paths, and question tenets that have been generally received. But conversation accustoms us to hear a variety of sentiments, obliges us to exercise patience and attention, and gives freedom and elasticity to our disquisitions. A thinking man, if he will recollect his intellectual history, will find that he has derived inestimable benefit from the stimulus and surprise of colloquial suggestions; and, if he review the history of literature, will perceive that minds of great acuteness and ability have commonly existed in a cluster.

It follows that the promoting the best interests of mankind eminently depends upon the freedom of social communication. Let us figure to ourselves a number of individuals who, having stored their minds with reading and reflection, are accustomed, in candid and unreserved conversation, to compare their ideas, suggest their doubts, examine their mutual difficulties and cultivate a perspicuous and animated manner of delivering their sentiments. Let us suppose that their intercourse is not confined to the society of each other, but that they are desirous extensively to communicate the truths with which they are acquainted. Let us suppose their illustrations to be not more distinguished by impartiality and demonstrative clearness than by the mildness of their temper, and a spirit of comprehensive benevolence. We shall then have an idea of knowledge as perpetually gaining ground, unaccompanied with peril in the means of its diffusion. Their hearers will be instigated to impart their acquisitions to still other hearers, and the circle of instruction will perpetually increase. Reason will spread, and not a brute and unintelligent sympathy.

✳✳✳✳✳

Book IV, Chapter VI: *Of Sincerity*

The powerful recommendations attendant upon sincerity are obvious. It is intimately connected with the general dissemination of innocence, energy, intellectual improvement, and philanthropy.

Did every man impose this law upon himself, did he regard himself as not authorized to conceal any part of his character and conduct, this circumstance alone would prevent millions of actions from being perpetrated in which we are now induced to engage by the prospect of secrecy and impunity. We have only to suppose men obliged to consider, before they determined upon an equivocal action, whether they chose to be their own historians, the future narrators of the scene in which they were acting a part, and the most ordinary imagination will instantly suggest how essential a variation would be introduced into human affairs. It has been justly observed that the popish practice of confession is attended with some salutary effects. How much better would it be if, instead of an institution thus equivocal, and which has been made so dangerous an instrument of ecclesiastical despotism, every man were to make the world his confessional, and the human species the keeper of his conscience?

There is a further benefit that would result to me from the habit of telling every man the truth, regardless of the dictates of worldly prudence and custom. I should acquire a clear, ingenuous and unembarrassed air. According to the established modes of society, whenever I have a circumstance to state which would require some effort of mind and discrimination to enable me to do it justice, and state it with the proper effect, I fly from the talk, and take refuge in silence or equivocation. But the principle which forbad me concealment would keep my mind for ever awake, and for ever warm. I should always be obliged to exert my attention, lest, in pretending to tell the truth, I should tell it in so imperfect and mangled a way as to produce the effect of falsehood. If I spoke to a man of my own faults or those of his neighbour, I should be anxious not to suffer them to come distorted or exaggerated to his mind, or to permit what at first was fact to degenerate into satire. If I spoke to him of the errors he had himself committed, I should carefully avoid those inconsiderate expressions which might convert what was in itself beneficent into offence; and my thoughts would be full of that kindness, and generous concern for his welfare, which such a talk necessarily brings along with it. Sincerity would liberate my mind, and make the eulogiums I had occasion to pronounce, clear, copious and appropriate. Conversation would speedily exchange its present character of listlessness and insignificance, for a Roman boldness and fervour; and, accustomed, at first by the fortuitous operation of circumstances, to tell men of things it was useful for them to know, I should speedily learn to study their advantage, and never rest satisfied with my conduct till I had discovered how to spend the hours I was in their company in the way which was most rational and improving.

✳✳✳✳✳

Book IV, Chapter X: *Of Self-Love And Benevolence*

The system of disinterested benevolence proves to us that it is possible to be virtuous, and not merely to talk of virtue; that all which has been said by philosophers and moralists respecting impartial justice is not an unmeaning rant; and that, when we call upon mankind to divest themselves of selfish and personal considerations, we call upon them for something they are able to practise. An idea like this reconciles us to our species; teaches us to regard, with enlightened admiration, the men who have appeared to lose the feeling of their personal existence, in the pursuit of general advantage; and gives us reason to expect that, as men collectively advance in science and useful institution, they will proceed more and more to consolidate their private judgement, and their individual will, with abstract justice, and the unmixed approbation of general happiness.

10. Mary Wollstonecraft, excerpts from *Letters Written during a Short Residence in Sweden, Norway, and Denmark* (1796).

Mary Wollstonecraft (1759–1797) was a major radical voice of the revolutionary age, remembered today primarily as a path-breaking feminist. Her ideas and writings on gender and revolutionary cultural politics were central, formative references for Brown and his circle, who frequently discussed her books. Brown's Alcuin *(1798), published before he wrote his longer fictions, rehearses many of the arguments in Wollstonecraft's* Vindication of the Rights of Woman *(1792) about the social factors that disempower women. Although less well known than her* Vindication, *the* Letters Written during a Short Residence *is regarded by some scholars today as the most important Anglophone travel narrative after Laurence Sterne's* Sentimental Journey *(1768; see the excerpt in Related Texts). Certainly they had an impact on Wollstonecraft's future husband, William Godwin, who wanted to meet their author after reading them.*

These excerpts from the narrative's Letters 19 and 23, concerning the prevalence of commercial fraud and the mercantile culture of the German city of Hamburg, provide suggestive parallels with Arthur Mervyn's *views of the mercantile city and its corruption as well as with Brown's characteristic, Wollstonecraft-derived emphasis on the domination of women as a structural feature of the social order. Wollstonecraft's sketch of Hamburg additionally dramatizes the impact of French elite refugees on Protestant urban culture, similar to the effects of the Caribbean Francophone refugees in* Arthur Mervyn *and the "Portrait of an Emigrant" sketch also in this volume's Related Texts.*

Wollstonecraft's dysfunctional relationship with U.S. adventurer Gilbert Imlay seems to be referenced in the backstory of Achsa Fielding in Brown's novel. Despite her rejection by Imlay and following her suicide attempt in response to this rejection (all recounted in Godwin's 1798 Memoirs of Wollstonecraft*), Mary agreed to undertake this extraordinary voyage as an unaccompanied woman vested with important business authorizations and traveled through northern Europe in a difficult attempt to rescue Imlay's speculative investment and possibly renew his affection. Her impatience with Imlay's involvement in mercantile speculation and fraud is clearly expressed in Letter 23, where the narrator addresses Imlay directly as "you." Overall, Wollstonecraft's travel narrative involves numerous precedents for the depiction of mercantile corruption in the context of revolutionary shipping and smuggling that plays such an important role in the background of* Arthur Mervyn.

*****

LETTER XIX.

[. . .] It moves my gall to discover some of the commercial frauds practiced during the present war. In short, under whatever point of view I consider society, it appears to me that an adoration of property is the root of all evil. Here it does not render the people enterprising, as in America, but thrifty and cautious. I never, therefore, was in a capital where there was so little appearance of active industry; and as for gaiety, I looked in vain for the sprightly gait of the Norwegians, who in every respect appear to me to have got the start of them. This difference I attribute to their having more liberty: a liberty which they think their right by inheritance, whilst the Danes, when they boast of their negative happiness, always mention it as the boon of the Prince Royal, under the superintending wisdom of Count Bernstorff. Vassalage is nevertheless ceasing throughout the kingdom, and with it will pass away that sordid avarice which every modification of slavery is calculated to produce.

If the chief use of property be power, in the shape of the respect it procures, is it not among the inconsistencies of human nature most incomprehensible, that men should find a pleasure in hoarding up property which they steal from their necessities, even when they are convinced that it would be dangerous to display such an enviable superiority? Is not this the situation of serfs in every country? Yet a rapacity to accumulate money seems to become stronger in proportion as it is allowed to be useless.

Wealth does not appear to be sought for amongst the Danes, to obtain the excellent luxuries of life, for a want of taste is very conspicuous at Copenhagen; so much so that I am not surprised to hear that poor Matilda offended the rigid Lutherans by aiming to refine their pleasures. The elegance which she wished to introduce was termed lasciviousness; yet I do not find that the absence of gallantry renders the wives more chaste, or the husbands more constant. Love here seems to corrupt the morals without polishing the manners, by banishing confidence and truth, the charm as well as cement of domestic life. A gentleman, who has resided in this city some time, assures me that he could not find language to give me an idea of the gross debaucheries into which the lower order of people fall; and the promiscuous amours of the men of the middling class with their female servants debase both beyond measure, weakening every species of family affection.

I have everywhere been struck by one characteristic difference in the conduct of the two sexes; women, in general, are seduced by their superiors, and men jilted by their inferiors: rank and manners awe the one, and cunning and wantonness subjugate the other; ambition creeping into the woman's passion, and tyranny giving force to the man's, for most men treat their mistresses as kings do their favourites: *ergo* is not man then the tyrant of the creation?

[. . .] I have before mentioned that the men are domestic tyrants, considering them as fathers, brothers, or husbands; but there is a kind of interregnum between the reign of the father and husband which is the only period of freedom and pleasure that the women enjoy. Young people who are attached to each other, with the consent of their friends, exchange rings, and are permitted to enjoy a degree of liberty together which I have never noticed in any other country. The days of courtship are, therefore, prolonged till it be perfectly convenient to marry: the intimacy often becomes very tender; and if the lover obtain the privilege of a husband, it can only be termed half by stealth, because the family is willfully blind. It happens very rarely that these honorary engagements are dissolved or disregarded, a stigma being attached to a breach of faith which is thought more disgraceful, if not so criminal, as the violation of the marriage-vow.

Do not forget that, in my general observations, I do not pretend to sketch a national character, but merely to note the present state of morals and manners as I trace the progress of the world's improvement. Because, during my residence in different countries, my principal object has been to take such a dispassionate view of men as will lead me to form a just idea of the nature of man. And, to deal ingenuously with you, I believe I should have been less severe in the remarks I have made on the vanity and depravity of the french, had I travelled towards the north before I visited France.

✳✳✳✳✳

LETTER XXIII.

[. . .] Hamburg is an ill, close-built town, swarming with inhabitants; and, from what I could learn, like all the other free towns, governed in a manner which bears hard on the poor, whilst narrowing the minds of the rich; the character of the man is lost in the Hamburger. Always afraid of the encroachments of their Danish neighbours, that is, anxiously apprehensive of their sharing the golden harvest of commerce with them, or taking a little of the trade off their hands—though they have more than they know what to do with—they are ever on the watch, till their very eyes lose all expression, excepting the prying glance of suspicion.

The gates of Hamburg are shut at seven, in the winter, and nine in the summer, lest some strangers, who come to traffic in Hamburg, should prefer living, and consequently—so exactly do they calculate—spend their money out of the walls of the Hamburger's world. Immense fortunes have been acquired by the *per-cents* arising from commissions nominally only two and a half; but mounted to eight or ten at least, by the secret *manoeuvres* of trade, not to include the advantage of purchasing goods wholesale, in common with contractors, and that of having so much money left in their hands—not to play with, I can assure you. Mushroom fortunes have started up during the war; the men, indeed, seem of the species of the fungus; and the insolent vulgarity which a sudden influx of wealth usually produces in common minds is here very conspicuous, which contrasts with the distresses of many of the emigrants, "fallen, fallen from their high estate," such are the ups and downs of fortune's wheel. Many emigrants have met, with fortitude, such a total change of circumstances as scarcely can be paralleled, retiring from a palace to an obscure lodging with dignity; but the greater number glide about, the ghosts of greatness, with the *croix de St. Louis* ostentatiously displayed, determined to hope, "though heaven and earth their wishes crossed." Still good breeding points out the gentleman; and sentiments of honour and delicacy appear the offspring of greatness of soul when compared with the groveling views of the sordid accumulators of *cent. per cent.*

Situation seems to be the mould in which men's characters are formed: so much so, inferring from what I have lately seen, that I mean not to be severe when I add—previously asking why priests are in general cunning and statesmen false?—that men entirely devoted to commerce never acquire or lose all taste and greatness of mind. An ostentatious display of wealth without elegance, and a greedy enjoyment of pleasure without sentiment, embrutes them till they term all virtue of an heroic cast, romantic attempts at something above our nature, and anxiety about the welfare of others, a search after misery in which we have no concern. But you will say that I am growing bitter, perhaps personal. Ah! shall I whisper to you, that you yourself are strangely altered since you have entered deeply into commerce—more than you are aware of; never allowing yourself to reflect, and keeping your mind, or rather passions, in a continual state of agitation? Nature has given you talents which lie dormant, or are wasted in ignoble pursuits. You will rouse yourself and shake off the vile dust that obscures you, or my understanding, as well as my heart, deceives me egregiously—only tell me when. But to go farther a-field.

[. . .] At Altona, a president of one of the *ci-devant* parliaments keeps an ordinary, in the French style; and his wife with cheerful dignity submits to her fate, though she is arrived at an age when people seldom relinquish their prejudices. A girl who waits there brought a dozen *double louis d'or* concealed in her clothes, at the risk of her life, from France, which she preserves lest sickness or any other distress should overtake her mistress, "who," she observed, "was not accustomed to hardships." This house was particularly recommended to me by an acquaintance of yours, the author of the American Farmer's Letters.[1] I generally dine in company with him: and the gentleman whom I have already mentioned is often diverted by our declamations against commerce, when we compare notes respecting the characteristics of the Hamburgers. "Why, madam," said he to me one day, "you will not meet with a man who has any calf to his leg; body and soul, muscles and heart, are equally shrivelled up by a thirst of gain. There is nothing generous even in their youthful passions; profit is their only stimulus, and calculations the sole employment of their faculties, unless we except some gross animal gratifications which, snatched *at spare moments*, tend still more to debase the character, because, though touched by his tricking wand, they have all the arts, without the wit, of the wing-footed god."

Perhaps you may also think us too severe; but I must add that the more I saw of the manners of Hamburg, the more was I confirmed in my opinion relative to the baleful effect of extensive speculations on the moral character. Men are strange machines; and their whole system of morality is in general held together by one grand principle which loses its force the moment they allow themselves to break with impunity over the bounds which secured their self-respect. A man ceases to love humanity, and then

---

[1] "Author of the American Farmer's Letters": John Dickinson, *Letters from a Farmer in Pennsylvania: To the Inhabitants of the British Colonies* (Philadelphia and London, 1774).

individuals, as he advances in the chase after wealth; as one clashes with his interest, the other with his pleasures: to business, as it is termed, everything must give way; nay, is sacrificed, and all the endearing charities of citizen, husband, father, brother, become empty names. But—but what? Why, to snap the chain of thought, I must say farewell. Cassandra was not the only prophetess whose warning voice has been disregarded. How much easier it is to meet with love in the world than affection!

11. Laurence Sterne, excerpt from *A Sentimental Journey through France and Italy* (1768).

Scholars have noted that Arthur Mervyn's *stagecoach scene, set during a ride through the slave state of Maryland to Baltimore in Chapter II.17, is intended to provoke reflections on slavery and race. It is also important to note, in this connection, that the passage draws on the then well-known starling scene and stagecoach ambience of Laurence Sterne's* Sentimental Journey, *invoking Sterne's influential mobilization of sensibility and associative sentiment for abolitionist discourses. Brown's stylistic allusions to Sterne, in Mervyn's "sentimentalized" outbursts in the novel's last section, arguably link this Sternean reflection to Mervyn's own voice as it takes over the narrative from Dr. Stevens and organizes the romance's conclusion after Chapter II.16.*

Laurence Sterne (1713–1768) was a key reference for writers of the revolutionary period. His novel The Life and Opinions of Tristram Shandy *(1759–1769) became a standard source for the prose stylistics of enlightened sensibility that are frequently emulated and referenced by Brown's Woldwinite models. A* Sentimental Journey, *Sterne's final narrative, is a sequel to* Tristram Shandy *that follows that novel's character Yorick on a voyage to the continent and was primarily understood as a showcase for the representation of sensibility and its progressive cultural implications. The excerpt here provides most of the episode concerning the pet starling, an emblem of slavery that provides the precedent for the pet monkey named "Dominique" in Brown's novel. The passage begins with the starling's appearance as a literalization of the narrator Yorick's anxieties about being imprisoned in the Bastille and develops into a polemic on slavery as the imprisoned black bird is shifted from owner to owner as a token of social domination, without ever being freed. As critic Markman Ellis has noted, Sterne's engagement with issues concerning slavery and abolition stem from his acquaintance and correspondence with black writer Ignatius Sancho and became a familiar reference point for abolitionists in the 1790s.*

*****

THE PASSPORT.

The Hotel at Paris.

[. . .] I was interrupted in the hey-day of this soliloquy, with a voice which I took to be of a child, which complained "it could not get out."—I look'd up and down the passage, and seeing neither man, woman, nor child, I went out without farther attention.

In my return back through the passage, I heard the same words repeated twice over; and, looking up, I saw it was a starling hung in a little cage.—"I can't get out,—I can't get out," said the starling.

I stood looking at the bird: and to every person who came through the passage it ran fluttering to the side towards which they approach'd it, with the same lamentation of its captivity—"I can't get out," said the starling—God help thee! said I, but I'll let thee out, cost what it will; so I turned about the cage to get to the door; it was twisted and double twisted so fast with wire, there was no getting it open without pulling the cage to pieces—I took both hands to it.

The bird flew to the place where I was attempting his deliverance, and thrusting his head through the trellis press'd his breast against it as if impatient—I fear, poor creature! said I, I cannot set thee at liberty—"No," said the starling— "I can't get out—I can't get out," said the starling.

I vow, I never had my affections more tenderly awakened; nor do I remember an incident in my life, where the dissipated spirits, to which my reason had been a bubble, were so suddenly call'd home. Mechanical as the notes were, yet so true in tune to nature were they chanted, that in one moment they overthrew all my systematic reasonings upon the Bastile; and I heavily walk'd upstairs, unsaying every word I had said in going down them.

Disguise thyself as thou wilt, still, slavery! said I—still thou art a bitter draught; and though thousands in all ages have been made to drink of thee, thou art no less bitter on that account.—'tis thou, thrice sweet and gracious goddess, addressing myself to LIBERTY, whom all in public or in private worship, whose taste is grateful, and ever wilt be so, till NATURE herself shall change—no *tint* of words can spot thy snowy mantle, or chymic power turn thy sceptre into iron—with thee to smile upon him as he eats his crust, the swain is happier than his monarch from whose court thou art exiled—Gracious Heaven! cried I, kneeling down upon the last step but one in my ascent—grant me but health, thou great Bestower of it, and give me but this fair goddess as my companion—and shower down thy mitres, if it seems good unto thy divine providence, upon those heads which are aching for them.

11. Laurence Sterne, excerpt from *A Sentimental Journey through France and Italy*

THE CAPTIVE.

PARIS.

THE bird in his cage pursued me into my room; I sat down close to my table, and leaning my head upon my hand, I began to figure to myself the miseries of confinement. I was in a right frame for it, and so I gave full scope to my imagination.

I was going to begin with the millions of my fellow-creatures born to no inheritance but slavery; but finding, however affecting the picture was, that I could not bring it near me and that the multitude of sad groups in it did but distract me.—

—I took a single captive, and having first shut him up in his dungeon, I then look'd through the twilight of his grated door to take his picture.

I beheld his body half wasted away with long expectation and confinement, and felt what kind of sickness of the heart it was which arises from hope deferr'd. Upon looking nearer I saw him pale and feverish: in thirty years the western breeze had not once fann'd his blood—he had seen no sun, no moon, in all that time—nor had the voice of friend or kinsman breathed through his lattice—his children—

—But here my heart began to bleed—and I was forced to go on with another part of the portrait.

He was sitting upon the ground upon a little straw, in the furthest corner of his dungeon, which was alternately his chair and bed: a little calendar of small sticks were laid at the head, notch'd all over with the dismal days and nights he had pass'd there—he had one of these little sticks in his hand, and with a rusty nail he was etching another day of misery to add to the heap. As I darkened the little light he had, he lifted up a hopeless eye towards the door, then cast it down—shook his head, and went on with his work of affliction. I heard his chains upon his legs, as he turn'd his body to lay his little stick upon the bundle—He gave a deep sigh—I saw the iron enter into his soul—I burst into tears—I could not sustain the picture of confinement which my fancy had drawn—I started up from my chair, and calling La Fleur, I bid him bespeak me a *remise*, and have it ready at the door of the hotel by nine in the morning.

—I'll go directly, said I, myself to Monsieur Le Duke de Choiseul.

La Fleur would have put me to bed; but not willing he should see anything upon my cheek, which would cost the honest fellow a heart ache—I told him I would go to bed by myself—and bid him go do the same.

THE STARLING.

ROAD TO VERSAILLES.

I GOT into my *remise* the hour I proposed: La Fleur got up behind, and I bid the coachman make the best of his way to Versailles.

As there was nothing in this road, or rather nothing which I look for in travelling, I cannot fill up the blank better than with a short history of this self-same bird, which became the subject of the last chapter.

Whilst the Honourable Mr. **** was waiting for a wind at Dover it had been caught upon the cliffs, before it could well fly, by an English lad who was his groom; who not caring to destroy it, had taken it in his breast into the packet—and by course of feeding it, and taking it once under his protection, in a day or two grew fond of it, and got it safe along with him to Paris.

At Paris the lad had laid out a livre in a little cage for the starling, and as he had little to do better the five months his master stay'd there, he taught it, in his mother's tongue, the four simple words—(and no more)—to which I own'd myself so much it's debtor.

Upon his master's going on for Italy—the lad had given it to the master of the hotel—But his little song for liberty, being in an *unknown* language at Paris—the bird had little or no store set by him—so La Fleur bought both him and his cage for me for a bottle of Burgundy.

In my return from Italy I brought him with me to the country in whose language he had learn'd his notes—and telling the story of him to Lord A—Lord A begg'd the bird of me—in a week Lord A gave him to Lord B—Lord B made a present of him to Lord C— and Lord C's gentleman sold him to Lord D's for a shilling—Lord D gave him to Lord E— and so on—half round the alphabet—From that rank he pass'd into the lower house, and pass'd the hands of as many commoners—But as all these wanted to *get in*—and my bird wanted to get out—he had almost as little store set by him in London as in Paris.

12. Mathew Carey, excerpts from *A Short Account of the Malignant Fever, Lately Prevalent in Philadelphia: with a statement of the Proceedings that took place on the subject, in different parts of the United States. By Mathew Carey. Third Edition, Improved. Philadelphia: Printed by the Author.* (November 30, 1793).

Carey's Short Account *was a tremendously popular overview of the yellow fever epidemic. Published immediately after the epidemic ended, it went through four editions in the space of a few months in late 1793 and early 1794. Mathew Carey (1760–1839) was an enterprising Irish-Catholic émigré writer and successful, influential printer-bookseller. He left Ireland as a young man to avoid prosecution for criticizing the Irish penal code and* worked with Benjamin Franklin in Paris before arriving in Philadelphia in 1784. At present, the Short Account *is most often discussed in light of Absalom Jones and Richard Allen's rebuttal of Carey's accusations, added to the third edition, against black laborers who were the earliest volunteers to organize a response to the epidemic after the breakdown of civil order in September 1793. After Jones and Allen's pamphlet, Carey changed the fourth (February 1794) and later editions slightly by adding an apologetic footnote, included here in square brackets.*

The excerpts printed here (from the third edition to which Jones and Allen responded) highlight Carey's comments on themes and concerns that are noted in different ways in Arthur Mervyn, *above all the instability of the city's mercantile and financial institutions at a time when waves of refugees from the Haitian revolution were beginning to arrive and the overwhelming challenges posed by the breakdown of civic and moral order at the height of the fever in September–October. Carey remains noncommittal on a theory that Brown and his friends rejected, the then-common notion, with obvious xenophobic implications, that Africans and the French had some intrinsic immunity to the disease. For more on this theory, see the Introduction and the discussion of Jones and Allen in Related Text 13. Like Brown, and Jones and Allen, Carey places great emphasis on the destructive effects of fear, anxiety, and panic, which do much to amplify the biological and social damage of the crisis. In later editions that appeared up to 1830, Carey comments that* Arthur Mervyn's *depiction of the epidemic in Chapters 15–23 "gives a vivid and terrifying picture, probably not too highly coloured, of the horrors of that period."*

*****

CHAP. I *State of Philadelphia previous to the appearance of the malignant fever—with a few observations on some of the probable consequences of that calamity.*

BEFORE I enter on the consideration of this disorder, it may not be improper to offer a few introductory remarks on the situation of Philadelphia previous to its commencement, which will reflect the light on some of the circumstances mentioned in the course of the narrative.

The manufactures, trade, and commerce of this city, had, for a considerable time, been improving and extending with great rapidity. From the period of the adoption of the federal government, at which time America was at the lowest ebb of distress, her situation had progressively become more and more prosperous. Confidence, formerly banished, was universally restored. Property of every kind, rose to, and in some instances beyond, its real value: and a few revolving years exhibited the interesting spectacle of a young country, with a new form of government, emerging from a state which approached very near to, anarchy, and acquiring all the flexibility and nerve of the best-toned and oldest nations.

In this prosperity, which revived almost-extinguished hopes of four millions of people, Philadelphia participated in an eminent degree. Numbers of new houses, in almost every street, built in a very neat, elegant style, adorned, at the same time that they greatly enlarged the city. Its population was extending fast. House rent had risen to an extravagant height; it was in many cases double, and in some treble what it had been a year or two before; and, as is generally the case, when a city is advancing in prosperity, it far exceeded the real increase of trade. The number of applicants for houses, exceeding the number of houses to be let, one bid over another; and affairs were in such a situation, that many people, though they had a tolerable run of business, could hardly do more than clear their rents, and were, literally, toiling for their landlords alone.* Luxury, the usual, and perhaps inevitable concomitant of prosperity, was gaining ground in a manner very alarming to those who considered how far the virtue, the liberty, and the happiness of a nation depend on its temperance and sober manners.—Men had been, for some time, in the improvident habit of regulating their expenses by prospects formed in sanguine hours, when every probability was caught at as a certainty, not by their actual profits, or income. The number of coaches, coachees, chairs, etc., lately set up by men in the middle rank of life, is hardly credible. Not to enter into a minute detail, let it suffice to remark, that extravagance, in various shapes, was gradually eradicating the plain and wholesome habits of the city. And although it were presumption to attempt to scan the decrees of heaven, yet few, I believe will pretend to deny, that something was wanting to humble the price of a city, which was running on in full career, to the goal of prodigality and dissipation.

However, from November 1792, to the end of last June, the difficulties of Philadelphia were extreme. The establishment of the bank of Pennsylvania, in embryo for the most part of that time, had arrested in the two other banks such a quantity of the circulating specie, as embarrassed almost every kind of business; to this was added the distress arising from the very numerous failures in England, which had extremely harassed several of our capital merchants. During this period, many men experienced as great difficulties as were ever known in this city.** But the opening, in July, of the bank of Pennsylvania, conducted on the most generous and enlarged principles, placed business on its former favourable footing. Every man looked forward to this fall as likely to produce a vast extension of trade. But how fleeting are all human views! How uncertain all plans sounded on earthly appearances! All these flattering prospects vanished "like the baseless fabric of a vision."

In July, arrived the unfortunate fugitives from Cape François. And on this occasion, the liberality of Philadelphia was displayed in a most respectable point of light. Nearly 12,000 dollars were in a few days collected for their relief. Little, alas! did many of the contributors, then in easy circumstances, imagine, that a few weeks would leave their wives and children dependent on public charity, as has since

---

* The distress arising from this source, was perhaps the only exception to the general observation of the flourishing situation of Philadelphia.

** It is with great pleasure, I embrace this opportunity of declaring that the very liberal conduct of the Bank of the United States, at this trying season, was the means of saving many a deserving and industrious man from ruin.

unfortunately happened. An awful instance of the rapid and warning vicissitudes of affairs on this transitory stage.

About this time, this destroying scourge, the malignant fever, crept in among us, and nipped in the bud the fairest blossoms that imagination could storm. And oh! what a dreadful contrast has since taken place! Many women, then in the lap of ease and contentment, are bereft of beloved husbands, and left with numerous families of children to maintain, unqualified for the arduous task—many orphans are destitute of parents to foster and protect them—many entire families are swept away, without leaving "a trace behind"—many of our first commercial houses are totally dissolved, by the death of the parties, and their affairs are necessarily left in so deranged a state, that the losses and distresses, which must take place, are beyond estimation. The protests of notes for a few weeks past, have exceeded all former examples; for a great proportion of the merchants and traders having left the city, and been totally unable, from the stagnation of business, and diversion of all their expected resources, to make any provision for payment, most of their notes have been protested, as they became due.***

*****

CHAP. V. *General despondency. Deplorable scenes. Frightful view of human nature. A noble and exhilarating contrast.*

THE consternation of the people of Philadelphia at this period was carried beyond all bounds. Dismay and affright were visible in almost every person's countenance. Most of those who could, by any means, make it convenient, fled from the city. Of those who remained, many shut themselves up in their houses, and were afraid to walk the streets. The smoke of tobacco being regarded as a preventative, many persons, even women and small boys, had segars constantly in their mouths. Others placing full confidence in garlic, chewed it almost the whole day; some kept it in their shoes. Many were afraid to allow the barbers or hair-dressers to come near them, as instances had occurred of some of them having shaved the dead—and many having engaged as bleeders. Some, who carried their caution pretty far, bought lancets for themselves, not daring to allow themselves to be bled with the lancets of the bleeders. Some houses were hardly a moment in the day, free from the smell of gunpowder, burned tobacco, nitre, sprinkled vinegar, &c. Many of the churches were almost deserted, and some wholly closed. The coffee house was shut up, as was the city library, and most of the public offices—three out of the four daily papers were

---

*** The Bank of the United States, on the 15th of October, passed a resolve, empowering the cashier to renew all discounted notes, when the same drawers and indorsers were offered, and declaring that no notes should be protested, when the indorsers bound themselves in writing, to be accountable in the same manner as in cases of protest.

dropped,* as were some of the other papers.—Many were almost incessantly purifying, scouring, and whitewashing their rooms. Those who ventured abroad, had hand-kerchiefs or sponges impregnated with vinegar or camphor at their noses, or smelling-bottles with the thieves' vinegar. Others carried pieces of tarred rope in their hands or pockets, or camphor bags tied round their necks. The corpses of the most respectable citizens, even of those who did not die of the epidemic, were carried to the grave, on the shafts of a chair, the horse driven by a negro, unattended by a friend or relation, and without any sort of ceremony. People hastily shifted their course at the sight of a hearse coming towards them. Many never walked on the foot-path, but went into the middle of the streets, to avoid being infected in passing by houses wherein people had died. Ac-quaintances and friends avoided each other in the streets, and only signified their re-gard by a cold nod. The old custom of shaking hands fell into such general disuse, that many shrunk back with affright at even the offer of the hand. A person with a crape, or any appearance of mourning, was shunned like a viper. . . .

[. . .] Who, without horror, can reflect on a husband, married perhaps for twenty years, deserting his wife in the last agony—a wife unfeelingly, abandoning her hus-band on his death bed—parents forsaking their only children—children ungratefully flying from their parents, and resigning them to chance, often without an enquiry after their health or safety—masters hurrying off their faithful servants to Bushhill, even on suspicion of the fever, and that at a time, when, like Tartarus, it was open to every visitant, but never returned any—servants abandoning tender and humane masters, who only wanted a little care to restore them to health and usefulness—who, I say, can even now think of these things without horror? Yet they were daily ex-hibited in every quarter of our city; and such was the force of habit, that the parties who were guilty of this cruelty, felt no remorse themselves—nor met with the exe-cration from their fellow-citizens, which such conduct would have excited at any other period. Indeed, at this awful crisis, so much did *self* appear to engross the whole attention of many, that less concern was felt for the loss of a parent, a husband, a wife, or an only child, than, on other occasions, would have been caused by the death of a servant, or even a favourite lap dog.

This kind of conduct produced scenes of distress and misery, of which few parallels are to be met with, and which nothing could palliate, but the extraordinary public panic, and the great law of self preservation, the dominion of which extends over the whole animated world. Many men of affluent fortunes, who have given daily em-ployment and sustenance to hundreds, have been abandoned to the care of a negro, after their wives, children, friends, clerks, and servants, had fled away, and left them to their fate. In many cases, no money could procure proper attendance. With the poor, the case was, as might be expected, infinitely worse than with the rich. Many of these have perished, without a human being to hand them a drink of water, to ad-

---

* It would be improper to pass over this opportunity of mentioning that the Federal Gazette, printed by Andrew Brown, was uninterruptedly continued and with the usual industry, during the whole calamity, and was of the utmost service, in conveying to the citizens of the United States authentic intelligence of the state of the disorder, and of the city generally.

minister medicines, or to perform any charitable office for them. Various instances have occurred, of dead bodies found lying in the streets, of persons who had no house or habitation, and could procure no shelter.

✶✶✶✶✶

CHAP. VII. *Magnanimous offer. Wretched Sate of Bush-hill. Order introduced there.*

[. . .] On the 16th, the managers of Bushhill, after personal inspection of the state of affairs there, made report of its situation, which was truly deplorable. It exhibited a picture of human misery as ever existed. A profligate, abandoned set of nurses and attendants (hardly any of good character could at that time be procured) rioted on the provisions and comforts, prepared for the sick, who (unless at the hours when the doctors attended) were left almost entirely destitute of every assistance. The dying and dead were indiscriminately mingled together. The ordure and other evacuations of the sick, were allowed to remain in the most offensive state imaginable. It was, in fact, a great human slaughter house, where numerous victims were immolated at the altar of riot and intemperance. No wonder, then, that a general dread of the place prevailed through the city, and that a removal to it was considered as the seal of death. In consequence, there were various instance of sick persons locking their rooms, and resisting every attempt to carry them away. At length, the poor were so much afraid of being sent to Bushhill, that they would not acknowledge their illness, until it was no longer possible to conceal it. For it is to be observed, that the fear of the contagion was so prevalent, that as soon as any one was taken ill, an alarm was spread among the neighbors, and every effort was used to have the sick person hurried off to Bushhill, to avoid spreading the disorder. The cases of poor people forced in this way to that hospital, though labouring under only common colds, and common fall fevers, were numerous and afflicting. They were not wanting instances of persons, only slightly ill, being sent to Bushhill, by their panic-struck neighbors, and embracing the first opportunity of running back to Philadelphia.

✶✶✶✶✶

CHAP. XIV. *Disorder fatal to the doctors—to the clergy—to drunkards— to filles de joie—to maid servants— to the poor—and in close streets.— Less destructive to the French—and to the negroes.*

[. . .] From the effects of this disorder, the French settled in Philadelphia, have been in a very remarkable degree exempt. To what this may be owing, is a subject deserving particular investigation.* By some it has been ascribed to their despising the danger.

---

* The frequent use the French make of *lavements* [enemas], at all times, may probably account for their escaping so very generally as they did. These purify the bowels, help to discharge the foul

But, though this may have had some effect, it will not certainly account for it altogether; as it is well known that many of the most courageous persons in Philadelphia, have been among its victims. By many of the French, the prevalence of the disorder has been attributed to the vast quantities of crude and unwholesome fruits brought to our markets, and consumed by all classes of people.

When the yellow fever prevailed in South Carolina, the negroes, according to that accurate observer, Dr. Lining, were wholly free from it. "There is something very singular in the constitution of the negroes," says he, "which renders them not liable to this fever; for though many of them were as much exposed as the nurses to this infection, yet I never knew one instance of this fever among them, though they are equally subject with the white people to the bilious fever".** The same idea prevailed for a considerable time in Philadelphia; but it was erroneous. They did not escape the disorder; however, the number of them that were seized with it, was not great; and, as I am informed by an eminent doctor, "it yielded to the power of medicine in them more easily than in the whites." The error that prevailed on this subject had a very salutary effect; for, at an early period of the disorder, hardly any white nurses could be procured; and, had the negroes been equally terrified, the sufferings of the sick, great as they actually were, would have been exceedingly aggravated. At the period alluded to, the elders of the African church met, and offered their services to the mayor, to procure nurses for the sick, and to assist in burying the dead. Their offers were accepted; and Absalom Jones and Richard Allen undertook the former department, that of furnishing nurses, and William Gray, the latter—the interment of the dead. The great demand for nurses, afforded an opportunity for imposition, which was eagerly seized by some of the vilest of the blacks. They extorted two, three, four, and even five dollars a night for attendance, which would have been well paid by a single dollar. Some of them were even detected in plundering the houses of the sick.[†] But it is wrong to cast a censure on the whole for this sort of conduct, as many people have done. The services of Jones, Allen, and Gray, and others of their colour, have been very great, and demand public gratitude.

On examining the books of the hospital at Bushhill, it appears that there were above fifteen blacks received there, of whom three fourths died. There may have been more, as the examination was made very cursorily.

*****

---

matter, and remove costiveness [constipation], which is one of the most certain supports of this and other disorders.

** Essays and observations, vol. II. page 407.

[†] [Note added to fourth edition, 1794, in response to Jones and Allen's defense of the free black community: "The extortion here mentioned, was very far from being confined to the negroes: many of the white nurses behaved with equal rapacity."]

CHAP. XVI. *Desultory facts and reflexions.—A collection of scraps.*

[. . .] Several classes of people were highly benefited by the public distress. Coffin-makers had a large demand, and in general high prices for their work. Most of the retail stores being shut up, those that remained open, had an uncommon demand; as the whole of the business was divided among a few. Those who had carriages to hire, to transport families to the country, received whatever they pleased to demand. The holders of houses at from three, to twenty miles from the city, who chose to rent the whole or part of them, had high rents. The two notaries, who protested for the banks, profited highly by the absence of the merchants and traders. . . .

[. . .] The effect of fear in predisposing the body for the yellow fever and other disorders, and increasing their malignance, when taken, is well known.

*****

CHAP. XVII. *Another collection of scraps.*

THOSE who reflect on the many revolting cases of cruelty and desertion of friends and relations which occurred in Philadelphia, however, cannot be surprised, that in the country, and in various towns and cities, inhumanity should be experienced by Philadelphians from strangers. The universal consternation extinguished in people's breasts the most honourable feelings of human nature; and in this case, as in various others, the suspicion operated as injuriously as the reality. Many travelers from this city, exhausted with fatigue and with hunger, have been refused all shelter and all sustenance, and have fallen victims to the fears, not to the want of charity, of those whom they applied for relief. Instances of this kind have occurred on almost every road leading from Philadelphia. People under suspicion of having this disorder, have been forced by their fellow travelers to quit the stages, and perished in the woods without a possibility of procuring any assistance. At Easton, in Maryland, a wagon-load of goods from Philadelphia, was actually burned; and a woman, who was with it, was tarred and feathered.

[. . .] A poor man was taken sick on the road at a village not far from Philadelphia. He lay calling for water, a considerable time in vain. At length, an old woman brought a pitcher full, and not daring to approach him, she laid it at a distance, desiring him to crawl to it, which he did. After lying there about forty-eight hours, he died; and the body lay in a state of putrefaction for some time, until the neighbours hired two black butchers to bury him, for twenty-four dollars. They dug a pit to windward—with a fork, hooked a rope about his neck—dragged him into it and at as great a distance as possible, cast earth into the pit to cover him.

[. . .] A drunken sailor lay in the street for a few hours asleep, and was supposed by the neighbours to be dead with the disorder; but they were too much afraid, to make personal examination. They sent to the committee for a cart and a coffin. The carter took the man by the heels, and was going to put him into the coffin. Handling him roughly, he awoke, and damning his eyes, asked him what he was about? The carter let him drop in a fright, and ran off as if a ghost was at his heels.

13. Absalom Jones and Richard Allen, excerpt from *A Narrative of the Proceedings of the Black People, during the Late Awful Calamity in Philadelphia, in the Year 1793: And a Refutation of Some Censures, Thrown upon Them in Some Late Publications* (Philadelphia: Printed for the authors, by William W. Woodward, 1794).

Absalom Jones (1746–1818) and Richard Allen (1760–1831) were key African American ministers and abolition activists in the early republic and figureheads of Philadelphia's (the nation's first) free black community in the 1790s. Allen was born into slavery under a Philadelphia Quaker, then sold to a middling Delaware farmer who allowed him to attend Methodist meetings where he drew strength from religious faith and community. The antislavery message of these evangelicists also converted Allen's new master, and he allowed Allen to purchase his own and his brother's freedom in 1780. Jones was likewise born into slavery in Delaware, moved to Philadelphia with his master at age fifteen, and after long efforts purchased his freedom in 1784 before becoming a minister. Both studied at Quaker Anthony Benezet's (Society of) Friends' Free African School. In response to the St. Georges' Methodist Episcopal Church's refusal to desegregate prayers, in 1787 they together founded the Free African Society, the first African American mutual aid society in U.S. history. From this institutional base, each in turn created the new nation's first two African American churches: Allen's Bethel African Episcopal Church (1793) and Jones' St. Thomas' African Episcopal Church (1794).

Jones and Allen's leadership in founding the earliest African American civic institutions was linked to public interventions and strategy on the politics of slavery. Both protested the passage of the 1793 Fugitive Slave Act, which provided a juridical mechanism for seizing and resubjugating runaway slaves. When George Washington signed the act into law in February 1793, Allen and Jones began working with the Pennsylvania Abolition Society (PAS) to expand the informal Underground Railroad network that was already helping runaway slaves elude masters and slave hunters. Their organizational experience as leaders of the city's free black institutions, as well as their work with PAS members such as Dr. Benjamin Rush and Isaac Hopper, led to the free black community's initiative in becoming the first citizen volunteers to work as emergency nurses and undertakers during the 1793 yellow fever epidemic. When the outbreak passed, they were dismayed to see Mathew Carey's widely read Short Account of the Malignant Fever *(see the excerpts in Related Texts) publicize rumors that some blacks had used their positions to extort money for services and steal from the helpless. In response to Carey's accusations, Jones and Allen wrote* A Narrative *and paid for its publication, despite the refusal of many white printers to publish the pamphlet.*

A Narrative *seeks initially to discount the notion that Africans were immune to the yellow fever, since that idea negated the deadly risks African Americans took when the city was falling into chaos. Many whites believed that Africans (and French immigrants) were immune to the fever. What was not understood at that time is that immunity results from surviving an initial infection. Since many Africans in the U.S. had survived first contacts with the disease in Africa, the Middle Passage, or New World landfalls, the immunity they acquired in this manner was misinterpreted as an ethno-racial characteristic. Similarly, many of the French and other Caribbean transplants who came to the U.S. via the Caribbean, like Dr. Jean Devèze or Dr. Edward Stevens, had also survived earlier infections and developed immunity. Many other Africans, however, especially those born in America, lacked this protection and suffered the same mortality rates as the rest of the population. Additionally, the white community rarely witnessed African American illness, since blacks associated hospitals with slave prisons and rarely used them. Instead, many sought care provided by other blacks familiar with African herbal medicines. Interestingly, Jones and Allen's strategic commitment to Dr. Benjamin Rush's controversial, violent, and ineffective method of bleeding and purging marks their distance from non-Christian Africans who avoided these treatments at the same time that African knowledge was surviving and passing into wider practice via French and other Caribbean doctors who learned it from their contacts on Caribbean plantations.*

Throughout these excerpts from A Narrative, *Jones and Allen emphasize the selflessness and civic generosity of black nurses and undertakers in contrast to the selfishness and panicked withdrawal of whites. The full implication of this contrast emerges when the main body of the pamphlet is read in connection with its concluding sections, which are not included here. After including a testimony from Mayor Matthew Clarkson, Allen and Jones attach "An Address to Those Who Keep Slaves, and Approve the Practice" that argues that God disapproves of slavery. The pamphlet then concludes with a final note "To the People of Color," advising slaves not to lose faith in God because this faith may help them maintain an "affectionate regard" for their masters and win their liberty peacefully through righteous persuasion (as Allen had done). They argue that freed African Americans should show gratitude, not rancor, toward their former masters and should remember that many whites have also worked to create the conditions for emancipation. Thus these concluding remarks highlight Allen and Jones's larger goals for the pamphlet beyond the immediate motivation of challenging and correcting relatively minor inaccuracies in Carey's account.*

The ministers use the larger opportunity created by this riposte to Carey to reassure the educated, white community that it has nothing to fear from the abolition of slavery and to calm white anxieties about black revenge, a fear that was raised to crisis levels in 1793 by accounts of massacres in Haiti. Allen and Jones insist that whites need not fear blacks, even if the latter have the upper hand, as demonstrated by their civic benevolence during the epidemic. The detailed accounting of personal and financial sacrifices by Philadelphia blacks implies that whites have a debt, both monetary and moral, to a black community that has given of itself for the common good and that this debt can be repaid by the civil emancipation of blacks, that is, the abolition of slavery and extension of citizen status to all. Jones and Allen use gothic-sentimental images of families being destroyed by the epidemic to forge a sympathetic link to one of the most powerful images in abolitionist and later U.S. culture: the multigenerational trauma and social damage created when slavery breaks up black families and produces fear and denial of black-white family mixture.

While the passages urging black benevolence and brotherhood toward whites have left Jones and Allen open to criticism for their lack of radicalism, it is important to remember two things. First, A Narrative *was written for a primarily white audience; it was in-*

tended to garner support for abolition by mobilizing white public opinion against a neg-
ative legal environment recently worsened by the 1793 Fugitive Slave Act and thereby to
denormalize slavery in white minds. Jones and Allen (like Brown's novel) make a point of
emphasizing the idea that mental predispositions may affect one's health and memorably
dramatize the situation of whites who effectively worried themselves to death during the
epidemic. This emphasis also functions as a political allegory, pointing out that the dom-
inant white community's fear and paranoia is as important a factor in the outcome of
black emancipation as the attitudes and behaviors of the black community. As the Span-
ish painter Goya put it in 1798, "the sleep of reason produces monsters."

Second, while Allen and Jones were conducting strategic legal projects and writing a
pamphlet like this one, they were also busy creating an illegal Underground Railroad net-
work in collaboration with mainly Quaker whites, such as Isaac Hopper and Thomas
Harrison (see the Related Text on Hopper in this volume). Viewed from this perspective, A
Narrative *is only superficially a reaction to Carey's accusations. It is better understood as a*
progressive action, a path-breaking instance of antiracist black ministerial civil (dis)obe-
dience that establishes a precedent for later figures such as Martin Luther King, Jr. and
Cornel West.

In Arthur Mervyn, *Brown acknowledges Jones and Allen's arguments by dramatizing*
the service of free blacks as nurses and undertakers, by implying in the first part's twin
mirror scenes that Mervyn's identity is bound up with that of his black counterparts, and
by having enlightened characters in the fever scenes, such as Medlicote, Estwick, and
Stevens, insist that a benevolent and caring disposition in the face of social change and
crisis is the best course of action. Mervyn's transformation in the course of the novel from
a naïve and easily manipulated Scots-Irish youth to a self-educating, cosmopolitan citizen
eager to embrace the dark-skinned Achsa Fielding enacts the white response that Jones
and Allen, and Brown alike, seek to achieve.

✶✶✶✶✶

IN consequence of a partial representation of the conduct of the people who were
employed to nurse the sick, in the late calamitous state of the city of Philadelphia, we
are solicited, by a number of those who feel themselves injured thereby, and by the
advice of several respectable citizens, to step forward and declare facts as they really
were; seeing that from our situation, on account of the charge we took upon us, we
had it more fully and generally in our power, to know and observe the conduct and
behavior of those that were so employed.

Early in September, a solicitation appeared in the Public papers, to the people of
colour to come forward and assist the distressed, perishing, and neglected sick; with
a kind of assurance, that people of our colour were not liable to take the infection,
upon which we and a few others met and consulted how to act on so truly alarming
and melancholy an occasion. After some conversations, we found a freedom to go
forth, confining in him who can preserve in the midst of a burning fiery furnace, sensible that it was our duty to do all the good we could to our suffering fellow mortals.
We set out to see where we could be useful. The first we visited was a man in Emsley's

alley, who was dying, and his wife lay dead at the time in the house, there were none to assist but two poor helpless children. We administered what relief we could, and applied to the overseers of the poor to have the woman buried. We visited upwards of twenty families that day—they were scenes of woe indeed! The Lord was pleased to strengthen, and remove all fear from us, and disposed our hearts to be as useful as possible.

In order the better to regulate our conduct, we called on the mayor next day, to consult with him how to proceed, so as to be most useful. The first object he recommended, was a strict attention to the sick, and the procuring of nurses. This was attended to by Absalom Jones and William Gray; and, in order that the distressed might know where to apply, the mayor advertised the public that upon application to them they would be supplied. Soon after, the mortality increasing, the difficulty of getting a corpse taken away, was such, that few were willing to do it, when offered great rewards. The black people were looked to. We then offered our services in the public papers, by advertising that we would remove the dead and procure nurses. Our services were the production of real sensibility;—we sought not fee nor reward, until the increase of the disorder rendered our labour so arduous that we were not adequate to the service we had assumed. The mortality increasing rapidly, obliged us to call in the assistance of five* hired men, in the awful discharge of interring the dead. They, with great reluctance, were prevailed upon to join us. It was very uncommon, at this time, to find any one that would go near, much more, handle, a sick or dead person.

Mr. Carey, in page 106 of his third edition, has observed, that, "for the honor of human nature, it ought to be recorded, that some of the convicts in the gaol, a part of the term of whose confinement had been remitted as a reward for their peaceable, orderly behavior, voluntarily offered themselves as nurses to attend the sick at Bush-Hill; and have, in that capacity, conducted themselves with great fidelity, &c." Here it ought to be remarked, (although Mr. Carey hath not done it) that two thirds of the persons, who rendered these essential services, were people of colour, who, on the application of the elders of the African church, (who met to consider what they could do for the help of the sick) were liberated, on condition of their doing the duty of nurses at the hospital at Bush-Hill; which they as voluntarily accepted to do, as they did faithfully discharge, this severe and disagreeable duty. —May the Lord reward them, both temporally and spiritually.

When the sickness became general, and several of the physicians died, and most of the survivors were exhausted by sickness or fatigue; that good man, Doctor Rush, called us more immediately to attend upon the Sick, knowing we could both bleed; he told us we could increase our utility, by attending to his instructions, and accordingly directed us where to procure medicine duly prepared with proper directions how to administer them, and at what stages of the disorder to bleed; and when we found ourselves incapable of judging what was proper to be done, to apply to him,

---

* Two of whom were Richard Allen's brothers.

and he would, if able, attend them himself, or end Edward Fisher, his pupil, which he often did; and Mr. Fisher manifested his humanity, by an affectionate attention for their relief. —This has been no small satisfaction to us; for, we think, that when the instruments, in the hand of God, for saving the lives of some hundreds of our suffering fellow mortals.

We feel ourselves sensibly aggrieved by the censorious epithets of many, who did not render the least assistance in the time of necessity, yet are liberal of their censure of us, for the prices paid for our services, when no one knew how to make a proposal to any one they wanted to assist them. At first we made no charge, but let it to those we served in removing their dead, to give what they thought fit—we set no price, until the reward was fixed by those we had served. After paying the people we had to assist us, our compensation is much less than many will believe.

We do assure the public, that *all* the money we have received, for burying, and for coffins which we ourselves purchased and procured, has not defrayed the expense of wages which we had to pay to those whom we employed to assist us. The following statement is accurately made:

CASH RECEIVED.

The whole amount of Cash we received
for burying the dead, and for burying
beds, is,   £ 233 10 4

CASH PAID.

For coffins, for which we have
received nothing   £33 0 0

For the hire of five men, 3 of
them 70 days each, and the
other two, 63 days each,
at 22/6 per day   378 0 0
                                411 0 0

Debts due us, for which we expect
but little,   £110 0 0

From this statement, for the truth of
which we solemnly vouch, it is evident,
and we sensibly feel the operation
of the fact, that we are out of
pocket,   £ 177 9 8

Besides the cost of hearses, maintenance of our families for 70 days, (being the period of our labours) and the support of the five hired men, during the respective times of their being employed; which expences, together with sundry gifts we occasionally made to poor families, might reasonably and properly be introduced, to shew our actual situation with regard to profit—but it is enough to exhibit to the public, from the above specified items, *of Cash paid and Cash received*, without taking into view the other expences, that, by the employment we were engaged in, we have lost £177 9 8.

But, if the other expences, which we have actually paid, are added to that sum, how much then may we not say we have suffered! We leave the public to judge.

It may possibly appear strange to some who know how constantly we were employed, that we should have received no more Cash than £ 233 10 4. But we repeat our assurance, that this is the fact, and we add another, which will serve the better to explain it: We have buried *several hundreds* of poor persons and strangers, for which service we have never received, nor never asked any compensation.

We feel ourselves hurt most by a partial, censorious paragraph, in Mr. Carey's second edition, of his account of the sickness, &c. in Philadelphia; pages 76 and 77, where he asperses the blacks alone, for having taken the advantage of the distressed situation of the people. That some extravagant prices were paid, we admit; but how came they to be demanded? The reason is plain. It was with difficulty persons could be had to supply the wants of the sick, as nurses;—applications became more and more numerous, the consequence was, when we procured them at six dollars per week, and called upon them to go where they were wanted, we found they were gone elsewhere; here was a disappointment; upon enquiring the cause, we found, they had been allured away by others who offered greater wages, until they got from two to four dollars per day. We had no restraint upon the people. It was natural for people in low circumstances to accept a voluntary, bounteous reward; especially under the loathsomness of many of the sick, when nature shuddered at the thoughts of the infection, and the talk assigned was aggravated by lunacy, and being left much alone with them. Had Mr. Carey been solicited to such an undertaking, for hire, *Query*, "What would *he* have demanded?" but Mr. Carey, although chosen a member of that band of worthies who have so eminently distinguished themselves by their labours, for the relief of the sick and helpless—yet, quickly after his election, left them to struggle with their arduous and hazardous talk, by leaving the city. 'Tis true Mr. Carey was no hireling, and had a right to flee, and upon his return, to plead the cause of those who fled; yet, we think, he was wrong in giving so partial and injurious an account of the black nurses; if they have taken advantage of the public distress? Is it any more than he hath done of its desire for information. We believe he has made more money by the sale of his "scraps" than a dozen of the greatest extortioners among the black nurses. The great prices paid did not escape the observation of that worthy and vigilant magistrate, Mathew Clarkson, mayor of the city, and president of the committee—he sent for us and requested we would use our influence, to lessen the wages of the nurses, but on informing him the cause, i.e. that of the people over-bidding one another, it was concluded unnecessary to attempt any thing on that head; therefore it was left to the people concerned. That there were some few black people guilty of plundering the distressed, we acknowledge; but in that they only are pointed out, and made mention of, we esteem partial and injurious; we know as many whites who were guilty of it; but this is looked over, while the blacks are held up to censure.—Is it a greater crime for a black to pilfer, than for a white to privateer?

We wish not to offend, but when an unprovoked attempt is made, to make us blacker than we are, it becomes less necessary to be over cautious on that account; therefore we shall take the liberty to tell of the conduct of some of the whites.

We know, six pounds was demanded by, and paid, to a white woman, for putting a corpse into a coffin; and forty dollars was demanded, and paid, to four white men, for bringing it down the stairs.

Mr. and Mrs. Taylor both died in one night; a white woman had the care of them; after they were dead she called on Jacob Servoss, esq. for her pay, demanding six pounds for laying them out; upon seeing a bundle with her, he suspected she had pilfered; on searching her, Mr. Taylor's buckles were found in her pocket, with other things.

An elderly lady, Mrs. Malony, was given into the care of a white woman, she died, we were called to remove the corpse, when we came the women was laying so drunk that she did not know what we were doing, but we know she had one of Mrs. Malony's rings on her finger, and another in her pocket.

Mr. Carey tells us, Bush-Hill exhibited as wretched a picture of human misery, as ever existed. A profligate abandoned set of nurses and attendants (hardly any of good character could at that time be procured) rioted on the provisions and comforts, prepared for the sick, who (unless at the hours when the doctors attended) were left almost entirely destitute of every assistance. The dying and dead were indiscriminately mingled together. The ordure and other evacuations of the sick, were allowed to remain in the most offensive state imaginable. Not the smallest appearance of order or regularity existed. It was in fact a great human slaughter house, where numerous victims were immolated at the altar of intemperance.

It is unpleasant to point out the bad and unfeeling conduct of any colour, yet the defence we have undertaken obliges us to remark that although "hardly any of good character at that time could be procured" yet only two black women were, at this time in the hospital, and they were retained and the others discharged when it was reduced to order and good government.

The bad consequences many of our colour apprehend from a partial relation of our conduct are, that it will prejudice the minds of the people in general against us—because it is impossible that one individual, can have knowledge of all, therefore at some future day, when some of the most virtuous, that were upon most praise-worthy motives, induced to serve the sick, may fall into the service of a family that are strangers to him, or her, and it is discovered that it is one of those stigmatised wretches, what may we suppose will be the consequence? It is not reasonable to think the person will be abhored, despised, and perhaps dismissed from employment, to their great disadvantage, would not this be hard? and have we not therefore sufficient reason to seek for redress? We can with certainty assure the public that have seen more humanity, more real sensibility from the poor blacks, than from the poor whites. When many of the former, of their own accord rendered services where extreme necessity called for it, the general part of the poor white people were so dismayed, that instead of attempting to be useful, they in a manner hid themselves—A remarkable instance of this—A poor afflicted dying man, stood at his chamber window, praying and beseeching every one that passed by, to help him to a drink of water; a number of white people passed, and instead of being moved by the poor man's distress, they hurried as fast as they could out of the sound of his cries—until at length a gentleman, who seemed to be a foreigner came up, he could not pass by, but had not resolution enough to go into the house, he held eight dollars in his hand, and offered it to several as a reward for giving the poor man a drink of water, but was refused by every one, until a poor black man came up, the gentleman offered the eight dollars to him, if he would relieve the poor man with a little water, "Master" replied the good natured fellow, "I will supply the gentleman with water, but surely I will not take your money for it" nor could he be prevailed upon to accept his bounty: he went in, supplied the poor object with water, and rendered him every service he could.

A poor black man, named Sampson, went constantly from house to house where distress was, and no assistance without fee or reward; he was smote with the disorder, and died, After his death his family were neglected by those he had served.

Sarah Bass, a poor black widow, gave all the assistance she could, in several families, for which she did not receive any thing; and when any thing was offered her, she left it to the option of those she served.

A woman of our colour, nursed Richard Mason and son, when they died, Richard's widow considering the risk the poor woman had run, and from observing the fears that sometimes rested on her mind, expected she would have demanded something considerable, but upon asking what she demanded, her reply was half a dollar per day. Mrs. Mason, intimated it was not sufficient for her attendance, she replied it was enough for what she had done, and would take no more. Mrs. Mason's feelings were such, that she settled an annuity of six pounds a year, on her, for life. Her name is Mary Scott.

An elderly black woman nursed —— — with great diligence and attention; when recovered he asked what he must give for her services—she replied "a dinner master on a cold winter's day," and thus she went from place to place rendering every service in her power without an eye to reward.

A young black woman, was requested to attend one night upon a white man and his wife, who were very ill, no other person could be had—great wages were offered her—she replied, I will not go for money, if I go for money God will see it, and may be make me take the disorder and die, but if I go, and take no money, he may spare my life. She went about nine o'clock, and found them both on the floor; she could procure no candle or other light, but staid with them about two hours, and then left them. They both died that night. She was afterward very ill with the fever—her life was spared.

Caesar Cranchal, a black man, offered his services to attend the sick, and said, I will not take your money, I will not sell my life for money. It is said he died with the flux.

A black lad, at the Widow Gilpin's, was intrusted with his young master's keys, on his leaving the city, and transacted his business, with greatest honesty, and dispatch, having unloaded a vessel for him in the time, and loaded it again.

A woman, that nursed David Bacon, charged with exemplary moderation, and said she would not have any more.

It may be said, in vindication of the conduct of those, who discovered ignorance or incapacity in nursing, that it is, in itself, a considerable art, derived from experience, as well as the exercise of the finer feelings of humanity—this experience, nine tenths of those employed, it is probable were wholly strangers to.

We do not recollect such acts of humanity from the poor white people, in all the round we have been engaged in. We could mention many other instances of the like nature, but think it needless.

It is unpleasant for us to make these remarks, but justice to our colour, demands it. Mr. Carey pays William Gray and us a compliment; he says, our services and others of their colour, have been very great &c. By naming us, he leaves these others, in the hazardous state of being classed with those who are called the "vilest." The few that were discovered to merit public censure, were brought to justice, which ought to have sufficed, without being canvassed over in his "Trifle" of a pamphlet—which causes us to be more particular, and endeavour to recall the esteem of the public for our friends, and the people of colour, as far as they may be found worthy; for we conceive, and experience proves it, that an ill name is easier given than taken away. We have many unprovoked enemies, who begrudge us the liberty we enjoy, and are glad to hear of any compliant against our colour, be it just or unjust; in consequence of which we are more earnestly endeavouring all in our power, to warn, rebuke, and exhort our African friends, to keep a conscience void of offence towards God and man; and, at the same time, would not be backward to interfere, when stigmas or oppression appear pointed at, or attempted against them, unjustly; and, we are confident, we shall stand justified in the fight of the candid and judicious, for such conduct.

Mr. Carey's first, second, and third editions, are gone forth into the world, and in all probability, have been read by thousands that will never read his fourth—consequently, any alteration he may hereafter make, in the paragraph alluded to, cannot have the desired effect, or atone for the past; therefore we apprehend it necessary to publish our thoughts on the occasion. Had Mr. Carey said, a number of white and black Wretches eagerly seized on the opportunity to extort from the distressed, and some few of both were detected in plundering the sick, it might extenuate, in a great degree, the having made mention of the blacks.

We can assure the public, there were as many white as black people, detected in pilfering, although the number of the latter, employed as nurses, was twenty times as great as the former, and that there is, in our option, as great a proportion of white, as of black, inclined to such practices. It is rather to be admired, that so few instances of pilfering and robbery happened, considering the great opportunities there were for such things: we do not know of more than five black people, suspected of any thing clandestine, out of the great number employed; the people were glad to get any person to assist them—a black was preferred, because it was supposed, they were not so likely to take the disorder, the most worthless were acceptable, so that it would have been no cause of wonder, if twenty causes of compliant occurred, for one that hath. It has been alledged, that many of the sick, were neglected by the nurses; we do not wonder at it, considering their situation, in many instances, up night and day, without any one to relieve them, worn down with fatigue, and want of sleep, they could not in many cases, render that assistance, which was needful: where we visited, the causes of compliant on this score, were not numerous. The case of the nurses, in many instances, were deserving of commiseration, the patient raging and frightful to behold; it has frequently required two persons, to hold them from running way, other have made attempts to jump out of a window, in many chambers they were nailed down, and the door was kept locked, to prevent them from running away, or breaking their necks, others lay vomiting blood, and screaming enough to chill them with horror. Thus were many of the nurses circumstanced, alone, until the patient died, then called away to another scene of distress, and thus have been for a week or ten days left to do the best they could without any sufficient rest, many of them having some of their dearest connections sick at the time, and suffering for want, while their husband, wife, father, mother, &c. have been engaged in the service of the white people. We mention this to shew the difference between this and nursing the common cases, we have suffered equally with the whites, our distress hath been very great, but much unknown to the white people. Few have been the whites that paid attention to us while the black were engaged in the other's service. We can assure the public we have taken four and five black people in a day to be buried. In several instances when they have been seized with the sickness while nursing, they have been turned out of the house, and wandering and destitute until taking shelter wherever they could (as many of them would not be admitted to their former homes) they have languished alone and we know of one who even died in a stable. Others acted with more tenderness, when their nurses were taken sick they had proper care taken of them at their houses. We know of two instances of this.

It is even to this day a generally received opinion in this city, that our colour was not so liable to the sickness as the white. We hope our friends will pardon us for setting this matter in its true state.

The public were informed that in the West-Indies and other places where this terrible malady had been, it was observed the blacks were not affected with it—Happy would it have been for you, and much more so for us, if this observation had been verified by our experience.

When the people of colour had the sickness and died, we were imposed upon and told it was not with the prevailing sickness, until it became too notorious to be denied, then we were told some few died but not many. Thus were our services extorted *at the peril of our lives*, yet you accuse us of extorting *a little money from you*.

The bill of mortality for the year 1793, published by Matthew Whitehead and John Ormrod, clerks, and Joseph Dolby, sexton, will convince any reasonable man that will examine it that as many coloured people died in proportion as others. In 1792, there were 67 of our colour buried, and in 1793 it amounted to 305; thus the burials among us have increased more than fourfold was not this to a great degree the effects of the services of the unjustly vilified black people?

Perhaps it may be acceptable to the reader to know how we found the sick affected by the sickness; our opportunities of hearing and seeing them have been very great. They were taken with a chill, a headach, a sick stomach, with pains in their limbs and back this is the way the sickness in general began, but all were not affected alike, some appeared but slightly affected with some of these symptoms, what confirmed us in the opinion of a person being smitten was the colour of their eyes. In some it raged more furiously than in others—some have languished for seven and ten days, and appeared to get better the day, or some hours before they died, while others were cut off in one, two, or three days, but their complaints were similar. Some lost their reason and raged with all the fury madness could produce, and died in strong convulsions. Others retained their reason to the last, and seemed rather to fall asleep than die. We could not help remarking that the former were of strong passions, and the latter of a mild temper. Numbers died in a kind of dejection, they concluded they must go (so the phrase for dying was) and therefore in a kind of fixed determined state of mind went off.

It struck our minds with awe, to have application made by those in health, to take charge of them in their sickness, and of their funeral. Such applications have been made to us; many appeared as though they thought they must die, and not live, some have lain on the floor, to be measured for their coffin and grave. A gentleman called one evening, to request a good nurse might be got for him, when he was sick, and to superintend his funeral, and gave particular directions how he would have it conducted, it seemed a surprising circumstance, for the man appeared at the time, to be in perfect health, but calling two or three days after to see him, found a woman dead in the house, and the man so far gone, that to administer any thing for his recovery, was needless—he died that evening. We mention this, as an instance of the dejection and despondence, that took hold on the minds of thousands, and are of opinion, it aggravated the case of many, while others who bore up chearfully, got up again, that probably would otherwise have died.

When the mortality came to its greatest stage, it was impossible to procure sufficient assistance, therefore many whose friends, and relations had left them, died unseen, and unassisted. We have found them in various situations, some laying on the floor, as bloody as if they had been dipt in it, without any appearance of their having had, even a drink of water for their relief; others laying on a bed with their clothes on, as if they had came in fatigued, and lain down to rest; some appeared, as if they had fallen dead on the floor, from the position we found them in.

Truly our task was hard, yet through mercy, we were enabled to go on.

One thing we observed in several instances—when we were called, on the first appearance of the disorder to bleed, the person frequently, on the opening a vein before the operation was near over, felt a change for the better, and expressed a relief in their chief complaints; and we made it a practice to take more blood from them, than is usual in other cases; these in a general way recovered; those who did omit bleeding any considerable time, after being taken by the sickness, rarely expressed any change they felt in the operation.

We feel a great satisfaction in believing, that we have been useful to the sick, and thus publicly thank Doctor Rush, for enabling us to be so. We have bled upwards of eight hundred people, and do declare, we have not received to the value of a dollar and a half, therefor: we were willing to imitate the Doctor's benevolence, who sick or well, kept his house open day and night, to give that assistance he could in this time of trouble.

Several affecting instances occurred, when we were engaged in burying the dead. We have been called to bury some, who when we came, we found alive; at other places we found a parent dead, and none but little innocent babes to be seen, whose ignorance led them to think their parent was asleep; on account of their situation, and their little prattle, we have been so wounded and our feelings so hurt, that we almost concluded to withdraw from our undertaking, but seeing others so backward, we still went on.

An affecting instance.—A woman died, we were sent for to bury her, on our going into the house and taking the coffin in, a dear little innocent accosted us, with, mamma is asleep, don't wake her; but when she saw us put her in the coffin, the distress of the child was so great, that it almost overcame us; when she demanded why we put her mamma in the box? We did not know how to answer her, but committed her to the care of a neighbour, and left her with the heavy hearts. In other places where we have been to take the corpse of a parent, and have found a group of little ones alone, some of them in a measure capable of knowing their situation, their cries and the innocent confusion of the little ones, seemed almost too much for human nature to bear. We have picked up little children that were wandering they knew not where, whose (parents were cut off) and taken them to the orphan house, for at this time the dread that prevailed over people's minds was so general, that it was a rare instance to see one neighbour visit another, and even friends when they met in the streets were afraid of each other, much less would they admit into their houses the distressed orphan that had been where the sickness was; this extreme seemed in some instances to have the appearance of barbarity; with reluctance we call to mind the many opportunities there were in the power of individuals to be useful to their fellow-men, yet through the terror of the times was omitted. A black man riding through the street, saw a man push a woman out of the house, the woman staggered and fell on her face in the gutter, and was not able to turn herself, the black man thought she was drunk, but observing she was in danger of suffocation alighted, and taking the woman up found her perfectly sober, but so far gone with the disorder that she was not able to help herself; the hard hearted man that threw her down, shut the door and left her—in such a situation she might have perished in a few minutes: we heard of it, and took her to Bush-Hill. Many of the white people, that ought to be patterns for us to follow after, have acted in a manner that would make humanity shudder. We remember an instance of cruelty, which we trust, no black man would be guilty of: two sisters orderly, decent white women were sick with the fever, one of them recovered so as to come to the door; a neighbouring white man saw her, and in an angry tone asked her if her sister was dead or not? She answered no, upon which he replied, damn her, if she don't die before morning, I will make her die. The poor woman shocked at such an expression, from this monster of a man, made a modest reply, upon which he snatched up a tub of water, and would have dashed it over her, if he had not been prevented by a black man; he then went and took a couple of fowls out of a coop, (which had been given them for nourishment) and threw them into an open alley; he had his wish, the poor woman that he would make die, died the night. A white man threatened to shoot us, if we passed by his house with a corpse: we buried him three days after.

We have been pained to see the widows come to us, crying and wringing their hands, and in very great distress, on account of their husbands' death; having nobody to help them, they were obliged to come to get their husbands buried, their neigh-bours were afraid to go to their help or to condole with them, we ascribe such un-friendly conduct to the frailty of human nature, and not to wilful unkindness or hardness of heart.

Notwithstanding the compliment Mr. Carey hath paid us, we have found reports spread, of our taking between one, and two hundred beds, from houses where people died; such slanderers as these, who propagate such wilful lies are dangerous, although unworthy notice. We wish if any person hath the least suspicion of us, they would endeavour to bring us to the punishment which such atrocious conduct must de-serve; and by this means, the innocent will be cleared from reproach, and the guilty known.

We shall now conclude with the following old proverb, which we think applicable to those of our colour who exposed their lives in the late afflicting dispensation:—

> God and a soldier, all man do adore,
> In time of war, and not before;
> When the war is over, and all things righted,
> God is forgotten, and the soldier slighted.

14. Three Abolitionist Addresses from Brown's Circle.

Although Brown never seems to have formally joined an abolition society, his closest friends and associates were significant leaders and organizers of antislavery societies in Connecticut, New York, and Pennsylvania. Nearly every member of the New York Friendly Club, the discussion group that included Brown, was an officer in an abolition society, and in 1803–1805 Brown and his lifelong friend Thomas Pym Cope together planned an abolitionist History of Slavery *that was never completed.*

During the 1790s the U.S. abolitionist movement entered a new phase for three main reasons. First, black revolution and massacres of whites in Haiti (then known as San Domingo or St. Domingue) provided a concrete example of what could happen elsewhere if slavery were not quickly abolished. Older moral arguments against slavery took on new geopolitical urgency as the black revolution not only introduced the threat of violence but also upset the balance of power in the Caribbean between European imperial states, which had direct, important effects on the economy and territorial ambitions of the United States. Despite the Constitution's attempt to regulate the question of slavery in the 1780s, the multitude of problems it created remained irresolvable.

Second, abolition activists developed innovative institutional and regional networking practices that increased their effectiveness. Throughout the 1790s, abolitionist societies de-veloped new constitutions and improved committee structures that advocated for legal change; worked with the free black community to provide material assistance in housing, health, and education; and provided legal and illegal help to runaway slaves. The multi-ple state organizations began to coordinate their activities and set a national agenda at conventions like the Philadelphia meeting that Brown's close friends Smith, Dunlap, and Miller attended in May 1797.

Third, the outlook and theory of the abolition societies was significantly transformed by a younger generation of recent college graduates and men like the Friendly Club's members, who not only joined the movement but took on central administrative roles in the newly restructured societies. These men revitalized the somewhat aging membership of many societies and brought with them the progressive political sociology of favorite writers such as Thomas Paine, William Godwin, and Mary Wollstonecraft. The older abolitionist arguments that relied primarily on religious reasoning, mainly from the Quakers, were now fused with the secular slogans of the bourgeois enlightenment. These are the ideas that animate Brown's treatment of Arthur Mervyn, who struggles to free himself from the social prejudice of nonbourgeois birth; and from this perspective the novel systematically aligns itself with abolitionist claims and arguments.

These selections, from three abolitionist addresses by Brown's close friends, forcefully articulate the new, politicized viewpoint of the younger abolitionists. They claim that past behavior has no authority for justifying slavery and that it ought to be immediately abolished. Slavery belongs to the older, feudal order of rule by warriors that is unacceptable to a civilizing Enlightenment. There are no moral, social, cultural, or physical justifications for keeping Africans in positions of inferiority. The writers actively promote the idea of monogenesis, the idea that all humans belong to the same race, and dispute physiognomic notions of polygenesis—the belief that there are several separate human races, such as a "white" one, an African one, etc. The present behavior of Africans, be it violent or immoral, is simply the predictable consequence of the social conditions in which they have been unjustly placed. Because humans are formed by their social and cultural environment, Africans will change and "improve" under conditions of freedom, just as Europeans have done. A postslavery society can overcome racial divisions by empowering Africans in the practice of active citizenship, and racial prejudice may be usefully overcome by creating a mixed-race society through intermarriage.

The first address, by Connecticut-based Theodore Dwight (1764–1846), is perhaps the most surprising, given its unexpected celebration of black slave insurgency in Haiti and a notable lack of anxiety about that revolution's violence. Arguing that white plantation owners have simply reaped what they have sown, especially with their Cain-like exile from the island, Dwight rejects the idea that the Haitian Creoles deserve any help based on a shared "whiteness" with U.S. citizens. Black violence is "the language of truth" and merely the outgrowth of divinely inspired yearning for freedom, a spirit that is sympathetically circulated and amplified from individual to region to nation-state (and implicitly the globe). Only the immediate abolition of slavery will prevent a similar outbreak in the United States. These are strong words from a white lawyer who, within a few short years, will become a leading member of the arch-conservative wing of the Federalist Party.

Dr. Elihu Hubbard Smith (1771–1798) was one of Brown's first and closest non-Quaker friends. More than anyone else, Smith encouraged and even financially supported Brown's career as a professional writer, and Brown often draws on Smith as a source for characters and episodes in his fictions. Arthur Mervyn*'s benevolent character Dr. Maravegli, for example, is based on Smith's care of the Venetian Dr. Giambattista Scandella, who died from yellow fever in Smith and Brown's apartment in 1798. Smith's* Discourse *offers a Godwinian analysis of slavery as a particular form of domination by political and* *religious institutions; so that he sees "race" as a category constructed by these premodern institutions and not as a biological essence. Conceptualizing slavery literally as a socially transmitted civic disease, Smith argues that it can be cured by providing a therapy of just benevolence.*

Samuel Miller (1769–1850), a Presbyterian minister and later author of A Brief Retrospect of the Eighteenth Century *(1803), presents the basic contradiction between the continuation of slavery and the principles of citizenship. Miller explicitly rejects notions of racial polygenesis, which could be used to support the argument that freed slaves are fundamentally different from whites and should be returned to Africa, and argues instead that the nation's best hope after abolition is to integrate freed slaves fully within American society. Like Smith, Miller sees slavery and racism as historical diseases that cripple "our political body."*

*****

a) Theodore Dwight, excerpts from *An Oration, Spoken before "The Connecticut Society, for the Promotion of Freedom and the Relief of Persons Unlawfully Holden in Bondage." Convened in Hartford on the 8th day of May, A.D. 1794.* Hartford: Hudson and Goodwin, 1794.

[. . .] It being then acknowledged, that the enslaving of Africans was wrong in the first instance, it must necessarily follow, that the continuance of it is wrong: for a continued succession of unjust actions, can never gain the pure character of justice. If it was originally wrong, it never ceased to be wrong for a moment since; and length of time, instead of sactioning [sic], aggravates the transgression. [. . .] And what is the real ground of this difference, in the administration of justice, between white men, and negroes? Simply this—the white men can appeal to the laws of their country, and enforce their rights. The negroes whom our fathers, and ourselves have enslaved, have no tribunal to listen to their complaints, or to redress their injuries. Forced from their country, their friends, and their families, they are dragged to the sufferance of slavery, of torture, and of death, with no eye, and no arm, but the eye and arm of God, to pity, and to punish their wrongs. Society recognizes their existence only for the purposes of injustice, oppression, and punishment.

By doing strict justice to the negroes, I presume is meant, totally to abolish slavery, and place them on the same ground, with free white men.

[. . .] From France, turn your attention to the island of St. Domingo. A succession of unjust, and contradictory measures, in both the national and colonial governments, at length highly exasperated the negroes, and roused their spirits to unanimity and fanaticism. Seized by the phrenzy of oppressed human nature, they suddenly awoke from the lethargy of slavery, attacked their tyrannical masters, spread desolation and blood over the face of the colony, and by a series of vigorous efforts, established themselves on the firm pillars of freedom and independence. Driven from their houses and possessions, by new and exulting masters, the domestic tyrants of that island wander over the face of the earth, dependent on the uncertain hand of

Charity for shelter, and for bread. To the honour of Americans, it is true, that in this country, they have realized the most liberal humanity. But by a dispensation of Providence which Humanity must applaud, they are forced to exhibit, in the most convincing manner, this important truth—that despotism and cruelty, whether in the family, or the nation, can never resist the energy of enraged and oppressed man, struggling for freedom.

These evils may perhaps appear distant from us; yet to some of our sister states they are probably nigh, even at the doors. Ideas of liberty and slavery, have taken such strong hold of the negroes, that unless their situation is suddenly ameliorated, the inhabitants of the southern states, will have the utmost reason to dread the effects of insurrection. And with the example of the West-Indies before their eyes, they will be worse than mad, if they do not adopt effectual measures to escape their danger. To oppress the slaves by force when in a state of rebellion, or to hold them in their present condition, for any considerable length of time in future, will be beyond their strength. Courage and discipline, form but a feeble front, to check the onset of freedom. [. . .] And when hostilities are commenced, where shall they look for auxiliaries, in such an iniquitous warfare? Surely no friend to freedom and justice will dare to lend them his aid.

[. . .] Who then can charge the negroes with injustice, or cruelty, when "they rise in all the vigour of insulted nature," and avenge their wrongs? What American will not admire their exertions, to accomplish their own deliverance? Every friend to justice and freedom, while his heart bleeds at the recital of the devastation and slaughter, which necessarily attend such convulsions of liberty, must thank his God for the emancipation of every individual from the miseries of slavery. This is the language of freedom; but it is also the language of truth—a language which ever grates on the ears of tyrants, whether placed at the head of a plantation, or the head of an empire. [. . .] For the same principles, which lead nations to the attainment of freedom, urge individuals to pursue the same important object; and the struggles of the latter, are as often marked with desperation, as the efforts of the former. Indeed, from individuals, the spirit is generally communicated to states, and from states to nations. And since the mighty, and majestic course of Freedom has begun, nothing but the arm of Omnipotence can prevent it from reaching to the miserable Africans. But let the domestic tyrants of the earth, tremble at the approaches of such a destructive enemy.

*****

b) Elihu Hubbard Smith, excerpts from *A Discourse, Delivered April 11, 1798, At the Request of and Before The New-York Society for Promoting the Manumission of Slaves, and Protecting Such of Them as Have Been or May Be Liberated. By E. H. Smith, a Member of the Society. New-York: Printed by T. & J. Swords, No. 99 Pearl-Street.*

[. . .] The most hasty outline of the history of slavery must commence with the formation of Society: the history of man is the history of slavery.

In the rude ages of the world, as in the most refined, superior force and superior cunning have equally been practiced, and have both succeeded in enslaving one portion of the human race to another. What individual strength and personal address accomplished, in respect to one or a few, in the infancy of society, has been since extended and perpetuated by multiform combinations both of power and art. Ignorance, and credulity and fear, the companions of ignorance, furnished ample opportunity for successful enterprize, where direct violence must have been hazardous and uncertain. Mental slavery, therefore, was of early origin and quick growth; it was assiduously cultivated; and the bands of superstition restrained those who would easily have shaken off the fetters of subjection. So important were these two methods of holding men in bondage to each other, so consentaneous in their principles, and so co-ordinate in their birth, that, in the outset, they not infrequently united in the same person: the same person was at once king and pontiff. As society advanced, the agents of this tyranny were augmented; a seeming division of powers took place, while a real union was maintained; to one party was committed the execution of their joint devices; to the other was entrusted the more silent and specious diffusion of opinions favourable to their views. The first subdued opposition in the field; the last undermined it in the family; and while the king led his chiefs to combat, the pontiff, surrounded by his priests, invested with the security of inviolable sanctity, refined his cunning, multiplied his wiles, and at length succeeded in subjugating the prince as well as the people. This was sometimes a delicate task; but the fear which even the most powerful despots entertain of their slaves, favoured the sacerdotal usurpation; and they were held by the interest who secretly derided the pretensions of the prelacy.

As the state of society improved, the cultivators of superstition subtilized and perfected their arts. They saw and obeyed the necessity of governing less in appearance, while they redoubled their exertions, by converting to their aid all the errors of judgment, all the violences of passion, and all the phenomena of nature, to hold an ampler tyranny over the minds of men. Unable absolutely to impede the progress of knowledge, they laboured to distort it to their own purposes; or, failing of success, imposed a more powerful obstacle, by exerting their influence for the destruction of the intractable sovereign, and enlightened philosopher.

While nations were exclusively ruled by the priesthood, or by tyrants who united in their own persons the offices of monarch and high-priest, no safe means of obtaining and consolidating authority were neglected. Afterwards, upon a separation of the two functions of enslaving the bodies and subjugating the minds of men, the leaders of opinion strenuously supported all the outrages of the despot who was subservient to their wishes; and, whether he ground with the iron edge of oppression his own subjects, or the subjects of another, whether his capricious frenzy doomed his own territories, or the dominions of a neighbouring prince, to desolation, alike sustained his fury and panegyrized his injustice. Under such circumstances, is it wonderful that slavery became widely diffused; that the sword and the robe alone were deemed worthy the ambition of the great; that all the arts which nourish and bless mankind were despised as servile; that men became worshippers of men, and eagerly acknowledged themselves the servants of one, that they might more securely tyrannize over many.

Nor was this state of things limited to monarchies. Forms of government rather varied the application of the spirit of despotism, than destroyed it.

[. . .] In the existing circumstances of society, encumbered as we are with this mighty evil, which slavery has cast upon us, we are only free to chuse, amid [a] variety of embarrassments. There is no fear that even this factitious right of property, so much insisted on, will not be sufficiently respected. Alas! there is no hope but that it will long continue triumphantly to oppose all the efforts of benevolence. But, were it justly insisted on, what demons of malignant cruelty paralize the senses and the reason of legislators? Do they not see the ruin which surrounds us? Are they unconscious of the poison which hovers over every roof, lurks in every house, and infects every cup? Wait they till the venders of pestilence, till the manufacturers of plagues, relinquish their productive and desolating craft, before they labour for the restoration of health, for the prevention of disease? What! will they foster the fury, relax the fetters which partially confine her, and imp her with new wings, that she may more vigorously pursue the work of devastation?—You, yes you, the Legislators of America, you are the real upholders of slavery! You, yes you, Legislators of this Commonwealth, you foster and protect it here! Is it not recognized by your laws? and in the very face of your Constitution? of that instrument which you maintained by your arms, and sealed with your blood? Have not those laws authorized, systematized, and protected, and do they not now protect it? If you fear the clamors of the enslavers of men, or if you acknowledge the justice of their claims to compensation, it is you who sanction, you who uphold the crime. It is you who are deaf to the demands of justice, the signs of humanity, the representations of policy, the calls of interest, the suggestions of expediency, the warning voice of domestic tranquility. It is you who shut the ear, who close the eye, who clench the hand, insensible to every motive which most determine men to hear, to see, and to act. You perpetrate, you perpetuate, you immortalize injustice—and all "for so much trash as may be grasped thus." The opposers of justice do not read, think, reason, feel,—they do not so much as listen. They admit but one idea, that of gain from the labour of their slaves; they are occupied but with one care, that of maintaining their authority. And you nourish that gain, you cherish that care, you defend with double mounds that monstrous authority, at the hazard, if not with the sacrifice, of all the dearest interests of society, of its very existence. These you hazard, when the remedy is obvious, certain, easy to be obtained, and safe to be applied. Mad insensibility! the little interests of the moment, the gratifications of vanity, and the contests of passion, a market, a palace, or a strip of land, engross your thoughts and dissipate your treasures, while the welfare of a nation sleeps unregarded, while thousands of your fellow-beings, children of the same father, and inheritors of the same destiny, eat the bitter bread of slavery, writhe under the lash of cruelty, and sink into the untimely grave amid the taunts of oppression!—Amen! so be it! and so shall be the retribution!*

---

* It is but justice to the last House of Representatives of this State to inform the reader, in this place, that they passed a bill providing for the gradual abolition of slavery, and by a considerable majority. The bill, however, was rejected by the Senate.

[. . .] The experience of many years, evidence palpable to the most hardened and obstinate sense, has demonstrated the capacity of the Blacks. The very vices of which they stand so bitterly accused, demonstrate it. They, alike all men else, are the creatures of education, of example, of circumstances, of external impressions. Make them outcasts and vagabonds, thrust them into the society of drunkards and of thieves, shut them from the fair book and salutary light of knowledge, degrade them into brutes, and trample them into dust, and you must expect them to be vile and wretched, dissolute and lawless, base and stupid. Madmen! would you "gather grapes of thorns, or figs of thistles?"

But, notwithstanding the degraded condition of the Africans, and their descendants among us,—a condition to which they have been reduced, or in which they have been retained, by those who reproach them with it, and would offer it as an excuse for their own inhumanity and injustice,—still they exhibit many examples of humble, but of cheering virtue. We not only see them irreproachably employed in various mechanic occupations; but, in some few instances, elevated to the illustrious offices of the instructors in learning, and inculcators of morality. The desk, and the pulpit, have witnessed their triumphs over all the efforts of blind and malignant prejudice. Already they begin to feel their own worth as men; already are they impressed with some just sense of the nature of those exertions which are making in their behalf; already have they attained to some conception of that prudent and virtuous conduct which is the best reward for all our toils; already may they challenge the palm from many of their whiter brethren. Perceive you not that spirit of improvement—slow though it be, yet visible—which diffuses itself among them? Observe you not their growing knowledge, their increasing industry, their softening manners, their correcter morals? Hear you not that sigh, wakened by your benevolent sympathy? Mark you not that tear of grateful joy, silently descending? See you not that sable figure, that casts himself at your feet, that kisses your hand, that clasps your knees, "fathers and benefactors of our race," that exclaims—"the sons of Africa feel your virtue at their souls;—their hearts, their hands, their lives, are devoted to your service."

'Go, hapless progeny of a violated parent! cultivate peace, order, knowledge. Let your patience grow with your wrongs. Let your hearts learn forgiveness, your hands labour for your tyrants, your lives refute their calumnies. Go! assured, that, as for us, we have well considered what awaits us,—the extent of surrounding obstacles, and their duration, and have resolved, never to quench our zeal, to withhold our care, to intermit our labours, never to drop the language of persuasion, and forget the tone of justice, till we behold you disenthralled of bonds, reinstated in your rights, blessed with science, and adorned with virtue.'

*****

c) Samuel Miller, excerpts from *A Discourse Delivered April 12, 1797 at the Request of and Before the New-York Society for Promoting the Manumission of Slaves, and Protecting Such of Them as Have Been or May Be Liberated.* New York: T. and J. Swords, 1797.

[. . .] That, in the close of the eighteenth century, it should be esteemed proper and necessary, in any civilized country, to institute discourse to oppose the slavery and commerce of the human species, is a wonderful fact in the annals of society! But that this country should be America, is a solecism only to be accounted for by the general inconsistency of the human character. But, after all the surprise that Patriotism can feel, and all the indignation that Morality can suggest on this subject, the humiliating tale must be told—that in this free country—in this country, the plains of which are still stained with blood shed in the cause of liberty,—in this country, from which has been proclaimed to distant lands, as the basis of our political existence, the noble principle, that "ALL MEN ARE BORN FREE AND EQUAL,"—in this country there are slaves!—men are bought and sold! Strange indeed! that the bosom which glows at the name of liberty in general, and the arm which has been so vigorously exerted in vindication of human rights, should yet be found leagued on the side of oppression, and opposing their avowed principles!

[. . .] In the present age and country, none, I presume, will rest a defence of slavery on the ground of superior force; the right of captivity; or any similar principle, which the ignorance and the ferocity of ancient times admitted as a justifiable tenure of property. It is to be hoped the time is passed, never more to return, when men would recognize maxims as subversive to morality as they are of social happiness. Can the laws and rights of war be properly drawn into precedent for the imitation of sober and regular government? Can we sanction the detestable idea, that liberty is only an advantage gained by strength, and not a right derived from nature's God? Such sentiments become the abodes of demons, rather than societies of civilized men.

Pride, indeed, may contend, that these unhappy subjects of our oppression are an *inferior race of beings;* and are therefore assigned by the strictest justice to a depressed and servile station in society. But in what does this inferiority consist? In a difference of *complexion* and *figure?* Let the narrow and illiberal mind, who can advance such an argument, recollect whither it will carry him. In traversing the various regions of the earth, from the Equator to the Pole, we find an infinite diversity of shades in the complexion of men, from the darkest to the fairest hues. If, then, the proper station of the African is that of servitude and depression, we must also contend, that every Portuguese and Spaniard is, though in a less degree, inferior to us, and should be subject to a measure of the same degradation. Nay, if the tints of colour be considered the test of human dignity, we may justly assume a haughty superiority over our southern brethren of this continent, and devise their subjugation. In short, upon this principle, where shall liberty end? or where shall slavery begin? At what grade is it that the ties of blood are to cease? And how many shades must we descend still lower in the scale, before mercy is to vanish with them?

But, perhaps, it will be suggested, that the Africans and their descendents are inferior to their brethren in *intellectual capacity*, if not in complexion and figure. This is strongly asserted, but upon what ground? Because we do not see men who labour under every disadvantage, and who have every opening faculty blasted and destroyed by their depressed condition, signalize themselves as philosophers? Because we do not find men who are almost entirely cut off from every source of mental improvement, rising to literary honours? To suppose the Africans of an inferior racial character, because they have not thus distinguished themselves, is just as rational as to suppose every private citizen of an inferior species, who has not raised himself up to the condition of royalty. But, the truth is, many of the negroes discover great ingenuity, notwithstanding their circumstances so depressed, and so unfavourable to all cultivation. They become excellent mechanics and practical musicians, and, indeed, learn every thing their masters take the pains to teach them.* And how far they might improve in this respect, were the same advantages conferred on them that freemen enjoy, is impossible for us to decide until the experiment be made.

ARISTOTLE long ago said—"Men of little genius, and great bodily strength, are by nature destined to serve, and those of a better capacity to command. The natives of Greece, and of some other countries, being naturally superior in genius, have a natural right to empire; and the rest of mankind, being naturally stupid, are destined to labour and slavery."** What would this great philosopher have thought of his own reasoning, had he lived till the present day? On the one hand, he would have seen his countrymen, of whose genius he boasts so much, lose with their liberty all mental character; while, on the other, he would have seen many nations, whom he consigned to everlasting stupidity, shew themselves equal in intellectual power to the most exalted of human kind.

[. . .] But higher laws than those of common justice and humanity may be urged against slavery. I mean THE LAWS OF GOD, revealed in the scriptures of truth. This divine system, in which we profess to believe and to glory, teaches us, that *God has made of one blood all nations of men that dwell on the face of the whole earth.*

[. . .] There have not been wanting, indeed men, as ignorant as they were impious, who have appealed to the sacred scriptures for a defence of slavery.

[. . .] Many have been the proposals of benevolent men to remedy this grand evil, and to ameliorate the condition of the injured negroes. But, while I revere the very mistakes of those who have shewn themselves friends to human happiness, yet the most of these proposals appear to me incumbered with insuperable difficulties, and, in some points of view, to involve greater mischief than the original disorder designed to be cured. Immediately to emancipate *seven hundred thousand* slaves, and

---

* Having been, for two years, a monthly visitor of the African School in this city, I directed particular attention to the capacity and behaviour of the scholars, with a view to satisfy myself on the point in question. And, to me, the negro children of that institution appeared, in general, quite as orderly and quite as ready to learn, as white children.

** De Republ. lib.i,cap.5,6.

send them forth into society, with all the ignorance, habits, and vices of their degraded education about them, would probably produce effects more unhappy than any one is able to calculate or conceive. Nor does the plan appear much more plausible, which some have proposed, to collect, and send them back to the country from whence they or their fathers have been violently dragged; or, to form them into a colony, in some retired part of our own territory.[1] I shall not pronounce either of these impracticable; because one of them has been attempted by an European nation, and not altogether without success.[2] I shall not say, that such a removal would be less happy for the subjects of it, than their present condition; because, in particular instances, it might prove otherwise. But, in my view, the difficulties and objections attending such a plan, especially on a large scale, are far greater and more numerous than many sanguine speculators have seemed to suppose.

Perhaps no method can be devised, to deliver our country from the evil in question, more safe, more promising, and more easy of execution, than one which has been partially adopted in some of the states,[3] and hitherto with all the success that could have been expected. This plan is, to frame laws, which will bring about the emancipation in a GRADUAL MANNER; which will, at the same time, PROVIDE FOR THE INTELLECTUAL AND MORAL CULTIVATION of slaves, that they may be prepared to exercise the rights, and discharge the duties of citizens, when liberty shall be given them; and which, having thus fitted them for the station, will confer upon them, in due time, the privileges and dignity of other freemen. By the operation of such a plan, it is easy to see that slavery, at no great distance of time, would be banished in the United States; the mischiefs attending an universal and immediate emancipation would be, in a great measure, if not entirely, prevented; and beings, who are now gnawing the vitals, and wasting the strength of the body politic, might be converted into wholesome and useful members of it. Say not that they are unfit for the rank of citizens, and can never be made honest and industrious members of the community. Say not that their ignorance and brutality must operate as everlasting bars against their being elevated to this station. All just reasoning abjures the flimsy pretext. Make them freemen; and they will soon be found to have the manners, the character, and the virtues of freemen.*

---

[1] [Editors' Note: Miller refers to African or other recolonization proposals by Jefferson and others and rejects the idea in favor of a vision of a mixed-race society, which he articulates in the remainder of the address. Earlier, in a passage not included here, Miller quotes Jefferson's famous warning: "I tremble for my country when I remember that God is just—that his justice cannot sleep for ever—and that an exchange of circumstances is among probable events. The Almighty has no attribute which can take side with us in such a conflict" (Miller, 27).]

[2] [Editors' Note: Miller refers to the British scheme in 1792 to recolonize Sierra Leone with those who had formerly been slaves in the Caribbean and North America.]

[3] [Editors' Note: i.e., a reference to Pennsylvania's 1781 abolition law and the work of building black institutions and education there.]

* It is easy to foresee that many strong prejudices, and many feelings not altogether unnatural, will oppose the execution of this plan. The idea of admitting negroes to a state of political and social

15. Two Perspectives on Slavery from *The Monthly Magazine and American Review*

These two pieces on slavery and racial domination were published in the Monthly Magazine and American Review, *the magazine founded and edited by Brown's New York circle and in which Brown played a central editorial role. Both appeared during the months when* Second Part *was being written and use historical case studies from Roman and English history as evidence of ways in which the damage caused by slavery in the United States can be overcome. The first section comes from an article by "H.L.," possibly a pseudonym for Brown's childhood friend Joseph Bringhurst, Jr. H.L. uses the arguments linking population, territory, and economic resources that are most commonly associated today with Thomas Malthus'* An Essay on the Principle of Population, as It Affects the Future Improvement of Society with Remarks on the Speculations of Mr. Godwin, M. Condorcet, and Other Writers *(1798).*

Malthus refuted progressive claims that society can become more perfect by arguing that the increase of population will act as a conservative check on social change, since population growth creates a scarcity of resources. But H.L. turns Malthus on his head by arguing that miscegenation and the relative increase of the white population into an expanding frontier will allow for a transformation of American society through the peaceful abolition of slavery, just as slaves were incorporated into Roman society.

The second excerpt comes from an anonymous review of a section of William Eton's four volume A Survey of the Turkish Empire *(London, 1798). Because this is not a review of Eton's entire work, but a re-publication of a particular section, it is most likely that Brown, as editor, chose the fragment to highlight an argument with which he was in sympathy. Eton argues that the character of Greeks cannot be adduced from their present behavior as dominated peoples under the rule of the Ottoman Empire. Because of the legal and cultural divisions created by the ruling Turks in order to disempower and disenfranchise the Greeks, their human vitality is suppressed. Using England as his example, Eton argues that that the difference among peoples can be overcome through universal rights and miscegenation. Eton's argument can also be understood in the context of wider British romantic era interest in the theme of Greek independence (in the best-known example, the poet Byron dies in Greece for this cause). Brown's magazine most likely publishes the extract as a comparative example that helps explain African behavior under slavery and that projects the results of a full emancipation and incorporation of Africans as equal citizens.*

✳✳✳✳✳

---

equality with the whites, even after the best education they can receive, is not a very pleasant one to a great majority even of those who are warmly engaged for their emancipation. I shall not discuss the reasonableness of such feelings at present. It is sufficient to say, that our political body is labouring under a most hurtful and dangerous disease; and that the most skilful physician cannot restore it to health without the exhibition of some remedies which are more or less unpalatable.

a) H.L., "Thoughts on the Probable Termination of Negro Slavery in the United States of America," *The Monthly Magazine and American Review* 2:2 (February 1800).

[. . .] Domestic Slavery was greatly prevalent among the Romans, in the height of their power. Their system, in this respect, was remarkably similar to ours, except in the employment of their slaves, which did not essentially differ from that of servants and peasants in modern Italy and Spain. Their manners, religion, and government, were far less favorable to manumission than ours, and yet a slave, in the third generation, was rarely known. The mass of people in the cities, the knights, and finally the senators and governors of provinces were chiefly composed of the posterity of slaves.

Hence, when the limits of the empire became stationary, and war no longer supplied the markets with captives, the people insensibly mingled into one mass, with little distinction but those of property or profession. The progress to this state of things, with us, may be reasonably expected to be infinitely more rapid, from the greater prevalence of enlightened opinions, from the inferior proportion of the number of slaves to that of freemen,* and from causes peculiar to our selves, which obstruct their propagation or shorten their lives.

But however we determine as to the absolute number of slaves, at any given period, it is evident that their relative or proportionate number will decline. The southern States are, comparatively, deserts. A few districts on the seaboard are planted with rice, and maize, and tobacco; but the western regions are nearly unoccupied except by panthers and deer. These, however, will quickly be stocked by people who will migrate hither from the east and north. The new comers will bring with them habits, if not opinions, incompatible with slavery. They will till their fields and stock their corn with their own hands.

[. . .] As the proportion of freemen increases, it must be expected that every moral cause tending to annihilate servitude, will increase in force. . . . Comprehensive schemes of emancipation may possibly be dangerous when the number of slaves is *one half* or *one third* of the whole; but this danger is annihilated when it dwindles to a fifteenth or a twentieth.

*****

b) William Eton, "Interesting Account of the Character and Political State of the Modern Greeks. [From a Survey of the Turkish Empire, &c. by W. Eton, Esq.]." *The Monthly Magazine and American Review* 2:6 (May 1800).

[. . .] Every object, moral and physical, the fair face of nature and the intellectual energies of the [Greek] inhabitants, have alike been blasted and defiled by the harpytouch of Turkish tyranny.

---

* Some have computed the slaves in the Roman provinces to be half the inhabitants. In our southern states it is but little more than one third of the whole population.

[. . .] Of the defects of the Grecian character, some are doubtless owing to their ancient corruptions; but most of them take their rise in the humiliating state of depression in which they are held by the Turks. This degradation and servility of their situation, has operated for centuries, and has consequently produced an accumulated effect on the mind; but, were this weight taken off, the elasticity and vigour of the soul would have wide room for expansion; and, though it cannot be expected that they would at once rise to the proud animation of their former heroes, they would doubtless display energies of mind which the iron hand of despotism has long kept dormant and inert. It is rather astonishing that they have retained so much energy of character, and are not more abased, for, like noble coursers, they champ the bit, and spurn indignantly the yoke: when once freed from these, they enter the course of glory.

[. . .] It has been said, that long possession of a country gives an indisputable right of dominion, and that the right of the Turks to their possessions has been acknowledged by all nations in their treaties. As to treaties between the Turks and other nations, who had no right to dispose of the countries usurped by the Turks, they cannot be binding to the Greeks, who never signed such treaties, nor were consulted, or consented to their signing.

When one nation conquers another, and they become incorporated by having the same rights, the same religion, the same language, and by being blended together by intermarriages, a long series of years renders them one people. Who can, in England, distinguish the aborigines from the Romans, Saxons, Danes, Normans, and other foreigners? They are all Englishmen.

The Greeks were conquered by the Turks, but they were attacked (like all other nations they conquered) by them without provocation. It was not a war for injury or insult, for jealousy of power or the support of an ally, contests which ought to end when satisfaction or submission is obtained; it was a war having for its aim conquest, and for its principle a right to the dominion of the whole earth; a war which asserted that all other sovereigns were usurpers, and the deposing and putting them to death was a sacred duty. Do the laws of nations establish that such a conquest gives right of possession? They, on the contrary, declare such conquest usurpation.

The conquered were never admitted by the Turks to the rights of citizens or fellow subjects, unless they abjured their religion and their country: they became slaves; and as, according to their cowardly law, the Turks have a right, at all times, to put to death their prisoners, the conquered and their posterity for ever are obliged annually to *redeem their heads*, by paying the price set on them: they are excluded from all offices in the state. It is death for a conquered Greek to marry a Turkish woman, or even to cohabit with a common prostitute of that nation. They are, in every respect, treated as enemies. They are still called and distinguished by the name of their nation, and a Turk is never called a Greek, though his family should have been settled for generations in that country. The testimony of a Greek is not valid in the court of judicature, when contrasted with that of a Turk. They are distinguished by a different dress: it is death to wear the same apparel as a Turk: even their houses are painted a different colour: in fine, they are in the same situation they were the day they were conquered; totally distinct as a nation; and they have therefore the same right now as they then had, to free themselves from the barbarous usurpers of their country, whose conduct to all the nations they have conquered, merits the external execration of mankind.

16. Benjamin Nones vs. the *Gazette*

This polemical newspaper exchange from early August 1800 between an anonymous "Observer" in the Federalist Gazette of the United States *and Benjamin Nones (1757–1826), a Democratic-Republican society[1] and Jewish community activist, is a likely context for Brown's decision, late in the novel's composition, to give the character Achsa Fielding Jewish ethnicity and to end the novel with a romantic union between the Scots-Irish Mervyn and a dark-skinned, non-Christian emigrant. By concluding the novel with this affirmation of a Jewish character and an interracial marriage, and publishing it in a context that included heated exchanges like this one, Brown codes the novel's ending as an argument against the partisan racialization of political debate in his immediate environment and as a wider affirmation of progressive ethnic and class mixture in personal and civic relations.*

Additionally, given Nones' suggestion that all Jews and the less wealthy ought naturally to support republican causes, the conclusion of Brown's novel may be seen in this light as an oblique, discrete criticism of the Federalist administration in the key months leading up to the December 1800 national election that ended the Federalist party's domination of national politics. Brown made a brief visit to Philadelphia from New York in late August and would have been well aware of such a remarkable exchange appearing in the leading Philadelphia newspapers of the day. The exchange had an afterlife through the rest of the month when Nones' reply was distributed as a broadside on the streets of Philadelphia, reprinted elsewhere, and satirized in subsequent issues of the Gazette.

The exchange is best known for Benjamin Nones' landmark assertion and defense of Jewish civic identity in the U.S. When Nones was refused the right of response to insults against him in the final lines of the Gazette *article, he published his now-famous reply— defiantly declaring "I am a Jew . . . I am Republican . . . I am poor"—in the opposition newspaper, the Jeffersonian-identified* Aurora. *Nones was a French Sephardic Jew who came to the U.S. from Bordeaux at age twenty in 1777 to fight in the American Revolution, became naturalized in 1784, and settled in Philadelphia, where he was active in numerous civic organizations, serving for example as the president (1791–1799) of the Congregation Mikveh Israel, the first synagogue in Philadelphia.*

Nones was also an abolitionist, joining the Pennsylvania Society for Promoting the Abolition of Slavery and manumitting his one slave in summer 1793 before working to

---

[1] "Federalist . . . Democratic-Republican": in the political party terminology of the 1790s, Federalists are the more Anglophile, moneyed elite, and conservative party (the party of the Washington and Adams administrations), and Democratic-Republicans are the more socially and regionally heterogeneous Francophile party (which comes into power after 1800 in the Jefferson and Madison administrations). Democratic-Republican societies were local political action committees that were typically more radical in tone and spirit that the party's elite leaders such as Jefferson or Madison.

persuade other Jewish refugees from the black revolution in Haiti to free slaves they had brought to Philadelphia. One of Nones' three sons (who all became consuls) had a consular appointment to Haiti. Within this group, Nones would have been familiar to Brown's close abolitionist friends, to the African American ministers Richard Allen and Absalom Jones, as well as to the white co-organizers of the Underground Railroad, Thomas Harrison (listed in Nones' reply as one of his repaid creditors) and Isaac Hopper. In this letter to the Gazette, *Nones defends himself against a personalized slur but explicitly situates his claims in larger terms as part of the period's ongoing struggle for the civil emancipation of Jews in the United States and other postrevolutionary republics.*

For readers of Arthur Mervyn, *it is also instructive to consider the attack that provoked Nones' response, since the anonymous* Gazette *piece exemplifies the scurrilous style of antiworker, antiblack, and anti-Semitic slurs that was repeatedly employed by Federalist journalists in the partisan infighting of the late 1790s, especially in attacks on the Democratic-Republican societies that had been providing new mechanisms for egalitarian-minded social organization since they began to appear in 1793. That is, the* Gazette *piece is not primarily an attack on any of the individuals it insults, but a race-baiting account of a meeting of the True Republican Society of Pennsylvania (earlier called the Democratic Society of Pennsylvania) with a larger agenda that was clear to contemporary readers.*

The piece's larger argument, built on its appeal to ethnic and class stereotypes, is against the kind of mixed-ethnicity potential that the club and its principles make possible, and which are affirmed by Arthur Mervyn's *Woldwinite program. The attack is not an isolated gesture, but continues the earlier partisan mobilization of anti-Semitic slurs by Federalist journalists such as William Cobbett and John Fenno (the previous editor of the* Gazette*) that was a repeated feature of the decade's political newspaper wars.*

The Gazette's *caricatures are directed at the Society's social diversity and egalitarian goals, characterized as ridiculous openness to the "very* refuse *and* filth *of society." The "Citizen Sambo" character refers to Cyrus Bustil, a black Quaker and leader in the city's Free Black community who played an important role in responses to the 1793 fever epidemic and later organized a black school in his own home (Bustil was the great-great-grandfather of twentieth-century black activist and actor Paul Robeson). "Citizen I—s—l" is city politician Israel Israel, another democratic activist who was the object of Federalist anti-Semitic slurs on the basis of his family background, although he was not himself Jewish. George Lesher, owner of the tavern mentioned by name in Chapters 3, 14, and 19 of* Arthur Mervyn, *was a member of the same political society being attacked here and hosted meetings in support of Israel Israel at his tavern in 1798–1799. These meetings at Lesher's Tavern were chaired by radical John Barker, the same chairperson mocked here as "Citizen B—r," the tailor. "Citizen N— the Jew" refers of course to Benjamin Nones.*

*****

a) "An Observer," excerpts from "For the Gazette of the United States" (*The Gazette*, August 5, 1800).

Actuated by motives of curiosity, I attended the meeting of Jacobins,[2] on Wednesday evening last, at the State House. Diverted at the consummate ignorance and stupidity, as well as self importance of these miserable wretches, I will endeavour to recount the various and singular transactions of this *wonderful* meeting, almost altogether composed of the very *refuse* and *filth* of society. To prove this my assertion (if proof be necessary) let it be known, that a large proportion of this meeting was men of the most infamous and abandoned characters; men, who are notorious for the seduction of *black innocence*,[3] who have more than once been convicted in open court of wilful perjury, and men who with sacriligious hands have impiously dared to tear down from the sacred desk, the emblems of mourning in honour of our beloved Washington—When persons of such character assume to themselves the order and regulation of a *government*, soon may we expect anarchy, confusion and commotion to ensue.

This meeting was opened by the *great big little* citizen of Market Street in the following style, "Fellow citizens, its most eight o'clock; an't it most time to commence the meeting, shall our worthy and Republican say—hem, Citizen B—r take the chair." Aye, Aye, was the general response, whereupon from the *motley group* out pops little Johnny (Knight of the Thimble) and at his tail the lap stone boy, R.[4] as his journeyman, Pshaw I mean his secretary. When seated, Barker loudly thumps his cudgel upon the table and with an audible voice proclaims order; "order Gent.—hem—Fellow Citizens, order, posi-ti-vely we cant *recede* to business without some order; Brother R— read the minutes of the last assemblage." Here secretary Vizze seating himself upon the table near the *Rush light*[5] (for reader he has not very good

---

[2] "Jacobin": was an all-purpose synonym for "disreputable" or "subversive" when used in this manner by a conservative commentator in the late 1790s. The original reference is to the Jacobin faction of the French Revolution, which for conservatives became synonymous with revolutionary excesses after the 1793–1794 "Reign of Terror" that figures in Achsa Fielding's backstory.

[3] "The seduction of *black innocence*": in other words, well-known for advocating black emancipation. Nones, Benjamin Rush, and others present were also members of abolition societies.

[4] "Little Johnny . . . and . . . the lap stone boy, R.": John Barker was a tailor. "Lap stone boy" indicates that "R." is a shoemaker, since lap stones are emblems of that trade.

[5] "Rush light": a cheap candle substitute, a reed or rush dipped in fat or wax; here the term alludes to "The Rush-Light," a series of pamphlet attacks written February–September 1800 by conservative journalist William Cobbett, against Dr. Benjamin Rush's yellow fever treatments and progressive political associations. Thus the term provides a dig at Rush's influence in this club that avoids naming him directly, since in December 1797 Rush had won a large damage award against Cobbett for previous libels. The *Gazette* insults lower-status club members by name but avoids direct mention of an elite figure capable of striking back against such attacks. Rush's lawsuit ended Cobbett's career in the United States; surprisingly, he became famous as a laboring-class activist after returning to England. When the libel damages were finally paid in 1801, Rush distributed the money to poverty relief organizations.

eyes) after a great deal of coughing twisting and snuffing the candles, and a *little bit* of spelling here and there (having been no doubt accustomed to the din of Hammers) bawled out in a most ridicullus and blundering manner the aforesaid minutes. [. . .]

[. . .] A great noise—Chairman what's the matter?

Citizen I—s—l. Nothing only our friend Billy is a little *gone.*

Citizen B—r, (in a half whisper and shaking his head), Ah poor soul, I'm afraid that damn'd gin will be the death of him; but come let us *reconnoitre* the business;—I think Citizen F—n was going to move—

Citizen Sambo. Ah massa he be *shove off* already; he go away wid broder Bully—oh here he come.

[. . .] *Cit B—r.* Citizens before we sojourn, I will remark that I know Republicans are always a pertty much *barrassed* for the rhino,[6] but must *detrude* upon your ginerosity to night by exing you to launch out some of the *ready* for the citizen who provides for the room; I know Democrats hav'nt many *English Guineas* amongst them but I hope they have some *sipyenny bits* to night *at least,* and if they will *jist* throw them into *my hat* as they go along I shall be *defientially* obliged to them.*

Here I observed not a few gave an eleven penny bit and asked for a sipenny bit change, which they received. As for myself, I returned to my house as soon as possible, that I might enjoy my laugh, which be assured I did, and heartily too.

AN OBSERVER.[7]

Citizen N— the Jew. I hopsh you will consider dat de monish ish very scarch, and besides you know I'sh just come out by de Insholvent Law.[8]

Several. Oh yes let N— pass.

*****

---

[6] "Rhino": slang for money.

[7] Historian Jacob Rader Marcus suggests that Federalist journalist Joseph Dennie was behind this piece as author or editor, although there is no conclusive evidence for the attribution. See Marcus's discussion in *United States Jewry* I.527–28.

[8] "*I hopsh . . . de Insholvent Law*": the dialect speech given to Nones is based on anti-Jewish stereotypes in contemporary theater, for example in the character Ben Hassan in Susanna Rowson's *Slaves in Algiers* (1794). See Nathans, "A Much-Maligned People: Jews on and off the Stage in the Early American Republic."

b) Benjamin Nones, "To the Printer of the Gazette of the U.S." (*The Aurora*, August 13, 1800).

TO THE EDITOR.

MR. DUANE.[9]

I enclose you an article which I deemed it but justice to my character to present for insertion in the Gazette of the United States, in reply to some illiberalities which were thrown out against me in common with many respectable citizens in that paper of the 5th inst. When I presented it to Mr. Wayne,[10] he promised me in the presence of a third person, that he would publish it. I waited until this day, when finding it had not appeared, I called on him, when he informed me that he would not publish it. I tendered him payment if he should require it. His business appears to be to asperse and shut the door against justification. I need not say more:

I am &c. B. NONES.

Philadelphia Aug. 11, 1800.

———

To the Printer of the Gazette of the U.S.

SIR,

I hope, if you take the liberty of inserting calumnies against individuals, for the amusement of your readers, you will at least have so much regard to justice, as to permit the injured through the same channel that conveyed the slander, to appeal to the public in self defence.—I expect of you therefore, to insert this reply to your ironical reporter of the proceedings at the meeting of the republican citizens of Philadelphia, contained in your gazette of the fifth instant: so far as I am concerned in that statement. —I am no enemy Mr. Wayne to wit; nor do I think the political parties have much right to complain, if they enable the public to laugh at each others expence, provided it be managed with the same degree of ingenuity, and some attention as truth and candour. But your reporter of the proceedings at that meeting is as destitute of truth and candour, as he is of ingenuity, and I think, I can shew, that the want of prudence of this Mr. Marplot in his slander upon me, is equally glaring with his want of wit, his want of veracity, his want of decency, and his want of humanity.

I am accused of being a *Jew*; of being a *Republican*; and of being *Poor*.

I *am* a *Jew*. I glory in belonging to that persuasion, which even its opponents, whether christian, or Mahomedan, allow to be of divine origin—of that persuasion on which Christianity itself was originally founded, and must ultimately rest—which has preserved its faith secure and undefiled, for near three thousand years—whose

---

[9] William Duane, editor and publisher of the *Aurora*.

[10] Caleb P. Wayne, publisher-printer of the *Gazette*.

votaries have never murdered each other in religious wars, or cherished the theological hatred so general, so unextinguishable among those who revile them. A persuasion, whose, patient followers have endured for ages the pious cruelties of Pagans, and of christians, and persevered in the unoffending practice of their rites and ceremonies, amidst poverties and privations—amidst pains, penalties, confiscations, banishments, tortures, and deaths, beyond the example of any other sect, which the page of history has hitherto recorded.

To be of such a persuasion, is to me no disgrace; though I well understand the inhuman language, of bigotted contempt, in which your reporter by attempting to make me ridiculous, as a Jew, has made himself detestable, whatever religious persuasion may be dishonored by his adherence.

But I am a Jew. I am so—and so were Abraham, and Isaac, and Moses and the prophets, and so too were Christ and his apostles. I feel no disgrace in ranking with such society, however, it may be subject to the illiberal buffoonery of such men as your correspondents.

I am a *Republican!* Thank God, I have not been so heedless, and so ignorant of what has passed, and is now passing in the political world. I have not been so proud or so prejudiced as to renounce the cause for which I have *fought*, as an American throughout the whole of the revolutionary war, in the militia of Charleston, and in Polaskey's legion,[11] I fought in almost every action which took place in Carolina, and in the disastrous affair of Savannah,[12] shared the hardships of that sanguinary day, and for three and twenty years I felt no disposition to change my political, any more than my religious principles.—And which in spite of the witling scribblers of aristocracy, I shall hold sacred until death as not to feel the ardour of republicanism. —Your correspondent, Mr. Wayne cannot have known what it is to serve his country from principle in time of danger and difficulties, at the expence of his health and his peace, of his pocket and his person, as I have done; or he would not be as he is, a pert reviler of those who have so done—as I do not suspect you Mr. Wayne, of being the author of the attack on me, I shall not enquire what share you or your relations had in establishing the liberties of your country. On religious grounds I am a republican. Kingly government was first conceded to the foolish complaints, of the Jewish people, as a punishment and a curse; and so it was to them until their dispersion, and so it has been to every nation, who have been as foolishly tempted to submit to it. Great Britain has a king, and her enemies need not wish her the sword, the pestilence, and the famine.

In the history of the Jews, are contained the earliest warnings against kingly government, as any one may know who has read the fable of Abimelick,[13] or the exhorta-

---

[11] "Polaskey's legion": troops commanded by Casimir Pulaski (1746–1779), a Polish officer who fought and died in the American Revolution.

[12] "Disastrous affair of Savannah": the Battle of Savannah (1778), won by the British.

[13] "Abimelick": the Biblical character Abimilech (*Judges* 9:1), a bastard son whose name (signifying "my father, the king") was a direct claim to hereditary power that he wielded tyrannically. To seize

tions of Samuel.[14] But I do not recommend them to your reporter, Mr. Wayne. To him the language of truth and soberness would be unintelligible.

I am a Jew, and if for no other reason, for that reason am I a republican. Among the pious priesthood of church establishments, we are compassionately ranked with Turks, Infidels and Heretics. In the *monarchies* of Europe we are hunted from society—stigmatized as unworthy of common civility, thrust out as it were from the converse of men; objects of mockery and insult to froward children, the butts of vulgar wit, and low buffoonery, such as your correspondent Mr. Wayne is not ashamed to set us an example of. Among the nations of Europe we are inhabitants every where—but Citizens no where *unless in Republics*. Here, in France, and in the Batavian Republic alone, we are treated as men and as brethren. In republics we have *rights*, in monarchies we live but to experience *wrongs*. And why? because we and our forefathers have *not* sacrificed our principles to our interest or earned an exemption from pain and poverty, by the dereliction of our religious duties, no wonder we are objects of derision to those, who have no principles, moral, or religious, to guide their conduct.

How then can a Jew but be a Republican? in America particularly. Unfeeling & ungrateful would he be, if he were callous to the glorious and benevolent cause of the difference between his situation in this land of freedom, and among the proud and privileged law givers of Europe.

But I am *poor*, I am so, my family also is large, but soberly and decently brought up. They have not been taught to revile a christian, because his religion is not *so old* as theirs. They have not been taught to mock even at the errors of good intention, and conscientious belief. I hope they will always leave this to men as unlike themselves, as I hope I am to your scurrilous correspondent.

I know that to purse proud aristocracy *poverty is a crime* but it may *sometimes* be accompanied with honesty even in a Jew. I was a Bankrupt some years ago. I obtained my certificate, and I was discharged from my debts. Having been more successful afterwards, I called my creditors together, and eight years afterwards unsolicited I discharged all my old debts, I offered interest which was refused by my creditors, and they gave me under their hands without any solicitations of mine, as a testimonial of the fact (to use their own language) as a tribute due to my honor and honesty. This testimonial was signed by Messrs. J. Ball, W. Wister, George Meade, J. Philips, C. G. Paleske, J. Bispham, J. Cohen, Robert Smith, J. H. Leuffer, A. Kuhn, John Stille, S. Pleasants, M. Woodhouse, Thomas Harrison, M. Boraef, E. Laskey, and Thomas Allibone, &c.

I was discharged by the insolvent act, true, because having the amount of my debts owing to me from the French Republic, the differences between France and America

---

the throne he killed his seventy half-brothers but was himself killed by a rebellious woman after only three years in power.

[14] "Samuel": in 1 *Samuel* 12 the prophet Samuel in his farewell speech inveighs against the worship of kings and warns that rulers must be held accountable for their actions.

have prevented the recovery of what was due to me, in time to discharge what was due to my creditors. Hitherto it has been the fault of the political situation of the two countries, that my creditors are not paid; when peace shall enable me to receive what I am entitled to it will be my fault if they are not fully paid.

This is a long defence Mr. Wayne, but you have called it forth, and therefore, I hope you at least will not object to it. The Public will now judge who is the proper object of ridicule and contempt, your facetious reporter, or

Your Humble Servant,

BENJAMIN NONES.

17. Lydia Maria Child, excerpts from *Isaac T. Hopper: A True Life* (Boston: J. P. Jewett & Co., 1853).

Despite his relative obscurity today, Isaac Tatem Hopper (1771–1852) was one of the great progressive activists of the early Republic and antebellum era. Hopper was one of the central creators of the early Underground Railroad network that worked to free slaves in 1790s Pennsylvania, particularly after the Fugitive Slave Act of 1793 and may have provided a model for certain aspects of Brown's character Arthur Mervyn. Many of Hopper's efforts involved attempts to secure freedom for Haitian slaves who were brought to Philadelphia by masters fleeing revolution. Despite public anxieties that these "French negroes" might spread the seeds of violent black revolt, Hopper and other abolition activists actively sought to aid the foreign slaves and draw sympathy to their plight, as in the examples of "Romaine" and "Poor Amy" reprinted here.

Raised as a Presbyterian near Woodbury, New Jersey, Hopper moved to Philadelphia at age sixteen (1787), almost immediately became involved in abolitionist networks, apprenticed as a tailor, and converted to Quakerism at about age twenty-two (1793–1794). By the mid-1790s he was an active member of the Pennsylvania Abolition Society (PAS) and taught at the school for free blacks founded by Anthony Benezet. Inside the PAS, Hopper was known for his ironclad knowledge of laws concerning runaway slaves, especially 1790s laws about emancipation for slaves legally residing in Pennsylvania for a period of six months. After being trained in the late 1780s and early 1790s by Thomas Harrison, another Quaker tailor and abolitionist, in techniques for creating an illegal network to transport runaway slaves to freedom, Hopper was responsible for expanding its activity and creating a matrix of safe houses in and around Philadelphia.

Working closely with free black community leaders like Richard Allen and Absalom Jones, Hopper was an important link between the PAS's more elite membership and Philadelphia's blacks. His tailor shop became an unofficial office at which blacks could seek aid, and he was well known for his emergency interventions in sometimes-violent situations involving the attempted recapture of escaped slaves. From 1829 to his death in 1852, Hopper lived in New York City and ran a bookstore for the more progressive "Hicksite" wing of the Quakers but continued to play an important role in mentoring black abolitionists such as David Ruggles and Frederick Douglass. In New York he was also active in prison reform and, with his daughter, founded prisoner advocacy groups.

At present, very little is known about the early Underground Railroad and its relations to the PAS (unlike the antebellum network about which a great deal is known). This absence of historical records partly results from cultural differences between the denominational and regional groups that dominated the earlier and later phases of Underground Railroad activity. The later phase is tied to the work of New England mainline Protestants, such as William Lloyd Garrison, who brilliantly recognized the potential impact of mass-printed slave narratives and who never missed opportunities to publicize their activities in print. The earlier abolitionists, by contrast, mainly followed Quaker cultural styles that discouraged self-promotion. They consequently tended to organize their projects—especially illegal ones like the Underground Railroad—in discrete, unostentatious, nonpublicized ways.

Only in the 1840s, when the main channels of the Underground Railroad shifted westward from Philadelphia and the early mechanisms of its operation had been surpassed, was Hopper prevailed upon by Lydia Maria Child to publish accounts of his earlier activity, which then appeared in the abolitionist National Anti-Slavery Standard *as a biweekly column titled "Tales of Oppression." After Hopper's death in 1852, Child collected and slightly revised his recollections for publication in her* Isaac T. Hopper: A True Life *(1853). Child heard many of these stories from Hopper himself, since she knew him well and briefly lodged with his family. She explains that she edited Hopper's originals lightly because he "had a more dramatic way of telling a story than he had of writing it." A comparison of Child's and Hopper's texts confirms that she was, in fact, a nonobstructive editor who made slight stylistic changes without altering the substance of the original. The comparison is useful in that it also suggests that her role in editing Harriet Jacob's* Incidents in the Life of a Slave Girl *(1861) was similarly light handed. Hopper, of course, appears in Jacob's tale as the "Lawyer Hopper" who gives her advice about the best routes to travel to freedom, a fitting tale to summarize a figure whose life was spent in administering the Underground Railroad.*

Within the small circles of abolitionist Quaker Philadelphia in the 1790s, Hopper would have been intimately familiar to Brown. Brown and Hopper were the same age and lived only a few doors apart, Brown at 117–119 and Hopper at 88–90 South Second. Hopper's mentor Thomas Harrison lived around the corner, and Harrison had been on the same 1777 list of Quakers to be incarcerated in Virginia as Brown's father, except that Harrison was tipped off, managed to evade arrest, and then survived in hiding during the rest of the Revolution. It would have been hard to ignore Hopper; he was not only a well-known and dramatic figure who stood out to most people who met him but he also insisted on wearing the distinctive buttonless coats and broad-brimmed hats of Penn-era Quakers, long after this clothing style had become obsolete. The well-known writer Margaret Fuller later recounted with pleasure how Hopper's visit to a Boston abolitionist event made it particularly memorable.

Brown's fictions often refer elliptically to his acquaintances and Arthur Mervyn *seems to draw on Hopper's well-known personal style in legible ways, especially in the dramatization of Mervyn's selfless efforts to help others in the novel's* Second Part. *Readers of Hopper's anecdotes will recognize parallels between Hopper and Mervyn's idiosyncratic manner in scenes such as Mervyn's confrontation with the matron Mrs. Althorpe in*

421

Chapter II.2, with the angry Philip Hadwin in Chapter II.10 (see Hopper's "Poor Amy"), his intervention at Villars' brothel in Chapters II.11–12 (see "The Uncomplimentary Invitation"), or his nonjudgmental efforts to comfort the jailed and ruined Welbeck in Chapter II.13 ("The Magdalen"). When the novel's first part ends with Mervyn telling the reader that he has seen objects with very important implications in an attic crawlspace but cannot explain because "it appears to be my duty to pass them over in silence" (Chapter 23), Brown may be referring to the kinds of hiding places that Hopper's Underground Railroad used to safeguard runaway slaves.

*****

ROMAINE.

A Frenchman by the name of Anthony Salignac removed from St. Domingo to New-Jersey, and brought with him several slaves; among whom was Romaine. After remaining in New-Jersey several years, he concluded in 1802, to send Romaine and his wife and child back to the West Indies. Finding him extremely reluctant to go, he put them in prison some days previous, lest they should make an attempt to escape. From prison they were put into a carriage to be conveyed to Newcastle, under the custody of a Frenchman and a constable. They started from Trenton late in the evening, and arrived in Philadelphia about four o'clock in the morning. People at the inn where they stopped remarked that Romaine and his wife appeared deeply dejected. When food was offered they refused to eat. His wife made some excuse to go out, and though sought for immediately after, she was not to be found. Romaine was ordered to get into the carriage. The Frenchman was on one side of him and the constable on the other. "*Must* I go?" cried he, in accents of despair. They told him he must. "And alone?" said he. "Yes, you must," was the stern reply. The carriage was open to receive him, and they would have pushed him in, but he suddenly took a pruning knife from his pocket, and drew it three times across his throat with such force that it severed the jugular vein instantly, and he fell dead on the pavement.

As the party had travelled all night, seemed in great haste, and watched their colored companions so closely, some persons belonging to the prison where they stopped suspected they might have nefarious business on hand; accordingly, a message was sent to Isaac T. Hopper, as the man most likely to right all the wrongs of the oppressed. He obeyed the summons immediately; but when he arrived, he found the body of poor Romaine weltering in blood on the pavement.

Speaking of this scene forty years later, he said, "My whole soul was filled with horror, as I stood viewing the corpse. Reflecting on that awful spectacle, I exclaimed within myself, How long, O Lord, how long shall this abominable system of slavery be permitted to curse the land! My mind was introduced into sympathy with the sufferer. I thought of the agony he must have endured before he could have resolved upon that desperate deed. He knew what he had to expect, from what he had experienced in the West Indies before, and he was determined not to submit to the same misery and degradation again. By his sufferings he was driven to desperation; and he preferred launching into the unknown regions of eternity to an endurance of slavery."

An inquest was summoned, and after a brief consultation, the coroner brought in the following verdict: "Suicide occasioned by the dread of slavery, to which the deceased knew himself devoted."

Romaine and his wife were very good looking. They gave indications of considerable intelligence, and had the character of having been very faithful servants. His violent death produced a good deal of excitement among the people generally, and much sympathy was manifested for the wife and child, who had escaped.

The master had procured a certificate from the mayor of Trenton authorizing him to remove his slaves to the West Indies; but the jury of inquest, and many others, were of opinion that his proceedings were not fully sanctioned by law. Accordingly, Friend Hopper, and two other members of the Abolition Society, caused him to be arrested and brought before a magistrate; not so much with the view of punishing him, as with the hope of procuring manumission for the wife and child. In the course of the investigation, the friends of the Frenchman were somewhat violent in his defence. Upon one occasion, several of them took Friend Hopper up and put him out of the house by main force; while at the same time they let their friend out of a back door to avoid him. However, Friend Hopper met him a few minutes after in the street and seized him by the button. Alarmed by the popular excitement, and by the perseverance with which he was followed up, he exclaimed in agitated tones, "Mon Dieu! What is it you do want? I will do anything you do want."

"I want thee to bestow freedom on that unfortunate woman and her child," replied Friend Hopper.

He promised that he would do so; and he soon after made out papers to that effect, which were duly recorded.

*****

POOR AMY.

A Frenchman named M. Bouilla resided in Spring Garden, Philadelphia, in the year 1806. He and a woman, who had lived with him some time, had in their employ a mulatto girl of nine years old, called Amy. Dreadful stories were in circulation concerning their cruel treatment to this child; and compassionate neighbors had frequently solicited Friend Hopper's interference. After a while, he heard they were about to send her into the country; and fearing she might be sold into slavery, he called upon M. Bouilla to inquire whither she was going. As soon as he made known his business, the door was unceremoniously slammed in his face and locked. A note was then sent to the Frenchman, asking for a friendly interview; but he returned a verbal answer. "Tell Mr. Hopper to mind his own business."

Considering it his business to protect an abused child, he applied to a magistrate for a warrant, and proceeded to the house, accompanied by his friend Thomas Harrison and a constable. As soon as they entered the door, M. Bouilla ran up-stairs, and arming himself with a gun, threatened to shoot whoever advanced toward him. Being blind, however, he could only point the gun at random in the direction of their voices, or of any noise which might reach his ear. The officer refused to attempt his arrest under such peril; saying, he was under no obligation to risk his life. Friend Hopper expostulated with the Frenchman, explained the nature of their errand, and urged him to come down and have the matter inquired into in an amicable way. But he would not listen, and persisted in swearing he would shoot the first person who attempted to come near him. At last, Friend Hopper took off his shoes, stepped up-stairs very softly and quickly, and just as the Frenchman became aware of his near approach, he seized the gun and held it over his shoulder. It discharged instantly, and shattered the plastering of the stairway, making it fly in all directions. There arose a loud cry, "Mr. Hopper's killed! Mr. Hopper's killed!"

The gun being thus rendered harmless, the Frenchman was soon arrested, and they all proceeded to the magistrate's office, accompanied by several of the neighbors. There was abundant evidence that the child had been half starved, unmercifully beaten, and tortured in various ways. Indeed, she was such a poor, emaciated, miserable looking object, that her appearance was of itself enough to prove the cruel treatment she had received. When the case had been fully investigated, the magistrate ordered her to be consigned to the care of Isaac T. Hopper, who hastened home with her, being anxious lest his wife should accidentally hear the rumor that he had been shot.

He afterwards ascertained that Amy was daughter of the white woman who had aided in thus shamefully abusing her. He kept her in his family till she became well and strong and then bound her to one of his friends in the country to serve till she was eighteen. She grew up a very pretty girl, and deported herself to the entire satisfaction of the family. When her period of service had expired, she returned to Philadelphia, where her conduct continued very exemplary. She frequently called to see Friend Hopper, and often expressed gratitude to him for having rescued her from such a miserable condition.

*****

THE MAGDALEN.

Upon one occasion, Friend Hopper entered a complaint against an old woman, who had presided over an infamous house for many years. She was tried, and sentenced to several months imprisonment. He went to see her several times, and talked very seriously with her concerning the errors of her life. Finding that his expostulations made some impression, he asked if she felt willing to amend her ways. "Oh, I should be thankful to do it!" she exclaimed. "But who would trust me? What can I do to earn an honest living? Everybody curses me, or makes game of me. How *can* I be a better woman, if I try ever so hard?"

"I will give thee a chance to amend thy life," he replied; "and if thou dost not, it shall be thy own fault."

He went round among the wealthy Quakers, and by dint of great persuasion he induced one to let her a small tenement at very low rent. A few others agreed to purchase some humble furniture, and a quantity of thread, needles, tape, and buttons, to furnish a small shop. The poor old creature's heart overflowed with gratitude, and it was her pride to keep everything very neat and orderly. There she lived contented and comfortable the remainder of her days, and became much respected in the neighborhood. The tears often came to her eyes when she saw Friend Hopper. "God bless that good man!" she would say. "He has been the salvation of me."

*****

THE UNCOMPLIMENTARY INVITATION.

A preacher of the Society of Friends felt impressed with the duty of calling a meeting for vicious people; and Isaac T. Hopper was appointed to collect an audience. In the course of this mission, he knocked at the door of a very infamous house. A gentleman who was acquainted with him was passing by, and he stopped to say, "Friend Hopper, you have mistaken the house."

"No, I have not," he replied.

"But that is a house of notorious ill fame," said the gentleman.

"I know it," rejoined he; "but nevertheless I have business here."

His acquaintance looked surprised, but passed on without further query. A colored girl came to the door. To the inquiry whether her mistress was within, she answered in the affirmative. "Tell her I wish to see her," said Friend Hopper. The girl was evidently astonished at a visitor in Quaker costume, and of such grave demeanor; but she went and did the errand. A message was returned that her mistress was engaged and could not see any one. "Where is she?" he inquired. The girl replied that she was upstairs. "I will go to her," said the importunate messenger.

The mistress of the house heard him, and leaning over the balustrade of the stairs, she screamed out, "What do you want with me, sir?"

In very loud tones he answered, "James Simpson, a minister of the Society of Friends, has appointed a meeting to be held this afternoon, in Penrose store, Almond-Street. It is intended for publicans, sinners, and harlots. I want thee to be there, and bring thy whole household with thee. Wilt thou come?"

She promised that she would; and he afterward saw her at the meeting melted into tears by the direct and affectionate preaching.

Henri-François Riesener, *Portrait de*
Maurice Quay (1797-99). Musée du
Louvre. Reproduced by permission of
Erich Lessing/Art Resources, NY.

François-Xavier Fabre, *Portrait of a*
Mulatto (1809-10). Courtesy of
Arenski Fine Art, Ltd., London.

The two portraits reproduced here exemplify the revolutionary era's new visual modes
for representing individuals and status-group (class, gender, ethnicity) distinctions; these
provide visual analogues for Brown's literary portrait of Arthur Mervyn. Trained in the
studio of Jacques-Louis David, the stylistic and institutional center of politically-
engaged visual art in revolutionary France, Riesener and Fabre are self-consciously modern and Davidian in their use of single-person portraiture to represent previously marginalized social types with the new dignity of the citizen. Foregoing the use of external
accessories, such as furnishings or other objects to convey social distinctions, this spare
style of portraiture conveys character by asking the viewer to focus on the sitter's physiognomy, clothing, and hairstyle.

Maurice Quay was a bohemian artist and leader of the "Barbu" (bearded, primitive)
school, a subgroup in David's studio. His facial hair and clothing implicitly defend a
new democratization by alluding to laboring-class clothing and grooming, rejecting the
finery of the old regime. Fabre's anonymous sitter is probably a "free man of color" (possibly a wealthy planter from the West Indies), whose *à la mode* clothing suggests his
crossing of ethno-racial and class barriers within the context of the post-revolutionary
order. He wears his hair in the fashionable "Titus" cut, named after the Roman Emperor
Titus and first popularized in Paris and London after 1791 by the actor Talma. This
hairstyle was associated with the mood of emancipatory cultural transformation
throughout the theater of Atlantic revolutions as it frees the hair from the fussy, quasiaristocratic style of powdered wigs. By letting the hair flow *au naturel,* the Titus cut's
conscious unruliness was egalitarian; both Europeans and Africans, and women and
men could equally sport this hairstyle in the 1790s and 1800s, when it retained its association with the Roman and revolutionary iconography of the David school.

BIBLIOGRAPHY AND WORKS CITED

I. Writings by Brown.

Comprehensive bibliographies of Brown's writings and scholarship on Brown are available at the website of The Charles Brockden Brown Electronic Edition and Scholarly Archive: http://www.brockdenbrown.ucf.edu.

A. Novels

Brown, Charles Brockden, *Wieland; or The Transformation. An American Tale*. New York: Printed by T. & J. Swords for H. Caritat, 1798.

_____. *Arthur Mervyn; or, Memoirs of the Year 1793*. Philadelphia: H. Maxwell, 1799.

_____. *Edgar Huntly; or, Memoirs of a Sleep-Walker*. Philadelphia: H. Maxwell, 1799.

_____. *Ormond; or The Secret Witness*. New York: Printed by G. Forman for H. Caritat, 1799.

_____. *Memoirs of Stephen Calvert*. Published serially in *The Monthly Magazine*, Vols. 1–2 (New York: T. & J. Swords, June 1799–June 1800).

_____. *Arthur Mervyn; or, Memoirs of the Year 1793. Second Part*. New York: George F. Hopkins, 1800.

_____. *Clara Howard; In a Series of Letters*. Philadelphia: Asbury Dickens, 1801.

_____. *Jane Talbot; A Novel*. Philadelphia: John Conrad; Baltimore, M. & J. Conrad; Washington City, Rapin & Conrad, 1801.

_____. *The Novels and Related Works of Charles Brockden Brown*. Bicentennial edition. 6 vols. Sydney J. Krause and S.W. Reid, eds. Kent: Kent State UP, 1977–87. [The Kent State Bicentennial edition is the modern scholarly text of Brown's seven novels, plus the Wollstonecraftian dialogue *Alcuin* and the unfinished *Memoirs of Carwin*.]

B. Essays and Uncollected Fiction

_____. *Alcuin; A Dialogue*. New York: T. & J. Swords, 1798.

_____. *The Historical Sketches*. In the Allen-Dunlap biographies and *The Literary Magazine and American Register*, 1803–1806.

_____. *Literary Essays and Reviews*. Alfred Weber and Wolfgang Schäfer, eds. Frankfurt: Peter Lang, 1992.

_____. *Somnambulism and Other Stories*. Alfred Weber, ed. Frankfurt: Peter Lang, 1987.

_____. *The Rhapsodist and Other Uncollected Writings*. Harry R. Warfel, ed. Delmar, NY: Scholar's Facsimiles and Reprints, 1977.

C. Periodicals and Pamphlets

The three periodicals that Brown edited include hundreds of his own articles and miscellaneous pieces in a variety of genres (dialogues, essay-fictions, reviews, anecdotes, and other forms) and on a wide range of subjects, from literary, artistic, and musical culture to social and political questions, history, geopolitics, and different subfields of science. For a listing of these publications, consult the Comprehensive Bibliography at the website of The Charles Brockden Brown Electronic Archive and Scholarly Edition.

_____. *The Monthly Magazine and American Review.* Vols. 1–3. New York: T. & J. Swords, April 1799–December 1800.

_____. *An Address to the Government of the United States, on the Cession of Louisiana to the French.* Philadelphia: John Conrad, 1803.

_____. *Monroe's Embassy; or, the Conduct of the Government, in Relation to Our Claims to the Navigation of the Missisippi [sic], Considered.* Philadelphia: John Conrad, 1803.

_____. *The Literary Magazine and American Register.* Vols. 1–7. Philadelphia: C. & A. Conrad, 1803–1806.

_____. *The American Register, or General Repository of History, Politics, and Science.* Vols. 1–7. Philadelphia: C. & A. Conrad, 1807–1809.

_____. *An Address to the Congress of the United States, on the Utility and Justice of Restrictions upon Foreign Commerce.* Philadelphia: C. & A. Conrad, 1809.

II. Biographies of Brown and Diaries of his friends Smith, Dunlap, and Cope.

Besides the published biographies, an important resource is the unfinished biographical study by Daniel Edwards Kennedy now preserved at the Kent State Institute for Bibliography and Editing. Written between 1910 and 1945, this manuscript remains a source of much still unexplored information about Brown's life and career. The Smith and Dunlap diaries provide detailed reportage about Brown and his New York circle in the crucial period when Brown was writing his novels. Cope's diary documents Brown's never accomplished plan, in 1803–1806, to write an abolitionist History of Slavery.

Clark, David Lee. *Charles Brockden Brown: Pioneer Voice of America.* Durham: Duke UP, 1952.

Cope, Thomas P. *Philadelphia Merchant: The Diary of Thomas P. Cope, 1800–1851.* Edited and with an introduction and appendices by Eliza Cope Harrison. South Bend, IN: Gateway Editions, 1978.

Dunlap, William. *Diary of William Dunlap (1766–1839): The Memoirs of a Dramatist, Theatrical Manager, Painter, Critic, Novelist, and Historian.* 3 vols. Dorothy C. Barck, ed. New York: The New-York Historical Society, 1930.

_____. *The Life of Charles Brockden Brown.* 2 vols. Philadelphia: James P. Parke, 1815. [A first one-volume version drafted by Paul Allen, unpublished until the late twentieth century, is *The Life of Charles Brockden Brown, A Facsimile Reproduction*

(Columbia, SC: Faust, 1976). The *Historical Sketches* were first published post-humously in Dunlap and Allen.]

Kafer, Peter. *Charles Brockden Brown's Revolution and the Birth of American Gothic*. Philadelphia: U of Pennsylvania P, 2004.

Smith, Elihu Hubbard. *The Diary of Elihu Hubbard Smith (1771–1798)*. James E. Cronin, ed. Philadelphia: American Philosophical Society, 1973.

Warfel, Harry R. *Charles Brockden Brown: American Gothic Novelist*. Gainesville: U of Florida P, 1949.

III. Brown and *Arthur Mervyn* in the wider context of cultural and literary history.

Amfreville, Marc. *Charles Brockden Brown: La part du doute*. Paris: Belin, 2000.

Anthony, David. "Banking on Emotion: Financial Panic and the Logic of Male Submission in the Jacksonian Gothic." *American Literature* 76.4 (2004): 719–47.

Axelrod, Alan. *Charles Brockden Brown: An American Tale*. Austin: U of Texas P, 1983.

Baker, Jennifer J. *Securing the Commonwealth: Debt, Speculation, and Writing in the Making of Early America*. Baltimore: Johns Hopkins UP, 2006.

Bell, Michael Davitt. "'The Double-Tongued Deceiver': Sincerity and Duplicity in the Novels of Charles Brockden Brown." *Early American Literature* 9.2 (1974): 143–63.

Bennett, Charles E. "Charles Brockden Brown's 'Portrait of an Emigrant.'" *College Language Association Journal* 14 (1970): 87–90.

Block, James E. *A Nation of Agents: The American Path to a Modern Self and Society*. Cambridge: Harvard UP, 2002.

Bradfield, Scott. *Dreaming Revolution: Transgression in the Development of American Romance*. Iowa City: U of Iowa P, 1993.

Cahill, Edward. "An Adventurous and Lawless Fancy: Charles Brockden Brown's Aesthetic State." *Early American Literature* 36.1 (2001): 31–70.

Cavitch, Max. "The Man That Was Used Up: Poetry, Particularity, and the Politics of Remembering George Washington." *American Literature* 75.2 (June 2003): 247–74.

Chase, Richard. *The American Novel and Its Tradition*. New York: Doubleday, 1957.

Christophersen, Bill. *The Apparition in the Glass: Charles Brockden Brown's American Gothic*. Athens: U of Georgia P, 1993.

Cody, Michael. *Charles Brockden Brown and the Literary Magazine: Cultural Journalism in the Early American Republic*. Jefferson, NC: McFarland, 2004.

Crain, Caleb. *American Sympathy: Men, Friendship, and Literature in the New Nation*. New Haven: Yale UP, 2001.

Dauber, Kenneth. *The Idea of Authorship in America: Democratic Poetics from Franklin to Melville*. Madison: U of Wisconsin P, 1990.

Davidson, Cathy. *Revolution and the Word: The Rise of the Novel in America*. Expanded Edition. New York: Oxford UP, 2004.

Dawes, James. "Fictional Feeling: Philosophy, Cognitive Science, and the American Gothic." *American Literature* 76.3 (2004): 437–66.

Dillon, Elizabeth Maddock. *The Gender of Freedom: Fictions of Liberalism and the Literary Public Sphere*. Stanford: Stanford UP, 2004.

Dillon, James. "'The Highest Province of Benevolence': Charles Brockden Brown's Fictional Theory." *Studies in Eighteenth-Century Culture* 27 (1998): 237–58.

Doolen, Andy. *Fugitive Empire: Locating Early American Imperialism*. Minneapolis: U of Minnesota P, 2005.

Dykstra, Kristin A. "On the Betrayal of Nations: Jose Alvarez de Toledo's Philadelphia *Manifesto* (1811) and *Justification* (1816)." *The New Centennial Review* 4.1 (2004): 267–305.

Edmondson, Philip N. *The St. Domingue Legacy in Black Activist and Antislavery Writings in the United States, 1791–1862*. Dissertation. College Park: U of Maryland, 2003.

Elliott, Emory. *Revolutionary Writers: Literature and Authority in the New Republic, 1725–1810*. New York: Oxford UP, 1986.

Ferguson, Robert A. *Law and Letters in American Culture*. Cambridge: Harvard UP, 1984.

———. "Yellow Fever and Charles Brockden Brown: The Context of the Emerging Novelist." *Early American Literature* 14 (1980): 293–305.

Fiedler, Leslie A. *Love and Death in the American Novel*. New York: Criterion Books, 1960.

Fliegelman, Jay. *Prodigals and Pilgrims: The American Revolution against Patriarchal Authority*. Cambridge: Cambridge UP, 1982.

Goddu, Teresa. *Gothic America: Narrative, History, and Nation*. New York: Columbia UP, 1997.

Goudie, Sean X. *Creole America: The West Indies and the Formation of Literature and Culture in the New Republic*. Philadelphia: U of Pennsylvania P, 2006.

Gould, Philip. "Race, Commerce, and the Literature of Yellow Fever in Early National Philadelphia." *Early American Literature* 35 (2000): 157–86.

Grabo, Norman S. *The Coincidental Art of Charles Brockden Brown*. Chapel Hill: U of North Carolina P, 1981.

Haviland, Thomas P. "Preciosité Crosses the Atlantic." *PMLA: Publications of the Modern Language Association of America* 59.1 (1944): 131–41.

Hedges, William. "Charles Brockden Brown and the Culture of Contradictions." *Early American Literature* 9 (1974): 107–42.

Herdman, John. *The Double in Nineteenth-Century Fiction: The Shadow Life*. New York: St. Martin's Press, 1991.

Hinds, Elizabeth Jane Wall. *Private Property: Charles Brockden Brown's Gendered Economics of Virtue*. Newark, DE: U of Delaware P, 1997.

Kindermann, Wolf. *Man Unknown to Himself: Kritische Reflexion der Amerikanischen Aufklärung: Crèvecoeur, Benjamin Rush, Charles Brockden Brown*. Tübingen: G. Narr, 1993.

Larsson, David M. "Arthur Mervyn, Edgar Huntly, and the Critics." *Essays in Literature* 15 (1988): 207–19.

Lewis, R. W. B. *The American Adam: Innocence, Tragedy and Tradition in the Nineteenth Century.* Chicago: U of Chicago P, 1955.

Limon, John. *The Place of Fiction in the Time of Science: A Disciplinary History of American Writing.* Cambridge: Cambridge UP, 1990.

Lindberg, Gary. *The Confidence Man in American Literature.* New York: Oxford UP, 1982.

Lukasik, Christopher. "'The Vanity of Physiognomy': Dissimulation and Discernment in Charles Brockden Brown's *Ormond.*" *Amerikastudien/American Studies* 50.3 (2005): 485–505.

Mackenthun, Gesa. *Fictions of the Black Atlantic in American Foundational Literature.* New York: Routledge, 2004.

McNutt, Donald J. *Urban Revelations: Images of Ruin in the American City, 1790–1860.* New York: Routledge, 2006.

Okun, Peter. *Crime and the Nation: Prison Reform and Popular Fiction in Philadelphia, 1786–1800.* New York: Routledge, 2002.

Ringe, Donald A. *Charles Brockden Brown.* Revised Edition. Boston: Twayne; G. K. Hall, 1991.

Samuels, Shirley. *Romances of the Republic: Women, the Family, and Violence in the Literature of the Early American Nation.* New York: Oxford UP, 1996.

Shapiro, Stephen. *The Culture and Commerce of the Early American Novel: Reading the Atlantic World-System.* University Park: Pennsylvania State UP, 2008.

———. "'I Could Kiss Him One Minute and Kill Him the Next!': The Limits of Radical Male Friendship in Holcroft, CB Brown, and Wollstonecraft Shelley." In Walter Göbel, Saskia Schabio, and Martin Windisch, eds., *Engendering Images of Man in the Long Eighteenth Century,* 111–32. Trier: Wissenschaftlicher Verlag, 2001.

Simpson, Lewis P. "The Symbolism of Literary Alienation in the Revolutionary Age." *The Journal of Politics* 38.3 (200 Years of the Republic in Retrospect: A Special Bicentennial Issue; 1976): 79–100.

Slawinski, Scott Paul. *Validating Bachelorhood: Audience, Patriarchy and Charles Brockden Brown's Editorship of the* Monthly Magazine *and* American Review. New York: Routledge, 2005.

Strode, Timothy Francis. *The Ethics of Exile: Colonialism in the Fictions of Charles Brockden Brown and J. M. Coetzee.* New York: Routledge, 2005.

Teute, Fredrika J. "The Loves of the Plants; or, the Cross-Fertilization of Science and Desire at the End of the Eighteenth Century." In Robert M. Maniquis, ed., *British Radical Culture of the 1790s,* 63–89. San Marino: Huntington Library, 2002.

———. "A 'Republic of Intellect': Conversation and Criticism among the Sexes in 1790s New York." In Philip Barnard, Mark L. Kamrath, and Stephen Shapiro, eds., *Revising Charles Brockden Brown: Culture, Politics, and Sexuality in the Early Republic,* 149–81. Knoxville: U of Tennessee P, 2004.

Tompkins, Jane. *Sensational Designs: The Cultural Work of American Fiction, 1790–1860,* 62–93. New York: Oxford UP, 1985.

Verhoeven, W. M. "Opening the Text: The Locked-Trunk Motif in Late Eighteenth-Century British and American Gothic Fiction." In Valeria Tinkler-Villani, Peter Davidson, and Jane Stevenson, eds., *Exhibited by Candlelight: Sources and Developments in the Gothic Tradition,* 205–19. Amsterdam: Rodopi, 1995.

Warner, Michael. "Homo-Narcissism; or, Heterosexuality." In Joseph A. Boone and Michael Cadden, eds., *Engendering Men: The Question of Male Feminist Criticism,* 190–206. London: Routledge, 1991.

———. *Letters of the Republic: Publication and the Public Sphere in Eighteenth-Century America.* Cambridge: Harvard UP, 1990.

Waterman, Bryan. *Republic of Intellect: The Friendly Club of New York City and the Making of American Literature.* Baltimore: Johns Hopkins UP, 2007.

Watts, Steven. *The Romance of Real Life: Charles Brockden Brown and the Origins of American Culture.* Baltimore: Johns Hopkins UP, 1994.

Weyler, Karen A. *Intricate Relations: Sexual and Economic Desire in American Fiction, 1789–1814.* Iowa City: U of Iowa P, 2004.

Wood, Sarah. *Quixotic Fictions of the USA, 1792–1815.* New York: Oxford UP, 2005.

Ziff, Larzer. *Writing in the New Nation: Prose, Print, and Politics in the Early United States.* New Haven: Yale UP, 1991.

IV. Discussions primarily of *Arthur Mervyn.*

Amfreville, Marc. "The Theater of Death in Charles Brockden Brown's *Arthur Mervyn,*" *Litteraria Pragensia* 14.28 (2004).

Bernard, Kenneth. "*Arthur Mervyn*: The Ordeal of Innocence." *TSLL* 6 (1965): 441–59.

Berthoff, Warner B. "Adventures of the Young Man: An Approach to Charles Brockden Brown." *American Quarterly* 9 (1957): 421–34.

———. "Introduction." In Charles Brockden Brown, *Arthur Mervyn; or, Memoirs of the Year 1793,* vii–xxi. New York: Holt, Rinehart, and Winston, 1962.

Brancaccio, Patrick. "Studied Ambiguity: *Arthur Mervyn* and the Problem of the Unreliable Narrator." *American Literature* 42 (1970): 18–27.

Cohen, Daniel A. "*Arthur Mervyn* and His Elders: The Ambivalence of Youth in the Early Republic." *The William and Mary Quarterly* 43 (1986): 362–80.

Eiselein, Gregory. "Humanitarianism and Uncertainty in *Arthur Mervyn.*" *Essays in Literature* 22 (1995): 215–26.

Elliot, Emory. "Narrative Unity and Moral Resolution in *Arthur Mervyn.*" In Bernard Rosenthal, ed., *Critical Essays on Charles Brockden Brown,* 142–63. Boston: G. K. Hall, 1981.

Feeney, Joseph J. "Modernized by 1800: The Portrait of Urban America, Especially Philadelphia, in the Novels of Charles Brockden Brown." *Essays in Arts and Sciences* 11 (1982): 59–68.

Gado, Frank. "*Arthur Mervyn*: Mounting into Man." In Charles Brockden Brown, *Arthur Mervyn; or, Memoirs of the Year 1793, in Two Parts*, iii–xxiv. Albany: New College and UP, 1992.

Goudie, Sean X. "On the Origin of American Specie(s): The West Indies, Classification, and the Emergence of Supremacist Consciousness in *Arthur Mervyn*." In Philip Barnard, Mark L. Kamrath, and Stephen Shapiro, eds., *Revising Charles Brockden Brown: Culture, Politics, and Sexuality in the Early Republic*, 60–87. Knoxville: U of Tennessee P, 2004.

Grabo, Norman. "Historical Essay." In Charles Brockden Brown, *Arthur Mervyn; or, Memoirs of the Year 1793*. Vol. 3, *The Novels and Related Works of Charles Brockden Brown*, 447–75. Kent: Kent State UP, 1980.

Hale, Dorothy. "Profits of Altruism: *Caleb Williams* and *Arthur Mervyn*." *Eighteenth-Century Studies* 22 (1988): 47–69.

Harap, Louis. "Fracture of a Stereotype: Charles Brockden Brown's Achsa Fielding." *American Jewish Archives* 24 (1972): 187–95.

Hedges, William L. "Benjamin Rush, Charles Brockden Brown, and the American Plague Year." *Early American Literature* 7 (1973): 295–311.

Justus, James A. "Arthur Mervyn, American." *American Literature* 42 (1970): 304–24.

Larson, David M. "*Arthur Mervyn, Edgar Huntly*, and the Critics." *Essays in Literature* 15 (1988): 207–19.

Levine, Robert S. "*Arthur Mervyn*'s Revolutions." *Studies in American Fiction* 12 (1984): 145–60.

McAlexander, Patricia Jewell. "*Arthur Mervyn* and the Sentimental Love Tradition." *Studies in Literature* 9 (1976): 31–42.

McAuley, Louis Kirk. "'Periodical Visitations': Yellow Fever as Yellow Journalism In Charles Brockden Brown's *Arthur Mervyn*." *Eighteenth-Century Fiction* 19.3 (2007): 307–40.

Monahan, Kathleen Nolan. "Brown's *Arthur Mervyn* and *Ormond*." *Explicator* 45 (1987), 18–20.

Nelson, Carl W. "A Method for Madness: The Symbolic Patterns in *Arthur Mervyn*." *West Virginia University Philological Papers* 22 (1975): 29–30.

Orishima, Masashi. "Immersed in Palpable Darkness: Republican Virtue and the Spatial Topography of Charles Brockden Brown's *Arthur Mervyn*." *The Japanese Journal of American Studies* 13 (2002): 7–23.

Ostrowski, Carl. "'Fated to Perish by Consumption': The Political Economy of *Arthur Mervyn*." *Studies in American Fiction* 32.1 (2004): 3–20.

Patrick, Marietta. "The Doppelgänger Motif in *Arthur Mervyn*." *Journal of Evolutionary Psychology* 10 (1989): 360–71.

Person, Leland S. "My Good Mama: Women in *Edgar Huntly* and *Arthur Mervyn*." *Studies in American Fiction* April (1981): 33–46.

Russo, James. "The Chameleon of Convenient Vice: A Study of the Narrative of *Arthur Mervyn*." *Studies in the Novel* 11 (1979): 381–405.

Samuels, Shirley. "Infidelity and Contagion: The Rhetoric of Revolution." *Early American Literature* 22 (1987): 183–19.

————. "Plague and Politics in 1793: *Arthur Mervyn.*" *Criticism* (1985): 225–46.

Schloss, Dietmar. "Charles Brockden Brown's *Arthur Mervyn* and the Idea of Civic Virtue." In Alfred Hornung, Reinhard R. Doerries, and Gerhard Hoffman, eds., *Democracy and the Arts in the United States*, 171–82. Munich: Fink, 1996.

Smith-Rosenberg, Carroll. "Black Gothic: The Shadowy Origins of the American Bourgeoisie." In Robert Blair St. George, ed., *Possible Pasts: Becoming Colonial in Early America*, 243–69. Ithaca: Cornell UP, 2000.

Spangler, George M. "Charles Brockden Brown's *Arthur Mervyn*: A Portrait of a Young American Artist." *American Literature* 52 (1981): 578–92.

Tattoni, Igina. "'There Was No Room for Hesitation': The Revolution of Time in Charles Brockden Brown's *Arthur Mervyn.*" In Massimo Bacigalupo and Pierangelo Castagneto, eds., *America and the Mediterranean*, 559–65. Turin: Otto, 2003.

Traister, Bryce. "Libertinism and Authorship in America's Early Republic." *American Literature* 72.1 (2000): 1–30.

Van der Beets, Richard, and Paul Witherington. "My Kinsman, Brockden Brown: Robin Molineux and Arthur Mervyn." *American Transcendentalist Quarterly* 1 (1969): 13–15.

Waterman, Bryan. "*Arthur Mervyn*'s Medical Repository and the Early Republic's Knowledge Industries." *American Literary History* 15 (2003): 213–47.

Wawrzyniak, Anna. "A Journey through the Labyrinth of Distorted Image: Arthur Mervyn's Quest for Knowledge." *Interactions: Aegean Journal of English and American Studies/Ege Ingiliz ve Amerikan Incelemeleri Dergisi* 14.1 (2005): 279–87.

Witherington, Paul. "Benevolence and the 'Utmost Stretch': Charles Brockden Brown's Narrative Dilemma." *Criticism* 14 (1972): 175–91.

Wood, Sarah F. "Foul Contagion and Perilous Asylums: The Role of the Refugee in *Ormond* and *Arthur Mervyn.*" *Overhere: A European Journal of American Culture* 18.3 (1999): 82–92.

V. *Arthur Mervyn*'s early national and Atlantic context.

A. Philadelphia's late eighteenth-century urban space and social structure.

Alexander, John K. *Render Them Submissive: Responses to Poverty in Philadelphia, 1760–1800.* Amherst: U of Massachusetts P, 1980.

Blumin, Stuart. *The Emergence of the Middle Class: Social Experience in the American City, 1760–1900.* New York: Cambridge UP, 1989.

Branson, Susan. "St. Domingan Refugees in the Philadelphia Community in the 1790s." *Amerindians, Africans, Americans: Three Papers in Caribbean History*, 69–84. Mona: U of the West Indies, 1993.

————. *These Fiery Frenchified Dames: Women and Political Culture in Early National Philadelphia.* Philadelphia: U of Pennsylvania P, 2001.

Branson, Susan, and Leslie Patrick. "*Etrangers dans un pays étrange:* Saint-Domingan Refugees of Color in Philadelphia." In David P. Geggus, ed., *The Impact of the Hait-*

ian Revolution in the Atlantic World, 193–208. Columbia: U of South Carolina P, 2001.

Campbell, William Burke. *Old Towns and Districts of Philadelphia*. Philadelphia: City History Society of Philadelphia, 1942.

Carter, Edward C., II. "A 'Wild Irishman' under Every Federalist's Bed: Naturalization in Philadelphia, 1789–1806." *Proceedings of the American Philosophical Society*, 133.2, *Symposium on the Demographic History of the Philadelphia Region, 1600–1860* (1989): 178–89.

Foster, Kathleen A. *Captain Watson's Travels in America: The Sketchbooks and Diary of Joshua Rowley Watson, 1772–1818*. Philadelphia: U of Pennsylvania P, 1997.

Gilchrist, Agnes Addison. "Market Houses in High Street." *Transactions of the American Philosophical Society*, New Ser., 43.1 (1953): 304–12.

Graham, Robert Earle. "The Taverns of Colonial Philadelphia." *Transactions of the American Philosophical Society*, New Ser., 43.1 (1953): 318–25.

Griffin, Patrick. *The People with No Name: Ireland's Ulster Scots, America's Scots Irish, and the Creation of a British Atlantic World, 1689–1764*. Princeton: Princeton UP, 2001.

Klepp, Susan. *Philadelphia in Transition: A Demographic History of the City and Its Occupational Groups, 1720–1830*. New York: Garland, 1989.

Lemon, James T. *The Best Poor Man's Country; A Geographical Study of Early Southeastern Pennsylvania*. Baltimore: Johns Hopkins UP, 1972.

———. *Liberal Dreams and Nature's Limits: Great Cities of North America since 1600*. New York: Oxford UP, 1996.

Lyons, Clare A. *Sex among the Rabble: An Intimate History of Gender & Power in the Age of Revolution, Philadelphia, 1730–1830*. Chapel Hill: U of North Carolina P, 2006.

Meadows, R. Darrell. "Engineering Exile: Social Networks and the French Atlantic Community, 1789–1809." *French Historical Studies* 23.1 (2000): 67–108.

Meranze, Michael. *Laboratories of Virtue: Punishment, Revolution, and Authority in Philadelphia, 1760–1835*. Chapel Hill: U of North Carolina P, 1996.

Moreau de St. Méry, Médéric-Louis-Elie. *Voyage aux Etats-Unis d'Amérique, 1793–1798*. Stewart L. Mims. ed. New Haven: Yale UP, 1913. Eng. tr. Kenneth and Anna M. Roberts, *Moreau de St. Méry's American Journey* (New York: Doubleday & Company, 1947).

Newman, Simon P. *Embodied History: The Lives of the Poor in Early Philadelphia*. Philadelphia: U of Pennsylvania P, 2003.

Salinger, Sharon V. "Spaces, Inside and Outside, in Eighteenth-Century Philadelphia." *Journal of Interdisciplinary History* 26.1 (1995): 1–31.

———. *"To Serve Well and Faithfully": Labor and Indentured Servants in Pennsylvania, 1682–1800*. New York: Cambridge UP, 1987.

Schweitzer, Mary M. "The Spatial Organization of Federalist Philadelphia, 1790." *Journal of Interdisciplinary History* 24.1 (1993): 31–57.

Shammas, Carole. "The Space Problem in Early United States Cities." *The William and Mary Quarterly* 57.3. (2000): 505–42.

Smith, Billy G., ed. *Life in Early Philadelphia: Documents from the Revolutionary and Early National Periods.* University Park: Pennsylvania State UP, 1995.

———. *"The Lower Sort": Philadelphia's Laboring People, 1750–1800.* Ithaca, NY: Cornell UP, 1990.

———. "The Material Lives of Laboring Philadelphians, 1750 to 1800." *The William and Mary Quarterly* 38.2. (1981): 163–202.

Smith, Tom. *The Dawn of the Urban-Industrial Age: The Social Structure of Philadelphia, 1790–1830.* Dissertation. Chicago: U of Chicago, 1980.

Teitelman, S. Robert. *Birch's Views of Philadelphia, with Photographs of the Sites in 1960 and 1982.* Philadelphia: The Free Library of Philadelphia, 2000. Available at: http://www.ushistory.org/birch/index.htm.

Thompson, Peter. *Rum Punch and Revolution: Taverngoing and Public Life in Eighteenth-Century Philadelphia.* Philadelphia: U of Pennsylvania P, 1999.

B. The 1793 yellow fever epidemic.

Arnebeck Bob, *Destroying Angel: Benjamin Rush, Yellow Fever and the Birth of Modern Medicine.* Online book: http://www.geocities.com/bobarnebeck/fever1793.html.

Day, Stacey B. *Edward Stevens: Gastric Physiologist, Physician, and American Statesman.* Montreal: Cultural and Educational Productions, 1969.

Estes, J. Worth, and Billy G. Smith, eds. *A Melancholy Scene of Devastation: The Public Response to the 1793 Philadelphia Yellow Fever Epidemic.* Canton, MA: Published for the College of Physicians of Philadelphia and the Library Company of Philadelphia by Science History Publications, 1997.

Kopperman, Paul E. "'Venerate the Lancet': Benjamin Rush's Yellow Fever Therapy in Context." *Bulletin of the History of Medicine* 78.3 (2004): 539–74.

Kornfield, Eve. "Crisis in the Capital: The Cultural Significance of Philadelphia's Great Yellow Fever Epidemic." *Pennsylvania History* 51 (1984): 189–205.

Lee, Debbie. "Yellow Fever and the Slave Trade: Coleridge's *The Rime of the Ancient Mariner.*" *English Literary History* 65.3 (1998): 675–700.

Miller, Jacquelyn C. *The Body Politic: Passions, Pestilence, and Political Culture in the Age of the American Revolution.* Dissertation. New Brunswick: Rutgers U, 1995.

Pace, Antonio. "Giambattista Scandella and His American Friends." *Italica* 42.2 (1965): 269–84.

Pernick, Martin S. "Politics, Parties, and Pestilence: Epidemic Yellow Fever in Philadelphia and the Rise of the First Party System." *The William and Mary Quarterly* 29.4 (1972): 559–86.

Powell, J. M. *Bring Out Your Dead: The Great Plague of Yellow Fever in Philadelphia in 1793.* Reprinted with a new Introduction by Kenneth R. Foster, et al. Philadelphia: U of Pennsylvania P, 1993 [1949].

Taylor, P. Sean. *"We Live in the Midst of Death": Yellow Fever, Moral Economy, and Public Health in Philadelphia, 1793–1805.* Dissertation. Dekalb: Northern Illinois U, 2001.

C. Atlantic slavery, Caribbean slave revolution, and the Philadelphia free black community.

Anstey, Roger, and P. E. H. Hair, eds. *Liverpool, the African Slave Trade, and Abolition: Essays to Illustrate Current Knowledge and Research*. London: Historic Society of Lancashire and Cheshire: 1976.

Baucom, Ian. *Specters of the Atlantic: Finance Capital, Slavery, and the Philosophy of History*. Durham: Duke UP, 2005.

Blackburn, Robin. "Haiti, Slavery, and the Age of Democratic Atlantic Revolution." *The William and Mary Quarterly* 63.4 (2006): 643–74.

Brooks, Joanna, "The Early American Public Sphere and the Emergence of a Black Print Counterpublic." *The William and Mary Quarterly* 62.1 (2005): 67–92.

Dain, Bruce. *A Hideous Monster of the Mind: American Race Theory in the Early Republic*. Cambridge, MA Harvard UP, 2002.

David, C. W. A. "The Fugitive Slave Law of 1793 and Its Antecedents." *Journal of Negro History* 9.1 (1924): 18–25.

Davis, David Brion. "American Equality and Foreign Revolutions." *The Journal of American History* 76.3 (1989): 729–52.

Drexler, Michael. "Brigands and Nuns: The Vernacular Sociology of Collectivity after the Haitian Revolution." In Malini Johar Schueller and Edward Watts, eds., *Messy Beginnings: Postcoloniality and Early American Studies*, 175–99. New Brunswick, NJ: Rutgers UP, 2003.

Dubois, Laurent. *Avengers of the New World: The Story of the Haitian Revolution*. Cambridge: Harvard UP, 2004.

Garraway, Dorris. "Race, Reproduction and Family Romance in Moreau de Saint-Méry's *Description de la Partie Françoise de L'Isle Saint-Domingue*." *Eighteenth-Century Studies* 38.2 (2005): 227–46.

Geggus, David. "Jamaica and the Saint Domingue Slave Revolt, 1791–1793." *The Americas* 38.2 (1981): 219–33.

———. *Slavery, War, and Revolution: The British Occupation of Saint Domingue, 1793–1798*. Oxford: Clarendon P, 1982.

Hudson, Nicholas. "From 'Nation' to 'Race': The Origin of Racial Classification in Eighteenth-Century Thought." *Eighteenth-Century Studies* 29.3 (1996): 247–64.

Isani, Mukhtar Ali. "Far from 'Gambia's Golden Shore': The Black in Late Eighteenth-Century American Imaginative Literature." *The William and Mary Quarterly* 36.3 (1979): 353–72.

Linebaugh, Peter, and Marcus Rediker. *The Many-Headed Hydra: Sailors, Slaves, Commoners, and the Hidden History of the Revolutionary Atlantic*. London: Verso, 2000.

Matthewson, Tim. *A Proslavery Foreign Policy: Haitian-American Relations during the Early Republic*. Westport, CT: Praeger, 2003.

Meaders, Daniel. "Kidnapping Blacks in Philadelphia: Isaac Hopper's Tales of Oppression." *The Journal of Negro History* 80.2 (1995): 47–65.

———, ed. *Kidnappers in Philadelphia: Isaac Hopper's Tales of Oppression, 1780–1843*. New York: Garland, 1994.

Nash, Gary B. *Forging Freedom: The Formation of Philadelphia's Black Community, 1720–1840*. Cambridge: Harvard UP, 1988.

———. "Reverberations of Haiti in North America: Black Saint Dominguans in Philadelphia." *Pennsylvania History* 65 (1998): 44–73.

Newman, Richard S. *The Transformation of American Abolitionism*. Chapel Hill: U of North Carolina P, 2002.

Stewart, Michael A. Morrison, and James Brewar, eds. *Race and the Early Republic: Racial Consciousness and Nation-Building in the Early Republic*. Lanham, MD: Rowman & Littlefield, 2002.

White, Ashli. *"A Flood of Impure Lava": Saint Dominguan Refugees in the United States, 1791–1820*. Dissertation. New York: Columbia U, 2003.

Will, Thomas E. "Liberalism, Republicanism, and Philadelphia's Black Elite in the Early Republic: The Social Thought of Absalom Jones and Richard Allen." *Pennsylvania History* 69 (2002): 558–76.

Winch, Julie. *Philadelphia's Black Elite: Activism, Accommodation, and the Struggle for Autonomy, 1787–1848*. Philadelphia: Temple UP, 1993.

Zuckerman, Michael. *Almost Chosen People: Oblique Biographies in the American Grain*. Berkeley: U of California P, 1993.

D. The Sephardim and Philadelphia Jewish community.

Birmingham, Stephen. *The Grandees: America's Sephardic Elite*. New York: Harper & Row, 1971.

Calmann, Marianne. *The Carrière of Carpentras*. Oxford: Oxford UP, 1984.

Cohen, Robert. *Jews in Another Environment: Suriname in the Second Half of the Eighteenth Century*. Leiden: Brill, 1997.

Endelman, Todd M. *The Jews of Georgian England, 1714–1830: Tradition and Change in a Liberal Society*. Philadelphia: The Jewish Publication Society of America, 1979.

Israel, Jonathan I. *Diasporas with a Diaspora: Jews, Crypto-Jews and the World Maritime Empires (1540–1740)*. Leiden: Brill, 2002.

Kaplan, Yosef. "Political Concepts in the World of the Portuguese Jews of Amsterdam during the Seventeenth Century: The Problem of Exclusion and the Boundaries of Self-Identity." In Yosef Kaplan, Henry Méchoulan, and Richard H. Popkin, eds., *Menasseh Ben Israel and His World*, 45–62. Leiden: Brill, 1989.

Malino, Frances. *The Sephardic Jews of Bordeaux: Assimilation and Emancipation in Revolutionary and Napoleonic France*. Tuscaloosa: U of Alabama P, 1978.

Marcus, Jacob Rader. *United States Jewry, 1776–1985*. Vol. I. Detroit: Wayne State UP, 1989.

Moulinas, René. *Les Juifs du Pape: Avignon et le Comtat Venaissin*. Paris: Albin Michel, 1992.

Nathans, Heather S. "A Much-Maligned People: Jews on and off the Stage in the Early American Republic." *Early American Studies* 2.2 (2004): 310–42.

Pencak, William. *Jews and Gentiles in Early America, 1654–1800.* Ann Arbor: U of Michigan P, 2005.

Schappes, Morris. "Reaction and Anti-Semitism, 1795–1800." *Publications of the American Jewish Historical Society* 38 (1948): 109–37.

Szajkowski, Zosa. "The Comtadin Jews and the Annexation of the Papal Province by France, 1789–1791." *The Jewish Quarterly Review*, New Ser., 46.2 (1955): 181–93.

Wolf, Edwin, and Maxwell Whiteman. *The History of the Jews of Philadelphia from Colonial Times to the Age of Jackson.* Bicentennial Edition. Philadelphia: Jewish Publication Society of America, 1975.

Yogev, Gedalia. *Diamonds and Coral: Anglo-Dutch Jews and Eighteenth-Century Trade.* Leicester: Leicester UP, 1978.

E. Mercantile networks and the culture of commerce.

Braudel, Fernand. *Civilization and Capitalism: 15th–18th Century.* 3 vols., trans. Siân Reynolds. New York: Harper & Row, 1981–1984 [1979].

Chew, Richard S. "Certain Victims of an International Contagion: The Panic of 1797 and the Hard Times of the Late 1790s in Baltimore." *Journal of the Early Republic* 25 (2005): 565–613.

Ditz, Toby L. "Secret Selves, Credible Personas: The Problematics of Trust and Public Display in the Writing of Eighteenth-Century Philadelphia Merchants." In Robert Blair St. George, ed., *Possible Pasts: Becoming Colonial in Early America*, 219–42. Ithaca: Cornell UP, 2000.

———. "Shipwrecked; or, Masculinity Imperiled: Mercantile Representations of Failure and Gendered Self in Eighteenth-Century Philadelphia." *Journal of American History* 81.3 (1994): 51–80.

Doerflinger, Thomas M. *A Vigorous Spirit of Enterprise: Merchants and Economic Development in Revolutionary Philadelphia.* Chapel Hill: U of North Carolina P, 1986.

Dun, James Alexander. " 'What Avenues of Commerce, Will You, Americans, Not Explore!': Commercial Philadelphia's Vantage onto the Early Haitian Revolution." *The William and Mary Quarterly* 62.3 (2005): 473–504.

Gillingham, Harold E. *Marine Insurance in Philadelphia, 1721–1800.* Philadelphia: Privately printed, 1933.

Gould, Philip. *Barbaric Traffic: Commerce and Antislavery in the Eighteenth-Century Atlantic World.* Cambridge: Harvard UP, 2003.

Kingston, Christopher. "Marine Insurance in Britain and America, 1720–1844: A Comparative Institutional Analysis." *The Journal of Economic History* 67.2 (2007): 379–409.

Mann, Bruce H. *Republic of Debtors: Bankruptcy in the Age of American Independence.* Cambridge: Harvard UP, 2002.

Martin, David A. "Bimetallism in the United States before 1850." *The Journal of Political Economy* 76.3. (1968): 428–42.

Nechtman, Tillman. *Nabobs: Defining the Indian Empire and the British Nation in the Late Eighteenth Century.* Dissertation. Los Angeles: U of Southern California, 2005.

Spera, Elizabeth Gray Kogan. *Building for Business: The Impact of Commerce on the City Plan and Architecture of the City of Philadelphia, 1750–1800.* Dissertation. Philadelphia: U of Pennsylvania, 1980.

Sussman, Charlotte. *Consuming Anxieties: Consumer Protest, Gender, and British Slavery, 1713–1833.* Stanford: Stanford UP, 2000.

Wallerstein, Immanuel. "The Bourgeois(ie) as Concept and Reality." *New Left Review* 167 (1988): 91–106.

Winch, Julie. "'You Know I Am a Man of Business': James Forten and the Factor of Race in Philadelphia's Antebellum Business Community." *Business and Economic History* 26.1 (1997): 213–28.

F. Revolution debates and counterrevolutionary backlash in the American 1790s.

Cotlar, Seth. "The Federalists' Transatlantic Cultural Offensive of 1798 and the Moderation of American Political Discourse." In Jeffrey L. Pasley, Andrew W. Robertson, and David Waldstreicher, eds., *Beyond the Founders: New Approaches to the Political History of the Early American Republic*, 274–99. Chapel Hill: U of North Carolina P, 2004.

Chernow, Ron. *Alexander Hamilton.* New York: Penguin, 2004.

Elkins, Stanley, and Eric McKitrick. *The Age of Federalism: The Early American Republic, 1788–1800.* New York: Oxford UP, 1993.

Fischer, David Hackett. *The Revolution of American Conservatism: The Federalist Party in the Era of Jeffersonian Democracy.* New York: Harper & Row, 1965.

Foner, Philip S., ed. *The Democratic-Republican Societies, 1790–1800: A Documentary Sourcebook of Constitutions, Addresses, Resolutions, and Toasts.* Westport, CT: Greenwood P, 1976.

Hofstadter, Richard. *The Paranoid Style in American Politics and Other Essays.* New York: Knopf, 1966.

Koschnik, Albrecht. "The Democratic Societies of Philadelphia and the Limits of the American Public Sphere, circa 1793–1795." *The William and Mary Quarterly* 58.3 (2001): 615–36.

Miller, John C. *Crisis in Freedom: The Alien and Sedition Acts.* Boston: Little, Brown and Company, 1951.

Tise, Larry E. *The American Counterrevolution: A Retreat from Liberty, 1783–1800.* Mechanicsburg, PA: Stackpole Books, 1998.

White, Ed. "The Value of Conspiracy Theory." *American Literary History* 14.1 (2002): 1–31.

Wood, Gordon S. "Conspiracy and the Paranoid Style: Causality and Deceit in the Eighteenth Century." *The William & Mary Quarterly* 39 (1982): 401–41.

G. British radical-democratic novel in the 1790s: links between Woldwinites and Brown's circle.

Allen, B. Sprague. "William Godwin and the Stage." *PMLA* (Papers of the Modern Language Association) 35.3 (1920): 358–74.

Butler, Marilyn. *Jane Austen and the War of Ideas*. Oxford: Clarendon P, 1975.

Butler, Marilyn, and Janet Todd, eds. *The Works of Mary Wollstonecraft*. London: Pickering, 1989.

Clemit, Pamela. *The Godwinian Novel: The Rational Fictions of Godwin, Brockden Brown, Mary Shelley*. Oxford: Oxford UP, 1993.

Green, David Bonnell. "Letters of William Godwin and Thomas Holcroft to William Dunlap." *Notes and Queries* 3.10 (1956): 441–43.

Johnson, Nancy E. *The English Jacobin Novel on Rights, Property, and the Law*. New York: Palgrave Macmillan, 2004.

Juengel, Scott. "Godwin, Lavater, and the Pleasures of Surface." *Studies in Romanticism* 35 (1996): 73–97.

Kelly, Gary. *English Fiction of the Romantic Period, 1789–1830*. London: Longman, 1989.

———. *The English Jacobin Novel 1780–1805*. Oxford: Oxford UP, 1976.

Peacock, Thomas Love. "Memoir of Percy Bysshe Shelley." In *The Works of Thomas Love Peacock, Including His Novels, Poems, Fugitive Pieces, Criticisms, etc.*, III, 385–449. London: R. Bentley, 1875.

Steinman, Lisa M. "Transatlantic Cultures: Godwin, Brown, and Mary Shelley." *Wordsworth Circle* 32.3 (2001): 126–30.

Tompkins, J. M. S. *The Popular Novel in England, 1770-1800*. Lincoln: U of Nebraska P, 1961.

H. Sensibility, sentiment, physiognomy, and the gothic.

Barker-Benfield, G. J. *The Culture of Sensibility: Sex and Society in Eighteenth-Century Britain*. Chicago: U of Chicago P, 1992.

Barnes, Elizabeth. *States of Sympathy: Seduction and Democracy in the American Novel*. New York: Columbia UP, 1997.

Botting, Fred. *Gothic*. London: Routledge, 1995.

Burgett, Bruce. *Sentimental Bodies: Sex, Gender, and Citizenship in the Early Republic*. Princeton, NJ: Princeton UP, 1998.

Chapman, Mary, and Glenn Hendler. *Sentimental Men: Masculinity and the Politics of Affect in American Culture*. Berkeley: University of California Press, 1999.

Ellis, Kate Ferguson. *The Contested Castle: Gothic Novels and the Subversion of Domestic Ideology*. Chicago: U of Illinois P, 1989.

Ellis, Markman. *The Politics of Sensibility: Race, Gender, and Commerce in the Sentimental Novel*. Cambridge: Cambridge UP, 1996.

Epley, Steven. "Alienated, Betrayed, and Powerless: A Possible Connection between *Charlotte Temple* and the Legend of Inkle and Yarico." *Papers on Language & Literature* 38.2 (2002): 200–22.

Johnson, Claudia L. *Equivocal Beings: Politics, Gender, and Sentimentality in the 1790s—Wollstonecraft, Radcliffe, Burney, Austen.* Chicago: U of Chicago P, 1995.

Jones, Chris. *Radical Sensibility: Literature and Ideas in the 1790s.* London: Routledge, 1993.

Kilgour, Maggie. *The Rise of the Gothic Novel.* London: Routledge, 1995.

Mullan, John. *Sentiment and Sociability: The Language of Feeling in the Eighteenth Century.* Oxford: Clarendon P, 1988.

Rivers, Christopher. *Face Value: Physiognomical Thought and the Legible Body in Marivaux, Lavater, Balzac, Gautier, and Zola.* Madison: U of Wisconsin P, 1994.

Stafford, Barbara. *Body Criticism: Imagining the Unseen in Enlightenment Art and Medicine.* Cambridge: MIT Press, 1991.

Stern, Julia. *The Plight of Feeling: Sympathy and Dissent in the Early American Novel.* Chicago: U of Chicago P, 1997.

Todd, Janet. *Sensibility: An Introduction.* London; New York: Methuen, 1986.

Watt, James. *Contesting the Gothic: Fiction, Genre, and Cultural Conflict, 1764–1832.* Cambridge: Cambridge UP, 1999.

SHAKESPEARE
THE PLAYER

SHAKESPEARE

THE PLAYER

A Life in the Theatre

John Southworth

SUTTON PUBLISHING

First published in 2000 by
Sutton Publishing Limited · Phoenix Mill
Thrupp · Stroud · Gloucestershire · GL5 2BU

British Library Cataloguing in Publication Data
A catalogue record for this book is available from the British
Library

ISBN 0-7509-2312-1

Typeset in 11/14.5 Sabon.
Typesetting and origination by
Sutton Publishing Limited.
Printed and bound in England by
J. H. Haynes & Co. Ltd, Sparkford.

Dedicated in grateful and affectionate memory
to my former teachers at the Old Vic Theatre School

Michel Saint-Denis
Glen Byam Shaw and
George Devine

especially Glen, remembering his sensitive
and true productions of Shakespeare

Contents

	List of Illustrations	ix
	Acknowledgements	xi
1	*The Invisible Man*	1
2	*Killing the Calf*	14
3	*The Apprentice*	24
4	*Admiral's Man*	32
5	*The Rose, 1592*	51
6	*The Player Poet*	65
7	*Chamberlain's Man*	93
8	*He that Plays the King*	129
9	*The Globe, 1599–1601*	160
10	*Travelling Man*	196
11	*King's Man*	228
12	*Blackfriars*	254
13	*The Man Shakespeare*	277
	Appendices	
	A Recollections of Marlowe, Kyd and Peele in Shakespeare's early plays	285

Contents

B   Conjectural programme of performances of 'harey the vi' at the Rose in 1592/3   295

C   Correspondences in word, image or thought between Shakespeare's plays of 1593/4 and the Sonnets   297

D   Conjectural doubling plots for *Romeo and Juliet, Henry V* and *Troilus and Cressida*   301

Abbreviations   309

Notes   311

Further Reading   343

Index   345

List of Illustrations

	Page
The Droeshout engraving, 1623	xii
Stratford Guildhall	18
Illustration to *Henry VI, Part 1*	40
Portrait of Tamburlaine	43
Illustration from Kyd's *The Spanish Tragedie*	44
The murder of Thomas Arden	46
Imaginary portrait of Edward I	49
Reconstruction of the Rose theatre in 1592	52
Woodcut which illustrates *The Ballad of Titus Andronicus*	57
Illustration from *The Two Gentlemen of Verona*	73
Edward III	86
Henry Carey, Lord Hunsdon	94
William Kempe with his taborer	97
Shakespeare's principal fellows	99
Autograph of Samuel Gilburne	104
Illustration from *Romeo and Juliet*	109
Gild or Moot Hall, Ipswich	117
Town or Market Hall, Faversham	124
John Davies	130
Orford Castle, Suffolk	141
Illustration from *Richard II*	145
The Globe Theatre, 1616	162
Illustration from *Henry V*	165
Robert Armin as 'Blue John'	169
Illustrations from *Hamlet*	185
Guildhall, Hadleigh	207
St Mary's Guildhall, Coventry	211
Market or Town Hall, Henley-in-Arden	213
Market Hall and courthouse, Maidstone	244

Possible portrait of Shakespeare in *Pericles*   261
'Shakespeare the Player'   278
Engraving of Shakespeare   284

Plates between pages 180 and 181

1   Portrait engraving of Shakespeare by George Vertue, 1754
2   The Shakespeare memorial bust in Stratford church
3   Stratford Guildhall, upper chamber
4   Bankside, 1600
5   William Sly
6   Richard Burbage
7   Edward Alleyn
8   Tomb of John Gower in Southwark Cathedral
9   Jill Showell as Portia
10 'Wee Three Logerheads'
11 'What, the sword and the word?' *The Merry Wives of Windsor*, Stratford, 1955
12 Maldon Moot Hall
13 John Lowin
14 *King Lear* at Ipswich, 1974
15 'When shall we three meet again?' *Macbeth*, Ipswich, 1978
16 The Peacham drawing
17 Nathan Field
18 Old Moot Hall, Sudbury, Suffolk

Acknowledgements

I am indebted for the data on which my book is based to all those scholars who have toiled so devotedly in the field of research to establish the facts as we presently know them, especially Sir Edmund Chambers, whose six volumes of his *Elizabethan Stage* and *William Shakespeare* – from which I quote throughout, as acknowledged in the notes – have provided an invaluable source of reference.

I am likewise indebted to the many libraries that have assisted my studies, and here I want to make special mention of my friends at the Central Ipswich Branch of Suffolk Libraries (my home library) who have been so unfailingly helpful in obtaining the books I have needed through the Inter-Library Loan Scheme, and in meeting my other enquiries.

In the interpretation of the plays, I have learnt as much from the directors and actors I have worked with in productions of the plays down the years as I have from books. Though it is impossible for me to name them all individually, I thank them very sincerely.

A final word of acknowledgement is due to those libraries and museums that have kindly supplied photographs for the book's illustrations, and given me permission to reproduce them. Particular acknowledgement is made in the captions. In the few instances where I have been unable to trace the copyright owners, I offer apologies and assurance of future correction, if they will kindly get in touch with me.

John Southworth
Ipswich, February 2000

The Droeshout engraving, 1623 (Folger Shakespeare Library, Washington, DC)

ONE

The Invisible Man

The eyes that stare blankly out at us from the familiar Droeshout portrait of Shakespeare have little to tell us of the player that he was – or indeed of the man, however we choose to regard him. This should not surprise us. The artist's depiction of his features must have borne a reasonable likeness or it would not have been passed by Shakespeare's former fellows, Heminges and Condell, for inclusion in the First Folio of 1623, which they edited; but Droeshout had been only fifteen when Shakespeare died in 1616 and he is unlikely to have known him well, if at all.[1] He had probably based his engraving on an earlier portrait or sketch and, if so, whatever life the original may have had was lost in the copying.

But in fairness to Droeshout, we should bear in mind what Heminges and Condell's purpose had been in commissioning the portrait, which was to embellish a first collected edition of their friend's plays with an appropriately dignified image of their author. Shakespeare's renown as player and man of the theatre was not in question – not among those who had known him personally or had seen him perform; his reputation as dramatic poet was yet to be established. Seven years earlier in a bid to secure scholarly recognition for his own dramatic achievements, Ben Jonson had published his plays in a similarly impressive folio volume, which may have prompted Heminges and Condell to do the same for their former fellow. As they explain in their prefatory letters, the Shakespeare folio was intended as both memorial and rescue mission: 'to keepe the memory of so worthy a Friend, & Fellow alive, as was our SHAKESPEARE'; but also because whereas before 'you [the readers] were abus'd with deverse stolne, and surreptitious

1

copies, maimed, and deformed by the frauds and stealthes of injurious imposters, that expos'd them: even those are now offer'd to your view cur'd, and perfect in their limbes; and all the rest, absolute in their numbers, as he conceived them'.[2] (The 'rest', it should be said, comprised no less than eighteen plays that had never before appeared in print, including *The Tempest, Twelfth Night* and *Macbeth*, which, but for Heminges and Condell's initiative in searching out Shakespeare's manuscripts and the company's prompt books, might easily, probably would, have been lost for ever.) But, like Jonson, they would also have had a larger end in view. For the paradox is that at the highest point of their achievement in the English dramatic renaissance of the sixteenth and early seventeenth centuries, the status of playwrights had never been so low, or plays so little regarded as a literary form.

In 1605, at the lowest ebb of his fortunes, the proudly assertive Jonson, committed to prison with George Chapman for their part in the writing of a play called *Eastward Ho!* that had given offence to the authorities, was so far obliged to bow to the common opinion as to write cringingly to the Earl of Salisbury that the cause of their incarceration – '(would I could name some worthier) . . . is, a (the word irks me that our Fortunes hath necessitated us to so despised a course) a play, my Lord'.[3] In founding his now famous Oxford library in the years that followed, Sir Thomas Bodley was insistent on excluding plays from the newly published books that he wished to assemble on its shelves. Writing to the Bodleian's librarian in 1611/12, Sir Thomas assures him that even if 'some little profit might be reaped (which God knows is very little) out of some of our playbooks, the benefit thereof will nothing near countervail the harm that the scandal will bring unto the library when it shall be given out that we stuff it full of baggage books . . .'. In another letter, he puts playbooks in the same category of ephemera as almanacs and proclamations, and refers to them collectively as 'riff-raffs'. The 'baggage books' and 'riff-raffs' he thus dismisses as unworthy of attention would have included newly published quarto editions of plays by both Shakespeare and Jonson.[4] Even so cultured and frequent a playgoer as the poet John Donne, writing in 1604 or

1605 (years in which *Hamlet* and *Othello* were in performance at the Globe), does not even mention Shakespeare's name or that of any other dramatist in a catalogue of thirty-four works by thirty different authors of the time. As Professor Bentley concludes, 'he did not consider plays in the category of serious literature'.[5] Nor even, it would appear, of literature at all in the usual sense. Though Shakespeare the player, Shakespeare the theatre director and part-owner, would certainly have been known to him, Shakespeare the playwright and dramatic poet was seemingly invisible to him.

Plays of the period were, of course, written to be performed: heard, not read. Throughout the whole of the seventeenth century – and in spite of first Jonson's, then Heminges and Condell's, best editorial endeavours – plays continued to be primarily regarded, not as books and thus belonging to literature, but as public events in which a story was enacted by means of spoken words and the movement and gestures of actors on a stage to an audience assembled at a particular time and place. They existed temporally – in the two to three hours' traffic of the stage – not spatially in the way that a book exists and can be handled and shelved. In the theatre, the words were of great importance; at no period of theatrical history have they been of *more* importance (one went to hear a play, not see it); but they were written by their author to be memorised by actors, and came into their true, intended form only when spoken. We need to remember, too, that Shakespeare was one of those actors; he was writing for himself as a performer as well as for his fellows.

In this respect, the medium in which Shakespeare and other dramatists of the period worked – that of the popular theatre – had continuity with, and was itself an almost unique survival of, the age-old oral culture that had been dominant throughout the Middle Ages. By Shakespeare's time that popular culture of the harper-poets and itinerant interluders was in rapid disintegration and retreat before the advance of literacy and an increasing availability of printed books;[6] a profound shift in the cultural climate that had been in slow, inexorable progress since the fourteenth century but was then brought to a critical stage by more recent religious changes. The Bible

– previously reserved as reading matter to a Latin-speaking elite and communicated to an illiterate laity in the form of pictorial images, liturgical ritual and religious drama (all providing an essentially communal experience) – now became in its English translations generally available and subject to individual interpretation. The altar, where an action was performed and a sacrifice offered, gave place in importance to the pulpit, from which the scriptures were read and expounded, and to the chained Bible which people were encouraged to read for themselves – an essentially private act. In the religious compromise effected by the Elizabethan church settlement, the Eucharist survived, but more perhaps as a service to be read than as an action to be *done*, with the altar replaced by a removable table. The great *Corpus Christi* cycles of plays, that had survived long enough for Shakespeare to have seen at least one of them at Coventry, did not simply fall out of favour, as was once believed, but were actively suppressed in the interests of the new Protestant orthodoxy by an alliance of secular and ecclesiastical powers that within thirty years of Shakespeare's death was to close and demolish the theatres.[7] So far as the medium of Shakespeare's expression was concerned, it was an end-game that he and his fellows were playing.

Shakespeare's plays (and those of his fellow dramatists) were no more written for publication than were the *Corpus Christi* cycles or later morality plays and interludes, and their survival as texts was to prove just as chancy. Not only were they aimed at performance, rather than publication, but their publication was, in most circumstances, firmly resisted by the companies for which they had been written, including the Chamberlain's (later, King's) Men, in which Shakespeare became a sharer. This was because, in the absence of any enforceable copyright other than that of the stationers who printed them, the effect of such publication was to make the texts of the plays freely available for performance by rival companies to the financial loss of those who had commissioned and first performed them. (The plays belonged, not to the author, but to the company. Hence the importance of the playbook, and the book-keeper who was responsible for it.) Nevertheless, as we know, some of Shakespeare's more popular plays *did* find their way into print during his lifetime, for the most part in pirated editions, 'maimed and deformed', as Heminges and Condell put it, 'by the frauds and stealthes of injurious imposters', and it was in response to that specific situation that they had mounted their rescue mission. In normal circumstances, only when a play was thought to have exhausted its immediate potential in the theatre and had been dropped from the current repertoire was its publication authorised by the company concerned as a disposable capital asset.

But there was another, more telling reason for Shakespeare having remained invisible to so many of his contemporaries. It was not just the ephemerality of the medium in which he worked or the low status accorded to dramatists among other authors, but a deep-seated disdain on the part of the educated and armorial classes of his day, especially the literati among them, for all those who, like himself and his fellows, earned their living in the realm of public entertainment, whether as musicians, actors or playwrights. Quite simply, they were regarded as 'below the salt', to be patronised perhaps, but otherwise excluded from respectable society. Here was the real source of that discredit which Bodley believed would reflect upon his new library by the admittance of playbooks – irrespective of their quality. It was embodied in the vagrancy laws of the period where minstrels and players were routinely cited together as 'rogues and vagabonds', subject to a whipping if caught on the road without the protection afforded by their acceptance of a nominal, but nonetheless menial, status as servants of the monarch or other great lord. Quite apart from the extreme views of Puritans such as Stubbs and Gosson, for whom acting itself was an offence against God, and players the 'Devil's brood', such attitudes were a commonplace of moderate contemporary opinion.

Once, it may have been otherwise. 'Plaier', John de la Casa admits in 1615, 'was ever the life of dead poesie, and in those times, that Philosophy taught us morall precepts [he means the classical era], these acted the same in publicke showes'; but 'Player is now a name of contempt, for times corrupt men with vice, and vice is growne to a height of government'; for 'Players, Poets, and Parasites', he goes on, 'doe now in a man joyne hands [in Shakespeare? In Marlowe and Jonson, who at one time had also been players?]; and as Lucifer fell from heaven through pride: these have fallen from credit through folly: so that to chast eares they are as odious as filthy pictures are offensive to modest eyes'.[8]

Here, perhaps, are those 'public means which public manners breeds' referred to by Shakespeare himself in Sonnet 111:

> Thence comes it that my name receives a brand,
> And almost thence my nature is subdued
> To what it works in, like the dyer's hand.

Or, as Shakespeare's friend and admirer, John Davies of Hereford, was to bluntly express it in 1603, 'the stage doth staine pure gentle bloud'.[9] The same snobbish disdain for the occupation of player was to fester on until comparatively recent times.

The publication of the First Folio was not only, then, a work of fellowly piety to preserve the text of Shakespeare's plays and rescue them from the pirates; it also implied a claim for recognition of his genius as a dramatic poet, which, seven years after his death, remained largely unacknowledged. And the engraving Heminges and Condell commissioned Droeshout to make for it was designed to promote a reformed image of Shakespeare as poet and man of letters in circumvention of the contemporary prejudice against him as public entertainer. In the immediate term, their efforts met with only limited success;[10] but, as the book found its way into libraries (the earliest reference is to a copy bound by the Bodleian in 1624), it was to light a long fuse to an explosion of scholarly interest and a still-thriving academic industry – all centred, naturally enough, on the plays as literary texts. It is the Droeshout engraving – the only authenticated, contemporary portrait we possess – that has dominated the imagination of the book's users ever since.

The Droeshout engraving is immediately followed in the First Folio by Ben Jonson's tribute to his dead colleague and friend and, as if in acknowledgement of its limitations, the reader is urged by him to 'look/Not on his picture, but his book'.

The memorial bust of Shakespeare in Stratford church (of uncertain date but installed by 1623 at the latest) reinforces this message. (See Plate 2.) Beneath a carving of the now familiar figure, holding a quill in his right hand and resting his left on a sheet of paper, the passer-by is enjoined to stay, and

READ IF THOU CANST, WHOM ENVIOUS DEATH HATH PLAST,

WITH IN THIS MONUMENT SHAKSPEARE: WITH WHOME,

QUICK NATURE DIDE: WHOSE NAME DOTH DECK Y^S TOMBE,

FAR MORE THEN COST: SIEH ALL, Y^T HE HATH WRITT,

LEAVES LIVING ART, BUT PAGE, TO SERVE HIS WITT.

The inscription is misspelt and over-punctuated; nor does Shakespeare lie 'with in this monument' but under the floor of the church some yards away, but its purport is identical to that of Jonson's epitaph. If we seek the soul of Shakespeare, his 'living art', we have nowhere left to look but to the pages of his book; in that time and place, the theatre was not considered an acceptable option.

A long succession of biographers and scholars have since applied this advice in the most literal way by searching the speeches of the fictional characters he created, and the changing themes of his plays, for clues to Shakespeare's inner, emotional life, or his political and religious opinions. The method is not altogether without interest or value; but the material available to this kind of research is so large and so various that, like the Bible, it can be used selectively to support a multiplicity of contradictory views. So prone is it to subjective bias that all too often the portrait that emerges is found to be more reflective of the researchers' own preconceptions and prejudices, and of the values and assumptions of the period in which they are writing, than it is of Shakespeare; these look for Shakespeare in the mirror of his book and see only a cloudy image of themselves. In so far as such enquiries proceed from a belief that in writing his plays Shakespeare was primarily engaged in a form of self-expression, rather than in responding to the practical needs of the theatres he served and the changing demands and tastes of the public with whom he was in constant touch in the most intimate way possible – as an actor on the stage – they rest on a fallacious premise. This is not to deny that, like all great poets and writers, Shakespeare was able to mould whatever material came his way to an aesthetic expression of his own unique experience of life and of the world around him, or to do so in words that at their finest and best reach to universal truths; but, by definition, such intuitive insights are not to be found on the surface of his mimetic inventions; and unless we start from a true appreciation of his initial motivations in putting pen to paper, of choosing one theme, one treatment of a theme, one story rather than another, and always with a particular end in view – a play for a specific group of actors to perform in a specific theatre at a specific time that would give pleasure to a specific audience – we go badly astray. In search of his 'living art', we discover only a life. And is it really Shakespeare's?

Those unwilling or unable to accept the plain fact of his profession as player, or its necessary implications, have found 'evidence' for a whole series of alternative occupations to fill the so-called 'lost years' of his youth and early manhood: schoolmaster, soldier, sailor, butcher, glover, dyer, scrivener, lawyer, barber-surgeon – nothing is too far-fetched if it can serve to postpone the moment of his emergence, 'exelent in the qualitie he professes', as player. Others would avoid that moment of truth altogether by attributing the plays to some other contemporary figure considered to be more fitted by birth and education to be their author. Sir Francis Bacon, the earls of Rutland, Derby, Southampton and Oxford have been among the leading contenders for the coveted title. The mystery these set out to solve is of their own making, and the effect of their conjectures merely to muddy the waters of genuine research.

For those who focus on Shakespeare's poetry in isolation from the dramatic uses to which he put it, there is no mystery; or rather the mystery is seen as endemic to the nature of poetry itself, for as Keats explained in a letter,

> . . . the poetical Character . . . is not itself – it has no self – it is every thing and nothing. It has no character – it enjoys light and shade; it lives in gusts, be it foul or fair, high or low, rich or poor, mean or elevated. . . . A poet is the most unpoetical of anything in

existence; because he has no identity – he is continually in and filling some other Body. The Sun, the Moon, the Sea and Men and Women who are creatures of impulse are poetical and have about them an unchangeable attribute – the poet has none; no identity – he is certainly the most unpoetical of all God's creatures. . . .[11]

For Jorge Luis Borges likewise, 'There was no one in him; behind his face (which even through the bad paintings of those times resembles no other) and his words, which were copious, fantastic and stormy, there was only a bit of coldness, a dream dreamt by no one'. But Borges situates this quality of 'negative capability' not in Shakespeare's nature as poet, but in his predestined profession as actor. 'No one', he goes on to assert,

> has ever been so many men as this man who like the Egyptian Proteus could exhaust all the guises of reality. At times he would leave a confession hidden away in some corner of his work, certain that it would not be deciphered; Richard affirms that in his person he plays the part of many and Iago claims with curious words 'I am not what I am'.[12]

And certainly, if part of his peculiar genius as dramatist and poet lay in his capacity to identify with the thoughts and feelings of his characters, and to speak with their voices out of the situations in which he had placed them, that authorial gift cannot have been wholly unconnected with the actor's ability – which, as a senior member of the leading company of his day, he would also have enjoyed – to identify with the characters he played and to make the words of the playwright his own – which in his case, of course, they normally *were*. It is this protean component in Shakespeare's identity that leads so many biographers astray and confuses the critics.

I have said that in publishing the First Folio, Heminges and Condell had planted the seed for an extraordinary, if belated, awakening of scholarly interest in the plays, but the repercussions of it were to spread much further afield.

9

By the time of Shakespeare's death in 1616, the theatre to which he had contributed so greatly was already in decline; in 1642 the playhouses were closed by government decree, and were to remain closed for the nineteen long years of the interregnum, during which time they fell into ruin and were demolished. The companies disbanded and, apart from occasional scratch performances in private houses, makeshift booths or taverns, theatrical activity came to an end. Much that is now obscure and confusing in Shakespeare's life story is directly attributable to this break in tradition. When, at his restoration in 1660, Charles II licensed the building of two new theatres in the capital, they were of a very different type from those that Shakespeare had known and written for, and his plays had only a fitful presence in them. When occasionally revived, it was usually in 'improved' (that is to say, mutilated) versions that their author would have had difficulty in recognising as his own.

It was not, then, principally through the theatre that the great upsurge of interest in, and admiration for, his plays was mediated, but rather through publication of a long and continuing series of revised, annotated editions of the First Folio, to which many of the most learned men of the late seventeenth and eighteenth centuries contributed. And as more popular versions of these proliferated in the nineteenth century (lacking notes but often lavishly illustrated by imagined scenes from the plays), the 'book', to which Jonson had recommended the reader to look rather than its author's portrait, came to occupy an honoured place beside the Bible in every Victorian home. And the higher that Shakespeare's reputation as poet and author rose to a pinnacle of universal praise as National Bard, patriotic spokesman, secular prophet and moral exemplar, the more desirable it became to distance him from his theatrical roots and from his occupation as player; while Baconian eccentrics balked at any such connection, these were simply passed over by the mass of biographers as an incidental circumstance of his social situation at a particular period of his life that he was soon to transcend. The tendency was to delay his adoption of the base trade to as late as possible and contrive his retirement from it as early as possible.

In 1908, Thomas Hardy, replying to an appeal for a donation to a Shakespeare memorial that was to take the form of a national theatre, was able to reply that he did not think that Shakespeare

> appertains particularly to the theatrical world nowadays, if ever he did. His distinction as a minister of the theatre is infinitesimal beside his distinction as a poet, man of letters, and seer of life, and that his expression of himself was cast in the form of words for actors and not in the form of books to be read was an accident of his social circumstances that he himself despised.[13]

Recent scholarship, to which we are indebted for more detailed information about the theatrical conditions in which the plays were conceived and first performed than was previously available and, from the beginning of the twentieth century, the restoration to the plays in the theatre of a fuller, more accurate text and a better understanding and respect on the part of actors and directors for Shakespeare's intentions and methods in writing them, has gone some way to restore the balance. No one today would write about Shakespeare's plays without paying at least lip service to the theatrical context of their original creation or seek to deny (as Hardy did) its relevance to a more complete appreciation of them as works of art.

But the pattern of late entry to the players' profession and early retirement from it first set by Shakespeare's early biographers on the basis of imperfect knowledge and Warwickshire legend persists. And as the Droeshout engraving and the Stratford monument have continued to cast their baleful gaze over subsequent generations of readers, and a great, still burgeoning quantity of academic writing – ranging in quality from the brilliantly perceptive to the near-lunatic and barely comprehensible – has descended on the plays considered primarily as texts to be studied rather than as plays to be enjoyed, Shakespeare the player and man of the theatre has remained in the shadows. While literally millions of words have been devoted to authorial and textual problems, few have thought it worthwhile or necessary to treat in any detail of Shakespeare's consecutive career as player, or the possible ways in which his experience as an actor may have influenced his writing. The situation that confronted Heminges and Condell in 1623 has thus been exactly reversed. The unacknowledged dramatist whose reputation they sought to promote in face of scholarly neglect has come to occupy nearly all of the frame while the player and man of the theatre whose memory they revered is relegated to the margins.

Does any of this really matter? True, we do not know for certain how good a player Shakespeare was and, for the most part, can only conjecture as to the roles that he played. Again, the art of the actor, however accomplished, and the art of the theatre in general of which he was undoubtedly a master, are essentially ephemeral and, to that extent, beyond our recall. In these circumstances, it is not to be wondered at that his supreme achievement as dramatic poet, for which we have the firm evidence of the printed plays, is seen as of greater importance than any necessarily speculative estimate of his histrionic skills. But from an historical and biographical point of view, it is surely necessary to an adequate understanding of the period, the society in which he lived, and his place within it, to seek an authentic portrait of the man in the fullness of his being; and how can we hope to do this without taking due account of his professional occupation during much the greater part of his life – the occupation by which he was mainly known to his contemporaries? Rob a man of his profession or 'quality' (as the actor's profession was termed in his time) and you rob him of an essential part of his identity. And this is perhaps more true of the actor than anyone else. But there is another objection to those who regard Shakespeare's occupation as player as more or less peripheral to an appreciation of his genius as 'poet, man of letters, and seer of life'; for, in attempting to separate the two – the man from his works, the works from the context and original purpose of their creation – you distort and obscure the meaning of the works themselves.

Here, precisely, is the vacuum that lies at the heart of so much biographical and academic writing about Shakespeare, past and present. And how deeply alienating it can be to those who are brought to approach his plays for the first time in preparing for school examinations, when the incomparable music of his verses is reduced to numbered, chopped-up parcels of dead learning. 'Explain and discuss'!

Certainly, unless we place this fact of his occupation at the centre of our consideration of his life and works, we are left with an insoluble enigma; of how a well-educated but inexperienced young man from a small Warwickshire town with no theatrical background or training came to have such command of theatrical ways and means, such knowledge and understanding of the poetic and dramatic techniques of his predecessors and contemporaries as, in his earliest-known works, to have surpassed them in achievement and, in a few short years, gone on to write the greatest plays in the language.

To get to grips with the man himself, we have to go behind the literary legend, the invisible man of the Droeshout portrait and the Stratford monument; to make a big leap of historical imagination to put ourselves into that pre-literary, theatrical world that Shakespeare actually inhabited, when the words that he wrote in his London lodgings, or in the snatched intervals of repose on his visits home or on tour, were words to be acted, words for himself and his fellows to speak and be heard from a stage. This I attempt from the perspective of a fellow performer, a latter-day working actor, in the chapters that follow.

TWO

Killing the Calf

As all that is known with any degree of certainty concerning Shakespeare, is – *that he was born at Stratford upon Avon, – married and had children there, – went to London, where he commenced actor, and wrote poems and plays, – returned to Stratford, made his will, died, and was buried,* – I must confess my readiness to combat every unfounded supposition respecting the particular occurrences of his life.

George Steevens in a letter to Malone[1]

Half a century passed after Shakespeare's death before anyone thought it worthwhile to publish an account of his life. In the meantime, the country had been torn apart by civil war, the theatres closed and destroyed, and the world he had known turned upside down. The first such account (too brief to be described as anything more than a biographical sketch) was that of Thomas Fuller in his *History of the Worthies of England* (1662). Though Shakespeare's second daughter Judith had lived on until the Restoration, and there must then have been others in both Stratford and London who remembered him and would have been able to supply at least some outline of his early life and career, the normally assiduous Fuller appears to have taken little trouble to seek them out, and the half-page entry he devotes to Shakespeare in his *Worthies* is massively uninformative. He tells us correctly of his birth in Stratford but even the date of his death – for which he had only to glance at the monument in Holy Trinity church – is left a blank. In place of facts, he gives us generalities deriving from Jonson's eulogy about his natural genius and 'wood-notes wild'. Sketchy as it was, Fuller's

14

account remained the primary source for subsequent biographical entries in the seventeenth century.

John Aubrey's random jottings, made around 1681, had to wait over two hundred years for publication as *Brief Lives*. They contain interesting scraps of information from various stages of Shakespeare's life but, though conscientiously recorded, they had come to him only at second or third hand and are not to be taken at their face value. For example, on a visit to Stratford he was told by one of the locals that Shakespeare was the son of a butcher and had occasionally taken a turn at his father's craft; 'when he killed a calf', his informant assured him, 'he would do it in high style and make a speech'. We know now that William's father, John Shakespeare, was in fact a glover by trade and in later life something of a general merchant in agricultural produce. That he was ever personally involved in the slaughter of cattle seems improbable, and that his young son was allowed to carry out the butchery himself (in whatever style) even less likely. Either Aubrey's informant was having him on, or had picked up and misunderstood a genuine tradition from an earlier time, in which the act of killing a calf was mimicked in pantomime, or shadow play behind a curtain, by travelling showmen; a trick that William may have seen at a fair and performed for the amusement of his family and neighbours. There is a record from 1521 in the household accounts of Princess Mary (then six years old) of a 'man of Windsor' being rewarded for 'killing of a calf before my Lady's grace behind a cloth'.[2] That the adult Shakespeare was familiar with it, we know from *Hamlet* where, in answer to Polonius' boast that at university he had acted Julius Caesar and been killed in the Capitol, he has Hamlet reply, 'It was a brute part of him to kill so capital a calf there' (III.ii.104) – an ironic anticipation of Polonius' death behind a cloth – the arras behind which he has hidden to overhear the scene between Hamlet and Gertrude and through which he is killed by Hamlet's rapier. Aubrey was seemingly unaware of this background to the story he tells: a testimony to his accuracy as a reporter but to nothing else. The anecdote contains a true statement but we have to put it back into its original context to know what it means.

To set the record straight, the slaughter of those animals whose skins were used in the glover's trade (mainly pigs and goats) was the job of the butchers, whose shambles in Stratford was situated in Middle Row. Schoenbaum suggests that it was in visiting his uncle Henry's farm in Snitterfield that William may have witnessed a scene that was to stay with him and return to his mind in writing *Henry VI*.[3] Seeking an analogy to convey the young king's distress at the arrest of 'good Duke Humphrey' which has just taken place in his presence, and anticipating the old man's fate, he has Henry say of him that,

> . . . as the butcher takes away the calf,
> And binds the wretch, and beats it when it strains,
> Bearing it to the bloody slaughter-house;
> Even so, remorseless, have they borne him hence;
> And as the dam runs lowing up and down,
> Looking the way her harmless young one went,
> And can do nought but wail her darling's loss;
> Even so myself bewails good Gloucester's case
> With sad unhelpful tears, and with dimm'd eyes
> Look after him, and cannot do him good . . .
>
> (2 *Henry VI*, III.i.210–19)

If, as I later suggest, he was to play the part of Henry himself, these words would, at their first hearing, have come from his own lips. A later speech in the same play takes us into the shambles itself, for when Warwick is questioned about his suspicions as to the identity of the murderers, he asks in reply,

> Who finds the heifer dead, and bleeding fresh,
> And sees fast by a butcher with an axe,
> But will suspect 'twas he that made the slaughter?

and goes on,

> Who finds the partridge in the puttock's nest,
> But may imagine how the bird was dead,
> Although the kite soar with unblooded beak?
>
> (III.ii.187–92)

It is recollections such as these from Shakespeare's upbringing in a small country town, and observations from nature in the countryside around it, that give life and substance to the more rhetorical passages in his early plays, and mark them as his own.

I need to say a little more at this point about William's father. Deriving from yeoman stock in the nearby village of Snitterfield, John Shakespeare had moved to Stratford in about 1550. As we have seen, he was a glover and wittawer (dresser of soft leather) by trade. In the town his business had prospered so well that in the course of a few years he had been able to buy land and property, including the house in Henley Street that William was later to inherit. In 1559 he had married Mary Arden, the daughter of a well-to-do local farmer with connections to a gentry family of the same name that could trace its Warwickshire roots to before the Norman conquest. William, their eldest son, had been born in April 1564; the day of the month is unknown, but he was baptised in the Stratford parish church of Holy Trinity on the 26th. By then, John had already recommended himself to the town elders as a suitable candidate for municipal office, and in 1557 was serving as ale-taster, the first of a series of minor posts that was to lead, in 1568, to his election as Bailiff or Mayor. Thereafter, he was always addressed as *Master* Shakespeare. Though he was Bailiff only for a year, and was not, like some of his fellow burgesses, re-elected to the office, he acted as Chamberlain (treasurer) in several years both before and after his mayoralty, and went on to serve the town as alderman for nearly two more decades.

We have no firm evidence relating to William's education. Biographers mainly assume that he attended the King's New School in Stratford, which occupied an upper chamber of the Guildhall (Plate 3). As tuition there was free to the sons of burgesses and it was not far from his home in Henley Street, it would have been the natural place for him to go. Contrary to anti-Stratfordian arguments, his schooling there would have been sufficient to provide at least an adequate basis for the classical learning he was later to exhibit in the plays. Ben Jonson, who is patronising in his eulogy about Shakespeare's 'small Latine and lesse Greek', is known to have

Stratford Guildhall as it was before the restoration of 1892, with the Guild Chapel at centre (Shakespeare Birthplace Trust, Stratford-upon-Avon)

completed a similar course at Westminster School. Though, exceptionally, Jonson may have stayed on at Westminster a year or two longer, the normal age at which boys destined to go into one of the crafts or professions finished their grammar school education was fourteen or fifteen. At this age, William would have found himself in Stratford looking about for future employment. The year was 1578 or 1579.

Up to this time all had gone well with John Shakespeare and, as late as 1575, we learn of his extending his property in Henley Street by the purchase of an adjoining tenement with orchards and gardens; but between September 1576 and January 1577 something occurred that was to throw the current of his life completely off course. An application he had made to the College of Heralds for a coat of arms as 'gentleman' – an honour to which as former Bailiff of an incorporated town (one with a royal charter) he was fully entitled – was unaccountably abandoned. He was sued for debt, ceased to attend Council meetings, and failed to respond to repeated demands for payment of various dues and levies that were made upon him. Though treated with exceptional leniency by his Council colleagues, their patience finally ran out, and in 1586 two new aldermen were elected to take his place and that of another defaulter, because they did not 'Come to the halles when they be warned nor hathe not done of Longe tyme'.[4]

It would be tiresome to the reader to rehearse here the several contradictory theories that have been advanced to account for this dramatic change in John Shakespeare's fortunes. That they were at least in part religious is suggested by his inclusion in a list of those who failed to come monthly to church to receive Communion as the law required, and more explicitly by the discovery, after his death, of a 'spiritual testament' – a form of Catholic devotion originally composed by St Charles Borromeo of Milan – in the rafters of his Henley Street house. In this, among other evidence of his attachment to proscribed beliefs and forms of worship, he requests his friends and relations, 'lest by reason of my sins I be to pass and stay a long while in Purgatory, they will vouchsafe to assist and succour me with their holy prayers and satisfactory works, especially with the holy sacrifice of the Mass . . .'.[5] Printed copies of this document in English are known to have been brought from Milan and distributed in England by two Jesuit missionaries, Thomas Campion and Robert Persons, and both men are known to have passed through Warwickshire in 1580. Persons was entertained by Edward Arden, then head of the Arden family, at Park Hall; Campion by Sir William Catesby at Lapworth, for which Catesby was arrested and imprisoned in the Fleet.

The Elizabethan era has often been depicted retrospectively in rosy hues, but the England in which William grew up was riven by deep divisions and uncertainties in which politics and religion had become disastrously entangled; a time of plots and rumours, fears of foreign invasion and mounting paranoia, in which the unprincipled prospered while men of conscience such as Edward Arden could end up with their head stuck on the end of a pike on Tower Bridge. If

John Shakespeare was indeed sympathetic to the old religion of his youth, he was treading a dangerous path.

Traditional accounts of William's early life delay his entrance into the acting profession to as late as 1590, 'or a few years earlier', as one recent biographer vaguely puts it. But the craft of the player is not learnt in a day or even in a few years – a fact of which biographers in general and academics in particular appear blissfully unaware. In proposing that a mature young man in his middle twenties, with no previous training or experience, could come from the background I have indicated and, by 1592, advanced to a point where Henry Chettle (a man thoroughly versed in the ways of the theatre) could describe him in print as 'exelent in the qualitie he professes' (that of a player), and to have acquired a 'facetious grace in writting, that aprooves his Art',[6] is to assume the impossible. It betrays both a degree of contempt for the player's art and total disregard of theatrical conditions in the period, when the normal, if not invariable, routes of entry to the profession were either by patrimonial inheritance or apprenticeship at an early age (between ten and sixteen) to a senior member, usually a 'sharer', in one of the existing companies.

Richard Burbage followed his father into the Queen's men. Edward Alleyn is said by Fuller in his *Worthies* to have been 'bred a Stage-player'; his father was a London innkeeper and he may have begun his acting career playing minor roles with the companies that had used the inn for their performances. If we look at the list of 'Principall Actors in all these Playes' printed by Heminges and Condell at the front of their 1623 edition of Shakespeare's *Works* (reproduced on p. 99), we find that all those named of whose beginnings we have any information were involved in the apprenticeship system in one way or another – as masters or apprentices. Nicholas Tooley was Burbage's apprentice. In his will of 1605, Augustine Phillips bequeathed a legacy to Samuel Gilburne, 'my late apprentice'. John Rice was John Heminges' boy when, in 1607, he performed for James I at a Merchant Taylors' dinner; Alexander Cooke also acknowledged Heminges as his master. Robert Gough is first recorded playing a female role in *The Seven*

Deadly Sins in about 1590/1; Thomas Pope, who remembered Gough in his will of 1603, was probably his master. Robert Armin had begun as apprentice to a London goldsmith and is reputed to have been encouraged as a 'wag' by Queen Elizabeth's jester and player, Tarlton, who prophesied that he should 'enjoy my clownes sute after me', which in course of time he did. Of the twenty-six actors named, only William Ostler, Nathan Field, John Underwood and Richard Robinson are known to have entered the profession in any other way, and that was as singing boys in one of the royal chapels or children's companies.[7] Nor is there a single player in the whole period known to have been accepted into any of the companies in his early to middle twenties without previous training or experience, as is supposed of Shakespeare.

If apprenticeship was the normal pattern of recruitment for those boys and adolescents who had not been 'bred to the stage', as the evidence suggests, there is no reason to believe that Shakespeare, for all his later renown as poet and dramatist, would, as a player, have been treated any differently to other boys of his class and education, or would not have been obliged to climb the same arduous ladder to advancement.

The hoary legend of the young Shakespeare stealing a deer from the park of Sir Thomas Lucy and so arousing the enmity of its owner that he was 'oblig'd to leave his Business and Family in Warwickshire, for some time, and shelter himself in London', as propagated by Nicholas Rowe in 1709,[8] was demolished by Edmond Malone in his uncompleted *Life* published by Boswell in 1821;[9] that it survives at all in subsequent biographies may be due to its usefulness in absolving authors from the painful task of explaining how it came about that the gentle Shakespeare they like to depict could have brought himself to abandon his wife and young family without visible means of support in pursuance of his late-developing histrionic ambitions. But of course there is no real evidence that he did anything of the kind. The dates of his marriage to Anne Hathaway and births of their three children have no relevance to the time of his first departure from Stratford. 'All they prove', as John Dover Wilson pointed out, 'is that he must have been at home about August 1582, nine months before the birth of Susanna; in November of the same year for his marriage; and once again in the early summer of 1584, nine months before the birth of the twins', and, because it was in the summer that plays were normally suspended in London because of the plague, 'the dates referred to do not at all forbid us supposing Shakespeare to have been already a professional player at this period'.[10] Indeed, the fact of his marriage in 1582 gives added support to the hypothesis I am putting forward, for whereas it is easily understandable that an unencumbered boy of fifteen or sixteen should have entered the profession of his choice after completing his grammar school education a year or so earlier, as was normal in the period, it is far from easy to envisage circumstances that might have induced him to do so as a mature young man with family responsibilities.

Nor was there any lack of opportunity for him to have taken that step at the earlier age, for companies of players had been visiting Stratford from 1569 onwards, when he was five, and continued to come there throughout the whole period of his boyhood and adolescence. As troubles came upon him from 1576 onwards, John Shakespeare would have had good reason for wishing his son away from the town and, as alderman and justice, he was ideally placed to facilitate his engaging himself to one of their senior men. For we know that all such players' apprenticeships – whether effected by a simple contract of service or more formal indentures requiring the seal of some regulatory third party[11] – were concluded, not with the company as a constituent body, but with an individual 'sharer' by agreement of his fellows. For the sharers – those who had invested in the company's capital stock of costumes, props and playbooks – '*were* the company, and all the others in the troupe merely their employees'.[12] It is true that no record survives of William having been apprenticed in this way; nor are we given any later hint as to the company or player concerned, the payment of a premium, or the nature and term of his engagement. But neither are we afforded any other reliable information about him at the time and, if William's recruitment and subsequent life as an apprentice player remains a blank, the same is true of the vast majority of other boys of his age recruited into one or other of the numerous companies of players then on the road. By examining the Stratford records of those companies known to have visited the town in the period, it may however still be possible, by process of elimination, to arrive at a working hypothesis as to the one he had joined, and that in turn may lead us to the identity of the player whose responsibility it would have been to instruct him in the rudiments of his craft. Though based only in probabilities, such an investigation is unlikely to remain for long in the dark for, by following the footsteps of that company and player through their subsequent histories so far as these are known to us, we shall be able to test our conjectures by the destination to which they take us. If they bring us to a point where Shakespeare is known to have been when he first emerges from obscurity to public notice in the early 1590s, we shall have confirmation that we have been on the right track from the start. Even if it should later transpire that we have taken a wrong turning in the course of the journey, the attempt will still have been worth making if it suggests a more credible alternative – a more possible process of climbing – than the impossible leap to eminence with which we are usually presented.

THREE

The Apprentice

*. . . when we find a man of thirty already near the top of his
particular tree, we must assume some previous climbing.*

John Dover Wilson[1]

The date at which troupes of travelling players first included
Stratford in their itineraries is not precisely known but,
interestingly, the first such visitors to be recorded came there in
1568/9,[2] the year in which John Shakespeare served as Bailiff. Was
he instrumental in bringing them there?

The first to arrive were the Queen's players – not the more famous
company brought together by Walsingham in 1583 of which
Richard Tarlton, Elizabeth's jester, was the star attraction – but an
earlier troupe she had inherited from Edward VI and Queen Mary
of which little is known. That was in the summer of 1569. A month
or so later came Worcester's men, who looked for protection as
patron to William Somerset who had succeeded to his title as third
earl of Worcester in 1548 and lived until 1589. Protection was
needed from the vagrancy laws and within a few years was to
become an absolute necessity with the passing of the Act for the
Punishment of Vagabonds in 1572 which, among other things, laid
down that 'all Fencers Bearewards Comon Players in Enterludes &
Minstrels, not belonging to any Baron of this Realme or towards
any other honorable Personage of greater Degree . . . shalbee taken
adjudged and deemed Roges Vacabounds and Sturdy Beggers . . . to
be grevously whipped'.[3]

The procedure followed by the players on their arrival in incorporated towns where they hoped to perform, is well set out by a

man called Willis, written much later when he was aged seventy-five but relating back to the time of his boyhood in the late 1560s or early '70s in Gloucester.

> In the City of Gloucester the manner is (as I think it is in other like corporations) that when Players of Enterludes come to towne, they first attend the Mayor to enforme him what noble-mans servants they are, and so to get licence for their publike playing; and if the Mayor like the Actors, or would shew respect to their Lord and Master, he appoints them to play their first play before himselfe and the Aldermen and common Counsell of the City; and that is called the Mayors play, where every one that will comes in without money, the Mayor giving the players a reward as hee thinks fit to shew respect unto them. At such a play, my father tooke me with him and made mee stand betweene his leggs, as he sate upon one of the benches, where wee saw and heard very well.[4]

Normally, as at both Gloucester and Stratford, the 'mayor's play' was given in the 'town house' or guildhall. As we shall discover later, admission to this first performance was not everywhere free to the public as Willis tells us it was in Gloucester, and in many towns even councillors were expected to contribute to the reward. If the play was approved and received a licence, further public perform-ances followed – usually in the guildhall as before or, if that was not available, in a nearby inn. At these subsequent shows, attendance was charged in the form of a 'gathering' to which everyone present was expected to contribute.

At the tender age of five, the young Shakespeare may have been too young to stand between his father's legs as Willis had done; but as the Queen's and Worcester's men were succeeded by Leicester's in 1573 and Warwick's in 1575, we can be reasonably sure he was there in the Guildhall (with or without his father) to see and enjoy their plays.

From the point of view of William's joining one of these companies, the crucial period is between 1577 when he was thirteen and starting his last year or two of studies at the King's school, and

25

1580 when he was sixteen and had already left. Worcester's and Leicester's men were both to make return visits to the town in 1575/6, and Worcester's were there again at or around Christmas 1577 and at the same time of year in 1580. Derby's came in 1578/9, and three other companies – those of Lord Strange, Lord Berkeley and the Countess of Essex – in that or the following year. Of these six, three can be eliminated fairly easily. The visit of Leicester's troupe (probably in October 1576) is a little too early as William would then have been only twelve, and it was not to return until 1586/7, which is far too late. Berkeley's makes only rare appearances in the records elsewhere and sinks from view altogether in the vital period between 1586/7 and 1597. The Countess of Essex had inherited a company of players on her husband's death as recently as September 1576, but this is unlikely to have survived for long after 1579 when her secret marriage to Leicester was revealed to the Queen.[5] At first sight, the related troupes of the Earl of Derby and that of his son and heir, Ferdinando Lord Strange, offer the most promising alternatives as William's choice of company because of the connection with Strange's that he is known to have had in the early 1590s at the Rose and elsewhere; but Derby's men were to go into limbo in the upheavals of 1583, and the Strange's company of 1590–2 had little, if any, connection (apart from its patron) with the one that had visited Stratford and, in the 1580s, appears to have specialised in acrobatic displays at court for the Queen.

This leaves only Worcester's men, which is usually dismissed as being merely a provincial company in the period, its first recorded London appearance being not until 1602. But this early provincial status accords very well with the fact of Shakespeare's obscurity during his apprentice years, and though we lack all knowledge of its repertoire of plays – a particular loss in that Shakespeare in the decade of the 1580s is likely to have contributed to it, if only by way of revisions – we know a good deal of its personnel and history in the years immediately ahead. Moreover, while the visits to the town of Essex's, Derby's and Strange's men recorded above were unique in the period, Worcester's were there on no fewer than six occasions between 1569 and 1584, so there was ample opportunity for John

Shakespeare and his eldest son to have made the acquaintance and established personal relations with their leading men, including William's future 'master'.[6]

There is another important factor to be considered. Though, as Dover Wilson correctly discerned, the dates of Shakespeare's marriage and of the births of his children tell us nothing about the time of his *first* departure from Stratford, the fact that it was during the period of William's youth and early manhood that he met with, courted and finally married Anne Hathaway, giving her three children before 1586, does require that he remained in those years near enough to his home town to have paid fairly regular visits to it, and specifically to have been there in the summer of 1582 and again in 1584. Worcester's are the only one of the six troupes I have named whose movements would have enabled him to fulfil this requirement. The two Stanley companies of Derby and Lord Strange ranged particularly widely and spent much of their time in the north, especially the north-west, where the earl and his heir kept palatinate state in their manors of Lathom, Knowsley and New Park. Derby's men (as patronised by Henry Stanley, the fourth earl) disappear from the records in 1583, and Strange's (apart from their tumbling at court) were to make only intermittent visits to the south after that date until their amalgamation with the Admiral's in about 1590/1.

It is possible that William joined Worcester's men on their third visit to the town in 1577, but he was then only thirteen and we should allow him a little more time both to complete his education and get to know Anne. The company were performing in Coventry on 22 November 1580, and were in Stratford, probably for Christmas in that year, when William was sixteen. The most probable course of events is that he joined them then, having already paid court to Anne; that he consummated his betrothal to her in the summer of 1582, and returned to marry her later that year.

The impression of hurry and confusion that the records of their marriage produces – that the final date for posting the banns before the prohibited Christmas season was missed; that a special licence was thus required; that the application for it was made, not by the bridegroom as was usual, but by friends of the bride; and the clerk's mistake in confusing Anne Hathaway of Shottery with Anne Whately of Temple Grafton – is more readily explained by the simple circumstance of William's having been away from Stratford on tour when Anne's pregnancy became apparent, and his thus having to hurry home for the wedding ceremony as soon as he could, than by any of the more involved and romantic theories that have so far been advanced. We know that Worcester's men were in Coventry in 1582, though we are given no indication of the month.[7] As no evidence survives of where or exactly when the wedding took place, it is equally possible that Anne travelled to join him elsewhere in the diocese. (Stratford lay within the diocese of Worcester, whose bishop had granted the special licence.)

Moving forward, their first child was baptised in Holy Trinity church on 26 May 1583. William is unlikely to have been able to join in the celebrations, but we know that the company was at Stratford at some time in the following year, so he would have seen his daughter Susanna then, if not before. The company was recorded at Gloucester on 22 December 1583, at Leicester after 6 March 1584, and in Coventry also in 1584. If the players came from Leicester or Coventry to Stratford in April or May, that would be consistent with the birth of the twins in February 1585.[8] I am not intending to suggest that these were the *only* occasions when Shakespeare visited Stratford in the years immediately following his marriage to Anne – there were slack times in the company's year, as in Lent, and even apprentices were allowed occasional holidays – but simply to demonstrate that he was there (or could have been there) at those times when the subsequent births of his children require him to have been. Our conjectures having taken us thus far, let us now look a little more closely at Worcester's company in the period to discover who his fellows would have been and, if possible, the identity of the senior man among them to whom he was apprenticed.

At Southampton in June 1577, we are told that the company comprised ten men (sharers); and in the course of a contretemps with the Mayor of Leicester in March 1584, a licence was produced from the Earl of Worcester, dating from January of the previous year, in which they were named as Robert Browne, James Tunstall, Edward Alleyn, William Harryson, Thomas Cooke, Richard Johnes (Jones), Edward Browne and Rychard Andrewes. (Two others, not named in the licence – William Pateson and Thomas Powlton – are also mentioned and make up the complement of ten men referred to at Southampton.) As usual in such records, their apprentices and any hired men or other functionaries they had taken with them on tour were ignored.[9]

Of the ten sharers, two names immediately stand out: Robert Browne and Edward Alleyn. Browne, whose name is given first and may be taken therefore as the leader, was to achieve a European reputation as pioneer, from 1590 onwards, of the tours of English players to Germany and the Low Countries; Alleyn was soon to be recognised as the most accomplished player of his generation. Though some eighteen months younger than Shakespeare and only sixteen at the date of the 1583 patent, his listing in third place among the sharers is indicative of a remarkable and precocious talent. Richard Jones was later to accompany Browne to the continent, but little is known of the others. If Shakespeare was apprenticed to Browne as is probable, he is likely to have learnt as much, if not more, from the junior but already experienced Alleyn.

In the absence in the period of any other form of training, apprentices learnt on the job, playing minor roles in which they were coached by their masters, learning to fence, dance and play a variety of instruments, as well as making themselves generally useful on tour in the way that 'acting ASMs' were expected to do until comparatively recent times. Then, their duties would have included packing and unpacking the cart with props and costumes, setting out the benches for performances, providing refreshments for their masters and helping them with their changes. In Leicester, the players having defied a ban on their performing that night at their inn, 'went with their drum & trumppytts thorowe the Towne'.[10]

The young Shakespeare was to stay with Worcester's men for four or five years. And all that while he was learning the basics of his craft as a player – slowly and painfully as any such process of trial and error must be, but also, I am sure, with enthusiasm and a sense of joyful discovery. Like a present-day drama student thrown in at the deep end of a hectic repertory season or fit-up tour (but much less well equipped from a technical point of view), it would have been largely a matter of sink or swim. He might have had a similar experience in any number of companies, but could have chosen much worse than Worcester's, with the capable Browne as his mentor and Alleyn as model. Though sometimes today unjustly characterised as old-fashioned in his style of acting as contrasted with the later Burbage, Alleyn was no barnstormer and, among his many qualities as a player, the one that writers of his time picked out most often for comment was his exceptional grace of movement and speech.

We have no record whatever of the company's repertoire of plays at this time, though they would doubtless have included historical moralities of a similar kind to Tarlton's *Seven Deadly Sins* and the anonymous *Knack to Know a Knave*. We can be sure that William was already thinking he could do very much better and testing himself out in that way. At the same time, he was discovering England. I picture a sixteen-year-old lad on a cart, growing year by year into manhood, journeying out of the Arden of his childhood into ever more unfamiliar, distant regions, travelling ill-made roads in all weathers, sleeping in inns, hearing and memorising strange new dialects and forms of speech, meeting with every possible type and character of person; learning, most of all perhaps, from the audiences to which he played in guildhalls and inns: their varied responses, likes and dislikes, what 'held' and what did not, along with the more arcane mysteries of the player in holding successfully the mirror up to nature. From the very partial records that survive – and apart from its regular visits to the Midland towns of Stratford, Coventry, Gloucester and Leicester, as already noted – we find the company at Plymouth and Abingdon (Oxon) in 1580/1; Bridgwater (Somerset) on 19 September 1581 and 30 July 1582; Ipswich and Southampton in 1581/2; and Norwich, Doncaster and Hythe (Kent) in 1582/3.

It was no tired, cynical collection of old hacks that Shakespeare had joined, but a young, impetuous band of players with their future

before them. Browne was still near the beginnings of his distinguished career; Ned Alleyn was only fourteen in 1580. Impatient no
doubt of the ponderous deliberations of mayors and aldermen, their
defiance of the Leicester mayor in 1584, when they had played at
their inn in despite of his ban (for which they had later to apologise
and eat humble pie), was not the first or only such brush they had
with civic authority in the course of their travels. In spite of pleas to
the mayors involved that their disputatious behaviour should not be
reported to their patron, the earl of Worcester, word of it may
eventually have reached him. For having visited Stratford again in
1584, Maidstone in 1584/5, and made the long journey to York in
1585, the company appears to have been disbanded, and nothing
more is heard of it until 1589, when the third earl died and was
succeeded by his son. In the meantime, at least five of its former
sharers – Robert and Edward Browne, Ned Alleyn, Tunstall and
Jones – were recruited by Lord Charles Howard of Effingham on his
appointment by the Queen as Lord High Admiral in 1585, and from
thenceforward were known as Admiral's men. As Shakespeare would
still have had a year or two of his apprenticeship to serve (the normal
term for a youth of his age was seven years), he would almost
certainly have gone with them. He would thus have entered upon the
most exciting and fruitful of his apprentice years that were to have a
profound effect on his development as both player and playwright.

FOUR

Admiral's Man

It is extremely likely that he [Shakespeare] acted in Marlowe's plays, and developed much of his own power by learning Marlowe by heart.

Peter Levi[1]

We have only to look at the repertoire associated with the Admiral's men in the years between 1585 and 1590 to realise its significance for Shakespeare's biography; for among many other less familiar titles, we find Kyd's *The Spanish Tragedy* and three of Marlowe's plays: both parts of *Tamburlaine the Great* and *The Jew of Malta*. As performances of all four plays are believed to pre-date, and to have influenced the writing of Shakespeare's early plays, and none was published before 1590 (*Tamburlaine* in that year, the *Spanish Tragedy* in 1592, and the *Jew of Malta* not until 1633), it is axiomatic that he could only have seen and heard them in the theatre.[2] But for them to have impressed themselves on his mind in the way they did, how much more probable it is that he had *acted* in them. And if he had acted in them, he could only have done so as an Admiral's man. (I return to this point, and to a consideration of the parts he played in them, later in the chapter.)

In June 1585, the newly constituted company were in Dover, Folkestone and Hythe, and on 6 January 1586 played at court for the Queen. They then set out on a long tour that was to take them, among other towns, to Ipswich (on 20 February), Cambridge, Coventry, Leicester, Folkestone, Faversham and Hythe.[3] In January 1587, the Admiral's were reported by an agent of Secretary Walsingham, along with the Queen's, Leicester's and Oxford's men, as posting their bills in the City of London every day of the week, 'so that when the bells toll to the Lecturer, the trumpets sound to the stages to the Joy of the wicked faction of Rome'.[4] In May of that year they were back in Ipswich (a favourite port of call), Coventry and Leicester, as also at Norwich, York, Southampton, Exeter and Bath.[5]

In November 1587, a tragic accident occurred during a City performance of the second part of *Tamburlaine*, when a misfired pistol killed a pregnant woman and a child in the audience and 'hurt another man in the head very soore'. (The scene in question was identified by Chambers as the execution of the Governor of Babylon in *2 Tamburlaine*, V.i.)[6] This disaster may have resulted in a suspension of the company's activities. Needless to say, the Puritans made the most of it as a sign of God's displeasure and, apart from two court performances in the holiday season of 1588/9, there are no further records of the Admiral's men in London or on tour until November 1589, when they were to reappear at Ipswich. I believe it was during this long interval that Shakespeare – released from the pressures of daily performance and constant travel – began work on the first of his own acknowledged plays, and may have returned to Stratford in order to do so.

In his induction to *Bartholomew Fair* of 1614, Ben Jonson was to link *Titus Andronicus* with *Jeronimo* (an alternative title for Kyd's *Spanish Tragedy*) as, in the opinion of the type of playgoer who sticks to his own views come what may, 'the best plays yet', a judgement that 'hath stood still these five and twenty, or thirty years'.[7] If interpreted literally, this would take *Titus* back to between 1584 and 1589. And that it was written for the Admiral's men is indicated by the nature of its leading role, for if ever a role was tailor-made for Alleyn, it was Titus. He dominates the play in the same way that Hieronimo dominates the *Spanish Tragedy*, or Tamburlaine (another Alleyn role) the Marlowe plays. It is a part that demands of any actor who undertakes it a bravura performance, and Alleyn was then emerging as the finest actor of his day. But if Jonson's double-edged compliment to *Titus* and *Jeronimo* in *Bartholomew Fair* should suggest that the kind of dominance required was of the exaggerated, ranting style to be parodied by

Hamlet as 'out-heroding Herod', it should be remembered that Jonson himself, in a later epigram addressed to Alleyn, compares him to the two men of classical times who, in the period, represented an ideal of excellence in acting, 'skilful Roscius and grave Aesop', and tells him he is one,

> Who both their graces in thy self hast more
> Out-stript than they did all that went before:
> And present worth in all dost so contract
> As others speak, but only thou dost act.[8]

The influence that Alleyn (Plate 7) had upon Elizabethan acting in general has yet to be fully acknowledged. He did more than anyone else to raise it to the level from which the acting of Shakespeare's great tragic heroes was later to become possible for Burbage.[9]

If *Titus Andronicus* was regarded by Jonson as between twenty-five and thirty years old in 1614, and was written by Shakespeare for Alleyn and the Admiral's men, a date for its composition of 1587/8 appears likely, though because of the temporary disgrace into which the company had fallen, and a consequent depletion in its ranks, it may not have been performed before 1589/90.[10]

The Taming of the *Shrew* was once thought to have been a revision by Shakespeare of an anonymous play published in 1594 as *The Taming of* a *Shrew*; but, since the 1920s, scholars have been gradually coming round to the opposite view: that Shakespeare's play was written first, and that the one with the indefinite article in its title was a pirated version of Shakespeare's original – a 'memorial reconstruction' put together by a group of players who had acted in it some time before. In a closely reasoned introduction to his Arden edition of 1981, Brian Morris has persuasively argued for a date prior to 1592, and proposes 1589, which would make it the first of Shakespeare's comedies. In line with the earlier date I have given for Shakespeare's departure from Stratford, I would take the play back a year or two more, and thus roughly contemporary with the writing of *Titus*.

For its main plot, the *Shrew* draws on traditional stories that would have been familiar to Shakespeare from an early age; and for its subplot, the wooing of Bianca by Lucentio, it is clear he made use of Ariosto's Italian comedy, *I Suppositi*, as translated by George Gascoigne in 1566. In the induction to the play, a tinker called Christopher Sly, who tells us he is 'old Sly's son of Burton-heath' is discovered in a drunken stupor; Barton-on-the-Heath is an actual village some sixteen miles out of Stratford, where Shakespeare's aunt, Joan Lambert, lived. For a joke, Sly is put to bed in an inn and, when he wakes up, treated as if he were a lord who had dreamed what he believes to have been his former life as a tinker. Meantime, a band of players arrives and agrees to entertain Sly with a play – the *Taming of the Shrew* – the plot of which is itself driven by a whole series of pretended changes of identity.

It would have been wholly in the spirit of the comedy for Shakespeare to have taken the character's surname from the actor who played him, William Sly, a member of the combined Admiral's/ Strange's company from about 1590, who was later to join the Chamberlain's men with Shakespeare and to feature (in ninth place) in the First Folio list of 'Principall Actors in all these Playes'. (See Plate 5: there were Slys in Stratford as well as in London, but William was probably a descendant of the John Slye who had led one of Henry VIII's companies of interluders in the 1520s.)[11] So, in the final analysis, Sly is neither Christopher the tinker nor the lord that everyone pretends him to be in the play, but William Sly the player, purporting to be both – a theme of confusions of identity to which Shakespeare would return and put to a variety of uses. That the Second Player in the Induction – who would have doubled a part, probably the Tailor, in the play-within-a-play – was acted by John Sincler is clearly established by the prefix 'Sinklo', his usual nickname, that Shakespeare gives to his solitary line. We are to meet with him again in *Henry VI*, and it is interesting to find that several other players can be identified by Shakespeare's use of their forenames or abbreviated surnames as having future connections with the Admiral's men.[12] There can be little doubt that Petruchio was written for Alleyn and first played by him, but we can only guess at the part that Shakespeare took for himself. In 1587 he was twenty-three. I give him Lucentio because he opens the play proper and is there at the end to speak the final line – something that he liked to do, as many later and surer instances will show.

We should not overlook that 1588 was the year of the Armada, or that in 1587 the company's patron, Lord Howard, had been appointed by the Queen as supreme commander of the country's naval defences. In the frenzy of preparations to repel the Spanish invaders – reaching inland even to Stratford with the mustering of the trained bands – theatrical activity generally came to a halt. It was in an atmosphere of patriotic fervour, engendered first by the threat of the Armada and then by the scale and completeness of its destruction, that Shakespeare conceived and put into execution his ambitious plan for a series of plays that were to focus, not on one heroic figure from ancient history, as *Tamburlaine* and his own *Titus* had done, but on a 'quasi-Biblical' story of England 'from the original sin of Henry IV to the grand redemption of the Tudors'.[13] Their theme – as dramatised from the chronicles he was reading, especially Hall's – would have struck home to his contemporaries as highly relevant to the turbulent times through which they were living; that 'as by discord great thynges decaie and fall to ruine, so the same by concord be revived and erected', and England 'by union and agrement releved pacified and enriched'.[14]

But when the London playhouses reopened and touring resumed in September 1588, the Admiral's – with exception of the two court performances already mentioned (in December 1588 and February 1589) – remained in the doldrums; and while Shakespeare may reasonably be conjectured as working on the three parts of his *Henry VI* – perhaps with financial support from Alleyn – his fellows would have had to look elsewhere for their bread. Only Alleyn at this time appears to have had access to a ready supply of money. In January 1589 he purchased from Richard Jones (one of Worcester's men who had transferred to the Admiral's) his share in the company's stock of costumes and playbooks, which up to that time had been held on an equal basis with John Alleyn and Robert Browne, and the transaction was witnessed by another former Worcester sharer, James Tunstall. John Alleyn was Edward's elder brother, and was not a player. He is described in the bill of sale as 'citizen and inholder of London', and is said elsewhere to have 'dwelt with my very good lord, Charles Heawarde'. Chambers suggests that it may have been through him that Edward and his fellows of Worcester's company had come to be Admiral's men in the first place. If so, he may well have continued to act as intermediary between his brother and Howard, and to have supplied the cash, either from his own pocket or Howard's, that enabled Edward to make the above and other purchases that followed. As no new sharers are named as having been admitted, he appears to have been taking advantage of a difficult period in the company's history to draw financial control of its capital resources (and thus of its future profits) into his own hands.[15]

We know that by late October or early November 1589, the company had resumed playing in the City; for when, on 5 November, an order went out from the Lord Mayor that all the companies then in the City should cease playing because of the Martin Marprelate controversy – a pamphlet war between pro- and anti-theatre factions – the Admiral's were named as one of the companies affected. Robert Browne may also have sold out to Alleyn at this time, and one or two others may have done the same. Browne was in Holland in 1590. When the company reappears in provincial records, they were at Ipswich, a port often used by players travelling to the Low Countries. Alleyn and the others may have accompanied their former leader so far and given two farewell performances with him to raise money for his travel expenses.[16] The company's subsequent appearances at court on 28 December, 'shewinge certen feates of activitie' (an acrobatic display by the apprentices), and on 3 March with a play, was probably a reward for their prompt compliance with the closure order of 5 November (which a newly reconstituted Strange's had defied), and marks a return to favour in which their patron Howard may have been instrumental.[17]

From 1590, however, we find them working ever more closely with Strange's, and this may reflect the loss of Browne, Jones, perhaps others. But the subsequent confusion in the records of both City and provincial appearances – where the company is sometimes named as Strange's, sometimes as the Admiral's or Alleyn's, and sometimes as a combination of the two – can only be explained if we assume (with Chambers) a virtual amalgamation of which Alleyn was leader and principal player.[18]

There was in these years a good deal of fluctuation in the personnel of the companies generally. The formerly prestigious Leicester's men had been dissolved on the death of their patron in 1588, a year which also saw the passing of Richard Tarlton and the start of a steady decline in the fortunes of the Queen's men. The alliance of the Admiral's and Strange's – the latter strengthened by a number of experienced recruits from Leicester's including George Bryan and Thomas Pope – was thus enabled by 1590 to take prime position as the most popular and successful of all the noblemen's companies then on the road, in the City, or at court.

It was to achieve its finest hour at the Rose in 1592; but, in the meantime, Shakespeare would have rejoined his fellows and brought with him completed manuscripts of an early version of *Titus* (with its splendid new role for Alleyn) and the three parts of *Henry VI* to add to the company's repertoire. By 1588, he would have reached his twenty-fourth year and attained his freedom as a player. As he is unlikely at that time to have had the means to buy himself into the privileged position of sharer (had Alleyn been willing to admit him, which is far from certain), he would then have been employed as a 'hired man' or journeyman player on a small but regular salary. But whatever his status, with some seven years' solid acting experience behind him, he is likely to have been cast in increasingly important parts.

I give my reasons in the following chapter for believing that among these roles was the young king of the title in *Henry VI*. There is no obvious part for Alleyn (unless it was Talbot in Part One), but with availability of the additional forces brought to the alliance from Strange's, there would be no shortage of experienced men to take the many other good parts that the plays offer. (With Titus, Tamburlaine and Hieronimo among his roles in the current repertoire, Alleyn would doubtless have welcomed an occasional 'play out' and a rest.)

Many of the Strange's men and their apprentices would have been new to Shakespeare in 1590, but that in writing the plays he had

had in mind for the smaller parts some familiar fellows from the Admiral's is evident in his use of their first names or nicknames in the stage directions and speech prefixes of Parts Two and Three that eventually were to find their way into the First Folio.

'Bevis' of Part Two is otherwise unknown; but John Holland who plays a short scene with him as a fellow rebel in IV. ii is named in a 'plot' (a synopsis of scenes and characters posted backstage as an *aide-mémoire* for the actors) of Tarlton's *Seven Deadly Sins*, of which a single performance was to be given at the Rose on 6 March 1592.[19] In Part Three, the Messenger of I.ii.47 is assigned to 'Gabriel', and the Keepers of III.i to 'Sinklo' and 'Humfry'. 'Gabriel' was almost certainly Gabriel Spencer, 'Sinklo' a nickname for John Sincler (whom we have already encountered in the *Shrew*), and 'Humfry', a man called Humphrey Jeffes.[20] Like Holland, Sincler was to remain with the company, and went on to become the thin-faced actor of the Chamberlain's men, but there is no further trace of either Spencer or Jeffes in the English records between 1592 and 1597. We know, however, that Robert Browne, having returned from his first, exploratory trip to the continent in 1590, was to set out again with a full company of players for Germany in February 1592, for which he obtained a passport from the Admiral. The passport names Browne, Richard Jones, two others whose names are previously unknown (John Bradstreet and Thomas Sackville) '*avec leurs consortz*', and Howard refers to them collectively as '*mes Joueurs et serviteurs*' ('my players and servants').[21] The probability is that Spencer, Humphrey Jeffes and his brother Anthony (recorded in Germany in 1595) were included in the party as '*consortz*'. On their return to England in 1597, these three rejoined the Admiral's, and Spencer was to be killed in a duel with Ben Jonson in 1598.[22]

But in the meantime, the Admiral's company would have been left decidedly weak in numbers in relation to Strange's – especially as regards the proportion of senior men among them. By early 1593, when all the London theatres were closed by the plague and application was made to the Privy Council for a new licence for the company to travel, Alleyn was the only remaining Admiral's man to be so distinguished in a list of its sharers. At what precise point the combined company became, in effect, Strange's, and whether, or to what extent, Shakespeare transferred his allegiance from the Admiral to Strange is unknown. As his status was still that of a hired man, he may easily have come to feel somewhat out on a limb.

Having sketched the history of the Admiral's men so far, and indicated how Shakespeare's early plays may have come into being in the years between 1585 and 1590, it is time to look more closely at his contribution to the company's work as an actor, and to do this we shall need to retrace our steps a little. For if, as I suggested earlier, Shakespeare's identity as player is the key to a fuller understanding of him as a person and historical figure, the more we can learn of the parts that he played, both in other men's plays and his own, the more surely we can dispel those mists of invisibility that veil him from our view, and the nearer we can hope to get to the man himself.

One or two more or less reliable traditions of his later roles survive that we shall be examining in due course, and we have an important clue in some lines of John Davies of Hereford as to his playing 'Kingly parts'; but an actor, however talented, does not begin his career by playing kings or any other such leading roles. If he is to 'discover himself' in the sense of learning by trial and error

'Like captives bound to a triumphant car' (illustration to *Henry VI, Part 1* from the *Henry Irving Shakespeare*, 1892)

the nature and limits of his particular gifts, and so attain that mastery of his craft we know that Shakespeare came to possess (for Aubrey tells us on good authority that he 'did act exceedingly well'),[23] he requires above all else the opportunity of essaying a large variety of roles in as many different plays.

I have said that Shakespeare's familiarity with Kyd's *Spanish Tragedy* and several of Marlowe's plays (evident in his recollections of them in *Titus*, the *Shrew*, and the *Henry VI/Richard III* tetralogy) is more likely to derive from his having acted in those plays than in any other way as, of them all, only *Tamburlaine* had been published before 1592. This being so, the possibility arises that, by a close study of the sources of his recollections, we may be able to arrive at some knowledge of the particular parts that he played in the course of his apprenticeship and early career.

Actors' powers of recall are of several kinds and operate at varying levels of efficiency. The actor with visual memory is able to memorise his lines with remarkable speed and accuracy, and may even be able to tell you on what page of his written text they occur and their position on the page. Aural memory is by far the more common. Performing in a play brings to the actor a general familiarity with the text as a whole – for even while changing or resting off-stage, he needs to give half an ear to what is being spoken on stage if he is not to miss his entrance cues, though he is unlikely to be able to reproduce it with any great accuracy.[24] However, the lines of the part he is playing, having been committed to memory by dint of constant, spoken repetition in private study and rehearsal and subjected to that process of mimetic identification whereby the actor seeks to make them his own, may become integral to his personal thought processes and imagining, and the longer he continues to perform the part, the deeper they reach. In the receptive mind of a young player-poet like Shakespeare, the more familiar they become, the more likely they are to resurface – often quite unconsciously and not necessarily in any instantly recognisable form – in his future writing.

They are rarely of the word-for-word, literal kind that might be regarded as plagiaristic. More often, a striking expression is re-phrased and adapted to another, perhaps analogous character or situation, but with the retention of certain key words which enable us to identify its source; or a visual image deriving from a certain dramatic situation or stage picture is recycled as metaphor in a contrasting context. Thus, Hieronimo's line in the *Spanish Tragedy*, 'Sweet lovely Rose, ill pluckt before thy time', becomes in *Henry VI, Part Three*, 'How sweet a plant have you untimely cropp'd', and an image of Tamburlaine's entrance in the second part of the Marlowe play, drawn in a chariot by two of the African kings he has defeated in battle, is applied with memorable effect in the opening scene of *Henry VI* to the coffin of Henry V carried in procession by his former comrades, 'like captives bound to a triumphant car'. Taken together with other, more superficial similarities of phrase or image that are of no great significance in themselves and might easily – perhaps a little *too* easily – be dismissed as commonplace or accidental, they have much to tell us of an otherwise unknown chapter in Shakespeare's life as a young actor, the plays in which he appeared, and some of the parts he played in them. (For line references to the above, and many other quoted examples, see Appendix A, where they are set out, play by play, in tabular form.)

There are forty-seven named roles in the two parts of Marlowe's *Tamburlaine*, and many other unnamed, smaller roles which – however large the combined company may have been – would have necessitated a lot of doubling. And by 'doubling', I mean that most of the actors would have been required to take, not just two, but sometimes three or more roles in the course of a performance. Since 1586/7, when the Admiral's first acquired them, Shakespeare is thus likely to have been cast in many different parts in the two plays, starting perhaps with unnamed messengers and soldiers and, as time went by and he became more experienced and skilled, progressing to larger and more important roles. This in itself would account for the exceptionally large number of his recollections of *Tamburlaine* in his own early writings (see Section 1 of Appendix A). As the text of the plays would also have been available to him in their published form from 1590, some later verbal echoes might derive (in theory at least) from his reading. He seems, however, to have had a particular familiarity with the speeches of Theridamus, one of the three young

A portrait of Tamburlaine from Richard Knolles' *Generall Historie of the Turkes* (1603), which has been claimed as showing Edward Alleyn in the title role in Marlowe's play, *Tamburlaine the Great*

shepherds in whose company Tamburlaine is discovered in Scene 2 of Part One, and who accompanies him throughout most of the succeeding action. Many of Tamburlaine's recollected lines are spoken in the presence of Theridamus, and some are actually addressed to him. (It is as important for the actor to know his cues as it is to learn his own lines.) Shakespeare may also at some point have understudied Tamburlaine.

The impact of Marlowe's *Jew of Malta* on Shakespeare is more apparent in the influence that its machiavellian villain Barabas (as played by Alleyn) had on his conception of Aaron in *Titus* and of Richard III than in his recollections of its language (Section 2 of the Appendix). All three characters are outsiders; all three pursue their criminal careers with zestful energy and sardonic humour strongly reminiscent of the Vice of earlier morality plays. So far as they go, his memories of the play suggest that his own part was the kingly one of Ferneze, Governor of Malta, one of whose lines he echoes in the *Shrew*, and others in *Henry VI* and *Richard III*. This could only have been from memory as the text remained unpublished until after his death.

His recollections of the *Spanish Tragedy* (Section 3 of Appendix) go deeper and are more revealing. A speech in *Henry VI* and three in

Illustration from the title page of the 1615 edition of Kyd's *The Spanish Tragedie*

Richard III echo the Prologue to Kyd's tragedy, which is spoken by
the Ghost of Andrea, a young courtier whose death in battle prior to
the action of the play is seen to trigger a series of brutal murders by
which he is finally avenged. The only other character on stage
throughout the Prologue is the Spirit of Revenge, to whom Andrea
describes his journey through the underworld, for which Kyd draws
heavily on Virgil. Revenge tells him he has now arrived

> Where thou shalt see the author of thy death,
> Don Balthazar, the Prince of Portingale,
> Depriv'd of life by Bel-imperia –

who is Andrea's former lover. 'Heere sit we downe', Revenge continues,

> to see the misterie,
> And serve for Chorus in this Tragedie.   (I.i.87–91)

44

Two further recollections from later scenes between Andrea's Ghost and Revenge in *Titus* and *Henry VI* leave little doubt that Andrea was Shakespeare's part. And in view of the character's presence on stage throughout the whole of the play, occasional echoes from other scenes and speeches to be found in his subsequent writing require no further explanation. (Interestingly, one of the few roles in his own plays that Shakespeare is said by his first biographer to have played was the Ghost which – like that of Andrea but in a more powerful and realised form as both 'perturbed spirit' and 'Spirit of Revenge' – motivates the action in *Hamlet*. His acting of that role was reported to have been the 'top of his Performance';[25] if it was, the basis for it may well have been laid here.)

Shakespeare's debt to the *Spanish Tragedy* goes far beyond his occasional recycling of image and phrase. More significant parallels in character and plot development between that play and *Titus* in particular have often been pointed out, including the play-within-a-play device that he was to use also in the *Shrew*, and again in *Hamlet*.[26] The play that Hieronimo stages to effect his revenge on the murderers of his son in Act 4 was based on a story that was given a separate, full-length dramatisation (probably by Kyd himself) as *Soliman and Perseda*, though whether this was already in existence when the *Spanish Tragedy* was written – in line with Hieronimo's claim that,

> When in Tolleda there I studied,
> It was my chance to write a Tragedie . . .
> Which, long forgot, I found this other day –
>
> (IV.i.76–7, 79)

or was later in date, remains uncertain.[27]

But that *Soliman and Perseda* existed by the late 1580s, and that Shakespeare had acted in it, is indicated by a further series of recollections in *Henry VI* (Section 4 of Appendix). It is apparent from these that his role was that of another unfortunate lover, Erastus, in love with and loved in return by Perseda, who falls victim to the jealous enmity of the tyrant Soliman. Perseda avenges Erastus, and at the same time brings about her own death, by challenging Soliman to a duel in the disguise of a man. When, in dying, her identity is revealed, she offers Soliman a notorious poisoned kiss: 'A kisse I graunt thee, though I hate thee deadlie', which was to find an echo on the lips of Queen Margaret to the dying York.

Unlike the *Spanish Tragedy, Soliman and Perseda* was not to be included in the Rose season of 1592, and a description of Erastus in the play as 'not twentie yeares of age,/Not tall, but well proportioned in his lims' (III.i.18–19) takes it back to an earlier time. If Erastus was one of the first of Shakespeare's juvenile roles, it is understandable that some of its more striking images and phrases (eagles gazing against the sun, 'a sunshine day', 'dazzle mine eyes') should have stayed in his mind.

Marlowe and Kyd were not the only contemporary dramatists to have provided material for Shakespeare's acting. Two other plays, one said to be anonymous and the other by Peele, remain to be discussed before we bring the chapter to a close; but in the case of the first, the question of the role or roles that he played is complicated by the possibility of his authorship or part-authorship.

The plot of *Arden of Faversham* derives from an actual murder, and many of its details, including the names of its incompetent

The murder of Thomas Arden as depicted in the frontispiece to the 1633 quarto of the play

hitmen, Black Will and Shakebag, come from Holinshed's account of the real event in the second, posthumous edition of his *Chronicle*, which appeared in 1586 – a year in which the Admiral's men are on record as having visited Faversham in Kent, the scene of the murder. (In Faversham records, Shakebag's name is given as Loosebag.) The dark humour of the play – which mainly consists in the bungling and frustrated attempts of Black Will and Shakebag to waylay and kill Arden at the behest of his wife and her lover – is suggestive of both Marlowe and Kyd, but also of Shakespeare; one thinks especially of the prison scenes in *Measure for Measure* and the shady underworld of Falstaff and his cronies in *Henry IV*. Black Will boasts of having robbed a man at Gad's Hill, and after the murder Shakebag takes refuge with a 'bonny northern lass,/The widow Chambley' in Southwark, but ends up pushing her downstairs and cutting 'her tapster's throat'. He is finally burnt for his crimes 'in Flushing on a stage'. As Peter Levi remarks, 'the connection with Shakespeare is at least as obvious as that of Sir Thomas Lucy with Shallow'.[28]

Informed that Arden is sleeping in a certain house, Shakebag approaches it with a speech that would not have seemed wholly out of place in a later play of Shakespeare's on the theme of another, yet more terrible murder.

> Black night hath hid the pleasures of the day
> And sheeting darkness overhangs the earth,
> And with the black fold of her cloudy robe
> Obscures us from the eyesight of the world,
> In which sweet silence, such as we triumph.
> The lazy minutes linger on their time,
> Loth to give due audit to the hour,
> Till in the watch our purpose be complete
> And Arden sent to everlasting night.[29]

When, however, he and Black Will try the door, they find it is locked. Tragedy descends into bathos.

'Sheeting darkness', 'the lazy minutes linger on their time' bear a Shakespearean stamp. In the realism with which the social situation of the characters is depicted (not so distant from Shakespeare's own bourgeois background), the truthfulness of its psychology and the generosity of its treatment of the smallest roles (another Shakespearean trait), it is, as Keith Sturgess has said, very much an actor's play.[30] I believe it was written by Shakespeare with some unknown collaborator for the Admiral's men, and performed by them in Faversham, if not in 1586, in 1591/2 when they were also to be there.[31] The play was published in 1592 anonymously – as were the quartos of all of Shakespeare's early plays.

His later recollections of its lines (Section 5 of the Appendix), though particularly striking, are of little help in determining the part that he played as he would here, as likely as not, have been unconsciously echoing himself, for *Titus*, as we have seen, was written at about the same time and *Henry VI* a year or two later. It was probably either Shakebag or the Franklin (an invented character who fulfils, among other functions in the play, a choric role) – perhaps, on different occasions, both.

According to the Victorian scholar F.G. Fleay, some lines of Queen Elinor in George Peele's *Edward I*, addressed to Baliol, whom Edward has just appointed King of the Scots, indicate that he had played the title role in that play.

> Now brave John Baliol Lord of Gallaway,
> And king of Scots shine with thy goulden head,
> *Shake thy speres* in honour of his name,
> Under whose roialtie thou wearst the same.[32]

Unsurprisingly, Chambers found the conjecture 'not very convincing',[33] but Peele was renowned for his puckish sense of humour and, if it is not to be interpreted in the way that Fleay suggested, it seems an odd thing for Elinor to say. Why – unless with ironic intent – should she tell the Scots to *shake* their spears?[34]

Little is known of the play. Fleay assigns its first performance to 1591, by which time Shakespeare would have been sufficiently advanced in his profession to play the title role, with Alleyn perhaps as Lluellen. If written as late as this, the lines quoted in Section 6 of

Imaginary portrait of Edward I from G.W. Spencer's *History of England*, 1895

the Appendix would derive from Peele's recollection of *Titus*, rather than Shakespeare's of Peele, and may have been intended as a graceful tribute to their author. It was licensed in October 1593 as 'an enterlude entituled the Chronicle of Kinge Edward the firste surnamed Longeshank . . .' and a corrupt text was published shortly afterwards. A play called *Longshank* (probably the same) was acted fourteen times by the Admiral's men at the Rose in 1595/6, by which time, however, Shakespeare had left the company, and in 1602 it was sold by Alleyn with another old play for £4. ('Long-shanckes sewte' – described in Peele's text as of translucent appearance – is in the Admiral's inventory of 10 March 1598.)[35]

Shakespeare is thus seen to have enjoyed an actor/author relationship with three of the leading playwrights of his early years: Marlowe, Kyd and (less certainly) Peele – ironically, two of whom Greene was shortly to warn of the 'upstart Crow' that was coming

49

among them. By then, Shakespeare's talents as a player – if not his greater potential as poet and dramatist – would hardly have been news to them.

To summarise our findings, then, as to Shakespeare's roles in the course of his apprenticeship and early career as an Admiral's man, the indications are that in those plays that were familiar enough to him to be echoed in his own later writings he had played a variety of parts: probably including Theridamus in Marlowe's two *Tamburlaine* plays, Ferneze in *The Jew of Malta*, the Ghost of Andreas in Kyd's *Spanish Tragedy*, Erastus in *Soliman and Perseda*, and Shakebag or the Franklin (perhaps both) in *Arden of Faversham*, with the title role in Peele's *Edward I* as a possible late runner.

With a change of play usual every day and the large repertoire that the Admiral's would thus have needed to carry with them on tour, this could only be the merest sampling from all the parts that he would have been required to play over a period of seven years, though they are likely to have been among the more important. Even so, they represent a not-inadequate grounding in the versatility of skills in many types of role that he would then have been able to contribute to the performance of his own future plays. It is to these and, in the first place, his involvement as both player and dramatist in the climactic season at the Rose in 1592, that we now turn.

FIVE

The Rose, 1592

Shakespeare's memory has been fully vindicated from the charge
of writing the above play by the best critics.

      Bishop Thomas Percy of Titus Andronicus *in 1794*[1]

that Drum and trumpet Thing

      Maurice Morgann of Henry VI *in 1777*[2]

The occasion of Shakespeare's emergence from the obscurity of his apprentice years was the season at the Rose beginning 19 February 1592 that was to mark a high point in the alliance of Strange's and the Admiral's men; the several public acknowledgements of it were to be in effect his first press notices. He was to come to it – not as a 28-year-old tyro from the country, recently advanced from such mundane tasks as holding horses' heads at the playhouse door or call-boy, as has been seriously suggested – but as an accomplished actor with a twelve-year apprenticeship behind him, who was already becoming a little too old to play the young lovers of Marlowe and Kyd.

 The Rose, built and managed by an entrepreneur called Philip Henslowe on the south (Surrey) bank of the Thames (Plate 4), had only recently opened its doors after refurbishment when Alleyn and the combined company moved in, following a row between Alleyn and the Burbages (father and son) that had effectively closed the company's normal London venue, the Theatre in Shoreditch, to them. And the exceptionally full information we have of this season all derives from a diary kept by Henslowe for his own, mainly financial purposes, in which he noted in idiosyncratic shorthand the title of each day's play and his share of its takings.[3]

51

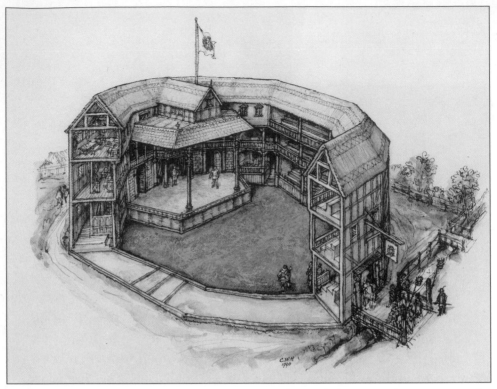

Reconstruction of the Rose theatre as refurbished and extended in 1592 (from a painting by C. Walter Hodges, by permission of the artist and the Museum of London)

In determining the nature and extent of Shakespeare's involvement (both as author and actor), much depends on the interpretation we give to two particular sets of entries. The first is a record of 'harey the vi' on 3 March, repeated at varying intervals thirteen times in the succeeding period to 23 June, when the season was interrupted by a Privy Council interdict occasioned by riots in the City;[4] the other relates to a play described as 'titus & vespacia', first recorded on 11 April and repeated six times during the same period. The first mention of each play is glossed as 'ne' – Henslowe's shorthand for 'new'.[5] When, after an interval of six months, the season was resumed for a further month, two more showings of 'harey the vi' are noted and three of 'titus', with no further mention of 'vespacia'.

Much scholastic ink has been expended on the question of whether Henslowe's 'titus and vespacia' in the first part of the season referred to Shakespeare's *Titus Andronicus*. Some editors, not wishing to accept such an early date for Shakespeare's play (the earliest published edition of which dates only from 1594), have conjectured that it was the title of an otherwise unrecorded play on the subject of the conquest of Jerusalem by the Roman emperors Vespasian and his son Titus in AD 90. But would Shakespeare have named his own protagonist 'Titus' if a play including that name in its title was already in the company's repertoire? More probably, *Titus and Vespasian* was Shakespeare's original title, of which the second name was misheard or misread by Henslowe as 'Vespacia'; the former pawnbroker is unlikely to have been able to boast much classical learning. But who, then, was Vespasian if he was not the father of Titus?

The significant clues were provided (as so often) by Chambers. The first is that a play about Shakespeare's Titus was taken to Germany at an indeterminate date by a company of English players, translated into German, and belatedly published in a collection of *Englische Comedien und Tragedien* in 1620 under a title which (when translated back into English) reads, *A Very Lamentable Tragedy of Titus Andronicus and the Haughty Empress*.[6] Though stripped to the barest essentials and in prose, this follows the plot and sequence of scenes in Shakespeare's play fairly closely, but varies from it mainly in that all the characters bar Titus himself bear different names, and that of Titus's son (Lucius in the surviving English text) appears as Vespasian. We have seen that Robert Browne led a break-away section of the Admiral's company to Germany in February 1592 (at just the same time that their remaining fellows were opening at the Rose in combination with Strange's), and we know that they took with them from the company's current repertoire several of Marlowe's plays because they were recorded as performing these at Frankfort Autumn Fair in September of that year.[7] The question thus arises: did they also take with them an early version of Shakespeare's *Titus* that was eventually to find its way into the *Englische Comedien und Tragedien* of 1620? The part of Titus's son in later, published texts of the play is too small to justify its naming as co-hero in the title; but in the German translation (and probably therefore in Shakespeare's original), it is of greater importance, and it is he, not Marcus, who enters with the crown in the opening scene to offer it to Titus. Also, Titus's quarrel with his sons and the killing of Mutius are omitted in the German version and there are signs in Shakespeare's published text that these were later additions.[8] That Henslowe's 'titus and vespacia' was indeed an equivalent title for Shakespeare's play in its original form gains further support from Chambers' second clue; for in a list of six play titles deriving from the Revels office in 1619, of which at least four, and probably five, of the plays are by Shakespeare, the sixth is given as 'Titus and Vespatian'.[9]

The interpretation is supported also by a re-examination of the famous Peacham drawing (shown in Plate 16) – the only contemporary illustration to survive of a Shakespeare play in performance. This shows seven characters strung out across the stage, of which the two central figures have usually been identified as Tamora, Queen of the Goths, pleading to Titus for the lives of her sons who are kneeling behind her, and this appears to be confirmed by the writing across the top of the picture which reads, 'Tamora pleading, written by Henry Peacham – author of the complete gentleman'. The difficulty is that the action as shown in the sketch fails to match at all exactly with the forty or so lines from *Titus* transcribed below it – or with any other scene in the play. But, as June Schlueter has recently pointed out,[10] it bears a much closer relation to an equivalent scene in the German *Very Lamentable Tragedy* which, as argued above, derives from Shakespeare's early version of *Titus*, named by Henslowe in 1592 as 'titus and vespacia'. In Shakespeare's revision, the stage is crowded with characters ('as many as can be'); in the *Lamentable Tragedy* there are only eight. In *Titus*, Tamora pleads for the life of one of her three sons; in the German play, there are two sons (as in the drawing) and neither is threatened. In the *Lamentable Tragedy*, Aetiopissa, the Queen, is not pleading for their lives but submitting herself and them to Titus, who is about to present them to the Emperor on his right. A stage direction reads, 'takes the Queen by the hand and leads her to the Emperor'; this, I suggest, is just about to happen. Somewhat differently to Dr Schlueter, I interpret the characters in the drawing as (from L to R) Vespasian; the Emperor (wearing German armour of an outdated kind); Titus with ceremonial spear and wearing a laurel wreath (as a stage direction stipulates); Queen Aetiopissa, described as 'lovely and of fair complexion'; her two sons (Helicates and Saphonus); and the Moor of the play (Morian), who is boasting of his valiant deeds in battle as he does in a soliloquy which immediately follows the scene I have described. Only a silent Andronica, Titus's daughter, is missing. All of which suggests that the play that Peacham saw, and sketched at a particular moment of performance, was not *Titus Andronicus* but the earlier *Titus and Vespasian* of which the *Lamentable Tragedy* is a translation, and that the quotations written below the drawing, as well as the reference above to 'Tamora pleading', were made by other and later hands.

The probable course of events was therefore as follows. The play was written by Shakespeare in 1587/8 as *Titus and Vespasian*, performed by the Admiral's/Strange's alliance under that title from 1590, and taken to the continent by Browne and his fellows in February 1592, where an abbreviated version was translated into German. During the six months' break in the Rose season from June to December 1592, Shakespeare revised his original text, reducing the part of Titus's son in size and importance and (to avoid confusion with the historical emperors, Vespasian and Titus) changing the character's name from Vespasian to Lucius. It was then performed at the Rose as *Titus Andronicus* (abbreviated by Henslowe to 'titus') for the remainder of the season, which came to an end in February 1593. (It seems that Henslowe himself was confused by the changes, for when, in January 1594, the play was revived by Sussex's men at the Rose, he refers to it nonsensically as 'titus & andronicus'.)[11]

That the play recorded by Henslowe as 'harey the vi' was not just *Henry VI, Part One*, as is usually assumed,[12] but comprised all three parts of the play in rotation is evidenced by the terms of Greene's bitter attack on Shakespeare which I shall quote in a moment: but is deducible also from the frequency of its performances and their financial returns. In the eighteen-week period from 19 February to 22 June, in which twenty-three plays were given one or more performances, *Henry VI* (in one or other of its parts) was acted on fourteen occasions – more often than any other, including Kyd's immensely popular *Spanish Tragedy* (with thirteen performances) and Marlowe's *Jew of Malta* (with ten).[13] By contrast, Greene's *Friar Bacon and Friar Bungay*, in spite of having opened the season, was thought to justify only three repeats in 1592, and his *Orlando Furiosa*, given two days later, none at all. (No wonder Greene was put out!) In financial terms, against an average return to Henslowe of £1 14s per performance, 'titus and vespacia', averaging £2 8s 6d over seven performances, was by far the most profitable, with the fourteen showings of 'harey the vi' achieving a more than respectable average of £2 0s 6d. (See Appendix B for a suggested breakdown of the way in which the three parts of the play were rotated to allow for five complete cycles of the trilogy to be given.)

When the season was interrupted in June 1592, the two companies (the Admiral's and Strange's) took to the road and toured independently.[14] When, after a six months' break, they came together again at the Rose, several new plays were added to their joint repertoire, including Marlowe's *Massacre at Paris* (described by Henslowe as 'the tragedy of the gvyes'). There was still no sign of *Richard III* though by then it would almost certainly have existed in manuscript, and may even have been in rehearsal when the season was interrupted once more; this time by the plague, and finally abandoned.[15] The last performance of the season – the *Jew of Malta* by the Admiral's – was on 1 February 1593, after which the London theatres were to remain closed for almost a year.

I have said that if ever a part was written for Alleyn, it was Titus. Though only twenty-one in 1587 (the year of the fatal shooting when *Tamburlaine* was in performance in the City), he would already have been playing the lead in that play, and Barabas in the *Jew of Malta*, for the actor/playwright Thomas Heywood was later to specify both these roles in praising him as 'the best of actors',

> Proteus for shapes, and Roscius for a tongue,
> So could he speake, so vary.[16]

This woodcut (which Halliwell-Phillipps describes as 'large and hideous') illustrates *The Ballad of Titus Andronicus*, which was published at about the same time as Shakespeare's play (1594). It may have been one of the sources for the latter but, more probably, derives from it (reproduced from *Some Account of the Antiquities, Coins, Manuscripts* etc. *Illustrative of the Life and Works of Shakespeare in the Possession of James Orchard Halliwell*, Brixton Hill, 1853, by permission of the Central Library, Manchester)

By 1587, when Shakespeare was writing *Titus*, Alleyn was indisputably the Admiral's leading player and the part could only have been meant for him.

As we do not have an extant text for Shakespeare's original version of *Titus* (Henslowe's 'titus & vespacia'), it is impossible to say what part he himself played in it, or in its subsequent revision as *Titus Andronicus*. In view of his close relationship with Alleyn as companion, and perhaps role model, of his apprentice years, it may have been that of Titus's elder brother, the tribune Marcus, played as an older man, Titus's son Vespasian (renamed Lucius in the revised text) having gone to a younger apprentice. If Marcus, it was the first of his 'old man' parts – 'thou reverend man of Rome', as Emillius addresses him.[17]

But if Titus was, in a sense, Shakespeare's tribute to Alleyn and an acknowledgement of his debt to him, in writing *Henry VI* he is likely to have had in mind a more central and significant role for himself, and I have already suggested that this was the young king of the title. In his mid-twenties, he was at the optimum age to embody all stages in the character's development – from the 'sweet prince', as yet uncrowned, who makes his first entrance in Act 3 of Part One to the mourning father and doomed king of Act 5, Part Three. Though the part is small in terms of lines (it has less than 200 in the whole of Part One), Henry remains throughout the focal figure, and his presence on stage in so many scenes would have enabled Shakespeare to influence their staging and the performances of his fellows in line with his intentions as author. (In the absence from the Elizabethan stage of a director as such, and the equal status of the sharers, the contribution that he was to make in this way to the success of these and all his future plays in the theatre can hardly be overestimated; it is an aspect of his creativity to which I return.)

It was in response to these performances of four of his plays and his involvement as actor in the season as a whole – for he would still have been playing his usual roles in *Tamburlaine*, the *Spanish Tragedy* and other plays in the Admiral's repertoire – that the first published notices of Shakespeare as player and dramatist come to light. The earliest was by Thomas Nashe and appeared in his *Pierce Penilesse his Supplication to the Divell*, which was entered in the Stationers' Register in August 1592:

> How would it have joyed brave *Talbot* (the terror of the French) to thinke that after he had lyne two hundred yeares in his Tombe, hee should triumphe againe on the Stage, and have his bones newe embalmed with the teares of ten thousand spectators at least, (at severall times) who, in the Tragedian that represents his person, imagine they behold him fresh bleeding?[18]

– as clear a reference as one could hope to find to *Henry VI, Part One*, where Talbot is likewise described as 'the Terror of the French' (I.iv.41), enjoying a 'triumph' (III.iii.5), and with his son, fresh bleeding (IV.vii). The capacity of the Rose is thought to have been between 2000 and 2400. At something less than capacity, five repetitions of Part One ('at severall times') accords very well with Nashe's 'ten thousand'.

But the proof that Henslowe's 'harey the vi' was indeed Shakespeare's *Henry VI* and comprised all three parts of the trilogy was to come from the disappointed playwright Robert Greene, who, lying on his squalid deathbed in the late summer of that same year, launched a blast of vituperation against players in general and one in particular whose plays had so recently triumphed over his own at the Rose. Addressing himself to three of his fellow authors (probably Marlowe, Nashe and Peele) that 'spend their wits in making plaies', he tells them they are

Base minded men all three of you, if by my miserie you be not warnd: for unto none of you (like mee) sought those burres to cleave: those Puppets (I meane) that spake from our mouths, those Anticks garnisht in our colours . . . trust them not: for there is an upstart Crow, beautified with our feathers, that with his *Tygers hart wrapt in a Players hyde*, supposes he is as well able to bombast out a blanke verse as the best of you: and beeing an absolute *Johannes fac totum*, is in his owne conceit the onely Shake-scene in a countrey.[19]

'Tygers hart wrapt in a Players hyde' is a slight adaptation of York's line to Queen Margaret in *Henry VI, Part Three* (I.iv.137), 'O tiger's heart wrapp'd in a woman's hide!' As the play had not been published in any form at that date, and the London theatres had been closed from 22 June until after Greene's death on 3 September, the only possible way he could have heard Shakespeare's original line so recently as to have remembered it, and turned it in the way that he did against its author, was in a performance of Part Three of the play from the stage of the Rose.

Greene's gibe hurt – as doubtless he intended it should – and, in December of the same year, it was followed by a graceful and equally famous apology from Henry Chettle, himself a prolific writer and reviser of plays for Henslowe who had edited Green's posthumous confessions for the press.

About three moneths since died M. *Robert Greene*, leaving many papers in sundry Booke sellers hands, among other his Groatsworth of wit, in which a letter written to divers playmakers, is offensively by one or two of them taken; and because on the dead they cannot be avenged, they wilfully forge in their conceites a living Author: and after tossing it to and fro, no remedy, but it must light on me. How I have all the time of my conversing in printing hindered the bitter inveying against schollers, it hath been very well knowne; and how in that I dealt, I can sufficiently proove. With neither of them that take offence was I acquainted, and with one of them I care not if I never be: The other, whome at that time I did not so much spare, as since I wish I had, for that as I have moderated the heate of living writers, and might have usde my owne discretion (especially in such a case) the Author beeing dead, that I did not, I am as sory as if the originall fault had beene my fault, because my selfe have seene his demeanor no lesse civill than he exelent in the qualitie he professes: Besides, divers of worship have reported his uprightnes of dealing, which argues his honesty, and his facetious grace in writting, that aprooves his Art.[20]

If Marlowe was one of the two who had taken offence – the person with whom Chettle was not acquainted and 'care not if I never be' – the other whose demeanour he had seen as 'no lesse civill than he exelent in the qualitie he professes' was unquestionably Shakespeare. And it is interesting to find that the terms that Chettle used in expressing his regret for Greene's intemperate words tell us more of the high regard in which Shakespeare's acting had come to be held than of his standing as author, for 'exelent in the qualitie he professes' clearly refers to his worth as a player, of which the facility and grace of his writing and 'uprightness of dealing' are merely said to 'aproove' – or, as we might put it now, confirm.

Neither *Titus* nor the *Henry VI* plays have been much appreciated for their qualities as dramatic poetry (unjustly so, as it seems to me, for they contain some magical lines), and in all the complex discussions of their origins as published texts as between their quarto and folio editions – of which came first and how the differences between them are best accounted for – the scholars, primarily concerned as they are with *literary* values, are in danger of losing the wood for the trees. For it is only when these texts have been performed, and (in the case of the *Henry VI/Richard III* tetralogy) performed in sequence as they were intended to be, that they have commanded recognition for their exceptional qualities as *plays*. It is when the scholars have turned their attention from textual niceties to the plays' structure that they have begun to be appreciated at their true worth as the work of a master craftsman.

In defiance of Mere's listing of *Titus* among Shakespeare's tragedies in 1598, and its inclusion by Heminges and Condell in the First Folio, *Titus* has been dismissed by a majority of critics and editors from the seventeenth century onwards as unworthy of Shakespeare's pen, as more 'a heap of Rubbish than a structure'; and as late as 1947 Dover Wilson was able to describe it as 'like some broken-down cart, laden with bleeding corpses from an Elizabethan scaffold, and driven by an executioner from Bedlam dressed in cap and bells'.[21]

I had the privilege of holding a spear in the definitive Peter Brook production at Stratford in 1955 with Olivier as Titus, and was able to witness at first hand how a play that had previously been regarded as virtually unactable and, in its succession of horrors, even something of a joke, could be lifted by a great performance in the title role to the status of high art which, in its finer moments, critics of the time did not hesitate to compare with *King Lear*. As George Rylands once wrote, Shakespeare's plays require, not so much interpretation, as collaboration from the actors who perform them, and this is perhaps more true of the early plays than any of the others. It was collaboration of precisely the kind that Shakespeare demands that Olivier brought to Titus, and it was enough, in combination with Brook's stylistically sensitive direction, to trigger a radical revision in both popular and critical opinions of the play. (Angus McBean's posed photographs of this production, often reproduced, though excellent in their way, do less than justice to the stark austerity of the decor or the visceral power of Olivier's performance at Stratford.)

Likewise with *Henry VI*. As Andrew Cairncross explains,[22] 'It became part of the Shakespeare "mythos" that anything unworthy of his genius or repulsive to the sensibilities of the critic's time should be removed from the canon, and fathered on some altern-ative writer, or even a "symposium" of writers, with Shakespeare possibly adding a few scenes or revising the whole. In *1 Henry VI*, "the revolting treatment of Joan", and the "mean and prosaical" style were sufficient grounds, along with two or three shreds of contemporary evidence and some "echoes" and inconsistencies in the play, for an elaborate theory involving the part authorship of Greene, Marlowe, and Nashe, or some of them.' Though the 'revision' theory of the play's origins had been demolished by Alexander in 1929, it was mainly as a consequence of a series of pioneering productions of all three plays of the trilogy in sequence, for which first credit must go to an American company in 1903, and to more recent productions at Birmingham, Stratford and the Old Vic[23] that critical opinion, after centuries of disparagement, began to revert to Dr Johnson's refreshingly commonsense views, that 'the diction, the versification, and the figures, are *Shakespeare*'s', and (in a note to *2 Henry VI*) that 'this play begins where the former ends, and continues the series of transactions, of which it presupposes the first already known' so that 'the second and third parts were not written without dependance on the first'.[24]

What Shakespeare achieves in these plays, as H.T. Price pointed out in his seminal study of their structure, is to impose 'upon a body of historical data a controlling idea, an idea that constructs the play'.[25] And we have only to look at their opening scenes to see how that controlling idea is planted and followed through in such a way as to command the immediate attention of the audience, to hold it through the two or three hours' 'traffic of the stage', and to lead it on into the next play in the series. This could only have been done by someone with hard-won practical experience of the theatrical medium in which he was working. By someone who had stood on a stage, known and shared the excitement of an audience gripped by the action of the play and the lines he was speaking. Or, conversely and perhaps even more instructively, had come to recognise the unmistakable signals put out by an audience whose attention is slipping away by default of its author, and been powerless to arrest it.

Nor should it ever be forgotten that he was so present on stage in all the first productions of his plays. He was in those circumstances his own collaborator, able to give a lead to his fellows by example in the kind of acting that each of them demanded. For, in so far as each in its own way was innovatory in aims and achievement, they required something new in the style of acting appropriate to them. And he would have been able to give his fellows that lead – not, as he was later to imagine Hamlet as doing, from the condescending heights of an amateur patron – but in just such a way that professional actors in all periods most respect, as one of themselves.

The parts that he played remain open to debate; but the nature and quality of his acting is of far more than incidental importance in arriving at a true estimate of his achievement as poet and playwright, or to an adequate account of his life. It is at the heart of both.

I said in Chapter 2 that the test of the hypothesis I have been putting forward in the previous chapters as to Shakespeare's early adoption of the profession of player and the identity of the company he first joined would come at the point of his emergence into the public arena as player and playwright. We have now reached and encompassed that point, and it will be for the reader to judge of its credibility.

A course has been plotted for Shakespeare's career through the obscure and shifting sands of Elizabethan theatre history that has brought it into line with what we know of his fellows and prevailing theatrical conditions in the period, and that also explains how, by long process of assimilation and practice as apprentice, he attained that excellence in his profession as player attested by Chettle. The choice of Worcester's men as his first company has been shown as consistent with the Stratford records, the dates of his marriage and subsequent births of his children; it has been seen as leading him as active participant into that crucial period of dramatic renaissance associated with Marlowe and Kyd, and the alliance of Strange's and the Admiral's men at the Rose. It has brought him into intimate working relations with the greatest actor of his time, Edward Alleyn, and the patronage of one of the Queen's most influential and powerful ministers, Howard of Effingham. If accepted, such a course disposes once and for all of the problem of the 'lost years'. An undeniable gain. It has provided a credible context in which his early plays were written and performed and has gone some way to explaining the nature and extent of the debt he owed to his predecessors. The evidence for it remains circumstantial and may never be proven. I submit that it explains too much that is incomprehensible in other, more traditional accounts of his early life (which, let it be said, are in truth equally conjectural) to be wholly mistaken.

SIX

The Player Poet

With this key, Shakespeare unlocked his heart

Wordsworth on the Sonnets

Did he? If so, the less Shakespeare he!

Browning's reply[1]

In the Middle Ages, poets were primarily tellers of stories. We know less, much less, of the author of *Piers Plowman* than we do of Shakespeare: only his name (William Langland), his parentage, and the approximate year of his birth (1332). His identity is subsumed in the character of Piers and the story of his dream, and the dreamer is a 'dramatic *persona* whose function, as in other medieval dream-poems, is to provide a link between the reader and the visions'.[2]

Chaucer's *Canterbury Tales* (from 1386) is a collection of stories told by a wonderfully diverse cast of characters to entertain each other as they make their way on pilgrimage to St Thomas's shrine. Gower's *Confessio Amantis* (1390–3) follows a similar pattern of story-telling set within a single, unifying frame. Shakespeare, as well as drawing on classical and Renaissance sources familiar from his schooldays, inherited and remained closely in touch with this literary tradition of the English medieval poets. He knew and loved their writings. There are traces of Chaucer's *Knight's Tale* in *The Two Gentlemen of Verona* and its successor *The Two Noble Kinsmen* (written much later with Fletcher), and he was not only to take the plot of *Pericles* from Gower but also to include the poet himself in his cast as the play's presenter. As a writer, we think and speak of him now as much, perhaps more often, as playwright than

65

we do as poet, but to his contemporaries he was simply a poet. That said it all. It was not just that he wrote largely in verse; poets were also understood to be tellers of stories and dreamers of dreams, and he was notably both.

'For God's sake', Richard II tells his followers in the hour of defeat,

> let us sit upon the ground
> And tell sad stories of the death of kings . . .

and the irony is, of course, that the play itself is another such story. In Macbeth's despairing vision, 'Life's but a walking shadow . . . a tale/Told by an idiot, full of sound and fury,/Signifying nothing'. The *Henry VI/Richard III* tetralogy is, as we have seen, a story of England and, like all the old stories and plays, ends with a moral and a prayer.

> England hath long been mad, and scarr'd herself . . .
> Now civil wounds are stopp'd; peace lives again.
> That she may long live here, God say Amen.[3]

The Comedy of Errors is set within the frame of Egeon's story of his life, with which it begins and ends. The imagery of dream and of dreaming pervades the plays at every stage of Shakespeare's writing. 'Am I a lord and have I such a lady', asks Christopher Sly, 'Or do I dream? Or have I dreamed till now?' 'Are you sure/That we are awake?' asks Demetrius. 'It seems to me/That yet we sleep, we dream.' And for Prospero, the world of reality is as insubstantial as the magical pageant he has conjured for the instruction of the play's lovers.

> We are such stuff
> As dreams are made on; and our little life
> Is rounded with a sleep.[4]

But if Shakespeare inherited a literary tradition of story-telling and dream poetry from the Middle Ages, he was also the bearer of another, more ancient and popular tradition: that of the minstrels and harper-poets who, like himself, were both author and performer of their songs and stories, and whose ancestry goes back to Homer.[5] It is to these, rather than to his own, more literary productions, that the revivified Gower of *Pericles* seems to refer.

> To sing a song that old was sung.
> From ashes ancient Gower is come,
> Assuming man's infirmities,
> To glad your ear, and please your eyes.
> It hath been sung at festivals,
> On ember-eves and holy-ales . . .   (I.i.1–6)

Like Shakespeare, the harper-poets had little interest in publication; books appeared to them more as a threat to their livelihood as performers than as a means of preserving their compositions for the enjoyment of future generations. It was for that very reason, and because they looked to near-illiterate magnates and the mass of the people for patronage and appreciation rather than to the learned, that they were despised by the literati of their time – just as Shakespeare's plays and those of his fellows were ignored or regarded as 'riff-raffs' by bookmen such as Sir Thomas Bodley. Their audience was as mixed as his own at the Rose or the Globe; typically comprising a lord or lady of the manor at table with family, steward and chaplain, one or two visiting neighbours, with a crowd of servants filling the benches and standing at the back of the hall – craftsmen, apprentices and labourers. The harper, with his tale of Sir Orfeo or Gawain, represented a popular oral tradition of performing poets, of which Shakespeare may be claimed as the greatest – possibly the last.

When the season at the Rose came to a premature end in February 1593 because of a serious outbreak of plague, there was an inevitable dispersal of the players who had been engaged in it. Some of them joined a new travelling company which, in the previous year, had succeeded in obtaining the patronage of Henry Herbert, earl of

Pembroke: Pembroke's men. They had spent the final months of 1592 in the Midlands, but on Boxing Day of that year, and on 6 January 1593, performed at court for the Queen. The new recruits from the former alliance, including a certain George Bevis who had played a rebel in *Henry VI, Part Two*, were to bring with them pirated versions of that play and its sequel, put together from memory with addition of some written parts they had collected of the longer speeches.[6] When their subsequent tour in the summer of 1593 proved unviable and the company went bust, these were sold to a publisher as *The First part of the Contention betwixt the two famous Houses of Yorke and Lancaster (Henry VI, Part 2)* and *The true Tragedie of Richard, Duke of Yorke (Henry VI, Part 3)*. (We know that Bevis was one of them because there is a jokey reference to him in Act 2, Scene 3 of the *Contention*.) Others, especially from the Admiral's, may have gone to join Browne and other of their former fellows in Germany.

The main part of Strange's, with Alleyn still at their head as leading man, hesitated for a while – hoping, perhaps, for a speedy lifting of the ban that had closed the London theatres to them – but finally gave up, and in April 1593 applied to the Privy Council for a new licence to travel. This was granted on 6 May 1593, naming Edward Alleyn ('servaunt to the right honorable the Lord Highe Admiral'), William Kempe, Thomas Pope, John Heminges, Augustine Phillips and George Bryan.[7] Significantly, Shakespeare's name is missing, and we have no further record of him until March 1595, when he appears in the accounts of the Queen's Treasurer as joint-payee with Kempe and Richard Burbage (all three 'servantes to the Lord Chamberleyne') for plays performed before the Queen at Greenwich the previous Christmas.[8] But he is likely to have been a sharer in the new company from June 1594, when it joined with a reconstituted Admiral's for a short season under Henslowe's management at Newington Butts; this closed after only ten performances, though not before Shakespeare's *Titus* and the *Shrew* had been given. What, then, had he been doing in the meantime?

Though we have no evidence of a quarrel between Shakespeare and Alleyn then or later, the most likely conjecture is that on the breaking of the alliance in February 1593 the two men had reached a natural parting of the ways. Alleyn, who in October 1592 had married Henslowe's step-daughter, Joan Woodward, and was already involved in business dealings with his father-in-law, was plainly set on a course of theatre ownership and management that was to lead within a few years to his amassing a large fortune and, in about 1603, to his retirement from the stage. Shakespeare would have had good reason to be grateful to him, and doubtless was, but his own immediate needs and ambitions were different. Not only was it essential for him, after his long apprenticeship, to find more adequate means of supporting his young family – Susanna would then have been nine and the twins just eight – he would have been seeking to accumulate sufficient capital to buy himself a share in one or other of the major companies that would guarantee a more stable income in the future and, at the same time, secure him a measure of aristic control over future productions of his plays – a position that Alleyn was either unable or unwilling to provide. The success he had had in the theatre with his early plays must have given him great confidence in his abilities, but the *Shrew* and Parts 2 and 3 of *Henry VI* were then in process of exploitation and deformation by pirates, and his manuscript of *Richard III* (which I believe had been written for Alleyn, and what a magnificent part it would have been for him) remained unperformed.

In the want of any other information, we must look to internal evidence presented by the poems and plays he wrote in the fifteen months that followed the closures of 1593 for clues to his situation in the period. In examining this, we shall find that in temporarily turning aside from active involvement with any of the surviving companies, he did not cease to be a player any more than he ceased to be a poet when he was acting. He was of that rare breed in his time (perhaps in any time), a player-poet.

Venus and Adonis was published in London by a former Stratford neighbour of Shakespeare's, Richard Field. As the book was registered at Stationers' Hall on 18 April 1593 and is known to have been on sale in the shops less than two months later, I find it hard to believe that it was wholly written in the seven-week interval between 1 February (when the Rose season was brought to an end) and 18 April. The poem is remarkable for the freshness and spontaneity of its verse, but the spontaneity is of the kind that conceals art and can only be achieved by hard and sustained labour. With Shakespeare, however – then in the springtime of his creativity – we can never be sure; we know that he could write very quickly ('without a blot') and usually did. If he had returned to his home in Stratford, at the heart of the Warwickshire countryside, in early February, and the poem was written in a concentrated burst of creative energy, it might help to account for the vivid observations of the life of nature that transfuse its classical setting with a sense of down-to-earth reality, expressed in 'true, plain words': the 'dive-dapper peering through a wave', the milch-doe with 'swelling dugs', the 'angry chafing boar', and Watt, the terrified 'purblind hare'.

That the poem was written by someone familiar with the dramatic requirements of the theatre is apparent from the very first stanza; for, with the minimum of introductory matter, he plunges us straight into action.

> Even as the sun with purple-coloured face
> Had tane his last leave of the weeping morn,
> Rose-cheeked Adonis hied him to the chase;
> Hunting he loved, but love he laughed to scorn.
> > Sick-thoughted Venus makes amain unto him,
> > And like a bold-faced suitor gins to woo him.

Of the poem's 1194 lines, nearly half are of direct speech and dialogue. That the poet was also a player is manifest in the extent to which he is able to enter into and identify with the characters in the story: the alluring goddess and the reluctant, embarrassed youth. These are individual people who are speaking, not poetic abstractions, and they are talking, not as in so many narrative poems to the reader, but to each other. Adonis becomes present to us in his first directly quoted speech – he is flat on his back with Venus pinning him down:

> 'Fie, no more of love!
> The sun doth burn my face, I must remove.'   (ll. 185–6)

But she stays where she is, and so does he. Goddess though she is, Venus, in her embodiment of conflicting human qualities and emotions – seductive beauty and self-willed determination, playfulness and dignity, tenderness and anger – becomes as real to us as Cleopatra.

Shakespeare's name is absent from the title page of the printed book but, in an obvious bid for personal patronage, appears at the end of a dedicatory letter addressed to Henry Wriothesley, earl of Southampton.

> Right Honourable, I know not how I shall offend in dedicating my unpolisht lines to your Lordship, nor how the worlde will censure mee for choosing so strong a proppe to support so weake a burthen, onelye if your Honour seeme but pleased, I account my selfe highly praised, and vowe to take advantage of all idle houres, till I have honoured you with some graver labour. But if the first heire of my invention prove deformed, I shall be sorie it had so noble a god-father: and never after eare so barren a land, for feare it yeeld me still so bad a harvest, I leave it to your Honourable survey, and your Honor to your hearts content which I wish may alwaies answere your owne wish, and the worlds hopefull expectation.
>
> > Your Honors in all dutie,
> > William Shakespeare[9]

It is more than possible that Southampton had visited the Rose and sat at the side of the stage during a performance of *Titus* or *Henry VI* in which Shakespeare had acted. The earl and the actor may thus have been known to each other by sight and even exchanged an occasional greeting. But in view of the social chasm that yawned in the period between members of the aristocracy and that lowest of life forms, the players, it is most unlikely (to put it no stronger) that their relationship was then, or ever, closer than that of master to servant, patron to client. Though the eighteen-year-old earl had the contemporary reputation of being well disposed towards poets and artists, it is doubtful, indeed, that Shakespeare would have cast his bread on the waters in his direction without some previous assurance that the dedicatee would regard his doing so with favour – or at least without taking offence – and preliminary soundings may have been made through Shakespeare's former patron as Admiral's man, Lord Howard. (Howard was intimate with Burghley, and Southampton was Burghley's ward.)

As Chambers pointed out, Elizabethan patrons were expected to put their hand in their pocket. That Southampton did so is indicated by the sequel; for when, in the following year, Shakespeare completed *The Rape of Lucrece* (that 'graver labour' he had promised), he was to dedicate that also to the earl in slightly warmer and more confident terms. But for all their flowery phrases and exaggerated expressions of devotion (quite normal and expected of literary dedications in the period), both of Shakespeare's published letters to Southampton end in due and proper form, 'Your Honors [Lordships] in all dutie'.

Whatever Shakespeare received for *Venus and Adonis* by way of donation ('The warrant I have of your Honourable disposition') would have gone some way, if not all the way, in providing the capital he needed to fulfil his ambition of purchasing a share in one of the companies.[10] The opportunity for that lay still in the future; through 1593, the theatre remained in disarray because of the plague. In the meantime he had other work to do. *The Rape of Lucrece* and the first of the Sonnets were already in hand, but his mind would also have been buzzing with the plays he would write for the company, as yet unknown, he was soon to join.

If we wanted to find an overall theme and title for Shakespeare's writing in 1593 and early 1594, it would have to be Love and Friendship. The narrative poems and Sonnets are often considered in isolation from the plays, which is a big mistake because the numerous similarities of thought and language that echo between them indicate that they were written in tandem and, when considered in that way, are mutually illuminating. (For some of the more obvious verbal correspondences, see Appendix C.)

If Shakespeare had looked to Kyd and his classical precursors for initial inspiration in the writing of *Titus*, and to the rough and rowdy tradition of the English interludes and Italian popular comedy for the *Shrew*, it was the near-contemporary prose dramas of John Lyly that provided his starting point for *The Two Gentlemen of Verona*. Like them, it is courtly in tone and draws on the ancient but currently fashionable Friendship Cult to demonstrate the way in which a Platonic relationship between two men (however sincere, even passionate) is liable to founder when subjected to the demands of Eros and exigencies of love and marriage.

The play begins with a parting of two such friends, Proteus and Valentine, who address each without inhibition as 'my loving Proteus', 'sweet Valentine'. Valentine is leaving to serve at the Emperor's court; Proteus stays behind to pursue his wooing of Julia. Valentine mocks at love,

> where scorn is bought with groans;
> Coy looks, with heart-sore sighs; one fading moment's mirth
> With twenty watchful, weary, tedious nights . . .   (I.i.29–31)

but on arrival at court, soon becomes a victim himself by falling in love with the Emperor's daughter, Silvia. Despatched by his father to join Valentine at court, Proteus (forgetting Julia) is attracted to the same girl, and betrays his friend by revealing to the Emperor Valentine's plan to elope with her. The triangular situation between these three is not dissimilar to the dimly discernible plot at the heart of the Sonnets, where the 'dark lady' is the disruptive factor, though here treated in lighter, comedic vein. With the arrival of the abandoned Julia disguised as a boy (the first occasion on which Shakespeare makes use of what was to be a favourite device), the trio of lovers becomes a quartet.

One immediately striking feature of the play as compared with its predecessors is the smallness of the cast. Clearly the crisis year of 1593 was not a time for large, unwieldy epics that would be unviable on tour – as Pembroke's men discovered to their cost that same summer. Of its thirteen named roles, at least four could be doubled, and four others are written for boys, playing the girls' parts and a quick-witted page called Speed. It could thus have easily been acted by a company of seven actors, four boys – and a dog, of which more in a moment.

Unlike the *Shrew* and *Henry VI*, the text has no 'rogue' references to its first performers – which is not surprising if, as I believe, he had begun to write it 'on spec'. But the insertion in the cast of the clownish servant Launce, at what Clifford Leech has shown to be a late, probably final, stage of composition,[11] suggests that Shakespeare made this important addition to the play in the early part of 1594, when he learned that William Kempe was to be one of his fellows in the Chamberlain's men. The character is an obvious precursor of Costard and Launcelot Gobbo, and has the stage persona of Kempe written all over it. He and Kempe had worked together before of course at the Rose, and Shakespeare would have known very well what he could do with such a role. Launce's interventions in the play are, for the most part, independent of plot, and his speeches – especially the soliloquies in which he plays off his mongrel Crab in

Launce: 'Friend', quoth I, 'you mean to whip the dog?' 'Ay, marry do I', quoth he (from the *Henry Irving Shakespeare*, 1892)

the same way that some music hall comedians of recent memory used an equally silent but expressive stooge – may have derived in part from one of Kempe's solo performances as clown, for which he was already famous. They provide the funniest moments in the play.

> When a man's servant shall play the cur with him, look you, it goes hard: one that I brought up of a puppy; one that I saved from drowning, when three or four of his blind brothers and sisters went to it . . . I was sent to deliver him as a present to Mistress Silvia, from my master; and I came no sooner into the dining chamber, but he steps me to her trencher, and steals her capon's leg. O, 'tis a foul thing, when a cur cannot keep himself in all companies . . . If I had not had more wit than he, to take a fault upon me that he did, I think verily he had been hanged for't. You shall judge: he thrusts me himself into the company of three or four gentleman-like dogs, under the Duke's table; he had not been there (bless the mark) a pissing while, but all the chamber smelt him. 'Out with the dog', says one; 'What cur is that?' says another; 'Whip him out', says the third; 'Hang him up', says the Duke. I, having been acquainted with the smell before, knew it was Crab; and goes me to the fellow that whips the dogs: 'Friend', quoth I, 'you mean to whip the dog?' 'Ay, marry do I', quoth he. 'You do him the more wrong', quoth I; ''twas I did the thing you wot of'. He makes me no more ado, but whips me out of the chamber. How many masters would do this for his servant?
>
> (IV.iv.1–30)

There could be no better illustration of the kind of collaboration that Shakespeare's fellow performers were able to offer, or the contribution they made to the richness and variety of his dramatic inventions. Apart from its obvious entertainment value, the particular service of Launce to the play is to anchor the romantic Arcadia which the other characters inhabit to the world of ordinary, everyday experience, thus providing a sub-text of affectionate mockery to which Crab contributes by simply remaining what he is: a dog.

At twenty-nine (a mature age in Elizabethan times) Shakespeare would have considered himself too old to play either of the two gentlemen. The role he had had in mind for himself, and probably did perform when the play eventually reached the stage, was that of the Emperor, or 'Duke' as he is invariably described in speech prefixes and stage directions; another of those 'kingly parts' that were to keep him in control at the centre of the action on stage without burdening himself with too many lines.

Shakespeare's 'dukes' are worthy of more detailed study than they usually receive. Often they are lumped together as among the least interesting of his characters and regarded as virtually indistinguishable. If approached with such preconceptions by the actor, they can indeed be very boring. But looked at more closely, they reveal important individual differences – not least in authority. Though described merely as 'duke', Silvia's father is in reality a monarch with absolute power, whose court is consistently referred to in the text as 'the Emperor's'.

We meet him first *en famille*. He enters (in II.iv) without fanfare as Silvia tells Valentine (as it might be the postman), 'Here comes my father'. In the scene that follows, Valentine addresses him as 'my lord', as today, in similarly informal circumstances, we might address a member of the royal family as 'ma'am' or 'sir'. His royalty is veiled by a manner of friendly courtesy, but it should nevertheless be apparent in Valentine's attitude towards him that this is the most powerful person in the play. The same is true of the subsequent scene (III.i) in which the Duke, by his assumption of the same urbane condescension (seeking advice as one gentleman to another) tricks Valentine into revealing his plan to elope with Silvia. Only then – and it should be as big a shock to the audience as it is to Valentine – does his true authority and power reveal itself in a splendid speech of barely controlled anger.

> Why, Phaeton, for thou are Merops' son
> Wilt thou aspire to guide the heavenly car?
> And with thy daring folly burn the world?
> Wilt thou reach stars, because they shine on thee?
> Go, base intruder, overweening slave,
> Bestow thy fawning smiles on equal mates,
> And think my patience (more than thy desert)
> Is privilege for thy departure hence . . .   (III.i.153–60)

This is far from being the most interesting or challenging of the kingly roles that Shakespeare was to write for himself, but no one can truly claim that it is either obvious or boring – or, for that matter, easy of performance.[12]

That the play was written quickly, and probably (as Leech argues) in a series of interrupted phases, in the intervals of which he was also working on other plays and poems, is suggested by its frequent inconsistencies in geography and loose ends in plot development of the kind that cause such worry to scholars but which audiences rarely notice. The play was not published till its inclusion in the First Folio of 1623 in a text deriving from Shakespeare's manuscript. There are no surviving performance records from the sixteenth or seventeenth centuries, but Meres' listing of it in first place among Shakespeare's comedies in 1598 tells us that it *had* been performed and was popular from an early date.

In *The Comedy of Errors*, the writing of which is thought to have followed that of the *Two Gentlemen* fairly closely, Shakespeare's intended role would again have been that of the 'Duke', and here also he uses the term in a generic sense to include a ruler or prince of royal blood; for as the Duke in question, named Solinus in the first line of the play, explains to Egeon,

> were it not against our laws,
> Against my crown, my oath, my dignity,
> Which princes, would they, may not disannul,
> My soul should sue as advocate for thee ...   (I.i.142–5)

The situation at the play's opening is that Egeon, a merchant of Syracuse, has fallen foul of the law of Ephesus, of which Solinus is ruler, by venturing into its territory in search of his wife and sons, from whom he was separated by a disaster at sea when the sons (identical twins) were still in their infancy. The law ordains that unless he can redeem himself by payment of a thousand crowns before the evening of the same day, his life is forfeit. It is Egeon's story of his misadventures as told to the Duke that frames the comedy within the play; and for the plot of the comedy, Shakespeare returned to his classical reading, adapting a Latin play by Plautus, the *Menaechmi*, to his own purposes. It was also a return to those confusions of identity he had mined so successfully in the *Taming of the Shrew*, but here the confusions take on a positively surreal quality.

Egeon's sons, Antipholus of Ephesus and his twin, Antipholus of Syracuse, separated from each other as well as from their parents by the accident at sea Egeon has already recounted, fortuitously find themselves in Ephesus at the same time, unbeknown to the other, each accompanied by a servant called Dromio, the two of whom are likewise identical twins. Antipholus and Dromio of Ephesus are resident in the city and known to its inhabitants; their twins of Syracuse are, like Egeon, visitors, and the people they meet are strangers to them. Once this latter pair have parted company, as happens very soon when Dromio is sent on an errand, we enter on a complex and beautifully constructed sequence of scenes in which servants mistake their masters, masters their servants, and the people they meet mistake both masters and servants for their twins, but in which (until the final scene) the two sets of twins are never confronted face to face with their respective doubles. The outcome is mounting disorder and panic as all involved try to understand the strange things that are happening to them, and are unable to do so.

An expert farceur, Ralph Lynn, once remarked that the essence of farce was *worry*. *The Comedy of Errors* is not a farce, but the elements of farce that it contains can only work their comedic effect if they are based in a real and credible uncertainty in the Antipholus twins as to their own identity. The visitor from Syracuse is not only threatened by the same law that has been seen to put his father in irons, so that he is obliged to adopt a false persona but, deprived of his parents and twin, feels himself to be

> like a drop of water
> That in the ocean seeks another drop,
> Who, falling there to find his fellow forth,
> (Unseen, inquisitive) confounds himself.
> So I, to find a mother and a brother,
> In quest of them, unhappy, lose myself.　　(I.ii.35–40)

Failing to find them, and meeting instead a succession of strangers would be bad enough: for him to encounter people he does not know but who *seem to know him* induces superstitious dread and fear of madness, from which he is saved by his discovery of a dawning love for one of the strangers, Luciana, who later turns out to be his brother's sister-in-law. His twin of Ephesus – who we do not meet until Act 3 – is found to be subject to another form of disorientation resulting from the jealousy of his wife Adriana, Luciana's sister.

> How comes it now, my husband,

she demands of him,

> > O, how comes it,
> That thou art then estranged from thyself?–
> Thyself I call it, being strange to me,
> That undividable, incorporate,
> Am better than thy dear self's better part.
> Ah, do not tear away thyself from me . . .   (II.ii.119–24)

But unfortunately it is not her husband she is addressing with her reproaches, as she thinks, but his Syracusian twin, who is, of course, bewildered by them. (It is interesting to find that these and several other of Adriana's lines provide cues for Shakespeare's meditations on the complexities of human relationships in the Sonnets – see Section 2 of Appendix C.)

If this were all, the play would by now have ceased to be a comedy, but the brothers' crises of identity are judiciously balanced by the involvement of their servants, the Dromios who, in their indignant responses to the many undeserved beatings they receive in the course of the play, remain (like Crab in the *Two Gentlemen*) joyously, irrepressibly themselves. These two characters have no equivalent in Shakespeare's principal source; in creating them, I believe he was again anticipating the presence of Kempe in the cast, and that he intended Kempe to play both parts, as their masters, the Antipholus twins, were also meant to be doubled. To do so presents difficult but not insurmountable problems, but the effort and ingenuity required in overcoming these brings rich rewards in terms of the credibility of the action, and thus of the audience's enjoyment of it.[13] The only other character we can safely associate with a particular actor – if at this stage only in Shakespeare's imagination – is Dr Pinch, the quack-physician, whose description by Antipholus of Ephesus as a 'hungry lean-fac'd villain;/A mere anatomy', 'A living dead man', 'with no-face (as 'twere) out-facing me' (V.i.238–45) brings to mind the unmistakably skeletal form of John Sincler, who as 'Sinklo' we have already encountered in the *Shrew* and *Henry VI*, and will meet with again in similar roles as a Chamberlain's man.

But basic to the comedy of errors and confusions throughout the play is the essential seriousness and potential tragedy of its opening scene in which Egeon tells his sad story to the Duke. Apart from *The Tempest*, this is the only play of Shakespeare's to preserve the unities of time, place and action – that is, if we accept Ephesus as a single place. The Duke's sentence of death on Egeon, failing payment of a fine that we have been told far exceeds his resources, is to be carried out on the evening of the same day. The progress of the sun in the sky and the movements of a clock dominate the action, to the moment in the final scene when 'the dial points at five', and Egeon and the Duke re-enter

> to the melancholy vale,
> The place of death and sorry execution
> Behind the ditches of the abbey here.   (V.i.120–2)

(It is from the abbey that the person who is to set all their misunderstandings to rights will emerge.) Unless those first and final scenes are played with due conviction and, in spite of its considerable length and convoluted form, Egeon's story commands the credibility of the audience, the rest of the play is doomed to failure; that it should do so is necessary to give edge to the ensuing comedy, especially its farcical elements, but also to enable the play's deeper meanings to resonate as Shakespeare intended they should. If, as an easy way out, it is guyed, the rest can easily degenerate, as it sometimes does, into a pointless romp. We do not know who Shakespeare had in mind to play Egeon, or who did eventually play him in the first recorded performance at Grays Inn on 28 December (Innocents' Day) 1594 – which, as it happened, turned out to be a comedy of errors in quite another sense[14] – but we can readily understand why he should have wanted to be in charge as the Duke.

We have seen how some of the thought that lies behind the characters and their relationships in the *Two Gentlemen* and *Comedy of Errors* points to the Sonnets. In our review of Shakespeare's writing in the period, we cannot fail to take these wonderful, if puzzling, poems into consideration, if only to bring out a little more clearly their connection with the plays.

Apart from his ostensibly successful marriage to Anne Hathaway, we know so little of Shakespeare's emotional life – of his loves and personal attachments – it is understandable that biographers have looked to the Sonnets to fill the gap. As the 154 poems that make up the completed series are unique among his works in featuring the authorial 'I' (or what is taken to be the authorial 'I'), they assume that he was here, to quote Wordsworth's phrase, 'unlocking his heart' for their inspection. The search is then on for the identity of the Fair Youth, the 'master-mistress' of his passion, to whom most are addressed. Of a long list of historical characters proposed, Henry Wriothesley, the young earl of Southampton to whom he had dedicated *Venus and Adonis* and was shortly to dedicate the *Rape of Lucrece*, has been and remains the front-runner. When they were first published sixteen years later, the Sonnets were also to carry a dedication:

TO . THE . ONLIE . BEGETTER . OF
THESE . INSUING . SONNETS.
Mr. W. H. ALL . HAPPINESSE.
AND . THAT. ETERNITIE.
PROMISED.
BY.
OUR . EVER-LIVING . POET.
WISHETH.
THE . WELL-WISHING.
ADVENTURER . IN.
SETTING.
FORTH.
T.T.

– about which the only certainty is that T.T. stands for Thomas Thorpe, the book's publisher. The dedication, then, was Thorpe's, not Shakespeare's, and the mysterious 'Mr W.H.' no more, perhaps, than a publisher's device to whip up speculation and increase his sales.

The riddles that remain have given rise to acres of print, and I do not mean to add to them. Those who make the assumptions on which they are based mostly forget, or do not want to accept, the simple fact of Shakespeare's occupation as a player and writer for the public theatres. The scrivener and versifier John Davies was not alone in believing that 'the stage doth staine pure gentle bloud'; it was, as we have seen, the common opinion of the time, an opinion of which Shakespeare could not fail to be aware and to have regretted.

> O, for my sake do you with Fortune chide,
> The guilty goddess of my harmful deeds,
> That did not better for my life provide
> Than public means which public manners breeds.
> Thence comes it that my name receives a brand,
> And almost thence my nature is subdued
> To what it works in, like the dyer's hand.   (111.1–7)

But we should take note that when read in context with the two preceding sonnets, 'harmful deeds' is seen to refer to the infidelities to which the poet has there confessed, and it is the brand his name has received, not the 'public means' in themselves, that have threatened to subdue his nature. Furthermore, though generally understood in an autobiographical sense as referring to the theatre, the 'public means which public manners breeds' is open to other interpretations, such as politics or the law; the deliberate ambiguity surrounding the poet's identity is thus preserved. His defiance of those who would drag him down by association should also be noticed:

> 'Tis better to be vile than vile esteemed
> When not to be receives reproach of being . . .
> No, I am that I am, and they that level
> At my abuses reckon up there own;

I may be straight though they themselves be bevel.
By their rank thoughts my deeds must not be shown,
  Unless this general evil they maintain:
  All men are bad and in their badness reign.

(121.1–2, 9–14)

But in view of the prevailing social prejudices, is it conceivable that such a branded individual could in any circumstances have formed an intimate friendship with Southampton or any other aristocratic nominee for the title of the Fair Youth to the extent of having shared a mistress with him? I think not. There is, perhaps, a kind of reverse snobbery at work in such claims. Because of their admiration for Shakespeare, the man and the poet, those who put them forward seek to exalt him by making him a familiar companion of the highest in the land; but in so doing, they not only contradict the known facts of his social situation, they deny the great and glorious thing that he was; of all the poets who ever lived, he is least in need of such promotion. Nor can we safely assume that in writing the poems in the first person he was simply engaged in a form of self-expression. John Kerrigan puts the truth of the matter best when he writes that 'The text is neither fictive nor confessional. Shakespeare stands behind the first person of his sequence as Sidney had stood behind Astrophil – sometimes near the poetic "I", sometimes farther off, but never without some degree of rhetorical projection. *The Sonnets are not autobiographical in a psychological mode.*'[15]

What seems to me most likely is that the first sixteen (perhaps nineteen) poems in the sequence were commissioned by the parents or guardians of a high-placed young man, probably unknown to Shakespeare except by repute, whom they wished to marry against his own inclinations, to be sent to him anonymously; that in fulfilling this demand, Shakespeare adopted the persona of a slightly older admirer of similar social status, and that both this assumed persona and that of the Fair Youth he had envisaged so took root in his imagination as to stimulate a continuation of the series, in which he was able to express (at one remove) his deep insights into love, friendship, the Friendship Cult and its betrayal. It was the way his creative imagination normally worked. The authorial 'I' was thus, like Langland's Piers, Sidney's Astrophil or Marlowe's Passionate Shepherd, in part an invented character in the story he was telling – along with the Fair Youth, the Dark Lady and the Rival Poet. This is not to deny that in writing the poems he drew on his own life experience and that of the people he had come into contact with in the theatre or elsewhere, though the characters in them are more likely to be amalgams of several such people than identifiable individuals. To try to pin them down in that way is thus a futile exercise that risks missing the point of what Shakespeare is really meaning to say. For the ambiguity in which both the poetic 'I' and his beloved are clothed – his withholding of their names and of any clue to their identity – is the secret of the unique appeal the Sonnets have always had to the reader who, whatever his or her own circumstances may be, is thereby enabled to respond directly to the poet's thoughts and feelings, and identify with them. He invites the collaboration of the reader in giving his lovers a face and an identity in the same way that he invites the actor to embody the characters of his plays, and his audience to 'piece out our imperfections with your thoughts'. He gives them room enough to put their imaginations to work, but never so much as to make them redundant.

There can be no question, then, of Shakespeare's sincerity. For all their technical brilliance and dexterity of word-play, the Sonnets are passionately sincere. But are they any more sincere than the heartfelt speeches he gives to the characters in his plays: to Romeo or Juliet, Hamlet or Lear? The tone of his poet's voice varies, occasionally falters but, as Muriel Bradbrook wrote, in all their variety of accomplishment, 'there is no variation in that capacity for a transfer of the whole centre of being into the life of another, which is the mark linking these sonnets to dramatic art'.[16]

To the Puritans of Shakespeare's time, plays were all lies, and the players who performed them retailers of lies, no better than deceiving whores – pretending to be what they were not, dissembling emotions they did not feel, and doing both for money. The prejudice survives in the common assumption that acting and sincerity are so mutually incompatible as to be, to all intents and purposes, opposites. But whatever may be said of the people in ordinary life who conceal or disguise their true identity or feelings in order to deceive and manipulate others, actors in their professional capacity make no such pretences, nor do they seek to deceive. Depending on their individual ability and command of their craft in holding the 'mirror up to nature', their acting may be true or false; but the actor *per se* is the most truthful person in existence for, whatever part he or she is playing, no one can be in any doubt as to who they are, or what they are doing on the stage. So it is with the poets and the stories they tell. So it was with Shakespeare. At the core of the Sonnets there is certainly the story of an intense, emotional attachment, but to interpret it as necessarily Shakespeare's is to confuse the story-teller with the story, the player with the play.

Curiously, the play that relates more closely to the Sonnets than any other belonging to this period of Shakespeare's 'resting' as a player is one that until recently has rarely been claimed as his, though his part-authorship has often been suspected: the anonymous *Edward III*.

It was entered in the Stationers' Register on 1 December 1595, and published in the following year, 'as it hath bin sundrie times plaied about the Citie of London'.[17] But no mention is made of its author or the company that played it; nor does any record survive of its performances in the City or elsewhere. Though no one claimed it as Shakespeare's before the second half of the seventeenth century, his familiarity with the play is evident, not only in the lines relating to the Sonnets quoted in Section 3 of Appendix C, but in numerous other less precise echoes or anticipations of image and language to be found in his recognised plays, both early and late.[18] Some of these correspondences might be accounted for by his having acted in the play, when the words he had spoken entered so deeply into his conscious or unconscious memory as to be later recycled in his writing in the same way that images and phrases from Marlowe and Kyd have been seen to resurface in *Titus* and *Henry VI*. But that could only have been prior to 1593 when the City theatres were closed, which is too early, and there would hardly have been time for him to have toured in the play any later than that. Moreover, the Edward/Countess scenes

Edward III

Edward III as depicted in the Temple edition of the play, 1897

of Acts 1 and 2, which provide what has always been seen as the most persuasive evidence of his authorship, stand out from the rest in the quality and style of their verse to so large a degree as to make such an explanation untenable.

One scene in particular – that between the king and his secretary (Act 2, Scene 1) – supplies such clear echoes of lines from the Sonnets as to indicate that they were written very close to each other in time.[19] The scene has also what I take to be a nice example of Shakespeare's self-deflatory humour: a mocking glance at himself where he is being most earnest, as in the Sonnets. The secretary (Lodowick) is ordered by the king to compose a poem in praise of the Countess and, after several pages of detailed instruction as to what it should say, succeeds only in producing two comically inappropriate lines. But a serious point is also being made about the futility of poetical comparisons and flattery – a central theme of the Sonnets to which he was shortly to return in *Love's Labour's Lost*.

It is significant, however, that in all those features in which the earlier *Arden of Faversham* has been claimed to be strong – characterisation, social realism and treatment of its minor roles, to which I would add coherent structure – *Edward III* is notably weak. After what would have been for Shakespeare a uniquely feeble opening, in which Edward's claim to the throne of France is introduced, the remainder of the first two acts is occupied by his attempted seduction of the Countess, the wife of one of his nobles, and only when her honour and courage have been shown to triumph over his lust do we cross to France for a confused account of the battles of Sluys, Crécy and Poitiers. The two parts of the play (Acts 1 and 2, and 3 to 5) fail to hang together, and the character of the king remains an enigma. The Countess lacks the outraged dignity that Shakespeare would have given her, and the other characters are little more than ciphers.[20]

The most likely explanation for Shakespeare's undoubted connection with the play is that during the latter part of 1593 or early 1594, Henslowe, in anticipation of the combined season of the Admiral's and Chamberlain's men at Newington Butts in June of the latter year, offered Shakespeare the part of Lodowick (doubling, perhaps, with King John of France in Part 2), and that Shakespeare accepted on condition that he could revise those scenes of the play in which he appeared, mainly Act 2. But the season failed and came to a premature end while *Edward III* was still in rehearsal. On the renewed separation of the two companies, it would then have gone to the Admiral's, with which Henslowe (through Alleyn) retained a close connection, and was played by them in the City prior to its publication in 1596. (That it was not performed after 1603 is explained by the play's uncomplimentary references to the Scots that would certainly have been taken as gravely offensive to King James and thus have landed its authors in jail.)

— * —

From the besieged Ardea all in post,
Borne by the trustless wings of false desire,
Lust-breathed Tarquin leaves the Roman host
And to Collatium bears the lightless fire,
Which in pale embers hid lurks to aspire
    And girdle with embracing flames the waist
    Of Collatine's fair love, Lucrece the chaste.

So begins the product of that 'graver labour' Shakespeare had promised Southampton. Again, we are plunged straight into action; but in contrast to the sunlit outdoors of *Venus and Adonis* with its frequent reminders of the vibrant life of nature in the background, here we are taken indoors at 'dead of night', where the tapestried walls of Lucrece's chamber are illumined only by the 'lightless fire' of Tarquin's torch and the hellish embers of his lust.

The scene is more obviously theatrical, but in a mode of sombre tragedy to which Shakespeare would not return until, some ten years later, he came to write *Othello* and *Macbeth*. For the story of Lucrece, he drew on the Latin of Ovid and Livy; but in putting it into English he was following in the footsteps of his medieval predecessors – of Chaucer, Gower and Lydgate – who had already made of it a familiar tale and established the figure of Lucrece as an admired moral exemplar. It was the nearest Shakespeare ever came to writing a tragedy in the unalloyed classical manner, and he goes so far in that direction as to indicate the formalised gestures, as laid down by classical writers on oratory, its performance would require.[21] The prose 'Argument' that precedes the poem in the published text may draw some of its details from Painter's translation of Livy in his *Pallace of Pleasure* (1566) and reads almost like a theatrical 'Plot'. Of its 1,855 lines, again nearly half (as in *Venus and Adonis*) are of direct speech, and some of its rhetorical set pieces – especially Lucrece's invocation to the Night in the aftermath of her rape – cry out for a great classical actress (a Sybil Thorndike or a Diana Rigg) to deliver:

> O comfort-killing Night, image of hell,
> Dim register and notary of shame,
> Black stage for tragedies and murders fell,
> Vast sin-concealing chaos, nurse of blame,
> Blind muffled bawd, dark harbour for defame!
>   Grim cave of death, whisp'ring conspirator
>   With close-tongued treason and the ravisher!

(ll. 764–70)

– and so on for a further thirty-eight tremendous stanzas of complaint. And this is followed by a beautifully sensitive scene between Lucrece and her maid – awe-struck by the intensity of her mistress' grief and not yet understanding its cause – that, without a word of alteration, might have graced a play for the stage if Shakespeare had chosen to write it.

The poem lacks the narrative flow and interplay of *Venus and Adonis*, and the unrelieved pain of its subject matter makes it the more difficult to read. It contains, as we might expect, a number of cross-references to *Venus* and the earlier Sonnets. Nothing could better illustrate Shakespeare's flexibility of mind and the many-sided nature of his creative imagination than that he was able to combine in so relatively short a period work on so many contrasting themes with such wide divergencies of mood.

The poem was published, again by Field, in May or June 1594, with another self-deprecatory dedication to Southampton.

To the Right Honourable, Henry Wriothesley, Earle of Southampton, and Baron of Titchfield.

The love I dedicate to your Lordship is without end: wherof this Pamphlet without beginning is but a superfluous Moity. The warrant I have of your Honourable disposition, not the worth of my untutored Lines makes it assured of acceptance. What I have done is yours, what I have to doe is yours, being part in all I have, devoted yours. Were my worth greater, my duety would shew greater, meane time, as it is, it is bound to your Lordship; To whom I wish long life still lengthned with all happinesse.

Though generally considered to be warmer in tone, the letter ends as before, 'Your Lordships in all duety, William Shakespeare'.[22]

Shakespeare was in exuberant mood when, probably in the early months of 1594, he came to write *Love's Labour's Lost* – the last of his plays belonging to the period. Like the *Two Gentlemen*, its ambience is courtly Arcadian. It tells a story of the King of Navarre and three of his young courtiers who vow to devote themselves to philosophy for three years in rural seclusion, and during that time to forgo the society of women; whereupon a Princess of France with her ladies promptly arrive on the scene with predictable results. The play fairly fizzles with word-play, and the popular element in it – represented not only by Kempe as Costard the clown, but also a supporting cast of richly comic characters for which Shakespeare clearly had other known actors in mind – is more pronounced than in the *Two Gentlemen*.

The high spirits of its author, which I attribute to his success in obtaining a share in the new company then in process of formation, the Lord Chamberlain's, overflow into good-humoured satire at the expense of figures in the literary-cum-political circles of the time, and their factional in-fighting. This has made of the play a happy hunting ground for scholars in search of hidden meanings; of a general theory that would throw light on Shakespeare's own allegiances in the period (an aim that no one yet has come near to achieving, if any such meaning is there to be found). Editions of the published text are thick with recondite notes in which every quibble and pun is subject to a learned essay. All this is doubtless necessary and valuable to the student, but should not be allowed to smother the spirit of uninhibited fun which, in an unimpeded reading or performance, is the play's dominant mood. We do not need to know that in the tortuously rhetorical speeches of the fantastical Spaniard Don Armado, Shakespeare may be satirising the prose style of some contemporary pedant to find them funny; or appreciate that Armado's page, Moth (a supercharged Speed from the *Two Gentlemen*), may relate to the personality of the mercurial Nashe to enjoy the comic interplay between them. The learned exhibitionism of the school-master Holofernes, the simple folly of the parson Sir Nathaniel, and the honest stupidity of Dull may or may not reflect the failings of particular individuals among Shakespeare's contemporaries (if they do, no two scholars agree as to their identity), but they can just as easily be taken and enjoyed as representative of varieties of pomposity to be as commonly encountered now as they would have been then. Most of the textual obscurity that remains derives from the particularity of Shakespeare's references to traditional songs, proverbs and stories familiar to his audience but which have since been forgotten, and the apparent inability he betrays (here more than in any other of his plays) to refuse any and every opportunity for a pun, however far-fetched; both of which would have been especially enjoyed by the groundlings. In a modern production, they can be pruned to advantage.

Both in its mockery (more affectionate than savage) of the inconstancy of the king and his friends in having so easily abandoned their vows of celibacy on the appearance of the ladies, and (more broadly) those who, through self-conceit and a desire to impress, mangle the language, the message of the play (in so far as it has one) lies in its assertion of the superiority of common sense over misapplied learning, and the ways of nature over artificiality of behaviour and expression. 'The words of Mercury' may be 'harsh after the songs of Apollo', but are just as necessary and desirable. The same message pervades the Sonnets. I give a few of the more obvious parallels in Section 4 of the Appendix; but it should not be overlooked that the scene in which the hypocrisy of the king and his companions is revealed (IV.iii), the crux of the plot, turns upon their secret composition of Sonnets and other poems of love. The more recondite references that have been alleged to the Marprelate and other controversies of the time remain conjectural, and the mention of the 'school of night', of which so much has been made, may, as likely as not, result from a misprint.

On the supposition that the play would have been 'caviare to the general', it is said to have been written for private performance in some nobleman's house (possibly Southampton's), where the larger than usual number of boys required to play Moth and the five female roles would have been available from among the resident choirboys and pages. On the contrary, I find it much more probable that Shakespeare wrote it for court or City performance, drawing on the resources of an existing company of players, including Kempe and other skilled men who would have brought their trained apprentices with them to play the boys' parts,[23] and that the company in question was the newly formed Chamberlain's men. In such a company, Shakespeare, at the age of twenty-nine or thirty, would have been ideally cast as Ferdinand, the king. The play was to remain generally popular. It was performed for the Queen at Christmas 1597 or 1598, and again for King James in 1605. According to the Second Quarto of 1631, it was also acted 'by his Majesties Servants at the Blacke-Friers and the Globe'.[24]

Shakespeare's period of inactivity as a player was over, and later in 1594 we find him with Kempe, Richard Burbage and others as a sharer-member of the Chamberlain's (ultimately King's) company, which he was to serve as poet and player for the rest of his career. He had used his enforced 'sabbatical' to write two lengthy narrative poems, a substantial number of sonnets, three plays, and found time to make important revisions to a fourth, not his own. As we embark in the following chapter on a survey of his future plays and the parts that he played in them, we must also take occasion to look more closely at the personalities of his fellow players and the theatrical conditions prevailing in the period that were to govern their collaboration. For though his own genius was to make by far the most significant and lasting contribution to the company's work, his fellows deserve more credit than they usually get for what was to be a unique theatrical enterprise; one that was to provide him with the ideal setting in which his outstanding abilities as dramatic poet were to grow to greatness.

SEVEN

Chamberlain's Man

However much we may think of him as a genius apart, to himself and to his age he appeared primarily as a busy actor associated with the leading stock-company of his time; . . . writing that his troupe might successfully compete with rival organizations; and, finally, as a theatrical proprietor, owning shares in two of the most flourishing playhouses in London. Thus his whole life was centred in the stage and his interests were essentially those of his 'friends and fellows', the actors, who affectionately called him 'our Shakespeare'.

J. Quincy Adams[1]

We do not know the exact circumstances surrounding the formation of the Chamberlain's men in 1594, or on what basis players were selected to become its original sharers. No doubt it was an honour to be asked, especially as the position was to carry with it the privileges of a Groom of the Chamber including protection from arrest; but a financial investment was also required in a capital fund from which costumes and props could be purchased as well as a repertoire of plays. To these last, Shakespeare would have been able to contribute in kind from the fruits of his labours in the preceding year which, as we have seen, included the *Two Gentlemen of Verona*, the *Comedy of Errors* and *Love's Labour's Lost*, along with the previously unperformed *Richard III*, over which he had presumably retained the rights. But others of his earlier plays that in course of time were to feature in the Chamberlain's programme would have had to be bought in from those who had first commissioned them: *Titus* (already in print) from Henslowe; the *Shrew* and *Henry VI* from Alleyn. It was, however, primarily as a player, rather than a dramatist, that he had been invited to join the new company, and for that reason he is unlikely to have been wholly exempt from the obligation to contribute to the considerable costs of setting it up; for it was on the basis of that initial stake in its capital that his subsequent share in the profits of the enterprise would, like those of his fellows, depend.

The Lord Chamberlain who had initiated the company by granting it his patronage was Henry Carey, Lord Hunsdon. It was not the first troupe of players to have looked to him for protection; a company known originally as Lord Hunsdon's men is recorded on tour and as giving occasional performances at court between 1564 and 1585 when, on Hunsdon's appointment to his high office, it became the Chamberlain's. But the last we hear of this earlier troupe is at Maidstone in 1590, and there is unlikely to have been any continuity between it and the one that Shakespeare joined in 1594.[2]

The decline of the Queen's players following the death of their chief attraction, Tarlton, in 1588, and the disbandment of Leicester's in the same year, had left a gap that needed to be filled: but more

Henry Carey, Lord Hunsdon (from a print in the British Museum)

94

immediately the new company may have owed its inception to the breaking of the Admiral's/Strange's alliance in February 1593 because of the plague, and the dispersal of its players. It was one of the Chamberlain's responsibilities, exercised through the Master of the Revels, to provide court entertainment of a quality to satisfy the high demands of the Queen. In the best of times this was no easy task, but by the autumn of 1593 it had become an impossible one. The Pembroke company had collapsed on tour in the course of the summer. Even Henslowe of the Rose was feeling the pinch: 'comend me harteley to all the reast of youre fealowes in generall', he wrote to Alleyn in August, 'for I growe poore for lacke of them'.[3] There were none of the usual plays at court that Christmas, and the sudden death of Ferdinando, earl of Derby (formerly Lord Strange), in April of the new year can only have added to the general uncertainty. With the plague easing, and the London playhouses starting to reopen in the summer of 1594, there was both need and opportunity for a new beginning.

It is interesting to find that the company's first appearance was in conjunction with Alleyn and a remnant of the Admiral's under Henslowe's management, and that the venue was an out-of-the-way theatre at Newington Butts – well outside the City limits. This was in June 1594, and Shakespeare's personal involvement is suggested by the presence of his *Taming of the Shrew* and *Titus Andronicus* among the plays performed. The season lasted only ten days and is usually put down as a failure, but may have been primarily intended as a try-out for the new company. At all events, it was out of that short season that the shape of the future Chamberlain's emerged, and it will be seen that with the notable exception of Alleyn (who had other irons in the fire), it included the more senior and experienced men from all the previously existing companies.

Richard Burbage (Plate 6) had begun his career in the 1580s with his father James as a Queen's man, and in 1590 is found playing important parts in a revival of the second part of Tarlton's *Seven Deadly Sins* by the Admiral's/Strange's alliance – probably at the Theatre, which his father had built. But his connection with that company and its

95

leading player, Edward Alleyn, is unlikely to have survived a bitter dispute that had broken out during the company's tenancy between the Burbages and Alleyns (Ned and his elder brother John, who was not a player) over division of the box office takings, in the course of which James had made slighting remarks about the Lord Admiral. This had resulted in Alleyn abandoning the Theatre for the Rose. It is equally unlikely then that Richard had played any part in the season at the Rose of 1592/3, when Shakespeare's *Henry VI* had attracted the praise of Nashe and the envy of Greene.[4]

Like his father, Richard was – in those young days at least – of a fiery temperament and, in the heat of another dispute involving James's business dealings, had wielded a 'broom staff' to see off an unwelcome visitor to the theatre yard and twisted another man's nose.[5] His date of birth is not recorded, but he was junior to his brother Cuthbert, born in 1566/7; at the time of the quarrel with Alleyn he would have been about twenty-two or twenty-three, and thus a mature twenty-six or seven when he found himself a fellow of Shakespeare's in the Chamberlain's. He was to succeed Alleyn as the leading player of his day, but in 1594 his great potential may not have been immediately apparent. Actors develop their individual powers in responding to the challenges that dramatists give them. As Alleyn had risen on the wings of Kyd's Hieronimo, Marlowe's Tamburlaine, Barabas and Faustus, Burbage was to reach even greater heights in essaying Shakespeare's Hamlet, Othello and Lear; in 1594 these roles were still some way in the future.

William Kempe, on the other hand, came to the company with an already established reputation as comedian and clown in the tradition of Tarlton, but he was also an experienced actor. He is first recorded as a Leicester's man in the Low Countries in 1586/7, from where he had made his way to Denmark, as attested by an Elsinore pay-roll. He was back in England by 1590, when Nashe dedicated his *Almond for a Parrat* to him, describing him as 'that Most Comicall and conceited Cavaleire Monsieur du Kempe, Jestmonger and Vice-gerent generall to the Ghost of Dicke Tarlton'.[6] After the death of Leicester, Kempe had joined the Admiral's, and had played one of the men of Goteham in the anonymous *A Knacke to know a*

William Kempe with his taborer on a dancing journey to Norwich, from his *Nine Daies Wonder* of 1600 (Folger Shakespeare Library, Washington, DC)

Knave at the Rose in 1592/3. When the play was published in 1594, it was described on its title page as 'Newlie set foorth, as it hath sundrie tymes bene played by ED. ALLEN and his Companie. With KEMPS applauded Merrimentes of the men of Goteham, in receiving the King into Goteham'. As the 'Merrimentes' occupy little more than a page of the printed text and read as only moderately amusing, the prominence of Kempe's name on the title page may be taken as a publishers' device (not entirely unknown today) to attract additional sales, and thus as an indication of Kempe's popular appeal at the time.[7] That Shakespeare knew him well, admired his skills, and anticipated working with him again in the not-so-distant future is strongly suggested by the roles of Launce, the Dromios and Costard that he had written for him in the previous year.

We cannot be sure of the exact number of founding sharers, but there were certainly eight and possibly ten. Along with Shakespeare, Burbage and Kempe, three others may be taken as certain as they are named at various times between 1594 and 1598 as receiving payment on behalf of the sharers as a whole for the company's court performances; these were George Bryan, Thomas Pope and John Heminges. Bryan and Pope were former Leicester's men who (along with Kempe) had accompanied their patron to the Low Countries in 1585 and, after their return and the death of Leicester in 1588, had transferred to Strange's and from Strange's, to the Alleyn-led alliance. Heminges had probably begun his career as a Queen's man but had transferred to Strange's by May 1593. All three were senior to Shakespeare – certainly in professional status.

To these original sharers, we should probably add the names of Augustine Phillips, William Sly, Richard Cowley and Henry Condell who, with those already mentioned, occupy the first nine places after Shakespeare himself in the list of 'Principall Actors in all these Playes' printed by Heminges and Condell at the front of their First Folio of 1623, reproduced opposite. All would have been familiar to Shakespeare as former colleagues from the Admiral's or the Admiral's alliance with Strange's. Phillips was another former Strange's man and, like Bryan and Pope, had been a sharer in that company. Sly we have already encountered playing the tinker 'Sly' in the *Shrew* back in 1587/8, and, so far as we know, had remained with the Admiral's ever since.[8] Of Condell and Cowley, I shall have more to say in a moment. Though our knowledge of all these fellows of Shakespeare, and of the roles that each of them played, is so limited, we should not underrate their abilities, or the significance of the contribution they made to the plays he wrote for them. They were all distinguished men in their day. Apart from Burbage and Kempe (of whom we know a good deal more than the others), Pope was famous for his playing of 'clowns' – in modern terms, as a character comedian – and, along with Phillips and Sly, was to receive valedictory praise from Thomas Heywood in his *Apology for Actors* of 1612, in that, though all three were then dead, 'their deserts yet live in the remembrance of many' – the best that can be said of any actor.[9]

Though the sharers, as we have seen, *were* the company in a legal and constitutional sense, they were not the *whole* of the company; rather, a nucleus of leading men who shared financial and managerial

The Workes of William Shakespeare,

containing all his Comedies, Histories, and
Tragedies: Truely set forth, according to their first
ORIGINALL.

The Names of the Principall Actors
in all these Playes.

 William Shakespeare.

Richard Burbadge.

John Hemmings.

Augustine Phillips.

William Kempt.

Thomas Poope.

George Bryan.

Henry Condell.

William Slye.

Richard Cowly.

John Lowine.

Samuell Crosse.

Alexander Cooke.

Samuel Gilburne.

Robert Armin.

William Ostler.

Nathan Field.

John Underwood.

Nicholas Tooley.

William Ecclestone.

Joseph Taylor.

Robert Benfield.

Robert Goughe.

Richard Robinson.

Iohn Shancke.

Iohn Rice.

Shakespeare's principal fellows, from the First Folio of 1623 (Shakespeare Folger Library, Washington, DC) responsibility for its success or failure. They did not appear in every play; nor did they always play the leading roles.[10] In the operation of a repertoire system of the kind to which they and other companies in the period all adhered, with daily rotation of plays and limited time for rehearsal, that would have been impossibly exhausting, and it would often have fallen to them to take (and often to double) smaller, but nonetheless important, subsidiary roles. But in casting the plays – doubtless in consultation with his fellows – Shakespeare and other dramatists like Ben Jonson who wrote for the company were able to draw on a much larger body of players, comprising apprentices and 'hired men'. Of these, the apprentices were of prime importance, for not only did they play all the younger female parts, but these were often among the leads. (We have only to think of Kate in the *Shrew*, Portia in the *Merchant of Venice*, Helena in *All's Well that Ends Well*, Juliet, Cleopatra and Cressida for the point to be made.) Nor were they limited to female parts, for in addition to the numerous messengers and servants that would necessarily have gone to them, there is reason to believe (as argued below for Romeo) that they played many of the male juvenile leads also.

Much confusion has surrounded the question of the age at which boys were apprenticed and the length of their apprenticeships, and the only certain conclusion to be drawn from currently available evidence is that both were extremely variable. The age is found to vary between ten and sixteen, and the term between three and twelve years; nor can we assume that the younger the boy, the longer the term; indeed, the opposite may well have been true. In the children's companies, such as the Queen's Revels in 1606, boys were contracted for only three years – presumably until their voices broke. In the Chamberlain's, where the usual age of recruitment was probably thirteen or fourteen, the term appears to have been seven or eight years to take the boys to their majority at twenty-one, but in one late instance extended to twelve.[11] During the whole period of their training, the boys were maintained by their individual masters and instructors, who were, however, entitled to charge the common funds of the company with an agreed amount in return for their services.[12] On completion of whatever term he had agreed to serve, the apprentice was normally employed as a 'hired man' (journeyman player) before becoming a sharer himself – though the final step was not guaranteed; it would have depended on the talents he had to offer and, as for Shakespeare himself who did not achieve it until he was thirty, the availability of a vacant place, for which he might have to wait a considerable time and still be required to pay a hefty premium as the price of his admission. As a hired man, he received a weekly wage which, like the sharers' expenses in the maintenance of their apprentices, was charged to the company, along with other production expenses, before division of the profits (if any) among the sharers.

In the absence of complete, printed texts of the plays when they were first performed, the actors had to make do in rehearsal with individual, hand-written parts and cues. As they were often required to double or treble parts, it was usually necessary to post a notice backstage to remind them of the sequence of characters and scenes in which they appeared. These were known as 'plots' and, fortunately, several have survived. One for the second part of Tarlton's *Seven Deadly Sins*, found among Alleyn's papers at Dulwich and dated to about 1590 (before Alleyn's break with the Burbages and move to the Rose), is especially valuable as it gives the names of most of the actors who were members of the alliance at the time, including the apprentices, along with the parts that they played.

By comparing the names in the plot with those in the Folio list of principal actors, it may be possible to recover the identities of some of the Chamberlain's original apprentices, as these are likely to have accompanied their masters into the new company at the time of its foundation. As nearly all the 'principal actors' are known to have been, in fact, sharers in the Chamberlain's or King's at one time or another, we may also be able to determine how many of the apprentices did eventually obtain that final promotion. One difficulty, however, is that while the sharers in the plot (such as Bryan, Pope and Phillips) appear under their surnames graced by the prefix 'Mr', and the hired men under surname and initial, the apprentices are referred to only by first names or nicknames, so we cannot always be certain of their identity.

In the plot, Harry, Kit and Vincent are recorded as playing small male roles, and Saunder, Nick, Robert, Ned, Will and T. Belt, female roles. 'Harry' and 'Kit' were very probably Henry Condell and Christopher Beeston. Both were to be named by Jonson as 'principall Comedians' in the cast of his *Every Man In his Humour* as performed by the Chamberlain's in 1598, but only Condell became a sharer – perhaps as previously suggested from the start, but certainly by 1603; Beeston (who was to be named by Phillips in his will as his 'servant') had by the latter year transferred to a reconstituted Worcester's.[13] 'Vincent' is unusual among players in the period as either Christian or surname; he is likely to have been the Thomas Vincent we know to have occupied the important post of book-keeper and prompter at the Globe, and may even have done so from the company's beginnings.[14]

Of the younger apprentices who had played women's parts in the *Deadly Sins*, 'Saunder' or 'Sander' is an obvious abbreviation of Alexander that also appears as a speech prefix in the pirated version of Shakespeare's *Shrew* – the one with the indefinite article, performed by Pembroke's; almost certainly, it relates to Alexander Cooke, who was to become a sharer in the later King's company (he is thirteenth in the Folio list of principal actors). He may have gone to Pembroke's as a boy on the breaking of the Admiral's/Strange's alliance early in 1593 but, when Pembroke's collapsed in the summer of the same year, would then have been free to join the Chamberlain's as Heminges' apprentice. Heminges was a freeman of the London Grocers and had used his privileges as such to apprentice Cooke for, having served his time, Cooke was to be received into that company in 1608. This does not imply (as some scholars have suggested) that either Heminges or Cooke led 'double lives' as players and grocers. The full-time nature of their commitment as players makes that very improbable and there is no evidence for it. It was, in fact, quite possible for a boy to be apprenticed as a grocer *to learn the craft of a player* if that was his master's usual occupation, as evidenced by the case of William Trigg, apprenticed to Heminges in 1626 for a term of twelve years for 'la arte d'une Stage player'.[15] If Cooke had entered into his apprenticeship with Heminges on the formation of the company in 1594 or a year or two later, and was enfranchised in 1608, he would have served a similar term. He features under his full name in the cast-lists of all of Jonson's plays, and one by Beaumont and Fletcher, acted by the King's between 1603 and 1613, probably playing the more mature women's parts, as he may also have done in Shakespeare's plays during the same period, for he would then have been in his late twenties or early thirties. He was to die young in 1614, leaving a young family. In his will, he was to appoint Heminges and Condell as trustees for his children, and requests them to take charge of the money he had left for them and 'see it saflye put into grocers hall'. He also refers to a sum of £50, 'which is in the hand of my fellowes as my share of the stock'.[16] This, then, was the premium he had paid on becoming a sharer, which after his death would be returned to his estate.

Nick was quite a common name among players of the period, but the 'Nick' of the plot was probably Nicholas Tooley, born in 1575. He may have begun his career in the Admiral's, playing several small servant roles with the prefix 'Nicke' in the Folio text of the *Shrew* when he was aged twelve or thirteen, and a female role in the *Deadly Sins* when he was fifteen. If so, he would have been nineteen at the formation of the Chamberlain's. His first, fully named appearance with the company was in Jonson's *The Alchemist* in 1610, but he is likely to have been active in Shakespeare's plays from a much earlier date, if not from the beginning. He never married, and was to die in the house of Richard Burbage's brother Cuthbert, referring in his will to Richard (who had predeceased him) as his 'late master'; he is named in nineteenth place in the Folio list. The 'Ro. Go.' of the plot is plainly Robert Gough, who was a beneficiary of Pope's will in 1603, and probably his apprentice, along with John Edmans (later a Queen Anne's man); they were to divide their former master's 'wearing apparrell and armes' between them. In the same year, Gough was to marry Phillips' sister, Elizabeth, and to witness his brother-in-law's will in 1605. He had three children, one of whom, Alexander, followed him into the profession. He is known to have played male roles in the King's, and was a sharer by 1619 – twenty-third in the Folio list. We can only guess at the other boys named in the plot: 'Will' as perhaps William Eccleston, who was a King's man at various times between 1610 and 1622, like Gough a sharer by 1619, and (in twentieth place) a 'Principall Actor'; 'Ned' as just possibly Shakespeare's younger brother Edmund who is said to have followed him into the profession, though in 1590 he would have been only ten. 'T. Belt' wholly escapes us.

Though not distinguishable in the plot, several others are likely to have been apprentices in the Chamberlain's from an early date. Samuel Crosse, though listed twelfth among the principal actors, did not survive long enough to be named in any of the Jacobean cast-lists, and may have been a victim of the plague which, though quiescent in the City in the late 1590s, rose to a new peak of virulence in 1603. Samuel Gilburne (in fourteenth place in the Folio list) is named in Phillips' will of 1605 as his 'late apprentice' and was bequeathed 40*s* in money, his master's velvet hose and white taffeta doublet, black taffeta suit, purple cloak, sword and dagger, and a bass viol. There is a fleeting reference to him as 'Gebon' (which is probably how his name was pronounced and known to

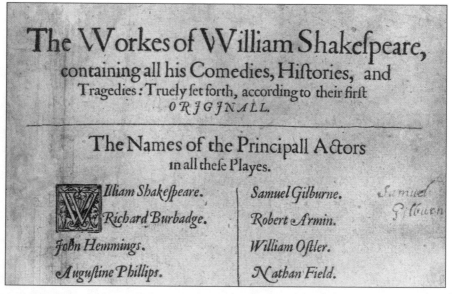

Autograph of Samuel Gilburne against his name in a copy of the First Folio (Folger Shakespeare Library, Washington, DC)

Shakespeare) in a rogue stage direction in *Henry V*, and touchingly, his signature has been found in a copy of the First Folio.

James Sandes appears in Phillips' will as his current apprentice, and was to receive the same amount of money as Gilburne, plus a 'Citterne, a Bandore and a Lute', but only at 'thexpiracon of his yeares in his Indentur or Aprenticehood'. The management of Sandes' apprenticeship was to be taken over by Sly, one of Phillips' executors, who when he came to make his own will in 1608 left him a munificent £40.[17]

It is impossible to be exact, but Burbage, Pope and Heminges all appear to have brought apprentices with them from their previous companies, and others were recruited. At the company's formation, there could hardly have been fewer than seven or eight boys apprenticed to one or other of the sharers. And as these moved slowly up the ladder to become hired men and often sharers in their turn, there would have been no lack of applicants to replace them.[18] It was a royal road to advancement in their profession and few appear to have fallen by the way. Once they had joined, the majority were to remain with the company for the rest of their active careers – and usually that meant for the rest of their lives.

Of the hired men of the *Deadly Sins* plot – those whose surnames and initials are given without the distinguishing 'Mr' – only R. Burbage, W. Sly, R. Cowley, J. Duke and J. Sincler joined the Chamberlain's; Burbage, Sly, perhaps Cowley, from the start. Richard Cowley was to be named by Shakespeare in a 'rogue direction' as playing Verges to Kempe's Dogberry in *Much Ado About Nothing*. John Duke appears with Christopher Beeston in the cast of Jonson's *Every Man In his Humour* in 1598 but, like Beeston, he was to leave the Chamberlain's for Worcester's by 1603 and was never a sharer. But where in the plot, we may ask, were Mr Heminges and W. Shakespeare who, by 1590, would both have been well-established as members of the Alleyn-led alliance? And where for that matter is Alleyn himself? Presumably taking a play 'out'; but for Heminges and Shakespeare we must look to the play's presenters: John Lydgate the poet and King Henry VI who, because they never leave the stage and it would be impossible for them to double, need no reminding of the parts they are playing or the sequence of scenes in which they appear.[19]

These then were Shakespeare's fellows when he started out in 1594 as a Chamberlain's man: eight, possibly ten sharers with their apprentices, and four or five regularly employed hired men including one or two player-musicians.[20] I have spent some time in establishing their identities – in so far as that is now possible – because the company was to be of unique importance in theatrical history; not only because Shakespeare belonged to it and wrote for it, but for its unparalleled success as a co-operative enterprise, which was to survive the passing of both its original sharers and principal playwright, and take it to the eve of the civil wars and the closure of the playhouses by the Puritans in 1642. It was something much more than a group of actors brought together for a particular production or, at best, for a season of plays (as the term 'company' is understood today), but rather a living, self-perpetuating community. Professor Baldwin wrote of it as the 'Shakespeare clan'; it would be more accurate to describe it as a family: a body of players with their musicians, tiremen and stage keepers working together on a permanent basis and, in many instances, living in close proximity to each other in the same suburb of the City; self-perpetuating because it contained within its structure both a school of acting and a natural means of progression whereby its members could advance in their profession so far as their abilities were sufficient to take them from being apprentices to hired men, and from hired men to sharers.[21] And for evidence that the relations of its members with each other were far closer than merely professional, we have only to read their wills; the way in which masters remember their apprentices and former apprentices, apprentices their masters, and the sharers their fellows. To refer to it as the 'Shakespeare clan' or the 'Shakespeare company' is to mistake both Shakespeare's place in it – always one of partnership, never of dominance – and the nature of the company itself, founded as it was on the equality of its sharers and leading men under its successive patrons.

One consequence of the general neglect by biographers and scholars of Shakespeare's professional activity as performer and man of the theatre has been to separate him from his fellows; because of his concurrent role as dramatist, to see him as somehow detached from them; choosing themes and subjects to explore in accordance with his personal interests or moods of the moment with little, if any, regard for the men who would be called upon to perform the plays and carry responsibility for their success or failure, whereas all the evidence from the period as to the position of the dramatist in relation to the troupe he served indicates a collaborative process.[22] Every aspect of the plays and their production – initial choice of theme and title, intended performance venues, size of cast, casting of the principal and apprentice roles, hired men to be employed – would necessarily have been subject to the agreement of his fellows. It is no denial of Shakespeare's genius as poet and dramatist to state that the plays he wrote for the company, from *Romeo and Juliet* to *Henry VIII*, were shaped and brought to the form in which they have come down to us as the result of a co-operative effort by the company as a whole, to which the youngest apprentice and the most junior hired man would have had a contribution to make; it is rather to affirm it.

In 1594, there was only one thing that the Chamberlain's men lacked to ensure the company's success, and that was a permanent home – a theatre in the capital they could call their own and that would serve as a base for all their future activities. That was to come their way five years later. In the meantime, they did what the companies had always done: they took to the road.

In the late summer of 1594, we find them at Marlborough, and there were doubtless visits to other Wiltshire and Berkshire towns; but on 8 October they were back in London, as attested by a letter from Lord Hunsdon to the Lord Mayor, requesting him, 'the time beinge such as, thankes be to god, there is nowe no danger of the sicknes', to suffer his 'nowe companie of Players' to exercise their quality at the Cross Keys inn in Gracechurch Street in the City.[23] Requests from the Lord Chamberlain were not lightly refused, and the probability is that the company performed there throughout the winter of 1594/5. Its repertoire would almost certainly have included *Titus* and the *Shrew* as these had been given at Newington Butts in June and were already in the repertoire. The opening scenes of the *Shrew*, set in an inn, would have made good use of the Cross Key's galleries and yard, which by this date had probably been covered to protect the groundlings from the worst of the weather. *The Comedy of Errors* is another virtual certainty for inclusion in the Cross Keys season because we know that a special performance of it was given on Innocents' Day (28 December) at Grays Inn, where a stage had been built and scaffolds set up 'to the top of the house'. *The Two Gentlemen* and *Love's Labour's Lost* are also likely to have received their first City performances during the course of the winter. There were good parts in all of these plays for several of the players we have identified as present in the company, including Burbage, Sly, 'Sinklo', Shakespeare as their respective 'dukes', and not least Kempe, who would already have been one of the company's big attractions. Only Alleyn would have been missed.

I have said that in forming the company, Hunsdon is likely to have been motivated in part by the need to supply quality entertainment to the Queen and the court, who had been starved of it throughout the time of plague. In writing to the Lord Mayor on its behalf in October – an unusual, though doubtless welcome, step for a patron to take – he may have had the same consideration in mind, for by bringing his players to the capital and ensuring a winter venue for them there, they would also have been available for duty at court. This is borne out by the record already quoted of a payment of £20 to William Kempe, William Shakespeare and Richard Burbage for performances at Greenwich on 26 and 28 December.[24]

In the meantime, Shakespeare would have been hard at work on the two plays that most editors agree were next in the sequence of his writing: *Romeo and Juliet* and *A Midsummer Night's Dream*. With these, Shakespeare was to enter on a new, more confident and lyrical phase that was to produce some of his most magical and universally popular plays. For the first time, he had a large company comprising many of the finest acting talents of the day at his disposal, supported by a more than adequate supply of enthusiastic apprentices of various ages, and a position among them that ensured

'I do remember an apothecary', *Romeo and Juliet*, V.i.37 (from the *Henry Irving Shakespeare*, 1892)

his voice would be heard. The five years that followed were also to see the creation of *King John, Richard II, The Merchant of Venice*, the two parts of *Henry IV, The Merry Wives of Windsor, Much Ado About Nothing, As You Like It*, and the second of the Roman plays, *Julius Caesar*. It was as though all the brakes and restrictions on his creativity he had suffered in the past were removed at a stroke. Though never exempt from those numerous hard choices and petty difficulties that theatrical conditions at all times impose on authors and players alike in bringing a new play to life on the stage, he now found himself with a straight path before him – one from which he was never to turn back.

Romeo and Juliet is the first of Shakespeare's undoubted masterpieces. The story was not new; orginating in folklore, it had gained wide currency in England through the publication of Arthur Brooke's poem, *Romeus*, in 1562. Its dramatic potential would have been obvious to Shakespeare's fellow sharers from the moment he first suggested it to them as a possible subject. Theatrically, the play has everything: 'a pair of star-crossed lovers', an Italian setting, sharply defined and believable characters, a nail-biting plot, and language ranging in tone from the grossly bawdy to the sublimely lyrical. In the frantic four days into which the plot is compressed, the whole life of a Renaissance city is brought before us in scenes of civil brawl, domestic turmoil, merriment, and sudden death. Nothing remotely like it had ever been put on the stage before.

It is a play of the summer, and is likely to have been first performed in James Burbage's Theatre, which lay across fields in the parish of St Leonard's, Shoreditch, just outside the Bishopsgate entrance to the City, in the summer of 1595. The Theatre's open thrust stage, closely encompassed by tiered galleries and a yard, accommodating some three thousand people all in intimate communication with the performers, offered an ideal venue for the expansive action of the play.

There were several doors at the back of the stage, one of them being used as a curtained entry point, from which, for example, Juliet could quickly appear to take the stage after the scene of the Romeo/Tybalt duel –

> Gallop apace, you fiery-footed steeds,
> Towards Phoebus' lodging. Such a waggoner
> As Phaeton would whip you to the west
> And bring in cloudy night immediately.　　　(III.ii.1–4)

– one of the most astonishing moments in the whole of Renaissance drama, which has the effect of changing the scene in an instant of time from Verona's sun-baked, blood-stained piazza, where the pronouncement of Romeo's banishment still hangs in the air, to the shadowed intimacy of Juliet's chamber. For the lovers, the time that keeps them apart cannot pass too quickly; when they are together they seek to delay it; this relativity of time is of the essence of the play. As audience, we are ahead of them both. We know how the story is to end because Shakespeare tells us in the Prologue, but nevertheless are kept in a state of suspenseful anxiety as we watch it unfold. He makes us care very much about the fate of all his characters.

The extreme youth of the lovers is vital to the play's credibility. Juliet's age is reduced by Shakespeare from sixteen in his immediate source to just short of fourteen, and was necessarily played by a boy of similar age. Romeo is young enough at the play's opening to be still in the thrall of calf-love; 'run through the ear with a love song', as Mercutio puts it, 'And is he a man to encounter Tybalt?' (II.iv.14–17). Plainly, he is not. At twenty-seven or eight, Richard Burbage would have been too mature a man to play the part convincingly or match with a thirteen-year-old Juliet. It would have gone to one of the older apprentices or younger sharers (Beeston, perhaps, or Condell), with Burbage as Mercutio and the comedian Pope as Capulet. That the small part of Peter, the Nurse's man, was intended for Kempe, we know from a 'rogue' direction in the Good Quarto text (at IV.v.99), 'Enter Will Kemp', copied no doubt from Shakespeare's manuscript, and that the Apothecary was written for his favourite thin man (John Sincler) is apparent from Romeo's description of him as a 'caitiff wretch', 'meagre' of looks, whose 'Sharp misery had worn him to the bones' (V.i.40 ff).

I have little doubt that the Chorus who speaks the Prologue and a linking narration after the masque (both in the form of a sonnet) was taken by Shakespeare in his dual capacity as poet and performer – a representative voice. It is a collective, not authorial, possessive he is using:

> Two households both alike in dignity
> (In fair Verona, where *we* lay *our* scene) . . .
>
> The fearful passage of their death-mark'd love . . .
> Is now the two hours' traffic of *our* stage;
> The which, if you with patient ears attend,
> What here shall miss, *our* toil shall strive to mend.

It was the first occasion on which he had begun a play with a prologue and spoken it himself, but it was not to be the last, and it did not preclude him – either here or later – from assuming other parts in the play that was to follow. The entrance of the Prince at an intermediate

111

point between the two choruses (at I.i.78) makes it unlikely, however, that this admittedly 'kingly' role was one of them; it is too similar in diction and insufficiently distinctive in character to make a viable double.[25] The disappearance of the Chorus from the play after the opening of Act 2, and the absence of a formal Epilogue,[26] suggest to me a change of mind: that Shakespeare had originally intended entering as poet at intervals throughout the play, but in the course of writing, finding further Chorus interjections unnecessary, rejected his initial idea in favour of doubling his choric role in the first two acts with that of the Friar, whose first entrance is in Act 2, Scene 3.

Friar Laurence is sometimes misconceived as a loquacious old dodderer who has nothing better to offer the desperate lovers than conventionally pious sentiments and a dubious 'magical potion'. When played in that way, the effect on the energy levels and pace of the performance can be near fatal. It is true that he speaks of his 'ancient ears', and his 'old feet' stumbling at graves; but Lady Capulet likewise refers to her 'old age' and she can be little more than twenty-eight. Like the passage of time, age in the play is relative. If the lovers are played as young as they should be, there is no need for the Friar to be more than middle-aged. He is the voice of prudence and conventional wisdom in the play, but also of good sense, and his strictures to the banished Romeo (in III.iii), if delivered with the authority and force that the situation requires, are necessary and effective in restoring the demoralised and near-hysterical youth to a semblance of manhood. However dubious the potion he prescribes for Juliet may appear to us now, it is, as he explains, a desperate remedy for a desperate situation, and it does in fact work; it is not his fault that the timing goes so disastrously wrong. Nor can we altogether blame him when, at a moment of crisis in the tomb, he loses his nerve. He does not have a superfluous line in the play, and his long, expository speech in the final scene – so often butchered in recent productions – is essential to the audience's understanding of the play's conclusion.[27]

There is a further consideration that may have weighed with Shakespeare in choosing to play the part himself, and it is one that introduces the more general question of the extent to which he was involved in directing this and other of his plays. He would have realised that the scenes in which, first Romeo, and then Juliet, come to the Friar's cell, positioned in the play as they are (Romeo's after the magical balcony scene), are ones in which the impetus of the performance might easily be lost, and that the necessarily limited experience of his young actors, however talented and well instructed, needed the stiffening of a seasoned adult for them to play against. If so, who better than himself?

The play was to make heavy demands on the company's apprentices – as the conjectural doubling plot I give in Appendix D demonstrates; for not only does it draw on them for its two leads and all the female characters, but also for most of its numerous servants, and Paris. It is sometimes assumed that, in the absence of a designated director, Elizabethan actors were left to find their own way about the stage; but, whatever may have happened elsewhere, in relation to Shakespeare and the Chamberlain's there is no call for any such unlikely assumption. As author, Shakespeare would have been present at morning rehearsals of his plays as a matter of course to explain how he had conceived the action, to elucidate his text where elucidation was needed, and choreograph movement on and off the stage. And that this was the normal practice is attested by Richard Flecknoe in his *Short Discourse of the English Stage* of 1664, where, looking back to that golden age of Shakespeare, Jonson, Beaumont and Fletcher, he tells us, 'It was the happiness of the Actors of those Times to have such Poets as these to instruct them, and write for them; and no less of those Poets to have such docile and excellent Actors to Act their Playes as a *Field* and *Burbidge*.'[28] The practice is confirmed by the testimony of a German scholar, Johannes Rhenanus, who, on a visit to England in 1611, observed that the English actors were 'daily instructed, as it were in a school, so that even the most eminent actors have to allow themselves to be taught their places by the dramatists, and this gives life and ornament to a well-written play, so that it is no wonder that the English players (I speak of skilled ones) surpass others and have the advantage over them'.[29] If this was true of men such as Burbage and Kempe, there can be no question whatever that it was true of the more junior members of the company.

113

As an actor himself, and one who, on most occasions, was to take part in the performances that followed, Shakespeare could not have been better placed to fulfil the function of instructor. The adult roles in his plays had been written for specific actors of experience with whom he enjoyed a ready rapport and mutual respect. It is the apprentices – especially here his Romeo and Juliet – who would have occupied most of his time in rehearsal, and his presence on stage with them as the Friar at critical moments of the performance would have been a further encouragement to them to give of their best. We know how good that best could be and, in particular, that a well-trained boy playing a female role was capable of winning an audience's complete belief in the truth of his impersonation.[30]

Not all the present-day functions of a director would have fallen to him, for Kempe, a renowned dancer in his day as well as the most popular comedian, would have been on hand to choreograph the masque;[31] Augustine Phillips, a versatile musician who was to bequeath four different instruments to his apprentices in his will of 1605, to organise the music; and Richard Burbage to arrange the fights. The book-keeper was, of course, in charge of the all-important prompt-copy, and was responsible for calling rehearsals, writing out the actors' parts and the backstage 'plot' to remind them of their entrance cues. A stage-keeper was in charge of any furniture required on stage, while the tireman looked after costumes and the smaller props. All the sharers would have had individual contributions to make to the preparation and performance of the plays, quite apart from their acting roles, and we know that Heminges came in time to carry most of the managerial and financial responsibility. It was a co-operative enterprise throughout: 'our scene', 'our stage', 'our toil'.

I have suggested that *Romeo and Juliet* was first performed in the summer season of 1595 at James Burbage's Theatre, the precise location of which has recently been confirmed as at the junction of Curtain Road and New Inn Yard, close to the present site of Liverpool Street Station.[32] We are not to suppose, however, that it enjoyed a continuous run of the kind we are accustomed to today; instead, single performances would have been slotted into the current repertoire with whatever frequency its popularity was found to justify.

If Shakespeare was so fully engaged in rehearsal and performance as I have claimed, we may justifiably wonder how he found time to write two new plays in each of the years between 1595 and 1599 as he is known to have done. The company's London seasons were not of course continuous through the year; apart from other interruptions (touring commitments, eruptions of plague and civil disturbance), the lack of indoor venues in the winter would have prevented that. But clearly he must often have been under considerable pressure. A rare intimation of that pressure emerges from a stray note of John Aubrey's, deriving from Kit Beeston (who may have shared lodgings with him in the period) through his son William, who was contemporary with Aubrey. 'He was not a company keeper', we are told, 'lived in Shoreditch, wouldnt be debauched, & if invited to writ; he was in paine'.[33]

If Shakespeare's coaching of the company's apprentices had contributed to the success of *Romeo and Juliet,* it was to be a crucial factor in the staging of *A Midsummer Night's Dream* in the autumn and winter of the same year: for out of a cast of twenty-two named characters, at least ten including five of the major roles were to be played by the same apprentices – a remarkable tribute to their abilities and Shakespeare's confidence in them.

The *Dream* is by general consensus Shakespeare's most lyrical play; it is also the most magical. Unusually, the plot appears to have been largely of his own invention, and may in part have been inspired by a request from some highly placed courtier to provide entertainment for a family wedding celebration; and certainly, its theme of the consummation of love in marriage would have made it an ideal choice for such an occasion. Of the various court weddings known to have taken place in the period, the one most likely to have occasioned it is that of Sir George Carey's daughter Elizabeth to Thomas, son of Lord Berkeley, at Blackfriars on 19 February 1596; Elizabeth was the granddaughter of Lord Hunsdon, the company's patron, whom Sir George was to succeed as Lord Chamberlain in 1597. Much has been made of some complimentary references in the play to the Queen as suggesting she was present, and that this was its first performance. It is also said that Sir George maintained a musical *schola* at the time on which Shakespeare might have drawn for his fairies. But as we have seen in relation to *Romeo*, Shakespeare had a sufficiency of boys in the company without any need to draw on outside resources, and the title page to the Quarto text of 1600 specifically states that it had been 'sundry times *publickely* acted, by the Right honourable, the Lord Chamberlaine his servants'.[34] As Stanley Wells points out, 'If Shakespeare's company could at any time muster enough boys for public performance, we have no reason to doubt that it could have done so from the start'.[35] We know, moreover, that the company was paid for court performances at Richmond that Christmas, both before and shortly after the date of the Carey wedding (on 26, 27 and 28 December 1595, and 6 January and 22 February 1596) and, as the *Dream* was almost certainly one of the plays performed, the references to the Queen could just as easily have been inserted then.[36]

It is of course a midsummer play; the lovers sleep out in the wood, and Titania lies on a 'bank where the wild thyme blows,/Where oxlips and the nodding violet grows', but is unique in that seven or eight of its nine scenes take place at night or in the early dawn, lit by moonlight. The moon, indeed, is the presiding luminary planet in the play, as its opening lines establish:

> Now, fair Hippolyta, our nuptial hour
> Draws on apace; four happy days bring in
> Another moon: but O, methinks, how slow
> This old moon wanes!

Though many of the later plays intended for performance in public theatres open to the elements such as the Rose and the Theatre contain night scenes, and the convention was one readily accepted by Elizabethan audiences, there would have been little point in writing a play in which such scenes predominate unless it was intended for indoor performance where the artificial light of candles would have aided its mysterious effect. It is difficult to imagine its being played on the open stage of the Theatre on dank afternoons in the depths of an English winter, by all accounts an exceptionally severe one.

The play was probably rehearsed in the late summer of 1595, using boys who were then appearing in *Romeo*, and acted indoors (both publicly and privately) during the autumn and winter that followed, with performances in the Theatre withheld until the spring and early summer of 1596. In view of the situation in London, where inns such as the Cross Keys were in process of being closed to the players by City ordinance and where James Burbage's plans to open an indoor playhouse in one of the buildings of the former Blackfriars' Priory had yet to reach fulfilment, the *Dream* may, in fact, have opened out of town, where indoor performance was the norm. We know that the company was in Cambridge and Ipswich before 29 September 1595, and that in Ipswich the players received a record reward from the town's bailiffs of 40s for their initial performance in the Guildhall.[37]

The ancient Guildhall in Ipswich would have been familiar to Shakespeare from his earlier visits to the town with Worcester's and the Admiral's men, and though space was limited there, the bailiffs'

The Gild or Moot Hall in Ipswich. In the fifteenth century, a Dutch carver had been paid to wainscot the interior of the upper floor, and a painter employed to decorate a cloth with the arms of the king, St George, and the Borough to cover the end wall behind a dais. It was demolished in 1812 (from a nineteenth-century print)

117

play was followed by others for the public at large to attend – probably in the same venue.

Accumulating indications from what has been said already of Shakespeare's roles in the plays suggest that he liked to be on stage at their opening (if not to open them himself), and that he usually contrived to be there again for their final scenes – leaving himself both time and opportunity to work with his fellows on other parts of the plays.[38] We have seen him doing just this in *Titus*, the *Comedy of Errors, Love's Labour's Lost*, and *Romeo*. And so, I believe, he did in the *Dream*, playing Theseus, to whom, though widely acknowledged King of Athens, he gives the lesser title of Duke, as with three of his previous 'kingly' roles.

With so many parts being played by the company's apprentices, the casting would have made only modest demands on the sharers. All we know of the boys who played the girls' parts is that Hermia was short in stature and Helena tall, and we find the same contrast between Hero and Beatrice in *Much Ado About Nothing*, Celia and Rosalind in *As You Like It*, and Maria and Viola in *Twelfth Night*. The two male lovers Lysander and Demetrius would have been drawn from the older apprentices (Romeo and Paris?), with Pope or Bryan as the pompous father, Egeus, and Heminges perhaps as Philostrate, the Master of Revels at Theseus' court. We can be more confident of three of the mechanicals: Cowley and Kempe as Quince and Bottom, and Sincler as Starveling; for Cowley and Kempe were to play in similar relation to each other as Verges and Dogberry in *Much Ado*, where Shakespeare records the actors' names, and 'Sinklo' as Starveling is in line with his casting in thin-man roles in all the plays in which we know him to have featured. This was not so much a matter of type-casting as that Shakespeare wrote these parts especially for him, as he wrote for other members of the company who are not so clearly distinguishable because we know too little about them as individuals; it is only by virtue of Sinklo's unusual physique that we are able to identify him in some of the parts that he played. In writing his plays, Shakespeare was engaged in creating roles for particular actors to inhabit, not character types to which they might be fitted. That is why, when embodied by sensitive performers, they come over still as human beings rather than as puppets of the dramatist's imagination.[39]

William Kempe is often dismissed or patronised as one of the blabbing clowns condemned by Hamlet as speaking 'more than is set down for them'; but we should take note of the progressively more complex roles that Shakespeare writes for him, from that of Launce in the *Two Gentlemen* with his simple but hilarious monologues, through the Dromios – a *tour de force* of doubling requiring extraordinary acting skills – to Bottom, who proves in the play to draw on surprising philosophical depths. And there were greater challenges for him ahead! Among the fairies, only Oberon requires more authority than a skilled apprentice could be expected to supply, and calls out for the experience and *élan* of Burbage; in the magical world of the wood, the disparity of age between Titania and himself would not have been a problem.

As the unashamedly lowbrow humour of Launce and Crab had done in the *Two Gentlemen*, the play of Pyramus and Thisbe, which the mechanicals are shown as rehearsing at intervals throughout the *Dream*, serves to anchor the courtly intrigues of the lovers in the plebeian realities of life as experienced by the artisans of Athens, and more immediately those of the groundlings who, in the summer of 1596, would have crowded the yard of the Theatre in Shoreditch. And there is surely here, on Shakespeare's part, an element of self-parody that would have delighted his fellows. For Peter Quince is not just the book-keeper for the play but also, it appears, the poet; receiving the idiotic objections to his text and suggestions for its improvement put forward by Bottom and the others with judicious gravity and, in the performance before the Duke that brings the comedy of the play to a glorious climax, speaking his own Prologue and making such a hash of it!

In this most fruitful and prolific period of his creativity, Shakespeare was now to switch the focus of his attention back to history. The date of *King John* is uncertain, but as I find it hard to believe that having once embarked on his second great history cycle beginning with *Richard II*, he would have wished to return to the much earlier reign of John before going on to continue the series with the two parts of *Henry IV*, I incline to date *John* the earlier: to

119

the winter of 1595/6 (following closely on the *Dream*), with *Richard* in the summer of 1596, and *Henry IV* in the winter that followed. I am referring here to their *production* dates.[40] As these plays were to provide him with some of the largest and most significant roles of his acting career, and in writing and performing them he was to pursue an intense and abiding interest in the nature and limits of kingship, I defer consideration of them to the following chapter, where I shall be looking at other of his 'kingly' parts and can relate them to each other. In what remains of the present chapter, I confine myself to the two remaining comedies of the period: *The Merchant of Venice* and *Much Ado About Nothing*.

A date sometime in the autumn of 1596 for the *Merchant*, proposed by Chambers, is supported by the later discovery that Antonio's 'wealthy Andrew dock'd in sand/Vailing her high top lower than her ribs/To kiss her burial' (I.i.27–9) derives her name from that of a Spanish galleon captured at Cadiz in 1596, the news of which reached England in July of that year. The historical *Andrew* had been captured when it ran aground in the approaches to Cadiz, and when brought to England narrowly escaped a similar fate on sands in the King's Channel off Chatham, suggesting to Shakespeare the fate of Antonio's *Andrew*.[41]

The play brings together two quite different stories – neither of Shakespeare's invention but deriving from ancient tradition. One concerns the wooing of Portia by Bassanio and the love-test of the caskets; the other that of a rapacious usurer (Shylock) who seeks the death of a rival merchant (Antonio) by imposing the forfeit of a pound of his flesh as penalty for failure to repay a loan he has made him by the due date. Nor was Shakespeare the first to bring the stories together. His immediate source is disputed and need not concern us. For all its fairy-tale improbabilities, his masterly handling of this material ensures that the play in performance carries its audience with it in ready suspension of disbelief. There is much true Shakespearean magic in the play that in later times has often been dimmed by miscast or routine productions, or over-familiarity on the part of jaded theatre critics.

As an exemplar of unstinting generosity to his friend, Antonio –
the merchant of the title – is the central figure, and the indications
are that Shakespeare played it. He is there at the play's beginning to
speak its opening lines and initiate the plot, returns for the pivotal
scene with Shylock to negotiate the loan, and again for the trial, but
otherwise remains largely on the margins of the action; a characteristic procedure that allowed him time (with a minimum of lines to
learn) to guide the players in rehearsal and also to be with them on
stage at critical moments of performance. When, in the final scene,
he appears once more to receive the unexpected but welcome news
of the safe return of three of his ships, he gives himself one of the
shortest lines in the play, 'I am dumb!', and has only three more
lines to add to it before the close.

Shakespeare would have been thirty-two in 1596; again, as for the
lovers in *Romeo* and the *Dream*, it is essential for Bassanio and
Portia to be appreciably younger, and the same is true for Bassanio's
companions, who would all have been drawn from the company's
apprentices and younger sharers.

Portia especially (Plate 9) needs to be played as she describes
herself in the scene of Bassanio's choosing of the caskets, as

> . . . an unlesson'd girl, unschool'd, unpractised,
> Happy in this, she is not yet so old
> But she may learn: happier than this,
> She is not bred so dull but she can learn . . . (III.ii.159–62)

She does, and gains in experience and authority through the play;
but from her opening scene with Nerissa, through all of the casket
scenes to this one and beyond, we need to see that she has still some
way to go in that learning process.

The play would have been performed in repertoire with *Romeo*
and the *Dream*, and the first performances of all three plays are near
enough together in time for the same pair of boys to have played
consecutively, on the one side, as the mute Rosalind of *Romeo*,
Helena and Portia (tall and fair), and on the other, as Juliet, Hermia
and Nerissa (small and dark in colouring). Older sharers would have

taken the Duke, Morocco, Tubal, and Portia's stately servant Balthazar: 'Madam, I go with all convenient speed' (III.iv.56) – one of the biggest laughs in the play if his exit is taken with due deliberation.[42] There is obvious scope for doubling. Perhaps Shakespeare wrote another role for his favourite thin man (Sinklo) in the proud, ridiculous figure of Arragon, confronting a jester's head on a stick. 'Did I deserve no more than a fool's head?', he asks into a resounding silence, 'Is that my prize? are my deserts no better?' (II.ix.59–60). That Kempe was Launcelot Gobbo is a near certainty, and represents a return to his original stage persona as rustic clown. If we were right to cast him and Cowley as Bottom and Verges in the *Dream*, the partnership may well have extended to what is here little more than a double-act for young and old Gobbo.

Shylock may equally well have gone to the veteran Bryan as to Burbage; neither would have been inhibited from playing him as the villain that Shakespeare intended – motivated by envy and malice throughout, caring more for his money than he does for his daughter. That he is a villain conceived in human terms, who even in the frustration of his evil purpose in the trial commands our pity in face of the cruel baiting he receives, is testimony (if one were needed) to Shakespeare's largeness of vision. Though a Jew, he is not represented as typical of his race or religion; on the contrary, he is described as a devil 'in the *likeness* of a Jew' (III.i.20).[43]

If, as proposed, its composition was completed in the late summer of 1596 – though naturally Shakespeare would have begun work on it some months earlier – the play would have fitted well into the company's autumn and winter seasons of that year, and would have been equally effective in both indoor and open-air venues. The play begins in daylight and the text is suggestive of exterior settings. Towards the end of Act 2, there is talk of evening and dinner. Jessica, Shylock's daughter, is stolen away in darkness, and it is nine o'clock when Antonio interrupts preparations for a masque to hurry Gratiano away to join Bassanio for his voyage to Belmont. For the Belmont scenes we are in daylight until the final act which, like that of the *Dream*, is set wholly outdoors and at night, lit by a fitful moon. On the open stages of the Theatre or its neighbour the

Curtain, the natural light of the afternoon would by then have been drawing in, and the introduction of candles and torches on stage, with perhaps Portia and Nerissa approaching through a darkening yard, would have had a magical effect.[44]

Portia:	That light we see is burning in my hall:
	How far that little candle throws his beams!
	So shines a good deed in a naughty world.
Nerissa:	When the moon shone we did not see the candle.
Portia:	So doth the greater glory dim the less . . . (V.i.89–93)

Here music sounds 'much sweeter than by day', differences between the lovers are resolved, and Antonio's and Lorenzo's fortunes are repaired. Only Shylock remains disturbingly outside the circle of love and reconciliation.

We cannot be sure of the theatre in which the *Merchant* was first performed. Though James Burbage had completed his purchase of a building in Blackfriars, he was prevented from opening it as an indoor theatre by an objecting petition from important residents of the estate – including, oddly enough, Sir George Carey who, in July of that year, was to succeed his father as Lord Hunsdon and the company's patron. To be patron of a highly regarded band of players was one thing; to have them as near neighbours in a public playhouse was quite another and not to be endured! As the City inns were also now closed to them, Shakespeare may again have taken the cast of his new play out of town for their final rehearsals and an opening in the Market Hall of Faversham in Kent, where we find them 'aboute Lamas' (1 August) receiving 16*s* from Mr Saker, the Mayor.[45]

If, as was usual elsewhere, the Mayor's performance at Faversham was followed by public shows in the same venue or, if that was not available, one of the town's inns, the company may still have been there or in the vicinity when Shakespeare received the dreadful news of the death of his eleven-year-old son Hamnet in Stratford. He would have hurried home to comfort Anne and Hamnet's surviving twin sister Judith, though it is hardly possible that he was in time for the funeral on 11 August.[46] The first London performance of the

The Town or Market Hall in Faversham dates from *c.* 1575 and, though much altered in the eighteenth century, retains a traditional structure (after a drawing by T.M. Baynes in 1830, by permission of the Centre for Kentish Studies, Maidstone)

Merchant, then, was probably one of those given at Whitehall for the Queen and court at Christmas or New Year 1596/7, for which Thomas Pope and John Heminges received the Queen's reward on behalf of their fellows.[47]

If Shakespeare had wished to express his grief at the death of Hamnet, it is hidden away in *Richard II* or *Henry IV*, which he went on to write in the year that followed; but I doubt that he allowed events in his personal life, whether distressful or joyful, to impinge in that immediate way on his writing. The actor goes on stage and fulfils his professional commitment to the play and his fellows whatever his state of mind or the nature of his role, and so, I believe, did Shakespeare in his work as a dramatist. If events of that kind were to find an echo in the plays, it would be very much later: perhaps this particular grief lingers in the haunting epitaph that Cymbeline's sons were to speak over Fidele:

Fear no more the heat o' the sun,
    Nor the furious winter's rages,
Thou thy worldly task has done,
    Home art gone and ta'en thy wages.
Golden lads and girls all must,
    As chimney-sweepers, come to dust . . .

Four histories in a row would have been too much of a good thing even for an Elizabethan audience, and between the second part of *Henry IV* and its sequel, *Henry V*, belongs one of the three most perfect comedies Shakespeare was ever to write: *Much Ado About Nothing*. It was not included in Meres' listing of his plays in *Palladis Tamia*, entered in the Stationers' Register on 7 September 1598, and we know that William Kempe, who is mentioned in Shakespeare's text as playing Dogberry, left the company early in 1599, which makes *Much Ado* a play for the autumn and winter of 1598/9, acted perhaps more often indoors than out. Again, there are several notable night scenes, including, of course, the setting of the watch; and when, in the penultimate scene of Act 5, Claudio and the Prince visit what they believe to be Hero's tomb they are followed by 'three or four with tapers'.

Though it would have gone down very well with that section of the public who are more attracted by easy laughs than subtleties of meaning, there is more in the title than first appears; certainly, 'much ado', but it is only late in the action that we discover it is all 'about nothing'. Like the *Merchant*, the play combines two separate stories of ancient origin: the attempted sabotage of a marriage that is due to take place between Hero and Claudio by means of a slander against Hero's reputation, involving impersonation of her by one of her gentlewomen, and the contrivance of a marriage between two notorious mockers against love and marriage (Beatrice and Benedick) by the spreading of false reports that each is secretly in love with the other. There is a satisfying symmetry here: a marriage threatened and a marriage achieved, and both by reports that are false; the first eventually revealed to be so, the second found after all to be true. The author of the second, more fortunate invention is the Prince of the play, Don Pedro, and all he intends is a mischievous joke against Benedick; the prime mover in the attempt to blacken Hero's name is the Prince's bastard brother, Don John, who is resentful of his brother's friendship with Claudio. The masterly way in which Shakespeare integrates the two stories and brings them to simultaneous climax in the church scene of the play must be left to the theatre-goer to enjoy.

Shakespeare's role is Leonato, the father of Hero, the slandered bride. He speaks the opening line of the play and is there at its close; if, at thirty-four, he was young for the part it was not by much, for Hero can be little more in age than fifteen, as was his own daughter, Susanna. The emotional drive of Leonato's speeches in the latter part of the play herald a new kind of dramatic utterance – new in his own work and that of any other – that was to find fuller expression in the great tragedies that lay ahead. This to Leonato's elder brother, Antonio, who had attempted to comfort him in his grief and anger on Hero's behalf:

> I pray thee cease thy counsel
> Which falls into mine ears as profitless
> As water in a sieve. Give not me counsel,
> Nor let no comforter delight mine ear
> But such a one whose wrongs do suit with mine.
> Bring me a father that so lov'd his child,
> Whose joy of her is overwhelm'd like mine,
> And bid him speak of patience;
> Measure his woe the length and breadth of mine,
> And let it answer every strain for strain,
> As thus for thus, and such a grief for such,
> In every lineament, branch, shape, and form.
> If such a one will smile and stroke his beard,
> Bid sorrow wag, cry 'Hem!' when he should groan,
> Patch grief with proverbs, make misfortune drunk
> With candle-wasters, bring him yet to me,
> And I of him will gather patience . . .   (V.i.3–19)

If Shakespeare can be said anywhere in his writing to have 'unlocked his heart', it was in speeches like this.

The part is of medium size (334 lines as against Benedick's 430, and the Prince's 320). While Benedick's wit and skill with words call out for Burbage, I give Shakespeare the smaller role the more confidently in the belief that the kingly part of Don Pedro, the Prince, should be played by an actor much younger than himself – one more of an age with Claudio, who is in his late teens or early twenties.[48] When Leonato and Antonio confront the two young men after the church scene in which Claudio has rejected Hero at the altar with the Prince's support, the normal deference they give to the Prince is overborne by indignation at his and Claudio's acceptance of Hero's guilt, and Antonio goes so far as to address them as 'Boys, apes, braggarts, Jacks, milksops!', and again as 'Scambling, outfacing, fashion-monging boys'. Leonato, who up to this point has tried to restrain his brother, answers a further refusal by the Prince to hear him with a curt 'No? Come, brother, away! I will be heard' and exits in anger.

The master-stroke by which Hero is finally vindicated is Shakespeare's invention of the incomparable Dogberry and his band of idiot watchmen, who are supposed to be guarding Leonato's house from intruders. By sheer chance, they overhear an incriminating conversation between the two rogues whom Don John had employed to stage the scene, witnessed by Claudio and the Prince, which has persuaded them of her unworthiness; but will they have the sense to make known their discovery of the plot, and do it in time? Anxiety remains.

The character of Dogberry, a pompous and very stupid local official who is nevertheless convinced of his own sagacity and importance, is one of the joys of the play. Here, there can be no doubt whatever that it was played by Kempe for Shakespeare prefaces some of his lines in his manuscript with the actor's name rather than that of the character, and these have found their way into the Quarto and Folio texts. And nothing could be more conclusive of Kempe's ability, for the part is not one for a 'clown' but for a true actor, in which the slightest hint of awareness in the performance that what he is saying may be considered funny – or indeed is anything less than the epitome of wisdom – kills the humour stone dead. I said earlier that Shakespeare was engaged in creating roles for actors, not character types to which they might be fitted. This is exemplified in Dogberry who, apart perhaps from sharing Bottom's self-conceit, has little in common with any of the previous characters that Kempe has played, and yet was specifically written for him.

Shakespeare was not much interested in the psychology of his characters, in their motivations or the 'whys' of their behaviour. There is no attempt to explain or justify Don John's 'discontent' – or, for that matter, why Iago hates Othello or Lear gives away his kingdom. Nor can they explain it themselves. Don John tells us, 'I am a plain-dealing villain . . . let me be that I am'. This, Shakespeare appears to be saying, is how things are; they are given to us as *data* we must accept if the story that follows is to make any sense. But these are just starting points. It is in the relations his characters are seen to have with each other, and the way these develop in response to changing circumstances and events, that the interest lies; and it is in the interchange of language between them – to be fully appreciated only when we hear it in performance – that the characters emerge in all their complexity of being. We know very well, of course, that they are not real – only characters in a play – but in watching the play we are persuaded to suspend that disbelief. Part of the illusion lies in their embodiment by the actors who inhabit them, but the more significant factor is the way in which they imitate life in their responses to each other and, in so doing, gain in awareness of themselves. 'All the world's a stage,/And all the men and women merely players', acting a series of roles; but conversely in Shakespeare's art, the players assume in their role-play with each other an uncanny resemblance to real men and women. Here also, *Much Ado* exemplifies the process, for as Claudio remains the rather shallow young man we suspect him to be from the beginning, and Dogberry as invincible in his ignorance and inviolable in his self-esteem, Beatrice and Benedick are transformed. As for Don John, Benedick has the last word;

> Think not on him till tomorrow; I'll devise thee brave
> punishments for him. Strike up, pipers!

EIGHT

He that Plays the King

To our English Terence Mr. Will: Shake-speare

Some say good *Will* (which I, in sport, do sing)
   Had'st thou not plaid some Kingly parts in sport,
Thou hadst bin a companion for a *King*;
And, beene a King among the meaner sort.
Some others raile; but raile as they thinke fit,
Thou hast no rayling, but, a raigning Wit:
   And honesty *thou sow'st, which they do reape;*
   So, to increase their Stocke which they do keepe.
               John Davies of Hereford, c. 1611[1]

He that plays the king shall be welcome; his Majesty shall have
tribute of me . . .

                          Hamlet, II.ii.318–19

While the old idea that each player in the Chamberlain's men had a characteristic 'line of parts' that was consistently adhered to in the casting of the plays is no longer accepted, we must allow that certain of the players came to be regarded as specialists in a certain broad category of role. The obvious examples are of Kempe and his successor Armin in 'clown' parts, and Sincler in 'thin-man' roles – though that, perhaps, was more of a physical limitation than a specialism. Was Shakespeare another in his playing of 'Kingly parts'? The first of the quotations above – from John Davies' *Scourge of Folly* – would seem to suggest so. 'If only you hadn't acted those kingly parts in plays', he is saying, 'you might have been a fit companion for kings, and have come to be regarded as something of a king yourself among ordinary people.' To judge of the reliability of Davies' evidence, we need to know a little more about him.

Born a year or two earlier than Shakespeare, he was the most renowned penman and writing master of his day, when the art of calligraphy was more valued than it is today, and a prolific versifier whose extant works fill two sizeable volumes. As a teacher of calligraphy, he numbered among his pupils the Earl of Northumberland and the Countess of Derby with their families, the Earl of Pembroke and, most exalted of all, King James's son and intended heir, Prince Henry. He is said by one of his pupils to have been a recusant Catholic. Apart from the epigram to Shakespeare, there are others in the same collection dedicated to Ben Jonson, Marston and Fletcher. He seems to have enjoyed a wide acquaintance with poets and other writers of the time including Nashe, Gabriel Harvey and Dekker, to all of whom he refers in his works. His attitude to the players – like most of his contemporaries – was ambivalent. He castigates them for their pride:

Contemporary portrait of John Davies of Hereford, *c.* 1562–1618 (from frontispiece to his *Complete Works*, published 1878)

130

But that which grates my *Galle*, and mads my *Muse*,
Is (ah that ever such just cause should *Bee*)
To see a *Player* at the put-downe *stewes**
Put up his *Peacocke's* Taile for al to see,
And for his hellish voice, as prowde as *hee*;
What *Peacocke* art thou prowd? Wherefore? because
Thou *Parrat*-like canst speake what is taught thee.
A *Poet* must teach thee from clause to clause,
Or thou wilt breake *Pronunciation's* Lawes.

– but praises them warmly in other respects, '*Players*, I love yee and your Qualitie', he tells us a few lines later,

As ye are Men, *that* pass-time not abus'd:
And some I love for *painting, poesie*,
And say fell *Fortune* cannot be excus'd,
That hath for better *uses* you refus'd:
Wit, Courage, good-shape, good partes, and all *good*,
As long as al these *goods* are no *worse* us'd,
And though the *stage* doth staine pure gentle *bloud*,
Yet generous yee are in minde and *moode*.[2]

And in the margin against the second line, 'And some I love for painting, poesie', Davies glosses the initials, 'W.S.R.B.': William Shakespeare and Richard Burbage, the latter known to have been a competent painter.

These are not Davies' only references to Shakespeare. In *Speculum Proditori* of 1616, he tells us, 'I knew a *Man*' – and by 'man' in this context was commonly meant an actor, as in 'Chamberlain's man' –

I knew a *Man*, unworthy as I am,
And yet too worthie for a *counterfeit*,

---

* As Davies explains in a note, the 'stewes' (brothels) 'once stoode where now Play-houses stand'.

Made once a *king*; who though it were in *game*,
Yet was it there where *Lords* and *Ladyes* met;
Who honor'd him, as hee had been the same,
And no subjective *dutie* did forget;
    When to him-selfe he smil'd, and said, lo here
    I have for noght, what *Kings* doe buy so deere.

No odds there was in shew (and but in show,
Kings are too often honour'd) save that *he*
Was but twelve gamesome *daies* to *king* it so:
And *kings*, more *yeares* of soveraigne misery.
His *raigne* was *short* and *sweet*, theirs *long* in *wo*.
He after liv'd: they, with or for *theirs*, die.
    He had a tast of *raigne*, with powre to leave;
    They cannot tast, but life must *take* or *give*.[3]

Grosart, his Victorian editor, interprets this as referring to 'private theatricals' in which Shakespeare had been invited to participate, but the place is more likely to have been the tiring house of one of the public theatres, and the 'twelve gamesome daies' a series of performances (not necessarily consecutive) in which he had played the part of a king. (We have seen that fourteen performances of *Henry VI* were given at the Rose in 1592.) That the players were accustomed to receive distinguished patrons in the tiring house appears from another quotation from the *Scourge of Folly*:

I came to English Aesop (on a tide)
    As he lay tirde (as tirde) before to play:

– meaning presumably 'attired', ready in costume –

I came unto him in his flood of pride;
He then was King, and thought I should obay.
And so I did, for with all reverence, I
As to my Soveraigne (though to him unknowne)
Did him approach; but loe, he casts his Eye,

> As if therein I had presumption showne:
> I, like a Subject (with submisse regard)
> Did him salute, yet he re-greeted mee
> But with a Nod, because his speech he spar'd
> For Lords and Knights that came his Grace to see.

Davies is greatly put out by Aesop's unceremonious nod, and takes it as cue for another attack on the players' pride. He blames himself for approaching Aesop in the way that he did when 'I well knew him (though he knew not me)'

> *To be a player, and for some new Crownes*
> *Spent on a Supper, any man may bee*
> *Acquainted with them, from their Kings to Clownes.*[4]

Again the ambivalence of his attitude comes to the fore – though in truth Aesop's casual acknowledgement of him may have been indicative of that state of mind that most actors experience in the half-hour or so before performance, in which (often quite unconsciously) they assume the manner of the character they are about to play, rather than intended as a deliberate snub. As to the identity of 'Aesop', he could just as well have been Burbage (who also played some notable kings including Richard III and Lear), but there can be little doubt of Davies' more intimate knowledge of Shakespeare, and genuine admiration for him in spite of what he saw as the unworthiness of his profession. It was with Shakespeare that he mainly associated 'kingly parts' and, as an almost exact contemporary, he was in a good position to know. With this in mind, let us briefly review Shakespeare's history plays up to 1599 and see what other indications we can find of the roles that he played in them.

In *Henry VI*, as I have already suggested, Shakespeare's part was almost certainly that of the young king, and in reading the play we find the character bears a curious stamp of detachment. From the opening scene of Part One, in which his presence is imagined off-

stage as an infant, Henry is presented as at once the fulcrum of
events and, by reason initially of his tender years and later of his
personal deficiencies of character, powerless to influence them. In
the bearpit of conflicting interests and self-seeking ambitions into
which the body politic has descended, his Christian virtues of piety
and desire for peace and reconciliation appear only as weakness,
and the few assertions of authority that he brings himself to make as
more disastrous in their effects than his more usual passivity.

His first entrance is in Act 3 of Part One, and his initial attempts
to reconcile his feuding uncles fall on deaf ears. In Part Two he
watches horrorstruck the innocent Humphrey arrested and taken
away, 'as the butcher takes away the calf . . . Bearing it to the
bloody slaughter-house', and is powerless to prevent it. When, in
Part Three at the culmination of his tragedy – which is also the
tragedy of England, with France lost and the country divided in
internecine strife – he is confronted by the murderous York, the poet
gives himself these lines:

> So flies the reckless shepherd from the wolf;
> So first the harmless sheep doth yield his fleece,
> And next his throat unto the butcher's knife.   (V.vi.7–9)

The image of the slaughter-house returns in force as an immediate
threat, and Henry goes on to ask – of York? the audience? perhaps
mainly himself –

> What scene of death hath Roscius now to act?

Roscius was, of course, the great Roman actor, cited by Elizabethans
as an ideal representative of the acting profession. The actor on
stage, performing the part of the deposed and threatened king,
becomes at this moment, in a deliberate confusion of identities, both
victim and observer in the scene of his own murder.

The play metaphor by which 'All the world's a stage,/And all the
men and women merely players' was not, of course, unique to
Shakespeare. It derived from the classical drama of Greece and

Rome, and had been employed before him by Kyd, Marlowe and many lesser writers. Indeed, by the 1590s, it may already have become something of a cliché. But no other dramatist had ever used it with more subtle, discreet or telling effect than Shakespeare was to do. We shall be considering his recourse to it more fully in the following chapter, but the sense of disjunction it here provides between actor and role – the sudden shock of self-awareness in the character as to who he is and what he is doing in relation to those around him – is not confined to Henry VI; we shall come to recognise it also in others of his characters and plays, notably in *Richard II* and *Hamlet*. It will be seen to have a particular relevance to Shakespeare's dual occupations as poet and performer.

Richard III had probably been written for Edward Alleyn, and when performed by the Chamberlain's men in its due place as sequel to the three *Henry VI* plays was to provide Burbage with one of his most famous roles. He is the joker in Shakespeare's pack of kings. A monstrous creation of unalloyed, unblushing villainy, whose demonic energy and black humour recall the Vice of the old interludes and moralities, he is a character with whom Richard explicitly associates himself in an aside:

> Thus, like the formal Vice, Iniquity,
> I moralize two meanings in one word.   (III.i.82–3)

In the opening speech of the play, he buttonholes the audience into complicity by telling them plainly what he is about, for

> . . . since I cannot prove a lover
> To entertain these fair well-spoken days,
> I am determined to prove a villain,
> And hate the idle pleasures of these days.
> Plots have I laid, inductions dangerous,
> By drunken prophecies, libels, and dreams,
> To set my brother Clarence and the King
> In deadly hate, the one against the other . . .   (I.i.28–35)

I have said that Shakespeare created roles for actors rather than character types; but with Richard he goes a step further, for Richard is himself an inveterate role-player, a man who invents a whole series of characters to play in the deception of others and achievement of his ultimate purpose to be King: to Clarence, the sympathetic brother; to Lady Anne, the impassioned lover; to the citizens of Act 3, the saintly recluse. He even takes it upon himself to prompt others in the art, and finds an equally adept performer in Buckingham.

Richard: Come, cousin, canst thou quake and change thy
      colour,
      Murder thy breath in middle of a word,
      And then again begin, and stop again,
      As if thou were distraught and mad with terror?

Buckingham: Tut, I can counterfeit the deep tragedian,
      Speak, and look back, and pry on every side,
      Tremble and start at wagging of a straw,
      Intending deep suspicion. Ghastly looks
      Are at my service like enforced smiles,
      And both are ready in their offices
      At any time to grace my stratagems.   (III.v.1–11)

The theatre imagery continues into Act 4, in which Richard's mother, the old Duchess of York, joins with the widows of Henry VI and Edward IV (Margaret and Elizabeth) in lamenting Richard's innocent victims, who now include Margaret's husband and son, Elizabeth's young sons, and Clarence. It is an extraordinary scene, and we must assume there were present in the company older apprentices or hired men who were capable of playing these three embittered women, in their passionate reproaches to each other and imprecations on Richard, in such a way as to compel belief in the truth of their performances. Margaret describes the events she has witnessed as a 'dire induction' (prologue) to the tragedy that is still to unfold; the Duchess speaks of 'Woe's scene, world's shame, grave's due by life usurp'd;/Brief abstract and record of tedious days' (IV.iv.27–8); and Margaret of 'this frantic play'; addressing her successor, Elizabeth, as

> . . . poor shadow, painted queen,
> The presentation of but what I was;
> The flattering index of a direful pageant . . .
> A queen in jest, only to fill the scene.   (IV.iv.83–5, 91)

It is in Act 4 that Richard attains the crown, and in this final role he is not so impressive; he makes mistakes, forgets his lines. When, on the eve of Bosworth, he is assailed by a long procession of ghosts of those he has murdered, his former confidence in his identity as villain is fractured by stirrings of conscience and, in the course of a tragi-comic sequence of questions and answers, incongruously recalling Launcelot Gobbo's debate with himself in the *Merchant* ('"Budge", says the fiend, – "Budge not!" says my conscience'), he is brought to the edge of despair.

> O coward conscience, how dost thou afflict me!
> The lights burn blue; it is now dead midnight.
> Cold fearful drops stand on my trembling flesh.
> What do I fear? Myself? There's none else by;
> Richard loves Richard, that is, I and I.
> Is there a murderer here? No. Yes, I am!
> Then fly. What, from myself? Great reason why,
> Lest I revenge? What, myself upon myself?
> Alack, I love myself. Wherefore? For any good
> That I myself have done unto myself?
> O no, alas, I rather hate myself
> For hateful deeds committed by myself.
> I am a villain – yet I lie, I am not! . . .   (V.iii.180–92)

The play has the longest cast-list of any in the canon and names some fifty-two speaking roles. Even when we have subtracted the female characters and boys who would have been played by apprentices (doubling as necessary with unnamed messengers and other minor roles as well as with each other), it could not have been played by less than a full complement of sharers with the addition of several hired men, and the only one of them who would not have been required to double was Burbage as Richard. This is true even of the shorter Quarto versions, in which several characters are combined and others excised altogether.[5] There is no part in the play for a clown other than Richard himself, who contains in his role as Vice both villain and joker. But this does not mean that Kempe would have had the day off! He was too versatile and useful an actor to be left aside in that way. He could have played the First Murderer (who is 'strong-framed' as Costard was said to be of 'great limb or joint') with Cowley or Sincler as his reluctant assistant in Act 1, Scene 4, and the nervously compliant Mayor of Act 3, Scene 7. A touch of humour in the playing of both would not have come amiss (nor would it today) in a play that has so much the character of a latter-day morality.

Shakespeare would not have been exempt from the general necessity for doubling, and I give him Clarence in Act 1 and Richmond in Act 5: Clarence because, though relatively small, the exceptional demands that the part makes of the actor in the handling of its verse are of the kind that, as author, he was ideally equipped to supply, and Richmond because it qualifies in every respect as one of those kingly roles with which he was especially associated, and which by now he would have acquired a practised skill in performing. The accuracy with which both parts are recollected in the reconstituted Quarto text of 1597 supports the view that he had played them.[6] Richmond is presented as quietly confident in the justice of his cause and the constancy of his supporters, whereas Richard is shown (with good reason) as distrustful of his. While Richmond commits his cause to God and contemplates the possibility of defeat with resignation, Richard can appeal only to the pride of his soldiers, and recommends that 'Our strong arms be our conscience, swords our law'. 'March on', he tells them in a last defiant throw,

> Let us to it pell-mell –
> If not to Heaven, then hand in hand to Hell!

From this time on, Shakespeare and Burbage were to divide the kingly parts between them, with Burbage taking the larger, more extrovert roles (Henry V, Antony and Lear) and Shakespeare most, if not all, of the others – Alonso, Duncan and John, as well as previously, the king or duke of the comedies.

King John, as we have seen, probably belongs to the winter of 1595/6, along with the *Dream* – though it could not be more different in feeling. If not in the first division of Shakespeare's plays, it must be placed near the top of the second. Written wholly in verse of a strikingly direct and muscular kind, its first two acts sweep through with only a single change of scene – from England to France at the end of Act 1.

The opening lines set the businesslike tone.

John:	Now say, Chatillon, what would France with us?
Chatillon:	Thus, after greeting, speaks the King of France,
	In my behaviour, to the majesty,
	The borrowed majesty, of England here.
Q. Eleanor:	A strange beginning – 'borrowed majesty'?
John:	Silence, good mother; hear the embassy.
Chatillon:	Philip of France, in right and true behalf
	Of thy deceased brother Geoffrey's son,
	Arthur Plantagenet, lays most lawful claim
	To this fair island . . .

The dubiety of John's claim to the English throne is signalled as clearly as Shakespeare dared in the political climate of the 1590s by the strange little scene with the Faulconbridge brothers that follows, in which the elder brother's title to his dead father's estate is preferred to that of the younger, to whom it had been bequeathed by the father's will; for by the same token, on King Richard's death, the crown should properly have gone to Geoffrey's son Arthur, and not to him. The elder brother, Philip, is recognised by Queen Eleanor and John, moreover, as the illegitimate son of Richard (the Lionheart), and is named thereafter as the Bastard.

In Act 2, set beneath the walls of Angers, the action takes the form of a series of formal exchanges between the opposing kings, enlivened by a slanging match in which Eleanor and Constance, Arthur's mother, trade insults, with ironic asides from the Bastard. To his disgust, Hubert, who first appears as spokesman for the citizens of Angers, brokers a marriage alliance between the two sides by which Arthur is granted nominal title to Brittany, and all John's territories in France are ceded to the French Dauphin.

> Mad world, mad kings, mad composition!

– the Bastard comments in his role as informal Chorus to the play.

Act 3 brings the intervention of the Pope's emissary, Cardinal Pandulph, who, in response to John's refusal to admit Stephen Langton to the see of Canterbury, imposes excommunication on him, the effect of which is to rekindle conflict between England and France and leads to John's imprisonment of Arthur.

Shakespeare, who would have been at this time under pressure to produce more plays for the still under-provided company, drew largely for his structure and sequence of scenes on the anonymous *Troublesome Reign of King John* (1591), which in turn looked back to John Bale's interlude of *King Johan*, a piece of blatant anti-papal propaganda, performed before Cranmer. But Shakespeare's treatment of John is very different to theirs. In Bale, he is a proto-Protestant martyr, poisoned by a monk; in the *Troublesome Reign*, a repentant sinner and, in his dying speech, a prophet;

> I am not he shall buyld the Lord a house,
> Or roote these Locusts from the face of earth:
> But if my dying heart deceave me not,
> From out these loynes shall spring a Kingly braunch
> Whose armes shall reach unto the gates of *Rome*,
> And with his feete treade downe the Strumpets pride,
> That sits upon the chaire of *Babylon*.[7]

Shakespeare is having none of this. His John is a usurper and a cold-blooded murderer – an unrepentant one at that. (When he changes his mind about Arthur, it is not through any moral considerations.) On the controversial question of relations with Rome, Shakespeare is careful to maintain a neutral position. The points at issue are clearly stated but not in such a way as to give offence to either party. The ludicrous scene in the *Troublesome Reign* in which the Bastard, in search of monastic gold, discovers a nun hiding in a chest and a friar in the nun's cupboard, is thankfully omitted, and Pandulph puts the case for the Pope in Act 3 fairly and with impressive authority.[8]

At the opening of Act 4, the action of the play, which up to this point has required a large, open stage and daylight for its performance, narrows in focus to Orford Castle and its surroundings.

Orford Castle, Suffolk, where the last two acts of *King John* are set, as it appeared in 1600. From its walls Arthur is said to have fallen to his death:

The wall is high, and yet I will leap down.
Good ground, be pitiful and hurt me not!
There's few or none do know me; if they did,
This ship-boy's semblance hath disguised me quite.
I am afraid, and yet I'll venture it.
If I get down and do not break my limbs,
I'll find a thousand shifts to get away.
As good to die and go as die and stay.   (IV.iii. 1–8)

(from John Norden's *Survey of the Manor of Sudbourne*, 1600–2, by permission of English Heritage (National Monuments Record))

It is in the dungeons of Orford – of which historically Hubert de Burgh was Keeper – that the play's most famous scene of Hubert's attempted blinding of Arthur is set.[9] The voice of the angel ('an angel spake') that heralds Pandulph's approach to the invading French in Scene 2 of Act 5 is, I suggest, a rumble of thunder, and the final scenes take place in gathering gloom, lit by lanterns. As John dies miserably in the orchard of Swineshead Abbey, Pandulph negotiates a peace, and the English nobles, who have deserted John for the French on the death of Arthur, return to their allegiance.

The play offers three magnificent roles – John, the Bastard and Hubert – as well as a number of meaty supporting parts including Pandulph, King Philip and Louis of France, and for the older apprentices, Eleanor and Constance. There is an obvious cameo for Sincler in the 'half-faced' Robert Faulconbridge, the Bastard's younger brother. Again, there is no part for a 'clown', but there is a small but fitting one for Kempe in the lion-clad Duke of Austria.

As the bluff and extrovert Bastard would surely have gone to Burbage, with Sly perhaps as Hubert, we cannot deny John to Shakespeare. (Again, he speaks the opening line and is there, though dead, at the close.) As in *Henry VI*, he is the focus of the action but in responding to events rather than initiating them; unsure of himself, dependent for the strength that he lacks on the support of others, notably Eleanor, Hubert and the Bastard. Deprived of that support – Eleanor disappears from the play after Act 3, and Hubert is disabled by his pity for Arthur – he flounders. Only the Bastard remains quixotically loyal to the end. There is no separation here between the man and his role, and little apparent interior life. He is given less than a dozen lines of soliloquy – and they are of the bleakest. This, an aside:

> Withhold thy speed, dreadful Occasion!
> O, make a league with me till I have pleased
> My discontented peers. What? Mother dead?
> How wildly then walks my estate in France!   (IV.ii.125–8)

And later in the scene, when he is left alone, he repeats despairingly, 'My mother dead!' For a title role, the part is small, barely 400 lines against the Bastard's 520. Though present on stage for much of the action, John is laconic in his responses or uncomfortably silent; he has no more than three or four lengthy speeches. The part is all in the acting: a fearful, haunted presence at the play's centre.

In his last, dying speeches, he compels our compassion.

> Poisoned, ill fare; dead, forsook, cast off,
> And none of you will bid the winter come
> To thrust his icy fingers in my maw,
> Nor let my kingdom's rivers take their course
> Through my burned bosom, nor entreat the north
> To make his bleak winds kiss my parched lips
> And comfort me with cold. I do not ask you much;
> I beg cold comfort. And you are so strait
> And so ungrateful, you deny me that.   (V.vii.35–43)

It is left to the Bastard to deliver the patriotic moral – a much-quoted plea for national unity.

> O, let us pay the time but needful woe,
> Since it hath been beforehand with our griefs.
> This England never did, nor never shall,
> Lie at the proud foot of a conquerer
> But when it first did help to wound itself.
> Now these her princes are come home again,
> Come the three corners of the world in arms
> And we shall shock them! Naught shall make us rue,
> If England to itself do rest but true.

Though popular in the Victorian period – largely, it would seem, for the opportunities it provided for spectacular scenic effects and antiquarian costuming – the play is not a fashionable choice among present-day directors. Its politics are perhaps too distant and its patriotism too overt. It awaits a contemporary interpretation that would do adequate justice to its considerable merits.

— ❖ —

In the sequence of Shakespeare's plays, *Richard II* follows directly on *King John*, and was probably staged at the Theatre in the summer of 1596. It is a summer play and again requires an open stage for its performance. It initiates the second of Shakespeare's great historical cycles (the 'Henriad') that was to take the story of England and its kings from the fall of Richard through the 'unquiet' reign of Henry IV to the triumphs of Henry V. And as the first three plays in the series (the second *Richard* and the two parts of *Henry IV*) were to appear within a period of little more than eighteen months, with *Henry V* joining them a year or two later, and as all four plays are likely to have been performed in repertoire thereafter in close proximity to each other, a continuity in the casting of its leading roles would have been highly desirable, if not essential. The Bolinbroke of *Richard*, for example, must surely have been played by the actor who was to be Henry IV, and whoever played Prince Hal in *Henry IV*, the title role in *Henry V*. Anything else would have been confusing to the public, and have resulted in one of the great bonuses enjoyed by the Chamberlain's men – the near-permanent status of its players – being needlessly thrown away. Given that Shakespeare and Burbage divided the kingly roles between them, the consequences are obvious and inescapable. If Burbage played the more showy part of Richard, Shakespeare would have taken Bolinbroke in the first of the plays. Shakespeare goes on to play the King, and Burbage Prince Hal, in Parts One and Two of *Henry IV*, with Shakespeare as Chorus and Burbage as King in *Henry V*. The fact that Hal, though mentioned as present off-stage as Bolinbroke's dissolute son, never appears in *Richard* may be taken, perhaps, as confirmation of this particular division, and that it was planned from the start.

Pre-eminently, Richard II is the Player King. Like Richard III, he is a role-player but, unlike him, is limited to a single role and believes in it with all his heart. Nevertheless, it remains a role; deprived of this assumed identity by the fact of Bolinbroke's usurpation, he is lost in uncertainty as to who or what he is.

In the opening scene of the play, surrounded by his court and all the panoply of royalty, he is superb. Heralded by trumpets, he takes

'Pale, trembling coward, there I throw my gage', *Richard II*, I.i.69 (illustration by Gordon Browne from the *Henry Irving Shakespeare*, 1892)

the chair of state upstage-centre and plays the impartial judge, epitome of kingly grace and power, to perfection.

> Old John of Gaunt, time-honoured Lancaster,
> Hast though according to thy oath and band
> Brought hither Henry Herford, thy bold son,
> Here to make good the boisterous late appeal,
> Which then our leisure would not let us hear,
> Against the Duke of Norfolk, Thomas Mowbray?

Bolinbroke (titled at the time as Hereford), who is Richard's cousin, has accused Mowbray of the murder of their uncle, Gloucester. Each announces his name and states his case as in a court of law. The hatred between them is palpable. Addressing Richard as 'gracious sovereign', 'most loving liege', 'dear, dear lord', they nevertheless reject his pleas for reconciliation and insist on their right to submit their quarrel to trial by combat. Reluctantly, the king agrees. The scene shifts to Coventry where, after elaborate, chivalric preliminaries have been completed, Richard suddenly announces that to prevent the spilling of his 'kindred's blood' he has decided to banish them both, Bolinbroke for six years, Mowbray for life. It is in the short scene that follows between Richard and his cronies that the façade of impartial royalty cracks. His fear and suspicion of Bolinbroke now emerge, and when news is brought of the mortal illness of 'time-honoured Lancaster', Bolinbroke's father, the falsity of his kingly performance in the earlier scenes of the play is shockingly revealed:

> Now put it, God, in the physician's mind
> To help him to his grave immediately.
> The lining of his coffers shall make coats
> To deck our soldiers for these Irish wars.
> Come, gentlemen, let's all go visit him.
> Pray God we make haste and come too late.   (I.iv.58–63)

The trial has been a sham, and Richard's impartiality as judge a lie; not only is Mowbray guilty of Gloucester's death, but Richard knows that he is for it was he who ordered it.

In *Henry VI*, Bolinbroke's usurpation of the throne was presented as the original sin whereby the seed of future factional strife that was to bring the country to its knees in the Wars of the Roses was planted. In stepping back in time to that historical moment in *Richard*, Shakespeare sees it very differently. The fault now lies in the king; in his unwillingness or incapacity to assume the responsibilities of the role he has inherited. He plays the part convincingly, knows his lines and delivers them with practised skill, but they are only words – eloquent but false.

The disparities and confusions that arise between man and his office, reality and image, actor and role, are a recurring preoccupation in Shakespeare's writing, and his life as a player (especially perhaps a player of kings) would have kept it in his thoughts. We find it in *Hamlet* –

> The time is out of joint; O cursed spite
> That ever I was born to set it right!

– and in *Lear* who, in giving away his kingdom, loses both his role and his reason. The last two acts of *Richard* are a sustained meditation on this theme in which the metaphor of the stage as microcosm of the world is variously employed.

The identity of king and kingdom – the belief that the king *was* England in a metaphysical sense, and that the well-being of the nation depended in a very real way on the moral worth of its ruler – was still current in the Elizabethan period as it had been dominant throughout the Middle Ages. Here, both king and kingdom are in deep trouble. Gaunt is dying, but sees that Richard also is mortally ill, and that

> Thy deathbed is no lesser than thy land,
> Wherein thou liest in reputation sick,
> And thou, too careless patient as thou art,
> Commit'st thy anointed body to the cure
> Of those physicians that first wounded thee.
> A thousand flatterers sit within thy crown

>Whose compass is no bigger than thy head,
>And yet encaged in so small a verge
>The waste is no whit lesser than thy land.   (II.i.95–103)

Richard angrily dismisses Gaunt's diagnosis, but a new, more pragmatic view of kingship is gaining ground that he will be unable to ignore. Just as the actor's success in the part he is playing is not simply dependent on the imaginative power and self-belief that he is able to bring to it, but also on the degree to which he is able to carry his audience along with him in that belief, so the king, playing what he believes is his divinely ordained role on the stage of the world, is likewise dependent on its acceptance by his subjects, and that in turn on the worldly power he has at his command.

On returning from Ireland to find Bolinbroke's invading army already landed, Richard is full of confidence in the sacred nature of his office and the nominal power of his kingly title. When he is told that twelve thousand of his Welsh soldiers have deserted, dispersed or fled, it is only momentarily that his confidence and courage fail. 'Am I not king?' he asks,

>Awake, thou coward! Majesty, thou sleepest.
>Is not the king's name twenty thousand names?
>Arm, arm, my name! A puny subject strikes
>At thy great glory. Look not to the ground.
>Ye favourites of a king, are we not high?
>High be our thoughts.   (III.ii.83–9)

But with news of further defections arriving every moment, he is forced to face the reality of the situation, and ends by placing both his crown and his person meekly into Bolinbroke's hands.

Though the self-absorption and role-playing continue, it is in the humiliation of his fall that Richard discovers a new voice and a more truthful eloquence that arouses our compassion.

>Cover your heads, and mock not flesh and blood
>With solemn reverence. Throw away respect,

> Tradition, form and ceremonious duty,
> For you have but mistook me all this while.
> I live with bread like you, feel want,
> Taste grief, need friends. Subjected thus,
> How can you say to me I am a king?   (III.ii.171–7)

His degradation is to go much further. Through York's tear-filled eyes, we are given a picture of the royal cousins riding together into London; Bolinbroke,

> Mounted upon a hot and fiery steed
> Which his aspiring rider seemed to know,
> With slow but stately pace kept on his course,
> Whilst all tongues cried 'God save thee, Bolinbroke!'

Richard following behind; and,

> As in a theatre the eyes of men
> After a well-graced actor leaves the stage
> Are idly bent on him that follows next,
> Thinking his prattle to be tedious,
> Even so or with much more contempt men's eyes
> Did scowl on Richard. No man cried 'God save him',
> No joyful tongue gave him his welcome home,
> But dust was thrown upon his sacred head . . .   (V.ii.8–30)

In all this, Bolinbroke is presented as the opposite pole to Richard; he is the man of action as against the self-regarding poet. He is at his most eloquent in his accusations of Mowbray in the opening scene. He returns in arms from banishment, not as usurper, but as Duke of Lancaster to reclaim his father's lands, which Richard has unjustly sequestered. At his first meeting with the humbled king, he kneels to him and treats him with respect. Thereafter, his attitude is wholly pragmatic. When Richard offers him the crown, he accepts it. In speech, he is increasingly taciturn. He has little more than 400 lines to Richard's 750. In the Deposition scene, Richard addresses him as

149

'silent king'. While Richard commands the stage with speeches of eloquent self-pity, Bolinbroke commands Richard in saying very little. It is a battle royal between the intoxicating spell of words and the unspoken realities of military and political power. One of Richard's few remaining supporters describes it later as a 'woeful pageant'. (The scene was cut from the first published text in deference to the Queen, who is reported to have said, 'I am Richard'. Though one may doubt the truth of the comparison, it would have made uncomfortable reading for her.) As Richard is effectively deposed by the desertion of his subjects, Bolinbroke is enthroned by their need to fill the consequent vacuum. He ascends the throne to the acclamations of his supporters with the flattest of lines: 'In God's name I'll ascend the regal throne.' In the end, he wishes Richard dead – and the sycophantic Exton is on hand to oblige. The sin is acknowledged by Henry as his, and will haunt him through the next two plays in the cycle. It is interesting and significant that Shakespeare chose to play this role. And it was not because he thought it was easy, because it is not.

Of the two old men of the play, Gaunt, with the marvellous speech in which he describes his dying vision of England, would probably have gone to Bryan or Heminges, and the somewhat comical York (the 'mad-cap Duke', as Hotspur later calls him) to Pope. The part of the senior Gardener may well have been Kempe's. The various lords and other subsidiary characters require careful casting and are easily distinguishable in performance, though they lack in the writing (no doubt deliberately so) the sharper edge that Shakespeare normally gives to his supporting roles as well as to many smaller ones.

Though Henry is the stronger of the two kings, and emerges as the victor in the struggle between them, the play and the tragedy are Richard's. Alone in prison, he searches for his lost identity.

> . . . play I in one person many people,
> And none contented. Sometimes am I king,
> Then treasons make me wish myself a beggar,
> And so I am. Then crushing penury
> Persuades me I was better when a king,
> Then am I kinged again, and by and by

Think that I am unkinged by Bolinbroke,
And straight am nothing. But whate'er I be
Nor I nor any man that but man is
With nothing shall be pleased till he be eased
With being nothing.   (V.v.31–41)

— ❋ —

I have proposed that *Richard II* was performed in the summer of 1596, and the *Merchant of Venice* in the autumn of that year. The twelve months that followed were to be an eventful and difficult period in the history of the company. As already recounted, the company's first patron, Lord Hunsdon, had died in July 1596, and was succeeded as Chamberlain by Sir William Brooke, Lord Cobham, and as patron by Sir George Carey, Hunsdon's son and heir. Early versions of the two parts of *Henry IV* under the title of *Sir John Oldcastle* were staged in the winter of 1596/7, but were objected to by Cobham on the grounds that the historical Oldcastle, whose name Shakespeare had borrowed for his principal buffoon, was an ancestor of his and highly regarded by the Puritan party as an early Protestant martyr. The plays were withdrawn for revision. But in March 1597, Cobham died and was succeeded as Chamberlain by Carey, the second Lord Hunsdon (whereupon the company reverted to their previous title, having been known as Hunsdon's in the interim). At the same time, Shakespeare was commissioned to produce an entertainment to celebrate their new patron's appointment as Knight of the Garter, and an early version of *The Merry Wives of Windsor*, probably comprising little more than the final masque of the play as we have it now, is thought to have been staged at Windsor for Carey's installation in May.[10]

Then, in July, all the London playhouses were closed by the Privy Council in reaction to the staging by Pembroke's men (probably at the Swan) of an allegedly seditious play by Jonson and Nashe, *The Isle of Dogs*, that landed its authors in gaol. The Chamberlain's took to the road, visiting Rye and Dover, Marlborough, Bath and Bristol, and the first authorised publication of any of Shakespeare's plays – the 'good'

151

Quarto of *Richard II* and the reconstituted text of *Richard III*, sold to the printer Andrew Wise in August and October of the same year – may well have been occasioned by a cash-flow crisis resulting from the July closures and a need for extra funds to finance the tour.

One other important change in the company's fortunes in 1597 should be mentioned. In February, James Burbage (Richard's father) died, leaving a financial muddle behind him, with the ground lease of the now ageing Shoreditch Theatre nearing its end, and his projected indoor playhouse at Blackfriars still in limbo. Consequently, when, in October, the London theatres were allowed to reopen, the company moved its operations in London from the Theatre to the Curtain, which stood nearby and in which the Burbage brothers had inherited an interest. It was probably there that the first London performances of the revised and renamed *Henry IV* plays were given.[11] It is quite possible, therefore, that like the *Dream* and the *Merchant*, they were premiered and brought to a high state of finish in the course of the company's autumn tour.[12] However that may have been, the necessity for revision resulting from the Oldcastle/Falstaff controversy ensured an exceptionally long gestation period for the plays, and this shows. They are among Shakespeare's greatest achievements; superbly crafted and breaking wholly new ground.

The lyricism of *Richard II* now gives place to a more realistic treatment of character; poetry to an alternation of strongly dramatic verse and rhythmical prose. At the same time, the focus widens from Richard's self-absorption and the verge of the court to the whole of England, in which every class and section of society is represented. The small scene between the carriers that opens Act 2 of Part One, set in the yard of a Rochester inn with its early morning bustle, lanterns and occupational jargon, is a good example of Shakespeare's widening vision in the plays, and comes straight from his own experience as a player on the road; it has little relation to plot, but contributes to the general impression we get of a continuum of energetic life at the ordinary, humdrum level enveloping the big events of the play and its significant relationships, which are those between the King and his son, Hal and Falstaff. The Boar's Head scenes in both parts, though dominated by Falstaff, Shakespeare's greatest comic creation, are models of accurate observation and reporting in which the meanest of the tavern servants, Francis the drawer, with his catch-phrase of 'Anon, anon, sir', is given his moment.

Prince: How old art thou, Francis?
Francis: Let me see, about Michaelmas next I shall be –
Poins: [*Within*] Francis!
Francis: Anon, sir – pray stay a little, my lord.
Prince: Nay but hark you, Francis, for the sugar thou gavest me, 'twas a pennyworth, was't not?
Francis: O Lord, I would it had been two!
Prince: I will give thee for it a thousand pound – ask me when thou wilt, and thou shalt have it.
Poins: [*Within*] Francis!
Francis: Anon, anon.
Prince: Anon, Francis? No, Francis, but tomorrow, Francis; or, Francis a-Thursday; or indeed, Francis, when thou wilt . . .

(1H4: II.iv.53–66)

(The Boar's Head and Rochester scenes would have found a perfect venue in inns along the roads to Dover and Bristol.)

In view of the number of named roles (42 in Part Two), he would be a brave person who attempted a doubling plot. Hotspur is a part that the best of actors have been glad to play, and in Glendower we have the first of a series of Welshmen of whom I shall have more to say in the following chapter. All we can say for sure of the smaller roles is that Sincler doubled Simon Shadow and the First Beadle in Part Two, where he is named in a stage direction as 'Sinklo' and addressed by Doll and the Hostess as 'paper-faced villain', 'starved bloodhound' and 'goodman bones' (V.iv). He would also have made an excellent Rumour. It is a 'company play' if ever there was one and would have been a joy to perform – as it still is!

Though he has no more than six out of nineteen scenes in Part One, and only three in Part Two, Shakespeare's role as the King is the hub around which the plays turn; and the tug-of-war between himself and Falstaff for the soul of Hal, their central and cohesive theme.

153

Historically, only two years have elapsed between the end of *Richard II* and the beginning of *Henry IV*, but in that time Henry's character has appreciably soured. We now find him testy, worried and ill. The burdens of office, his role as king, have taken their toll. The patience and courtesy of the man as shown in *Richard* – his kneeling to his defeated opponent, his treatment of the common people,

> How he did seem to dive into their hearts
> With humble and familiar courtesy

is revealed as having been a calculated strategy, as Richard had suspected. 'By being seldom seen', Henry now confides to Hal,

> I could not stir
> But like a comet I was wonder'd at,
> That men would tell their children, 'This is he!'
> (1H4: III.ii.46–8)

And in lines that follow, Richard is characterised as 'the skipping King', who

> ambled up and down
> With shallow jesters, and rash bavin wits,
> Soon kindled and soon burnt, carded his state,
> Mingled his royalty with cap'ring fools,
> Had his great name profaned with their scorns,
> And gave his countenance against his name
> To laugh at gibing boys . . .   (III.ii.60–6)

Henry's nightmare is that Hal is following the same path that led Richard to his ruin.

> . . . in that very line, Harry, standest thou,
> For thou hast lost thy princely privilege
> With vile participation. Not an eye
> But is a-weary of thy common sight,

Save mine, which hath desir'd to see thee more . . .
                    For all the world
As thou art to this hour was Richard then . . .
                              (III.ii.85–9, 93–4)

In Henry's apprehensive vision, Hal *is* Richard, and the fact that the actor playing Hal (Burbage), now standing before him, had been Richard in the earlier play would have made the point more effectively than any other casting could have done.

In effective opposition to the king in his struggle to retain the allegiance of his son stands Falstaff, and as Henry dominates the court scenes, which are wholly in verse, Falstaff dominates the world of the tavern, wholly in prose – prose of a quality that Shakespeare was never to surpass.

Falstaff has been described in many ways: as buffoon, vice, wit, liar, coward, toper, parasite, scoundrel, con-man and clown; he is all of these, and more. He contains, as has been said, multitudes, and yet remains irredeemably and consistently himself. So much has been written about him – not always in context – that he is in danger of being mythologised out of existence. The plain fact is, of course, that he is neither real nor fictional, but a role in a series of plays written for a particular actor who would have brought to his performance of the part his own unifying personality and presence that now we can only guess at. Though not as yet generally acknowledged, I believe that John Dover Wilson was right in assigning it to Kempe.[13]

There is no doubt that Kempe was the principal fool of the company, and one who had, through his playing of Dogberry and Peter – and probably also the Dromios, Launce and Bottom – demonstrated exceptional ability as a versatile character actor who kept to the lines his author gave him. Being large in limb, the part would have been (with the aid of padding) within his physical range. The self-defining function of the fool is to evoke laughter, and this is precisely Falstaff's function in the play.

Men of all sorts take a pride to gird at me. The brain of this foolish-compounded clay, man, is not able to invent anything that intends to laughter more than I invent, or is invented on me; I am not only witty in myself, but the cause that wit is in other men.

(2H4:I.ii.5–9)

To see him as the central figure is understandable but mistaken. For his humour, though spreading around him like a benign penumbra to everyone he meets, whether receptive or not, has a specific purpose and is directed to a particular person: it is to make Hal laugh, and so educate and humanise him. We see him storing up material to this end – observing people's behaviour, listening to their chatter, drawing them out as he does with Shallow, and making mental notes of the future use he can make of the results. 'I will devise matter enough out of this Shallow', he tells us in soliloquy,

to keep Prince Harry in continual laughter the wearing out of six fashions . . . O, you shall see him laugh till his face be like a wet cloak ill laid up! (2H4:V.i.75–7, 81–2)

There is calculation here – just as there is calculation in Hal's relation to Falstaff. For however much they enjoy their double-act together, the relationship between them is more one of mutual self-interest than affection. Both are playing a role. Hal's role is as prodigal son, sowing his wild oats. He loves Falstaff's humour, participates in it, feeds and grows on it as a human being. It is necessary to him as an escape from the repressive expectations of his father; but there is always a reservation in his performance of it, an awareness that when the moment comes he must and will reject it to assume his destiny as king. He makes no promises to Falstaff, but means to provide for him, and does. Falstaff's role is as buffoon to the Prince;[14] but he lacks the simplicity of the fool, for he too has a further objective in view: to provide for his future prosperity and comfort. He has misjudged his man. In rejecting Falstaff, Hal is also rejecting his *alter ego* as Richard. 'Master Shallow', Falstaff wryly observes when the penny finally drops, 'I owe you a thousand pound.'

There is a textual indication of Kempe's casting in the role. In the 'good' Quarto edition of Part Two, we find a rogue stage direction,

'Enter Will', after II.iv.18 – some 14 lines in advance of Falstaff's marked appearance, singing. The prompter would have been stationed at stage level. If, as is probable, Falstaff was intended to enter at the upper level, he would have needed an early signal to climb the backstage steps to be ready on cue for his entrance on the gallery; the song would have covered his descent to the stage.

But the clearest pointer to Kempe as Falstaff's original performer is in the Epilogue of Part Two. Though some recent editors like to divide this and apportion its several sections to different occasions and various speakers, it is included in full (with only slight variations) in both Quarto and Folio versions of the play, and hangs together very well. From Pope onwards, early editors attributed the whole to a 'Dancer'; they were right, for Kempe was famous for his dancing as well as for his fooling, and was the author of published jigs. As the play ends and all the characters left on stage exit, Falstaff hurriedly returns from the opposite side, having escaped from the guards who are escorting him to prison.

> First, my fear; then, my curtsy;

– he takes a bow to tumultuous applause –

> last, my speech. My fear, is your displeasure; my curtsy, my duty; and my speech, to beg your pardons. If you look for a good speech now, you undo me, for what I have to say is of my own making; and what indeed I should say will, I doubt, prove mine own marring.

This tells us plainly enough that it is not the play's author who is speaking, but one of the other actors and, from the terms of the apology he goes on to make, it is equally clear that it has to do with his previous performance as Sir John Oldcastle, and the 'displeasing play', the play of that name that Shakespeare has now revised and retitled.

> Be it known to you, as it is very well, I was lately here in the end of a displeasing play, to pray your patience for it, and to promise you a better. I meant indeed to pay you with this; which if like an

157

ill venture it come unluckily home, I break, and you, my gentle creditors, lose. Here I promised you I would be, and here I commit my body to your mercies . . .

In the final part of the speech, Kempe is part in, part out of character. He would still, of course, have been wearing his costume and padding as Falstaff. Though we are not told whether Falstaff is much of a dancer, Kempe is, and speaks as such. When he tells us that 'Oldcastle died martyr, and this is not the man', the identity of the speaker is put beyond doubt.

If my tongue cannot entreat you to acquit me, will you command me to use my legs? And yet that were but light payment, to dance out of your debt . . . One word more, I beseech you. If you be not too cloyed with fat meat, our humble author will continue the story, with Sir John in it, and make you merry with fair Katharine of France; where, for anything I know, Falstaff shall die of a sweat, unless already a be killed with your hard opinions; for Oldcastle died martyr, and this is not the man. My tongue is weary; when my legs are too, I will bid you good night.

The last line is cue for a jig and, as the musicians strike up, Kempe is joined on stage by the rest of the company, including Shakespeare, who take a dancing call. The play, as originally performed, thus ends on a much lighter note than the text may at first suggest; and if the audience are still upset by Falstaff's rejection (as so many critics have been), they are comforted in the knowledge that he is to be given a further lease of life in the play's sequel.

That, as we know now, was not to be, for he does not appear in *Henry V*, and the Falstaff of the *Merry Wives*, a few years later, has somehow lost the true flavour and bite of Shakespeare's original creation. The reasons for this have been much debated, but the most obvious one is that the player who had first acted the role, and become associated with it through its several incarnations, was no longer of the company, and that Shakespeare baulked at the necessity to introduce another actor in the part while the memory of its first performer was fresh in the public's mind. Here again, Kempe – and only Kempe of the senior sharers – fits the bill, for we know that he left the company in mysterious circumstances in 1599 to embark on his dancing journey to Norwich; see illustration on p. 97. (He is in the actor-list of Jonson's *Every Man in his Humour* of 1598 but not in that of his *Every Man out of his Humour* of 1599, and sold his share in the Globe shortly after the lease of 21 February 1599 was signed.)[15] It is not, however, true (as often stated) that he claimed to have danced himself out of the world, meaning the Globe. The claim was made by some unauthorised hack of a ballad-singer, the truth of which Kempe only half allows ('others guess righter'); for he had probably never been in the Globe. He had danced, as Falstaff, out of the Curtain.[16]

Enough has been said to indicate that stylistically the two *Henry IV* plays are very different to their immediate predecessor, and yet they retain a unity within the cycle of the Henriad. And as *Richard II* and *Henry IV* belong together, so *Henry V* will be found to belong with *Henry IV*. The shift in style and mood from *Richard* to its sequels is thus less a matter of Shakespeare's leaving behind a lyrical phase in his writing for one that is more prosaic and realistic than a deliberate shift in perspective – an adaptation of manner both to the varying events that history presented to him and the changing demands of the public. In the difficult conditions of 1596/7, the company badly needed a hit, Shakespeare pulled out all the stops to provide it and, having courted disaster with his first attempt, ended by writing a masterpiece. 'Uneasy lies the head that wears a crown.' In his role as Bolinbroke, the 'silent king' of *Richard II*, he had given the stage to Richard; as Henry IV he moves to its centre. The reconciliation scene between himself and Hal in Act 4 of Part Two is both the true dramatic crux of the whole and a perfect induction to the play that is to follow.

NINE

The Globe, 1599–1601

The Globe Theatre was a magical theatre, a cosmic theatre, a religious theatre, an actor's theatre, designed to give fullest support to the voices and the gestures of the players as they enacted the drama of the life of man within the Theatre of the World . . . His theatre would have been for Shakespeare the pattern of the universe, the idea of the Macrocosm, the world stage on which the Microcosm acted his parts. All the world's a stage. The words are in a real sense the clue to the Globe Theatre.

Frances A. Yates[1]

When, in October 1597, the London playhouses were allowed to reopen after the *Isle of Dogs* controversy, by which time the ground lease of the Shoreditch Theatre had run out, the company moved into its near neighbour, the Curtain. We know very little about the Curtain except that it was of the same age and had been used as an 'easer' to the Theatre, which suggests that it was a good deal smaller. Nevertheless, it provided a metropolitan base for the Chamberlain's company in the two years that followed, where Shakespeare's plays written in the period, including both parts of *Henry IV* and *Much Ado About Nothing*, received their first London performances. But whatever merits the Curtain possessed by reason of its intimacy were outweighed by its practical disadvantages, for like the Theatre it would now have been showing its age, and its more limited capacity would have greatly restricted the company's share of box office takings, on which the players largely depended.

The degree of frustration they were feeling in this situation is apparent in what happened next. For under cover of darkness, one night near the end of December 1598 or early in January 1599, a group of them, assisted by a dozen or so labourers under the supervision of a builder called Peter Street, entered Burbage's original building, the old Theatre, and proceeded to demolish its timbers. These they transported, presumably by barge, to a new site on the opposite, Surrey, side of the Thames, not far from the Rose in the parish of St Saviour's, Southwark, where they were to set about building the Globe. Though the owners of the land on which the Theatre had stood subsequently launched a writ of trespass against Richard and Cuthbert Burbage, who had inherited ownership of the theatre's structure from their father, the brothers had right on their side and, after several years of legal wrangling, were finally exonerated.

They were not, however, able to meet more than half the cost of the rebuilding from their own resources, so five others of the company's senior men – Heminges, Kempe, Phillips, Pope and Shakespeare – contributed 10 per cent each and so became, not only sharers in the company's profits as they had been from the beginning, but also co-owners ('housekeepers', as they were termed) of its theatre, and entitled to an additional share in half the gallery takings. (General admittance to the theatre was charged at a penny a head, which went to the company; for further admittance to one or other of the galleries an extra penny or twopence was charged, and traditionally this was divided equally between company and owners.) Such joint ownership by a company of players of the building in which they performed was unique in the period and has rarely, if ever, been repeated. It also placed them in the enviable position of exercising a controlling influence on the design of the new theatre. As plans of neither Theatre nor Globe have survived and we have only an exterior sketch of the Globe (reproduced overleaf), we can only guess at the nature and extent of the changes they effected, but in view of the rapid developments that had taken place in the drama since the earlier building – the first of its kind – had been erected back in 1576, they are likely to have been significant, especially as regards the internal architecture of the stage and proscenium in relation to the yard and galleries. We may take it as certain that, as a senior sharer and the company's resident author, Shakespeare's views in the matter would

Detail from Claes Janzs Visscher's engraving of London in 1616 showing the Globe Theatre – presumably as rebuilt in 1614 (Folger Shakespeare Library, Washington, DC)

have carried considerable weight. Though I have earlier objected to the expression 'Shakespeare's company' as sometimes used of the Chamberlain's men, it would be difficult to dispute Miss Yates' claim that the Globe was in large measure Shakespeare's theatre, reflecting his personal view of its function. This is borne out, I suggest, by the plays that he wrote specifically for it.

Most scholars who have studied *Henry V* agree that Shakespeare's reference in his Act 5 Chorus to the Earl of Essex as 'General of our gracious Empress' who is expected on his return from Ireland to bring out the sort of crowds on the streets of the City that welcomed

162

Henry on his triumphant return from France, dates the composition of the play to between 27 March 1599, when Essex left on his pacifying mission to Ireland, and his far from triumphant return on 28 September of the same year, which corresponds with the period when the Globe would have been under construction. As the company would have been eager to obtain use of their new playhouse as soon as possible, and we know that the builder, Street, later contracted to erect a similar structure (the Fortune) within a period of four months, the Globe would almost certainly have been ready for occupation by June or July 1599.

In *The Life of Henry the Fift*, as the play is entitled in the First Folio, Shakespeare reverted to the role of story-teller he had adopted and then abandoned half-way through in *Romeo and Juliet*. He enters as poet, invoking inspiration:

> O for a muse of fire, that would ascend
> The brightest heaven of invention,
> A kingdom for a stage, princes to act,
> And monarchs to behold the swelling scene!

But this was not to be. If all the world's a stage, the stage is here conversely an unworthy scaffold and a mere cockpit. 'Can this cockpit hold/The vasty fields of France?' he asks.

> Or may we cram
> Within this wooden O the very casques
> That did affright the air at Agincourt?

Given the 'flat unraised spirits' who have dared 'bring forth/So great an object', and the poverty of means at their disposal, they can only succeed with the active co-operation of the audience. But an apology for the players' presumption is followed by a series of uncompromising imperatives –

> Suppose within the girdle of these walls . . .
> Piece out our imperfections with your thoughts.
> Into a thousand parts divide one man . . .
> Think, when we talk of horses that you see them . . .

– that are to continue through the play in the choruses that precede each of the acts. Having played out his previous role in *Henry IV*, Shakespeare is freed to act as Chorus in its sequel, but he is more than Chorus in the traditional mode; rather, a magician, a Prospero-to-be, whose vision of the play's hero and his victories is to work directly on the audience's imagination in bringing him and them to immediate life on the stage. That is the kind of theatre the Globe is to be: a theatre of the imagination, an actor's theatre, a magical theatre.

I said earlier that *Henry V* belongs together with *Henry IV* as *Henry IV* explains and clarifies *Richard II*, for the 'warlike Harry' of *Henry V* is identical to the reformed Hal who makes his first appearance in Act 5 of *Henry IV, Part 2*:

> . . . Princes all, believe me, I beseech you,
> My father has gone wild into his grave,
> For in his tomb lie my affections;
> And with his spirits sadly I survive
> To mock the expectation of the world,
> To frustrate prophecies, and to raze out
> Rotten opinion, who hath writ me down
> After my seeming. (V.ii.122–9)

Hal has rejected Falstaff as the Christian is exhorted to expel the old Adam and, as Henry in the present play, he allows Bardolph to go to his death for stealing a pyx without a flicker of recognition that he had ever known him. In that, he is his father's son and fulfils his promises to him in full measure; but if his wildness now lies in his father's grave, the same cannot be said of his humanity. He is presented in *Henry V* as the ideal king, the ideal military commander, but if Shakespeare can be accused with some justification of idealising the Henry V of history – by most accounts a somewhat humourless fanatic – it was by making him more, rather than less, human. The common touch he has acquired as Hal – the ability to communicate with all classes and conditions of men and relate to them at their own level – never deserts him, and only in one confessed moment of anger ('I was not angry since I came to France/

Until this instant') does he lose a sense of proportion. He assumes the role of king he has inherited and it fits him like a glove, but it remains a role; he is not obsessed by its accidentals, as was Richard, nor reduced by its burdens like his father.

For all its interconnections with its predecessors in the Henriad, stylistically the play again breaks the mould. Deriving the main lines of its plot from Holinshed with hints from an earlier, cruder dramatisation (the anonymous *Famous Victories*), it is epical and episodic in form; but in its alternation between three contrasting worlds, each with its own distinctive set of characters – the English court, that of the opposing French, and the English army in the field – the play is unlike any other in the canon.

The thirteen nobles who comprise the English court are given only a fitful, shadowy presence in the play. They come and go, appear and

But tell the Dauphin I will keep my state,
Be like a king and show my sail of greatness,
When I do rouse me in my throne of France.

(I.ii.274–6)

(Illustration by Gordon Browne from the *Henry Irving Shakespeare*, 1892)

165

disappear as required by the exigencies of doubling and, with the exception perhaps of Exeter and Erpingham, have little opportunity of establishing themselves as individuals. The bishops who open the play after the first chorus are, more often than not, ruthlessly pruned in performance, and sometimes guyed (as in Olivier's classic film), but what they have to say is important in establishing the nature of Henry's reformation for those in the audience who have missed out on earlier performances of *Henry IV*. Of the six nobles who are named as appearing in the court scene that follows, only Westmorland and Exeter speak, and they have less than thirty lines between them. They provide an appropriately grave and distinguished audience for the bishops' justification of Henry's proposed invasion of France and the entrance of the French ambassadors, but do little more than dress the stage. (The imaginative Victorian illustration seen on previous page probably approximates to the scene's original staging.)

The French court is more strongly individualised, and functions in the play as a reverse image to the English. The figure of the French King (Charles VI), often misconceived as either mad or senile, requires an especially strong performance as Henry's principal opponent. Whatever the historical record may say, in Shakespeare's text he is an awe-inspiring, fearful ghost from the past, reliving terrible memories of the time

> When Cressy battle fatally was struck,
> And all our princes captived, by the hand
> Of that black name, Edward, Black Prince of Wales;

whose warning to his feckless and over-confident nobles that the English king is 'a stem'

> Of that victorious stock, and let us fear
> The native mightiness and fate of him   (II.iv.54–64)

falls on deaf ears to their ultimate cost.

It is from the third category of subsidiary characters – those belonging to the English army – that most of the comedy derives. There can be little doubt that Shakespeare had originally intended to bring Falstaff into this part of the play (as he had announced that he would in the Epilogue to *Henry IV*), but was forestalled by Kempe's sudden withdrawal from the company.[2] Pistol, whose popularity with the Elizabethan public must have been second only to that of Falstaff to judge by his naming on the title page of the pirated Quarto of 1600,[3] appears nonetheless, along with Bardolph of the fiery nose and a new character, Nym. The three of them are shown as setting out for France, having heard from Mistress Quickly the news of Falstaff's untimely death, which they attribute to a broken heart at his rejection by Hal.[4] But amusing as Pistol's antics in France prove to be, he and his companions are essentially satellites of Falstaff, and the introduction of the delightfully loquacious Welshman Fluellen and his fellow captains never quite succeeds in filling the gap left by the missing knight.

The Folio text of the play is thought by scholars to derive in the main from Shakespeare's authorial papers. Given the thousand-and-one unforeseen eventualities that arise in the course of production, it may never have reached the stage in the complete form in which it has come down to us; but provides nevertheless a valuable insight into the working of his mind in constructing a play in which his fellows are so used as to exploit their individual strengths to the full in the achievement of his dramatic purposes.

George Bryan, one of the more senior sharers, having left the company in 1597 to take up a full-time post as Ordinary Groom of the Chamber, and Kempe having also departed, Shakespeare would have had available to him in casting the play only eight of the original sharers, but an increasing number of former apprentices would by now have been swelling the number of hired men as they matured into young manhood, and there would have been much for them to do, along with the younger recruits. Though any attempt to assign with any exactness the fifty speaking parts and 'double' them effectively is inevitably doomed to failure, I have made a conjectural doubling plot, shown in Appendix D, which I hope will be of interest.

As Chorus, Shakespeare would have been in a position to double any number of the smaller parts. I have given him Bedford and Burgundy for the reasons given in my notes to the plot. In suggesting other doubles, I have borne in mind throughout the principle enunciated earlier that it is always easier and more effective to combine contrasting roles than those that are similar. At least one of these – the doubling of the French King and Montjoy the herald, which I have given to Condell – is, I believe, integral to Shakespeare's dramatic intentions.

A further word should be said at this point about an important new recruit to the company, Robert Armin. He was to take over some of Kempe's 'clown' parts, including Dogberry, but was a versatile character actor in his own right, as well as a published author, and the roles that Shakespeare was to write for him were significantly different from those he had created for Kempe.

He would almost certainly have played Fluellen. Originally a member of Lord Chandos' men, Armin's first known London performance was in an early version of his own play, the *Two Maids of More-clacke* in 1596, when he had demonstrated his versatility by quadrupling four roles: that of a natural fool called Blue John (a real person whom he had known in London and was to write about in his whimsical study of such innocents, *Foole upon Foole*), Tutch, a clever household fool, Tutch in the disguise of Blue John, and Tutch again in his impersonation of a Welsh knight. It has often been noted that Shakespeare's series of Welsh characters begins with a Welsh captain in *Richard II*, proceeds to Glendower in Part One of *Henry IV*, and thence to Fluellen. The likelihood is that Armin was spotted by Shakespeare in the *Two Maids*, joined the company immediately afterwards to play the Welsh captain and other minor roles in *Richard*, went with the company on tour and to the Curtain, playing Glendower, and from thence to the Globe as Fluellen.[5] If he was already a Chamberlain's man in 1596/7, there could be no question of his being brought in to fill the vacancy left by Kempe early in 1599, as is usually supposed; by then he would already have been an established member of the company, though not yet a sharer. I have assumed that Shakespeare would have made full use of his versatility in *Henry V*.

The play bears all the marks of a dual celebration. It celebrates and gives theatrical life to the memory of a remarkable king and his

Robert Armin as 'Blue John' from the title page of his play, *History of the two Maids of More-clacke*, as published in 1609 (British Library)

victories; but it is also a celebration of theatre, an opportunity for the players to demonstrate both their individual talents and their cohesion as an ensemble in an exciting new arena, the Globe. From the point of view of the scholar and the literary critic, it may not be among the more profound of Shakespeare's plays, but in the power of its language and richness of its characterisation it remains one of the most enjoyable and rewarding in performance.

That in writing *Henry V* Shakespeare was already thinking of Rome, and rereading his Plutarch, is suggested by the incidental references it contains to Roman history,[6] and the first performance of *Henry* at the Globe was soon to be followed by *Julius Caesar*, the second of his Roman plays and the first of his great tragedies.

The time of its production can be dated with exceptional precision by the report of a visit to London by a Swiss doctor from Basle, Thomas Platter, who was in England between 18 September and 20 October 1599:

On the 21st of September, after dinner, at about two o'clock, I went with my party across the water; in the straw-thatched house we saw the tragedy of the first Emperor Julius Caesar, very pleasingly performed, with approximately fifteen characters; at the end of the play they danced together admirably and exceedingly gracefully, according to their custom, two in each group dressed in men's and two [in] women's apparel.[7]

The performance he saw is unlikely to have been the first. If, as suggested, *Henry V* had appeared in June or July, *Caesar* is likely to have followed a few weeks later in July or August. (I return to his report of the dance.)

The language of the play has a classical austerity and directness with few rhetorical flourishes, which contributes to making it one of the most frequently quoted of Shakespeare's plays if *Hamlet* is excepted. The text is among the best and least polluted in the Folio, and there are no quartos (authorised or otherwise) to muddy the record. The familiar plot of friendship and its betrayal through allegiance to an abstract ideal of honour and freedom, and the terrible consequences of that betrayal, drives through with unparalleled urgency and power from the first scene to the last. It admits of no intervals or pauses for the shifting of scenery or extraneous 'business'.

If mute extras are omitted from the count, Platter's 'approximately fifteen characters' (by which I take him to mean actors) corresponds well enough with the size of the Globe company as previously estimated. With some forty speaking roles, doubling would have been as extensive as in *Henry V* but, because of the marked shift of direction and location that occurs in Act 3 – from concentration on the plot to assassinate Caesar to its effects, and from Rome to Sardis and Philippi – far less complex in its demands. The conspirators of the earlier part become in the main soldiers in the later, and of the twenty-one named characters in the first, only five survive into the second: Brutus, Cassius, Antony, Caesar (briefly as ghost), and the boy Lucius.

It is commonly assumed that Burbage played all the leading parts in Shakespeare's plays, by which is usually meant the largest, though the only ones we can be sure of from near-contemporary sources are Richard III, Hamlet, Lear and Othello. These are indisputably leads, but they do not entitle us to assume that he invariably took the lead; nor is the leading role invariably the largest.[8] Though Brutus is generally recognised as the first of Shakespeare's tragic heroes in that his fall can be attributed to a basic flaw of character and an interior conflict manifest in his Hamlet-like soliloquies, I believe the part would have gone to one of the younger men (perhaps Condell), and Burbage's skills reserved for the more extrovert Antony, whose long and subtly constructed oration in the Forum over the corpse of Caesar is the turning point of the play. Though briefly introduced with Caesar in Act 1, he has only seven lines prior to Caesar's death in Act 3, and only the third largest part with some 300 lines in all.

Age differences between the characters are important. Historically, Caesar was fifty-five at the time of his death and Antony about forty. Brutus is young enough to have been rumoured Caesar's bastard son. When Cicero is under discussion as a possible recruit to the conspiracy, Metellus suggests to Brutus and the others that his

> silver hairs
> Will purchase us a good opinion . . .
> Our youths and wildness shall no whit appear,
> But all be buried in his gravity.   (II.i.143–4, 147–8

Though 'wildness' is hardly applicable to Brutus, he is of the same generation as his fellow conspirators, while Antony is appreciably older. (In 1599, Burbage was thirty-two or thirty-three.) In that respect, the play is a conflict between youth and age, idealism and experience. With the entrance of Octavius in Act 4, the balance shifts. If Brutus is played young, as Shakespeare intended, even greater poignancy attaches to Caesar's dying words as Brutus advances to the kill, 'Et tu, Brute?', and as he strikes home, 'Then fall, Caesar'. In that moment, Brutus realises the true horror of what he is doing, and his character deteriorates rapidly to the washing of hands in Caesar's blood and the forced and mistimed rhetoric of the lines that follow:

171

Cassius:	How many ages hence
	Shall this our lofty scene be acted over
	In states unborn and accents yet unknown?
Brutus:	How many times shall Caesar bleed in sport
	That now on Pompey's basis lies along,
	No worthier than the dust? (III.i.111–16)

– that have the double-mirror effect of making the performance on stage appear more real than the ghastly actuality it reflects.

Shakespeare's portrait of Caesar has been criticised for its emphasis on the character's pride and arrogance, though in that he is merely following Plutarch. At this point in his life, Caesar's military triumphs, on which his reputation rests, are behind him. He is old, ill, prone to superstition, and tetchy; but as Brutus admits, 'I know no personal cause to spurn at him', and 'to speak truth of Caesar/ I have not known when his affections swayed/More than his reason' (II.i.11, 19–21). He is to be killed, not because he has given offence, but may do so in the future; not because any of his present words or actions can be faulted, but because the power that he enjoys renders him a potential threat to all that Brutus (the quintessential Roman) holds most dear. He is the serpent's egg that must be crushed before it hatches. Brutus' intentions are indeed honourable, but those of his fellows are less so, and their actions are to lead both him and Rome into evil and the destruction of all he had hoped to preserve. This is the core of the tragedy.

Shakespeare's problem with Caesar is that he has really nothing to do or say in the play except in responding to the weaknesses and deliberate provocations of others. He is, as Hazlitt noticed, like the man in the coffin at a funeral – an essential but passive character in the proceedings. The importunate warnings of the Soothsayer and Artemidorus are brushed aside with superb aplomb, and his proudest speeches are in contemptuous dismissal of the egregious flattery he encounters:

> I must prevent thee, Cimber:
> These couchings and these lowly courtesies
> Might fire the blood of ordinary men,
> And turn pre-ordinance and first decree
> Into the lane of children. Be not fond
> To think that Caesar bears such rebel blood
> That will be thawed from the true quality
> With that which melteth fools – I mean sweet words
> Low-crooked curtsies and base spaniel fawning.   (III.i.35–43)

The negative impression of Caesar is more apparent in reading than in the theatre. The true note of offended dignity and patrician hauteur, as opposed to arrogant boasting, can only be found in performance. For all its passivity – indeed the more compellingly for it – the role requires the charismatic presence of a great actor. And that, I believe, is what Shakespeare would have brought to it when the play was first staged, for there can be little doubt that he played it himself. Both in its 'kingliness' and curious blend of centrality and detachment, it is a characteristic Shakespeare role.

Platter's report of the dance that concluded the Globe performance – executed, we are told, with extreme grace by two men in women's clothes and two in men's – calls for a further comment. Technically, this was known as a 'jig', and sometimes incorporated elements of characterisation and song, but we need to disassociate the term from the vigorous Irish jig of today. The meaning of its occurrence here is to be found in the very special feeling that Shakespeare had for music, especially in alliance with dance, which to him was the ultimate expression of harmony among human beings, reflecting the movements of the planets and the music of the spheres. Frances Yates (in the quotation at the top of the chapter) was right to speak of the Globe as a 'cosmic theatre, a religious theatre', and the ceiling of the canopy that overhung the stage is said to have been painted blue and dotted with stars.[9] In the course of the play, we have witnessed an assassination that was also a betrayal of friendship (the worst of sins in Shakespeare's moral code), a poet

173

being torn to pieces by the mob, the suicides of Cassius and Brutus, the disruption of social coherence in the internecine clash of two Roman armies, and a near-total breakdown in human relations. The dance that brought the Globe performance to an end was an elegant coda to send the audience away in a calmer state of mind than they would otherwise have known; but more significantly also, a restoration of harmony to audience, players, and the theatre itself: that microcosm of the universe that the Globe represented.

After three consecutive histories and a tragedy, the company would have been pressing Shakespeare for a new comedy to take into the Globe and, if the traditional story is believed, the Queen was demanding another play about Falstaff – 'Falstaff in love' – and hers was a voice not to be denied. But if *The Merry Wives of Windsor* belongs to the winter of 1599, *As You Like It* is a play for all seasons but especially summer, and so we shall glance at that first.

Dr Johnson describes it with his usual exactness as a fable 'wild and pleasing'.[10] It is justly one of the three most popular comedies that Shakespeare wrote, and contains in Rosalind, its leading role, one of his most delightful female characters.

The play begins in fraternal strife in two separate households; that of a royal duke, where the place of the elder brother (Duke Senior) has been usurped by the younger (Duke Frederick), and the legitimate ruler expelled to take refuge in the Forest of Arden; the other, that of the sons of Sir Rowland de Boys, where the elder, Sir Oliver, is tyrannising over a younger, Orlando, for whom he has conceived an unreasoning hatred. At the ducal court, we find also two unhappy cousins and friends, Celia, the daughter of Duke Frederick, the usurper, and Rosalind, the daughter of his exiled brother. The plot – which Shakespeare derived in the main from a popular prose romance by Thomas Lodge – brings Orlando and Rosalind together at court on the occasion of a wrestling match in which Orlando has challenged a professional fighter, Charles, who has been secretly bribed by Sir Oliver to kill him; but Orlando, though young, is no weakling and, having been brought up among peasants and their rural sports, triumphs in the contest to the obvious admiration of Rosalind. Returning home, Orlando is warned by Adam, an old and sympathetic family retainer, of the murderous intentions of his brother towards him, and the two of them take flight in the direction of the Forest. Concurrently, Duke Frederick, resentful of Rosalind's friendship with his daughter, banishes her, and the two girls likewise depart towards Arden. Act 2 follows them there, where we meet Duke Senior, and find that not only has he accepted the fact of his exile with remarkable stoicism, but has come to appreciate the virtues of the simpler, rustic way of life that he and his loyal courtiers have of necessity adopted. 'Hath not old custom made this life more sweet', he asks them, 'Than that of painted pomp?'

> Are not these woods
> More free from peril than the envious court? . . .
> Sweet are the uses of adversity
> Which like the toad, ugly and venomous,
> Wears yet a precious jewel in his head;
> And this our life, exempt from public haunt,
> Finds tongues in trees, books in the running brooks,
> Sermons in stones, and good in everything.
>
> (II.i.2–4, 12–17)

The events that follow, and the course of Rosalind's courtship of Orlando (who improbably fails to see through her male disguise), must be left to Shakespeare to reveal in his own good time in the theatre. I shall focus here on the play's characters, and what I conjecture to have been their original casting – in particular, the role that Shakespeare chose for himself.

A tradition originating with an eighteenth-century antiquarian, William Oldys, and first published by Steevens in 1778, suggests that Shakespeare's part in the play was that of Sir Oliver's old retainer, Adam.

One of Shakespeare's younger brothers, who lived to a good old age, even some years, as I compute, after the restoration of *K.*

Charles II, would in his younger days come to London to visit his brother *Will*, as he called him, and be a spectator of him as an actor in some of his own plays.

Questioned in extreme old age by some Restoration actors, 'greedily inquisitive into every little circumstance' which the old man could relate of his brother, all that he could recollect was the 'faint, general, and almost lost ideas he had of having once seen him act a part in one of his own comedies, wherein being to personate a decrepit old man, he wore a long beard, and appeared so weak and drooping and unable to walk, that he was forced to be supported and carried by another person to a table, at which he was seated among some company, who were eating, and one of them sung a song'[11] – which fits, of course (perhaps a little too neatly), with the situation in Act 2, Scene 7 of *As You Like It*, where Orlando carries the exhausted Adam to the Duke's table in the forest, and Amiens sings 'Blow, blow, thou winter wind' (ll. 167ff.). Though Shakespeare had no younger brother who survived later than 1613 (when Richard was buried), Oldys' anecdote makes a good story and has been generally adopted (with suitable reservations) for want of anything better in the way of evidence, and even made the basis for a belief that Shakespeare the player specialised in 'old man' parts.

As Schoenbaum points out in a similar context, 'the wish is father to many a tradition', and on the face of it, this one is just as dubious as most other of the personal anecdotes of Shakespeare that Oldys relates. But it is just possible that it preserves in a roundabout, multi-handed way a substratum of truth. And though there is a tenable alternative in the beneficent duke of the play, whose kindly spirit is the presiding genius in the green, healing world of Arden, the role of Adam commends itself as more likely by its own innate qualities, its uniqueness among Shakespeare's many servant characters, and position in the play. He is present on stage at the opening in a scene with Orlando, and though he disappears from the action very early (after II.vii), as Caesar had done, there is opportunity for his return at the close – as we shall see in a moment. As previously, he gives himself time to work with his cast in rehearsal, and a small but important role in performance that will have a significant impact at critical stages. There is no doubt that, as Peter Levi remarks, 'Shakespeare's heart is in Adam'.[12]

With less than half the number of named characters than in the histories, the casting would have been well within the compass of the existing company. Orlando is young, handsome, athletic, warm-hearted, shy with girls, and not over-bright. If I was right in saying that Burbage at twenty-eight was too old for Romeo in 1595, he would certainly have been out of the running for Orlando at thirty-two. The part would have gone to one of the older apprentices, perhaps Kit Beeston, or Nick Tooley who would then have been twenty-four. For his female roles – Rosalind and Celia, a pert shepherdess called Phoebe, and the feisty goatherd Audrey – he would have drawn on the company's more recent recruits. The age of the boy-actor playing Rosalind presents something of a puzzle. He would have needed to be young enough to represent the charms of Rosalind as a girl convincingly, but sufficiently tall and assured in her male disguise as Ganymede to act as confidant and instructor in the arts of love to Orlando. With some 700 lines, the part is by far the longest and most complex of Shakespeare's heroines who disguise themselves as men, and would have required exceptional ability and experience.[13] He would have had a particular boy in mind when he wrote it.

Jaques is one of two 'odd men out' in the play; he looks at life aslant, a true eccentric. Though he inhabits the ducal court, respects the Duke, and is regarded by him with affectionate amusement, he never quite belongs in his world. I assign it to Burbage in a possible double with Duke Frederick.[14]

It is Duke Senior (as played perhaps by Phillips) who gives the cue for the most famous speech in the play – if not in the whole of Shakespeare –

> Thou seest, we are not alone unhappy:
> This wide and universal theatre
> Presents more woeful pageants than the scene
> Wherein we play in.

Jaques: All the world's a stage . . .   (II.vii.136ff.)

The speech has been criticised by certain scholars as no more than a series of trite commonplaces, coloured by Jaques' melancholy view of man's end; but in that context – the late summer of the company's opening season at the Globe – it is superbly right and effective and, despite its present over-familiarity, can still send a shiver of pleasurable anticipation down the spine when we hear its opening line. Though from the point of view of plot construction, it is merely filling-in time to allow Orlando to fetch Adam to the feast, it is a perfectly judged restatement of the message that had already gone out strongly from *Henry V*, and was to remain at the back of Shakespeare's mind in writing all his subsequent plays: that the theatre – the particular theatre in which the play is presently being performed – is a figure in miniature of that 'universal theatre' in which we all play a part, that by the power of imagination aims to bring the whole of life within its walls. *Totus mundus agit histrionem*, as the Globe's motto put it. We are all actors to one degree or another.

The other outsider in the forest is of course Touchstone, who no one seriously doubts would have gone to Armin as the first of a series of clever fools that Shakespeare was to write especially for him; like Jaques, the character has no precedent in Shakespeare's sources for the play. But the debt he owed to Armin – or, more accurately perhaps, the extent to which he was able to mould the actor's talents and personality to his own purposes in this new creation – has not been fully acknowledged. For not only does the character's name combine that of Armin's Tutch from his *Two Maids of More-clacke* with a contemporary court fool called Stone, but the style of his wit, in its blending of whimsical humour and word-play with scraps of learning (verse 'as well blancke as crancke', prose that passes for 'currant', as Armin describes it himself), is anticipated in his *Two Maids*, and echoed in his *Foole upon Foole* and *Quips for Questions* of the following year.[15] The combination in Touchstone of cleverness and folly would have been new to Shakespeare's audience, as it is unexpected by Jaques on first meeting him:

A fool, a fool! I met a fool i' th' forest . . .
Who laid him down and bask'd him in the sun,
And rail'd on Lady Fortune in good terms,
In good set terms, and yet a motley fool.   (II.vii.12, 15–17)

Kempe's fools had been either comic servants like Launce, the Dromios and Gobbo, or characters such as Bottom and Dogberry who remain blissfully unaware of their own foolishness. Touchstone is the first of the professional fools to appear in the plays.[16] He is 'motley' in two senses: in his conscious assumption of folly and the costume he wears; not the 'idiot's robe' Armin is seen to be wearing for his impersonation of the natural, Blue John, in the illustration on p. 169, but in its motley combination of colours.[17]

I doubt that Shakespeare intends us to take very seriously Rosalind's claims to magical knowledge; they are part of her ingenious device for bringing about a suitable occasion on which she can reveal herself to Orlando in her true gender – as the girl he loves and his prospective bride. The masque that ends the play is thus not, as sometimes presented, a true theophany comparable to that of Jupiter in *Cymbeline* or Diana in *Pericles*, but a theatrical event, a play-within-the-play that she has put together and rehearsed with the aid of her country friends. Realistically, the part of the god Hymen should most probably go to Corin (Heminges?), the wise old shepherd who met with her and Celia on their first arrival in the forest and found them a cottage in which to live, who is otherwise absent from the final scene; but the early disappearance of Adam from the play at the end of Act 2, when he is taken off by Duke Senior to recuperate in his cave, somehow requires that he should return before the end, and there is no other role in which he can do so more appropriately than as Hymen – especially as acted by Shakespeare. There are more songs in *As You Like It* than in any other of the plays, and music pervades it. As in Caesar – but this time as an integral part of the play – harmony is generally restored and celebrated in a stately dance in which not just two, but four, couples move about the stage in admirable and graceful combination with each other.

The Merry Wives of Windsor is a play of the winter and, though a variety of dates have been proposed, I think it most probable that the Folio text as we have it now was written in the summer of 1599, and first produced at the Globe in the winter of that year.

I mentioned earlier that it may owe its genesis to a previous event in the life of the company's patron, the second Lord Hunsdon, who in April 1597 was appointed Knight of the Garter, having recently succeeded Cobham as Lord Chamberlain. A tradition that the play was written by command of the Queen, 'who was so eager to see it Acted, that she commanded it to be finished in fourteen days' – first recorded by an unsuccessful playwright, John Dennis, in 1702 – is likely to have originated with a request from Hunsdon himself, who may perhaps have backed it with some hint of the pleasure it would give to the Queen.[18]

According to Leslie Hotson,[19] the play was first performed at a Garter feast in the presence of the Queen on St George's Day, 23 April 1597. The installation of the new knights (there were four others in addition to Hunsdon) was to take place as customary in St George's Chapel, Windsor, a month later, which fits with Mistress Quickly's instructions to the fairies in Act 5 of the play, to

> Search Windsor Castle, elves, within and out.
> Strew good luck, ouphes, on every sacred room,
> That it may stand till the perpetual doom
> In state as wholesome as in state 'tis fit,
> Worthy the owner and the owner it.
> The several chairs of order look you scour
> With juice of balm and every precious flower.
> Each fair instalment, coat, and several crest,
> With loyal blazon, evermore be blest!
> And nightly, meadow-fairies, look you sing,
> Like to the Garter's compass, in a ring . . .   (V.v.56–66)

But it is impossible to believe that the play as printed in the Folio could have been written and rehearsed in a fortnight – let alone ten days, as Dennis was later to assert. And there are problems in this

1   Shakespeare the player? A bearded Shakespeare in profile from a miniature by George
Vertue, dated 1754 (from the collection of Lois A. Gaeta, photograph supplied by courtesy
of the Shakespeare Centre Library, Stratford-upon-Avon)

2   The memorial bust in Holy Trinity Church (courtesy of Shakespeare Centre Library, Stratford-upon-Avon)

3   Stratford Guildhall, upper chamber, as it was about 1900. From the 1560s this had been used by the King's School which Shakespeare attended, and probably also by the companies of players who visited the town from 1569 onwards. The desks shown in the photograph are a later addition. In Shakespeare's time, the pupils would have sat on benches, and the same benches might also have been used by those attending the plays (Shakespeare Birthplace Trust, Stratford-upon-Avon)

4   Reconstructed view of London south of the Thames in about 1600, showing location of the Rose and the Globe (from a painting by C. Walter Hodges by permission of the artist and the Museum of London)

5   William Sly by an unknown artist (by permission of the Trustees of Dulwich Picture Gallery)

6   Richard Burbage. Burbage was a painter as well as an actor and this is said to be a self-portrait (by permission of the Trustees of Dulwich Picture Gallery)

7 Anonymous portrait of Edward Alleyn (by permission of the Trustees of Dulwich Picture Gallery)

8 The Tomb of John Gower in Southwark Cathedral (formerly, from 1539, the parish church of St Saviour) where Shakespeare's younger brother Edmund was buried in 1607. In the following year, Gower was to feature as presenter in *Pericles* (courtesy of the Dean and Chapter of Southwark Cathedral)

9   An 18-year-old Portia, Jill Showell, in Glen Byam Shaw's production of *The Merchant of Venice* for the Young Vic in 1950/51 (author's archive)

10   A seventeenth-century depiction of 'Wee Three Logerheads', probably featuring (left) Tom Derry, an innocent in the keeping of Anne of Denmark, and Muckle John, a fool at the court of Charles I, with marotte (courtesy of the Shakespeare Birthplace Trust, Stratford-upon-Avon)

11   'What, the sword and the word? Do you study them both, Master Parson?' (Shallow). *The Merry Wives of Windsor*, Act 3, Scene 1, Stratford-upon-Avon, 1955. L to R: the author as Rugby, Michael Denison (Caius), Edward Atienza (Shallow), Patrick Wymark (Host), William Devlin (Sir Hugh), Ralph Michael (Page), Geoffrey Sassé (Simple), Geoffrey Bayldon (Slender). (Photograph by Angus McBean, author's collection)

12 The Moot Hall in Maldon as it was *c.* 1890. It was built as a private house and acquired by the town in 1576. The classical-style portico is much later in date and replaced a gallery from which proclamations were read (photograph by courtesy of the Maldon Society)

13 John Lowin in 1640. He lived until 1659, and in 1604 would still have been in early manhood. He is said by a Restoration writer to have played Henry VIII, and to have been instructed in the part by 'Mr Shakespeare himself'. (Ashmolean Museum, Oxford)

14 'When thou dost ask me blessing, I'll kneel down/And ask of thee forgiveness' (*King Lear*, V.iii.10–11). Sally Knyvette as Cordelia and the author as Lear in a production by Giles Block at Ipswich Arts Theatre in 1974 (photograph by Paul Levitton)

15 'When shall we three meet again?' (*Macbeth*, I.i). The Weird Sisters in a production by the author at Ipswich Arts Theatre in 1978, as played by John Dallimore, Pat Wainwright and John Matshikiza.

16 The Peacham drawing of 1595(?) (from the Portland Papers at Longleat by permission of the Marquis of Bath)

17 Nathan Field was the son of a clergyman. According to Cuthbert Burbage (Richard's brother), he came to the King's company from the Children of the Chapel in 1608/9. He later joined Lady Elizabeth's men but returned to the King's in 1615. Ben Jonson claimed him as 'his schollar'. He is seventeenth in the Folio list of Principal Actors after William Ostler (from an anonymous portrait in Dulwich Picture Gallery, by permission of the Trustees).

18 The Old Moot Hall in Cross Street, Sudbury, dates from the fourteenth century. This postcard view shows what it looked like before restoration in the 1940s (reproduced from Barry L. Wall, *Sudbury through the Ages*, 1870, Ipswich, n.d.)

early date for the play. As Chambers pointed out, the inclusion of Nym among Falstaff's cronies, and his naming as 'Corporal', would have made little sense if he had not previously been seen on the battlefield in *Henry V*,[20] which we can date rather precisely to the early summer of 1599. Nor does the play as a whole suggest that it was written for a courtly rather than a popular audience.

The most likely explanation for these incompatibilities in the evidence is that put forward by G.R. Hibbard: that Shakespeare was indeed comissioned to provide an after-dinner entertainment for the Garter feast of 1597, but that it consisted in a masque of the kind that Elizabeth is known to have enjoyed, featuring the legendary Herne the Hunter, a Fairy Queen and satyrs, which he could have put together rather quickly, and this was later utilised by him with his usual economy to form the final act of the play he was to write for the Globe in 1599.[21]

However that was, the play as we have it now is unique in the canon in drawing on the bourgeois life of a small country town that must have been close to Shakespeare's own experience of Stratford. There are links with the court as represented by the nearby Castle, and the character of Fenton who is said to have kept company with the 'wild prince and Poins' of *Henry IV*; but the main focus of the play is on the wives of the title in their humbling of Falstaff. In their combination of all the wifely virtues with wit, resourcefulness and an unfailing *joie de vivre*, they are set from the start to win hands down in their contest with the fat knight. They are depicted with such affectionate realism as to suggest they were based on real women very close to Shakespeare. They are matched in truth of observation and credibility by their husbands: George Page, the solid, well-to-do townsman, whose prejudices are tempered by toleration and love of fair play; and Frank Ford, who is not so consumed by his jealousy as to learn from his mistakes and, in the end, to beg pardon for them. Page's daughter, Anne, demonstrates in her reply to the proposition that she should marry the ludicrous French physician Caius – 'I had rather be set quick i' th' earth/And bowled to death with turnips' – that she has inherited much of her mother's spirit and wit. The other inhabitants of this small world are comic eccentrics. Bardolph, Nym and Pistol come in the wake of Falstaff from *Henry V*. They bring their familiar humours with them, but are given little scope for further development. Justice Shallow and his nincompoop nephew Slender – whose courtship of Anne Page is one of the joys of the play – are visitors from the Gloucestershire of *Henry IV*. In the persons of Mistress Quickly (another importation from the Henriad) and Dr Caius, much typical Shakespeare humour is made of their mistreatment of the language. The facetious host of the Garter inn is a still-recognisable portrait of his occupational kind. The play is written largely in prose and bowls along at exemplary pace with hardly a dull moment and many incidental delights, such as Sir Hugh's Latin lesson for the Pages' small son William (IV.i), and Caius' servant Rugby, whose only fault in Quickly's estimation is that he is 'given to prayer; he is somewhat peevish that way' (I.iv.12–13).

Scholarly criticism has been largely taken up with matters of dating and Shakespeare's treatment of Falstaff, which some nineteenth-century critics considered to be a degradation of his original conception of the character in *Henry IV*. Recent editors have rightly pointed out that it is not so much Falstaff who has changed as the context in which he appears, and his function in the play.[22] I do think, however, that though much of his spirit and wit remain, Shakespeare was missing Kempe in the role.

Otherwise, the casting of the play, with its relatively modest number of characters (twenty-two named roles with three or four additional children) would have presented little difficulty. Kempe's immediate replacement is unknown. Burbage would have brought real passion to his playing of Ford, and thus have provided a necessary ballast to the play's more farcical situations and scenes. Sir Hugh Evans, the parson, would almost certainly have gone to Armin as the last in a series of Welsh parts that had begun with his Welsh Captain in *Richard II* (see note 21 above). From Simple's description of him as having 'but a little wee face, with a little yellow beard', there cannot be much doubt that Slender was Sincler's part, with Pope, Sly and Cowley as Pistol, Bardolph and Nym (as in *Henry V*), and Cowley in a possible double of Nym and Shallow. The two wives, Anne, Quickly, Fenton and the servants would all have gone to apprentices of various ages, and there appears to have been an infusion of very young boys to play Robin, William and any extra fairies that were required.[23]

Shakespeare's part in the play could only, I think, have been Page. Though small in terms of lines (some 150), he makes an appearance in half the twenty-two scenes, and the fact of the character's normality among so many eccentrics gives it a special position; he is a yardstick of good sense against which we can measure the others' follies and self-deceptions. He might easily have been dull or sententious but is not allowed to become so. The reader may find this over-fanciful, but just as I have suggested that Shakespeare drew on the important women in his life for the wives, I think he may have drawn on his father for Page. John Shakespeare would now have been in his sixties. It will be remembered that back in 1568 he had made an approach to the College of Arms for a grant of arms that would have entitled him to the status and name of gentleman, but that as troubles engulfed him it had been allowed to lapse. In 1596, when William had begun to enjoy the first fruits of his success, he had renewed the application on behalf of his father and himself, and been successful in obtaining it; in 1599 John had less than two more years to live. (The names were common enough, but is it only coincidence that the Pages' children are named as Anne and William?) The background of the play is so close to what we know of Shakespeare's early life in Stratford that I feel sure there was for him a personal, nostalgic interest in the writing of it that lends a warmth to the whole, and makes it something much more attractive and appealing than it would otherwise have been. His participation as Page would have been at one with that.

The play has been most often presented as a midsummer romp, but a careful reading of the text reveals that the action was originally conceived as taking place in winter. As reward for his watching, Mistress Quickly promises Rugby a companionable, bedtime 'posset' (a milk-drink curdled with wine or ale) 'at the latter end of a sea-coal fire' (I.iv.8); Page queries Sir Hugh's appearance at Frogmore for his duel with Caius, 'youthful still – in your doublet and hose this raw rheumatic day?' (III.i.44); and at the conclusion of the play, his wife proposes,

> Good husband, let us every one go home,
> And laugh this sport o'er by a country fire;
> Sir John and all.

In recent theatrical history, Glen Byam Shaw was the first to return to a midwinter interpretation in his definitive Stratford production of 1955, with Angela Baddeley and Joyce Redman as the wives and Christmas-card settings and costumes by Motley, in which the company sweated through a hot Stratford summer (see Plate 11). Though there have been good productions since, it gave both room to the warmth at the heart of the play and a crispness to the comedy that I doubt has been surpassed.

Hamlet belongs to 1600 and *Twelfth Night* to 1600/1, and these two plays were to bring the present period of Shakespeare's writing to a close.[24] In their different ways, they bring him near to the peak of his achievement as a dramatic poet, and provide him also with two of his finest and most challenging acting roles.

Hamlet is the second of his great tragedies, but in the degree to which it has entered the mainstream of European thought and literature, and its language and imagery become part of the mindset and expression of English speakers everywhere, it is of course unique. The influence it has had, and continues to have, makes it all the more difficult for us to see it, as we must try to do here, in its original context as a theatrical event – a play among others, written for a specific group of actors to perform in a particular theatre (the Globe) at a given moment of Shakespeare's and the Chamberlain's history.

It has been described as the most problematic of his plays. Many of the supposed problems as seen from the study are found to disappear when we put it back where it primarily belongs – on the stage; but there is one problem at least that need never arise: the identity of the role he wrote for himself. For here tradition, and consideration of those other factors I have proposed as affecting his choice of parts, point in the same direction; it was that of the Ghost, the ghost of Hamlet's father, the former king.

Nicholas Rowe tells us in 1709 that

'Thou wretched, rash, intruding fool, farewell./I took thee for thy better', *Hamlet*, III.iv.30–1 (from the *Henry Irving Shakespeare*, 1892)

His Name is Printed, as the Custom was in those Times, amongst those of the other Players, before some old Plays, but without any particular Account of what sort of Parts he us'd to play; and tho' I have inquir'd, I could never meet with any further Account of him this way, than that the top of his Performance was the Ghost in his own *Hamlet*.[25]

The information, along with most of the other anecdotes Rowe retails of Shakespeare's life, had come to him through the great Restoration actor, Thomas Betterton (*c.* 1635–1710), as he himself acknowledged, and though many of these stories, apparently gathered in the course of a visit by the actor to Stratford early in the Restoration period, are found to be little better than gossip – dubious at best, some demonstrably false – the probability of this one being true is strengthened by the indications we have already uncovered of

Shakespeare having played similar spectral roles in Kyd's *Spanish Tragedy* and, more recently, *Julius Caesar*. The opening scene on the battlements of Elsinore in *Hamlet* has been justly praised for its imaginative power in creating an atmosphere of impending doom and fear among the watchers, into which the Ghost enters with awe-inspiring effect. One has only to compare it with the equivalent scene in Kyd, featuring the Ghost of Andrea, to realise how much Shakespeare as poet would have learnt from his playing of that role, and that the secret of his greater success with the Ghost in *Hamlet* lies in its economy of means; for while Kyd's Ghost immediately embarks on a long, detailed account of his journey through the underworld, Shakespeare's is initially silent, and it is not until Scene 5 of Act 1, when he finds himself alone with his son, that he confides:

> But that I am forbid
> To tell the secrets of my prison-house,
> I could a tale unfold whose lightest word
> Would harrow up thy soul, freeze thy young blood,
> Make thy two eyes like stars start from their spheres,
> Thy knotted and combined locks to part,
> And each particular hair to stand an end
> Like quills upon the fretful porpentine.
> But this eternal blazon must not be
> To ears of flesh and blood . . .   (I.v.13–22)

– which, in its reticence, is all the more chilling.

To watch these scenes in rehearsal (as I have had the privilege of doing on several occasions) is to realise something else about the Ghost, related to this economy of description, that Shakespeare the player would have understood very well; that much of the effectiveness of the performance depends on its economy of movement; the extent to which the actor can bring to it a preternatural stillness, an immobility of posture in repose in contrast to the progressively more fevered reactions of the watchers. As indicated in Shakespeare's text and stage directions, it goes 'slow and stately' by them; it 'spreads its arms', it lifts its head,

186

> and did address
> Itself to motion like as it would speak.
> But even then the morning cock crew loud,
> And at the sound it shrunk in haste away
> And vanished from our sight.   (I.ii. 216–20)

When it does find a voice, we are often treated to sonorous, actorly tones, but the voice should surely be similarly detached from life and human emotion, unpractised, hollow of tone. (The curious thing is that the more these scenes with the Ghost are subjected, in later stages of the rehearsal process, to technological resources of the modern stage in the way of ghostly lighting, dry ice and electronic sound effects, the more the excitement engendered by Shakespeare's words and imaginative acting tends to be lost, and what was initially – and may remain in essence – thrillingly real is reduced in performance to mere spectacle and incoherence.)

If Shakespeare played the Ghost, it is unlikely to have been his only part in the play. There are eighteen named roles to be filled, along with at least five unnamed Players, the Grave-digger and his mate, a Captain, a Lord, a Priest or Minister, English Ambassadors, sailors and messengers – some thirty speaking parts in all, of which at least ten would have been doubled. The Ghost, who disappears from the action after the Closet scene (III.iv), is one of them.

The clue to the identity of Shakespeare's second role is to be found in the basic dramatic and moral structure of the play, which, reduced to its simplest terms, is the story of a king murdered by his brother and avenged by his son. It is the closely entwined triangular situation, deriving from Shakespeare's sources (including the lost *Ur-Hamlet* that once had a place in the company's repertoire) that dictates the 'idea' of the play and also its casting. The moral disparity between the brother-kings is stressed from the start. 'So excellent a king', says Hamlet of his father in the first of his soliloquies, 'that was to this/Hyperion to a satyr'; but Claudius' real offence in Hamlet's eyes lies not in his difference from his father but in his likeness; in the inescapable fact that they are brothers; that the marriage of Claudius with Hamlet's mother (Gertrude) is not just over-hasty but *incestuous*, and the murder of his father, *fratricidal*. Failing the unlikely presence in the company of two brothers of the right approximate age, the simplest and most effective way in which this blood relationship between the two can be realised on stage is for the parts to be doubled and, if we look in detail at the text and sequence of scenes, we find that Shakespeare has gone to some trouble to make that possible. If, then, he played the Ghost, as generally accepted, it is highly likely that he played Claudius also. Too often, *Hamlet* has been seen as a 'one-man tragedy, one vast part meant for a great actor'.[26] We need perhaps to stand the play on its head to see it afresh; not as one vast part for a great actor, but three parts of varied length for *two* great actors – Burbage and Shakespeare.

That Hamlet was indeed Burbage's part is attested to by an anonymous elegy following the actor's death in 1619:

> Hee's gone & with him what a world are dead . . .
> No more young Hamlett, ould Heironymoe.
> Kind Leer, the greved Moore, and more beside,
> That lived in him, have now for ever dy'de.[27]

All the world's a stage. We never lose sight of that theme for very long in the plays, and *Hamlet* brings it back to our attention in the most insistent manner possible, for not only does Shakespeare introduce a play-within-the-play (as Kyd had done before him in the *Spanish Tragedy*) and uses it to test the truth of the Ghost's accusation against Claudius, but daringly brings in a troupe of travelling players to peform it under Hamlet's direction. But there is more to it than that, for as Anne Righter points out,

> *Hamlet* is a tragedy dominated by the idea of the play. In the course of its development the play metaphor appears in a number of forms. It describes the dissembler, the Player King, the difference between appearance and reality, falsehood and truth, and the theatrical nature of certain moments of time. The relationship of world and stage is reciprocal: the actor holds a mirror up to nature, but the latter in its turn reflects the features of the play.[28]

The speech of the First Player, whom Hamlet greets as his 'old friend' and invites to give a taste of his quality on the players' arrival, has been sadly misunderstood and misplayed as parody. But its significant theme – the slaughter of Priam by one of his sons – is Hamlet's choice, not the Player's. And though abused by literary critics as 'bombast', 'bad verse' and similar terms, Hamlet is clearly of a different opinion for the speech is one that he 'chiefly loved' – to the extent that he has committed it to memory, and is able to quote a dozen of its opening lines in giving the Player his cue, which he takes up thus:

> Anon he finds him,
> Striking too short at Greeks. His antique sword,
> Rebellious to his arm, lies where it falls,
> Repugnant to command. Unequal match'd,
> Pyrrhus at Priam drives, in rage strikes wide;
> But with the whiff and wind of his fell sword
> Th'unnerved father falls . . .   (II.ii.464–70)

If this is bombast, it is very good bombast – the kind of bombast that Shakespeare might have written if he had set himself to do it. If the speech is elevated in style it is because, as Harold Jenkins explains, it 'has to stand out from the drama which surrounds it and which is already removed from ordinary life; and this . . . demands a style which rises above normal theatrical elevation as the latter does above natural speech'.[29] But it is not the style or content of the speech, with which he is already familiar, but the commitment and depth of feeling that the Player brings to it that astounds Hamlet, and acts as a spur to his future actions.[30] To guy the speech in the manner of an old-fashioned 'ham' for cheap laughs, as has regrettably been done, is not just artistically inept, but loses the main point of the scene, which is to bring Hamlet to the point of resolution.

As Brutus enjoins the conspirators in *Caesar* –

> Let not our looks put on our purposes,
> But bear it as our Roman actors do,
> With untir'd spirits and formal constancy   (II.i.224–6)

– so Hamlet takes strength from the Player's commitment to his role. The mirror throws back a reverse image: the world reflects the stage.

> O what a rogue and peasant slave am I!
> Is it not monstrous that this player here,
> But in a fiction, in a dream of passion,
> Could force his soul so to his own conceit
> That from her working all his visage wann'd,
> Tears in his eyes, distraction in his aspect,
> A broken voice, and his whole function suiting
> With forms to his conceit? And all for nothing!
> For Hecuba!
> What's Hecuba to him, or he to her,
> That he should weep for her? . . .
> Yet I,
> A dull and muddy-mettled rascal, peak
> Like John-a-dreams, unpregnant of my cause,
> And can say nothing – no, not for a king,
> Upon whose property and most dear life
> A damn'd defeat was made . . .   (II.ii.544–54, 561–6)

In admitting the centrality of the play metaphor in *Hamlet*, we must beware however of confusing two quite different levels of reality which may, as Anne Righter has said, touch at certain points but should not be confused. For though the actors on stage who represent the Players are players themselves, they are nevertheless assuming roles in a play; and while the company of which they are members has points of similarity with the Chamberlain's men – such as the occasional need to travel and competition from 'little eyases' – it is *not* the Chamberlain's men, and the city from which it is said to have come could hardly have been London. There are indications that in the admittedly jocular terms in which Hamlet greets them –

He that plays the king shall be welcome – his Majesty shall have tribute of me, the adventurous knight shall use his foil and target, the lover shall not sigh gratis, the humorous man shall end his part in peace, the clown shall make those laugh whose lungs are tickle a th' sear, and the lady shall say her mind freely – or the blank verse shall halt for't.   (II.ii.318–24)

– Shakespeare has in mind, not his own or any other contemporary troupe, but earlier interluders of the 'half-dozen men and a boy' tradition, in which it was accepted that each actor would specialise in a particular type of role (the King, the Knight, etc.) and rarely depart from it except in doubling.

Nor should we assume that in Hamlet's instructions to the Players, and his admonitions to them to avoid over-acting on the one hand and tameness on the other, Shakespeare was addressing his fellows of the Chamberlain's, as is commonly supposed, rather than making a generally applicable statement of principle;[31] or that the tone of patronising superiority adopted by Hamlet represents in the slightest degree one that Shakespeare in his own person would ever have used to his fellows. On the contrary, his intention throughout the scene is one of disassociation – of the 'double mirror' effect. For if, as Hamlet tells us, 'the purpose of playing . . . both at the first and now, was and is to hold as 'twere the mirror up to nature', it is by putting the Players *as players* on stage, so that they and their play become part of the picture the mirror reflects, that Shakespeare achieves the illusion of making the larger action appear more real than it would otherwise have done. The more he can strip away illusion from the play-within-the-play and from those who perform it, the more readily the audience will accept the play as a whole and those who carry it forward as a true reflection of reality. Here is magic of a high order, in which the players themselves are complicit. Illusion within illusion.

> The play's the thing
> Wherein I'll catch the conscience of the King.

— ✳ —

The play that was to bring this extraordinary series of variations on the theme of reality and illusion to a joyful conclusion is one that has continued to delight audiences ever since, and has established itself (with *Much Ado* and *As You Like It*) as one of Shakespeare's three most popular comedies: *Twelfth Night, or What You Will*.

It has to be said that for the most part the scholars have made heavy weather of it, beginning in the eighteenth century with Dr Johnson. Though he found the play 'in the graver part elegant and easy, and in some of the lighter scenes exquisitely humorous', he considered the 'natural fatuity' of Sir Andrew (though 'drawn with great propriety') as 'not the proper prey of a satirist', and the 'marriage of Olivia and the succeeding perplexity, though well enough contrived to divert on the stage' as wanting credibility and failing to 'produce the proper instruction required in the drama, as it exhibits no just picture of life'.[32] Academics and scholarly editors generally continue to look for 'instruction' in the plays, and are disabled in their appreciation of comedy by a predisposition to interpret it as satire. *Twelfth Night* is comedy in its purest form, with an underlay of wistful romance, that requires no other justification for its existence than the pleasure it gives.

The circumstances in which Shakespeare came to write it and the occasion of its first performance point us in the right direction. Late in December 1600, it was announced by the Lord Chamberlain, Hunsdon (also the company's patron), that a visit was shortly to be made to the now-ageing Queen by a young and admired Italian nobleman, Don Virginio Orsino, duke of Bracciano, and the search was on for a play to entertain him that 'shalbe best furnished with rich apparell, have greate variety and change of Musicke and daunces, and of a Subject that may be most pleasing to her Majestie'. The date proposed for the performance was 6 January 1601, the feast of Epiphany, the last of the twelve days of Christmas, a period when the court gave itself over to hectic enjoyment, and a Lord of Misrule was appointed to oversee the festivities, along with the Master of Revels. Clearly at such short notice (less than two weeks), there was no opportunity for Shakespeare or anyone else to write and rehearse a new play especially for the occasion; it was a question of choosing from what the principal companies already had on offer or could bring up to scratch in the time available. Was it merely coincidence that Shakespeare's new comedy (probably with the original title of

What You Will) was already in rehearsal? It is difficult to think of any other contemporary comedy that might have been thought a more appropriate choice. Doubtless after a discreet enquiry as to whether the gesture would be acceptable to the Queen and her guest, the Duke of the play was named Orsino in the visitor's honour and, with the addition of one or two dances, which it otherwise lacks, the play was duly performed at Whitehall on the day appointed. It has been known ever since as *Twelfth Night*.[33]

As befits its festive occasion, the play is filled with music and song. It begins with music, and the now familiar, hauntingly beautiful lines –

> If music be the food of love, play on,
> Give me excess of it, that, surfeiting,
> The appetite may sicken, and so die.
> That strain again, it had a dying fall:
> O, it came o'er my ear like the sweet sound
> That breathes upon a bank of violets,
> Stealing and giving odour.

That Shakespeare spoke them in the character of Orsino admits of little doubt; the part would have been for him a return to the kingly dukes of his earlier comedies and, at thirty-six, he was at the optimum age to play it. Orsino is seriously in love with a young and beautiful neighbour, Olivia, who, in her mourning for a beloved brother, is unresponsive. Complications arise with the appearance of Viola, whom we first meet as survivor of a shipwreck in which she too has lost a beloved brother (or so she believes). Having made her way to Orsino's court disguised as a boy (Cesario), she is promptly recruited by Orsino as intermediary in his courtship of Olivia. It is the tangles of love between these three – Orsino for Olivia, Viola for Orsino, Olivia for Cesario – that take up most of the action. But a secondary plot, in which Olivia's bucolic and troublesome kinsman Sir Toby Belch and her gentlewoman Maria take the lead in a conspiracy to humble the pompous household steward, Malvolio, is important also in providing the play's broader, more uninhibited humour. Sir Toby is the self-appointed Lord of Misrule in Olivia's household in direct opposition to its puritanical steward, and Feste the clown is his jester. Along with Sir Andrew Aguecheek, a simple-minded knight whom Sir Toby is gulling for his money, these three constitute (as Feste points out) a personification of the then popular image of 'We three' – comprising two fools and an ass, or (as illustrated in Plate 10) a marotte.

The later arrival on the scene of Viola's supposedly drowned brother, Sebastian, who in appearance is identical to her in her disguise as Cesario and of Sebastian's friend Antonio, and the further confusions of identity that follow on their various meetings with each other, are wonderfully managed to bring the comedy of the play to an uproarious climax. Malvolio, who has been tricked into a belief that Olivia is in love with *him*, exits promising revenge on 'the whole pack of you'.

Orsino is a typical Shakespeare role. He opens the play, initiates the basic plot situation as between himself, Olivia and Viola, and contrives an early exit in Act 2 to return only for the play's resolution, and to speak the final lines. Malvolio, in his combining of self-love and gullibility, is a unique invention. He dominates the comedy – and to some extent the play. The part is not one for a clown or recognised comedian, whom we expect to be funny, but for a leading actor of 'straight' or tragic roles; it would surely have gone to Burbage. Sir Toby is again a fresh creation, and more than a surrogate Falstaff. Though buffoon in the sense of dependant, he lacks both Falstaff's massive bulk and his wit, but compensates with his sense of fun and unfailing belief in his own dignity. Though an inveterate toper, there is no compelling reason for him to be fat at all, and he has been played with success as a trim, soldierly figure; it was a part for Pope or for Cowley. He and Sir Andrew make a splendid double-act. Sir Andrew, thin of face, a bloodless 'clodpole' with hair that hangs 'like flax on a distaff', is a close relation of Slender in the *Merry Wives*; the latest in that long series of thin-man parts that we have traced from as far back as the *Shrew* and *Henry VI* in having been played by John Sincler.[34] If there had been any doubt that Armin was of the company to play Touchstone in *As You Like It*, there can be none at all about his participation here as Feste, for the peculiar style of his wit is reproduced in full measure, and the character bears the same marks of independence and freedom of spirit as Touchstone. Both are professional jesters, dependent on no one but themselves, without emotional ties. Nor are they confined to any one place for, as Feste explains, 'Foolery, sir, does walk about the orb like the sun, it shines everywhere' (III.i.39–40). Here, too, in his impersonation of Sir Topas, is more evidence of Armin's versatility, and of his skill as a singer which, though strangely missing from *As You Like It*, he had previously demonstrated as Tutch in the *Two Maids of More-clacke*. I forbear even to guess at the names of the boys who played Olivia, Viola and Maria; but they would doubtless have been drawn from that same exceptionally gifted group who had previously been cast (and were still performing) as Kate in *Henry V*, Portia in *Caesar*, Rosalind and Celia in *As You Like It*, Ophelia in *Hamlet*, and as the 'merry wives'. Shakespeare would have spent much of his rehearsal time with them. For all its boisterous Twelfth-night humour, there is, as I have said, an underlay of wistful romance in the play, of which Orsino in his opening lines sets the tone, and we hear it again from Viola, which must stand with Rosalind, Helena and Imogen as one of the most beautiful parts he wrote for his boys. Even Sir Andrew is given his moment of nostalgic sadness: 'I was adored once too'.

We have seen that *Twelfth Night* was written for performance in the winter, and there is at least a possibility that, like the *Merry Wives*, its action was conceived as taking place in that season, and specifically at Christmas. The indications of this are ambiguous; the song of 'the wind and the rain', with which Feste brings the play to an end, is perhaps more suggestive of an English summer than an Illyrian winter, and the orchard location of the central 'letter scene' may likewise point in another direction. Nevertheless, the midnight carousal of Act 2, Scene 3, with its burning of sack, singing of catches and 'On the twelfth day of December' (a version or concealed reference to the well-known carol, 'The Twelve Days of Christmas') give the impression of a traditional Christmas festivity. If played in that way and (where possible) in that season, the play gains an added dimension of enjoyment and a consistency entirely at one with its title.[35]

TEN

Travelling Man

By far the most popular place for performances outside London was the Townhall, and a surprising amount of detailed evidence survives concerning the conditions in which performances were given in this favourite building.

Glynne Wickham[1]

For a variety of reasons largely outside its control, the period 1601 to 1604 was a difficult one for the company. It was to see a first significant slackening in Shakespeare's production of new plays, and a return by him and his fellows to an earlier pattern of performance in which appearances at court (wherever the court happened to be at the time) alternated with extensive provincial tours; one in which their seasons at the Globe were frequently disrupted – often for months at a time – by political events and, most of all, by the plague.

The first such interruption to their playing in London was occasioned by the abortive Essex rebellion of 1601, which followed closely on the company's performance of *Twelfth Night* at court on 6 January. Having failed miserably in Ireland, and incurred Elizabeth's grave displeasure by his early, unauthorised return in the previous September, the arrogant and headstrong earl now planned to recover the situation by taking forcible possession of the person of the Queen, and occupying Whitehall. As cover and justification for this desperate adventure, he hoped to provoke the London mob into riot, and to that end the Chamberlain's men were commissioned to give a special performance of the 'deposing and killing of Richard II' (presumably Shakespeare's play) at the Globe on the eve of the intended rising. In ignorance of what was afoot, but somewhat naively perhaps, the company agreed to this proposal on the promise of a larger than normal fee, as the play was not in their current

196

repertoire and would have needed fresh rehearsal. But when, on the day following the performance (8 February), the earl and his supporters took to the streets with the cry, 'For the Queen! For the Queen! The crown of England is sold to the Spaniard. A plot is laid for my life', the Londoners were more bewildered than alarmed and failed to respond. Whereupon, the earl and his men returned lamely to Essex House, where they were quickly surrounded by the Queen's guards and arrested. The players were left with some explaining to do, which Augustine Phillips as their spokesman did so effectively, when called before a commission of enquiry ten days later, that they escaped without apparent penalty, and we find them performing again at court within a few days. It is hardly to be supposed, however, that their public performances at the Globe were allowed to continue uninterrupted – at least until after the earl's execution on the twenty-fourth of the month. Having completed their season at court, the sharers may well have decided to travel for a while. There is a record of rewards to three unnamed companies at Oxford (the town, not the university) in 1600/1, and the Chamberlain's may have been one of them – perhaps with *Hamlet*.[2]

Though she reacted to it with her customary courage, and had to be discouraged at the age of sixty-eight from going out into the street to see whether any rebel dared fire a shot at her, the whole episode was a shock to the Queen, and the relevance of Richard's deposition to her own situation, if lost on the Londoners, was not lost upon her. When, in August of the same year, William Lambarde, her Keeper of the Records, presented her with an account of the historical documents in his care and she happened on some pages relating to Richard's reign, she remarked to him, 'I am Richard II, know you not that?'; and when Lambarde in reply spoke of Essex and his 'wicked imagination', she went on to say, 'He that will forget God, will also forget his benefactors; this tragedy was played forty times in open streets and houses'.[3] A reminder of the thin ice on which Shakespeare was often walking in his history plays.

If the company's unwitting involvement in the Essex affair left any shadow of doubt over the players' loyalty in Elizabeth's mind, it was soon dispelled. For by the end of the year there are records of the company's court appearances on Boxing Day and 27 December; a performance attended by the Queen, with her *candidae auditrices* (maids of honour, dressed always in white), at Lord Hunsdon's house in Blackfriars on the 29th and others at Whitehall on New Year's Day and 14 February 1602. Unfortunately, no mention was made of the plays presented, but they would probably have included a repeat performance of *Twelfth Night* as this was also given at the Middle Temple for its fellows' annual feast on 2 February, as noted by John Manningham in his *Diary*.[4]

The year that followed (1602) was to be the last full year of Elizabeth's reign – a time of increasing anxiety in the life of the nation. Though sound in health and with a mind as clear as ever, the Queen was now showing the inevitable signs of advancing age in an uncertain temper and sense of loneliness as so many of her loyal servants were passing, or had passed away, most affectingly Burghley in 1598. She was now given to pacing her privy chamber with a rusty old sword in her hand, which occasionally she would 'thrust into the arras in great rage'. An era was felt by all to be coming to an end.

Only two plays by Shakespeare can be assigned to this and the following year (1602/3) – *Troilus and Cressida* and *All's Well that Ends Well*[5] – and, for reasons that will appear later, it is doubtful whether either would have been deemed appropriate for performance at the Globe or at court until very much later – if at all.

The company were performing as usual at Whitehall on Boxing Day 1602. On 14 January 1603 the Queen and her court made a final journey in pouring rain to Richmond, which she spoke of as the 'warm box' to which she could 'best trust her sickly old age', and it was there the company travelled on 2 February to give what would be their last performance for her – if she was well enough to see it. She was suffering from a bad cold and was severely depressed. As the weeks passed she became no better. Refusing medicine, she lay for four days on cushions in her privy chamber until, too weak to protest, she was finally carried to her bed, where she died in the early hours of 24 March.

The playhouses were closed in respect and were to remain dark until after her funeral at the end of April. Within a week, James VI of

Scotland was on his way south to enter on his inheritance as James I of Great Britain but, as he paused at the border town of Berwick on 8 April, the shadow of an old enemy was starting to fall across London with news of a recurrence of bubonic plague in the borough of Stepney, down by the docks. On 5 May, Henslowe at the Rose noted in his diary that 'we leafte of playe now at the Kynges cominge', and when, on the 19th of the month, the new king graciously took the former Lord Chamberlain's servants into his own service, the letters patent effecting their change of status contained an ominous qualification: that those named were 'freely to use and exercise the Arte and faculty of playinge . . . *when the infection of the plague shall decrease . . .*'.[6] Almost a year was to go by before any such decrease occurred. In the meantime, the infection intensified and spread; from 18 deaths in the City in the week prior to 12 May, to a weekly total of 158 in June, 917 in July, rising to an appalling peak of 3,035 (including outlying parishes) in the final week of August.[7] Not only was the plague to close the London playhouses and cast a blight on the life of the City throughout 1603, as it had done ten years earlier in 1593, but it was to throw a lengthening shadow forwards over much of the country during the remainder of Shakespeare's life and career. As we have seen, the company had never altogether ceased to travel during part of each year, and the royal patent of 1603 was to give them a renewed licence and authority for continuing to do so. For not only did it authorise them to exercise their art for the king's 'Solace and pleasure when wee shall thincke good to see them', but 'aswell within theire nowe usual howse called the Globe within our County of Surrey, *as alsoe within anie towne halls or Moute halls or other conveniente places within the liberties and freedome of anie other Cittie, universitie, towne, or Boroughe whatsoever within our said Realmes and domynions*'.[8] While continuing to make regular use of the Globe whenever plague restrictions allowed, they were to take full advantage of this larger freedom in the years ahead.

Before we move on to consider a further chapter in the history of the company, it is time to focus more especially on that portion of Shakespeare's professional life that lay outside the capital. For, contrary to the impression that is usually given by his biographers and editors, the fact is that a substantial part of his career as player and poet from 1580 (as previously proposed) or, more traditionally, from the middle or late 1580s – at a conservative estimate between ten and sixteen years in total – was spent 'on the road'.

He was, to begin with, a Warwickshire man; it was in Stratford that he maintained a permanent home and, until his purchase of an apartment in the Blackfriars Gatehouse in 1613 (within three years of his death), was never more than a lodger in London; nor, in contrast to most of his fellow dramatists in the period, did he ever write a 'London play'. Throughout most of his active years as a player, the guildhalls of such provincial centres as Coventry, Gloucester, Ipswich and Dover would have been almost as familiar to him as the Rose, the Curtain or the Globe itself. If we want to arrive at a balanced view of the theatre scene in which he spent his career, we need to give more careful attention to those alternative indoor venues than is generally afforded by traditional accounts.[9] Nor should we underestimate the importance of Shakespeare's position in relation to his patrons. Though we speak loosely of the Chamberlain's/King's men as 'London companies', the actual status of the players was invariably recorded in official documents as that of 'Servants to the Lord Chamberlain' or 'Servants to the King'. When the monarch moved away from London as Elizabeth and James frequently did – either to one of the outlying palaces or further afield – and the players were summoned to perform at court, they were expected to follow them there as a matter of course. Their position as members of the royal household defined their identity.[10]

From 1599, Shakespeare's company was of course unique in that it possessed a venue in the capital to which it alone had access, and which, from that time forward, naturally served as a base for its subsequent travels; but this does not imply that the company was ever resident there for more than a few months at a time, or – irrespective of the exigencies brought about by the plague and other exceptional circumstances prevailing in London – that it ever ceased to be what it had been from its beginnings: a company of travelling players.

Because no records of the company's performances at the Globe, such as those that Henslowe made in his diary for the Admiral's men at the Rose, have survived, and only a very partial record of their performances elsewhere, it is difficult, perhaps impossible, to establish a seasonal pattern. It has been claimed that, apart from those years in which recurrences of the plague prevented it, the players acted in London between mid-September and late June, and toured in the summer months of July and August when the state of the roads was more favourable to travel.[11] Against this is the fact that – until the opening of the Blackfriars indoor playhouse (which became available to them only in 1609) – their public performances in the capital were limited to the Globe, where audiences were in part exposed to the vagaries of the weather, and which in the depths of the English winter must often have been freezingly cold, impossible to heat, and difficult of access across the Thames. Would it not have been odd, to say the least, if the players had chosen to abandon their own purpose-built theatre at that very time of the year – the summer months of July and August – when it was likely to provide the most favourable conditions for enjoyment of the plays by a majority of London playgoers, and when, therefore, such performances were likely to have been most profitable to them?[12] If there was ever a normal pattern, which has yet to be established, it is likely to have been more complex than that suggested by the Oxford editors, and (allowing for variations from year to year) probably comprised Christmas at court, a Lenten break, Easter and high summer seasons at the Globe, with provincial tours in both early summer and autumn.[13]

A recent, detailed study of the plague years in relation to Shakespeare's output of plays in the period has shown that during the eight years between 1603 and 1611 the London playhouses, including the Globe, are likely to have been closed to the players for at least 68 months in total – that is, for two-thirds of the time.[14] Whatever the pattern of London residence and touring in the years prior to 1603, and from 1611, may have been, it would clearly have been disrupted throughout the whole of that period of recurrent plague, and to have resulted in more touring than was normal. It is significant, however, that between Easter 1611 and June 1613 – during which time the Blackfriars indoor theatre was available in addition to the Globe, and the plague was no longer a problem – the company continued to tour; in 1611 they were at Shrewsbury; in 1612 at New Romney (on 21 April) and Winchester; and in 1612/13 at Folkestone, Oxford, Stafford and Shrewsbury.[15]

Contrary, then, to the common assumption that from 1599 the Chamberlain's/King's men travelled out from their base in London into the provinces only when obliged to do so by the plague, the evidence suggests that such touring was always conceived – both by the players themselves and those who policed them – as a normal component in the annual round of their activities. And the more one studies in detail the varying pattern of the company's movements in each succeeding year, the more impressed one becomes by the evident flexibility and resourcefulness of the players in keeping their enterprise afloat in the face of so many difficulties. To maintain an ongoing establishment of some twenty men and boys, to meet the essential expenses of play production, weekly wages for the hired men, accommodation on tour, and still apparently make a profit for its sharers throughout so long a period (as their continuing prosperity attests) was an extraordinary achievement in itself. Bearing in mind Shakespeare's involvement as player and sharer in every aspect of the company's activity – travelling long distances on horseback or perched on a wagon over ill-made roads in all seasons – it is hardly surprising to find that his production of plays slackens. Prior to 1604, he had written twenty-six plays, including *Measure for Measure*; in the final twelve years of his life, he was to produce only eleven more if we include *Pericles* and *Henry VIII*, which may not all have been his. Do we need to seek any other explanation?

The belief that the Chamberlain's/King's men travelled only by force of necessity imposed by the plague is not the only unwarranted assumption to have distorted our understanding of the company's touring, and the estimate we make of its artistic and financial importance. Though in the absence of performance records from the Globe, we are ready enough to assume that, when not recorded as performing elsewhere, they were in occupation of their London base, the notices of their provincial visits are read as one-off events – as their only stopping places on each particular tour. Similarly, the rewards they received from local Chamberlains, as recorded in their accounts, are interpreted as the sum total of their receipts in each town. Given the economic realities of touring (then as now), which require that to reduce the heavy expenses of travel and accommodation, the legs between stops be kept as short as possible, and that whatever demand that exists in towns along the way is exploited to the full, such a narrow interpretation of the sparse records to have survived appears very unlikely. (Would the players really have travelled so far for so little?) If we look more closely at the records for 1603 in relation to the mass of evidence of other provincial touring in the period, we shall find that all such assumptions are equally open to question.

Apart from the possibility of a few days' playing at the Globe and elsewhere between the Queen's funeral on 28 April and the suspension of 5 May in anticipation of James's arrival in the capital, the London playhouses were to remain closed throughout the whole of 1603, and until May 1604.

With the exception of Kent, to which the plague had already spread, much of the rest of the country was still open to the players, but the further they travelled from the capital the more likely they were to find a welcome. Unfortunately, the Chamberlains' records of the companies' visits to their towns are, for the most part, not precisely dated, but merely group them together (sometimes in chronological order, sometimes not) as occurring within their annual accounting period which normally, but not invariably, ran from Michaelmas (29 September) to Michaelmas, or its octave (6 October). All we can say for certain, therefore, of the 1603 tour on the basis of those records that survive is that in the period between 19 May, when they were appointed 'Servants to the King', and the first few weeks of the new fiscal year in early October, the company was at various times at Bath, Shrewsbury, Coventry, Ipswich, Maldon and Oxford.[16] It takes no great knowledge of geography to realise that these places are widely spread over much of southern and middle England, but a glance at a map is enough to suggest a probable route. Starting from the nearest point to London, the little port of Maldon on the Blackwater estuary in Essex (where exceptionally the fiscal year began on 6 January, and their visit is thus recorded in 1603/4, rather than 1602/3 as elsewhere), they are likely to have travelled north to Ipswich, then in a rotary movement northwest through Coventry to Shrewsbury, from Shrewsbury southwards to Bath, and from Bath to Oxford, where they arrived early in the new fiscal year, beginning there at Michaelmas. We have thus both a probable starting point and terminus for the players' tour in this year. But were these the *only* towns with a suitable venue in which they could perform in the course of such a long and circuitous journey? Of course they were not.

The counties of Essex and Suffolk were curiously detached from London in the Elizabethan and Jacobean periods, and the roads through Chelmsford and Colchester to Maldon and Ipswich notoriously bad.[17] The first leg of their journey, therefore, is more likely to have been accomplished by sea on one of the small coastal vessels that plied between the east coast ports and London, bringing supplies of food to the capital and returning with whatever cargo they could find. On its return journey, there would have been room enough in one of these boats for the twenty or so players with costumes and props for the three or four plays they would have taken with them. (At Plymouth in 1618/19, Lady Elizabeth's men were to number twenty; the King's in 1603 could hardly have managed with less.)[18]

Their first performance in Maldon would have been at the Moot Hall, acquired in 1576, which survives in part (Plate 12).[19] This first performance was known as the 'mayor's play', and was attended, not only by the mayor in person, but also by his councillors, the town's principal officers and justices. It was rewarded by the Maldon Chamberlains with 15s. That the players should submit themselves to the mayors of the towns they visited for their approval in this way was not just a matter of custom but a legally binding obligation, imposed on them by a royal proclamation of Elizabeth's in 1559.[20] The Chamberlains' reward was a tangible sign of that approval, and normally carried with it a licence to give further public performances in the town. But the official reward for this 'mayor's play' was not the only income the players might expect to receive from it. In some towns, admittance to the mayor's play for ordinary members of the public who were able to find a place when the mayor and his men had taken their seats was free (as at Gloucester)[21] but in many others an additional charge was made by the players in the form of a 'gathering', the proceeds of which often exceeded the amount of the reward. At Bath (which the company was to visit later this year), the Queen's men in 1586/7 had received a civic reward of 19s 4d and also, to 'make it up', 26s 8d 'that was gathered at the benche', making a total return of £2 6s.[22] At Leicester, the phrase 'more than was gathered' occurs regularly against a whole series of rewards from the 1550s onward. That these extra gatherings are rarely mentioned, however, should not surprise us, as whatever was gathered directly from the public in that way would have gone straight to the players, and was thus of little interest to the Chamberlains, who were only accountable for payments from the town chest. Similarly, receipts from gatherings at the subsequent public performances that, in all but the smallest towns, followed the mayor's play – more often than not in the same venue – are ignored in the official accounts, and for the same reason. If they are mentioned at all it is only by way of restriction. At Gloucester, for example, by a civic ordinance of 1580, the total number of performances permitted to a company was ruled to depend on the status of its patron: the Queen's players were allowed three performances in three days; those of a baron or noble of greater rank, two plays in two days; and players whose patron was of lesser rank, only one.[23] At Norwich from the 1580s, licences are variously given for two, three or four days – and, more rarely, for as long as a week or eight days.[24] In these respects, the recorded rewards for players on tour are generally deceptive, for when gatherings at the mayor's play and subsequent performances are taken into account, the sum of what the players received in the course of each visit to a town is likely to have been two or more times as much as the stated reward – depending on the number of performances given – and thus far less 'paltry' than is often suggested.[25]

The small size of Maldon may only have justified one or two public shows, after which the company travelled on – probably again by sea – to Ipswich. Here, Shakespeare (along with most of his fellows) would have been on familiar ground, for if my account of his apprentice years is accepted, he had visited it with various companies on at least seven prior occasions.[26] They would have played, as previously, in the ancient Moot Hall on the Cornhill, and if the building shown on p. 117 looks small to have housed a production of *Hamlet*, or even of *All's Well* (which by now may also have been in the company's repertoire), together with the large audience that either play would have attracted, we should remember that before the fairly recent introduction of fire regulations, theatre managers generally were able to pack a surprising number of people, sitting on benches or standing, into the most confined of spaces, and that the mayor's play would have been followed by as many others as the demand for places warranted. And having arranged the seating to their liking and set up their props in the largest chamber the hall had to offer – in Ipswich, presumably the Council Chamber on the upper floor – they would have been reluctant to uproot themselves and move elsewhere.[27] The town's reward for the mayor's play was the sizeable sum of 26*s* 8*d*, and this is likely to have been matched several times over by gatherings at this and subsequent performances which here might easily have extended to a week.[28]

There were a number of other Suffolk boroughs, as well as manor houses, to the east and north of Ipswich likely to have welcomed a visit from the newly appointed King's men when their Ipswich run had come to an end, but whose records for the period have not survived.[29] The players, it is true, would have been in no hurry to return to plague-stricken London, but they had a long journey before them, and on this occasion may have decided to stay with a predetermined route that was to take them in a north-westerly direction to their next recorded venue in Coventry. From this point on, they would, of course, have required horses and a covered wagon to transport them with their precious costumes and other belongings across country. Unless they had been able to ship horses and a wagon from London, they would have purchased these in Ipswich. (When, in March 1615, Lady Elizabeth's players, comprising seven sharers and seven boys, arrived in Coventry, they had five horses between them.[30] The King's men would have needed more. Wagons are mentioned in other accounts.[31])

Setting out from Ipswich, then, a likely route to Coventry would have taken them through Hadleigh, Sudbury, Boxford, Haverhill and Cambridge; but until Cambridge, only Hadleigh and Sudbury preserve records, as well as buildings from the period in which they might have performed. At Hadleigh, they would have played in the fifteenth-century Guildhall which stands to this day in a remarkable state of preservation, and perhaps even more remarkably, retains many of its original functions as both centre of local administration and communal meeting place.

The Guildhall is actually a complex of small to medium-sized buildings of varying date, joined together. When I visited it (as it happens on a Sunday), its offices were closed but a wedding anniversary celebration was in full swing in the original hall on the ground floor. What I take to have been used as a communal hall in the early seventeenth century is a handsome upper chamber, some 80 feet in length by 22½ feet wide,

The Guildhall, Hadleigh, as it is today (pen and ink drawing by Geoff Pleasance, by permission of the artist)

with an open king-post roof, which, allowing for an unraised acting area of about 20 by 15 feet, might have accommodated an audience of some 250 people sitting on benches, with standing room at the back. Timber beams in the side walls still show scorch marks made by the candles that had once been affixed to them. Though no mention is made in the town's surviving records of payments to visiting players, an agreement made with a shoemaker called John Allen on his appointment as 'overseer of the poor' in January 1599 indicates that the hall was then being used for performances by them, albeit on certain conditions, for Allen is instructed

> that he shall not suffer any playes to be made within the guildhall without consent of syx of the Cheife Inhabitants of the towne under ther handwriting/and further that all such playes as shall be made there may be ended in the daye time and also that if any hurte or dammage be made by the saide playes or weddings kept there, that then the saide John Allen shall repaire & make the saide houses in as good sorte as they are nowe at his owne costs and charges.[32]

– the fulfilment of which conditions should not have proved too difficult for the King's own servants, with their leading poet. There was no mayor's reward because at this date in its history the town had no mayor, so Shakespeare and his fellows would have been dependent on whatever was 'gathered at the benche'.

That companies of players visited Sudbury and were rewarded by its mayor is attested by the town's records. Lord Oxford's men were there on 17 April 1585, Leicester's on 2 June of the same year, and Strange's in 1592, receiving rewards of 5s, 6s 8d, and 3s 4d respectively. The King's men are known to have performed in the town six years later (in 1609/10) when, oddly enough, they were given only 5s as against Leicester's reward of 6s 8d twenty-four years earlier, but unfortunately the relevant accounts for the years 1593 to 1606 are missing.[33] In 1603, they would have played either in the Old Moot Hall in Cross Street of fourteenth-century origin (Plate 18) – or its sixteenth-century replacement on Market Hill, which has since been demolished. For while most of the hall's official functions were transferred from Cross Street to Market Hill when the new hall was built in the reign of Queen Mary, the original building continued to be used by the town for feasts and plays well into the seventeenth century, as attested by a mural depicting the arms of James I over a chimney breast in the lower chamber of the fifteenth-century building shown on the left of the illustration.[34]

In theory at least, the absolute terms of the company's royal patent, so recently received – to exercise their art 'within the liberties and freedome of anie other Cittie, universitie, towne, or Boroughe whatsoever' – should have overridden long-standing Cambridge University statutes barring professional players from performing within five miles of the town centre, which had resulted in even the Queen's men having been turned away on more than one occasion; but, if it did, the surviving Town Treasurers' books have nothing to say of any reward. So in spite of the claim made by the pirated quarto of *Hamlet* (Q1), dated 1603, that the play had been acted by 'his Highnesse servants . . . in the two Universities of Cambridge and Oxford', a question mark remains over Cambridge. If the company did succeed in playing there at this time, it would not have been in any of the colleges but in the town's Guildhall. For while the undergraduates were encouraged to act in both Latin and English plays in their college halls (with consequent large expenditure on the replacement of window glass), the university authorities were steadfast in their opposition to any exposure of the students to the corrupting influence of professional players, Shakespeare not excepted. When, in 1605/6, Worcester's men were given permission by the Mayor to perform in the Guildhall, entrusted with the key, and order given to 'buyld theire Stage & take downe the glass windowes there' (a sensible precaution), he was overruled by the Vice Chancellor, and the players sent on their way under threat of a hefty fine.[35] Nevertheless, we know that the Chamberlain's men had performed there in 1594/5, receiving 40s, and that one or two other companies had also managed to do so at various times, so we cannot altogether exclude the possibility of an unrecorded visit by the King's. As the Guildhall measured only 22 by 17½ feet, however, and would hardly have afforded room for more than the Mayor and his guests, the mayor's play would have been followed by other performances – perhaps at Chesterton or elsewhere in the town.[36] When, in 1580, the great Lord Burghley, the university's Chancellor, wrote to John Hatcher, the Vice-Chancellor, to put in a good word for Lord Oxford's players (and was politely refused), he mentioned that they intended a stay of four or five days.[37] Perhaps the King's men escaped opposition and notice by arriving in the long vacation?

Moving on through Northamptonshire (doubtless stopping more than once on the way) the company arrived in Coventry in what by now would have been late summer. And here we find our next firm record: a Chamberlain's reward of 40*s* – the most generous they were to receive anywhere on this particular tour, but which undoubtedly would again have been greatly increased by gatherings. Though not specifically mentioned, there can be little doubt of the venue – the magnificent St Mary's Guildhall[38] – which, despite subsequent 'restorations' and the terrible blitz suffered by the city in the Second World War, has retained much of its original glory to the present.

The Victorian print reproduced opposite may act as a salutary corrective to those who write in a derogatory way of the company's out-of-town performance venues as necessarily 'makeshift'. This is not to deny that in the smaller guildhalls the players would have been hard-pressed to make the best of the limited space at their disposal, but here, as in other cities, they encountered conditions which, in terms of spaciousness, comfort and splendour, rivalled any of the London playhouses including the Globe; to which, indeed (if conjectural reconstructions of their stages are to be trusted), the Coventry hall bears some resemblance – as in the disposition of doors at the upper end, and the gallery above. With this advantage: that in Coventry neither actors nor audience would have been at the mercy of the elements.

Dating from the late fourteenth and early fifteenth centuries, the hall is some 76 feet long by 30 feet wide. In some respects the appearance of the hall in 1603 would have differed from that shown in the illustration. In 1581, for a visit by the Earl of Leicester, a substantial screen (partly of stone) was erected to conceal the three arched doorways at the south end of the hall, of which the centre

St Mary's Guildhall, Coventry, as it appeared after the restoration of 1824 (reproduced from Benjamin Poole's *Coventry: its history and antiquities*, 1870, by courtesy of Coventry City Archives)

one led to the kitchen and those on each side to enclosed chambers (originally buttery and pantry) which might have been used by the players as changing rooms. The screen, which would have facilitated entrances and exits for the players, had gone by 1824 and has not been replaced. The original hall also featured an extensive dais at the north and opposite end of the hall, occupying almost a third of the total floor space, which disappeared in 1755 when the rest of the floor was boarded over and raised to the level of the dais. Here the more important guests would have sat at the front, with doubtless the Mayor and Master of the Trinity Guild sitting together at centre on the Guild chair which, in the illustration, stands against the west wall. The rest of the audience sat on benches (which, when not in use in the hall, were stored in the Undercroft) or stood at the back. The floor has since been lowered and the dais restored.

After over 100 miles of travel – mainly by horse and wagon – the players would have been in need of a rest. From Coventry, it is only 17 miles to Stratford, and Shakespeare would not have come so far without paying a visit to Anne and his daughters. Susanna would then have been twenty, and Judith eighteen. He may well have taken some of the company with him – especially the younger boys. New Place, which he had bought in 1597, was the second largest house in the town and could have accommodated most of them.

Setting out from Stratford to their next recorded stop at Shrewsbury, there are several routes they might have taken; the most likely being along what is now the A34 through Henley-in-Arden. There they would have played – not at the Guildhall which, like many other of the smaller halls of religious origin had been sequestered by the crown early in Edward VI's reign, and in 1603 was in private hands – but at the Market House or Townhall, demolished in 1793.

Like the Guildhall that still stands in Thaxted, Essex, it rested on wooden beams, and was open at ground level to give shelter to traders. The hall proper was, as usual, on the upper floor, and was described in the eighteenth century as extensive. In 1609, it was laid down by the Court Leet, which met there, that 'neither Master Bailiff nor any other inhabitant shall licence or give leave to any players to play within the Towenhale upon pain to forfeit 40s.';

The Market or Town Hall of Henley-in-Arden, demolished in 1793, can just be glimpsed to the left of the Town Cross in this old drawing from William Cooper's *Henley-in-Arden, an Ancient Market Town*, 1946 (reproduced by courtesy of Warwickshire Record Office, Warwick)

which tells us that it had been visited by players *prior* to 1609, and we know that despite the prohibition they continued to come, because players are reported there again in 1615.[39]

From Henley, the company would have gone on through the Forest of Arden, the heart of England, to Bromsgrove, perhaps, and Bewdley, across the Severn at Bridgnorth, and so to Shrewsbury; a

213

journey of some 60 miles as the crow flies, but at the pace of a horse-drawn wagon on country roads – stopping several times to perform and spend the night – must have taken them not less than a week. (Was *As You Like It* one of the plays they had brought with them? There is an indication later that it may have been; if so, it would of course have been especially appropriate on this leg of their journey.)

Performances at Shrewsbury were in the Booth Hall, which had been rebuilt in 1512 but has since disappeared. We know from the town's records that the major companies were accustomed to stay for several days, and that the mayor's play – for which, on this occasion, the company received a reward of 20*s* – was normally followed by a run of public shows, probably in the same hall and at night.[40]

The next stage of their journey to Bath (over 100 miles to the south) would necessarily have taken them through Ludlow and Gloucester, at both of which it was usual for travelling companies to stop and perform (as they probably did), but where the Chamberlains' accounts have since been lost so we cannot confirm it. The Gloucester accounts are entirely missing between 1596 and 1629, but the procedure by which visiting players were required to obtain a licence from the mayor has already been quoted from a contemporary witness (see p. 25), and is confirmed by a civic ordinance of 1580.[41]

It soon becomes apparent from the surviving records that the companies' hosts in the towns they visited were prepared to spend both time and money in meeting the players' needs. In the first place, the hall where they were to play would have had to be cleared of its usual furniture and fittings. At nearby Bristol (which the King's men are also likely to have visited on this tour, but where again the relevant accounts are missing), 20*d* was expended in 1573/4 for a visit by Leicester's men in 'taking down the table in the mayers courte and setting yt up agayne after the said players were gonne'.[42] Having cleared the space, it was often necessary in the larger halls to erect a platform stage at one end, as at Gloucester in 1567/8, where a man called Batty was paid 8*s* for '103 quarters of elme bourdes for a skaffold for playors to playe one', and 2*s* for a 'peece of tymber to sett under the bourdes'.[43] Many of the performances, here as elsewhere, took place in the evening. At Bristol where the Mayor's Audits that survive are unusually detailed, a sum of

22*s* was paid in 1577/8 to 'my Lord of Leycesters Players at the end of their Play in the yeld [guild] hall before master mayer and the Aldremen and for lyngkes to geve light in the evenyng',[44] which I read as a matinee for the Mayor and aldermen, and an evening show for the public on the same day. Links were torches of pitch and tow, more often used to give light in the streets; at Gloucester in 1561/2, 3*d* was paid for a pound of candles.[45] In the winter fires were lit in the chamber, as for Leicester's men at Ipswich on 21 February 1565.[46] At Bristol, in 1576, we hear of a need to strengthen the Guildhall door, and for 'mending the cramp of Iren which shuttyth the barre, which cramp was stretchid with the presse of people at the play of my lord Chamberleyns Servauntes in the yeld hall before master mayer and thaldremen'.[47] The crush of spectators in confined spaces inevitably resulted in other damage. At Bristol again, in 1581, after a performance by Strange's men, the 'mending of 2 fowrmes which were taken owt of St Georges Chapple and set in the yeld hall at the play, and by the disordre of the people were broken', cost 2*s* 5*d*.[48] At Leicester in 1608, 2*s* was paid for 'mending the glasse Wyndowes att the towne hall more then was given by the playors who broake the same', and at Barnstaple in 1592/3 there was even damage to a ceiling.[49]

That the mayors and their aldermen were not generally resentful of all this extra expense and inconvenience, but took it in their stride as an acceptable price to be paid for the rare pleasures that the players brought to their towns, is attested by frequent references to drinks with the players after the show: at Coventry in 1608, Lord Compton's men were entertained in the parlour with wine, sugar and bread; at Gloucester in 1559/60, the Queen's were given a 'banket' costing 5*s* 7*d*, and in 1565/6 the same company was treated to 'wine and chirries' at 'Mr Swordbearers'.[50]

For Shakespeare and the King's in 1603, Gloucester's Mayor is unlikely to have been any less hospitable. And so fortified, perhaps, they would have journeyed to Bath, and from there to their last recorded venue at Oxford, stopping several more times on the way to perform. At Bath, they received a generous mayor's reward of 30*s*, and at Oxford, 20*s*. In both cities, the fiscal year began and ended at Michaelmas or a week or two later. It appears from the dating of the

Chamberlains' accounts that the company was at Bath towards the end of the fiscal year 1602/3 (probably in late September), and arrived in Oxford early in the next, 1603/4 – about the middle of October.[51] We have seen that in Bath in 1587, a reward of 19*s* 4*d* to the Queen's men had been supplemented by 26*s* 8*d* 'gathered at the bench', making a sizeable total of 46*s*. For the King's in 1603, it could hardly have been less and, if we add the gatherings at subsequent performances, the company's receipts from the visit as a whole are likely to have reached a most useful sum. They would almost certainly have played at the old Guildhall, whch continued to be used as such until the 1620s when it was converted into a shambles (for the slaughter of cattle), the external dimensions of which were 56 by 24 feet.[52]

The Editor of the Oxford city records has it that the players stayed there at the King's Head in Cornmarket and that the plays were acted in its yard, but the once common belief that players at this time normally performed in inn yards has since been largely exploded.[53] Efforts by the university authorities to bar professional players from the city had proved, if anything, rather less successful here than in Cambridge, and in 1586 exemption had been made by the Mayor ('onlie at this tyme') for Essex's men to perform in the 'Guylde Hall courte'.[54] The likelihood is that the King's, armed with their new patent, were similarly treated, and that by the 'courte' was meant – not, as Salter thought, an outside yard – but a large chamber in the Guildhall normally used by magistrates or visiting judges. (Many guildhalls in the period were alternatively named as 'Court' halls and chiefly used for that purpose.) Was this the occasion when *Hamlet* was acted at Oxford – as claimed in the quarto of 1603? Another possibility, as we shall find in a moment, is *Troilus and Cressida*.

On 21 October of this year, Joan Alleyn, wife of the player Edward Alleyn, who was then on a visit to Sussex, wrote as follows to her husband:

My entire and well-beloved sweetheart, still it joys me – and long, I pray God, may I joy – to hear of your welfare, as you of ours. Almighty God be thanked, my own self (yourself) and my mother and whole house are in good health, and about us the sickness doth cease. . . . All the companies be come home, and well, for aught we know, but that Brown of the Boar's Head is dead, and died very poor. . . . All of your own company [the Admiral's] are well at their own houses.[55]

Similarly optimistic news of an easing of the plague in London (where, in fact, deaths, though falling, were still occurring at the rate of several hundred a week) may have reached the players in Oxford, along with a report that the court was intending to return to Hampton Court for Christmas. As it happened, court and players had earlier crossed paths. After his coronation on 25 July, the King had set out on a progress to the West Country, which had taken him to Woodstock, near Oxford, in September; but plague having by then already reached Oxford, he and the court proceeded to Winchester, and in late October to Wilton, near Salisbury – home of the young Earl of Pembroke. Anticipating, along with other companies, an early lifting of the closure order on the London playhouses as the severity of the plague diminished with the approach of winter, and also perhaps in expectation of a royal summons to perform at Hampton Court during the Christmas season, the players left Oxford to return to the capital. On arrival, however, discovering that the infection was still rampant in Southwark, they took refuge in the pleasant suburb of Mortlake on the river, where Augustine Phillips had a house. It was there apparently that the summons eventually reached them – not for Hampton Court but for Wilton. And so they were obliged to retrace their steps in double-quick time the way they had come. It was in Wilton on 2 December that they were to give their first performance for King James, and where Heminges, as payee for his fellows, was justly compensated with an exceptional reward of £30, 'for the paynes and expences of himself and the rest of the company in coming from Mortelake in the countie of Surrie unto the courte aforsaid and there presenting before his Majestie one playe'.[56] A later unconfirmed but reliable report, deriving from Wilton, has it that the play was *As You Like It*, and confirms (if confirmation were needed) that 'we have the man Shakespeare with us'.[57]

But no sooner had the company arrived at Wilton and given this, and perhaps one or two other performances, than there was yet another change of plan. It was decided that the King and the court should spend Christmas at Hampton Court after all, and Queen Anne was to leave for the capital only five days later,[58] followed by the King, the now weary players, and the rest of the court. There are varying estimates of the importance of the players' new, high-sounding status as 'servants of the King'. One thing is clear: it was no sinecure.

At Hampton Court, Heminges was again the payee for performances on Boxing Day, 27, 28 and 30 December 1603, and on New Year's Day (two plays) and 2 February 1604, with an eighth at Whitehall on 19 February. Though no titles are recorded, a letter from Dudley Carleton to John Chamberlain describes one as 'a play of Robin goode-fellow' (almost certainly, *A Midsummer Night's Dream*),[59] and Jonson's tragedy *Sejanus*, in which both Burbage and Shakespeare had leading roles, was probably another. For the plays between 26 December and 1 January, the company's reward had been £53, and for those on 2 and 19 February, a further £20.[60] (£10 per play was to be the normal payment for court performances throughout the whole of the reign.)

During the previous eight months, the company had travelled over 600 miles. Against a meagre total of six visits recorded in surviving accounts, the actual number of places in which they stopped to perform is more likely to have been (at a conservative estimate) in the region of twenty (one every ten days), and the number of performances given (averaging three in each town) about sixty. Similarly, when additional gatherings at the mayor's play and subsequent shows are taken into account (generally amounting to at least twice the stated reward), the sum of their recorded rewards (£7 11s 8d, averaging about 22s a visit) needs to be doubled, and then multiplied by a factor of sixty, to arrive at an approximate estimate of their total receipts from the tour: £132. Compared to the £10 per play they received for their court performances, this is still a relatively modest amount, but it would at least have met their expenses and kept the company solvent, which £7 11s 8d would certainly not have done.

What cannot be calculated is the pleasure and enrichment the players brought to the thousands of people who packed their guildhalls throughout a large swathe of the country to see and hear their performances; nor the satisfaction that Shakespeare and his fellows would have derived from that.[61] As King's men, this was the first of a series of extensive tours they were to undertake; in 1605, they were in Oxford again, at Saffron Walden in Essex, and Barnstaple, Devon; in 1606, at Marlborough and Oxford, in the Midlands as far as Leicester, and Maidstone and Dover in Kent; in 1607, at Oxford, Barnstaple, and Dunwich in Suffolk; and so on in almost every year to the end of Shakespeare's career.

In attempting to follow in Shakespeare's footsteps on this first of his tours as a King's man, and describing some of the venues in which he performed and the conditions he is likely to have found in them, we have come to grips with the concrete realities that surrounded his life as a travelling player which, as we have seen, occupied a substantial part of his career both before and after 1603. In doing so, we have hopefully come a little nearer to understanding the colour and texture of what his real life would have been as opposed to the myths of the popularisers and the 'cloud-capp'd towers' of literary theory erected by some academics. As poet, dramatist and player, the audience he served lay across the whole of the country, and not just in London. Though the Globe was important to him – both as symbol and, in a practical way, as an ideal venue for the performance of his plays – it had no exclusive claim on him. He remained at heart a 'travelling man'. But this, of course, is only half the story. It is time to return to the plays.

I said earlier that only two plays can with any reasonable assurance of probability be dated to the period 1602/3: *Troilus and Cressida* and *All's Well that Ends Well*. For the reasons advanced by G.K. Hunter and others, *All's Well* cannot be later than 1604, and I think that Chambers was right in putting it a little earlier into 1602/3.[62] I find it hard to believe that Shakespeare would have written a play that begins with a dying king after the accession of James I. Its composition belongs, with *Troilus*, to the last year of Elizabeth's reign and, if so, it would have been an obvious choice for the 1603 tour. With only fifteen named characters, including at least five boys' roles, and with little necessity for doubling, it would easily have been within the compass of a travelling troupe, and makes no demands in its staging that the smallest guildhall would not have been able to supply. It may even have been written for touring. Many of its more intimate scenes – if not exactly lost – would have been in peril of being so on the larger, more exposed stage of the Globe, while they are likely to have been most effective in the smaller, more enclosed setting of a guildhall. Then again, Shakespeare's use of cornets, a softer wind instrument than the more usual trumpets, to greet the entrance of the King at I.ii and II.i indicate an indoor venue, though the play is too early in date for Blackfriars.[63]

To scholars, it is the first of what have become known as the 'problem plays', but its sole intractable problem, as I see it, lies in its combination of a fairy-tale plot (Helena's near-magical cure for the King's illness, and the 'bed-trick' whereby she substitutes herself for Bertram's intended bed-mate, Diana) with the depth and realism of its character-drawing and rich complexity of language. In both, it represents an advance for Shakespeare: in its use of folk elements, it is a first, perhaps hesitant, approach to that sublimation of human conflict and suffering through faith in an ultimate, providential reordering to be found more fully realised in his later romances; in its observation of character and individuality of speech, it leaves all the earlier comedies behind it. It belongs to its time, the last troubled days of Elizabeth's reign and the approach of a still-unknown Jacobean era, but it does not succumb to those uncertainties; rather, it rises above them. To be part of it – to see it from the inside, as it were, as I have had the privilege of doing on two long-separated occasions – is to become increasingly aware of its distinctive qualities and beauty.

Helena is the heart of the play, and unique among Shakespeare's lovers in that all that happens turns upon her. The play tells a love story, but the love is all hers; the object of her love – the callow, immature, insufferable Bertram – is everything to her but very little in the play. It is one of those data that Shakespeare gives for our necessary acceptance that perhaps in some earlier phase of his boyhood (for he and Helena have grown up together), and perhaps again in the person who starts to emerge in the final scene, there is something in Bertram, someone who is worth loving. We have to take that on trust if the play is to make sense. The plot follows Helena's rise from humble beginnings as an orphaned physician's daughter in the Countess's household, where she occupies the position of serving woman, to one high in the King's favour through the esoteric knowledge of the healer's art which her father has bequeathed to her, and her own determination; and its sole motivation is love – to put herself on the same plane as the young count so that he is able to see her as the person she really is, not as she appears, and to return her love. In that respect, the play is as much about class and the nature of kingship as the true fount of honour and rank, as it is about sexual fulfilment and marriage – a theme that could not have been all that distant from Shakespeare's awareness of his own situation as a not very much more than menial servant of the King's, for so he was regarded by most of his contemporaries. Hence his invisibility to them, as Helen to Bertram. And the bed-trick, which Victorian moralists found so shocking, and which is not exactly in accord with feminist principles either, should be seen, not as a young Chambers among others saw it – as the ignoble means by which a young girl should get a handsome young man in her bed – or not predominantly that, but as a necessary sealing through consummation of the rite of marriage which Bertram has obstinately withheld from her.[64] She is perhaps the toughest and most determined of Shakespeare's heroines.

One of the reasons why so many actors find that acting in Shakespeare brings them more fulfilment than in plays by any other author, alive or dead, is that he always gives them, along with marvellous lines and formidable challenges, room to contribute something of themselves. This seems especially true of the parts he wrote for himself – and the King of France in this play is surely one of them. In writing such parts, he knew in advance exactly what he as a player could and would bring to them: a natural distinction of manner and personality, great authority, a total absence of self-pity in his early scenes, and a quirky sense of humour.

Both Helena and Bertram (like nearly all of Shakespeare's lovers) need to be played very young, and would have gone to apprentices: Helena by necessity, Bertram in order to match with her. Helena is seen to be emerging from girlhood into womanhood. 'I have those hopes of her good', the Countess tells us, 'that her education promises her dispositions'; she is still in process of achieving her goodness (I.i.36ff.). Like Portia, we see her mature and grow in confidence as the play proceeds. Bertram is described by his mother as an 'unseason'd courtier', and by the King as a 'proud, scornful boy'. When Lafew, the old lord to whose immediate charge the Countess has entrusted him, says of him in an aside, 'I am sure thy father drank wine; but if thou be'st not an ass, I am a youth of fourteen' (II.iii.99), he may be glancing at Bertram's actual age. (In modern terms, he might be played as a cocky sixteen- or seventeen-year-old; he too must be seen to develop – if only by way of humiliation.)

Parolles, Bertram's unworthy but self-appraising buffoon, is the second largest part in the play (after Helena) and carries the comic sub-plot of his own unmasking. It would probably have gone to Burbage who, like all the really great tragedians, was also an accomplished comedy actor. Both he and the crusty, good-hearted Lafew, who at last takes Parolles into his service, are new, joyful creations in Shakespeare's gallery of living portraits. Heminges would have been disappointed if he had not been given Lafew. Lavatch, the clown of the play, is one of the saddest of Shakespeare's household fools. 'A shrewd knave and an unhappy', Lafew remarks of him (IV.v.60); but he has his moments, and Armin would have made the most of them. The speeches of the First and Second Lords in Paris – to be identified with the Dumaine brothers of Florence – are somewhat confusedly distinguished in Shakespeare's text by the letters E and G, which probably refer to two of the company's older apprentices, Ecclestone and Gough.

The citizens of Ipswich and Shrewsbury would have thronged to see the play, and rewarded the players generously with their applause and contributions to the 'gatherings'. As the Epilogue (doubtless spoken by Shakespeare as the King) says in bringing the play to its end,

Ours be your patience then and yours our parts;
Your gentle hands lend us and take our hearts.

There is no mention of *All's Well* in performance records, or of a published version in the Stationers' Register, until its appearance in the First Folio of 1623, and yet, as recent productions have shown, it is eminently actable. One can only suppose, as suggested above, that in the early years of James I, its opening theme of a sickening king would have made its London production untactful to say the least. So far as the capital was concerned, it had missed its moment.

The same may also be true of *Troilus and Cressida* – but for different reasons. Here, however, we are given some clues. The play was first registered for publication on 7 February 1603 by a Master Roberts: 'to print when he hath gotten sufficient aucthority for yt, The booke of Troilus and Cresseda as yt is acted by my lord Chamberlens Men, 6d.'[65] Clearly, he had not at that time received the permission he needed, though the play was already in performance; we are not told where, but in February or March of that year, when the Queen lay mortally ill at Richmond, there is only one realistic possibility, and that is the Globe.

Contrary to recent scholarly opinion, which has it that the play is of a sophisticated kind, 'highly satirical at times, experimental in genre and attuned to an avant-garde idiom . . . rather like the play that Hamlet describes to the First Player as "caviar to the general"; it "pleased not the million"',[66] I make no doubt that it was written for a popular audience at the Globe and would have been a roaring success with the groundlings in particular. It has everything we know that they liked: a railing fool in Thersites supplying scatalogical humour, a compelling plot of love betrayed, chivalric display and processions, scenes of combat and murder, with drums and trumpets a-plenty. Nor would its basis in Greek history and legend have been at all likely to put them off. A lost play with the title of *Troy* had been acted at the Rose in 1596, and Chettle and Dekker's *Troilus and Cressida* (of which only a fragment survives) had been given by the Admiral's men in 1599. They would have been keen to see what Shakespeare and the Chamberlain's were to make of it. True, there are some long speeches with serious intent from Nestor and Ulysses (some of the longest in the canon), but even here we are on a knife-edge of parody, where eloquence teeters on the brink of a merely comic loquacity.

The immense potential that the play has for popular entertainment has been demonstrated beyond all possible doubt by the success of recent revivals. Were the mixed audiences at the Globe any more sophisticated in their tastes than an average audience at Stratford or the National? I take leave to doubt it. Is the play any more select in its appeal than *Hamlet*? But no sooner had it received its first few performances than the London playhouses were closed by the death of the Queen, then again by the imminent coming of James, and finally by the plague – all within a matter of weeks. When, in May, the players received their royal mandate as the King's servants and took to the road, would they not have taken their latest popular success with them? Though its cast has been described as too large for public performance, the conjectural doubling plot I give in Appendix D demonstrates that it was well within the resources of fifteen men, four boys, and one mute player-musician – no more than was required for *Hamlet* or *Henry V*. Though we should take note that, despite its epic structure, a surprising number of its scenes require no more than two or three people to be on stage together, and that the silent procession of warriors in Act 1, Scene 2 could have passed through the body of the hall, viewed (or merely imagined) by Cressida and Pandarus on stage, it may still have been too large in its demands for the smaller guildhalls; it would, however, have come into its own in Coventry. And if, as Professor Alexander conjectured, it found an ideal audience in one of the Inns of Court, it is likely to have received an equally enthusiastic reception from the undergraduates of Oxford and Cambridge, if the company was allowed to perform for them on its visits in 1603. Roberts' qualification of his Stationers' entry, that he intended to print the play only when 'he hath gotten sufficient aucthority for it', may have resulted from the players' reluctance to release a play for publication while it was still enjoying a successful run at the Globe or was intended for revival; but when, for the Christmas season of 1603/4, the company was at last able to return to London, the atmosphere at court and in the City was found to have changed and become more repressive. (It was in 1604/5 that Ben Jonson was clapped in gaol, in imminent danger of losing his ears, for his contribution to *Eastword Ho!* on account of some mildly satirical humour it contained at the expense of the Scots.) In short, the play was suppressed.[67] In 1609, it was to be re-entered in the Register and published by another printer, but its description on the title page, as 'acted by the Kings Majesties servants at the Globe', was rapidly expunged in a second, revised impression, to which was added a publisher's blurb claiming it as a 'new play, never stal'd with the Stage, never clapper-clawd with the palmes of the vulger, and yet passing full of the palme comicall'. Having been banned from the stage, it received the dubious puff of an appeal to a minority of allegedly enlightened readers, who were urged to buy it because 'when hee [Shakespeare] is gone, and his Commedies out of sale, you will scramble for them, and set up a new English Inquisition'.[68] The writer need not have worried.

Because of their innate need to categorise, the play has been troublesome to scholars and literary critics. It has been variously described as comedy, tragedy, tragi-comedy, history, satire or, more judiciously, as a unique blend of elements from all the more admitted genres. 'There is no one of Shakespeare's plays harder to characterize', Coleridge confessed; one scarcely knows 'what to say of it'.[69] Even Hemings and Condell found it difficult to place, eventually describing it as a tragedy and putting it in the First Folio between the histories and tragedies. Only the imperturbable Dr Johnson was to keep his critical cool:

> This play is more correctly written than most of *Shakespeare's* compositions, but it is not one of those in which either the extent of his views or elevation of his fancy is fully displayed. As the story abounded with materials, he has exerted little invention; but he has diversified his characters with great variety, and preserved them with great exactness. His vicious characters sometimes disgust, but cannot corrupt, for both *Cressida* and *Pandarus* are detested and contemned. The comick characters seem to have been the favourites of the writer, they are of the superficial kind,

and exhibit more of manners than nature, but they are copiously filled and powerfully impressed.[70]

He is unduly hard, I think, on Cressida and Pandarus. Though presented as flawed, Cressida evokes more pity than condemnation, and Pandarus is too funny to have been detested by his creator. Though an out-and-out reprobate (as his Epilogue makes clear), he is a likeable one and, as one of the 'favourites of the writer', fully deserves the billing he is given on the revised title page of the 1609 quarto: 'The Famous Historie of Troylus and Cresseid. Excellently expressing the beginning of their loves, with the conceited wooing of Pandarus Prince of Licia', which strongly suggests (in contradiction of the statement in the blurb) that the play *had* been performed, and that Pandarus had proved a notable success. I see him as one of those middle-aged men of indeterminate sexuality that one used to meet with in theatrical boarding houses, taking an inordinate interest in the love affairs of the younger lodgers. His love-song for Helen and Paris, in which he accompanies himself on the lute, is a delight.

> Love, love, nothing but love, still love, still more!
>   For, O, love's bow
>   Shoots buck and doe.
>   The shaft confounds
>   Not that it wounds,
> But tickles still the sore.
>
> These lovers cry, 'O! O!', they die!
>   Yet that which seems the wound to kill
> Doth turn 'O! O!' to 'Ha, ha, he!'
>   So dying love lives still.
> 'O! O!' a while, but 'Ha, ha, ha!'
>   'O! O!' groans out for 'Ha, ha, ha! –
> Heigh ho! (III.i.109–21)

When, just before this, Helen remarks on his 'fine forehead', perhaps (as Bevington suggests) caressing it, I am reminded of Dr Rowe's enthusiastic comment on the Droeshout portrait of Shakespeare: 'What a powerful impression it gives . . . what a forehead, what a brain!'[71] And indeed, I think it probable that Shakespeare played the part. With a little under 400 lines, it is just the size of role that he preferred, and (as with the Friar in *Romeo*), nearly all of his scenes are with the company's apprentices – here with Troilus and Cressida, Helen and Paris – to whom he would have been able to give his support. After the pseudo-heroic Prologue, with its echoes of *Henry V*, he opens the play with Troilus, brings the lovers together, watches helpless as Cressida is taken away, but is absent from all of the action in the Greek camp, returning only for the Epilogue. (For some further suggestions on casting, see my doubling plot in Appendix D.)

Though the play is sometimes read as expressive of a mood of world-weary cynicism on Shakespeare's part, or (more reasonably) as an attempt to rival the recently devised genre of comical satire for which Jonson and Marston had set the fashion,[72] I see it rather as a case of Shakespeare stretching his wings; as a final anarchic fling in a number of different directions before settling himself to the more profound and integrated themes that he was to address in the years ahead. *Troilus* needs to be played with a light touch, with due weight given to its more lyrical and serious passages. To the literary scholar, it may present an impossibly intransigent medley of contradictory styles, tendencies and moods; in the theatre, it is rarely less than entertaining, and at best a triumphant success.

ELEVEN

King's Man

Shakespeare was not stung into tragedy by any Dark Lady. He
was not depressed into tragedy by the fall of Essex, who
threatened revolution and chaos in England, to Shakespeare's
horror and alarm; the cruelty of anarchy was a thought that
haunted the poet like a nightmare. He did not degenerate into
tragedy in a semi-delirium of cynicism and melancholy, ending in
a religious crisis. Shakespeare *rose* to tragedy in the very height
and peak of his powers, nowhere else so splendidly displayed, and
maintained throughout his robust and transcendent faith in God
and his creature Man.

C.J. Sisson[1]

When Shakespeare and his fellows returned to London in the
footsteps of Queen Anne in December 1603, they found
themselves in an atmosphere very different from the one they had left
in May to embark on their countrywide tour. To begin with, London –
epecially that part of it about the Globe with which they were most
familiar – had been ravaged by the plague. The fact that no one
famous in history or literature had succumbed (the court and those
wealthy enough to own country estates where they could take refuge
would naturally have escaped) has led historians and literary scholars
to underestimate its effects, but Stowe's estimate of a death toll within
the city and liberties of over 38,000 in a population of some 200,000
faces us with the stark reality. And among the humbler citizens of
Bankside – those among whom the players customarily lived and
moved, travelling from their lodgings to the theatre every day for
rehearsals and shows – there must have been many a once-familiar

face that would then have been missing. In the Christmas season of 1603/4 the crisis was not by any means over. Hampton Court may have been relatively safe, but in the city the death rate was still running at 74 per week at the end of December, and it was not until February that it fell below 30.[2] Nor can we safely assume that the company itself was altogether free of loss in the period, especially among the younger apprentices and hired men. John Sincler may have been one such victim. He is mentioned (as appearing under his nickname of Sinklo) in the prologue to Marston's *The Malcontent*, which was probably one of the plays acted at court that Christmas, but from this time on his name is absent from the records, and the thin-man parts that Shakespeare had written for him and of which he had made a speciality, disappear from the plays. Given the family feeling we have seen to have existed among the players, and the close personal relationships they enjoyed with each other, such losses would have been felt very deeply – not least by Shakespeare himself.

But the most far-reaching change that confronted them on their return to the capital was the presence of their new patron and principal employer in the person of James. In character and tastes, he could hardly have been more different to the old Queen, whose partialities they had come to know so well and to cater for so expertly, whereas in James they were dealing with a largely unknown quantity. By any standard, Elizabeth was a well-educated woman who liked to show off her knowledge of Latin and other languages, but whose tastes in humour inclined to the low-brow and whose favourite fools had been Tarlton and Kempe. All that the players would have known of James at this time is that he was a recognised scholar whose particular interest and expertise lay in the realm of theology, and who was given to instructing his subjects in lengthy treatises as to their moral behaviour.

The King's attitude to the players and to the theatre in general is a subject of continuing controversy. He had demonstrated an intention to retain, even to enhance, the existing system of court patronage of the drama by his speedy appointment of the former Chamberlain's men as his personal servants, and by the exceptionally broad patent he had given them. The summons to Wilton in November 1603, and the eight further performances he had commissioned on his return to Hampton Court in December, provide additional evidence of that intention, while the reward of £30 to them at Wilton as compensation for the long journey they had made and, even more remarkably, of a further donation of £30 via Richard Burbage in January 1604, 'for the mayntenaunce and releife of himselfe and the rest of his company being prohibited to presente any playes publiquelie in or neere London' because of the plague, were unprecedented.[3] There is no question either that the number of performances given at court by the company between 1603 and Shakespeare's death in 1616 was to far exceed that of the previous reign: according to Chambers' reckoning, 177 by the King's men in thirteen years as against 31 by the Chamberlain's in nine, though this may in part by accounted for by the enhanced status of the company under James. But the actual pleasure he took in the performances was not always evident to his contemporaries, and remains in doubt; nor was he always personally present at them, being represented on occasion by the Queen or young Prince Henry. These other members of the royal family may, indeed, have been more enthusiastic playgoers – and behind the scenes more friendly to the players – than he was. By 1604, two of the company's principal competitors at court and elsewhere, the Admiral's men and Worcester's, had also been raised in nominal status to the position of royal servants: the Admiral's being named thereafter as the Prince's players, and Worcester's as the Queen's.

If 1603 had been a difficult year for the company, 1604 was to be, if anything, worse. The theatres remained closed throughout Lent, and though the Privy Council authorised their reopening for Easter (Easter Day this year was 8 April), by May deaths from the plague were again on the rise, and the probability is that the Globe was only intermittently open through much of the summer. But if in London the plague lingered on – rising to a weekly peak of 34 in June – in the rest of the country it was to spread more widely and increase in virulence so that the possibility of another lengthy provincial tour was no longer an option.

In March, ten of the company's leading players, along with a similar number from the Queen's and Prince's companies, had each been issued with 4½ yards of red cloth to take part in the King's long-deferred coronation procession through London. It has been pointed out that the King's men were not at this time grooms of the chamber, but only became so five months later, and that the cloth they received was of the lowest grade awarded to crown servants to wear on such occasions.[4] In August, Phillips and Heminges with ten of their fellows were appointed grooms, and roped in to attend on the Spanish Ambassador for eighteen days at the Queen's palace, Somerset House, which had been placed at the Ambassador's disposal during negotiations for an important new peace treaty with Spain. There is no suggestion that they were required to perform; their duties appear to have been merely those of liveried attendants. They were each paid two shillings a day for this service, which, though no more than the guards received, would have helped to eke out their dwindling resources.

The appointment of twelve of the players as grooms represents an increase of three to the nine who were named in the patent of the previous year, and indicates the advancement of three former hired men or apprentices to the position of sharers. The chosen three were probably John Lowin, Samuel Crosse and Alexander Cooke, listed in eleventh, twelfth and thirteenth places in the Folio list of 'Principall Actors'. As we have seen (pp. 102–4), Crosse and Cooke had been with the company, initially as apprentices, since its inception as the Chamberlain's in 1594, but if Crosse was indeed one of the three, he must have died fairly soon afterwards (another victim, perhaps, of the plague) for there is no subsequent record of him; he would have been replaced by another long-serving apprentice, Nicholas Tooley – then about thirty years old.

Lowin (Plate 13) had joined the company from Worcester's in 1603 and, as suggested in my doubling plot for *Troilus* (Appendix D), may already have toured with the play in that year. Both he and Cooke are named as principal tragedians in Jonson's *Sejanus*, performed for the court at Christmas, and Lowin went on to replace Kempe as Falstaff and to play Henry VIII.[5]

With the approach of colder weather and a general easing of the plague throughout the country in September and October 1604, the players set out on their customary autumn tour. Only a few provincial records survive from this year, but we know them to have been at Barnstaple (probably for the Michaelmas Fair), and they would hardly have gone so far without playing also in Exeter, Bristol, and towns along the way.[6]

But by the end of October they were back in the capital, receiving a summons to perform at court, and from the Revels accounts of that holiday season, we discover that Shakespeare had occupied his time in the previous year in writing two new plays.

Othello and *Measure for Measure* are of special interest as being the first of Shakespeare's Jacobean plays; and though in writing them he would have kept in mind the likes and dislikes of his regular public at the Globe and elsewhere, he would also have felt a pressing need to please the company's new, still unpredictable patron. All the speculation about the possibility or Shakespeare having experienced some form of emotional crisis or romantic disappointment in the previous period that turned him away from light-hearted comedy towards darker and more tragic themes in the years that followed can be dismissed as so much moonshine, based in a fundamental misunderstanding of his writing as motivated primarily by a need for self-expression, rather than by a combination of theatrical demands with a creative urge to understand and explore human nature in all its many aspects. One of the first of his plays had been an historical tragedy, *Titus*, whose protagonist is a figure of heroic dimensions. My own view is that he had always intended to return to such themes, and that in writing the more complex comedies and the tragedies that date from this time, he was rising to the best and finest potentialities that he knew to be in him, rather than sinking in a mood of despondency and disillusion to a more pessimistic view of the world. Not that he would have been unaware of or unaffected by the changes around him. The swashbuckling Elizabethan era (if it was ever truly that) had predeceased the Queen. This was a new, more challenging world in which he found himself. But the accession of James, with his moral preoccupations, arrogant interpretation of his kingly role, and (as time would reveal) increasingly inept performance of it, is more likely to have been a spur to his creativity than a discouragement of it.

For all their obvious differences, *Othello* and *Measure for Measure* possess these characteristics in common: both have relatively small casts and both appear to have been written for indoor performance, in which the intimacy and intensity of their best scenes would have found a more appropriate setting than in the daylit, open spaces of the Globe. The first recorded performance of *Othello* was for the King and the court at Whitehall on 1 November 1604. The choice of day (Hallowmas or All Saints, the eve of All Souls) was perhaps no more than coincidental, but could not have been more apt; for *Othello* is a play of contrasting light and darkness and the struggle between them, in which the love of Othello for Desdemona is poisoned at source through the malign, driving ambition of Iago. I suggested earlier that in writing *Troilus* and *All's Well*, Shakespeare was already preparing for a drastic shift in the focus of his artistic and spiritual vision. At some point along the long road he had come since he and his fellows set out on their 1603 tour, he had found the story he had been looking for that was to release a new flood of creative energy that was to take him to greater heights of dramatic achievement than any he had attained before. The sense of urgency is palpable in the opening scene. There is no question here of the play being plot-driven or character-driven. From the moment that Iago and his stooge Roderigo burst upon the scene in mid-flow, we are in the vice-like grip of a plot that *is* the play –

> *Roderigo*:   Tush, never tell me, I take it much unkindly
> That thou, Iago, who hast had my purse,
> As if the strings were thine, shouldst know of this.
>
> *Iago*:   'Sblood, but you will not hear me.
> If ever I did dream of such a matter,
> Abhor me –

And there we remain – however painful the experience may be in repetition – until the play's exhausted and terrible end.

It is a commonplace to say that *Othello* – though not the greatest of Shakespeare's tragedies – is the best of them in terms of the total credibility of its characters and assured skill of its construction. In these respects, it is not only foremost among the tragedies but also perhaps the most technically accomplished of all his plays. My impression is that he wrote it quickly, but only after a long period of gestation for which the previous two years of travel and restricted London activity had provided space. Sometimes in the plays, we sense that he was feeling his way in the creation of his characters and the casting of them; in *Othello*, they enter fully formed and assigned from the start.

There was no longer any doubt about Burbage – as there may have been initially in *Hamlet*. His ability to throw himself into a role, and to identify with it wholly throughout the length of each performance, is well attested. 'Oft have I seene him' – an obituarist was to write –

> leap into the grave,
> Suiting the person which he seem'd to have
> Of a sadd lover with soe true an eye,
> That theer I would have sworne, he meant to dye.
> Oft have I seene him play this part in jeast,
> Soe lively, that spectators, and the rest
> Of his sad crew, whilst he but seem'd to bleed,
> Amazed, thought even then hee dyed in deed.[7]

Othello demands this kind of totally committed acting. It is a great tragic role in the tradition of Titus, Kyd's Hieronimo, Marlowe's Tamburlaine and Faustus as played by Alleyn; but with this difference, for here the burden of dominance is shared. There are *two* great parts in *Othello*; the other of course is Iago, and it is only when both are acted with equal weight and conviction that the play achieves the full effect in performance that Shakespeare intended.

Unusually, Shakespeare gives us Iago's exact age – twenty-eight; but rather than narrowing the field of possibility to Condell or Cooke as the actor for whom it was written – both men being now of that approximate age – I take it as a signal that the player concerned was somewhat older (as Burbage had been for Hamlet). Why else should Shakespeare have felt a need to state it so precisely? Shakespeare himself was at this time only forty, and who else could have brought to it the same degree of understanding and authority? The part is larger than any other I have given him – larger, indeed, than Othello; nor does it conform to any of the previous categories he had made his own, such as his kingly or presenter roles. But if ever there was an occasion for breaking the mould of what had been done before, it was this. Iago opens the play and is there at the end, though stubbornly silent. It has all the marks of detachment – though here of the most chilling and inhuman kind – that distinguish many of the parts to which Shakespeare was drawn. I give Brabantio to Heminges, his brother Gratiano to Sly, and the Duke to Phillips – if he was well enough at this time to take it, for he was to die in the following May – with Condell, perhaps, as Cassio, Armin as the Clown, and Cowley as Roderigo. Emilia may have gone to Cooke or to Tooley, and Desdemona to a more recent recruit – possibly (as suggested below) to William Ostler.

The first court performance of *Othello* – which could hardly have failed to be sensational – took place, as I have said, on 1 November. Going from one extreme to another of Shakespeare's dramatic range, it was followed a few days later by a revival of the *Merry Wives,* and the ready availability of both plays so soon after the company's return from travel suggests that they were drawn from its current repertoire, and that *Othello* had been premiered on tour, if not at the Globe in the previous summer. But nearly two months were to pass before the players were to make their next appearance at court with *Measure for Measure,* and as this was to be followed by a whole series of revivals extending to the eve of Lent, involving a good deal of recasting to take account of changes in the company that had occurred in the interim, much of this time would have been spent in rehearsal.

The first thing to say about *Measure for Measure* is that for all its serious concerns and darker moments, it remains from first to last a comedy, and was meant to be played as such. The day of its first court performance – which is likely to have been its premiere – may be significant in this respect: it was acted before the King in the banqueting hall at Whitehall on St Stephen's day – the start of the Christmas holiday season. Again, Shakespeare was to play a leading part, but one that was more familiar to him; that of Vincentio, the Duke of the play who, like his previous dukes, is plainly a ruler with regal authority. Was this Shakespeare's device for shielding himself from accusations of *lèse-majesté*? Nevertheless, when, in the opening moments of the play, King James, seated in a position of honour in his palace of Whitehall, was confronted by Shakespeare in this kingly role, a frisson of anxiety may have gone through the audience of courtiers as to how he might react. Shakespeare anticipates this, and plays on it in the scene that follows. Any obvious relation between the spectator King and the fictional Duke is avoided by Shakespeare's setting of the story in Vienna, from which, it appears, the Duke is about to depart on urgent, undisclosed business elsewhere, leaving his deputy Angelo to rule in his place; but teasingly, he invites the comparison a few moments later when he has the Duke inform Angelo that he wishes to leave the city privately and unattended because, although he 'loves the people', he does not 'like to stage me to their eyes', which, as everyone in the audience would have known, was exactly James's reaction to the crowds who had thronged to see him on his journey south. Thereafter, however, reality and drama part company, for it shortly transpires that the Duke has not departed the city at all, but has remained behind to keep a hidden eye on Angelo, whom he intends to put to the test with the suspicion that he is not the man he appears, or believes himself to be.

This opening scene sets the key. Like *All's Well*, the play draws on a traditional story, and though Shakespeare improvises brilliantly to retain our credibility and keep us in suspense, there is a playfulness in his treatment of it that is often missed in performance. This is especially true of the Duke, and the way the part is played determines the whole. We may accept the impenetrability of his disguise as a friar as a not uncommon stage convention, and there can be no doubt of his serious purpose, but why does he complicate matters by concealing for so long Angelo's fall from grace in attempting to blackmail the beautiful Isabella into sleeping with him by threatening the life of her brother? And why, having saved the brother (Claudio), does he go to such lengths to hide the fact that he has done so – if not simply to maintain suspense and contrive a more effective ending? For if the play is plot-driven, there can be no question as to who is driving the plot. It is the Duke himself in the person of Shakespeare in his dual capacity of Player King at his most quixotic and Player Poet, controlling it all. Much of the comedy is what we might now describe as black, but it is comedy nonetheless, and however truly the other players act their parts – and I am not suggesting they should be acted for anything less than their full dramatic value – the audience knows that all will be well because the Duke is in charge.

Isabella is the latest in Shakespeare's series of young, strong-minded heroines, whose beauty and shining sincerity bring out the best and the worst of the various men she encounters – depending on their predispositions.[8]

With Condell as Angelo, I conjecture Heminges to have been cast as Escalus, and Burbage as Lucio, a 'fantastic'. The smaller comic characters fulfil an equivalent function in the play to the mechanicals in the *Dream* or Dogberry's watch in *Much Ado* (if, that is, they are not too drastically cut); by their inane incursions into the action, they keep the play on an appropriately comedic level. I see Lowin as Elbow, Cowley as Froth, Armin as Pompey the clown, and Sly as Barnardine. In recent times, the play has often been plunged in Stygian gloom, with undue emphasis given to its darker elements and a repressive 'Jacobean atmosphere'. There could be no surer way of killing the comedy, or of obscuring Shakespeare's meaning. For though the play draws its title from an Old Testament source, implying 'measure for measure' in the sense of an eye for an eye and a tooth for a tooth, the Duke stands the old harsh maxim on its head by exemplifying Christian charity in fullest, overflowing measure by forgiving all who have sinned – the penitent and impenitent alike. Even Barnardine, the condemned criminal who obstinately refuses to yield his head when one is required to substitute for that of the redeemed Claudio, is finally let off the hook.

— ✳ —

It is apparent from the series of revivals of the company's earlier successes that followed the first performance of *Measure for Measure* that the players were pulling out all the stops in their effort to reinforce the favourable impression they had made on their new patron with *As You Like It*, the *Dream* and *Othello*. *Measure* on Boxing Day was succeeded two days later (in its usual slot on Innocents' Day) by the *Comedy of Errors*. In the New Year came *Love's Labour's Lost*, *Henry V* on 7 January, and on the next day, Jonson's comedy, *Every Man Out of his Humour*. Three weeks later (by special request?) the last play's precursor, *Every Man In his Humour*, was given with Shakespeare in a principal role, and on 10 February (a Sunday) the *Merchant of Venice*. An interesting pointer to King James's personal tastes is provided by his choice of the *Merchant* for a repeat performance on Shrove Tuesday – the eve of Lent.[9]

After a Lenten break, during which (one hopes) Shakespeare may have been able to manage a week or two's rest with his family in Stratford, the Globe reopened for an Easter season in April, when *Measure for Measure* and *Othello* would have received public performance along with the recent revivals of Jonson's and Shakespeare's comedies.

But the plague was still present in London. In July, there was already talk of a prorogation of the session of Parliament due to meet in September, and by the first week of October, when the weekly death toll had risen again to 30, another closure order went out from the Privy Council, and the theatres were to remain shut for the rest of the year. This was, however, a usual time for the company to travel, and an autumn tour may already have been planned, if not begun. Fortunately, an exact date for the players' visit to Oxford in this year is recorded as 9 October so we know that by then they were well on their way.[10] It was probably on this occasion that Jonson's *Volpone* was performed in the university city, as claimed on the dedication page of the play's 1607 edition, along with *Othello* and *Measure*. The players appear not to have travelled further west at this time, but to have returned on a roundabout route taking in possibly Cambridge, where Jonson also claimed *Volpone* to have received 'love and acceptance', and certainly Saffron Walden in Essex on the final leg of their journey.[11]

National events were now to play a part in keeping the London theatres closed, for on 5 November 1605 the Gunpowder Plot was uncovered, and it was not until 15 December that permission was given for their reopening. Ten plays were acted at court during the Christmas season of 1605/6, though we have no record of their titles. Nor do we have any direct information as to Shakespeare's personal reactions to the current political turmoil. Or to the witchhunt and ruthless purge of Catholics (some guilty but mostly innocent) that followed. That some of the victims would have been known to him personally – especially in and around Stratford, where a jury of citizens was summoned to root out alleged sympathisers – seems very likely. All we have to go on – and it is surely enough – are the plays that he wrote in the period: *King Lear* and *Macbeth*.

Though the stories they tell are completely different, the two plays have much in common. They both feature great but flawed heroes whose downfall is primarily brought about through self-indulgence of their moral failings: ambition in the one, pride and its concomitant vice, self-absorption, in the other. They continue Shakespeare's return, begun in *Othello*, to a more classical type of drama in which one or two characters dominate the whole. Macbeth has a partner in evil; Lear stands alone. They may not be the best of Shakespeare's plays but they are undoubtedly among the very greatest, and more profoundly disturbing. In them, Shakespeare confronts head-on the mystery of evil, and though Lear is finally destroyed by it, he achieves true majesty in the course of his struggle, whereas Macbeth follows an opposite curve; starting from a position of nobility and honour, his progression is all downhill. If the fatalism of *Macbeth* is redeemed by the poetic splendour of its language, *Lear* is the more terrible of the plays but also, in a paradoxical way, the more life-enhancing.

Much scholarly argument has turned on the question of when they were written and which of the two came first. It is more than possible, however, that in the 24 weeks between 5 November 1605 and a reopening of the Globe after the Lenten break on 21 April

1606, Shakespeare – working at white heat – had been able to complete them both, and that both were premiered at the Globe in the course of that Easter season.[12]

That Burbage played Lear is a matter of record – and who could refuse him Macbeth? But what of the other roles, and especially Shakespeare's? In *Lear*, I give him Gloucester – mainly because I cannot conceive of his entrusting the part to anyone else, or that any other actor in the company could have played it so well; especially with Burbage in the heart-stopping scene with the mad Lear, when he has been blinded.

> *Gloucester*: The trick of that voice I do well remember:
> Is't not the King?
> *Lear*: Ay, every inch a king:
> When I do stare, see how the subject quakes . . .
> *Gloucester*: O! let me kiss that hand.
> *Lear*: Let me wipe it first; it smells of mortality.
> *Gloucester*: O ruin'd piece of Nature! This great world
> Shall so wear out to naught. Dost thou know me?
> *Lear*: I remember thine eyes well enough. Dost thou
> squiny at me?
> No, do thy worst, blind Cupid; I'll not love . . .
> (IV.vi.106–8, 131–6)

In modern productions, the Fool – in spite of being addressed by Lear as 'pretty knave', 'lad' and 'boy' – often goes to an older actor. This may lend the role a certain added pathos, but is not, I think, Shakespeare's intention. Historically, it is usually assigned to Armin, but Armin at this date would have been too mature a man to play it. It would have been given to one of the company's younger apprentices (perhaps Armin's apprentice) as a double with Cordelia – one of those doubles that transcends economic necessity to fulfil an important dramatic function in the play. Armin's versatility and expert knowledge of contemporary fools would have been more valuably employed as Edgar – especially in his assumed identity as Poor Tom.[13] It is, of course, Cordelia's genuine love for her father, which shines out in the later scenes of their reconciliation (Plate 14), that makes it impossible for her to take any part in the phoney love-test of the first act, which sets the tragedy in motion.

Regan and Goneril are parts for those older apprentices or former apprentices (Cooke and Tooley?) who appear to have gone on playing the more mature women's roles well into their thirties. I see Condell as Kent, Cowley and Sly as Cornwall and Albany, Gough or Gilburne perhaps as Edmund, Lowin as Oswald, and Heminges as the Old Man of Act IV, Scene 1. With over twenty speaking roles to be covered, a fair amount of doubling was required.

All of that small minority of scholars who have given serious consideration to the parts that Shakespeare took in his own plays agree that King Duncan in *Macbeth* was one of them – doubling, perhaps, with the Doctor attending on Lady Macbeth in Act 5.[14] It is a nice example of the 'Kingly parts' he played 'in sport' and, with only 69 lines, would have afforded welcome respite from the other, much larger roles he was playing in the period. Small as it is, it requires an actor of gentle, charismatic presence.

Macbeth is the only play of Shakespeare's in which the powers of darkness are given material form, and their appearance at the start must have sent a shiver of very real dread through the play's early audiences. Since then the figure of the witch has been conventional-ised, and so often guyed as to become merely risible, and present-day directors must find an alternative way of evoking the same effect (Plate 15). It is, however, only in stage directions and speech prefixes that they are described as 'witches'; to Banquo they 'look not like th'inhabitants o'th'earth,/And yet are on't' (I.iii.41–2), and Macbeth refers to them as 'weird sisters', meaning 'weyard', sisters of fate. In Jacobean English, 'hag' or 'witch' could mean, not only what it does today, but also a demon *disguised* as a witch. Though they have no power in the play to take Macbeth further along the path to treason and murder than he consents in his heart to go, they lead him on to damnation and death with half-truths and deceitful prophecies. But of course it is Lady Macbeth who pushes him over the edge into absolute evil, for if Macbeth is practised on by demons, his remorseless wife is possessed by them at her own invitation. We do

241

not know who played the role in the first production – I suspect Tooley or Cooke – but it requires a strong performance from a very good actor. We may no longer believe in the powers of demons but the play can still convince us they are real. It is the nearest that Shakespeare came to writing a morality play. Good triumphs in the end but at fearful cost.

There are some thirty speaking parts in all, requiring extensive doubling. Nevertheless, with apprentices doubling the smaller women's roles with boys and servants, and the Weird Sisters appearing also as the murderers, Seyton and the drunken Porter, it would still have been possible to stage the play with a dozen actors, three or four apprentices and a few additional soldiers. Even today, the tighter the ensemble and the more completely the company is involved from start to finish, the greater the total effect is likely to be.

On 4 May 1605, Augustine Phillips had made his will, and died a few days later. He was one of the senior men of the company, a skilled musician and composer of jigs, a family man whose youngest daughter had married Robert Gough, and a respected figure in and beyond his profession whose advocacy with the authorities had saved the company from possible disgrace at the time of the Essex affair. His bequests to his fellows give a picture in little of the company's personnel and rankings – probably as it had been a few years earlier when the will was originally drafted, as two of the beneficiaries (Beeston and Fletcher) were no longer active in the company in 1605. Five pounds in gold were to be divided among the hired men; with thirty shillings each in gold to Shakespeare, Condell and 'to my servaunte' Christopher Beeston; and twenty shillings each to Lawrence Fletcher, Armin, Cowley, Cooke and Tooley (in that order). His late apprentice, Samuel Gilburne, was to receive forty shillings and items from his wardrobe including 'my purple Cloke, sword and dagger', and his present apprentice, James Sandes, forty shillings with his musical instruments, comprising a bass viol, cittern, bandore and lute – but only 'at thexpiracon of his yeares in his Indentur or Apprenticehood'. Heminges, Burbage and Sly were appointed 'overseers' of the will, each to receive for their pains a 'boule of silver of the valew of ffyve poundes apeece'. Gough is named as one of two witnesses to Phillips' signature.[15] He would have been much missed by all of his fellows.

During the early months of 1606, concurrent with the trial of the Jesuit Provincial, Fr Garnet, and further rumours of treason and plots, the plague in London continued to cause anxiety as the weekly total of deaths veered between single numbers and the twenties. Then, in the middle of July, there was a leap to 50, and by the end of that month to 66. Again, the Globe and other playhouses were closed, and probably remained so for eight or nine months until Easter 1607.

In 1606 the company was recorded at Oxford, Marlborough, and in Kent, and in the summer, Heminges was rewarded on behalf of his fellows for 'three playes before his Majestie and the kinge of Denmarke at Greenwich and Hampton Court'.

The Danish king was in England between 15 July and 11 August to visit his sister, Queen Anne, but during the first two weeks of his stay, the queen was still recuperating from childbirth at Greenwich. The players were at Oxford between 28 and 31 July, having travelled perhaps by way of Marlborough. The queen having been churched on 3 August, they were summoned to Greenwich for two performances there between the 3rd and the 5th. They would then have accompanied the royal entourage to Hampton Court, where a third performance was given and Heminges was paid.[16] As the plague in London was still on an upward curve, rising to a weekly death toll of 85 in August, 116 in early September, to reach a peak of 141 at the beginning of October, the company would have gone from Hampton Court as directly as possible into Kent.

Again we have only a partial record of the towns in which they played: Maidstone, Faversham, and finally Dover, which they reached on 30 August.[17] At Maidstone, an unusual entry in the Chamberlains' accounts reads, 'payd to the kinges players by mr maior & to the trompettors, £2 5s' – more than twice the usual reward. Though the Royal Corps of Trumpets and Drums is often found on tour independently, and their combining with the players here may only have been coincidental, the fact that Maidstone would probably have

Performances at Maidstone took place in one of the town's market or courthouse buildings demolished in the eighteenth century but recorded in this early drawing (Maidstone Museum)

been the company's first stop after leaving Hampton Court on 8 August suggests that a section of the royal band accompanied them at least so far, and that the play was *Lear*, in which, apart from stipulated sennets, flourishes and drums, two trumpeters are required to appear and play on stage in Act 5. Their participation would have added an authentic touch of royal pageantry to the performance.

The writing of *Antony and Cleopatra* and *Coriolanus* belongs in all probability to the latter part of this year during which the Globe remained closed. Nine plays were given at court during the Christmas season of 1606/7 which extended from 26 December to 27 February in the second week of Lent, and *Antony* may well have been one of them.[18] We know that *Lear* was performed on St Stephen's day (26 December) before the King; not the most obvious choice of play for

244

such a festive occasion, and, if the choice was that of James, one that would indicate that his taste in such matters was more discerning than he has usually been given credit for.

The Globe and other metropolitan theatres may have opened briefly at Easter 1607, for Easter and the early summer of 1608, and for one or two months in the early part of 1610; otherwise the whole of that three-year period was a blank so far as London was concerned. It is true that from the middle of December 1607 to May 1608, the weekly totals of plague deaths remained in single figures, but as the plague eased, Londoners had the Great Freeze to contend with, when the Thames froze over and conditions in the exposed theatres would have been impossibly cold both for the players and those who may have struggled across the ice in the hope of seeing them. Then in June 1608, the plague toll returned to double figures, rose steadily to a further peak of 147 in September, and remained at a prohibitively high level for the rest of that year and throughout the whole of 1609.

In 1608/9, Thomas Dekker was to describe the situation in London as one in which:

> Pleasure itself finds now no pleasure but in sighing and bewailing the miseries of the time . . . Play-houses stand (like taverns that have cast out their masters) the doors locked up, the flags (like their bushes) taken down; or rather like houses lately infected, from whence the affrighted dwellers are fled, in hope to live better in the country. . . . Playing vacations are diseases now as common and as hurtful to them as the Foul Evil to a Northern Man or the Pox to a Frenchman. . . . To walk every day into the fields is wearisome; to drink up the day and night in a tavern, loathsome, to be ever riding upon that beast with two heads (lechery) most damnable, and yet to be ever idle is detestable.

Only, he tells us, across the river in the Bear Garden, is any diversion to be found. 'The company of the Bears hold together still; they play their tragicomedies as lively as ever they did: the pied bull here keeps atossing and a roaring when the Red Bull [a theatre in Clerkenwell] dares not stir.'[19]

How would Shakespeare have reacted to this bleak situation? It is not a question that biographers often ask – let alone attempt to answer. At this point in their narratives they usually take refuge in generalities, or write in vague terms of Shakespeare distancing himself from his profession as player and from the company he served. I shall be looking more closely at the question of Shakespeare's alleged retirement, and the various dates that have been advanced for it in the following chapter; but it can be said here that if Shakespeare ever did withdraw from acting and his close involvement in the day-to-day activities of the company, which I doubt, we can be sure that it would not have been *now*; not (if my estimate of his character is anywhere near the mark) at this moment of crisis when, to all those involved, the very survival of the company and all that he and his fellows had worked to achieve and to build in the preceding fourteen years must have seemed under imminent threat of extinction.

One important advantage that Shakespeare enjoyed in the period in contrast to a free-lance playwright like Dekker – who, in consequence of the London closures, had been reduced to the necessity of pamphleteering in order to scrape a living – lay in his permanent attachment to a single company, the King's, and the continuing demand that was made upon it throughout the plague years for court entertainment, especially the provision of new plays which, as its principal author, he was expected to supply. We find the company at Whitehall on eleven occasions in the winter of 1607/8 – sometimes performing twice on the same day; giving twelve plays for the King, Queen, Prince Henry and the Duke of York (again at Whitehall) in 1608/9; and thirteen more in 1609/10. These 36 performances – not all of them of plays by Shakespeare, of course, though a good many were – produced £380 in rewards, along with two grants-in-aid totalling a further £70; the second of which (on 10 March 1610) was paid to Heminges 'for himselfe and the reste of his companie beinge restrayned from publique playinge within the citie of London in the tyme of infeccon durioge the space of sixe weekes in which tyme they practised pryvately for his majesties service'.[20] Nor did the company cease to travel. On 6 September 1607 we find them at Oxford again, and in the same year at Barnstaple, and receiving a modest reward of

6s 8d from the Chamberlains of the lost city of Dunwich on the Suffolk coast (now under the encroaching sea); in 1608 at Marlborough and Coventry; and in 1609 at Ipswich, and Hythe and New Romney in Kent. Though on all these extensive tours they would have been dodging the plague – and, as they moved from place to place, may sometimes have been paid *not* to perform – the few records that have survived the passing of four hundred years can represent (as in 1603) only a small proportion of the number of towns which they actually visited and in which they played, and the official rewards they received (rarely more than a pound in each) the merest fraction of their total receipts when additional gatherings at these and subsequent performances are taken into account. When compared with their usual takings at the Globe, their income from such visits would not have been large but, in conjunction with payments for their court performances, sufficient to keep the company together and operational on the proverbial shoe-string with the hope of better times to come; a not unfamiliar state of being to professional companies in this country, now as then.

If, as I have conjectured, *Antony and Cleopatra* was premiered in London in a court performance during the Christmas season of 1606 and featured in a brief season at the Globe at Easter 1607, it would almost certainly have gone with the company on the series of tours to Oxfordshire, Suffolk and Devon that occupied the rest of that year. Though clearly belonging to the sequence of tragedies of unparalleled power and invention on which Shakespeare was then embarked, it is different in both structure and aims from its immediate predecessors. Structurally, it represents a return to the looser, chronicle pattern of story-telling he had previously employed in his English history plays; in subject, it continues his account of the Roman world as reflected by Plutarch, and picks up the story of Antony where he had left it in *Julius Caesar*. He shows us, in a succession of vividly realised episodes, what some twenty years of power, political intrigue, and hard drinking had done to him; more importantly he shows him in love, for *Antony and Cleopatra* is as much a tragedy of love as was *Romeo and Juliet*.

For all its epic dimensions, this is a very personal, even intimate, play that is not helped by overblown, grandiose production. Its scenes are many and for the most part short, and there is rarely need for more than half a dozen characters to be on stage together. That is why it is perfectly valid for us to envisage it as equally (if not more) effective in the restricted surroundings of the Dunwich guildhall as on the open stage of the Globe.

It goes without saying that Antony would have been for Burbage; it is also apparent that Shakespeare had at his disposal at the time a boy player of remarkable ability for whom Cleopatra was written. Peter Levi has suggested that this was William Ostler, who had begun his career with the Chapel company (a children's troupe) with which he had taken a part in Jonson's *Poetaster* in 1601.[21] He is first recorded as a King's man in 1610 but is likely to have joined the company earlier. (He is given sixteenth place, after Robert Armin, in the Folio list of principal actors.) He was later to marry Thomasine, Heminges' daughter, but died still relatively young in 1614. In an epigram in his *Scourge of Folly* of *c.* 1611, our old acquaintance, John Davies of Hereford, describes him as 'the Roscius of These Times' and a 'King of Actors', who

> . . . if thou plaist thy dying part as well
> As thy stage parts, thou hast no part in hell[22]

– which, of course, is where he assumes the majority of players to be headed!

If, as is quite possible, Ostler had already played Desdemona, he would have been well practised in the art of dying. But whether it was he or another recent recruit who played Cleopatra in the original production, he would have been in command of the bewildering mood changes, tricks and shifting strategies, as also the depths of true feeling, of which the character shows herself to be capable, and that makes her one of the two or three most complex and fascinating female roles that Shakespeare ever wrote.

I believe that his own part in the play was Enobarbus. It has the

distinctive characteristic of detachment and is of the medium size
(some 350 lines) that he preferred. Present on the sidelines in all the
more significant scenes and situations, his chief function in the play
is that of a witty, intelligent and perceptive observer of the action
throughout; it is one of Shakespeare's presenter roles. Alone among
the characters, he is able to give clear, objective expression to
Cleopatra's motives and, on occasion, to put Antony right about
them. When Antony speaks of her as 'cunning', he corrects him:

> Alack, sir, no, her passions are made of nothing but the finest part
> of pure love. We cannot call her winds and waters sighs and tears;
> they are greater storms and tempests than almanacs can report.
> This cannot be cunning in her; if it be, she makes a shower of rain
> as well as Jove. (I.ii.144–9)

His retrospective descriptions of her more spectacular self-
dramatisations are so graphic as to bring them on stage, and make
us feel we were there.

> The barge she sat in, like a burnish'd throne
> Burn'd on the water: the poop was beaten gold;
> Purple the sails, and so perfumed that
> The winds were love-sick with them; the oars were silver,
> Which to the tune of lutes kept stroke, and made
> The water which they beat to follow faster,
> As amorous of their strokes. . . . (II.ii.191–7)

In character, Enobarbus is another of Shakespeare's originals –
combining the soldierly virtues of courage, honour and good humour
with an intensely personal devotion to Antony. When, at the end of
Act 3, he takes the sensible decision to desert his cause, realising it is
doomed to failure, he is so unforgiving of himself as to die of grief.
As with Mercutio in *Romeo*, it becomes dramatically necessary to
remove him from the play at this point if the denouement – in its
concentration on the two lovers – is to achieve its fullest tragic and

poetic dimensions. Which it does. The apparent simplicity of the play's first four acts is deceptive; its cumulative effect is superb.

If *Antony and Cleopatra* is a tragedy of love, *Coriolanus* is a tragedy of honour; the story of a man who, by reason of an austere Roman upbringing by his formidable mother Volumnia, places an ideal of soldierly pride above all other virtues, even patriotism, to his own ultimate destruction. It is a powerful, intense drama, closely based, like *Antony*, on Lord North's translation of Plutarch. But it has contemporary relevance also. The corn riots in Rome reported by Plutarch are paralleled by food shortages and civil disorder in England throughout the Elizabethan and Jacobean periods, resulting from the replacement of tillage by pasture and enclosures of common land. Prices generally were rising; there was a dearth of corn in 1607 and 1608, and the former year saw a popular insurrection in the Midlands. Though the causes of the future civil war between King and Parliament were more constitutional and religious than social in origin, it is difficult not to see in the picture of civil unrest and class warfare that Shakespeare gives us in the play's opening scene an awful prognostication of what was to come. It is in the context of a divided and fractious population that the personal tragedy of Coriolanus is framed.

A reference in the first scene to the 'coal of fire upon the ice' (l. 172) suggests that the play was written in the hard winter of 1607/8 when, as we have seen, the Thames froze – for the first time in over forty years – and there are reports of fires having been lit on the ice. And this fits with stylistic and other slight indications of date, as well as an entry in the Stationers' Register in May 1608.[23] It may have been premiered at court in February 1608, and staged at the Globe at Easter or early summer of that year. It is a play of violent action. It begins, like *Julius Caesar*, with a mob of mutinous citizens 'over the stage', and proceeds to some of the most blood-bespattered battle scenes that Shakespeare ever devised. It is clear from the stage directions, which make good claim to derive from his original manuscript, that it was written for the Globe, and demands all the space that the Globe's open stage – possibly also its yard – could provide. He was not to know that the company's London venue was

to be available to it only for a few weeks, and that further performances there would be inhibited by the plague for a year and a
half. It is doubtful whether more than a handful of the guildhalls
that he and his fellows were to visit in the months that followed
would have been able to accommodate it.

Shakespeare is careful to preserve a balance of sympathies as
between the opposing parties: between the riotous citizens and their
arrogant rulers, and later between Coriolanus and his fellow
patricians. The plebs are more realistically drawn than in *Caesar*,
and though they are just as fickle and bloody-minded, they are given
more justification for being so. Coriolanus is seen at his worst in his
relations with them but, in his natural environment of war, wins
respect for his courage, his modesty – based as this appears to be in
an egocentric disdain for publicity – and occasional bursts of
generosity towards his defeated foes. The role would have gone by a
now well-founded right to Burbage. Volumnia is the strongest of
Shakespeare's older women and would have been a gift to one of the
former apprentices who specialised in such parts. She has created in
her son a monster of self-willed fanaticism, and the scene (V.iii) in
which she turns aside his determination to destroy Rome out of
revenge for what he sees as its ingratitude to him by an appeal to the
filial debt that he owes her, is the best in the play. She succeeds, but
only at the cost of Coriolanus' own death at the hands of the
Volscians who, in sparing Rome, he has betrayed. 'Kill, kill, kill, kill,
kill him!', they cry (echoing the mad Lear), in a final horrific scene
as they cut him down and trample him under foot.

There is not much human warmth or humour in the play, and
most of the little that Shakespeare allows in his stark retelling of the
story is given to Menenius Agrippa. This elderly patrician, despite
his loyalty to Coriolanus and admiration for him, is the voice of
moderation and humanity in the play. I have little doubt that it was
Shakespeare's role, and that his performance of it would have done
much to ameliorate the play's otherwise chilling effect.

This, however, was not quite the end of the road in Shakespeare's
exploration of the darker, more destructive sides of human nature
on which he had first embarked in *Othello*. That was to come with

Timon of Athens, which exists only in an imperfect, disjointed text which Chambers was probably correct in characterising as a first, unrevised draft. As such, I shall not do Shakespeare the injustice of discussing it as if it were anything more – though tidied-up versions have been staged with success in recent years. One thing that may be said of it with reasonable certainty – arising from its locales, use of space and stage directions – is that, like *Coriolanus*, it was intended for the open stage of the Globe. In a rare indulgence in conjecture, Chambers went on to suggest that the reason for its being unfinished is that Shakespeare 'dealt with it under conditions of mental and perhaps physical stress, which led to a breakdown'.[24] But as we have no grounds for doubting that during this whole period Shakespeare continued his normal activities, travelling with the company on its more than usually lengthy travels, playing his usual roles in its now rich repertoire of earlier plays including comedies, I think it more likely that the play was left unfinished because, by 1609, it would have become apparent to him that production at the Globe was no longer a viable option in the foreseeable future, and by the time of the Globe's reopening, he had found other, more promising themes to explore. Like *Troilus and Cressida*, it had missed its moment.

It can be admitted, however, that this is unlikely to have been a happy time in Shakespeare's personal life. Not only would he have lost friends and fellows to the plague but, towards the end of December 1607, his younger brother Edmund who had followed him to London to become a player, died when only twenty-eight years old. We know nothing of the circumstances, whether Edmund was, or ever had been, a member of the company, or how close the brothers were. All we really know about him is that earlier in 1607 an illegitimate son of his named Edward had been buried at St Giles, Cripplegate; and that when his own death followed four months later, someone (it was almost certainly William) arranged and paid for an expensive funeral in St Saviour's, Southwark, with burial in the church and a 'forenoon knell of the great bell'.[25] Nor was this to be the last of his griefs in the year that followed.

There is one other play belonging to the period 1607/8 still to be mentioned: *Pericles*. But this too only survives in an imperfect text –

one so unsatisfactory to Heminges and Condell, who would have played in it, that they omitted it from the First Folio altogether. As it represents the beginnings of another of those sea changes in Shakespeare's shifting perspectives on the world of his time, it will be best to defer consideration of it to the following chapter.

TWELVE

Blackfriars

The latter part of his Life was spent, as all Men of good Sense will wish theirs may be, in Ease, Retirement, and the Conversation of his Friends. He had the good Fortune to gather an Estate equal to his Occasion . . . and is said to have spent some Years before his Death at his native Stratford.

Nicholas Rowe, 1709[1]

He . . . waited until 1613 before acquiring his first London property. It is sometimes said that he had already retired, and that he purchased the Blackfriars gatehouse purely as an investment . . . . We think otherwise: in 1613 he was still in his forties, the gatehouse was conveniently close to the Blackfriars theatre, and had he not pledged to pay his share of this theatre's rent for twenty-one years? . . . He could not foresee in 1613 that he had only three more years to live; he might reasonably hope to continue his London career.

E.A.J. Honigmann and Susan Brock[2]

On the basis of the vague statement quoted above from Shakespeare's first biographer Rowe in the eighteenth century – qualified as it is by that notorious let-out, 'is said' – it has been almost universally accepted that Shakespeare retired from active involvement in the theatre to his home in Stratford at some time between 1610 and 1613. Chambers points out that his name does not appear in any of Jonson's cast lists after *Sejanus* in 1603 but, as he is named in only one other before that date (*Every Man in his Humour* in 1598), and as the lists are retrospectively compiled and far from complete, this tells us very little. In 1610 Shakespeare was only forty-six. Actors, then as now, do not retire in their forties (or

254

ever) if there is still work for them to do. As indeed there was for Shakespeare. In 1610 there were definite signs that the plague was at last releasing its hold on London, and that the Globe might become available to the company again on a more regular basis, requiring new plays with which it might hope to recoup the losses of the previous seven years. In 1608 Burbage had finally succeeded in gaining access for the company to the Blackfriars indoor playhouse in which he and his brother had inherited an interest from their father, and which in the meantime they had been able to extend to take in some adjacent property. In 1600, following objections by wealthy neighbours to its use by the then Chamberlain's men, it had been leased to 'little eyases' – the Children of the Chapel Royal; but in 1608 that company had been closed down by the authorities and, previous objections to the adult company having meanwhile evaporated or been overridden, the King's were invited to take over the lease. A syndicate was formed by seven of the company's sharers, including Shakespeare, each committing himself to pay his share of the rent for twenty-one years. Though no longer exempt from City ordinances as once it had been, and the plague was to deny the use of it to them for a further eighteen months, the company now had a prestigious indoor playhouse north of the river that would provide a haven from the severities of winter weather. Shakespeare's plays of the period 1608 to 1613 show no signs of any withdrawal on his part from the hurly-burly of production, and continue to throw up parts for him to act.

Throughout the whole of his active career as a player, he had lived as a lodger in London. In 1597 he was recorded as resident in Bishopsgate ward, a short distance from the Theatre and Curtain, but by 1599 had crossed the river to the Liberty of the Clink in Southwark, near the Globe. In 1604, and for some time before and after that year, he 'lay in the house' of Christopher Mountjoy, a French milliner, in Cripplegate, not far from St Paul's – as we know from a court case that arose in 1612 concerning a disputed will, in which he was called and gave testimony as a witness. It was not until March 1613 that he purchased a house of his own, and unsurprisingly it was in Blackfriars itself, a short walk away from the company's new playhouse, and from a ferry at Puddle Wharf that would have taken him across the Thames to the Globe. Those biographers who by this time have packed him off to Stratford, as nearly all of them have, to enjoy its 'open fields and cool water meadows' (as Chambers puts it), are at a loss to account for this London purchase, and describe it as 'an investment pure and simple'. But why here, and why now? True, the purchase was hedged about with peculiarities which have not as yet been fully explained; for though, with the help of a short-term mortgage, he was the sole buyer, legal ownership was shared with three others: his fellow, John Heminges, William Johnson, perhaps the former Admiral's man who was landlord of the nearby Mermaid tavern in Bread street, and a certain John Jackson, who may have been the Hull shipowner of that name who frequented the Mermaid when he was in London. What was going on here? Shakespeare's gatehouse, which lay by, and in part over, a 'great gate' that in pre-Reformation times had led to the Prior's house of the Dominican friary, had previously been occupied by a succession of Catholic recusants, and in 1598 had been searched for hidden priests on a report of its containing 'many places of secret conveyance'.[3] Was Shakespeare taking a leaf out of his father's book in deliberately muddying the legal waters to circumvent a possible confiscation of the property? One would like to know more about the John Robinson, who was later to be mentioned in Shakespeare's will as 'dwelling' in the house, and may have rented from him one or more of its rooms.

Shakespeare was present in the Globe (he was probably on stage) when, three months later, on 29 June 1613 during a performance of *Henry VIII*, a cannon fired from an upper gallery set fire to the straw thatching of the roof and rapidly spread to consume the whole building. As one of the theatre's original 'householders', he contributed his share to the cost of its reconstruction; it was open again by 30 June 1614 – exactly a year later. Also in 1613, he collaborated with Richard Burbage in the making of an *impresa*, a painted chivalric device with appropriate motto, for the Earl of Rutland to bear in a tourney at court in celebration of the King's accession. And though there are indications during these years of visits to Stratford of the kind he had been accustomed to make throughout his career, there is no evidence of any protracted stay. According to one account, it was in London that he caught the fever from which he was to die. When, in 1709, Rowe claimed that Shakespeare's last years were spent at Stratford in 'Ease, Retirement, and the Conversation of his Friends . . . as all Men of good Sense will wish theirs may be', he was simply transposing into Shakespeare's biography what he and similarly placed men of his time regarded as a desirable close to a lifetime of literary endeavour. He had no conception or understanding of Shakespeare as a player who, however fulfilled as poet and dramatist he may then have been, would still have been committed to the continuing life of his plays on the stage.

During the long shut-down of the London theatres, lasting from July 1608 to 1610, the company would necessarily have been solely occupied in court entertainment and travel. *Pericles* had first been performed at the Globe in the early summer of 1608. When, at the end of July, the weekly death toll from plague rose to 50 and proceeded inexorably upwards, the players would have lost no time in preparing to tour – if they were not already planning to do so. But the horrors of the plague are likely to have been brought home to them in a more personal way by the passing of their old comrade, William Sly. Latterly, Sly had lived in Cripplegate as a lodger in the family home of Robert Browne of German fame, from where he was buried at St Leonard's, Shoreditch, on 14 August. That his death was sudden and unexpected we know from the fact that only five days earlier he had joined with his fellows in purchasing a share in the new Blackfriars playhouse, and that his will was nuncupative (declared orally) and signed only with a mark. (There were 79 plague deaths in the City that week.)

News of his mother's decline would have reached Shakespeare by early August when he and his fellows were planning their autumn tour; it may well have been instrumental in taking them in the direction of Stratford. Mary Shakespeare – now in her late sixties or early seventies – is a shadowy figure in the background of

Shakespeare's life. Is there perhaps a trace of her character in the Countess of *All's Well* or Volumnia? In creating these strong but compassionate women, he clearly had a model in mind, and it is more than likely to have been his mother. Whether he was able to be at her bedside when she died in the first week of September, or to accompany her coffin to Stratford churchyard for burial on the 9th, we do not know; but that the company was in Warwickshire about this time is documented. Provincial records for the period are as usual sparse and mostly uncertain. The only exact date we have is for Coventry on 29 October, where, in the great St Mary's Guildhall, *Pericles* would have found an ideally spacious, medieval setting. A visit to Marlborough in Wiltshire (dated in an accounting period ending 9 December 1608) must also belong to this year.[4]

Twelve plays, almost certainly including *Pericles*, were given at court in the Christmas season of 1608/9. In 1609, while plague continued to rage unabated in London, the company were at Ipswich on 9 May, receiving their customary reward of 26*s* 8*d*; and that despite a civic ordinance of the previous year that 'Noe freeman or their servants or apprentises shall resort to any Playes to be holden within this Town under perill of fforfaiture for every offence, 12*d*.' Evidently, the King's men were made an exception, and from this time forward only companies with royal patrons were allowed, and in some years none at all.[5] The Protestant Puritan party which, in the course of the coming decades, was to close all the English provincial guildhalls to the players, and by 1642 the London playhouses also, was already gaining power in the towns and starting to exert its baleful influence. From Ipswich, the players would have travelled by boat around the coast to the port of Hythe in Kent, where they performed on 16 May, and at New Romney on the following day.[6] Further visits, dated only by fiscal year, which may thus refer either to the latter part of 1609 (from Michaelmas) or to the first nine months of 1610, are recorded in indeterminate order at Oxford, Shrewsbury, Stafford and the little town of Sudbury in Suffolk. They were back in London, however, for Christmas 1609/10, giving thirteen plays for the King and royal family 'in the tyme of the holidayes and afterwardes'.[7] It is probable that *Cymbeline* was one of them.

We know that the Globe was open again in the spring of 1610 because the visiting Prince Lewis Frederick of Württemberg saw a performance of *Othello* there on 30 April.[8] Plague deaths in that year remained about or below 20 a week until the beginning of July when, to general dismay, they rose to 38, and upwards thereafter to a peak of 99 in the final week of August. Once more the theatres closed, and the company resumed their travels until Christmas 1610/11, when they were back at Whitehall performing fifteen plays. By then, though they were not to know it at the time, the worst of the plague was over, and it was not to return in any significant way during the remainder of Shakespeare's life.

For 1611 we are fortunate to have two more detailed reports from London: one made by a quack doctor named Simon Forman of his visits to the Globe in the early summer, and a Revels account of the plays at court between 1 November 1611 and 23 February 1612.[9] From these we learn that after the usual Lenten closure, the Globe reopened for an Easter season in late March or early April, during which *Macbeth* and *Cymbeline* were performed, and that, by the following Christmas, *The Winter's Tale*, *The Tempest*, and *The Two Noble Kinsmen* (to which Shakespeare may have contributed scenes) had been added to the company's repertoire. From Easter 1610, the Blackfriars playhouse would also have been available to the players, though that too would have been closed by the plague during the latter part of the year until Easter 1611. As noted already, between April 1611 and June 1613, when the players had two London theatres at their disposal – one indoors, one outdoors, for all kinds of weather – and the threat of the plague had finally receded, they continued to embark on extensive, countrywide tours, which puts paid to the myth that the company only travelled out of London when driven by the plague. In 1611, they are included in a general entry as having visited Shrewsbury. In 1612, they were back at New Romney (on 21 April) and at Winchester, and between Michaelmas 1612 and Michaelmas 1613, at Oxford, Folkestone, Stafford and Shrewsbury – we do not know in what order.[10]

— ✳ —

The transition between the tragedies and Shakespeare's last romances is, as Chambers puts it, 'not an evolution but a revolution'.[11] It is a near total change of emphasis from the negative aspects of human nature to the positive; from the deadly sins of pride, self-absorption, ruthless ambition, envy, false conceptions of honour and of bounty – leading to death and despair – to the healing virtues of patience, fidelity, contrition and forgiveness – leading to reconciliation and hope. That of course is too simple. The denouements of *Lear, Macbeth* and *Antony and Cleopatra* are far from being wholly pessimistic; a kind of human splendour shines out from the fall of their flawed heroes. 'Ripeness', we are told in *Lear*, 'is all'. There is an ultimate victory of good over evil – however arbitrary it may sometimes appear. Nor do the final comedies blink at man's potentialities for evil or self-destruction; but their final message is very different, echoing Julian of Norwich; that whatever disasters people may bring upon themselves and others, or fate may have in store for them, 'All thing shall be well . . . Thou shalt see thyself that all manner thing shall be well'.[12] Stylistically, the change from *Coriolanus* to *Pericles* is as great as that between *Love's Labour's Lost* and *Romeo and Juliet*, or *Richard II* and *Henry IV*.

Pericles, as I have said, survives only in a pirated, plainly corrupted text – omitted from the First Folio presumably because its editors were unable to trace a better. And yet we know the play was a great success when first produced in its original form in 1608; and, when further London performances were prevented by the plague, the pirated text appeared in a record number of printed quartos – three before Shakespeare's death in 1616, and a further three between then and 1635. Late in 1608, there was published moreover a prose version of the story, based in part on Shakespeare's play by George Wilkins, as today a successful film is often followed by a 'book of the film', in obvious response to popular demand. Wilkins' treatment carries the title of 'The Painfull Adventures of Pericles Prince of Tyre. Being the true History of the Play of Pericles, as it was lately presented by the worthy and ancient Poet John Gower', and is accompanied by a woodcut of Gower, which I believe may be a portrait of Shakespeare in that role. If so, it would, of course, be unique as a representation of him in action as a player. That he played the role is (to my own mind at least) beyond doubt. I have already written of his fondness for the old English poets, and Gower would have been familiar to him, not only from his published verse, but from his tomb in Southwark, where he is shown reclining with his head resting on a pile of his books (Plate 8), and from which, in the opening speech of the play, he is imagined as rising.

> To sing a song that old was sung,
> From ashes ancient Gower is come,
> Assuming man's infirmities,
> To glad your ear, and please your eyes.

It is another, and one of the best, of Shakespeare's presenter roles, and the archaism of the rhyming couplets that he speaks is, of course, a deliberate impersonation of Gower – not, perhaps, without a touch of affectionate satire. It may be this assumed manner of speech – along with the simplicity of the play's story-telling and the rarity of its stage productions until comparatively recent times – that has led scholars into theories of multiple authorship (once so

Possible portrait of Shakespeare in the role of Gower in *Pericles* from the title-page of Wilkins' 'Painfull Adventures of Pericles Prince of Tyre'. Note Gower's square-cut beard and medieval costume. He is carrying a bunch of fragrant herbs in his left hand. Does the lectern with an open book on it suggest that his speeches in the play were read?

fashionable in respect of his earlier work) in which the best of the scenes are attributed to Shakespeare and the rest to some other less accomplished hand or hands. But having both directed and acted in the play, I can only say that no such division of authorship is apparent on closer acquaintance, and in almost every scene one finds images, characters and snatches of dialogue that have Shakespeare's unique impress upon them:

> The blind mole casts
> Copp'd hills towards heaven, to tell the earth is throng'd
> By man's oppression, and the poor worm doth die for't.
>
> (I.i.101–3)

The wise old counsellor, Helicanus (a beautiful part for Heminges) in an exchange with Pericles in a rare moment of anger:

Pericles: Helicanus
           Thou hast mov'd us; what seest thou in our looks?
Helicanus: An angry brow, dread lord.
Pericles: If there be such a dart in princes' frowns,
           How durst thy tongue move anger to our face?
Helicanus: How dares the plants look up to heaven, from whence
           They have their nourishment?
Pericles: Thou know'st I have power
           To take thy life from thee.
Helicanus: I have ground the axe myself;
           Do you but strike the blow.

> (I.ii.51–9)

And the humour of the three down-to-earth but kindly Fishermen who find and succour Pericles when he has been cast ashore after shipwreck:

Fisherman 3:   Master, I marvel how the fishes live in the sea.
Fisherman 1:   Why, as men do a-land: the great ones eat up
                the little ones. I can compare our rich misers to

nothing so fitly as to a whale: a' plays and
tumbles, driving the poor fry before him, and at
last devours them all at a mouthful. Such whales
have I heard on a'th' land, who never leave
gaping till they swallow'd the whole parish,
church, steeple, bells and all.   (II.i.26–34)

– all three examples from the first two acts, which are generally
denied to Shakespeare.

I said earlier of *Timon of Athens* that the most likely reason for its
remaining unfinished is that the Globe, for which it was planned,
was closed by the plague; that it had missed its moment. That may
have been true but is not, I think, the whole explanation. It is
possible also that in the course of writing *Timon*, Shakespeare tired
of its protagonist's imprecations upon a corrupt and ungrateful
world, and felt the need to refresh his spirit in that other world of
folk-tale and myth from which he had already drawn in *All's Well*
and *Measure for Measure*, but had never as yet wholly succeeded in
reconciling with his more realist aims of holding the mirror up to
nature and the complexities of human personality and behaviour.
For *Pericles*, while starting from a situation of impending
degradation and evil, soon escapes with its hero into the story of an
epic journey encompassing the Mediterranean world of its time –
vaguely that of the post-classical, early Middle Ages.

Pericles' fortunes rise and fall. He marries a king's daughter and
has a child by her he names Marina, but his wife is thought to have
died in giving birth to her during a storm at sea, and in course of
time Marina is lost to him also. But he is the antithesis of Timon in
that in face of all the disasters that befall him, he refuses to be
overcome or embittered by them. At the climax of an earlier storm
that has wrecked his ship and cast him ashore, he has a speech that
recalls Lear but also marks a significant difference in their respective
attitudes to the forces of nature that threaten them both:

Yet cease your ire, you angry stars of heaven!
Wind, rain, and thunder, remember, earthly man

> Is but a substance that must yield to you;
> And I, as fits my nature, do obey you . . .
>
> Let it suffice the greatness of your powers
> To have bereft a prince of all his fortunes;
> And having thrown him from your wat'ry grave,
> Here to have death in peace is all he'll crave.
>
> (II.i.1–11)

– this again from the supposedly non-Shakespearean second act. But no one, so far as I am aware, has sought to deny Shakespeare the final act of the play in which all that Pericles has seemingly lost is restored to him, with its beautiful and moving recognition scene on board a ship at anchor, in which he and Marina find each other again.

> O Helicanus, strike me, honour'd sir!
> Give me a gash, put me to present pain,
> Let this great sea of joys rushing upon me
> O'erbear the shores of my mortality,
> And drown me with their sweetness. O, come hither,
> Thou that beget'st him that did thee beget;
> Thou wast born at sea, buried at Tharsus,
> And found at sea again. O Helicanus,
> Down on thy knees! thank the holy gods as loud
> As thunder threatens us: this is Marina.
>
> (V.1.190–9)

The story is very old, deriving from that of Apollonius of Tyre, but it is Gower's version of it in his *Confessio Amantis* that Shakespeare gives us, with interesting correspondences to the medieval Saints' play of *Mary Magdalene*. Shakespeare's original contribution is in his introduction of the themes of patience, redemption through suffering, loss and recovery, which was to set the keynote for his later romances.[13] The text abounds in verbal obscurities, irregularities of rhythm and rhyme, mislineation, prose printed as verse and verse as prose – mainly arising from its having been 'reported', that is to say, surreptitiously taken down in a form

of shorthand by a publisher's nark during one of its first performances at the Globe in 1608. The wonder is that so much that is
good has been preserved.

Of its eighteen named roles (five of them female) and some dozen
other speaking parts, only Pericles and Helicanus continue through
the whole of the action, the rest being confined to particular scenes
or sections of the play, which makes it readily amenable to doubling.
As Pericles, Burbage would have been mature for the dashing young
prince of the first three acts, but perfectly cast in the fourth, with
Condell perhaps doubling the two kings of contrasting character, the
evil Antiochus of Act 1 with the affable Simonides of Act 2, and
Armin as Fisherman and Bawd.

The sea is never far away in the play; nor is the sound of music
which, as in a similar situation in *Lear*, accompanies Pericles'
awakening from a near-fatal lethargy. I would like to see it performed
in an amphitheatre open to the sky and, if possible, near to the sea. It
is a play for the summer.

The first recorded performance of *Cymbeline* was that seen by
Forman at the Globe before September 1611, probably in April of
that year; but the consensus of recent scholarly opinion accords with
that of Chambers in putting its composition two years earlier in
1608/9. Though intended for the Globe, it could not have been
performed there until 1610 at the earliest. The probability is that it
was premiered during the long tour of 1609/10, and acted at court
in the Christmas season of 1609.[14]

It is an extraordinary play that has evoked wildly variant responses
from the critics, ranging from Dr Johnson's – that though it has
'many just sentiments, some natural dialogues, and some pleasing
scenes',

> they are obtained at the expense of much incongruity. To remark
> the folly of the fiction, the absurdity of the conduct, the confusion
> of the names, and manners of different times, and the impossi-
> bility of the events in any system of life, were to waste criticism
> upon unresisting imbecility, upon faults too evident for detection,
> and too gross for aggravation –

to Hazlitt's 'one of the most delightful of Shakespeare's historical plays', and Swinburne's rhapsodical praise of Imogen as 'woman above all Shakespeare's women . . . the woman best beloved in all the world of song and all the tide of time'.[15]

The plot of *Cymbeline* is put together by Shakespeare from an incongruous selection of historical, pseudo-historical, and fictional sources including Geoffrey of Monmouth, Holinshed and Boccaccio's *Decameron*. It has a strongly fairy-tale atmosphere. There is an intemperate king (Cymbeline), practised upon by a malign, hypocritical Queen, stepmother to Imogen, Cymbeline's only daughter; a flawed hero in Posthumus whom Imogen has married in defiance of her father's wishes, and who is banished in consequence; the story of Posthumus' wager in Rome with a smooth, Italian villain named Iachimo on the question of Imogen's chastity, with unfortunate consequences that take up most of Act 2; an appropriately named boaster called Cloten, son to the Queen by a previous marriage, whom the King had wanted Imogen to marry; a tale of two princes, Cymbeline's sons, stolen as infants from the cradle, growing up in a cave in the Welsh mountains unaware of their true identity, thinking the man who has brought them up, a banished lord named Belarius, to be their father – and quite a lot more. The scene shifts between Cymbeline's palace, Rome, and the Welsh mountains, and the whole is set in a context of political strife between Britain and Rome, culminating in a Roman invasion. One point that all the critics and commentators agree upon is that it is very entertaining. And at the centre of it all is the courageous, faithful Imogen – the truest and most appealing of the many fine roles that Shakespeare created for his boy actors.

His own role, of course, would have been that of the King. Who else at this time might have undertaken it? For though the company's original apprentices would by now have been in their twenties and thirties, and there were plenty of young recruits to take their places – Ostler, Underwood and Field among them – there are no recorded replacements for the older men, and with the loss of Pope, Phillips and Sly, those who were left would have been hard-pressed to cover all the more mature parts in the plays. As a player, Shakespeare would have been more valuable to the company in this period of its history than perhaps ever before. Posthumus needs to be more of an age with Imogen, and would have gone to one of the younger men – perhaps Field (Plate 17). With Lowin as Iachimo, Condell as Pisanio, Armin doubling as Cloten and the First Gaoler, and Heminges as Jupiter in Posthumus' vision, Burbage would have been most valuably employed as Belarius who, having previously abducted the King's sons, returns with them in Act 4 to save the British cause from defeat.

In spite of its moments of near-tragedy and horror, the play has more humour in it than may appear on the page, and the smiles that greet the more improbable coincidences of the final scene, as Shakespeare weaves his magic in bringing the play's disparate elements into a coherent unity, would not, I think, have surprised or displeased him. The scene is one of his most brilliant technical achievements. But what gradually arises in the audience is not just admiration for the dramatist's skill but also a deepening sense of genuine wonder: that out of such a mishmash of mixed intentions, disordered emotions and strange events, the good and the just should be seen to prevail.

The Winter's Tale, deriving as it does in the main from a prose romance by Robert Greene first published in 1588, is a more simply organised, co-ordinated play than *Cymbeline*; but, as its title suggests, explores the same territory of folk-tale and romance. It has many parallels with *Pericles*: at the centre of both, there is a wide gap of time in which infants grow up; in each, a ruler believes mistakenly his wife to be dead, and there is a royal daughter, separated from her father, who is finally reunited with him.[16] Shakespeare's themes, as in all his plays of the period, are of the loss of harmony through human frailty and sin; its recovery by means of an acceptance of suffering, and sincere contrition; of death and regeneration. All this is worked out in terms of the play's theatrical life on the stage, in which music and dance play a prominent role. The rhythms and texture of the verse, and the imagery that it employs, affect the auditors' emotions at a deep, subliminal level. However improbable the stories may appear on the page, they are peopled by men and women of real flesh and blood. Leontes, King of Sicilia, is jealous of his wife, Hermione's affection for his friend and guest Polixenes, King of Bohemia. Jealousy in Shakespeare's plays is nearly always murderous. Leontes commands Camillo, one of his lords, to poison Polixenes, but Camillo warns the intended victim and procures his escape. Hermione is imprisoned and gives birth to a daughter, whom Leontes orders should be taken to some desert place, beyond his dominions, and there abandoned. The story of Hermione's vindication and her seeming death, of Leontes' repentance and the eventual restoration to him of both his wife and the daughter, Perdita, he had abandoned, must be left to the playgoer to enjoy in the theatre. It is a beautiful play that carries the audience with it every step of the way – I would say a perfect one if there were not an even better to come.

Probably written in the latter part of 1610, it was seen by Forman at the Globe on 15 May 1611 and performed at court on 5 November of that year, having been toured to Shrewsbury and doubtless other towns west. Like *Pericles*, it has eighteen named roles (six of them female) but offers less scope for doubling. If, as I have previously suggested, Burbage played Ford in the *Merry Wives* and Othello, he would have been on familiar ground with Leontes, and brought to it the passion and commitment the character demands. There is no immediately obvious part for Shakespeare – or rather, there are several that might have been his, and we must make a difficult choice between them. Polixenes is of an age with Leontes, and this, of course, would not have been the first occasion when Burbage and he had played together as kings. The small chorus role of Time is another possibility as standing, both in character and function, apart from the rest of the action. Carrying an hourglass, he introduces the second half of the play (Acts 4 and 5), speaking antique rhyming couplets reminiscent of Gower, announcing a lapse in time of sixteen years. It offers a nostalgic indulgence in theatrical cliché Shakespeare would have enjoyed, and the speech has several allusions that hint at a parallel identity for the speaker as author:

> Your patience this allowing,
> I turn my glass, and give *my scene* such growing
> As you had slept between . . .

> A shepherd's daughter,
> And what to her adheres, which follows after,
> Is *th' argument* of Time.

But Time is not the only character to use imagery deriving from the drama. Camillo, the wise old man who serves in turn both Leontes and Polixenes as counsellor, tells Florizel, Polixenes' son and Perdita's lover, when contriving their flight together,

> it shall so be my care
> To have you royally appointed, as if
> *The scene you play were mine.*   (IV.iv.592–4)

And a little later, Perdita responds to his advice to disguise herself with,

> I see the play so lies
> That I must bear a part.   (655–6)

Camillo, the fourth largest role with 300 lines, opens the play with a visiting Bohemian lord and is there (largely silent) at the end. It is one of Shakespeare's 'old man' roles, and also bears the character of a benevolent contriver in the mould of Friar Laurence and the Duke of *Measure for Measure*. When we look at the likeliest allocation of other principal parts, we find it supports this casting, for Polixenes requires little more than kingly bearing and authority which Condell would have been able to supply, and Time would have fitted what little we know of Cowley's ecentric but more limited talents. Heminges is usually relegated to a solely managerial function in this later period of the company's history on the basis of a report (in a popular ballad) of his being distressed and 'stuttering' when the Globe burnt down in 1613; but if a man is not allowed to show distress and stutter when a theatre in which he has just been acting and has a substantial financial stake, burns down before his eyes without being judged as 'past it' as an actor, it would be a poor outlook for a good many of us! The Old Shepherd who finds Perdita as a baby and brings her up as his daughter would have been an excellent part for him. With Armin as his clownish son and Lowin as the roguish pedlar Autolycus, all the senior men would thus have been well used. The two mature women's parts (Hermione and her doughty friend and ally Paulina) would probably have gone to Tooley and Cooke, and there remains scope for both the older apprentices and hired men in doubling the various Lords and Gentlemen, and for the younger recruits as Mamillius (Leontes' young son who dies of grief for his mother), Perdita and her sister shepherdesses, with Field perhaps as Florizel.

I said earlier that in writing these final plays Shakespeare was feeling his way to a more consistent reconciliation of the folkloric material that had always attracted him (now more than ever) with his other, realist aims of fidelity to nature and psychological truth and, if we read the plays in sequence, we see evidence of his growing confidence in achieving just that. The process culminates in *The Tempest*, which can make good claim to be his most beautifully constructed play. Its earliest recorded performance was at court at Hallowmas (1 November) before the King in 1611,[17] but there is nothing to suggest that this was its premiere – though it may have been. In the best of conditions, first nights are chancy, nervous occasions, and in 1611 the *Tempest* was to open the season. In the busy banqueting hall at Whitehall where the play was given, there cannot have been much time or opportunity to rehearse. Without previews or follow-up performances, when faults could be corrected or the staging improved, this, like nearly all Shakespeare's court performances, was a one-off affair before the company's patron, who was also of course the King. Instinct and experience tell me that the players would have made very sure they were well practised to cope with any emergencies or unforeseen responses and that here, as on prior occasions of a similar kind, the play had been premiered elsewhere – perhaps on the Shrewsbury tour of that year and possibly also in private performance at Blackfriars, which at last was available to use by the company.

The Tempest is too well known to require more than a sentence or two of description. The action begins with a shipwreck – echoing those of *Pericles* and the *Winter's Tale* – in which a party of noblemen including Antonio, usurping Duke of Milan, and his ally the King of Naples are cast on the shore of a remote island whch they believe to be uninhabited. But here, as we learn in the second scene, Prospero, the rightful ruler of Milan, is already in occupation with his daughter Miranda, and is responsible for having raised the tempest by use of the magical power he has acquired in exile to bring those who had usurped his duchy, and consigned him and his infant daughter to the mercies of the sea twelve years before, within reach of his vengeance. These events, that at an earlier period of Shakespeare's writing would probably have occupied an act at least in chronicle form, he here condenses into a duologue between Prospero and the now twelve-year-old Miranda (of which Prospero has by far the greater part) that recapitulates the past and brings it on stage in the most masterly way. As Roy Walker has written of the Peter Brook production in the 1950s, which he describes as a breakthrough in theatrical understanding of the play, 'the brief opening scene on a ship heaving wildly in a storm at sea became the image of a storm in the mind of a man who has suffered notorious wrong and nursed his anger through long years of exile on bitter fantasies of superhuman revenge'.[18]

So much for the initial situation of disharmony and loss. The action that follows is a profound meditation on the conflict of good and evil – both in the souls of men and human affairs – expressed in purely theatrical terms. As such, it defies interpretation of the allegorical or symbolical kind which so many critics (and some directors) have attempted to impose on it. Of all Shakespeare's plays, it makes the most insistent call to be seen and heard for what it is rather than 'read' for what it represents; it represents only itself, and we should be more than content with that. And yet all the themes I have mentioned as filling Shakespeare's mind in these last romances are here: loss of harmony and its recovery, the final victories of forgiveness over revenge, love over hate, life over death. If taken at this spiritual level throughout – as I am sure that it was under Shakespeare's firm hand as 'instructor' – 'questions of credibility are not answered, they simply never arise. This is a contest of ape and essence for possession of a man's soul, played out like a master-game of chess. The final disclosure of Ferdinand and Miranda at chess becomes . . . a summing of what has been happening throughout . . . the war-game has ended in a love-match'.[19]

Though it was once supposed that by Prospero's breaking of his magician's staff and drowning of his book, as well as by his epilogue –

> Now my charms are all o'erthrown,
> And what strength I have's mine own,
> Which is most faint . . .
>
> As you from crimes would pardon'd be,
> Let your indulgence set me free.

– Shakespeare was signalling his retirement from the stage, it is virtually certain that the part was played by Burbage; his own role was probably that of Alonso, King of Naples, whose grief at what he believes to be the loss of his son Ferdinand in the wreck is poignantly expressed in his silences and refusal to be comforted. 'You cram these words into mine ears against/The stomach of my sense', he complains in his one substantial speech in this earlier part of the play.

> O thou mine heir
> Of Naples and of Milan, what strange fish
> Hath made his meal on thee?   (II.i.102–9)

With little more than a hundred lines, he is there as usual at both beginning and end. It was another of Shakespeare's kingly roles. The play is remarkable (among many things) for the originality of the two semi-human creatures Shakespeare invents as ministers of Prospero's magic. Ariel is described as an 'airy spirit'; Caliban as a 'salvage and deformed slave'. King and courtiers are not the only survivors of the tempest. Stephano is a 'drunken butler' and his companion, Trinculo, a professional jester. And one of Shakespeare's master strokes is to keep all three groups – Prospero and Miranda, the usurping duke and his party, and the two comic servants – apart from each other until the final act. With Ariel, Miranda, Ferdinand, and the masqueing spirits going to apprentices or hired men, there would have been little need for doubling. I see Condell as Antonio, Lowin as Caliban, and Cowley as Stephano. There is another charming 'old man' part for Heminges in Gonzalo and, in Trinculo, a last and very funny jester for Armin.

Like *Pericles*, the play is never far from the sea, nor from the sounds of music, for as Caliban explains,

> the isle is full of noises,
> Sounds and sweet airs, that give delight, and hurt not.
> Sometimes a thousand twangling instruments
> Will hum about mine ears; and sometimes voices,
> That, if I then had wak'd after long sleep,
> Will make me sleep again . . .   (III.ii.133–8)

There is little more to be said of Shakespeare's final years with the company. As a writer, he was apparently content to let his younger colleagues – notably John Fletcher – have their day in supplying the new plays that would still have been required. He was roped in, however, to contribute to *Henry VIII* (first recorded in performance on the occasion of the destruction of the first Globe in June 1613) and *The Two Noble Kinsmen*, which may date from the latter part of that year. But there is not the slightest indication that he had ceased to act; nor is there any sign in the actor lists or other records of the company during these years of the introduction of an actor of comparable age and experience who could have taken over his customary roles in those earlier plays of his we know to have been still in the repertoire or revived in the period: *Macbeth* in 1611; *Much Ado About Nothing, The Tempest, The Winter's Tale, Henry IV, Othello* and *Julius Caesar* – all revived in 1613 as part of the festivities surrounding the marriage of Princess Elizabeth to the Elector Palatine.

I say he had been roped in to contribute scenes to *Henry VIII* but it may have been he who did the roping in; for if we look at the particular scenes that have been most usually attributed to him (I.i and ii; II.iii and iv; III.ii to line 203; and V.i) we find that all but two feature Wolsey and, in sum, contain nearly all of that role, and certainly the best of it. With Burbage as Buckingham and Lowin as Henry (in which we are told by a Restoration writer he was instructed by Shakespeare) he was the obvious choice to play the Cardinal. And having agreed to do so, might he not also have felt, with justification, that he could produce some rather better lines to speak than Fletcher had been able to do, and gone on to rewrite, not only his own lines as Wolsey, but the whole of the scenes in which he appeared – and one or two others as well? Fletcher was adept at rhetorical speeches, but was he as good as this?

> Nay then, farewell!
> I have touched the highest point of all my greatness,
> And from that full meridian of my glory
> I haste now to my setting. I shall fall
> Like a bright exhalation in the evening,
> And no man see me more. (III.ii.222–7)

Similar questions arise in relation to the *Two Noble Kinsmen*, though here the division of scenes between the two authors appears to have been more deliberately planned. But again we notice that those scenes generally attributed to Shakespeare (the whole of Act I; III.i; and V.i, iii and iv) contain the most and the best of a particular character – Theseus, Duke of Athens; but, in this instance, it is not only the one most likely to have been played by Shakespeare (he is 'kingly', present from the start, speaks the closing lines, and is of optimum size) but one he had played before in *Midsummer Night's Dream*, where he had been accompanied, as here, by Hippolyta, queen of the Amazons and his wife to be.

The company continued to tour. In 1614, they were back in Coventry, and in April 1615 were recorded in Nottingham,[20] which, so far as we know (and that is very little), was the furthest north they were ever to travel. I see no reason whatever to doubt that Shakespeare was as usual in company with his fellows, playing his usual parts in their recent successes. Though none of their titles were recorded, they performed seven plays at court in the holiday season of 1613/14, sixteen in 1614/15, and a further fifteen in 1615/16. Many of these, of course, would have been revivals.

It was probably in November or December of 1615 that Shakespeare gave instructions for the drafting of his will. This is generally assumed to have been executed in Stratford by the Warwick solicitor, Francis Collins, but the handwriting remains to be positively identified and may belong instead to any number of others including Collins' clerk and Shakespeare himself; nor do we have any evidence as to where it was written. If Shakespeare had summoned Collins for the purpose, it is more likely to have been to London, where he would then have been working, than to Stratford. As Shakespeare attests in the opening preamble that he is in 'perfect health & memorie god be praysed', there are no grounds for believing that he was ill at the time.

The holiday season at court extended that winter from 1 November 1615 to 12 February 1616 (Shrove Tuesday, the last day before Lent), with a final performance on 1 April (Easter Monday). According to John Ward, who was Vicar of Stratford from 1662 to 1681 – just early enough to have met Shakespeare's younger daughter Judith before her death at the age of seventy-seven – and writing nearly half a century before Rowe, 'Shakespear, Drayton, and Ben Jhonson, had a merry meeting, and itt seems drank too hard, for Shakespear died of a feavour there contracted'.[21] Such a meeting could only, of course, have occurred in London, and it was just of the kind that we might expect a group of theatre friends and colleagues to enjoy together at the conclusion of a busy season. As such, it may well have taken place on the evening of Shrove Tuesday or quite shortly afterwards. Shakespeare had probably intended to return to Stratford for the first few weeks of Lent, as was his custom, and the fever would have hurried him home. Did John Robinson, his lodger at Blackfriars, seeing his state of health, accompany him? It would be good to think so, and certainly someone of that name was present in Stratford a few weeks later to witness his will. It was not until 25 March that Collins was summoned to the bedside to make those amendments to the earlier draft consequent upon Judith's marriage to the Stratford vintner Thomas Quiney in the previous month. A need for some haste at that point is indicated by the use of the draft for all but the first of the will's three pages, with small corrections and additions being made between the lines. Shakespeare's bequests of money to John Heminges, Richard Burbage and Henry Condell – whom he describes as 'my ffellowes', not *former* fellows – to buy them rings, remain unaltered. When, on 1 April, his old company came together in London to give the final performance of the season for the King at Whitehall, their thoughts would all have been with him. He was to linger on for another three weeks, and died on his birthday, 23 April. He was just fifty-two.

THIRTEEN

The Man Shakespeare

Shakespeare was the least of an egotist it was possible to be. He was nothing in himself; but he was all that others were, or that they could become. He not only had in himself the germs of every faculty and feeling, but he could follow them by anticipation, intuitively, into all their conceivable ramifications, through every change of fortune, or conflict of passion, or turn of thought. He had 'a mind reflecting ages past', and present . . . He had only to think of anything in order to become that thing, with all the circumstances belonging to it.

William Hazlitt, 1818[1]

When, in the 1890s, the historian William Cory visited Wilton House, home of the earls of Pembroke, he was told of the letter that an earlier Lady Pembroke had written to her son, asking him to bring James I from Salisbury to see *As You Like It*, and telling him 'we have the man Shakespeare with us'; a curious expression if we did not know that by 'man' in this context was meant an actor as Shakespeare had been first a 'Chamberlain's man' and then a 'King's man', for this is how he was generally known in his time. In 1592, Chettle was to speak of him as 'exelent in the qualitie he professes', and 'qualitie' in such a context was used of the *acting* profession. In 1602, when York Herald challenged the grant to his father and himself by Garter King-of-Arms of a coat of arms and the right to call themselves gentlemen, it was on the grounds that the author of some two dozen of the finest plays in the English language, including *Romeo and Juliet*, *Henry V* and *Hamlet*, was merely a player, as a sketch in his notes of the arms in question, with the words 'Shakespeare the Player' underneath them, makes abundantly clear.[2]

277

Shakespear ỹ Player
by Garter

The sketch of 1602 (Folger
Shakespeare Library, Washington, DC)

In the first chapter we discovered how – precisely as player – he was to remain invisible to so many of his contemporaries, and especially the literary establishment of his day to whom, if he was known at all, it was chiefly as 'sweet Mr Shakespeare', the author of *Venus and Adonis* and the Sonnets. But how *much* of a player was he, and how important was the fact of his profession to *him*? It will be clear from the preceding chapters that it took up a very great deal of his time and his life, and was important enough for him to have abandoned a promising career as narrative and lyric poet, aiming at publication, in order to pursue this other profession, devoting all his energies to the writing, production and performance of plays for the looked-down-upon public theatres of his day. For the three activities hung together, and I doubt that he ever stopped to distinguish them in his own mind, or to think of his acting career as separate from his writing career, or his writing and acting careers as separate from his responsibilities for their production and the 'instruction' of his fellows. He was not, as generally envisaged and presented by academic authors, a great dramatist who did some acting on the side; he was not a university, part-time or amateur actor, happy enough to indulge himself on the stage for a few months, or even for one or two

278

years, in order to gain experience before getting on with the serious business of life, which, in his case, is assumed to have been the writing of plays; but a full-time, wholly committed, professional player and man of the theatre for whom the text of a play was not an end in itself (like any other book) but a means to an end – a performance on stage with himself as author, enabler and player. Contrary to Rowe's unfounded assertion, and the statements of those who have accepted it at face value, he was not a dramatist who became an actor for a time and, having made his pile, gave it up to enjoy rural retirement and the 'Conversation of his Friends', but an actor who became a dramatist, and never stopped performing, even after he had stopped writing plays, until fatal illness intervened.

He was not unique in that total commitment. I have presented him in his dual capacity of Player Poet as heir to an ancient European tradition of performing poets and minstrels; but we could find his fellows also among the great dramatists of classical Greece and Rome who were equally involved in the staging and performance of their works, and doubtless those in other periods and cultures who, like him, were written down in their own time on account of that involvement as 'merely players'. Nor was he unique in this respect among his contemporaries. Among Shakespeare's fellows, Robert Armin and Nathan Field are both known to have written and published successful plays and, among the dramatists, Jonson – possibly Marlowe also – spent some years as players. But the man whose career parallels that of Shakespeare most nearly is Thomas Heywood, a prolific and popular dramatist whose distinguished career as a player can be traced in the records between 1598 and 1619, but who, as late as 1640, was told in an epigram that 'grovelling on the stage' did not become his then advanced years.[3] 'Grovelling' was how the literati of his time thought about acting, and how many of their successors have continued to think until comparatively recent times (some still do). Little wonder then that Shakespeare's first biographers had so little to say about his acting, and contrived his entrance into that profession as late as possible and his exit from it as early as possible.

It was not so much the activity of acting itself that presented such people with a problem, but the fact that it was done for money (hence the 'grovelling'); that Shakespeare and his fellows were professionals. Shakespeare's professionalism is summed up in his title and status of 'sharer'. It is a concept that, even today, some academics find hard to take hold of. It means, of course, that he shared in the profits of the enterprise – so much is clear; but it also implies a willingness to share in its work – in every aspect of its work; and if he was allowed, indeed encouraged, by reason of his immense contributions as author and instructor, to take a somewhat smaller part in the performance of the plays than his gifts as a player would otherwise have merited, that is not to say that he would ever have expected to be excused from involvement altogether; or, more importantly, would have *wanted* to be so excused. Nor, as has been seriously proposed, would he have been left at home to write another masterpiece while his fellows slogged their way around the country earning the company's bread. Nor would he have *wanted* to be!

How *good* a player was he, and how good were his fellows? For the answer to both questions, we only need to look again at Shakespeare's professionalism. He would only have cast himself in certain parts if he had felt his talents as a player were equal to them – and his fellows agreed. He would not have written the parts that he did for his fellows if they were beyond their capacity to peform. Dramatists do not write good plays for bad or indifferent actors and, if they do, the results can only be disastrous for both: the better the play, the worse the result. Good actors and good direction can make a poor play appear much better than it is; bad or indifferent actors can only drag a good play down. One has sat through too many bad or inadequate performances of Shakespeare's plays to make any mistake about this. An unactable play is a bad play. Shakespeare was not writing for posterity, for some future generation of super-actors who would one day, hopefully, attain the skills his writing required, but for his fellows in the then and there: for Burbage, Cowley, Sly and the rest, and the results were put to the test in the immediate term. They were not found wanting. The 'devil of progress in the arts' would have it that what was seen on the stage of the Globe, or in the provincial guildhalls in which the company performed four hundred years ago, was necessarily inferior to what we might see today at Stratford or the National; but why should we believe it? The players were speaking in an idiom and at a pace much nearer to the rhythms of natural speech in their time than their modern successors, and in a style of verse to which both they and their audience were more thoroughly attuned. They were trained from an early age in the technical disciplines required; today they are not, and are too often left to pick them up for themselves wherever they can. The spaces in which they acted were generally more intimate (even when larger) than they are today, and the theatres more designed for hearing than seeing. Audiences, if less inhibited in expressing their approval and disapproval, were better and more practised listeners, and more practised also, perhaps, in using their imaginations.

I have said that actors develop with the parts they are given to play, and as they develop, the dramatist is encouraged to challenge them further. Burbage at twenty or thirty would not have been able to meet the challenge of Othello or Lear any more than Shakespeare would have been able to write those plays at a similar age. By the 1600s, they could and they did. They developed together, along with the rest of their fellows, in a unique theatrical partnership of poet and players.

So much for 'the man Shakespeare'. What of 'Shakespeare the man'? To see him, to try to understand him as a player, takes us some of the way in dispelling the invisibility that often surrounds him, but we have further to go before we can greet him as a fellow human being, and displace the myth. Players, though they have an indefinable something about them they recognise in each other, are as individually different in character and personality as the members of any other profession or craft. What kind of person was he? Gentle or forceful? Quietly confident in his own genius or restlessly ambitious? Extrovert or introvert? Religious or sceptical? A devoted husband or a bit of a rake?

Having come with me so far, year by year, through the various turns of Shakespeare's career, and the detailed history of the company of which he was a member for the final twenty years of his life, the reader may agree with me in saying that the characteristic that most impresses itself on one's mind is his apparently limitless energy. To write thirty-six plays of such variety, scope and achievement; to have at least a guiding hand – probably a decisive hand – in shaping their realisation on stage; acting in most, if not all of them, travelling hundreds of miles in each year to take them to halls large and small throughout the country; to build with his fellows their own theatre in London, to see it destroyed, and build it again within a year – is to leave one without any doubt whatsoever of his exceptional energy and commitment. It was, I believe, a contained energy, and a quiet but deep-seated commitment to the theatre he loved. I cannot imagine that he ever wasted his energy in shouting or railing to get what he wanted, however important he felt it to be. 'Some others raile', Davies tells us,

> but raile as they thinke fit
> Thou hast no rayling, but, a raigning Wit.

His plays are suffused with his wit – even the tragedies; the light that it throws flickers low in *Coriolanus* and goes out in *Timon*, but otherwise is always there. He was a naturally witty man, who liked always to see the humorous side of things, and was never over-solemn about his work or anything else. He had learnt how 'to care and not to care'.

'Shakespeare was the least of an egotist it was possible to be . . . He had only to think of anything in order to become that thing, with all the circumstances belonging to it.' This, of course, is where his writing and acting joined hands: the ability to enter into his characters and by living within them, to give them life. In both, he was drawing on the same mental and intuitive resources, applying them in different ways. If I am not to be accused of attempting to pluck out the heart of his mystery, I must leave it there. It goes without saying that he was acutely sensitive to the people around him – endlessly curious, ever receptive of their thoughts, feelings and experiences, and all this acquired understanding, as well as what he could obtain from books, was fed into that fund of knowledge from which his creative imagination drew. He was in love with the English language.

We have Chettle's word (although at second hand) for his 'uprightness of dealing, which argues his honesty', and Aubrey's that 'he was not a company keeper' and 'wouldnt be debauched'. The distinction of his mind was, I believe, reflected in his outward manners and appearance in such a way as to make his casting as kings and royal personages almost inevitable, and to draw from John Davies the statement I have quoted that, were it not for his association with the stage, he might have been 'companion for a King' and 'King among the meaner sort'; the latter he surely was. He had the rare gift of 'presence' on stage.

But he was too good an actor to allow himself to become typecast in such roles, and contrived in his writing to give himself also parts such as Friar Laurence, Adam and Pandarus which enabled him to extend his acting range in a number of other directions. If, as we have seen, the one characteristic that all his roles hold in common is a certain detachment from the central action of the plays, the detachment lay in the plays' conceptual structure – providing time and opportunity to exercise his directorial function in their rehearsal – rather than his performance of them, which was as whole-hearted and committed as that of Burbage in *Hamlet* or *Lear*.

In religion, the invariably sympathetic treatment that he gives to the many friars and nuns who feature in the plays, and the detailed knowledge he betrays of their orders and ways of life – in striking contrast to his fellow dramatists (Marlowe and Greene in particular) who routinely hold them up to parody and ridicule – tells us that he was Catholic in his sympathies. Nor did he ever seek to conceal them – even from his royal patrons. Doubtless he obeyed the law when he had to; not otherwise. I see no reason to doubt the unequivocal statement by an Anglican minister of honest repute that 'He dyed a papist'.[4] To what degree he had lived as one, we have insufficient information to judge.

He was not a saint, and was not without faults, but we have no knowledge of what they were. We know that he was late in paying his rates, but so are a good many others for various reasons. He would not have been human had he not been tempted to mitigate the long periods of celibacy that he spent away from Anne – in London or elsewhere on his travels – by an occasional sexual adventure, but if he did indulge himself in that way, we have no evidence of it, or that he was ever anything but faithful to her – despite the 'second-best bed' of his will, which probably had some special, personal significance for them both.

Engraving by Gordon Browne from the Chandos portrait (reproduced from the frontispiece to the *Henry Irving Shakespeare*, 1892)

One other thing we know from the plays, that strangely enough has not been much remarked on or appreciated, is the interest and confidence he had in the young, as demonstrated by the opportunities he provided for the young apprentices of the company to shine in his plays – more than any other dramatist then, before or since. He loved music, played the lute, and saw music and dance in combination as the supreme expression of that ultimate harmony in the universe that he thought about and longed for all his life; a longing that became a faith, and one that permeates the last romances, 'that all thing shall be well and all manner of thing shall be well'.

He knew very little of his aristocratic patrons and the other famous men and women of his day; he was most at home with his fellows, and they, apart from his family and one or two of his Stratford neighbours, were the only people to be named in his will. To them he was simply and proudly, 'Our Shakespeare'.

Appendix A

Recollections of (1) *Tamburlaine the Great*, (2) *The Jew of Malta*, (3) *The Spanish Tragedy*, (4) *Soliman and Perseda*, (5) *Arden of Faversham*, and (6) *Edward I* in Shakespeare's early plays (*Titus Andronicus, The Taming of the Shrew, Henry VI,* and *Richard III*).

SECTION 1: TAMBURLAINE

PART ONE

Meander at I.i.41:
. . . misled by dreaming prophecies

Clarence at R3: I.i.54:
He hearkens after prophecies and dreams

Cosroe at II.i.1 – opening line of scene:

Thus far are we towards Theridamus

K. Edward at 3H6: V.iii.1 – opening line of scene:

Thus far our fortune keeps an upward course

Meander at II.ii.22:
This country swarms with vile outrageous
   men

Gloucester at 1H6: III.i.11:
The manner of thy vile outrageous crimes

Meander at II.ii.73:
Fortune herself doth sit upon our crests

Stanley at R3: V.iii.80:
Fortune and Victory sit upon thy helm
Richard at V.iii.352:
Upon them! Victory sits on our helms

Theridamus at II.v.58–60:
I think the pleasure they enjoy in heaven
Cannot compare with kingly joys in earth;
To wear a crown . . .
Tamburlaine at II.vii.28–9
The perfect bliss and sole felicity,
The sweet fruition of an earthly crown

Richard at 3H6: I.ii.29–31:
How sweet a thing it is to wear a crown,
Within whose circuit is Elysium
And all that poets feign of bliss and joy

King of Morocco at III.i.51–2:
For neither rain can fall upon the earth,
Nor sun reflex his virtuous beams thereon

Pucelle at 1H6: V.iv.87–8:
May never glorious sun reflex his beams
Upon the country where you make abode

285

Agydas at III.ii.85–7:
            . . . the late-felt frowns
That sent a tempest to my daunted thoughts,
And makes my soul divine her overthrow

Clarence at R3: I.iv.44:
O then began the tempest in my soul

Tamburlaine at III.iii.44–5:
I that am term'd the Scourge and Wrath
 of God,
The only fear and terror of the world

French General (of Talbot) at 1H6: IV.ii.15–16:
Thou ominous and fearful owl of death,
Our nation's terror and their bloody scourge

Bejazeth at III.iii.236–8:
Now will the Christian miscreants be glad,
Ringing with joy their superstitious bells
And making bonfires for my overthrow

York at 2H6: V.i.3:
Ring bells aloud; burn bonfires clear and bright

Tamburlaine at IV.ii.8–9:
The chiefest god, first mover of that sphere
Enchas'd with thousands ever-shining lamps

K. Henry at 2H6: III.iii.19:
O thou eternal Mover of the heavens

Tamburlaine at IV.iv.29–31:
I glory in the curses of my foes,
Having the power from the empyreal heaven
To turn them all upon their proper heads

Buckingham at R3: V.i.20–2:
That high All-seer which I dallied with
Hath turn'd my feigned prayer on my head,
And given in earnest what I begg'd in jest

First Virgin at V.ii.18–19:
Pity old age, within whose silver hairs
Honour and reverence evermore have reign'd

K. Henry at 2H6: V.i.162:
Old Salisbury, shame to thy silver hair

PART TWO

Sigismund at I.ii.5–6:
I here present thee with a naked sword;
Wilt thou have war, then shake this blade
 at me

Clifford at 2H6: IV.viii.16, 18:
Who hateth him [the King] . . .
Shake he his weapon at us, and pass by

Callapine at 1.iii.41–2:
And, as thou rid'st in triumph through the
 streets,
The pavement underneath thy chariot
 wheels . . .

Gloucester at 2H6: II.iv.11, 13–14:
The abject people . . .
That erst did follow thy proud chariot wheels
When thou didst ride in triumph through the
 streets

Tamburlaine at I.iv.19:
. . . all the wealthy kingdoms I subdu'd

Cardinal at 2H6: I.i.153:
. . . all the wealthy kingdoms of the west

Tamburlaine at I.iv.25–31:
Their hair . . .
Which should be like the quills of
    porcupines
As black as jet, and hard as iron or steel,
Bewrays they are too dainty for the wars.
Their fingers made to quaver on a lute,
Their arms to hang about a lady's neck,
Their legs to dance and caper in the air

York [of Cade] at 2H6: III.i.362–5:
. . . his thighs with darts
Were almost like a sharp-quill'd porpentine
And, in the end being rescu'd, I have seen
Him caper like a wild Morisco

Richard at R3: I.i.12–13:
He capers nimbly in a lady's chamber
To the lascivious pleasing of a lute

Tamburlaine at II.iv.1, 7:
Black is the beauty of the brightest day . . .
Ready to darken earth with endless night

Bedford at 1H6: I.i.1:
Hung be the heavens with black, yield day to
night

Theridamus at II.iv.121:
If words might serve, our voice hath
   rent the air

Edward at 2H6: V.i.139:
Ay, noble father, if our words will serve

Olympia [to Theridamus] at IV.ii.33–5:
        . . . draw your sword
Making a passage for my troubled soul,
Which beats against this prison to get out

Clarence at R3: I.iv.36–8:
. . . often did I strive
To yield the ghost, but still the envious flood
Stopp'd in my soul, and would not let it
   forth

Stage direction at IV.iii.1:
Enter Tamburlaine, drawn in his chariot
by the Kings of Trebizon and Soria, with bits
in their mouths, reins in his left hand, and
in his right hand a whip with which he
scourgeth them

Exeter at 1H6: I.i.19, 22:
Upon a wooden coffin we attend . . .
Like captives bound to a triumphant car

Tamburlaine at IV.iii.20–1:
        . . . draw
My chariot swifter than the racking clouds

Richard at 3H6: II.i.26–7:
Three glorious suns . . .
Not separated with the racking clouds

Orcanes at IV.iii.32:
O thou that sway'st the region under earth

Pucelle at 1H6: V.iii.10–11:
. . . ye familiar spirits that are cull'd
Out of the powerful regions under earth

Orcanes at IV.iii.42: Haling him headlong to the lowest hell	*Bedford at 1H6: I.i.149:* I'll hale the Dauphin headlong from his throne
Amyras at V.iii.250: Meet heaven and earth, and here let all things end	*Young Clifford at 2H6: V.ii.40, 42:* O let the vile world end . . . Knit heaven and earth together

SECTION 2: THE JEW OF MALTA

Prologue to the play is spoken by 'Machevill'	*Richard at 3H6: III.ii.193:* I can . . . . . . set the murderous Machiavel to school
Barabas at I.ii.197–8: And henceforth wish for an eternal night, That clouds of darkness may enclose my flesh	*Margaret at R3: I.iii.267–9:* Witness my son, now in the shade of death, Whose bright out-shining beams thy cloudy wrath Hath in eternal darkness folded up
Barabas at I.ii.241–2: . . . Things past recovery Are hardly cur'd with exclamations	*Richard at R3: II.ii.103:* But none can help our harms by wailing them
Barabas at II.iii.20–1: We Jews can fawn like spaniels when we please, And when we grin, we bite	*Margaret at R3: I.iii.289–90:* O Buckingham, take heed of yonder dog! Look when he fawns, he bites
Ferneze [of his son] at III.ii.11–12: . . . My Lodowick slain! These arms of mine shall be thy sepulchre	*Talbot [of his son] at 1H6: IV.vii.32:* Now my old arms are young Talbot's grave *Father [of his son] at 3H6: II.v.114–15:* These arms of mine shall be thy winding- sheet; My heart, sweet boy, shall be thy sepulchre

Ferneze at III.ii.35:
And with my prayers pierce impartial
  heavens
	Margaret at R3: I.iii.195:
	Can curses pierce the clouds and enter
	  heaven?

Ferneze at III.v.2–4:
Ferneze: What wind drives you thus
into Malta-road?
Basso: The wind that bloweth all the world
besides,
Desire of gold

Hortensio at Shr.: I.ii.47ff.:
Hortensio: . . . what happy gale
Blows you to Padua here from old Verona?
Petruchio: Such wind as scatters young men
through the world
To seek their fortunes farther than at home

Calymath [to Ferneze and others] at V.ii.1–2:
Now vail your pride, you captive Christians,
And kneel for mercy to your conquering foe

Katherina at Shr.: V.ii.177–8:
Then vail your stomachs, for it is no boot,
And place your hands below your husband's
foot

SECTION 3: THE SPANISH TRAGEDY

Ghost of Andrea at I.i.12–13:
But in the harvest of my summer joys
Death's winter nipped the blossoms of my
bliss

Gloucester at 2H6: II.iv.1–4:
Thus sometimes hath the brightest day a cloud;
And after summer evermore succeeds
Barren winter, with his wrathful nipping cold:
So cares and joys abound, as seasons fleet

Ghost of Andrea at I.i.27–8:
Then was the ferryman of hell content
To pass me over to the slimy strand

Clarence at R3: I.iv.31–2:
                    . . . reflecting gems,
That woo'd the slimy bottom of the deep

Ghost of Andrea at I.i.55–6:
In keeping on my way to Pluto's court,
Through dreadful shades of ever-glooming
night

Clarence at R3: I.iv.45–7:
I pass'd . . .
With that sour ferryman which poets write of,
Unto the kingdom of perpetual night

Ghost of Andrea at I.i.65, 71:
Where bloody Furies shakes their whips
of steel . . .
And all foul sins with torments overwhelmed

Clarence at R3: I.iv.57–9:
'Seize on him, Furies! Take him into torment!'
With that, methoughts, a legion of foul fiends
Environ'd me, and howled in my ears

Viceroy at I.iii.5:
Then rest we here awhile in our unrest

Duchess of York at R3: IV.iv.29:
Rest thy unrest on England's lawful earth

Hieronimo at III.xiii.29:
Thus therefore will I rest me in unrest

Aaron at Tit.:IV.ii.31:
But let her rest in her unrest awhile

Horatio at I.iv.36:
There laid him down and dewed him with
  my tears

Q. Margaret at 2H6: III.ii.338–9:
        . . . Give me thy hand
That I may dew it with my tears

Ghost of Andrea at I.v.1:
Come we for this from depth of underground

Hume at 2H6: I.ii.79:
A spirit rais'd from depth of under ground

Pedringano at II.i.89:
I swear to both by Him that made us all

Richard at 3H6: II.ii.124:
By Him that made us all, I am resolv'd

King of Spain at II.iii.17–18:
I'll grace her marriage with an uncle's gift,
And this it is: in case the match go forward . . .

*Q. Margaret [of a proposed marriage] at 3H6:
III.iii.58:*
If that go forward, Henry's hope is done

Lorenzo [murdering Horatio] at II.iv.55:
Ay, thus and thus! These are the fruits of love

K. Edward [in another sense] at 3H6: III.ii.58:
But stay thee – 'tis the fruits of love I mean

Lorenzo [of Bel-imperia] at II.iv.63:
Come, stop her mouth. Away with her

Chiron [to Lavinia] at Tit.: II.iii.185:
Nay, then, I'll stop your mouth

Hieronimo at II.v.17:
O speak, if any spark of life remain

Richard at 3H6: V.vi. 66–7:
If any spark of life be yet remaining,
Down, down to hell

Hieronimo at II.v.46:
Sweet lovely rose, ill-plucked before thy time

Q. Margaret at 3H6: V.v.60:
How sweet a plant have you untimely cropp'd

Hieronimo at II.v.53:
Seest thou those wounds that yet are bleeding
  fresh?

Lady Anne at R3: I.ii.55–6:
        . . . See, see dead Henry's wounds
Open their congeal'd mouths and bleed afresh

Ghost of Andrea at II.vi.4–6:
              . . . Bel-imperia,
On whom I doted more than all the world
Because she loved me more than all the
  world

Chiron at Tit.: II.i.71–2:
I care not, I, knew she and all the world:
I love Lavinia more than all the world

Pedringano at III.iii.16:
Here therefore will I stay and take my stand

1 Watchman at 3H6: IV.iii.1:
Come on, my masters, each man take his stand

Pedringano at III.iii.37:
Who first lays hand on me, I'll be his priest
[meaning to kill him; administer the last rites]

Suffolk [in same sense] at 2H6: III.i.272:
Say but the word and I will be his priest

Lorenzo at III.iv.78:
Now stands our fortune on a tickle point

York at 2H6: I.i.216–17:
                    . . . the state of Normandy
Stands on a tickle point

Hieronimo at III.vii.32–3 [reading letter]:
. . . I write, as mine extremes required,
That you would labour my delivery

Clarence at R3: I.iv.235–6:
. . . he . . . swore with sobs
That he would labour my delivery

Bel-imperia at III.ix.12:
Well, force perforce, I must constrain myself

York at 2H6: I.i.259:
And force perforce I'll make him yield the
    crown

Lorenzo at III.x.1:
Boy, talk no further; thus far things go well
[opening line of scene]

K. Edward at 3H6: V.iii.1:
Thus far our fortune keeps an upward
    course
[opening line of scene]

Portingale 1 at III.xi.1–3:
Portingale 1: By your leave, sir.
Hieronimo: Good leave have you. Nay, I
    pray you go,
For I'll leave you, if you can leave me, so

K. Edward at 3H6: III.ii.33–5:
K. Edward: Lords, give us leave . . .
Richard: Ay, good leave have you, for you will
    have leave
Till youth take leave and leave you to the
    crutch

Hieronimo at III.xii.31:

. . . Hieronimo, beware; go by, go by

*Sly at Shr.: Induction.i.7 [deliberate
    quotation]:*
Go by, Saint Jeronimy, go to thy cold bed and
    warm thee

Hieronimo at II.v.1–2:
What outcries pluck me from my naked bed,
And chill my throbbing heart with trembling fear

Hieronimo at III.xii.70–1:
Give me my son . . .
Away! I'll rip the bowels of the earth
He diggeth with his dagger

Titus at Tit.: IV.iii.5, 11–12:
She's gone, she's fled. Sirs, take to your tools . . .
Tis you must dig with mattock and with spade
And pierce the inmost centre of the earth

Hieronimo at III.xiii.86–7:
He draweth out a bloody napkin
O no, not this! Horatio, this was thine,
And when I dyed it in your dearest blood . . .

Q. Margaret at 3H6: I.iv.79–81:
Look, York, I stain'd this napkin with the blood
That valiant Clifford with his rapier's point
Made issue from the bosom of the boy

Hieronimo at IV.iv.122–4:
And here behold this bloody handkercher,
Which at Horatio's death I weeping dipped
Within the river of his bleeding wounds

York at 3H6: I.iv.157–9:
This cloth thou dipp'dst in blood of my sweet
  boy,
And I with tears do wash the blood away.
Keep thou the napkin . . .

Hieronimo at III.xiv.118:
Pocas palabras, mild as the lamb
[*pocas palabras* is Spanish for 'few words']

Sly at Shr.: Induction.i.5:
Therefore *paucas pallabris*, let the world slide

SECTION 4: SOLIMAN AND PERSEDA

Erastus at I.iv.136:
As storms that fall amid a sun shine day

Richard at 3H6: II.i.187:
Ne'er may he live to see a sunshine day

Erastus at II.i.189,212:
. . . bid them bring some store of crowns with
them . . . What store of crowns have you
  brought?

Son at 3H6: II.v.56–7
This man . . .
May be possessed with some store of crowns

Ferdinando [to Erastus] at II.i.244:
Dasell mine eyes, or ist Lucinas chaine?

Edward at 3H6: II.i.25:
Dazzle mine eyes, or do I see three suns?

Piston [to Erastus] at II.i.291–2:
Hetherto all goes well; but, if I be taken –
I, marry, sir, then the case is altered . . .

Warwick at 3H6: IV.ii.1:
Trust me, my lord, all hitherto goes well
K. Edward at 3H6: IV.iii.31:
Ay, but the case is alter'd

Erastus at III.i.85–7:
As ayre bred Eagles, if they once perceive
That any of their broode but close their sight
When they should gase against the glorious
  Sunne

Richard at 3H6: II.i.91–2:
Nay, if thou be that princely eagle's bird,
Show thy descent by gazing 'gainst the sun

Perseda at V.iv.67:
A kisse I graunt thee, though I hate thee
  deadlie

Q. Margaret at 3H6: I.iv.84–5:
Alas, poor York! but that I hate thee deadly,
I should lament . . .

SECTION 5: ARDEN OF FAVERSHAM

Mosby at i.325:
The rancorous venom of thy mis-swol'n
  heart

Aaron at Tit.: V.iii.13:
The venomous malice of my swelling heart

Franklin [alone on stage] at iv.45:
Then fix his sad eyes on the sullen earth

Eleanor at 2H6: I.ii.5:
Why are thine eyes fix'd to the sullen earth

Black Will [to Alice] at xiv.79:
Patient yourself; we cannot help it now

Titus [to Tamora] at Tit.: I.i.121:
Patient yourself, madam, and pardon me

Mosby at xiv.96–7:
        . . . will you two
Perform the complot that I have laid?

Tamora at Tit.: II.iii.264–5:
        . . . too late I bring this fatal writ,
The complot of this timeless tragedy

Alice at xiv.310:
Ah, neighbours, a sudden qualm came
  over my heart

Gloucester at 2H6: I.i.54:
Some sudden qualm hath struck me at the
  heart

SECTION 6: EDWARD I

Lluellen at iv.20–1 (ll.853–4):
Tell them the Chaines that Mulciber erst made,
To tie Prometheus lims to Caucasus . . .

Aaron at Tit.: II.i.16–17
And faster bound to Aaron's charming eyes
Than is Prometheus tied to Caucasus

Edward at x.201 (l. 1796):
Fast to those lookes are all my fancies tide

Appendix B

Conjectural Programme of Performances of 'harey the vi' at the Rose between 3 March 1592 and 31 January 1593 (based on Henslowe's Diary in Foakes and Rickert, pp. 16–20)

General note: A play was performed on every weekday with the exception of Good Friday (24 March) and two other days, drawing on a repertoire of 23 plays performed in varying sequence and at varying intervals, the same play being rarely repeated in any one week. The longer intervals between performances of 'harey the vi' on 16 and 28 March, 21 April and 4 May (11 and 12 days respectively against an average elsewhere of 5) are interpreted as allowing for a more extended period of rehearsal in which the following play in the trilogy was brought up to scratch. (I assume that the leading roles would already have been familiar to the actors who played them from their having previously toured in the plays.) Performances took place in the afternoons.

Date	Interval between performances		Henslowe's share of the takings	
Friday, 3 March 1592		FIRST PERFORMANCE, Henry VI, Part 1	£3 16s 8d	
Tuesday, 7 March	3 days	SECOND PERFORMANCE, Part 1	£3	
Saturday, 11 March	3 days	THIRD PERFORMANCE, Part 1	£2 7s 6d	
Thursday, 16 March	4 days	FOURTH PERFORMANCE, Part 1	£1 11s 6d	(1)
Tuesday, 28 March (Easter Tuesday)	11 days	FIRST PERFORMANCE, Henry VI, Part 2	£3 8s	
Wednesday, 5 April	7 days	SECOND PERFORMANCE, Part 2	£2 1s	
Thursday, 13 April	7 days	THIRD PERFORMANCE, Part 2	£1 6s	(2)
Friday, 21 April	7 days	FOURTH PERFORMANCE, Part 2	£1 13s	
Thursday, 4 May (Ascension Day)	12 days	FIRST PERFORMANCE, Henry VI. Part 3	£2 16s	(3)

Date	Interval	Performance	Price	Note
Sunday, 7 May	2 days	SECOND PERFORMANCE, Part 3	£1 2s	(4)
Sunday, 14 May (Whit Sunday)	6 days	THIRD PERFORMANCE, Part 3	£2 10s	
Friday, 19 May	4 days	FOURTH PERFORMANCE, Part 3	£1 10s	
Thursday, 25 May	5 days	FIFTH PERFORMANCE, Part 3	£1 4s	
Monday, 12 June	17 days	New sequential cycle begins with FIFTH PERFORMANCE OF Henry VI, Part 1	£1 12s	
Monday, 19 June	6 days	FIFTH PERFORMANCE, Henry VI, Part 2	£1 11s	
Thursday, 22 June		Season interrupted by riots in City		
Friday, 29 December	6 months	Season resumes		
Tuesday, 16 January 1593		New cycle begins with (?) SIXTH PERFORMANCE of Henry VI, Part 1	£2 6s	
Wednesday, 31 January	14 days	(?) SIXTH PERFORMANCE of Henry VI, Part 2	£1 6s	
Wednesday, 7 February		Season interrupted by plague and abandoned		

Notes to Appendix B

1. To produce a regular sequence of four performances for each of the trilogy in this early part of the season, Henslowe's 'harey' is here interpreted as referring to *Henry VI*. Note diminishing returns with each repeat of Part 1.

2. Again, note diminishing returns.

3. This, and the performances on 7, 14 and 25 May were consecutive with 'titus and vespacia'. On 4 and 25 May, 'harey the vi' followed 'titus'; on 7 and 14 May, it preceded 'titus'. Performances of these plays are often linked also with 'Jeronimo' (*The Spanish Tragedy*) or *The Jew of Malta*. All six plays belonged primarily to the Admiral's.

4. Either Henslowe has mistaken the date or, exceptionally, the play was performed on a Sunday, as in the following week on Whit Sunday.

Appendix C

Correspondences in word, image or thought between Plays of 1593/4 and the Sonnets

Section 1: The Two Gentlemen of Verona

Proteus at I.i.42–3:
Yet writers say: as in the sweetest bud
The eating canker dwells

Sonnet 70.7:
For canker vice the sweetest buds doth love
Sonnet 35.4:
And loathsome canker lives in sweetest bud

Lucetta at I.ii.139:
I see things too, although you judge I wink

Sonnet 43.1:
When most I wink, then do mine eyes best see

Speed and Valentine at II.i.65–8:
Speed: If you love her, you cannot see her.
Valentine: Why?
Speed: Because Love is blind. O that you had mine
eyes, or your own eyes had the lights they were wont
to have

Sonnet 137.1–2:
Thou blind fool, Love, what dost thou to mine eyes
That they behold and see not what they see?
Sonnet 148.1–2:
O me, what eyes hath love put in my head,
Which have no correspondence with true sight!
(See also 113.1–4)

Proteus at II.ii.16–18:
    What, gone without a word?
Ay, so true love should do: it cannot speak,
For truth hath better deeds than words to grace it

Sonnet 69.8–10:
. . . seeing farther than the eye hath shown.
They look into the beauty of thy mind,
And that in guess they measure by thy deeds

Section 2: The Comedy of Errors

Adriana at II.i.87–8:
His company must do his minions grace,
Whilst I at home starve for a merry look

Adriana at II.ii.110–11:
Ay, ay, Antipholus, look strange and frown,
Some other mistress hath thy sweet aspects

Adriana at II.ii.119–23:
How comes it now, my husband, O, how comes it,
That thou are then estranged from thyself? –
Thyself I call it, being strange to me,
That undividable, incorporate,
Am better than thy dear self's better part

Antipholus of Syracuse at III.ii.47–51:
Sing, siren, for thyself, and I will dote;
Spread o'er the silver waves thy golden hairs,
And as a bed I'll take thee, and there lie,
And in that glorious supposition think
He gains by death that hath such means to die

Antipholus of Syracuse at III.ii.61–2:
It is thyself, mine own self's better part,
Mine eye's clear eye, my dear heart's dearer heart

Sonnet 47.3:
When that mine eye is famished for a look
Sonnet 75.9–10:
Sometime all full with feasting on your sight,
And by and by clean starved for a look

Sonnet 89.8:
I will acquaintance strangle and look strange

Sonnet 39.1–4:
O, how thy worth with manners may I sing
When thou art all the better part of me?
What can mine own praise to mine own self bring,
And what is't but mine own when I praise thee?

Sonnet 92.9–12:
Thou canst not vex me with inconstant mind,
Since that my life on thy revolt doth lie.
O, what a happy title do I find,
Happy to have thy love, happy to die!

Sonnet 46.12–14:
The clear eye's moiety and the dear heart's part:
As thus – mine eye's due is thy outward part,

Section 3: Edward III

And my heart's right thy inward love of heart

Lodowick at II.i.10–12:
His cheeks put on their scarlet ornaments,
But no more like her oriental red
Than brick to coral or live things to dead

Sonnet 142.5–7:
. . . not from those lips of thine,
That have profaned their scarlet ornaments
And sealed false bonds of love as oft as mine

King Edward at II.i.143–6:
Compar'st thou her to the pale queen of night,
Who, being set in dark, seems therefore light?
What is she, when the sun lifts up his head,
But like a fading taper, dim and dead?

Sonnet 7.1–4:
Lo, in the orient when the gracious light
Lifts up his burning head, each under eye
Doth homage to his new-appearing sight,
Serving with looks his sacred majesty

King Edward at II.i.164–5:
Who smiles upon the basest weed that grows,
As lovingly as on the fragrant rose

Sonnet 94.11–12:
But if that flower with base infection meet,
The basest weed outbraves his dignity

Sonnet 95.1–3:
How sweet and lovely dost thou make the shame
Which, like a canker in the fragrant rose,
Doth spot the beauty of thy budding name

Warwick at II.i.450–1:
Dark night seems darker by the lightning flash;
Lilies that fester smell far worse than weeds

Sonnet 94.13–14 (continues from above):
For sweetest things turn sourest by their deeds;
Lilies that fester smell far worse than weeds

Section 4: Love's Labour's Lost

Princess at II.i.13–16:

Good Lord Boyet, my beauty, though but mean,
Needs not the painted flourish of your praise:
Beauty is bought by judgement of the eye,
Not utter'd by base sale of chapmen's tongues

Princess at IV.i.1–2:

Was that the king, that spurr'd his horse so hard
Against the steep-up rising of the hill?

Berowne at IV.iii.230–7:

Of all complexions the cull'd sovereignty
Do meet, as at a fair, in her fair cheek;
Where several worthies make one dignity,
Where nothing wants that want itself doth seek.
Lend me the flourish of all gentle tongues, –
Fie, painted rhetoric! O! she needs it not:
To things of sale a seller's praise belongs;
She passes praise; then praise too short doth blot.

Sonnet 21.1–2, 13–14:

So is it not with me as with that Muse,
Stirred by a painted beauty to his verse . . .
Let them say more that like of hearsay well;
I will not praise that purpose not to sell

Sonnet 7.5:

And having climbed the steep-up heavenly hill

Sonnet 82.5–14:

Thou are as fair in knowledge as in hue,
Finding thy worth a limit past my praise;
And therefore art enforced to seek anew
Some fresher stamp of the time-bettering days.
And do so, love; yet when they have devised
What strained touches rhetoric can lend,
Thou, truly fair, wert truly sympathized
In true plain words by thy true-telling friend:
And their gross painting might be better used
Where cheeks need blood; in thee it is abused.

Appendix D

Conjectural Doubling Plots

1. Romeo and Juliet

2. Henry V

3. Troilus and Cressida

KEY

CAPITALS denote character speaks in scene

Lower-case letters denote character is mute in scene

S = Sharer

HM = Hired Man

HM/A = Hired Man or Apprentice

A = Apprentice

PM = Player-musician

Extras are drawn from stage keepers, tiremen and gatherers (stage, wardrobe and box-office staff)

Plot 1: *Romeo and Juliet (characters in approximate order of appearance)*

ACTOR	ACT 1 (1–4)	MASQUE (1.5)	ACT 2	ACT 3	ACT 4	ACT 5 (1–2)	TOMB (5.3)	(Notes)
S1 (Shakespeare)	CHORUS		CHORUS/FRIAR	FRIAR	FRIAR	FRIAR	FRIAR	
S2 (Sly?)	SAMPSON	CAP SERV		Tyb man	CAP SERV		WATCH	(1)
HM1	GREGORY	CAP SERV		Tyb man	CAP SERV		CAP SERV	
HM2 (Sincler?)	ABRAM	Masquer		Mont man		APOTHECARY/	Mont man	(2)
S3 (Cowley?)	BALTHASAR	Masquer		Mont man		BALTHASAR	BALTHASAR	
S4 (Condell?)	BENVOLIO	Masquer	BENVOLIO	BENVOLIO			Benvolio	
HM3	TYBALT	TYBALT		TYBALT/		FRIAR JOHN/	WATCH	
S5 (Pope?)	CAPULET	CAPULET		CAPULET	CAPULET		CAPULET	(3)
A1	L CAPULET	L CAPULET		L CAPULET	L CAPULET		L CAPULET	
S6 (Heminges?)	MONTAGU	Masquer		MONTAGU			MONTAGU	
A2	L MONTAGU	ANTHONY		L MONTAGU/			WATCH	(4)
S7 (Phillips?)	PRINCE	Masquer		PRINCE			PRINCE	
A3	ROMEO	ROMEO	ROMEO	ROMEO		ROMEO	ROMEO	
A4	PARIS	Masquer		PARIS	PARIS		PARIS	
A5	NURSE	NURSE	NURSE	NURSE	NURSE		Nurse	(3)
A6	JULIET	JULIET	JULIET	JULIET	JULIET		JULIET	
S8 (Burbage?)	MERCUTIO	MERCUTIO	MERCUTIO	MERCUTIO/			Watch	
A7		POTPAN		Tyb man	Cap serv		Cap serv	
S9 (Bryan?)	CAP SERV (?)	COUSIN CAP/		CITIZEN			Watch	
S10 (Kempe)	Prince's train	Masquer	PETER	Peter	PETER		Peter	(5)
A8	Prince's train	'Susan G'/		Prince's train	Cap serv		Prince's train	(6)
A9	Prince's train	'Nell'/		Prince's train	Cap serv		Page to Paris	
A10	Prince's train	'Rosaline'/		Mercutio's page	Cap serv		Mon man	
Musicians 3+	Citizens	Musicians		Citizens	MUSICIANS			
Extras 5+	Citizens	Torchbearers		Citizens			Prince's train	

Notes

1. Sampson and Gregory remain in character while playing all Capulet servants and Tybalt's men.
2. Abram and Balthasar remain in character while playing Montagu men. As masquers, their faces remain covered throughout the scene.
3. The older women's roles are played by senior apprentices, some of whom may have become hired men.
4. All the mute masquers are disguised by masks and cloaks.
5. Kempe (as Peter?) may also have played the illiterate Capulet servant of Act 1, Scene 2.
6. Susan Grindstone, Nell and Rosaline are brought on stage to provide dancing partners for the masquers.

Plot 2: Henry V (sharers listed first)

ACTOR	1.1	1.2	2.1	2.2	2.3	2.4	3.1	3.2	3.3	3.4	3.5	3.6	3.7	4.1	4.2	4.3	4.4	4.5	4.6	4.7	4.8	5.1	5.2	Notes
S1 (Shakespeare)	CHO	Bed	CHO	BED			CHO		Bed					CHO		Bed			Bed	Bed		CHO	BUR	(1)
S2 (Burbage)		HEN		HEN			HEN		HEN			HEN		HEN		HEN			HEN	HEN	HEN		HEN	
S3 (Phillips?)		WES		WES			Wes	MAC	MAC		BOU		BOU	BAT		WES		BOU		Bou	WES		WES	
S4 (Heminges?)		EXE		EXE		EXE	Exe		Exe							EXE			EXE	EXE	EXE		EXE	
S5 (Pope?)			PIS		PIS			PIS	Pis			PIS		PIS			PIS		Her	Her	HER	PIS	EPI	(2)
S6 (Cowley?)			NYM		NYM			NYM	Nym				lor	ERP		Erp						lor	lor	
S7 (Sly?)			BAR		BAR			BAR	Bar		lor			WIL	GRA		FER			WIL	WIL		lor	
S8 (Condell?)	CAN	CAN		SCR		FrK	sol				FrK	MON				MON				MON			FrK	(3)
S9 (Armin?)	ELY	ELY		Cla			Flu	FLU	Flu			FLU		FLU						FLU	FLU	FLU	lor	(4)
HM1 (Sincler?)		Cla				DAU	sol		sol		DAU	sol	DAU		DAU			DAU		sol	sol		Cla	
HM2		AMB		CAM		CON	sol		GOV		CON		CON	COU	CON	YOR		CON		sol	sol		Hun	
HM3		Glo				Bri	Glo	JAM	Jam		BRI	GLO		GLO		GLO			Glo	GLO	GLO		Glo	
HM4		att				Ber	sol	GOW	Gow			GOW	sol	GOW		Gow			GOW	GOW	GOW	GOW	lor	
A1 (Gilburne?)		War		War					sol		RAM	Ram	RAM		RAM	SAL		RAM		War	WAR		War	(5)
A2		Amb		sol		MES				ALI		sol	MES		MES				Orl	Orl	sol		ALI	
A3			HOS		HOS		sol		sol		ORL	Orl	ORL		ORL			ORL	Orl	Orl			ISA	
A4			BOY		BOY			BOY		KAT							BOY		pri	pri	sol		KAT	(6)
Mute extras (3+)		att		sol			sol		cit		sol	sol	sol	sol	sol	sol			sol	sol	sol		att	(7)

Notes

1. Shakespeare would have been able to slip in and out of the scenes in which Bedford appears (including 3.1 and 4.1) with a minimum of fuss; he is always at hand to swell a scene and add the odd line when required. A change of costume to armour as the action moves from England to France would have been equally appropriate to Bedford and Chorus. He would have changed to a robe for Burgundy. Bedford is named in the initial stage direction to 5.2 but is not among those deputed to negotiate the details of the treaty, as he would surely have been if Shakespeare had finally intended him to be present. Huntingdon (a mute character who appears nowhere else in the play) looks like a late substitution.

2. The Epilogue goes to Pope as Pistol in the same way that the Epilogue to *Henry IV* had gone to Kempe as Falstaff. Both refer to the author as a separate person, which would have come strangely from Shakespeare.

3. Montjoy, as herald, is the voice of the French King. 'Where is Montjoy the herald?', asks the King at 3.5.36. Where indeed? 'Speed him hence:/Let him greet England with our sharp defiance'. And on his first appearance in the following scene, Montjoy, having identified himself by his habit, begins, 'Thus says my king' (3.6.117). I am indebted for this and other doubles to John Barton, who directed me in both parts for the Elizabethan Theatre Company in 1953.

4. I have assumed that by 1599 Armin would have become a sharer.

5. In the Folio text of the opening stage direction to 3.7, Rambures appears as 'Gebon', and 'Ge' is given the first line of 4.5, in which Rambures also appears but is otherwise silent. 'Gebon' may have been Shakespeare's approximation of the name of Samuel Gilburne, mentioned in Phillips' will of 1605 as his 'late apprentice'. Apprentices 1, 2 and 3 would all have been drawn from the company's older apprentices, some of whom may by this time have achieved the status of hired men. There are indications that those who played girls' parts in their young years sometimes grew up to play older women on occasion, but usefully could double these with male roles.

6. The only boy actor required in the cast. Like Apprentice 2, he would have needed some knowledge of French.

7. The extras fit in as attendants, soldiers, citizens or French prisoners as required.

Plot 3: Troilus and Cressida (sharers listed first as in 1603 patent)

ACTOR	1.1	1.2	1.3	2.1	2.2	2.3	3.1	3.2	3.3	4.1	4.2	4.3	4.4	4.5	5.1	5.2	5.3	5.4	5.5	5.6	5.7	5.8	5.9	5.10	5.11	Notes
S1 Fletcher	AEN	Aen	AEN							AEN	AEN	Aen	AEN	AEN	AEN	AEN							Myr		AEN	(1)
S2 Shakespeare	PAN	PAN					PAN	PAN			PAN		PAN				PAN						Myr		PAN	(2)
S3 Burbage	PRO		ULY			ULY			ULY						ULY	ULY			ULY					ULY		
S4 Phillips			AGA			AGA			AGA					AGA	AGA				AGA					AGA		
S5 Heminges					PRI												PRI									(3)
S6 Condell		Hec			HEC				CAL					HEC		CAL	HEC	HEC		HEC			HEC			(4)
S7 Sly		Hls	MEN	ALE	HLS				MEN					MEN							MEN	MEN	Myr			(5)
S8 Armin				THE		THE			THE						THE	THE		THE			THE	THE				
S9 Cowley			NES			NES			NES					NES	NES				NES	NES	NES			NES		
HM Lowin				ACH		ACH			ACH					ACH	ACH				ACH	ACH	ACH		ACH			(6)
HM/A 1	TRO	Tro			TRO			TRO			TRO	TRO	TRO	TRO		TRO	TRO	TRO		TRO	TRO				TRO	(7)
HM/A 2				AJA		AJA			AJA					AJA	AJA				AJA	AJA	AJA			AJA		
HM/A 3				PAT		PAT			PAT					PAT	PAT				Pat				Myr			(8)
HM/A 4			Dio			DIO			DIO	DIO		Dio	DIO	DIO	DIO	DIO		DIO		DIO	DIO			DIO		
HM/A 5		Par			PAR		PAR			PAR		PAR	PAR	PAR								PAR			PAR	
A1		CRE						CRE			CRE		CRE	CRE		CRE			sol							
A2	Boy	BOY			CAS			BOY									CAS		SER			BAS	Myr		Bas	(9)
A3	sol	sol					HEL			tor			att	att					sol	sol						
PM 1		Dei					SER			DEI		Dei	DEI	tru			AND		sol				tru		Dei	
PM2		Ant					mus			Ant		Ant	tru	tru					sol	Myr			tru		Ant	

Notes

1. Fletcher was appointed a King's servant by the patent of 1603, and being known to the King – having previously appeared with a company of English players on tour in Scotland – is listed first. He seems not to have joined the company on a permanent basis but, in this plague year of 1603, I think it at least possible that he went with them on tour.

2. There is no necessity for Shakespeare to double until Act 5, when he would have been needed as a Myrmidon. The Myrmidons wear distinctive cloaks and concealing helmets, possibly masks.

3. Heminges has only two scenes as Priam. As Company Manager, he would have had much to do off-stage – especially on tour. But he too would have been needed as a Myrmidon.

4. Calchas has nothing to say in 2.3, and I have left him offstage. In 5.2 we hear his voice from off; he does not appear.

5. When doubling Trojan and Greek characters (as Sly briefly does here), any possibility of confusion is avoided by the use of distinctive costumes and armour for the opposing armies. There is no need for Helenus to be present in 4.5, or for Menelaus in 5.10, though both are named in stage-directions by some editors.

6. John Lowin may have been brought in as a replacement for Thomas Pope, who was ill when the 1603 patent was drawn up, and died later this year.

7. The apprentices who play the younger male roles (HM/A 1 to 5) have been with the company since its formation in 1594. They would now have been in their middle to late twenties, and some would have achieved their 'freedom' and been employed as hired men.

8. I have hesitated as to whether to include Patroclus among the older apprentices or the boys. He is addressed by Achilles as 'sweet Patroclus', and by Thersites as 'boy', 'fool' and ruder terms. He has the gift of mimicry and is old enough to enjoy kissing Cressida. He kisses her twice.

9. I have assumed that A2 has some instrumental skill and doubles as a musician in 3.1. Player-musician 1 is young enough to play Andromache. PM 2 is an older man with a good presence but is mute throughout. Both need to be expert trumpeters.

Abbreviations

The following abbreviations are used in the notes that follow. Other works and sources are cited in full on first reference to them in each set of notes. Place of publication is London except where otherwise stated.

Bentley, JCS   G.E. Bentley, *The Jacobean and Caroline Stage*, 7 vols., Oxford, 1941–68

Bentley, PDST   G.E. Bentley, *The Profession of Dramatist in Shakespeare's Time, 1590–1642*, Princeton, 1971

Bentley, PPST   G.E. Bentley, *The Profession of Player in Shakespeare's Time, 1590–1642*, Princeton, 1984

Chambers, ES   E.K. Chambers, *The Elizabethan Stage*, 4 vols., Oxford, 1923

Chambers, WS   E.K. Chambers, *William Shakespeare, A Study of Facts and Problems*, 2 vols., Oxford, 1930

Fripp   Edgar I. Fripp (ed.), *Minutes and Accounts of the Corporation of Stratford-upon-Avon and Other Records, 1553–1620*, vols 2 and 3, 1924–6

Halliwell-Phillipps J.O. Halliwell-Phillipps, *The Visits of Shakespeare's Company of Actors to the Provincial Cities and Towns of England*, Brighton, 1887

Jonson   *Ben Jonson*, ed. C.H. Herford, P. and E. Simpson, 11 vols, Oxford, 1925–52

MLR   *Modern Language Review*

MSC   *Malone Society Collections*

 II, Part 3   for 'Players at Ipswich', ed. E.K. Chambers, pp. 258–84, Oxford, 1931

 VII   *Records of Plays and Players in Kent, 1450–1642*, ed. G.E. Dawson, Oxford, 1965

 XI   *Records and Plays and Players in Norfolk and Suffolk, 1330–1642*, ed. John Wasson, Oxford, 1980–1

MSR   *Malone Society Reprints*

Murray   John Tucker Murray, *English Dramatic Companies, 1558–1642*, 2 vols, 1910, reprinted New York, 1963

Nungezer	Edwin Nungezer, *A Dictionary of Actors*, New York, 1929, reprinted 1968
PMLA	*Publications of the Modern Language Association of America*
REED	*Records of Early English Drama*. General editor: A.F. Johnston. Toronto, 1979 –
Bristol	*Bristol*, ed. Mark C. Pilkington, 1997
Cambridge	*Cambridge*, ed. A.H. Nelson, 2 vols, 1989
Coventry	*Coventry*, ed. R.W. Ingram, 1981
Cumb, West, Glos	*Cumberland, Westmorland, Gloucestershire*, ed. A. Douglas and P. Greenfield, 1986
Devon	*Devon*, ed. John M. Wasson, 1986
Hereford and Worcester	*Herefordshire, Worcestershire*, ed. David N. Klausner, 1990
Newcastle	*Newcastle upon Tyne*, ed. J.J. Anderson, 1982
Norwich	*Norwich 1540–1642*, ed. David Galloway, 1984
Shropshire	*Shropshire*, ed. J.A.B. Somerset, 2 vols, 1994
Somerset	*Somerset including Bath*, ed. James Stokes, with R.J. Alexander, 2 vols, 1996
Schoenbaum, CDL	S. Schoenbaum, *William Shakespeare, A Compact Documentary Life*, Oxford, 1977
Schoenbaum, SL	S. Schoenbaum, *Shakespeare's Lives*, Oxford, revd edn, 1993
Southworth, EMM	John Southworth, *The English Medieval Minstrel*, Woodbridge, 1989
Southworth, F & J	John Southworth, *Fools and Jesters at the English Court*, Stroud, 1998
SQ	*Shakespeare Quarterly*
SS	*Shakespeare Survey*
Wills	E.A.J. Honigmann and Susan Brock, *Playhouse Wills, 1558–1642*, Manchester and New York, 1993

Notes

Chapter 1: *The Invisible Man*

1. Schoenbaum, CDL, p. 315.
2. Quoted from Chambers, WS, II, pp. 228–30.
3. I am drawing here on Bentley, PDST, pp. 38–9.
4. *Ibid.*, pp. 51–3.
5. *Ibid.*, pp. 50–1.
6. For the harper-poets, see Southworth, EMM, chapters 3 and 7.
7. See H.C. Gardiner, *Mysteries' End*, Yale, 1946 (reprinted Anchor, 1967).
8. Quoted from *Harrison's Description of England in Shakspere's Youth*, ed. F.F. Furnivall with additions by Mrs C.C. Stopes, IV (Supplement, 1908), p. 367.
9. From *Microcosmos* in *The Complete Works of John Davies of Hereford*, ed. A.B. Grosart (1878), I, p. 82. Davies qualifies this statement in the next line with, 'Yet generous yee are in minde and moode'.
10. Bentley describes the effect of the Jonson and Shakespeare folios on the reputation of dramatists as a rise 'from an exceedingly low status to a

moderately low one'; *op. cit.* (n. 3), p. 57. For the Bodleian copy referred to below, see Schoenbaum (n. 1), p. 315.
11. Letter to Richard Woodhouse of 27 October 1818, in *The Letters of John Keats*, ed. Maurice Buxton Forman (Oxford, 3rd edn, 1947), pp. 227–8.
12. Jorge Luis Borges, *Labyrinths* (Penguin, 1970), pp. 284–5.
13. As quoted by Kenneth Muir in *Shakespeare the Professional and Related Studies* (1973) from Florence E. Hardy, *Life of Thomas Hardy* (1962), p. 341.

Chapter 2: *Killing the Calf*

1. Quoted from Schoenbaum, SL, p. 120.
2. *Letters and Papers of Henry VIII* (HMSO), III, Part 2, p. 1100.
3. Schoenbaum, CDL, p. 74.
4. Fripp, III, p. 170.
5. Quoted from Schoenbaum, CDL, p. 47.
6. Quoted from Chambers, WS, II, p. 189.
7. I have been drawing here on the actors' biographies in Chambers,

ES, II, pp. 295–350. See also Bentley's study of apprenticeship in PPST. Professor Bentley writes (p. 122): 'there is no doubt that the acting troupes used the apprentice system to train and hold their boy actors'.

8. Shakespeare, *Works*, ed. Rowe (1709), I, p. v.

9. Shakespeare, *Works*, ed. Malone (1821), II, Section IX. Malone concludes (p. 166): 'All these circumstances decidedly prove, in my apprehension, that this anecdote is a mere fiction. . . . It is, I think, much more probable, that his own lively disposition made him acquainted with some of the principal performers who visited Stratford . . . and that there he first determined to engage in that profession.'

10. John Dover Wilson, *The Essential Shakespeare, A Biographical Adventure* (Cambridge, 1937), pp. 42–3.

11. For the distinction between the two, see Chambers, WS, II, pp. 84–5.

12. Bentley, PPST, p. 26.

Chapter 3: The Apprentice

1. *The Essential Shakespeare, A Biographical Adventure* (Cambridge, 1937), p. 43.

2. The municipal year in Stratford ran from Michaelmas (29 September) to Michaelmas, and the Chamberlains' accounts were presented retrospectively. Confusingly,

however, certain entries are found to be subsequent to the accounting periods to which they are attributed. For dates throughout the chapter, I draw on Fripp, II and III, and Murray, I, pp. 43–57.

3. *The Statutes of the Realm*, ed. A. Luders *et al.*, IV, Part 1 (1819), p. 591. Also in Chambers, ES, IV, p. 270.

4. REED: *Cumb, West, Glos*, pp. 362–3.

5. For Essex' and Berkeley's men, see Chambers, ES, II, pp. 102–4. Robert Devereux, second earl of Essex, had a company from 1581 which visited Stratford in 1583–4 and 1587. Berkeley was named at Stratford as 'Bartlett' or 'Bartlite'.

6. On the occasion of their first visit in 1569, when John Shakespeare was Mayor and therefore in a position to determine the amount of their reward, they received a mere shilling in contrast to the thirteen shillings awarded later to Leicester's players. But in subsequent years, though remaining well below the level that Leicester's continued to command, their rewards were to rise to a more respectable 3s 4d or 5s. As I explain in Chapter 10, the mayor's reward was only a part of the income they would expect to receive in the course of such visits.

7. REED: *Coventry*, pp. 293, 298.

8. For Gloucester, see REED: *Cumb, West, Glos*, p. 309; for Leicester, Murray, II, p. 302; and for Coventry, REED: *Coventry*, p. 302.

9. For a full and revealing account of the dispute that gave rise to these records, see Chambers, ES, II, pp. 221–4.
10. *Ibid.*, p. 223.

Chapter 4: Admiral's Man

1. *The Life and Times of William Shakespeare* (1988), p. 61.
2. Unlike non-dramatic poetry, which often circulated in manuscript before publication, playscripts were jealously guarded by the companies that had commissioned and owned them to protect them from rival companies and pirates.
3. For Kent towns, see MSC VII under appropriate towns and dates; for Ipswich, MSC II, Part 3, p. 274; other towns, Murray, I, p. 141.
4. Murray, I, p. 112. Plays and players were regarded by Puritans as in direct competition with Protestant preachers of sermons (given in the afternoons when plays were performed in the open-air theatres) and thus in league with the 'papists'.
5. Murray, I, pp. 141–2.
6. Chambers, ES, II, p. 135.
7. Jonson, VI, p. 16.
8. Jonson, VIII, pp. 56–7.
9. See William A. Armstrong, 'Shakespeare and the Acting of Edward Alleyn' in SS 7 (1954, reprinted 1974), pp. 82–9.
10. J.C. Maxwell in his 1961 Arden edition stated that 'there does not seem to be anything that flatly contradicts a date of about 1589/90'

(p. xxiv). Eugene M. Waith in his Oxford edition of 1984 concludes that 'by a conservative estimate, it was first performed in the years 1590–2' (p. 20). Jonathan Bate, in his Arden edition of 1995 (pp. 69–79) is alone among the play's recent editors in dating its first performance to as late as 1594. I return to consider the play's performance history in the following chapter.

11. He is mentioned by name as visiting Worcester in REED: *Hereford and Worcester*, pp. 494, 499. For Shakespeare's use of other actors' names subsequently to find their way into the Folio texts of his plays, see Alison Gaw, 'Actors' Names in Basic Shakespeare Texts' in PMLA 40 (1925), pp. 530–50; and Karl P. Wentersdorf, 'Actors' Names in Shakespearean Texts' in *Theatre Studies* (1976/7), pp. 18–30.
12. 'Par', which appears as a speech prefix at IV.ii.71, is probably meant to indicate the player of the Pedant, and may be either an abbreviation for Thomas Parsons, who was acting with the Admiral's in 1598, or a reference to William Parr, recorded in a 'plot' of *Tamar Cam*, a lost play performed by the Admiral's in 1602, who is 'not known to have been associated with any company except this one and its derivatives' (Bentley, JCS, II, p. 520). He was to become a personal friend of Alleyn's. Similarly, 'Fel', prefixing the one-line role of the

Haberdasher at IV.iii.63, is likely to have been William Felle, who is described in *Henslowe's Diary* in 1599 as William Bird's 'man'; Bird was a member of the Admiral's company in 1597, and both he and his man (apprentice?) may go back to this earlier time. Among the many named servants of Petruchio in IV.i, 'Peter' is given several short speeches and, as Dover Wilson pointed out, is almost certainly the first name of an actor as he makes another, speechless entrance at IV.iv.68 as a servant to Tranio. The forename is rare among players of the time. He may be Alleyn's servant, Peter, sent with a message and a horse to Henslowe in 1593 (*Henslowe's Diary*, ed. Greg, II, p. 302). For such a large cast all available supernumeraries would have been roped in. The still rarer 'Curtis' – improbably given to the steward of Petruchio's estate near Verona – is more than likely that of the actor Curtis Greville, who is later recorded as a King's man, playing small parts in *The Two Noble Kinsmen* of 1613 (Chambers, WS, I, p. 530). See also the New Cambridge edition of the play, ed. Sir Arthur Quiller–Couch and John Dover Wilson (Cambridge, 1928, reprinted 1968), pp. 115–20, and for biographies of the actors named, Chambers, ES, II, pp. 295–350.

13. Andrew S. Cairncross in his Arden edition of *Henry VI, Part One* (1962), p. xli.

14. Edward Hall, *The Union of the Two Noble and Illustre Famelies of Lancastre and Yorke* (1548), as quoted by Cairncross, *op. cit.*, p. xlii.

15. See Chambers, ES, II, pp. 137–8.

16. MSC II, Part 3, p. 276. Only the fiscal year is stated (1589/90), but from the position of the entries in the Chamberlain's accounts, they appear to have taken place no earlier than the end of October and would probably therefore have followed the City prohibition of 5 November. They received £1 for the first performance and 10*s* for the second.

17. Chambers, WS, I, p. 41; II, p. 306.

18. Chambers, WS, I, pp. 48–9.

19. The plot, which was found among Alleyn's papers at Dulwich, relates to a somewhat earlier revival of the play at the Theatre or Curtain in 1590/1.

20. These are all commonly described as 'minor players', but Spencer at least was famous enough in his day to be mentioned by Thomas Heywood in his *Apology for Actors* of 1612 along with Singer, Pope, Phillips and Sly: that 'though they be dead, their deserts yet live in the remembrance of many' (p. 43). Though Shakespeare only names them as playing very small, unnamed parts, they may of course have doubled these with larger roles that he had no particular reason to record.

21. That Howard was willing to supply such a document indicates that he took a closer interest in his players,

and was more helpful to them, than is often suggested.

22. See Willem Schrickx, 'English Actors at the Courts of Wolfenbüttel, Brussels and Graz during the Lifetime of Shakespeare' in SS 33 (1980), pp. 153–9.

23. Quoted from Chambers, WS, II, p. 253.

24. The texts of Shakespeare's plays as memorially reconstructed by actors in pirated editions, such as the quartos of *Henry VI, Parts Two and Three (First Part of the Contention* and *The true Tragedie)*, are mainly of this approximate kind.

25. Nicholas Rowe in the biographical introduction to Shakespeare, *Works* (1709) I, p. vi.

26. See F.S. Boas (ed.), *The Works of Thomas Kyd* (Oxford, 1901), pp. lxxviii–lxxx, and Eugene M. Waith's introduction to his Oxford edition of *Titus* (1984), pp. 37–8. For the use that Shakespeare made of it in his later writings, Boas, pp. lxxxii–iii. Shakespeare may also have acted in an old play about Hamlet (the so-called *Ur-Hamlet*), possibly by Kyd, that was being performed in 1589, and in which the Ghost wore a visard (mask) and cried 'like an oister wife, "Hamlet, revenge"'. A later performance of it was given by a combination of the Admiral's and Chamberlain's men in a small theatre at Newington Butts on 11 June 1594, in which Shakespeare is likely to have taken part, and this may have influenced his own later treatment of the story more directly. See Chambers, WS, I, pp. 411–12.

27. It was not licensed for publication till 1592, and the only surviving copies date from 1599. See Boas (n. 26 above), pp. liv–lxi.

28. *The Life and Times of William Shakespeare* (1988), p. 62.

29. Scene 5, 1–9; Cf. *Macbeth*, II.i.49–64; also *The Rape of Lucrece*, ll. 162–8.

30. In his introduction to the text of the play in *Three Elizabethan Domestic Tragedies* (Penguin English Library, 1969), p. 25.

31. For the Faversham visits, see Murray, I, p. 141; MSC VII, p. 62. The visit of 1586 appears in Murray and Chambers (ES, II, p. 135) only. I cannot do justice to the case for Shakespeare's authorship here. The usual tests fail in that being so early nothing of the play would have been known to Heminges and Condell, or to Mears; nor does it appear to have been revived by the Chamberlain's men. It is true that it is quite unlike anything else that Shakespeare was to write; but in a curious way, this may also be taken as an argument in its favour, for how often did Shakespeare ever repeat himself?

32. F.G. Fleay, *A Chronicle History of the Life and Work of William Shakespeare* (1886), p. 14; *King Edward the First by George Peele 1593*, ed. W.W. Greg, MSR (1911), ll. 759–62; my italics.

33. Chambers, ES, III, pp. 460–1.

34. In Elizabethan drama, a shaking of weapons is usually taken as a gesture of rejection or defiance. In *Tamburlaine*, the Christian general Sigismund presents a doubtful ally with a naked sword and tells him, 'Wilt thou have war, then shake this blade at me;/If peace, restore it to my hands again' (2 *Tam*: I.ii.6–7); Tamburlaine defies Mahomet by burning his sacred books and challenging him to send his vengeance 'on the head of Tamburlaine/That shakes his sword against thy majesty' (2 *Tam*: V.i.193–4). In Shakespeare (according to Onions), the commonest meanings of 'shake' are 'lay aside, get rid of, discard', and in *Henry VI*, Old Clifford instructs those of Cade's rebels who hate the king and 'honours not his father/Henry the Fifth . . . Shake he his weapon at us, and pass by' (2H6: IV.viii.16–18). He has not many takers.

35. Chambers, as n. 33 above.

Chapter 5: The Rose, 1592

1. As quoted by Eugene M. Waith in his Oxford edition of *Titus* (1984), p. 12.

2. Quoted from the Arden edition of *Henry VI, Part 1*, ed. Andrew S. Cairncross (1962, reprinted 1986), p. xxxviii.

3. *Henslowe's Diary*, ed. R.A. Foakes and R.T. Rickert (Cambridge, 1961), pp. 16–21. According to Chambers (ES, II, p. 139), the fluctuating sum of his takings 'seems to have represented half the amount received for admission to the galleries of the house; the other half, with the payments for entrance to the standing room in the yard, being divided amongst such of the players as had a share in the profits'.

4. I have excluded an indeterminate entry of 'harey' on 16 March as this might refer to a play Henslowe names elsewhere as 'harey of cornwell'.

5. The same gloss is given to 'the second pte of tamber' (a lost play called *Tamar Cham*) on 28 April, 'the taner of denmarke' (another lost play) on 23 May, and 'a knacke to know a knave' (on 10 June), which is extant and contains a reference to Titus as having 'made a conquest on the Goths', thus tending to confirm that Shakespeare's *Titus* was already in existence by this date and known to the author of the *Knack* (see Chambers, WS, I, p. 316). Henslowe's 'ne' does not, of course, preclude the possibility that the plays so marked had been premiered out of London. It may simply mean that they were new to Henslowe, or the Rose.

6. Chambers, WS, I, pp. 318–19; translated from German to English in E. and H. Brennecke, *Shakespeare in Germany 1590–1700* (Chicago, 1964), pp. 18–51.

7. Chambers, ES, II, p. 274.

8. Waith (n. 1 above), pp. 32–3, 39. W.W. Greg noted that 'Mutius seems to be an extra son, for Titus had twenty-five and lost twenty-two, yet brought four to Rome'; quoted from Geoffrey Bullough, *Narrative and Dramatic Sources of Shakespeare* (1966), VI, p. 6, n. 3.

9. Chambers, WS, I, pp. 312–22; II, p. 346.

10. June Schlueter in 'Rereading the Peacham Drawing' in SQ (Summer 1999), pp. 171–83.

11. *Henslowe's Diary* (n. 3 above), p. 21.

12. Perhaps as a hangover from the old revision theory of the plays' origins, whereby it was believed that Parts 2 and 3 were written in advance of Part 1 for another company, Pembroke's men, and published by them as *The First part of the Contention betwixt the two famous Houses of Yorke and Lancaster* and *The true Tragedie of Richard Duke of Yorke*, which Shakespeare was thought to have later revised. However, in 1929 Peter Alexander convincingly demonstrated that the *Contention* and the *True Tragedie* were, in fact, memorial reconstructions of Shakespeare's plays pirated by actors – probably a break-away group from the Admiral's/Strange's alliance following the closure of the Rose season in February 1593. There is no evidence that Shakespeare had anything to do with Pembroke's men as either author or actor. Cf.

similarly comprehensive references to Parts 1 and 2 of *Henry IV* as simply *Henry IV* as noted by A.R. Humphreys in his Arden edition of Part 2 of that play (1966), p. xvi.

13. I derive these, and the figures that follow, from Chambers, ES, II, pp. 121–2.

14. Strange's men were at Oxford on 6 October and Coventry on 1 November; the Admiral's at Leicester on 19 December. While Strange's were performing at Hampton Court for the Queen on 31 December and 1 January 1593, the Admiral's were back at the Rose in the *Knack to Know a Knave* (on 31 December) and the *Jew of Malta* (on 1 January). This suggests that, though in alliance, the companies had retained performance right in the smaller-cast plays in their respective repertoires while joining forces only, perhaps, for the bigger productions, which would certainly have included *Titus* and the *Henry VI* plays.

15. I agree, however, with Chambers that, in view of Henslowe's manifest imprecision in his use of titles, it is not inconceivable that the play performed as *Buckingham* by Sussex's men at the Rose when the theatres reopened at the end of 1593 was Shakespeare's *Richard III*. It opened on 30 December, and three more performances were given in January 1594. If Buckingham is not the lead role in Shakespeare's play, it is the second lead. The fact that Sussex's company also gave two

performances of 'titus & andronicous' (undoubtedly Shakespeare's *Titus*) in the same short season (it closed on 6 February) suggests that the prompt-books of both *Titus* and *Richard III* had been retained by Henslowe on the breaking of the Admiral's/Strange's alliance (as he may have been entitled to do), and passed by him to Sussex's men for performance a year later. See Chambers, WS, I, pp. 303–4, 497–8; *Henslowe's Diary* (n. 3 above), pp. 20–1.

16. Prologue to the *Jew of Malta* at the Cockpit theatre, 1633, in *Works of Christopher Marlowe*, ed. C.F. Tucker Brooke (Oxford, 1910), p. 239.

17. V.iii.136. T.W. Baldwin in his *Organization and Personnel of the Shakespearean Company* (Princeton, 1927) gives the part to Heminges, the older actor of the later Chamberlain's company; but we need to remember that at this early date Shakespeare's fellows, including Heminges, Brian and Pope, cannot have been a great deal older than he was. Alleyn was younger, and Heminges went on to outlive him by fourteen years. It was a young company throughout.

18. As quoted by Chambers, WS, II, p. 188. Was Nashe's 'Tragedian' Edward Alleyn? As principal player of the company and foremost tragedian of his day, it would seem more than likely. But if so, he was much smaller in stature than his imposing portrait at Dulwich (Plate 7) suggests. For, on first meeting Talbot, the Countess of Auvergne – expecting 'some Hercules/ A second Hector' – is surprised to find a person she is overheard to describe as 'a silly dwarf', 'this weak and writhled shrimp' (II.iii.18–22). The part is usually assigned to Burbage, but there is no evidence that he was one of the company at this date. In view of the quarrel between Alleyn and Richard's father, James, that had brought the company to the Rose in the first place, it is most unlikely that he was.

19. From *Greenes Groats-worth of Wit* (1592) as quoted by Chambers, WS, II, p. 188.

20. From *Epistle* to *Kind-Harts Dreame* (n.d.); quoted by Chambers, WS, II, p. 189.

21. Quoted by J.C. Maxwell in his Arden edition of *Titus* (1953, 3rd edn of 1961), p. xxxiv.

22. In his 1962 Arden edition of *1 Henry VI*, p. xxviii.

23. At San Francisco in 1903, and again in 1935 (including *Richard III*); at Stratford in 1906 by Sir Frank Benson; by the Birmingham Repertory Theatre (*2 and 3 Henry VI*) in 1952, and later (*1 to 3 Henry VI*) at the Old Vic; by the RSC in heavily adapted versions by John Barton and Peter Hall as *The Wars of the Roses* in 1963; and again by the RSC, including *Richard III* but extensively edited to form three

plays as *The Plantagenets* by Adrian Noble, in 1988/9. The British theatre has yet to do justice to the four plays of the tetralogy by performing them in due sequence and in full. Perhaps the new, restored Globe will oblige?

24. *Johnson on Shakespeare*, ed. Walter Raleigh (Oxford, 1908, reprinted 1965), pp. 144, 136.

25. Hereward T. Price, *Construction in Shakespeare* (Michigan, 1951), p. 26, as quoted by Cairncross (n. 2 above), p. xli.

Chapter 6: The Player Poet

1. Quoted from *Schoenbaum, SL*, p. 182.

2. J.F. Goodridge, *Piers the Ploughman* (Penguin Classics, 1966 edn), p. 9.

3. For *Richard II*, III.ii.155–6; *Macbeth*, V.v.24–8; *Richard III*, V.v.23, 40–1.

4. For Sly, *Taming of the Shrew*, Ind., ii, 69–70; Demetrius, *Midsummer Night's Dream*, IV.i.192–4; Prospero, *Tempest*, IV.i.156–8.

5. For an account of their medieval history, see Southworth, EMM, chapters 3 and 7.

6. For the rehearsal of new plays, none of the players was provided with a complete copy of the text (as yet unpublished), but only with a transcript of their own speeches and cues. Once the actors had learnt their lines, these would often have been discarded. It may have been some of these that Bevis and his

fellows got hold of and incorporated in their pirated versions of the plays. For the company, see Chambers, ES, II, p. 128; Mary Edmond, 'Pembroke's Men' in *Review of English Studies*, NS, Vol. XXV, No. 98 (1974), pp. 129–30.

7. The wording is given in full by Chambers, WS, II, pp. 312–13.

8. Chambers, ES, IV, pp. 164–5.

9. Quoted from Chambers, WS, I, pp. 543–4.

10. The unreliable Davenant is credited by Rowe with a story that Southampton had given to Shakespeare 'a thousand pounds, to enable him to go through with a Purchase which he heard he had a mind to' (cited in Schoenbaum, SL, p. 65). Even if essentially true, the amount of the gift has been inflated beyond credibility in the retelling. In 1605, Edward Alleyn valued his 'share of aparell' in the Admiral's at £100 (Chambers, ES, II, p. 298). Southampton's gift could hardly have been more than that, and may have been less.

11. See Leech's introduction to his 1969 Arden edition of the play, pp. xxvi–xxx.

12. Professor T.W. Baldwin betrays his ignorance of the actor's craft when he opines that Shakespeare chose such roles because they required of him 'comparatively little acting to do' (*Organization and Personnel of the Shakespearean Company*, Princeton, 1927, p. 262). One has

only to see how poorly they are played in some modern productions to realise how mistaken the Professor was in his estimate of their inherent difficulty.

13. When the Ephesian Dromio and his master try unsuccessfully to gain admittance to their house (in III.i), we hear the voice of the Syracusan Dromio from within (either imitated by an actor backstage or spoken upstage by his twin), but there is no need for them to appear together. The only occasion on which they meet is in the final scene, where clearly look-alike doubles are required, but Antipholus and Dromio of Syracuse, who are the last to arrive on stage, have only 26 lines between them in the rest of the play, and the scene is kept as short as Shakespeare could reasonably make it, with the Abbess having all the longer speeches. By then, the light in an open-air performance on Innocents' Day in the winter would have been failing. If it is objected that the audience would be initially confused by such doubling, the answer is that they are meant to be confused, and it is from that general confusion that the essential humour of the play arises.

14. See the account printed by R.A. Foakes in his Arden edition of 1962, pp. 115–17.

15. *The Sonnets and A Lover's Complaint* (Penguin, 1986), p. 11. My italics.

16. *Shakespeare, The poet in his world* (1978, University Paperback edn, 1980), p. 79.

17. Chambers, WS, I, p. 515.

18. For a detailed study of these, see Eric Sams, *Shakespeare's Edward III* (New Haven and London, 1996), pp. 185–7 and notes.

19. For a deeper relationship between them, see Kerrigan (n. 15 above), pp. 293–5.

20. For a detailed synopsis and more sympathetic appreciation of the play and its themes, see Sams (n. 18 above), pp. 3–12.

21. See ll. 111, 793–4, 1660–6, 1720, and notes on these lines by John Roe in his New Cambridge edition of *The Poems* (Cambridge, 1992).

22. Chambers, WS, I, p. 546. Sir Edmund comments (*ibid.*, pp. 61–2): 'A super-subtle criticism detects a great advance in the poet's intimacy with his patron between the two addresses, which I am bound to say is not apparent to me'. If, as I believe, Shakespeare had received a financial reward from Southampton for *Venus and Adonis*, any increase of warmth discernible in the second letter is adequately explained, for then his patron could indeed be said to have made an investment in Shakespeare's future, so that 'what I have to doe is yours, being part in all I have' becomes no more than the literal truth of his situation at the time.

23. To play with conviction a Princess of France or one of her ladies was

not something that any intelligent choirboy or page could pick up in a matter of days or weeks; it was the result of years of continuous instruction from as early an age as eight. Though the London theatres had been closed since February 1593, the companies had continued to tour so the apprentices' training need not have been interrupted.

24. Chambers, WS, I, pp. 331–2.

Chapter 7: Chamberlain's Man

1. *A Life of William Shakespeare* (1923), pref., p. ix; quoted from Schoenbaum, SL, pp. 505–6.
2. Chambers, ES, II, p. 193. When, in July 1596, Henry Carey died and was succeeded as Lord Hunsdon by his son, Sir George Carey, and as Chamberlain by Lord Cobham, the company was to be known briefly once more as Lord Hunsdon's. It was only in March 1597, when Cobham died and was succeeded in turn by Sir George in his father's old office as Chamberlain, that the company was able to resume its former title.
3. Chambers, WS, II, p. 314.
4. He may, however, have appeared as the young Richard (afterwards Gloucester) in Part 3 of *Henry VI* at the Theatre before the dispute with Alleyn, and thus have prepared the ground for one of the most famous of his later roles, that of Richard III in Shakespeare's play.

5. A full account of the latter dispute is given by Chambers in ES, II, pp. 387–93.
6. *The Works of Thomas Nashe*, ed. R.B. McKerrow, revised F.P. Wilson (Oxford, 1958), III, p. 341.
7. That the *Knacke* was an Admiral's play, and that it was the Admiral's company that Kempe had joined on his return from the continent (not Strange's, as is usually stated), is proven by performance records for 31 December 1592 and 1 January 1593, for on those dates the *Knacke* and the *Jew of Malta* (another Admiral's play) were in performance at the Rose while Strange's were performing at court; see *Henslowe's Diary*, ed. Foakes and Rickert, p. 19, and Chambers, WS, II, p. 311.
8. On negative evidence, Chambers (ES, II, p. 340) assumes he was a Strange's man, though the record he quotes from an inventory of costumes belonging to the Admiral's in March 1598 after he had transferred to the Chamberlain's ('Perowes sewt, which Wm Sley were') indicates the contrary.
9. For biographical information, above and below, I have drawn mainly on Chambers, ES, II, pp. 295–350, and WS, II, pp. 71–87; Nungezer, *Dictionary*; and Bentley, JCS, II. For the players' wills, see *Wills*.
10. See Bentley, PPST, p. 221, para 2. In the *Seven Deadly Sins*, 'Mr Bryan' plays the part of a Councillor to Burbage's leading role as Goboduc,

and Warwick in a concluding scene with Henry VI and Sincler as his Keeper. (Was Warwick Bryan's part in *Henry VI, Part 3* as the Keeper was Sincler's?) In another plot (for *The Battle of Alcazar, c.* 1598), a 'Mr Charles' has three supporting roles, and 'Mr Sam', six (*ibid.*, pp. 213, 230–1).

11. See Bentley, PPST, pp. 118–26. William Trigg, a leading player of women's roles in the Caroline period, was thirteen or fourteen when apprenticed to John Heminges for a period of twelve years to learn 'la arte d'une Stage player'; he would thus have been twenty-five or twenty-six before achieving his freedom. Some of the guilds (and the Grocers may have been one of them) withheld enfranchisement until the apprentice was twenty-four – as ordained by the Statute of Artificers of 1563, Section 19.

12. In 1597, Henslowe 'bought' a boy, James Bristow, for £8 – presumably from a player to whom James had initially been apprenticed on payment of a premium – and received 3s a week from the Admiral's in respect of his services; Chambers, ES, II, pp. 153, 155.

13. In the Induction to Marston's *The Malcontent* of 1603, Condell appears under his own name, and is asked for as 'Harry Condell' (Revels edn, l. 11.) Beeston went on to a successful career as actor-manager in the Jacobean and Caroline theatre. He is thought to have provided information to John Aubrey regarding Shakespeare's mode of life in the time they had worked together as Chamberlain's men. To this I return.

14. In 1592, he is recorded as a Pembroke's man (Mary Edmond in *Review of English Studies*, 25, 1974, p. 131), but in 1593 the company had collapsed on the road, which may have prompted his move to the Chamberlain's and change of occupation.

15. See n. 11 above. Heminges had probably achieved his freedom of the Grocers by performing at their feasts – a means of entry for which there is long precedent among entertainers. Among other Chamberlain's men and 'principal actors' known to have enjoyed the freedom of one or other of the London guilds were Robert Armin and John Lowin of the Goldsmiths, John Shank of the Weavers, and James Burbage of the Joiners. Robert Armin (who succeeded Kempe in his clown roles) is on record as apprenticing another player in the same craft, as Heminges had apprenticed Cooke. There is no evidence that any of these men practised at any time the crafts of which they were nominally 'free'.

16. See *Wills*, pp. 94–6.

17. *Ibid.*, pp. 73, 80. The specific mention of Sandes' 'Indenture' is interesting in view of what has been said above (n. 15). Chambers (WS,

II, p. 85) reluctantly allows that Phillips may have been a member of the London Company of Minstrels and Musicians, and that Sandes may have followed him into that indistinct profession; but the ability to play musical instruments was, if not *de rigueur*, common among players of the time, and Phillips could just as easily have been free of any one of the guilds, and used it (as Heminges had done) to hold his apprentice. To have taken over from him in the way that he did, Sly must have belonged to the same guild.

18. Among later recruits to be named in the Folio as sharers and principal actors were John Lowin (from 1603), William Ostler (1610), Nathan Field (1615, a former pupil of Ben Jonson's) – all of whom we shall meet again in later chapters – John Underwood (1608), Richard Robinson (1611) and John Rice (before 1607, another of Heminges' apprentices). Of these, Ostler, Field, Underwood and Robinson had begun their careers as children in one of the royal chapels or Queen's Revels, and joined the King's men as adolescents.

19. The text of neither part of the *Seven Deadly Sins* has survived. Though described by Henslowe in his *Diary* as 'Four Plays in One', it is clear from the plot that the second part comprised only three plays, preceded by a Prologue, in which Pride, Wrath and Covetousness (presumably the subjects of Part 1) are ejected from the stage by Envy,

Sloth and Lechery, the subjects of Part 2. It is at this point that Henry VI (as played, I believe, by Shakespeare), who has been asleep, perhaps dreaming, in a tent, wakes up and is joined by J. Sincler as the Keeper. The Prologue's author may here have been drawing on Act 3, Scene 1 of Shakespeare's *Henry VI, Part 3*, which also features Henry VI and Sincler as a Keeper, and for an Epilogue – in which Henry is joined by others including 'warders' and Warwick, played by Bryan – made use of other speeches from that play.

20. The player-musicians included William Tawyer, the trumpeter of the *Dream* (V.i.125) and Jack Wilson, the lutenist and singer of 'Sigh no more, ladies' in *Much Ado* (II.iii.36); but we cannot claim these two as necessarily original members of the company as their names (unlike those previously cited from rogue directions and speech prefixes) are more likely to derive from the prompt books of later revivals than from Shakespeare's original manuscripts. See Alison Gaw, 'Actors' Names in Basic Shakespearean Texts' in PMLA, 40 (1925), pp. 532–3.

21. When, in the early 1950s, the then directors of the Old Vic (Michel Saint-Denis, Glen Byam Shaw and George Devine) had proposed a similar organisational structure for the company that was intended to form the basis for a future National Theatre, incorporating a school and

youth theatre (the Young Vic) which were already in existence, the Old Vic governors were advised by various well-known theatre people of the time that such a structure, though long established and notably successful in other European capitals, would be inimical to 'English theatrical tradition', and in consequence it was shamefully abandoned; an indication of the depth of ignorance prevailing at the time (and which regrettably still largely prevails both in and out of the profession) concerning our own theatrical history in the period of its finest achievements.

22. See Bentley, PDST, *passim*.
23. Chambers, ES, IV, p. 316. He concedes that 'where heretofore they began not their Plaies till towards fower a clock, they will now begin at two, & have don betwene fower and five, and will nott use anie Drumes or trumpettes att all for the callinge of peopell together . . .'.
24. Chambers, WS, II, p. 319; for the amount, ES, IV, pp. 164–5. As the Admiral's were also paid for a court performance on the 28th and, as previously stated, the Chamberlain's performance of the *Comedy of Errors* at Grays Inn was given on the same evening, the second of the two Greenwich dates is usually taken to be a mistake for the 27th. This may be so; but the *Comedy* is Shakespeare's shortest play, and the distance between Greenwich and the City is not so great as to make it

impossible for the players to have gone by river from an afternoon performance at Greenwich to Grays Inn where, we are told, the audience did not arrive until 9 p.m. and where the festivities were further delayed by a 'disordered Tumult and Crowd upon the stage' (*Gesta Grayoram*, as quoted by R.A. Foakes in his Arden edition of the play, pp. 115–17). The Admiral's performance may have followed that of the Chamberlain's on the same evening. The Christmas season was harvest-time for the players and they would have needed to make the most of it.

25. It is sometimes supposed that it is easier and more practicable to double parts that are similar in age, diction, character or appearance than those which are contrasting in one or more of these respects; as an actor himself, Shakespeare would have known that the opposite is true. The more different the parts, the easier it is for the actor to make the necessary distinctions between them by drawing on contrasting facets of his own personality. If he is able to do this, there is also less risk of confusing the audience. In a non-naturalistic theatre such as Shakespeare's, in which 'doubling' (by which is meant playing more than one part, perhaps three or more) is an accepted convention, there is no requirement for the actor to conceal his identity when performing duplicate roles; simply to make them true to themselves in all their differences.

26. Of the other five plays that open with a Prologue (*Henry IV, Part 2, Henry V, Henry VIII, Troilus and Cressida*, and *Pericles*), all but *Troilus* end with a formal Epilogue.

27. I am indebted to T.J.B. Spencer's defence of the Friar in his Penguin edition of the play (1967), pp. 8, 36. The character may have been based by Shakespeare on one of the recusant priests he had met with in Stratford during the period of his father's return to the Catholicism of his youth in the late 1570s or early '80s. Cf. Greene's paltry treatment of the thirteenth-century English Franciscan, Roger Bacon, in his *Friar Bacon and Friar Bungay* of about 1589.

28. As quoted by William A. Armstrong, 'Actors and Theatres', in SS 17 (1964), p. 196.

29. From Preface by Rhenanus to *Speculum Aistheticum* of 1613, as cited and translated by David Klein, 'Notes on "Did Shakespeare Produce His Own Plays?"' in MLR 57 (October 1962), p. 556. For other references to the poet's function at rehearsals, see Klein, pp. 556–60.

30. See Bentley, PPST, pp. 113–16.

31. He was the author of a number of published jigs – a lost performance art involving characterisation and song, as well as dance. Marston's *Scourge of Villainy* (Satire XI.31) of 1598 has the lines,

A hall, a hall!
Room for the spheres, the orbs celestial
Will dance Kempe's jig (Nungezer, p. 218)
that echo Capulet's,

A hall, a hall, give room! And foot it, girls!
More light, you knaves, and turn the tables up. (I.v.26–7)

32. In the course of an English Heritage survey by Simon Blatherwick, as reported in *The Times* of 11 January 1999, p. 3.

33. Chambers, WS, II, p. 252. According to the way it is punctuated, these phrases can be, and sometimes are, interpreted as meaning 'Lived in Shoreditch; wouldn't be debauched, and, if invited [to be debauched], replied he was in pain'. But is anyone normally *invited* to be debauched? And if someone was so invited, would they normally excuse themselves by saying they were *in pain*? I find it easier to believe that Shakespeare was often in pain in writing his plays.

34. Chambers, WS, I, p. 356. My italics.

35. Introduction to his Penguin edition of 1967, p. 13.

36. For the court performances, Chambers, WS, II, p. 321.

37. Chambers, WS, II, p. 320; MSC 2, Part 3, p. 279. The amount of their reward was twice as much as that received by the Queen's, and four times that by the Admiral's men in 1596/7.

38. My personal experience suggests that if one can get the play started in the right way, even at the cost of a disproportionate amount of

rehearsal time, the chances of its staying on course to the end are vastly improved. To have Shakespeare on stage for both opening and concluding scenes would have been double insurance!

39. On the basis of some lines in *Hamlet*, Professor Baldwin (*Organization and Personnel of the Shakespearean Company*, Princeton, 1927, pp. 230ff.) proposed that each of the players had a set line of parts ('player king', 'adventurous knight', 'humorous man' etc.) that was consistently adhered to in the casting of the plays. Apart from the thin man, Sincler (in a category of his own), and to some extent Kempe or Armin as clowns and Shakespeare in his kingly parts, there is no real evidence of this; nor does the theory take into account the frequent necessity for doubling, especially in the histories. Great credit is nevertheless due to Baldwin who, virtually alone among serious scholars, attempted to throw some much-needed light on the matter. Though my own suggestions as to casting rarely accord with his, I have consulted them throughout, and am indebted to his discussion of the problems.

40. Andrew Gurr, in his New Cambridge edition of *Richard II* of 1984, among other scholars, dates the play to 1595 partly on the basis of a letter written by Sir Edward Hoby on 7 December of that year to Lord Burleigh, inviting him to 'visit poore Channon rowe where as late as it shal please you a gate for your supper shal be open: & K. Richard present him selfe to your vewe' (pp. 1–2). Hoby is known to have been a collector of historical portraits, and the letter reads to me more like an invitation to view a recent acquisition of that kind (not necessarily of the *second* Richard) than a two or three-hour performance of Shakespeare's play, of which Burleigh and Hoby were apparently to be the only auditors. How late would the players have been expected to remain in waiting for Burleigh? and how late would Burleigh have been expected to stay?

41. See Chambers, WS, I, p. 373: *The Merchant of Venice*, ed. John Russell Brown (Arden edn, 1955, reprinted 1964), pp. xxv–vii.

42. It is interesting to find that nearly all of Shakespeare's Balthasars (in the *Comedy of Errors, Romeo*, and here) are obvious doubles for one or other of the sharers. The Balthasar of *Much Ado* is the exception.

43. The attitude of Elizabethan playwrights to the Jews in general is more complex than is often supposed; nor were they unaware or uncritical of hypocrisy in the behaviour of Christians towards them. In Robert Wilson's *Three Ladies of London*, a popular morality of the 1580s, the Jew Gerontus is depicted as a paragon of upright dealing and generosity, in pointed contrast to Mercatore, a

Christian merchant who, having borrowed money of the Jew, seeks to avoid repayment by fraud, perjury in a Turkish court, and finally apostasy. Gerontus is so appalled by the merchant's willingness to deny his religion that he remits the debt as, in Shakespeare's play, Antonio remits a part of the fine imposed on Shylock. Mercatore later boasts that he has 'cosen'd' the Jew. The Turkish judge in the case concludes that 'Jews seek to excel in Christianity and Christians in Jewishness'. The text of the play is in Dodsley's *Old English Plays*, ed. W.C. Hazlitt, VI (1874).

44. The skilful use that Shakespeare makes of the natural dimming of light in the late afternoon of autumn and winter days in the theatres where his plays were performed has not always been noticed or appreciated. The hour at which his final scenes are said to take place is often found to correspond, more or less exactly, with the actual time a 2 o'clock performance would by then have reached in the theatre. In the *Comedy of Errors*, the Duke's doom on Egeon is timed to take effect at five in the evening and that is the hour of its final scene; the play of the Nine Worthies in Act 5 of *Love's Labour's Lost* is intended, as Holofernes says, for the 'posterior of the day'; and when, in the last act of the *Tempest*, Prospero asks of Ariel, 'How's the day?', the spirit replies, 'On the sixth

hour'. Sometimes, as in the *Merchant*, candles and other lights are introduced, and I see no reason to doubt that they were practical. In Act 5 of *Romeo*, Paris and Romeo enter the darkness of the cemetery accompanied by torchbearers, and the Friar carries a lantern. The fairies in Act 5 of the *Dream* are commanded, 'Through the house give glimmering light/By the dead and drowsy fire' and, as the New Cambridge edition notes, this is explained by a stage direction in the Bad Quarto text of the *Merry Wives* (probably descriptive of performance) instructing the pretend fairies of that play to enter with 'waxen tapers on their heads', which, as Mistress Page explains, 'at the very instant of Falstaff's and our meeting, they will at once display to the night' (V.iii.14–16). (If the tapers were fixed to their heads with bands, both sets of fairies would have been free to dance 'hand-in-hand'.) The final scene of *Othello* begins with Desdemona asleep in bed and the entrance of Othello 'with a light'. These are not just tokens to the audience that a degree of darkness is to be imagined, but more probably actual lights that on a shadowed stage would both have illumined the action to some extent and, more importantly, added to the atmosphere that Shakespeare wished to create.

45. The year is given by Chambers (in WS, II, p. 321) under a heading of 1597 but, as he points out

elsewhere, the Faversham visit must have been in 1596 because the company is named there as Lord Hunsdon's players and it was only known by that title between 22 July 1596, when the first Lord Hunsdon died, and 5 March 1597, when his son succeeded him as Chamberlain. See also MSC VII, p. 63, where the entry is correctly placed in 1595/6.

46. Victorian scholars liked to date *King John* to this year because they thought that Shakespeare's rather idealised portrait of young Arthur in that play was his memorial to Hamnet; but I am one of those who consider that if *John* had been completed after rather than before his son's death, he would have written about Arthur in a different way, or perhaps not at all.

47. Chambers, WS, II, p. 321. The dates were 26 and 27 December, 1 and 6 January, and 6 and 8 February. The three pairs of dates suggest that three plays were given, and each in turn repeated a day or two later, to allow more of the Queen's household and guests to see them than could easily be accommodated at a single performance.

48. I am indebted here to Baldwin, who assigns it with probability to Condell.

Chapter 8: He that Plays the King

1. From *The Scourge of Folly*, Epigram 159, in *The Complete Works of John Davies of Hereford*, ed. Alexander B. Grosart (2 vols, privately printed, 1878), II, p. 26.

2. From *Microcosmos* (1603) in *Complete Works* (*op. cit.*), I, p. 82.

3. From *Speculum Proditori* in *Complete Works* (note 1 above), II, p. 18.

4. From *Scourge of Folly,* Epigram 180, *Complete Works,* II, p. 28.

5. I have previously suggested that the play was originally written for the Admiral's/Strange's alliance at the Rose in 1592/3. When revived by Shakespeare for the Chamberlain's in 1595/6, it became necessary to reduce its length and the number of its roles. It is now generally accepted as probable that the prompt-book of this revised text was somehow lost (perhaps on tour) and, Shakespeare's original manuscript not being readily to hand, was reconstructed from memory by the actors, including Shakespeare, for its publication in the Quarto edition of 1597. By 1623, Shakespeare's manuscript had resurfaced and was used by Heminges and Condell in combination with the published Quarto for their fuller version of the play in the First Folio. See Antony Hammond's introduction to his Arden edition of 1981, pp. 1–50.

6. See previous note. Hammond describes Clarence as a 'gift' part: 'Into his dream Shakespeare poured the most impassioned, lyrically active verse in the play. Most other characters are assigned a single tone of voice, but apart from Richard

Clarence alone is allowed the span of the poet's abilities' (Introduction, p. 111). Note also the recollections in the dream speech of the Ghost of Andrea from the *Spanish Tragedy*, as listed in Section 3 of Appendix A. As the ghosts in the last act of *Richard*, including that of Clarence, are not individualised in manner or diction, and announce in a ritual way who they are on appearance, Shakespeare's presence on stage as Richmond, sleeping in his tent, would not have created any difficulty. Probably, the ghosts wore identical shrouds and masks and spoke in diguised spectral voices, and thus could have been played by any of the actors who happened to be available. They are shades from a classical Hades, rather than spirits from a Catholic Purgatory who (like the Ghost in *Hamlet*) retain much of their human personalities and concerns.

7. Quoted from Geoffrey Bullough, *Narrative and Dramatic Sources of Shakespeare*, IV, p. 148.

8. Of the speech in question (III.i.263ff.), contrary to those who see in it a parody of riddling casuistry, Dr Johnson comments, 'I am not able to discover here any thing inconsequent or ridiculously subtle. The propositions that the voice of the church is the voice of heaven, and that the Pope utters the voice of the church, neither of which Pandulph's auditors would deny, being once granted, the argument used is irresistible; nor is it easy, notwithstanding the gingle, to enforce it with greater brevity or propriety'. I am indebted for this quotation, and other points in my discussion, to John Dover Wilson's introduction to the New Cambridge edition of the play (1936, reprinted 1954), pp. lvii–lxii.

9. For this location, see John Wasson, *Suffolk in the History Plays of Shakespeare*, Xth Harry Clement Memorial Lecture at Keynes Hall, King's College, Cambridge (Suffolk Federation of WEA, 1974), pp. 4–7.

10. For this timing of events, I am drawing on that proposed by A.R. Humphreys in his Arden edition of Part One of *Henry IV* (1960); see especially pp. xiii–xv. For the *Merry Wives*, see following chapter.

11. John Marston in his *Scourge of Villanie* of 1598 speaks of 'Curtaine plaudeties' in connection with *Romeo and Juliet*, which, in 1597, would still have been in the company's repertoire (quoted in Chambers, WS, II, pp. 195–6).

12. The possibility of 'out of town' openings for these and other of Shakespeare's plays was not seriously considered by Chambers, being out of the sphere of his experience of theatre in the period when he wrote, the early 1900s, when such an expedient was rarer than it has since become. There are, however, distinct advantages, as later producers have discovered, in opening plays in the course of a pre-

London provincial tour – especially from the point of view of the author, who is thereby enabled to put his work to the test of an audience and introduce whatever changes are required in the light of that experience in a gradual, unpressured way.

13. This was first proposed by Professor H.D. Gray, 'The Roles of William Kempe', in MLR 25 (1930), pp. 265–7, and taken up by Professor Wilson in *The Fortunes of Falstaff* (Cambridge, 1943), pp. 124–5. The discussion that follows draws (with amendment) on that in Southworth, F & J, pp. 131–3.

14. I am using the term 'buffoon' in the specialised sense of the medieval *scurra*, a type of court fool distinguished by his innate cleverness and talent to amuse, typically literate and belonging to the minor armorial class. For some historical precedents see Southworth, F & J, 'buffoons' as indexed.

15. Chambers, ES, II, p. 326.

16. *Kemps Nine Daies Wonder: Performed in a Morrice from London to Norwich* (1600), ed. G.B. Harrison (Bodley Head Quartos, 1923), p. 3.

Chapter 9: The Globe, 1599–1601

1. From *Theatre of the World* (1969), p. 189.

2. Critics have argued that for him to have done so required Falstaff to reform and that this would have been contrary to the character's essential nature as previously established; but it would have been quite in character for him to have *pretended* reform, and so convinced the king of his sincerity as to be included in his army. In substituting Falstaff for his original name of Oldcastle, Shakespeare was drawing on a minor character in Part One of *Henry VI*, who is denounced as a 'cowardly knight' in that play; but he may also have had it in mind from Holinshed that the historical Fastolfe, a lieutenant in service of the Duke of Exeter, was appointed to command the garrison of Harfleur after its capture by the king, which would have provided ample scope for further backsliding on the part of Sir John. In the event, he had no choice but to insert the scene in which his earlier death is reported by Mistress Quickly (II.iii), and to suppress the fact of Fastolfe's appointment.

3. *The Chronicle History of Henry the fift, With his battell fought at Agin Court in France, Togither with Auntient Pistoll. As it hath bene sundry times playd by the Right honorable the Lord Chamberlaine his servants.*

4. In so doing they sentimentalise Falstaff. He dies of a 'quotidian tertian', not of a broken heart. However he got there, he is doubtless in Arthur's bosom. Theobald's emendation in Quickly's speech of the Folio's 'and a Table of greene fields' to 'a babbled of green fields'

was inspirational but may have been mistaken, as a slight rearrangement of the speech renders it unnecessary without changing a word: 'For after I saw him fumble with the sheets and play wi'th' flowers, and smile upon his fingers' ends *and a table of green fields,* I knew there was but one way, for his nose was as sharp as a pen . . .'. 'Table' was the Tudor term for small, alabaster plaques depicting devotional subjects, including the decapitated head of St John the Baptist on a salver, of the type manufactured in Nottingham for private use of the laity up to the time of the Reformation. These were brightly painted, and surviving examples on which some traces of paint remain show a green field in the lower background, dotted with daisies (see Francis Cheetham, *English Medieval Alabasters,* Oxford, 1984, pp. 317–32). John the Baptist was of course Sir John's name saint, and he dies calling on God.

5. This sequence of events is supported by his description of himself in the first edition of his *Foole upon Foole* – published in 1600 but written a year or so earlier, as also in his *Quips upon Questions* of similar date – as 'Clonnico de *Curtanio* Snuffe', and in a later edition of *Foole upon Foole* in 1605, as 'Clonnico del *Mondo* Snuffe'. See Chambers, ES, II, p. 300.

6. See II.iv.37 for the 'Roman Brutus'; Fluellen's references to the 'Roman disciplines' and wars in III.ii; to

Pompey the Great at IV.i.70; and, most pertinently, the chorus to Act 5, where 'the senators of th'antique Rome/With the plebeians swarming at their heels,/Go forth and fetch their conquering Caesar in' (ll. 26–8).

7. As quoted in David Daniell's Arden edition of 1998, p. 12. The German original is in Chambers, ES, II, pp. 364–5.

8. For Burbage's roles, see Chambers, ES, II, pp. 308–9. In Jonson's actor lists, his name appears in first place in the tragedies, in *Every Man Out of his Humour* (1599), *Volpone* (1605?), and *The Alchemist* (1610), but in only sixth place in the earlier *Every Man in his Humour* (1598) behind Shakespeare, Phillips, Condell, Sly and Kempe.

9. This would have given particular point to Caesar's line, 'The skies are painted with unnumbered sparks' (III.i.63); and it may be significant that, in the night before the murder when the conspirators are due to meet, the skies are covered with cloud so that Brutus is unable to tell the time from 'the progress of the stars'; he is losing his way.

10. Quoted by Alan Brissenden in his Oxford edition of the play (1993), p. 1.

11. Quoted from Chambers, WS, II, p. 278.

12. *The Life and Times of William Shakespeare* (1988), p. 209.

13. There is some confusion in the Folio text as to the relative heights of

Rosalind and Celia. At I.ii.262, Celia is said to be the taller of the two, but at I.iii.111 Rosalind claims to be 'more than common tall', while at IV.iii.87 Celia is described as 'low'. This may indicate a change of cast during what is likely to have been an extended run or, perhaps to share the load, the two young actors involved exchanged roles on occasion.

14. There is only one difficult change: from Jaques to Frederick between II.vii and III.i, which would require Jaques to make an early exit from II.vii – perhaps at the end of his 'seven ages' speech or during Amiens' song. Or was there a pause in the action at this point?

15. For more about Armin, see Leslie Hotson, *Shakespeare's Motley* (1952), pp. 84–128; Charles S. Felver, *Robert Armin, Shakespeare's Fool* (Kent State University Bulletin, Research Series V, Ohio, 1961; Southworth, F & J, for Armin, pp. 133–6, and Stone, 139–40. My quotation is from Armin's preface to his 1608 edition of the *Two Maids of More-clacke*: 'I commit it into your hands to be scan'd, and you shall find verse, as well blancke, as crancke, yet in the prose let it passe for currant. I would have againe inacted *John* myselfe, but *Tempora mutantur in illis. . . .*'

16. Some scholars have found inconsistency in his early scenes as to the kind of fool Touchstone is intended to be; on his first entrance,

for example, he is referred to by Celia as a 'natural'; but this is surely Celia's attempt at a deliberate put-down, which the clown takes in his stride and immediately demonstrates is unfounded. The part as written was, I believe, conceived from the start as for Armin. In view of his skill as a singer, which he had demonstrated in the *Two Maids*, it is odd, however, that he is not given any songs to sing.

17. It probably comprised doublet and hose, and was of the kind supplied by the Queen to her court fools Hoyden and Shenton in 1574/5, which included 'canyons' (thigh-fitting extensions of trunk hose, reaching to the knee), doublets of striped sackcloth, and a coat of wrought velvet, 'paned' in red, green and yellow (see Southworth, F & J, p. 113 and Chapter 17, 'The Fools' Motley').

18. For Dennis, see Chambers, WS, II, p. 263.

19. *In Shakespeare versus Shallow* (1931), pp. 119–22.

20. Chambers, WS, I, p. 434.

21. See Hibbard's introduction to his Penguin edition of the play (1973), pp. 48–50. A further point that Professor Hibbard makes in support of this hypothesis is Shakespeare's treatment of the Welsh parson, Sir Hugh Evans. Shakespeare's Welsh parts in the period form a sequence which I have earlier traced from *Richard II* to *Henry V* and associated with the arrival and

advance in the company of Robert Armin. Hibbard points out that not only do the parts become progressively bigger and more important, but they also become more obviously Welsh. The Welsh Captain of *Richard II* is the smallest and betrays no trace of an accent; Glendower is susceptible to being spoken with a Welsh lilt but his pronunciation is not apparent in the writing; Fluellen, with his confusion of 'p's and 'b's, 'look you's' and verbal repetitions is unmistakably Welsh, and Sir Hugh goes further in the same comedic direction: 'Trib, trib, fairies. Come. And remember your parts. Be pold, I pray you. Follow me into the pit, and when I give the watch-'ords, do as I pid you. Come, come; trib, trib' (V.iv). 'Evans', the Professor concludes, 'must be the last term in the series; and *The Merry Wives of Windsor* must have followed *Henry V*' (*ibid.*, p. 49). It should also be noticed that there is no trace of Sir Hugh's peculiarities of pronunciation in his part as satyr in the masque, and that in a similar way Quickly's malapropisms and other idiosyncrasies of speech disappear from her lines as the Fairy Queen, indicating that the masque was written first, and for a different occasion.

22. See Hibbard, *op. cit.*, pp. 42–6; and H.J. Oliver in his Arden edition of 1971, pp. lxvii–lxx.

23. A clue to the actors playing the Host and, less certainly, Falstaff, is provided by the 'bad' quarto text (Q1) published in 1602, which most editors agree is a pirated report of a performance supplied in part by two of the original performers, identified by the exceptional accuracy with which their lines are reported. As only two actors, Kit Beeston and John Duke, are known to have left the company between 1598 (when they are listed by Jonson as appearing in *Every Man in his Humour*) and 1602, by which time they had joined Queen Anne's men – and it is hardly conceivable that any others would have risked their employment in such a way for what was doubtless a paltry fee – the finger of suspicion points to them. Were they, in fact, fired for their disloyalty? If the suspects are so obvious to modern editors four hundred years later, they would have been even more apparent to their fellows at the time. Interestingly, Oliver (n. 22 above, p. xxvii, n. 2) suggests that the actor who played the Host may also have understudied Falstaff which, if so, would let one of them off the hook!

24. For the dating of *Hamlet*, see Chambers, WS, I, pp. 423–4; Harold Jenkins, Arden edition (1982), pp. 1–13. For *Twelfth Night*, Chambers, WS, I, p. 405; Leslie Hotson, *The First Night of 'Twelfth Night'* (1954).

25. As quoted in Chambers, WS, II, p. 265.

26. Levi (n. 12 above), p. 218.

27. Quoted from Chambers, ES, II, p. 309. But the casting is not without its problems; there is a discrepancy of age. The impression we get of the character from all that is said about him in the earlier part of the play is of a very young man; a fellow-student and contemporary of Rosencrantz and Guildenstern at Wittenberg at a time when university education normally began earlier and finished sooner than it does today. He is consistently referred to as 'young Hamlet'; and yet, in Act 5, the Grave-digger tells us that he came to his work thirty years ago – 'that very day that young Hamlet was born' (V.i.143); and, in the midst of the duel, Gertrude comments to Claudius that Hamlet is 'fat and scant of breath' (V.ii.290), which, even if 'fat' is interpreted as 'out of condition', is a strange thing to say of an eighteen or nineteen-year-old youth who assures Horatio of his 'continual practice' (V.II.207). It sounds very much as if Shakespeare had originally intended the part for a much younger actor but, in the course of writing the play, changed his mind, and decided (whatever the reason) to give it to the 33-year-old Burbage.

28. *Shakespeare and the Idea of the Play* (1962), pp. 158–9.

29. In his 1982 Arden edition, p. 479, citing Schlegel.

30. The role would have gone to one of Shakespeare's senior fellows – probably Phillips or Heminges – who would have had experience of the earlier, more rhetorical style of verse employed by Kyd and Marlowe, and had worked with Alleyn, its finest exponent. But if a memory of Alleyn was present to the player – and had been present also perhaps to Shakespeare when he wrote it – it is far more likely to have been intended as a tribute than a parody. See William Armstrong, 'Shakespeare and the Acting of Edward Alleyn' in SS 7 (1954), pp. 82–9.

31. G.B. Harrison, in his notes to the Penguin edition of 1937, p. 170, goes so far as to say that 'Both the attack on the ranting tragedian and the conceited clown are directed against individuals', and that 'The latter is obviously Will Kempe'; whereas there is not a scrap of evidence to suggest that any such 'ranting tragedian' would have been tolerated for a moment in the Chamberlain's company, or that Kempe was either conceited or had ever indulged in the sort of behaviour Hamlet is deploring.

32. *Johnson on Shakespeare*, ed. Walter Raleigh (Oxford, 1908, 1965 edn), p. 93.

33. I have been drawing here on Leslie Hotson (n. 24 above), p. 180 and *passim*, and remain unconvinced by the objections to Hotson's hypothesis made in recent editions of the play. Chambers dates it before *Hamlet* to 1600/1 (WS, I, pp. 404–7). It may be, as T.W. Craik

remarks, 'downright simplicity' to suggest, along with John Downes in 1708, that it was called *Twelfth Night* because 'it was got up on purpose to be Acted on Twelfth Night' (Arden, 1975, p. xxxiv); perhaps I am very simple, but this still seems to me the most likely explanation.

34. Cf. Sir Toby's reference to Andrew as playing the viol-de-gamboys (I.iii.25) and (in relation to his hair) 'I hope to see a housewife take thee between her legs and spin it off' (I.iii.99–101), with the passage in the Induction to Marston's *The Malcontent* (1604), in which Sincler features under his own name and, when Sly invites him to sit between his legs, refuses on the grounds that 'the audience then will take me for a viol-de-gamboy, and think that you play upon me' (Revels edition, 1975, p. 9, ll. 20–1). Some academics dismiss the possibility of Sincler having played the role because it is too important for a 'small-part' or 'bit' player. But, as in any half-decent repertory company, members of the Chamberlain's were allowed, and doubtless encouraged, to develop, and the parts that Shakespeare wrote for them were as small or as large as he wanted them to be.

35. I am indebted for this idea to John Harrison's production at the Nottingham Playhouse in January 1957, with designs by Voytek, in which I had the good fortune to play Sir Andrew.

Chapter 10: Travelling Man

1. From *Early English Stages, 1300 to 1660*, Vol. 2 (1576–1660), Part 1 (1963), p. 183.

2. H.E. Salter, *Oxford Council Acts, 1583–1626* (Oxford, 1928), p. 382. For this possibility, see Chambers, ES, II, pp. 205–7.

3. Chambers, WS, II, pp. 326–7.

4. *Ibid.*, pp. 327–8.

5. For this dating, see Chambers, WS, I, pp. 443, 451. David Bevington suggests late in 1601 for *Troilus* (Arden edition of 1998, p. 11), and G.K. Hunter, 1603/4 for *All's Well* (Arden, 1959, p. xxv).

6. Chambers, ES, II, p. 208; my italics.

7. I am indebted for these figures to the table given by Professor Leeds Barroll in his *Politics, Plague, and Shakespeare's Theater, The Stuart Years* (Ithaca and London, 1991), p. 223.

8. As cited above (n. 6); again, my italics.

9. As Glynne Wickham discovered, the great majority of performances by players in general in the period, including all localities, were given indoors. See *Early English Stages* (n. 1 above), pp. 176–9.

10. According to the records collated by Chambers (WS, II, pp. 319–43), they were at Richmond in 1595, 1598/9, 1600 and 1602/3; at Greenwich in 1594, 1605/6, 1611/12 and 1613; at Hampton Court in 1603/4 and 1605/6; and at Wilton in 1603.

11. Stanley Wells, Gary Taylor *et al.*, *William Shakespeare, A Textual Companion* (Oxford, 1987), p. 90.

12. The Oxford editors argue that during the summer months of July and August, 'the smart set left London for their country estates' and that Queen Elizabeth chose this time of year for her annual progresses; but I doubt that the movements of the 'smart set' – or, for that matter, the court – had much effect on business at the Globe, which was a popular theatre seating upwards of 2000 people and largely dependent for its success on a popular audience, most of whom would have had to cross the river to get to it. There is, of course, no evidence for the scholarly assumption that Shakespeare did not accompany his fellows on tour. How would he have been replaced as player in such a tight-knit ensemble, operating without subsidy and with only occasional help from its patrons? Precise dates for the companies' appearances in provincial towns are so infrequent that it is unsafe to draw any firm conclusions from them, but they do not uphold the Oxford editors' claim that, ignoring plague years, 'the summer months account for almost every datable reference to a provincial performance by a London company [?] with which Shakespeare was – or may have been – associated'. On a cursory survey, I find the Admiral's men at Ipswich on 20 February 1586 and 26 May 1587, and at Shrewsbury on 3 February 1592. Strange's men were at Exeter on 17 April 1580, and Leicester's (another contender for the title of Shakespeare's first company) at Exeter on 23 March 1586, at Maidstone on 23 January 1587, Dover on 4 March, Bristol between 9 and 15 April, and Plymouth on 15 May of the same year. Conversely, the Admiral's were at the Rose throughout the summers of 1597 and 1598, in which years they appear not to have travelled at all. In February 1600, they bought a drum and trumpets to 'go into the country', but were back at the Rose between 2 March and 13 July. For the later, plague-free period between 1611 and 1625 (focusing on a single city), the Prince's men were at Coventry on 7 November 1614 and 13 December 1622; the King's men on 10 January 1620; and Lady Elizabeth's men on 4 January 1618, 5 January 1620, and 24 January 1622; all these were so-called 'London companies'.

13. The great majority of court performances recorded at Whitehall or outlying palaces are found to occur in the Christmas holiday period between 26 December and Shrove Tuesday, the eve of the Lenten season, during which playing was inhibited in the City – though not necessarily in the county of Surrey, where the Globe and most other public playhouses were situated. It

follows, therefore, that at Christmas each year, through January to the beginning of Lent in February or March, the players would necessarily have been stationed in or about London, but that, until the opening of the Blackfriars indoor playhouse in 1609, performances at the Globe would have been restricted in most years by the severity of the weather. The evidence for Lent is ambiguous but in general suggests – at least in the Stuart period – a cessation of playing (see Barroll, n. 7 above, pp. 211–16). Shakespeare may have used this opportunity to pay what Aubrey claimed to have been an annual visit to his home in Stratford (Chambers, WS, II, p. 253). But, if he did, he would have needed to be back in London for the final weeks of Lent to oversee rehearsals for a short Easter season at the Globe, as in 1611 (Chambers, *ibid.*, pp. 337–41) – plague and weather permitting. This, I propose, is likely to have normally been followed by a spring tour to one of the nearer English regions (as in 1612 when the company were at New Romney in Kent on 21 April), a summer season at the Globe (as in July 1601, and 1613 until 29 June when the Globe burnt down), and a further, more lengthy tour in the autumn (as in 1594, when the players were at Marlborough in September, and in 1597 at Bristol between 11 and 17 September), before returning to the capital as usual for Christmas.

14. See Barroll (n. 7 above), p. 19, and the table shown on p. 173. Cf. the plague records given by Chambers in ES, IV, pp. 345–51.
15. See Chambers, WS, II, pp. 336–42.
16. *Ibid.*, pp. 328–9.
17. See *The Counties of Britain, A Tudor Atlas by John Speed*, with commentaries by Alasdair Hawkyard (paperback edn, 1995), p. 77.
18. REED: *Devon*, p. 267.
19. I am indebted here, as elsewhere throughout the chapter, to Robert Tittler's *Architecture and Power, The Town Hall and the English Urban Community, c. 1500–1640* (Oxford, 1991); see especially pp. 139–50 and, for a partial listing of civic halls in the period, 160–8.
20. For the text of the proclamation, Chambers, ES, IV, pp. 263–4.
21. See Willis's account quoted above, p. 25. The same appears to have been true at Newcastle upon Tyne, where there are several references to rewards for 'free' plays, which (perhaps in compensation for the loss of a gathering) seem especially generous, ranging from 40s to £3. In 1593, the Earl of Sussex' men were awarded 'full paymente of £3 for playing a free play commanded by mr maiore' but only 20s is entered in the accounts (REED: *Newcastle*, p. 92). If the play was free, who contributed the remaining £2? The councillors? As payments to other companies are, however, equally generous as those that are

said to be free, I infer that all such mayors' plays in Newcastle were probably free so far as the public was concerned. In Leicester, and perhaps elsewhere, the councillors (the '24' and the '48') were certainly expected to contribute to the reward (see Chambers, ES, I, pp. 334–5).

22. REED: *Somerset*, I, p. 14.

23. REED: *Cumb, West, Glos*, pp. 306–7.

24. REED: *Norwich*; see, for examples, pp. 90 (2 days), 115 (4 days), 117 (3 days), 142 (3 days in one week, 5 in the next), 156 (a week).

25. Compare Henslowe's daily taking at the Rose which, for typical periods in 1595, varied between 3s and 73s, averaging (according to Dr Greg's calculations) 30s. These amounts, of course, represent only his share of the total box office receipts as the theatre's owner. If the company (the Admiral's) received an equal or slightly greater share than Henslowe, we see that the difference between the daily income of a company on tour and one in London was not so great and, on occasion, may even have been to the advantage of the tourists. (The King's men and the Admiral's are not, however, strictly comparable as the King's owned their own theatre in London which the Admiral's did not.) See Chambers, ES, II, pp. 142–3.

26. As a Worcester's man in 1581/2 and June 1583; as Admiral's man in February and again in May 1586, and twice more with the same company in 1589/90; and with the Chamberlain's (perhaps as suggested earlier in the *Dream*) in 1595. For these records, see 'Players at Ipswich', ed. Chambers, in MSC II, Part 3, pp. 272–81.

27. On this point, with specific reference to Ipswich, see Wickham (n. 1 above), pp. 178–9, and for touring venues generally in the period, 176–90.

28. Chambers (ES, I, p. 335) points out that the rewards entered in the accounts are generally round sums; 'where they are broken, they probably went to make up the results of the "gatherings" to round sums'. If, as elsewhere, the gathering at the mayor's play in Ipswich exceeded the reward, it could easily have resulted in a payment of £3 for that single performance.

29. See John Wasson, *Suffolk in the History Plays of Shakespeare* (Xth Harry Clement Memorial Lecture at Keynes Hall, King's College, Cambridge, 15 June 1974, published by Suffolk WEA, 1974), pp. 3–4. There were thirteen borough towns in Suffolk in the period, of which only four have retained records of payments to players, and of those, all four record visits by companies of which Shakespeare was a member. As Professor Wasson asks, 'Could Shakespeare by some accident have visited only those boroughs which were going to preserve their records?' (p. 4).

30. REED: *Coventry*, pp. 393–4.
31. At Faversham in 1596/7, a wagon belonging to 'Lord Bartlettes [i.e. Berkeley's] players' was misused by 'certen persons', who were fined 15s 9d for their offence (Murray, II, p. 274).
32. MSC XI, p. 163.
33. *Ibid.*, pp. 196–8.
34. Since the 1940s, the building has been in private hands, and is not open to visitors. See Barry L. Wall, *Sudbury through the Ages* (Ipswich, n.d.), pp. 44–7.
35. REED: *Cambridge*, I, pp. 403–4.
36. *Ibid.*, II, pp. 723–7, including plans of the hall, since demolished.
37. *Ibid.*, I, pp. 290–1.
38. Sometimes referred to familiarly as 'the Mayor's house', as quoted, for example, in REED: *Coventry*, p. 567. It had also been used for rehearsals of the *Corpus Christi* plays. The same identification of the mayor's house with the Guildhall may also be true elsewhere, though the former is usually interpreted by REED editors as a separate building. When, for example, in this year of 1603, James I visited Newcastle on his way south, and was officially received in the 'Mayors house, where he was richly entertained' (REED: *Newcastle*, p. 140), it is surely the Guildhall that was meant.
39. See William Cooper, *Henley-in-Arden, An Ancient Market Town and its Surroundings* (1946, reprinted with illustrations, Buckingham, 1992), pp. 74–5.
40. REED: *Shropshire*, II, p. 382.
41. REED: *Cumb, West, Glos*, pp. 306–7.
42. REED: *Bristol*, p. 85. I take the 'mayers courte' to refer to the 'yelde hall' or Guildhall mentioned in the previous entry, relating to the same occasion. The building has since been demolished.
43. REED: *Cumb, West, Glos*, p. 300.
44. REED: *Bristol*, p. 115.
45. REED: *Cumb, West, Glos*, p. 299.
46. MSC II, Part 3, p. 263.
47. REED: *Bristol*, p. 112.
48. *Ibid.*, p. 122.
49. Murray, II, p. 310; REED: *Devon*, p. 46.
50. REED: *Coventry*, p. 374; REED: *Cumb, West. Glos*, pp. 298, 300.
51. As Chambers notes (WS, II, p. 329), the order of entries at Oxford appears not to have been chronological, so we can infer nothing from the lowly position of the relevant entry on the page, especially as it is the only report of a visit by players in the year.
52. REED: *Somerset*, I, p. 19; II, pp. 490–1.
53. See Wickham (n. 1 above), pp. 186–90.
54. See Salter (n. 2 above), pp. xxiv–v, 26, 386. Neither the Bath nor Oxford guildhalls survive to the present.
55. Quoted from Barroll (n. 7 above), p. 110.
56. Chambers, WS, II, p. 329.
57. *Ibid.*
58. Barroll (n. 7 above), p. 113.

59. Chambers, WS, II, pp. 329–30.
60. Chambers, ES, IV, pp. 168–9.
61. As any actor who has taken part in a 'fit-up' tour of this kind will confirm, the rewards to be obtained from playing in the audience's familiar surroundings, where they come together as an existing community, rather than in a theatre where the actor is on familiar ground and the audience are visitors to it and un-known to each other, are very special, and compensate for the rigours of travel and generally spartan nature of conditions backstage.
62. G.K. Hunter in his Arden edition of 1959 (as reprinted, 1967), pp. xviii–xxv; Chambers, WS, I, pp. 449–52.
63. As suggested by W.J. Lawrence in *Shakespeare's Workshop* (Oxford, 1928), p. 60.
64. See Chambers' early essay on the play, dating from the period 1904/8, reprinted in his *Shakespeare: a Survey* (1925), pp. 200–7.
65. Chambers, WS, I, p. 438.
66. David Bevington in his Arden edition of 1998, p. 19.
67. See E.A.J. Honigmann, 'Shakespeare suppressed: the unfortunate history of *Troilus and Cressida*' in *Myriad-minded Shakespeare: Essays on the tragedies, problem comedies and Shakespeare the man* (London and New York, 1989, 2nd edn, 1998), pp. 112–29.
68. Chambers, WS, II, pp. 216–17.
69. As quoted by Bevington (n. 66 above), p. 4.

70. *Johnson on Shakespeare*, ed. W. Raleigh (Oxford, 1908, reprinted 1965), p. 184.
71. As quoted by Schoenbaum, CDL, p. 315.
72. See, for example, Oscar James Campbell, *Shakespeare's Satire* (Hamden and London, 1943, reprinted New York, 1963), pp. 98–120.

Chapter 11: King's Man

1. From *Mythical Sorrows of Shakespeare* (1934), pp. 27–8, as quoted by Schoenbaum, SL, p. 527.
2. For these and subsequent plague figures, see Leeds Barroll, *Politics, Plague and Shakespeare's Theater* (Ithaca and London, 1991), pp. 223–6.
3. Quoted from Chambers, ES, IV, pp. 168–9.
4. See Barroll (n. 2 above), pp. 49, 59. It is not certain that any of them were actually required to walk in the procession.
5. For Lowin's roles, see Chambers, WS, II, pp. 72, 263–4; ES, II, pp. 328–9.
6. The Barnstaple accounts covered the period 1604/5, and were dated from Michaelmas to Michaelmas. We know, however, with unusual accuracy, that the company were at Oxford on 9 October 1605, having travelled from London where the playhouses had only recently been closed. Almost certainly, therefore,

the visit to Barnstaple would have taken place in the previous year at Michaelmas 1604. See REED: *Devon*, pp. xii–xiii, 48. For Oxford, see also n. 10 below.

7. Quoted from Chambers, ES, II, p. 309.

8. Though it is clear from the first scene in the convent (I.iv) that she is still merely a postulant to the Poor Clares (a strictly enclosed contemplative order) and would not at that stage have been clothed in its habit or vowed to its rule, some modern directors have insisted on dressing Isabella as a fully fledged nun, which has the unfortunate effect of making the Duke's tentative proposal of marriage in the final act appear, not only mistimed (which it is, as he himself realises immediately afterwards), but positively sacrilegious, which it is not.

9. For these dates and titles, see Chambers, WS, II, pp. 331–2.

10. H.E. Salter, *Oxford Council Acts, 1583–1626* (Oxford, 1928), p. 390.

11. REED: *Cambridge*, II, p. 985; Halliwell-Phillipps, p. 27.

12. Chambers (WS, I, pp. 468, 475) gives a date 'early in 1606' for both plays; Kenneth Muir (Arden, 1972 edn, pp. xiii–xxii) puts *Macbeth* between 1603 and 1606, inclining to the latter date, and *Lear* (Arden, 1972, p. xxi) a year earlier to the winter of 1604/5.

13. I have written more largely of Armin, including this particular

casting, in Southworth, F & J, pp. 133–6 and n. 35.

14. When the present book was at an advanced stage of writing, there appeared Professor Park Honan's biography (*Shakespeare, A Life*, Oxford, 1998) reporting on recent computer studies involving the lexicon or vocabulary of Shakespeare's *dramatis personae*, which appear to confirm his playing of Duncan as well as a number of other roles that I have proposed as his on different grounds in previous chapters; namely, Chorus in *Henry V*, Friar Laurence and Chorus in *Romeo and Juliet*, Theseus in the *Dream*, Leonato in *Much Ado*, the title role in *Henry IV*, the King in *All's Well*, Adam in *As You Like It* and the Ghost in *Hamlet*. See Honan, pp. 204–5 and n. 10.

15. *Wills*, pp. 72–5.

16. For these dates, see Chambers, WS, II, p. 333, and Barroll (n. 2), p. 148.

17. MSC VII, pp. 117, 65, 49.

18. For this dating, see Chambers, WS, I, pp. 476–8.

19. Extracted from Dekker's *Work for Armorers* (printed 1609), as quoted by Barroll (n. 2 above), p. 176.

20. Chambers, WS, II, pp. 335–6; ES, IV, pp. 174–6.

21. *The Life and Times of William Shakespeare* (1988), p. 279.

22. Quoted from Chambers, ES, II, p. 331.

23. See Philip Brockbank's Arden edition of 1976, pp. 24–9; Chambers, WS, I, pp. 478–80.

24. Chambers, WS, I, pp. 482–3.
25. Chambers, WS, II, p. 18.

Chapter 12: Blackfriars

1. Nicholas Rowe, 'Some Account of the Life . . . of Mr William Shakespeare' in Shakespeare, *Works*, ed. Rowe (1709), I, p. xxxv, as quoted by Schoenbaum, CDL, p. 279.
2. *Wills*, pp. 8–9.
3. See Chambers, WS, II, pp. 154–69, quoting from 166.
4. REED: *Coventry*, p. 373; for Marlborough, Halliwell-Phillipps, p. 29.
5. MSC II, Part 3, pp. 282–4; Nathaniel Bacon, *The Annalls of Ipswiche: The Lawes, Customes and Government of the Same* (1654), ed. W.H. Richardson (Ipswich, 1884), p. 434.
6. MSC VII, pp. 88, 141.
7. Chambers, WS, II, p. 336.
8. *Ibid.*
9. *Ibid.*, pp. 337–42.
10. *Ibid.*, pp. 341–4.
11. Chambers, WS, I, p. 86.
12. Dame Julian of Norwich, *Revelations of Divine Love*, Chapter 32.
13. See F.D. Hoeniger's introduction to his Arden edition of 1963, especially pp. lxxxvi–xci.
14. Chambers, WS, I, pp. 484–7; see also J.M. Nosworthy's Arden edition of 1955, pp. xiv–xvii.
15. As quoted by Nosworthy (*op. cit.*), pp. xl–xlii.
16. Here, and througout this section, I am indebted to J.H.P. Pafford's Arden edition of 1963.
17. Chambers, WS, II, p. 342.
18. In a personal communication to the author.
19. *Ibid.*
20. Chambers, WS, II, p. 345.
21. *Ibid.*, p. 250.

Chapter 13: The Man Shakespeare

1. From *Lectures on the English Poets* (1818), pp. 92–3, as quoted in Schoenbaum, SL, pp. 185–6.
2. See Schoenbaum, CDL, pp. 227–32.
3. *To Mr Thomas Heywood*
   Thou hast writ much and art
       admir'd by those
   Who love the easie ambling of thy
       prose;
   But yet thy pleasingest flight was
       somewhat high,
   When thou didst touch the angels
       Hyerarchie;
   Fly that way still, it will become thy
       age
   And better please then groveling on
       the stage.

   Quoted from Nungezer, *Dictionary*, p. 191.
4. Archdeacon Richard Davies, for whom see Chambers, WS, II, pp. 255–7.

Further Reading

Numerous biographies of Shakespeare and books about his plays are published every year, and most have something useful to say as well as much that is debatable. The following very selective list is of those I have found most useful in writing my own, or relate in a particular way to its themes.

Leeds Barroll, *Politics, Plague and Shakespeare's Theatre, The Stuart Years*, Ithaca and London, 1991.

G.E. Bentley, *The Jacobean and Caroline Stage*, 7 vols, Oxford, 1941–68 – especially Vol. 2 for the information it contains about the later careers of Shakespeare's fellows.

G.E. Bentley, *The Profession of Player in Shakespeare's Time, 1590–1642*, Princeton, 1984.

E.K. Chambers, *William Shakespeare, A Study of Facts and Problems*, 2 vols, Oxford, 1930 – the essential reference work.

Christopher Devlin, *Hamlet's Divinity and Other Essays*, London, 1963 – for the religious background to the plays.

Peter Levi, *The Life and Times of William Shakespeare*, London, 1988 – a poet's biography.

Kenneth Muir, *Shakespeare the Professional and Related Studies*, London, 1973 – especially the lead essay.

S. Schoenbaum, *William Shakespeare, A Compact Documentary Life*, Oxford, 1977.

Ian Wilson, *Shakespeare: The Evidence*, London, 1993.

Index

Shakespeare's plays, and also those that are anonymous or of disputed authorship, are indexed under their titles; other plays under the name of their main author. Principal entries are indicated by bold type, illustrations by italics.

Abingdon, Oxon., 30
Adams, J. Quincy, quoted 93
Admiral, the, *see* Howard, Lord Charles
Admiral's men, 27, 31, 32–40, 42, 47–50,
  56, 68, 87, 95, 96–7, 103, 223, 230
  see also Howard, Lord Charles;
  Admiral's/ Strange's alliance;
  Prince's men
Admiral's/Strange's alliance, **37–8**, 51,
  55, 95–6, 98, **101–6**
Aesop (Aesopus Claudius), Roman
  tragic actor, 34
Alexander, Peter, cited 62, 224
Allen, John (of Sudbury), 208
Alleyn, Edward, player, 20, **29–31**,
  33–4, *Plate 7*, 35, 36–9, 43, 48,
  51, **56–7**, **68–9**, 94, 95, 96, 97,
  105, 135
Alleyn (née Woodward), Joan, 69,
  quoted 216–17
Alleyn, John (Edward's elder brother),
  36–7, 96
All's Well that Ends Well, 198, **219–23**
Andrewes, Richard, player, 29
Anne of Denmark, Queen, 218, 230, 242
  see also Queen's men
Antony and Cleopatra, 244, **247–50**

Apollonius of Tyre, 264
apprentices and apprenticeship, 20–3,
  29–31, **100–5**
  see also boy players, quality of; and
  under names of individual boys
Arden, Edward, 19
Arden of Faversham, 46, *46–8*
Ariosto, Lodovico, *I Suppositi*, 35
Armada, the, 36
Armin, Robert, player and author, 21,
  129, **168**, *169*, **178–9**, 182,
  194–5, 222, 235, 237, 240, 242,
  265, 267, 270, 273
  Foole upon Foole, 168, 178
  *History of the Two Maids of More-
  clacke*, 168, 178, 195
  Quips for Questions, 178
As You Like It, 118, **174–9**, 217
Aubrey, John, 15, 41, 115

Baddeley, Angela, 184
Baldwin, T.W., cited 106
Bale, John, *King Johan*, 140
Barnstaple, Devon, 215, 232, 246
Barton-on-the-Heath, Warwicks., 36
Bath, 33, 151, 203–4, 205, **215–16**
  Guildhall, 216

Beeston, Christopher, player, 102, 115, 177, 242

Beeston, William (Christopher's son), player, 115

Belt, T., apprentice player, 102, 104

Bentley, E.C., quoted 3

Berkeley's men, 26

Betterton, Thomas, 185

Bevis, George, player, 39, 68

Bible, the, 3–4, 10

Blackfriars
  estate, 115, 123, 198
  Gatehouse, **255–6**
  Priory, 117
  theatre, 92, 255, 259

Boccaccio's *Decameron*, 266

Bodley, Sir Thomas, quoted 2

Borges, Jorge Luis, quoted 9

Borromeo, St Charles, 19

boy players, quality of, 112–13, 114, 115, 177, 195, 248
  see also apprentices and apprenticeship; and under names of individual boys

Bradbrook, Muriel, quoted 84

Bradstreet, John, player, 39

Bridgwater, Som., 30

Bristol, 151, 214, 214–15
  Guildhall, 215

Brook, Peter, 61, 271

Brooke, Arthur, author of *Romeus*, 109

Brooke, Sir William, Lord Cobham; Lord Chamberlain, 1596/7, 151

Browne, Edward, player, 29, 31

Browne, Robert, player, 29–31, 36, 37, 39, 68, 257

Browning, Robert, quoted 65

Bryan, George, player, 38, 68, **98**, 118, 122, 150, 167

Burbage, Cuthbert (Richard's elder brother), 96, 103, 161

Burbage, James (Richard's father), player, 51, 95–6, 117, 123, 152

Burbage, Richard, player, 20, 51, 68, **95–6**, *Plate* 6, 103, 111, 114, 119, 122, 133, 135, 138–9, 142, 144, 155, 161, 170–1, 173–4, 177, 182, **188**, 194, 218, 222, 230, **234**, 237, 240, 242, 248, 255, 256, 265, 267, 268, 272, 274, 276

Burghley, Lord (William Cecil), 72, 210

Cairncross, Andrew, quoted 62

Cambridge, 32, 117, **209–10**, 238
  Guildhall, 209

Campion, Thomas, 19

Carey, Sir George, *see* Hunsdon, Lord

Carey, Henry, *see* Hunsdon, Lord

Carleton, Dudley, quoted 218

Catesby, Sir William, 19

Cecil, Robert, earl of Salisbury, 2

Chamberlain's men, 90, 91, **93–109**, 113, 116, *passim* to 199, 215 (1576), 223
  see also King's men; Hunsdon's men

Chambers, E.K. (Sir Edmund), cited 33, 37, 48, 53–4, 72, 120, 181, 219, 221, 230, 252, 254, 256, 265

Charles I (as Duke of York), 246

Charles II, 10

Chaucer, Geoffrey, *The Canterbury Tales*, 65, 88

Chettle, Henry, 20, **59–60**
  Troilus and Cressida, 223

Children of the Chapel Royal, 248, 255

Cobham, Lord, *see* Brooke, Sir William

Coleridge, Samuel Taylor, quoted 225

College of Heralds, 18, 183, 277

Collins, Francis, 275

Comedy of Errors, The, 66, **77–81**, 108, 238

Condell, Henry, player, 98, 102, 103, 235, 241, 242, 265, 267, 269, 273, 276

   see also Heminges and Condell (as editors)

Contention, First part of the, betwixt the two famous Houses of Yorke and Lancaster (pirated text of *Henry VI, Part 2*), 68

Cooke, Alexander ('Saunder'), player, 20, **102–3**, 231, 235, 241, 242, 270

Cooke, Thomas, player, 29

Coriolanus, 244, **250–1**

Corpus Christi (mystery) plays, 4

Cory, William, 277

Countess of Essex's men, 26

Court, the players at
   Greenwich, 68, 108, 243
   Hampton Court, 218, 243
   Richmond, 116, 198
   Whitehall, 124, 193, 196, 198, 218, 233, 236, 246, 259, 270, 276
   Wilton, 217
   Windsor, 151, 180

Coventry, 4, 27–8, 32, 33, 203–4, 206, **210–12**, 215, 247, 258, 274
   St Mary's Guildhall, 210–12, *211*

Cowley, Richard, player, 98, 105, 118, 122, 182, 194, 235, 237, 241, 242, 269, 273

Cross Keys inn (theatre), 107–8, 117

Crosse, Samuel, player, 104, **231**

Curtain theatre, 122–3, 152, 159, 160

Cymbeline, 124–5, 179, 258, 259, **265–7**

Davies, John, of Hereford, 6, 40, 82, **129–33**, *130*, 248, 282, 283

Dekker, Thomas, quoted 245, 246

de la Casa, John, quoted 5–6

Denmark, 96
   king of, 243

Dennis, John, 180

Derby's men, 26–7

director, Shakespeare as, 58, 63, **112–14**, 278–9

Doncaster, Yorks., 30

Donne, John, 2–3

'double-mirror' effect, 172, 188, 191

doubles and doubling, **42**, 79–80, 112, 122, 137–8, 153, 166, 167–8, 170, 187–8, 240, 241, 242, 265
   see also Appendix D

Dover, Kent, 32, 151, 243

dramatists, low status of, 2–3

Drayton, Michael, 275

Droeshout, Martin, and his engraving, *xii*, **1**, 6

Duke, John, player, 105

Dunwich, Suffolk, 247

Eccleston, William, player, 104, 222

Edmans, John, player, 103

Edward III, 85–7

Edward VI, 24

Elector Palatine, 273

Elizabeth, Princess (daughter of James I), 273
   see also Lady Elizabeth's men

Elizabeth I, Queen, 21, *passim* (as the Queen) to 180–1, 192–3, **196–8**
   see also Queen's men

Englische Comedien und Tragedien, 53

Essex, Earl of (Robert Devereux, 2nd earl), 162–3, 196–7
   see also Essex's men; Countess of Essex's men

Essex's men, 216

Eucharist, the, 4
Exeter, 33

*Famous Victories of Henry the fifth,
The*, 165
Faversham, Kent, 32, 47, 48, 123, 243
  Market Hall, 123, *124*
Ferdinando, Lord Strange, 26, *95*
  see also Strange's men
Field, Nathan, player, 21, 267, *Plate 17,*
  270, 279
Field, Richard, 69
First Folio (1623), **1–2**, 6, 10, 20, 39,
  61, 77, 98, 99, *104*, 105, 163,
  225, 253, 260
  see also Heminges and Condell (as
  editors)
Fleay, F.G., cited 48
Flecknoe, Richard, *Short Discourse of
  the English Stage*, quoted 113
Fletcher, John, 273, 274
Fletcher, Lawrence, player, 242, 305,
  n.1
Folkestone, Kent, 32, 259
Forman, Simon, 259, 268
Fortune theatre, 163
Frankfort Autumn Fair, 53
Friendship Cult, 73, 83
Fuller, Thomas, 14–15, 20

Garnet, Fr Henry, 243
Gascoigne, George, 35
gatherings, 25, **204–5**, 206, 208, 210,
  216, 218, 247
Geoffrey of Monmouth, 266
Germany, 29, 39, 53, 68
Gilburne (Gebon?), Samuel, player, 20,
  104–5, 241, 242
Globe theatre, 92, 102, **160–2**, *Plate 4,*
  162, 164, 173–4, 178, *passim* to

end but see especially 199, 219,
  223, 224, 256
Gloucester, 25, 28, 205, 214, 215
  Booth (Bothall) or town hall, 25
Goodridge, J.F., quoted 65
Gough (née Phillips), Elizabeth, 103
Gough, Robert, player, 20–1, **103**, 222,
  241, 242–3
Gower, John, 65, *Plate 8*, 67, 88,
  260–1, *261*
  Confessio Amantis, 65, 264
Great Freeze, 245, 250
Greene, Robert, 56, **59–60**, 267
  Friar Bacon and Friar Bungay, 56
  Groats-worth of Wit, 59–60
  Orlando Furiosa, 56
Grocers, London Company of, 102–3
  and n.15
Grooms of the Chamber, 93, 167, 231
guildhalls, 25
  see also town halls, and under
  relevant cities or towns
Gunpowder Plot, 239

Hadleigh, Suffolk, 207–8
  Guildhall, *207*
Hall, Edward, quoted 36
Hamlet, 15, 45, 129, 147, **184–91**, 216,
  223
Hardy, Thomas, quoted 11
harper-poets, 3, 67
  see also minstrels
Harryson, William, player, 29
Hatcher, John, 210
Hathaway, Anne, *see* Shakespeare, Anne
Hazlitt, William, cited 172, 266, 277
Heminges, John, player, 20, 68, **98**,
  102–3, 105–6, 114, 118, 124,
  150, 161, 179, 217, 218, 222,
  231, 235, 237, 241, 242, 243,

246, 256, 262, 267, **269**, 273, 276
  as editor, *see also* under Heminges
    and Condell
Heminges and Condell (as editors), **1–2,**
  5, 20, 61, 98, 225, 253
  see also First Folio
Henley-in-Arden, Warwicks., 212–13
  Market House or Town Hall, *213*
Henry, Prince (son of James I), 230
  see also Prince's men
Henry IV, 47, 119–20, 151, **152–9**, 273
  Part I, 152
  Part 2, 156–8, 159, 164
Henry V, 159, **162–9**, 238
Henry VI, 16, 36, 38, 43, 45, 55–6,
    57–8, 59, **60–1**, **62–3**, 94, 133–5
  'harey the vi' (Henslowe), 52, 55–6,
    59
  Henry VI, Part 1, 42, 55, 58
  Henry VI, Part 2, 16, 62, 68, 69
  Henry VI, Part 3, 42, 59, 68, 69
Henry VI/Richard III tetralogy, 61, 66
Henry VIII (with Fletcher), 256, **273–4**
Henslowe, Philip, 51, 53, 68, 69, 87,
  94, 95
  Diary, 51–6, 199
Herbert, Henry, 2nd earl of Pembroke,
  67–8
  see also Pembroke's men
Herbert, William, 3rd earl of Pembroke,
  217
Heywood, Thomas, player and author,
  56, 98, 279
  Apology for Actors, 98
Hibbard, G.R., cited 181
hired men, 100–1, 105, 167
Holinshed, Raphael, 47, 165, 266
Holland, 37
  see also Low countries
Holland, John, player, 39

Honigmann, E.A.J. (with Susan Brock),
  quoted 254
Hotson, Leslie, quoted 180
housekeepers, 161
Howard, Lord Charles, of Effingham,
  Lord Admiral, 31, 36, 37, 39–40,
  72, 96
  see also Admiral's men
Hunsdon, Lord (Lord Chamberlain)
  1585–96: Henry Carey, 1st Lord
    Hunsdon, 94, 94–5, 107–8, 115,
    151
  1597–1603: Sir George Carey, 2nd
    Lord Hunsdon, 115–16, 123, 151,
    180, 192, 198
  see also Chamberlain's men;
    Hunsdon's men
Hunsdon's men
  1564–85: 94
  1596–97: 151
Hunter, G.K., cited 219
Hythe, Kent, 30, 32, 247, 258

Innocents' Day, 80–1, 108, 238
interludes and interluders, 3, 35, 73
Ipswich, Suffolk, 30, 32, 33, 37, 117,
  203–4, **206**, 215, 247, 258
  Moot or Guildhall, 117–18, *117*

Jackson, John, 256
James I, 20, 87, 92, 199, 217, **229–30,**
  232–3, 236, 245, 270, 276, 277
  see also King's men
Jeffes, Anthony (Humphrey's younger
  brother), player, 39
Jeffes, Humphrey, player, 39
Jenkins, Harold, quoted 189
jigs, 158, **173–4**
Johnson, Dr Samuel, quoted 62, 174,
  192, 225–6, 265

Johnson, William, 256

Jones, Richard, player, 29, 31, 36, 39

Jonson, Ben, 1, 2, 6, 14, 17–18, 33–4,
39, 225, 227, 275
The Alchemist, 103
Bartholomew Fair, 33
Eastward Ho! 2, 225
Every Man In his Humour, 102, 105,
159, 238
Every Man Out of his Humour, 159,
238
The Isle of Dogs, 151, 160
The Poetaster, 248
Sejanus, 218, 231
Volpone, 238

Julian of Norwich, 260

Julius Caesar, **169–74**, 273

Keats, John, quoted 8–9

Kempe, William, player, 68, 74–5, 79,
90, 91, **96–7**, 97, 111, 114, 118,
119, 122, 125, **127–8**, 129, 138,
142, 150, 155, **156–9**, 161

Kerrigan, John, quoted 83

King John, 119–20, **139–43**

King Lear, 147, **239–41**, *Plate 14*,
244–5, 260

King's men (formerly Chamberlain's),
199, 200, 202, *passim* to end

Knack to Know a Knave, The, 30, 96–7

Kyd, Thomas, 32, 43–6
Soliman and Perseda, **45–6**
The Spanish Tragedy (*Jeronimo*), 32,
33, 42, **43–5**, 44, 56, 186

Lady Elizabeth's men, 204, 206
see also Elizabeth, Princess

Lambarde, William, 197

Lambert, Joan (Shakespeare's aunt), 35

Langland's *Piers Plowman*, 65

Leech, Clifford, cited 74, 77

Leicester (town), 28, 29, 31, 32, 33,
205, 215, 219

Leicester, Earl of (Robert Dudley), 26,
38, 210
see also Leicester's men

Leicester's men, 25–6, 32, 38, 96, 98,
208, 214, 215

Levi, Peter, quoted 32, 47, 177, 248

Lewis Frederick of Württemberg,
Prince, 259

Livy, 88

Lodge, Thomas, 174

London and vicinity
City, 33, 37, 52, 85, 107–8, 199
Cripplegate, 252, 255, 257
Grays Inn, 80, 108
Mortlake, 217
Shoreditch, 51, 110, 115
Southwark, 47, 161, 217, 252, 255
see also Blackfriars; Court

Longshank, see Peele's *Edward I*

Lord Chamberlain, *see* Hunsdon, Lord;
Brooke, Sir William
see also Chamberlain's men

Lord Chandos' men, 168

Lord Compton's men, 215

Lords of Misrule, 192, 193

Love's Labour's Lost, **89–92**, 108, 238

Low Countries, 29, 96, 98
see also Holland

Lowin, John, player, **231**, *Plate 13*, 237,
241, 267, 270, 273, 274

Lucy, Sir Thomas, 21, 47

Lydgate, John, 88

Lyly, John, 73

Lynn, Ralph, 78

Macbeth, 2, 66, 239–40, **241–2**, *Plate
15*, 259, 273

Maidstone, Kent, 31, 94, 243–4, *244*
Maldon, Essex, **203–4**
  Moot Hall, 204, *Plate 12*
Malone, Edmond, 21
Manningham, John, *Diary*, 198
Marlborough, Wilts., 107, 151, 243, 247, 258
Marlowe, Christopher, 32, 42–3, 59–60
  The Jew of Malta, 32, **43**, 56
  Massacre at Paris, 56
  Tamburlaine the Great, 32, 33, **42–3**
Marston, John, 227
  The Malcontent, 229
Martin Marprelate controversy, 37, 91
Mary Magdalene (medieval Saints' play), 264
Mary, Queen
  as princess, 15
  as queen, 24
Master of the Revels, 95, 192
mayor's (or bailiff's) play, 25, **204–5**, 206, 214, 218
Measure for Measure, 47, 232–3, **235–7**
Merchant of Venice, The, **120–4**, *Plate 9*, 137, 238
Meres, Francis, in *Palladis Tamia*, 77, 125
Merry Wives of Windsor, The, 151, 158, 174, **180–4**, *Plate 11*, 235
Midsummer Night's Dream, A, 66, 108, **115–19**, 121, 218
minstrels, 5, 67
  see also harper-poets
Morgann, Maurice, quoted 51
Morris, Brian, cited 34
Motley (designers), 184
Mountjoy, Christopher, 255
Much Ado About Nothing, 105, 118, **125–8**, 160, 273

music in the plays, 114, 123, **173–4**, 179, 193, 265

Nashe, Thomas, 58, 59, 90, 96
  Almond for a Parrat, 96
  Pierce Penilesse his Supplication to the Divell, 58
Newington Butts theatre, 68, 98
New Romney, Kent, 247, 258, 259
Norwich, 30, 33, 159, 205
Nottingham, 274

Oldys, William, quoted 175–6
Olivier, Laurence, 61–2
Orford Castle, Suffolk, 141–2, *141*
Orsino, Don Virginio, 192–3
Ostler (née Heminges), Thomasine, 248
Ostler, William, player, 21, 235, **248**
Othello, **232–5**, 259, 273
Ovid, 88
Oxford (city), 203–4, **215–16**, 238, 243, 246, 258, 259
  Guildhall, 216
Oxford's (Lord) men, 32, 208, 210

Painter's *Pallace of Pleasure*, 88
Pateson, William, player, 29
Peacham drawing, *Plate 16*, 54–5
Peele, George, 48–50, 59
  Edward I, **48–9**
Pembroke's men, 67–8, 73, 102, 151
  see also Herbert, Henry, 2nd earl of Pembroke
Percy, Bishop Thomas, quoted 51
Pericles, 65, 67, 179, 252, 257, **260–5**
Persons, Robert, 19
Phillips, Augustine, player, 20, 68, **98**, 103, 104–5, 114, 161, 177, 197, 217, 231, 235, 242–3

plague, 56, 67, 95, 199, 201–2, 203, 216–17, 228–9, 230, 238, 243, 245, 251, 255, 257, 259
Platter, Thomas, 169–70, 173–4
Plautus' *Menaechmi*, 78
'play metaphor', **134–5**, 136–7, 147–51, 177–8, 188–91
player-musicians, 106 and note
players, disdain for, **5–6**, 20, 82–3, 130–1, 132–3, 209, 279
'plots', 39, **101–6**
Plutarch, 169
Plymouth, 30, 204
Pope, Thomas, player, 21, 38, 68, **98**, 103, 111, 118, 124, 150, 161, 182, 194; for his death, Appendix D, Plot 3, n. 6
Powlton, Thomas, player, 29
Price, H.T., quoted 62
Prince's (Prince Henry's, formerly Admiral's) men, 230
Privy Council, 39, 52, 68, 151, 238
publication of plays, **4–5**, 67, 151–2
Puritans, 33, 84–5, 106, 151, 258

Queen's men
    of Elizabeth I: 20, 32, 38
    of Anne of Denmark (formerly Worcester's), 230
Queen's Revels (children's company), 100
Quiney, Thomas, 276

Rape of Lucrece, The, 72, **87–9**
Red Bull theatre, 245
Redman, Joyce, 184
Rhenanus, Johannes, quoted 113
Rice, John, player, 20
Richard II, 66, 119–20, **144–51**, 152, 196

Richard III, 43, 44, 56, 69, 93, **135–8**, 152
Righter, Anne, quoted 188, 190
Rigg, Diana, 88
Roberts, Master (publisher), 223, 224
Robinson, John, 256, 275
Robinson, Richard, player, 21
rogues and vagabonds, 5, 24
Romeo and Juliet, 108, **109–14**, 121
Roscius (Roman actor), 34, 134
Rose theatre, 26, 39, 46, 51, 52, *Plate 4*, 52–6, 58–9
Rowe, Nicholas, 21, 184–5, 254, 257, 279
Royal Corps of Trumpets and Drums, 243–4
Rutland, Earl of, 256
Rye, Sussex, 151
Rylands, George, cited 61

Sackville, Thomas, player, 39
Saffron Walden, Essex, 238
Salisbury, Earl of, *see* Cecil, Robert
Sandes, James, player, 105, 242
Schlueter, June, cited 54
Schoenbaum, S., cited 16, 176
Shakespeare (née Hathaway), Anne, 21–2, 27–8, 283
Shakespeare, Edmund (younger brother), 104, 252
Shakespeare, Edward (nephew), 252
Shakespeare, Hamnet (son), 123
Shakespeare, Henry (uncle), 16
Shakespeare, John (father), 15, 17, 18–20, 22, 24–5, 26–7, 183
Shakespeare, Judith (second daughter), 14, 275, 276
Shakespeare (née Arden), Mary, mother, 17, 257–8
Shakespeare, Susanna (elder daughter), 22, 28

sharers, 20, **22**, 95–8, 114, 167, 280
  see also under names of individual
    players
Shaw, Glen Byam, 184
Shrewsbury, 203–4, **214**, 258, 259
  Booth Hall, 214
Sincler, John ('Sinklo'), player, 35, 39,
    80, 111, 118, 122, 129, 142, 153,
    182, 194, 229
'Sinklo', *see* Sincler, John
Sir John Oldcastle (early version of
    Shakespeare's *Henry IV*), 151
  see Henry IV
Sisson, C.J., quoted 228
Sly, William, player, 35, *Plate 5*, **98**,
    105, 142, 182, 235, 237, 241,
    242, **257**
Slye, John, interluder, 35
Somerset, William, 3rd earl of
    Worcester, 24, 28, 31
  see also Worcester's men
Sonnets, 72, 73, 79, **81–5**, 89
  Sonnet 111, 6
  Sonnet 121, 82–3
Southampton (Hants), 28, 30, 33
Southampton, Earl of, *see* Wriothesley,
    Henry
Spencer, Gabriel, player, 39
Stafford, 258, 259
Stanley, 4th earl of Derby, 27
  see Derby's men
Steevens, George, quoted 14, 175
Stone, a professional fool, 178
Strange's men, 26–7, 37–8, 51, 56, 68,
    98, 215
  see also Ferdinando, Lord Strange;
    Admiral's/Strange's alliance
Stratford-upon-Avon and vicinity,
    14–23, 24–8, 31, 36, 183, 212,
    239, 257

Guildhall, 17, *18*, 25
Holy Trinity church, 7, 17, 28
Henley Street, 17–19
King's New School, 17, *Plate 3*, 25
New Place, 212
Shakespeare memorial bust, 7, *Plate 2*
Shambles, 16
Snitterfield, 16, 17
Street, Peter, 161, 163
Sturgess, Keith, cited 48
Sudbury, Suffolk, **208–9**, 258
  Old Moot Hall, *Plate 18*
Swinburne, Algernon Charles, quoted 266

Taming of a Shrew, The (pirated text of
    Shakespeare's play), 34, 102
*Taming of **The** Shrew, The* **34–6**, 43,
    45, 66, 68, 69, 94, 95, 103, 108
Tarlton, Richard, player and
    playwright, 21, 24, 38
  Seven Deadly Sins, 20–1, 39, 95,
    101–6
Tempest, The, 2, 66, 259, **270–3**
Theatre, the, 51, 95–6, **110**, 114, 116–17,
    122–3, 144, 152, 160–1
theatres, *see* Blackfriars, Cross Keys,
    Curtain, Fortune, Globe,
    Newington Butts, Red Bull, Rose
Thorndike, Sybil, 88
Thorpe, Thomas, 82
Timon of Athens, 251–2
Titus Andronicus, 33–4, 38, 43, 45,
    53–5, 56–7, *57*, 60–2, 68, 93, 95,
    108
  'titus and vespacia' (Henslowe), 52–6
Tooley, Nicholas, player, 20, **103**, 177,
    231, 235, 241, 242, 270
tours and touring, 30–1, 32–3, 68, 107,
    117, 151, **199–219**, 231–2, 238,
    243–4, 246–7, 257–8, 259, 274

seasonal pattern, 200–1, notes 12
  and 13
town halls or houses, 25, 196
  see also guildhalls and under names
    of relevant towns or cities
Trigg, William, player, 102 and note
Troilus and Cressida, 198, **223–7**
Troublesome Reign of King John, The,
    140–1
Troy (anon. play at the Rose), 223
True Tragedie of Richard, Duke of
    Yorke, The (pirated text of *Henry*
    VI, Part 3), 68
Tunstall, James, player, 29, 31, 36
Twelfth Night, 2, 118, **191–5**, 198
Two Gentlemen of Verona, The, 65,
    73–7, 108
Two Noble Kinsmen, The (with
    Fletcher), 65, 259, 273, **274**
type-casting, 118–19, 128, 129–30

Underwood, John, player, 21

Venus and Adonis, **69–72**, 89
Very Lamentable Tragedy of Titus
    Andronicus and the Haughty
    Empress, A, *see* under *Titus*
    Andronicus, 'titus and vespacia'
Vice of the moralities, 43, 135, 138

Vincent, Thomas, player and prompter, 102

Walker, Roy, quoted 271–2
Walsingham, Sir Francis, 32
Ward, John, 275
Warwick's men, 25
'We three', image of, 194, *Plate 10*
Wells, Stanley, cited 116
Whateley, Anne, 28
Wickham, Glynne, quoted 196
Wilkins, George, 260–1
Willis, R., quoted 24–5
Wilson, John Dover, quoted 21–2, 24,
    61, 155
Wilton, Wilts., 217
Winchester, Hants, 259
Winter's Tale, The, 259, **267–70**, 273
Wise, Andrew, 152
Woodward, Joan, *see* Alleyn, Joan
Worcester, Earl of, see Somerset,
    William
Worcester's men, 24–31, 102, 105, 230
  see also Queen's men
Wordsworth, William, quoted 65
Wriothesley, Henry, earl of
    Southampton, 71–2, 81, 83, 89

Yates, Frances A., quoted 160, 162, 173
York, 31, 33